2004
POET'S MARKET

1,800+ PLACES TO PUBLISH YOUR POETRY

EDITOR
NANCY BREEN

ASSISTANT EDITOR
VANESSA LYMAN

WRITER'S DIGEST BOOKS
CINCINNATI, OH

Important Market Listing Information

● Listings are based on questionnaires completed by editors and on subsequent verified copy. Listings are not advertisements *nor* are markets necessarily endorsed by the editors of this book.

● Information in the listings comes directly from the publishers and is as accurate as possible. However, publications and editors come and go, and poetry needs fluctuate between the publication date of this directory and the date of purchase.

● If you are a poetry publisher and would like to be considered for a listing in the next edition, send a SASE (or SAE and IRC) with your request for a questionnaire to *Poet's Market*—QR, 4700 East Galbraith Road, Cincinnati OH 45236 or e-mail us at poetsmarket@fwpubs.com. Questionnaires received after February 15, 2004, will be held for the 2006 edition.

● *Poet's Market* reserves the right to exclude any listing that does not meet its requirements.

Complaint Procedure

If you feel you have not been treated fairly by a market listed in *Poet's Market*, we advise you to take the following steps:

• First, try to contact the market. Sometimes one phone call or letter can quickly clear up the matter. Document all your communications with the market.

• When you contact us with a complaint, provide the details of your submission, the date of your first contact with the market, and the nature of your subsequent communication.

• We will file a record of your complaint and further investigate the market.

• The number and severity of complaints will be considered when deciding whether or not to delete a market from the next edition of *Poet's Market*.

Editorial Director, Writer's Digest Books: Barbara Kuroff
Managing Editor, Writer's Digest Books: Alice Pope
Production Editor: Michael Schweer

Writer's Market website: www.writersmarket.com
Writer's Digest Books website: www.writersdigest.com

International Standard Serial Number 0883-5470
International Standard Book Number 1-58297-187-0

Attention Booksellers: This is an annual directory of F&W Publications. Return deadline for this edition is December 31, 2004.

Contents

From the Editor

As I write this it's late April and National Poetry Month 2003 is drawing to a close. I celebrated in a number of ways: bought some books and magazines, attended a few readings, even *wrote* some poetry. And I spoke to gatherings in local bookstores and at the library about how to submit poems for publication. Sometimes audience members' eyes glazed over as I droned on about submission guidelines, copyrights, and formatting manuscripts. Other times the air seemed charged with their enthusiasm, and I found myself admiring the passion of their desire to share their work.

The nuts-and-bolts details of publishing poetry are, indeed, pretty dry, especially after the "rush" of creating the poetry itself. However, being practical (and professional) is part of the process, too. And it's an indispensable part if you're serious about getting your work into print.

So hunker down, grit your teeth if necessary, and learn everything about the submission process, from manuscript preparation to studying markets. Absorb these practices and they'll become automatic. Then you can devote your energies to what you love best—writing your poems.

To help you balance the right brain/left brain demands of creating and submitting poetry, we've combined the hard data of market listings with a variety of articles and Insider Reports. See what the editors of *Verse*, *Threepenny Review*, *Colorado Review*, and *Skanky Possum* have to say about their journals and the submissions they receive. Find out more about the history of the chapbook and the importance of this literary gem to contemporary poetry. Sharpen your marketing instincts by learning how to spot poetry publishers and contests you should avoid.

Read what **Ray Gonzalez** has to say about the influence of cultural roots and locale in poetry. Sit in as **Marvin Bell** discusses one of his poems. As a further bonus, read Bell's **32 Statements About Writing Poetry** for unique perspectives and advice. See what **Lisel Mueller** has to say about her belated start in poetry, what **Margo Stever** recommends about making time for writing. Know any children or teens who write? Read up on **markets for young poets** and pass along this valuable information. And learn how **Ken Waldman** combines his poetry and fiddling skills into a one-of-a-kind spoken word performance.

We hope these articles provide inspiration, instruction, maybe even revelation (not to mention distraction for those times when you're just not in the mood to write). And we hope the wide range of listings in this edition of *Poet's Market* provide plenty of fruitful opportunities to share *your* work.

Nancy Breen
poetsmarket@fwpubs.com

What's Different in 2004?

Poetry samples

Since *Poet's Market* was founded in 1985 by the late Judson Jerome (legendary poetry columnist for *Writer's Digest*), many market listings have included poetry samples selected by the editors and publishers of those markets. The samples were valued by our readers and were part of the *Poet's Market* tradition. The selected poets seemed to appreciate having their moment in the spotlight.

However, times change. Because of a number of important reasons, poetry samples are no longer part of the market listings. The factors we took into consideration include the decreasing number of samples editors are submitting for their listings, the logistics of ironing out rights for samples that *are* submitted, space constraints, and the significant jump in magazine- and publisher-oriented websites that include samples of complete poems (as opposed to the six-line excerpts our listings offered).

We know many of our readers will miss seeing the poetry samples, but we hope you'll continue to find *Poet's Market* an invaluable resource despite this change. The good news is the absence of poetry samples opened up space for about 50 additional publishing opportunities we couldn't have included otherwise, plus all listings feature the same detailed information and comments from editors you've come to expect.

New listing symbols

We've tweaked the symbols that appear in our listings to increase their benefit to your marketing efforts. The (⊞) symbol now signals markets that are truly *new*—established in the last three years and never before in *Poet's Market*. The (◩) symbol indicates any established market that did not appear in the 2003 edition of *Poet's Market*, whether it was in the book previously or not. We hope this distinction will help you better target markets for your work.

Canadian postal codes

The mail addresses for all Canadian markets now include the two-letter abbreviations for provinces and territories (for example, AB instead of Alberta and SK instead of Saskatchewan) as recommended by the Canadian Postal Service. For your easy reference, we've printed a chart of these codes on the inside back cover of this book, along with the U.S. two-letter abbreviations. (For more about Canadian postal regulations, see www.canadapost.ca.)

Getting Started (and Using This Book)

Delving into the pages of *Poet's Market* indicates a commitment—you've decided to take that big step and begin submitting your poems for publication. Good for you! How do you *really* begin, though? Here are eight quick tips to help make sense of the marketing/submission process. Follow these suggestions, study the markets in this book carefully, and give proper attention to the preparation of your manuscript. And remember, you're already pursuing your dream of seeing your poems in print.

1. **Read. And read. Then read some more.** You'll never develop your skills if you don't immerse yourself in poetry of all kinds. It's essential to study the masters; however, from a marketing standpoint, it's equally vital to read what your contemporaries are writing and publishing. Read journals and magazines, chapbooks and collections, anthologies for a variety of voices; scope out the many poetry sites on the Internet. Develop an eye for quality, then use that eye to assess your own work. Don't rush to publish until you know you're writing the best poetry you're capable of producing.

2. **Know what you like to write—and what you write best.** Ideally you should be experimenting with all kinds of poetic forms, from free verse to villanelles. However, there's sure to be a certain style with which you feel most comfortable, that conveys your true "voice." Whether you're into more formal, traditional verse or avant-garde poetry that breaks all the rules, you should identify which markets publish work similar to yours. Those are the magazines and presses you should target to give your submissions the best chance of being read favorably—and accepted! (See the Subject Index beginning on page 539 to get an idea of how some magazines and presses specify their needs.)

3. **Learn the "biz."** Poetry may not be a high-paying writing market, but there's still a right way to go about the "business" of submitting and publishing poems. Learn all you can by reading writing-related books and magazines. Read the articles and interviews in this book for plenty of helpful advice. Surf the Internet for a wealth of sites filled with writing advice, market news, and informative links. (See Websites of Interest on page 509 for some leads.)

4. **Research those markets.** Start by studying the listings in *Poet's Market*. Each gathers the names, addresses, figures, editorial preferences, and other pertinent information all in one place. (The Publishers of Poetry section begins on page 27, with the Contests & Awards section following on page 423. Also, the indexes at the back of this book provide insights to what a publication or publisher might be looking for.)

   You're already reading a variety of published poetry (or at least you should be). That's the best way to gauge the kinds of poetry a market publishes. However, you need to go a step further. It's best to study several issues of a magazine/journal or several of a press's books to get a feel for the style and content of each. If the market has a Web address (when available, websites are included in the contact information for each listing in this book), log on and take a look. Check out the site for poetry samples, reviews and other content, and especially guidelines! If a market isn't online, send for guidelines and sample copies. Guidelines give you the lowdown on what an editor expects of submissions, the kind of "insider information" that's too valuable to ignore.

5. **Start slowly.** As tempting as it may be to send your work straight to *The New Yorker* or *Poetry*, try to adopt a more modest approach if you're just starting out. Most listings in this book show symbols that reflect the level of writing a magazine or publisher would prefer to receive. The (◻) symbol indicates a market that welcomes submissions from beginning or unpublished poets. As you gain confidence and experience (and increased skill in your writing), move on to markets coded with the (◐) symbol. Later, when you've built a publication history, submit to the more prestigious magazines and presses (the ◑ markets). Although it may tax your patience, slow and steady progress is a proven route to success.

6. **Be professional.** Professionalism is not something you should "work up to." Make it show in your first submission, from the way you prepare your manuscript to the attitude you project in your communications with editors.

   Follow guidelines. Submit a polished manuscript. (See Frequently Asked Questions on page 7 for details on manuscript formatting and preparation.) Choose poems carefully with the editor's needs in mind. *Always* include a SASE (self-addressed stamped envelope) with any submission or inquiry. Such practices show respect for the editor, the publication, and the process; and they reflect *your* self-respect and the fact that you take your work seriously. Editors love that; and even if your work is rejected, you've made a good first impression that could help your chances with your next submission.

7. **Keep track of your submissions.** First, do *not* send out the only copies of your work. There are no guarantees that your submission won't get lost in the mail, misplaced in a busy editorial office, or vanish into a black hole if the market winds up closing shop. Create a special file folder for poems you are submitting. Even if you use a word processing program and store your manuscripts on disk, keep a hard copy file as well.

   Second, establish a tracking system so you always know which poems are where. This can be extremely simple: index cards, a chart made up on the computer, or even a simple notebook used as a log. (You can photocopy an enlarged version of the Submission Tracker on page 6 or use it as a model to design your own.) Note the titles of the poems submitted (or the title of the manuscript, if submitting a collection); the name of the publication, press, or contest; date sent; and date returned *or* date accepted. Additional information you may want to log includes the name of the editor/contact, date the accepted piece is published, the pay received, rights acquired by the publication or press, and any pertinent comments.

   Without a tracking system you risk forgetting where and when pieces were submitted. This is even more problematic if you simultaneously send the same poems to different magazines. And if you learn of an acceptance at one magazine, you must notify the others that the poem you sent them is no longer available. You have a bigger chance of overlooking someone without an organized approach. This causes hard feelings among editors you may have inconvenienced, hurting your chances with these markets in the future.

   Besides, a tracking system gives you a sense of accomplishment, even if your acceptances are infrequent at first. After all, look at all those poems you've sent out! You're really working at it, and that's something to be proud of.

8. **Learn from rejection.** No one enjoys rejection, but every writer faces it. The best way to turn a negative into a positive is to learn as much as you can from your rejections. Don't let them get you down. A rejection slip isn't a permission slip to doubt yourself, condemn your poetry, or give up.

   Look over the rejection. Did the editor provide any comments about your work or reasons why your poems were rejected? Probably he or she didn't. Editors are extremely busy and don't necessarily have time to comment on rejections. If that's the case, move on to the next magazine or publisher you've targeted and send your work out again.

   If, however, the editor *has* commented on your work, pay attention. It counts for something that the editor took the time and trouble to say anything, however brief, good, or bad. And consider any remark or suggestion with an open mind. You don't have to agree, but you shouldn't automatically disregard it, either. Tell your ego to sit down and be quiet, then use the editor's comments to review your work from a new perspective. You might be surprised how much you'll learn from a single scribbled word in the margin; or how encouraged you'll feel from a simple "Try again!" written on the rejection slip.

Keep these eight tips in mind as you prepare your poetry manuscript, and keep *Poet's Market* close at hand to help you along. Believe in yourself and don't give up! As the 1,800+ listings in this book show, there are many opportunities for beginning poets to become published poets. Why shouldn't you be one of them?

GUIDE TO LISTING FEATURES

Below is an example of the market listings you'll find in the Publishers of Poetry section. Note the callouts that identify various format features of the listing. The front inside cover of this book contains a key to the symbols used at the beginning of all listings.

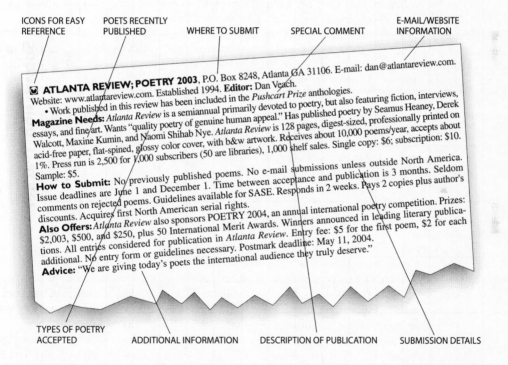

ICONS FOR EASY REFERENCE   POETS RECENTLY PUBLISHED   WHERE TO SUBMIT   SPECIAL COMMENT   E-MAIL/WEBSITE INFORMATION

☑ **ATLANTA REVIEW; POETRY 2003**, P.O. Box 8248, Atlanta GA 31106. E-mail: dan@atlantareview.com. Website: www.atlantareview.com. Established 1994. **Editor:** Dan Veach.
• Work published in this review has been included in the *Pushcart Prize* anthologies.
Magazine Needs: *Atlanta Review* is a semiannual primarily devoted to poetry, but also featuring fiction, interviews, essays, and fine art. Wants "quality poetry of genuine human appeal." Has published poetry by Seamus Heaney, Derek Walcott, Maxine Kumin, and Naomi Shihab Nye. *Atlanta Review* is 128 pages, digest-sized, professionally printed on acid-free paper, flat-spined, glossy color cover, with b&w artwork. Receives about 10,000 poems/year, accepts about 1%. Press run is 2,500 for 2,000 subscribers (50 are libraries), 1,000 shelf sales. Single copy: $6; subscription: $10. Sample: $5.
How to Submit: No previously published poems. No e-mail submissions unless outside North America. Issue deadlines are June 1 and December 1. Time between acceptance and publication is 3 months. Seldom comments on rejected poems. Guidelines available for SASE. Responds in 2 weeks. Pays 2 copies plus author's discounts. Acquires first North American serial rights.
Also Offers: *Atlanta Review* also sponsors POETRY 2004, an annual international poetry competition. Prizes: $2,003, $500, and $250, plus 50 International Merit Awards. Winners announced in leading literary publications. All entries considered for publication in *Atlanta Review*. Entry fee: $5 for the first poem, $2 for each additional. No entry form or guidelines necessary. Postmark deadline: May 11, 2004.
Advice: "We are giving today's poets the international audience they truly deserve."

TYPES OF POETRY ACCEPTED   ADDITIONAL INFORMATION   DESCRIPTION OF PUBLICATION   SUBMISSION DETAILS

ⓘ ***For More Information***

If you're interested in writing for greeting card companies, WritersMarket.com (www.writersmarket.com), the online subscription-based companion to *Writer's Market*, includes a section devoted to the greeting card/giftware industry. If you write song lyrics as well as poetry, *Songwriter's Market* (Writer's Digest Books) is an ideal resource for this field and is available through your local library or bookstore, or can be ordered directly through the publisher at (800)448-0915 or www.writersdigest.com.

Submission Tracker

Poem Title	Publication/ Contest	Editor/Contact	Date Sent	Date Returned	Date Accepted	Date Published	Pay Received	Comments

Frequently Asked Questions

There are important questions we hear regularly at *Poet's Market*, so it made sense to provide our readers with a handy FAQ section ("frequently asked questions"). The following answers provide the expert knowledge you need to submit your poetry like a pro.

Important Note: Most basic questions such as "How many poems should I send?", "How long should I wait for a reply?", and "Are simultaneous submissions okay?" can be answered by simply reading the listings in the Publishers of Poetry section. See the introduction to that section for an explanation of the information contained in the listings. Also, see the Glossary of Listing Terms on page 511.

Is it okay to submit handwritten poems?

Usually no. Now and then a publisher or editor makes an exception and accepts handwritten manuscripts. However, check the preferences stated in each listing. If no mention is made of handwritten submissions, assume your poetry should be typed or computer-printed.

How should I format my poems for submission to magazines and journals?

If you're submitting poems by regular mail (also referred to as *land mail*, *postal mail*, or *snail mail*), follow this format:

Poems should be typed or computer-printed on white 8½ × 11 paper of at least 20 lb. weight. Left, right, and bottom margins should be at least one inch. Starting ½ inch from the top of the page, type your name, address, telephone number, and e-mail address (if you have one), and number of lines in the poem in the *upper right* corner, individual lines, single spaced. Space down about six lines and type the poem title, either centered or flush left. The title may appear in all caps or in upper and lower case. Space down another two lines (at least) and begin to type your poem. Poems are usually single spaced, although some magazines may request double-spaced submissions. (Be alert to each market's preferences.) Double space between stanzas. Type one poem to a page. For poems longer than one page, type your name in the *upper left* corner; on the next line type a key word from the title of your poem, the page number, and indicate whether the stanza begins or is continued on the new page (i.e., NEEDING SLEEP, Page 2, continue stanza *or* begin new stanza).

If you're submitting poems by e-mail:

First, make sure the publication accepts e-mail submissions. This information, when available, is included in all *Poet's Market* listings. In most cases include poems within the body of your e-mail, *not* as attachments. This is the preference of many editors accepting e-mail submissions because of the danger of viruses, the possibility of software incompatibility, and other concerns. Editors who consider e-mail attachments taboo may even delete the message without ever opening the attachment.

Of course, other editors do accept, and even prefer e-mail submissions as attachments. This information should be clearly stated in the market listing. If it's not, you're probably safer submitting your poems in the body of the e-mail. (All the more reason to pay close attention to details given in the listings.)

Note, too, the number of poems the editor recommends including in the e-mail submission. If no quantity is given specifically for e-mails, go with the number of poems an editor recommends submitting in general. Identify your submission with a notation in the subject line. Some editors simply want the words "Poetry Submission" while others want poem titles. Check the market listing for preferences. If you're uncertain about any aspect of e-mail submission formats, double-check the website (if available) for information or contact the publication for directions.

If you're submitting poems by disk:

Submit poems by disk *only* when the publication indicates this is acceptable. Even then, if no formatting preferences are given, contact the publisher for specifics before sending the disk. Always include a hardcopy (i.e., printed copy) of your submission with the disk.

What is a chapbook? How is it different from a regular poetry book?

A chapbook is a booklet averaging 24-50 pages in length (some may be shorter), usually digest sized (5½×8½, although chapbooks can come in all sizes, even published within the pages of a magazine). Typically a chapbook is saddle-stapled with a soft cover (card or special paper); however, chapbooks can also be produced with a plain paper cover the same weight as the pages, especially if the booklet is photocopied.

A chapbook is a much smaller collection of poetry than a full-length book (which runs anywhere from 50 pages to well over 100 pages, longer for "best of" collections and retrospectives). There are probably more poetry chapbooks being published than full-length books, and that's an important point to consider. Don't think of the chapbook as a poor relation to the full-length collection. While it's true a chapbook won't attract big reviews, qualify for major prizes, or find national distribution through large bookstores, it's a terrific way for a poet to build an audience (and reputation) in increments, while developing the kind of publishing history that may eventually attract the attention of a book publisher. (See In Praise of the Humble Chapbook on page 17 for advice and perspectives on chapbook publication.)

Although some presses consider chapbook-length submissions, many choose manuscripts through competitions. Check each publisher's listing for requirements, send for guidelines or visit the website (absolutely vital if a competition is involved), and check out some sample chapbooks the press has already produced (these are usually available from the publisher). Chapbook publishers are usually just as choosy as book publishers about the quality of work they accept. Submit your best work in a professional manner. (See the Chapbook Publishers Index on page 516 for markets that consider chapbook manuscripts.)

How do I format a collection of poems to submit to a book/chapbook publisher?

Before you send a manuscript to a book/chapbook publisher, request guidelines (or consult the publisher's website, if one is available). Requirements vary regarding formatting, query letters and samples, length, and other considerations. Usually you will be using 8½×11 20 lb. paper; left, right, and bottom margins of at least one inch; your name and title of your collection in the top left corner of every page; one poem to a page (although poems certainly may run longer than one page); and pages numbered consecutively. Individual publisher requirements may include a title page, table of contents, credits page (indicating where previously published poems originally appeared), and biographical note.

If you're submitting your poetry book or chapbook manuscript to a competition, you *must* read and follow the guidelines. Failure to do so could disqualify your manuscript. Guidelines for a competition may call for a special title page, a minimum and maximum number of pages, the absence of the poet's name anywhere in the manuscript, and even a special entry form to accompany the submission.

What is a cover letter? Do I have to send one? What should it say?

A cover letter is your introduction to the editor, telling him a little about yourself and your work. Most editors indicate their cover letter preferences in their listings in the Publishers of Poetry section. If an editor states that a cover letter is "required," absolutely send one! It's also better to send one if a cover letter is "preferred." Experts disagree on the necessity and appropriateness of cover letters, so use your own judgment when preferences aren't clear in the listing.

A cover letter should be professional but also allow you to present your work in a personal manner. (See the fictional cover letter on page 10 as an example.) Keep your letter brief, no more than one page. Address your letter to the correct contact person. (Use "Poetry Editor" if no contact name appears in the listing.) Include your name, address, phone number, and e-mail address (if available). If a biographical note is requested, include 2-3 lines about your job, interests, why you write poetry, etc. Avoid praising yourself or your poems in your letter (your submission should speak for itself). Include titles (or first lines) of the poems you're submitting. List a few of your most recent publishing credits, but no more than five. (If you haven't published any poems yet, you may skip this. However, be aware that some editors are interested in and make an effort to publish new writers.) Show your familiarity with the magazine to which you're submitting—comment on a poem you saw printed there, tell the editor why you chose to submit to her magazine, mention poets the magazine has published. Use a business-style format for a professional appearance, and proofread carefully; typos, misspellings, and other errors make a poor first impression. Remember that editors are people, too. Respect, professionalism, and kindness go a long way in poet/editor relationships.

What is a SASE? An IRC (with SAE)?

A SASE is a self-addressed stamped envelope. Don't let your submission leave home without it! You should also include a SASE if you send an inquiry to an editor. If your submission is too large for an envelope (for instance, a bulky book-length collection of poems), use a box and include a self-addressed mailing label with adequate return postage paper clipped to it.

An IRC is an International Reply Coupon, enclosed in place of a SASE with manuscripts submitted to foreign markets. Each coupon is equivalent in value to the minimum postage rate for an unregistered airmail letter. IRCs may be exchanged for postage stamps at post offices in all foreign countries that are members of the Universal Postal Union (UPU). When you provide the adequate number of IRCs and a self-addressed envelope (SAE), you give a foreign editor financial means to return your submission (U.S. postage stamps cannot be used to send mail *to* the United States from outside the country). Purchase price is $1.75 per coupon. Call your local post office to check for availability (sometimes only larger post offices sell them).

To save trouble and money, poets sometimes send disposable manuscripts to foreign markets and inform the editor to discard the manuscript after it's been read. Some enclose an IRC and SAE for reply only; others establish a deadline after which they will withdraw the manuscript from consideration and market it elsewhere.

How much postage does my submission need?

As much as it takes; you do *not* want your manuscript to arrive postage due! Purchase a postage scale or take your manuscript to the post office for weighing. Remember you'll need postage on two envelopes: the one containing your submission and SASE, and the return envelope itself. Submissions without SASEs usually will not be returned (and possibly may not even be read).

First Class Postage is 37 cents for the first ounce, 23 cents for each additional ounce up to 13 ounces. So, if your submission weighs in at five ounces, you'll need to apply $1.29 in postage. Note that three pages of poetry, a cover letter, and a SASE can be mailed for one First-Class stamp using a #10 (business-size) envelope; the SASE should be either a #10 envelope folded in thirds or a #9 envelope. Larger envelopes may require different rates, so check with your post office.

Mail over 13 ounces is sent Priority Mail automatically. Priority Mail Flat Rate, using the envelope provided by the Postal Service, costs $3.85 regardless of weight or destination. If sending a bulky manuscript (a full-length book manuscript, for instance), check with the post office for rates. (There's lots of valuable information on the USPS website at www.usps.gov; the Canadian site is www.canadapost.ca.)

Perry Lineskanner
1954 Eastern Blvd.
Pentameter, OH 45007
(852)555-5555
soneteer@trochee.vv.cy

April 24, 2004

Spack Saddlestaple, Editor
The Squiggler's Digest
Double-Toe Press
P.O. Box 54X
Submission Junction, AZ 85009

Dear Mr. Saddlestaple:

Enclosed are three poems for your consideration for *The Squiggler's Digest*: "His Tired Feet," "Boogie Lunches," and "Circling Piccadilly."

Although I'm a long-time reader of *The Squiggler's Digest*, this is my first submission to your publication. However, my poetry has appeared in other magazines, including *The Bone-Whittle Review*, *Bumper Car Reverie*, and *Stock Still*. I've won several awards through the annual *Buckeye Versefest!* contests and my chapbook manuscript was a finalist in the competition sponsored by Hollow Banana Press. While I devote a great deal of time to poetry (both reading and writing), I'm employed as a coffeehouse manager—which inspires more poetry than you might imagine!

Thank you for the opportunity to submit my work. Your time and attention are much appreciated, and I look forward to hearing from you.

Sincerely,

Perry Lineskanner

An example of what to include in a cover letter. Note: The names used in this letter are intended to be fictional; any resemblance to real people, publications, or presses is purely coincidental.

For complete U.S. Postal Service information, including rates and increases, a postage calculator, and the option to buy stamps online with a credit card, see their website at www.usps.gov. Canadian Postal Service information is available at www.canadapost.ca.

What does it mean when an editor says "no previously published" poems? Does this include poems that have appeared in anthologies?

If your poem appears *anywhere* in print for a public audience, it's considered "previously" published. That includes magazines, anthologies, websites and online magazines, and even programs (say for a church service, wedding, etc.). See the following explanation of rights, especially *second serial (reprint) rights* and *all rights* for additional concerns about previously published material.

What rights should I offer for my poems? What do these different rights mean?

Usually editors indicate in their listings what rights they acquire. Most journals and magazines license *first rights* (a.k.a. *first serial rights*), which means the poet offers the right to publish the poem for the first time in any periodical. All other rights to the material remain with the poet. (Note that some editors state that rights to poems "revert to authors upon publication" when first rights are acquired.) When poems are excerpted from a book prior to publication and printed in a magazine/journal, this is also called *first serial rights*. The addition of *North American* indicates the editor is the first to publish a poem in a U.S. or Canadian periodical. The poem can still be submitted to editors outside of North America or to those who acquire reprint rights.

When a magazine/journal licenses *one-time rights* to a poem (also known as *simultaneous rights*), the editor has *nonexclusive* rights to publish the poem once. The poet can submit that same poem to other publications at the same time (usually markets that don't have overlapping audiences).

Editors/publishers open to submissions of work already published elsewhere seek *second serial (reprint) rights*. The poet is obliged to inform them where and when the poem previously appeared so they can give proper credit to the original publication. In essence, chapbook or book collections license reprint rights, listing the magazines in which poems previously appeared somewhere in the book (usually on the copyright page or separate credits page).

If a publisher or editor requires you to relinquish *all rights*, be aware that you are giving up ownership of that poem or group of poems. You cannot resubmit the work elsewhere, nor can you include it in a poetry collection without permission or negotiating for reprint rights to be returned to you. Before you agree to this type of arrangement, ask the editor first if she is willing to acquire first rights instead of all rights. If she refuses, simply write a letter withdrawing your work from consideration. Some editors will reassign rights to a writer after a given amount of time, such as one year.

With the growth in Internet publishing opportunities, *electronic rights* have become very important. These cover a broad range of electronic media, including online magazines, CD recordings of poetry readings, and CD-ROM editions of magazines. When submitting to an electronic market of any kind, find out what rights the market acquires upfront (many online magazines also stipulate the right to archive poetry they've published so it's continually available on their websites).

What is a copyright? Should I have my poems copyrighted before I submit them for publication?

Copyright is a proprietary right that gives you the power to control your work's reproduction, distribution, and public display or performance, as well as its adaptation to other forms. In other words, you have legal right to the exclusive publication, sale, or distribution of your poetry. What's more, your "original works of authorship" are protected as soon as they are "fixed in a tangible form of expression," or written down. Since March 1989, copyright notices are no longer required to secure protection, so it's not necessary to include them on your poetry manuscript. Also, in many editors' minds copyright notices signal the work of amateurs distrustful and paranoid about having work stolen.

If you still want to indicate copyright, use the (c) symbol or the word *copyright*, your name, and the year. Furthermore, if you wish you can register your copyright with the Copyright Office for a $30 fee. (Since paying $30 per poem is costly and impractical, you may prefer to copyright a group of poems for that single fee.) Further information is available from the U.S. Copyright Office, Library of Congress, Washington DC 20559-6000. You can also call the Copyright Public Information Office at (202)707-3000 between 8:30 a.m. and 5:00 p.m. weekdays (EST). Copyright forms can be ordered from (202)707-9100 or downloaded from www.loc.gov/copyright (this Library of Congress website includes advice on filling out forms, general copyright information, and links to copyright-related websites).

Special note regarding Copyright Office mail delivery: The "effective date of registration" for copyright applications is usually the day the Copyright Office actually receives all elements of the application (application form, fee, and copies of work being registered). Because of security concerns, all USPS and private-carrier mail is being screened off-site prior to arrival at the Copyright Office. This can add 3-5 days to delivery time and could, therefore, impact the effective date of registration.

Four Editors Discuss Turn-Ons, Turnoffs, and Slush Pile Trends

BY WILL ALLISON

Each of the magazine editors participating in this roundtable—Brian Henry of *Verse*, Wendy Lesser of *Threepenny Review*, David Milofsky of *Colorado Review*, and Dale Smith of *Skanky Possum*—published two or more poems that were selected for the 2002 edition of *The Best American Poetry*, the country's most widely read poetry anthology.

(For more information on the magazines featured in this interview, please see the individual listings in the Publishers of Poetry section, page 27.)

Who reads the poetry submissions at your magazine, and what criteria are used in choosing the poems you publish?

Brian Henry, **Verse:** Most submissions go through the *Verse* office at the University of Georgia, where I teach. I quickly go through them all, to see what is coming in and who is submitting, then pass them along to my assistant editors. I occasionally make notes on submissions that I think deserve close attention. The assistant editors read the poems and discuss them (about 100 poems each week) at weekly editorial meetings. For a poem to make it past the assistant editors, it first must be interesting—it literally must catch someone's interest. If the poem does not engage the readers on the levels of language or content, it will be returned. Poems that stand out in their style or content fare better in the initial process than poems that resemble so many other poems that come in. Poems that employ traditional or nonce form with flair or great skill tend to fare well, as do successful experimental poems. About 5% of the submissions come back to me, and about 10% of those (or ½% of the total) are strong enough for me to forward them to my co-editor, Andrew Zawacki, with a recommendation to publish them. He and I generally agree on submissions, so if one of us thinks something should be in the magazine, it almost always is accepted.

Wendy Lesser, **Threepenny Review:** All manuscripts—poetry, fiction, and nonfiction—are read by one of the two editors, myself and Francie Lin (my longtime associate editor). Particularly promising material is read by both of us. Since we receive more than 100 manuscripts a week (and a manuscript might include up to five poems), we can't give detailed attention to everything, so treasures may occasionally slip by us—but we do read all the unsolicited manuscripts that follow our guidelines (that is, they should come by regular mail, not e-mail; they should include a SASE; and they should not be sent to us during the June-September reading break). All of these guidelines are available on the "submissions" page of our website, www.threepennyreview.com.

David Milofsky, **Colorado Review:** We have three first readers who are graduate interns in poetry at the *Review*. Their job is essentially to skim the best work from the nearly 6,000 submissions we receive each year, but we do ask them to be generous since they are not making final decisions. Poems that survive are then sent to either Jorie Graham or Donald Revell, our senior

---

WILL ALLISON*'s short stories have appeared or are forthcoming in* Kenyon Review, Shenandoah, American Short Fiction, Florida Review, *and other magazines. He can be reached at willalliso@aol.com.*

poetry editors. Occasionally, we have a guest editor like Forrest Gander who will also see poems. I also read a number of submissions and generally but not always defer to the judgments of our poetry editors. I'm referring here obviously to the so-called slush pile. Many poems are also sent directly to the poetry editors or to me and do not go through the process described above.

Dale Smith, **Skanky Possum***:* I edit *Skanky Possum* with my wife, the poet Hoa Nguyen. One of us reads everything received in the mail. Mostly, since our time and budget are limited (we publish only twice a year), we make decisions based on what fits thematically or formally with each issue. There aren't many firm requirements. We assume familiarity with our magazine and with the writers we have published. Affinity for the nocturnal rummaging of *Didelphis marsupialis* is a plus. It's also important for us to choose work that achieves the upper limit of poetic vitality and beauty designated by our adjective "skanky."

What are the most common reasons you turn poems away?

Brian Henry, **Verse***:* Poetry is a language art, and for a poem to engage our attention, it must do so through language. Many of the poems submitted to *Verse* could work just as well in prose, which we consider a flaw; and though we publish a lot of prose poems and we recently devoted two large issues to prose, we do look for poems that earn their lines and line breaks. So at one level, we have high expectations for the way a poem is written.

A lot of the poems we receive are competently written—most likely the result of the prevalence of graduate creative writing programs and their emphasis on craft—but do not contain a concept, idea, atmosphere, argument, or tone that we find essential. Most poems do not distinguish themselves. We want every poem published in *Verse* to demand and maintain our interest on the levels of language and content, however a poem defines its own content.

Wendy Lesser, **Threepenny Review***:* Basically, [because] we don't think they are good enough. Sometimes we have to turn things away because they are tailored to a past issue (in other words, we might have just published a tribute to W. G. Sebald, and then someone sends us a poem about W. G. Sebald, which we can't use because we've just done that). More often, though, it is simply the quality of the poetry as poetry that makes us turn it down.

David Milofsky, **Colorado Review***:* Poems that are imitative in the extreme or trendy in some other way stand out for me. I should also say that since we try to be eclectic, it concerns me when we seem to be taking too many poems that hew to one school or another. But for the most part, poems that are mannered or have brilliant surfaces without being truly accomplished or moving are unlikely to appeal to me.

Dale Smith, **Skanky Possum***:* We reject poems if they're over-long, typed in a small typeface, mailed without a SASE, or e-mailed to us. If they fail to achieve a certain possum logic or if they condescend to that marsupial intelligence, we toss them from the litter for the fire ants to eat.

On another note, we are always looking for reviews, essays, and commentary for our web newsletter, *The Possum Pouch* (www.skankypossum.com/pouch.htm). It's updated every two months and will soon be re-organized into a blog format. The goal there is to generate writing about poetry and to extend discussion of issues important to contemporary poetics.

What trends are you seeing in the slush pile? For example, did you notice any changes in submissions following the September 11 attacks, and, if so, did those changes last?

Brian Henry, **Verse***:* We have received a lot of September 11 poems. One poet sent a batch the week after the attacks and wrote on the envelope "9/11 poems: open immediately!" We generally do not let such imperatives sway us; that submission was read no sooner or later than the others that arrived that week. We still receive September 11 poems, but the quality of those poems has improved, probably because of the time that has passed, which has allowed poets to reflect more deeply on the event and to revise their poems.

Wendy Lesser, **Threepenny Review***:* Yes, we noticed an immediate flow of September 11 material, almost all of which was unusable. (The notable exception was Frank Bidart's poem "Curse," which alluded to the events without naming them exactly. We did publish that, generating both controversy and acclaim.) We are still getting some of this stuff, but mostly there is no discernible trend at the moment—just the usual batches of spiritual awakening, sad family event, relationship breakup, or nature stuff.

David Milofsky, **Colorado Review***:* Since I don't generally read the slush pile, I can't answer this intelligently, but long lines seem to be in this year, as they have been for a while. I can't say that 9/11 has had much impact on the submissions I've seen.

Dale Smith, **Skanky Possum***:* We've seen few responses in poems to September 11. Which is probably good. It will take a while for that to settle, collectively and privately. We received from one writer a clipping from a Kansas news column about a possum fry early in the last century whereat hundreds of our totem friends were slaughtered in celebration of a Midwest holiday. Others in our slush pile simply can't grip the fur on mamma possum's back tight enough.

How would you characterize your level of commitment to publishing new and emerging poets? Do you take into consideration a poet's publication history (or lack thereof)?

Brian Henry, **Verse***:* We have a strong and enduring commitment to emerging poets. We published a feature in 1999 on younger American poets, and every issue of *Verse* includes poems by a number of new or emerging poets. One of the main reasons I founded Verse Press was to foster the work of new poets. We also try to have as many books by emerging poets reviewed as possible, as first or second books are often overlooked by critics.

We notice if a poet has published in magazines that we admire or have published in, and that does make us more likely to read the work more carefully. We actually take unpublished poets more seriously than widely published poets whose work has appeared in magazines we've never heard of.

Wendy Lesser, **Threepenny Review***:* We try not to take it into account at all. I am always pleased when it turns out that we are publishing someone for the first time—this happens about three or four times a year—but we make no specific effort to do this. That is, we are open to new poets but we do not favor them particularly. In recent years, some of the best poems have been by our newer poets—Anna Ziegler and Karen Bjorneby, for instance, both wrote poems that ended up on our website and received lots of praise from readers.

David Milofsky, **Colorado Review***:* Publishing new poets is extremely important to us and we try to reserve a significant amount of space in each issue for people who have not published with us before. This is something I track in each issue and frequently correspond with our poetry editors about, though it's not really necessary since they share the same value. I do feel that with all successful magazines it's a problem, since more and more established writers are sending to us and also deserve publication.

Dale Smith, **Skanky Possum***:* Every issue presents established poets along with newer names. We look at how a particular poem contributes to the larger conversations our writers engage in.

We're looking for some skank, of course, anywhere we can get it. Not your ordinary kind of skankiness, but down and dirty, waddling-across-your-yard-into-the-gutter skank. Anyone, green or grizzled with words, can hop in our pouch. But somewhere in their poem there'd better be a little whiff of you-know-what.

Work from your magazine has been selected for the annual *Best American Poetry* anthology. Do such honors typically surprise you? Or do you have a sense, as you're publishing a poem, that it will be one that draws attention? And what does it mean to you as an editor to have work selected for such anthologies?

Brian Henry, **Verse:** I was delighted the first time it happened for *Verse* under my editorship (in *The Best American Poetry 1997*), but I don't get too exercised about it now. There are so many magazines out there, I think it would be foolish to expect to be in every edition of *The Best American Poetry* unless one edits an ultra-established magazine like *Poetry* or *The New Yorker*. And being in *The Best American Poetry* does not make a magazine better than a magazine not included in the anthology. Because the editor of *The Best American Poetry* changes every year, the editorial focus changes, which means a magazine like *Verse*, because it is not a catchall or mainstream poetry magazine, will be overlooked by certain editors. *Verse* also publishes a lot of special features by non-U.S. poets, which means we could have a year in which very few poems by U.S. poets appear in the magazine. From a practical standpoint, appearing in *The Best American Poetry* results in more submissions, maybe a few more subscriptions.

Wendy Lesser, **Threepenny Review:** It's always great to get things into the anthologies, and it doesn't surprise me now, because it's been happening for so many years. We usually have things in *Best American Poetry*, the *Puschart Prize*, and other anthologies; I would say that at least one of our poems (generally more than that) gets anthologized somewhere every year. It's a nice form of recognition, for the magazine and for the poets.

David Milofsky, **Colorado Review:** I seldom have a sense as to which poem will be honored, but we've been designated often enough now that it's not really a surprise when we're included in a prize anthology like *Best American* or the *Pushcart Prize*. As an editor I can only say that it's very gratifying to be recognized; at the same time, I think there's a lot of fine work that goes unrecognized, in our magazine and elsewhere. That is, prizes are great and we love to receive them, but we're under no illusion that all the good work is in prize anthologies. And of course the real honor is to the poets whose poems are chosen, not to the editors who are fortunate enough to print the poems.

Dale Smith, **Skanky Possum**: *Skanky Possum* is about as low-fi as it gets in publishing (each issue is Xeroxed, stapled, and bound with hand-painted covers), so yes, we were surprised that so many poems were chosen for the prestigious *BAP 2002*. But our poets have given us consistently good work for many years. That they should be so publicly recognized now by the mainstream print world is wonderful, and I'm happy to have participated in that process. We're honored, too, by Robert Creeley's commitment to our little marsupial movement. I feel that we've finally let ourselves down out of a tree, or crawled up out of the gutter, so to say, onto the highway of the American culture industry.

In Praise of the Humble Chapbook

BY VIVÉ GRIFFITH

They can be held easily in the hand, tucked graciously into a bag, slipped safely into a pocket. They can be read in one sitting. They are inexpensive to produce and purchase, and thus provide a perfect means for getting more new poetry into the world. Their compressed form encourages innovation. Their established relationship with the fine letter press makes them a vehicle for collaboration between artists and writers. They are so easy to read and pass around that conversations and communities are built around them.

These unique gifts of the poetry chapbook indicate why it has long played a vital and important role in American poetry. Many discussions treat these slim volumes as full-length books in waiting, almost-books, even practice books. But as a chapbook author and a chapbook fan, I see in that approach a diminishment of what the form has to offer. These approachable, accessible books serve their art today as they have since their inception hundreds of years ago.

Early editions

The word chapbook derives from the "chapmen" of England and Scotland, itinerant agents who traveled from town to town peddling small books for a few pence apiece. I love the image of these men of yore with their packs stuffed full of stories. The original chapbooks were often made from one piece of paper folded into a single gathering, and they generally ran 24 pages, roughly the same length of today's chapbook. Quality varied, but their popularity was secure.

It was through these chapbooks that the stories we still tell today were spread and savored. Chapbooks told the tale of Tom Thumb, Mother Hubbard, and Jack the Giant Killer. They contained abridged forms of Don Quixote and Robinson Crusoe. They were often illustrated with a few crude woodcuts, and they captured the imagination from the 16th to 19th centuries.

It's impossible to point to the moment chapbooks entered the American poetry scene, because they've almost always been around as pamphlets, artists' books, and self-published books. Thus, they are inseparable from how poetry developed in our culture. Alice Quinn, Executive Director of the Poetry Society of America (PSA) and poetry editor at *The New Yorker* magazine, believes the chapbook has played a key role in American poetry. "They have had a long and fabulous history," she says.

Some of that history rises from the chapbook's close relationship with experimental work. Historically, poetic movements that didn't find their voices being heard in the mainstream press turned to self-publishing. And that self-publishing often took the form of chapbooks. It still does today. I've seen chapbooks sitting next to the register in little coffeehouses or for sale after readings by local poets. I've had a poetic acquaintance slip me a chapbook after chatting over our latest projects. The result is inevitably one of being treated to something I couldn't have found elsewhere.

The growth of chapbook publishing

To poet Joshua Beckman, this through-the-back-door sensibility is how chapbooks make their greatest impact. It's less important that they be sold in bookstores across the country than that

---

VIVÉ GRIFFITH *lives in Austin, Texas, where she teaches poetry in the community. Her poetry and stories have appeared in* Gettysburg Review, Black Warrior Review, *and elsewhere.*

they are distributed hand-to-hand, that they make the direct connection between poet and reader. "Publishing a chapbook provides an opportunity to be part of a poetic community," he says, "and to become part of a dialogue with other people who are writing."

While many chapbooks have been and are being published off the radar, chapbook publication by established presses and organizations has grown steadily for 50 years. Quinn points to long-standing series like the Pocket Poet Series from San Francisco's City Lights Books. Though not titled a "chapbook," these tiny books that first sold for $1 each brought the words of Lawrence Ferlinghetti, Allen Ginsberg, Diane di Prima, and others directly to readers both serious and curious.

Ferlinghetti's *Pictures of the Gone World*, first published in 1955, runs 27 pages, and the lines move helter-skelter across the page. Maybe this could have been part of a full-length, full-

Advice About Chapbook Preparation

Here are specific things to keep in mind when preparing your own chapbook:

1) **Make it coherent**. This is perhaps even more important for the chapbook than for the full-length collection. The compressed form dictates that what's inside not be simply a disconnected sampling. For this reason, the chapbook is especially friendly to the poetry sequence and the long poem. If you are not working with a sequence, consider what elements will help the poems speak to one another.

I have chapbooks on my shelf that contain poems linked by subject matter—the life of Christ, a difficult relationship with a mother, a year spent as a foreigner in Japan. But subject matter is not the only means of creating coherence. Sometimes a strong sense of voice, music, or form can connect a chapbook.

2) **Pay a lot of attention to order**. Because the chapbook can be and often is read in one sitting, the flow from one poem to the next is extremely important. Readers are less likely to pick it up and read from a random spot.

Sarabande's Sarah Gorham says the successful chapbooks she's seen have a real sense of narrative arc. They have a clear beginning, middle, and end. Offer the reader a sense of completion when the chapbook ends.

3) **Work with the physical form**. Eavan Boland says, "Because the chapbook is brief in the space it sets out and often handsome in the frame it offers, it raises the reader's expectations in a subtle way." The reader is holding in his hand an object that suggests it is complete in itself. Think about the placement of poems on a page. Think about integrating artwork and the visual, especially if you are self-publishing.

The Center for Book Arts in New York City runs an annual chapbook competition that relates to their mission of keeping alive the tradition of letter press and fine press printing. Executive Director Rory Golden says the connection between the letter press and the poet is obvious. "Poets appreciate the attention to the work and the fine object."

4) **Be willing to play**. The chapbook finds its roots in the experimental. While many contests are geared toward seeing the chapbook as a step toward a full-length book, many chapbook readers are still looking to the chapbook as a way of rooting out the new and interesting. Chapbooks open up dialogues. They create communities. Treat them with that possibility.

Editor's note: If you're interested in self-publishing a chapbook, take a carefully assembled collection of your poems to several local printers to discuss format, paper, coverstock, and costs. Get several quotes, and don't overlook "quick print" shops. Don't forget to discuss how your home computer can save you money (from typesetting and laying out the chapbook yourself to having it printed directly from your disk).

size book, but there's something perfect about its incarnation in these small pages. There is a narrative, and there is a sense of form, and the chapbook holds them both. Its ultimate adaptability may partly account for the recent explosion in chapbook publication.

Take, for example, Sarabande Book's launch of their Quarternote Series featuring such poetic superstars as James Tate, Frank Bidart, and Louise Glück. Editor Sarah Gorham explains, "We wanted to add some of our favorite poets to our list without infringing on their established publishing contracts." Chapbooks were allowable within those contracts, and Sarabande could publish a complete piece by each poet. In addition, choosing chapbooks as its medium gave Sarabande other benefits.

"Our philosophy was to make this series accessible to students," says Gorham, "and the low price makes it possible for people to buy them. Plus, the chapbook is highly collectible, and we hope to be able to offer a boxed set at some point."

The bulk of the expansion in chapbook publishing still comes in providing a forum for new and emerging poets. This isn't surprising. Despite a corresponding burgeoning in first-book publications, there is far more good poetry being written than there are means of disseminating it. Book contests are glutted with submissions, and journals can't keep up with the amount of work coming in. Plenty of poetry languishes for years out of sight of readers, and this isn't good for the individual poet, nor for poetry as a whole.

Poet Eavan Boland has judged several chapbook contests for emerging poets. She says, "In the work of a new poet, [chapbooks] serve both as a sampling and shape of the first book which is to come. They allow the new poet to assemble the very best of their work in an intense and representative way."

The PSA recently inaugurated a series of four annual chapbook fellowships, confirming the respect chapbooks garner today. Four distinguished poets will choose a manuscript each for publication, and the published chapbooks will be sent to approximately 350 top PSA contributors, as well as being available for sale. In this forum the chapbook is guaranteed a national readership.

Program Associate Brett Fletcher Lauer says, given what the PSA was already doing with its Norma Farber First Book Award and other awards, the chapbook "seemed like the most organic form for opening the field and presenting more poets to the public."

Quinn explains the original intent was to have a festival featuring 20 new American poets. "We thought it would be exciting and dramatic if a few of the poets were at a very early stage in their careers and if we could publish them for the first time ourselves," she says. "We knew it would mean a great deal to these poets if their manuscripts were selected by tremendously distinguished poets, so we asked John Ashbery, Eavan Boland, Carl Phillips, and C.D. Wright to be the judges. Their choices and our original sixteen make up our list of twenty." The PSA received nearly 700 manuscripts, and clearly the chapbooks they publish will provide a luminous introduction for the new writer.

Value of chapbook publication

On any level, chapbook publication has great value. When Kent State University Press published my chapbook *Weeks in This Country* in 2000, I knew it would help facilitate the career I was building as a writer. However, the experience was much larger than I ever imagined.

It started years before I won the contest. In fact, it started with the very first chapbook I put together. As a new writer, I took on creating a chapbook manuscript as a way of consolidating work that felt, until then, rather scattershot. We tend to write poem by poem, without a larger conception of what we are creating. The first time I made a collection of my poems, I realized I had never looked objectively at what I had written. I had to identify themes, find connections, see what fit and didn't fit. Once I had done that, I started thinking about my future work as part of a larger whole.

Beckman says, "Once you have the idea of a book available as an option, your imagination is expanded in terms of what you can do with your poetry. You see the chapbook as an imagined future for it." He goes on to say, "Each time you put together a book, you are doing something interesting and challenging for your own work."

With *Weeks in This Country*, I knew I had been writing for several years around themes of travel. When I pulled the poems together into a cohesive whole, I found the group was stronger than the poems standing alone. And when Maggie Anderson, editor of Kent State's chapbook series, called me to say they wanted to publish my chapbook, I was thrilled.

One of the great gifts publishing a chapbook offers the young writer is the chance to experience the publishing process firsthand, even before she has a full length collection. In finalizing my chapbook with the press, I made edits based on Anderson's suggestions. I collected endorsements for the back cover. I wrote a synopsis for marketing materials, dealt with an author photo and an acknowledgements page. There were readings and signings and all the things I thought I wouldn't experience until I had a full-length book.

As important was the chance to have my poems read by people who weren't sitting next to me at a workshop table or related to me by blood. Chapbooks may not appear in bookstore windows, and they are rarely reviewed in newspapers and journals. But they inevitably get work out into the world. By definition they are a means of sharing poetry, and I found handing my poems to another person in published form gave them a power and validation they hadn't had before.

Even a small run chapbook accomplishes this, and the fact that a chapbook is so cheap and accessible encourages people to give poetry a try. Friends, friends of friends, new acquaintances, strangers, and distant relatives read my book. I really believe that even if we write for ourselves, the future of poetry asks that we conceive of our work as something to be shared. This is why the chapbook exists.

Those of us interested in the future of poetry in America must be grateful for that existence and the ease with which the chapbook puts work into the world. Quinn, who worked at Knopf for 15 years before going to *The New Yorker*, says, "Poetry is very popular now. You just have to get it into people's hands." With the humble, friendly chapbook, there is a perfect fit.

Poet Beware!

BY VICTORIA STRAUSS

There are many legitimate markets and opportunities for poets. There are also many schemes and pitfalls. Some appeal to your ego, some to your frustration—and all want your money.

Vanity anthologies

Dozens of vanity anthology companies target poets. Unlike true anthologies, where writers are paid for their contributions, contributors to vanity anthologies pay the publisher.

Most vanity anthologizers operate more or less the same way. They place ads in writers' magazines and elsewhere announcing a free poetry contest, with cash prizes for the finalists and guaranteed publication for finalists and semi-finalists.

Problem is, the contest isn't a real contest. It's a marketing ploy designed to draw in paying customers. Everyone who submits receives a glowing, ego-boosting letter declaring them a semi-finalist. They're then given opportunities to spend money: $50 or more for the anthology, plus anywhere from $20 to several hundred dollars for extras such as adding a biography, having the poem read onto audio tape, having the poem mounted on a plaque or embossed on a coffee mug, joining poets' societies, and attending expensive poetry conferences (celebrity hosts often lend these events a misleading veneer of respectability).

Vanity anthology companies usually fulfill their publishing promises, so if you're just looking to see your poem in print, you may consider this a reasonable deal. But if you want a genuine publishing credit, the anthologies are not the place to obtain it. Since everyone who enters is eligible for publication, the overall quality of the published poems is poor. Anthology credits are not respected by publishing professionals. Nor do the anthologies get wide exposure. Despite the companies' claims, vanity anthologies aren't reviewed, nor are they purchased by libraries or stocked in bookstores. Nearly all are sold to the contributors themselves or their friends and family.

Subsidy publishers

A subsidy publisher charges a fee to print your book, plus provide additional services such as distribution and warehousing. For poets frustrated by the difficulty of selling poetry collections, this can look like a tempting alternative.

Be aware, though, that subsidy publishers are not in business to sell your book to the public; they're in business to sell their services to you. Most charge hugely inflated fees, and despite their promises do little or nothing to market books. (Why should they? They've already made a fat profit on what they charged you.) Worse, some subsidy publishers engage in fraudulent practices, from offering terrible contracts and producing shoddy books to printing a fraction of the promised print run (or taking your money and then failing to print anything at all). Plus, because subsidy publishers will publish anyone who can pay, subsidy-published books aren't

VICTORIA STRAUSS *is the author of six fantasy novels, including* The Arm of the Stone *and* The Garden of the Stone *(HarperCollins Eos). She serves as the vice-chair of the Writing Scams Committee for the Science Fiction and Fantasy Writers of America and maintains the Writer Beware literary scams warning website (www.sfwa.org/beware/).*

respected. A subsidy-published book won't be stocked by bookstores, and it's not likely to be reviewed.

A better alternative is one of the print-on-demand (POD) self-publishing services. These provide reliable publication for a fraction of the cost; and, in addition, make your book easy to order online and through the catalogue of a major wholesaler such as Ingram. You'll still have to market your book yourself and struggle for respect (many people regard POD self-publishing the same way they do subsidy publishing). But you're much more likely to get your money's worth.

Internet-based publishers

The power of the Internet and the ease of print-on-demand technology have made it simple for almost anyone to set up as a publisher. Many of these small presses, unlike larger houses, are eager to consider poetry collections. However, caution is definitely in order.

Some of these presses are just vanity publishers in disguise. They charge "setup" fees, or fees for adjunct services such as editing and design. Often you won't discover this until you receive the contract.

Others are "author mills," publishers that turn a profit by publishing enormous numbers of writers and selling just a hundred or so books from each. Author mills often present themselves as "traditional" because they don't require you to pay anything. As with the vanity anthologies, however, their books are marketed not to the public but to authors (who are pressured to buy their own books for resale) and their friends and family. Also, because author mills need a constant flow of new writers, they tend to accept just about everything that's submitted, regardless of quality. An author mill will put your collection in print, but it won't give you a professional publishing credit.

Even when Internet-based publishers are well intentioned, they're often run by people without publishing experience, resulting in poorly edited, unprofessional-looking books. To make matters worse, Internet-based publishers often offer terrible, non-standard contracts and are prone to running into financial and other difficulties, vanishing suddenly without a trace and leaving writers high and dry.

Do some careful checking before choosing an Internet-based publisher:

- How long has the publisher been around? Look for evidence that it has been in business a year or more, and that it has a backlist of published books. This indicates at least some stability, as well as the capacity to take a book all the way through the production process.
- Are the books edited, professionally produced, and of good physical quality? Order a couple so you can check.
- Do you have to pay? Small publishers may not be able to afford advances, but they shouldn't charge authors. Any money required as part of the publication process, including pre-purchase or pre-sale requirements, signals a publisher that relies on its authors as its main income source. It therefore doesn't have much incentive to get its books before the public.
- Are the books reasonably priced? Internet-based publishers often price their books very high—a real disincentive for readers.
- Can the books be obtained easily? A small press may have trouble getting bookstores to stock its books, but they should at least be available through the catalogue of a major wholesaler and from online booksellers. Books that can be bought only from the publisher's website or from authors won't sell many copies.
- Contact some of the publisher's authors and ask them about their experiences.

Reading fees

A small reading fee ($5 or $10) is easy to rationalize; it helps defray the expenses of the publication that's asking for it, and it won't break your pocketbook.

However, while there are some sincere, struggling publications that charge reading fees in order to survive, just as many are simply trying to turn an extra profit. Given how hard it is to tell the difference—not to mention the number of publications that *don't* charge—reading fees are usually best avoided. (Note that a reading fee isn't the same as a contest entry fee—see below.)

Contests

The lure of contests is strong. There are prizes to be won and sometimes publication to be had. Once again, though, caution is in order.

Some contests are just schemes to sell you merchandise, as with the vanity anthologies described earlier. Watch out also for "contest mills" that make a profit on the front end, via entry fees. Some advertise enormous prizes ($15,000 for the winner, $10,000 for second place, etc.) with correspondingly high entry fees ($25 or $30). Read the fine print and you may discover the contest owner reserves the right to award prizes on a pro rata basis (i.e., prize amounts are determined by the number of entrants, guaranteeing a profit for the owner no matter what). Other contest mills are run by magazines or e-zines that conduct a dozen or more contests a year, or by Internet-based groups that offer monthly contests and advertise under several different names and URLs to draw more entrants. Such contests aren't likely to employ rigorous judging standards. The prizes are nice if you win, but winning doesn't mean much professionally.

Other contests are outright fakes, run by crooked literary agencies as part of an editing or fee-charging scam, or by vanity publishers looking for paying customers.

Some questions to ask before entering:

- Who's running the contest? If it's an organization you don't recognize, verify that it's legitimate. If you can't confirm this, pass the contest over.
- Who's doing the judging? Some contests protect judges' privacy, so not naming judges isn't necessarily a warning sign. Still, if you know who the judges are, you can better assess the contest's prestige.
- How often is the contest offered? If there's a contest every month, or many contests every quarter, it may be just a money-making scheme.
- Is the entry fee appropriate? Contrary to popular belief, an entry fee (or a "reading" fee associated with entry) isn't a sign of a questionable contest. Many legitimate contests charge a fee to cover expenses and fund the prize. However, the fee should be appropriate to the contest. Anything over $15 should prompt some careful checking.
- What's the prize? The contest rules should make clear exactly what the prizes are. (And there should be contest rules, clearly stated; if not, be cautious.) Be suspicious of contests that offer enormous cash prizes (see above).

    Contests that offer publication are very appealing. However, publication isn't necessarily a sign of legitimacy. Many fake contests offer publication to winners. If the contest is sponsored by a book or chapbook publisher, carefully research the publisher before entering. Never enter a contest that requires you to accept a publishing contract—some vanity publishers trap clients this way. And there should never be an extra cost associated with a publication prize.
- Read the fine print! Contests sometimes require entrants to give up various rights, such as first publication or the right to sell the entry elsewhere. Some require you to give up copyright. And if you enter a contest online, you may be giving permission for your entry to be published on the company's website, whether you win or not.

Literary agents

Successful literary agents rarely represent poets. Unless you're already famous, poetry collections are a tough sell—plus, the poetry market simply isn't lucrative enough to make it worth most agents' while.

Beware, therefore, of literary agents whose guidelines say they accept poets or poetry collections. Nearly always, they're unscrupulous operators looking to make a living not from selling books to publishers, but from charging fees to clients. Most have no track record of sales to paying publishers.

And finally . . .

If you run across something you're not sure about, industry watchdog groups can help. Preditors & Editors (www.anotherealm.com/prededitors/) provides lists of publishers and literary agents, with warnings about those that aren't reputable. Writer Beware (www.sfwa.org/beware/) tracks contests, publishers, and literary agents; you can e-mail the staff, and they'll let you know if they've received complaints.

Pitfalls for poets are many and various. But if you do your research, keep your wits about you, and look before you leap, you'll be fine. Happy writing!

Helpful Websites

The following websites include specific information about questionable poetry publishers and awards. For additional websites important to poets, see Websites of Interest in the Resources section at the back of this book.

- Answers to frequently asked questions about poetry awards from the Academy of American Poets: *www.poets.org/awards/faq.cfm*
- Poets will find warnings and other valuable publishing information on the Preditors & Editors website: *www.anotherealm.com/prededitors/*
- Writer Beware tracks contests, publishers, and literary agents: *www.sfwa.org/beware*
- Online "Scam Kit" from The Writer's Center: *www.writer.org/scamkit.htm*

Promote Yourself and Your Work: Five Quick Tips

Whether you're a poet, editor of a magazine, or publisher with a book to sell, you want the public to know about you and what you have to offer. Here are some tips for promoting your work and increasing your audience:

1. Get involved in readings. If you're a poet, contact bookstore and coffeehouse managers to let them know you're available for readings. Find out when and where open mic readings are being held; go, sign up, and read some of your poems. If you're the editor of a magazine, organize a reading of local poets appearing in your latest issue. Be sure to provide plenty of copies for sale at the reading (and perhaps at the bookstore or coffeehouse on a permanent basis). If you're a publisher, talk to the author of your latest poetry book about scheduling a "circuit" of publicity readings within a convenient radius of his/her hometown. Arrange for a book signing to follow the readings.

2. Make connections. Explore networking, and not just locally. Groups and associations in your own area are important (and easy to reach). However, don't overlook such opportunities as state poetry societies, publishing- or poetry-oriented organizations with national affiliations, and writer's newsletters (whether their readership is county-wide or country-wide). Tap into the Internet for an overwhelming array of networking possibilities, from online forums and bulletin boards to poetry websites of every description.

3. Contact the media. Send out press releases, especially to community newspapers—often they're very open to printing newsy tidbits (such as a poet's latest award or print appearance), and they may be on the lookout for feature story possibilities (such as a small local press or literary journal). Also, the calendar sections of newspapers are ideal to promote readings and book signings. Be sure to provide all the necessary details, including your contact information.

Don't overlook TV and radio stations, which may broadcast arts and entertainment calendars at various times during the day. There may also be locally produced TV or radio programs willing to feature a poet, editor, or publisher with area connections. Contact the appropriate producer (be polite, not pushy).

Again, turn to the Internet—many electronic newsletters for writers carry all kinds of announcements about poets and poetry publishers. Check and follow their submission guidelines.

4. Get a business card. Business cards are easy to design on the computer; you can even buy special stock for printing them out yourself, or you can take your design to your local quick-print center (costs are usually quite reasonable for a generous quantity of cards). Be sure to include all pertinent information and try to make the card eye-catching but professional. And don't be shy about passing cards out everywhere to everyone.

5. Create a website. Even a basic website can be extremely valuable, whether you're a poet who wants to post some samples of your work or a press with several chapbooks to promote. A website can be as complicated or as simple as you wish. There are plenty of books and software programs available to help, even if you're a first-timer with few computer skills. There's also a lot of free information on the Web, from tutorials to HTML guides. Enter the words "basic web development" or "beginner web development" (include quotation marks) or similar phrases in your favorite search engine to call up all the resources you'll need.

Important Market Listing Information

• Listings are based on questionnaires completed by editors and on subsequent verified copy. Listings are not advertisements *nor* are markets necessarily endorsed by the editors of this book.

• Information in the listings comes directly from the publishers and is as accurate as possible. However, publications and editors come and go, and poetry needs fluctuate between the publication date of this directory and the date of purchase.

• If you are a poetry publisher and would like to be considered for a listing in the next edition, send a SASE (or SAE and IRC) with your request for a questionnaire to *Poet's Market*—QR, 4700 East Galbraith Road, Cincinnati OH 45236 or e-mail us at poetsmarket@fwpubs.com. Questionnaires received after February 15, 2004, will be held for the 2006 edition.

• *Poet's Market* reserves the right to exclude any listing that does not meet its requirements.

Complaint Procedure

If you feel you have not been treated fairly by a market listed in *Poet's Market*, we advise you to take the following steps:

• First, try to contact the market. Sometimes one phone call or letter can quickly clear up the matter. Document all your communications with the market.

• When you contact us with a complaint, provide the details of your submission, the date of your first contact with the market, and the nature of your subsequent communication.

• We will file a record of your complaint and further investigate the market.

• The number and severity of complaints will be considered when deciding whether or not to delete a market from the next edition of *Poet's Market*.

The Markets

Publishers of Poetry

Look around. You'll find poetry being published in a variety of ways: in magazines; in literary and academic journals; in books and chapbooks produced by both large and small presses; in anthologies assembled by poetry societies and other groups; on CDs and tapes that feature poets reading their own work; and on the Internet in sites ranging from individual web pages to sophisticated digital publications. There are probably others as well, not to mention new cutting-edge opportunities not yet widely known.

In this edition of *Poet's Market* we've striven to gather as much information about these markets as possible. Each listing in the Publishers of Poetry section gives an overview of the various activities for a single operation as described by the editors/publishers we queried. These include magazines/journals, books/chapbooks, contests, workshops, readings, organizations, and whatever else the editor/publisher thinks will be of interest to you. For those publishers with projects at different addresses, or who requested their activities to be broken out into the appropriate sections of the book, we've cross-referenced the listings so the overview will be complete.

HOW LISTINGS ARE FORMATTED

To organize all this information within each listing, we follow a basic format:

Symbols. Each listing begins with symbols that reflect various aspects of that operation: (▣) this market is newly established and new to this edition; (✖) this market did not appear in the 2003 edition; (✚) this is a Canadian or (▦) international market; ($) this is a cash-paying market (as opposed to one that pays in copies); (▢) this market welcomes submissions from beginning poets; (◨) this market prefers submissions from skilled, experienced poets, will consider work from beginning poets; (◕) this market prefers submissions from poets with a high degree of skill and experience; (◎) this market has a specialized focus (listed in parentheses after title); and (⊘) this market is currently closed to *all* submissions. (Keys to these symbols are listed on the inside front cover of this book; they also appear in blurbs at the bottom of pages scattered throughout each section.)

Contact Information. Next you'll find all the information you need to contact the market, as provided by each editor/publisher: names (in bold) of all operations associated with the market (with areas of specialization noted in parentheses where appropriate); regular mail address; telephone number; fax number; e-mail address; website address; year the market was established; the name of the person to contact (with that person's title in bold); and membership in small press/publishing organizations (when provided).

Magazine Needs: This is an important section to study as you research potential markets. Here you'll find the editor's or publisher's overview of the operation and stated preferences (often in his or her own words), plus a list of recently published poets; production information about the market (size of publication, printing/binding methods, art/graphics); statistics regarding the number of submissions the market receives vs. the number accepted; and distribution and price information.

How to Submit: Another important section. This one gets down to specifics—how many poems to send; minimum/maximum number of lines; preferences regarding previously published poems and simultaneous submissions, as well as electronic submissions; payment, rights, and response times; and a lot more.

Book/Chapbook Needs and How to Submit: Same as the information for magazines with added information tailored to book/chapbook publishers.

Also Offers: Check this section for contests, conferences/workshops, readings, or organizations sponsored by or affiliated with the market.

Advice: In this section you'll find direct quotes from editors and publishers about everything from pet peeves to tips on writing to views on the state of poetry today.

GETTING STARTED, FINDING MARKETS

If you don't have a publisher in mind, just begin reading through the listings, possibly making notes as you go (don't hesitate to write in the margins, underline, use highlighters; it also helps to flag markets that interest you with Post-it Notes). Browsing the listings is an effective way to familiarize yourself with the information presented and the publishing opportunities available.

If you have a specific market in mind, however, begin with the General Index. This is where *all* listings are alphabetized (i.e., all the markets included within a single listing). For instance, what if you want to check out Pickle Gas Press? If you turn to the "P" listings in the Publishers of Poetry section, you won't find this publisher. The information appears as part of *The Aardvark Adventurer* listing (along with *The Armchair Aesthete*). In the General Index, though, Pickle Gas Press is listed individually along with the page number for *The Aardvark Adventurer* so you can go straight to the source for the information you need. (Sound confusing? Try it, it works.)

The General Index also lists markets from the 2003 edition that don't appear in this book, along with a two-letter code explaining the absence (see the introduction to the General Index on page 549 for an explanation of these codes). In addition, markets that have changed names since the 2003 edition are listed in the General Index, cross-referenced to the new titles.

REFINE YOUR SEARCH

In addition to the General Index, we provide several more specific indexes to help you refine your marketing plan for your poems. The editors/publishers themselves have indicated how and where they want their listings indexed, and not every listing appears in one of these specific indexes. Therefore, use these indexes only to supplement your other research efforts:

Chapbook Publishers Index provides a breakdown of markets that publish chapbooks.

Book Publishers Index indicates markets looking for book-length collections of poetry.

Openness to Submissions Index breaks out markets according to the symbols (▢ ◪ ◪ ◉) that appear at the beginning of each listing, signposts indicating the level of writing a market prefers to see. (For an explanation of these symbols, see the previous page or the inside front cover of this book.)

Geographical Index sorts markets by state. Some markets are more open to poets from their region, so use this index when you're pinpointing local opportunities.

Subject Index groups markets into categories according to areas of interest. These include all specialized markets (appearing with the ◉ symbol) as well as broader categories such as online markets, poetry for children, markets that consider translations, and others. Save time when looking for a specific type of market by checking this index first.

THE NEXT STEP

Once you know how to interpret the listings in this section to identify markets for your work, the next step is to start submitting your poems. See Getting Started (and Using This Book) on page 3 and Frequently Asked Questions on page 7 for advice, guidelines about preparing your manuscript, and proper submission procedures.

ADDITIONAL INFORMATION

The Publishers of Poetry section includes five Insider Reports: **Ray Gonzalez** discusses landscape, memory, and the complexity of our Mexican-American border culture. **Marvin Bell** talks about the influence of great teachers as well as the inspiration for one of his best-known poems. **Lisel Mueller** reflects on her "late start" in publishing poetry. **Margo Stever** examines a busy life immersed in every aspect of writing and publishing poetry. *Poet's Market* Assistant Editor Vanessa Lyman reports on the **market for young poets.** And **Ken Waldman** recounts how he became Alaska's Fiddling Poet. In addition, as a special bonus we feature **Marvin Bell's "32 Statements About Writing Poetry."**

This section includes the covers of eight literary magazines reflecting the range of print publications being produced today. Such images tell a lot about a publication's style and content, as do the accompanying comments by editors regarding why the cover images were selected. (When evaluating a potential market for your work, consider everything that makes up the product—the poets being published, style and quality of content, guidelines, editorial comments, cover art, and even ads.)

And remember, the opportunities in the Publishers of Poetry section are only part of the picture. Be sure to look at the sections that follow (Contests & Awards, Conferences & Workshops, Organizations, and Publications of Interest) for additional market leads, competitions, and educational and informational sources of special interest to poets.

◙ A SMALL GARLIC PRESS (ASGP); AGNIESZKA'S DOWRY (AgD), 5445 Sheridan #3003, Chicago IL 60640. E-mail: marek@asgp.org. or ketzle@asgp.org. Website: http://asgp.org. Established 1995. **Co-Editors:** Marek Lugowski, katrina grace craig.

Magazine Needs: *Agnieszka's Dowry (AgD)* is "a magazine published both in print and as a permanent Internet installation of poems and graphics, letters to Agnieszka. The print version consists of professionally crafted chapbooks. The online version comprises fast-loading pages employing an intuitive if uncanny navigation in an interesting space, all conducive to fast and comfortable reading. No restrictions on form or type. We use contextual and juxtapositional tie-ins with other material in making choices, so visiting the online *AgD* or reading a chapbook of an *AgD* issue is required of anyone making a submission." Single copy: $2 plus $2 shipping, if ordered from website by an individual. Make checks payable to A Small Garlic Press.

How to Submit: Submit 5-10 poems at a time, by e-mail to Katja and Marek simultaneously. "Please inform us of the status of publishing rights." E-mail submissions only, plain text ("unless you are in prison—prisoners may make submissions by regular mail and we will waive the requirements that they read a print issue.") Sometimes comments on rejected poems. Guidelines available on website only. Responds online or by SASE usually in 2 months. Pays 1 contributor's copy. Acquires one-time rights where applicable.

Book/Chapbook Needs & How to Submit: A Small Garlic Press (ASGP) publishes up to 3 chapbooks of poetry/year. Query with a full online ms, ASCII (plain text) only.

Also Offers: "We also offer on our webpage extensive discussions of our policies and submission guidelines. We are in the process of organizing Twice Twenty-Two, an open un-mike in Chicago on the 22nd of each month in the evenings—more details on website as things develop."

◖ ◎ THE AARDVARK ADVENTURER; THE ARMCHAIR AESTHETE; PICKLE GAS PRESS (Specialized: humor), 31 Rolling Meadows Way, Penfield NY 14526. (585)388-6968. E-mail: bypaul@netacc.net. Established 1996. **Editor:** Paul Agosto.

Magazine Needs: *The Aardvark Adventurer* is "a quarterly family-fun newsletter-style zine of humor, thought, and verse. Very short stories (less than 500 words) are sometimes included." Prefers "light, humorous verse; any style; any 'family acceptable' subject matter; length limit 32 lines. Nothing obscene, overly forboding, no graphic gore or violence." Has published poetry by Paul Humphrey, Ray Gallucci, Max Gutmann, and Theone DiRocco. *The Aardvark Adventurer* is 6-12 pages, 8½×14, photocopied, corner-stapled, with many playful b&w graphics. Receives about 500 poems/year, accepts about 40%. Press run is 150 for 100 subscribers. Single copy: $2; subscription:

$5. Sample: $2. Make checks payable to Paul Agosto. "Subscription not required but subscribers given preference."

Magazine Needs: Also publishes *The Armchair Aesthete*, a quarterly digest-sized zine of "fiction and poetry of thoughtful, well-crafted concise works. Interested in more fiction submissions than poetry though." Line length for poetry is 30 maximum. *The Armchair Aesthete* is 40-60 pages, digest-sized, quality desktop-published, photocopied, card cover, includes ads for other publications and writers' available chapbooks. Each issue usually contains 10-15 poems and 9-14 stories. Receives about 300 poems/year, accepts about 25-30%. Subscription: $10/year. Sample postpaid: $3. Make checks payable to Paul Agosto.

How to Submit: For both publications, accepts previously published poems and simultaneous submissions, if indicated. Accepts e-mail submissions, include in body of message. Cover letter preferred. Time between acceptance and publication is up to 9 months. Seldom comments on rejected poems. *The Aardvark Adventurer* occasionally publishes theme issues, but *The Armchair Aesthete* does not. Guidelines available by SASE for both publications. Responds in 2 months. Pays 1 contributor's copy. Acquire one-time rights. The staff of *The Aardvark Adventurer* reviews books and chapbooks of poetry in 100 words. The staff of *The Armchair Aesthete* occasionally reviews chapbooks. Send materials for review consideration.

Advice: "*The Aardvark Adventurer* is a perfect opportunity for the aspiring poet, a newsletter-style publication with a very playful format."

⬤ ABBEY; ABBEY CHEAPOCHAPBOOKS, 5360 Fallriver Row Court, Columbia MD 21044. E-mail: greisman@aol.com. Established 1970. **Editor:** David Greisman.

Magazine Needs & How to Submit: *Abbey*, a quarterly, aims "to be a journal but to do it so informally that one wonders about my intent." Wants "poetry that does for the mind what that first sip of Molson Ale does for the palate. No pornography or politics." Has published poetry and artwork by Richard Peabody, Vera Bergstrom, D.E. Steward, Carol Hamilton, Harry Calhoun, Wayne Hogan, and Cheryl Townsend. *Abbey* is 20-26 pages, magazine-sized, photocopied. Publishes about 150 of 1,000 poems received/year. Press run is 200. Subscription: $2. Sample: 50¢. Guidelines are available for SASE. Responds in 1 month. Pays 1-2 copies.

Book/Chapbook Needs & How to Submit: *Abbey Cheapochapbooks* come out 1-2 times/year averaging 10-15 pages. For chapbook consideration query with 4-6 samples, bio, and list of publications. Responds in 2 months. Pays 25-50 copies.

Advice: The editor says he is "definitely seeing poetry from two schools—the nit'n'grit school and the textured/reflective school. I much prefer the latter."

★ ⊞ ◗ ◎ ABIKO ANNUAL WITH JAMES JOYCE FW STUDIES (Specialized: translations), 8-1-7 Namiki, Abiko-shi, Chiba-ken 270-1165 Japan. Phone/fax: 011-81-471-84-5873. E-mail: hce@jcom.home.ne.jp. Website: http://members.jcom.home.ne.jp/hce. Established 1988. **Contact:** Dr. Tatsuo Hamada.

Magazine Needs: *Abiko* is a literary-style annual journal "heavily influenced by James Joyce's *Finnegan's Wake*. We publish all kinds, with an emphasis like Yeats's quote: 'Truth seen in passion is the substance of poetry!' We prefer poetry like Eliot's or Donne's. We include originals and translations from Japanese and other languages." Has published poetry by Eileen Malone, James Fairhall, and Danetta Loretta Saft. *Abiko Annual* is about 350 pages, 14.8cm × 21cm, perfect-bound, coated paper cover. Press run is 300 for 50 subscribers of which 10 are libraries. Sample: $25.

How to Submit: Submission guidelines available on website. Send materials for review consideration.

Advice: "Please remember U.S. postage does not work in Japan with SAEs! Send 2 International Reply Coupons."

◗ ◎ ABLE MUSE (Specialized: form/style); ERATOSPHERE, 467 Saratoga Ave., #602, San Jose CA 95129-1326. Phone/fax: (801)729-3509. E-mail: submission@ablemuse.com. Website: www.ablemuse.com. Established 1999. **Editor:** Alex Pepple.

Magazine Needs: *Able Muse: a review of metrical poetry* "spotlights formal poetry via a quarterly online presentation, in the supportive environment of art, photography, essays, interviews, book reviews, fiction, and a literary forum. Also includes electronic books of poetry. *Able Muse* exclusively publishes formal poetry. We are looking for well-crafted poems of any length or subject that employ skillful and imaginative use of meter, or meter and rhyme, executed in contemporary idiom, that reads as naturally as your free-verse poems. Do not send us free-verse, greeting card verse, or poetry campaigning for the revival of archaic language." Has published poetry by Mark Jarman, A.E. Stallings, Rhina P. Espaillat, A.M. Juster, Annie Finch, and Leslie Monsour. Receives about 800 poems/ year, accepts about 10%. Publish 20 poems/issue.

How to Submit: Submit 1-5 poems at a time. No previously published poems or simultaneous submissions. Accepts e-mail and disk submissions. "E-mail is the preferred medium of submission, but we also welcome snail mail, or submit directly from the website with the automated online submission form." Cover letter preferred. Time between acceptance and publication is 4-10 weeks. Often comments on rejected poems. Occasionally publishes theme issues. Guidelines and a list of upcoming themes available by e-mail or on website. Responds in 1 month. Sometimes sends prepublication galleys. Acquires first rights. Reviews books of poetry. Send materials for review consideration.

Also Offers: "*Eratosphere* is provided online for the posting and critique of poetry and other literary work. It is a 'virtual' workshop! Literary online chats also provided featuring the scheduled appearance of guest celebrity poets."

Advice: "Despite the rush to publish everything online, most of web-published poetry has been free verse. This is surprising given formal poetry's recent rise in popularity in the number of print journals that exclusively publish formal poetry. *Able Muse* attempts to fill this void bringing the best contemporary formalists online. Remember, content is just as important as form."

◙ ◎ ABRAXAS MAGAZINE; GHOST PONY PRESS (Specialized: lyric poetry), P.O. Box 260113, Madison WI 53726-0113. (608)238-0175. E-mail: abraxaspress@hotmail.com or ghostp onypress@hotmail.com. Website: www.geocities.com/Paris/4614. *Abraxas* established in 1968 by James Bertolino and Warren Woessner; Ghost Pony Press in 1980 by editor/publisher Ingrid Swanberg. **Contact:** Ingrid Swanberg (for both presses).

Magazine Needs & How to Submit: *Abraxas* no longer considers unsolicited material, except as announced as projects arise. Interested in poetry that is "contemporary lyric, experimental, and poetry in translation." Does not want to see "political posing; academic regurgitations. Please include poem in the original language along with submissions of translations." Has published poetry by William Stafford, Ivan Argüelles, Denise Levertov, César Vallejo, and Andrea Moorhead. *Abraxas* is up to 80 pages (160 pages, double issues), digest-sized, flat-spined (saddle-stapled with smaller issues), litho-offset, original art on matte card cover, with "unusual graphics in text, original art and collages, concrete poetry, exchange ads only, letters from contributors, essays." Appears "irregularly, 9- to 12-month intervals or much longer." Press run is 600 for 500 subscribers of which 150 are libraries. Subscription: $16/4 issues, $20/4 issues Canada, Mexico, and overseas. Sample: $4 ($8 double issues). *Abraxas* will announce submission guidelines as projects arise. Pays 1 copy plus 40% discount on additional copies.

Book/Chapbook Needs & How to Submit: To submit to Ghost Pony Press, inquire with SASE plus 5-10 poems and cover letter. Accepts previously published material for book publication by Ghost Pony Press. Editor sometimes comments briefly on rejected poems. Submissions by post only; no e-mail submissions. No promised response time. "We currently have a considerable backlog of mss." Payment varies per project. Send SASE for catalog to buy samples. Has published three books of poetry by próspero saíz including *the bird of nothing & other poems*; 168 pages, 7 × 10, sewn and wrapped binding, paperback available for $20 (signed and numbered edition is $35), as well as *Zen Concrete + Etc.*, by d.a. levy; 268 pages, magazine-sized, perfect-bound, illustrated, paperback for $27.50.

Advice: "Ghost Pony Press is a small press publisher of poetry books; *Abraxas* is a literary journal publishing contemporary poetry, criticism, and translations. Do not confuse these separate presses!"

$▢ ACM (ANOTHER CHICAGO MAGAZINE); LEFT FIELD PRESS; CHICAGO LITERARY PRIZE, 3709 N. Kenmore, Chicago IL 60613. Website: www.anotherchicagomag.com. Established 1977. **Poetry Editor:** Barry Silesky.

● Work published in *ACM* has been frequently included in *The Best American Poetry* and *Pushcart Prize* anthologies.

Magazine Needs: Published in May and November, *ACM* is a literary biannual, with emphasis on quality, experimental, politically aware prose, fiction, poetry, reviews, cross-genre work, and essays. No religious verse. Has published prose and poetry by Albert Goldbarth, Michael McClure, Jerome Sala, Nadja Tesich, Wanda Coleman, Charles Simic, and Diane Wakoski. *ACM* is 220 pages, digest-sized, offset-printed, with b&w art and ads. Appreciates traditional to experimental verse with an emphasis on message, especially poems with strong voices articulating social or political concerns. Press run is 2,000 for 500 subscribers of which 100 are libraries. Single copy: $8.

How to Submit: Submit 3-4 typed poems at a time. Accepts simultaneous submissions; no previously published poems. Reads submissions from February 1 through August 31. Responds in 3 months, has 3- to 6-month backlog. Sends prepublication galleys. Pays "if funds permit," and/or 1 contributor's copy and 1 year subscription. Acquires first serial rights. Reviews books of poetry in 250-800 words. Send materials for review consideration.

Also Offers: Sponsors Chicago Literary Prize. Deadline: December.

Advice: "Buy a copy—subscribe and support your own work."

◻ ◎ **THE ACORN; EL DORADO WRITERS' GUILD (Specialized: regional, Western Sierra),** P.O. Box 1266, El Dorado CA 95623-1266. E-mail: acorn@edwg.org. Website: www.edwg.c om. Established 1993. **Editors:** Julie Ellis, Nicholas Rotondo, and Frank J. Severson.

Magazine Needs: *the ACORN* is a quarterly journal of the Western Sierra, published by the El Dorado Writers' Guild, a nonprofit literary organization. It includes "fiction and nonfiction, history and reminiscence, story and legend, and poetry." Wants poetry "up to 30 lines long, though we prefer shorter. Focus should be on western slope Sierra Nevada. No erotica, pornography, or religious poetry." Has published poetry by Taylor Graham, Sherman Pearl, Muriel Varvin, Patricia Wellingham-Jones. *the ACORN* is 44 pages, digest-sized, offset-printed, saddle-stapled, light card cover. Receives about 400 poems/year, accepts about 15%. Press run is 200 for 110 subscribers. Subscription: $16. Sample: $4.

How to Submit: Submit 3-5 poems, neatly typed or printed, at a time. Accepts previously published poems (indicate where published), but no simultaneous submissions. E-mail submissions encouraged; "prefer attachment in MSWord format. However, in body of message is acceptable." Cover letter with short (75-word) bio and publication credits preferred. "Our issues favor topical items suitable for the season." Deadlines are February 1, May 1, August 1. "January is our contest issue." Guidelines available for SASE, by e-mail, on website. Time between acceptance and publication is 1 month. "Five editors score the poems for content, form, and suitability. Graphics editor selects to fit space available." Often comments on rejected poems. Responds within 1 month after deadline. Pays 2 copies.

Also Offers: Sponsors annual contest. 1st Prize: $100, 2nd Prize: $50. Entry fee: $10/3 poems, 40 lines maximum/poem. Deadline: December 31. All winning entries are published in the contest edition of *the ACORN* in January. Send SASE for complete rules.

Advice: "If your poetry is about nature, be accurate with the species' names, colors, etc. If you describe a landscape, be sure it fits our region. Metered rhyming verse had better be precise. (We have an editor with an internal metronome!) Slant rhyme and free verse are welcome. Avoid trite phrases."

⊕ ◪ **ACUMEN MAGAZINE; EMBER PRESS; THE LONG POEM GROUP NEWSLET-TER,** 6 The Mount, Higher Furzeham, Brixham, South Devon TQ5 8QY England. Press established 1971. *Acumen* established 1984. **Poetry Editor:** P. Oxley.

Magazine Needs: *Acumen* appears 3 times/year (in January, May, and September) and is a "small press publisher of a general literary magazine with emphasis on good poetry." Wants "well-crafted, high quality, imaginative poems showing a sense of form. No experimental verse of an obscene type." Has published poetry by Elizabeth Jennings, William Oxley, Gavin Ewart, D.J. Enright, Peter Porter, Kathleen Raine, and R.S. Thomas. *Acumen* is 100 pages, A5, perfect-bound. "We aim to publish 120 poems out of 12,000 received." Press run is 650 for 400 subscribers of which 20 are libraries. Subscription: $45 surface/$50 air. Sample copy: $15.

How to Submit: Submit 5-6 poems at a time. Accepts simultaneous submissions, if not submitted to UK magazines; no previously published poems. Responds in 1 month. Pays "by negotiation" and

1 copy. Staff reviews books of poetry up to 300 words, single format or 600 words, multi-book. Send materials for review consideration to Glyn Pursglove, 25 St. Albans Rd., Brynmill, Swansea, West Glamorgan SA2 0BP Wales. "If a reply is required, please send IRCs. One IRC for a decision, 3 IRCs if work to be returned."

Also Offers: Publishes *The Long Poem Group Newsletter,* established in 1995, which features short articles about long poems and reviews long poems. Free for large SASE (or SAE with IRC).

Advice: "Read *Acumen* carefully to see what kind of poetry we publish. Also read widely in many poetry magazines, and don't forget the poets of the past—they can still teach us a great deal."

◯ ADASTRA PRESS, 16 Reservation Rd., Easthampton MA 01027-2536. Established 1980. **Publisher:** Gary Metras.

Book/Chapbook Needs: "Adastra is primarily a chapbook publisher using antique equipment and methods, i.e., hand-set type, letterpress printed, hand-sewn bindings. Any titles longer than chapbook length are by special arrangement and are from poets who have previously published a successful chapbook or two with Adastra. Editions are generally released with a flat-spine paper wrapper, and some titles have been bound in cloth. Editions are limited, ranging from 200-400 copy print runs. Some of the longer titles have gone into reprint and these are photo-offset and perfect-bound. Letterpress chapbooks by themselves are not reprinted as single titles. Once they go out of print, they are gone. Instead, I have released *The Adastra Reader, Collected Chapbooks, 1979-1986* (1987), and am assembling *The Adastra Reader II, Collected Chapbooks, 1987-1992.* These anthologies collect the first twelve chapbooks and the second twelve, respectively, and I am now planning the third series. I am biased against poems that rhyme and/or are religious in theme. Sequences and longish poems are always nice to present in a chapbook format. There are no guidelines other than these. Competition is keen. Less than .5% of submissions are accepted." Poets published include *Digger's Blues* by Jim Daniels, *The First Thing* by Anna Kirwan, *Breaking the Voodoo* by M.L. Liebler, *Boto* by Susan Edwards Richmond, *Enough Said* by Kiev Rattee, and *Millrat* by Mike Casey. Publishes 2-4 chapbooks/year. Sample hand-crafted chapbook: $6 postpaid.

How to Submit: "I am overcommitted and will not read new submissions this or next year."

◯ ADEPT PRESS; SMALL BRUSHES, P.O. Box 391, Long Valley NJ 07853-0391. Established 1999. **Editor:** Jan Epps Turner.

• *Small Brushes* will not be reading submissions until May 15, 2004.

Magazine Needs: Published quarterly, *Small Brushes* wants "to be another showcase for good poetry from many voices. We prefer poems of 36 lines or fewer, and we are unlikely to use any poem over 42 lines. We want poetry of all forms springing from important human emotions, ethics, and realizations. We value unity, coherence, emphasis, and accessibility. We will not use material containing vulgarity, explicit sexual references, or words or descriptions that might reasonably offend anyone. We avoid issues of a narrow religious, social, or political nature." Has published poetry by Richard R. Faschan, Paul Truttman, B.Z. Niditch, Kelley Jean White, Arlene L. Mandell, and John P. Kristofco. *Small Brushes* is 28 pages, digest-sized, desktop-published, photocopied and saddle-stapled, with parchment cover, color graphics. Receives over 1,000 poems/year, accepts about 20%. Publishes about 50 poems/issue. Press run is 100 for contributors, subscriptions, and shelf sales. Single copy: $3; subscription: $10/year (4 issues). Sample: $2. Make checks payable to Adept Press.

How to Submit: Submit 3-4 poems at a time. No previously published poems or simultaneous submissions. Cover letter requested. "Please include a brief bio in your cover letter, place your name and address at the top of each manuscript page and type or print clearly. Please send SASE for our comments or contact." Reads submissions after May 15, 2004. Submit seasonal poems 2 months in advance. Time between acceptance and publication is up to 18 months. Seldom comments on rejected poems. Guidelines available for SASE. Responds in up to 3 months. Sometimes sends prepublication galleys. Pays 1 copy/published poem. Rights remain with authors and artists.

Advice: "We look for poetry of literary quality and selections of humor and nostalgia that we like. Overly sentimental or overly personal poems do not, as a rule, work for us. Read poetry, including the masters. Ignore the trends. Write from your own experiences and deep feelings."

◯ THE ADIRONDACK REVIEW, P.O. Box 46, Watertown NY 13601. E-mail: editors@adirondackreview.org. Website: www.adirondackreview.org. Established 2000. **Editor:** Colleen Ryor.

Magazine Needs: *The Adirondack Review* is a quarterly online literary journal dedicated to quality free verse poetry and short fiction as well as book and film reviews, art, photography, and interviews. "We are open to both new and established writers. Our only requirement is excellence. We would like to publish more French and German poetry translations as well as original poems in these languages. We publish an eclectic mix of voices and styles, but all poems should show attention to craft. We are open to beginners who demonstrate talent, as well as established voices. The work should speak for itself." Wants well-crafted, thoughtful writing full of imagery. Does not want religious, overly sentimental, horror/gothic, rhyming, greeting card, pet-related, humor, or science fiction poetry. Recently published poetry by Walt McDonald, Lee Upton, D.C. Berry, Denise Duhamel, James Reidel, and R.T. Smith. *The Adirondack Review* is published online. Accepts about 3-5% of poems submitted. Publishes about 30 poems/issue.

How to Submit: Submit 2-7 poems at a time. Accepts simultaneous submissions. Accepts e-mail submissions; no fax or disk submissions. "All submissions should be pasted into the body of an e-mail (no attached files, please)." Cover letter is preferred. Reads submissions year round. Submit seasonal poems 3 months in advance. Time between acceptance and publication is 1-3 months. Seldom comments on rejected poems. Guidelines available on website. Responds in 1 month. Acquires first or one-time rights. Reviews books of poetry. Poets may send materials for review consideration "but query by e-mail first."

Advice: "Get your hands on all the good writing you can, including international, past, contemporary, web-based, and print. Read much, write well, and send us what you love."

ADVOCATE, PKA's PUBLICATION, 1881 Co. Rt. 2, Prattsville NY 12468. (518)299-3103. Established 1987.

Magazine Needs: *Advocate* is a bimonthly advertiser-supported tabloid, 12,000 copies distributed free, using "original, previously unpublished works, such as feature stories, essays, 'think' pieces, letters to the editor, profiles, humor, fiction, poetry, puzzles, cartoons, or line drawings." Wants "nearly any kind of poetry, any length, but not religious or pornographic. Poetry ought to speak to people and not be so oblique as to have meaning only to the poet. If I had to be there to understand the poem, don't send it. Now looking for horse-related poems, stories, drawings, and photos." Accepts about 25% of poems received. Sample: $4.

How to Submit: No previously published poems or simultaneous submissions. Time between acceptance and publication is an average of 6 months. "Occasionally" comments on rejected poems. Responds in 2 months. Pays 2 copies. Acquires first rights only.

Advice: "All submissions and correspondence must be accompanied by a self-addressed, stamped envelope with sufficient postage."

AFRICAN VOICES (Specialized: ethnic, people of color), 270 W. 96th St., New York NY 10025. (212)865-2982. Fax: (212)316-3335. E-mail: general@africanvoices.com. Website: www.africanvoices.com Established 1992. **Poetry Editor:** Layding Kaliba.

Magazine Needs: *African Voices* is a quarterly "art and literary magazine that highlights the work of people of color. We publish ethnic literature and poetry on any subject. We also consider all themes and styles: avant-garde, free verse, haiku, light verse, and traditional. We do not wish to limit the reader or author." Accepts poetry written by children. Has published poetry by Reg E. Gaines, Maya Angelou, Jessica Care Moore, Asha Bandele, Tony Medina, and Louis Reyes Rivera. *African Voices* is about 48 pages, magazine-sized, professionally printed, saddle-stapled, paper cover, with b&w photos and illustrations. Receives about 100 submissions/year, accepts about 30%. Press run is 20,000 for 5,000 subscribers of which 30 are libraries, 40% shelf sales. Single copy: $4; subscription: $12. Sample: $5.

How to Submit: Submit no more than 2 poems at any one time. Accepts previously published poems and simultaneous submissions. Accepts submissions by e-mail (in text box), by fax, and by postal mail. Cover letter and SASE required. Seldom comments on rejected poems. Guidelines available for SASE or on website. Responds in 3 months. Pays 2 copies. Acquires first or one-time rights. Reviews books of poetry in 500-1,000 words. Send materials for review consideration, attn. Layding Kaliba.

Also Offers: Sponsors periodic poetry contests and readings. Send SASE for details.

Advice: "We strongly encourage new writers/poets to send in their work. Accepted contributors are encouraged to subscribe."

■ $◐ **AGNI**, Boston University, 236 Bay State Rd., Boston MA 02215. (617)353-7135. Fax: (617)353-7134. E-mail: agni@bu.edu. Website: www.bu.edu/agni. Established 1972. **Editors:** Askold Melnyczuk and Eric Grunwald.
   ● Work published in *AGNI* has been regularly included in *The Best American Poetry* and *Pushcart Prize* anthologies.
Magazine Needs: *AGNI* is a biannual journal of poetry, fiction, and essays "by both emerging and established writers. We publish quite a bit of poetry in forms as well as 'language' poetry, but we don't begin to try and place parameters on the 'kind of work' that *AGNI* selects." Wants readable, intelligent poetry—mostly lyric free verse (with some narrative and dramatic)—that somehow communicates tension or risk. Has published poetry by Adrienne Rich, Seamus Heaney, Maxine Scates, Rosanna Warren, Chinua Achebe, and Ha Jin. *AGNI* is typeset, offset-printed, and perfect-bound. Publishes about 40 poems/issue. Circulation is 1,500 for subscription, mail order and bookstore sales. Subscription: $17. Sample: $10, $12 for 30th Anniversary Poetry Anthology.
How to Submit: "Our reading period runs October 1st until February 15. Please submit no more than five poems at a time. No fancy fonts, gimmicks. Send SASE, no preformatted reply cards. No work accepted via e-mail. Brief, sincere cover letters." Accepts simultaneous submissions; no previously published poems. Pays $10/page, $150 maximum, plus 2 copies and one-year subscription. Acquires first serial rights.

◖ **THE AGUILAR EXPRESSION**, 1329 Gilmore Ave., Donora PA 15033. (724)379-8019. E-mail: XAeol@stargate.net. Established 1986. **Editor/Publisher:** Xavier Aguilar.
Magazine Needs: *Aguilar Expression* appears annually in October. "In publishing poetry, I try to exhibit the unique reality that we too often take for granted and acquaint as mediocre. We encourage poetics that deal with *now*, which our readers can relate to." Has published poetry by Martin Kich and Gail Ghai. *Aguilar Expression* is 4-20 pages, photocopied on 8½ × 11 sheets. Receives about 20-30 poems/month, accepts about 5-10. Circulation is 300. Sample: $8. Make checks payable to Xavier Aguilar.
How to Submit: "We insist that all writers send a SASE for writer's guidelines before submitting." Submit up to 3 poems at a time in a clear, camera-ready copy, 30-line limit, any topic/style. Does not accept e-mail submissions. Cover letter, including writing background, and SASE for contact purposes, required with submissions. Reads mss in January, February, March. Manuscripts received in any other months will be discarded unopened. "Send copies; mss will not be returned." Responds in 2 months. Pays 2 copies.

◑ **AHSAHTA PRESS; SAWTOOTH POETRY PRIZE**, MFA Program in Creative Writing, Boise State University, 1910 University Dr., Boise ID 83725. (208)426-2195. Fax: (208)426-4373. E-mail: ahsahta@boisestate.edu. Website: http://ahsahtapress.boisestate.edu. Director: Janet Holmes. **Contact:** Editor.
Book/Chapbook Needs: Ahsahta Press has been publishing contemporary poetry of the American West since 1976. "It has since expanded its scope to publish poets nationwide, seeking out and publishing the best new poetry from a wide range of aesthetics—poetry that is technically accomplished, distinctive in style, and thematically fresh." Has published *Corpus Socius*, by Lance Phillips; *Esse*, by David Mutschlecner; *Fictional Teeth*, by Linda Dyer; *The Widow's Coat*, by Miriam Sagan as well as work by Wyn Cooper, Craig Cotter, Sandra Alcosser, and Cynthia Hogue.
How to Submit: Submit only during their March 1 through May 31 reading period. Send complete ms and SASE for reply. Accepts multiple and simultaneous submissions. Responds in up to 3 months. Forthcoming, new, and backlist titles available from website. Most backlist titles: $9.95; most current titles: $12.95.
Also Offers: Sawtooth Poetry Prize publishes a book-length collection of poetry judged by a nationally recognized poet (2001 judge was Brenda Hillman). Publishes a letterpress broadside series drawn from Ahsahta Press authors. Beginning in 2002, will publish 1 letterpress chapbook/year. Query first.
Advice: "Ahsahta seeks distinctive, non-imitative, unpredictible, and innovatively crafted work. Please check out our website for examples of what we publish."

◐**ALASKA QUARTERLY REVIEW**, University of Alaska Anchorage, 3211 Providence Dr., Anchorage AK 99508. Phone/fax: (907)786-6916. E-mail: ayaqr@uaa.alaska.edu. Website: www.uaa. alaska.edu/aqr. Established 1981. **Executive Editor:** Ronald Spatz.

• Poetry published in *Alaska Quarterly Review* has been selected for inclusion in *The Best American Poetry*, *Pushcart Prize,* and *Beacon's Best* anthologies.

Magazine Needs: *Alaska Quarterly Review* "is a journal devoted to contemporary literary art. We publish both traditional and experimental fiction, poetry, literary nonfiction, and short plays." Has published poetry by Kim Addonizio, Tom Lux, Pattiann Rogers, John Balaban, Albert Goldbarth, Jane Hirshfeld, Billy Collins, and Dorianne Laux. Wants all styles and forms of poetry with the most emphasis perhaps on voice and content that displays "risk," or intriguing ideas or situations. Publishes two double-issues/year, each using between 40-125 pages of poetry. *Alaska Quarterly Review* runs between 224 and 300 pages, digest-sized, professionally printed, perfect-bound, card cover with color or b&w photo. Receives up to 3,000 submissions/year, accepts 40-90. Circulation is 2,500 for 500 subscribers of which 32 are libraries. Subscription: $10. Sample: $6.

How to Submit: Does not accept fax or e-mail submissions. Manuscripts are *not* read from May 15 through August 15. Responds in up to 4 months, sometimes longer during peak periods in late winter. Pay depends on funding. Acquires first North American serial rights. Guest poetry editors have included Stuart Dybek, Jane Hirshfield, Stuart Dischell, Maxine Kumin, Pattiann Rogers, Dorianne Laux, Peggy Shumacher, Nancy Eimers, Michael Ryan, and Billy Collins.

◐ ◎ **ALBATROSS; THE ANABIOSIS PRESS (Specialized: nature)**, 2 South New St., Bradford MA 01835. (978)469-7085. E-mail: rsmyth@mva.net. Website: http://members.mva.net/ rsmyth/anabiosis. **Editor:** Richard Smyth.

Magazine Needs: *Albatross* appears "as soon as we have accepted enough quality poems to publish an issue—about one a year. We consider the albatross to be a metaphor for an environment that must survive. This is not to say that we publish only environmental or nature poetry, but that we are biased toward such subject matter. We publish mostly free verse, 200 lines/poem maximum, and we prefer a narrative style, but again, this is not necessary. We do not want trite rhyming poetry which doesn't convey a deeply felt experience in a mature expression with words." Also publishes interviews with established writers. Has published poetry by Carol Hamilton, Joanna Catherine Scott, Rina Ferrarelli, Serge Lecomte, and Simon Perchik. *Albatross* is 28 pages, digest-sized, laser-typeset, linen cover, with some b&w drawings. Subscription: $5/2 issues. Sample: $3.

How to Submit: Submit 3-5 poems at a time. "Poems should be typed single-spaced, with name, address, and phone number in upper left corner." No simultaneous submissions. Accepts e-mail submissions if included in body of message. Name and address must accompany e-mail submissions. Cover letter not required; "We do, however, need bio notes and SASE for return or response." Guidelines available for SASE and on website. Responds in up to 1 month, has 3-month backlog. Pays 1 copy. Acquires all rights. Returns rights provided that "previous publication in *Albatross* is mentioned in all subsequent reprintings."

Also Offers: Holds a chapbook contest. Submit 20 pages of poetry, any theme, any style. Deadline is June 30 of each year. Include name, address, and phone number on the title page. Charges $10 reading fee (check payable to Anabiosis Press). Winner receives $100 and at least 50 copies of his/ her published chapbook. All entering receive a free copy of the winning chapbook. Also publishes the Anabiosis Press Pocket Book series. These are $5 \times 3\frac{1}{2}$, laser typeset with linen cover. Initial print run of 100. Send 350 lines of poetry, preferably from a single long poem. Guidelines on website or for SASE.

Advice: "We expect a poet to read as much contemporary poetry as possible. We seek deeply felt experiences expressed maturely in a unique style of writing. We want to be moved. When you read our poetry, we hope that it moves you in the same way that it moves us. We try to publish the kind of poetry that you would want to read again and again."

⭐ ◐ **ALDEN ENTERPRISES; POETIC VOICES MAGAZINE**, 2206 Bailey St. NW, Hartselle AL 35640-4219. E-mail: editor@poeticvoices.com (for Robin Travis-Murphree) or poetryeditor @poeticvoices.com (for Ursula T. Gibson). Website: www.poeticvoices.com. Established 1997. **Executive Editor (Alden Ent.):** Robin Travis-Murphree. **Submissions Editor (*Poetic Voices*):** Ursula T. Gibson.

Magazine Needs: E-mailed to subscribers monthly, *Poetic Voices* is "informational and educational in content. Articles include feature interviews, columns on the mechanics of writing, questions on writing and publishing, information on organizations useful to poets, contest and award opportunities, publishing opportunities, workshops and conferences, book reviews and more. We are open to most forms, styles, and subjects. No pornography, scatology, racial slurs, or dehumanizing poems." Accepts poetry written by children. Has published poetry by Lyn Lifshin, David Lehman, Michael McClure, Kevin Stein, Molly Peacock, Afaa Weaver, and others. *Poetic Voices* is an electronic magazine containing 30-60 pages published online. Receives about 1,200 poems/year, accepts about 10%. Circulation is "over 22,000 poets in 28 countries each month."

How to Submit: Submit up to 4 poems/month by e-mail, text in body of message, to Ursula T. Gibson. Accepts previously published poems and simultaneous submissions. Cover letter preferred. Often comments on rejected poems. Guidelines available for SASE or on website. Responds in 2 months. Acquires one-time rights. Reviews books and chapbooks of poetry and other magazines in 200-500 words. Poets may send material for review consideration to Robin Travis-Murphree.

Advice: "Make sure you read and follow guidelines. Make sure your work is neatly presented. There is nothing worse than receiving messy work or work that does not conform to the guidelines."

$ 🖋 ◎ ◉ ALIVE NOW (Specialized: spirituality, themes); POCKETS (Specialized: Christian, children, themes); DEVO'ZINE (Specialized: Christian, youth, themes); WEAVINGS; THE UPPER ROOM, 1908 Grand Ave., P.O. Box 340004, Nashville TN 37203-0004. E-mail: alivenow@upperroom.org. Website: www.alivenow.org or www.upperroom.org. This publishing company brings out about 30 books/year and 5 magazines: *The Upper Room, Alive Now, Pockets, Devo'Zine,* and *Weavings.* Of these, three use unsolicited poetry.

Magazine Needs & How to Submit: *Pockets, Devotional Magazine for Children,* which comes out 11 times/year, circulation 90,000, is for children 6-12. "Offers stories, activities, prayers, poems—all geared to giving children a better understanding of themselves as children of God. Some of the material is not overtly religious but deals with situations, special seasons and holidays, and ecological concerns from a Christian perspective." Uses 3-4 pages of poetry/issue. Sample free with 7½ × 10½ SAE and 4 first-class stamps. Accepts e-mail submissions; include text in body of message. Ordinarily 24-line limit on poetry. Upcoming themes and guidelines available for SASE and on website. Pays $25-50.

Magazine Needs & How to Submit: *Alive Now* is a bimonthly, circulation 70,000, for a general Christian audience interested in reflection and meditation. Buys 20 poems/year, avant-garde and free verse. Submit 5 poems, 10-45 lines. Guidelines and upcoming themes available for SASE and on website. "Poems **must** relate to themes." Pays $25 and up.

Magazine Needs & How to Submit: *Devo'Zine: Just for Teens* is a bimonthly devotional magazine for youth ages 13-18. Offers meditations, scripture, prayers, poems, stories, songs, and feature articles to "aid youth in their prayer life, introduce them to spiritual disciplines, help them shape their concept of God, and encourage them in the life of discipleship." Ordinarily 20-line limit on poetry. Guidelines and upcoming themes available for SASE and on website. Pays $25.

Also Offers: *The Upper Room* magazine does not accept poetry.

✪ ◯ ◎ THE ALLEGHENY REVIEW (Specialized: undergraduate students); THE AL-LEGHENY REVIEW AWARD IN POETRY, Box 32, Allegheny College, Meadville PA 16335. (814)332-5386. E-mail: review@allegheny.edu. Website: http://review.allegheny.edu. Established 1983. **Faculty Advisor:** Christopher Bakken.

Magazine Needs: "Each year *The Allegheny Review* compiles and publishes a review of the nation's best undergraduate literature. It is entirely composed of and by college undergraduates." *The Alle-*

MARKET CONDITIONS are constantly changing! If you're still using this book and it's 2005 or later, buy the newest edition of *Poet's Market* at your favorite bookstore or order directly from Writer's Digest Books (800)448-0915 or www.writersdigest.com.

gheny Review is digest-sized, flat-spined, professionally printed, b&w photo on glossy card cover. Single copy: $4. Sample: $4 and 11 × 18 SASE.

How to Submit: Submit 5 poems. No fax or e-mail submissions. "Each poem should have author's name and address clearly indicated. Only submissions accompanied by a SASE should expect a response from the editors." Submissions should be accompanied by cover letter "stating which college the poet is attending, year of graduation, and a very brief bio." Call or e-mail for current deadlines. Responds in early March.

Also Offers: "Submissions for *The Allegheny Review* Award in Poetry are read in the Fall semester of each year. All submissions accompanied by an entry fee receive an one-year subscription to the journal and are considered for publication. In March a nationally-recognized poet awards $250 to the contest winner." Guidelines available by e-mail or on website. *The Allegheny Review* also welcomes b&w art submissions. Send copies (not originals) and SASE.

Advice: "Familiarize yourself with any journal to which you submit your work for publication and send only your very best work. While *The Allegheny Review* has no particular stylistic preferences, you will have a better sense of the kind of writing we tend to publish if you do. And when you submit, please take enough pride in your work to do so professionally. Handwritten or poorly typed and proofed submissions definitely convey an impression—a negative one."

★ $ ◨ ALLIGATOR JUNIPER, Prescott College, 301 Grove Ave., Prescott AZ 86301. (520)778-2090, ext. 2012. E-mail: aj@prescott.edu. Website: www.prescott.edu/highlights/aj.html. Established 1995. **Contact:** Poetry Editor.

Magazine Needs: *Alligator Juniper* is a contest publication appearing annually in May. "We publish work based only on artistic merit." Has published poetry by Elton Glaser and Fatima Lim-Wilson. *Alligator Juniper* is 200 pages with b&w photography. Receives about 1,200-1,500 poems/year, accepts about 6-20 poems. Press run is 1,500 for 600 subscribers; 200 distributed free to other reputable journals, MFA programs, and writers' colonies. Subscription: $12/2 years (2 issues). Sample: $7.50. "We publish one issue per year and it's always a contest, requiring a $10 fee which allows us to pay a $500 first prize in each category—fiction, poetry, creative nonfiction, and photography. All entrants receive a copy of the next issue."

How to Submit: Submit up to 5 poems at a time with reading fee. Include SASE for response only; mss are not returned. "All entrants receive a personal letter from one of our staff regarding the status of their submissions." Accepts simultaneous submissions; no previously published poems. No e-mail or fax submissions. Cover letter required. Postmark deadline: October 1. "We read and select what we will publish from all the work submitted so far that calendar year." Reading fee: $10/entry (5 poems or 5 pages of poetry). Time between acceptance and publication is 3-5 months. "Finalists are selected in-house and passed on to a different guest judge each year." Occasionally publishes theme issues. Guidelines available for SASE, by e-mail, or on website. Responds in 5 months. Each year, one winner receives $500 plus 4 copies; all other poets whose work is selected for publication receive payment in copies only.

★ ◐ THE ALSOP REVIEW, 122 Broad Creek Rd., Laurel DE 19956. E-mail: alsop@alsoprevie w.com. Website: www.alsopreview.com/. Established 1998. **Editor:** Jamie Wasserman. **Founder:** Jaimes Alsop.

Magazine Needs: *The Alsop Review* "aims to merge the print and Web world, to bring established print writers to the Web and highlight those writers whose reputations are still word-of-mouth." Wants "well-crafted verse with a strong voice. No pornography; overtly religious work, greeting card verse, or sloppy writing." Has published poetry by Lola Haskins, Gwendolyn MacEwen, A.E. Stallings, and Kim Addonizio. Receives about 1,000 poems/year, accepts about 2%.

How to Submit: Submit 3-5 poems at a time. Accepts simultaneous submissions; no previously published poems. Cover letter preferred. "Submissions may only be sent via e-mail in body of message." Time between acceptance and publication is 1 month. Seldom comments on rejected poems. Guidelines are available by e-mail or on website. Responds in 1 month. Acquires first rights.

Also Offers: *The Alsop Review* "sponsors annual poetry and fiction contests, and runs the most popular workshop on the Web (The Gazebo)."

N ◐ ◎ **AMAZE: THE CINQUAIN JOURNAL (Specialized: American cinquain)**, 10529 Olive St., Temple City CA 91780. E-mail: cinquains@hotmail.com. Website: www.amaze-cinquain.c om. Established 2002. **Editor:** Deborah P. Kolodji. **Webmaster:** Lisa Janice Cohen.

Magazine Needs: *Amaze: The Cinquain Journal* is a biannual literary journal (in both print and online webzine format) devoted to the cinquain poetry form. "The webzine is published on a continuous flow basis, as we accept submissions for the current issue. The print version is published two months after submissions close for the webzine." Wants American cinquains as invented by Adelaide Crapsey (5 lines with a 2-4-6-8-2 syllable pattern) and cinquain variations (mirror cinquains, crown cinquains, cinquain sequences, etc.). Does not want any poetry not based upon the American cinquain nor "grammar-lesson" cinquains based upon parts of speech. Nothing hateful, racist, or sexually explicit. Recently published poetry by an'ya, Ann K. Schwader, Michael McClintock, naia, and Denis Garrison. The print version of *Amaze* is 40-50 pages, digest-sized, photocopied, saddle-stapled, card stock cover with photograph/artwork. Receives about 1,500 poems/year, accepts about 200. Publishes about 100 poems/issue. Press run is 100-200 for 25 subscribers. Single copy: $6.00 US, $7.50 non-US; subscription: $12 US, $15 non-US. Make checks payable to Deborah P. Kolodji, or pay online through PayPal.

How to Submit: Submit 1-10 poems at a time. Line length for poetry is 5. Accepts previously published poems; no simultaneous submissions. Accepts e-mail submissions; no fax or disk submissioins. E-mail submissions preferred, with poems in the body of the e-mail. Do not send attachments. Include SASE with postal submissions. Reads submissions "on a continuous flow." Time between acceptance and publication is 3 weeks for webzine, up to 8 months for print journal. "Poems are evaluated on quality, form, and content." Often comments on rejected poems. Guidelines available for SASE or on website. Responds in up to 6 weeks. Acquires one-time rights.

🌐 ◐ **AMBIT**, 17 Priory Gardens, Highgate, London N6 5QY England. Phone: 0181-340-3566. Website: www.ambit.co.uk. **Editor:** Martin Bax. **Poetry Editors:** Martin Bax, Carol Ann Duffy, and Henry Graham. Prose Editors: J.G. Ballard and Geoff Nicholson. Art Editor: Mike Foreman.

Magazine Needs: *Ambit* is a 96-page quarterly of avant-garde, contemporary and experimental work. Subscription: £24 individuals, £35 institutions (UK); £26 ($52) individuals, £37 ($74) institutions (overseas). Sample: £6.

How to Submit: Submit up to 6 poems at a time, typed double-spaced. No previously published poems or simultaneous submissions. Pay is "variable plus 2 free copies. SAE vital for reply." Staff reviews books of poetry. Send materials for review consideration, attn. review editor.

Also Offers: Website includes names of editors and poetry and prose selected from the magazine's latest number.

Advice: "Read a copy of the magazine before submitting!"

◖ **AMERICA; FOLEY POETRY CONTEST**, 106 W. 56th St., New York NY 10019. (212)581-4640. Fax: (212)399-3596. Website: www.americapress.org. Established 1909. **Poetry Editor:** Paul Mariani

Magazine Needs: *America* is a weekly journal of opinion published by the Jesuits of North America. Primarily publishes articles on religious, social, political, and cultural themes. *America* is 36 pages, magazine-sized, professionally printed on thin stock, thin paper cover. Circulation is 39,000. Subscription: $48. Sample: $2.75.

How to Submit: "Because of a large backlog, we are only accepting poems submitted for the Foley Poetry Contest." The annual Foley Poetry Contest offers a prize of $1,000 and 2 contributor copies, usually in June. No fax submissions. Send SASE for rules. "Poems for the Foley Contest should be submitted between January and April. Poems submitted for the Foley Contest between July and December will be returned unread."

Advice: "*America* is committed to publishing quality poetry as it has done for the past 90 years. We encourage more established poets to submit their poems to us."

★ ☐ ◎ **THE AMERICAN COWBOY POET MAGAZINE (Specialized: cowboy)**, Dept. PM, P.O. Box 326, Eagle ID 83616. (208)888-9838. Fax: (208)888-2986. E-mail: icpg@cowboyrudy. com. Website: www.cowboyrudy.com/icpg1.htm. Established 1988 as *The American Cowboy Poet Newspaper*, magazine format in January 1991. **Publisher:** Rudy Gonzales. **Editor:** Rose Fitzgerald.

Magazine Needs: *The Amercian Cowboy Poet Magazine* is a quarterly "about real cowboys" using "authentic cowboy poetry. Must be clean—entertaining. Submissions should avoid 'like topics.' We will not publish any more poems about Old Blackie dying, this old hat, if this pair of boots could talk, etc. We do not publish free verse poetry. Only traditional cowboy poetry with rhyme and meter." Also publish articles, including a "Featured Poet," stories of cowboy poetry gatherings, and news of coming events. Subscription: $12/year US, $15 Canada, $20 Overseas. Sample: $3.50.

How to Submit: Cover letter required with submissions. Guidelines available for SASE, by e-mail, or on website. Editor always comments on rejected poems. Staff reviews related books and tapes of poetry. Send material for review consideration.

THE AMERICAN DISSIDENT(Specialized: political, social issues), 1837 Main St., Concord MA 01742. E-mail: enmarge@aol.com. Website: www.geocities.com/enmarge. Established 1998. **Editor:** G. Tod Slone.

Magazine Needs: *The American Dissident* appears 2 times/year to "provide an outlet for critics of America." Wants "well-written dissident work (poetry and short 250-750 word essays) in English, French, or Spanish. Submissions should be iconoclastic and anti-obfuscatory in nature and should criticize some aspect of the American scene." *The American Dissident* is 56 pages, digest-sized, offset-printed, perfect-bound, card cover, with sociopolitical cartoons. Press run is 200. Single copy: $7. Subscription: $14.

How to Submit: Submit 3 poems at a time. Accepts simultaneous submissions; no previously published poems. No e-mail submissions. "Include SASE and cover letter containing short bio (Manifest humility! Don't list credits and prizes), including de-programing and personal dissident information and specific events that may have pushed you to reject indoctrination and stand apart from your friends and/or colleagues to speak the rude truth." Time between acceptance and publication up to 9 months. Almost always comments on rejected poems. Guidelines available for SASE. Responds in 1 month. Pays 1 copy. Acquires first North American serial rights. Reviews books and chapbooks of poetry and other magazines in 250 words, single book format. Send materials for review consideration.

Advice: "Poets are not on the edge where they ought to be. They've become too gregarious, comfortable, inbred, self-congratulating, and incapable of acting or speaking as individuals. It is time poets force themselves to stand alone against the herd and permit courage and action to prevail over fear and inaction. They need to harness the wondrous energy produced when courage triumphs over fear. Poets must speak out against corruption and suppression of the first amendment, especially in the poet's immediate surroundings. Do not send general critique, but rather personal-experience verse or prose. *The American Dissident* seeks that rare poem of rude truth that risks, be it ostracism from other poets, loss of reading invitations, chapbook contacts, poetry prizes, money, or even job. No pain, no gain; no fear, no risk . . . no visceral indignation!"

AMERICAN LITERARY REVIEW, University of North Texas, P.O. Box 311307, Denton TX 76203-1307. (940)565-2755. E-mail: americanliteraryreview@yahoo.com. Website: www.engl.unt. edu/alr. **Editors:** Corey Marks. **Poetry Editors:** Bruce Bond and Corey Marks.

Magazine Needs: *American Literary Review* is a biannual publishing all forms and modes of poetry and fiction. "We are especially interested in originality, substance, imaginative power, and lyric intensity." Has published poetry by Matthew Rohrer, Dara Wier, Pattiann Rogers, Donald Revell, Laura Kasischke, and David Biespiell. *American Literary Review* is about 120 pages, digest-sized, attractively printed, perfect-bound, color card cover with photo. Subscription: $10/year, $18/2 years. Sample: $6 (US), $7 (elsewhere).

How to Submit: Submit up to 5 typewritten poems at a time. No fax or e-mail submissions. Cover letter with author's name, address, phone number, and poem titles required. Guidelines available for SASE and on website. Responds in 2 months. Pays 2 contributor's copies.

Also Offers: Sponsors poetry and fiction contest in alternating years. Next poetry contest will be in 2004. Send SASE for details.

AMERICAN RESEARCH PRESS (Specialized: paradoxism); "FLORENTIN SMARA-NDACHE" AWARD FOR PARADOXIST POETRY, P.O. Box 141, Rehoboth NM 87322. E-mail: M_L_Perez@yahoo.com. Website: www.gallup.unm.edu/~smarandache/ebooksliterature.htm. Established 1990. **Publisher:** Minh Perez.

Book/Chapbook Needs: American Research Press publishes 2-3 poetry paperbacks per year. Wants experimental poetry dealing with paradoxism. No classical poetry. See website for poetry samples. Has published poetry by Al. Florin Tene, Anatol Ciocanu, Nina Josu, and Al Bantos.

How to Submit: Submit 3-4 poems at a time. No previously published poems or simultaneous submissions. Cover letter preferred. Submit seasonal poems 1 month in advance. Time between acceptance and publication is 1 year. Seldom comments on rejected poems. Responds to queries in 1 month. Pays 100 author's copies. Order sample books by sending SASE.

Also Offers: Sponsors the "Florentin Smarandache" Award for Paradoxist Poetry. Free e-books available on website.

$⬚ THE AMERICAN SCHOLAR, 1606 New Hampshire Ave., NW, Washington DC 20009. (202)265-3808. Established 1932. Website: www.pbk.org/americanscholar.htm. **Poetry Editor:** Robert Farnsworth. **Associate Editor:** Sandra Costich.

   • Poetry published here has also been included in the 2002 *Pushcart Prize* anthology.

Magazine Needs: *American Scholar* is an academic quarterly which uses about 5 poems/issue. "The usual length of our poems is 34 lines." The magazine has published poetry by John Updike, Philip Levine, and Rita Dove. What little poetry is used in this high-prestige magazine is accomplished, intelligent, and open (in terms of style and form). Study before submitting. Sample: $8; subscription: $25/year, $48/2 years, $69/3 years.

How to Submit: Submit up to 4 poems at a time; "no more for a careful reading. Poems should be typed, on one side of the paper, and each sheet should bear the name and address of the author and the name of the poem." Guidelines available for SASE. Responds in 4 months. Always sends prepublication galleys. Pays $50/poem and 3 contributor's copies. Acquires first rights only.

[N] ○ AMERICAN SOUP MAGAZINE. E-mail: americansoupmagazine@yahoo.com. Website: http://americansoupmagazine.tripod.com. Established 2003. **Founder/Publisher/Editor:** Tanya Shlosman. **Co-Founder/Editor:** Kayla Sheaffer.

Magazine Needs: *American Soup Magazine* is a bimonthly online literary journal. "All poetry submitted will be considered for publication. We would like to see unusual poetry that is willing to be experimental." Does not want greeting card poems. Recently published poetry by Kimberly Richardson and J.R. Corbin. *American Soup Magazine* is published online only. Anticipates publishing up to 30 poems/issue.

How to Submit: Submit 2 poems at a time. Line length for poetry is open. Accepts previously published poems and simultaneous submissions. Accepts e-mail submissions **only** (no attachments); no fax or disk submissions. Cover letter is preferred. Reads submissions all year. Submit seasonal poems 4 months in advance. Time between acceptance and publication is 1 month. Poems are circulated to an editorial board. "We have three editors who read submitted work." Guidelines available by e-mail or on website. Responds in up to 3 weeks. Author retains all rights.

Advice: "Don't be intimidated by literary publishers, everyone has to start somewhere. Keep writing no matter how many rejection slips you may receive."

◎ AMERICAN TANKA (Specialized: form/style, tanka), P.O. Box 120-024, Staten Island NY 10312. E-mail: editor@americantanka.com. Website: www.americantanka.com. Established 1996. **Contact:** Editor.

Magazine Needs: *American Tanka* appears annually each spring and is devoted to single English-language tanka. Wants "concise and vivid language, good crafting, and echo of the original Japanese form." Does not want anything that is not tanka. Has published poetry by Sanford Goldstein, Marianne Bluger, Michael McClintock, Michael Dylan Welch, Jane Reichhold, and George Swede. *American Tanka* is 95-120 pages, digest-sized, perfect-bound, glossy cover, with b&w original drawings. Single copy: $12; subscription: $20.

How to Submit: Submit up to 5 poems at a time; "submit only once per reading period." No previously published poems or simultaneous submissions. Accepts submissions in e-mail text box and through online submission form. Reads manuscripts from September 15 to February 15. Guidelines available for SASE, by e-mail, or on website. Responds in up to 2 months. Acquires first North American serial rights.

Advice: "Become familiar with the tanka form by reading both translations and English-language tanka. In your own tanka, be natural and concrete and vivid. Avoid clichés, overcrowded imagery, or attempting to imitate Japanese poems."

AMERICAN TOLKIEN SOCIETY; MINAS TIRITH EVENING-STAR; W.W. PUBLICATIONS (Specialized: science fiction/fantasy, Tolkien), P.O. Box 7871, Flint MI 48507-0871. Established 1967. **Editor:** Philip W. Helms.

Magazine Needs & How to Submit: Journals and chapbooks use poetry of fantasy about Middle-Earth and Tolkien. Accepts poetry written by children. Has published poetry by Thomas M. Egan, Anne Etkin, Nancy Pope, and Martha Benedict. *Minas Tirith Evening-Star* is digest-sized, offset from typescript, with cartoon-like b&w graphics. Press run is 400 for 350 subscribers of which 10% are libraries. Single copy: $3.50; subscription: $12.50. Sample: $3. Make checks payable to American Tolkien Society. No simultaneous submissions; previously published poems "maybe." Cover letter preferred. "We do not return phone calls unless collect." Editor sometimes comments on rejected poems. Occasionally publishes theme issues. Guidelines available for SASE. Responds in 2 weeks. Sometimes sends prepublication galleys. Pays contributor's copies. Reviews related books of poetry; length depends on the volume, "a sentence to several pages." Send materials for review consideration.

Book/Chapbook Needs & How to Submit: Under the imprint of W.W. Publications, publishes collections of poetry 50-100 pages. For book or chapbook consideration, submit sample poems. Publishes 2 chapbooks/year.

Also Offers: Membership in the American Tokien Society is open to all, regardless of country of residence, and entitles one to receive the quarterly journal. Dues are $12.50 per annum to addresses in US, $12.50 in Canada, and $15 elsewhere. Sometimes sponsors contests.

THE AMHERST REVIEW, Box 2172, Amherst College, P.O. Box 5000, Amherst MA 01002-5000. E-mail: review@amherst.edu. **Editor-in-Chief:** Samuel Masinter.

Magazine Needs: *The Amherst Review*, appearing in April, is an annual (inter)national literary magazine seeking quality submissions in fiction, poetry, nonfiction, and photography/artwork. "All kinds of poetry welcome." *The Amherst Review* is 80 pages, 5×8, soft cover with photography, art, and graphics. Receives 800-900 mss/year, accepts approximately 30. Sample: $6. Make checks payable to *The Amherst Review*.

How to Submit: Accepts simultaneous submissions; no previously published poems. No e-mail submissions. Reads submissions from September through March only. Magazine staff makes democratic decision. Guidelines available for SASE. Responds in April. Pays 1 copy.

$ ANCIENT PATHS (Specialized: religious, Christian). P.O. Box 7505, Fairfax Station VA 22039. E-mail: skylar.burris@gte.net. Website: www.LiteratureClassics.com/ancientpaths/. Established 1998. **Editor:** Skylar H. Burris.

Magazine Needs: *Ancient Paths* is published semiannually in Spring and Fall "to provide a forum for quality Christian literature. It contains poetry, short stories, and art." Wants "traditional rhymed/metrical forms or free verse; Christian images, issues, events or themes. I seek poetry that makes the reader both think and feel. No 'preachy' poetry or obtrusive rhyme; no stream of conscious or avant-garde work; no esoteric academic poetry." Has published poetry by Giovanni Malito, Ida Fasel, Diane Glancy, Walt McDonald, and Donna Farley. *Ancient Paths* is 40 pages, digest-sized, photocopied, side-stapled, cardstock cover, with b&w art. Receives about 400 poems/year, accepts about 10%. Press run is 175 for about 55 paid subscribers, 30 individual copy sales; 80 distributed free to churches, libraries, and authors. Subscription: $7/1 year; $13/2 years. Sample: $3. Make checks payable to Skylar Burris.

How to Submit: Submit up to 5 poems at a time, single-spaced. Line length for poetry is 60 maximum. Accepts previously published poems and simultaneous submissions. Accepts e-mail submissions, but regular mail submissions preferred. "E-mail submissions should be pasted directly into the message, single spaced, one poem per message, using a small or normal font size, with name and address at the top of each submission. Use subject heading: ANCIENT PATHS SUBMISSION, followed by your title." Cover letter not required. "Name, address, and line count on first page. Note if the poem is previously published and what rights (if any) were purchased." Time between acceptance and publication is up to a year. Often comments on rejected poems. Guidelines available for SASE. Responds in "3-4 weeks if rejected, longer if being seriously considered." Pays $1/poem and

The artwork created by Ontario, Canada artist Wendy Lu "expresses the theme of *Ancient Paths* well," says Skylar Burris, editor. "It conveys the Christian content of the magazine as well as a sense of tradition, and it does so in an elegant, subtle way." Burris designed the Spring 2002 cover.

1 copy. Acquires one-time or reprint rights. Reviews other magazines and chapbooks in 100 words. The online journal contains original content not found in the print edition. "Easter and Christmas poems needed for online seasonal issues. Authors published online will receive one free copy of the printed publication (no cash payment for online publication)." Contact Skylar H. Burris.

Advice: "Read the great religious poets: John Donne, George Herbert, T.S. Eliot, Lord Tennyson. Remember not to preach. This is a literary magazine, not a pulpit. This does not mean you do not communicate morals or celebrate God. It means you are not overbearing or simplistic when you do so."

◪**ANHINGA PRESS; ANHINGA PRIZE**, P.O. Box 10595, Tallahassee FL 32302-0595. (850)521-9920. Fax: (850)442-6323. E-mail: info@anhinga.org. Website: www.anhinga.org. Established 1972. **Poetry Editors:** Rick Campbell.

Book/Chapbook Needs: The press publishes "books and anthologies of poetry. We want to see contemporary poetry which respects language. We're inclined toward poetry that is not obscure, that can be understood by any literate audience." Has published *The Secret History of Water* by Silvia Curbelo as well as works by Naomi Shibab Nye, Robert Dana, Lola Haskins, and Ruth L. Schwartz (the 2000 Anhinga Prize winner).

How to Submit: Considers simultaneous submissions. Accepts submissions on disk and by postal mail (no e-mail). Include SASE with all submissions.

Also Offers: The annual Anhinga Prize awards $2,000 and publication to a book-length poetry ms. Send SASE for rules. Submissions accepted February 15 to May 1. Entry fee: $20. Past judges include William Stafford, Louis Simpson, Henry Taylor, Hayden Carruth, Marvin Bell, Donald Hall, and Joy Harjo. "Everything we do is on our website."

Advice: "Write good poetry. Read contemporary poetry. Not necessarily in that order."

◪**ANTHOLOGY; ANTHOLOGY, INC.**, P.O. Box 4411, Mesa AZ 85211-4411. E-mail: info@a nthology.org. Website: www.anthology.org. Executive Editor: Sharon Skinner. **Poetry Editor:** Trish Justrich.

Magazine Needs: *Anthology* appears every 2 months and intends to be "the best poetry, prose, and art magazine." Wants "poetry with clear conceit. Evocative as opposed to provocative. We do not dictate form or style but creative uses are always enjoyed. Graphic horror and pornography are not encouraged." Accepts poetry written by children. Has published poetry by Terry Thomas, Jack Evans,

Lynn Veach Sadler, Dlyn Fairfax Parra, Gerri Green, and Jon Wesick. *Anthology* is 28-32 pages, magazine-sized, saddle-stapled, b&w drawings and clip art inside. Press run is 1,000 for 150 subscribers of which 10 are libraries, with 50-75 distributed free to local coffeehouses, beauty parlors, doctors' offices, etc. Single copy: $3.95; subscription: $20 (6 issues). Make checks payable to *Anthology*.

How to Submit: Submit up to 5 poems at a time with SASE. Line length for poetry is 100 maximum. Accepts previously published or simultaneous submissions. "Do not send handwritten work or unusual fonts." Include name and address on each page of submission. Time between acceptance and publication is up to 8 months. Guidelines available for SASE and on website. Responds in 3 months. Pays 1 copy. Acquires one-time rights.

Also Offers: Sponsors annual contest with cash and other prizes for both poetry and short stories. Entry fee: $1/poem required. Send SASE for guidelines.

Advice: "Send what you write, not what you think an editor wants to hear. And always remember that a rejection is seldom personal, it is just one step closer to a yes."

🌑 ◎ **THE ANTHOLOGY OF NEW ENGLAND WRITERS; ROBERT PENN WARREN POETRY AWARDS (Specialized: form, free verse); NEW ENGLAND WRITERS CONFERENCE; VERMONT POETS ASSOCIATION; NEWSCRIPT (Specialized: membership/subscription)**, P.O. Box 5, Windsor VT 05089. (802)674-2315. Fax: (802)674-2556. E-mail: newvtpoet@aol.com. Website: http://hometown.aol.com/newvtpoet/myhomepage/business.html. Established 1986. **Editor:** Frank Anthony. **Associate Editor:** Susan Anthony.

Magazine Needs: *The Anthology of New England Writers* appears annually in November. All poems published in this annual are winners of their contest. Wants "unpublished, original, free verse poetry only; 10-30 line limit." Open to *all* poets, not just New England. Also accepts poetry written by teenagers. Has published poetry by Richard Eberhart, Rosanna Warren, David Kirby, and Vivian Shipley. *Anthology* is 44 pages, digest-sized, professionally printed, perfect-bound, colored card cover, with b&w illustrations. Press run is 425. Single copy: $4.95. Make checks payable to New England Writers.

How to Submit: Submit 3-9 poems at a time with contest reading fee (3 poems: $6; 6 poems: $10; 9 poems: $15). Include 3×5 card with name, address, and titles of poems. No previously published poems or simultaneous submissions. Reads submissions postmarked January through June 15 only. Guidelines available for SASE or by e-mail. Responds 6 weeks after June 15 deadline. Sends prepublication galleys. Pays 1 copy. All rights revert to author upon publication.

Also Offers: Sponsors an annual free verse contest with The Robert Penn Warren Poetry Awards. Awards $300 for first, $200 for second, and $100 for third. Also awards 10 Honorable Mentions ($20 each), 10 Commendables, and 10 Editor's Choice. Entry fee: $6/3 poems. Winners announced at the New England Writers Conference in July. All submissions are automatically entered in contest. The New England Writers/Vermont Poets Association was established in 1986 "to encourage precision and ingenuity in the practice of writing and speaking, whatever the form and style." Currently has 500 members. Writing information is included in the biannual newsletter, *NewScript*. Meetings are held several times/year. Membership dues: $10, $7 senior citizens and students. Send SASE or e-mail for additional information. Also sponsors the annual New England Writers Conference with nationally known writers and editors involved with workshops, open mike readings, and a writer's panel. 2001 date: July 21. Conference lasts one day and is "affordable," and open to the public.

$ ANTIETAM REVIEW, Washington County Arts Council, 41 S. Potomac St., Hagerstown MD 21740-5512. (301)791-3132. Fax: (240)420-1754. E-mail: winnie@antietamreview.com. Website: http://antietamreview.com. Established 1980. **Managing Editor:** Winnie Wagaman. **Poetry Editor:** Paul Grant.

● Public Radio's series *The Poet and the Poem* recognized *The Antietam Review* as an "outstanding contributor to American Letters."

Magazine Needs: *The Antietam Review* appears annually in June and looks for "well-crafted literary quality poems." Needs 25 poems/issue, up to 30 lines each. Has published poetry by Ace Boggess, Joshua Poteat, and Susan Printz Robb. *Antietam Review* is 76 pages, magazine-sized, saddle-stitched, glossy paper with glossy card cover and b&w photos throughout. Press run is 1,000. Sample: $6.30 back issue, $8.40 current.

How to Submit: Submit 3 typed poems at a time. "We prefer a cover letter stating other publications, although we encourage new and emerging writers. We do not accept previously published poems and reluctantly take simultaneous submissions." No fax or e-mail submissions accepted. "We read from September 1 through February 1 annually." Guidelines available for #10 SASE and on website. Pays $25/poem, plus 2 copies. Acquires first North American serial rights.

Also Offers: Sponsors a Summer Literary Contest. Send #10 SASE for details.

★ ✂ ⌀ **THE ANTIGONISH REVIEW**, P.O. Box 5000, Antigonish NS B2G 2W5 Canada. (902)867-3962. Fax: (902)867-5563. E-mail: TAR@stfx.ca. Website: www.antigonishreview.com. Established 1970. **Editor:** Allan Quigley. **Poetry Editor:** Peter Sanger.

Magazine Needs: *The Antigonish Review* appears quarterly and "tries to produce the kind of literary and visual mosaic that the modern sensibility requires or would respond to." Wants poetry not over "80 lines, i.e., 2 pages; subject matter can be anything, the style is traditional, modern, or post-modern limited by typographic resources. Purpose is not an issue." No "erotica, scatalogical verse, excessive propaganda toward a certain subject." Has published poetry by Andy Wainwright, W.J. Keith, Michael Hulse, Jean McNeil, M. Travis Lane, and Douglas Lochhead. *The Antigonish Review* is 150 pages, digest-sized, flat-spined with glossy card cover, offset-printing, using "in-house graphics and cover art, no ads." Receives 2,500 submissions/year; about approximately 10%. Press run is 850 for 700 subscribers. Subscription: $24. Sample: $4.

How to Submit: Submit 5-10 poems at a time. No simultaneous submissions or previously published poems. Include SASE (or SAE and IRCs if outside Canada). Accepts fax submissions. No e-mail submissions. Time between acceptance and publication is up to 8 months. Editor sometimes comments on rejected poems. Guidelines available for SASE or by e-mail. Responds in 2 months. Pays 2 copies. Acquires first North American serial rights.

$ ⌀ **THE ANTIOCH REVIEW**, P.O. Box 148, Yellow Springs OH 45387. (937)769-1365. Website: www.antioch.edu/review. Established 1941. **Poetry Editor:** Judith Hall.

● Work published in this review has been frequently included in *The Best American Poetry* and *Pushcart Prize* anthologies.

Magazine Needs: *The Antioch Review* "is an independent quarterly of critical and creative thought . . . For well over 50 years, creative authors, poets and thinkers have found a friendly reception . . . regardless of formal reputation. We get far more poetry than we can possibly accept, and the competition is keen. Here, where form and content are so inseparable and reaction is so personal, it is difficult to state requirements or limitations. Studying recent issues of *The Review* should be helpful. No 'light' or inspirational verse." Has published poetry by Harryette Mullen, Colette Inez, Jacqueline Osherow, and Richard Howard. Receives about 3,000 submissions/year, publishes 16 pages of poetry in each issue, and has about a 6-month backlog. Circulation is 5,000, with 70% distributed through bookstores and newsstands. Large percentage of subscribers are libraries. Subscription: $35. Sample: $6.

How to Submit: Submit 3-6 poems at a time. No previously published poems. Reads submissions September 1 through May 1 only. Guidelines available for SASE or on website. Responds in 2 months. Pays $10/published page plus 2 copies. Reviews books of poetry in 300 words, single format.

$ ◎ **ANTIPODES (Specialized: regional, Australia)**, 8 Big Island, Warwick NY 10990. E-mail: kane@vassar.edu. Established 1987. **Poetry Editor:** Paul Kane.

Magazine Needs: *Antipodes* is a biannual of Australian poetry, fiction, criticism, and reviews of Australian writing. **Wants work from Australian poets only.** No restrictions as to form, length, subject matter, or style. Has published poetry by Les Murray, Jan Owen, and John Kinsella. *Antipodes* is 180 pages, magazine-sized, perfect-bound, with graphics, ads, and photos. Receives about 500 submissions/year, accepts about 10%. Press run is 500 for 200 subscribers. Subscription: $25. Sample: $17.

How to Submit: Submit 3-5 poems at a time. No previously published poems or simultaneous submissions. Cover letter with bio note requested. Prefers submission of photocopies which do not have to be returned. Seldom comments on rejected poems. Responds in 2 months. Pays $50/poem plus 1 copy. Acquires first North American serial rights. Staff reviews books of poetry in 500-1,500 words. Send materials for review consideration.

✪ ▱ ◎ **APALACHEE REVIEW; APALACHEE PRESS (Specialized: themes)**, P.O. Box 10469, Tallahassee FL 32302. Established 1971. **Editors:** Laura Newton, Mary Jane Ryals, and Michael Trammell.

Magazine Needs: Has published poetry by David Kirby, Peter Meinke, Alfred Corn, and Virgil Suarez. *Apalachee Review* is 160 pages, digest-sized, professionally printed, perfect-bound, card cover. There are 55-95 pages of poetry in each issue. "Every year we do an issue on a special topic. Past issues include Dental, Revenge, Cocktail Party, and Noir issues." Press run is 700 for 350 subscribers of which 75 are libraries. Subscription: $15. Sample: $5.

How to Submit: Submit clear copies of 3-5 poems, name and address on each. Accepts simultaneous submissions. "We don't read during the summer (June 1 through August 31)." Sometimes comments on rejected poems. Publishes theme issues. Guidelines and a list of upcoming themes available for SASE. Pays 2 copies. Staff reviews books of poetry. Send materials for review consideration.

▱ **APPLES & ORANGES POETRY MAGAZINE; LA GRANDE POMME AWARD.** E-mail: editor@aopoetry.com. Website: www.aopoetry.com. Established 1997. **Editor:** Tom Fallon.

Magazine Needs: *Apples & Oranges Poetry Magazine* appears online. "All poetry forms accepted from international and U.S. poets. See Submission Guide at www.aopoetry.com/aopmsubmit.html." Wants "any poetry form: free verse, prose poems, traditional poetry, experimental forms. Satire, the erotic, humorous, serious religious poetry okay." Does not want greeting card, pornographic, or discriminatory poetry. Recently published poetry by Brendan O'Neill, Kucinta Setia, Ruth Daigon, Miguel de Asen, Anupama Bhargava, Elisha Porat, and Kristen Lindquist. Receives about 2,000 poems/year, accepts about 10%. Publishes about 50 poems/issue.

How to Submit: Poets should submit 3-5 poems at a time. No simultaneous submissions or previously published poems. Cover letter is preferred. "E-mail submissions only: poems in the body of the message. No attachments. See Submission Guide." Reads submissions January 1 to July 1. Time between acceptance and publication is 3 months. "The three-month selection period allows multiple readings of each submission." Never comments on rejected poems. Guidelines available on website. Responds in 3 months. Acquires one-time rights.

Also Offers: La Grande Pomme Award of $300 granted to poetry published in *Apples & Oranges* by an international or US poet during the year.

Advice: "Beginning poets should read *Poet's Market* and the *Apple's & Oranges* submission guide before e-mailing poems to the magazine. And *Apples & Oranges* unequivocally supports a poet's freedom to explore poetic form in any direction."

▱ ◎ **APROPOS (Specialized: subscribers)**, Ashley Manor, 450 Buttermilk Rd., Easton PA 18042. Established 1989. **Editor:** Ashley C. Anders.

Magazine Needs: *Apropos* publishes all poetry submitted by subscribers except that judged by the editor to be pornographic or in poor taste. *Apropos* is 90 pages, desktop-published, digest-sized, plastic ring bound, with heavy stock cover. $25 for 6 issues. Sample: $3.

How to Submit: Submit 1 poem at a time. Line length for poetry is 40 maximum—50 characters/line. Editor prefers to receive sample of poetry prior to acceptance of subscription. Samples will not be returned. Accepts previously published poems; no simultaneous submissions. Guidelines available for SASE. All poems are judged by subscribers. Prizes for regular issues are $50, $25, $10, and $5.

🌐 ▱ **AQUARIUS**, Flat 4, Room B, 116 Sutherland Ave., Maida-Vale, London W9 2QP England. **Poetry Editor:** Eddie Linden.

Magazine Needs & How to Submit: *Aquarius* is a literary biannual publishing poetry, fictional prose, essays, interviews, and reviews. "Please note the magazine will not accept work unless writers have bought the magazine and studied the style/form of the work published." Single copy: $10; subscription: $50 (US); special issue on the poets/writers George Barker and W.S. Graham available for £6 plus £1.25 p&p in United Kingdom. Payment is by arrangement.

◪ $ ▱ **ARC: CANADA'S NATIONAL POETRY MAGAZINE; THE CONFEDERATION POETS PRIZE; POEM OF THE YEAR CONTEST**, P.O. Box 7219, Ottawa ON K1L 8E4 Canada. E-mail: arc.poetry@cyberus.ca. Website: www.cyberus.ca/~arc.poetry. Established 1978. **Co-Editors:** Rita Donovan and John Barton.

● *Arc* received both gold and silver National Magazine Awards in 2001.

Magazine Needs: *Arc* is a biannual of poetry, poetry-related articles, interviews, and book reviews. "Our tastes are eclectic. Our focus is Canadian, but we also publish writers from elsewhere." Has published poetry by Evelyn Lau, Michael Crummey, Erin Mouré, Patricia Young, and Joelene Heathcote. *Arc* is 120 pages, perfect-bound, with varnished 4-color cover, artwork and ads. Receives about 500 submissions/year, accepts approximately 40-50 poems. Press run is 1,500 for 1,000 subscribers. Single copy/sample copy: $11.50 Canadian/Canada; $16 Canadian/US; $18 Canadian/overseas. Subscription (4 issues): $38 Canadian/Canada; $50 Canadian/US; $64 Canadian/overseas.

How to Submit: Submit 5-8 poems, single spaced, with name and address on each page. No previously published poems or simultaneous submissions. Cover letter required. Guidelines available for SAE and IRC and on website; upcoming themes on website and in publication. Responds in 3-6 months. Pays $30 Canadian/page plus 2 copies. Acquires first Canadian serial rights.

Also Offers: The Confederation Poets Prize is an annual award of $100 for the best poem published in *Arc* that year. *Arc* also sponsors a "Poem of the Year Contest." Awards first prize of $1,000, second prize of $750 and third prize of $500. Deadline in June 30.

⊞ $☑ ARC PUBLICATIONS, Nanholme Mill, Shaw Wood Rd., Todmorden, Lancashire OL14 6DA United Kingdom. Phone: (01706)812338. Website: www.arcpublications.co.uk. Established 1969. **Partners:** Tony Ward, Angela Jarman, and Rosemary Jones.

Book/Chapbook Needs: ARC publishes 8 paperback books of poetry/year. Wants "literary, literate, contemporary poetry. No religious or children's verse. We specialize not only in contemporary poetry of the U.K. but also in poetry written in English from across the world." Has published books of poetry by Andy Brown (U.K.), Michael S. Harper (U.S.), Eva Lipska (Poland), Sarah Day (Australia), and Jaqueline Brown (U.K.). Their books are 64-100 pages, digest-sized, offset litho and perfect-bound with card covers in 2-3 colors.

How to Submit: Query first with 10 sample poems and a cover letter with brief bio and publication credits. "No submissions replied to if there is no IRC." Accepts previously published poems and simultaneous submissions. Mss are read by at least 2 editors before possible acceptance. Seldom comments on rejected poems. Guidelines available for SASE. Responds to queries in up to 4 months. Pays 7-10% royalties and 5 author's copies (out of a press run of 600). Send SASE (or SAE and IRCs) for current list to order samples.

Advice: "Poets should have a body of work already published in magazines and journals, and should be acquainted with our list of books, before submitting."

ARCTOS PRESS; HOBEAR PUBLICATIONS, P.O. Box 401, Sausalito CA 94966-0401. (415)331-2503. E-mail: runes@aol.com. Website: http://members.aol.com/RUNES. Established 1997. **Editor:** CB Follett.

Book/Chapbook Needs: Arctos Press, under the imprint HoBear Publications, publishes 1-2 paperbacks each year. "We publish quality books and anthologies of poetry, usually theme-oriented, in runs of 1,000, paper cover, perfect-bound." Has published *GRRRRR, A Collection of Poems About BEARS* (anthology), *Prism*, Poems by David St. John; *Fire Is Favorable to the Dreamer*, poems by Susan Terris; and others.

How to Submit: "We do not accept unsolicited mss unless a current call has been posted in *Poets & Writers* and/or elsewhere, at which time up to 5 poems related to the theme should be sent." Accepts previously published poems (if author holds the rights) and simultaneous submissions ("if we are kept informed"). Accepts submissions by post only. Guidelines and upcoming themes available on website and for SASE. Pays 1 copy; discounts available on additional copies.

FOR EXPLANATIONS OF THESE SYMBOLS,
SEE THE INSIDE FRONT COVER OF THIS BOOK.

Also Offers: *Runes, A Review of Poetry* (see separate listing in this section).

◑ARIES: A JOURNAL OF CREATIVE EXPRESSION, Dept. of Languages and Literature, 1201 Wesleyan St., Fort Worth TX 76105-1536. (817)531-4907. Fax: (817)531-6503. E-mail: aries_jo urnal@yahoo.com. Website: http://web.txwes.edu/languagesliterature/aries.html. Established 1973. **General Editor:** Stacia Dunn Neeley.

Magazine Needs: *Aries* appears annually in June publishing quality poetry, b&w art, fiction, essays, and one-act plays. Wants poetry in all forms up to 50 lines. "Special needs: Spanish language poetry and translation thereof (send *both* versions)." Does not want erotica. Recently published poetry by Virgil Suarez, Richard Robbins, Susan Smith Nash, and Lynn Veach Sadler. *Aries* is 60 pages, digest-sized, offset-printed, perfect-bound, heavy cardstock cover, with b&w art (1500 dpi scans). Receives about 600 poems/year, accepts about 10%. Press run is 300 for 100 subscribers of which 3 are libraries, 125 shelf sales; 50 distributed free to contributors. Single copy: $6; subscription: $6. Sample: $6. Make checks payable to *Aries* general editor, Stacia Neeley.

How to Submit: Submit 1-5 poems at a time. Line length for poetry is 3 minimum, 50 maximum. Accepts simultaneous submissions; no previously published poems. No fax, e-mail, or disk submissions. Cover letter is required. "Blind submissions only: cover letter with titles; no identifying marks on submissions." Reads submissions September 1-January 31 only. Time between acceptance and publication is 3-5 months. "Three editors read every submission blindly. Personal response to *every* submission accompanied by a SASE or functioning e-mail address." Always comments on rejected poems. Guidelines available in magazine, by e-mail, or on website. Responds in up to 6 months. Pays 1 contributor's copy. Acquires first rights.

Advice: "Write in the voice that's most comfortable for you. Our editors tend to choose works where 'there's something at stake.' "

◢ ◎ ARJUNA LIBRARY PRESS; JOURNAL OF REGIONAL CRITICISM (Specialized: surrealism, science fiction/fantasy, spirituality, symbols), 1025 Garner St. D, Space 18, Colorado Springs CO 80905-1774. Library established 1963; press established 1979. **Editor-in-Chief:** Count Prof. Joseph A. Uphoff, Jr.

Magazine Needs: "The Arjuna Library Press is avant-garde, designed to endure the transient quarters and marginal funding of the literary phenomenon (as a tradition) while presenting a context for the development of current mathematical ideas in regard to theories of art, literature, and performance; photocopy printing allows for very limited editions and irregular format. Quality is maintained as an artistic materialist practice." Publishes "surrealist prose poetry, visual poetry, dreamlike, short and long works; no obscene, profane (will criticize but not publish), unpolished work." Has published work by B.Z. Niditch, Siddartha Panda, Chris Volkay, Jabran W. Downs, Nicole Danielle Holoboff, and Julia Skinner. *Journal of Regional Criticism* is published on loose photocopied pages of collage, writing, and criticism, appearing frequently in a varied format. Press run is 1 copy each. Reviews books of poetry "occasionally." Send materials for review consideration. "Upon request will treat material as submitted for reprint, one-time rights."

Book/Chapbook Needs & How to Submit: Arjuna Library Press publishes 6-12 chapbooks/year, averaging 50 pages. Sample: $2.50. Currently accepting one or two short poems, with a cover letter and SASE, to be considered for publication. Accepts submissions by post only. Guidelines available by SASE.

Advice: "Trying to win awards by satisfying requirements is craft, the effort of an artisan. This is a good way to learn and is like copying the work of the old masters such as painters do. If a poet has a personal goal, instead, and practices without overbearing reference or influence, as the work improves or succeeds the awards will be automatic. They will be offered and need not be sought after."

◖ ◎ ARKANSAS REVIEW: A JOURNAL OF DELTA STUDIES (Specialized: regional), P.O. Box 1890, State University AR 72467-1890. (870)972-3043. Fax: (870)972-3045. E-mail: delta @toltec.astate.edu. Website: www.clt.astate/arkreview. Established 1968 (as *Kansas Quarterly*). **General Editor:** William M. Clements. **Creative Materials Editor:** Tom Williams.

Magazine Needs: Appearing 3 times/year, the *Arkansas Review* is "a regional studies journal devoted to the seven-state Mississippi River Delta. Interdisciplinary in scope, we publish academic articles, relevant creative material, interviews, and reviews. Material must respond to or evoke the experiences and landscapes of the seven-state Mississippi River Delta (St. Louis to New Orleans)." Has published poetry by Walt McDonald, Gordon Osing, and Colleen McElroy. *Arkansas Review* is 92 pages, magazine-sized, photo offset-printed, saddle-stapled, 4-color cover, with photos, drawings, and paintings. Receives about 500 poems/year, accepts about 5%. Press run is 600 for 400 subscribers of which 300 are libraries, 20 shelf sales; 50 distributed free to contributors. Subscription: $20. Sample: $7.50. Make checks payable to ASU Foundation.

How to Submit: No limit on number of poems submitted at a time. No previously published poems or simultaneous submissions. Accepts submissions by postal mail, as e-mail attachment, in e-mail text box, and on disk. Cover letter with SASE preferred. Time between acceptance and publication is about 6 months. Poems are circulated to an editorial board. "The Creative Materials Editor makes the final decision based—in part—on recommendations from other readers." Often comments on rejections. Occasionally publishes theme issues. Guidelines available by e-mail or for SASE. Responds in 4 months. Pays 5 copies. Acquires first rights. Staff reviews books and chapbooks of poetry in 500 words, single and multi-book format. Send materials for review consideration to William M. Clements. ("Inquire in advance.")

★ ✂ $ ⊘ ARSENAL PULP PRESS, 103-1014 Homer St., Vancouver BC V6B 2W9 Canada. E-mail: contact@arsenalpulp.com. Website: www.arsenalpulp.com. Established 1980. Publishes 1 paperback book of poetry/year. Only publishes the work of Canadian poets; currently closed to all submissions.

⊘ ARSENIC LOBSTER, 1800 Schodde Ave., Burley ID 83318. Established 2000. **Editors:** Jen Hawkins.

Magazine Needs: *Arsenic Lobster*, which appears biannually in April and October, "prints succulent poems for toxic people. Honed lyricism, stripped narrative." Wants "surgical steel punk, arterial ink, ecstatic gremlins, and hysterical saints. Be charlie-horse hearted and heavily quirked." Does not want "marmalade, hyacinths, or the art of gardening. No cicadas, wheelbarrows, or fond reflections on the old county fair. Nothing about Tai Chi. Nothing written with a cat on your lap." Has published poetry by John Oliver Simon, Cecilia Woloch, Margaret Aho, Rebecca Loudon, Rob Cook, and J.P. Dancingbear. *Arsenic Lobster* is 35 pages, digest-sized, saddle-stapled, illustrated card stock cover. Publishes about 30 poems/issue. Press run is 300. Single copy $4; subscription: $8/year. Make checks payable to Jen Hawkins.

How to Submit: Submit 4-7 poems at a time. Accepts previously published poems and simultaneous submissions. ("Please inform us.") No fax, e-mail, or disk submissions. "Free verse poems and biographical cover letters (not credit lists) preferred; SASE a must." Reads submissions all year. Time between acceptance and publication is 6 months. Responds in 1 month. Pays 1 contributor's copy. Acquires first/one-time rights. Reviews chapbooks and other magazines/journals. Send materials for review consideration, Attn: Jen Hawkins.

⊘ ART TIMES: COMMENTARY AND RESOURCE FOR THE FINE & PERFORMING ARTS, P.O. Box 730, Mount Marion NY 12456-0730. Phone/fax: (845)246-6944. E-mail: poetry@art timesjournal.com. Website: www.arttimesjournal.com. **Poetry Editor:** Raymond J. Steiner.

Magazine Needs: *Art Times* is a monthly tabloid newspaper devoted to the arts. Focuses on cultural and creative articles and essays, but also publishes some poetry and fiction. Wants "poetry that strives to express genuine observation in unique language; poems no longer than 20 lines each." *Art Times* is 20-26 pages, newsprint, with reproductions of artwork, some photos, advertisement-supported. Receives 300-500 poems/month, accepts about 40-50/year. Circulation is 24,000, of which 5,000 are subscriptions; most distribution is free through galleries, theatres, etc. Subscription: $15/year. Sample: $1 with 9×12 SAE and 3 first-class stamps.

How to Submit: Submit 4-5 typed poems at a time, up to 20 lines each. "All topics; all forms." Include SASE with all submissions. No e-mail submissions. Has an 18-month backlog. Guidelines available for SASE. Responds in 6 months. Pays 6 copies plus 1-year subscription.

★ ⊘ ARTISAN, A JOURNAL OF CRAFT, P.O. Box 157, Wilmette IL 60091. E-mail: artisanjnl @aol.com. Website: http://members.aol.com/artisanjnl. Established 1995. **Editor:** Joan Daugherty.

Magazine Needs: *artisan* is a tri-quarterly publication based on the idea that "anyone who strives to express themselves with skill is an artist and artists of all kinds can learn from each other. We want poetry that is vital, fresh, and true to life; evocative. Nothing trite, vague, or pornographic." Has published poetry by Virgil Suarez, Joan Payne Kincaid, and Evelyn Perry. *artisan* is 36 pages (including cover), magazine-sized, saddle-stapled with card stock cover, with minimal graphics and ads. Receives about 450 poems/year, accepts about 10%. Press run is 300 for 100 subscribers; 100 distributed free to coffeehouses and local libraries. Subscription: $18. Sample: $6. Make checks payable to artisan, ink.

How to Submit: Submit 2-3 poems at a time. No previously published poems or simultaneous submissions. Accepts e-mail submissions and queries in attached file, ASCII text format. Cover letter not necessary, however "if you send a cover letter, make it personal. We don't need to see any writing credentials; poems should stand on their own merit." Guidelines available for SASE or on website. Responds in up to 8 months. Pays 2 copies. Acquires first rights.

Also Offers: *artisan* sponsors an annual poetry contest. 1st prize: $200, 2nd prize: $100. Prize winners and works meriting honorable mention are published in an upcoming issue. Entry fee is $5/poem. Postmark deadline: December 31.

✕ $ ◪ ARTS & LETTERS JOURNAL OF CONTEMPORARY CULTURE, Campus Box 89, Georgia College & State University, Milledgeville GA 31061. (478)445-1289. E-mail: al@gcsu.edu. Website: http://al.gcsu.edu. Established 1999. **Editor:** Martin Lammon. **Poetry Editor:** Susan Atefat-Peckham.

● Work published in *Arts & Letters Journal* has received two Pushcart Prizes

Magazine Needs: *Arts & Letters Journal of Contemporary Culture* is a biannual journal devoted to contemporary arts and literature, featuring ongoing series such as The World Poets, Translation Series, and The Mentors Interview Series. Wants work that is of the highest literary and artistic quality. Does not want genre fiction, light verse. Recently published poetry by Margaret Gibson, Marilyn Nelson, Stuart Lishan, R.T. Smith, Laurie Lamon, and Miller Williams. *Arts & Letters Journal of Contemporary Culture* is 180 pages, offset-printed, perfect-bound, glossy cover with varied artwork, also internal b&w photographs and color prints; includes ads. Receives about 4,000 poems/year, accepts about .5%. Publishes about 10 poems/issue. Press run is 1,500 for 1,000 subscribers of which 12 are libraries. Single copy: $8 for current issue plus $1 postage; subscription: $15 for 2 issues (one year). Sample: $5 plus $1 postage for back issue. Make checks payable to Georgia College & State University.

How to Submit: Submit 5 poems at a time. No previously published poems. "Simultaneous submissions are accepted if we are notified immediately of publication elsewhere." No fax, e-mail, or disk submissions. Cover letter is preferred. Include SASE. Reads submissions September 1 through April 30. Poems are circulated to an editorial board. "Poems are screened, discussed by group of readers, then if approved, submitted to Poetry Editor for final approval." Seldom comments on rejected poems. Guidelines available in magazine, for SASE, by e-mail, or on website. Responds in 2 weeks. Always sends prepublication galleys. Pays $10/published page, $50 minimum, plus 2 contributor's copies. Acquires one-time rights. Reviews books of poetry in 2,000 words, multi-book format. Query first to Martin Lammon.

Also Offers: Annual Arts & Letters Prize for Poets ($1,000, publication, and visit to campus for awards program) and annual Arts & Letters Workshops (May of each year, one-week residential workshops in several genres, including poetry).

✕ ◪ ASCENT, Dept. of English, Concordia College, 901 S. Eighth St., Moorhead MN 56562. E-mail: olsen@cord.edu. Established 1975. **Editor:** W. Scott Olsen.

Magazine Needs: *Ascent* appears 3 times/year, using poetry that is "eclectic." Has published poetry by Kate Coles, Sydney Lea, Wendy Bishop, Larry Watson, and Scott Cairns. *Ascent* is 100 pages, digest-sized, professionally printed and perfect-bound with matte card cover. Receives more than 1,000 poems/year, accepts approximately 5%. Press run is 750 for 750 subscribers of which 90 are libraries. Subscription: $12/year. Sample: $5.

How to Submit: Submit 3-6 poems at a time. Always sends prepublication galleys. Pays 2 copies.

Advice: "Poems are rejected or accepted from 2 weeks to 5 months. Acceptances are usually published within the year."

▧ ▨ ◩ ◎ **ASCENT: ASPIRATIONS FOR ARTISTS MAGAZINE**, 1560 Arbutus Dr., Nanoose Bay BC V9P 9C8 Canada. (250)468-7313. E-mail: ascentaspirations@shaw.ca. Website: www.bcsupernet.com/users/ascent. Established 1997. **Editor:** David Fraser.

Magazine Needs: *Ascent: Aspirations for Artists Magazine* appears quarterly and is "a quality electronic publication specializing in poetry, short fiction, essays, and visual art. *Ascent* is dedicated to encouraging aspiring poets and fiction writers. We accept all forms of poetry on any theme. Poetry needs to be unique and to touch the reader emotionally with relevant human, social, and philosophical imagery." Does not want poetry "that focuses on mainstream overtly religious verse." Recently published poetry by Janet Buck and Taylor Graham. *Ascent* is 40 pages, published online with photographs and paintings. Receives about 200 poems/year, accepts about 20%. Publishes about 10 poems/issue.

How to Submit: Submit 1-5 poems at a time. Accepts previously published poems and simultaneous submissions. Accepts e-mail submissions (prefers electronic submissions within the body of the e-mail or as attachment in Word); no disk submissions. Reads submissions all year on a quarterly basis. Time between acceptance and publication is 3 months. Editor makes decisions on all poems. Seldom comments on rejected poems. Occasionally publishes theme issues. List of upcoming themes available on website. Responds in 3 months. Acquires one-time rights.

Advice: "Write with passion for your material. In terms of editing, always proofread to the point where what you submit is the best it possibly can be. Never be discouraged if your work is not accepted; it may be just not the right fit for the current publication."

◕ **ASHEVILLE POETRY REVIEW**, P.O. Box 7086, Asheville NC 28802. (828)649-0217. E-mail: editor@ashevillereview.com. Website: www.ashevillereview.com. Established 1994. **Founder/Managing Editor:** Keith Flynn.

Magazine Needs: *Asheville Poetry Review* appears "every 200 days. We publish the best regional, national, and international poems we can find. We publish translations, interviews, essays, historical perspectives, and book reviews as well." Wants "quality work with well-crafted ideas married to a dynamic style. Any subject matter is fit to be considered so long as the language is vivid with a clear sense of rhythm." Has published poetry by Robert Bly, Yevgeny Yevtushenko, Eavan Boland, and Fred Chappell. *Asheville Poetry Review* is 160-180 pages, digest-sized, perfect-bound, laminated, full-color cover, b&w art inside. Receives about 2,500 poems/year, accepts about 5-10%. Press run is 1,000. Subscription: $22.50/1 year, $43.50/2 years. Sample: $13. "We prefer poets purchase a sample copy prior to submitting."

How to Submit: Submit 3-5 poems at a time. Accepts simultaneous submissions; no previously published poems. No submissions by e-mail. Cover letter required. Include comprehensive bio, recent publishing credits, and SASE. Submission deadlines: January 15 and July 15. Time between acceptance and publication is up to 7 months. Poems are circulated to an editorial board. Seldom comments on rejected poems. Publishes theme issues occasionally. Guidelines and upcoming themes available for SASE. Responds in up to 7 months. Pays 1 copy. Rights revert back to author upon publication. Reviews books and chapbooks of poetry. Send materials for review consideration.

◕ **ATLANTA REVIEW; POETRY 2004**, P.O. Box 8248, Atlanta GA 31106. E-mail: dan@atlantareview.com. Website: www.atlantareview.com. Established 1994. **Editor:** Dan Veach.

● Work published in this review has been included in the *Pushcart Prize* anthologies.

Magazine Needs: *Atlanta Review* is a semiannual primarily devoted to poetry, but also featuring fiction, interviews, essays, and fine art. Wants "quality poetry of genuine human appeal." Has published poetry by Seamus Heaney, Derek Walcott, Maxine Kumin, and Naomi Shihab Nye. *Atlanta Review* is 128 pages, digest-sized, professionally printed on acid-free paper, flat-spined, glossy color cover, with b&w artwork. Receives about 10,000 poems/year, accepts about 1%. Press run is 2,500 for 1,000 subscribers (50 are libraries), 1,000 shelf sales. Single copy: $6; subscription: $10. Sample: $5.

How to Submit: No previously published poems. No e-mail submissions unless outside North America. Issue deadlines are June 1 and December 1. Time between acceptance and publication is 3 months. Seldom comments on rejected poems. Guidelines available for SASE. Responds in 2 weeks. Pays 2 copies plus author's discounts. Acquires first North American serial rights.

Also Offers: *Atlanta Review* also sponsors POETRY 2004, an annual international poetry competition. Prizes: $2,004, $500, and $250, plus 50 International Merit Awards. Winners announced in leading literary publications. All entries considered for publication in *Atlanta Review*. Entry fee: $5 for the first poem, $2 for each additional. No entry form or guidelines necessary. Postmark deadline: May 11, 2004.

Advice: "We are giving today's poets the international audience they truly deserve."

$◙ THE ATLANTIC MONTHLY, Dept. PM, 77 North Washington St., Boston MA 02114. Website: www.theatlantic.com. Established 1857. **Poetry Editor:** Peter Davison. **Assistant Poetry Editor:** David Barber.

● Poetry published here has been included in every volume of *The Best American Poetry*.

Magazine Needs: *The Atlantic Monthly* publishes some of the most distinguished poetry in American literature, including work by Andrew Hudgins, Stanley Kunitz, Rodney Jones, Galway Kinnell, Philip Levine, Richard Wilbur, Donald Hall, and W.S. Merwin. Has a circulation of 500,000, of which 5,800 are libraries. Receives some 60,000 poems/year, accepts about 30-35, has an "accepted" backlog of 6-12 months. Sample: $4.95.

How to Submit: Submit 3-5 poems with SASE. No simultaneous submissions. No fax or e-mail submissions. Publishes theme issues. Responds in 3 weeks. Always sends prepublication galleys. Pays about $4/line. Acquires first North American serial rights only.

Advice: Wants "to see poetry of the highest order; we do *not* want to see workshop rejects. Watch out for workshop uniformity. Beware of the present tense. Be yourself."

◙ THE AUROREAN: A POETIC QUARTERLY; THE UNROREAN; ENCIRCLE PUBLICATIONS, P.O. Box 219, Sagamore Beach MA 02562. Phone/fax: (508)833-0805. E-mail: cafpoet3 7@aol.com. Press established 1992. Magazine established 1995. **Editor:** Cynthia Brackett-Vincent.

Magazine Needs: *The Aurorean*, which appears in March, June, September, and December, seeks to publish "poetry that is inspirational (but not religious), meditational, or reflective of the Northeast. Strongly encouraged (but not limited to) topics: positiveness, recovery, and nature. Maximum length: 40 lines. No hateful, overly religious or poetry that uses four-letter words for four-letter words' sake. Use mostly free-verse; occasional rhyme; I am biased toward haiku and well-written humor. I'm *always* in need of short (2-6 lines), seasonal poems. For seasonal poems, please note specific deadlines in our guidelines." Welcomes submissions from both beginning and experienced poets. Accepts poetry written by children. Has published poetry by Rod Farmer, Robert K. Johnson, Robin Merrill, Alice Persons, and Pearl Mary Wilshaw. *The Aurorean* is 36 pages of poetry, 5 pages of contributor's bios, digest-sized, professionally printed, perfect-bound with papers and colors varying from season to season. Open to exchange ads. Press run is 550. Single copy: $6 US, $7 international. Subscription: $21 US, $25 international. Make checks payable to Encircle Publications or *The Aurorean*.

How to Submit: Submit 3-5 poems at a time. No previously published poems or simultaneous submissions. No e-mail or fax submissions. Cover letter strongly preferred with first submission. "Poems folded individually can not be read. Fold cover letter separately, then entire batch of poems together." Sometimes comments on rejected poems. Guidelines available for SASE. Authors notified when ms received if SASE or e-mail address included. Responds on acceptance in up to 3 months. Always sends prepublication galleys. Pays 3 copies/poem with an-up-to 50-word bio in the "Who's Who" section. Also features a "Poet-of-the-Quarter" each issue with publication of up to 3 poems and an extended bio (100 words). The "Poet-of-the-Quarter" receives 10 copies and a 1-year subscription. Reviews chapbooks of poetry published in the last 6 months. Send material for review consideration to the editor (cannot be acknowledged or returned).

Also Offers: "New contests for *The Aurorean:* each issue an independent judge picks Best-Poems-of-Last-Issue; winner receives $20. Send entries for Poetic-Quote-of-the-Season (cannot be acknowledged or returned); 4 lines maximum, quote by not-too-obscure poet." Source must be cited. Winner receives 2 free issues. "New broadsheet, *The Unrorean*, will appear 2/year . . . experimental, risque, and for poems that might not fit *The Aurorean*. Still, nothing hateful. SASE for return/reply. No proofs, acknowledgements, deadlines, or bio listings. 11 × 17; laser-printed. $2 each postpaid." Pays one copy/poem published. Unless otherwise requested, work sent to *The Aurorean* will also be considered for the broadsheet.

Advice: "Study *Poet's Market*. Be familiar with any journal before submitting."

$ ◻ AUSABLE PRESS, 1026 Hurricane Rd., Keene NY 12942-9719. E-mail: editor@ausablepre ss.com. Website: www.ausablepress.com. Established 1999. **Editor:** Chase Twichell. Member: CLMP.

Book/Chapbook Needs & How to Submit: Ausable Press wants poetry "that investigates and expresses human consciousness in language that goes where prose cannot." Does not want children's poetry or poetry for children, light verse, inspirational poetry, illustrated poetry, or journal entries. Recently published poetry by William Matthews, C.K. Williams, Steve Orlen, Julianne Buchsbaum, and James Richardson. Publishes 4-6 paperback or hardback titles/year. Number of pages varies, offset-printed, paper and cloth editions. "Please send SASE for submission guidelines or visit our website (www.ausablepress.com)." Accepts unsolicited mss in June and July only. **Charges reading fee of $20.** Responds to queries in 1 week; to mss in up to 4 months. Pays royalties of 5-8%, advance of $1,000 and 20 author's copies (out of a press run of 2,000).

Advice: "This is not a contest. Ausable Press is under no obligation to publish any of the manuscripts submitted. Response time can be as long as 3-4 months, so please be patient."

◎ AVOCET, A JOURNAL OF NATURE POEMS (Specialized: nature, spirituality), P.O. Box 8041, Calabasas CA 91372-8041. E-mail: patricia.j.swenson@csun.edu. Website: www.csun. edu/~pjs44945/avocet.html. First issue published fall 1997. **Editor:** Patricia Swenson.

Magazine Needs: *Avocet* is a quarterly poetry journal "devoted to poets seeking to understand the beauty of nature and its interconnectedness with humanity." Wants "poetry that shows man's interconnectedness with nature; discovering the Divine in nature." Does not want "poems that have rhyme or metrical schemes, cliché, abstraction, and sexual overtones." Has recently published poetry by Donna J. Waidtlow, Fred Boltz, Joan Goodwin, Paul B. Roth, Sharron Kollmeyer, and Judy Snow. *Avocet* is 30 pages, 4¼ × 5½, professionally printed, saddle-stapled, card cover, with some illustrations. Single copy: $5; subscription: $20. Make checks payable to Pat Swenson.

How to Submit: Submit up to 5 poems at a time. Accepts previously published poems if acknowledged; no simultaneous submissions. Accepts e-mail submissions with name, city, state, and e-mail address; include submission in body of message, no attachments. Cover letter required including SASE. Time between acceptance and publication is up to 6 months. Responds in 8 weeks. Pays 1 contributor's copy.

★ ◎ THE AWAKENINGS REVIEW (Specialized: people living with mental illness), University of Chicago, Center for Psychiatric Rehabilitation, 7230 Arbor Dr., Tinley Park IL 60477. (708)614-4770. Fax: (708)614-4780. E-mail: rklundin@uchicago.edu. Website: www.ucpsychrehab.o rg. Established 1999. **Editor:** Robert Lundin.

Magazine Needs: *The Awakenings Review* appears biannually to publish works by people living with mental illness: consumers, survivors, family members, ex-patients. Wants "meaningful work, good use of the language. Need not be about mental illness." Recently published poetry Joan Rizzo, Wanda Washko, Ben Beyerlein, and Trish Evers. *The Awakenings Review* is 150 pages, digest-sized, perfect-bound, b&w, glossy cover, with some art/graphics. Receives about 800 poems/year, accepts about 20%. Publishes about 80 poems/issue. Press run is 1,000 for 100 subscribers of which 2 are libraries, 600 shelf sales; 300 are distributed free to contributors, friends. Single copy $15; subscription: $30. Sample: $10. Make checks payable to *Awakenings Review*.

How to Submit: Submit 5 poems at a time. No previously published poems or simultaneous submissions. Does not accept e-mail submissions. Cover letter is preferred. Include SASE and short bio. Submit seasonal poems 6 months in advance. Time between acceptance and publication is 8 months. Poems are read by a board of editors. Often comments on rejected poems. Poet "must live with mental illness: consumer, survivor, family member, ex-patient." Occasionally publishes theme issues. Guidelines are available in magazine, for SASE, by e-mail. Responds in 1 month. Always sends prepublication galleys. Pays 4 contributor's copies. Acquires first rights. Send materials for review consideration.

Advice: "Include a cover letter with your publishing experience. We value knowing your relationship to mental illness: consumer, survivor, family member, friend, professional."

◔ AXE FACTORY REVIEW; CYNIC PRESS, P.O. Box 40691, Philadelphia PA 19107. E-mail: cynicpress@yahoo.com. *Axe Factory* established 1986. Cynic Press established 1996. **Editor/Publisher:** Joseph Farley.

Magazine Needs: *Axe Factory* is published 1-4 times/year and its purpose is to "spread the disease known as literature. The content is mostly poetry and essays. We now use short stories too." Wants "eclectic work. Will look at anything but suggest potential contributors purchase a copy of magazine first to see what we're like. No greeting card verse." Accepts poetry written by children. "Parents should read magazine to see if they want their children in it as much material is adult in nature." Has published *River Architecture: poems from here & there* by Louis McKee and poetry by Taylor Graham, A.D. Winans, Normal, and John Sweet. *Axe Factory* is 20-40 pages, magazine-sized, saddle-stapled, neatly printed with light card cover. Press run is 100. Current issue: $9; sample: $8; subscription: $24 for 4 issues. Make checks payable to Cynic Press or Joseph Farley.

How to Submit: Submit up to 10 poems. Accepts previously published poems "sometimes, but let me know up front" and simultaneous submissions. Cover letter preferred "but not a form letter, tell me about yourself." Often comments on rejected poems. Pays 1-2 copies. " 'Featured poet' receives more." Reserves right to anthologize poems under Cynic Press; all other rights returned. Several anthologies planned; upcoming themes available for SASE, by e-mail, and in publication. Reviews books of poetry in 10-1,000 words. Send materials for review consideration.

Book/Chapbook Needs & How to Submit: Cynic Press occasionally publishes chapbooks. Published *Yellow Flower Girl* by Xu Juan, *Under the Dogwoods* by Joseph Banford, *Ceiling of Mirrors* by Shane Allison, and *13 Ways of Looking at Godzilla* by Michael Hafer. Send $10 reading fee with ms. No guarantee of publication. All checks to Cynic Press. Contest information available by e-mail.

Advice: "Writing is a form of mental illness, spread by books, teachers, and the desire to communicate."

▣ ◪ ◎ BABEL: The multilingual, multicultural online journal and community of arts and ideas (Specialized: bilingual/foreign language). E-mail: malcolm@towerofbabel.com. Website: www.towerofbabel.com. Established 1995. Editor-in-Chief: Malcolm Lawrence.

Magazine Needs: "*Babel* is an electronic zine which publishes regional reports from international stringers all over the planet, as well as features, round table discussions, fiction, columns, poetry, erotica, travelogues, and reviews of all the arts and editorials. We are an online community involving an extensive group of over 50 artists, writers and programmers, and over 150 translators representing (so far) 36 of the world's languages. We encourage poetry from all over the planet, especially multicultural poetry as well as multilingual poetry or poetry which has been translated into or from another language, so long as it is in English at least. We also encourage gay/lesbian, bisexual, and pansexual writers. Please, God, no more Bukowski wannabe's. Poetry is not a Darwinian competition. It is an expression of who you are. We're not interested in male-bashing or female-bashing poetry. There's a difference between the person who broke your heart and half of the human race. Please don't confuse poetry with therapy. If you do have to bash something, bash the real enemy: corporations. The more they keep us bashing each other, the more they know we won't have the energy to bash them." Has published poetry by Federico Garcia Lorca, Leila Imam-Kulieva, Yves Jaques, and Suzanne Gillis. Receives about 100 poems/year, accepts approximately 5%.

How to Submit: Submit no more than 10 poems at a time. Accepts previously published poems and simultaneous submissions. E-mail submissions only. Cover letter required. "Please send submissions with a résumé/cv or biography as a Microsoft Word or RTF document attached to e-mail." Time between acceptance and publication varies; "usually no more than a month or two depending on how busy we are." Seldom comments on rejected poems. Obtain guidelines via website. Responds in 2-4 weeks. Reviews books and chapbooks of poetry and other magazines, single and multi-book format. Open to unsolicited reviews. Poets may also send books for review consideration.

Advice: "We would like to see more poetry with first-person male characters written by female poets as well as more poetry with first-person female characters written by male poets. The best advice we could give to writers wanting to be published in our publication is simply to write passionately."

◯ BABYSUE®, P.O. Box 33369, Decatur GA 30033. Established 1985. Website: www.babysue.com. and www.LMNOP.com. **Editor/Publisher:** Don W. Seven.

Magazine Needs: *babysue* appears twice/year publishing obtuse humor for the extremely open-minded. "We are open to all styles, but prefer short poems." No restrictions. Has published poetry by Edward Mycue, Susan Andrews, and Barry Bishop. *babysue* is 32 pages, offset-printed. "We print prose, poems, and cartoons. We usually accept about 5% of what we receive." Subscription: $16 for 4 issues. Sample: $4.

How to Submit: Accepts previously published poems and simultaneous submissions. Deadlines are March 30 and September 30 of each year. Seldom comments on rejected poems. Responds "immediately, if we are interested." Pays 1 copy. "We do occasionally review other magazines."

Advice: "We have received no awards, but we are very popular on the underground press circuit and sell our magazine all over the world."

◼◪◍ BACCHAE PRESS; SCOW BAY BOOKS; BACCHAE PRESS POETRY CHAPBOOK CONTEST, 10 Sixth St., Suite 215, Astoria OR 97103. E-mail: rbrown@oregonreview.com. Website: www.oregonreview.com. Established 1992. **Publisher/Editor:** Robert Brown.

Book/Chapbook Needs: Under the imprints Bacchae Press and Scow Bay Books, publishes poets who are in transition from smaller to larger publishers. Publishes 2 paperbacks and 4 chapbooks/year. Wants "high quality, literary poetry by poets who read and reflect. No greeting card verse." Books are usually 60-90 pages, offset-printed, perfect-bound, heavy card stock cover, with art/graphics. Chapbooks are usually 28 pages, offset-printed, saddle-stapled, heavy card stock cover.

How to Submit: Query first with 5 sample poems and cover letter with brief bio and publication credits. Accepts previously published poems and simultaneous submissions. No fax or e-mail submissions. Time between acceptance and publication is 6-12 months. Poems are circulated to an editorial board. Seldom comments on rejected poems. Responds to queries in 1 month; to mss in 2 months. Pays 25 author's copies (out of a press run of 300-500). Order sample books/chapbooks by sending $5 to Bacchae Press.

Also Offers: Sponsors the annual Bacchae Press Poetry Chapbook Competition. Winner receives 25 copies of the chapbook, scheduled to be published in August. Submit 16-24 typed ms pages., no more than 1 poem/page. "With your submission, include a brief bio, acknowledgements, and a SASE for return of your manuscript and/or contest results." Entry fee: $9, includes copy of the winning chapbook. Deadlines: April 15. Winners will be announced in June.

◍ BARDSONG PRESS; CELTIC VOICE ANNUAL CONTESTS (Specialized: Celtic-themed), P.O. Box 775396, Steamboat Springs CO 80477-5396. Fax: (970)879-2657. E-mail: celts@bardsongpress.com. Website: www.bardsongpress.com. Established 1997. **Editor:** Ann Gilpin. Member: SPAN, PMA, CIPA.

Book/Chapbook Needs: At Bardsong Press "our quest is to encourage and celebrate Celtic heritage and culture through poetry, short stories, essays, creative nonfiction, and historical novels. We are looking for poetry that reflects the ageless culture, history, symbolism, mythology, and spirituality that belongs to Celtic heritage. Any style or format is welcome. If it is not Celtic-themed, don't submit it." Bardsong Press publishes 1 paperback/year. Book is usually offset-printed, perfect-bound.

How to Submit: Query first, with a few sample poems and cover letter with brief bio and publication credits. Book mss may not include previously published poems. Responds to queries in 1 month; to mss in 3 months. Pays 25 author's copies (out of a press run of 500). Order sample books by sending $11.95 to Bardsong Press.

Also Offers: "We also sponsor an annual 'Celtic Voice' writing contest which usually includes a poetry category. Entry fee is $10. Small cash award and copies of anthology in which poem is published." Guidelines available for SASE, by e-mail, or on website. Deadline is September 30.

Advice: "Please follow the publisher's guidelines; neatness counts, too."

$◍ BARNWOOD PRESS; BARNWOOD, P.O. Box 146, Selma IN 47383. (765)288-0149. Fax: (765)285-3765. E-mail: tkoontz@bsu.edu. Website: www.barnwoodpress.org. Established 1975. **Editor:** Tom Koontz.

Magazine Needs: *Barnwood* appears online "to serve poets and readers by publishing excellent poems." Does not want "expressions of prejudice such as racism, sexism." Has published poetry by Bly, Goedicke, Friman, and Stafford. Receives about 1,500 poems/year, accepts about 2%.

How to Submit: Submit 1-3 poems at a time. Accepts simultaneous submissions; no previously published poems. Accepts submissions by postal mail only. "SASE or no response." Reads submissions September 1 through May 31 only. Time between acceptance and publication is 1 day. Seldom comments on rejected poems. Responds in 1 month. Pays $25/poem. Acquires one-time rights.

Book/Chapbook Needs & How to Submit: Barnwood Press publishes 1 paperback and 1 chapbook of poetry/year. Has recently published *The White Poems* by Barbara Crooker and *Whatever You Can Carry* by Stephen Herz. Chapbooks are usually 12-32 pages, size varies, offset printed and saddle-stapled with paper cover and cover art. Query first with a few sample poems and cover letter with brief bio and publication credits. Responds to queries and mss in 1 month. Payment varies. Order sample books or chapbooks by sending price of book plus $2.50.

Advice: "Emphasize imagination, passion, engagement, artistry."

BARROW STREET; BARROW STREET PRESS, P.O. Box 2017, Old Chelsea Station, New York NY 10113-2017. E-mail: info@barrowstreet.org. Website: www.barrowstreet.org. Established 1998. **Editors:** Patricia Carlin, Peter Covino, Lois Hirshkowitz, Melissa Hotchkiss.
• Poetry published in *Barrow Street* has been selected for inclusion in *The Best American Poetry 2000, 2001* and *2002*.

Magazine Needs: "*Barrow Street*, a poetry journal appearing twice yearly, is dedicated to publishing new and established poets." Wants "poetry of the highest quality; open to all styles and forms." Has published poetry by Kim Addonizio, Lyn Hejinian, Brian Henry, Jane Hirshfield, Phillis Levin, and Molly Peacock. *Barrow Street* is 96-120 pages, digest-sized, professionally printed and perfect-bound with glossy cardstock cover with color and photography. Receives about 3,000 poems/year, accepts about 3%. Press run is 1,000. Subscription: $15/1 year, $28/2 years, $42/3 years. Sample: $8.

How to Submit: Submit up to 5 poems at a time. Accepts simultaneous submissions (when notified); no previously published poems. Cover letter with brief bio preferred. Reads submissions year round. Poems are circulated to an editorial board. Seldom comments on rejected poems. Publishes theme issues occasionally. Guidelines available for SASE or on website. Responds in approximately 6 months. Always sends prepublication galleys. Pays 2 copies. Acquires first rights.

Book/Chapbook Needs & How to Submit: Barrow Street Press was established in 2002. Recently published *Sellah* by Joshua Corey. Submit ms to Barrow Street Press Book Contest. Publication of ms in book form and $1,000 awarded to "best previously unpublished manuscript of poetry in English." Manuscript should be single-spaced and on white 8½ × 11 paper. Photocopies acceptable. Include 2 title pages and acknowledgement page listing where any poem has appeared in a publication. Author's name, address, and daytime phone should appear on first title page only. Include SASE for notification and $25 entry fee. Make checks payable to Barrow Street. Deadline in 2003 was July 1. See website for current guidelines.

Advice: "Submit your strongest work."

BATHTUB GIN; PATHWISE PRESS, P.O. Box 2392, Bloomington IN 47402. E-mail: charter@bluemarble.net. Website: http://home.bluemarble.net/~charter/ginmain.htm. Established 1997. **Editor:** Christopher Harter.

Magazine Needs: *Bathtub Gin*, a biannual appearing in April and October, is "an eclectic aesthetic . . . we want to keep you guessing what is on the next page." Wants poetry that "takes a chance with language or paints a vivid picture with its imagery . . . has the kick of bathtub gin, which can be experimental or a sonnet. No trite rhymes . . . Bukowski wannabes (let the man rest) . . . confessional (nobody cares about your family but you)." Has published poetry by Kell Robertson, Mark Terrill, Carmen Garmain, and Lindsay Wilson. *Bathtub Gin* is approximately 60 pages, digest-sized, laser-printed, saddle stapled, 80 lb. coverstock cover, includes photography, collages, line drawings. "We feature a 'News' section where people can list their books, presses, events, etc." Receives about 1,200 poems/year, accepts about 5%. Press run is 250 for 50 subscribers, 60 shelf sales; 10 distributed free to reviewers, other editors, and libraries. Subscription: $8. Sample: $5; foreign orders add $2; back issues: $3.50. Make checks payable to Christopher Harter.

How to Submit: Submit 4-6 poems at a time. Include SASE. Accepts previously published poems and simultaneous submissions. Accepts submissions by postal mail and by e-mail (include ms in text box). "Three to five line bio required if you are accepted for publication . . . if none [given], we make one up." Cover letter required. Reads submissions July 1 through September 15 and January

1 through March 15 only. Time between acceptance and publication is up to 4 months. Often comments on rejected poems. Guidelines available for SASE, by e-mail, on website, and in publication. Responds in 2 months. Pays 1 contributor's copy. "We also sell extra copies to contributors at a discount, which they can give away or sell at full price."

Book/Chapbook Needs & How to Submit: Pathwise Press's goal is to publish chapbooks, broadsides, and "whatever else tickles us." Has published *Bone White/Raven Black* by John Gohmann, *You Write Your Life Like Fiction* by Gordon Annand, and *Living Room, Earth* by Carmen Germaine. For publishing guidelines, send SASE or visit website.

Advice: "Submission etiquette goes a long way. Always include a cover letter. I receive too many submissions with no cover letter to explain what the poems are for (*Bathtub Gin* or a chapbook or what?). Make sure the poems are neat and without typos; if you don't care about your submission, why should I?"

⭐ ◎ ∅ **WILLIAM L. BAUHAN, PUBLISHER (Specialized: regional)**, P.O. Box 443, Old County Rd., Dublin NH 03444. Fax: (603)563-8026. E-mail: info@bauhanpublishing. Website: www.bauhan.com/. Established 1959. Editor: William L. Bauhan. Publishes poetry and art, especially New England regional books. *Currently accepts no unsolicited poetry.*

◑ **BAY AREA POETS COALITION (BAPC); POETALK**, P.O. Box 11435, Berkeley CA 94712-2435. E-mail: poetalk@aol.com. Established 1974. Direct submissions to Editorial Committee. Coalition sends quarterly poetry journal, *Poetalk*, to over 300 people. Also publishes an annual anthology (25th edition: 120 pages, out in Spring 2004), giving one page to each member of BAPC (minimum 6 months) who has had work published in *Poetalk* during the previous year.

Magazine Needs: *Poetalk* publishes approximately 70 poets each issue. BAPC has 150 members, 70 subscribers, but *Poetalk* is open to all. No particular genre. Short poems (under 35 lines) are preferred. "Longer poems of outstanding quality accepted. Rhyme must be well done." Has published poetry by Barry Ballard, Carol Hamilton, Kevin Roddy, Fred Ostrander, and Mona Locke. Membership: $15/year of *Poetalk*, copy of anthology and other privileges; extra outside US. Also offers a $50 patronage, which includes a subscription and anthology for another individual of your choice, and a $25 beneficiary/memorial, which includes membership plus subscription for friend. Subscriptions: $6/year. *Poetalk* is 36 pages, digest-sized, photocopied, saddle-stapled with heavy card cover. Send SASE with 83¢ postage for a free complimentary copy.

How to Submit: Submit up to 4 poems, typed and single-spaced, with SASE, no more than twice a year. "Manuscripts should be clearly typewritten and include author's name and mailing address on every page. Include e-mail address if you have one." Accepts simultaneous and previously published work, but must be noted. Response time is up to 4 months. Pays 1 copy. All rights revert to authors upon publication.

Also Offers: BAPC holds monthly readings (in Berkeley, CA) and a yearly contest, etc. Send SASE in early September for contest guidelines, or request via e-mail.

Advice: "If you don't want suggested revisions you need to say so clearly in your cover letter or indicate on each poem submitted."

◑ ◎ **BAY WINDOWS (Specialized: gay/lesbian)**, 631 Tremont St., Boston MA 02118. E-mail: rKikel@baywindows.com. Website: http://BayWindows.com. Established 1983. **Poetry Editor:** Rudy Kikel.

Magazine Needs: *Bay Windows* is a weekly gay and lesbian newspaper published for the New England community, regularly using "short poems of interest to lesbians and gay men. Poetry that is 'experiential' seems to have a good chance with us, but we don't want poetry that just 'tells it like it is.' Our readership doesn't read poetry all the time. A primary consideration is giving pleasure. We'll overlook the poem's (and the poet's) tendency not to be informed by the latest poetic theory,

OPENNESS TO SUBMISSIONS: ◖ beginners; ◑ beginners and experienced; ◕ mostly experienced, few beginners; ◎ specialized; ∅ closed to all submissions.

if it does this: pleases. Pleases, in particular, by articulating common gay or lesbian experience, and by doing that with some attention to form. I've found that a lot of our choices were made because of a strong image strand. Humor is always welcome—and hard to provide with craft. Obliquity, obscurity? Probably not for us. We won't presume on our audience." Has published poetry by Scott Wiggerman, Dennis Rhodes, David Eberly, Christina Hutchins, Sunita K. Singhi, and Mina Kumar. "We try to run four poems each month." Receives about 300 submissions/year, accepts about 1 in 10, has a 3-month backlog. Press run is 24,000 for a circulation of 60,000. Single copy: 50¢; subscription: $40. Sample: $3.

How to Submit: Submit 3-5 poems at a time, "up to 30 lines are ideal; include short biographical blurb and SASE. No submissions via e-mail, but poets may request info via e-mail." Responds in up to 6 months. Pays 1 copy "unless you ask for more." Acquires first rights. Editor "often" comments on rejected poems. Reviews books of poetry in about 750 words—"Both single and omnibus reviews (the latter are longer)."

★ ◑ ◎ **BEACON STREET REVIEW (Specialized: graduate-level writers)**, Dept. of Writing, Literature, and Publishing, 120 Boyleston St., Emerson College, Boston MA 02116. E-mail: beaconstreetreview@hotmail.com. Established 1986. **Contact:** Poetry Editor.

Magazine Needs: *Beacon Street Review* appears biannually "to publish the best prose (fiction and nonfiction) and poetry we receive; to publish specifically the poetry that evidences the highest degree of creative talent and seriousness of effort and craft. Facile poetry that is not polished and crafted and poems that lack a strange sense of the 'idea' will not be ranked highly. Submissions from Emerson students as well as writers across the country are welcomed and encouraged." Has published poetry by Charlotte Pence, John McKernan, and Paul Berg. *Beacon Street Review* is 96-104 pages, digest-sized, offset-printed and perfect-bound with 4-color, matte finish cover with art/photo. Receives about 700 poems/year, accepts about 4%. Press run is 1,000; 200 distributed free to Emerson College students. Subscription: $10/year (2 issues), $18/2 years (4 issues). Sample: $6.

How to Submit: Submit 3-5 poems at a time. Accepts simultaneous submissions; no previously published poems. No fax, e-mail, or disk submissions. Cover letter required. "Poets should include four copies of each poem. The poet's name and address should not appear on those copies but should appear on the cover letter with all titles clearly listed." Reads submissions year round but responds only during early December and early April. Time between acceptance and publication is 2 months. Poems are circulated to an editorial board. "We have reading boards who read and rate all poems, submitting ranks and comments to a poetry editor. The poetry editor and the editor-in-chief confer with those ranks and comments in mind and then make final decisions." Send SASE for guidelines. Responds in 2 months. Pays 3 copies. Acquires first rights. Staff reviews of poetry in 250 words, single book format. Send materials for review consideration to editor-in-chief.

Also Offers: Sponsors the Editor's Choice Awards. Selected by local established poets, the award gives a cash prize for the best poem published in *Beacon Street Review* during the year.

★ ◑ ◎ **BEAR CREEK HAIKU (Specialized: haiku/senryu; poems under 5 lines)**, P.O. Box 3787, Boulder CO 80307. Established 1991. **Editor:** Ayaz Daryl Nielsen.

Magazine Needs: *Bear Creek Haiku* appears irregularly in an extra-small format, publishing poems of 5 lines or less. Wants especially haiku/senryu plus poetry of any form and style no longer than 5 lines. Recently published poetry by Carol Schwalberg, Miriam Sagan, Kelly Jean White MD, Ron Hughes, and Ed Markowski. *Bear Creek Haiku* is 12 pages, Xeroxed on legal-sized colored paper that is cut in thirds, stacked three-high, folded in the middle, and stapled (finished size is $2\frac{1}{2} \times 7$ inches). Includes sumi ink artwork by Laurel A. Starkey. Receives about 1,000 poems/year, accepts about 15%. Publishes about 11-15 poems/issue. Press run is 20-30, distributed free to poets. Single copy: free for SASE; subscription: $5/year. Make checks payable to Daryl Nielsen.

How to Submit: Submit 5-20 poems at a time. Line length for poetry is 1 minimum, 5 maximum. Accepts previously published poems and simultaneous submissions. No fax, e-mail, or disk submissions. "Name and address on each page, with several haiku on each page. Keep your mailing expenses to 2 First-Class stamps, one of which is on the SASE." Reads submissions year round. Submit seasonal poems anytime. Time between acceptance and publication varies, averages 6 months. "If a poem is remotely close, we'll ask poet about revision—and have published the original and revised poem together. Appreciate poetic interaction, albeit usually brief." Often comments on rejected poems. Responds in 1 month. Pays 1 contributor's copy. Acquires first rights.

Also Offers: "Beginning in '03 and continuing yearly, will publish an anthology including all poets published the prior year, one copy to each poet. Am considering a series of chapbooks, format as yet undecided for anthologies and chapbooks. Will contact potential victims about chapbooks."

Advice: "Would appreciate receiving your own personal favorites, be they simultaneously submitted or published elsewhere or never before seen. Write, create your poems—the heart, spirit, shadow, ancestors, an occasional editor, and etc. will benefit deeply."

$ 回 THE BEAR DELUXE (Specialized: nature/ecology), P.O. Box 10342, Portland OR 97296-0342. (503)242-1047. Fax: (503)243-2645. E-mail: bear@orlo.org. Website: www.orlo.org. Established 1993. **Editor:** Tom Webb. **Contact:** poetry editor.

• Note: *The Bear Deluxe* is published by Orlo, a nonprofit organization exploring environmental issues through the creative arts.

Magazine Needs: *The Bear Deluxe*, formerly *Bear Essential*, is a semiannual that "provides a fresh voice amid often strident and polarized environmental discourse. Street-level, non-dogmatic, and solution-oriented, *The Bear Deluxe* presents lively creative discussion to a diverse readership." Wants poetry with "innovative environmental perspectives, not much longer than 50 lines. No rants." Has published poetry by Judith Barrington, Robert Michael Pyle, Mary Winters, Stephen Babcock, Carl Hanni, and Derek Sheffield. *Bear Deluxe* is 60 pages, 11×14, newsprint with brown Kraft paper cover, saddle-stapled, with lots of original graphics and b&w photos. Receives about 1200 poems/year, accepts about 20-30. Press run is 19,000 for 750 subscribers of which 20 are libraries, 18,000 distributed free on the streets of the Western US and beyond. Subscription: $16. Sample: $3. Make checks payable to Orlo.

How to Submit: Submit 3-5 poems at a time up to 50 lines each. Accepts previously published poems and simultaneous submissions, "so long as noted." Accepts e-mail submissions, "in body of message. We can't respond to e-mail submissions but do look at them." Poems are reviewed by a committee of 7-9 people. Publishes 1 theme issue/year. Guidelines and a list of upcoming themes available for SASE. Responds in 6 months. Pays $10/poem, 5 copies (more if willing to distribute), and subscription. Acquires first or one-time rights.

$ 🖉 回 BEAR STAR PRESS; DOROTHY BRUNSMAN POETRY PRIZE (Specialized: regional), 185 Hollow Oak Dr., Cohasset CA 95973. (530)891-0360. E-mail: bspencer@bearstarpres s.com. Website: www.bearstarpress.com Established 1996. **Publisher/Editor:** Beth Spencer.

Book/Chapbook Needs: Bear Star Press accepts work by poets from Western and Pacific states ("Those in West of Central time zone"). "Bear Star is committed to publishing the best poetry it can attract. Each year it sponsors a contest open to poets from Western and Pacific states, although other eligibility requirements change depending on the composition of our list up to that point. From time to time we add to our list other poets from our target area whose work we admire." Wants "well-crafted poems. No restrictions as to form, subject matter, style or purpose." Has published *Poems in Which* by Joseph Di Prisco, *The Archival Birds* by Melissa Kwaswy, *The Bandsaw Riots* by Arlitia Jones, *Closet Drama* by Kandie St. Germain, and *The Book of Common Betrayals* by Lynne Knight. Publishes 1-2 paperbacks and occasionally chapbooks. Books are usually 35-75 pages, size varies, professionally printed, and perfect-bound. Chapbooks are usually $7; full-length collections, $12.

How to Submit: "Poets should enter our annual book competition. Other books are occasionally solicited by publisher, sometimes from among contestants who didn't win." Accepts previously published poems and simultaneous submissions. "Prefer single-spaced manuscripts in plain font such as Times New Roman. SASE required for results. Manuscripts not returned but are recycled." Generally reads submissions September through November. Guidelines available for SASE or on website. Contest entry fee: $16. Time between acceptance and publication is up to 9 months. Poems are circulated to an editorial board. "I occasionally hire a judge. More recently I have taken on the judging with help from poets whose taste I trust." Seldom comments on rejected poems. Responds to queries regarding competitions in 1-2 weeks. Contest winner notified February 1 or before. Contest pays $1,000 and 25 author's copies (out of a press run of up to 750).

Advice: "Send your best work, consider its arrangement. A 'Wow' poem early on keeps me reading."

✦ ◯ ◎ **BELHUE PRESS (Specialized: gay)**, 2501 Palisade Ave., Suite A1, Riverdale, Bronx NY 10463. E-mail: belhuepress@earthlink.net. Website: www.perrybrass.com. Established 1990. Editor: Tom Laine.

Book/Chapbook Needs: A small press specializing in gay male poetry, publishing 3 paperbacks/year—no chapbooks. "We are especially interested in books that get out of the stock poetry market." Wants "hard-edged, well-crafted, fun and often sexy poetry. No mushy, self pitying, confessional, boring, indulgent, teary or unrequited love poems—yuck! Poets must be willing to promote book through readings, mailers, etc." "We have a $10 sample and guideline fee. Please send this before submitting any poetry. We have had to initiate this due to a deluge of bad, amateur, irrelevant submissions. After fee, we will give constructive criticism when necessary."

How to Submit: Query first with 6 pages of poetry and cover letter. Accepts previously published poems and simultaneous submissions. Time between acceptance and publication is 1 year. Often comments on rejected poems. Will request criticism fees "if necessary." Responds "fast" to queries and submitted mss. No payment information provided. Sample: $9.95.

Advice: "The only things we find offensive are stupid, dashed off, 'fortune cookie' poems that show no depth or awareness of poetry. We like poetry that, like good journalism, tells a story."

◑ **BELLINGHAM REVIEW; 49TH PARALLEL POETRY AWARD**, M.S. 9053, Western Washington University, Bellingham WA 98225. E-mail: bhreview@cc.wwu.edu. Website: www.wwu.edu/~bhreview/. Established 1975. **Editor:** Brenda Miller. **Contact:** Poetry Editor.

Magazine Needs: *Bellingham Review* appears twice/year. "We want well-crafted poetry but are open to all styles," no specifications as to form. Has published poetry by David Shields, Tess Gallagher, Gary Soto, Jane Hirshfield, Albert Goldbarth, R.T. Smith, and Rebecca McClanahan. *Bellingham Review* is digest-sized, perfect-bound, with art and matte cover. Each issue has about 60 pages of poetry. Circulation is 1,500. Subscription: $14/year, $27/2 years. Sample: $7. Make checks payable to The Western Foundation/*Bellingham Review*.

How to Submit: Submit 1-3 poems at a time with SASE. Accepts simultaneous submissions with notification. No fax or e-mail submissions. Reads submissions October 1 through February 1 only. Guidelines available for SASE or on website. Responds in 2 months. Pays 1 copy, a year's subscription plus monetary payment (if funding allows). Acquires first North American serial rights.

Also Offers: The 49th Parallel Poetry Award, established in 1983, awards a $1,000 first prize plus publication and a year's subscription to the *Bellingham Review*. Submissions must be unpublished and may be entered in other contests. "Include a 3×5 card with title, author's name, and address. Author's name must not appear anywhere on the manuscript. Entry fee is $15 for up to 3 poems." No fax or e-mail submissions. "Entries must be postmarked between December 1 and March 15." Guidelines available for SASE or website. Most recent award winner was Kerri Webster, 2002. Judge was Mark Doty. Winners will be announced in summer.

◑ **BELLOWING ARK; BELLOWING ARK PRESS**, P.O. Box 55564, Shoreline WA 98155. (206)440-0791. Established 1984. **Editor:** Robert R. Ward.

Magazine Needs: *Bellowing Ark* is a bimonthly literary tabloid that "publishes only poetry which demonstrates in some way the proposition that existence has meaning or, to put it another way, that life is worth living. We have no strictures as to length, form or style; only that the work we publish is to our judgment life-affirming." Does not want "academic poetry, in any of its manifold forms." Has published poetry by James Hobbs, Len Blanchard, Paula Milligan, Esther Cameron, Margaret Hodge, and Jacqueline Hill. *Bellowing Ark* is 32 pages, tabloid-sized, printed on electrobright stock with b&w photos and line drawings. Circulation is 1,000, of which 275 are subscriptions and 500 are sold on newsstands. Subscription: $15/year. Sample: $3.

How to Submit: Submit 3-6 poems at a time. "Absolutely *no* simultaneous submissions." Accepts submissions by postal mail and on disk only. Responds to submissions in up to 12 weeks and publishes within the next 1 or 2 issues. Occasionally will criticize a ms if it seems to "display potential to become the kind of work we want." Sometimes sends prepublication galleys. Pays 2 copies. Reviews books of poetry. Send materials for review consideration.

Book/Chapbook Needs & How to Submit: Bellowing Ark Press publishes collections of poetry by *invitation only*.

⬤ ◎ **BELL'S LETTERS POET (Specialized: subscribers)**, P.O. Box 2187, Gulfport MS 39505-2187. E-mail: jimbelpoet@aol.com. Established 1956. **Publisher/Editor:** Jim Bell.

Magazine Needs: *Bell's Letters Poet* is a quarterly which you must buy ($5.50/issue, $22 subscription) to be included. "Many say they stop everything the day it arrives," and judging by the many letters from readers, that seems to be the case. Though there is no payment for poetry accepted, many patrons send cash awards to the poets whose work they especially like. Poems are "four to 20 lines in good taste." Wants "clean writing; no vulgarity, no artsy vulgarity." Has published poetry by Dawn Zapletal, Virginia Ditomas, Dolores Malaschak, and Patrick Flavin. *Bell's Letters Poet* is about 60 pages, digest-sized, photocopied on plain bond paper (including cover) and saddle-stapled. Sample: $5. "Send a poem (20 lines or under, in good taste) with your sample order and we will publish in our next issue."

How to Submit: Submit 4 poems at a time. No simultaneous submissions. Accepts previously published poems "if cleared by author with prior publisher." Accepts submissions by regular mail only. Accepted poems by subscribers go immediately into the next issue. Guidelines available for SASE and in publication. Deadline for poetry submissions is 2 months prior to publication. Reviews books of poetry by subscribers. "The Ratings" is a competition in each issue. Readers are asked to vote on their favorite poems, and the "Top 40" are announced in the next issue, along with awards sent to the poets by patrons. *Bell's Letters Poet* also features a telephone and e-mail exchange among poets, a birth-date listing, and a profile of its poets.

Advice: "Tired of seeing no bylines this year? Subscription guarantees a byline in each issue."

⬤ **THE BELOIT POETRY JOURNAL; CHAD WALSH POETRY PRIZE**, 24 Berry Cove Rd., Lamoine ME 04605-4617. (207)778-0020. E-mail: sharkey@maine.edu (for information only). Website: www.bpj.org. Established 1950. **Editor:** Marion K. Stocking.

- Poetry published in *The Beloit Poetry Journal* has also been included in *The Best American Poetry* (1994, 1996, 2000, and 2002) and *Pushcart Prize* anthologies.

Magazine Needs: *The Beloit Poetry Journal* is a well-known, long-standing quarterly of quality poetry and reviews. "We publish the best poems we receive, without bias as to length, school, subject, or form. It is our hope to discover the growing tip of poetry and to introduce new poets alongside established writers. We publish occasional chapbooks to diversify our offerings, most recently *Poets Under Twenty-Five*. These are almost never the work of one poet." Wants "fresh, imaginative poetry, with a distinctive voice. We tend to prefer poems that make the reader share an experience rather than just read about it, and these we keep for up to four months, circulating them among our readers, and continuing to winnow for the best. At the quarterly meetings of the Editorial Board we read aloud all the surviving poems and put together an issue of the best we have." Has published poetry by Bei Dao, Albert Goldbarth, Patricia Goedicke, Glori Simmons, and Janet Holmes. *The Beloit Poetry Journal* averages 48 pages, digest-sized, saddle-stapled, and attractively printed with tasteful art on the card cover. Circulation is 1,250 for 725 subscribers of which 225 are libraries. Subscription: individuals $18/year, institutions $23/year. Sample (including guidelines): $5. Guidelines without sample available for SASE.

How to Submit: Submit any time, without query, any legible form. "No previously published poems or simultaneous submissions. Any length of ms, but most poets send what will go in a business envelope for one stamp. Don't send your life's work." No e-mail submissions. Pays 3 copies. Acquires first serial rights. Editor reviews books by and about poets in an average of 500 words, usually single format. Send materials for review consideration.

Also Offers: The journal awards the Chad Walsh Poetry Prize ($3,000 in 2002) to a poem or group of poems published in the calendar year. "Every poem published in 2004 will be considered for the 2004 prize."

Advice: "We are always watching for new poets, fresh insights, live forms and language."

◼ ◻ **BETWEEN WHISPER AND SHOUT PUBLISHING; PURDUE INK POETRY.** E-mail: KXZX@hotmail.com. Website: http://geocities.com/bws5000/index.html. Established 1999. **Editor:** Kate Zielinski.

Magazine Needs: Between Whisper and Shout Publishing and *Purple Ink Poetry* are looking for well written poetry. Wants "poetry from new or experienced poets. Any form or style is welcome as well as any purpose. No pornography, epic, or extremely violent poems are even considered." Submit 2-3 poems at a time. Line length for poetry is 40 maximum. Accepts previously published poems and simultaneous submissions. Accepts e-mail submissions *only*. "Include all poems in the body of the e-mail; no attachments please! Include e-mail address. Poet may include a brief bio to be posted with submission(s)." Reads submissions constantly, but "site updates are done every other month." Submit seasonal poems 2 months in advance. Editor reads all submissions and chooses according to available space on the website and the quality of the poems. Seldom comments on rejections.

Advice: "Send in poetry that you are proud of and never, ever be afraid of rejection; it fuels better work in the future."

$ 🖉 ◎ BIBLE ADVOCATE (Specialized: Christian, religious), P.O. Box 33677, Denver CO 80233. E-mail: bibleadvocate@cog7.org. Website: www.cog7.org/BA. Established 1863. **Associate Editor:** Sherri Langton.

Magazine Needs: *Bible Advocate*, published 10 times/year, features "Christian content—to advocate the Bible and represent the church." Wants "free verse, some traditional; 5-20 lines, with Christian/Bible themes." Does not want "avant garde poetry." *Bible Advocate* is 24 pages, magazine-sized with most poetry set up with 4-color art. Receives about 30-50 poems/year, accepts about 10-20. Press run varies for 13,500 subscribers with all distributed free.

How to Submit: Submit no more than 5 poems at a time, 5-20 lines each. Accepts previously published poems (with notification) and simultaneous submissions. Accepts e-mail submissions with text included in body of message; no attachments. "No fax or handwritten submissions, please." Cover letter preferred. Time between acceptance and publication is up to 12 months. "I read them first and reject those that won't work for us. I send good ones to editor for approval." Seldom comments on rejected poems. Publishes theme issues. Guidelines and upcoming themes available for SASE and on website. Responds in 2 months. Pays $20 and 2 contributor's copies. Acquires first, reprint, electronic, and one-time rights.

Advice: "Avoid trite, or forced rhyming. Be aware of the magazine's doctrinal views (send for doctrinal beliefs booklet)."

◎ 🖉 BIBLIOPHILOS (Specialized: bilingual/foreign language, ethnic/nationality, political, social issues, writing), 200 Security Building, Fairmont WV 26554. (304)366-8107. Established 1981. **Editor:** Gerald J. Bobango.

Magazine Needs: "*Bibliophilos* is an academic journal, for the literati, illuminati, amantes artium, and those who love animals; scholastically oriented, for the liberal arts. Topics include fiction and nonfiction; literature and criticism, history, art, music, theology, philosophy, natural history, educational theory, contemporary issues and politics, sociology, and economics. Published in English, French, German, Romanian." Wants "traditional forms, formalism, structure, rhyme; also blank verse. Aim for concrete visual imagery, either in words or on the page. No inspirational verse, or anything that Ann Landers or Erma Bombeck would publish." Accepts poetry written by children, ages 10 and up. Has published poetry by Lenore M. Coberly, Thomas Michael McDade, Virgil Suarez, Albert Russo, Belle Randall, Jack Lloyd Packard, and Edward Locke. *Bibliophilos* is 68 pages, digest-sized, laser photography printed and saddle-stapled with light card, includes clip art, ads. Receives about 200 poems/year, accepts about 33%. Press run is 300 for 175 subscribers. Subscription: $18/year, $35/2 years. Sample: $5.25. Make checks payable to *The Bibliophile*. West Virginia residents please add 6% sales tax.

How to Submit: Closed to unsolicited submissions. Query first with SASE and $5.25 for sample and guidelines. Then, if invited, submit 3-5 poems at a time. Accepts previously published poems and simultaneous submissions. Cover letter with brief bio preferred. Time between acceptance and publication is up to 1 year. Often comments on rejected poems. Guidelines available for SASE. Responds in 2 weeks. Pays 2 copies. Acquires first North American serial rights. Staff reviews books and chapbooks of poetry in 750-1,000 words, single book format. Send materials for review consideration.

Also Offers: Sponsors poetry contest. Send SASE for rules. 1st Prize $25 plus publication.

Advice: "Study our listing in *Poet's Market*, and read the entire thing! Then take our advice, and don't get snotty when we refuse to make an exception for you or don't answer you when you send unsolicited material. And do *not* send 'what is the status of my stuff' letters, once something is accepted."

N M ◎ BIG CITY LIT (Specialized: themes); LYRIC RECOVERY FESTIVAL™; HEAD-WATERS/HUDSON PRESS; THE AUTHOR'S WATERMARK, INC., P.O. Box 1141, Cathedral Station, New York NY 10025. (212)865-3443 or (212)864-2823. E-mail: editors@nycBigCityLit.com. Website: www.nycBigCityLit.com. Established 2000. **Senior Editors:** Nicholas Johnson and Maureen Holm.

Magazine Needs: "Professionally edited, NYC's premier online literary monthly offers a cohesive, theme-based poetry anthology (Feature) and special hand-picked, non-theme section (Twelve-12), plus city-specific Bridge City Lit (foreign language) and Big City, Little (personal vantage). Also in every issue: Fiction/Short Prose; Bookshelf (first chapters); essays; articles, interviews; book reviews, event listings and reviews, Series on Series (self-profile), Other Arts (dance, theatre, etc.); Legal Forum and Free Expressions sections (commentary/analysis)." Wants all forms of poetry; multi-part; ekphrasis; narrative; dramatic monlogue; translations; experimental. Does not want "dominant paradigm domestic joys/sorrows; childhood reminiscence ('I remember when we used to . . .'); self-therapy; missives to/from the muse; shock value, polemic; body-part erotica." Recently published poetry by James Ragan, David Yezzi, Mervyn Taylor, Alice B. Fogel, Rob Wright, and Adam Merton Cooper. *Big City Lit* appears online and in print format; print version is 28-40 pages, magazine-sized, laser-printed, saddle-stapled, full-color cover on 60 lb. glossy, includes art/graphics and ads. Receives about 3,000 poems/year, accepts about 15%. Publishes about 30 poems/issue. Press run is 15,000. Single copy: $10. Make checks payable to Headwaters Press.

How to Submit: Submit 3-5 poems at a time. Line length for poetry is 2 minimum, 600 maximum. Accepts previously published poems and simultaneous submissions if disclosed. Accepts e-mail and disk submissions; no fax submissions. Cover letter is required. Send hard copy, or e-mail with copy pasted in the body of the message. "No attachments except as subsequently requested." Reads submissions year round. Submit seasonal poems 3 months in advance. Time between acceptance and publication is up to 6 months. Poems are circulated to an editorial board. "All editors, including guests, recommend and recruit. Final decisions are made by senior editors Johnson and Holm." Often comments on rejected poems. Regularly publishes theme issues. List of upcoming themes available on website. Guidelines available in magazine or on website. Responds in 2 weeks. Always sends prepublication galleys. No payment. Rights revert to author; retains "broad license to reprint consistent with applicable law." Reviews books and chapbooks of poetry and other magazines/journals in 300-1,200 words, single book and multi-book format. Poets may send materials for review consideration to the attention of the Articles Editor.

Book/Chapbook Needs & How to Submit: Headwaters/Hudson Press publishes digest-sized compilations from the online magazine, full-format newsstand versions, and monographs; also, chapbooks and full-length poetry collections. Publishes 2 books, 6 chapbooks, and 6 anthologies/year. Manuscripts are selected from the magazine, through open submissions, and through competition. See website for rules and guidelines. Books/chapbooks are 16-56 pages, laser-printed, saddle-stapled, full-color or b&w cover with art/graphics. Query first, with a few sample poems and a cover letter with brief bio and publication credits. Book/chapbook mss may include previously published poems. Responds to queries in 2 weeks; to mss in 1 month. Pays royalties of 7%, 20 author's copies (out of a press run of 100). Order sample books/chapbooks by contacting Headwaters Press.

Also Offers: The Lyric Recovery Festival™, featuring contest winners as well as music, dance, and theatre, is produced by philophonema™ biannually (in spring) at Carnegie's Weill Hall. Headwaters Press publishes the anthology of 20-24 award-winning poems. The top prize ($1,000) at LyR 2002 went to a poem by Bertha Rogers selected by Alfred Corn. The judge for LyR 2000 was Dana Gioia.

Advice: "Poetry lies the more shallow-exposed in another's speech the deeper it lies in one's own. The diffident listener has first corrupted his own dialogue between poet and poem, thus, corrections must begin there. Extreme deference to the poem during the compositional dialogue and unobtrusive service during delivery are indispensable to its retrieval from the nonverbal nether into the speech-illumined world . . . When we try to override the poems' ego-free will by force of intellect—syntactical pushing and shoving or recalcitrant insistence on clever purport—it refuses to debate, flees, or worse, squats impassive on the page. Triteness is the revenge of the poem bullied, misquoted, or ignored." (From "Ego-Free, The Poem Aloft," an essay by Maureen Holm).

◎ **BILINGUAL REVIEW PRESS; BILINGUAL REVIEW/REVISTA BILINGÜE (Special-ized: ethnic/Hispanic, bilingual/Spanish)**, Hispanic Research Center, Arizona State University, Box 872702, Tempe AZ 85287-2702. (480)965-3867. Journal established 1974, press in 1976. **Managing Editor:** Karen Van Hooft.

Magazine Needs: "We are a small press publisher of U.S. Hispanic creative literature and of a journal containing poetry and short fiction in addition to scholarship." *Bilingual Review/Revista Bilingüe,* published 3 times/year, contains some poetry in most issues. "We publish poetry by and/ or about U.S. Hispanics and U.S. Hispanic themes. We do not publish translations in our journal or literature about the experiences of Anglo-Americans in Latin America. We have published a couple of poetry volumes in bilingual format (Spanish/English) of important Mexican poets." Has published poetry by Alberto Ríos, Martín Espada, Judith Ortiz Cofer, and Marjorie Agosín. *Bilingual Review/ Revista Bilingüe* is 96 pages, 7×10, offset-printed and flat-spined, with 2-color cover. Accepts less than 10% of hundreds of submissions received each year. Press run is 1,000 for 700 subscribers. Subscriptions: $25 for individuals, $40 for institutions. Sample: $9 individuals/$14 institutions.

How to Submit: Submit "two copies, including original if possible, with loose stamps for return postage." Cover letter required. Pays 2 copies. Acquires all rights. Reviews books of US Hispanic literature only. Send materials, Attn: Editor, for review consideration.

$ ◪ ◎ **BIRCH BROOK PRESS (Specialized: nature, sports/recreation)**, P.O. Box 81, Delhi NY 13753. (212)353-3326 (messages only). Website: www.birchbrookpress.info. Established 1982. **Contact:** Tom Tolnay. Member: American Academy of Poets, Small Press Center, American Typefounders Fellowship.

Book/Chapbook Needs: Birch Brook "is a letterpress book printer/typesetter/designer that uses monies from these activities to publish several titles of its own each year with cultural and literary interest." Specializes in literary work, flyfishing, baseball, outdoors, anthologies, books about books. Has published *The Moonlit Door*, by Frank Fagan; *Shadwell Hills*, by Rebecca Lilly; *Contemporary Martyrdom*, by John Popielaski; *Longing for Laura*, by A.M. Juster; *Beowulf*, by Bertha Rogers; *Walking the Perimeters of the Plate Glass Window Factory*, by Jared Smith. Publishes 4-6 paperbacks and/or hardbacks per year. The press specializes "mostly in anthologies with specific subject matter. Birch Brook Press occasionally publishes one or two books annually by individuals with high-quality literary work on a co-op basis." Books are "handset letterpress editions printed in our own shop."

How to Submit: Query first with sample poems or send entire ms. "Must include SASE with submissions." Occasionally comments on rejected poems. Authors may obtain sample books by sending SASE for catalog. Guidelines also available for SASE. Pays from $5-20 for publication in anthology.

Advice: "Send your best work, and see other Birch Brook Press books."

◪ **THE BITTER OLEANDER; FRANCES LOCKE MEMORIAL AWARD**, 4983 Tall Oaks Dr., Fayetteville NY 13066-9776. (315)637-3047. Fax: (315)637-5056. E-mail: bones44@ix.netcom. com. Website: www.bitteroleander.com. Established 1974. **Editor/Publisher:** Paul B. Roth.

● Poetry published in *The Bitter Oleander* has been included in *The Best American Poetry*.

Magazine Needs: *The Bitter Oleander* appears biannually in April and October, publishing "imaginative poetry; poetry in translation; serious language." Wants "highly imaginative poetry whose language is serious. We prefer short poems of no more than 30 lines. Highly interested in translations. Has published poetry by Christine Boyka Kluge, Robert Bly, Alan Britt, Duane Locke, Silvia Scheibli, Anthony Seidman, and Charles Wright. *The Bitter Oleander* is 128 pages, digest-sized, offset-printed, perfect-bound with glossy 4-color cover, cover art, ads. Receives about 10,000 poems/year, accepts about 1%. Press run is 1,500; 1,000 shelf sales. Single copy: $8; subscription: $15. Make checks payable to Bitter Oleander Press.

How to Submit: Submit up to 5 poems at a time with name and address on each page. No previously published poems or simultaneous submissions. No e-mail submissions unless outside U.S. Cover letter preferred. Does not read mss during July. Time between acceptance and publication is 6 months. Guidelines available for SASE and on website. "All poems are read by the editor only and all decisions are made by this editor." Often comments on rejected poems. Responds within a month. Pays 1 copy.

Also Offers: Sponsors the Frances Locke Memorial Award, awarding $1,000 and publication. Submit any number of poems. Entry fee: $10/5 poems, $2 each additional poem. Open to submissions March 15 through June 15 only.

Advice: "We simply want poetry that is imaginative and serious in its performance of language. So much flat-line poetry is written today that anyone reading one magazine or another cannot tell the difference."

◐ ◎ BLACK BEAR PUBLICATIONS; BLACK BEAR REVIEW (Specialized: social issues), 1916 Lincoln St., Croydon PA 19021-8026. E-mail: BBReview@earthlink.net. Website: http://BlackBearReview.com. Established 1984. **Poetry and Art Editor:** Ave Jeanne (editor@blackbearreview.com). **Business Manager:** Ron Zettlemoyer.

Magazine Needs: *Black Bear Review* is a semiannual international literary and fine arts magazine in print and online. Seeks "well-crafted poetry that mirrors the intensities of life. We seek energetic poetry, avant-garde, free verse and haiku which relate to a social awareness. We seldom publish the beginner, but all submissions are judged on the poem rather than the poet. No traditional poetry is used. The underlying theme of Black Bear Publications is social concerns, but the review is interested also in environmental, war/peace, ecological, human rights, poverty, discrimination, apathy, and minorities themes. We would like to receive more ideas on mental health, life styles, and current political topics." Has recently published poetry by A.D. Winans, John Grey, Alan Catlin, and Carlos Martinez. *Black Bear Review* is 64 pages, digest-sized, perfect-bound, offset from typed copy on white stock, with line drawings, collages, and woodcuts. Circulation is 500 for 300 subscribers of which 15 are libraries. Subscription: $12, $18 overseas. Sample: $6; back copies when available are $5 (overseas add $3/copy). Make checks payable to Ron Zettlemoyer.

How to Submit: Submit no more than 5 poems by e-mail. "Surface mail submissions of poetry are not considered and will not be returned. E-mail submissions are answered within a week, use Arial or Times New Roman font. Include snail mail address. No attached files considered." Simultaneous submissions are not considered. Time between acceptance and publication is 6 months. Guidelines available on website. Pays 1 copy. Acquires first North American serial rights and electronic rights, "as work may appear on our website."

Book/Chapbook Needs & How to Submit: Publishes 2 chapbooks/year. "Publication is now on a subsidy basis." Consideration for chapbook series requires a **reading fee of $15**, complete ms, and cover letter sent via snail mail. Guidelines available on website. For book publication, requires that "Black Bear Publications has published the poet and is familiar with his/her work." Author receives one-half print run. Recently published *Tracers* by Gerald Wheeler.

Also Offers: "Our yearly poetry competition offers cash awards to poets." **Deadline:** November 30. Guidelines available on website. "Our website is designed and maintained by Ave Jeanne and is updated regularly to meet the diverse needs of our readers to keep writers informed of editorial needs, and to keep the socially concerned informed of current topics and resources. *Bear Facts* is our online newsletter, which readers can subscribe to at no charge. Details can be found on website. Mark Zettlemoyer, *Bear Facts* Editor (MarkZett@earthlink.net.)"

Advice: "We appreciate a friendly, brief cover letter. All submissions are handled with objectivity and timeliness. Keep e-mail submissions professional. We frequently suggest poets keep up with the current edition of *Poet's Market*. We make an effort to keep our readers informed and on top of the small press scene. Camera-ready ads are printed free of charge as a support to small press publishers. Ad space for relevant advertising is also available on the website. We do suggest poets and artists read issues before submitting to absorb the flavor and spirit of our publication. Send your best! Visit our applauded website. *Black Bear* will continue to print in our paperback format as well as art and poems online. We are financially supported by our poets, artists, and readers."

★ ⊘ BLACK THISTLE PRESS, 491 Broadway 6th Floor, New York NY 10012. (212)219-1898. Fax: (212)431-6044. E-mail: bthistle@ix.netcom.com. Website: www.blackthistlepress.com. Established 1990. **Publisher:** Ms. Hollis Melton. "We are no longer accepting submissions because we are not publishing new projects at this time."

$ ⊘ BLACK WARRIOR REVIEW; WARRIOR WEB, P.O. Box 862936, Tuscaloosa AL 35486-0027. (205)348-4518. E-mail: bwr@ua.edu. Website: http://webdelsol.com/bwr. Established 1974. **Poetry Editor:** Braden Phillips-Welborn. **Editor:** Dan Kaplan.

● Poetry published in *Black Warrior Review* has been included in the 1997, 1999, and 2000 volumes of *The Best American Poetry* and *Pushcart Prize* anthologies.

Magazine Needs: *Black Warrior Review* is a biannual review appearing in March and October. Has published poetry by W.S. Merwin, Anne Carson, Mark Doty, Jane Miller, Medbh McGuckian, Jane Houlihan, and C.D. Wright. *Black Warrior Review* is 200 pages, digest-sized. Press run is 2,000. Subscription: $14/year, $25/2 years, $30/3 years. Sample: $8. Make checks payable to the University of Alabama.

How to Submit: Submit 3-6 poems at a time. Accepts simultaneous submissions if noted. No electronic submissions. Responds in 4 months. Pays $25-50 and year subscription. Acquires first rights. Reviews books of poetry in single or multi-book format. Send materials for review consideration.

Also Offers: Awards one $500 prize annually to a poet whose work appeared in either the fall or spring issue. Also offers $1,500 Black Warrior Chapbook Contest. Submit 10-25 pages of unpublished poetry along with name, phone number, e-mail, SASE, and $10 entry fee. Make checks payable to University of Alabama. All entrants will receive a 1-year subscription. All entries must be postmarked between January 1 and May 1. Send to above address but label it Black Warrior Chapbook Contest.

Advice: "Subscribe or purchase a sample copy to see what we're after. For 30 years, we've published new voices alongside Pulitzer Prize winners. Freshness and attention to craft, rather than credits, impress us most. Our chapbook contest is a rare opportunity for new and experienced writers alike."

N ◖ **BLACKWIDOWS WEB OF POETRY**, 177 U St., Springfield OR 97477. E-mail: sunris2 set@aol.com. Established 2001. **Contact:** J. Margiotta, chief editor. **Editors:** Matthew Wilson and Lynelle Rasmussen.

Magazine Needs: *Blackwidows Web of Poetry* appears 3 times/year. "We are a growing magazine striving to open the door to beginning poets, dedicated to publishing great poetry." Wants well-crafted poetry, all styles and forms. "We love unique, strong imagery; love, nature, humorous, etc. Rhyming must be great. We encourage all the subject matters, art accompanied by poems is welcome." Does not want overly sexual, political, racist/violent poetry. Recently published poetry by Matthew Wilson, James Burdick, Thomas Paul Sterner/Howe, Rachel Fuchs, and Mike Lerma. *Blackwidows Web of Poetry* is 40-60 pages, digest-sized, laser-printed and photocopied, saddle-stapled, color cover on 65 lb. cardstock with smooth finish, includes b&w art and graphics. Receives about 250 poems/year, accepts about 40%. Publishes about 50-65 poems/issue. Press run is 150 for 30 subscribers; 25 are distributed free to coffeehouses, local areas of interest. Single copy: $6; subscription: $15. Make checks payable to J. Margiotta.

How to Submit: Submit 5 poems at a time. Line length for poetry is 3 minimum, 30 maximum. Accepts previously published poems and simultaneous submissions. No fax, e-mail, or disk submissions. Cover letter is required. "Cover letter should include a brief bio, name, address, and phone number as well. SASE is required." Reads submissions all year. Submit seasonal poems 3 months in advance. Time between acceptance and publication is 4 months. Poems are circulated to an editorial board. "Poems are circulated among three people at the present time. Poems are in review for opinion, style, content, originality, punctuation, etc." Often comments on rejected poems. "We recommend you invest in a copy to see what we're all about, but it's not required. We appreciate all your support now and in the future." Occasionally publishes theme issues. List of upcoming themes available for SASE. Guidelines available for SASE. Responds in 1 month or less. Sometimes sends prepublication galleys. Pays 1 contributor's copy. Acquires one-time rights. Reviews other magazines/journals.

Advice: "Trust yourself, write what you know, keep your pen alive, and revise, revise!"

◖ **BLEEDING HEARTS MAGAZINE; BLEEDING HEARTS ANTHOLOGY**, P.O. Box 882, Delhi CA 95315. Established 1996. **Poetry Editor:** Spector 6.

Magazine Needs: *Bleeding Hearts Magazine* appears quarterly and is "a free-for-all blitz of the surreal and the all too real; a mesh of art, insanity, fiction, and poetry. Each issue also features interviews, contests, and giveaways. All submissions considered. No rants or juvenile angst." Accepts poetry by young poets, but cautions that "children shouldn't be allowed to read this rag." Recently published poetry by Ben Pleasants, M. Schepler, Angelique X, Jonathyn Sinistre, Promethius Twig, and Charlotte Shai. *Bleeding Hearts Magazine* is 64 pages, magazine-sized, digital output, saddle-stapled, full color cover, with heavy, graphically intense content, with ads. Receives about 200 poems/year, accepts about 20%. Publishes about 20 poems/issue. Press run is 500 for 150 subscribers of which 20 are libraries, 200 shelf sales; 50 distributed free to various sources. Single copy: $5 plus s&h; subscription: $20 plus s&h. Sample: $5 plus s&h. Make checks payable to C.D. Wofford.

How to Submit: Submit 5 poems at a time maximum. Line length for poetry is 100 maximum. Accepts previously published poems and simultaneous submissions. Accepts submissions on disk and by postal mail; no e-mail submissions. Cover letter is preferred. "Include SASE if you wish your submissions returned." Reads submissions year round. Submit seasonal poems 4 months in advance. Time between acceptance and publication is usually months. "All poems are read by the poetry editor. Those under consideration are then reviewed by the poetry staff and a final decision is made." Never comments on rejected poems. "Should poet request criticism, a $5 charge/piece is applicable." Guidelines available in magazine and for SASE. Responds in up to 2 months. Pays 1 contributor's copy. Acquires one-time rights. Reviews books and chapbooks of poetry in 360-400 words. Send materials/chapbooks for review consideration to *Bleeding Hearts*, Attn: Spector 6.

Book/Chapbook Needs & How to Submit: Bleeding Hearts Publications/B.H.E. publishes 1 anthology/year, oversize chapbook format. Anthologies are usually 24 pages, digital output, saddle-stapled, 4-color cover, with heavy art/graphics. "Our anthologies are only created with material that we have previously published in *Bleeding Hearts Magazine*—material which stands over the top." Pays 1 contributor's copy (out of a press run of 100). Order sample anthologies by sending $25 to C.D. Wofford.

Advice: "This journal is designed to be a platform for art; as such, the editorial role at Bleeding Heart is solely to place deserving works, regardless of style or content, where they will hopefully be seen and appreciated. And we like cheese that is smooth and creamy."

THE BLIND MAN'S RAINBOW, P.O. Box 1557, Erie PA 16507-0557. E-mail: editor@bmrpoetry.com. Website: www.bmrpoetry.com. Established 1993. **Editor:** Melody Sherosky.

Magazine Needs: *Blind Man's Rainbow* is a quarterly publication "whose focus is to create a diverse collection of quality poetry and art." Wants "all forms of poetry (Beat, rhyme, free verse, haiku, etc.), though excessively long poems are less likely to be accepted. All subject matter accepted." Does not want "anything excessively sexual or violent." Accepts poetry written by children though they are held to the same standards as adults. *The Blind Man's Rainbow* is 20-24 pages, magazine-sized, photocopied and side-stapled, paper cover with art, line drawings inside. Receives about 500 submissions a month. Subscription: $10 US, $14 foreign. Sample: $3 US, $4 foreign. Make checks payable to Melody Sherosky.

How to Submit: Submit 2-10 poems at a time with name and address on each poem. Include SASE. Accepts previously published poems and simultaneous submissions, "but it is nice to let us know." Accepts submissions on disk and by post only; no e-mail. Cover letter preferred. "Submissions only returned if requested and with adequate postage." Time between acceptance and publication is up to 6 months. Often comments on rejected poems. Guidelines available for SASE, by e-mail or on website. Responds in 3 months. Pays 1 copy. Acquires one-time rights.

BLUE COLLAR REVIEW; PARTISAN PRESS; WORKING PEOPLE'S POETRY COMPETITION (Specialized: social issues, working class), P.O. Box 11417, Norfolk VA 23517. E-mail: redart@infi.net. Website: www.partisanpress.org. *Blue Collar Review* established 1997. Partisan Press established 1993. **Editor:** A. Markowitz. **Co-Editor:** Mary Franke.

Magazine Needs: *Blue Collar Review* (*Journal of Progressive Working Class Literature*) is published quarterly and contains poetry, short stories, and illustrations "reflecting the working class experience, a broad range from the personal to the societal. Our purpose is to promote and expand working class literature and an awareness of the connections between workers of all occupations and

USE THE GENERAL INDEX in the back of this book to find the page number of a specific market. Also, markets listed in the 2003 edition but not included in this edition appear in the General Index with a code explaining their absence from the listings.

the social context in which we live. Also to inspire the creativity and latent talent in 'common' working people." Wants "writing of high quality which reflects the working class experience from delicate internal awareness to the militant. We accept a broad range of style and focus—but are generally progressive, political/social. Nothing racist, sexist-misogynist, right wing, or overly religious. No 'bubba' poetry, nothing overly introspective or confessional, no academic/abstract or 'Vogon' poetry. No simple beginners rhyme or verse." Has published poetry by Jeff Vande Zande, Joya Lonsdale, Antler, Jim Daniels, Kathryn Kirkpatrick, Marge Piercy, Alan Catlin, and Rob Whitbeck. *Blue Collar Review* is 56 pages, digest-sized, offset-printed and saddle-stapled with colored card cover, includes b&w illustrations and literary ads. Receives hundreds of poems/year, accepts about 30%. Press run is 350 for 200 subscribers of which 8 are libraries, 50 shelf sales. Subscription: $15/year. Sample: $5. Make checks payable to Partisan Press.

How to Submit: Submit up to 4 poems at a time; "no complete manuscripts please." Accepts previously published poems and simultaneous submissions. Accepts submissions by e-mail (include in text box) and by post. Cover letter preferred. "Poems should be typed as they are to appear upon publication. Author's name and address should appear on every page. Overly long lines reduce chances of acceptance as line may have to be broken to fit the page size and format of the journal." Time between acceptance and publication is 3 months to 1 year. Poems are reviewed by editor and co-editor. Seldom comments on rejected poems. SASE for response. Responds in 3 months. Sends prepublication galleys only upon request. Pays 1-3 copies. Reviews of chapbooks and journals accepted.

Book/Chapbook Needs & How to Submit: Partisan Press looks for "poetry of power that reflects a working class consciousness and which moves us forward as a society. Must be good writing reflecting social/political issues, militancy desired but not didactic screed." Publishes about 3 chapbooks/year and are not presently open to unsolicited submissions. "Submissions are requested from among the poets published in the *Blue Collar Review*." Has published *Dictation* by Anne Babson and *Dreambuilders* by Armando Zuniga. Chapbooks are usually 20-60 pages, digest-sized, offset-printed and saddle-stapled with card or glossy cover. Sample chapbooks are $5 and listed on website.

Also Offers: Sponsors the Working People's Poetry Competition. Entry fee: $15 per entry. Prize: $100 and 1-year subscription to *Blue Collar Review*. Deadline: May 1. Winner of the 2001 Working People's Poetry Competition was Luis Cuauhtemoc Berriozabal. "Include cover letter with entry and make check payable to Partisan Press."

Advice: "Don't be afraid to try. Read a variety of poetry and find your own voice. Write about reality, your own experience, and what moves you."

◉ BLUE LIGHT PRESS; THE BLUE LIGHT POETRY PRIZE AND CHAPBOOK CONTEST, P.O. Box 642, Fairfield IA 52556. (641)472-7882. E-mail: bluelightpress@aol.com. Established 1988. **Chief Editor:** Diane Frank.

Book/Chapbook Needs: Publishes 2 paperbacks, 3 chapbooks/year. "We like poems that are imagistic, emotionally honest, and uplifting, where the writer pushes through the imagery to a deeper level of insight and understanding. No rhymed poetry." Has published poetry by Kate Gray, Viktor Tichy, Tom Centolella, Michael Angelo Tata, Christopher Buckley, and Diane Averill. Christopher Buckley's *Against the Blue* is 32 pages, digest-sized, professionally printed and flat-spined with elegant matte card cover. Cost is $8 plus $2 p&h. Also published 3 anthologies of visionary poets.

How to Submit: Does not accept e-mail submissions. Guidelines available for SASE or by e-mail. Has an editorial board. "We work in person with local poets, have an ongoing poetry workshop, give classes, and will edit/critique poems by mail—$30 for 4-5 poems. We also have an online poetry workshop. Send an e-mail for guidelines."

Also Offers: Sponsors the Blue Light Poetry Prize and Chapbook Contest. "The winner will be published by Blue Light Press, receive a $100 honorarium and 50 copies of his or her book, which can be sold for $8 each, for a total of $500." Submit ms of 10-24 pages, typed or printed with a laser or inkjet printer, between March 1, 2004 and May 1, 2004. Entry fee: $10. Make checks payable to Blue Light Press. Include SASE. No ms will be returned without a SASE. Winner will be announced on or before September 1, 2004, and the book will be published in April, 2005. Send SASE for more information.

Advice: "Read some of the books we publish, especially one of the anthologies. We like to publish poets with a unique and expanded vision and gorgeous or unusual language. Stay in the poem longer and see what emerges in your vision and language."

BLUE MESA REVIEW, Dept. of English, Humanities Bldg. #217, University of New Mexico, Albuquerque NM 87131-1106. (505)277-6155. Fax: (505)277-5573. E-mail: bluemesa@unm.edu. Website: www.unm.edu/~bluemesa. Established 1989 by Rudolfo Anaya. **Editor:** Julie Shigekuni. **Fiction Editor:** Dan Mueller. **Poetry Editor:** Amy Beeder.

Magazine Needs: *Blue Mesa Review* is an annual review of poetry, short fiction, creative essays, and book reviews. Wants "all kinds of free, organic verse; poems of place encouraged. Limits: four poems or six pages of poetry; one story; one essay. We accept theoretical essays as well as fiction, poetry, and nonfiction." Has published poetry by Virgil Suarez, David Axelrod, Paula Gunn Allen, and Brian Swann. *Blue Mesa Review* is about 250 pages, digest-sized, professionally printed and flat-spined with glossy cover, photos, and graphics. Receives about 1,000 poems/year, accepts about 10% or less. Press run is 1,000 for 600 shelf sales. Sample: $12.

How to Submit: "Please submit two copies of everything with your name, address and telephone number on each page. Fax numbers and e-mail addresses are also appreciated." No previously published poems or simultaneous submissions. No fax or e-mail submissions. Cover letter required. Accepts mss from July 1 through October 1 only. Poems are then passed among readers and voted on. Guidelines available on website. Reports on mss by mid-December to mid-January. Pays 2 copies.

BLUE MONK POEMS & STORIES; BLUE MONK PRESS, P.O. Box 53103, New Orleans LA 70153-3103. (504)495-2102. E-mail: editors@bluemonkpress.com. Website: www.bluem onkpress.com. Established 1999. **Editors:** Joseph Kees, Brian Kees.

Magazine Needs: *Blue Monk Poems & Stories* is a biannual journal of poems, stories, and art. "We are open to any subject matter, style, or purpose. For the most part, we do not like rhyming poetry." Recently published poetry by Gordon Massman, I. Urquiza Vincente, Janet Buck, Nick Antosca, Jimmy Ross, and John Sweet. *Blue Monk* is 100 pages, digest-sized (also appears online), typeset, flat-spined, with quality card stock cover with art, also photos, paintings, and mixed media reproductions, offers three pages of ads. Receives about 1,000 poems/year, accepts about 10%. Publishes about 40 poems/issue. Press run is 1,000 for 50 subscribers of which 2 are libraries, 600 shelf sales; 200 are distributed free to artists/contributors/reviewers. Single copy: $5; subscription: $8.50. Sample: $4. Make checks payable to Blue Monk Press.

How to Submit: Submit 3-6 poems at a time. Accepts previously published poems and simultaneous submissions. Accepts e-mail and disk submissions. Include SASE and short bio. Reads submissions all year. Time between acceptance and publication is 6 months. Poems are circulated to an editorial board. Seldom comments on rejected poems. Guidelines available in magazine, for SASE, or on website. Responds in 2 months. Pays 2 contributor's copies. Acquires first North American serial rights and anthology rights. Reviews books and chapbooks of poetry and other magazines/journals in 500-1,000 words, single book format. Poets may send materials for review consideration to Brian Kees/Joseph Kees at Blue Monk Press.

Book/Chapbook Needs & How to Submit: Blue Monk Press publishes work "that badgers and pisses on the page and makes you spill your wine. Our work is fiendish and hopefully truthful." Publishes 1 chapbook/year. Chapbooks are usually 50-70 pages, typeset, saddle-stapled, with quality card stock cover and art/graphics. Responds to queries in 3 months; to mss in 6 months. Pays royalties of 15-20%. Order sample chapbooks by sending $5 to Blue Monk Press.

Advice: "We publish poetry for splintered skulls and out-of-tune pianos."

THE BLUE MOUSE; SWAN DUCKLING PRESS, P.O. Box 586, Cypress CA 90630. E-mail: swduckling@aol.com. Established 1998. **Editor:** Mark Bruce.

Magazine Needs: *The Blue Mouse* appears quarterly. Wants "poetry based on personal experience. Short poems in which common experience is related in an uncommon way." Does not want "abstract, philosophical musings, literary rehashes, Gramma's oven poetry, doggerel, cowboy poetry, smut, Bukowski imitators." Recently published poetry by Katya Giritsky, Lyn Lyfshin, Michael Kramer, Rachel Rose, and B.Z. Niditch. *The Blue Mouse* is 20 pages, copied, stapled, with blue cover, no artwork. Receives about 100 poems/year, accepts about 30. Publishes about 15 poems/issue. Press run is 350 for 10 subscribers; 340 are distributed free to coffeehouses and poetry readings. Single copy: $1.50; subscription: $6. Make checks payable to Swan Duckling Press.

How to Submit: Submit 4 poems at a time. Line length is 2 minimum, 35 maximum. No previously published poems or simultaneous submissions. Accepts e-mail submissions; no disk submissions. Cover letter is preferred. "Remember SASE. One poem per page, typed or typeset." Time between acceptance and publication is 6 months. "I am a one-man editorial board. If I like it, it goes in. Be prepared to edit." Often comments on rejected poems. Guidelines available for SASE or by e-mail. Responds in 6 months. Pays 2 contributor's copies. "Poet keeps copyrights."

Book/Chapbook Needs & How to Submit: Swan Duckling Press publishes 4 chapbooks/year. Manuscripts are selected through annual competition. **Deadline:** Competition opens in July, ends October 31. **Entry fee:** $15, includes subscription to *Mouse* and copy of winning chapbook. Chapbook mss may include previously published poems. "Other than contest, chapbooks are published by invitation *only*."

Advice: "Don't think we're related to that cartoon mouse down the road. Our mouse is gaining respect because we choose good, compelling poems. Don't send mediocre stuff."

N ◯ THE BLUE REVIEW, 23 Berkeley Dr., Athens OH 45701. E-mail: editors@corbapress.com. Website: www.corbapress.com/blue.htm. Established 2002. **Editors:** Paul Hina and A. Scott Britton.

Magazine Needs: "We publish subversive and unique pieces from writers that perpetuate interesting ideas in their work and a strong desire to share their curiosities and ideals." Open to almost anything, "as long as it seems truthful. If you don't feel like you are being honest with a poem, then don't waste our time." Does not want pornography, rhyming, or children's poetry. *The blue Review* is 30 pages, digest-sized, photocopied, saddle-stapled, with colored coverstock. Receives about 200 poems/year, accepts about 5%. Publishes about 2-4 poems/issue. Press run is 100 for 95 subscribers; 5 are distributed free to contributing writers. Single copy: $3 (plus $1 s&h); subscription: $10 for 4 issues (plus $2 s&h). Make checks payable to Paul Hina.

How to Submit: Submit 3-5 poems at a time. Line length is open. Accepts previously published poems and simultaneous submissions. Accepts e-mail submissions only; no disk submissions. Reads submissions all year. Time between acceptance and publication is 4-6 weeks. Seldom comments on rejected poems. Guidelines available on website. Responds in up to 6 weeks. Pays 1 contributor's copy. Acquires one-time rights.

Advice: "*The blue Review* has been created for those of us who have grown tired of the modern literary conventions. Our review has been invented to perpetuate subversive and mindful literary works that would otherwise fall through the cracks of an increasingly less tolerant publishing community. *The blue Review* is here to supply the writer-as-artist with the voice that has, for far too long, been absent from bookstores and many prominent small press publications."

◯ BLUE UNICORN, A TRIQUARTERLY OF POETRY; BLUE UNICORN POETRY CONTEST, 22 Avon Rd., Kensington CA 94707. (510)526-8439. Established 1977. **Poetry Editors:** Ruth G. Iodice, John Hart, and Fred Ostrander.

Magazine Needs: *Blue Unicorn* wants "well-crafted poetry of all kinds, in form or free verse, as well as expert translations on any subject matter. We shun the trite or inane, the soft-centered, the contrived poem. Shorter poems have more chance with us because of limited space." Has published poetry by James Applewhite, Kim Cushman, Patrick Worth Gray, Joan LaBombard, James Schevill, and Gail White. *Blue Unicorn* is "distinguished by its fastidious editing, both with regard to contents and format." *Blue Unicorn* is 56 pages, narrow digest-sized, finely-printed, saddle-stapled, with some art. Features 40-50 poems in each issue, all styles, with the focus on excellence and accessibility. Receives over 35,000 submissions/year, accepts about 200, has a year's backlog. Single copy: $6, foreign add $2; subscription: $14/3 issues, foreign add $6.

How to Submit: Submit 3-5 typed poems on 8½×11 paper. No simultaneous submissions or previously published poems. "Cover letter OK, but will not affect our selection." Guidelines available for SASE. Responds in 3 months (generally within 6 weeks), sometimes with personal comment. Pays 1 copy.

Also Offers: Sponsors an annual contest with small entry fee, with prizes of $150, $75, $50, and sometimes special awards; distinguished poets as judges, publication of 3 top poems and 6 honorable mentions in the magazine. Entry fee: $6 for first poem, $3 for others to a maximum of 5. Write for current guidelines. Criticism occasionally offered.

Advice: "We would advise beginning poets to read and study poetry—both poets of the past and of the present; concentrate on technique; and discipline yourself by learning forms before trying to do without them. When your poem is crafted and ready for publication, study your markets and then send whatever of your work seems to be compatible with the magazine you are submitting to."

BLUELINE (Specialized: regional), Dept. PM, English Dept., Potsdam College, Potsdam NY 13676. Fax: (315)267-2043. E-mail: blueline@potsdam.edu. Established 1979. **Editor-in-Chief:** Rick Henry and an editorial board. Member: CLMP.

Magazine Needs: Appearing in May, *Blueline* "is an annual literary magazine dedicated to prose and poetry about the Adirondacks and other regions similar in geography and spirit." Wants "clear, concrete poetry pertinent to the countryside and its people. It must go beyond mere description, however. We prefer a realistic to a romantic view. We do not want to see sentimental or extremely experimental poetry." Usually uses poems of 75 lines or fewer, though "occasionally we publish longer poems" on "nature in general, Adirondack Mountains in particular. Form may vary, can be traditional or contemporary." Has published poetry by L.M. Rosenberg, John Unterecker, Lloyd Van Brunt, Laurence Josephs, Maurice Kenny, and Nancy L. Nielsen. *Blueline* is 200 pages, digest-sized, with 90 pages of poetry in each issue. Press run is 600. Sample copies: $4 for back issues.

How to Submit: Submit 3 poems at a time. Include short bio. No simultaneous submissions. Submit September 1 through November 30 only. Occasionally comments on rejected poems. Guidelines available for SASE or by e-mail. Responds in 10 weeks. Pays 1 copy. Acquires first North American serial rights. Reviews books of poetry in 500-750 words, single or multi-book format.

Advice: "We are interested in both beginning and established poets whose poems evoke universal themes in nature and show human interaction with the natural world. We look for thoughtful craftsmanship rather than stylistic trickery."

$ BOA EDITIONS, LTD., 260 East Ave., Rochester NY 14604. (585)546-3410. Website: www.boaeditions.org. Established 1976. **Poetry Editor:** Thom Ward. Has published some of the major American poets, such as W.D. Snodgrass, John Logan, Isabella Gardner, Richard Wilbur, and Lucille Clifton. Also publishes introductions by major poets of those less well-known. For example, Gerald Stern wrote the foreword for Li-Young Lee's *Rose*. Guidelines available for SASE and on website. Pays advance plus 10 copies.

BOGG PUBLICATIONS; BOGG, (Specialized: form/style, experimental, humor), 422 N. Cleveland St., Arlington VA 22201-1424. Established 1968. **Poetry Editors:** John Elsberg (USA), George Cairncross (UK: 31 Belle Vue St., Filey, N. Yorkshire YO 14 9HU England), Wilga Rose (Australia: 13 Urara Rd., Avalon Beach, NSW 2107 Australia), and Sheila Martindale (Canada: P.O. Box 23148, 380 Wellington St., London, Ontario NGA 5N9 Canada).

Magazine Needs: Appearing twice/year, *Bogg* is "a journal of contemporary writing with an Anglo-American slant. Its contents combines innovative American work with a range of writing from England and the Commonwealth. It includes poetry (to include haiku, prose poems, and experimental/visual poems), very short experimental or satirical fiction, interviews, essays on the small press scenes both in America and in England /the Commonwealth, reviews, review essays, and line art. We also publish occasional free-for-postage pamphlets." The magazine uses a great deal of poetry in each issue (with several featured poets)—"poetry in all styles, with a healthy leavening of shorts (under ten lines). Seeks original voices." Accepts all styles, all subject matter. "Some have even found the magazine's sense of play offensive. Overt religious and political poems have to have strong poetical merits—statement alone is not sufficient." *Bogg* started in England and in 1975 began including a supplement of American work; it now is published in the US and mixes US, Canadian, Australian, and UK work with reviews of small press publications from all of those areas. Has published work by Hugh Fox, Ann Menebraker, John M. Bennett, Marcia Arrieta, Harriet Zinnes, and Steve Sneyd. *Bogg* is 72 pages, typeset, saddle-stapled, in a digest-sized format that leaves enough white space to let each poem stand and breathe alone. There are about 50 pages of poetry/issue. Receives over 10,000 American poems/year, accepts about 100-150. Press run is 850 for 400 subscribers of which 20 are libraries. Single copy: $5.50; subscription: $15 for 3 issues. Sample: $3.50.

Roaming the Southwest

When Ray Gonzalez was growing up in the desert Southwest, he walked down the street in his native El Paso, Texas, and stared across the border, perplexed. Mexico, a mile away, may have been home to his grandparents, but it was a place the young Gonzalez could not easily grasp.

Photo by Ida Steven

Ray Gonzalez

In poems, essays, and short stories, Gonzalez has made it his life's work to explore his perplexity and frequent frustration. Throughout his wide range of work these past thirty years, he seems to have gained more understanding of his desert roots and how this place, the border, says as much about America itself as do the cities of Boston, New York, and Washington, D.C.

Gonzalez has chronicled more prolifically than any other contemporary poet the evolution and complexity of our Mexican-American border culture. And the more he writes, the more clearly Gonzalez can see how the tense relationship between Mexico and America creates in his writing a combination of anger, beauty, loneliness, and fear.

As both editor and writer, Gonzalez has enabled readers of mainstream literature to become more familiar with both this territory and the plethora of Chicano/a writers. In the 12 anthologies he's edited, Gonazlez has given new and highly regarded Chicano/a literary artists a voice that otherwise may not have surfaced with such consistency. He's also been poetry editor of *The Bloomsbury Review* since 1982 and, in 1998, started the literary magazine, *LUNA*, at the University of Minnesota where he's professor of English.

Gonzalez was born in 1952 near the Chihuahua desert. His vast publishing record (eight books of poetry, two books of fiction, one memoir, and one book of personal essays) testifies to his belief that "writing makes living necessary and worthwhile." His honors include a 2002 Western Heritage Award for Best Book of Short Fiction for *The Ghost of John Wayne and Other Stories* (University of Arizona Press); the 2001 Minnesota Book Award for Poetry; the 1997 PEN/Oakland Josephine Miles Book Award for *The Heat of Arrivals* (BOA Editions); a 2002 National Book Critic's Circle Award Notable Book Citation; and a Pulitzer Prize nomination in poetry for *The Hawk Temple at Tierra Grande* (BOA Editions). In 2003 he received a Lifetime Achievement Award in Literature from the Southwest Regional Border Library Association in El Paso, Texas.

In recent years Gonzalez has experimented with different ways of addressing his landscape and personal memory. Some of the subject matter that informs his poems has found its way into his essays and short stories. Gonzalez believes the heart of his writing—his exploration of family, the desert, and the problems in reconciling the past and present—needs as much room as possible. "That calls for writing in several genres, the constant going back and forth from poem to essay to story, and from story to essay to poem," he says. "I encourage poets to try all combinations just to see if what's good for a poem might be good for an essay, too."

Writers who complain about not having material at their disposal or claim writer's block may be missing an opportunity. "The idea is to get down words. If you're a poet and you're having trouble with a poem, write out your notes or thoughts all in prose at first," Gonzalez says. "Get everything possible down. Even many more words than you'd ever need. Then go back and look for ways of transforming that material into a poem. Look for the special elements that poetry hands us. Maybe that material will be a prose poem or maybe it'll be a short lyric poem. Let it take its natural course."

Gonzalez's poems are always filled with big contrasts, relying on strict combinations of image, metaphor, and sound so that song-like, unusual rhythms take shape. In one poem he may invoke an animal (like the spider in "See This" or the hawks in "Two Hawks Over Conchiti, New Mexico") to add a calming lyrical effect yet present an image of destruction or disappearance. In another poem, he might rely on images of fossils to derive a rhythmical chant or litany.

Gonzalez insists poetry should be filled with contrasts in order to give depth and meaning to what one is writing. "I can look at the sky and see more than just a plain sky. If you're a poet, you should see something more—and you should let that sky be a springboard into something more in the writing. Be adventurous."

The persistent urgency in Gonzalez's poems is, in part, due to his feeling that Chicano literature has always taken a backseat to "canon literature." There was a "Latino Boom" in the 1980s and early 1990s, but commercial publishing's fascination with many of these writers seems to have waned. Not true with Gonzalez, whose authorial voice looms larger with each book, essentially because he's determined to find fresh ways of circulating among poetry, stories, and essays. That notion of getting a dynamic poem out in the world that speaks of the vivid Mexican-American past and present fuels Gonzalez's oeuvre.

He's considered one of the most restless and significant American poets now writing. "My work is read by kids in the barrio, by executives, or by professors of English, and there's something for anyone to pick up," says Gonzalez. "Although I tend to write a lot about my place in the world, we all come from a 'place.' Still, no subject matter seems untouchable to me. You have to stretch as a poet."

Gonzalez's "stretching" is also what the essays and stories are all about. How does he suggest going from one genre to another—say, from a poem to an essay? Or from an essay to a poem?

If he finds subject matter he wants to use in both a poem and an essay, Gonzalez might exploit a situation to get both types of writing moving. One example might be "going back to El Paso and finding a lot of change in scenery," he says. The subject matter might include rattlesnakes, trash cans, an ocotillo field, or a speaker imagining a demon in an alley. The exploited "situation" might involve traveling, driving around to see these things, something Gonzalez loves to do.

In his poem, "The Face at Pacudora," the speaker's movements bring him to imagine how strange his nearly lost landscape has become. The movement is essential because it allows details to build, as with this stanza:

I opened my eyes and fought
the headache so I could see
the dark alley behind my grandmother's
house where trash cans were flipped
over by the wind, the demon
chasing me into a crowd of red
monkeys at the end of the lane.

> Gonzalez's original use of traveling and driving in *The Underground Heart: A Return to a Hidden Landscape* (University of Arizona Press), his collection of personal essays, allows his subject matter to become multi-dimensional and far situated from mere travelogue. Gonzalez's roaming the Southwest grants him access to peculiarities in the landscape, and the reader keenly experiences "white rain," *huevos rancheros*, the dust and heat of Juarez, Mexico, and the air among salt cedars, cottonwoods, and broken adobe walls.
>
> "What I knew I could do was let all the traveling and observing I have done overlap from my poems into my essays and stories," Gonzalez says. In the end, though, he pays most attention to the "music" his poems or essays are creating.
>
> "I spend more time mastering language in a poem or an essay than I do playing with the subject matter," he says. "I know that language counts for most everything, since I cherish poetry and simply reading aloud as a kind of musical event—regardless of what a piece of writing is *about*."
>
> —*Jeffrey Hillard*

How to Submit: Submit 6 poems at a time. No simultaneous submissions. Cover letters preferred. "They can help us get a 'feel' for the writer's intentions/slant." SASE required or material discarded ("no exceptions.") Prefer typewritten manuscripts, with author's name and address on each sheet. "We will reprint previously published material, but with a credit line to a previous publisher." Guidelines available for SASE. Responds in 1 week. Pays 2 copies. Acquires one-time rights. Reviews books and chapbooks of poetry in 250 words, single book format. Send materials to relevant editor (by region) for review consideration.

Book/Chapbook Needs & How to Submit: Their occasional pamphlets and chapbooks are by *invitation only*, the author receiving 25% of the print run, and you can get chapbook samples free for digest-sized SASE. "At least 2 ounces worth of postage."

Advice: "Become familiar with a magazine before submitting to it. Long lists of previous credits irritate me. Short notes about how the writer has heard about *Bogg* or what he or she finds interesting or annoying in the magazine I read with some interest."

🖉 **BOMBAY GIN**, Naropa University, 2130 Arapahoe Ave., Boulder CO 80302. (303)546-3540. Fax: (303)546-5297. E-mail: bgin@naropa.edu. Website: www.naropa.edu/gin.html. Established 1974. **Contact:** Judith Huntera.

Magazine Needs: "*Bombay Gin*, appearing in June, is the annual literary magazine of the Jack Kerouac School of Disembodied Poetics at Naropa University. Produced and edited by MFA students, *Bombay Gin* publishes established writers alongside those who have been previously unpublished. It has a special interest in works that push conventional literary boundaries. Submission of poetry, prose, visual art, and works involving hybrid forms and cross-genre exploration are encouraged." Recent issues have included works by Lisa Jarnot, Anne Waldman, Wang Ping, Thalia Field, Anselm Hollo, and Alice Notley. *Bombay Gin* is 124 pages, digest-sized, professionally printed, perfect-bound with color card cover, includes art and photos. Receives about 300 poems/year, accepts about 5%. Press run is 500, 400 shelf sales; 100 distributed free to contributors. Single copy: $10. Sample: $5.

How to Submit: "Submit up to 3 pages of poetry or up to 8 pages of prose/fiction (12 pt. Times New Roman). Art may be submitted as slides, negatives, or prints." No previously published poems or simultaneous submissions. Accepts disk submissions (PC format). Cover letter preferred. Reply with SASE only. Deadline: December 1. Submissions read December 15 through March 15. Guidelines available for SASE or on website. Notification of acceptance/rejection: April 15. Pays 2 copies. Acquires one-time rights.

⭐🖉 **THE BOOKPRESS: THE NEWSPAPER OF THE LITERARY ARTS**, The DeWitt Bldg., 215 N. Cayuga St., Ithaca NY 14850. (607)277-2254. Fax: (607)275-9221. E-mail: bookpress

@clarityconnect.com. Website: www.thebookery.com/Bookpress. Established 1990. **Editor/Publisher:** Jack Goldman.

Magazine Needs: *Bookpress* appears 8 times/year, each month except January, June, July, and August. As for poetry, the editor says, "The only criterion is a commitment to the aesthetic power of language. Avoid the hackneyed and formulaic." Has published poetry by Phyllis Janowitz, Kathleen Gemmell, and A.R. Ammons. *The Bookpress* is a 12-page tabloid. Receives about 50 poems/year, accepts about 10%. Press run is 6,500 for 300 subscribers of which 15 are libraries. Subscription: $12/year. Sample copies free.

How to Submit: No previously published poems or simultaneous submissions. Accepts e-mail submissions, include in body of message. Cover letter preferred. Reads submissions August 1 through April 1 only. SASE required. Time between acceptance and publication is 1 month. Often comments on rejected poems. Guidelines available for SASE. Responds in 3 months. Pays 2 copies. Acquires first North American serial rights. Reviews books of poetry. Length of reviews varies, typically between 1,500-2,000 words, sometimes longer. Poets may send material for review consideration.

BORDERLANDS: TEXAS POETRY REVIEW (Specialized: regional, translations, bilingual/foreign language), P.O. Box 33096, Austin TX 78764. E-mail: cgilbert@austin.rr.com or borderlands_tpr@hotmail.com. Website: www.borderlands.org. Established 1992. **Contact:** editor.

Magazine Needs: *Borderlands* appears twice/year publishing "high-quality, outward-looking poetry by new and established poets, as well as brief reviews of poetry books and critical essays. Cosmopolitan in content, but particularly welcomes Texas and Southwest writers." Wants "outward-looking poems that exhibit social, political, geographical, historical, feminist, or spiritual awareness coupled with concise artistry. We also seek poems in two languages (one of which must be English), where the poet has written both versions. Please, no introspective work about the speaker's psyche, childhood, or intimate relationships." Has published poetry by Walter McDonald, Naomi Shihab Nye, Mario Susko, Wendy Barker, Larry D. Thomas, and Reza Shirazi. *Borderlands* is 100-150 pages, digest-sized, offset, perfect-bound, with 4-color cover, art by local artists. Receives about 2,000 poems/year, accepts about 120. Press run is 1,000. Subscription: $18/year; $34/2 years. Sample: $12.

How to Submit: Submit 5 typed poems at a time. No previously published poems or simultaneous submissions. No e-mail submissions. Include SASE (or SAE and IRCs) with sufficient postage to return poems. Seldom comments on rejected poems. Guidelines are available for SASE and on website. Responds in 6 months. Pays 1 copy. Acquires first rights. Reviews books of poetry in one page. Also uses 3- to 6-page essays on single poets and longer essays (3,500-word maximum) on contemporary poetry in some larger context (query first). Address poetry submissions to "Editors, *Borderlands*."

Also Offers: The Writers' League of Texas is a state-wide group open to the general public. Established in 1981, the purpose of the Writers' League of Texas is "to provide a forum for information, support, and sharing among writers; to help members improve and market their skills; and to promote the interests of writers and the writing community." Currently has 1,600 members. Annual membership dues are $45. Send SASE for more information to: The Writers' League of Texas, 1501 W. 5th St., Suite E-2, Austin TX 78703.

BORDERLINES; ANGLO-WELSH POETRY SOCIETY, Nant Y Brithyll, Llangynyw, Powys SY21 OJS United Kingdom. Established 1977. **Editor:** Kevin Bamford. **Editor:** Dave Bingham.

Magazine Needs: *Borderlines* is published biannually to encourage reading and writing of poetry. "We try to be open-minded and look at anything. We do not normally publish very long poems. Most poems fit on one page. No poems about poems; unshaped recitals of thoughts and/or feelings." Has published poetry by Peter Abbs, Mike Jenkins, and Vuyelwa Carlin. *Borderlines* is 40-48 pages, digest-sized, neatly printed and saddle-stapled with light card cover, art on cover only. Receives about 600 poems/year, accepts about 16%. Press run is 200 for 100 subscribers of which 8 are libraries. Single copy: £1.50; subscription: £3, other EU countries £4, non-EU countries £5. Make checks payable to Anglo-Welsh Poetry Society.

How to Submit: Cover letter preferred. "Please write name and address on each poem sheet."

Time between acceptance and publication is up to 6 months. Seldom comments on rejected poems. Guidelines available for SASE (or SAE and IRC). Responds in 6 weeks. Sometimes sends prepublication galleys. Pays 1 copy.

Also Offers: "The Anglo-Welsh Poetry Society is a group of people interested in the reading, writing, and promotion of poetry, particularly in the Marches—the Anglo-Welsh border country. It is based in the border counties of Shropshire and Montgomeryshire, though there are members all over the country. A core group of members meets on the first Tuesday of the month at the Loggerheads pub in Shrewsbury. Other meetings such as readings, workshops, poetry parties are arranged at intervals over the course of the year. A monthly newsletter gives information of interest to members on events, publications, competitions, and other news of the poetry world." Membership fee for AWPS is £7.50/year.

$ ▨ ▢ ◎ BORDIGHERA, INC.; VOICES IN ITALIAN AMERICANA; VIA FOLIOS; THE BORDIGHERA POETRY PRIZE; ANIELLO LAURI AWARD (Specialized: ethnic/nationality, Italian-American), P.O. Box 1374, Lafayette IN 47902-1374. (561)297-3861. Fax: (561)297-2657. E-mail: atamburri@fau.edu. Established 1990. **Editors:** Anthony Julian Tamburri, Paolo Giordano, and Fred Gardaphé.

Magazine Needs: *Voices in Italian Americana* (*VIA*) is "a semiannual literary and cultural review devoted to the dissemination of information concerning the contributions of and about Italian Americans to the cultural and art worlds of North America." Open to all kinds of poetry. Has published poetry by Daniela Gioseffi, David Citino, Felix Stefanile, and Dana Gioia. *VIA* is about 200 pages, digest-sized, docutech printed, perfect-bound with glossy paper cover, includes art and ads. Receives about 150 poems/year, accepts about 25%. Press run is 500 for 300 subscribers of which 50 are libraries, 50 shelf sales; 50 distributed free to contributors. Subscription: $20 individual; $15 student/senior citizen; $25 institutional; $30 foreign. Sample: $10. Make checks payable to Bordighera, Inc.

How to Submit: No previously published poems or simultaneous submissions. Accepts e-mail and disk submissions. Cover letter required. Reads submissions October 1 through May 31 only. Time between acceptance and publication is 3 months. Poems are circulated to an editorial board. Often comments on rejected poems. Publishes theme issues occasionally. Guidelines and upcoming themes available for SASE. Responds in 6 weeks. Always sends prepublication galleys. Acquires all rights. Rights returned upon publication. "But in subsequent publications, poet must acknowledge first printing in *VIA*." Reviews books and chapbooks of poetry in 500-1,000 words, single book format. Send materials for review consideration to Fred Gardaphé, Center for Italian Studies, State University of New York, Stony Brook NY 11794-3358.

Book/Chapbook Needs & How to Submit: Bordighera, under the imprint *VIA* Folios, has published *The Silver Lake of Love Poems* by Emmanuel di Pasquale, *Going On* by Daniela Gioseffi, *Sardinia/Sardegna* by Robert Lima, and *The Book of Madness and Love* by Arthur L. Clements. Publishes 5 titles/year with the print run for each paperback being 550. Books are usually 50-75 pages, 8½×5½, docutech printed and perfect-bound with glossy paper cover and art. Query first, with a variety of sample poems and a cover letter with brief bio and publication credits. Responds to queries in 2 weeks; to mss in 6 weeks. Pays 10% royalties. Offers subsidy arrangements. Poets are required to subsidize 50% of publishing costs. "Author regains subsidy through sales with 50% royalties up to subvention paid, 10% thereafter."

Also Offers: Sponsors the Bordighera Poetry Prize, which awards book publication and $2,000, and the Aniello Lauri Award, which awards $150 plus publication in *Voices in Italian Americana*. Contest rules available for SASE.

◐ BORN MAGAZINE, P.O. Box 1313, Portland OR 97207-1313. E-mail: editor@bornmagazine.org. Website: www.bornmagazine.org. Established 1996. **Editor:** Anmarie Trimble. **Contributing Editors:** Jennifer Grotz, Bruce Smith, Tenaya Darlington.

Magazine Needs: *Born Magazine* appears quarterly as "an experimental online revue that marries literary arts and interactive media. We publish six to eight multimedia 'interpretations' of poetry and prose each issue, created by interactive artists in collaboration with poets and writers." Wants poems suited to "interpretation into a visual or interactive form. Due to the unusual, collaborative nature of our publication, we represent a variety of styles and forms of poetry." Recently published poetry by

Nick Flynn, Annie Kantar, Eliot Khalil Wilson, Thomas Swiss, Paisley Rekdal, Cate Marvin, Michele Glazer, and Philip Jenks. Publishes about 6-8 poems/online issue.

How to Submit: Submit 2-5 poems at a time. Accepts previously published poems; no simultaneous submissions. Accepts e-mail submissions. "Prefer electronic submissions as Word documents or .txt files. Also accept hard copies; electronic format on disk or via e-mail will be required upon acceptance." Reads submissions year round. Submit seasonal poems 4 months in advance. Time between acceptance and publication is 1-3 months. "Poems must be accepted by the editor and one contributing editor. Selected works are forwarded to our art department, which chooses an artist partner to work with the writer. Artist and writer collaborate on a concept, to be realized by the artist." Never comments on rejected poems. Guidelines available on website. Responds in 3 weeks to e-mail queries. Always sends prepublication galleys. No pay. "We can offer only the experience of participating in a collaborative community, as well as a broad audience. (We receive approximately 20,000-30,000 unique visitors to our site per month.)" Acquires one-time rights.

Advice: "We accept new and previously published work. *Born*'s mission is to nurture creativity and collaboration between different artistic genres to further the development of new literary art forms on the Web."

✦ $☺ **BOSTON REVIEW**, E53-407, MIT, 30 Wadsworth St., Cambridge MA 02139-4307. (617)253-3642. Fax: (617)252-1549. E-mail: bostonreview@mit.edu. Website: www.polisci.mit.edu/BostonReview/. Established 1975. **Poetry Editors:** Mary Jo Bang and Timothy Donnelly.

• Poetry published by this review has been included in *The Best American Poetry* (1998 and 2000 volumes).

Magazine Needs: *Boston Review* is a bimonthly tabloid format magazine of arts, culture, and politics which uses about 30 poems/year, for which they receive about 3,000 submissions. "We are open to both traditional and experimental forms. What we value most is originality and a strong sense of voice." Has published poetry by Gilbert Sorrentino, Heather McHugh, Richard Howard, Allen Grossman, Cole Swenson, Tan Lin, and Claudia Rankine. Circulation is 20,000 nationally including subscriptions and newsstand sales. Single copy: $3.50; subscription: $17. Sample: $4.50.

How to Submit: Submit 3-5 poems at a time. Submissions and inquiries are accepted via regular mail only. Cover letter with brief bio encouraged. Has a 6-12 month backlog. Responds in 3 months. Pays $40/poem plus 5 copies. Acquires first serial rights. Reviews books of poetry. Only using *solicited* reviews. Publishers may send materials for review consideration.

Also Offers: Sponsors an annual poetry contest. Awards publication and $1,000. Submit up to 5 unpublished poems, no more than 10 pages total, with postcard to acknowledge receipt. Deadline: June 1. Entry fee: $15. Guidelines available for SASE.

◎ **BOTTOM DOG PRESS, INC. (Specialized: regional, working class literature)**, P.O. Box 425, Huron OH 44839. (419)433-3573. Website: http://members.aol.com/lsmithdog/bottomdog/ . **Director:** Larry Smith. **Associate Editors:** David Shevin, Laura Smith.

Book/Chapbook Needs & How to Submit: Bottom Dog Press, Inc. "is a nonprofit literary and educational organization dedicated to publishing the best writing and art from the Midwest." Bottom Dog poets include Jeff Gundy, Ray McNiece, Maj Ragain, David Kherdian, and Sue Doro. Publishes the Working Lives and Midwest Series. See website for guidelines.

$◙ **BOULEVARD**, PMB 325, 6614 Clayton Rd., Richmond Heights MO 63117. Website: www.boulevardmagazine.com. Established 1985. **Editor:** Richard Burgin.

• Poetry published in *Boulevard* has been frequently included inclined in *The Best American Poetry* and *Pushcart Prize* anthologies.

Magazine Needs: *Boulevard* appears 3 times/year. "*Boulevard* strives to publish only the finest in fiction, poetry, and nonfiction (essays and interviews; we do not accept book reviews). While we

---

THE SUBJECT INDEX in the back of this book helps you identify potential markets for your work.

frequently publish writers with previous credits, we are very interested in publishing less experienced or unpublished writers with exceptional promise. We've published everything from John Ashbery to Donald Hall to a wide variety of styles from new or lesser known poets. We're eclectic. Do not want to see poetry that is uninspired, formulaic, self-conscious, unoriginal, insipid." No light verse. Has published poetry by Amy Clampitt, Molly Peacock, Jorie Graham, and Mark Strand. *Boulevard* is 200 pages, digest-sized, professionally printed, flat-spined, with glossy card cover. Their press run is 3,500 with 1,200 subscribers of which 200 are libraries. Subscription: $12/3 issues, $20/6 issues, $25/9 issues. Sample: $7 plus 5 first-class stamps and SASE. Make checks payable to Opojaz, Inc.

How to Submit: Submit up to 5 poems at a time. Line length for poetry is 200 maximum. No previously published poems. "*Boulevard* does allow, even encourages, simultaneous submissions, but we want to be notified of this fact." Does not accept fax or e-mail submissions. All submissions must include an SASE. Author's name and address must appear on each submission, with author's first and last name on each page. Cover letters encouraged but not required. Reads submissions October 1 through April 30 only. Editor sometimes comments on rejected poems. Responds in about 2 months. Pays $25-250/poem, depending on length, plus 1 copy. Acquires first-time publication and anthology rights.

Advice: "Write from your heart as well as your head."

$ ⬛ BOVINE FREE WYOMING. E-mail: submissions@bovinefreewyoming.com. Website: www.bovinefreewyoming.com. Established 2000. **Co-Editor:** Vickie L. Knestaut.

Magazine Needs: *Bovine Free Wyoming* is a quarterly electronic publication of literature. "We want to see quality poetry that appeals to a general reading audience. We do not want to see poetry that alienates the average reader." Recently published poetry by Michael A. Arnzen, Matt Mason, Deborah Bacharach, John Grey, Dn Muranaka, and Roger Pfingston. *Bovine Free Wyoming* is published in html format. Receives about 400 poems/year, accepts about 10%. Publishes about 10 poems/issue.

How to Submit: Submit 4 poems at a time. Line length for poetry is open. Accepts previously published poems and simultaneous submissions. Accepts e-mail submissions; no fax or disk submissions. Cover letter is required. "Please review submission guidelines before making a submission." Reads submissions year round. Submit seasonal poems 3 months in advance. Time between acceptance and publication is 3 months. Poems are circulated to an editorial board. "Staff reads and rates poems. Poems that score a certain rating or more are accepted for publication." Seldom comments on rejected poems. Guidelines available on website. Responds in 1 month. Always sends prepublication galleys. Pays $10. Acquires one-time electronic rights.

Advice: "It may be old hat, but it still needs to be said: Proof your work and know your market. If a poet doesn't care enough to send clean copies that adhere to the guidelines, then why should an editor care enough to publish it?"

⬛ BRANCHES; UCCELLI PRESS; BEST OF BRANCHES, P.O. Box 85394, Seattle WA 98145-1394. E-mail: editor@branchesquarterly.com. Website: www.branchesquarterly.com. Established 2001. **Editor:** Toni La Ree Bennett.

Magazine Needs: *Branches* is a quarterly online journal "dedicated to publishing the best of known and unknown artists and authors, presenting, when possible, verbal and visual art together in a way that expands their individual meaning." Wants poetry that is "educated but not pretentious. Seeking an eclectic, sophisticated mix of poetry, short prose, art, photos, fiction, essays, translations. No rhyming unless specific form. No greeting card verse, no openly sectarian religious verse (spirituality okay)." Recently published poetry by John Amen, Janet Buck, A.E. Stallings, Richard Jordan, Corrine de Winter, and John Sweet. *Branches* is published online, equivalent to about 30 pages in print. *Best of Branches* is an annual print version. Receives about 2,000 poems/year, accepts about 5%. Publishes about 25 poems/issue.

How to Submit: Submit 3-5 poems at a time. Accepts simultaneous submissions; no previously published poems "unless by invitation." Accepts fax and e-mail submissions; no disk submissions. Cover letter is strongly encouraged. "Preferred method of submission is to e-mail work in body of message to submit@branchesquarterly.com. Send art/photos as jpeg attachments. Submitters must be willing to have their work appear with other verbal or visual art of editor's choosing." Reads submissions continually; see website for issue deadlines. Submit seasonal poems 3 months in advance. Time between acceptance and publication is up to 3 months. Seldom comments on rejected poems. Guidelines available on website. Responds in 6 weeks. Always sends prepublication galleys (online only). Pays 1 contributor's copy of *Best of Branches* annual print version to those who will be published in it. Acquires first rights and retains right to archive online unless otherwise negotiated.

Also Offers: $25 cash contest each issue for Best Visual (art, photo, etc.) Response to a Verbal Piece and Best Verbal Response to a Visual Piece. See website for details.

Advice: "*Branches* is a place where 'the undefined and exact combine' (Verlaine). Artists live in a privileged, neglected place in our society. We are expected to make concrete the fluid, to tell the future, to work without recompense, and walk around naked. I'm looking for solid craftsmanship and an honest attempt to articulate the undefined."

THE BREAD OF LIFE MAGAZINE (Specialized: religious), 209 MacNab St. N., P.O. Box 395, Hamilton ON L8N 3H8 Canada. (905)529-4496. Fax: (905)529-5373. Website: www.thebre adoflife.ca. Established 1977. **Editor:** Fr. Peter Coughlin.

Magazine Needs: *The Bread of Life* is "a Catholic charismatic magazine, published bimonthly and designed to encourage spiritual growth in areas of renewal in the Catholic Church today." It includes articles, poetry, and artwork. *The Bread of Life* is 34 pages, magazine-sized, professionally printed and saddle-stapled with glossy paper cover, includes original artwork and photos. Receives about 50-60 poems/year, accepts approximately 25%. Press run is 3,600 for subscribers only. "It's good if contributors are members of *The Bread of Life*."

How to Submit: Accepts previously published poems and simultaneous submissions. Cover letter preferred. Publishes theme issues. Send SAE with IRCs for upcoming themes.

$ BREAKAWAY BOOKS (Specialized: sports), P.O. Box 24, Halcottsville NY 12438-0024. (212)898-0408. E-mail: Garth@breakawaybooks.com. Website: www.breakawaybooks.com. Established 1994. **Publisher:** Garth Battista.

Book/Chapbook Needs & How to Submit: Breakaway Books publishes "sports literature—fiction, essays, and poetry on the athletic experience." Wants "Poetry on sports only—for intelligent, literate athletes; book-length collections or book-length poems only." Accepts previously published poems and simultaneous submissions. Accepts e-mail submissions; no disk submissions. Query first, with a few sample poems and a cover letter with brief bio and publication credits. Responds to queries in 2 weeks; to mss in 2 months. Seldom comments on rejections. Pays royalties of 7-12%.

THE BRIAR CLIFF REVIEW, Briar Cliff College, 3303 Rebecca St., Sioux City IA 51104-2340. E-mail: emmons@briarcliff.edu. Website: www.briarcliff.edu/administrative/publications/bccr evie/bcreview.htm. Established 1989. **Managing Editor:** Tricia Currans-Sheehan. **Poetry Editor:** Jeanne Emmons.

  ● *The Briar Cliff Review* received the 1999 Columbia Scholastic Association Gold Crown and the 2000 Associated Collegiate Press Peacemaker Award.

Magazine Needs: *The Briar Cliff Review*, appearing in April, is an attractive annual "eclectic literary and cultural magazine focusing on (but not limited to) Siouxland writers and subjects." Wants "quality poetry with strong imagery; especially interested in regional, Midwestern content with tight, direct, well-wrought language. No allegorical emotional landscapes." Has published poetry by Sandra Adelmund, Vivian Shipley, Charles Atkinson, and Michael Carey. *The Briar Cliff Review* is 64 pages, magazine-sized, professionally printed on 80 lb. dull text paper, perfect-bound, four-color cover on dull stock, b&w and color photos inside. Receives about 600 poems/year, accepts about 15. Press run is 1,000, all shelf sales. Sample: $10.

How to Submit: Submissions should be typewritten or letter quality, with author's name and address on the first page, with name on following pages. Accepts simultaneous submissions, but expects prompt notification of acceptance elsewhere; no previously published poems. No fax or e-mail submissions. Cover letter with short bio required. "No manuscripts returned without SASE." Reads submissions August 1 through November 1 only. Time between acceptance and publication is up to 6 months. Seldom comments on rejected poems. Responds in 6 months. Pays 2 copies. Acquires first serial rights.

Also Offers: *The Briar Cliff Review* also sponsors a contest. Send 3 poems with a $10 reading fee by November 1. Prize is $500 and publication.

BRICKHOUSE BOOKS, INC.; NEW POETS SERIES, INC./CHESTNUT HILLS PRESS; STONEWALL SERIES (Specialized, Stonewall only: gay/lesbian/bisexual), 541 Piccadilly Rd., Baltimore MD 21204. (410)830-2869 or 828-0724. Fax: (410)830-3999. E-mail: charriss@towson.edu. Website: www.towson.edu/harriss/. Established 1970. **Editor/Director:** Clarinda Harriss. NPS, along with Chestnut Hills Press, Stonewall is now a division of BrickHouse Books.

Book/Chapbook Needs: BrickHouse and The New Poets Series, Inc. brings out first books by promising new poets. Poets who have previously had book-length mss published are not eligible. Prior publication in journals and anthologies is strongly encouraged. Wants "excellent, fresh, non-trendy, literate, intelligent poems. Any form (including traditional), any style." BrickHouse Books and New Poets Series pay 20 author's copies (out of a press run of 1,000), the sales proceeds going back into the corporation to finance the next volume. "BrickHouse has been successful in its effort to provide writers with a national distribution; in fact, The New Poets Series was named an Outstanding Small Press by the prestigious Pushcart Awards Committee, which judges some 5,000 small press publications annually." Chestnut Hills Press publishes author-subsidized books—"High quality work only, however. Chestnut Hills Press has achieved a reputation for prestigious books, printing only the top 10% of mss Chestnut Hills Press and New Poets Series receive." Chestnut Hills Press authors receive proceeds from sale of their books. The Stonewall series publishes work with a gay, lesbian, or bisexual perspective. New Poets Series/Chestnut Hills Press has published books by Chester Wickwire, Ted McCrorie, Sharon White, Mariquita McManus, and Jeff Mann. Brickhouse publishes 64-112 page works. Chapbooks: $8. Full-length books: $10.

How to Submit: Do not query by phone or fax; e-mail or postal mail queries only. Send a 50- to 55-page ms, $10 reading fee and cover letter giving publication credits and bio. Indicate if ms is to be considered for BrickHouse, New Poets Series, Chestnut Hills Press or Stonewall. Accepts simultaneous submissions. No e-mail submissions. Cover letters should be very brief, businesslike and include an accurate list of published work. Editor sometimes comments briefly on rejected poems. Responds in up to 1 year. Mss "are circulated to an editorial board of professional, publishing poets. BrickHouse is backlogged, but the best 10% of the mss it receives are automatically eligible for Chestnut Hills Press consideration," a subsidy arrangement. Send $5 and a 7×10 SASE for a sample volume.

BRIDGES: A JOURNAL FOR JEWISH FEMINISTS AND OUR FRIENDS (Specialized: ethnic, women/feminism, social issues), P.O. Box 24839, Eugene OR 97402. (541)343-7617. E-mail: clare@bridgesjournal.org. Website: www.bridgesjournal.org. Established 1990. **Managing Editor:** Clare Kinberg.

Magazine Needs: The biannual *Bridges* is "a showcase for Jewish women's creativity and involvement in social justice activism." Wants "anything original by Jewish women, not purely religious." Has published poetry by Emily Warn, Willa Schneberg, and Ellen Bass. *Bridges* is 128 pages, 7×10, professionally printed on 50% recycled paper, perfect-bound, with 2-color cover, b&w photos inside. Receives about 200 poems/year, accepts about 20. Press run is 3,000 for 1,500 subscribers of which 70 are libraries, 300 shelf sales; 200 distributed free to exchanges, board members, funders. Subscription: $18/year. Single: $9. Sample: free.

How to Submit: Submit 6-10 poems at a time. No previously published poems or simultaneous submissions. Cover letter preferred with 40 word bio. Time between acceptance and publication is 6 months. Poems are circulated to an editorial board. "Two poetry readers and sometimes others decide on poems." Often comments on rejected poems. Publishes theme issues. Guidelines available for SASE. Responds in 9 months. Sometimes sends prepublication galleys. Pays 5 copies. Sometimes reviews books of poetry. Send materials for review consideration.

BRIGHT HILL PRESS; WORD THURSDAYS READING SERIES; WORD THURSDAYS LITERARY WORKSHOPS; RADIO BY WRITERS; SHARE THE WORDS HIGH-SCHOOL POETRY COMPETITION; WORD AND IMAGE GALLERY, P.O. Box 193, 94 Church St., Treadwell NY 13846-0193. (607)829-5055. Fax: (607)746-7274. E-mail: wordthur@catskill.net. Website: www.brighthillpress.org. Established 1992. **Editor-in-Chief/Founding Director:**

Bertha Rogers. Member: Council of Literary Magazines and Presses, NYC.

Book/Chapbook Needs: Bright Hill Press publishes 2-3 paperbacks and 1 chapbook annually chosen through competition. **Considers mss submitted through competition only.** (See separate listings for Bright Hill Press Poetry Book Award and Chapbook Award in the Contests & Awards section.) Also publishes anthology. No beginners; no unpublished poets/writers. Recently published poetry by Claudia M. Reder, Beth Copeland Vargo, Richard Deutch, Matthew J. Spireng, Lisa Harris, and Judith Neeld.

Also Offers: Words Thursdays (reading series); Radio by Writers (a Catskills radio series heard on WJFF, the Sullivan Co. NPR affiliate); Share the Words High-School Annual Oral Poetry Competition; Word and Image gallery at the Bright Hill Center; Speaking the Words Tour and Festival; and the Word Thursdays Literary Workshops for Kids and Adults. See website for further information. (Also administers the New York State Council on the Arts Literary Curators website at www.nyslittree .org).

Advice: "Read poetry; read fiction. Send your poetry/fiction out for publication; when it comes back, revise it and send it out again."

📕 ◎ BRILLIANT CORNERS: A JOURNAL OF JAZZ & LITERATURE (Specialized: jazz-related literature), Lycoming College, Williamsport PA 17701. (570)321-4279. Fax: (570)321-4090. E-mail: bc@lycoming.edu. Website: www.lycoming.edu/BrilliantCorners. Established 1996. **Editor:** Sascha Feinstein.

Magazine Needs: *Brilliant Corners*, a biannual, publishes jazz-related poetry, fiction, and nonfiction. "We are open to length and form, but want work that is both passionate and well crafted—work worthy of our recent contributors. No sloppy hipster jargon or improvisatory nonsense." Has published poetry by Amiri Baraka, Jayne Cortez, Yusef Komunyakaa, Philip Levine, Colleen McElroy, and Al Young. *Brilliant Corners* is 100 pages, digest-sized, commercially printed and perfect-bound with color card cover with original artwork, ads. Accepts about 5% of work received. Press run is 800 for 200 subscribers. Subscription: $12. Sample: $7.

How to Submit: Submit 3-5 poems at a time. Previously published poems "very rarely, and only by well established poets"; no simultaneous submissions. No e-mail or fax submissions. Cover letter preferred. Reads submissions September 1 through May 15 only. Seldom comments on rejected poems. Responds in 2 months. Pays 2 copies. Acquires first North American serial rights. Staff reviews books of poetry. Send materials for review consideration.

🌐 📕 THE BROBDINGNAGIAN TIMES, 96 Albert Rd., Cork, Ireland. Phone: 353-21-4311227. Established 1996. **Editor:** Giovanni Malito.

Magazine Needs: *The Brobdingnagian Times* appears quarterly. "Its purpose and contents are international and eclectic. We wish to present a small sample of what is happening out there in the 'world' of poetry." Open to all kinds of poetry of 40 lines or less. "Translations are very welcome. Not very partial to rhyming forms." Has published poetry by Miroslav Holub, Leonard Cirino, Ion Codescru, John Martone, and John Millet. *The Brobdingnagian Times* is 8 pages, A3 sheet folded twice, photocopied from laser original. Receives about 300 poems/year, accepts about 10%. Press run is 250 for 65 subscribers, variable shelf sales; 12 distributed free to writers' groups. Subscription: $5 or equivalent in loose stamps. Sample: $1 or postage. Make checks payable to Giovanni Malito.

How to Submit: Submit 4-8 poems at a time. Line length for poetry is 1 minimum, 40 maximum. Accepts previously published poems and simultaneous submissions. Cover letter preferred. "SASE is required. If IRCs are not convenient then loose stamps for trade with Irish stamps are fine." Time between acceptance and publication is up to 6 months. Often comments on rejected poems. Publishes occasional theme issues as supplements. Guidelines and upcoming themes available for SASE. Responds in 1 month. Pays 1 copy. Acquires one-time rights. Staff reviews books and chapbooks of poetry in 300-500 words, single book format. Send materials for review consideration.

Book/Chapbook Needs & How to Submit: The Brobdingnagian Times Press is open to any type of prose and/or poetry and publishes 2-4 chapbooks/year. Chapbooks are usually "palmtop" in size, photocopied from laser original and side-stapled with slightly heavier stock colored paper, cover art only. "The palmtops are quite small. They may be one long poem (8 pages) or several (8-16) short poems (less than 6 lines) or something in between. Collections (unless haiku/senryu) must be more or less themed." Responds to queries in 1 week; to mss in up to 3 weeks. Pays 50 author's copies (out of a press run of 100). "Poets outside of Ireland are asked to cover the postage." Order sample chapbooks by sending 2 IRCs.

Advice: "Nerve and verve and the willingness to edit: these are three qualities a poet must possess."

✖ $ ◎ BROOKS BOOKS PRESS; MAYFLY (Specialized: haiku), (formerly High/Coo Press), 3720 N. Woodridge Dr., Decatur IL 62526. (217)877-2966. E-mail: brooksbooks@q-com.com. Website: www.family-net.net/~brooksbooks. Established 1976. **Editors:** Randy and Shirley Brooks.
   ● Their books have received the National Haiku Society of America Merit Awards.

Magazine Needs: Appearing in winter and summer, *Mayfly* publishes haiku exclusively. Wants "well-crafted haiku, with sensual images honed like a carved jewel, to evoke an immediate emotional response as well as a long-lasting, often spiritual, resonance in the imagination of the reader." Publishes no poetry except haiku. Has published haiku by George Swede, Peggy Lyles, Lee Gurga, and Masajo Suzuki. *Mayfly* is 16 pages, 3½×5, professionally printed on high-quality stock, saddle-stapled, one haiku/page. Publishes 32 of an estimated 1,800 submissions. Subscription: $8. Sample: $4; or send $17 (Illinois residents add 7½% tax) for the *Midwest Haiku Anthology* which includes the work of 54 haiku poets. A Macintosh computer disk of haiku-related stacks is available for $10.

How to Submit: Submit no more than 5 haiku/issue. No previously published poems or simultaneous submissions. Accepts e-mail submissions. Submission deadlines are May 15 and November 15. Guidelines available for SASE. Pays $10/poem; no copies.

Book/Chapbook Needs & How to Submit: Brooks Books, formerly High/Coo Press, publishes English language haiku books, chapbooks, magazines, and bibliographies. "Our goal is to feature the individual haiku as literary event, and to celebrate excellence in the art through collections by the best contemporary writers practicing the art of haiku." Has published *Almost Unseen: Selected Haiku of George Swede*, dual-language books of haiku by contemporary Japanese Writers, chapbooks, and haiga web collections. Brooks Books considers mss "by invitation only."

Advice: "Publishing poetry is a joyous work of love. We publish to share those moments of insight contained in evocative haiku. We aren't in it for fame, gain, or name. We publish to serve an enthusiastic readership."

◐ BRYANT LITERARY REVIEW, Faculty Suite F, Bryant College, Smithfield RI 02917. Website: http://web.bryant.edu/~blr. Established 2000. **Editor:** Tom Chandler. Member: CLMP.

Magazine Needs: *Bryant Literary Review* appears annually in May and publishes poetry, fiction, photography, and art. "Our only standard is quality." Recently published poetry by Michael S. Harper, Mary Crow, Cathleen Calbert, and Allison Joseph. *Bryant Literary Review* is 125 pages, digest-sized, offset-printed, perfect-bound, 4-color cover, with art or photo. Receives about 2,500 poems/year, accepts about 1%. Publishes about 25 poems/issue. Press run is 2,500. Single copy: $8; subscription: $8.

How to Submit: Submit 3-5 poems at a time. Cover letter is required. "Include SASE; please submit only *once* each reading period." Reads submissions September 1-December 31. Time between acceptance and publication is 5 months. Seldom comments on rejected poems. Guidelines available on website and in publication. Responds in 3 months. Pays 2 contributors copies. Acquires one-time rights.

Advice: "No abstract expressionist or l-a-n-g-u-a-g-e poems, please. We prefer accessible work of depth and quality."

$ ◐ ◎ BUGLE: JOURNAL OF ELK COUNTRY AND THE HUNT (Specialized: animals, nature/rural/ecology, elk conservation), Rocky Mountain Elk Foundation, P.O. Box 8249, Missoula MT 59807-8249. (406)523-4570. Fax: (406)543-7710. E-mail: bugle@rmef.org. Website: www.elkfoundation.org. Established 1984. **Assistant Editor:** Lee Cromrich.

Magazine Needs: *Bugle* is the bimonthly publication of the nonprofit Rocky Mountain Elk Foundation, whose mission is to ensure the future of elk, other wildlife, and their habitat. "The goal of *Bugle* is to advance this mission by presenting original, critical thinking about wildlife conservation, elk ecology, and hunting." Wants "high quality poems that explore the realm of elk, the 'why' of hunting, or celebrate the hunting experience as a whole. Prefer one page. Free verse preferred. No 'Hallmark' poetry." Has published poetry by Mike Fritch, John Whinery, and Ted Florea. *Bugle* is 130 pages, magazine-sized, professionally printed on coated stock and saddle-stapled with full-color glossy cover containing photos, illustrations, ads. Receives about 50 poems/year, accepts about 10%. Press run is 132,000. Subscription: $30 membership fee. Sample: $5.95. Make checks payable to Rocky Mountain Elk Foundation.

How to Submit: "Poets may submit as many poems as they'd like at a time." Accepts simultaneous submissions. Accepts e-mail (prefer attached file in Word), fax, and disk submissions. Cover letter preferred. Time between acceptance and publication varies. "Poems are screened by assistant editor first, those accepted then passed to editorial staff for review and comment, final decision based on their comments. We will evaluate your poem based on content, quality, and our needs for the coming year." Rarely comments on rejected poems. Publishes special sections. Guidelines available for SASE, by fax, by e-mail, and on website. Responds in 3 months. "The Rocky Mountain Elk Foundation is a nonprofit conservation organization committed to putting membership dollars into protecting elk habitat. So we appreciate, and still receive, donated work. However, if you would like to be paid for your work, our rate is $100 a poem, paid on acceptance. Should your poem appear in *Bugle*, you will receive three complimentary copies of the issue." Acquires first North American serial rights. Staff reviews other magazines.

Advice: "Although poetry has appeared periodically in *Bugle* over the years, it has never been a high priority for us, nor have we solicited it. A lack of high-quality work and poetry appropriate for the focus of the magazine has kept us from making it a regular feature. However, we've decided to attempt to give verse a permanent home in the magazine. . . . Reading a few issues of *Bugle* prior to submitting will give you a better sense of the style and content of the magazine."

◐ BUTTON MAGAZINE, P.O. Box 26, Lunenburg MA 01462. E-mail: Aiolia@worldnet.att.net. Website: http://moonsigns.net. Established 1993. **Editor:** Sally Cragin. **Contact:** Maude Piper.

Magazine Needs: *Button* "is New England's tiniest magazine of fiction, poetry, and gracious living." Wants "poetry about the quiet surprises in life, not sentimental, and true moments carefully preserved. Brevity counts." Has published poetry by William Corbett, Amanda Powell, Brendan Galvin, Jean Monahan, Diana Der-Hovanessian, Kevin McGrath, and Sappho ("Hey, we have a fabulous translator in Julia Dubnoff!"). *Button*, published annually, is 30 pages, 4¼ × 5½, saddle-stapled, card stock 4-color cover with illustrations that incorporate one or more buttons. Press run is 1,200 for more than 500 subscribers; 750 shelf sales. Subscription: $5/4 issues, $25/lifetime. Sample: $2 and a first class stamp.

How to Submit: Submit no more than 2 poems at a time. No previously published poems. Cover letter required. Time between acceptance and publication is up to 6 months. Poems are circulated to an editorial board. Often comments on rejected poems. Guidelines available by e-mail. Responds in 4 months. Pays honorarium, subscription, and at least 5 copies. Acquires first North American serial rights.

Advice: "Read good work by giants in the field. Eradicate 'I'. Revise. Wait. Revise some more. Wait some more. Keep submissions at least 6 months apart so you can revise. Wait. Revise."

$ ◐ ◎ BYLINE MAGAZINE; BYLINE LITERARY AWARDS (Specialized: writing), P.O. Box 5240, Edmond OK 73083-5240. (405)348-5591. E-mail: MPreston@bylinemag.com. Website: www.bylinemag.com (features guidelines, contest listings, subscription info, and sample column or article from magazine). Established 1981. **Poetry Editor:** Sandra Soli. **Editor:** Marcia Preston.

Magazine Needs: *ByLine* is a magazine for the encouragement of writers and poets, using 8-10 poems/issue about writers or writing. Has published poetry by Judith Tate O'Brien, Katharyn Howd Machan, and Henry B. Stobbs. *ByLine* is magazine-sized, professionally printed, with illustrations, cartoons, and ads. Has more than 3,000 subscriptions and receives about 2,500 poetry submissions/year, of which about 100 are used. Subscription: $22. Sample: $4.

How to Submit: Submit up to 3 poems at a time, no reprints. No e-mail or fax submissions, please. Guidelines available for SASE or on website. Responds within 6 weeks. Pays $10/poem. Acquires first North American serial rights.

Also Offers: Sponsors up to 20 poetry contests, including a chapbook competition open to anyone. Send #10 SASE for details. Also sponsors the *ByLine* Short Fiction and Poetry Awards, which is open only to subscribers. Prize: $250. Send SASE for guidelines.

Advice: "We are happy to work with new writers, but please read a few samples to get an idea of our style. We would like to see more serious poetry about the creative experience (as it concerns writing)."

⬛ **CALIFORNIA QUARTERLY; CALIFORNIA STATE POETRY SOCIETY,** P.O. Box 7126, Orange CA 92863-7126. (949)854-8024. E-mail: jipalley@aol.com. Established 1972. **Editors:** Julian Palley and Kate Ozbirn.

Magazine Needs: *California Quarterly* is the official publication of the California State Poetry Society (an affiliate of the National Federation of State Poetry Societies) and is designed "to encourage the writing and dissemination of poetry." Wants poetry on any subject, 60 lines maximum. "No geographical limitations. Quality is all that matters." Has published poetry by Michael L. Johnson, Lyn Lifshin, and Joanna C. Scott. *California Quarterly* is 64 pages, digest-sized, offset-printed, perfect-bound, heavy paper cover with art. Receives 3,000-4,000 poems/year, accepts about 5%. Press run is 500 for 300 subscribers of which 24 are libraries, 20-30 shelf sales. Membership in CSPS is $20/year and includes a subscription to *California Quarterly.* Sample (including guidelines): $5. Guidelines available for SASE.

How to Submit: Submit up to 6 "relatively brief" poems at a time; name and address on each sheet. Include SASE. Prefer no previously published poems. Accepts submissions by post only; no e-mail submissions. Seldom comments on rejected poems. Responds in up to 8 months. Pays 1 copy. Acquires first rights. Rights revert to poet after publication.

Also Offers: CSPS also sponsors an annual poetry contest. Awards vary. All entries considered for *California Quarterly.*

Advice: "Since our editor changes with each issue, we encourage poets to resubmit."

⬛ ⬛ **CALLALOO (Specialized: ethnic),** Dept. of English, Texas A&M University, 4227 TAMU, College Station TX 77843-4227. (979)458-3108. Fax: (979)458-3275. E-mail: callaloo@tam u.edu. Website: http://callaloo.tamu.edu. Established 1976. **Editor:** Charles H. Rowell.

• Poetry published in *Callaloo* has been frequently included in volumes of *The Best American Poetry.*

Magazine Needs: *Callaloo: A Journal of African Diaspora Arts & Letters*, published quarterly, is devoted to poetry dealing with the African Diaspora, including North America, Europe, Africa, Latin and Central America, South America, and the Caribbean. Has published poetry by Ai, Aimé Césaire, Lucille Clifton, Rita Dove, Toi Derricotte, Yusef Komunyakaa, Nathaniel Mackey, and Edimilson de Almeida Pereira. *Callaloo* features about 15-20 poems (all forms and styles) in each issue along with short fiction, interviews, literary criticism, and concise critical book reviews. Circulation is 1,600 subscribers of which half are libraries. Subscription: $39, $107 for institutions.

How to Submit: Submit complete ms in triplicate. Include cover letter with name, mailing address, e-mail address if available, and SASE. No fax or e-mail submissions. Responds in 6 months. Pays copies.

⬛ ⬛ **CALYX, A JOURNAL OF ART & LITERATURE BY WOMEN (Specialized: women, lesbian, multicultural); CALYX BOOKS,** P.O. Box B, Corvallis OR 97339-0539. (541)753-9384. Fax: (541)753-0515. E-mail: calyx@proaxis.com. Established 1976. **Senior Editor:** Beverly McFarland. **Managing Editor:** Micki Reaman.

Magazine Needs: *Calyx* is a journal edited by a collective editorial board. Publishes poetry, prose, art, book reviews, and interviews by and about women. Wants "excellently crafted poetry that also has excellent content." Has published poetry by Maurya Simon, Diane Averill, Carole Boston Weatherford, and Eleanor Wilner. *Calyx* appears 3 times every 18 months and is 6×8, handsomely printed on heavy paper, flat-spined, glossy color cover, 128-144 pages, of which 50-60 are poetry. Poems tend to be lyric free verse that makes strong use of image and symbol melding unobtrusively with voice and theme. Single copy: $9.50. Sample: $11.50.

How to Submit: Send up to 6 poems with SASE and short bio. "We accept copies in good condition and clearly readable. We focus on new writing, but occasionally publish a previously published piece." Accepts simultaneous submissions, "if kept up-to-date on publication." No fax or e-mail submissions. *Calyx* is open to submissions October 1 through December 31 only. Mss received when not open to reading will be returned unread. Guidelines available for SASE or e-mail. Responds in

9 months. Pays 1 copy/poem and subscription. Send materials for review consideration.

Book/Chapbook Needs & How to Submit: Calyx Books publishes 1 book of poetry/year. All work published is by women. Recently published *Black Candle* by Chitra Divakaruni. However, Calyx Books is closed for ms submissions until further notice.

Advice: "Read the publication and be familiar with what we have published."

$ **THE CAPILANO REVIEW**, 2055 Purcell Way, North Vancouver BC V7J 3H5 Canada. (604)984-1712. E-mail: tcr@capcollege.bc.ca. Website: www.capcollege.bc.ca/dept/TCR/. Established 1972. **Editor:** Sharon Thesen.

Magazine Needs: *The Capilano Review* is a literary and visual arts review appearing 3 times/year. Wants "avant-garde, experimental, previously unpublished work, poetry of sustained intelligence and imagination. We are interested in poetry that is new in concept and in execution." Has published poetry by bill bissett, Phyllis Webb, and Michael Ondaatje. *The Capilano Review* comes in a handsome digest-sized format, 115 pages, flat-spined, finely printed, semi-glossy stock with a glossy full-color card cover. Circulation is 1,000. Sample: $9 prepaid.

How to Submit: Submit 5-6 poems, minimum, with cover letter and SAE and IRC (no US postage). No simultaneous submissions. No e-mail or disk submissions. Responds in up to 5 months. Pays $50-200, subscription, plus 2 copies. Acquires first North American serial rights.

Advice: "*The Capilano Review* receives several manuscripts each week; unfortunately the majority of them are simply inappropriate for the magazine. The best advice we can offer is to read the magazine before you submit."

$ **CAPPER'S; BRAVE HEARTS (Specialized: inspirational, humor, themes)**, 1503 SW 42nd St., Topeka KS 66609-1265. (785)274-4300. Fax: (785)274-4305. Website: www.cappers.c om. Established 1879. **Editor:** Ann Crahan.

Magazine Needs & How to Submit: *Capper's* is a biweekly tabloid (newsprint) going to 240,000 mail subscribers, mostly small-town and rural families. Wants short poems (4-16 lines preferred, lines of one-column width) "relating to everyday situations, nature, inspirational, humorous. Most poems used in *Capper's* are upbeat in tone and offer the reader a bit of humor, joy, enthusiasm, or encouragement." Accepts poetry written by children, ages 12 and under and 13-19. Has published poetry by Elizabeth Searle Lamb, Robert Brimm, Margaret Wiedyke, Helena K. Stefanski, Sheryl L. Nelms, and Claire Puneky. Send $1.95 for sample. Uses 6-8 poems in each issue. Not available on newsstand. Submit 5-6 poems at a time, 14-16 lines. No simultaneous submissions. No e-mail or fax submissions. Returns mss with SASE. Publishes seasonal theme issues. Upcoming themes available for SASE. Responds in 3 months. Pays $10-15/poem. Additional payment of $5 if poem is used on website. Acquires one-time rights.

Magazine Needs & How to Submit: *Brave Hearts* is an inspirational magazine appearing quarterly in February, May, August, and November. Features themes and humorous poems. "Poems should be short (16 lines or less)." Sample: $4.95. Does not accept poetry by children. Guidelines and themes available for SASE. Accepts submissions by postal mail only. Pays on acceptance and 1 copy.

Advice: "Poems chosen are upbeat, sometimes humorous, always easily understood. Short poems of this type fit our format best."

THE CARIBBEAN WRITER (Specialized: regional, Caribbean); THE DAILY NEWS PRIZE; THE CANUTE A. BRODHURT PRIZE; THE CHARLOTTE AND ISIDOR PAIEWONSKY PRIZE; DAVID HOUGH LITERARY PRIZE; THE MARGUERITE COBB MCKAY PRIZE, University of the Virgin Islands, RR 02, P.O. Box 10,000, Kingshill, St. Croix, USVI 00850. (340)692-4152. Fax: (340)692-4026. E-mail: qmars@uvi.edu. Website: www.TheCarib beanWriter.com. Established 1987. **Editor:** Marvin E. William. **Contact:** Ms. Quilin Mars.

 • Poetry published in *The Caribbean Writer* has been included in the 2002 *Pushcart Prize* anthology.

Magazine Needs: *The Caribbean Writer* is a literary anthology, appearing in July, with a Caribbean focus. The Caribbean must be central to the literary work or the work must reflect a Caribbean heritage, experience or perspective. Has published poetry by Virgil Suarez, Thomas Reiter, Kamau Brathwaite, and Opal Palmer Adisa. *The Caribbean Writer* magazine is over 300 pages, digest-sized, handsomely printed on heavy stock, perfect-bound, with glossy card cover, using advertising and b&w art by Caribbean artists. Press run is 1,200. Single copy: $12 plus $4 postage; subscription: $20. Sample: $7 plus $4 postage. Guidelines are available for SASE. (Note: postage to and from the Virgin Islands is the same as within the US.)

How to Submit: Submit up to 5 poems. Accepts simultaneous submissions; no previously published poems. Accepts submissions by e-mail (attached file), on disk, and by post; no fax submissions. Blind submissions only: name, address, phone number, and title of ms should appear in cover letter along with brief bio. Title only on ms. Deadline is September 30 of each year. Publishes theme issues. Guidelines available for SASE, by e-mail, on website, and in publication. Pays 2 copies. Acquires first North American serial rights. Reviews books of poetry and fiction in 1,000 words. Send materials for review consideration.

Also Offers: The magazine annually awards the Daily News Prize ($300) for the best poem or poems, The Marguerite Cobb McKay Prize to a Virgin Island author ($100), the David Hough Literary Prize to a Caribbean author ($500), the Canute A. Brodhurst Prize for Fiction ($400), and the Charlotte and Isidor Paiewonsky Prize ($200) for first-time publication.

CARN; THE CELTIC LEAGUE (Specialized: foreign language, ethnic). Phone/fax: (0)1624 877918. E-mail: b.moffat@advsys.co.im. Website: www.manxman.co.im/cleague. Established 1973. **Editor:** Patricia Bridson. **Contact:** J.B. Moffat.

Magazine Needs: *Carn* is a magazine-sized quarterly, press run 2,000. "The aim of our quarterly is to contribute to a fostering of cooperation between the Celtic peoples, developing the consciousness of the special relationship which exists between them, and making their achievements and their struggle for cultural and political freedom better known abroad."

How to Submit: "Contributions to *Carn* come through invitation to people whom we know as qualified to write more or less in accordance with that aim. We would welcome poems in the Celtic languages if they are relating to that aim. If I had to put it briefly, we have a political commitment, or, in other words, *Carn* is not a literary magazine." Accepts submissions by e-mail only. Reviews books of poetry only if in the Celtic languages.

THE CAROLINA QUARTERLY; THE CHARLES B. WOOD AWARD, CB #3520 Greenlaw Hall, University of North Carolina, Chapel Hill NC 27599-3520. (919)962-0244. E-mail: cquarter@unc.edu. Website: www.unc.edu/depts/cqonline. Established 1948. **Contact:** Poetry Editor.

Magazine Needs: *Carolina Quarterly* appears 3 times/year publishing fiction, poetry, reviews, nonfiction and graphic art. No specifications regarding form, length, subject matter, or style of poetry. Considers translations of work originally written in languages other than English. Has published poetry by Denise Levertov, Richard Wilbur, Robert Morgan, Ha Jin, and Charles Wright. *The Carolina Quarterly* is about 90 pages, digest-sized, professionally-printed and perfect-bound, one-color matte card cover, a few graphics and ads. Receives about 6,000 poems/year, accepts about 1%. Press run is 900 for 200 library subscriptions and various shelf sales. Subscription: $12, $15 (institution). Sample: $5.

How to Submit: Submit 1-6 poems at a time. No previously published poems or simultaneous submissions. No submissions by e-mail. SASE required. Poems are circulated to an editorial board. "Manuscripts that make it to the meeting of the full poetry staff are discussed by all. Poems are accepted by majority consensus." Seldom comments on rejected poems. Responds in 4 months. "Poets are welcome to write or phone about their submission's status, but please wait about four months before doing so." Pays 2 contributor's copies. Acquires first rights. Reviews books of poetry. Send materials for review consideration (attn: Editor).

Also Offers: The Charles B. Wood Award for Distinguished Writing is given to the author of the best poem or short story published in each volume of *The Carolina Quarterly*. Only those writers *without* major publications are considered and the winner receives $500.

CAROLINA WREN PRESS (Specialized: women, ethnic, gay/lesbian, social issues), 120 Morris St., Durham NC 27701. (919)560-2738. Fax: (919)560-2759. E-mail: carolina@carolinawrenpress.org. Website: www.carolinawrenpress.org. Established 1976. **Contact:** David Kellogg.

Book/Chapbook Needs: Publishes 1 book/year "through our chapbook series. Primarily women and minorities, though men and majorities also welcome." Has published poetry by George Elliott Clarke, Andrea Selch, Evie Shockley, and Erica Hunt.

How to Submit: Currently are not accepting any unsolicited mss. Send standard SASE for catalog or order online. See website for yearly chapbook contest guidelines and deadlines.

⬤ ◎ **CATAMOUNT PRESS; COTYLEDON (Specialized: short free verse poems, haiku, tanka)**, 2519 Roland Rd. SW, Huntsville AL 35805-4147. Established 1992. **Editor:** Georgette Perry.

Magazine Needs: *Cotyledon*, established in 1997 and published 4 times/year, is a miniature magazine. Wants poems up to 8 lines. Nature and the environment are favorite subjects, but a variety of subject matter is needed. Poets recently published include Don Wentworth, Carl Mayfield, Judy Snow, Patricia G. Rourke, David Chorlton, and Julie Dunlop. *Cotyledon* is 16 pages, $3\frac{1}{2} \times 4\frac{1}{4}$, photocopied, saddle-stapled, with bond cover and b&w art. Sample: $1 or 3 unattached first class stamps.

How to Submit: Submit 3-6 poems at a time with cover letter and SASE. Accepts previously published poems if identified as such. Send three unattached first-class stamps for a sample *Cotyledon*, guidelines, and news of press offerings and plans. Responds in 2 months. Pays at least 2 copies.

Book/Chapbook Needs & How to Submit: "Catamount Press publishes very few chapbooks, so please do not submit a ms. Get acquainted with us first by submitting to *Cotyledon*, or querying."

Advice: "Casual, hand-written cover letters are fine. *Cotyledon* is not 'academic.' This doesn't mean it's an easy market. Standards are high. Include an SASE adequate for return of the poems. No need to mail poems flat unless you want them back that way. I hate to disappoint people and reject poems, but it's part of the game. If it turns out that *Cotyledon* isn't the right home for your poems, there are plenty of other places out there. Hang tough and send them out again."

$⬤ **CC. MARIMBO**, P.O. Box 933, Berkeley CA 94701-0933. Established 1996. **Editor:** Peggy Golden.

Book/Chapbook Needs: CC. Marimbo "promotes the work of underpublished poets/artists by providing a well-crafted, cheap (people's prices) and therefore affordable/accessible, collection." Publishes 2-3 poetry titles per year. "Books are issued as 'minichaps' to introduce underpublished poets/artists to the public. Runs done by alphabet, lettered A-Z, AA-ZZ, etc. Short poems for the small format, styles, and content welcome in whatever variation. We do not want to see already published work, unless poems previously in print in magazines (attributed), i.e., poems OK, reprintable books not OK." Has published poetry by David Stone, Phil Hackett, and Marie Kazalia. Chapbooks are usually 40 pages, $4\frac{1}{4} \times 5\frac{1}{4}$, offset-printed and photocopied, mainly handsewn binding with matt cover, includes art/graphics according to project.

How to Submit: Query first, with a few sample poems and cover letter with brief bio and publication credits, include SASE. Line length for poetry is 25 maximum. Responds in 3 months to queries; 6 months to mss. Pays 5 author's copies (out of a press run of 26), additional copies paid for larger press runs. "Author gets 10% of cover price on all copies sold, except for copies sold to author." Order sample chapbooks by sending $5 (5¢ for p&h).

Advice: "We must keep seeking."

★ $⬤ **CEDAR HILL PUBLICATIONS; CEDAR HILL REVIEW**, P.O. Box 15, Mena AR 71953. (501)394-7029. E-mail: mjaffe@mail.sdsu.edu. Established 1996. Managing Editor: Gloria Doyle. Senior Editor: Christopher Presfield. **Poetry Editor:** Maggie Jaffe.

Magazine Needs: *Cedar Hill Review* "favors contemporary themes and engaged poetry." Has published poetry by Ernest Cardenal, Virgil Suarez, Michael McIrvin, Adrian C. Louis, Sharon Doubiago, and Yvette Hatrak. *Cedar Hill Review* is 64 pages, digest-sized, professionally printed and perfect-bound with laminated cover, includes cover art. Receives about 2,000 poems/year, accepts approximately 10%. Press run is 300 for 200 subscribers of which 10 are libraries; 50 distributed

---

THE GEOGRAPHICAL INDEX in the back of this book helps you locate markets in your region.

free to institutions. Single copy: $6; subscription: $15. Sample: $4. Make checks payable to Cedar Hill Publications.

How to Submit: Submit 5 poems at a time, September through May, to Maggie Jaffe at 3730 Arnold Avenue, San Diego CA 92104-3444, (619)294-4924. Accepts previously published poems and simultaneous submissions. Cover letter required. Responds in up to 6 months. Acquires all or one-time rights. Returns rights upon publication. Reviews books of poetry and occasionally other journals.

Book/Chapbook Needs & How to Submit: Cedar Hill Publications "seeks to publish the best sound North America has to offer." Publishes 10 paperbacks and 2 chapbooks/year. Books are usually 64-80 pages, digest-sized, professionally printed and perfect-bound with laminated cover with art. "Must appear in *Cedar Hill Review* for book consideration." Responds to queries and mss in 3 months.

N: ◑ CENTER: A JOURNAL OF THE LITERARY ARTS, Center for the Literary Arts, 202 Tate Hall, University of Missouri, Columbia MO 65211-1500. (573)882-4971. E-mail: cla@missouri. edu. Website: www.missouri.edu/~cla. Established 2000. **Contact:** Poetry Editor.

Magazine Needs: *Center: A Journal for the Literary Arts* appears annually in April. Wants well crafted verse of any kind. Also interested in seeing sequences, part or whole. Recently published poetry by Annie Finch, Maura Stanton, Floyd Skloot, Simon Perchik, and Barbara Lefcowitz. *Center: A Journal* is 100+ pages, digest-sized, perfect-bound, with four-color card cover, 3 ads for literary journals. Receives about 1,000 poems/year, accepts about 30. Publishes about 20-35 poems/issue. Press run is 500 for 100 subscribers. Single copy: $6 (current issue). Sample: $3 (back issue). Make checks payable to *Center: A Journal*.

How to Submit: Submit 3-6 poems at a time. Accepts simultaneous submissions; no previously published poems. Accepts e-mail submissions from international poets only. Cover letter is preferred. Reads submissions September-April. "Please note that we go into production in mid-December. To be considered for current issue, send by November." Time between acceptance and publication is up to 5 months. "An editorial board of experienced writers in our creative writing program reviews all submission as they arrive." Seldom comments on rejected poems. Guidelines available for SASE or on website. "Response depends on submission period. Spring submissions can take as much as 9 months. Fall submissions will hear in 2-3 months." Acquires first North American serial rights; rights revert to poets upon publication.

Advice: "Some great poems will be overlooked by harried readers, but we do our best to read submissions with care."

◯ CHAFF, P.O. Box 632, McHenry IL 60051-0632. E-mail: jordantyoung@yahoo.com. Established 1996. First issue 1997. **Editor/Co-publisher:** Jordan Taylor Young.

Magazine Needs: *Chaff* is a semiannual publication "dedicated to the Lord, for the express purpose of reaching out to a lost and dying world, as well as uniting Christian poets through the publication of their work." Wants "free verse poetry—rhyme and meter only if exceptional quality—romance, nature, aging, friendship, family life, animals, senior citizens, social issues, children, and humor. Nothing satanic, obscene, violent, sensual, erotic, or homosexual." *Chaff* is 20-30 pages, digest-sized, laser-printed and stapled. Press run is 50-100. Single copy: $10. Poetry may be complemented by appropriate photographs, illustrations, or scripture. In addition, *Chaff* includes a "Featured Poet" segment, consisting of a short bio and photograph.

How to Submit: Submit no more than 6 poems; **there is a reading fee of $2 per poem.** Make checks payable to Jordan Taylor Young, editor. Accepts previously published poems and simultaneous submissions. Accepts e-mail submissions; no fax submissions. Cover letter and SASE required. Responds in 1 month. Guidelines available for SASE and by e-mail. Pays 2 copies, 3 copies to Featured Poet.

Advice: "Often poets are not recognized for their artistry, separated like chaff from wheat. The name *Chaff* stems from the editors' deep conviction that we are like chaff, and separated from God we can do nothing! This publication oftentimes finds its way into nursing homes and prisons. Be mindful of this as you select the appropriate uplifting poems for submission. We aspire to helping new and beginning poets to find their own voices through the publication of their work. 'For where your treasure is, there will your heart be also.' (Matthew 6:21)."

◐ **CHAFFIN JOURNAL**, Dept. of English, Case Annex 467, Eastern Kentucky University, Richmond KY 40475-3102. (859)622-3080. Established 1998. **Editor:** Robert W. Witt.

Magazine Needs: *The Chaffin Journal* appears annually. Publishes quality short fiction and poetry by new and established writers/poets. Wants any form, subject matter, or style. Does not want "poor quality." Recently published poetry by Pat Boran, James Doyle, Corey Mesler, Simon Perchik, Philip St. Clair, and Virgil Suarez. *The Chaffin Journal* is 120 pages, digest-sized, offset-printed, perfect-bound, plain cover with title only. Receives about 200 poems/year, accepts about 25%. Publishes about 40-50 poems/issue. Press run is 300 for 65 subscribers of which 3 are libraries, 180 shelf sales; 40-50 are distributed free to contributors. Single copy: $5; subscription: $5 annually. Make checks payable to *The Chaffin Journal*.

How to Submit: Submit 5 poems at a time. Accepts simultaneous submission; no previousy published poems. No fax, e-mail, or disk submissions. Cover letter is preferred. "Submit typed, double-spaced pages with only one poem per page. Enclose SASE." Reads submissions June 1 through November 1. Time between acceptance and publication is 6 months. Poems are reviewed by the general editor and 2 poetry editors. Never comments on rejected poems. Guidelines available in magazine. Responds in 3 months. Pays 1 contributor's copy. Acquires one-time rights.

✿ ○ ◎ **CHALLENGER INTERNATIONAL; ISLAND SCHOLASTIC PRESS (Specialized: teen/young adult)**. (250)991-5567. E-mail: lukivdan@hotmail.com. Website: http://challengerinternational.20m.com/index.html. Established 1978. **Editor:** Dan Lukiv.

Magazine Needs: *Challenger international*, a literary quarterly, contains poetry, short fiction, novel excerpts, and black pen drawings. Open to "any type of work, especially by teenagers (*Ci*'s mandate: to encourage young writers, and to publish their work alongside established writers), providing it is not pornographic, profane, or overly abstract." *Ci* has published poetry from Canada, the US, Switzerland, Russia, Malta, Italy, Slovenia, Ireland, Korea, and Columbia. *Ci* is about 20 pages, magazine-sized, photocopied and side-stapled. Press run is 50. *Ci* is distributed free to McNaughton Center-secondary alternate-students.

How to Submit: Accepts previously published poems and simultaneous submissions. Cover letter required with list of credits, if any. Accepts only e-mail submissions. "Sometimes we edit to save the poet rejection." Responds in 4 months. Pays 1 copy.

Book/Chapbook Needs & How to Submit: Island Scholastic Press publishes chapbooks of work by authors featured in *Ci*. Pays 3 copies. Copyright remains with author. Distribution of free copies through McNaughton Center.

Advice: "We like visual poetry that makes sense."

⊕ ◐ ◎ **CHAPMAN (Specialized: ethnic/nationality); CHAPMAN PUBLISHING**, 4 Broughton Place, Edinburgh EH1 3RX Scotland. Phone: (0131)557-2207. Fax: (0131)556-9565. E-mail: editor@chapman-pub.co.uk. Website: www.chapman-pub.co.uk. Established 1970. **Editor:** Joy Hendry.

Magazine Needs: "*Chapman* magazine is controversial, influential, outspoken, and intelligent. Established in 1970, it has become a dynamic force in Scottish culture covering theatre, politics, language, and the arts. Our highly-respected forum for poetry, fiction, criticism, review, and debate makes it essential reading for anyone interested in contemporary Scotland. *Chapman* publishes the best in Scottish writing—new work by well-known Scottish writers in the context of lucid critical discussion. It also, increasingly, publishes international writing. With our strong commitment to the future, we energetically promote new writers, new ideas and new approaches." Has published poetry and fiction by Alasdair Gray, Liz Lochhead, Sorley MacLean, T.S. Law, Edwin Morgan, Willa Muir, Tom Scott, and Una Flett. *Chapman* appears 3 times/year in a digest-sized, perfect-bound format, 144 pages, professionally printed in small type on matte stock with glossy card cover, art in 2 colors. Press run is 2,000 for 900 subscribers of which 200 are libraries. Receives "thousands" of poetry submissions/year, accepts about 200, has a 4- to 6-month backlog. Single copy: £6; subscription: £18. Sample: £4 (overseas).

How to Submit: "We welcome submissions which must be accompanied by a SASE/IRC. Please send sufficient postage to cover the return of your manuscript. Do not send foreign stamps." Submit 4-10 poems at a time, one poem/page. "We do not usually publish single poems." No simultaneous submissions. Cover letter required. Responds "as soon as possible." Always sends prepublication galleys. Pays copies. Staff reviews books of poetry. Send materials for review consideration.

Book/Chapbook Needs: Chapman Publishing is currently not accepting submissions.

Advice: "Poets should not try to court approval by writing poems especially to suit what they perceive as the nature of the magazine. They usually get it wrong and write badly." Also, they are interested in receiving poetry dealing with women's issues and feminism.

$ ☑ CHAPULTEPEC PRESS, 111 E. University #3, Cincinnati OH 45219. (513)281-9248. E-mail: chapultepecpress@hotmail.com. Website: www.tokyorecords.com. Established 2001. **Contact:** David Garza.

Book/Chapbook Needs & How to Submit: Chapultepec Press publishes books of poetry/litera-ture, essays, social/political issues, art, music, film, library/archive issues, history, popular science, and bilingual. Wants "poetry/literature that works as a unit, that is caustic, fun, open-ended, worldly, mature, relevant, stirring, evocative. Bilingual. No poetry/literature collections without a purpose, that are mere collections." Publishes 5-7 books/year. Books are usually 5-50 pages, with art/graphics. Query first, with a few sample poems and cover letter with brief bio and publication credits. Responds to queries and mss in 1 month. Pays advance of $10-15 and 3-5 author's copies. Order sample books by sending $4 to David Garza.

Advice: "Write as if your life depends on it . . . because it does."

$ ☑ THE CHARITON REVIEW, Truman State University, Kirksville MO 63501. (816)785-4499. Established 1975. **Editor:** Jim Barnes.

Magazine Needs: *The Chariton Review* began in 1975 as a twice yearly literary magazine and in 1978 added the activities of the press (now defunct). The poetry published in the magazine is, accord-ing to the editor, "open and closed forms—traditional, experimental, mainstream. We do not consider verse, only poetry in its highest sense, whatever that may be. The sentimental and the inspirational are not poetry for us. Also, no more 'relativism': short stories and poetry centered around relatives." Has published poetry by Michael Spence, Kim Bridgford, Sam Maio, Andrea Budy, Charles Edward Eaton, Wayne Dodd, and J'laine Robnolt. There are 40-50 pages of poetry in each issue of the *The Chariton Review*, a digest-sized, flat-spined magazine of over 100 pages, professionally printed, glossy cover with photographs. Receives 8,000-10,000 submissions/year, accepts about 35-50, with never more than a 6-month backlog. Press run is about 600 for 400 subscribers of which 100 are libraries. Subscription: $9/1 year, $15/2 years. Sample: $5.

How to Submit: Submit 5-7 poems at a time, typescript single-spaced. No simultaneous submis-sions. Do *not* write for guidelines. Responds quickly; accepted poems often appear within a few issues of notification. Always sends prepublication galleys. Pays $5/printed page. Acquires first North American serial rights. Contributors are expected to subscribe or buy copies. Send materials for review consideration.

◎ CHARM CITY REVIEW (Specialized: middle and high school students), Ben Franklin Junior High School, 1201 Cambria St., Baltimore MD 21225. (410)396-1373. Fax: (410)396-8434. E-mail: wildwildcats@yahoo.com. Established 1999. **Advising Editor:** Kim LaVigueur.

Magazine Needs: *Charm City Review* appears annually in April. Publishes poetry, fiction, and b&w art by middle school and high school students from across the nation. Produced by junior high school students. Wants "all forms, all subject matters, all styles or purposes. Nothing risqué." Accepts poetry written by young writers ages 12-18. Recently published poetry by Matthew Gonzalez, Michael Townes, and Tamara Foulke. *Charm City Review* is 64 pages, digest-sized, side stapled, commercially printed, perfect-bound, matte cover, with b&w photos and art, ad swaps for other publications. Re-ceives about 180 poems/year, accepts about 65%. Publishes about 45 poems/issue. Press run is 1,000 for 320 subscribers; all distributed free to Baltimore City Public School Students, contributors and by request. Subscription: $2.95/year. Sample: $2.95. Make checks payable to Benjamin Franklin Junior High School.

How to Submit: Submit 3-5 poems at a time. Accepts previously published poems and simultaneous submissions. Accepts fax, e-mail and disk submissions. Cover letter is required. "If submitted on disk, please no Mac-based. Submit .doc or .txt." Reads submissions September 1 through March 15. Time between acceptance and publication is up to 7 months. Poems are circulated to an editorial

board who meets and votes on selections. Never comments on rejected poems. Responds in up to 7 months. Pays 2 contributors copies. Acquires one-time rights.
Also Offers: $25 Prize (one each per publication) to a poet, fiction writer, artist/photographer.
Advice: "Write about what you know/experience."

$ ⬛ THE CHATTAHOOCHEE REVIEW, Georgia Perimeter College, 2101 Womack Rd., Dunwoody GA 30338. (770)551-3019. Website: www.chattahoochee-review.org. Established 1980. **Editor-in-Chief:** Lawrence Hetrick. **Poetry Editor:** John Warwick.
Magazine Needs: *The Chattahoochee Review* is a quarterly of poetry, short fiction, essays, reviews, and interviews, published by Georgia Perimeter College. "We publish a number of Southern writers, but *Chattahoochee Review* is not by design a regional magazine. All themes, forms, and styles are considered as long as they impact the whole person: heart, mind, intuition, and imagination." Has published poetry by A.E. Stalling, Carolyne Wright, Coleman Barks, Ron Rash, and Fred Chappell. *Chattahoochee Review* is 140 pages, digest-sized, professionally printed on cream stock with reproductions of artwork, flat-spined, with one-color card cover. Recent issues feature a wide range of forms and styles augmenting prose selections. Press run is 1,250, of which 300 are complimentary copies sent to editors and "miscellaneous VIPs." Subscription: $16/year. Sample: $6.
How to Submit: Writers should send 1 copy of each poem and a cover letter with bio material. No simultaneous submissions. Time between acceptance and publication is up to 4 months. Publishes theme issues. Guidelines and a list of upcoming themes available for SASE. Queries will be answered in 1-2 weeks. Responds in 3 months. Pays $50/poem and 2 copies. Acquires first rights. Staff reviews books of poetry and short fiction in 1,500 words, single or multi-book format. Send materials for review consideration.

🌐 ⬜ ◎ CHERRYBITE PUBLICATIONS; REACH (Specialized: subscription), (formerly Helicon) Linden Cottage, 45 Burton Rd., Little Neston, Cheshire CH64 4AE England. E-mail: helicon @globalnet.co.uk. Website: www.cherrybite.co.uk. Established 1993. **Editor:** Shelagh Nugent.
Magazine Needs: *Reach* is a monthly publication which publishes poems of any style or length. Poets are strongly advised to study the magazine before submitting. Accepts poetry written by children. Has published poetry by Roger Harvey, Leigh Edwards, Tim Kik, Bery Elson, Rowena M. Love, Richard Bonfield, and Gloria Moreno-Cashillo. *Reach* is 52 pages, A5, saddle-stitched with card cover. Receives about 2,000 poems/year, accepts approximately 2%. Press run is 400. Single copy: $6 (cash); subscription: 31 IRCs; sample: $3 (cash). "Must buy at least one copy before submitting. The standard is high."
How to Submit: Submit only 2 poems at a time. All mss must be accompanied by a "submissions form" which can be found inside each current issue. Accepts previously published poems; no simultaneous submissions. No e-mail submissions; postal mail only. Cover letter required. Time between acceptance and publication is up to 6 months. Often comments on rejected poems. Guidelines and upcoming themes available on website, for SASE, and in publication. Responds in 2 weeks. Copyright remains with the author. Every month, readers vote to award £50.
Also Offers: Sponsors regular competitions and "several booklets of use to poets and writers." Publishes the *Competitions Bulletin*, a bimonthly magazine containing details of UK writing competitions. Send IRC for details.
Advice: "Never send submissions without studying a magazine first. Always send a cover letter."

⬜ CHILDREN, CHURCHES AND DADDIES; DOWN IN THE DIRT; SCARS PUBLICATIONS, 824 Brian Court, Gurnee IL 60031. E-mail: ccandd96@aol.com (*Children, Churches and Daddies*) and scarspub@aol.com (*Down in the Dirt*). Website: http://scars.tv. Established 1993. **Editor/Publisher:** Janet Kuypers. **Editor:** Alexandria Rand.
Magazine Needs: *Children, Churches and Daddies (the unreligious, non-family oriented literary magazine)* is published "on Soltices and Equinoxes and contains news, humor, poetry, prose, and essays. We specialize in electronic issues and collection books. We accept poetry of almost any genre, but we're not keen on rhyme for rhyme's sake, and we're not keen on religious poems (look at our current issue for a better idea of what we're like). We like gay/lesbian/bisexual, nature/rural/ecology, political, social issues, women/feminism. We do accept longer works, but within two pages for an individual poem is appreciated. We don't go for racist, sexist (therefore we're not into pornography

either), or homophobic stuff." Has published poetry by Rochelle Holt, Virginia Love Long, Pete McKinley, and Janine Canan. The print version of *Children, Churches and Daddies* is about 100 pages, magazine-sized, photocopied and saddle-stapled, cover, with art and ads. Receives hundreds of poems/year, accepts about 40%. Press run "depends." Sample: $5.50. Make checks payable to Janet Kuypers.

How to Submit: Prefers electronic submissions but accepts submissions by e-mail (either in text box or as attachment), on disk, or by postal mail. Submit via e-mail in body of message, explaining in preceding paragraph that it is a submission. Or mail floppy disk with ASCII text or Macintosh disk. Accepts previously published poems and simultaneous submissions. Seldom comments on rejected poems. Guidelines available for SASE, e-mail, or on website. Responds in 2 weeks.

Magazine Needs & How to Submit: *Down in the Dirt* appears "as often as work is submitted to us to guarantee a good-length issue." Does not want smut, rhyming poetry, or poetry already accepted for *Children, Churches and Daddies*. Has published work by I.B. Rad, Jennifer Rowan, Cheryl A. Townsend, Tom Racine, David-Matthew Barnes, and Michael Estabrook. *Down in the Dirt* is published electronically, either on the web or in e-book form (PDF files). Prefers e-mail submissions. Accepts disk submissions formatted for Macintosh. Guidelines and sample issues available on website, by e-mail, and for SASE. Accepts previously published material.

Also Offers: Scars Publications sometimes sponsors a book contest. Write or e-mail for information. "The website is a more comprehensive view of what *Children, Churches and Daddies* does. All the information is there." Also able to publish chapbooks. Write for more information.

★ ◎ CHILDREN'S BETTER HEALTH INSTITUTE; HUMPTY DUMPTY'S MAGAZINE; TURTLE MAGAZINE FOR PRESCHOOL KIDS; CHILDREN'S DIGEST; CHILDREN'S PLAYMATE; JACK AND JILL; CHILD LIFE (Specialized: children), 1100 Waterway Blvd., P.O. Box 567, Indianapolis IN 46206-0567. Website: www.cbhi.org/.

Magazine Needs: All magazines appear 8 times/year and include poetry with health-related themes. *Humpty Dumpty* is for ages 4-6; *Turtle* is for preschoolers, similar emphasis, uses many stories in rhyme—and action rhymes, etc.; *Children's Playmate* is for ages 6-8; *Jack and Jill* is for ages 7-10; *Child Life* is for ages 9-11; and *Children's Digest* is for ages 6-8. Sample: $1.75.

How to Submit: Guidelines available for SASE or on website. Responds in about 3 months. Pays $25 minimum. Acquires all rights. Staff reviews books of poetry. Send materials for review consideration.

Advice: "Writers who wish to appear in our publications should study current issues carefully. We receive too many poetry submissions that are about kids, not for kids. Or, the subject matter is one that adults think children would or should like. We'd like to see more humorous verse."

◢ CHIRON REVIEW; CHIRON BOOKS; KINDRED SPIRIT PRESS, 702 N. Prairie, St. John KS 67576-1516. (620)786-4955. E-mail: chironreview@hotmail.com. Website: www.geocities. com/SoHo/Nook/1748/. Established 1982 as *The Kindred Spirit*. **Editor:** Michael Hathaway.

Magazine Needs: *Chiron Review* is a quarterly tabloid using photographs of featured writers. No taboos. Accepts poetry written by children. Has published poetry by Vivian Shipley, Virginia Love Long, Patricia Cherin, Rene Banyan, francEye, and Frank Van Zant. Each issue "contains dozens of poems." Press run is about 1,000. Subscription: $14 US, $28 overseas. Sample: $5 US, $10 overseas or institutions.

How to Submit: Submit 3-6 poems at a time, "typed or printed legibly, not folded separately." No simultaneous submissions or previously published poems. No e-mail submissions; accepts postal mail only. Very seldom publishes theme issues. Guidelines and upcoming themes available for SASE or on website. Responds in 2 months. Pays 1 copy with a discount on additional copies. Acquires first-time rights. Reviews books of poetry in 500-700 words. Send materials for review consideration.

Book/Chapbook Needs & How to Submit: For book publication, query. Publishes 1-3 chapbooks/year, flat-spined, professionally printed, paying 25% of press run of 100-200 copies.

Also Offers: Personal Publishing Program is offered under the Kindred Spirit Press imprint. "Through special arrangements with a highly specialized printer, we can offer extremely short run publishing at unbelievably low prices." Information available for SASE.

$ ⬗ ◎ THE CHRISTIAN CENTURY (Specialized: Christian, social issues), Dept. PM, 104 S. Michigan Ave., Suite 700, Chicago IL 60603. (312)263-7510. Fax: (312)263-7540. Website: www.ChristianCentury.com. Established 1884. Named *The Christian Century* 1900, estab. again 1908, joined by *New Christian* 1970. **Poetry Editor:** Jill Peláez Baumgaertner.

Magazine Needs: This "ecumenical weekly" is a liberal, sophisticated journal of news, articles of opinion and reviews from a generally Christian point-of-view, using approximately 1 poem/issue, not necessarily on religious themes but in keeping with the literate tone of the magazine. Wants "poems that are not statements but experiences, that do not talk about the world, but show it. We want to publish poems that are grounded in images and that reveal an awareness of the sounds of language and the forms of poetry even when the poems are written in free verse." Does not want "pietistic or sentimental doggerel." Has published poetry by Jeanne Murray Walker, Ida Fasel, Kathleen Norris, Luci Shaw, J. Barrie Shepherd, and Wendell Berry. *Christian Century* is magazine-sized, printed on quality newsprint, using b&w art, cartoons and ads, about 30 pages, saddle-stapled. Sample: $3.

How to Submit: Submit poems of up to 20 lines, typed and double-spaced, 1 poem/page. Include your name, address and phone number on the first page of each poem. "Prefer shorter poems." No simultaneous submissions. Submissions without SASE or SAE and IRCs will not be returned. Pays usually $20/poem plus 1 copy and discount on additional copies. Acquires all rights. Inquire about reprint permission. Reviews books of poetry in 300-400 words, single format; 400-500 words, multi-book format.

CHRISTIAN GUIDE (Specialized: Christian), P.O. Box 14622, Knoxville TN 37914. E-mail: Godpoems@aol.com. Established 1989. **Poetry Editor:** Brian Long.

Magazine Needs: *The Christian Guide* is a regional, quarterly publication featuring articles, announcements, advertisements, photographs, and poetry. "We seek positive, accessible poetry that concerns itself with the interaction between God and the nature of (and surrounding) mankind in micro- or macrocosm. All poems themed to the gentler tenets of the devotion reciprocated between Heaven and Earth are welcomed, but only the most well-crafted will be accepted." Does not want forced, trite rhyme. Recently published poetry by Jill Alexander Essbaum, C.E. Chaffin, Teresa White, Dennis Greene, Christopher George, and Leo Yankevich. *The Christian Guide* has a varied number of pages, is magazine-sized with full-color cover with photographs and/or artwork, includes b&w and full-color ads. Publishes about 1-3 poems/issue. Press run is 25,000. Single copy or subscription: free for SASE.

How to Submit: Submit 1-5 poems at a time. Maximum length for poetry is 200 words. Accepts previously published poems and simultaneous submissions. Accepts e-mail submissions; no fax or disk submissions. Cover letter is required. "Include brief bio, list of publishing credits, and a SASE. For e-mail submissions, no attachments." Reads submissions year round. Submit seasonal poems 6 months in advance. Seldom comments on rejected poems. Occasionally publishes theme issues. List of upcoming themes available for SASE or by e-mail. Guidelines available for SASE or by e-mail. Responds in 3 months. Pays 2 contributor's copies. Acquires one-time rights.

Advice: "Subtlety. Subtlety. Subtlety. We are seeking poems that inspire awe, but do so by speaking to (and through) the reader with that 'small, still voice.' "

⬗ CHRISTIANITY AND LITERATURE, Dept. of English, University of Delaware, Newark DE 19716-2537. **Poetry Editor:** Prof. Jeanne Murray Walker.

Magazine Needs: *Christianity and Literature* is a quarterly scholarly journal publishing about 6-8 poems/issue. Press run is 1,350 for 1,125 subscribers of which 525 are libraries, 600 individuals. Single copy: $7; subscription: $25/1 year, $45/2 years. Make checks payable to CCL.

How to Submit: Submit 1-6 poems at a time. No previously published poems or simultaneous submissions. Accepts submissions by surface mail only. Cover letter is required. Submissions must be accompanied by SASE. Time between acceptance and publication is 3-4 months. "Poems are chosen by our poetry editor." Responds within 1 month. Pays 2 contributor's copies "and a dozen offprints to poets whose work we publish." Rights revert to poets upon written request. Reviews poetry collections in each issue (no chapbooks).

Advice: "We look for poems that are clear and surprising. They should have a compelling sense of voice, formal sophistication (though not necessarily rhyme and meter), and the ability to reveal the spiritual through concrete images. We cannot return submissions that are not accompanied by SASE."

$ ◐ ◎ CHRYSALIS READER (Specialized: spirituality, themes), Rt. 1 Box 4510, Dillwyn VA 23936-9609. Fax: (434)983-1074. E-mail: chrysalis@hovac.com. Established 1985. **Poetry Editor:** Robert F. Lawson. **Editor:** Carol S. Lawson.

Magazine Needs: *Chrysalis Reader* is published by the Swedenborg Foundation as a "contribution to the search for spiritual wisdom." Appearing annually in September, it is a "book series that challenges inquiring minds using literate and scholarly fiction, essays, and poetry. Nothing overly religious or sophomoric. Poetry that surprises, that pushes the language, gets our attention." Has published work by Robert Bly, Linda Pastan, Wesley McNair, Julia Randall, William Kloefkorn, and Virgil Suárez. *Chrysalis Reader* is 208 pages, 7×10, professionally printed on archival paper and perfect-bound with coated coverstock, illustrations, and photos. Receives about 1,000 submissions/year, accepts about 12 poems. Press run is 3,500. Sample: $10.

How to Submit: Submit no more than 5 poems at one time with SASE. No previously published poems; accepts simultaneous submissions "if notified immediately when work is accepted elsewhere." Reads submissions year-round. Time between acceptance and publication is typically 18 months. Upcoming themes include "Passages," "Letting Go," and "Relationships." Guidelines and upcoming themes also available for SASE. Responds in 3 months. Always sends prepublication galleys. Pays $25 and 3 copies. Acquires first-time rights. "We expect to be credited for reprints after permission is given."

Advice: "When time permits, editorial suggestions are offered in the spirit of all good literature. Purchase a back issue or request your favorite bookstore to order a reading copy so that you can better gauge what to submit."

$ ◐ CIMARRON REVIEW, 205 Morrill Hall, Oklahoma State University, Stillwater OK 74078-0135. E-mail: cimarronreview@yahoo.com. Website: http://cimarronreview.okstate.edu. Established 1967. Editor: E.P. Walkiewicz. **Poetry Editors:** Lisa Lewis, Ai.

Magazine Needs: *Cimarron* is a quarterly literary journal. "We take pride in our eclecticism. We like evocative poetry (lyric or narrative) controlled by a strong voice. No sing-song verse. No quaint prairie verse. No restrictions as to subject matter. We look for poems whose surfaces and structures risk uncertainty and which display energy, texture, intelligence, and intense investment." Among poets they have published are James Harms, Gerry LaFemina, Phillip Dacey, Holly Prado, Nin Andrews, and Kim Addonizio. *Cimarron Review*, 100-150 pages, digest-sized, perfect-bound, boasts a handsome design, including a color cover and attractive printing. Poems lean toward free verse, lyric, and narrative, although all forms and styles seem welcome. There are 15-25 pages of poetry in each issue. Circulation is 600 of which a third are libraries. Single copy: $7; subscription: $24/year ($28 Canada), $65/3 years ($72 Canada).

How to Submit: Submit 3-5 poems, name and address on each, typed single- or double-spaced. No simultaneous submissions. Accepts submissions by postal mail only. No response without SASE. Guidelines available on website. Responds in up to 6 months. Pays 2 copies and a subscription. Acquires first North American serial rights only. Reviews books of poetry in 500-900 words, single book format, occasionally multi-book. All reviews are assigned.

✦ ◉ CITY LIGHTS BOOKS, 261 Columbus Ave., San Francisco CA 94133. (415)362-8193. Fax: (415)362-4921. E-mail: staff@citylights.com. Website: www.citylights.com. Established 1953.

Book/Chapbook Needs & How to Submit: City Lights Books is the legendary paperback house that achieved prominence with the publication of Allen Ginsberg's *Howl* and other poetry of the "Beat" school. Publishes "poetry, fiction, philosophy, political and social history." Does not accept unsolicited mss. No inquiries or submissions by e-mail. "Before sending a book proposal, we urge you to look at our catalog to familiarize yourself with our publication. If you feel certain that your work is appropriate to our list, then please send a query letter that includes your résumé (with a list of previous publications and a sample of no more than 10 pages." Include SASE for response. Responds in 3 months. Guidelines available on website.

✦ ◐ ◎ THE CLAREMONT REVIEW (Specialized: teens/young adults), 4980 Wesley Rd., Victoria BC V8Y 1Y9 Canada. (250)658-5221. Fax: (250)658-5387. Website: www.theClaremontReview.com. Established 1991. **Contact:** Susan Field.

Magazine Needs: *The Claremont Review* is a biannual review which publishes poetry and fiction written by those ages 13 to 19. Each fall issue also includes an interview with a prominent Canadian writer. Wants "vital, modern poetry with a strong voice and living language. We prefer works that reveal something of the human condition. No clichéd language nor copies of 18th and 19th century work." Has published poetry by Jen Wright, Erin Egan, and Max Rosenblum. *The Claremont Review* is 110 pages, digest-sized, professionally printed and perfect-bound with an attractive color cover. Receives 600-800 poems/year, accepts about 120. Press run is 700 for 200 subscribers of which 50 are libraries, 250 shelf sales. Subscription: $15/year, $25/2 years. Sample: $8.

How to Submit: Submit poems typed one to a page with author's name at the top of each. Accepts simultaneous submissions; no previously published poems. Cover letter with brief bio required. Reads submissions September through June only. Always comments on rejected poems. Guidelines available for SASE (or SAE and IRC), on website, and in publication. Publishes theme issues; upcoming themes available on website and in publication. Responds in up to 6 weeks (excluding July and August). Pays 1 copy and funds when grants allow it. Acquires first North American serial rights.

Advice: "We strongly urge potential contributors to read back issues of *The Claremont Review*. That is the best way for you to learn what we are looking for."

CLARK STREET REVIEW (Specialized: form/style, narrative and prose poetry), P.O. Box 1377, Berthoud CO 80513. E-mail: clarkreview@earthlink.net. Established 1998. **Editor:** Ray Foreman.

Magazine Needs: Appearing 8 times/year, *Clark Street Review* publishes narrative poetry and short shorts—"to give writers and poets cause to keep writing by publishing their best work." Wants "narrative poetry under 100 lines that reach readers who are mostly published poets and writers. Subjects are open. No obscure and formalist work." Has published poetry by Steven Levi, Errol Miller, Ray Dickson, Michael Ketchek, and Al De Genova. *Clark Street Review* is 20 pages, digest-sized, photocopied, and saddle-stapled with paper cover. Receives about 500 poems/year, accepts about 10%. Press run is 200 for 90 subscribers. Subscription: $10 for 10 issues postpaid. Single copy: $2. Make checks payable to R. Foreman.

How to Submit: Submit 1-10 poems at a time. Line length for poetry is 30 minimum, 100 maximum. Accepts previously published poems and simultaneous submissions. "Disposable sharp copies. Maximum width—65 characters. SASE or e-mail address for reply. No cover letter." Time between acceptance and publication is 3 months. "Editor reads everything with a critical eye of 30 years of experience in writing and publishing small press work." Often comments on rejected poems. Publishes theme issues occasionally. Guidelines available for SASE and by e-mail. "If one writes narrative poetry, they don't need guidelines. They feel it." Responds in 3 weeks. Acquires one-time rights.

Advice: "*Clark Street Review* is geared to the more experienced poet and writer. There are tips throughout each issue writers appreciate. As always, the work we print speaks for the writer and the magazine. We encourage communication between our poets by listing their e-mail address. Publishing excellence and giving writers a cause to write is our only aim."

CLAY PALM REVIEW: ART AND LITERARY MAGAZINE, 8 Huntington St., Suite 307, Shelton CT 06484-5228. E-mail: claypalm@cs.com. Website: www.claypalmreview.com. Established 1999 (premier issue, spring/summer 2000). **Founder/Editor:** Lisa Cisero.

• **Clay Palm Review will be on hiatus until late 2004 and will not be accepting submissions.**

Magazine Needs: Has published poetry by Naomi Shihab Nye, Marge Piercy, Duane Locke, Virgil Suarez, and John Smelcer. *Clay Palm Review* is about 120 pages, "a bit larger than digest-sized," offset-printed and perfect-bound with glossy cover, includes colored artwork, b&w photography, short fiction, essays, interviews, collage, sculpture, and ads. Samples available for the discounted price of $7.95 (includes s&h). Both full issues, when purchased together, cost $14.95.

$ CLEANING BUSINESS MAGAZINE; CLEANING CONSULTANT SERVICES, INC. (Specialized: cleaning, self-employment), P.O. Box 1273, Seattle WA 98111. (206)622-4241. Fax: (206)622-6876. E-mail: wgriffin@cleaningconsultant.com. Website: www.cleaningconsultants.com. Established 1976. **Poetry Editor:** William R. Griffin.

Magazine Needs: *Cleaning Business Magazine* is "a monthly magazine for cleaning and maintenance professionals" and uses some poetry relating to their interests. "To be considered for publication in *Cleaning Business*, submit poetry that relates to our specific audience—cleaning and self-employment." Has published poetry by Don Wilson, Phoebe Bosche, Trudie Mercer, and Joe Keppler. *Cleaning Business Magazine* is 100 pages, magazine-sized, offset litho printed, using ads, art, and graphics. Receives about 50 poems/year, accepts about 10. Press run is 5,000 for 3,000 subscribers of which 100 are libraries, 500 shelf sales. Single copy: $5; subscription: $20. Sample: $3.

How to Submit: Accepts simultaneous submissions; no previously published poems. Accepts submissions by e-mail (attachment or in text box), by fax, or by regular mail. Guidelines available for SASE, by fax, and by e-mail. Pays $5-10 plus 1 copy.

Advice: "Poets identify a specific market and work to build a readership that can be tapped again and again over a period of years with new books. Also write to a specific audience that has a mutual interest. We buy poetry about cleaning, but seldom receive anything our subscribers would want to read."

CLÓ IAR-CHONNACHTA (Specialized: bilingual/foreign language, Irish), Indreabhán, Co. Galway, Ireland. Phone: +353-91-593307. Fax: +353-91-593362. E-mail: cic@iol.ie. Website: www.cic.ie. Established 1985. **Contact:** Róisin Ní Mhianáin, editor.

Book/Chapbook Needs: Publishes books of Irish language and bilingual poetry. Has published collections of poetry by Cathal Ó Searcaigh, Nuala Ní Dhomhnaill, Gabriel Rosenstock, Michael Davitt, Liam Ó Muirthile, Gearóid Mac Lochlainn, and Celia de Fréine.

How to Submit: Query by postal mail with 20 sample poems and a cover letter with brief bio and publication credits. Mss are read by an editorial panel. No payment information provided.

$ CLOUD RIDGE PRESS, 815 13th St., Boulder CO 80302. Established 1985. **Editor:** Elaine Kohler.

Book/Chapbook Needs: Cloud Ridge Press is a "literary small press for unique works in poetry and prose." Publishes letterpress and offset books in both paperback and hardcover editions. In poetry, publishes "strong images of the numinous qualities in authentic experience grounded in a landscape and its people." The first book, published in 1985, was *Ondina: A Narrative Poem* by John Roberts. The book is digest-sized, handsomely printed on buff stock, cloth bound in black with silver decoration and spine lettering, 131 pages 800 copies were bound in Curtis Flannel and 200 copies bound in cloth over boards, numbered, and signed by the poet and artist. This letterpress edition, priced at $18/cloth and $12/paper, is not available in bookstores but only by mail from the press. The trade edition was photo-offset from the original, in both cloth and paper bindings, and is sold in bookstores. The press plans to publish 1-2 books/year.

How to Submit: Since the press is not accepting unsolicited mss, writers should query first. Queries will be answered in 2 weeks and mss reported on in 1 month. Simultaneous submissions are acceptable. Royalties are 10% plus a negotiable number of author's copies. A brochure is free on request; send #10 SASE.

$ CLUBHOUSE JR. (Specialized: children, Christian), 8605 Explorer Dr., Colorado Springs CO 80920. Fax: (719)531-3499. Website: www.clubhousemagazine.org/club_jr/. Established 1988. **Associate Editor:** Suzanne Hadley. **Editor:** Annette Bourland.

• *Clubhouse Jr.* won the Evangelical Press Association Award for Youth Publication.

Magazine Needs: *Clubhouse Jr.* is a monthly magazine published by Focus on the Family for 4-8 year olds. Wants short poems—less than 100 words. "Poetry should have a strong message that supports traditional values. No cute, but pointless work." *Clubhouse Jr.* is 16-20 pages, magazine-sized, web-printed on glossy paper and saddle-stapled with 4-color paper cover, includes 4-color art. The magazine has 96,000 subscribers. Single copy: $1.50; subscription: $15/year. Sample: $1.25 with 8×10 SASE. Make checks payable to Focus on the Family.

How to Submit: Submit up to 5 poems at a time. Accepts simultaneous submissions; no previously published poems. Cover letter preferred. No submissions by fax of e-mail. Time between acceptance and publication is in up to 1 year. Seldom comments on rejected poems. Occasionally publishes theme issues. Guidelines available for SASE. Responds in up to 2 months. Pays $50-100. Acquires first rights.

◪ **COAL CITY REVIEW**, English Dept., University of Kansas, Lawrence KS 66045. E-mail: briandal@ukans.edu. Established 1989. **Editor:** Brian Daldorph.

Magazine Needs: Published in the fall, *Coal City Review* is an annual publication of poetry, short stories, reviews, and interviews—"the best material I can find." As for poetry, the editor quotes Pound: " 'Make it new.' " Does not want to see "experimental poetry, doggerel, five-finger exercises, or beginner's verse." Has published poetry by Michael Gregg Michaud, Phil Miller, Walt McDonald, Thomas Zri Wilson, VirgilSuarez, and Denise Low. *Coal City Review* is 100 pages, digest-sized, professionally printed on recycled paper and perfect-bound with light, colored card cover. Accepts about 5% of the material received. Press run is 200 for 50 subscribers of which 5 are libraries. Subscription: $10. Sample: $6.

How to Submit: Submit 6 poems at a time with name and address on each page. Accepts previously published poems occasionally; prefers not to receive simultaneous submissions. No submissions by e-mail. "Please do not send list of prior publications." Seldom comments on rejected poems. Guidelines available for SASE. Responds in up to 3 months. Pays 1 copy. Reviews books of poetry in 300-1,000 words, mostly single format. Send materials for review consideration.

Book/Chapbook Needs & How to Submit: *Coal City Review* also publishes occasional chapbooks and books as issues of the magazine but does not accept unsolicited chapbook submissions. Their most recent book is *Under the Fool Moon* by Gary Lechliter.

Advice: "Care more (much more) about writing than publication. If you're good enough, you'll publish."

$ ◪ **C/OASIS**. Fax: (603)971-5013. E-mail: poetmuse@swbell.net. Website: www.sunoasis.com/oasis.html. Established 1996. Editor: David Eide. **Contact:** Vicki Goldsberry Colker.

Magazine Needs: *C/Oasis* is a monthly online journal containing poems, stories, personal essays, articles for writers, and commentary. "The purpose is two-fold. Number one is to publish excellent writing and number two is to explore the web for all the best writing and literary venues. Not only does *C/Oasis* publish original material but it investigates the web each month to deliver the very best material it can find." Wants "poetry that has an active consciousness and has artistic intention. Open on form, length, subject matter, style, purpose, etc. It must deliver the active consciousness and artistic intention. No sing song stuff, fluff stuff, those who write poems without real artistic intent because they haven't given the idea a thought." Has published poetry by Richard Fein, Anne Babson, John Sweet, Rebecca Lu Kiernan, and Jeffrey Alfier. "I'm trying to find the right style for the Web. I was inspired by the literary magazine phenomena but find the Web to be a new medium. One that is terrific for poetry." Receives "hundreds" of poems/year, accepts about 5%.

How to Submit: Submit 5 poems at a time. Accepts previously published poems; no simultaneous submissions. Accepts fax and e-mail submissions; "try to include submission in ASCII plain-text in body of e-mail message." Time between acceptance and publication is about 1 week. "We usually get word back to writers within 3 months. Poems that the editors like are looked at and reviewed very carefully before being accepted or rejected." Rarely comments on poems. Guidelines available for e-mail or website. Responds in 1 month. Pays $10/poem. Acquires first, first North American serial, one time, and reprint rights.

Advice: "Seek to improve the writing; take poetry seriously, treat it as an art and it will treat you well."

◪ ◎ **COCHRAN'S CORNER (Specialized: subscribers)**, 1003 Tyler Court, Waldorf MD 20602-2964. E-mail: adacochran@hotmail.com. Established 1985. **Editor:** John Treasure.

Magazine Needs: *Cochran's Corner* is a "family type" quarterly open to beginners, preferring poems of 20 lines or less. Must be a subscriber to submit. "Any subject or style (except porn)." Accepts poetry written by children. Has published poetry by Jean B. York, Brian Duthins, C.J. Villiano, and Annette Shaw. *Cochran's Corner* is 58 pages, desktop-published, saddle-stapled, with matte

---

THE OPENNESS TO SUBMISSIONS INDEX in the back of this book lists markets according to the level of writing they prefer to see.

card cover. Press run is 500. Subscription: $20. Sample: $5 plus SASE.

How to Submit: Submit 5 poems at a time. Accepts simultaneous submissions and previously published poems. Guidelines available for SASE. Responds in 3 months. Pays 2 copies. Acquires first or one-time rights. Reviews books of poetry. Send materials for review consideration.

Also Offers: Sponsors contests in March and July; $5 entry fee for unlimited poems "if sent in the same envelope. We provide criticism if requested at the rate of $1 per page."

Advice: "Write from the heart, but don't forget your readers. You must work to find the exact words that mirror your feelings, so the reader can share your feelings."

★ ◖ THE COE REVIEW, Coe College, 1220 First Ave. NE, Cedar Rapids IA 52402. (319)399-8539. E-mail: CoeReview@coe.edu. Website: http://japox.coe.edu/coereview/default.htm. Established 1972. **Contact:** Charles Aukema.

Magazine Needs: Published annually in April, *Coe Review* is "a diverse magazine, valuing innovation, experimentation, and originality, preferring well-developed and tasteful content, but eclectic in selection." Has published poetry by James Galvin, Marge Piercy, Sara Lindsay, Douglas Powell, David Ray, and Christine Zawadiwsky. *The Coe Review* is 100-150 pages, flat-spined, digest-sized with matte card cover. "Each issue includes 4-8 reproductions of works of art, usually photographs, lithography, and etched prints." Circulation is about 500. Sample: $5.

How to Submit: Submit 3-5 poems at a time. No simultaneous submissions. Include "brief cover letter with biographical information and SASE. We only accept submissions from August 31 through March 15 due to the academic year." Guidelines available for SASE and on website. Pays 2 copies.

◖ COFFEE HOUSE PRESS, 27 N. Fourth St., Suite 400, Minneapolis MN 55401. (612)338-0125. Established 1984. **Senior Editor:** Christopher Fischbach.

- Coffee House Press books have won numerous honors and awards. As an example, *The Book of Medicines* by Linda Hogan won the Colorado Book Award for Poetry and the Lannan Foundation Literary Fellowship.

Book Needs: Publishes 12 books/year, 4-5 of which are poetry. Wants poetry that is "challenging and lively; influenced by the Beats, the NY School, LANGUAGE and post-LANGUAGE, or Black Mountain." Has published poetry collections by Victor Hernandez Cruz, Anne Waldman, Eleni Sikelianos, and Paul Metcalf.

How to Submit: Submit 8-12 poems at a time. Accepts previously published poems. Cover letter and vita required. "Please include a SASE for our reply and/or the return of your ms." Seldom comments on rejected poems. Responds to queries in 1 month; to mss in up to 8 months. Always sends prepublication galleys. Send SASE for catalog. Absolutely no phone, fax, or e-mail queries.

★ ◖ COLD MOUNTAIN REVIEW, English Dept., Appalachian State University, Boone NC 28608. (828)262-3098. Fax: (828)262-2133. E-mail: coldmountain@appstate.edu. Website: www.coldmountain.appstate.edu.

Magazine Needs: *Cold Moutain Review* is published twice/year by the English Department at Appalachian State University and features poetry, interviews with poets, book reviews, b&w line drawings and photographs. "We're open to diverse perspectives and styles." Has published poetry by Sarah Kennedy, Robert Morgan, Susan Ludvigson, Aleida Rodríguez, R.T. Smith, and Virgil Suarez. *Cold Mountain Review* is about 72 pages, digest-sized, neatly printed with 1 poem/page (or 2-page spread), perfect-bound, with light card stock cover. Publishes about 10% of the submissions received. For sample, send SASE or make donation to ASU Cold Mountain Review.

How to Submit: Accepts submissions by postal mail only. No simultaneous or previously published submissions. "Please include short biographical sketch, with name, address and phone/e-mail on each poem." Reads submissions year-round, though response is slower in summer. Reporting time is generally 3 months. Send SASE for guidelines. Pays 2 copies.

$ ◖ COLORADO REVIEW; COLORADO PRIZE FOR POETRY, Dept. of English, Colorado State University, Ft. Collins CO 80523. (970)491-5449. E-mail: creview@colostate.edu. Website: www.coloradoreview.com. Established 1955 as *Colorado State Review*, resurrected 1967 under "New Series" rubric, renamed *Colorado Review* 1985. **Editor:** David Milofsky. **Poetry Editors:** Jorie Graham and Donald Revell.

● Poetry published in *Colorado Review* has been frequently included in volumes of *The Best American Poetry.*

Magazine Needs: *Colorado Review* is a journal of contemporary literature that appears 3 times/ year combining short fiction, poetry, and personal essays. Has published poetry by Robert Creeley, Rebecca Wolff, Robert Haas, Maxine Chernoff, and Fanny Howe. *Colorado Review* is about 224 pages, digest-sized, professionally printed and notch-bound with glossy card cover. Press run is 1,500 for 1,000 subscribers of which 100 are libraries. Receives about 10,000 submissions/year, accepts about 2%. Subscription: $24/year. Sample: $10.

How to Submit: Submit about 5 poems at a time. No previously published poems or simultaneous submissions. No e-mail submissions. Submissions must include SASE for response. Reads submissions September 1 through May 1 only. Responds in 2 months. Pays $5/printed page for poetry. Acquires first North American serial rights. Reviews books of poetry and fiction, both single and multi-book format. Send materials for review consideration.

Also Offers: Also sponsors the annual Colorado Prize for Poetry, established in 1995, offering an honorarium of $1,500. Book as a whole must be unpublished though individual poems may have been published elsewhere. Submit a book-length ms on any subject in any form. Guidelines available for SASE. Entry fee: $25. Deadline: January 13. Most recent award winner was Robyn Ewing (2002). Judge was Fanny Howe. Winner announced in May.

★ ◯ COLUMBIA: A JOURNAL OF LITERATURE AND ART, 415 Dodge Hall, Columbia University, New York NY 10027. (212)864-4216. Fax: (212)854-7704. E-mail: columbiajournal@col umbia.edu. Website: www.columbia.edu/~tnf12. Established 1977. **Editor:** Tiffany Fung. **Poetry Editors:** Anna Ross and Ericka Pazcoguin.

Magazine Needs: *Columbia* appears semiannually and "will consider any poem that is eclectic and spans from traditional to experimental genre." Has published poetry by Jane Hirschfield, Christina Pugh, Richard Howard, Eamon Grennan, Mary Jo Salter, Matthew Rohrer, and Mark Doty. *Columbia* is 180 pages, digest-sized, offset printed with notch binding, glossy cover, includes art and ads. Receives about 2,000 poems/year, accepts approximately 2%. Press run is 2,000 for 50 subscribers of which 30 are libraries. Subscription: $15/year, $25/2 years. Sample: $8; back issue: $10. Make checks payable to *Columbia Journal.*

How to Submit: Submit up to 4 poems at a time. Accepts simultaneous submissions, when noted; no previously published poems. Cover letter preferred. Reads submissions September 1 through February 1 only. Poems are circulated to an editorial board. Seldom comments on rejected poems. "Solicits theme section for each issue." Upcoming themes available on website. Recent themes include Film and Writing; Reinventing Fairy Tales, Myth and Legends; and Beyond Sportswriting: Spectatorship, Exhaustion, Competition. Guidelines available for SASE, by fax, by e-mail, and on website. Responds in 6 months. Pays 2 copies. Acquires first North American serial rights.

Also Offers: Sponsors annual contest with an award of $250. Open to submissions January 1 though April 15. Entry fee: $12. Submit no more than 5 poems/entry. All entrants receive a copy of the issue publishing the winners.

◖ COMFUSION REVIEW, 304 S. Third St., San Jose CA 95112. Website: www.comfusionrevie w.com.

● **At press time we learned *Comfusion Review* is suspending publication.**

Magazine Needs: *Comfusion* appears quarterly; www.comfusion.ws reflects print publication. "Our purpose is to showcase new and established talent skillfully manifested within the medium of poetry. We want well-crafted material that is original and edgy. We encourage innovative formal and free verse poetry." Also accepts essays, fiction, and photography. "We do not want to see sappy-sentimental love or devotional poetry. And please, absolutely no inspirational." Recently published poetry by Jeffrey McDaniel, Samuel Maio, Genny Lim, David Holler, Ginger Pielage, and Marc David Pinate. *Comfusion* is 60-80 pages, magazine-sized, saddle-stapled, glossy cover, with art/graphics and ads. "Many poems that go unprinted in our yearly publication are featured on our website." Receives about 120 poems/year, accepts about 10%. Publishes 5-10 poems/issue. Press run is 5,000 for 500 subscribers; 4,500 distributed free to independent book stores and cafes. Single copy: $3.95; subscription: $15. Sample bundle: $5. Make checks payable to Lotus Foundation.

How to Submit: No longer accepting unsolicited submissions. "We do, however, continue to solicit and publish poetry." Time between acceptance and publication is up to 1 year. Poems are circulated to an editorial board. Responds in up to 5 months. Pays 2 contributor's copies. Acquires one-time rights.

Advice: "Poets should take into account a broad spectrum of poetic tradition as refracted through the spectrum of their own personal irreverance and respect. Please don't insult your collective readers' intelligence by attempting to speak in the voice of the 'common man.' But feel free to make sure we know what you're talking about."

$⊘ COMMON GROUND REVIEW; COMMON GROUND POETRY CONTEST, 43 Witch Path #3, West Springfield MA 01089. Website: http://members.cox.net/cgreview/. Established 1999. **Editor:** Larry O'Brien.

Magazine Needs: *Common Ground Review* appears biannually publishing poetry and original artwork. Wants poetry with strong imagery; well-written free or traditional forms. No greeting card verse, overly sentimental, or political poetry. Recently published poetry by James Doyle, Martin Galvin, Lyn Lifshin, Virgil Suarez, and Rennie McQuilken. *Common Ground Review* is 40-58 pages, digest-sized, high quality photocopied, saddle-stapled, original artwork/card cover, with 4-6 pages original artwork. Receives about 1,000 poems/year, accepts less than 10%. Publishes about 35 poems/issue. Press run is 125-150. Single copy: $6.30. Sample: $6.30. Make checks payable to *Common Ground Review.*

How to Submit: Submit 1-5 poems at a time. Line length for poetry is 40 maximum. No previously published poems or simultaneous submissions. No submissions by fax, e-mail, or on disk. Cover letter is required. "Poems single-spaced, include name, address, phone, e-mail address, brief biography, SASE (submissions without SASE will be discarded)." Reads submissions all year. Submit seasonal poems 6 months in advance. Time between acceptance and publication is 4-6 months. Poems are circulated to an editorial board. "Editor reads and culls submissions. Final decisions made by editorial board." Seldom comments on rejected poems. Guidelines available in magazine, for SASE, by e-mail, or on website. Responds in 2 months. Pays 1 contributor's copy. Acquires one-time rights.

Also Offers: Annual contest. Awards 1st Prize: $100, 2nd Prize: $50, and 3rd Prize: $25. **Entry fee:** $10 for 1-3 unpublished poems. **Deadline:** February 28.

Advice: "Read journal before submitting. Beginning poets need to read what's out there, get into workshops, and work on revising. Attend writers' conferences. Listen and learn."

◎ COMMON THREADS; OHIO HIGH SCHOOL POETRY CONTESTS; OHIO POETRY ASSOCIATION (Specialized: membership, students), 3520 State Route 56, Mechanicsburg OH 43044. (937)834-2666. Website: www.crosswinds.net/~opa. Established 1928. **Editor:** Amy Jo Zook. Ohio Poetry Association (Michael Lepp, treasurer, 1798 Sawgrass Dr., Reynoldsburg OH 43068), is a state poetry society open to members from outside the state, an affiliate of the National Federation of State Poetry Societies.

Magazine Needs: *Common Threads* is the Ohio Poetry Association's biannual poetry magazine, appearing in April and October. Only members of OPA may submit poems. Does not want to see poetry which is highly sentimental, overly morbid, religiously coercive, or pornograpic—and nothing over 40 lines. "We use beginners' poetry, but would like it to be good, tight, revised. In short, not first drafts. Too much is sentimental or prosy when it could be passionate or lyric. We'd like poems to make us think as well as feel something." Accepts poetry written by children "if members or high school contest winners." Has published poetry by David Shevin, Cathryn Essinger, Timothy Russell, Yvonne Hardenbrook, Henry B. Stobbs, and Dalene Stull. *Common Threads* is 52 pages, digest-sized, computer-typeset, with matte card cover. "Ours is a forum for our members, and we do use reprints, so new members can get a look at what is going well in more general magazines." Annual dues including 2 issues *Common Threads*: $15. Senior (over 65): $12. Single copies: $2.

How to Submit: Accepts previously published poems, if "author is upfront about them. All rights revert to poet after publication." Accepts submissions by regular mail only. Frequently publishes seasonal poems. Guidelines available on website.

Also Offers: Ohio Poetry Association sponsors an annual contest for unpublished poems written by high school students in Ohio with categories of traditional, modern, and several other categories.

March deadline, with 3 money awards in each category. For contest information write Ohio Poetry Association, % Elouise Postle, 4761 Willow Lane, Lebanon OH 45036. "We publish student winners in a book of winning poems before reprinting their work in *Common Threads*. Also, we have a quarterly contest open to all poets, entry fee, two money awards and publication. Write to Janeen Lepp, 1798 Sawgrass Dr., Reynoldsburg OH 43068 (#10 SASE) or e-mail janeenlepp@juno.com for dates and themes." (Also see separate listing for Ohio Poetry Association in the Organizations section.)

★ $ ✉ ◎ COMMONWEAL (Specialized: religious, Catholic), 475 Riverside Dr., New York NY 10115. Fax: (212)662-4183. Website: www.commonwealmagazine.org. **Poetry Editor:** Rosemary Deen.
Magazine Needs: *Commonweal* appears every 2 weeks, circulation 20,000, is a general-interest magazine for college-educated readers by Catholics. Prefers serious, witty, well-written poems of up to 75 lines. Does not publish inspirational poems. Subscription: $44. Sample: $3.
How to Submit: Considers simultaneous submissions. Does not accept fax or e-mail submissions. Reads submissions September 1 through June 30 only. Pays 50¢ a line plus 2 copies. Acquires all rights. Returns rights when requested by the author. Reviews books of poetry in 750-1,000 words, single or multi-book format.

◐ ◎ A COMPANION IN ZEOR (Specialized: science fiction/fantasy), 1622 Swallow Crest Dr., Apt. B., Edgewood MD 21040-1751. Fax: (410)676-0164. E-mail: karen@simegen.com or cz@simegen.com. Website: www.simegen.com/sgfandom/rimonslibrary/cz/. Established 1978. **Editor:** Karen MacLeod.
Magazine Needs: *A Companion in Zeor* is a science fiction/fantasy fanzine appearing irregularly on the Internet. "Material used is now limited to creations based solely on works (universes) of Jacqueline Lichtenberg and Jean Lorrah. No other submission types considered. Prefer nothing obscene. Homosexuality not acceptable unless very relevant to the piece. Prefer a 'clean' publication image." Accepts poetry written by young writers over 13; "Copyright release form (on the web) available for *all* submissions."
How to Submit: Accepts submissions on disk, by fax, by e-mail (in text box), or by regular mail. Cover letter preferred with submissions; note whether to return or dispose of rejected mss. Guidelines available for SASE, by fax, by e-mail, and on website. Sometimes sends prepublication galleys. Acquires first rights. "Always willing to work with authors or poets to help in improving their work." Reviews books of poetry. Poets may send material for review consideration.

◢ THE COMSTOCK REVIEW; COMSTOCK WRITERS' GROUP INC.; MURIEL CRAFT BAILEY MEMORIAL PRIZE; JESSE BRYCE NILES MEMORIAL CHAPBOOK AWARD, 4956 St. John Dr., Syracuse NY 13215. (315)488-8077. E-mail: poetry@comstockreview.org. Website: www.comstockreview.org. Established 1987 as *Poetpourri*, published by the Comstock Writers' Group, Inc. **Contact:** Peggy Sperber Flanders, managing editor.
Magazine Needs: *The Comstock Review* appears biannually; Volume I in summer, Volume II in winter. Uses "well-written free and traditional verse. Metaphor and fresh, vivid imagery encouraged. Poems over 40 lines discouraged. No obscene, obscure, patently religious, or greeting card verse. Few Haiku." Has published poetry by E.G. Burrows, Barbara Crooker, William Greenway, Virgil Suarez, Susan Terris, Sue Ellen Thompson, and Ryan G. Van Cleave. *The Comstock Review* is about 100 pages, digest-sized, professionally printed, perfect-bound. Press run is 600. Subscription: $16/year; $28/2 years; $9/issue. Samples through year 2001: $6.
How to Submit: Submit 3-6 poems at a time; name, e-mail/phone, and address on each page; unpublished poems only. No e-mail submissions. "We prefer no simultaneous submissions." Cover letter with short bio preferred. Poems are read January 1 through March 15 only; acceptances mailed out mid-April. "Rejections may receive editorial commentary and may take slightly longer." Guidelines available for SASE, on website, and in publication. Pays 1 copy. Acquires first North American serial rights.
Also Offers: Offers the Muriel Craft Bailey Memorial Prize yearly with $1,000 1st Prize, $250 2nd Prize, $100 3rd Prize, honorable mentions, publication of all finalists. Entry fee: $3/poem. 40-line limit. No simultaneous submissions or previously published material (includes both print and elec-

tronic publications). Annual deadline: postmark by July 1. May offer discounted awards edition to entrants. Before submitting, send SASE or check website for current rules. Judge for 2003: David St. John; judge for 2002: Kelly Cherry. Also offers the Jesse Bryce Niles Memorial Chapbook Award of $1,000 plus publication and 50 copies. Each entrant receives a copy of the winning chapbook. Submissions read September 1 through 30. Complete rules, entry fee amount, and length requirements available on website.

CONCHO RIVER REVIEW; FORT CONCHO MUSEUM PRESS, P.O. Box 10894, Angelo State University, San Angelo TX 76909. (915)942-2273. Fax: (915)942-2155. E-mail: bradleyjw @hal.lamar.edu. Website: www.angelo.edu. Established 1984. **Editor:** James A. Moore. **Poetry Editor:** Jerry Bradley.

Magazine Needs: *Concho River Review* is a literary journal published twice/year. "Prefer shorter poems, few long poems accepted; particularly looking for poems with distinctive imagery and imaginative forms and rhythms. The first test of a poem will be its imagery." Short reviews of new volumes of poetry are also published. Has published poetry by Walt McDonald, Robert Cooperman, Mary Winters, William Wenthe, and William Jolliff. *Concho River Review* is 120-138 pages, digest-sized, professionally printed and flat-spined, with matte card cover. Accepts 35-40 of 600-800 poems received/year. Press run is 300 for about 200 subscribers of which 10 are libraries. Subscription: $14. Sample: $5.

How to Submit: "Please submit 3-5 poems at a time. Use regular legal-sized envelopes—no big brown envelopes; no replies without SASE. Type must be letter-perfect, sharp enough to be computer scanned." Accepts submissions by e-mail (attachment). Responds in 2 months. Pays 1 copy. Acquires first rights.

Advice: "We're always looking for good, strong work—from both well-known poets and those who have never been published before."

CONCRETE WOLF, P. O. Box 10250, Bedford NH 03110-0250. E-mail: editors@concretewol f.com. Website: www.concretewolf.com. Established 2001. **Editors:** Brent Allard and Lana Ayers. Member: CLMP.

Magazine Needs: *Concrete Wolf* appears quarterly. "We like to see fresh perspectives on common human experiences, with careful attention to words. No specifications as to form, subject matter, or style. Poems that give the impression the poet is in the room." Does not want "poetry that is all head or preaches rather than speaks." Recently published poetry by Martha Miller, Brian Moreau, Wunjo, Frank Bogan, Gertrude F. Bantle, and Nancy Brady Cunningham. *Concrete Wolf* is 85 pages, magazine-sized, duplex-printed, perfect-bound, matte card stock cover, with b&w art. Receives about 200 poems/month, accepts about 15%. Publishes about 70 poems/issue. Press run is 1,000 for 75 subscribers of which 5 are libraries, 30% shelf sales; 10% are distributed free to writing organizations. Single copy: $10; subscription: $35. Sample: $7. Make checks payable to *Concrete Wolf*.

How to Submit: Submit up to 5 poems at a time. Line length for poetry is 300 maximum. Accepts previously published poems and simultaneous submissions. Accepts submissions by postal mail only. Reads submissions year round. Time between acceptance and publication is up to 9 months. "Poetry is individually reviewed by two editors and then discussed. Poems agreed upon by both editors are accepted." Often comments on rejected poems. Guidelines available for SASE, in publication, and on website. Responds in up to 6 months. Pays 2 contributor's copies. Acquires one-time rights.

Also Offers: Holds annual chapbook contest; write for details. Website will occasionally post writing exercises. Future plans include a supplementary CD of poets reading their work.

Advice: "Poetry exists for everyone, not just the academic. Remember that poetry is work that requires crafting."

★ $ CONFLUENCE PRESS (Specialized: regional), 500 Eighth Ave., Lewis-Clark State College, Lewiston ID 83501. (208)792-2336. Fax: (208)792-2850. E-mail: conpress@lcsc.edu. Website: www.confluencepress.com. Established 1975. **Poetry Editor:** James R. Hepworth.

● "We have received four Western States Book Awards and two awards from The Pacific Northwest Booksellers within the last decade."

Book/Chapbook Needs: Confluence is an "independent publisher of fiction, poetry, creative nonfiction, and literary scholarship. We are open to formal poetry as well as free verse. No rhymed doggerel, 'light verse,' 'performance poetry,' 'street poetry,' etc. We prefer to publish work by poets who live and work in the northwestern United States." Has published poetry by John Daniel, Greg Keeler, Nancy Mairs, and Sherry Rind. Prints about 2 books/year.

How to Submit: "Please query before submitting manuscript." Query with 6 sample poems, bio, and list of publications. No fax or e-mail submissions. Responds to queries in 6 weeks. Pays 10% royalties plus copies. Acquires all rights. Returns rights if book goes out of print. Send SASE for catalog to order samples.

$ ⊘ ◎ CONFRONTATION MAGAZINE, English Dept., C.W. Post Campus of Long Island University, Brookville NY 11548-1300. (516)299-2720. Fax: (516)299-2735. E-mail: mtucker@liu.edu. Established 1968. **Editor-in-Chief:** Martin Tucker. **Poetry Editor:** Michael Hartnett.

Magazine Needs: *Confrontation Magazine* is "a semiannual literary journal with interest in all forms. Our only criterion is high literary merit. We think of our audience as an educated, lay group of intelligent readers. We prefer lyric poems. Length generally should be kept to two pages. No sentimental verse." Has published poetry by Karl Shapiro, T. Alan Broughton, David Ignatow, Philip Appleman, Jane Mayhall, and Joseph Brodsky. *Confrontation* is about 300 pages, digest-sized, professionally printed, flat-spined, with a press run of 2,000. Receives about 1,200 submissions/year, accepts about 150, has a 6- to 12-month backlog. Subscription: $10/year. Sample: $3.

How to Submit: Submit no more than 10 pages, clear copy. No previously published poems. Accepts queries by e-mail, but not submissions. Do not submit mss June through August. "Prefer single submissions." Publishes theme issues. Upcoming themes available for SASE. Responds in 2 months. Sometimes sends prepublication galleys. Pays $5-50 and 1 copy with discount available on additional copies. Staff reviews books of poetry. Send materials for review consideration.

Also Offers: Basically a magazine, they do on occasion publish "book" issues or "anthologies." Their most recent "occasional book" is *Clown at Wall*, stories and drawings by Ken Bernard.

Advice: "We want serious poetry, which may be humorous and light-hearted on the surface."

$ ⊘ THE CONNECTICUT POETRY REVIEW, P.O. Box 818, Stonington CT 06378. Established 1981. **Poetry Editors:** J. Claire White and Harley More.

Magazine Needs: *The Connecticut Poetry Review* is a "small press annual magazine. We look for poetry of quality which is both genuine and original in content. No specifications except length: 10-40 lines." Has published such poets as John Updike, Robert Peters, Diane Wakoski, and Marge Piercy. Each issue seems to feature a poet. The flat-spined, large digest-sized journal is "printed letterpress by hand on a Hacker Hand Press from Monotype Bembo." Most of the 45-60 pages are poetry, but they also have reviews. Receives over 2,500 submissions/year, accepts about 20, has a 3-month backlog. Press run is 400 for 80 subscribers of which 35 are libraries. Sample: $3.50.

How to Submit: Reads submissions April through June and September through December only. Responds in 3 months. Pays $5/poem plus 1 copy.

Advice: "Study traditional and modern styles. Study poets of the past. Attend poetry readings and write. Practice on your own."

⊘ CONNECTICUT REVIEW, Southern Community State University, 501 Crescent St., New Haven CT 06473. (203)392-6737. Fax: (203)392-5748. E-mail: ctreview@southernct.edu. Website: www.southernct.edu. Established 1968. **Editor:** Vivian Shipley.

• Poetry published in this review has been included in *The Best American Poetry* and *The Pushcart Prize* anthologies, has received special recognition for Literary Excellence from Public Radio's series *The Poet and the Poetry*, and has won the Phoenix Award for Significant Editorial Achievement from the Council of Editors of Learned Journals (CELJ).

Magazine Needs: *Connecticut Review*, published biannually, contains essays, poetry, articles, fiction, b&w photographs, and color artwork. Has published poetry by Robert Phillips, Maria Gillan, Colette Inez, Maxine Kumin, Diana der Hovanessians, Dave Smith, Dana Gioia, and Marilyn Nelson. *Connecticut Review* is 208 pages, digest-sized, offset-printed, perfect-bound, with glossy 4-color cover and 8-color interior art. Receives about 2,500 poems/year, accepts about 5%. Press run is 3,000 of which 400 are libraries, with 1,000 distributed free to Connecticut State libraries and high schools. Sample: $8. Make checks payable to Connecticut State University.

How to Submit: Submit 3-5 typed poems at a time with name, address, and phone in the upper

insider report

The importance of great teachers

Talking to Marvin Bell is a seminar in itself. His conversation is peppered with advice from his "32 Statements About Writing Poetry" (see page 124) and wisdom gained throughout a long, distinguished literary career.

As a professor at the University of Iowa's fabled Writers' Workshop (his tenure began in 1965), Bell's students have included John Irving, Lee Blessing, Denis Johnson, Sandra Cisneros, Patricia Hampl, Rita Dove, and James Tate. His own writing has produced 17 books of poetry, including *Nightworks: Poems 1962-2000* (Copper Canyon Press, 2000), and won him such honors as the American Academy of Arts and Letters Award in Literature, Guggenheim and National Endowment for the Arts fellowships, and Senior Fulbright appointments to Yugoslavia and Australia. In 2000, Bell was named Iowa's first Poet Laureate.

Marvin Bell

Photo by Jason Bell

Bell describes the Writers' Workshop as a program of about 110 graduate students. There are five sections of the Graduate Fiction Workshop and four sections of the Graduate Poetry Workshop. Each section has about 12 students, and each semester the students choose another teacher. Bell says the students are "self-motivated. These young writers are pretty far along. They have written and read quite a lot."

Each Writers' Workshop faculty member leads a section of the Graduate Fiction or Poetry Workshop plus a reading seminar or a craft class called "Form of Poetry" or "Form of Fiction." Student work is discussed in weekly workshop sessions where the writers receive feedback from the group. Students also meet individually with their professors.

Instead of scheduling regular conferences, Bell's students simply call him when they want his review of their work. They meet informally, often at a coffee shop. Bell might offer suggestions as to how a poem could be focused or expanded. "I try to fill their heads with possibilities. My job is giving them permission to go in new directions. I encourage them to surrender to the materials and to let the writing lead them."

Bell cites two teachers as having had an enormous impact on his own development as a poet. An early class with John Logan at the downtown center of the University of Chicago was particularly influential. Logan was "an emotional teacher," says Bell. "He was supportive, and he took us seriously at a time when we needed to be taken seriously. He read our poems aloud so beautifully, we thought we were good."

Through Logan, Bell joined a group called "The Poetry Seminar," whose members included Dennis Schmitz, Charles Simic, Bill Knott, and Naomi Lazard. Logan also guided Bell to the Writers' Workshop at the University of Iowa, where Bell met Donald Justice, who taught the Graduate Poetry Workshop. "If you're going to be serious about any art form, sooner or later, you have to run into a great teacher," says Bell, who describes Justice as "a master craftsman and a precise critic of poetry. He instilled in his students a respect for craft. He was a more intellectual teacher than Logan."

Through the years of his teaching at the Writers' Workshop, Bell has been able to pass along his love of writing as well as the ideas educators such as Logan and Justice shared with him. He tries to impress upon his students that writing is valid in and of itself. "Writing is getting into motion in the presence of language. It's a process of discovery. And the imagination is a survival mechanism. What is important about writing is the writing. Being published and receiving recognition is secondary, a bonus."

One of Bell's well-known and beloved works is "To Dorothy," a now-classic love poem Bell wrote to his wife in 1975. "To Dorothy" demonstrates Bell's idea that "repetition may be the essence of poetry."

"To Dorothy"

You are not beautiful, exactly.
You are beautiful, inexactly.
You let a weed grow by the mulberry
and a mulberry grow by the house.
So close, in the personal quiet
of a windy night, it brushes the wall
and sweeps away the day till we sleep.

A child said it, and it seemed true:
"Things that are lost are all equal."
But it isn't true. If I lost you,
the air wouldn't move, nor the tree grow.
Someone would pull the weed, my flower.
The quiet wouldn't be yours. If I lost you,
I'd have to ask the grass to let me sleep.

"If you think about it, rhyme is repetition, rhythm is repetition," says Bell. "An argument could be made that even metaphor is a form of repetition. In the second stanza of 'To Dorothy,' I repeat nearly everything.

"One way to extend a poem is simply to use things again. Sometimes a poet will say the same thing twice, and the second time, thanks to what has come up in the meantime, will carry more weight. I mention the tree, the weed, the wind, and the quiet in both stanzas. At the end, the quiet is the same sleep that ended the first stanza, but now it carries a deeper meaning."

How was Bell inspired to write this poem? "I set out to write a love poem to Dorothy. Christmas was coming and I had visions of having it secretly printed and secretly framed.

"I wrote the first stanza. Then I was casting about, looking at abandoned poems for something to keep me going. I had taught a week in Keokuk, Iowa. In the classroom, hanging from a chalkboard, there were pieces of paper with words and pictures on them. One said, 'Things that are lost are all equal.' I included it in a poem about that schoolroom, but that poem didn't want to get up and dance. Now I thought I could use that line again and this time argue with it."

Bell points out that poets who attempt to write love poems face a problem. "I once asked a high school class, 'What's the problem?' One of the kids answered, 'You're in love!' The bigger problem is that love poems are all over the place, including on greeting cards. Yet one wants to write something original."

Of the imagery in "To Dorothy," Bell explains, "I wanted supporting material from the physical world. I took the quiet, the mulberry tree, the weed, the wind. Weeds?—I like weeds. There was a mulberry so close to the house, we had to eventually cut it down so it wouldn't ruin the foundation. I like the quiet, and Dorothy doesn't like the wind. So I took the things at hand. It's a great advantage to include the physical world in a poem. I like ideas with dirt on their shoes."

Whenever someone asks how he knows when a poem is finished, Bell replies, "When everything in it is used up. This poem is an example. Everything is used, and nearly everything in it has a twin."

—Julianne Hill

left corner on 8½×11 paper with SASE for reply only. Accepts submissions by postal mail only. Guidelines available for SASE. Pays 2 copies. Acquires first or one-time rights.

CONNECTICUT RIVER REVIEW; ANNUAL CONNECTICUT RIVER REVIEW POETRY CONTEST; BRODINSKY-BRODINE CONTEST; WINCHELL CONTEST; LYNN DECARO HIGH SCHOOL COMPETITION; CONNECTICUT POETRY SOCIETY, P.O. Box 4053, Waterbury CT 06704-0053. E-mail: editorcrr@yahoo.com. Website: http://pages.prodigy.net/mmwalker/cpsindex.html. Established 1978. **Editor:** Sue Halloway.

Magazine Needs: Published by the Connecticut Poetry Society, *Connecticut River Review* appears annually in July or August. Looking for "original, honest, diverse, vital, well-crafted poetry; any form, any subject. Translations and long poems accepted." Has published poetry by Marilyn Nelson (CT Poet Laureate), Claire Zoghb, and Vivian Shipley. *Connecticut River Review* is attractively printed, digest-sized, perfect-bound, and contains about 100 pages of poetry, has a press run of about 300 with 175 subscriptions of which 5% are libraries. Receives about 2,000 submissions/year, accepts about 100. Single copy: $7; subscription: $14. CPS membership (including subscription): $25.

How to Submit: Submit up to 3 poems at a time. "Complete contact information typed in upper right corner, SASE required." No previously published poems. Accepts simultaneous submissions if notified of acceptance elsewhere." Cover letter with current bio appreciated. Reads submissions from October 1 to April 15. Guidelines available with SASE, by e-mail, and in publication. Responds in up to 6 weeks. Pays 1 copy. "Poet retains copyright."

Also Offers: Annual *Connecticut River Review* Poetry Contest has a $10 entry fee and 3 poem limit. Deadline: April 30. The Brodinsky-Brodine Contest has a $2 entry fee/poem and awards publication in the *Connecticut River Review*. Entries must be postmarked between May 1 and July 31. The Winchell Contest has a $2 entry fee/poem and awards publication in the *Connecticut River Review*. Entries must be postmarked between October 1 and December 31. The Lynn DeCaro Competition (for Connecticut high school students only) has no entry fee and awards publication in the *Connecticut River Review*. Entries must be postmarked between September 1 and February 27. Affiliated with the National Federation of State Poetry Societies, the Connecticut Poetry Society currently has 150 members. Sponsors conferences, workshops. Publishes *Newsletter*, a bimonthly publication, also available to nonmembers for SASE. Members or nationally known writers give readings that are open to the public. Sponsors open-mike readings. Membership dues are $25/year. Members meet monthly. Send SASE for additional information.

COPIOUS MAGAZINE, #276, 2416 Main St., Vancouver BC V5T 3E2 Canada. E-mail: editor@copiousmagazine.com. Website: www.copiousmagazine.com. Established 2000. **Editor:** Andrea Grant.

Magazine Needs: *Copious Magazine* appears biannually, featuring poetry, artwork, b&w photographs, pulp fiction novel covers, interviews, music, and *The Minx* comic. "I want poems that have that aching knife twist in them. Themes of nocturne, superheroes, mythology, and fairy tales. Larger than life, poems about people. *Copious* features 'the doyenne,' the vixen of *film noir* and hardboiled pulp novels. She defies social expectations as seduction melds with her tragic side - a strong female force! Love poems are always nice, Native Indian themes also." Does not want rhyming, horror, overly sentimental poetry. Accepts poetry written by children. Has published poetry by Ace Boggess, B.M. Bradley, Andrea MacPherson, and Laurel Ann Bogen. *Copious Magazine* is 46 pages, digest-sized, professionally-printed, glossy cover, with contributed artwork and photos, pulp fiction pictures, and ads for related industries or of reader interest. Publishes about 20 poems/issue. Press run is 1,000 and growing. Single copy: $5; subscription: $10 US/$20 Canada. Sample: $4. Make checks payable to *Copious Magazine*.

How to Submit: Submit 3-5 poems at a time. Accepts previously published poems and simultaneous submissions. Accepts e-mail submissions (in text box). Cover letter is required. "Please provide a short bio, send SASE." Reads submissions year round. Submit seasonal poems 6 months in advance. Time between acceptance and publication is up to 1 year. Often comments on rejected poems. Occasionally publishes theme issues. Guidelines and upcoming themes available in magazine, for SASE, by e-mail, or on website. Responds in up to 1 year. Pays 1 copy. Acquires one-time rights; reserves right to republish in future anthologies. Send materials for review consideration to Andrea Grant.

Advice: "The best poetry comes from the heart and has that haunting little twist. Don't be afraid to take risks."

◎ COPPER CANYON PRESS; HAYDEN CARRUTH AWARD, P.O. Box 271, Port Townsend WA 98368. (877)501-1393. Fax: (360)385-4985. E-mail: poetry@coppercanyonpress.org. Website: www.coppercanyonpress.org. Established 1972. **Editor:** Sam Hamill.

Book/Chapbook Needs: Copper Canyon publishes books of poetry. Has published books of poetry by Lucille Clifton, Hayden Carruth, Carolyn Kizer, Olga Broumas, Ruth Stone, and Jim Harrison.

How to Submit: Currently accepts no unsolicited poetry. E-mail queries and submissions will go unanswered.

Also Offers: Copper Canyon Press publishes 1 volume of poetry each year by a new or emerging poet through its Hayden Carruth Award. "For the purpose of this award an emerging poet is defined as a poet who has published not more than two books." Winner receives $1,000 advance, book publication with Copper Canyon Press, and a 1-month residency at the Vermont Studio Center. Each unbound ms submitted should be a minimum of 46 typed pages on white paper, paginated consecutively with a table of contents. Author's name or address must not appear anywhere on ms (this includes both title and acknowledgements pages). Please do not staple or paper-clip ms. Include $20 handling fee (check payable to Copper Canyon Press), submission form (available on website), and SASE for notification (mss will be recycled, not returned). Deadline: postmarked between November 1 and November 30, 2003. No entries by e-mail or fax. Winner announced February 21, 2004. Winners include Sascha Feinstein's *Misterioso*, Rebecca Wee's *Uncertain Grace*, Jenny Factor's *Unraveling at the Name*, and Peter Pereira's *Saying the Word*. Past judges include Jane Miller (2000), Marilyn Hacker (2001), Gregory Orr (2002). Further guidelines available for SASE and on website.

◪ ◎ CORRECTION(S): A LITERARY JOURNAL (Specialized: poetry from prisoners only); CORRECTION(S) CHAPBOOK CONTEST, P.O. Box 1234, New York NY 10276. Established 2001. **Editor:** K. Adams.

Magazine Needs: "*Correction(s)* is a biannual journal dedicated to the poetics and vision of prisoners." Wants "good writing with a sense of one's own poetics." Does not want blatant pornography. Recently published poetry by David Bowman, Spoon Jackson, Christopher Presfield, and Elmo Chattam. *Correction(s)* is 90 pages, digest-sized, perfect-bound, glossy and card stock cover, sometimes with art/graphics. Publishes 25-30 poems/issue. Single copy price: free (prisoners), $8 (everyone else). Make checks payable to *Correction(s)*.

How to Submit: Submit 3-8 poems at a time. Accepts simultaneous submissions, no previously published poems. Accepts disk submissions; no fax or e-mail submissions. Cover letter is preferred. "Include SASE and brief bio. Handwritten submissions are accepted. Please print as neatly as possible." Reads submissions "all year/all time." Time between acceptance and publication is about 6 months. Often comments on rejected poems. Will occasionally publish theme issues. "Lifers issue and Death Row issue forthcoming 2004." Upcoming themes and guidelines are available for SASE. Responds in 2 months. Pays 2 contributor's copies. Reviews books and chapbooks of poetry and other magazines/journals. Send materials for review consideration to *Correction(s)*.

Book/Chapbook Needs & How to Submit: Correction(s) Press "seeks to publish quality literature written by prisoners." Publishes one paperback, one chapbook/year. Selects chapbook through competition (see **Also Offers** below). Chapbooks are usually 30-45 pages, perfect-bound, varied covers, sometimes with art/graphics. Responds to queries in up to 10 weeks; to mss in up to 1 year. Pays 30 author's copies. Guidelines available for SASE.

Also Offers: The *Correction(s)* Chapbook Contest accepts submissions in poetry and short fiction. Handwritten mss accepted. Manuscript must not exceed 60 handwritten (45 typed) pages for poetry; 50 handwritten (35 typed) pages for short fiction. **Contest open to prisoners only.** Prize is 30 copies and publication in *Correction(s)*. Entry fee: $1. Deadline: January 1, 2004. Winners will be notified by May 2004.

★ ◎ **THE CORTLAND REVIEW**, 2061 NE 73rd St., Seattle WA 98115. E-mail: tcr@cortlandre view.com. Website: www.cortlandreview.com. Established 1997. **Editor-in-Chief:** Guy Shahar. **Contact:** Poetry Submission Reader.

Magazine Needs: *The Cortland Review* is an online literary magazine only (no print version) "publishing in text and audio, and its free. We publish poetry, essays, interviews, fiction, book reviews, etc." Has published poetry by W.S. Merwin, Charles Simic, Yehuda Amichai, Dick Allen, Linda Pastan, Billy Collins, David Lehman, Marge Piercy, and R.T. Smith.

How to Submit: Submit 3-5 poems at a time. No previously published poems or simultaneous submissions. *The Cortland Review* "prefers online submissions through our online submission form. Please visit website for full submission guidelines. Snail mail is also acceptable." Cover letter required. Time between acceptance and publication is up to 1 year, sometimes longer. Seldom comments on rejected poems. Guidelines available at www.cortlandreview.com/submission_guidelines.php.htm. Always sends prepublication galleys. Acquires first rights. Staff reviews books and chapbooks of poetry and other magazines in 100 words, multi-book format. Send materials for review consideration.

★ ✂ $ ✎ ◎ **COTEAU BOOKS; THUNDER CREEK PUBLISHING CO-OP (Specialized: Canadian, children)**, 401-2206 Dewdney Ave., Regina SK S4R 1H3 Canada. (306)777-0170. Fax: (306)522-5152. E-mail: coteau@coteaubooks.com. Website: www.coteaubooks.com. Established 1975. **Publisher:** Geoffrey Ursell. **Managing Editor:** Nik L. Burton. **Contact:** Acquisitions Editor.

Book/Chapbook Needs: Coteau is a "small literary press that publishes poetry, fiction, drama, anthologies, criticism, young adult novels—by Canadian writers only." Has published *A Secret Envy of the Unsaved* by Rebecca Frederickson, *Silence of the Country* by Kristjana Gunnars, and *The Names Leave the Stones* by Steven Michael Berzensky.

How to Submit: Writers should submit 30-50 poems "and indication of whole ms," typed with at least 12 point type; simultaneous and American submissions not accepted. Accepts e-mail submissions (send as .txt file attachments maximum 20 pages). No fax submissions. Cover letter required; include publishing credits and bio and SASE (or SAE and IRC) for return of ms. Queries will be answered and mss responded to in 4 months. Always sends prepublication galleys. Authors receive 10% royalty and 10 copies. Catalog (for ordering samples) free for 9×12 SASE (or SAE and IRC).

Also Offers: Website includes title and ordering information, author interviews, awards, news and events, submission guidelines and links.

Advice: "Generally, poets should have a number of publishing credits, single poems or series, in literary magazines and anthologies before submitting a manuscript."

◎ **COTTONWOOD; COTTONWOOD PRESS**, 400 Kansas Union-Box J, University of Kansas, Lawrence KS 66045. (913)864-3777. E-mail: cottonwd@ukans.edu. Website: www.falcon.cc.uka ns.edu/~cottonwd. Established 1965. **Poetry Editor:** Philip Wedge.

Magazine Needs: *Cottonwood* is published biannually. Wants "strong narrative or sensory impact, non-derivative, not 'literary,' not 'academic.' Emphasis on Midwest, but publishes the best poetry received regardless of region. Poems should be 60 lines or fewer, on daily experience, *perception."* Has published poetry by Rita Dove, Virgil Suarez, Walt McDonad, and Luci Tapahonso. *Cottonwood* is 112 pages, digest-sized, flat-spined, printed from computer offset, with photos, using 10-15 pages of poetry in each issue. Receives about 4,000 submissions/year, accepts about 30, have a maximum of 1-year backlog. Press run of 500-600, with 150 subscribers of which 75 are libraries. Single copy: $8.50. Sample: $5.

How to Submit: Submit up to 5 pages of poetry at a time. No simultaneous submissions. Sometimes provides criticism on rejected mss. Responds in up to 5 months. Pays 1 copy.

Book/Chapbook Needs & How to Submit: The press "is auxiliary to *Cottonwood Magazine* and publishes material by authors in the region. Material is usually solicited." The press published *Violence and Grace* by Michael L. Johnson and *Midwestern Buildings* by Victor Contoski.

Advice: "Read the little magazines and send to ones you like."

$ 🔘 COUNTRY WOMAN; REIMAN PUBLICATIONS (Specialized: women, humor), 5925 Country Lane, Greendale WI 53129. Established 1970. **Executive Editor:** Kathy Pohl. **Managing Editor:** Kathleen Anderson.

Magazine Needs: *Country Woman* "is a bimonthly magazine dedicated to the lives and interests of country women. Those who are both involved in farming and ranching and those who love country life. In some ways, it is very similar to many women's general interest magazines, and yet its subject matter is closely tied in with rural living and the very unique lives of country women. We like short (4-5 stanzas, 16-20 lines) traditional rhyming poems that reflect on a season. No experimental poetry or free verse. Poetry will not be considered unless it rhymes. Always looking for poems that focus on the seasons. We don't want rural putdowns, poems that stereotype country women, etc. All poetry must be positive and upbeat. Our poems are fairly simple, yet elegant. They often accompany a high-quality photograph." Has published poetry by Hilda Sanderson, Edith E. Cutting, and Ericka Northrop. *Country Woman* is 68 pages, magazine-sized, printed on glossy paper with much color photography. Receives about 1,200 submissions of poetry/year, accepts about 40-50. Backlog is 3 months. Subscription: $17.98/year. Sample: $2.

How to Submit: Submit up to 6 poems at a time. Photocopy OK if stated not a simultaneous submission. Responds in 3 months. Pays $10-25/poem plus 1 copy. Acquires first rights (generally) or reprint rights (sometimes).

Also Offers: Holds various contests for subscribers only.

Advice: "We're always welcoming submissions, but any poem that does not have traditional rhythm and rhyme is automatically passed over."

🔘 CRAB CREEK REVIEW, P.O. Box 840, Vashon Island WA 98070. E-mail: editor@crabcreekreview.org. Website: www.crabcreekreview.org. Established 1983. **Editorial Collective:** Eleanor Lee, Harris Levinson, Laura Sinai, and Terri Stone.

Magazine Needs: Published biannually, *Crab Creek Review* publishes "an eclectic mix of energetic poems, free or formal, and more interested in powerful imagery than obscure literary allusion. Wit? Yes. Punch? Sure. Toast dry? No thank you. Translations are welcome—please submit with a copy of the poem in its original language, if possible." Has published poetry by Pauls Toutonghi, Molly Tenenbaum, Judith Skillman, Derek Sheffield, David Lee, and Kevin Miller. *Crab Creek Review* is an 80 to 120-page, perfect-bound paperback. Subscription: $10 (2 issues). Sample: $5.

How to Submit: Submit up to 5 poems at a time. No fax or e-mail submissions. Include SASE ("without one we will not consider the work"). Responds in up to 4 months. Pays 2 copies. Guidelines available for SASE or on website.

$ 🔘 CRAB ORCHARD REVIEW; CRAB ORCHARD AWARD SERIES IN POETRY, English Dept., Faner Hall, Southern Illinois University at Carbondale, Carbondale IL 62901-4503.

MARKETS LISTED in the 2003 edition of *Poet's Market* that do not appear this year are identified in the General Index with a code explaining their absence from the listings.

Website: www.siu.edu/~crborchd. Established 1995. **Poetry Editor:** Allison Joseph. **Managing Editor:** Jon C. Tribble.

- *Crab Orchard Review* received a 2002 Literary Award and a 2002 Operating Grant from the Illinois Arts Council. Poetry from *Crab Orchard Review* has also appeared in *The Best American Poetry 1999, 2000,* and *2001* and *Beacon Best of 1999* and 2000.

Magazine Needs: *Crab Orchard Review* appears biannually in June and January. "We are a general interest literary journal publishing poetry, fiction, creative nonfiction, interviews, book reviews, and novel excerpts." Wants all styles and forms from traditional to experimental. No greeting card verse; literary poetry only. Has published poetry by Victoria Chang, Jesse Lee Kercheval, Robert Wrigley, Virgil Suarez, Marilyn Hacker, and Timothy Liu. *Crab Orchard Review* is 280-300 pages, digest-sized, professionally printed and perfect-bound with photos, usually glossy card cover containing color photos. Receives about 9,000 poems/year, accepts about 1%. Each issue usually includes 35-40 poems. Press run is 2,000 for 1,100 subscribers of which 400 are libraries; 100 distributed free to exchange with other journals; remainder in shelf sales. Subscription: $15. Sample: $8.

How to Submit: Submit up to 5 poems at a time. Accepts simultaneous submissions with notification; no previously published poems. No fax or e-mail submissions. Cover letter preferred. "Indicate stanza breaks on poems of more than one page." Reads submissions April to November for our Spring/Summer special issue, December to April for regular, non-thematic Fall/Winter issue. Time between acceptance and publication is 6-12 months. Poems are circulated to an editorial board. "Poems that are under serious consideration are discussed and decided on by the managing editor, and poetry editor." Seldom comments on rejected poems. Publishes theme issues. Theme for Spring/Summer 2004 issue is "Immigration, Migration, and Exile." Deadline: November 1, 2003. Upcoming themes available for SASE, on website, and in publication. Guidelines available for SASE, on website, and in publication. Responds in up to 8 months. Pays $15/page, $50 minimum plus 2 copies and 1 year's subscription. Acquires first North American serial rights. Staff reviews books of poetry in 500-700 words, single book format. Send materials for review consideration to managing editor Jon C. Tribble.

Also Offers: Sponsors the Crab Orchard Award Series in Poetry. The publisher of the books will be Southern Illinois University Press. The competition is open from October 1 to November 16 for US citizens and permanent residents. "The Crab Orchard Award Series in Poetry, launched in 1997, is committed to publishing two book-length manuscripts each year. We also run an annual fiction/nonfiction contest." Books are usually 50-70 pages, 9×6, perfect-bound with color paper covers. Entry fee: $25/submission (each entrant receives a subscription to *Crab Orchard Review*). 1st and 2nd Prize winners each receive a publication contract with Southern Illinois University Press. In addition, the 1st Prize winner will be awarded a $2,000 prize and $1,500 as an honorarium for a reading at Southern Illinois University at Carbondale; also, the 2nd Prize winner will receive $1,500 as an honorarium for a reading at Southern Illinois University at Carbondale. Both readings will follow the publication of the poets' collections by Southern Illinois University Press. 2002 winner was Elton Glaser for *Pelican Tracks*, second place winner was Patricia Jabbeth Wesley for *Becoming Ebony*. 2002 First Book winner was Chad Davidson for *Consolation Miracle*. Also, first book competition for the publication of a poet's first book. Reads for this prize from May 15, 2003 to June 15, 2003 (first book). All questions regarding the Award Series in Poetry should go to Jon C. Tribble, series editor, Crab Orchard Award Series in Poetry. Details available for SASE.

Advice: "Please include SASE with all submissions—let us know whether or not you want poems recycled or returned. Don't send SASEs that are smaller than number 10 envelopes."

◖CRAZYHORSE; CRAZYHORSE FICTION AND POETRY AWARDS, Dept. of English, College of Charleston, 66 George St., Charleston SC 29424. (843)953-7740. E-mail: crazyhorse@cofc .edu. Established 1960. **Poetry Editors:** Paul Allen and Carol Ann Davis.

Magazine Needs: *Crazyhorse* appears biannually and publishes fine fiction, poetry, and essays. "Send your best words our way. We like to print a mix of writing regardless of its form, genre, school, or politics. We're especially on the lookout for writing that doesn't fit the categories." Does not want "writing with nothing at stake. Before sending, ask 'What's reckoned with that's important for other people to read?'" Recently published poetry by David Wojahn, Mary Ruefle, Nance Van Winkle, Andrew Hudgins, James Grinwis, and Lola Haskins. *Crazyhorse* is 150-200 pages, 8¾×8½, perfect-bound, 4-color glossy cover. Receives about 8,000 poems/year. Publishes about 40 poems/issue. Press run is 1,500. Single copy: $8.50; subscription: $15 for 1 year/2 issues, $25 for 2 years, $40 for 3 years. Sample: $5. Make checks payable to *Crazyhorse*.

How to Submit: Submit 3-5 poems at a time. Accepts simultaneous submissions; no previously published poems. No fax, e-mail, or disk submissions. Cover letter is preferred. Reads submissions year round. "We read slower in summer." Time between acceptance and publication is 6 months. Seldom comments on rejected poems. Guidelines available in magazine, for SASE, or by e-mail. Responds in 3 months. Sometimes sends prepublication galleys. Pays 2 contributor's copies plus a year's subscription (2 issues). Acquires first rights.

Also Offers: The Crazyhorse Fiction and Poetry Awards: $500 and publication in *Crazyhorse*. Send SASE for details.

Advice: "Feel strongly; then write."

⦿ THE CREAM CITY REVIEW, P.O. Box 413, Dept. of English, University of Wisconsin at Milwaukee, Milwaukee WI 53201. (414)229-4708. E-mail: creamcity@uwm.edu. Website: www.uwm.edu/Dept/English/CCR. **Editor:** Erica Wiest. **Poetry Editors:** Beth Bretel and Jennifer Dworshack-Kinter.

  • Poetry published in this review has been included in the 1996 and 1997 volumes of *The Best American Poetry*.

Magazine Needs: *The Cream City Review* is a nationally distributed literary magazine published twice/year by the university's Creative Writing Program. "We seek to publish all forms of writing, from traditional to experimental. We strive to produce issues which are challenging, diverse and of lasting quality. We are not interested in sexist, homophobic, racist or formulaic writings." Has published poetry by William Harrold, Maxine Chernoff, Kate Braverman, Billy Collins, Bob Hicok, and Allison Joseph. They do not include sample lines of poetry; "Best to buy a copy—we publish the best from new and established writers. We like an energetic mix." *The Cream City Rewview* is averaging 200 pages, digest-sized, perfect-bound, with full-color cover on 70 lb. paper. Press run is 1,000 for 450 subscribers of which 40 are libraries. Single copy: $8; subscription: $15/1 year, $28/2 years; institutional subscription: $25/year. Sample: $5.

How to Submit: "Include SASE when submitting and please submit no more than five poems at a time." Accepts simultaneous submissions when notified. "Please include a few lines about your publication history and other information you think of interest." Reads submissions September 1 through April 1 only. Editors sometimes comment on rejected poems. Accepts submissions by regular mail only. Guidelines available for SASE. Responds in up to 6 months. Payment includes 1-year subscription. Acquires first rights. Reviews books of poetry in 1-2 pages. Send materials to the poetry editors for review consideration.

Also Offers: Sponsors an annual contest for poems under 100 lines. Submit 3 poems/entry. Entry fee: $10. Awards $100 plus publication; all entries considered for publication.

★ ⦿ CREATIVE ARTS BOOK COMPANY; DONALD S. ELLIS POETRY BOOKS, 833 Bancroft Way, Berkeley CA 94710. (510)848-4777. Fax: (510)848-4844. E-mail: staff@creativeartsbooks.com. Website: www.creativeartsbooks.com. Established 1968. **Publisher:** Donald S. Ellis.

  • Publications by Creative Arts Book Company have won the American Book Award and the Fred Cody/BABRA Award

Book/Chapbook Needs & How to Submit: Creative Arts Book Company publishes general and literary fiction, poetry, nonfiction, memoir/biography, and mystery/suspense. Recently published poetry by Deborah Major, George Tsongas, Morton Marcus, Sandy Diamond, Al Young, John Oliver Simon, Gloria Frym, Francisco Alarcon, and Gary Young. Publishes 6 poetry books/year. Manuscripts selected through open submission. Books are 80-250 pages, trade paper with 4-color gloss covers, includes art/graphics. Send complete ms, cover letter, brief bio, publication credits, and SASE (for return of ms if desired). Book mss may include previously published poems. Responds to mss in 3 months. Pays royalties/advance.

⦿ CREATIVE JUICES; FORESTLAND PUBLICATIONS, 423 N. Burnham Highway, Lisbon CT 06351. E-mail: forestland1@juno.com. Website: www.geocities.com/geraldinepowell/index.html. Established 1989 (Forestland Publications). **Editor:** Geraldine Hempstead Powell.

Magazine Needs: *Creative Juices*, published bimonthly, features poetry, arts, photos, "something to inspire everyone's creative juices." Wants "any style or subject, 50 lines or less." Does not want pornography. Accepts poetry written by children aged 10 or older. Press run is 100 for 65 subscribers, 30 shelf sales. Receives about 1,000 poems/year, accepts about 350. Single copy: $3; subscription: $20/year; $35/2 years. Sample: $3 and SASE. Make checks payable to Geraldine Powell.

How to Submit: Submit 3-5 poems at a time. Accepts simultaneous submissions. Time between acceptance and publication is up to 3 months. Submissions reviewed by editor. Often comments on rejected poems. Guidelines available for SASE, on website, by fax, in publication, or by e-mail. Responds in 1 month. Sometimes sends prepublication galleys. Pays 1 or more copies. Acquires first North American serial or one-time rights. Always returns rights. Reviews books of poetry. Send materials for review consideration.

Book/Chapbook Needs & How to Submit: Forestland Publications publishes 4-6 chapbooks/year. Has published Nancy Manning's *Amethyst Garden* and Reneeta Renganathan's *Sleeping Alone*. Chapbooks are usually 5×7, 20 pages. Send up to 20 poems, **$15 reading fee**, and cover letter with brief bio and publication credits. Responds to mss in 1 month. Obtain sample chapbooks by sending SASE with 2 stamps and $3.

○ **CREATIVITY UNLIMITED PRESS®; ANNUAL CREATIVITY UNLIMITED PRESS® POETRY COMPETITION**, 30819 Casilina, Rancho Palos Verdes CA 90275. E-mail: sstockwell@earthlink.net. Established 1978. **Editor:** Shelley Stockwell.

Book/Chapbook Needs: Creativity Unlimited® uses poetry submitted to their contest in published texts. Prize of $25 and possible publication. Deadline: December 31. "Short, clever, quippy, humor, and delightful language encouraged. No inaccessible, verbose, esoteric, obscure poetry. Limit two pages per poem, double-spaced, one side of page."

How to Submit: "Poems previously published will be accepted provided writer has maintained copyright and notifies us." Accepts e-mail submissions. Often uses poems as chapter introductions in self-help books. Comments on rejected poems. Pays 1 copy.

Advice: "We are interested in *humorous* poetry."

○ **CREOSOTE**, Department of English, Mohave Community College, 1977 W. Acoma Blvd., Lake Havasu City AZ 86403. Established 2000. **Editor:** Ken Raines.

Magazine Needs: *Creosote* is an annual publication of poetry, fiction, and literary nonfiction appearing in May. Has "a bias favoring more traditional forms, but interested in any and all quality poems." Has "a bias against confessional and beat-influenced poetry, but will consider everything." Recently published poetry by William Wilborn, Ruth Moose, and Star Coolbrooke. *Creosote* is 48 pages, digest-sized, saddle stapled, card cover. Receives about 150-200 poems/year, accepts about 10%. Publishes about 15 poems/issue. Press run is 500 for 30 subscribers of which 5 are libraries, 200 shelf sales; 100+ are distributed free to contributors and others. Single copy: $4. Sample: $2. Make checks payable to Mohave Community College.

How to Submit: Submit up to 5 poems at a time. Line length for poetry is open. Accepts simultaneous submissions "but please notify us ASAP if accepted elsewhere"; no previously published poems. Accepts disk submissions; no fax or e-mail submissions. Cover letter is preferred. "Disk submissions must be accompanied by a hard copy." Reads submissions September 1-February 28. Time between acceptance and publication is 2-3 months. Poems are circulated to an editorial board. "All work which passes initial screening is considered by at least 2 (usually more) readers." Seldom comments on rejected poems. Guidelines are available for SASE. Responds in 6 months "at most, usually sooner." Pays 2 contributor's copies. Acquires one-time rights. Occasionally reviews books of poetry in 250-500 words. Send materials for review consideration to Ken Raines, editor.

Advice: "Love words. Resist the urge to pontificate. Beware a self-congratulatory tone. Shun sloppy expression."

★ ⊕ ○ ◎ **CRESCENT MOON PUBLISHING; PASSION (Specialized: anthology, gay/lesbian, love/romance/erotica, occult, religious, spirituality, women/feminism)**, P.O. Box 393, Maidstone, Kent ME14 5XU United Kingdom. Phone: 01622-729593. E-mail: jrobinson@crescentmoon.org.uk. Website: www.crescentmoon.org.uk. Established 1988. **Editor:** Jeremy Robinson.

Magazine Needs: "We publish a quarterly magazine, *Passion* ($4 each, $17 subscription). It features poetry, fiction, reviews, and essays on feminism, art, philosophy, and the media. Many American poets are featured, as well as British poets such as Jeremy Reed, Penelope Shuttle, Alan Bold, D.J. Enright, and Peter Redgrove. Contributions welcome."

Book/Chapbook Needs: Crescent Moon publishes about 25 books and chapbooks/year on arrangements **subsidized by the poet.** Wants "poetry that is passionate and authentic. Any form or length." Not "the trivial, insincere or derivative. We are also publishing two anthologies of new American poetry each year entitled *Pagan America*." Has also published studies of Rimbaud, Rilke, Cavafy, Shakespeare, Beckett, German Romantic poetry and D.H. Lawrence. Books are usually about 76 pages, flat-spined, digest-sized. Anthologies now available ($8.95 or $17 for 2 issues of *Pagan America*) include: *Pagan America: An Anthology of New American Poetry*; *Love in America: An Anthology of Women's Love Poetry*; *Mythic America: An Anthology of New American Poetry*; and *Religious America: An Anthology of New American Poetry.*

How to Submit: Submit 5-10 poems at a time. Cover letter with brief bio and publishing credits required ("and please print your address in capitals"). Send SASE (or SAE and IRCs) for upcoming anthology themes. Responds to queries in 1 month, to mss 2 months. Sometimes sends prepublication galleys.

Advice: "Generally, we prefer free verse to rhymed poetry."

★ $◎ CRICKET; SPIDER, THE MAGAZINE FOR CHILDREN; LADYBUG, THE MAGAZINE FOR YOUNG CHILDREN; BABYBUG, THE LISTENING AND LOOKING MAGAZINE FOR INFANTS AND TODDLERS (Specialized: children); CICADA (Specialized: teens), P.O. Box 300, Peru IL 61354-0300. Website: www.cricketmag.com. *Cricket* estab. 1973. *Ladybug* estab. 1990. *Spider* estab. 1994. *Babybug* estab. 1995. *Cicada* estab. 1998. **Editor-in-Chief:** Marianne Carus.

Magazine Needs: *Cricket* (for ages 9-14) is a monthly, circulation 73,000, using "serious, humorous, nonsense rhymes" for children and young adults. Does not want "forced or trite rhyming or imagery that doesn't hang together to create a unified whole." Sometimes uses previously published work. *Cricket* is 64 pages, 8×10, saddle-stapled, with color cover and full-color illustrations inside. *Ladybug*, also monthly, circulation 131,000, is similar in format and requirements but is aimed at younger children (ages 2-6). *Spider*, also monthly, circulation 78,000, is for children ages 6-9. Format and requirements similar to *Cricket* and *Ladybug*. *Cicada*, appearing bimonthly, circulation 16,000, is a magazine for ages 14 and up publishing "short stories, poems, and first-person essays written for teens and young adults." Wants "serious or humorous poetry; rhymed or free verse." *Cicada* is 128 pages, digest-sized, perfect-bound with full-color cover and b&w illustrations. *Babybug*, published at 6-week intervals, circulation 48,000, is a read-aloud magazine for ages 6 months to 2 years; premier issue published January 1995. *Babybug* is 24 pages, 6¼×7, printed on cardstock with nontoxic glued spine and full-color illustrations. The magazines receive over 1,200 submissions/month, use 25-30, and have up to a 2-year backlog. Sample of *Cricket*, *Ladybug*, *Spider*, or *Babybug*: $5; sample of *Cicada*: $8.50.

How to Submit: Do not query. Submit no more than 5 poems—up to 50 lines (2 pages max.) for *Cricket*; up to 20 lines for *Spider* and *Ladybug*, up to 25 lines for *Cicada*, up to 8 lines for *Babybug*, no restrictions on form. Guidelines available for SASE and on website. Responds in 4 months. Payment for all is up to $3/line and 2 copies. "All submissions are automatically considered for all five magazines."

Also Offers: *Cricket* and *Spider* hold poetry contests every third month. *Cricket* accepts entries from readers of all ages; *Spider* from readers ages 10 and under. Current contest themes and rules appear in each issue.

◖ CRUCIBLE; SAM RAGAN PRIZE, Barton College, College Station, Wilson NC 27893. (252)399-6456. E-mail: tgrimes@barton.edu. Established 1964. **Editor:** Terrence L. Grimes.

Magazine Needs: *Crucible* is an annual published in November using "poetry that demonstrates originality and integrity of craftsmanship as well as thought. Traditional metrical and rhyming poems are difficult to bring off in modern poetry. The best poetry is written out of deeply felt experience which has been crafted into pleasing form. No very long narratives." Has published poetry by Robert

Grey, R.T. Smith, and Anthony S. Abbott. *Crucible* is 100 pages, digest-sized, professionally printed on high-quality paper with matte card cover. Press run is 500 for 300 subscribers of which 100 are libraries, 200 shelf sales. Sample: $7.

How to Submit: Submit 5 poems at a time between Christmas and mid-April only. No previously published poems or simultaneous submissions. Responds in up to 4 months. "We require three unsigned copies of the manuscript and a short biography including a list of publications, in case we decide to publish the work." Pays contributor's copies.

Also Offers: Send SASE for guidelines for contests (prizes of $150 and $100), and the Sam Ragan Prize ($150) in honor of the former Poet Laureate of North Carolina.

Advice: Editor leans toward free verse with attention paid particularly to image, line, stanza, and voice. However, he does not want to see poetry that is "forced."

CURBSIDE REVIEW, P.O. Box 667189, Houston TX 77266-7189. (713)529-0198. E-mail: rcastl2335@aol.com. Established 2000. **Co-Editors/Publishers:** Carolyn Adams and R.T. Castleberry.

Magazine Needs: *Curbside Review* appears monthly. "Our motto on the masthead is from W.B. Yeats: 'Our words must seem to be inevitable.' " Wants mature, crafted work in all styles and forms, "though we prefer modern free verse and prose poetry. We like intensity, dark humor, and wit." Recently published poetry by Larry D. Thomas, Robert Phillips, Lorenzo Thomas, Virgil Suarez, and Lyn Lifshin. *Curbside Review* is 4 pages, magazine-sized, copier-printed, folded. Receives about 1,200 poems/year, accepts about 20%. Publishes about 10 poems/issue. Press run is 400; all distributed free to local poetry groups and events, local independent bookstores. Single copy: free with #10 SASE.

How to Submit: Submit 5 poems at a time. Line length for poetry is 50 maximum. Accepts simultaneous submissions; no previously published poems. No fax, e-mail, or disk submissions. Cover letter is preferred. "We have a strict 'don't ask, don't tell' policy on previously published/simultaneous submissions. We read continuously throughout the year." Submit seasonal poems 4 months in advance. Time between acceptance and publication varies. Poems are circulated to an editorial board. "We often take more than one poem from writers, so publication is ongoing. Rather than reject, we often ask for revisions on promising poems." Never comments on rejected poems. Guidelines available in magazine, for SASE, or by e-mail. Responds in 3 months. Pays 2 contributor's copies. Acquires one-time rights.

Advice: "We publish *poetry* only. Since a sample copy is free, please take advantage of that to read it for a sense of our style."

CURRENT ACCOUNTS; BANK STREET WRITERS; BANK STREET WRITERS COMPETITION, 16-18 Mill Lane, Horwich, Bolton, Lancashire BL6 6AT England. Phone/fax: (01204)669858. E-mail: bswscribe@aol.com. Website: http://hometown.aol.co.uk/bswscribe/myhom epage/newsletter.html. Established 1994. **Editor:** Rod Riesco.

Magazine Needs: *Current Accounts* is a biannual publishing poetry, fiction, and nonfiction by members of Bank Street Writers and other contributors. Open to all types of poetry; maximum 100 lines. Accepts poetry written by children. Has published poetry by Pat Winslow, M.R. Peacocke, and Gerald England. *Current Accounts* is 52 pages, A5, photocopied, saddle-stapled, card cover with b&w or color photo or artwork. Receives about 300 poems/year, accepts about 5%. Press run is 50 for 3 subscribers, 30 shelf sales; 8 distributed free to competition winners. Subscription: UK £4. Sample: UK £2. Make checks payable to Bank Street Writers (sterling checks only). "No requirements, although some space is reserved for members."

How to Submit: Submit up to 6 poems at a time. Unpublished poems preferred; no simultaneous submissions. Accepts e-mail submissions in text box. Cover letter required and SAE or IRC essential for postal submissions. Guidelines available for SASE, by fax, by e-mail, and on website. Time between acceptance and publication is 6 months. Seldom comments on rejected poems. Responds in 1 month. Pays 1 contributor's copy. Acquires first rights.

Also Offers: Sponsors the annual Bank Street Writers Poetry and Short Story Competition. Submit poems up to 40 lines, any subject or style. Deadline: October 31. Entry fee: £2/poem. Entry form available for SAE and IRC. Also, the Bank Street Writers meets once a month and offers workshops, guest speakers and other activities. Write for details.

Advice: "We like originality of ideas, images, and use of language. No inspirational or religious verse unless it's also good in poetic terms."

⬭ ◎ **CURRICULUM VITAE LITERARY SUPPLEMENT; SIMPSON PUBLICATIONS (Specialized: themes, Nature/Rural/Ecology, Political, Women/Feminism)**, Grove City Factory Store, P.O. Box 1309, Grove City PA 16127. E-mail: simpub@hotmail.com. Established 1995. **Managing Editor:** Amy Dittman.
Magazine Needs: *Curriculum Vitae Literary Supplement* appears biannually in January and July and is "a thematic zine, but quality work is always welcome whether or not it applies to our current theme. We'd like to see more metrical work, especially more translations, and well-crafted narrative free verse is always welcome. However, we do not want to see rambling Bukowski-esque free verse or poetry that overly relies on sentimentality. We are a relatively new publication and focus on unknown poets." *Curriculum Vitae Literary Supplement* is 40 pages, digest-sized, photocopied, saddle-stapled, with a 2-color card stock cover. Receives about 500 poems/year, accepts about 75. Press run is 1,000 for 300 subscribers of which 7 are libraries, 200 shelf sales. Subscription: $6 (4 issues). Sample: $4.
How to Submit: Submit 3 poems at a time. "Submissions without a SASE cannot be acknowledged due to postage costs." Accepts previously published poems and simultaneous submissions. Accepts e-mail submissions (as attachment). Cover letter "to give us an idea of who you are" preferred. Time between acceptance and publication is 8 months. Poetry is circulated among 3 board members. Often comments on rejected poems. Publishes theme issues. Guidelines and upcoming themes available for SASE or by e-mail. Responds within 1 month. Pays 2 contributor's copies plus 1-year subscription.
Book/Chapbook Needs & How to Submit: Simpson Publications also publishes about 5 chapbooks/year. Interested poets should query.
Also Offers: "We are currently looking for poets who would like to be part of our Poetry Postcard series." Interested writers should query to The *CVLS* Poetry Postcard Project at the above address for more information.

⭐ ◖ **CUTBANK**, English Dept., University of Montana, Missoula MT 59812. (406)243-6156. E-mail: cutbank@selway.umt.edu. Website: www.umt.edu/cutbank. Established 1973. **Contact:** poetry editor.
Magazine Needs: *CutBank* is a biannual literary magazine which publishes regional, national and international poetry, fiction, interviews, and artwork. Has published poetry by Richard Hugo, Dara Wier, Sandra Alcosser, and Jane Hirshfield. There are about 100 pages in each issue, 25 pages of poetry. Press run is 500 for 250 subscribers of which 30% are libraries. Single copy: $6.95; subscription: $12/2 issues. Sample: $4.
How to Submit: Submit 3-5 poems at a time, single-spaced with SASE. Simultaneous submissions discouraged but accepted with notification. "We accept submissions from August 15 through March 15 only. Deadlines: Fall issue, November 15; Spring issue, March 15." Guidelines are available for SASE or by e-mail. Responds in up to 3 months. Pays 2 copies. All rights return to author upon publication.

◖ ◎ **CYCLE PRESS; INTERIM BOOKS; CAYO MAGAZINE (Specialized: regional, Florida Keys)**, 715 Baker's Lane, Key West FL 33040. Established 1968. **Contact:** Kirby Congdon.
Magazine Needs & How to Submit: *Cayo* is a biannual, irregular regional literary magazine focusing on the Florida Keys. *Cayo* is 40 pages, magazine-sized, offset printed and saddle-stapled with self-cover, includes photography. Receives about 100 poems/year, accepts approximately 20%. Press run is 1,000 for 100 subscribers, 400 shelf sales; 500 distributed free to sponsors/contributors. Single copy: $3; subscription: $16. Sample: $4. Submit 3 poems at a time. Accepts previously published poems and simultaneous submissions. Cover letter preferred. SASE required. Reads submissions July through August and October through April only. Time between acceptance and publication is 3-6 months. Poems are circulated to an editorial board. "The poetry editor finalizes his choices with the publisher and editor-in-chief." Often comments on rejected poems. Responds in 3 months. Pays 2 copies. Acquires one-time rights.
Book/Chapbook Needs: Cycle Press and Interim Books publish poems that are "contemporary in experience and thought. We concentrate on single poems, rather than more elaborate projects, for the

author to distribute as he sees fit—usually in numbered copies of 50 to 300 copies." Wants "provocative, uncertain queries; seeking resolutions rather than asserting solutions. No nineteenth century platitudes." Books are usually 6-12 pages, 5×8, computer-generated with hand-sewn binding.

How to Submit: Submit 3 poems at a time. Accepts simultaneous submissions. Cover letter preferred. "If spelling, punctuation and grammer are secondary concerns to the author. I feel the ideas and experience have to be secondary too." Time between acceptance and publication is 2 months. Often comments on rejected poems. "No requirements except a feeling of rapport with the author's stance."

Advice: "Use English correctly. Proof-read your text. Avoid forcing your statements to fit the convenience of the words; balance your ideas with what the poem is trying to tell you."

$⦿ DANA LITERARY SOCIETY ONLINE JOURNAL, P.O. Box 3362, Dana Point CA 92629-8362. Website: www.danaliterary.org. Established 2000. **Editor:** Ronald D. Hardcastle.

Magazine Needs: *Dana Literary Society Online Journal* appears monthly. Contains poetry, fiction, and nonfiction. "All styles are welcome—rhyming/metrical, free verse, and classic—but they must be well-crafted and throught-provoking. We want no pornography. Neither do we want works that consist of pointless flows of words with no apparent significance." Recently published poetry by A.B. Jacobs, C. David Hay, Raymond H.V. Gallucci, and Melvin Sandberg. *Dana Literary Society Online Journal* is equivalent to approximately 40 printed pages. Receives about 600 poems/year, accepts about 10%. Publishes about 5 poems/issue.

How to Submit: Submit up to 3 poems at a time. Line length for poetry is 120 maximum. Accepts previously published poems and simultaneous submissions. Accepts submissions by regular mail only. Time between acceptnce and publication is 3 months. Poems are selected by Society director and *Online Journal* editor. Often comments on rejected poems. Guidelines available on website. Responds in 2 weeks. Pays $25 for each poem accepted. Acquires right to display in *Online Journal* for one month.

Advice: "View the poetry on our website. We desire works that are well-crafted and thought-provoking. Neither pornography nor meaningless flows of words are welcome."

🌐 ◯ ◎ DANDELION ARTS MAGAZINE; FERN PUBLICATIONS (Specialized: membership/subscription), 24 Frosty Hollow, East Hunsbury, Northants NN4 0SY England. Fax: 01604-701730. Established 1978. **Editor/Publisher:** Mrs. Jacqueline Gonzalez-Marina M.A.

• Fern Publications subsidizes costs for their books, paying no royalties.

Magazine Needs: *Dandelion Arts Magazine*, published biannually, is "a platform for new and established poets and prose writers to be read throughout the world." Wants poetry "not longer than 35-40 lines. Modern but not wild." Does not want "bad language poetry, religious or political, nor offensive to any group of people in the world." Has published poetry by Andrew Duncan, Donald Ward, Andrew Pye, John Brander, and Gerald Denley. *Dandelion* is about 25 pages, A4, thermal binding with b&w and color illustrations, original cover design, some ads. Receives about 200-300 poems/year, accepts about 40%. Press run is up to 1,000 for about 100 subscribers of which 10% are universities and libraries, some distributed free to chosen organizations. Subscription: £12 (UK), £18 (Europe), £20 (US), £25 (ROW). Sample: half price of subscription. Make checks payable to J. Gonzalez-Marina.

How to Submit: Poets must become member-subscribers of *Dandelion Arts Magazine* and poetry club in order to be published. Submit 4-6 poems at a time. Accepts simultaneous submissions; no previously published poems. Cover letter required. "Poems must be typed out clearly and ready for publication, if possible, accompanied by a SAE or postal order to cover the cost of postage for the reply. Reads submissions any time of the year. Time between acceptance and publication is 2-6 months. "The poems are read by the editor when they arrive and a decision is taken straight away." Some constructive comments on rejected poems. Guidelines available for SASE (or SAE and IRC). Responds within 3 weeks. Reviews books of poetry. Send materials for review consideration.

Also Offers: *Dandelion* includes information on poetry competitions and art events.

Book/Chapbook Needs & How to Submit: Fern Publications is a subsidy press of artistic, poetic, and historical books and publishes 2 paperbacks/year. Books are usually 50-80 pages, A5 or A4, "thermal bound" or hand finished. Query first with 6-10 poems. Requires authors to subscribe to *Dandelion Arts Magazine*. Responds to queries and mss in 3 weeks. "All publications are published at a minimum cost agreed beforehand and paid in advance."

Advice: "Consider a theme from all angles and to explore all the possibilities, never forgetting grammar! Stay away from religious, political, or offensive issues."

$ ☑ JOHN DANIEL AND COMPANY, PUBLISHER; FITHIAN PRESS, a division of Daniel & Daniel, Publishers, Inc., P.O. Box 21922, Santa Barbara CA 93121-1922. (805)962-1780. Fax: (805)962-8835. E-mail: dandd@danielpublishing.com. Website: www.danielpublishing.com. Established 1980. Reestablished 1985.

Book/Chapbook Needs: John Daniel, a general small press publisher, specializes in literature, both prose, and poetry. "Book-length mss of any form or subject matter will be considered, but we do not want to see pornographic, libelous, illegal, or sloppily written poetry." Has published *Go Where the Landshed Takes You* by Jane Glazer, *Wafer Tender* by Mary Agnes Dalrymple, and *Signs of Life* by Kathleen Bird Metcalfe. Publishes about 4 flat-spined poetry paperbacks, averaging 80 pages, each year. Press runs average between 500-1,000. For free catalog of either imprint, send #10 SASE.

How to Submit: Send 12 sample poems and bio. Responds to queries in 2 weeks, to mss in 2 months. Accepts simultaneous submissions. No fax or e-mail submissions. Always sends prepublication galleys. Pays 10% royalties of net receipts. Acquires English-language book rights. Returns rights upon termination of contract.

Also Offers: Fithian Press books (50% of his publishing) are subsidized, the author paying production costs and receiving royalties of 60% of net receipts. Books and rights are the property of the author, but publisher agrees to warehouse and distribute for one year if desired.

Advice: "We receive over five thousand unsolicited manuscripts and query letters a year. We publish only a few books a year, of which fewer than half were received unsolicited. Obviously the odds are not with you. For this reason we encourage you to send out multiple submissions and we do not expect you to tie up your chances while waiting for our response. Also, poetry does not make money, alas. It is a labor of love for both publisher and writer. But if the love is there, the rewards are great."

★ ⊕ �ോ ◎ DARENGO; SESHAT: CROSS-CULTURAL PERSPECTIVES IN POETRY AND PHILOSOPHY (Specialized: translation), P.O. Box 9313, London E17 8XL United Kingdom. Phone/fax: (44)181-679-4150. Darengo established 1989. *Seshat* established 1997. **Editor/Proprietor:** Terence DuQuesne. **Editor:** Mark Angelo de Brito.

Magazine Needs: *Seshat*, published biannually, "provides a focus for poetry enthusiasts by publishing high-quality poems in English and in translation. It also prints prose articles which highlight connections between the poetic, the philosophical, and the spiritual. *Seshat* is committed to the view that poetry and other art-forms are vitalizing and raise consciousness and thus should not be regarded as minority interests. Poetry is not merely an aesthetic matter: it can and should help to break down the barriers of class, race, gender, age, and sexual preference. *Seshat* is named for the Egyptian goddess of sacred writing and measurement." Has published poetry by Sappho, Anthony James, Martina Evans, Ellen Zaks, and Dwina Murphy-Gibb. *Seshat* is 80 pages, offset-printed with stitched binding, laminated paper cover, includes graphics. Press run is 200. Single copy: £10 (payable in sterling only plus £5 postage outside UK); subscription: £20.

How to Submit: Submit up to 5 poems at a time. Accepts previously published poems; no simultaneous submissions. Accepts disk submissions. Cover letter required. Time between acceptance and publication is 3 months. Often comments on rejected poems. Guidelines available for SASE (or SAE and IRC). Responds in 2 weeks. Always sends prepublication galleys. Pays 1 contributor's copy, more on request. Poets retain copyright. Reviews books and chapbooks of poetry and other magazines in 1,000 words. Send materials for review consideration.

Book/Chapbook Needs & How to Submit: Darengo currently does not accept unsolicited mss.

⊘ ◎ DEAD FUN (Specialized: gothic/horror), P.O. Box 752, Royal Oak MI 48068-0752. E-mail: terror@deadfun.com. Website: www.deadfun.com. **Editoress:** Kelli.

Magazine Needs: *Dead Fun* "remains but is currently on an indefinite hiatus, therefore not accepting submissions at this time." Has published poetry by Ben Wilensky and Chris Albanese. *Dead Fun* is about 50 pages, digest-sized, photocopied and stapled with cardstock cover, includes pen and ink drawings, charcoal art, photography, as well as ads for zines, bands, and "anything relative." Sample: $3 plus $1.03 postage (inside US) or IRC. Make money orders payable to Kelli or send well-concealed cash.

How to Submit: Guidelines available for SASE, on website, or by e-mail. Responds in 6 weeks or a few days for e-mail requests. Pays 1 contributor's copy. Staff reviews books of poetry in approximately 40 words.

DEAD METAPHOR PRESS; DEAD-WALL REVIEW, P.O. Box 2076, Boulder CO 80306-2076. (303)875-5288. Established 1992. **Contact:** Richard Wilmarth.

Book/Chapbook Needs: Publishes 1-2 chapbooks of poetry and prose/year through an annual chapbook contest. "No restrictions in regard to subject matter and style." Has published poetry by John McKernan, Tracy Davis, Aimée Grunberger, Mark DuCharme, Maureen Foley, and Patrick Pritchett. Chapbooks are usually 20-80 pages, sizes differ, printed, photocopied, saddle-stapled or perfect-bound, some with illustrations. Sample: $6.

How to Submit: Submit 24 pages of poetry or prose with a bio, acknowledgments. Manuscripts are not returned. "Entries must be typed or clearly reproduced and bound only by a clip. Do not send only copy of manuscript." Accepts previously published poems and simultaneous submissions. Does not accept fax or e-mail submissions. SASE for notification. Guidelines and booklist available for SASE. **Reading fee:** $12. Deadline: October 31. Winner receives 20 copies, discounted additional copies available. For sample chapbooks, send $6.

Magazine Needs & How to Submit: *Dead-Wall Review* is a new magzine from DMP. Send poetry and fiction. No reading fee if under five pages. No guidelines."

DEBUT REVIEW, P.O. Box 266461, Kansas City MO 64126-6461. E-mail: Mikloren30@aol.com. Established 1999. **Editor:** Michael Lorenzo.

Magazine Needs & How to Submit: *Debut Review* appears annually to "showcase the work of a select few talented poets." *Debut Review* is "somewhere between 25-30 pages, printed in a somewhat informal manner, but highly professsional. I prefer one-page poems; nothing trite, unpolished or vulgar."

DECOMPOSITIONS (Specialized: horror), 4209 33rd Ave., Cincinnati OH 45209. (513)924-1512. E-mail: brosenberger@earthlink.net. Website: http://home.earthlink.net/~brosenber ger/decompositions.html. Established 2001. **Head Cheese:** Brian Rosenberger.

Magazine Needs: *Decompositions* is a monthly e-zine devoted to dark poetry with a focus on horror, psychological or graphic. "It just has to be dark. A sense of humor is also welcomed." Does not want "the literary version of *Scream* or works cursed by typos." Recently published poetry by Scott Urban, Kurt Newton, Michael Arnzen, John Lawson, Gary West, and Jarrett Keene. *Decompositions* is published online only, includes art/graphics. Receives about 100 poems/year, accepts about 60. Publishes about 5 poems/issue.

How to Submit: Submit 10 poems at a time. No line length for poetry but prefers shorter work. Accepts previously published poems and simultaneous submissions. Accepts e-mail submissions; no fax or disk submissions. Cover letter is preferred. "Reprints are OK, but I would like to know where they first appeared. Also accepts art and horror film reviews as long as the reviews are done as poems." Reads submissions year round. Submit seasonal poems 3 months in advance. Time between acceptance and publication is 2-4 months. "Either it fits what I am looking for or it doesn't. I do try to comment on all work submitted. It would be in your best interest to check out an issue before you submit." Guidelines available for SASE, by e-mail, or on website. Responds in up to 3 weeks. "No payment, only exposure." Acquires one-time rights.

DESCANT (Specialized: themes), Box 314, Station P, Toronto ON M5S 2S8 Canada. (416)593-2557. E-mail: descant@web.net. Website: www.descant.on.ca. Established 1970. **Editor-in-Chief:** Karen Mulhallen.

Magazine Needs: *Descant* is "a quarterly journal of the arts committed to being the finest in Canada. While our focus is primarily on Canadian writing we have published writers from around the world." Has published are Lorna Crozier, Eric Ormsby, and Jan Zwicky. *Descant* is 140 pages, over-sized digest format, elegantly printed and illustrated on heavy paper, flat-spined with colored, glossy cover. Receives 1,200 unsolicited submissions/year, accepts less than 100, has a 2-year back-log. Press run is 1,200. Sample: $8.50 plus postage.

How to Submit: Submit typed ms of no more than 6 poems, name and address on first page and last name on each subsequent page. Include e-mail address or SASE with Canadian stamps or SAE and IRCs. No previously published poems or simultaneous submissions. Guidelines and upcoming themes available online or for SASE (or SAE and IRC). Responds within 4 months. Pays "approximately $100." Acquires first rights.

Advice: "The best advice is to know the magazine you are submitting to. Please read the magazine before submitting."

DESCANT: FORT WORTH'S JOURNAL OF POETRY AND FICTION, English Dept., Box 297270, Texas Christian University, Fort Worth TX 76129. Fax: (817)257-6239. E-mail: descant @tcu.edu. Website: www.eng.tcu.edu/journals/descant/index.html. Established 1956. **Editor:** Dave Kuhne.

Magazine Needs: *descant* appears annually during the summer months. Wants "well-crafted poems of interest. No restrictions as to subject matter or forms. We usually accept poems 60 lines or fewer but sometimes longer poems." *descant* is more than 100 pages, digest-sized, professionally printed and bound with matte card cover. "We publish 30-40 pages of poetry per year. We receive probably 3,000 poems annually." Press run is 500 for 350 subscribers. Single issue: $12, $18 outside US. Sample: $6.

How to Submit: No simultaneous submissions. No fax or e-mail submissions. Reads submissions September through April only. Responds in 6 weeks. Pays 2 copies.

Also Offers: The Betsy Colquitt Award for poetry, $500 prize awarded annually to the best poem or series of poems by a single author in an issue. Complete contest rules and guidelines available for SASE or by e-mail.

DEVIL BLOSSOMS, P.O. Box 5122, Seabrook NJ 08302-3511. Established 1997. E-mail: theeditor@asteriuspress.com. Website: www.asteriuspress.com. **Editor:** John C. Erianne.

Magazine Needs: *Devil Blossoms* appears irregularly, 1-2 times/year, "to publish poetry in which the words show the scars of real life. Sensual poetry that's occasionally ugly. I'd rather read a poem that makes me sick than a poem without meaning." Wants poetry that is "darkly comical, ironic, visceral, horrific; or any tidbit of human experience that moves me." Does not want religious greetings, 'I'm-so-happy-to-be-alive' tree poetry. Has published poetry by M.E. Grow, John Sweet, Lisa Palmer, Joanne Lowery, and Stephen S. Nam. *Devil Blossoms* is 24 pages, 7×10, saddle-stapled, with a matte-card cover and ink drawings (cover only). Receives about 10,000 poems/year, accepts about 1%. Press run is 750, 200 shelf sales. Single copy: $5; subscription: $14. Make checks payable to John C. Erianne.

How to Submit: Submit 2-5 poems at a time. Accepts simultaneous submissions. Accepts e-mail submissions; include in body of message, no attachments. Cover letter preferred. Time between acceptance and publication is up to 6 months. "I promptly read submissions, divide them into a 'no' and a 'maybe' pile. Then I read the 'maybes' again." Seldom comments on rejected poems. Guidelines available on website. Responds in up to 2 months. Pays 1 contributor's copy. Acquires first rights.

Advice: "Write from love; don't expect love in return, don't take rejection personally and don't let anyone stop you."

DIAL BOOKS FOR YOUNG READERS (Specialized: children), 345 Hudson St., New York NY 10014. Website: www.penguinputnam.com. **Contact:** Submissions.

Book/Chapbook Needs & How to Submit: Publishes some illustrated books of poetry for children. Has published poetry by J. Patrick Lewis and Nikki Grimes. Do not submit unsolicited mss. Query first with sample poems and cover letter with brief bio and publication credits. SASE required

---

VISIT THE WRITER'S DIGEST WEBSITE at www.writersdigest.com for books, markets, newsletter sign-up, and a special poetry page.

with all correspondence. Accepts simultaneous submissions; no previously published poems. Send queries to Attn: Submissions. Responds to queries in 2-4 months. Payment varies.

🌐 Ⓜ ◎ DIALOGOS: HELLENIC STUDIES REVIEW (Specialized: Greek culture),

Dept. of Byzantine and Modern Greek Studies, King's College, Strand Campus, London WC2R 2LS England. Fax: 0044-020-7848-2830. E-mail: david.ricks@kcl.ac.uk. Website: www.frankcass.com. Established 1994. **Co-Editors:** David Ricks and Michael Trapp.

Magazine Needs: *Dialogos* is an annual of "Greek language and literature, history and archaeology, culture and thought, present and past." Wants "poems with reference to Greek or the Greek world, any period (ancient, medieval, modern), translations of Greek poetry." Does not want "holiday pictures or watery mythological musings." Has published poetry by Homer (translated by Oliver Taplin) and Nikos Engonopoulos (translated by Martin McKinsey). *Dialogos* is 150 pages, professionally printed and bound. Receives about 50 poems/year, accepts about 2%. Press run is 500 for 150 subscribers of which 100 are libraries. Sample: $45. Make checks payable to Frank Cass & Co. Ltd.

How to Submit: Submit 6 poems at a time. No previously published poems or simultaneous submissions. No e-mail or fax submissions. Time between acceptance and publication is 1 year. Poems are circulated to an editorial board of 2 editors. Seldom comments on rejected poems. Responds within 2 months. Always sends prepublication galleys. Pays 1 copy and 25 offprints. Acquires all rights. Returns rights. Reviews books of direct Greek interest, in multi-book review. Send materials for review consideration.

Ⓜ ◎ JAMES DICKEY NEWSLETTER (Specialized: membership/subscription, nature/rural/ecology),

1753 Dyson Dr., Atlanta GA 30307. Fax: (404)373-2989. E-mail: joycepair@mindspring.com. Website: www.jamesdickey.org. Established 1984. **Editor:** Joyce M. Pair.

Magazine Needs: *James Dickey Newsletter* is a biannual newsletter published in the spring and fall devoted to critical articles/studies of James Dickey's works/biography and bibliography. "Publishes a few poems of high quality. No poems lacking form or meter or grammatical correctness." Has published poetry by Linda Roth, Paula Goff, and John Van Peenen. *James Dickey Newsletter* is 30 pages of ordinary paper, neatly offset (back and front), with a card back-cover, stapled top left corner. Subscription to individuals: $12/year (includes membership in the James Dickey Society), $14 to institutions in the US; outside the US send $14/year individuals, $15.50 institutions. Sample available for $3.50 postage.

How to Submit: Contributors should follow MLA style and standard ms form, sending 1 copy, double-spaced. Cover letter required. Accepts e-mail submissions (in text box) and fax submissions. "However, if a poet wants written comments/suggestions line by line, then mail ms with SASE." Pays 3 copies. Acquires first rights. Reviews "only works on Dickey or that include Dickey."

Advice: "We accept only grammatically correct, full sentences (except rarely a telling fragment). No first person narratives."

◉ THE DIDACTIC,

11702 Webercrest, Houston TX 77048. Established 1993. **Editor:** Charlie Mainze.

Magazine Needs: *The Didactic* is a monthly publishing "only, only didactic poetry. That is the only specification. Some satire might be acceptable as long as it is didactic."

How to Submit: Accepts previously published poems and simultaneous submissions. Time between acceptance and publication is about a year. "Once it is determined that the piece is of self-evident quality and is also didactic, it is grouped with similar or contrasting pieces. This may cause a lag time for publication." Responds "as quickly as possible." Pay is "nominal." Acquires one-time rights. Considering a general review section, only using staff-written reviews. Send materials for review consideration.

N ◯ DIGRESS MAGAZINE,

4372 4th St., Riverside CA 92501. (909)218-8152. E-mail: Mable@digressonline.com. Website: http://digressonline.com. Established 2001. **Contact:** Annie Knight (Mable).

Magazine Needs: *Digress* is an art, music, and literary magazine "that promotes and celebrates independent artists and the creative process, which is felt by the editor to be just as important as the creative work produced. Past issues of *Digress* have featured beginning-to-up-and-coming authors in fiction, nonfiction, and poetry, along with reviews of art shows, band performances, CDs, books, and spoken-word events." *Digress* is 11 × 17 with a varied number of newsprint pages, includes artwork/graphics. Press run is 10,000. Sample: free for SASE.

How to Submit: Accepts previously published poems and simultaneous submissions. Accepts e-mail submissions. Cover letter is preferred. "Include brief bio with your thoughts regarding your writing process and the reason you write." Time between acceptance and publication is 3 months. Always comments on rejected poems. Guidelines available by e-mail. Responds in 2 months. Sends prepublication galleys upon request. Pays 2 contributor's copies. Acquires all rights.

Advice: "Just send it! I'm a struggling writer myself, so I understand the pain of rejection that is, unfortunately, essential to becoming a published writer."

DINER; POETRY OASIS INC., P.O. Box 60676, Greendale Station, Worcester MA 01606-2378. (508)853-4143. Website: http://spokenword.to/diner. Established 2000. **Editors:** Eve Rifkah and Abby Millager.

Magazine Needs: *Diner* appears biannually in May and October. Each issue publishes 2 feature poets. "Our taste is eclectic, ranging from traditional forms through all possibilities of style. We want to see poems that take risks, play/push language with an ear to sound." Accepts translations. Has published poetry by Gray Jacobik, Rosmarie Waldrop, Judith Hemschemeyer, and John Hodgen. *Diner* is 104 pages, digest-sized, perfect-bound, glossy card cover with photo; features b&w graphics. Publishes about 50 poems/issue. Press run is 500. Single copy: $10; subscription: $18. Sample: $8. Make checks payable to Poetry Oasis.

How to Submit: Submit no more than 5 poems. Accepts simultaneous submissions; no previously published poems. Accepts e-mail submissions from abroad only. Cover letter and SASE required. Responds in up to 6 months. Pays 1 copy. Reviews books by poets from Central New England.

Also Offers: The *Diner* Annual Poetry Contest. Send entries to the contest % Christine Cassidy, 51 Park St., Mansfield MA 02048. First place, $500; second place, $100; third place, $50; plus 3 honorable mentions. All winning poems published in Fall/Winter edition of *Diner*. "Do not list your name on submitted poems. Send a cover letter with name, address, e-mail, and titles of poems." Entry fee: $10 for 3 poems or $22 to include a 1-year subscription. Deadline: January 31. Past judges were X.J. Kennedy and Mary Ruefle.

THE DISTILLERY, Motlow State Community College, P.O. Box 88100, Lynchburg TN 37352-8500. (931)393-1700. Fax: (931)393-1761. Established 1994. **Editor:** Dawn Copeland.

Magazine Needs: *The Distillery* appears twice/year and publishes "the highest quality poetry, fiction, and criticism. We are looking for poetry that pays careful attention to line, voice, and image. We like poems that take emotional risks without giving in to easy sentimentality or staged cynicism." Has published poetry by Walter McDonald, Thomas Rabbitt, Virgil Suarez, and John Sisson. *Distillery* is 88 pages, digest-sized, professionally printed on matte paper, perfect-bound, color cover, b&w photography. Receives about 800 poems/year, accepts approximately 2%. Press run is 750. Subscription: $15/year (2 issues). Sample: $7.50.

How to Submit: Submit 4-6 poems at a time with SASE. Accepts simultaneous submissions "if poet informs us immediately of acceptance elsewhere"; no previously published poems. Cover letter preferred. Reads submissions August 15 through May 15 only. Time between acceptance and publication is 6-12 months. Poems are circulated to an editorial board. "Poems are read by three preliminary readers then passed to the poetry editor." Seldom comments on rejected poems. Guidelines available for SASE. Responds in 3 months. Pays 2 copies. Acquires first North American serial rights.

Advice: "We continue to publish the best poetry sent to us, regardless of name or reputation. We like poets who look as if they would write poems even if there were no magazines in which to publish them."

DMQ REVIEW; THE MUSES AWARD, (formerly Disquieting Muses). E-mail: editors@dmq review.com. Website: www.dmqreview.com. **Editor-in-Chief:** J.P. Dancing Bear. **Managing Editor:** C.J. Sage. **Editor:** D.E. Shephard.

Magazine Needs: *DMQ Review* appears quarterly as "a quality online magazine of poetry presented with visual art." Wants "lyricality, intriguing themes; unique, strong imagery; metaphor; and fresh, concise language over a base of smarts and discovery. We are interested in finely crafted poetry, formal or free verse." Does not want "narratives without interesting imagery or underlying musicality." Recently published poetry by Jane Hirshfield, William Logan, John Kennedy, Sidney Wade, Robley Wilson, and John Brehm. *DMQ Review* is published online; art/photography appears with the poetry. Receives about 3,000-5,000 poems/year, accepts about 1%. Publishes about 10-20 poems/ issue.

How to Submit: Submit 3 poems at a time. Accepts simultaneous submissions (with notifications only); no previously published poems. E-mail submissions only. "Paste poems in the body of an e-mail only; no attachments will be read. Please read and follow complete submissions guidelines on our website." Reads submissions year round. Time between acceptance and publication is 1-3 months. Poems circulated to an editorial board. Seldom comments on rejected poems. Responds in up to 2 months. Acquires first rights.

Also Offers: The Muses Award, an annual prize of $100 for the best poem to first appear in *DMQ Review* during the year. No entry fee or special entry process. "Our editors will select a winner from all poems first published in the magazine. To be eligible, contributors must simply adhere to all regular submission guidelines as outlined in our Guidelines page and, if using a pen name, include their legal name with the submission. Previously published poems are ineligible for the award." Also nominates 6 poems/year for the Pushcart Prize. "We also consider submissions of visual art, which we publish with the poems in the magazine with links to artists' sites."

Advice: "Send your best work. To delight is great; to instruct is fine. To surprise and dazzle with innovation, with craft, with your depth and courage to stand out in a crowd? Fantastic."

N Ø DOUBLE ROOM: A JOURNAL OF PROSE POETRY AND FLASH FICTION. E-mail: double_room@hotmail.com. Website: www.webdelsol.com/Double_Room. Established 2002. **Co-editors:** Mark Tursi, Peter Conners. Web Designer: Cactus May. Publisher: Michael Neff, Web del Sol.

Magazine Needs: *Double Room* is a biannual online literary journal devoted entirely to the publication and discussion of prose poetry and flash fiction. Each issue also features contemporary artwork. "Because we wish to create a solid dialogue regarding the pp/ff forms, we are currently only publishing work and discussion by established writers or newer writers whose work has been recommended by established writers. At this time, we do not accept open submissions. All such policy changes will be noted on our website." Recently published poetry by Cole Swensen, Rosmarie Waldrop, Nin Andrews, Sean Thomas Dougherty, Holly Iglesias, and Christopher Kennedy. *Double Room* is published online only, with art/graphics solicited by the editors. Publishes about 50 poems/issue.

How to Submit: All work is solicited by the editors. "All potential contributors are presented with submission guidelines upon first contact by the editors." Guidelines available on website. Acquires first North American serial rights. Reviews books and chapbooks of poetry. E-mail the editors for review guidelines.

Advice: "In addition to publishing the pp/ff forms, *Double Room* seeks to push them to the forefront of literary consideration by offering a Discussion On The Forms section in which contributors are asked to comment on a question related to the genre. Because we are seeking to construct a valuable resource for writers, scholars, and all interested, we are—initially, anyway—looking to publish writers who have long written and considered these forms. Thus our solicit-only submission policy. Please read, enjoy, and utilize the offerings we provide in *Double Room*, and keep an eye on our Submissions section for up-to-date changes in editorial policy."

$ ◎ DOVETAIL: A JOURNAL BY AND FOR JEWISH/CHRISTIAN FAMILIES (Specialized: interfaith marriage), 775 Simon Greenwell Lane, Boston KY 40107. (502)549-5499. Fax: (502)549-3543. E-mail: DI-IFR@Bardstown.com. Website: www.dovetailinstitute.org. Established 1991. **Editor:** Mary Rosenbaum.

Magazine Needs: *Dovetail*, published bimonthly, provides "strategies and resources for interfaith couples, their families and friends." Wants poetry related to Jewish/Christian marriage issues, no general religious themes. Has published work by Janet Landman, Donald R. Stoltz, and Eric Wolk Fried. *Dovetail* is 12-16 pages, magazine-sized, stapled, includes 1-5 ads. Receives about 10 poems/ year, accepts about 1%. Press run is 1,000 for 700 subscribers. Single copy: $5; subscription: $29.95. Make checks payable to DI-IFR.

How to Submit: Submit 1 poem at a time. Accepts previously published poems and simultaneous submissions. Accepts e-mail (in text box). Time between acceptance and publication is up to 1 year. Poems are circulated to an editorial board. "Clergy and other interfaith professionals review draft issues." Seldom comments on rejected poems. Publishes theme issues. Guidelines and upcoming themes available for SASE, by e-mail, by fax. Responds in 1 month. Pays $10-20 plus copies. Acquires first North American serial rights. Reviews other magazines in 500 words, single and multi-book format.

Advice: "We get 20 inappropriately denomination-oriented poems for every one that actually relates to interfaith marriage. Don't waste your time or ours with general Christian or 'inspirational' themes."

DREAM FANTASY INTERNATIONAL (Specialized: dreams/fantasy/horror), (formerly *Dream International Quarterly*), 809 W. Maple St., Champaign IL 61820-2810. (217)359-5056. E-mail: LLaquez3605@aol.com. Established 1981. **Editor-in-Chief/Publisher:** Charles I. (Chuck) Jones. **Senior Poetry Editor:** Carmen M. Pursifull.

Magazine Needs: "Poetry must be dream-inspired and/or dream-related. This can be interpreted loosely, even to the extent of dealing with the transitory as a theme. Nothing written expressly or primarily to advance a political or religious ideology. We have published everything from neo-Romantic sonnets to stream-of-consciousness, a la 'Beat Generation.'" Accepts poetry written by teens. Has published poetry by Carmen M. Pursifull, Professor Richard Arnold, Dr. Edward P. Fisher, Karen Jean Matsko Hood, William S. Mayo, Dr. Edward L. Smith. *Dream Fantasy International* is 120-150 pages, magazine-sized, with vellum cover and drawings. Receives 300 poems/year, accepts about 30. Press run is 300 for 20 subscribers. Subscription: $56/year, $112/2 years. Sample: $14. All orders should be addressed to Chuck Jones, Editor-in-Chief/Publisher, *Dream Fantasy International*, 411 14th St., #H-1, Ramona CA 92605-2769. All checks/money orders should be in US Funds and made payable to Charles I. Jones.

How to Submit: Submit up to 3 typed poems at a time. Accepts previously published poems and simultaneous submissions. Accepts e-mail submissions as attachments. Cover letter including publication history, if any. "As poetry submissions go through the hands of two readers, poets should enclose 2 loose stamps, along with the standard SASE." Do not submit mss in September or October. Time between acceptance and publication is up to 2 years. Comments on rejected poems if requested. Guidelines available for large SASE with 2 first-class stamps plus $2. Responds in 2 weeks. Sometimes sends prepublication galleys. Occasionally pays 1 copy, "less postage. Postage/handling for contributor's copy costs $4.50." Also, from time to time, "exceptionally fine work has been deemed to merit a complimentary copy." Acquires first North American serial or non-exclusive reprint rights.

Advice: "Avoid 'sing-song,' greeting card-type poetry. Rhyming poetry only if particularly adept and experienced with such poetry."

DREAM HORSE PRESS. E-mail: dreamhorsepress@yahoo.com. Website: www.dreamhorsepress.com. Established 1999.

● **"The press currently reads submissions that are entered in its contests ONLY. Please see website for details and instructions. Do not submit outside of contests; unsolicited submissions will be recycled unread."**

(See listing for The Dream Horse Press National Poetry Chapbook Prize in the Contests & Awards section.)

DREXEL ONLINE JOURNAL, Dept. of English & Philosophy, MacAlister Hall, Drexel University, Philadelphia PA 19104. (215)895-6469. Fax: (215)895-1071. E-mail: doj@drexel.edu. Website: www.drexel.edu/doj. Established 2001. **Poetry Editors:** Lynn Levin and Valerie Fox.

Magazine Needs: *Drexel Online Journal* is "a general interest, somewhat literary bimonthly. No limitations as to form; but if it rhymes, it should be unobtrusive (unless it is deliberately obtrusive rhyme). Recently published poetry by Barbara Daniels, Lewis Warsh, Brian Aldis, Lydia Cortes, Besnik Mustafaj, Jenn McCreary, and Michael McGoolaghan. *Drexel Online Journal* is published online. Accepts about 5% of poems received. Publishes about 5 poems/issue. Sample available free online at www.drexel.edu/doj.

How to Submit: Submit 1-6 poems at a time. Cover letter is preferred. "SASE should be included. Electronic submissions are not taken." Reads submissions year round. Submit seasonal poems 3

32 Statements About Writing Poetry (Work-in-Progress)

by Marvin Bell

1. Every poet is an experimentalist.

2. Learning to write is a simple process: read something, then write something;
read something else, then write something else.
And show in your writing what you have read.

3. There is no one way to write and no right way to write.

4. The good stuff and the bad stuff are all part of the stuff.
No good stuff without bad stuff.

5. Learn the rules, break the rules, make up new rules, break the new rules.

6. You do not learn from work like yours as much as you learn
from work unlike yours.

7. Originality is a new amalgam of influences.

8. Try to write poems at least one person in the room will hate.

9. The I in the poem is not you but someone who knows a lot about you.

10. Autobiography rots.

11. A poem listens to itself as it goes.

12. It's not what one begins with that matters;
it's the quality of attention paid to it thereafter.

13. Language is subjective and relative, but it also overlaps; get on with it.

14. Every free verse writer must reinvent free verse.

15. Prose is prose because of what it includes;
poetry is poetry because of what it leaves out.

16. A short poem need not be small.

17. Rhyme and meter, too, can be experimental.

18. Poetry has content but is not strictly about its contents.
A poem containing a tree may not be about a tree.

19. You need nothing more to write poems than bits of string and thread
and some dust from under the bed.

20. At heart, poetic beauty is tautological: it defines its terms and exhausts them.

21. The penalty for education is self-consciousness. But it is too late for ignorance.

22. What they say "there are no words for"—that's what poetry is for.
Poetry uses words to go beyond words.

23. One does not learn by having a teacher do the work.

24. The dictionary is beautiful; for some poets, it's enough.

25. Writing poetry is its own reward and needs no certification.
Poetry, like water, seeks its own level.

26. A finished poem is also the draft of a later poem.

27. A poet sees the differences between his or her poems
but a reader sees the similarities.

28. Poetry is a manifestation of more important things. On the one hand, it's poetry!
On the other, it's just poetry.

29. Viewed in perspective, Parnassus is a very short mountain.

30. A good workshop continually signals that we are all in this together, teacher too.

31. This Depression-Era jingle could be about writing poetry:
Use it up / wear it out / make it do / or do without.

32. Art is a way of life, not a career.

months in advance. Time between acceptance and publication is 2 months. Poems are circulated to an editorial board. "We currently have two readers who go by consensus." Often comments on rejected poems. Guidelines available on website. Responds in 6 weeks. Pay varies. Acquires first rights. Reviews books of poetry. Send materials for review consideration to Book Editor, *Drexel Online Journal*, Dept. of English and Philosophy, MacAlister Hall, Drexel University, Philadelphia PA 19104.

Advice: "We like original work. Read widely."

THE DRIFTWOOD REVIEW (Specialized: regional, Michigan), P.O. Box 2042, Bay City MI 48707. Established 1996. **Poetry Editor:** Jeff Vande Zande.

Magazine Needs: "An annual publication, *The Driftwood Review* strives to publish the best poetry and fiction being written by Michigan writers—known and unknown. We consider any style, but are particularly fond of poetry that conveys meaning through image. Rhyming poetry stands a poor chance." Has published poetry by Daniel James Sundahl, Danny Rendleman, Anca Vlasopolos, Terry Blackhawk, and Linda Nemec Foster. *The Driftwood Review* is 100-125 pages, digest-sized, professionally-printed, perfect-bound with glossy card cover containing b&w artwork. Receives about 500 poems/year, accepts about 5-7%. Press run is 200 for 75 subscribers. Subscription: $6.

How to Submit: Submit 3-5 poems at a time. No previously published poems or simultaneous submissions. Cover letter preferred. "Cover letter should include a brief bio suitable for contributors notes. No SASE? No reply." Reads submissions January 1 through September 15 only. Time between acceptance and publication is 9 months. Seldom comments on rejected poems. "Will comment on work that's almost there." Responds in 3 months. Pays 1 copy and includes the opportunity to advertize a book. Acquires first North American serial rights. Staff reviews chapbooks of poetry by Michigan writers only in 500 words, single book format. Send chapbooks for review consideration.

Also Offers: Sponsors an Editor's Choice Award.

Advice: "Strive to express what you have to say with image."

DWAN (Specialized: gay/lesbian/bisexual), Box 411, Swarthmore PA 19081-0411. E-mail: dwanzine@hotmail.com. Website: www.geocities.com/dwanzine/. Established 1993. **Editor:** Donny Smith.

Magazine Needs: Published every 2 to 3 months, *Dwan* is a "queer poetry zine; some prose; some issues devoted to a single poet or a single theme ('Jesus' or 'Mom and Dad,' for instance)." Wants "poetry exploring gender, sexuality, sex roles, identity, queer politics, etc. Heterosexuals usually welcome." Accepts translations and poetry in Spanish. Has published poetry by Melanie Hemphill, Susana Cattaneo, and Fabián Iriarte. *Dwan* is 20 pages, digest-sized, photocopied on plain white paper, and stapled. Receives 400-500 pages of poetry/year, accepts less than 10%. Press run is 100. Sample available for $2 (free to prisoners). Make checks payable to Donny Smith.

How to Submit: Submit 5-15 poems typed. Accepts previously published poems and simultaneous submissions. Accepts e-mail submissions, "no attachments." Cover letter required. Time between acceptance and publication is 6-18 months. Often comments on rejected poems. Guidelines available on website. Responds in 3 months. Pays copies. The editor reviews books, chapbooks, and magazines usually in 25-150 words. Send materials for review consideration.

Advice: "Be honest in your writing. Work hard. Read a lot."

ÉCRITS DES FORGES; ESTUAIRE; ARCADE (Specialized: women only); EXIT (All Specialized: foreign language, French), 1497 Laviolette, Trois-Rivières QC G9A 5G4 Canada. (819)379-9813. Fax: (819)376-0774. E-mail: ecrits.desforges@tr.cgocable.ca. Established 1971. **Président:** Gaston Bellemare. **Directrice Générale:** Maryse Baribeau.

Magazine Needs: Écrits des Forges publishes 3 poetry journals each year: *Estuaire* appears 5 times/year and wants poetry from well-known poets; *Exit* appears 4 times/year and wants poetry from beginning poets; and *Arcade* appears 3 times/year and wants poetry from women only. All three publications only accept work in French. Wants poetry that is "authentic and original as a signature." "We have published poetry from more than a thousand poets coming from most of the francophone's countries: André Romus (Belgium), Amadou Lamine Sall (Sénégal), Nicole Brossard, Claudine Bertrand, Denise Brassard, Tony Tremblay, and Jean-Paul Daoust (Québec)." The 3 journals are 88-108 pages, digest-sized, perfect-bound with art on cover, includes ads from poetry publishers. Receives more than 1,000 poems/year, accepts less than 5%. Press run for *Estuaire* is 750 for 450 subscribers of which 250 are libraries. Press run for *Arcade* is 650 for 375 subscribers of which 260 are libraries. Press run for *Exit* is 500 for 110 subscribers of which 235 are libraries. Subscription for *Estuaire* is $45 plus p&h; for *Arcade* is $27 plus p&h; for *Exit* is $36 plus p&h. Samples: $10 each. For *Exit* make checks payable to Éditions Gaz Moutarde. For *Estuaire* and *Arcade*, make checks payable to the respective publication.

How to Submit: Submit 10 poems at a time. No previously published poems or simultaneous submissions. "We make decisions on submissions in February, May, September, and December." Time between acceptance and publication is 3-12 months. Poems are circulated to an editorial board. "Nine persons read the submissions and send their recommendations to the editorial board." *Arcade* publishes theme issues. Upcoming themes are listed in the journal. Guidelines available by e-mail. Responds in 5 months. Pays "10% of the market price based on number of copies sold." Acquires all rights for 1 year. Retains rights to reprint in anthology for 10 years. Staff reviews books and chapbooks of poetry and other magazines on 1 page, double-spaced, single book format. Send materials for review consideration.

Book/Chapbook Needs & How to Submit: Écrits des Forges inc. publishes poetry only—40-50 paperbacks/year. Books are usually 80-88 pages, digest-sized, perfect-bound with 2-color cover with art. Query first with a few sample poems and cover letter with brief bio and publication credits. Responds to queries in 3-6 months. Pays royalties of 10-20%, advance of 50% maximum, and 25 author's copies. Order sample books by writing or faxing.

Also Offers: Sponsors the International Poetry Festival/Festival international de la poésie. "150 poets from 30 countries based on the 5 continents read their poems over 10-day period in 70 different cafés, bars, restaurants, etc. 30,000 persons attend. All in French." For more information, see website: www.fiptr.com.

⊘ EDGEWISE PRESS, INC., 24 Fifth Ave., #224, New York NY 10011. (212)982-4818. Fax: (212)982-1364. E-mail: epinc@mindspring.com. Website: www.edgewise.com. **Editor:** Richard Milazzo. Has published Mary de Rachewiltz, Alan Jones, Cid Corman, and Nanni Cagnone. Order sample books by sending $10, plus $2 p&h. Currently closed to all submissions.

⊘ EDGZ, Edge Publications, P.O. Box 799, Ocean Park WA 98640. Established 2000. **Publisher/Editor:** Blaine R. Hammond.

Magazine Needs: *Edgz* appears semiannually in March and September and publishes "poetry of all sorts of styles and schools. Our purpose is to present poetry with transpersonal intentions or applications and to put poets on a page next to other poets they are not used to appearing next to." Wants "a broad variety of styles with a transpersonal intent. *Edgz* has two main reasons for existence: My weariness with the attitude that whatever kind of poetry someone likes is the only legitimate poetry; and my desire to present poetry addressing large issues of life: meaning; oppression; exaltation; and whatever else you can think of. Must be engaged; intensity helps." Does not want "anything with a solely personal purpose; dense language poetry, which I'm not good at; poetry that does not take care with the basics of language, or displays an ignorance of modern poetry. No clichés, gushing, sentimentalism, or lists of emotions. Nothing vague or abstract. No light verse, but humor is fine" Accepts poetry by children; "I do not have a children's section, but do not discriminate by age." Has published poetry by David Small Bird, David Campiche, Randy Fingland, Naomi Ruth Lowinski, Patricia Ann Treat, and Ruth Moon Kempher. *Edgz* is digest-sized, laser-printed, saddle-stapled or perfect-bound (depends on number of pages), 94 lb. card stock cover with art/graphics (not comix). Printed on paper "made of no virgin wood fibers." 2003 prices are single copy: $7; subscription: $13 (2 issues). Sample: $3.50 when available. Make checks payable to Edge Publications.

How to Submit: Submit 3-5 poems at a time; "a longer poem may be submitted by itself." No limits on line length. Accepts simultaneous submissions; no previously published poems. Accepts submissions by postal mail only. "I don't mind more than one poem to a page or well-traveled submissions; these are ecologically sound practices. I like recycled paper. Submissions without SASE will be gratefully used as note paper. Handwritten OK if poor or incarcerated." Reads submissions all year. Deadlines: February 1 and August 1 for winter and summer issues. Time between acceptance and publication is 1-6 months. Often comments on rejections "as I feel like it. I don't provide criticism

services." Guidelines available for SASE. Responds in up to 6 months. Pays 1 copy per published piece with discounts on additional copies. Acquires first rights plus anthology rights ("just in case").
Advice: "It is one thing to require subscriptions in order to be published. It is something else to charge reading fees. In a world that considers poetry valueless, reading fees say it is less than value-less—editors should be compensated for being exposed to it. I beg such editors to cease the practice. I advise everyone else not to submit to them, or the practice will spread. My most common rejection note is 'to personal for my thematic focus.' "

EIDOS: SEXUAL FREEDOM & EROTIC ENTERTAINMENT FOR CONSENTING ADULTS (Specialized: erotica), P.O. Box 990095, Boston MA 02199-0095. E-mail: eidos@eidos .org. Website: www.eidos.org. Established 1982. **Poetry Editor:** Brenda Loew.
Magazine Needs: "Our website publishes erotic literature, poetry, photography, and artwork. Our purpose is to provide an alternative to women's images and male images and sexuality depicted in mainstream publications like *Playboy, Penthouse, Playgirl,* etc. We provide a forum for the discussion and examination of two highly personalized dimensions of human sexuality: desire and satisfaction. We do not want to see angry poetry or poetry that is demeaning to either men or women. We like experimental, avant-garde material that makes a personal, political, cultural statement about mutually respectful eroticism and sexuality." Has published poetry by Nancy Young, Miriam Carroll, Linwood M. Ross, Ann Tweedy, and Mona J. Perkins. *Eidos* is now publishing online only. Receives hundreds of poems/year, accepts approximately 10-20.
How to Submit: Only accepts sexually-explicit erotic material. Length for poetry is 1-page maxi-mum, format flexible. Must be 18 or over; age statement required. Accepts simultaneous submissions; no previously published poems. "Poets must submit their work e-mail." Publishes bio information as space permits. Comment or criticism provided as often as possible. Acquires first North American serial rights.
Advice: "There is so much poetry submitted for consideration that a rejection can sometimes mean a poet's timing was poor. We let poets know if the submission was appropriate for our publication and suggest they resubmit at a later date. Keep writing, keep submitting, keep a positive attitude."

$ THE EIGHTH MOUNTAIN PRESS, 624 SE 29th Ave., Portland OR 97214. E-mail: eighthmt@pacifier.com. Established 1985. **Editor:** Ruth Gundle.
Book/Chapbook Needs: Eighth Mountain is a "small press publisher of literary works by women." Has published poetry by Lucinda Roy, Maureen Seaton, Irena Klepfisz, Almitra David, Judith Bar-rington, and Elizabeth Woody. Publishes 1 book of poetry averaging 128 pages every few years. "Our books are handsomely designed and printed on acid-free paper in both quality trade paperbacks and library editions." Initial press run for poetry is 2,500.
How to Submit: "We expect to receive a query letter along with a few poems. A résumé of published work, if any, should be included. Work should be typed, double-spaced, and with your name on each page. If you want to know if your work has been received, enclose a separate, stamped postcard." Accepts submissions by postal mail and by e-mail (in text box). Responds within 6 weeks. SASE (#10 envelope) must be included for response. "Full postage must be included if return of the work submitted is desired." Pays 7-8% royalties. Acquires all rights. Returns rights if book goes out of print.

88: A JOURNAL OF CONTEMPORARY AMERICAN POETRY, % Hollyridge Press, P. O. Box 2872, Venice CA 90294. (310)712-1238. Fax: (310)828-4860. E-mail: T88AJournal@aol.c om. Website: www.hollyridgepress.com. Established 1999. **Managing Editor:** Ian Wilson. Member: PMA.
Magazine Needs: *88: A Journal of Contemporary American Poetry* appears annually, includes essays on poetry and poetics, also reviews. Wants mainstream, lyric, lyric narrative, prose poems, experimental. "Will consider work that incorporates elements of humor, elements of surrealism. No light verse, limericks, children's poetry." *88* is 176 pages, digest-sized, printed on-demand, perfect-bound, 4-color soft cover, with very limited art/graphics, ads. Publishes about 80 poems/issue. Single copy: $13.95.
How to Submit: Submit 5 poems at a time. No previously published poems or simultaneous submis-sions. No fax, e-mail, or disk submissions. Cover letter is required. Poems should be typed, single

spaced on one side, indicate stanza breaks if poem is longer than one page. Name and address should appear on every page. "Unsolicited submissions accompanied by a proof-of-purchase coupon clipped from the back of the journal are read year round. Without proof-of-purchase, unsolicited submissions are considered March 1 through May 31 only. Unsolicited submissions received outside these guidelines will be returned unread. Submissions sent without SASE will be discarded." Time between acceptance and publication is up to 9 months. "Managing editor has the final decision of inclusion, but every poem is considered by an editorial board consisting of contributing editors whose suggestions weigh heavily in the process." Guidelines available in magazine, on website, and for SASE. Responds in up to 6 months. Sometimes sends prepublication galleys. Pays 1 copy. Acquires one-time rights. Reviews books of poetry in 500-1,000 words, single book and multi-book format. Send materials for review consideration to Ian Wilson, managing editor. Also accepts essays on poetics and contemporary American poetry and poets, 5,000 words maximum.

Advice: "We believe it's important for poets to support the journals to which they submit. Because of print-on-demand, *88* is always available. We recommend becoming familiar with the journal before submitting."

EKPHRASIS (Specialized: ekphrastic verse); FRITH PRESS; OPEN POETRY CHAPBOOK COMPETITION, P.O. Box 161236, Sacramento CA 95816-1236. E-mail: frithpress @aol.com. Website: www.hometown.aol.com/ekphrasis1. *Ekphrasis* established Summer 1997, Frith Press 1995. **Editors:** Laverne Frith and Carol Frith.

• David Hamilton's "The Least Hinge" was winner of the 2002 Open Poetry Chapbook Competition. "Poems from *Ekphrasis* have been featured in *Poetry Daily*."

Magazine Needs: *Ekphrasis*, appearing in March and September, is a biannual "outlet for the growing body of poetry focusing on individual works from any artistic genre." Wants "poetry whose main content is based on individual works from any artistic genre. Poetry should transcend mere description. Form open. No poetry without ekphrastic focus. No poorly crafted work. No archaic language." Nominates for Pushcart Prize. Has published poetry by Jeffrey Levine, Peter Meinke, David Hamilton, Barbara Lefcowitz, Joseph Stanton, and Anne Finch. *Ekphrasis* is 40-50 pages, digest-sized, photocopied and saddle-stapled. Subscription: $12/year. Sample: $6. Make checks payable, in US funds, to Laverne Frith.

How to Submit: Submit 3-7 poems at a time with SASE. Accepts previously published poems "infrequently, must be credited"; no simultaneous submissions. Accepts submissions by postal mail only. Cover letter required including short bio with representative credits and phone number. Time between acceptance and publication is up to 1 year. Seldom comments on rejected poems. Guidelines available for SASE and on website. Responds in 4 months. Pays 1 copy. Acquires first North American serial or one-time rights.

Book/Chapbook Needs & How to Submit: Frith Press publishes well-crafted poems—all subjects and forms considered—through their annual Open Poetry Chapbook Competition. Submit 16-24 pages of poetry with **$10 reading fee** (US funds). Include cover sheet with poet's name, address, phone number, and e-mail. Previously published poems must be credited. "No poems pending publication elsewhere." Deadline: October 31. Winner receives $100, publication, and 50 copies of their chapbook.

Advice: "With the focus on ekphrastic verse, we are bringing attention to the interconnections between various artistic genres and dramatizing the importance and universality of language. Study in the humanities is essential background preparation for the understanding of these interrelations."

ELECTRIC VELOCIPEDE (Specialized: science fiction), P.O. Box 421, South Bound Brook NJ 08880. E-mail: evzine@aol.com. Website: http://members.aol.com/evzine. Established 2001. **Editor:** John Klima.

Magazine Needs: *Electric Velocipede* appears biannually as a "small science fiction zine in the

---

THE ◎ **SYMBOL** indicates a market with a specific or unique focus. This specialized area of interest is listed in parentheses behind the market title.

steampunk tradition" featuring short fiction and poetry. "Looking for things in the style of Jeffrey Ford, China Mieville, Jeff VanderMeer, Alex Irvine, and Paul DiFillippo." Does not want overly graphic violence or sexuality; "no unicorns." Recently published poetry by Norman Partridge, B.A. Chepaitis, Steve Sawicki, Kevin L. Donihe, Christina Sng, and Jonathan Brandt. *Electric Velocipede* is 36 pages, "direct to printer at copier from computer files," stapled, cardstock cover (110 lb.) with "usually found art," includes some design elements for each story/poem, ads for other small press publishers. Receives about 30 poems/year, accepts about 50% ("a lot of what I have is solicited"). Publishes about 8 poems/issue. Single copy: $3; subscription: $10 for 4 issues. Make checks payable to John Klima.

How to Submit: Submit up to 5 poems at a time. Line length for poetry is 50 maximum. Accepts previously published poems and simultaneous submissions. Accepts e-mail submissions; no fax or disk submissions. Cover letter is preferred. Reads submissions year round. Submit seasonal poems 6 months in advance. Time between acceptance and publication is 6 months. "I read the poems. I publish what I like." Often comments on rejected poems. Guidelines available in magazine, for SASE, by e-mail, or on website. Responds in 3 months. Pays 5 contributor's copies. Acquires one-time rights "with permission to place poem on website for 6 months. This is not a condition for publication, rather a request I make of the author. If they don't want to, they're still in the issue, they're just not online." Poets may send materials for review consideration to John Klima. "I have not done a poetry review, but since I do all the reviews, it's not out of the question. I try to do theme reviews, but sometimes the topic isn't there for me, so I review something I've had a strong reaction to that I've recently read."

Advice: "Either read previous issues or look online at what's been posted there."

$☑ ELLIPSIS MAGAZINE, Westminster College of Salt Lake City, 1840 S. 1300 East, Salt Lake City UT 84105. (801)832-2321. E-mail: Ellipsis@westminstercollege.edu. Website: www.west minstercollege.edu/ellipsis. Established 1967. **Faculty Advisor:** Natasha Sajé. **Contact:** Poetry Editor (rotating editors).

Magazine Needs: *Ellipsis* is an annual appearing in April. Needs "good literary poetry, fiction, essays, plays, and visual art." Has published work by Allison Joseph, Molly McQuade, Virgil Suarez, Maurice Kilwein-Guevara, Richard Cecil, and Ron Carlson. *Ellipsis* is 120 pages, digest-sized, perfect-bound, with color cover. Press run is 2,000 with most copies distributed free through college. Sample: $7.50.

How to Submit: Submit 3-5 poems or prose to 3,000 words. No previously published submissions. No fax or e-mail submissions. Accepts simultaneous submissions if notified of acceptance elsewhere. Include SASE and brief bio. Reads submissions August 1 to November 1. Responds in up to 5 months. Pays $10/poem, plus 1 copy.

Also Offers: "All accepted poems are eligible for the *Ellipsis* Award which includes a $100 prize. Past judges have included Jorie Graham, Sandra Cisneros, Phillip Levine, and Stanley Plumly." Also, Westminster College hosts Writers@Work, an annual literary conference, which sponsors a fellowship competition and features distinguished faculty. (See separate listing for Writers@Work in the Conferences & Workshops section).

▨ ☑ EMPLOI PLUS; DGR PUBLICATION, 1256 Principale N. St. #203, L'Annonciation QC J0T 1T0 Canada. Phone/fax: (819)275-3293. Established 1988 (DGR Publication), 1990 (*Emploi Plus*). **Publisher:** Daniel G. Reid.

Magazine Needs: *Emploi Plus*, published irregularly, features poems and articles in French or English. Has published poetry by Robert Ott. Recently published *Alexiville, Planet Earth* by D.G. Reid. *Emploi Plus* is 12 pages, 7 × 8½, photocopied, stapled, with b&w drawings, and pictures, no ads. Press run is 500 distributed free. Sample: free.

How to Submit: *Does not accept unsolicited submissions.*

$☑ EMRYS JOURNAL, P.O. Box 8813, Greenville SC 29604. Website: www.emrys.org. Established 1982. **Editor:** Jeanine Halva-Neubauer. **Contact:** Poetry Editor.

Magazine Needs: *Emrys Journal* is an annual appearing in April. Publishes "the accessible poem over the fashionably sophisticated, the touching dramatic or narrative poem over the elaborately meditative, the humorous poem over the ponderously significant, the modest poem over the showily learned." Has published poetry by Kristin Berkey-Abbott, Adriano Scopino, John Popielaski, J. Morris, and Terri McCord. *Emrys Journal* is up to 120 pages, digest-sized, handsomely printed, flat-spined. Press run is 400 for 250 subscribers of which 10 are libraries. "About 10 poems are selected for inclusion." Single copy: $12.

How to Submit: Submit up to 5 poems, no more than 25 pages total. Include SASE. No previously published poetry. Reads submissions August 15 through December 1, 2003 only. Accepts submissions by postal mail only. Time between acceptance and publication is up to 8 months. Guidelines available for SASE, on website, and in publication. Responds in 6 weeks. Pays $25/published poem and 5 copies.

ENITHARMON PRESS, 26B Caversham Rd., London NW5 2DU United Kingdom. Phone: (20)7482 5967. Fax: (20)7284 1787. E-mail: books@enitharmon.co.uk. Established 1967. **Poetry Editor:** Stephen Stuart-Smith.

Book/Chapbook Needs: Enitharmon is a publisher of fine editions of poetry and literary criticism in paperback and some hardback editions, about 15 volumes/year averaging 100 pages. Has published books of poetry by John Heath-Stubbs, Ted Hughes, David Gascoyne, Thom Gunn, Ruth Pitter, and Anthony Thwaite.

How to Submit: "Substantial backlog of titles to produce, so no submissions possible before 2006."

EOTU EZINE OF FICTION, ART & POETRY; CLAM CITY PUBLICATIONS, 2102 Hartman, Boise ID 83704. (208)322-3408. E-mail: editor@clamcity.com for inquiries; submissions@clamcity.com for poetry submissions. Website: www.clamcity.com/eotu.html. Established 2000 online; started as print zine in late 1980s. **Contact:** Larry Dennis.

Magazine Needs: *EOTU Ezine* appears bimonthly online, specializing in fiction, art, and poetry. "All fiction, art, and poetry needs to be published to have meaning. We do what we can to make that happen. We are open to all genres, though we tend toward literary and speculative work, science fiction, fantasy, and horror because that's where the editor's tastes lie. Since we are not funded by advertising or subscription sales, we aren't really audience driven. Each issue is a reflection of what the editor is into at the time. We are more an artistic endeavor than a business." Recently published poetry by Stephanie Scarborough, Delores Fleming, Barbara J. Petoskey, and Scott E. Green. "Present circulation is about 10,000 page views per issue."

How to Submit: Line length for poetry is 30 maximum. Accepts previously published poems; no simultaneous submissions. Accepts e-mail submissions. Send in body of e-mail message with no formatting; put title of work, "poem," or "poetry submission" in subject line. Include brief bio. Seldom comments on rejected poems. Occasionally publishes theme issues. "We have been known to do theme issues, but they aren't usually decided upon until 2-4 months before publication. Writers should check our guidelines page on the website for current themes." Guidelines available on website. Responds in up to 3 months. Pays $5/poem. Acquires one-time online rights; when a poem is published in an issue, it will remain in the current issue for 2 months and then archived.

Advice: "As far as we have been able to tell through our years of zine publishing, there are only two tips a beginning writer must follow to succeed: 1) Read a few issues of any magazine you are thinking of sending work to; and 2) read and follow submission guidelines. If you do only these two things, you will go far."

EPICENTER, P.O. Box 367, Riverside CA 92502. E-mail: poetry@epicentermagazine.org. Website: www.epicentermagazine.org. Established 1994. **Contact:** Rowena Silver.

Magazine Needs: *Epicenter* is a biannual poetry and short story forum open to all styles. "*Epicenter* is looking for ground-breaking poetry, essays, and short stories from new and established writers. No angst-ridden, sentimental, or earthquake poetry. We are not adverse to graphic images if the work is well presented and contains literary merit." Has published poetry by Doug Shy, Virgil Suarez, Lon Risley, Max Berkovitz, Stan Nemeth, and Vicki Solheid. *Epicenter* is 44 pages, digest-sized, and saddle-stapled with semi-glossy paper cover and b&w graphics. Receives about 1,000 submissions/year, accepts about 5%. Press run is 400 for 250 shelf sales. Single copy: $5. Sample: $5.75. Make checks payable to Rowena Silver.

How to Submit: Submit up to 5 poems. Include SASE with sufficient postage for return of materials. Accepts previously published poems and simultaneous submissions. Accepts e-mail submissions (as attachment or in e-mail). Seldom comments on rejected poems. Guidelines available for SASE, by e-mail, on website, in publication. Pays 1 copy. Acquires one-time and electronic rights.

$ ✉ EPOCH, 251 Goldwin Smith, Cornell University, Ithaca NY 14853. (607)255-3385. Website: www.arts.cornell.edu/english/epoch.html. Established 1947. **Editor:** Michael Koch. **Poetry Editor:** Nancy Vieira Couto.

Magazine Needs: *Epoch* has a distinguished and long record of publishing exceptionally fine poetry and fiction. Has published work by such poets as John Bensko, Jim Daniels, Allison Joseph, Maxine Kumin, Heather McHugh, and Kevin Prufer. *Epoch* appears 3 times/year in a digest-sized, professionally printed, flat-spined format with glossy color cover, 128 pages, which goes to 1,000 subscribers. Accepts less than 1% of the many submissions received each year. Sample: $5. Subscription: $11/year domestic, $15/year foreign.

How to Submit: No simultaneous submissions. Reads submissions between September 15 and April 21. Responds in up to 10 weeks. Occasionally provides criticism on mss. Pays 3 copies and $5-10/page. "We pay more when we have more!" Acquires first serial rights.

✪ ◯ ETHEREAL GREEN, 5753 Ridgeway Dr. #3, Haslett MI 48840. E-mail: etherealgreen2@at tbi.com. Established 1996. **Contact:** Sarah Hencsie.

Magazine Needs: *Ethereal Green*, published in June and December, strives "to feed readers unknown talent." Contains poetry and art. Wants "Shakespearian, nature, and children's poetry. Poems should be less than 30 lines." Does not want "religious, ethnic, or edited poems." *Ethereal Green* is 10-20 pages, approximately digest-sized, with cover art. Receives hundreds of poems/year, accepts about 50%. Press run is 200 for about 60 subscribers, 60% shelf sales. Subscription: $30. Sample: $7. Make checks payable to Sarah C. Hencsie.

How to Submit: Submit 3-7 typed poems at a time. SASE absolutely required. Accepts previously published poems and simultaneous submissions. Accepts e-mail submissions (no attachments). Cover letter required; "if no cover letter is submitted, submission will be automatically rejected." **Reading fee:** $1/poem. Time between acceptance and publication is 3-10 months. Poems are circulated to an editorial board with "poems edited twice; once by publisher and again by select editors on board." Always comments on rejected poems. Guidelines available for SASE and by e-mail. Responds in 4 months. Sometimes sends prepublication galleys. Pays 1 copy. Acquires first North American serial or one-time rights.

⊕ ◔ ◎ EUROPEAN JUDAISM (Specialized: religious, ethnic), Kent House, Rutland Gardens, London SW7 1BX England. Established 1966. **Poetry Editor:** Ruth Fainlight.

Magazine Needs: *European Judaism* is a "twice-yearly magazine with emphasis on European Jewish theology/philosophy/literature/history, with some poetry in every issue. It should preferably be short and have some relevance to matters of Jewish interest." Has published poetry by Linda Pastan, Elaine Feinstein, Daniel Weissbort, and Dannie Abse. *European Judaism* is a glossy, elegant, digest-sized, flat-spined magazine, rarely art or graphics, 110 pages Has a press run of 950, about 50% of which goes to subscribers (few libraries). Subscription: $27.

How to Submit: Submit 3-4 poems at a time. No material dealt with or returned if not accompanied by SASE (or SAE with IRCs). "We cannot use American stamps. Also, I prefer unpublished poems, but poems from published books are acceptable." Cover letter required. Pays 1 copy.

$ ✉ ◎ EVANGEL; LIGHT AND LIFE COMMUNICATIONS (Specialized: religious, Christian), P.O. Box 535002, Indianapolis IN 46253-5002. Established 1897. **Editor:** J. Innes.

Magazine Needs: *Evangel* is a weekly adult Sunday school paper. "Devotional in nature, it lifts up Christ as the source of salvation and hope. The mission of *Evangel* is to increase the reader's understanding of the nature and character of God and the nature of a life lived for Christ. Material that fits this mission that isn't more than one page will be considered." No rhyming work. *Evangel* is 8 pages, digest-sized (2 8½×11 sheets folded), printed in 4 color and unbound with photos and graphics used. Accepts approximately 5% of poetry received. Press run is approximately 20,000 for 19,000 subscribers. Subscription: $2.25/quarter (13 weeks).

How to Submit: Submit no more than 5 poems at a time. Accepts simultaneous submissions. Cover letter preferred. Seldom comments on rejected poems. "Poetry must be typed on 8½×11 inch white paper. In the upper left-hand corner of each page, include your name, address, phone number, and social security number. In the upper right-hand corner of cover page, specify what rights you are offering. One-eighth of the way down the page, give the title. All subsequent material must be double-spaced, one-inch margins." Submit seasonal material one year in advance. Guidelines and sample available for #10 SASE; "write 'guidelines request' on your envelope so we can sort it from the submissions." Responds in up to 2 months. Pays $10 plus 2 copies on publication. Acquires one-time rights.

Advice: "Poetry is used primarily as filler. Send for sample and guidelines to better understand what and who the audience is."

THE EVANSVILLE REVIEW, 1800 Lincoln Ave., Evansville IN 47722. Phone/fax: (812)488-1042. Established 1989. **Editor:** Jacqueline Musser and Elisabeth Meyer. **Contact:** Caroline Cuervo.
- Poetry published in *The Evansville Review* has been included in *Best American Poetry* (2001) and the *Pushcart Prize* anthology (2002).

Magazine Needs: *The Evansville Review* appears annually in April and publishes "prose, poems and drama of literary merit." Wants "anything of quality." No experimental work or erotica. Has published poetry by John Updike, Willis Barnstone, Vivian Shipley, Robert Bly, and Tess Galagher. *The Evansville Review* is 200 pages, digest-sized, perfect-bound, includes art on cover only. Receives about 1,000 poems/year, accepts approximately 2%. Publish 45 poems/issue. Press run is 3,000; all distributed free to students and attendees at conferences. Sample: $5 for 1, $8 for 2, $10 for 3.

How to Submit: Submit 5 poems at a time. Accepts previously published poems and simultaneous submissions. Cover letter required. Include SASE for reply for return and brief bio. Reads submissions September 1 through December 10 only. Time between acceptance and publication is 3 months. Poems are circulated to an editorial board. Seldom comments on rejected poems. Guidelines available for SASE. Responds in 5 months. Pays 2 copies. Rights remain with poet. "We are not copywritten."

Also Offers: "2003 is the first year for the Willis Barnstone translation prize. *The Evansville Review* will award $500 to the best translation of a poem. Entry fee is $5 per poem." 2003 Judge: Willis Barnstone.

EVENT, Douglas College, P.O. Box 2503, New Westminster BC V3L 5B2 Canada. (604)527-5293. Fax: (604)527-5095. E-mail: event@douglas.bc.ca. Website: http://event.douglas.bc.ca. Established 1971. **Poetry Editor:** Gillian Harding-Russell.

Magazine Needs: *Event* appears 3 times/year and is "a literary magazine publishing high-quality contemporary poetry, short stories, creative nonfiction, and reviews. In poetry, we tend to appreciate the narrative and sometimes the confessional modes. In any case, we are eclectic and always open to content that invites involvement. We publish mostly Canadian writers." Has published poetry by Tom Wayman, Lorna Crozier, Russell Thornton, Don McKay, A.F. Moritz, Marlene Cookshaw, and Tim Bowling. *Event* is 136 pages, digest-sized, finely printed and flat-spined with glossy cover. Press run is 1,300 for 700 subscribers of which 50 are libraries. Subscription: $22/year, $35/2 years. Sample back issue: $5.35; current issue: $8.49. Prices include GST. US subscribers please pay in US funds. Overseas and institutions: $32/year, $48/2 years. Sample: $9.

How to Submit: Submit 5 poems at a time. No previously published poems. No fax or e-mail submissions. Brief cover letter with publication credits required. Include SASE (Canadian postage only) or SAE and IRCs. "Tell us if you'd prefer your manuscript to be recycled rather than returned." Time between acceptance and publication is within 1 year. Comments on some rejected poems. Responds in 1-6 months. Pays honorarium. Acquires first North American print rights.

EXIT 13 (Specialized: geography/travel), % Tom Plante, P.O. Box 423, Fanwood NJ 07023-1162. (908)889-5298. E-mail: exit13magazine@yahoo.com. Established 1987. **Editor:** Tom Plante.

Magazine Needs: *Exit 13* is a "contemporary poetry annual" using poetry that is "short, to the point, with a sense of geography." Has published poetry by Ruth Holzer, Richard Krech, Joel Lewis, Lyn Lifshin, Don Thompson, and Louise Murphy. *Exit 13*, #11, was 72 pages. Press run is 300. Sample: $7.

How to Submit: Accepts simultaneous submissions and previously published poems. Accept submissions by postal mail and by e-mail (no attachments). Guidelines available for SASE and in publication. Responds in 4 months. Pays 1 copy. Acquires one-time and possible anthology rights.

Advice: "*Exit 13* looks for adventure, a living record of places we're experienced. Every state, region, country, and ecosystem is welcome. Write about what you know and have seen. Send a snapshot of an 'Exit 13' road sign and receive a free copy of the issue in which it appears."

◐ ◎ EXPERIMENTAL FOREST PRESS (Specialized: bilingual/foreign language, political, social issues), 223 A Bosler Ave., Lemoyne PA 17043. (717)730-2143. E-mail: xxforest@yahoo .com. Established 1999. **Co-Editors:** Jeanette Trout and Kevyn Knox.

Magazine Needs: *Experimental Forest* is published bimonthly "to show the world that there is more out there than meets the eye. Please, no sappy love poetry!" Has published poetry by Richard Kostelanetz, John M. Bennett, Taylor Graham, T. Kilgore Splake, Marty Esworthy, and Snow. *Experimental Forest* is 60 pages, digest-sized, stapled, b&w artwork on coverstock, also inside art. Receives about 1,000 poems/year, accepts about 20%. Publishes 30 poems/issue. Press run is 250 for 25 subscribers of which 5 are libraries, 75 shelf sales; 25 distributed free to fellow editors. Single copy: $5; subscription: $21.50/year. Sample: $5. Make checks payable to Jeanette Trout and/or Kevyn Knox.

How to Submit: Submit up to 5 poems at a time. Accepts e-mail submissions; no fax submissions. Cover letter preferred. "We prefer to have a short bio for our contributors page. We also require a SASE." Time between acceptance and publication is 6 months. Often comments on rejected poems. Publishes theme issues occasionally. A list of upcoming themes available for SASE. Responds in 2 months. Pays 1 copy. Acquires one-time rights.

Also Offers: Sponsors a poetry contest every fall with a $100 1st Prize and a short story contest each spring with a $100 1st Prize. Guidelines available for SASE or by e-mail.

Advice: "We accept poetry of any style or subject. We look for poetic voices that have something fresh and new to say. Remember, we are called '*Experimental' Forest*."

Ⓝ ◐ EYE DIALECT, P.O. Box 67, Athens GA 30603. E-mail: staff@contemporarypoetry.com. Website: www.contemporarypoetry.com/dialect/. Established 1999. **Editor-in-Chief:** RJ McCaffery. **Poetry Editor:** Kristina Van Sant.

Magazine Needs: *Eye Dialect* appears 3 times/year and features "poetry, essays, fiction, reviews, and whatever else we can squeeze in. *Eye Dialect*'s aesthetic is informed by two main goals and its structure: We're interested in juxtaposing emerging voices with more established writers; also, we're not afraid to republish good work if it has only previously appeared in difficult-to-find print media. After all, good writing should not be a disposable single-use flash pop. We've laid out the site to follow a 'ring' structure, in which there are no 'archived issues' per se, but only new works added to an easily accessible body of writing. All types of poetry are welcome but must pay attention to Sound and Sense and thus adhere to Coleridge's dictum of having the Best Words in their Best Order." Recently published poetry by Linda Sue Park, Curtis Bauer, Robert Fanning, and Jennifer Wallace. *Eye Dialect* is published online. Receives about 800 poems/year, accepts about 1%. Publishes about 12 poems/issue.

How to Submit: Submit 4-6 poems at a time. Line length is open. Accepts previously published poems ("but only if previously published in smaller print journals—we do not accept any poems which have already been published/republished on the Web") and simultaneous submissions. Accepts e-mail submissions; no disk submissions. Cover letter is preferred. "Please send submissions in the body of the e-mail. We do not open attachments of any kind." Reads submissions year round. Time between acceptance and publication is 1 month. "Submissions are reviewed by all editors. Final decisions are usually made within a month and notifications to the writers are made via e-mail." Often comments on rejected poems. Guidelines available on website. Responds in 1 month. No payment. Acquires first rights or one-time rights. Reviews books and chapbooks of poetry and other magazines/journals in 2,000 words or less. Poets may send materials for review consideration to RJ McCaffery.

Advice: "This is the final stage of your poetry's life cycle—it becomes *for* others, and no longer a private document. Make sure the poem really is for others before you send it out into the world."

◐ FAILBETTER.COM, 63 Eighth Ave., #3A, Brooklyn NY 11217. E-mail: submissions@failbett er.com. Website: www.failbetter.com. Established 2000. **Editor:** Thom Didato. Member: CLMP.

Magazine Needs: *failbetter.com* is an online literary journal "in the spirit of a traditional print journal, dedicated to publishing literary fiction, poetry, and artwork. While the Web plays host to hundreds, if not thousands, of genre-related literary sites (i.e., science fiction and horror, many of which have merit), *failbetter.com* is not one of them. We place a high degree of importance on originality, believing that even in this age of trends it is still possible." Publishes translations and interviews. Recently published poetry by Barry Ballard, Harold Bowes, Suzanne Burns, Amy Eisner, Jon Lapree, and Kathryn Rantala. *failbetter.com* is published exclusively online with art/graphics. Receives about 600 poetry submissions/year, accepts about 9-12. Publishes 3-4 poets/issue.

How to Submit: Submit 4-6 poems at a time. Line length for poetry is open. "We are not concerned with length: One good sentence may find a home here; as the bulk of mediocrity will not." Accepts simultaneous submissions; no previously published poems. Encourages e-mail submissions. "All e-mail submissions should include title in header. All poetry submissions must be included in the body of your e-mail. Please do not send attached files. If for whatever reason you wish to submit a MS Word attachment, please query first." Submissions also accepted by regular mail. "Please note, however, any materials accepted for publication must ultimately be submitted in electronic format in order to appear on our site." Cover letter is preferred. Reads submissions year round. Time between acceptance and publication ranges from up to 4 months. Poems are circulated to an editorial board. Often comments on rejected poems. "It is not unusual to ask poets re-submit, and their subsequent submissions have been accepted." Guidelines available on website. Responds in 3 weeks to e-mail submissions; up to 3 months for submissions by regular mail. "We will not respond to any e-mail inquiry regarding receipt confirmation or status of any work under consideration." No payment. Acquires exclusive first-time Internet rights; works will also be archived online. All other rights, including opportunity to publish in traditional print form, revert to the artist. Nominates work for Pushcart consideration.

Also Offers: *failbetter presents*, a New York-based reading series featuring both established and emerging poets and fiction writers. Inquiries regarding reading series can be made at failbetterpresents@yahoo.com.

Advice: "With a readership of 30,000, *failbetter* simply offers to expose poets' works to a much broader world-wide audience than the typical print journal. For both established and emerging poets our advice remains the same: We strongly recommend that you not only read the previous issue, but also sign up on our e-mail list (subscribe@failbetter.com) to be notified of future publications. Most importantly, know that what you are saying could only come from you. When you are sure of this, please feel free to submit."

⚪ THE FAIRFIELD REVIEW, 544 Silver Spring Rd., Fairfield CT 06430-1947. (203)256-1960. E-mail: fairfieldreview@hpmd.com. Website: www.farifieldreview.org. Established 1997. **Editors:** Janet and Edward Granger-Happ.

Magazine Needs: *The Fairfield Review* appears 2-3 times/year as an e-zine featuring poetry and short stories from new and established authors. "We prefer free style poems, approachable on first reading, but with the promise of a rich vein of meaning coursing along under the consonants and vowels." Does not want "something better suited for a Hallmark card." Accepts poetry written by children; requires parents' permission/release for children under 18. Recently published poetry by Taylor Graham, Kelley Jean White, and Michael Zack. *Fairfield Review* is 20-30 pages published online (HTML). Receives about 350 poems/year, accepts about 8%. Publishes about 10 poems/issue.

How to Submit: Submit 3 poems at a time. Line length for poetry is 75 maximum. Accepts previously published poems with permission; no simultaneous submissions. Accepts e-mail and disk submissions. Cover letter is preferred. "We strongly prefer submission via e-mail or e-mail attachment. Notifications are sent exclusively via e-mail. An e-mail address is required with all submissions. Reads submissions continually. Time between acceptance and publication is up to 1 year. Poems are circulated to an editorial board. Often comments on rejected poems, if requested and submitted via e-mail. Guidelines are available on website. Responds in up to 4 months. Always sends prepublications galleys (online only). Acquires first rights, right to retain publication in online archive issues, and the right to use in "Best of *The Fairfield Review*" anthologies. Reviews books of poetry. "We consider reviews of books from authors we have published or who are referred to us."

Also Offers: "We select poems from each issue for 'reader's choice' awards based on readership frequency."

Advice: "Read our article on 'Writing Qualities to Keep in Mind.' "

⚫ ◎ **FANTASTIC STORIES OF THE IMAGINATION (Specialized: science fiction/fantasy)**, P.O. Box 329, Brightwaters NY 11718. Established 1992. **Editor:** Edward J. McFadden. (Published by DNA Publications. Send all business-related inquiries and subscriptions to DNA Publications, P.O. Box 2988, Radford VA 24143.)

Magazine Needs: *Fantastic Stories* is a quarterly magazine "filled with fiction, poetry, art, and reviews by top name professionals and tomorrow's rising stars." Wants all forms and styles of poetry "within our genres—fantasy and science fiction. Best chance is 20 lines or less. No crude language or excessive violence. No pornography, horror, western, or romance. Poems should be typed with exact capitalization and punctuation suited to your creative needs." Has published poetry by Nancy Springer, Jane Yolen, and John Grey. *Fantastic Stories* is 72 pages, magazine-sized and saddle-stapled with a full-color cover, and b&w art throughout. Receives about 150 poetry submissions/year, accepts about 15-25 poems. Subscription: $16/4 issues, $27/8 issues. Sample: $4.95.

How to Submit: Accepts simultaneous submissions. Cover letter required; include credits, if applicable. Often comments on rejected poems. Guidelines available for SASE. Responds in 4 months. Pays 1-2 copies and 50¢ a line. Acquires first North American serial rights. Also "reserves the right to print in future volumes of *The Best of Fantastic Stories* anthology."

$ ⚫ ◎ **FARRAR, STRAUS & GIROUX/BOOKS FOR YOUNG READERS (Specialized: children)**, 19 Union Square W., New York NY 10003. (212)741-6900. Website: www.fsgbooks.com. Established 1946. **Contact:** Children's Editorial Department

Book/Chapbook Needs: Publishes one book of children's poetry "every once in a while," in trade hardcover only. Open to book-length submissions of children's poetry only. Has published Valerie Worth's *Peacock and Other Poems*; Tony Johnston's *An Old Shell*; and Helen Frost's *Keesha's House* (a novel in poems).

How to Submit: Query first with sample poems and cover letter with brief bio and publication credits. Accepts previously published in magazines and simultaneous submissions. Seldom comments on rejected poems. Send SASE for reply. Responds to queries in up to 2 months, to mss in up to 4 months. "We pay an advance against royalties; the amount depends on whether or not the poems are illustrated, etc." Also pays 10 copies.

⚫ **FAULTLINE**, Dept. of English & Comparative Literature, University of California—Irvine, Irvine CA 92697-2650. (949)824-1573. E-mail: faultline@uci.edu. Website: www.humanities.uci. edu/faultline. Established 1991. **Editor:** Lorene Delany-Ullman. **Contact:** Poetry Editor.

● Poetry published by this journal has also been selected for inclusion in a *Pushcart Prize* anthology.

Magazine Needs: On shelves in May, *Faultline* is an annual journal of art and literature occasionally edited by guest editors and published at the University of California, Irvine. Has published poetry by Larissa Szporluk, Jennifer Clarvoe, Lee Upton, and Homero Aridjis. *Faultline* is approximately 120 pages, digest-sized, professionally printed on 60 lb. paper, perfect-bound with 80 lb. coverstock and featuring color and b&w art and photos. Receives about 1,500 poems/year, accepts about 5%. Press run is 1,000. Single copy: $10. Sample: $5.

How to Submit: Submit up to 5 poems at a time. Accepts simultaneous submissions, "but please note in cover letter that the manuscript is being considered elsewhere." No fax or e-mail submissions. Cover letter preferred. Do not include name and address on ms to assist anonymous judging. Reads submissions September 1 to March 1 only. Poems are selected by a board of up to 6 readers. Seldom comments on rejected poems. Guidelines available for SASE and on website. Responds in 3 months. Pays 2 copies. Acquires first or one-time rights.

⊕ ⚫ **FEATHER BOOKS; THE POETRY CHURCH MAGAZINE; CHRISTIAN HYMNS & SONGS (Specialized: membership/subscription, Christian, religious)**, P.O. Box 438, Shrewsbury, SY3 0WN United Kingdom. Phone/fax: (01743)872177. E-mail: john@waddysweb.free uk.com. Website: www.waddysweb.freeuk.com. Feather Books established 1982. *The Poetry Church Magazine* established 1996. **Contact:** Rev. John Waddington-Feather, editor.

Magazine Needs: *The Poetry Church Magazine* appears quarterly and contains Christian poetry and prayers. Wants "Christian or good religious poetry—usually around 20 lines, but will accept longer." Does not want "unreadable blasphemy." Accepts poetry written by children over ten. Has published poetry by Laurie Bates, Joan Smith, Idris Caffrey, Walter Nash, and the Glyn family. *The Poetry Church Magazine* is 40 pages, digest-sized, photocopied, saddle-stapled with laminated cover and b&w cover art. Receives about 1,000 poems/year, accepts about 500. Press run is 1,000 for 400 subscribers of which 10 are libraries. Single copy free; subscription: £8 ($15 US). Sample: £3 ($5.50 US). Make checks payable in sterling to Feather Books. Payment can also be made through website.

How to Submit: *The Poetry Church Magazine* "publishes only subscribers poems as they keep us solvent." Submit 2 typed poems at a time. Accepts previously published poems and simultaneous submissions. Accepts e-mail submissions in attached file. Cover letter preferred with information about the poet. All work must be submitted by mail with SASE (or SAE and IRC). Time between acceptance and publication is 4 months. "The editor does a preliminary reading; then seeks the advice of colleagues about uncertain poems." Guidelines available for SASE (or SAE and IRC), by e-mail, or by fax. Responds within 1 week. Pays 1 copy. Poets retain copyright.

Book/Chapbook Needs & How to Submit: Feather Books publishes the Feather Books Poetry Series, books of Christian poetry, and prayers. Has recently published poetry collections by the Glyn family, Walter Nash, David Grieve, and Rosie Morgan Barry. "We have now published 181 poetry collections by individual Christian poets." Books are usually photocopied and saddle-stapled with laminated covers. "Poets' works are selected for publication in collections of around 20 poems in our Feather Books Poetry Series. We do not insist, but most poets pay for small run-offs of their work, e.g., around 50-100 copies for which we charge $270 per fifty. If they can't afford it, but are good poets, we stand the cost. We expect poets to read our *Poetry Church Magazine* to get some idea of our standards."

Also Offers: Feather Books also publishes *Christian Hymns & Songs*, a quarterly supplement by Grundy and Feather. And, each winter and summer, selected poems appear in *The Poetry Church Anthology*, the leading Christian poetry anthology used in churches and schools. Began a new chapbook collection, the "Christianity and Literature Series," which focuses on academic work. "The first, just published, is a paper by Dr. William Ruleman, of Wesley College, Tennessee, entitled *W.H. Auden's Search for Faith*. Other numbers include *Six Contemporary Women Christian Poets*, by Dr. Patricia Batstone; *In a Quiet Place: J.B. Priestley & Religion*, by Michael Nelson; *'The Dream of the Rood,' 'The Wanderer,' 'The Seafarer': Three Old English Early Christian Poems of the 8th Century*, newly translated by Reverend John Waddington-Feather, with an introduction by Professor Walter Nash, and *Women Hymn-Writers of the 19th Century*, by Dr. E.L. Edmonds."

Advice: "We find it better for poets to master rhyme and rhythm before trying free verse. Many poets seem to think that if they write 'down' a page they're writing poetry, when all they're doing is writing prose in a different format."

◖ **FEELINGS OF THE HEART**, 11477 Pinehurst Place W., Gulfport MS 39502-1022. Phone/fax: (228)864-0766 (call to ensure line is free before faxing). E-mail: aharnischfitchie@juno.com. Website: www.feelingsoftheheart.net. Established 1999. **Editor/Publisher/Founder:** Alice M. Harnisch-Fitchie.

Magazine Needs: *Feelings of the Heart* appears biannually as the Winter/Spring issue and the Summer/Fall issue. Wants "*good* poetry from the heart." Recently published poetry by Vernon A. Fitchie, Elijah St. Ives, Frank L. Kunkel, Richard Sponougle, Geneva Jo Anthony, McGuffy Ann Morris, and Gary Edwards. *Feelings of the Heart* is 50 pages, magazine-sized, computer-printed, stapled, artist cover, with ads from other publications. Receives about 100 poems/year, accepts about 95%. Publishes 20+ poems/issue. Press run is 100 for over 100 subscribers. Single copy: $6; subscription: $18/year, $34/2 years. Sample: $4.50. Make checks payable to Alice M. Fitchie.

How to Submit: Submit 5 poems at a time with "name and address on every poem submitted." Line length for poetry is 20-40. Accepts previously published poems and simultaneous submissions. Accepts e-mail and disk submissions, up to 5 poems per e-mail but only 3 e-mail per day. Cover letter is required. "Please enclose SASE or IRC with all correspondence." Submit seasonal poems 2 months in advance. Time between acceptance and publication is 2 weeks. Poems "are read by me, the editor, and decided by the poetic intent of poetry submitted." Often comments on rejections. Guidelines available for SASE or on website. Responds in 2 weeks with SASE. Sometimes sends

prepublication galleys. Acquires first rights. Reviews books and chapbooks of poetry and other maga-zines in 200 words or less, single book format. Poets may send materials for review consideration.
Advice: "Send poetry that you believe in, not something you just scribbled on a napkin. You should appear to be a well-crafted writer even if you aren't."

◐ ◎ FEMINIST STUDIES (Specialized: women/feminism), 0103 Taliaferro Hall, University of Maryland, College Park MD 20742. (301)405-7415. Fax: (301)405-8395. E-mail: femstud@u mail.umd.edu. Website: www.feministstudies.org. Established 1969. **Contact:** Creative Writing Editor.
Magazine Needs: *Feminist Studies* appears 3 times/year and "welcomes a variety of work that focuses on women's experience, on gender as a category of analysis, and that furthers feminist theory and consciousness." Has published poetry by Janice Mirikitani, Paula Gunn Allen, Cherrie Moraga, Audre Lorde, Valerie Fox, and Diane Glancy. *Feminist Studies* is 250 pages, elegantly printed, flat-spined paperback. Press run is 8,000 for 7,000 subscribers, of which 1,500 are libraries. There are 4-10 pages of poetry in each issue. Sample: $15.
How to Submit: "All subscribers should send one copy (no SASE) to the above address. Work will not be returned." No simultaneous submissions; will only consider previously published poems under special circumstances. No fax or e-mail submissions. Manuscripts are reviewed twice a year, in May and December. Deadlines are May 1 and December 1. Authors will receive notice of the board's decision by July 10 and February 10. Guidelines are available on website. Always sends prepublication galleys. Pays 2 copies. Commissions reviews of books of poetry. Send materials for review consideration to Claire G. Moses.

$ ◐ ◎ FIELD: CONTEMPORARY POETRY AND POETICS; FIELD TRANSLATION SERIES; FIELD POETRY PRIZE; FIELD POETRY SERIES; OBERLIN COLLEGE PRESS, 10 N. Professor St., Oberlin College, Oberlin OH 44074. (440)775-8408. Fax: (440)775-8124. E-mail: oc.press@oberlin.edu. Website: www.oberlin.edu/~ocpress. Established 1969. **Poetry Editors:** David Young and Martha Collins.
• Work published in *FIELD* has been frequently included in volumes of *The Best American Poetry*.
Magazine Needs: *FIELD* is a literary journal appearing in October and April with "emphasis on poetry, translations, and essays by poets." Wants the "best possible" poetry. Has published poetry by Marianne Boruch, Miroslav Holub, Charles Wright, Billy Collins, Jon Loomis, Charles Simic, and Sandra McPherson. *FIELD* is digest-sized, flat-spined, has 100 pages, rag stock with glossy card color cover. Although most poems fall under the lyrical free verse category, you'll find narratives and formal work here on occasion, much of it sensual, visually appealing, and resonant. Press run is 1,500, with 400 library subscriptions. Subscription: $14/year, $24/2 years. Sample: $7.
How to Submit: Submit up to 5 poems at a time. Include cover letter and SASE. Reads submissions year-round. No previously published or simultaneous submissions. Does not accept fax or e-mail submissions. Seldom comments on rejected poems. Responds in 2 months. Time between acceptance and publication is up to 6 months. Always sends prepublication galleys. Guidelines available for SASE, by e-mail, on website. Pays $15/page plus 2 copies. Staff reviews books of poetry. Poets and publishers may send books for review consideration.
Book/Chapbook Needs & How to Submit: Publishes books of translations in the *FIELD* Translation Series, averaging 150 pages, flat-spined and hardcover editions. Query regarding translations. Pays 7½-10% royalties and author's copies. Also has a *FIELD* Poetry Series. Has published *Ill Lit* by Franz Wright; and *The Pleasure Principle* by Jon Loomis. This series is by invitation only. Write for catalog to buy samples.
Also Offers: Sponsors the *FIELD* Poetry Prize, the winning ms will be published in the *FIELD* poetry series and receive $1,000 award. Submit mss of 50-80 pages with a $22 reading fee in May only. Contest guidelines available for SASE.

★ ⊠ ◐ FILLING STATION, P.O. Box 22135, Bankers Hall, Calgary AB T2P 4J5 Canada. (403)234-0336. E-mail: editor@fillingstation.ca. Website: www.fillingstation.ca. Established 1993. **Managing Editors:** Natalie Simpson. **Contact:** Carmen Derkson or Trevor Spellor.
Magazine Needs: Appearing 3 times/year (February, June, and October), *filling Station* is a maga-

zine of contemporary writing featuring poetry, fiction, interviews, reviews and other literary news. "We are looking for all forms of contemporary writing. No specific objections to any style." Has published poetry by Fred Wah, Larissa Lai, Margaret Christakos, Robert Kroetsch, Ron Silliman, Susan Holbrook, and Paula Tatarunis. *filling Station* is 80 pages, magazine-sized, perfect-bound with card cover and includes photos, artwork and ads. Receives about 100 submissions for each issue, accepts approximately 10%. Press run is 600 for 100 subscribers, 250 shelf sales. Subscription: $20/ 1 year, $35/2 years. Sample: $7.

How to Submit: Submit typed poems with name and address on each page. Accepts simultaneous submissions; no previously published poems. Accepts submissions by postal mail, as an e-mail attachment, or in e-mail text box (include mailing address). Cover letter required. Deadlines are November 15, March 15, and July 15. Seldom comments on rejected poems. Guidelines available for SASE, by e-mail, on website, and in publication. Responds in 6 months. Pays 1-year subscription. Acquires first North American rights. Reviews books of poetry in both single and multi-book format. Send materials for review consideration.

Advice: "You stop between these 'fixed' points on the map to get an injection of something new, something fresh that's going to get you from point to point. . . . We want to be a kind of connection between polarities: a link. We'll publish any poem or story that offers a challenge: to the mind, to the page, to writers and readers."

◐ FINISHING LINE PRESS; MM REVIEW; NEW WOMEN'S VOICES CHAPBOOK SERIES; FINISHING LINE PRESS OPEN CHAPBOOK COMPETITION, P.O. Box 1016, Cincinnati OH 45201-1016. E-mail: finishinglbooks@aol.com. Established 1998. **Editor:** C.J. Morrison (and occasionally guest editors). **Contact:** Poetry Editor.

Magazine Needs & How to Submit: "We are publishing chapbooks only and have suspended publishing *MM Review* for the next two years to focus on chapbook publication."

Book/Chapbook Needs & How to Submit: Finishing Line Press seeks to "discover new talent" and hopes to publish chapbooks by both men and women poets who have not previously published a book or chapbook of poetry. Has published *Looking to the East with Western Eyes* by Leah Maines; *Like the Air* by Joyce Sidman; *Startling Art* by Dorothy Sutton; *Foreign Correspondence* by Timothy Riordan; *Man Overboard* by Steven Barza. Publishes 20 poetry books/year; plans to publish up to 30 in 2004. Chapbooks are usually 25-30 pages, digest-sized, laser-printed and saddle-stapled with card cover with textured matte wrapper, includes b&w photos. Submit ms of 16-24 pages with cover letter, bio, acknowledgements and **$12 reading fee.** Responds to queries in 3-4 weeks, to mss in 3-4 months. Pay varies; pays in copies. "Sales profits, if any, go to publish the next new poet." Obtain sample chapbooks by sending $6.

Also Offers: Sponsors New Women's Voices chapbook competition. Entry fee: $12. Deadline: December 31. Finishing Line Press Open Chapbook Competition. Open to all poets regardless of past publications. Deadline: June 30.

Advice: "We are very open to new talent. If the poetry is great, we will consider it for a chapbook."

🌐 ◐ FIRE, Field Cottage, Old Whitehill, Tackley, Kidlington, Oxfordshire OX5 3AB United Kingdom. Website: www.poetical.org. Established 1994. **Editor:** Jeremy Hilton.

Magazine Needs: *Fire* appears 3 times/year "to publish little-known, unfashionable or new writers alongside better known ones." Wants "experimental, unfashionable, demotic work; longer work encouraged. Use of rhyme schemes and other strict forms *not* favored." Accepts poetry written by children. Has published poetry by Phillip Levine, Marilyn Hacker, Adrian C. Louis, Tom Pickard, Allen Fisher, Gael Turnbull, and David Hart. *Fire* is up to 180 pages, A5. Receives about 400 poems/ year, accepts about 35%. Press run is 300 for 230 subscribers of which 20 are libraries. Single copy: £4, add £1 postage Europe, £2 postage overseas. Subscription (3 issues): £7, add £2 postage Europe, £4 postage overseas.

How to Submit: Accepts previously published poems; no simultaneous submissions. Cover letter

---

◪ INDICATES A MARKET that did not appear in the 2003 edition.

preferred. Time between acceptance and publication "varies enormously." Often comments on rejected poems. Guidelines available for SASE and on website. Responds in 2 months. Sometimes sends prepublication galleys, "but rarely to overseas contributors." Pays 1 copy.

Advice: "Read a copy first. Don't try to tailor your work to any particular style, format, or formula. Free expression, strongly imaginative work preferred."

N © **FIREBUSH (Specialized: humor and experimentation)**, P.O. Box 1287, Spokane WA 99210. E-mail: LiteraryFirebush@aol.com. Established 2002. **Editors:** Jason Olsen and David Metzger.

Magazine Needs: *Firebush* is a biannual journal of poetry, review, opinions, and art. "We're not interested in cute kids who've appeared on Oprah or former presidents." Recently published poetry by Christopher Howell, Jonathan Johnson, Rhoda Janzen, James Grabill, and Philip Dacey. *Firebush* is about 55-60 pages, side-stapled, cardstock cover with b&w art, includes line art cartoons and drawings. Accepts about 5-10% of work submitted. Publishes about 30 poems/issue. Single copy: $4; subscription: $8/year. Make checks payable to Jason Olsen.

How to Submit: Submit 3-6 poems at a time. No previously published poems or simultaneous submissions. No fax, e-mail, or disk submissions. Cover letter is preferred. Reads submissions year round. Time between acceptance and publication is up to 6 months. "Poems are read and discussed by the four-person editorial board." Seldom comments on rejected poems. Guidelines available for SASE or by e-mail. Responds in up to 2 months. Pays 1 contributor's copy. Reviews books of poetry in single book format. Poets may send materials for review consideration to the editors.

Also Offers: "We're very open to reader response/reader opinions, and letters are considered for publication."

⬛ © **FIREWEED: POETRY OF OREGON (Specialized: regional)**, 5204 N. Gay Ave., Portland OR 97212. (503)285-8717. E-mail: fireweedmag@attbi.com. Established 1989. **Editors:** Shelley Reece, Sydney Thompson, and Pat Vivian.

Magazine Needs: *Fireweed* publishes the work of poets living in Oregon or having close connections to the region. However, poems need not be regional in subject; any theme, subject, length or form is acceptable. Publishes poetry by young writers over age 13; "Poetry must be intelligent and engaging—no limericks." Has published poetry by Carlos Reyes, James Grabill, Dan Raphael, Paulann Peterson, B.T. Shaw, and Judith H. Montgomery. *Fireweed* is 60 pages, digest-sized, laser printed and saddle-stapled with card cover. "We receive several hundred poems and publish about one quarter or one fifth of them." Press run is 250 for 180 subscribers of which 20 are libraries, 25 shelf sales. Subscription: $12. Sample: $6.

How to Submit: Submit 3-5 poems at a time, name and address on each page. Accepts simultaneous submissions; no previously published poems. Cover letter with brief bio required. Often comments on rejected poems. Does not publish guidelines for poets but will answer inquiries with SASE. Responds in up to 6 months. Pays 2 copies. Acquires first North American serial rights. Reviews books of poetry by Oregon poets in 500-750 words, single format. Oregon poets may send material for review consideration.

Advice: "Go for what's fresh, creative, and original. We like poems that express depth of feeling and avoid the pitfalls of sentimentality. Please be odd, but accessible. We prefer poems that are noted in experience over intellectual ruminations."

◪ **FIRST CLASS; FOUR-SEP PUBLICATIONS**, P.O. Box 86, Friendship IN 47021. E-mail: christopherm@four-sep.com. Website: www.four-sep.com. Established 1994. **Editor:** Christopher M.

Magazine Needs: *First Class* appears in May and November and "publishes excellent/odd writing for intelligent/creative readers." Wants "short postmodern poems, also short fiction." No traditional work. Has published poetry by Bennett, Locklin, Roden, Splake, Catlin, and Huffstickler. *First Class* is 60 pages, 4½ × 11, printed, saddle-stapled with colored cover. Receives about 1,500 poems/year, accepts about 30. Press run is 300-400. Sample (including guidelines): $6 or mini version $1. Make checks payable to Christopher M.

How to Submit: Submit 5 poems at a time. Accepts previously published poems and simultaneous submissions. Does not accept fax or e-mail submissions. Cover letter preferred. Time between acceptance and publication is 2-4 months. Often comments on rejected poems. Guidelines available for

SASE, on website, and in publication. Responds in 3 weeks. Pays in 1 copy. Acquires one-time rights. Reviews books of poetry. Send materials for review consideration.

Also Offers: Chapbook production available.

Advice: "Belt out a good, short, thought-provoking, graphic, uncommon piece."

★ ⊕ ○ FIRST TIME; INTERNATIONAL HASTINGS POETRY COMPETITION, The

Snoring Cat, 16 Marianne Park, Dudley Rd., Hastings, East Sussex TN35 5PU England. Phone/fax: 01424 428855. E-mail: firsttime@carefree.net. Established 1981. **Editor:** Josephine Austin.

Magazine Needs: *First Time*, published biannually in April and October, is open to "all kinds of poetry—our magazine goes right across the board—which is why it is one of the most popular in Great Britain." *First Time* is digest-sized, 80-100 pages, saddle-stapled, contains several poems on each page, in a variety of small type styles, on lightweight stock, glossy one-color card cover. Subscription: $13. Sample: $2 plus postage. "Please send dollars."

How to Submit: Submit 6 poems with name and address of poet on each. Poems submitted must not exceed 30 lines. No previously published poems. Does not accept e-mail submissions. Cover letter and SAE required. Time between acceptance and publication is up to 2 months. "Although we can no longer offer a free copy as payment, we can offer one at a discounted price of $3 and postage."

Also Offers: The annual International Hastings Poetry Competition for poets 18 and older offers awards of £150, £75, and £50; £2/poem entry fee.

Advice: "Keep on 'pushing your poetry.' If one editor rejects you then study the market and decide which is the correct one for you. Try to type your own manuscripts as longhand is difficult to read and doesn't give a professional impression. Always date your poetry — ©1997 and sign it. Follow your way of writing, don't be a pale imitation of someone else—sooner or later styles change and you will either catch up or be ahead."

◐ 5 AM, P.O. Box 205, Spring Church PA 15686. Established 1987. **Editors:** Ed Ochester and

Judith Vollmer.

Magazine Needs: *5 AM* is a poetry publication that appears twice/year. Open in regard to form, length, subject matter, and style. However, they do not want poetry that is "religious or naive rhymers." Has published poetry by Virgil Suarez, Nin Andrews, Alicia Ostriker, Edward Field, Billy Collins, and Denise Duhamel. *5 AM* is a 24-page, offset tabloid. Receives about 5,000 poems/year, accepts about 2%. Press run is 1,000 for 550 subscribers of which 25 are libraries, about 300 shelf sales. Subscription: $15/4 issues. Sample: $5.

How to Submit: No previously published poems or simultaneous submissions. Seldom comments on rejected poems. Responds within 6 weeks. Pays 2 copies. Acquires first rights.

★ $○ FIVE POINTS; JAMES DICKEY PRIZE FOR POETRY, Georgia State University,

University Plaza, Atlanta GA 30303-3083. (404)651-0071. Fax: (404)651-3167. Website: www.webd elsol.com/Five-Points. Established 1996. **Associate Editor:** Megan Sexton.

Magazine Needs: *Five Points* appears 3 times/year and "publishes quality poetry, fiction, nonfiction, interviews and art by established and emerging writers." Wants "poetry of high quality which shows evidence of an original voice and imagination." Has published poetry by Charles Wright, Kate Daniels, and Philip Levine. *Five Points* is about 200 pages, digest-sized, professionally printed and perfect-bound with 4-color card cover, includes b&w photos and ads. Receives about 2,000 poems/year, accepts about 5%. Press run is 2,000 for about 1,000 subscribers of which 10% are libraries, 40% shelf sales. Single copy: $7. Sample: $7.

How to Submit: Submit no more than 3 poems at a time. No previously published poems. No simultaneous submissions. Accepts 2 sumisssions per reading period. Cover letter preferred. Reads submissions September 1 through May 30 only. Time between acceptance and publication is 3 months. Poems are circulated to an editorial board. "First reader culls poems then send them to the final reader." Seldom comments on rejected poems. Guidelines available for SASE. Responds in 3 months. Always sends prepublication galleys. Pays $50/poem plus 2 copies and 1-year subscription. Acquires first North American serial rights.

Also Offers: Sponsors the James Dickey Prize for Poetry which awards $1,000 and publication in the Spring issue. Entry fee: $15 domestic, $20 foreign for up to 3 poems, no more than 50 lines each.

Entries must be typed. Fee includes 1-year subscription. Deadline: November 30. Complete contest guidelines available for SASE.

⊕ ⊘ FLAMING ARROWS, County Sligo VEC, Riverside, Sligo, Ireland. Phone: (+353)7147304. Fax: (+353)7143093. E-mail: leoregan@eircom.net. Established 1989. **Editor:** Leo Regan, A.E.O.

Magazine Needs: *Flaming Arrows*, published annually in January, features poetry and prose. Wants "cogent, lucid, coherent, technically precise poetry. Poems of the spirit, mystical, metaphysical but sensuous, tactile, and immediate to the senses." Has published poetry by Sydney Bernard Smith, Medbh McGuckian, Ben Wilensky, James Liddy, and Ciaran O'Driscoll. *Flaming Arrows* is 80-102 pages, A5, offset-printed, perfect-bound or saddle-stapled, with 2-color coverstock. Receives about 500 poems/year, accepts about 6%. Press run is 600 for 150 subscribers of which 30 are libraries, 180 shelf sales; 100 distributed free to writer's groups, contributors, literary events. Issues 2 and 3 are $6; issues 4, 5, and 6 are $3; postage $1.25. Make checks payable to County Sligo VEC.

How to Submit: Submit 5 poems "typed, A4, in 10 or 12 pt. for scanning or discs for Word 7 in Windows 95." Accepts previously published poems and simultaneous submissions. Cover letter required. Time between acceptance and publication is 10 months. Responds in 3 months. Pays 1 copy, additional copies at cost. Include SASE with IRC.

Advice: "Inspection of previous issues, especially 2, 3, 5, or 6 will inform prospective contributors of style and standard required."

✖ ⊕ $⊡ ⊘ FLARESTACK PUBLISHING; OBSESSED WITH PIPEWORK, 41 Buckleys Green, Alvechurch, Birmingham B48 7NG United Kingdom. Phone: 0121 445 2110. E-mail: flare.stack@virgin.net. Established 1995. **Editor:** Charles Johnson.

Magazine Needs: *Obsessed with Pipework* appears quarterly. "We are very keen to publish strong new voices—'new poems to surprise and delight' with somewhat of a high-wire aspect. We are looking for original, exploratory poems—positive, authentic, oblique maybe—delighting in image and in the dance of words on the page." Does not want "the predictable, the unfresh, the rhyme-led; the clever, the sure-of-itself. No formless outpourings, please." No full-length collection mss. Has published "Searching For Salsa" by Jennifer Ballerini and poetry by David Hart, Jennifer Compton, Susan Wicks, Carol Burns, Lucille Gang Shulklapper, and Maria Jastrzebska. *Obsessed With Pipework* is 49 pages, A5, photocopied and stapled with card cover, ads "by arrangement." Receives about 1,500 poems/year, accepts about 10%. Press run is 70-100. Single copy: £3.50; subscription: £12. Sample: £2 if available. Make checks payable in pounds to Flarestack Publishing.

How to Submit: Submit maximum of 6 poems at a time. No previously published poems or simultaneous submissions. Cover letter preferred. Accepts e-mail and fax submissions. "If sending by e-mail, send a maximum 3 poems in the body of the message, as attached files may become lost or corrupted." Time between acceptance and publication is 6 months maximum. Often comments on rejected poems. Guidelines available for SASE, by fax, or by e-mail. Responds in 2 months. Pays 1 copy. Acquires first rights.

Book/Chapbook Needs: Flarestack Publishing ("talent to burn") aims to "find an audience for new poets, so beginners are welcome, but the work has to be strong and clear." Publishes 12 chapbooks/year. Chapbooks are usually 12-40 pages, A5, photocopied and stapled with card cover.

How to Submit: Query first with a few sample poems (6 maximum) and cover letter with brief bio and publication credits. "Normally we expect a few previous magazine acceptances, but no previous collection publication." Responds to queries in 6 weeks; to mss in 2 months. Pays royalties of 25% plus 6 author's copies (out of a press run of 50-100). Order sample chapbooks by sending £3.50.

Advice: "Most beginning poets show little evidence of reading poetry before writing it! Join a poetry workshop. For chapbook publishing, we are looking for *coherent* first collections that take risks, make leaps, and come clean."

$ ⊘ ◎ FLESH AND BLOOD: QUIET TALES OF DARK FANTASY & HORROR (Specialized: horror, dark fantasy, off-beat, supernatural), 121 Joseph St., Bayville NJ 08721. E-mail: HorrorJack@aol.com. Website: www.fleshandbloodpress.com. Established 1997. **Senior Editor:** Jack Fisher.

Magazine Needs: Appearing 4 times/year, *Flesh and Blood* publishes work of dark fantasy and the supernatural. Wants surreal, bizarre, and avant-garde poetry. No "rhyming or love poems, epics, killers, etc." Has published poetry by Charles Jacob, Mark McLaughlin, Kurt Newton, Wendy Rathbone, J.W. Donnelly and Donna Taylor Burgess. *Flesh and Blood* is 50-52 pages, digest-sized, saddle-stapled with glossy full-color cover, includes art/graphics and ads. Receives about 200 poems/year, accepts about 10%. Publishes 4-6 poems/issue. Press run is 500 for 400 subscribers, 100 shelf sales; 50 distributed free to reviewers. Subscription: $15. Sample: $4.50. Make checks payable to Jack Fisher.

How to Submit: Submit up to 5 poems at a time. Line length for poetry is 3 minimum, 30 maximum. Accepts previously published poems; no simultaneous submissions. Accepts e-mail submissions (include text in body of e-mail). Cover letter preferred. "Poems should be on separate pages, each with the author's address. Cover letter should include background credits." Time between acceptance and publication is up to 10 months. Guidelines available for SASE or on website. Responds in 2 months. Pays $10-20/poem and 1 copy.

Advice: "Be patient, professional, and courteous."

FLINT HILLS REVIEW, Department of English, Box 4019, Emporia State University, Emporia KS 66801. Fax: (620)341-5547. E-mail: webbamy@emporia.edu. Website: www.emporia.edu/fhr/index.htm. Established 1995. **Contact:** Editors.

Magazine Needs: Published annually in late summer, *Flint Hills Review* is "a regionally focused journal presenting writers of national distinction alongside new authors." Open to all forms except "rhyming, sentimental or gratuitous verse." Has published poetry by E. Ethelbert Miller, Elizabeth Dodd, Walt McDonald, and Gwendolyn Brooks. *Flint Hills Review* is about 100 pages, digest-sized, offset-printed and perfect-bound with glossy card cover with b&w photo, also includes b&w photos. Receives about 2,000 poems/year, accepts about 5%. Single copy: $7.

How to Submit: Submit 3-5 poems at a time. Accepts simultaneous submissions; no previously published poems. Accepts submissions by e-mail (in text box), by fax, or postal mail. Cover letter with SASE required. Reads submissions January through March only. Time between acceptance and publication is about 1 year. Seldom comments on rejected poems. Occasionally publishes theme issues. Guidelines and a list of upcoming themes available for SASE or on website. Pays 1 copy. Acquires first rights.

Also Offers: Sponsors the annual Bluestem Press Award. See listing in the Contests & Awards section of this book.

Advice: "Send writing with evidences of a strong sense of place."

FLOATING BRIDGE PRESS (Specialized: regional, Washington State), P.O. Box 18814, Seattle WA 98118. E-mail: ppereira5@aol.com. Website: www.scn.org/arts/floatingbridge. Established 1994. **Contact:** editor.

Book/Chapbook Needs: Floating Bridge press is "supported by Seattle Arts Commission, King County Arts Commission, Washington State Arts Commission, and the Allen Foundation for the Arts." The press publishes chapbooks and anthologies by Washington state poets, selected through an annual contest. Recently published *The End of Forgiveness* by Joseph Green, *X: a poem* by Chris Forhan, *Sonnets from the Mare Imbrium* by Bart Baxter, and *Blue Willow* by Molly Tenenbaum. In 1997 the press began publishing *Pontoon*, an annual anthology featuring the work of Washington state poets. *Pontoon* is 96 pages, digest-sized, offset-printed and perfect-bound with matte cardstock cover. For a sample chapbook or anthology, send $7 postpaid.

How to Submit: For consideration, Washington poets (only) should submit a chapbook ms of 20-24 pages of poetry with $10 entry fee and SASE (for results only). The usual reading period is November 1 to February 15. Accepts previously published individual poems and simultaneous submissions. Author's name must not appear on the ms; include a separate page with title, name, address, telephone number, and acknowledgments of any previous publication. Mss are judged anonymously and will not be returned. In addition to publication, the winner receives $500, 50 copies, and a reading in the Seattle area. All entrants receive a copy of the winning chapbook. All entrants will be considered for inclusion in *Pontoon*, a poetry anthology.

FLUME PRESS, California State University at Chico, 400 W. First St., Chico CA 95929-0830. (530)898-5983. E-mail: flumepress@csuchico.edu. Website: www.csuchico.edu/engl/flumepress. Established 1984. **Poetry Editor:** Casey Huff.

Book/Chapbook Needs: Flume Press publishes poetry chapbooks. "We have few biases about form, although we appreciate control and crafting, and we tend to favor a concise, understated style, with emphasis on metaphor rather than editorial commentary." Has published chapbooks by Tina Barr, Luis Omar Salinas, Pamela Uschuk, Martha M. Vertreace, John Brehm, and David Graham.

How to Submit: Chapbooks are chosen from an annual competition. $20 entry fee (each entrant receives a copy of the winning chapbook). Submit 24-32 pages, including title, contents, and acknowledgments. Considers simultaneous submissions. Sometimes sends prepublication galleys. Winner receives $500 and 25 copies. Sample: $8. **Postmark deadline:** December 1.

FLYWAY, A LITERARY REVIEW, 206 Ross Hall, Iowa State University, Ames IA 50011-1201. Fax: (515)294-6814. E-mail: flyway@iastate.edu. Website: www.flyway.org. Established 1961. **Editor-in-Chief:** Stephen Pett.

Magazine Needs: Appearing 3 times/year, *Flyway* "is one of the best literary magazines for the money; it is packed with some of the most readable poems being published today—all styles and forms, lengths and subjects." The editor shuns elite-sounding free verse with obscure meanings and pretty-sounding formal verse with obvious meanings. *Flyway* is 112 pages, digest-sized, professionally printed and perfect-bound with matte card cover with color. Press run is 600 for 400 subscribers of which 100 are libraries. Subscription: $18. Sample: $7.

How to Submit: Submit 4-6 poems at a time. Cover letter preferred. "We do not read mss between the end of May and the end of August." May be contacted by fax. Publishes theme issues (Native American, Latino, Arab American). Responds in 6 weeks (often sooner). Pays 2 copies. Acquires first rights.

Also Offers: Sponsors an annual award for poetry, fiction, and nonfiction. Details available for SASE or on website.

FOR CRYING OUT LOUD, INC. (Specialized: women survivors of sexual abuse), 46 Pleasant St., Cambridge MA 02139. E-mail: fcol_snlc@hotmail.com. Established 1985. **Contact:** Survivors Newsletter Collective.

Magazine Needs: *For Crying Out Loud* appears quarterly "to provide a forum for the voices of women survivors of childhood sexual abuse. Each issue focuses on a theme. Recent themes include Trust; Justice; Memory; and Incest, Politics, and Power. We publish poetry by women abuse survivors, often (though not always) on topics related to abuse and healing from abuse, any form or style." Does not want poetry that is anti-survivor or anti-woman. *For Crying Out Loud* is 12 pages, magazine-sized, offset-printed in b&w, side-stapled, paper cover, with occasional line drawings and clip art. Receives about 75 poems/year, accepts about 25%. Publishes 4 poems/issue. Press run is 400 for 200 subscribers of which 10 are libraries, 20 shelf sales; 50 are distributed free to Cambridge, MA Women's Center. Single copy: $3; subscription: $10/4 issues, $18/8 issues, $25/12 issues. Sample: $3. Make checks payable to Survivors Newsletter Collective.

How to Submit: Submit 3-6 poems at a time. Accepts previously published poems and simultaneous submissions. No fax, e-mail, or disk submissions. Cover letter is preferred. Reads submissions year round. Submit seasonal poems 3 months in advance. Time between acceptance and publication is 3 months. "The newsletter is edited by an editorial collective which votes on all submissions." Never comments on rejected poems. Regularly publishes theme issues. List of upcoming themes available for SASE. Guidelines available in magazine or for SASE. Responds in 3 months; **does not return submitted work.** Pays 1 contributor's copy plus a year's subscription. Acquires one-time rights. Reviews books and chapbooks of poetry and other magazines/journals in 500 words, single book format. "We often review books and other resources that we feel will be of interest to our readers." Poets may send materials for review consideration to Survivors Newsletter Collective.

Advice: "Our mission is to break the silence around childhood sexual abuse and to empower survivors of abuse. We are interested in poetry (and prose of up to 500 words) that is related to this mission. We especially like to see work that is related to the theme of a particular issue."

THE FORMALIST; HOWARD NEMEROV SONNET AWARD (Specialized: form, metrical), 320 Hunter Dr., Evansville IN 47711. Website: www2.evansville.edu/theformalist/. Established 1990. **Editor:** William Baer.

Magazine Needs: *The Formalist*, appearing biannually in Spring/Summer and Fall/Winter, is "dedicated to contemporary *metrical* poetry written in the great tradition of English-language verse. We're looking for well-crafted poetry in a contemporary idiom which uses meter and the full range of traditional poetic conventions in vigorous and interesting ways. We're especially interested in sonnets, couplets, tercets, ballads, the French forms, etc. We're not, however, interested in haiku (or syllabic verse of any kind) or sestinas. Only rarely do we accept a poem over 2 pages, and we have no interest in any type of erotica, blasphemy, vulgarity, or racism. Finally, we suggest that those wishing to submit to *The Formalist* become familiar with the journal beforehand. We are also interested in metrical translations of the poetry of major, formalist, non-English poets—from the ancient Greeks to the present." Has published poetry by Derek Walcott, Richard Wilbur, John Updike, Maxine Kumin, X.J. Kennedy, and W.D. Snodgrass. *The Formalist* is 128 pages, digest-sized, offset-printed on bond paper and perfect-bound, with colored card cover. Subscription: $14/year; $26/2 years (add $7/year for foreign subscription). Sample: $7.50.

How to Submit: Submit 3-5 poems at a time. No simultaneous submissions, previously published work, or disk submissions. A brief cover letter is recommended and a SASE is necessary for a reply and return of ms. Responds within 2 months. Guidelines available for SASE or on website. Pays 2 copies. Acquires first North American serial rights.

Also Offers: The Howard Nemerov Sonnet Award offers $1,000 and publication in *The Formalist* for the best unpublished sonnet. The final judge for 2003 was Dana Gioia. Entry fee: $3/sonnet. Postmark deadline: June 15. Guidelines available for SASE.

◐ FORPOETRY.COM, E-mail: submissions@forpoetry.com. Website: www.ForPoetry.com. Established March 1999. **Editor:** Jackie Marcus.

Magazine Needs: *ForPoetry.Com* is a web magazine with daily updates. "We wish to promote new and emerging poets, with or without MFAs. We will be publishing established poets, but our primary interest is in publishing excellent poetry, prose, and reviews. We are interested in lyric poetry, vivid imagery, open form, natural landscape, philosophical themes but not at the expense of honesty and passion: model examples: Robert Hass, James Wright, Charles Wright's *The Other Side of the River*, Montale, Neruda, Levertov, and Louise Glück. No city punk, corny sentimental fluff, or academic workshop imitations." Has published poetry by Sherod Santos, John Koethe, Jane Hirshfield, Erin Believ, and Kathy Fagan. "We receive lots of submissions and are very selective about acceptances, but we will always try to send a note back on rejections."

How to Submit: Submit no more than 2 poems at a time. Accepts simultaneous submissions; no previously published poems. E-mail submissions only; include text in body of message, no attachments. Cover letter preferred. Reads submissions September through May only. Time between acceptance and publication is 2-3 weeks. Poems are circulated to an editorial board. "We'll read all submissions and then decide together on the poems we'll publish." Comments on rejected poems "as often as possible." Guidelines available on website. Responds in 2 weeks. Reviews books and chapbooks of poetry and other magazines in 800 words.

Advice: "As my friend Kevin Hull said, 'Get used to solitude and rejection.' Sit on your poems for several months or more. Time is your best critic."

◯ ◎ 4*9*1 NEO-NAIVE IMAGINATION (Specialized: neo-naive), 3234 Cross Timbers Ln., Garland TX 75044. E-mail: stompdncr@aol.com or juanbeaumontez@aol.com. Website: www.4 91.20m.com. Established 1997. **Editor:** Donald Ryburn. **Assistant Editor:** Juan Beauregard-Montez.

Magazine Needs: *4*9*1 Neo-Naive Imagination* appears continuously as an online publication and publishes poetry, art, photography, essays, and interviews. Wants "poetry of neo-naive genre. No academic poetry, limited and fallacious language." Accepts poetry written by children. Has published poetry by Duane Locke and Jesus Morales-Montez.

How to Submit: Submit 3-6 poems at a time. Accepts previously published poems and simultaneous submissions. E-mail, fax, disk, and CD-ROM submissions preferred; include e-mail submissions in body of message. "No attachments accepted or opened." Note "submission" in subject area. "Would like to hear the poets own words not some standard format." Cover letter with picture and SASE preferred. Time between acceptance and publication varies. Response time varies. Payment varies. Acquires first or one-time rights. Reviews books and chapbooks of poetry and other magazines. Send materials for review consideration.

Also Offers: Sponsors a series of creative projects. Write for details or visit the website.

★ ◑ **FOUR WAY BOOKS**, Box 535, Village Station, New York NY 10014. (212)619-1105. Fax: (212)406-1352. E-mail: four_way_editors@yahoo.com. Website: www.fourwaybooks.com. Established 1993. **Director:** Martha Rhodes.

• Four Way Books has received gifts from the Greenwall Fund of The Academy of American Poets and from the Carnegie Foundation

Book/Chapbook Needs & How to Submit: Four Way Books publishes poetry and short fiction. Wants full-length (book length: 48-100 pages) poetry mss. Does not want individual poems or poetry intended for children/young readers. Recently published poetry by D. Nurkse, Noelle Kocot, Susan Wheeler, Nancy Mitchell, Henry Israeli, and Paul Jenkins. Publishes 8 poetry books and 1 anthology/year. Manuscripts are selected through open submission and through competition. Books are 70 pages, offset-printed digitally, perfect-bound, paperback binding with art/graphics on covers. Book mss may include previously published poems. See Four Way Books website for complete submission guidelines. Responds to queries in 4 months. Payment varies. Order sample books from Four Way Books online or through bookstores.

Also Offers: Four Way Books runs two biennial contests, The Intro Prize and The Levis Prize (see separate listings in the Contests & Awards section).

Advice: "Four Way Books is a not-for-profit organization dedicated to encouraging, supporting, and promoting the craft of writing and identifying and publishing writers at decisive stages in their careers."

◑ **FOURTEEN HILLS: THE SFSU REVIEW,** Creative Writing Dept., San Francisco State University, 1600 Holloway Ave., San Francisco CA 94132. (415)338-3083. Fax: (415)338-7030. E-mail: hills@sfsu.edu. Website: www.14hills.com. Established 1994. **Contact:** Poetry Editor.

Magazine Needs: *Fourteen Hills* is semiannual appearing in December and May. "We are seeking high quality, innovative work." Has published poetry by Alice Notley, CD Wright, Sherman Alexie, and Virgil Suarez. *Fourteen Hills* is 170 pages, digest-sized, professionally printed and perfect-bound with glossy card cover. Receives about 900 poems/year, accepts approximately 5-10%. Press run is 600 for 125 subscribers of which 25 are libraries. Single copy: $7; subscription: $12/year, $21/2 years. Sample: $5.

How to Submit: Submit 5 poems at a time. Accepts simultaneous submissions but please indicate if this is the case; no previously published poems. Cover letter preferred. Reads submissions August-September for the fall issue; January-February for the spring. "The editorial staff is composed entirely of graduate students from the Creative Writing Program at SFSU." Seldom comments on rejected poems. Guidelines available in publication and on website. Responds in 6 months. Always sends prepublication galleys. Pays 2 copies.

Advice: "Please read an issue of *Fourteen Hills* before submitting."

◑ ◎ **FREE FOCUS (Specialized: women/feminist); OSTENTATIOUS MIND (Specialized: form/style)**, P.O. Box 7415, JAF Station, New York NY 10116. *Free Focus* established 1985. *Ostentatious Mind* established 1987. **Poetry Editor:** Patricia D. Coscia.

Magazine Needs: *Free Focus* "is a literary magazine only for creative women, who reflect their ideas of love, nature, beauty, and men and also express the pain, sorrow, joy, and enchantment that their lives generate. *Free Focus* needs poems of all types on the subject matters above. Nothing X-rated, please. The poems can be as short as two lines or as long as two pages. The objective of this magazine is to give women poets a chance to be fullfilled in the art of poetry, for freedom of expression for women is seldom described in society." Has published poetry by Nicole Provencher, Mead, Judy Klare. *Ostentatious Mind* "is a co-ed literary magazine for material of stream of consciousness and experimental poems. The poets deal with the political, social, and psychological." Has published poetry by Mead, Katisha Burt, Stephen Kaplan. Both magazines are printed on 8 × 14 paper, folded in the middle and stapled to make a 10-page (including cover) format, with simple b&w drawings on the cover and inside. The two magazines appear every 6-8 months. Sample of either is $6.

How to Submit: Submit only 3 poems at a time. Poems should be typed neatly and clearly on white typing paper. Accepts simultaneous submissions and previously published poems. Publishes theme issues. Guidelines and upcoming themes available for SASE and in publication. Responds "as soon as possible." Sometimes sends prepublication galleys. Pays 1 copy.

Advice: "I think that anyone can write a poem who can freely express intense feelings about their experiences. A dominant thought should be ruled and expressed in writing, not by the spoken word, but the written word."

FREE LUNCH, P.O. Box 717, Glenview IL 60025-0717. Website: www.poetsfreelunch.org. Established 1988. **Editor:** Ron Offen.

Magazine Needs: *Free Lunch* is a "poetry journal interested in publishing the whole spectrum of what is currently being produced by American poets. Features a 'Mentor Series,' in which an established poet introduces a new, unestablished poet. Mentor poets are selected by the editor. Mentors have included Maxine Kumin, Billy Collins, Lucille Clifton, Donald Hall, Carolyn Forché, Wanda Coleman, Lyn Lifshin, and Stephen Dunn. Especially interested in experimental work and work by unestablished poets. Hope to provide all serious poets living in the US with a free subscription. For details on free subscription send SASE. Regarding the kind of poetry we find worthwhile, we like metaphors, similes, arresting images, and a sensitive and original use of language. We are interested in all genres—experimental poetry, protest poetry, formal poetry, etc. No restriction on form, length, subject matter, style, purpose. No aversion to form, rhyme." Poets published include Thomas Carper, Jared Carter, Billy Collins, David Wagoner, Donald Hall, D. Nurkse, and Cathy Song. *Free Lunch*, published 2 times/year, is 32-40 pages, digest-sized, attractively printed and designed, saddle-stapled, featuring free verse that shows attention to craft with well-knowns and newcomers alongside each other. Press run is 1,200 for 1,000 free subscriptions and 200 paid of which 15 are libraries. Subscription: $12 ($15 foreign). Sample: $5 ($6 foreign).

How to Submit: "Submissions must be limited to three poems and are considered only between September 1 and May 31. Submissions sent at other times will be returned unread. Although a cover letter is not mandatory, I like them. I especially want to know if a poet is previously unpublished, as I like to work with new poets." Accepts simultaneous submissions; no previously published poems. Editor comments on rejected poems and tries to return submissions in 2 months. Guidelines available for SASE. Pays 1 copy plus subscription.

Also Offers: A prize of $200 is awarded to one poem in each issue of *Free Lunch*. The winning poem of the Rosine Offen Memorial Award is selected solely by the Board of Directors of Free Lunch Arts Alliance. Winners announced in next issue.

Advice: "Archibald MacLeish said, 'A poem should not mean/ But be.' I have become increasingly leery of the ego-centered lyric that revels in some past wrong, good-old-boy nostalgia, or unfocused ecstatic experience. Not receptive to poems about writing poems, other poems, poetry reading, etc. Poetry is concerned primarily with language, rhythm, and sound; fashions and trends are transitory and to be eschewed; perfecting one's work is often more important than publishing it."

FREEFALL, Undead Poets Press, 15735 Kerstyn St., Taylor MI 48180. (248)543-6858. E-mail: mauruspoet@yahoo.com. Established 1999. **Editor/Publishers:** Marc Maurus and T. Anders Carson.

Magazine Needs: *freefall* appears biannually, publishing the quality work of beginners as well as established poets. "Free verse or formal poetry is okay, and our acceptance policy is broad. No concrete, shape, or greeting card verse. No gratuitous language or sex. No fuzzy animals or syrupy nature poems." Recently published poetry by T. Anders Carson, Kristin Hatch, Mary Hedger, Ann Holdreith, and Cara Jane Houlberg. *freefall* is 40 pages, digest-sized, laser-printed, saddle-stapled, card stock cover. Receives about 200 poems/year, accepts about 50%. Publishes about 30-40 poems/issue. Press run is 250 for 50 subscribers of which 10 are libraries, 25 shelf sales; 25 are distributed free to small press reviewers. Single copy: $5; subscription: $7.50. Sample: $5. Make checks payable to Marc Maurus.

How to Submit: Submit 5-10 poems at a time. Line length for poetry is 3 minimum, 80 maximum. Accepts previously published poems with notification; no simultaneous submissions. Accepts e-mail submissions; no fax or disk submissions. Cover letter is preferred. "Snail mail preferred, please send SASE. E-mail submissions in body, not attached." Reads submissions all year. Submit seasonal poems 6 months in advance. Time between acceptance and publication is 6 months. Poems are circulated to an editorial board. "If a poem is high quality, I accept it right away, poor work is rejected immediately, and those on the fence are circulated to as many as 3 other guest editors." Often comments on rejected poems. ***Poems may be sent for critique only for $2 each plus SASE.*** Guidelines are available for SASE. Responds in 2 weeks. Always sends prepublication galleys. Pays 2 contributor's copies. Acquires first rights; rights always revert to author on publication. Reviews chapbooks of poetry and other magazines/journals in 500 words, single book format. Send materials for review consideration to Marc Maurus.

Advice: "We prefer to see crafted work, not unedited one-offs. We welcome as much formal verse as we can because we feel there is a place for it."

✖ ⊠ $⊘ FREEFALL MAGAZINE, Alexandra Writers' Centre Society, 922 Ninth Ave. SE, Calgary AB T2G 0S4 Canada. Phone/fax: (403)264-4730. E-mail: awcs@telusplanet.net. Website: www.alexandrawriters.org. Established 1990. **Editor:** Sharon Drummond. **Managing Editor:** Sherring Amsden. Member: AMPA.

Magazine Needs: Published in March and October, "*FreeFall's* mandate is to encourage the voices of new, emerging, and experienced writers and provide an outlet for their work. Contains: fiction, nonfiction, poetry, interviews related to writers/writing; artwork and photographs suitable for b&w reproduction." Wants "poems in a variety of forms with a strong voice, effective language, and fresh images." Has published poetry by Anne Burke, Lyle Weiss, Myrna Garanis, Liz Rees, Bob Stamp, Judith Robb. *FreeFall* is 40-44 pages, magazine-sized, "xerox digital" printing and saddle-stapled with 60 lb. paper cover, includes art/graphics. Receives about 50-60 poems/year, accepts about 20%. Publishes 12-18 poems/issue. Press run is 350 for 270 subscribers of which 20 are libraries, 80 shelf sales; 30 distributed free to contributors, promotion. Single copy: $8.50 US, $7.50 Canadian; subscription: $14 US, $12 Canadian. Sample: $6.50 US, $5.50 Canadian.

How to Submit: Submit 2-5 poems at a time. Line length for poetry is 60 maximum. No previously published poems or simultaneous submissions. Accepts disk submissions (ASCII, text format) with hard copy but no fax or e-mail submissions. Cover letter with 2-line bio and SASE required. Reads submissions March through April and October through November only. Time between acceptance and publication is 6 months. Poems are circulated to an editorial board. "All submissions read by four editors." Seldom comments on rejected poems. Occasionally publishes theme issues. Guidelines and upcoming themes available for SAE and IRC, by e-mail, in publication, or on website. Responds in 3 months. Pays $5 Canadian/page and 1 copy. Acquires first North American serial rights.

Also Offers: See website for information about the Alexandra Writers' Centre Society activities and services and for additional information about *FreeFall* magazine. Hosts an annual fiction and poetry contest with October 1 deadline.

The theme for the Spring 2002 issue of *FreeFall Magazine* was "community." The editors say Brent Rambie's artwork captures a juxtaposition between the shopkeeper and the man-of-the-street "that demonstrates a natural energy between man and his environment that is universal." Rambie, a Canadian artist renowned for his treatment of people and landscape, also designed the cover.

⊕ ⊘ **FREEXPRESSION**, P.O. Box 4, West Hoxton NSW 2171 Australia. Phone: (02)9607 5559. Fax: (02)9826 6612. E-mail: freexpression@bigpond.com.au. Established 1993. **Managing Editor:** Peter F. Pike.

Magazine Needs: *FreeXpresSion* is a monthly publication containing "creative writing, how-to articles, short stories, and poetry including cinquain, haiku, etc., and bush verse." Open to all forms. "Christian themes OK. Humorous material welcome. No gratuitous sex; bad language OK. We don't want to see anything degrading." Has published poetry by Ron Stevens, John Ryan, and Ken Dean. *FreeXpresSion* is 28 pages, magazine-sized, offset-printed and saddle-stapled with paper cover, includes b&w graphics. Receives about 1,500 poems/year, accepts about 50%. Press run is 500 for 300 subscribers of which 20 are libraries. Single copy: $3.50 AUS; subscription: $35 AUS ($55 overseas airmail). For sample, send large SAE with $1 stamp.

How to Submit: Submit 3-4 poems at a time. Accepts previously published poems and simultaneous submissions. Accepts submissions on disk, by fax, by postal mail, and by e-mail (include in body of message). Cover letter preferred. "Very long poems are not desired but would be considered." Time between acceptance and publication is 2 months. Seldom comments on rejected poems. Publishes theme issues. Guidelines available by fax, for SAE and IRC, by e-mail, and in publication. Upcoming themes available by e-mail and in publication. Responds in 2 months. Sometimes sends prepublication galleys. Pays 1 copy, additional copies available at half price. Acquires first Australian rights only. Reviews books of poetry in 500 words. Send materials for review consideration.

Also Offers: Sponsors annual contest with 2 categories for poetry: blank verse (up to 40 lines), traditional verse (up to 80 lines). 1st Prize in blank verse: $200, 2nd Prize: $100. 1st Prize in traditional rhyming poetry: $250, 2nd Prize: $150, 3rd Prize: $100. *FreeXpresSion* also publishes books up to 200 pages through subsidy arrangements with authors.

Advice: "Keep it short and simple."

Ⓝ ⊘ **FRIGATE: THE TRANSVERSE REVIEW**. E-mail: editor@frigatezine.com. Website: www.frigatezine.com. Established 2000.

Magazine Needs & How to Submit: **"Unsolicited manuscripts not welcome. Query editor@frigatezine.com after reading guidelines posted on site."**

★ ◯ ◎ **FRODO'S NOTEBOOK (Specialized: poetry by teens 13-19)**, 23 N. Pine St., Jacobus PA 17407. E-mail: editors@frodosnotebook.com. Website: www.frodosnotebook.com. Established 1998. **Redactor in Chief:** Daniel Klotz. **Senior Poetry Editor:** Tina Dischinger. Member: the Words Work Network (WoW Net at www.wow-schools.net).

Magazine Needs: *Frodo's Notebook* is an online international quarterly of poetry, fiction, and essays by teens. Wants all styles, particularly narrative and personal poems. Does not want unfinished work or work by writers over 19 years of age. *Frodo's Notebook* is published online only. Receives about 1,000 poems/year, accepts about 70. Publishes about 15 poems/issue. Sample: all issues available online at no cost.

How to Submit: No previously published poems or simultaneous submissions. Accepts e-mail submissions; no fax or disk submissions. Cover letter is required. "Carefully read submission guidelines available on the website." Reads submissions year round. Time between acceptance and publication is 2-3 months. Poems are circulated to an editorial board. "Senior poetry editor makes final selection from a pool of submissions which has been narrowed down by other editors." Often comments on rejected poems. Guidelines available on website. Responds in up to 6 weeks. Acquires first rights. Reviews books of poetry and other magazines/journals in 1,500 words, single book format. Poets may send materials for review consideration to Daniel Klotz.

Advice: "Your chances of acceptance skyrocket if you take the time to revise and edit very carefully, being sure to eliminate clichés."

⊕ ◖ **FROGMORE PAPERS; FROGMORE POETRY PRIZE**, 18 Nevill Rd., Lewes, East Sussex BN7 1PF England. Website: www.frogmorepress.co.uk. Established 1983. **Poetry Editor:** Jeremy Page.

Magazine Needs: *Frogmore Papers* is a biannual literary magazine with emphasis on new poetry and short stories. "Quality is generally the only criterion, although pressure of space means very long work (over 100 lines) is unlikely to be published." Has published "Other Lilies" by Marita

Over and "A Plutonian Monologue" by Brian Aldiss and poetry by Carole Satyamurti, John Mole, Linda France, Elizabeth Garrett, John Harvey, and John Latham. *Frogmore Papers* is 42 pages, saddle-stapled with matte card cover, photocopied in photoreduced typescript. Accepts 3% of the poetry received. Their press run is 300 for 120 subscribers. Subscription: £7 ($20). Sample: £2 ($5). (US payments should be made in cash, not check.)

How to Submit: Submit 5-6 poems at a time. Considers simultaneous submissions. Editor rarely comments on rejected poems. Responds in 6 months. Pays 1 copy. Staff reviews books of poetry in 2-3 sentences, single book format. Send materials for review consideration to Catherine Smith, 24 South Way, Lewes, East Sussex BN7 1LU England.

Also Offers: Sponsors the annual Frogmore Poetry Prize. Write for information.

Advice: "My advice to people starting to write poetry would be: Read as many recognized modern poets as you can and don't be afraid to experiment."

$⊚ FROGPOND: INTERNATIONAL HAIKU JOURNAL; HAIKU SOCIETY OF AMERICA; HAIKU SOCIETY OF AMERICA AWARDS/CONTESTS (Specialized: form/style, haiku and related forms; translation), P.O. Box 122, Nassau NY 12123. Fax: (708)810-8992. E-mail: ithacan@earthlink.net. Website: www.octet.com/~hsa/. Established 1978. **Contact:** John Stevenson, associate editor. Editor: Jim Kacian (P.O. Box 2461, Winchester VA 22604-1661. E-mail: redmoon@shental.net.)

Magazine Needs: *Frogpond* is the international journal of the Haiku Society of America and is published triannually (February, June, October). Wants "contemporary English-language haiku, ranging from 1-4 lines or in a visual arrangement, focusing on a moment keenly perceived and crisply conveyed, using clear images and non-poetic language." Also accepts "related forms: senryu, sequences, linked poems, and haibun. It welcomes translations of any of these forms." Accepts poetry written by children. Has published work by Stephen Addiss, LeRoy Gorman, Martin Lucas, Yasuhiko Shigemoto, and Max Verhart. *Frogpond* is 96 pages, digest-sized, perfect-bound, and has 60 pages of poetry. Receives about 20,000 submissions/year, accepts about 500. *Frogpond* goes to 800 subscribers, of which 15 are libraries, as well as to over a dozen foreign countries. Sample back issues: $7. Make checks payable to Haiku Society of America.

How to Submit: Submit 5-10 poems, with 5 poems per 8½ × 11 sheet, with SASE (send submissions to John Stevenson, associate editor, at address mentioned above). No simultaneous submissions. Accepts submissions by e-mail (as attachment or in text box), on disk, by fax, or by regular mail. Information on the HSA and submission guidelines available for SASE. Responds "usually" in 3 weeks or less. Pays $1/accepted item. Poetry reviews usually 1,000 words or less. "Authors are urged to send their books for review consideration."

Also Offers: *Supplement* publishes longer essays, articles, and reviews from quarterly meetings and other haiku gatherings. *Supplement* is 96 pages, digest-sized, perfect-bound. *HSA Newsletter*, edited by Mark Brooks, appears 4 times/year and contains reports of the HSA Quarterly meetings, regional activities, news of upcoming events, results of contests, publications activities, and other information. A "best of issue" prize is awarded for each issue through a gift from the Museum of Haiku Literature, located in Tokyo. The Society also sponsors The Harold G. Henderson Haiku Award Contest, the Gerald Brady Senryu Award Contest, the Bernard Lionel Einbond Memorial Renku Contest, the Nicholas A. Virgilio Memorial Haiku Competition for High School Students and the Merit Book Awards for outstanding books in the haiku field.

Advice: "Submissions to *Frogpond* are accepted from both members and nonmembers, although familiarity with the journal will aid writers in discovering what it publishes."

◙ FULLOSIA PRESS; THE ROCKAWAY PARK PHILOSOPHICAL SOCIETY, P.O. Box 280, Ronkonkoma NY 11779. E-mail: deanofRPPS@aol.com. Website: http://RPPS_FULLOSIA_PRESS.tripod.com. Established 1971. **Contact:** jd collins.

Magazine Needs: *Fullosia Press* appears online monthly, presenting news, information, satire, and right-conservative perspective. Wants any style of poetry. "If you have something to say, say it. We consider many different points of view." Does not want "anti-American, anti-Christian." Accepts poetry by children with parental approval. Recently published poetry by Peter Vetrano, Angeline Hawkes-Craig, Dr. Kelley White, Peter Layton, and Alice Fritchie. *Fullosia Press* is published online only. Receives about 50 poems/year, accepts about 40%. Publishes a varied number of poems/issue. Single copy: $5 and SASE—free online. Sample: $5. Subscription: $20/year; free online. Make checks payable to RPPS-Fullosia Press.

How to Submit: Accepts fax, e-mail (in text box), and disk submissions. Cover letter is required. "Electronic submission by disk to address; e-mail preferred. Final submission by disk or e-mail only." Reads submissions when received. Submit seasonal poems 1 month in advance. Time between acceptance and publication varies. "I review all poems: (1) do they say something; (2) is there some thought behind it; (3) is it more than words strung together?" Always comments on rejected poems. Guidelines and upcoming themes available for SASE, by e-mail, on website, and in publication. Responds in 1 month. Acquires one-time rights. Reviews books and chapbooks of poetry and other magazines/journals. Send materials for review consideration to RPPS-Fullosia Press.

Advice: "Say what you have in mind without tripping over your own symbolism. We like poems which are clear, concise, to the point; American traditional heroes; Arthurian legend; American states. Everybody sings about Texas, has anyone written a poem to New Jersey?"

$☐ THE FUNNY PAPER; F/J WRITERS SERVICE, P.O. Box 10135, Kansas City MO 64171-0135. E-mail: felixkc@sbcglobal.net. Website: www.angelfire.com/biz/funnypaper. Established 1985. **Editor:** Felix Fellhauer.

Magazine Needs: *The Funny Paper* appears 5 times/year "to provide readership, help and the opportunity to write for money to budding authors/poets/humorists of all ages." Accepts poetry written by children, ages 8-15. Wants "light verse; space limited; humor always welcome. No tomes, heavy, dismal, trite work, or pornography." *The Funny Paper* is 10 pages, magazine-sized, photocopied on colored paper and unbound, includes clip art and cartoons. Receives about 300 poems/year, accepts about 10%. Single copy: $2, subscription: $10/year. Make checks payable to F/J Writers Service.

How to Submit: Submit 1-2 poems at a time. Line length for poetry is 16 lines maximum. Accepts submissions by postal mail and by e-mail (include in body of message). "We encourage beginners; handwritten poems OK. Submissions not returned." Seldom comments on rejected poems. Publishes contest theme issues regularly. Guidelines and upcoming themes available for SASE, in publication, by e-mail, or on website. Pays $5-25/published poem and 1 copy. Acquires one-time rights.

Also Offers: Sponsors contests with $100 prize. Guidelines available for SASE or on website.

Advice: "When trying for $100 prize, take us seriously. The competition is fierce."

☐ ◎ FURROW—THE UNDERGRADUATE LITERARY AND ART REVIEW (Specialized: undergraduates only); THE ORCHARD PRIZE FOR POETRY, UWM Union Box 194, University of Wisconsin-Milwaukee, P.O. Box 413, Milwaukee WI 53201. (414)229-3405. E-mail: furrow@csd.uwm.edu. Established 1999. **Poetry Editor:** Emily Hall. **Executive Editor:** Jenny Jacobson.

Magazine Needs: *Furrow—The Undergraduate Literary and Art Review* appears 2 times/year. "We simply want to see poetry that does not take for granted any of the prescribed aesthetic functions of a poem. A poem should have a certain felicity of expression and originality but also be sort of dangerous and fun. We want wild associations, pungent images, and layered meanings. For the most part, we are not interested in poetry that reinforces traditional styles or what is fashionable in poetry." Has published poetry by Erika Mueller, Sarah Schuetze, Mike Krull, Daniel John Frostman, Russ Bickerstaff, and Donald V. Kingsbury. *Furrow* is 45-70 pages, digest-sized, perfect-bound, card stock cover. Receives about 400 poems/year, accepts about 10%. Publishes about 15 poems/issue. Press run is 400 for 25 subscribers of which 5 are libraries, 300 shelf sales; 1 each distributed free to contributors. Single copy: $3; subscription: $6 (2 issues). Sample: $4. Make checks payable to *Furrow*.

How to Submit: Submit 3-5 poems at a time. Accepts simultaneous submissions; no previously published poems. Accepts e-mail and disk submissions. "Please include SASE and cover letter stating school, year in school, brief bio note (no more than 5 sentences), and contact information (address, phone, e-mail)." Reads submissions year round, "although we only publish a spring and a fall issue." Submit seasonal poems 2 months in advance. Time between acceptance and publication is 1-2 months. "Submissions are read by a single editor, acceptances notified upon approval of undergraduate status." Seldom comments on rejected poems. Guidelines available for SASE. Responds in 2 months.

Pays 1 contributors copy/accepted piece. Acquires one-time rights. Reviews books and chapbooks of poetry and other magazines in 3,000 words maximum, single book format. Send materials for review consideration to Brett Kell.

Advice: "We would like to think that our poets at least have the decency to want to change poetry and make it their own."

$◻ FUTURES MYSTERIOUS ANTHOLOGY MAGAZINE, 902 W. Fifth St., Winona MN 55987-5120. (612)724-4023. Fax: (612)729-5138. E-mail: babs@fmam.biz. Website: www.fmam.biz. Established 1997. **Editor:** R.C. Hildebrandt.

Magazine Needs: *Futures Mysterious Anthology Magazine* is a quarterly magazine containing short stories, poetry, artwork and "inspiration for artists of all kinds." "We want creative people with the fire to fly!" Do not want to receive gratuitous profanity or pornography. Has published poetry by R.C. Hildebrandt, Simon Perchik, Kristin Masterson, Karen Davenport, and Ally Reith. *FMAM* is 130 pages, magazine-sized, with 2-color semigloss cover, includes art and ads. Receives about 250 poems/year, accepts about 10%. Publishes 5-10 poems/issue. Press run is 3,000. Single copy: $10.95; subscription: $52. Sample (including guidelines): $8.

How to Submit: Submit up to 5 poems at a time. Maximum length per poem is 1½ pages. Rarely accepts previously published poems. Accepts submissions in e-mail text box and by postal mail. Cover letter with complete contact info and bio required. "Capitalize the first letter of each word in the title, no underline, brackets, or unnecessary quotation marks. One poem per page. Author's name (only) beneath each poem." Time between acceptance and publication is up to 2 years (notifies within 30 days prior to publication). All rights revert to author following one-time publication. "Works and bios may be edited for length and clarity." Time between acceptance and publication is up to 6 months. Often comments on rejected poems. "If you want to assure a critique of your work, you may enclose a SASE and $3 with your request." Occasionally publishes theme issues. Guidelines available on website. Responds in 6 weeks. Pays up to $50 "for best of the year."

Also Offers: There are 2 Publisher's Choice Awards per issue (not necessarily for poetry). Winners receive $25 plus an award certificate and "their caricature done by our cartoonist James Oddie."

Advice: "If it is flat on the page, it is not a poem. You have to make an impact in few words. In poetry the line is really all—like a commercial—you have to make an emotional statement in a flash."

★ ⊕ ◗ GALAXY PRESS, 71 Recreation St., Tweed Heads N.S.W., 2485 Australia. Phone: (07)5536-1447. Established 1978. **Editor:** Lance Banbury.

Book/Chapbook Needs: Galaxy Press publishes "high seriousness about the opportunities of culture at the latter end of the twentieth century, including personal or experimental responses." Wants "poetry equally concerned with form and content." Has published work by Sheila Williams and Will H. Ogilvie. Books are usually 16-20 pages, 15×21cm, offset/lithograph printed, glossy color card cover, includes art. Press run is 100. Obtain sample books or chapbooks by "written request."

How to Submit: Accepts previously published poems and simultaneous submissions. Cover letter preferred. Often comments on rejected poems. Responds to queries in 2 weeks. Pays 10 copies.

Advice: "Sincerity is important but so is the vehicle in which it is conveyed, which ideally should be disciplined and contemporary, to whatever extent possible and in regard to personal understanding of postmodernism."

◗ GARGOYLE MAGAZINE; PAYCOCK PRESS, P.O. Box 6216, Arlington VA 22206-0216. (202)234-3287. E-mail: atticus@atticusbooks.com. Website: www.atticusbooks.com. Established 1976. **Co-Editors:** Richard Peabody and Lucinda Ebersole.

Magazine Needs: *Gargoyle Magazine* appears annually "to publish the best literary magazine we can. We generally run short one page poems. We like wit, imagery, killer lines. Not big on rhymed

---

NEED HELP? To better understand and use the information in these listings, see the introduction to this section.

verse or language school." Has published poetry by Kim Addonizio, Nin Andrews, Kenneth Carroll, Bruce A. Jacobs, Priscilla Lee, and Eileen Tabios. *Gargoyle* is 175 pages, digest-sized, offset printed and perfect-bound, color cover, includes photos, artwork and ads. Accept approximately 10% of the poems received each year. Press run is 2,000. Subscription: $20 for 2; $25 to institutions. Sample: $10. Make checks payable to Atticus Books.

How to Submit: Submit 5 poems at a time. Accepts simultaneous submissions. Prefers e-mail submissions in Microsoft Word or WordPerfect format. Accepts submissions by postal mail also. Reads submissions Memorial Day through Labor Day only. Time between acceptance and publication is 5 months. Poems are circulated to an editorial board. "The two editors make some concessions but generally concur." Often comments on rejected poems. Responds in 2 months. Always sends prepublication galleys. Pays 1 copy and ½ off additional copies. Acquires first rights

Book/Chapbook Needs & How to Submit: Paycock Press has published 9-10 books since 1976 and are not currently seeking mss.

GECKO, P.O. Box 6492, Destin FL 32550. E-mail: geckogalpoet@hotmail.com. Established 1998. **Editor:** Rebecca Lu Kiernan.

Magazine Needs & How to Submit: "Due to the overwhelming response of *Poet's Market* readers and personal projects of the editor, we are currenly closed to unsolicited manuscripts. We hope to change this in the future when an assistant will assume some of the editor's duties."

GENERATOR; GENERATOR PRESS (Specialized: visual poetry), 3503 Virginia Ave., Cleveland OH 44109. (216)351-9406. E-mail: generatorpress@msn.com. Website: www.genera torpress.com. Established 1987. **Editor:** John Byrum.

Magazine Needs: *Generator* is an annual magazine "devoted to the presentation of all types of experimental poetry, focusing on language poetry and 'concrete' or visual poetic modes."

Book/Chapbook Needs: Generator Press also publishes the Generator Press chapbook series. Approximately 1 new title/year.

How to Submit: Currently not accepting unsolicited manuscripts for either the magazine or chapbook publication.

GENTLE READER, 8 Heol Pen-y-Bryn, Penyrheol, Caerphilly, Mid Glam, South Wales CF83 2JX United Kingdom. Phone: (029)20 886369. E-mail: lynneejones@tiscali.co.uk. Established 1994. **Editor:** Lynne E. Jones.

● Editor will return from sabbatical and resume producing *Gentle Reader* after January 2004.

Magazine Needs: Published quarterly, *Gentle Reader* is "a short story magazine to encourage mostly new and unpublished writers worldwide. Poems provide food for thought and sometimes light relief." Wants "general easy to read verse, not too long, that appeals to a wide audience. Nothing obscure, odd, or esoteric." Accepts haiku. *Gentle Reader* is 48 pages, A5, desktop-published and stapled with paper cover, includes clip art and scanned photos, reciprocal ads from other small presses. Receives about 50 poems/year, accepts up to 80%. Press run is 80 for 65 subscribers of which 5 are libraries. Single copy: £2.50, overseas £3.50; subscription: £8.50, overseas £12.00. Sample: £2.00. Make checks payable (in sterling) to L.E. Jones.

How to Submit: Submit 2-3 poems at a time. Line length for poetry is 12 minimum, 30 maximum. Accepts previously published poems and simultaneous submissions. Accepts submissions by postal mail and by e-mail (as attachment or in text box; use slashes to indicate line breaks). "Include IRCs please for reply and return of work." Cover letter preferred. Time between acceptance and publication is up to 1 year. Guidelines available for SAE and IRC and by e-mail. Responds in 2 months. Acquires first British serial rights. Staff reviews other magazines in 50 words, single book format. Send materials for review consideration.

Advice: "Keep it simple."

THE GENTLE SURVIVALIST (Specialized: ethnic, nature, inspirational), P.O. Box 4004, St. George UT 84770. E-mail: gentle-survivalist@yahoo.com. Website: www.infowest.com/ gentle/. Established 1991. **Editor/Publisher:** Laura Martin-Bühler.

Magazine Needs: *The Gentle Survivalist* is a quarterly newsletter of "harmony—timeless truths and wisdom balanced with scientific developments for Native Americans and all those who believe in the Great Creator." Wants poetry that is "positive, inspirational, on survival of body and spirit, also man's interconnectedness with God and all His creations. Nothing sexually oriented, occult, negative, or depressing." Welcomes poetry in Spanish with English translation. Newsletter subjects vary dramatically from environmental illness, Eastern medicine, and common household toxins to avoid to money-saving tips and ideas on writing a personal history. Accepts poetry written by young poets. Has published poetry by Keith Moore and C.S. Churchman. "We print four poems average per issue." Press run is 200. Subscription: $20. Sample: $5.

How to Submit: Submit 4 poems at a time. Accepts previously published poems and simultaneous submissions. No e-mail submissions. Cover letter required; "just a note would be fine. I find noteless submissions too impersonal." Time between acceptance and publication is up to 4 months. For written evaluation and editing, send $5. "Written evaluation money is returned if writing is inappropriate or rejected. Evaluation and editing does not guarantee writing will be published." Guidelines are available for SASE and on website; no guidelines mailed without sample request and $5. "Folks need to see what they are getting into and I need to weed out frivolous submitters." Responds within 2 months. Does not return poetry. Pays 1 copy.

Also Offers: Sponsors annual contest. Awards a 1-year subscription to the winner. Winner announced in Spring issue.

Advice: "To succeed, one must not seek supporters, but seek to know whom to support. *The Gentle Survivalist* receives a great deal of poetry that is too general in nature. We seek poems of inspiration about God, Man, and our interconnectedness with all living."

$ THE GEORGIA REVIEW, The University of Georgia, Athens GA 30602-9009. (706)542-3481. Website: www.uga.edu/garev. Established 1947. **Editor:** T.R. Hummer. **Contact:** The Editors.

Magazine Needs: *Georgia Review* appears quarterly. "We seek the very best work we can find, whether by Nobel laureates and Pulitzer Prize-winners or by little-known (or even previously unpublished) writers. All manuscripts receive serious, careful attention." Has published poetry by Peter Davison, Rita Dove, Stephen Dunn, Philip Levine, Linda Pastan, and Pattiann Rogers. "We have featured first-ever publications by many new voices over the years, but encourage all potential contributors to become familiar with past offerings before submitting." *The Georgia Review* is 208 pages, 7×10, professionally printed, flat-spined with glossy card cover. Uses 60-70 poems/year, less than one-half of one percent of those received. Press run is 5,500. Subscription: $24/year. Sample: $7.

How to Submit: Submit 3-5 poems at a time. No simultaneous submissions. Rarely uses translations. No submissions accepted from May 15 through August 15. Occasionally publishes theme issues. Guidelines available for SASE and on website. Responds in 4 months. Always sends prepublication galleys. Pays $3/line, 1-year subscription, and a copy of issue in which work appears. Acquires first North American serial rights. Reviews books of poetry. "Our poetry reviews range from 500-word 'Book Briefs' on single volumes to 5,000-word essay reviews on multiple volumes."

Advice: "Needless to say, competition is extremely tough. All styles and forms are welcome, but response times can be slow during peak periods in the fall and late spring."

GERONIMO REVIEW; MAOMAO PRESS. E-mail: geronimoreview@ATT.net. Website: http://home.att.net/~geronimoreview. Established 1998. **Editor:** g. bassetti.

Magazine Needs: At this time *geronimo review* appears randomly as a zine. "Submit whatever strikes your fancy. Literally. Anything. *geronimo review* will publish on its website virtually everything submitted. Overt pornography, hate speech, etc. taken under editorial advisement." Has two submission categories—Open (these submissions are graded "mercilessly" by both editors and readers) and Amateur ("graded on an appropriate scale"). Wants "politics and political satire. *Anything* of unusual excellence, especially the short lyric." Recently published poetry by Mark C. Peery, dada rambass, zeninubasho, geronimo bassetti, and Élan B. Yergmoul.

How to Submit: Submit 3 poems at a time. Line length for poetry is 100 maximum (or the length demanded by the poem). Accepts simultaneous submissions; no previously published poems. Accepts submissions by e-mail only (as Word attachment or in text box). Reads submissions all year. Time between acceptance and publication is 2 weeks. Guidelines available on website. Responds in 3 weeks. Acquires all rights; returns to poet "on request." Reviews books and chapbooks of poetry and other magazines in 250-500 words, single book format. Send materials for review consideration to *geronimo review*.

Book/Chapbook Needs & How to Submit: MaoMao Press will publish essays on and reviews of poetry in the future. "Not presently accepting book submissions—watch our website."

Also Offers: Plans anthology of *geronimo review* material. "We hope to publish in printed form the cream of the crop sometime in the next year." Also publishing essays on Shakespearean sonnets which address the question of authorship.

Advice: "Don't be Susan Wheeler. Be in the tradition of Yeats, Frost, Carroll, Stevens, and be really original and inspire strong reactions."

GESTALTEN (Specialized: form/style), 15 St. Croix Place, Apt. M, Greensboro NC 27410. Website: www.brokenboulder.com. Established 1996. **Co-Editors:** Adam Powell and Paul Silvia.

Magazine Needs: *gestalten* appears 2 times/year and publishes experimental poetry from new and established writers. "We want experimental, abstract, collage, visual, language, asemic, found, system, proto, non, and simply strange forms of poetry. Coherence and words are optional. No vampire poetry; religious/inspirational poetry; Bukowski rip offs; no poems containing the word 'poetry'." Has published poetry by John Lowther, Spencer Selby, Peter Ganick, John M. Bennett, Michael Lenhart, and the Atlanta Poet's Group. *gestalten* is a 40 page saddle-stapled journal with full-color cover, includes "tons" of art/graphics and a few small-press ads. Receives about 500 poems/year, accepts about 20%. Publish 50 poems/issue. Press run is 100 for 80 subscribers. Subscription: $7/2 issues. Sample: $4. Make checks payable to Broken Boulder Press.

How to Submit: Submit 5-20 poems at a time. No previously published poems or simultaneous submissions. No fax or e-mail submissions. Cover letter preferred. "SASE required. No e-mail submissions, please. We like casual and quirky cover letters." Time between acceptance and publication is up to 8 months. Always comments on rejected poems. Guidelines available for SASE and on website. Responds in 3 weeks. Sometimes sends prepublication galleys. Pays 5 copies. Acquires one-time rights.

Advice: "You can't do anything new until you know what's already been done. For every hour you spend writing, spend five hours reading other writers."

GIN BENDER POETRY REVIEW, P.O. Box 406, Huntington TX 75949. E-mail: ginbender@yahoo.com (inquiries); submissions@ginbender.com (submissions). Website: www.ginbender.com. Established 2002. **Founder/Chief Editor:** T.A. Thompson.

Magazine Needs: *Gin Bender Poetry Review* is a literary webzine appearing 3 times/year and featuring both experienced and new writers. Wants poetry "from traditional to experimental." Does not want rhyme, sad love stories, greeting card verse. Recently published poetry by Janet Buck, Christopher Mulrooney, Duane Locke, Taylor Graham, Sean Brown, and Corey Mesler. *Gin Bender Poetry Review* is published online only. Receives about 400 poems/year, accepts about 10%. Publishes about 20 poems/issue. Sample: free online.

How to Submit: Submit 3-5 poems at a time. No previously published poems or simultaneous submissions. Accepts e-mail submissions; no fax or disk submissions. Cover letter is preferred. "We prefer e-mail submissions but also accept snail mail submissions with SASE." Reads submissions year round. Time between acceptance and publication is 4 months. Poems are circulated to an editorial board. "Submissions are read by an editorial staff of three people." Seldom comments on rejected poems. Guidelines available on website. Responds in up to 6 weeks. Acquires first rights.

Advice: "Send us something that will grasp our soul with vehemence."

$ GINNINDERRA PRESS, P.O. Box 53, Charnwood ACT 2615 Australia. E-mail: smgp@cyberone.com.au. Website: www.ginninderrapress.com.au. Established 1996. **Publisher:** Stephen Matthews.

Book/Chapbook Needs: Ginninderra Press works "to give publishing opportunities to new writers." Has published poetry by Alan Gould and Geoff Page. Books are usually up to 72 pages, A5, laser printed and saddle-stapled or thermal-bound with board cover, sometimes includes art/graphics.

How to Submit: Query first, with a few sample poems and cover letter with brief bio and publication credits. Accepts previously published poems; no simultaneous submissions. No fax or e-mail submisions. Time between acceptance and publication is 2 months. Seldom comments on rejected poems. Responds to queries in 1 week; to mss in 2 months. Pays royalties of 12½%.

GLASS TESSERACT. E-mail: editor@glasstesseract.com. Website: www.glasstesseract.com. Established 2001. **Editor:** Michael Chester.

Magazine Needs: *Glass Tesseract* appears once or twice a year in hardcopy and online and publishes poems and short stories. "Our purpose is to help bring works of art into the world. Our interests are eclectic." Wants poetry that is "rich in imagery, emotion, ideas, or the sound of language. We are open to all forms from rhyming sonnets to unrhymed, open-ended anything—so long as we feel that the poem is a work of art. We don't want sentimental, moralizing, devotional, cute, coy, or happy face poems." Recently published poetry by J.P. Dancing Bear, Rebecca Lu Kiernan, Corrine Lee, and Fernand Roqueplan. The hardcopy of *Glass Tesseract* is 48-96 pgs., digest-sized, laser-printed, spiral-comb bound, linen paper, color frontispiece, cover with art, some issues with b&w line art illustrations. Publishes about 24-48 poems/issue. "Each issue will also be provided on the website as a read-only pdf file, free to all readers to download to their computers for viewing, printing, or copying to CD. Furthermore, a special rotating selections menu displays poems selected from past, present, and future issues." Hard copy: $12. Enquire by e-mail about availability and new mailing address prior to sending a check. Make checks payable to *Glass Tesseract*.

How to Submit: Submit up to 10 poems at a time. Accepts simultaneous submissions and, occasionally, reprints. Accepts e-mail submissions only. Cover letter is optional. Reads submissions year round. Time between acceptance and publication is up to 1 year except for online publication on rotating selections menu (not guaranteed to all). "Poems are reviewed initially by one or more consulting editors and, before acceptance, by the editor. We are particularly alert to strong poems that differ from our own preferred styles." Sometimes comments on rejected poems. Guidelines are available in magazine, by e-mail, or on website. Responds in up to 4 months. Sometimes sends prepublication galleys. Pays 1 hardcopy of the magazine. Acquires one-time rights which revert to author upon publication.

Advice: "Steep yourself in the best enduring poetry found in anthologies or taught in literature classes—then go your own way. Experiment until you find your voice. Keep reading other poets in the magazines that interest you for your own poems."

GOOD FOOT, P.O. Box 681, Murray Hill Stn., New York NY 10156. E-mail: submissions@goodfootmagazine.com. Website: www.goodfootmagazine.com. Established 2000. **Editors:** Amanda Lea Johnson, Katherine Sarkis, Carmine Simmons, Matthew Thorburn.

Magazine Needs: *Good Foot* appears biannually and publishes "an eclectic mix of the finest poetry written by established and emerging poets. We welcome a wide cross-section of work without restriction: both free and formal, experimental and traditional, original and in translation, all styles and schools. Our only standard for selection is the quality of the work." Recently published poetry by Rachel Hadas, Matthea Harvey, David Lehman, David Trinidad, Paul Violi, and Susan Wheeler. *Good Foot* is about 100 pages, 7×8.5, professionally offset-printed, perfect-bound, 2-3 color matte card cover, with b&w photos/artwork and back page ads. Receives about 800 poems/year, accepts about 10%. Publishes about 50 poems/issue. Press run is 500. Single copy: $8; subscription: $14. Sample: $8. Make checks payable to *Good Foot Magazine*.

How to Submit: Submit 3 poems at a time. Accepts simultaneous submissions ("with timely notice of acceptance elsewhere"); no previously published poems. Accepts submissions by e-mail (in text box, no attachments), on disk, and by postal mail. Cover letter is preferred. "Include brief bio in cover letter. Include SASE." Reads submissions year round. Submit seasonal poems 6 months in advance. Time between acceptance and publication is 6 months. Poems are circulated to an editorial board ("read by all four editors"). Seldom comments on rejected poems. Guidelines available on website. Responds in up to 2 months. Sometimes sends prepublication galleys. Pays 1 contributor's copy. Acquires first North American serial rights. Reviews books of poetry ("reviews not included in every issue but upcoming issues may include them"). Send materials for review consideration to the attention of the editors.

GOOSE LANE EDITIONS (Specialized: regional, Canada), 469 King St., Fredericton NB E3B 1E5 Canada. (506)450-4251. Website: http://gooselane.com. Established 1954. **Editorial Director:** Laurel Boone.

Book/Chapbook Needs: Goose Lane is a small literary press publishing Canadian fiction, poetry, and nonfiction. Writers should be advised that Goose Lane considers mss by Canadian poets only. Receives approximately 400 mss/year, publishes 10-15 books yearly, 3 of these being poetry collections. Has published *Wanting the Day* by Brian Bartlett as well as *Coastlines: The Poetry of Atlantic Canada* edited by Anne Compton, Laurence Hutchman, Ross Leckie, and Robin McGrath.

How to Submit: Not currently reading unsolicited submissions. "Call to inquire whether we are reading submissions." Guidelines available for SASE. Always sends prepublication galleys. Authors may receive royalty of up to 10% of retail sale price on all copies sold. Copies available to author at 40% discount.

Advice: "Many of the poems in a manuscript accepted for publication will have been previously published in literary journals such as *The Fiddlehead, The Dalhousie Review, The Malahat Review,* and the like."

$ GRAIN; SHORT GRAIN CONTEST, P.O. Box 67, Saskatoon SK S7K 3K1 Canada. (306)244-2828. Fax: (306)244-0255. E-mail: grainmag@sasktel.net. Website: www.grainmagazine. ca. Established 1973. **Editor:** Elizabeth Philips. **Poetry Editor:** Séan Virgo.

• Grain was voted Saskatchewan Magazine of the Year, Western Magazine Awards 2001.

Magazine Needs: "*Grain,* a literary quarterly, strives for artistic excellence and seeks poetry that is well-crafted, imaginatively stimulating, distinctly original." Has published poetry by Lorna Crozier, Don Domanski, Cornelia Haeussler, Partrick Lane, Karen Solie, and Monty Reid. *Grain* is 128-144 pages, digest-sized, professionally printed. Press run is 1,800 for 1,600 subscribers of which 100 are libraries. Receives about 1,200 submissions of poetry/year, accepts 80-140 poems. Subscription: $26.95/1 year, $39.95/2 years, for international subscriptions provide $4 postage for 1 year, $8 postage for 2 years in US dollars. Sample: $9.95 plus IRC.

How to Submit: Submit up to 8 poems, typed on 8½×11 paper, single-spaced, one side only. No previously published poems or simultaneous submissions. Cover letter required. Include "the number of poems submitted, address (with postal or zip code), and phone number. Submissions accepted by regular post only. No e-mail submissions." Reads submissions August 15 through May 30 only. Guidelines available for SASE (or SAE and IRC), by fax, by e-mail, in publication, or on website. Responds in 3 months. "Response by e-mail if address provided (ms recycled). Then IRCs or SASE not required." Pays $40/page—up to five pages or a maximum of $175— and 2 copies. Acquires first North American serial rights.

Also Offers: Holds an annual Short Grain Contest. The four categories include Prose Poems (a lyric poem written as a prose paragraph or paragraphs in 500 words or less), Dramatic Monologues, Postcard Stories (also 500 words or less), or Long Grain of Truth (creative nonfiction, 5,000 words or less). "Twelve prizes of $500; three equal prizes in each category." Entry fee of $22 allows up to two entries in the same category, and includes a 1-year subscription. Additional entries are $5 each. "U.S. and international entrants send fees in U.S. funds ($22 for two entries in one category plus $4 to help cover postage)." Entries are normally accepted between September 1 and January 31. Also sponsors the Anne Szumigalski Editor's prize for poetry, $500 annually.

Advice: "Only work of the highest literary quality is accepted. Read several back issues."

GRASSLANDS REVIEW, P.O. Box 626, Berea OH 44017. E-mail: GrasslandsReview@aol.c om. Website: www.grasslandsreview.blogspot.com. Established 1989. **Editor:** Laura B. Kennelly.

Magazine Needs: *Grasslands Review* is a biannual magazine "to encourage beginning writers and to give adult creative writing students experience in editing fiction and poetry; using any type of poetry; shorter poems stand best chance." Has published poetry by William Virgil Davis, Kim A. Jaxtheimer, Rich Murphy, Stephen Kopel, Rob Carraway, and Eve Pekkala. *Grasslands Review* is 80 pages, digest-sized, professionally printed, photocopied, saddle-stapled with card cover. Accepts 30-50 of 600 submissions received. Press run is 200. Subscription (2 issues): $10 for individuals, $20 institutions. Sample: $5 for older issues, $6 for more recent.

How to Submit: Submit only during October and March, no more than 5 poems at a time. No previously published poems or simultaneous submissions. No e-mail submissions. Short cover letter preferred. Send #10 SASE for response. Editor comments on submissions "sometimes." Responds in 4 months. Sometimes sends prepublication galleys. Pays 1 copy.

Also Offers: Sponsors annual Editors' Prize Contest. Prize: $100 and publication. Deadline: September 30. Entry fee: $12 for 5 poems, $1/poem extra for entries over 5 poems. Entry fee includes 1-year subscription. Send SASE for reply.

Ⓩ GRAYWOLF PRESS, 2402 University Ave., Suite 203, Saint Paul MN 55114. E-mail: wolves @graywolfpress.org (for book catalog requests only). Website: www.graywolfpress.org. Established 1974. **Contact:** Editorial Department.

● Poetry published by Graywolf Press has been included in the 2002 *Pushcart Prize* anthology.

Book/Chapbook Needs: Graywolf Press does not read unsolicited mss. Considers mss *only* by poets widely published in journals of merit. Has published poetry by Jane Kenyon, David Rivard, Vijay Seshadri, John Haines, Eamon Grennan, Tess Gallagher, Tony Hoagland, William Stafford, Linda Gregg, Carl Phillips, and Dana Gioia. Sometimes sends prepublication galleys. No e-mail submissions or queries.

Ⓩ GREEN BEAN PRESS, P.O. Box 237, Canal Street Station, New York NY 10013. Phone/fax: (718)965-2076. E-mail: gbpress@earthlink.net. Website: www.greenbeanpress.com. Established 1993. **Editor:** Ian Griffin.

Book/Chapbook Needs: Green Bean Press publishes 6-8 chapbooks and 2-4 full-length books/year. Chapbooks are usually 20-30 pages, priced $5-6; occasional graphics; cover art sometimes provided by author, other times by publisher." Average press run is 125, pays 10 copies and 10% of list price royalty. Full-length books can range from 78-300 pages, usually digest-sized, list prices $10-16. Catalog available online only. Average press run is 600. Has published *From the Scenic Outlook the Battlefield Churns Beautifully* by Thomas M. Cassidy and *The West End* by Jessica Maich.

How to Submit: No unsolicited mss are read for full-length books. For chapbooks query first, with 5-10 sample poems and cover letter with brief bio and publication credits by mail, fax, or e-mail. "Not the entire manuscript, please." E-mail submissions preferred in body of e-mail, no attachments. Responds to queries in 1 month and mss in 2 months. Pays 10% author's copies and 10% of net sales.

Ⓩ GREEN HILLS LITERARY LANTERN, Truman State University, Division of Language & Literature, Kirksville MO 63501. (660)785-4513. E-mail: jksmith@grm.net or jbeneven@truman.e du. **Co-editors:** Joe Benevento (poetry) and Jack Smith (fiction).

Magazine Needs: *Green Hills Literary Lantern*, an annual journal of Truman State University appearing in summer or early fall, is open to short fiction and poetry of "exceptional quality." Wants "the best poetry, in any style, preferably understandable. There are no restrictions on subject matter, though pornography and gratuitous violence will not be accepted. Obscurity for its own sake is also frowned upon. Both free and formal verse forms are fine, though we publish more free verse overall. No haiku, limericks, or anything over two pages." Has published poetry by Jim Thomas, Phillip Dacey, Susan Terris, Louis Philips, Francine Tolf, and Julie Lechevsky. *Green Hills Literary Lantern* is 200-300 pages, digest-sized, professionally printed and perfect-bound with glossy, 4-color cover. Receives work by more than 200 poets/year and publishes about 10% of the poets submitting—less than 10% of all poetry received. Press run is 500. Sample: $7.

How to Submit: Send fiction to Jack Smith, *Green Hills Literary Lantern*, P.O. Box 375, Trenton MO 64683 and poetry to Joe Benevento, *Green Hills Literary Lantern*, Truman State University, Division of Language & Literature, Kirksville MO 63501. Submit 3-7 poems at a time, typed, 1 poem/page. Accepts simultaneous submissions but not preferred; no previously published poems. No fax or e-mail submissions. Cover letter with list of publications preferred. Often comments on rejected poems. Guidelines available for SASE or by e-mail. Responds within 4 months. Always sends prepublication galleys. Pays 2 copies. Acquires one-time rights.

Advice: "Read the best poetry and be willing to learn from what you encounter. A genuine attempt is made to publish the best poems available, no matter who the writer. First time poets, well-established poets, and those in-between, all can and have found a place in the *Green Hills Literary Lantern*. We try to supply feedback, particularly to those we seek to encourage."

● **GREEN MOUNTAINS REVIEW**, Johnson State College, Johnson VT 05656. (802)635-1350. Fax: (802)635-1294. E-mail: gmr@badger.jsc.vsc.edu. Established 1975. **Poetry Editor:** Neil Shepard.

• Poetry published in *Green Mountains Review* has been included in *The Best American Poetry* and the *Pushcart Prize* anthology.

Magazine Needs: *Green Mountains Review* appears twice/year and includes poetry (and other writing) by well-known authors and promising newcomers. Has published poetry by Carol Frost, Sharon Olds, Carl Phillips, David St. John, and David Wojahn. *Green Mountains Review* is digest-sized, flat-spined, 150-200 pages. Of 3,000 submissions they publish 30 authors. Press run is 1,800 for 200 subscribers of which 30 are libraries. Subscription: $14/year. Sample back issue: $5, current issue $8.50.

How to Submit: Submit no more than 5 poems at a time. Accepts simultaneous submissions. Reads submissions September 1 through March 1 only. Editor sometimes comments on rejection slip. Publishes theme issues. Guidelines and upcoming themes are available for SASE. Responds in up to 6 months. Pays 2 copies plus 1-year subscription. Acquires first North American serial rights. Send materials for review consideration.

● **GREENHOUSE REVIEW PRESS**, 3965 Bonny Doon Rd., Santa Cruz CA 95060. Established 1975. Publishes a series of poetry chapbooks and broadsides. "Unsolicited mss are not accepted."

■ ● **GREEN'S MAGAZINE**, P.O. Box 3236, Regina SK S4P 3H1 Canada. Established 1972. **Editor:** David Green.

Magazine Needs: *Green's Magazine* is a literary quarterly with a balanced diet of short fiction and poetry. Publishes "free/blank verse examining emotions or situations." Does not want greeting card jingles or pale imitations of the masters. Accepts poetry written by children. Has published poetry by Robert L. Tener, B.Z. Niditch, Nannette Swift Melcher, Ruth Moon Kempher, Giovanni Malito, and Ian Pilarczyk. *Green's* is 96 pages, digest-sized, typeset on buff stock with line drawings, matte card cover, saddle-stapled. Press run is 300. Subscription: $15. Sample: $5.

How to Submit: Submit 4-6 poems at a time. Prefers typescript, complete originals. No simultaneous submissions. "If © used, poet must give permission to use and state clearly the work is unpublished." Time between acceptance and publication is usually 6 months. Comments are usually provided on rejected mss. Guidelines available for SAE and IRC. Responds in 2 months. Pays 1 copy. Acquires first North American serial rights. Occasionally reviews books of poetry in "up to 150-200 words."

Advice: "Would-be contributors are urged to study the magazine first."

● **THE GREENSBORO REVIEW; GREENSBORO REVIEW LITERARY AWARDS**, English Dept., Room 134, McIver Bldg., University of North Carolina, P.O. Box 26170, Greensboro NC 27402. (336)334-5459. E-mail: jlclark@uncg.edu. Website: www.uncg.edu/eng/mfa. Established 1966. **Editor:** Jim Clark. **Contact:** Poetry Editor.

• Work published in this review has been consistently anthologized or cited in *Best American Short Stories, New Stories from the South, Pushcart Prize*, and *Prize Stories: The O. Henry Award*.

Magazine Needs: *The Greensboro Review* appears twice yearly and showcases well-made verse in all styles and forms, though shorter poems (under 50 lines) seem preferred. Has published poetry by Stephen Dobyns, Thomas Lux, Stanley Plumly, Alan Shapiro, and Bruce Smith. *The Greensboro Review* is 128 pages, digest-sized, professionally printed and flat-spined with colored matte cover. Uses about 25 pages of poetry in each issue, about 1.5% of the 2,000 submissions received for each issue. Subscription: $10/year, $25/3 years. Single/sample: $5.

How to Submit: "Submissions (no more than five poems) must arrive by September 15 to be considered for the Spring issue (acceptances in December) and February 15 to be considered for the Fall issue (acceptances in May). Manuscripts arriving after those dates will be held for consideration with the next issue." No previously published poems or simultaneous submissions. No fax or e-mail submissions. Cover letter not required but helpful. Include number of poems submitted. Guidelines available for SASE, on website, and in publication. Responds in 4 months. Always sends prepublication galleys. Pays 3 copies. Acquires first North American serial rights.

Also Offers: Sponsors an open competition for *The Greensboro Review* Literary Awards, $500 for both poetry and fiction each year. Deadline: September 15. Guidelines available for SASE, on website, and in publication.
Advice: "We want to see the best being written regardless of theme, subject, or style."

GSU REVIEW; GSU REVIEW ANNUAL WRITING CONTEST, Georgia State University, Campus Box 1894, Atlanta GA 30303. (404)651-4804. Fax: (404)651-1710. E-mail: kchaple@e mory.edu. Website: www.gsu.edu/~wwwrev/. Established 1980. **Editor:** Katie Chaple. **Poetry Editor:** Josephine Pallos.
Magazine Needs: *GSU Review* is a biannual literary magazine publishing fiction, poetry, and photography. Wants "original voices searching to rise above the ordinary. No subject or form biases." Does not want pornography or Hallmark verse. Has published poetry by Gary Sange, Virgil Suarez, Earl Braggs, Charles Fort, Kenneth Chamlee, and Dana Littlepage Smith. *GSU Review* is 112 pages. Press run is 2,500 for 500 subscribers, 600 shelf sales; 500 distributed free to students. Single copy: $5; subscription: $8.
How to Submit: Submit up to 3 poems, "each *no longer* than two pages in length." Name, address, and phone/e-mail must appear on each page of ms. Include SASE and cover letter with 3- to 4-line bio. Accepts simultaneous submissions; no previously published poems. No submissions by e-mail. Time between acceptance and publication is 3 months. Seldom comments on rejected poems. Guidelines available for SASE and by e-mail. Responds in up to 10 weeks. Pays 1 copy.
Also Offers: Sponsors the *GSU Review* Annual Writing Contest, an annual award of $1,000 for the best poem; copy of issue to all who submit. Submissions must be previously unpublished. Submit up to 3 poems on any subject or in any form. "Specify 'poetry' on outside envelope." Guidelines available for SASE and by e-mail. Accepts inquiries via fax and e-mail. Postmark deadline: January 31. Competition receives 200 entries. Past judges include Sharon Olds, Jane Hirschfield, Anthony Hecht, and Phillip Levine. Winner will be announced in the Spring issue.
Advice: "Avoid cliched and sentimental writing but as all advice is filled with paradox—write from the heart. We look for a smooth union of form and content."

GUERNICA EDITIONS INC.; ESSENTIAL POET SERIES, PROSE SERIES, DRAMA SERIES; INTERNATIONAL WRITERS (Specialized: regional, translations, ethnic/nationality), P.O. Box 117, Toronto ON M5S 2S6 Canada. (416)658-9888. Fax: (416)657-8885. E-mail: guernicaeditions@cs.com. Website: www.guernicaeditions.com. Established 1978. **Poetry Editor:** Antonio D'Alfonso.
Book/Chapbook Needs: "We wish to bring together the different and often divergent voices that exist in Canada and the U.S. We are interested in translations. We are mostly interested in poetry and essays on pluriculturalism." Has published work by Eugénio de Andrade (Portugal), Eugenio Cirese (Italy), Antonio Porta (Italy), Pasquale Verdicchio (Canada), Robert Flanagan (Canada), and Brian Day (Canada).
How to Submit: Query with 1-2 pages of samples. Send SASE (Canadian stamps only) or SAE and IRCs for catalog.
Advice: "We are interested in promoting a pluricultural view of literature by bridging languages and cultures. Besides our specialization in international translation."

$ GULF COAST: A JOURNAL OF LITERATURE AND FINE ART, Dept. of English, University of Houston, Houston TX 77204-3012. (713)743-3223. Website: www.gulfcoastmag.org. Established 1986. **Poetry Editors:** Miho Nonaka, Michael Dumanis, and Todd Samuelson.
Magazine Needs: *Gulf Coast* is published twice/year in October and April. While the journal features work by a number of established poets, editors are also interested in "providing a forum for new and emerging writers who are producing well-crafted work that takes risks." Each issue includes

HAVE A COLLECTION OF POETRY you want to publish? See the Chapbook Publishers Index or Book Publishers Index in the back of this book.

poetry, fiction, essays, interviews, and color reproductions of work by artists from across the nation. Has recently published poetry by Beckian Fritz Goldberg, Billy Collins, Nick Flynn, Bruce Smith, Judy Jordan, and Bob Hicok. *Gulf Coast* is 230 pages, 7×9, offset-printed, perfect-bound. Single copy: $7; subscription: $12/year, $22/2 years.

How to Submit: Submit up to 4 poems at a time. Accepts simultaneous submissions with notification; no previously published poems. Cover letter with previous publications, "if any," and a brief bio required. Does not read submissions June through August. Guidelines available for SASE, in publication, or on website. Responds in 6 months. Pays 2 copies and $15 per poem. Returns all rights (except electronic) upon publication.

Also Offers: Annual poetry and fiction contest with $1,000 awards and publication. Contact *Gulf Coast* for more information.

⬤ **GULF STREAM MAGAZINE**, English Dept. Florida International University, 3000 NE First St., North Miami Campus, North Miami FL 33181. (305)919-5599. E-mail: Gulfstrm@fiu.edu. Website: www.fiu.edu/~gulfstrm. Established 1989. **Editor:** John Dufresne. **Associate Editor:** Terri Carrion.

Magazine Needs: *Gulf Stream* is the biannual literary magazine associated with the creative writing program at FIU. Wants "poetry of any style and subject matter as long as it is of high literary quality." Has published poetry by Gerald Costanzo, Naomi Shihab Nye, Jill Bialosky, and Catherine Bowman. *Gulf Stream* is 96 pages, digest-sized, flat-spined, printed on quality stock, glossy card cover. Accepts less than 10% of poetry received. Press run is 750. Subscription: $9. Sample: $5.

How to Submit: Submit no more than 5 poems and include cover letter. Accepts simultaneous submissions (with notification in cover letter). Accepts submissions by postal mail, but prefers by e-mail. Reads submissions September 15 through February 1 only. Editor comments on submissions "if we feel we can be helpful." Publishes theme issues. Guidelines available by e-mail, on website, in publication. Responds in 3 months. Pays 2 copies and 2 subscriptions. Acquires first North American serial rights.

$ ⬜ ◎ **HADROSAUR TALES (Specialized: science fiction/fantasy)**, P.O. Box 8468, Las Cruces NM 88006-8468. (505)527-4163. E-mail: hadrosaur.productions@verizon.net. Website: http://hadrosaur.com. Established 1995. **Editor:** David L. Summers.

Magazine Needs: "*Hadrosaur Tales* is a literary journal that appears 3 times/year and publishes well written, thought-provoking science fiction and fantasy." Wants science fiction and fantasy themes. "We like to see strong visual imagery; strong emotion from a sense of fun to more melancholy is good. We do not want to see poetry that strays too far from the science fiction/fantasy genre." Has published poetry by Mario Milosevic, Christina Sng, Lisa Joyce Cohn, and K.S. Hardy. *Hadrosaur Tales* is about 100 pages, digest-sized, printed on 60 lb. white paper, perfect-bound with black drawing on card stock cover, uses cover art only, includes minimal ads. Receives about 100 poems/year, accepts up to 25%. Press run is 200 for 40 subscribers. Single copy: $6.95; subscription: $10/year. Sample: $6.95. Make checks payable to Hadrosaur Productions.

How to Submit: Submit 1-5 poems at a time. Accepts previously published poems. No longer accepts simultaneous submissions. Accepts e-mail submissions either in text box or as attachment (RTF format only). Cover letter preferred. "For electronic mail submissions, please place the word, 'Hadrosaur' in the subject line. Submissions that do not include this are subject to being destroyed unread. Poetry will not be returned unless sufficient postage is provided." Time between acceptance and publication is 1 year. Often comments on rejected poems. Occasionally publishes theme issues. Guidelines available for SASE, by e-mail, and on website. Upcoming themes available for SASE. Responds in 1 month. Sends prepublication galleys on request. Pays $2/poem plus 2 copies. Acquires one-time rights.

Advice: "I select poems that compliment the short stories that appear in a given issue. A rejection does not necessarily mean that I disliked your poem, only that the given poem wasn't right for the issue. Keep writing and submitting your poetry."

⬤ **HAIGHT ASHBURY LITERARY JOURNAL**, 558 Joost Ave., San Francisco CA 94127. Established 1979-1980. **Editors:** Indigo Hotchkiss, Alice Rogoff, and Conyus.

Magazine Needs: *Haight Ashbury* is a newsprint tabloid that appears 1-3 times/year. Use "all forms including haiku. Subject matter sometimes political, but open to all subjects. Poems of background—prison, minority experience—often published, as well as poems of protest and of Central America. Few rhymes." Has published poetry by Molly Fisk, Laura del Fuego, Dancing Bear, Lee Herrick, Janice King, and Laura Beausoleil. Haight Ashbury Literary Journal is 16 pages with graphics and ads. Press run 2,500. $35 for a lifetime subscription, which includes 3 back issues. Subscription: $12/4 issues. Sample: $3.

How to Submit: Submit up to 6 poems. "Please type one poem to a page, put name and address on every page and include SASE. No bios." Each issue changes its theme and emphasis. Guidelines and upcoming themes available for SASE. Responds in 4 months. Pays 3 copies, small amount to featured writers. Rights revert to author. An anthology of past issues, *This Far Together*, is available for $15.

N **⊘** **◎** **HAIJINX (Specialized: haiku, haiga, haibun, and renku); HAIJINX PRESS; JOHN CROOK AWARD; HAIJINX WEEKLY WIRE**, P.O. Box 200097, Austin TX 78720-0097. E-mail: submissions@haijinx.com. Website: www.haijinx.com. Established 2000. **Editor-in-Chief/Publisher:** Mark Brooks.

● Poetry published in *haijinx* was selected for inclusion in *The Red Moon Anthology 2002*

Magazine Needs: *haijinx* is a biannual haiku journal "that primarily focuses on modern interpretations of the haikai poetic and artistic tradition, including the role of humor in haiku. We accept original, unpublished haiku (preferably between five and ten at a time), haibun, haiga, renku, and sumi-e. Non-English works may be submitted with translation. We place emphasis on the haikai tradition and recommend a review of past issues before submission." Does not want "poems that overemphasize syllable-counting to the complete exclusion of other formal attributes and issues of content. Five, seven, and five English syllables does not automatically make a haiku, much less a good one." Recently published poetry by John Barlow, Penny Harter, William J. Higginson, Jim Kacian, Dhugal Lindsay, and Peggy Willis Lyles. *haijinx* is 176-208 pages, digest-sized, offset-printed, perfect-bound, glossy heavy stock cover with 4-color artwork (typically haiga), with art/graphics (b&w as well as some color, typically 4 pages/issue) and ads. Receives about 4,000 poems/year, accepts about 300. Press run is 250. Single copy: $15; subscription: $29. Make checks payable to haijinx press.

How to Submit: Submit 5-10 poems at time. Accepts previously published poems; no simultaneous submissions. Accepts e-mail and disk submissions; no fax submissions. Cover letter is preferred. "E-mail submissions highly preferred; otherwise, SASE required." Reads submissions year round, with deadlines of April 1 and October 1. Time between acceptance and publication is 2-3 months. Poems are circulated to an editorial board. "Submissions are divided amongst the editors. An editor selects haiku for further consideration. Those anonymous haiku are evaluated by the entire seven-person editorial board. Those selected are held until April or October. The editorial board then reevaluates those held haiku for final placement in the issue." Seldom comments on rejected poems. Guidelines available in magazine, for SASE, by e-mail, or on website. Responds in up to 4 months. Sometimes sends prepublication galleys. Pays $2/issue **to subscribers only**. Acquires first rights plus reprint rights ("right to reprint, or authorize reprint, in any form"). Reviews books and chapbooks of poetry and other magazines/journals.

Book/Chapbook Needs & How to Submit: haijinx press plans to publish chapbooks and books starting in late 2003. Contact before submitting mss.

Also Offers: Annual John Crook Award for haiku with humor; send SASE for guidelines; *haijinx weekly wire*, weekly e-mail with haiku news and contest information.

Advice: "*haijinx* attempts to find a balance between content and form within haiku and within haikai in general. The haiku published will vary in content, but they will typically have some sort of humor, no matter how slight. This humor will be constructive, rather than satiric or destructive. These haiku will typically be written with an eye towards the haikai tradition, including formal elements."

⊘ **◎** **HAIKU HEADLINES: A MONTHLY NEWSLETTER OF HAIKU AND SENRYU (Specialized: haiku and senryu)**, 1347 W. 71st St., Los Angeles CA 90044-2505. (323)778-5337. Established 1988. **Editor/Publisher:** Rengé/David Priebe.

Magazine Needs: *Haiku Headlines* is "America's oldest monthly publication dedicated to the genres of haiku and senryu only." Prefers the 5/7/5 syllabic discipline, but accepts irregular haiku and senryu which display pivotal imagery and contrast. Has published haiku by Dorothy McLaughlin, Jean Calkins, Günther Klinge, and Mark Arvid White. *Haiku Headlines* is 8 pages, magazine-sized, corner-stapled and punched for a three-ring binder. "Each issue has a different color graphic front page. The back page showcases a Featured Haiku Poet with a photo-portrait, biography, philosophy, and six of the poet's own favorite haiku." *Haiku Headlines* publishes 100 haiku/senryu a month. Has 225 subscribers of which 3 are libraries. Single copy: $2 US, $2.25 Canada, $2.50 overseas; subscription: $24 US, $27 Canada, $30 overseas.

How to Submit: Haiku/senryu may be submitted with 12 maximum/single page. Unpublished submissions from subscribers will be considered first. Nonsubscriber submissions will be accepted only if space permits and SASE is included. Guidelines available for SASE. Responds in 2 months. Pays subscribers half price rebates for issues containing their work; credits applicable to subscription. Nonsubscribers are encouraged to prepay for issues containing their work.

Also Offers: Monthly Readers' Choice Awards of $25, $15, and $10 are shared by the "Top Three Favorites." The "First Timer" with the most votes receives an Award of Special Recognition ($5).

HANDSHAKE; THE EIGHT HAND GANG (Specialized: science fiction, horror), 5 Cross Farm, Station Rd. N., Fearnhead, Warrington, Cheshire WA2 OQG United Kingdom. Established 1992. **Contact:** J.F. Haines.

Magazine Needs: *Handshake*, published irregularly, "is a newsletter for science fiction poets. It has evolved into being one side of news and information and one side of poetry." Wants "science fiction/fantasy poetry of all styles. Prefer short poems." Does not want "epics or foul language." Has published poetry by L.A. Hood, Steve Sneyd, Andrew Darington, Geoff Stevens, and Bruce Boston. *Handshake* is 1 sheet of A4 paper, photocopied with ads. Receives about 50 poems/year, accepts up to 50%. Press run is 60 for 30 subscribers of which 5 are libraries. Subscription: SAE with IRC. Sample: SAE with IRC.

How to Submit: Submit 2-3 poems, typed and camera-ready. No previously published poems or simultaneous submissions. Cover letter preferred. Time between acceptance and publication varies. Editor selects "whatever takes my fancy and is of suitable length." Seldom comments on rejected poems. Publishes theme issues. Responds ASAP. Pays 1 copy. Acquires first rights. Staff reviews books or chapbooks of poetry or other magazines of very short length. Send materials for review consideration.

Also Offers: *Handshake* is also the newsletter for The Eight Hand Gang, an organization for British science fiction poets, established in 1991. They currently have 60 members. Information about the organization is found in their newsletter.

HANDSHAKE EDITIONS; CASSETTE GAZETTE, Atelier A2, 83 rue de la Tombe Issoire 75014, Paris, France. Phone: 33.1.43.27.17.67. Fax: 33.1.43.20.41.95. E-mail: jim_haynes@wanadoo.fr. Established 1979. **Publisher:** Jim Haynes.

Magazine Needs & How to Submit: *Cassette Gazette* is an audiocassette issued "from time to time. We are interested in poetry dealing with political/social issues and women/feminism themes." Poets published include Yianna Katsoulos, Judith Malina, Elaine Cohen, Amanda Hoover, Roy Williamson, and Mary Guggenheim. Single copy: $10 plus postage. Pays in copies.

Book/Chapbook Needs & How to Submit: Handshake Editions does not accept unsolicited mss for book publication. New Book: "a bilingual English/Spanish edition by Cuban poet, Pablo Armando Fernandez to be co-published with Mosaic Press, Toronto" in early 2001.

Advice: Jim Haynes, publisher, says, "I prefer to deal face to face."

$ HANGING LOOSE PRESS; HANGING LOOSE, 231 Wyckoff St., Brooklyn NY 11217. Website: www.hangingloosepress.com. Established 1966. **Poetry Editors:** Robert Hershon, Dick Lourie, Mark Pawlak, and Ron Schreiber.

Magazine Needs: *Hanging Loose* appears in April and October. The magazine has published poetry by Sherman Alexie, Paul Violi, Donna Brook, Kimiko Hahn, Ron Overton, Jack Anderson, and Ha Jin. *Hanging Loose* is 120 pages, flat-spined, offset on heavy stock with a 4-color glossy card cover. One section contains poems by high-school-age poets. *Hanging Loose* "concentrates on the work of new writers." Sample: $9.

How to Submit: Submit 4-6 "excellent, energetic" poems. No simultaneous submissions. "Would-be contributors should read the magazine first." Responds in 3 months. Pays small fee and 2 copies.
Book/Chapbook Needs & How to Submit: *Hanging Loose* Press does not accept unsolicited book mss or artwork.

HANGMAN BOOKS, 11 Boundary Rd., Chatham, Kent ME4 6TS England. Website: www.hangmanbooks.com. Established 1982. **Editor:** Jack Ketch. **Administrator:** Juju Hamper.
Book/Chapbook Needs: Hangman publishes selected books of poetry. Recently published work by Billy Childish. Wants "personal" poetry, "underground" writing, "none rhyming, none political."
How to Submit: When submitting a ms, send sufficient IRCs for return.

$ HANOVER PRESS, LTD.; THE UNDERWOOD REVIEW, P.O. Box 596, Newtown CT 06470-0596. Established 1994. **Editor:** Faith Vicinanza.
Magazine Needs: *The Underwood Review* appears annually and publishes poetry, short stories, essays, and b&w artwork including photographs. Wants "cutting-edge fiction, poetry, and art. We are not afraid of hard issues, love humor, prefer personal experience over nature poetry. We want poetry that is strong, gutsy, vivid images, erotica accepted. No religious poems; no 'Hallmark' verse." Accepts poetry written by young poets, high school and above. Has published poetry by Elizabeth Thomas, Sandra Bishop Ebner, Leo Connellan, Richard Cambridge, Michael Brown, and Vivian Shipley. *The Underwood Review* is 120-144 pages, digest-sized, offset-printed and perfect-bound with card cover with computer graphics, photos, etc. Receives about 2,000 poems/year, accepts up to 3%. Press run is 1,000. Subscription: $13. Sample: $13. Make checks payable to Hanover Press, Ltd./Faith Vicinanza.
How to Submit: Submit up to 3 poems at a time. Accepts simultaneous submissions; no previously published poems. Accepts disk submissions. Cover letter with short bio (up to 60 words) preferred. Time between acceptance and publication is up to 8 months. Guidelines available for SASE and in publication. Responds in 5 months. Pays 2 copies. Acquires one-time rights.
Book/Chapbook Needs & How to Submit: Hanover Press, Ltd. seeks "to provide talented writers with the opportunity to get published and readers with the opportunity to experience extraordinary poetry." Has published *Crazy Quilt* by Vivian Shipley; *Short Poems/City Poems* by Leo Connellan; *We Are What We Love* by Jim Scrimgeour; *What Learning Leaves* by Taylor Mali; *Dangerous Men* by David Martin; and *The Space Between* by Sandra Bishop Ebner. Publishes 5 paperbacks/year. Books are usually digest-sized, offset-printed and perfect-bound with various covers, include art/graphics. Query first with a few sample poems and cover letter with brief bio and publication credits. Responds to queries in 4 months; to mss in 6 months. Pays 10% author's copies (100 out of a press run of 1,000 typically). Order sample books by sending $11.
Advice: "Poets so often just mass submit their work without being familiar with the literary journal and its preferences. Please don't waste an editor's time or your postage."

HARD ROW TO HOE; POTATO EYES FOUNDATION (Specialized: rural literature), P.O. Box 541-I, Healdsburg CA 95448. (707)433-9786. **Editor:** Joe E. Armstrong.
Magazine Needs: *Hard Row to Hoe,* taken over from Seven Buffaloes Press in 1987, is a "book review newsletter of literature from rural America with a section reserved for short stories (about 2,000 words) and poetry featuring unpublished authors. The subject matter must apply to rural America including nature and environmental subjects. Poems of 30 lines or less given preference, but no arbitrary limit. No style limits. Do not want any subject matter not related to rural subjects." Has published poetry by James Fowler, John Perrault, Jennifer Rudsit, Ruth Daniels. *Hard Row to Hoe* is 12 pages, magazine-sized, side-stapled, appearing 3 times/year, 3 pages reserved for short stories and poetry. Press run is 300. Subscription: $8/year. Sample: $3.
How to Submit: Submit 3-4 poems at a time. No simultaneous submissions. Accepts previously published poems only if published in local or university papers. Guidelines available for SASE. Editor comments on rejected poems "if I think the quality warrants." Pays 2 copies. Acquires one-time rights. Reviews books of poetry in 600-700 words. Send materials for review consideration.

HARP-STRINGS POETRY JOURNAL; EDNA ST. VINCENT MILLAY "BALLAD OF THE HARP WEAVER" AWARD; VERDURE PUBLICATIONS, P.O. Box 640387, Bev-

erly Hills FL 34464-0387. Fax: (352)746-7817. E-mail: verdure@digitalusa.net. Established 1989.
Editor: Madelyn Eastlund.

Magazine Needs: *Harp-Strings* appears quarterly. Wants "narratives, lyrics, prose poems, haibun, ballads, sestinas, and other traditional forms. Nothing 'dashed off,' trite, broken prose masquerading as poetry." Recently published poetry by Ruth Harrison, Nancy A. Henry, Robert Cooperman, Russell H. Strauss. *Harp-Strings* is 16-20 pages, digest-sized, saddle-stapled, professionally printed on quality colored matte stock with matte card cover. Accepts about 1% of poems received. Publishes about 12-16 poems/issue. Press run is 200 for 105 subscribers. Subscription: $12. Sample: $3.50.

How to Submit: Submit 3-5 poems at a time. Line length for poetry is 14 minimum, 80 maximum ("more often find 40-60 line poems have best chance"). Accepts previously published poems "but such poems should be accompanied with previous credit line." No simultaneous submissions. Accepts fax and e-mail submissions; no disk submissions. Cover letter is preferred with information on poet or poems. "Always an SASE—lately poets seem to forget. *Harper Strings* does use brief contributor notes." Reads submissions in February; May; August; November. "We do not hold poems until the next issue unless a poem is so good and we have no room in which case we so inform the author." Uses accepted poems in the next issue being planned following that reading period. Seldom comments on rejected poems. "A poem might not be right for us, but right for another publication. Rejection does not imply poem needs revisions." Responds at the end of each reading period. Pays 1 contributor's copy. Acquires one-time rights.

Also Offers: Sponsors the Edna St. Vincent Millay "Ballad of the Harp Weaver" Awards (narrative from 40 to 100 lines, annual deadline: August 15). Entry fee: 1-3 poems for $5. Make checks payable to Madelyn Eastlund. One cash award of $50 and publication.

Advice: "One thing that I've noticed in the past year or two is the number submissions with *no SASE*, submissions stuffed into very small envelopes, failure to put the poet's name with each poem submitted . . . And evidently, they don't pay attention to what the magazine lists as 'needs' because we get haiku, tanka, and other short verse. We also get 8-12 poems submitted with a note that 'this is from my book,' or worse—we get manuscripts, especially by e-mail, and must return them because we are not a press. It looks like many 'gun shot' their submissions."

$☉ HARPUR PALATE; MILTON KESSLER MEMORIAL PRIZE FOR POETRY, Dept. of English, Binghamton University, P.O. Box 6000, Binghamton NY 13902-6000. E-mail: hppoetry@hotmail.com (submissions only). Website: http://harpurpalate.binghamton.edu. Established 2000.
Poetry Editors: Anne Rashid and Thomas Rechtin.

Magazine Needs: *Harpur Palate* appears biannually. "We're dedicated to publishing the most eclectic mix of poetry and prose, regardless of style, form, and genre." Wants experimental, blank verse, free verse, haiku, lyrical, narrative, prose poem, sonnet, tanka, villanelle, speculative poetry, and metapoetry. "No light verse, pretentious attitudes, or violence for violence's sake." Recently published poetry by Virgil Suárez, Ryan G. Van Cleave, B.H. Fairchild, Tony Medina, Allison Joseph, and Bejamin Vogt. *Harpur Palate* is 100-120 pages, digest-sized, offset-printed, perfect-bound, matte or glossy cover. Receives about 700 poems/year, accepts about 35. Publishes about 10-15 poems/issue. Press run is 400-500 of which 50 are shelf sales; 50-100 distributed free to journals in exchange program, award anthologies, contributors, creative writing programs. Single copy: $7.50; subscription: $14/year, 2 issues. Sample: $7.50. Make checks payable to *Harpur Palate*.

How to Submit: Submit 3-5 poems at a time. "No line restrictions, poems must be 10 pages or less." Accepts simultaneous submissions "but we must be notified immediately if the piece is taken somewhere else"; no previously published poems. Accepts e-mail submissions; no fax or disk submissions. Cover letter is required. "E-mail submissions should be sent as .rtf file attachments (Rich Text Format) *only*. Please include your cover letter in the body of the e-mail." Reads submissions August 1-October 15 (winter issue); January 1-March 15 (summer issue). Time between acceptance and publication is 2 months. Poems are circulated to an editorial board. "Poetry board consists of first and second readers. Poems accepted for publication have been approved by a first reader and second reader and are selected by the Final Selection Committee consisting of all poetry readers, poetry editors, and managing editors." Seldom comments on rejected poems. Guidelines available for SASE or on website. Responds in up to 3 months, hopefully sooner. Pays $5-10 when funding available, and 2 contributors copies. Acquires first North American serial rights.

Also Offers: The Milton Kessler Memorial Prize for Poetry. Prize: $500 and publication in the winter issue of *Harpur Palate*. "Contest opens on July 1." **Postmark deadline:** October 1. "Poems in any style, form or genre are welcome as long as they are 1) no more than 3 pages and 2) previously unpublished. The entry fee is $10/5 poems. You may send as many poems as you wish, but no more than 5 poems per envelope. Please send checks drawn on a US bank or money orders made out to *Harpur Palate*. IMPORTANT: Checks *must* be made out to *Harpur Palate*, or we will not be able to process your check!" Complete guidelines available for SASE or on website. "We publish a Writing By Degrees supplement featuring fiction and poetry in the winter issue. Writing By Degree is a creative writing conference run by graduate students in Binghamton's Creative Writing Program."

Advice: "Please don't take rejection as a sign that we don't like your work. We receive so many quality submissions that there's no way we can publish them all. We're always open to form poetry, experimental poetry, metapoetry, and speculative poetry."

HARTWORKS; D.C. CREATIVE WRITING WORKSHOP, 601 Mississippi Ave. SE, Washington DC 20032-3899. (202)297-1957. E-mail: hartwrites@yahoo.com. Established 2000. **Executive Director:** Nancy Schwalb, D.C. Creative Writing Workshop.

• Although this journal doesn't accept submissions from the general public, it's included here as an outstanding example of what a literary journal can be (for anyone of any age).

Magazine Needs: *hArtworks* appears 3 times/year. "We publish the poetry of Hart Middle School students (as far as we know, Hart may be the only public middle school in the U.S. with its own poetry magazine) and the writing of guest writers such as Nikki Giovanni, Alan Cheuse, Arnost Lustig, and Henry Taylor, along with an interview between the kids and the grown-up pro. Also publishes work by our writers-in-residence who teach workshops at Hart, and provide trips to readings, slams, museums, and plays." Wants "vivid, precise, imaginative language that communicates from the heart as well as the head." Does not want "poetry that only 'sounds' good; it also needs to say something meaningful." Recently published poetry by DeAngelo Thomas, Terrell Hill, Delonte and Reggie Williams, Claudia Butler, Jessica Young, and James Saunders. *hArtworks* is 60 pages, magazine-sized, professionally-printed, saddle-stapled, card cover, with photography. Receives about 800 poems/year, accepts about 20%. Publishes about 60 poems/issue. Press run is 500 for 75 subscribers of which 2 are libraries, 100 shelf sales; 100 distributed free to writers, teachers. Single copy: $1; subscription: $5. Sample: $2. Make checks payable to D.C. Creative Writing Workshop.

How to Submit: "Writers-in-residence solicit most submissions from their classes and then a committee of student editors makes the final selections. Each year, our second issue is devoted to responses to the Holocaust."

Advice: "Read a lot; know something about how other writers approach their craft. Write a lot; build an understanding of yourself as a writer. Don't be so stubborn you settle into the same old poem you perfected in the past. Writing is not some static machine, but a kind of experience, a kind of growing."

HAWAI'I PACIFIC REVIEW, 1060 Bishop St., Honolulu HI 96813. (808)544-1108. Fax: (808)544-0862. E-mail: pwilson@hpu.edu. Website: www.hpu.edu. Established 1986. **Editor:** Patrice Wilson.

Magazine Needs: Published by Hawai'i Pacific University, *Hawai'i Pacific Review* is an annual literary journal appearing in August or September. Wants "quality poetry, short fiction, and personal essays from writers worldwide. Our journal seeks to promote a world view that celebrates a variety of cultural themes, beliefs, values, and viewpoints. We wish to further the growth of artistic vision and talent by encouraging sophisticated and innovative poetic and narrative techniques." Has published poetry by Wendy Bishop, B.Z. Niditch, Rick Bursky, Virgil Suarez, and Linda Bierds. *Hawai'i Pacific Review* is 80-120 pages, digest-sized, professionally printed on quality paper, perfect-bound, with coated card cover; each issue features original artwork. Receives 800-1,000 poems/year, accepts up to 30-40. Press run is approximately 500 for 100 shelf sales. Single copy: $8.95. Sample: $5.

How to Submit: Submit up to 5 poems, maximum 100 lines each. 1 submission/issue. "No hand-written manuscripts." Accepts simultaneous submissions with notification; no previously published poems. No fax or e-mail submissions. Cover letter with 5-line professional bio including prior publications required. "Our reading period is September 1 through December 31 each year." Seldom comments on rejected poems. Guidelines available for SASE or by e-mail. Responds within 3 months. Pays 2 copies. Acquires first North American serial rights.

Advice: "We'd like to receive more experimental verse. Good poetry is eye-opening; it investigates the unfamiliar or reveals the spectacular in the ordinary. Good poetry does more than simply express the poet's feelings; it provides both insight and unexpected beauty. Send us your best work!"

$ 🖉 HAYDEN'S FERRY REVIEW, Box 871502, Arizona State University, Tempe AZ 85287-1502. (480)965-1243. Website: www.haydensferryreview.com. Established 1986.
• Poetry published in *Hayden's Ferry Review* has been included in the *Pushcart Prize* anthologies (2001 and 2002).

Magazine Needs: *Hayden's Ferry* is a handsome literary magazine appearing in December and May. Has published poetry by Dennis Schmitz, Raymond Carver, Maura Stanton, Ai, and David St. John. *Hayden's Ferry Review* is digest-sized, 120 pages, flat-spined with glossy card cover. Press run is 1,300 for 200 subscribers of which 30 are libraries, 800 shelf sales. Accepts about 3% of 5,000 submissions annually. Subscription: $10. Sample: $6.

How to Submit: "No specifications other than limit in number (six)." No electronic submissions. Submissions circulated to two poetry editors. Editor comments on submissions "often." Guidelines available for SASE. Responds in 3 months of deadlines. Deadlines: February 28 for Spring/Summer issue; September 30 for Fall/Winter. Sends contributor's page proofs. Pays $25/page (maximum $100) and 2 copies.

⭐ 🖉 HAZMAT REVIEW; CLEVIS HOOK PRESS, P.O. Box 30507, Rochester NY 14603-0507. Website: www.hazmatlitreview.org. Established 1996. **Contact:** Editor.

Magazine Needs: *HazMat Review* is a biannual literary review, "about 70% poetry; 25% short story; 5% misc. (essays, review, etc.). *HazMat Review* stands for 'hazardous material,' which we believe poetry most definitely may be!" Wants "your best material; take chances; political pieces welcome; also experimental and/or alternative; especially welcome pieces that show things are not what they appear to be. We think poetry/fiction of the highest quality always has a chance. New Age, witches, ghosts, and goblins, vampires, probably not." Has published poetry by Eileen Myles, Marc Olmstead, Steve Hirsch, Jim Cohn, bobby johnson, Thom Ward, Lawrence Ferlinghetti, and Anne Waldman. *HazMat Review* is 96 pages, digest-sized, professionally printed and perfect-bound with glossy color or b&w cover, sometimes includes photographs or original art. Receives about 700 poems/year, accepts up to 20%. Press run is 500 for 60 subscribers of which 5 are libraries, 100 shelf sales; 100 distributed free to coffeehouses for publicity. Single copy: $12; subscription: $20/year. Sample: $7.

How to Submit: Submit 3 poems at a time. Accepts previously published poems; no simultaneous submissions. Accepts disk submissions. Cover letter preferred. SASE requested. Time between acceptance and publication is up to 1 year. Poems are circulated to an editorial board. "Editors pass promising material to staff readers for second opinion and suggestions, then back to editors for final decision." Often comments on rejected poems. Guidelines available for SASE. Responds in 3 months. Pays 1-2 copies. Acquires one-time rights. Staff reviews chapbooks of poetry. "Best chance for fiction, 2,500 words or less."

Advice: "We are encouraged by the renewed interest in poetry in recent years. If at all possible, read the magazine first before submitting to get a feel for the publication."

⭐ 🖉 HEELTAP; PARIAH PRESS, 604 Hawthorne Ave. E., St. Paul MN 55101. Established 1985 (Pariah Press); 1997 (*Heeltap*). **Editor:** Richard Houff.

Magazine Needs: *Heeltap* appears 2 times/year. Contains "social issues: people connecting with people/surviving chaos and government brain washing/re-establishing a literate society and avoiding the corporate machine." Very open to all kinds of poetry. "We don't believe in censorship." Does not want "early to mid-19th century rhyme about mother's lilacs, etc." Recently published poetry by Tom Clark, Gerald Locklin, Albert Huffstickler, Theodore Enslin, Charles Plymell, and Marge Piercy. *Heeltap* is 48-64 pages ("varies depending on finances"), digest-sized, laser/high speed-printed, saddle-stapled, cardstock cover (covers done by Mama Rue Day), ads for books and chapbooks from individuals and publishers. Receives about 10,000 poems/year, accepts about 2-5%. Publishes varied number of poems/issue. Press run is 500 for 50 subscribers of which 20 are libraries, 300 shelf sales. Single copy: $5; subscription: 4 issues/$18. Sample: $5 postage paid. "We encourage poets to buy samples." Make checks payable to Richard Houff.

How to Submit: Currently backlogged and closed to all submissions.

Book/Chapbook Needs & How to Submit: Pariah Press publishes *only* solicited material. Published 12 titles in 2000 ("varies depending on cash flow"). Chapbooks are 24 pages, laser/high speed-printed, saddle-stapled, with cover that varies from 150 lb. glossy to card stock, art/graphics on cover only. No unsolicited mss. "We solicit established poets and writers to send a complete manuscript." Responds to queries in 2 months. Pays 50 author's copies (out of a press run of 100). Order sample books/chapbooks by sending $5 (postage paid) to Richard Houff.

Advice: "The beginning poet should study the classics, from the early Greek tradition to the present. On the current scene, try to be yourself. Draw inspiration from others and you'll eventually find your voice. Let Bukowski rest—there are thousands of clones. Buk wouldn't approve."

Ø HELIKON PRESS, 120 W. 71st St., New York NY 10023. Established 1972. **Poetry Editors:** Robin Prising and William Leo Coakley. "Try to publish the best contemporary poetry in the tradition of English verse. We read (and listen to) poetry and ask poets to build a collection around particular poems. We print fine editions illustrated by good artists. Unfortunately we cannot encourage submissions."

★ Ø HELIOTROPE, P.O. Box 20037, Spokane WA 99204. E-mail: gribneal@omnicast.net. Website: www.Heliotropesoltice.com. Established 1996. **Editors:** Tom Gribble and Iris Gribble-Neal.

Magazine Needs: *Heliotrope*, published annually in January, is "an outlet for poetry, fiction, prose and criticism." Wants "poetry of any form, length, subject matter, style or purpose with no restrictions." Has published poetry by Bill Tremblay, Carlos Reyes, and Rane Arroyo. *Heliotrope* is 100 pages, digest-sized, perfect-bound with glossy cover with art. Press run is 200-300 for 75 subscribers. Subscription: $8. Make checks payable to Tom Gribble/*Heliotrope*.

How to Submit: Submit 5 poems at a time. No previously published poems or simultaneous submissions. Accepts e-mail submissions; include text in body of message. Cover letter preferred. Reads submissions June 21 through September 21 only. Poems are circulated to an editorial board. Seldom comments on rejected poems. Responds 2 months after end of reading period. Sometimes sends prepublication galleys. Pays 1 copy.

Advice: "We are open to all writers."

$ ◎ HERALD PRESS; PURPOSE; STORY FRIENDS; ON THE LINE; WITH (Specialized: religious, children), 616 Walnut Ave., Scottdale PA 15683-1999. (724)887-8500. Send submissions or queries directly to the editor of the specific magazine at address indicated.

Magazine Needs & How to Submit: *Herald Press*, the official publisher for the Mennonite Church in North America, seeks also to serve a broad Christian audience. Each of the magazines listed has different specifications, and the editor of each should be queried for more exact information. *Purpose*, editor James E. Horsch, a "religious young adult/adult monthly in weekly parts," press run 13,000, its focus: "action oriented, discipleship living." It is digest-sized with two-color printing throughout. Buys appropriate poetry up to 12 lines. *Purpose* uses 3-4 poems/week, receives about 2,000/year of which they use 150, has a 10- to 12-week backlog. Guidelines and a free sample are available for SASE. Mss should be double-spaced, one side of sheet only. Accepts simultaneous submissions. Responds in 2 months. Pays $7.50-20/poem plus 2 copies. *On the Line*, edited by Mary C. Meyer, a monthly religious magazine, for children 9-14, "that reinforces Christian values," press run 6,000. Sample free with SASE. Wants poems 3-24 lines. Submit poems "each on a separate 8½×11 sheet." Accepts simultaneous submissions and previously published poems. Responds in 1 month. Pays $10-25/poem plus 2 copies. *Story Friends*, edited by Susan Reith Swan, is for children 4-9, a "monthly magazine that reinforces Christian values," press run 6,500, uses poems 3-12 lines. Send SASE for guidelines/sample copy. Pays $10. *With*, Editorial Team, Box 347, Newton KS 67114, (316)283-5100. This magazine is for "senior highs, ages 15-18," focusing on empowering youth to radically commit to a personal relationship with Jesus Christ, and to share God's good news through word and actions." Press run 4,000, uses a limited amount of poetry. Poems should be 4-50 lines. Pays $10-25. Staff reviews books or chapbooks of poetry in 200-800 words. Send materials for review consideration.

◐ **HIDDEN OAK**, P.O. Box 2275, Philadelphia PA 19103. E-mail: hidoak@att.net. Established 1999. **Editor:** Louise Larkins.
Magazine Needs: *Hidden Oak* appears 3 times/year. "Hidden Oak seeks well-crafted poems which make imaginative use of imagery to reach levels deeper than the immediate and personal. Both traditional forms and free verse are accepted. Especially welcome are poems which include time-honored poetic devices and reveal an ear for the music of language." *Hidden Oak* is 60-68 pages, digest-sized, photocopied, stapled, original art/photograph on cover, with several b&w drawings. Receives about 500 poems/year, accepts up to 40%. Publishes about 50-60 poems/issue, usually 1 on a page. Press run is 80-100. Single copy: $4; subscription: $11. Sample: $3. Make checks payable to Louise Larkins.
How to Submit: Submit 3-6 poems at a time. Line length for poetry is 30 maximum. Accepts previously published poems; no simultaneous submissions. Accepts e-mail submissions; no disk submissions. Cover letter is preferred. Include SASE. Also accepts small b&w drawings, whether or not they are poem-related. Submit seasonal poems 2-3 months in advance. Time between acceptance and publication is up to 3 months. Seldom comments on rejected poems. Might publish theme issues in the future. Guidelines available for SASE or by e-mail. Responds in 1 week. Pays 1 copy. Does not review books or chapbooks.

$◐ ◎ **HIGH PLAINS PRESS (Specialized: regional, American West)**, P.O. Box 123, Glendo WY 82213. (307)735-4370. Fax: (307)735-4590. Website: www.highplainspress.com. Established 1985. **Poetry Editor:** Nancy Curtis.
Book/Chapbook Needs: High Plains Press considers books of poetry "specifically relating to Wyoming and the West, particularly poetry based on historical people/events or nature. We're mainly a publisher of historical nonfiction, but do publish one book of poetry every year." Has published *Close at Hand* by Mary Lou Sanelli and *Bitter Creek Junction* by Linda Hasselstrom.
How to Submit: Query first with 3 sample poems (from a 50-poem ms). Accepts fax submissions. Responds in 2 months. Time between acceptance and publication is up to 24 months. Always sends prepublication galleys. Pays 10% of sales. Acquires first rights. Catalog available on request; sample books: $5.
Advice: "Look at our previous titles."

★ ◐ ◎ **HIGHLIGHTS FOR CHILDREN (Specialized: children)**, 803 Church St., Honesdale PA 18431. (570)253-1080. E-mail: editorial@highlights-corp.com. Established 1946. **Contact:** Beth Troop.
Magazine Needs: *Highlights* appears every month using poetry for children ages 2-12. Wants "meaningful and/or fun poems accessible to children of all ages. Welcome light, humorous verse. Rarely publish a poem longer than 16 lines, most are shorter. No poetry that is unintelligible to children, poems containing sex, violence, or unmitigated pessimism." Accepts poetry written by children. "We print, but do not purchase, from individuals under age 16." Has published poetry by Ruskin Bond, Aileen Fisher, Eileen Spinelli, and Carl Sandburg. *Highlights* is generally 42 pages, magazine-sized, full-color throughout. Receives about 300 submissions/year, accepts up to 30. Press run is 2.5 million for approximately 2.2 million subscribers. Subscription: $29.64/year (reduced rates for multiple years).
How to Submit: Submit typed ms with very brief cover letter. Please indicate if simultaneous submission. No e-mail submissions. Editor comments on submissions "occasionally, if ms has merit or author seems to have potential for our market." Responds "generally within 1 month." Always sends prepublication galleys. Payment: "money varies" plus 2 copies. Acquires all rights.
Advice: "We are always open to submissions of poetry not previously published. However, we purchase a very limited amount of such material. We may use the verse as 'filler,' or illustrate the verse with a full-page piece of art. Please note that we do not buy material from anyone under 16 years old."

⊕ $◐ ◎ **HIPPOPOTAMUS PRESS (Specialized: form); OUTPOSTS POETRY QUARTERLY; OUTPOSTS ANNUAL POETRY COMPETITION**, 22 Whitewell Rd., Frome, Somerset BA11 4EL England. Phone/fax: 01373-466653. *Outposts* established 1943, Hippopotamus Press established 1974. **Poetry Editor:** Roland John.

Magazine Needs: "*Outposts* is a general poetry magazine that welcomes all work either from the recognized or the unknown poet." Wants "fairly mainstream poetry. No concrete poems or very free verse." Has published poetry by Jared Carter, John Heath-Stubbs, Lotte Kramer, and Peter Russell. *Outposts* is 60-120 pages, A5, litho printed and perfect-bound with laminated card cover, includes occasional art and ads. Receives about 46,000 poems/year, accepts approximately 1%. Press run is 1,600 for 1,200 subscribers of which 400 are libraries, 400 shelf sales. Single copy: $8; subscription: $26. Sample (including guidelines): $6. Make checks payable to Hippopotamus Press. "We prefer credit cards because of bank charges."

How to Submit: Submit 5 poems at a time. "IRCs must accompany U.S. submissions." Accepts simultaneous submissions; no previously published poems. Accepts fax submissions. Cover letter required. Time between acceptance and publications is 9 months. Seldom comments on rejected poems, "only if asked." Occasionally publishes theme issues. Upcoming themes available for SASE (or SAE and IRC). Responds in 2 weeks plus post time. Sometimes sends prepublication galleys. Pays £8/poem plus 1 copy. Copyright remains with author. Staff reviews books of poetry in 200 words for "Books Received" page. Also uses full essays up to 4,000 words. Send materials for review consideration, attn. M. Pargitter.

Book/Chapbook Needs & How to Submit: Hippopotamus Press publishes 6 books/year. "The Hippopotamus Press is specialized, with an affinity with Modernism. No Typewriter, Concrete, Surrealism." For book publication query with sample poems. Accepts simultaneous submissions and previously published poems. Responds in 6 weeks. Pays 7½-10% royalties plus author's copies. Send for book catalog to buy samples.

Also Offers: The magazine also holds an annual poetry competition.

◖ HIRAM POETRY REVIEW, P.O. Box 162, Hiram OH 44234. (330)569-7512. Fax: (330)569-5166. E-mail: greenwoodwp@hiram.edu. Established 1966. **Poetry Editor:** Willard Greenwood.

Magazine Needs: *Hiram Poetry Review* is an annual publication appearing in spring. "Since 1966, *Hiram Poetry Review* has published distinctive, beautiful, and heroic poetry. We're looking for works of high and low art. We tend to favor poems that are pockets of resistance in the undeclared war against 'plain speech,' but we are interested in any work of high quality." Circulation is 400 for 300 subscriptions of which 150 are libraries. Although most poems appearing here tend to be lyric and narrative free verse under 50 lines, exceptions occur (a few longer, sequence or formal works can be found in each issue). Subscription: $9/1 year; $23/3 years.

How to Submit: Query or send 3 to 5 poems and a brief bio. Accepts simultaneous submissions. Does not accept e-mail submissions or poems over 3 single-spaced pages in length. Reads submissions year-round. Responds in up to 6 months. Pays 2 copies. Acquires first North American serial rights; returns rights upon publication. Reviews books of poetry in single or multi-book format, no set length. Send materials for review consideration.

$ ◖ ◎ HODGEPODGE SHORT STORIES & POETRY (Specialized: subscribers), P.O. Box 6003, Springfield MO 65801. E-mail: fictionpub@aol.com. Established 1994. **Editor:** Vera Jane Goodin. **Contact:** Poetry Editor.

Magazine Needs: *Hodgepodge* appears quarterly to "provide a showcase for new as well as established poets and authors; to promote writing and offer encouragement." Open to all kinds of poetry. Accepts poetry written by children (but makes no special allowance for them). Has published poetry by Gloria Trapold Bradford and William Sowell. *Hodgepodge* is a 24- to 32-page chapbook, photocopied and saddle-stapled with self cover, includes clip art. Receives about 100 poems/year, accepts up to 50%. Press run is about 100 for about 100 subscribers. Single copy: $3; subscription: $12 US/ $15 foreign. Sample: $3. Make checks payable to Goodin Communications. "Potential contributors either need to purchase a copy or be annual subscribers."

WAIT! Don't mail your submission or correspondence without enclosing a SASE (self-addressed stamped envelope). If sending outside your own country, include SAE and IRCs (International Reply Coupons) instead.

How to Submit: Submit up to 4 poems at a time. Accepts previously published poems and simultaneous submissions. Accepts e-mail submissions; include text in body of message, no attachments. SASE required for return of poems. Time between acceptance and publication is 3 months. Seldom comments on rejected poems. Guidelines available for SASE and in publication. Responds in 3 months. Pays $1/poem. Acquires one-time rights. Staff reviews books and chapbooks of poetry and other magazines in 250 words, single and multi-book format. Send materials for review consideration to Review Editor.

Also Offers: Sponsors a Best-of-the-Year Contest. Any poem published in *Hodgepodge* is eligible for the contest. 1st Place $30, 2nd Place $15, 3rd Place free subscription. Also awards honorable mentions and certificates. "Judging is done by staff, but readers are asked for input."

$☑ THE HOLLINS CRITIC, P.O. Box 9538, Hollins University, Roanoke VA 24020-1538. (540)362-6275. Website: www.hollins.edu/academics/critic. Established 1964. **Editor:** R.H.W. Dillard. **Poetry Editor:** Cathryn Hankla.

Magazine Needs: *The Hollins Critic*, appears 5 times/year, publishing critical essays, poetry, and book reviews. Uses a few short poems in each issue, interesting in form, content or both. Has published poetry by William Miller, R.T. Smith, David Huddle, Margaret Gibson, and Julia Johnson. *The Hollins Critic* is 24 pages, magazine-sized. Press run is 500. Subscription: $6/year ($7.50 outside US). Sample: $1.50.

How to Submit: Submit up to 5 poems, must be typewritten with SASE, to Cathryn Hankla, poetry editor. Reads submissions September through May. Submissions received between June 1 and September 1 will be returned unread. Responds in 6 weeks. Pays $25/poem plus 5 copies.

☑ HOME PLANET NEWS, Box 415, Stuyvesant Station, New York NY 10009. Established 1979. **Co-Editor:** Enid Dame. **Co-Editor:** Donald Lev.

Magazine Needs: *Home Planet News* appears 3 times/year. "Our purpose is to publish lively and eclectic poetry, from a wide range of sensibilities, and to provide news of the small press and poetry scenes, thereby fostering a sense of community among contributors and readers." Wants "honest, well-crafted poems, open or closed form, on any subject. Poems under 30 lines stand a better chance. We do not want any work which seems to us to be racist, sexist, agist, anti-Semitic, or imposes limitations on the human spirit." Has published poetry by Layle Silbert, Robert Peters, Lyn Lifshin, and Gerald Locklin. *Home Planet News* is a 24-page tabloid, web offset-printed, includes b&w drawings, photos, cartoons and ads. Receives about 1,000 poems/year, accepts up to 3%. Press run is 1,000 for 300 subscribers. Subscription: $10/4 issues, $18/8 issues. Sample: $3.

How to Submit: Submit 3-6 poems at a time. No previously published poems or simultaneous submissions. Cover letter preferred. "SASEs are a must." Reads submissions February 1 through May 31 only. Time between acceptance and publication is 1 year. Seldom comments on rejected poems. Occasionally publishes theme issues. "We announce these in issues." Guidelines available for SASE, "however, it is usually best to simply send work." Responds in 4 months. Pays 1-year gift subscription plus 3 copies. Acquires first rights. All rights revert to author on publication. Reviews books and chapbooks of poetry and other magazines in 1,200 words, single and multi-book format. Send materials for review consideration to Enid Dame. "Note: we do have guidelines for book reviewers; please write for them. Magazines are reviewed by a staff member."

Advice: "Read many publications, attend readings, feel yourself part of a writing community, learn from others."

☑ HOMESTEAD REVIEW, Box A-5, 156 Homestead Ave., Hartnell College, Salinas CA 93901. (831)755-6943. Fax: (831)755-6751. E-mail: mtabor@jafar.hartnell.cc.ca.us. Website: www.hartnell.cc.ca.us/Homestead_Review. Established 1985. **Editor:** Maria Garcia Tabor.

Magazine Needs: *Homestead Review* appears biannually (December and May). Wants to see "avant-garde poetry as well as fixed form styles of remarkable quality and originality. We do not want to see Hallmark-style writing or first drafts." Accepts poetry written by children. Recently published poetry by Ray Gonzalez, Kathryn Kirkpatrick, Dana Garrett, Virgil Suarez, Morton Marcus, and Hilary Mosher Buri. Receives about 1,000 poems/year, accepts about 15%. Publishes about 65 poems/issue. Press run is 500 for 300 subscribers of which 300 are libraries; 200 are distributed free to poets, writers, bookstores. Single copy: $10, subscription: $20/year. Make checks payable to *Homestead Review.*

How to Submit: Submit 3 poems at a time. No previously published poems or simultaneous submissions. No fax, e-mail, or disk submissions. Cover letter is required. "A brief bio should be included in the cover letter." Reads submissions all year. Submit seasonal poems 3 months in advance. Time between acceptance and publication is 2 months. "Manuscripts are read by the staff and discussed. Poems/fiction accepted by majority consensus." Often comments on rejected poems. Guidelines available for SASE. Responds in 2 months. Pays 1 contributor's copy. Acquires one-time rights.

Also Offers: "We accept short fiction, book reviews, and b&w photography/art, and interviews."

Advice: "Poetry is language distilled; do not send unpolished work. Join a workshop group if at all possible."

🌐 ◗ HQ POETRY MAGAZINE (THE HAIKU QUARTERLY); THE DAY DREAM

PRESS, 39 Exmouth St., Kingshill, Swindon, Wiltshire SN1 3PU England. Phone: 01793-523927. Website: www.nogs.dial.pipex.com/HQ.htm. Established 1990. **Editor:** Kevin Bailey.

Magazine Needs: *HQ Poetry Magazine* is "a platform from which new and established poets can speak and have the opportunity to experiment with new forms and ideas." Wants "any poetry of good quality." Accepts poetry written by children. Has published poetry by Al Alvarez, D.M. Thomas, James Kirkup, Cid Corman, Brian Patten, and Penelope Shuttle. *HQ Poetry magazine* is 48-64 pages, A5, perfect-bound with art, ads, and reviews. Accepts about 5% of poetry received. Press run is 500-600 for 500 subscribers of which 30 are libraries. Subscription: £10 UK, £13 foreign. Sample: £2.80.

How to Submit: No previously published poems or simultaneous submissions. Cover letter and SASE (or SAE and IRCs) required. Time between acceptance and publication is 3-6 months. Often comments on rejected poems. Responds "as time allows." Pays 1 copy. Reviews books of poetry in about 1,000 words, single book format. Send materials for review consideration.

Also Offers: Sponsors "Piccadilly Poets" in London, and "Live Poet's Society" based in Bath, Somerset England. Also acts as "advisor to *Poetry on the Lake* Annual Poetry Festival in Orta, Italy."

◖ HUBBUB; VI GALE AWARD; ADRIENNE LEE AWARD, 5344 SE 38th Ave., Portland

OR 97202. Established 1983. **Editors:** L. Steinman and J. Shugrue.

Magazine Needs: Appearing once/year (usually in November/December), *Hubbub* is designed "to feature a multitude of voices from interesting contemporary American poets. We look for poems that are well-crafted, with something to say. We have no single style, subject, or length requirement and, in particular, will consider long poems. No light verse." Has published poetry by Madeline DeFrees, Cecil Giscombe, Carolyn Kizer, Primus St. John, Shara McCallum, and Alice Fulton. *Hubbub* is 50-70 pages, digest-sized, offset-printed and perfect-bound, cover art only, usually no ads. Receives about 1,200 submissions/year, accepts up to 2%. Press run is 350 for 100 subscribers of which 12 are libraries, about 150 shelf sales. Subscription: $5/year. Sample: $3.35 (back issues), $5 (current issue).

How to Submit: Submit 3-6 typed poems (no more than 6) with SASE. No previously published poems or simultaneous submissions. Guidelines available for SASE. Responds in 4 months. Pays 2 copies. Acquires first North American serial rights. "We review two to four poetry books/year in short (three-page) reviews; all reviews are solicited. We do, however, list books received/recommended." Send materials for consideration.

Also Offers: Outside judges choose poems from each volume for two awards: Vi Gale Award ($100) and Adrienne Lee Award ($50). There are no special submission procedures or entry fees involved.

◗ ◎ HUNGER MAGAZINE; HUNGER PRESS (Specialized: form, language-image experimentation), 1305 Old Route 28, Phoenicia NY 12464. (845)688-2332. E-mail: hunger@huc.rr. com. Website: www.hungermagazine.com. Established 1997. **Publisher/Editor:** J.J. Blickstein.

Magazine Needs: *Hunger Magazine* is an international zine based in the Hudson Valley and appears 2 times/year. "*Hunger* publishes mostly poetry but will accept some microfiction, essays, translations, cover art, interviews, and book reviews. Although there are no school/stylistic limitations, our main focus is on language-image experimentation with an edge. We publish no names for prestige and most of our issues are dedicated to emerging talent. Well known poets do grace our pages to illuminate possibilities. No dead kitty elegies; Beat impersonators; Hallmark cards; 'I'm not sure if I can write poems'. All rhymers better be very, very good. We have published poetry by Amiri Baraka, Paul Celan, Robert Kelly, Anne Waldman, Janine Pommy Vega, Antonin Artaud, and Clayton Eshleman." *Hunger* is 75-100 pages, magazine-sized, saddle-stapled with glossy full-color card cover, uses original artworks and drawings. Accepts about 10% of submissions. Press run is 250-500. Single issue: $8 and $1 p&h ($11 foreign); subscription: $16 ($21 foreign). Back issue: $8. Chapbooks: $5. Make checks payable to Hunger Magazine & Press.

How to Submit: "Send 3-10 pages and SASE." Accepts simultaneous submissions, if notified; no previously published poems. Accepts e-mail submissions and queries; include text in body of message "unless otherwise requested." Brief cover letter with SASE preferred. "Manuscripts without SASEs will be recycled. Please proof your work and clearly indicate stanza breaks." Time between acceptance and publication is up to 1 year. Guidelines available for SASE, by e-mail, on website, or in publication. Responds in up to 6 months, depending on backlog. Sends prepublication galleys upon request. Pays 1-3 copies depending on amount of work published. "If invited to be a featured poet we pay a small honorarium and copies." Acquires first North American serial rights.

Advice: "Please follow submission guidelines! Please be familiar with magazine content. The brief descriptions found in *Poet's Market* can only give one a general account of what a journal publishes. Do your research! Young poets, spend as much time reading as you do writing. Please no unsolicited book-length manuscripts."

⊘ THE HURRICANE REVIEW, (formerly *Half Tones to Jubilee*), English Dept., Pensacola Junior College, 1000 College Blvd., Pensacola FL 32504. (850)484-1447. Fax: (850)484-1149. E-mail:mwernicke@pjc.edu. Established 1986. **Faculty Editor:** Marian Wernicke.

Magazine Needs: *The Hurricane Review* is an annual literary journal appearing in September that features poetry and short fiction. Seeks poetry of "any style, any length. No biases other than quality, although we are not a market for inspirational or greeting card verse." Has published poetry by R.T. Smith, Sue Walker, Larry Rubin and Simon Perchik. *The Hurricane Review* is 100 pages, digest-sized, perfect-bound with matte card cover, professionally printed. Receives about 1,000 poems/year, accepts approximately 50-60. Press run is 500. Subscription: $4. Sample: $4.

How to Submit: Submit 3-5 poems at a time. No previously published work or simultaneous submissions. SASE mandatory. Cover letter with bio and/or publication history preferred. Reads submissions August 1 through May 15 only. Responds in 3 months, faster when possible. Pays 2 copies. Acquires first rights.

Advoce "As David Kirby says, a poem should be well punctuated and give evidence of careful proofreading. It should be understandable to a reader who is not the poet."

⊘ ◎ IAMBS & TROCHEES (Specialized: forms/metrical verse only); IAMBS & TROCHEES ANNUAL POETRY CONTEST, 6801 19th Ave. 5H, Brooklyn NY 11204. (718)232-9268. E-mail: carwill@prodigy.net. Website: www.iambsandtrochees.com. Established 2001. **Editor/Publisher:** William F. Carlson.

Magazine Needs: *Iambs & Trochees* appears biannually in spring and fall. Welcomes "poetry written in the great tradition of English and American literature. We will consider rhymed verse, blank verse, and metrically regular verse of any type, along with poems written in the various fixed forms. These include (but are not limited to) the sonnet, the villanelle, the ballade, the triolet, and the ottava rima. We are open to all genres: lyric, elegiac, satiric, narrative, or anything else. We have no restrictions on subject matter, nor do we demand that our writers follow any specific approach or ideology when handling their material. Our concern is strictly with the intrinsic aesthetic merit of a poem." Does not want free verse, syllabic verse. Recently published poetry by Alfred Dorn, Rhina Espaillat, Samuel Maio, Rachel Hadas, Jared Carter, and X.J. Kennedy. *Iambs & Trochees* is 64-124 pages, 7×9, digitally-printed, perfect-bound, paper cover. Single copy: $8; subscription: $15/year (2 issues). Sample: $8. Make checks payable to Iambs & Trochees Publishing.

How to Submit: No previously published poems or simultaneous submissions. Accepts e-mail and disk submissions; no fax submissions. Include SASE for return of poems not accepted. Time between acceptance and publication is 2 months. Submission deadline: January 30 (Spring) and August 30 (Fall/Winter). Poems are circulated to an editorial board. "We select poems on how well they are crafted." Seldom comments on rejected poems. Guidelines available in magazine or on website.

Responds in 2 months. Pays 1 contributor's copy. Acquires first North American serial rights. Reviews books of poetry *only* in 1,500 words.

Also Offers: Sponsors annual poetry contest for metrical poetry. Offers 3 awards of $300, $150, and $50. No entry fee. Guidelines available for SASE or on website.

Advice: "We feel keeping a beautiful tradition alive is possible by presenting poems in the classic tradition."

☑ IBBETSON ST. PRESS, 25 School St., Somerville MA 02143-1721. (617)628-2313. E-mail: dougholder@post.harvard.edu. Website: http://homepage.mac.com/rconte. Established 1999. **Editor:** Doug Holder. **Co-Editors:** Dianne Robitaille, Richard Wilhelm, Linda H. Conte, Marc Widershien, Robert K. Johnson.

Magazine Needs: Appearing biannually in June and November, *Ibbetson St. Press* is "a poetry magazine that wants 'down to earth' poetry that is well-written; has clean, crisp images; with a sense of irony and humor. We want mostly free verse, but open to rhyme. No maudlin, trite, overly political, vulgar for vulgar's sake, poetry that tells but doesn't show." Has published poetry by Robert K. Johnson, Don Divecchio, Ed Galing, Brian Morrissey, and Oliver Cutshaw. *Ibbetson St. Press* is 30 pages, magazine-sized, desktop-published with plastic binding and cream coverstock cover, includes b&w prints and classified ads. Receives about 300 poems/year, accepts up to 40%. Press run is 100 for 20 subscribers. Single copy: $5; subscription: $7. Sample: $2. Make checks payable to Ibbetson St. Press.

How to Submit: Submit 3-5 poems at a time. Accepts previously published poems and simultaneous submissions. Accepts submissions by postal mail only. Cover letter required. Time between acceptance and publication is up to 5 months. Poems are circulated to an editorial board. "Three editors comment on submissions." Guidelines available by SASE. Responds in 2 weeks. Pays 1 copy. Acquires one-time rights. Reviews books and chapbooks of poetry and other magazines in 250-500 words. Send materials for review consideration.

Book/Chapbook Needs & How to Submit: "We also publish chapbooks by newer, little exposed poets of promise. In some cases we pay for all expenses, in others the poet covers publishing expenses." Has published *The Life of All Worlds* by Marc Widershien, *In the Bar Apocalypse Now* by Gary Duehr, *Small World* by Jonathon Roses, *Slow as a Poem* by Linda Haviland Conte, and *Inaccessibility of the Creator* by Jack Powers. Chapbooks are usually 20-30 pages, magazine-sized, photocopied with plastic binding, white coverstock cover, includes b&w prints. "Send complete manuscript for consideration, at least 20-30 poems with or without artwork." Responds to queries in 1 month. Pays 50 author's copies (out of a press run of 100). Order sample books or chapbooks by sending $5.

Advice: "Please buy a copy of the magazine you submit to—support the small press. In your work, be honest. Don't affect."

$ ☑ THE ICONOCLAST, 1675 Amazon Rd., Mohegan Lake NY 10547-1804. Established 1992. **Editor/Publisher:** Phil Wagner. Member: CLMP.

Magazine Needs: *The Iconoclast* is a general interest literary publication appearing 6 times/year. Wants "poems that have something to say—the more levels the better. Nothing sentimental, obscure, or self-absorbed. Try for originality; if not in thought, then expression. No greeting card verse or noble religious sentiments. Look for the unusual in the usual, parallels in opposites, the capturing of what is unique or often unnoticed in an ordinary, or extraordinary moment. What makes us human—and the resultant glories and agonies. Our poetry is accessible to a thoughtful reading public." Has published poetry by Richard Hoffman, Graal Braun, and Andrew Sunshine. *The Iconoclast* is 40-64 pages, journal-sized, photo offset on #45 white wove paper, with b&w art, graphics, photos and ads. Receives about 2,000 poems/year, accepts up to 3%. Press run is 500-2,000 for 335 subscribers. Subscription: $15 for 8 issues. Sample: $2.50.

How to Submit: Submit 3-4 poems at a time. Time between acceptance and publication is 4-12 months. Sometimes comments on rejected poems. Guidelines available for SASE. Responds in 1 month. Pays 1 copy per published page or poem, 40% discount on extras, and $2-5 per poem for first North American rights on acceptance. Reviews books of poetry in 250 words, single format.

⬤ ◎ **THE IDIOT (Specialized: humor)**, P.O. Box 69163, Los Angeles CA 90069. E-mail: idiotsubmission@yahoo.com. Website: www.theidiotmagazine.com. Established 1993. **President for Life:** Sam Hayes. **Mussolini to My Hitler:** Brian Campbell.

Magazine Needs: *The Idiot* is a biannual humor magazine. "We mostly use fiction, articles, and cartoons, but will use anything funny, including poetry. Nothing pretentious. We are a magazine of dark comedy. Death, dismemberment, and religion are all subjects of comedy. Nothing is sacred. But it needs to be funny, which brings us to . . . Laughs! I don't want whimsical, I don't want amusing, I don't want some fanciful anecdote about childhood. I mean belly laughs, laughing out loud, fall on the floor funny. If it's cute, give it to your sweetheart or your puppy dog. Length doesn't matter, but most comedy is like soup. It's an appetizer, not a meal. Short is often better. Bizarre, obscure, and/ or literary references are often appreciated but not necessary." Has published poetry by Caitlin Ahearn, Freud Pachenko, and Stuffy Legs & Patches. *The Idiot* is 48 pages, digest-sized, profession-ally printed and staple-bound with glossy cover. Receives about 250 submissions/year, accepts up to 3-4. Press run is 300. Subscription: $10. Sample: $6.

How to Submit: Accepts previously published poems and simultaneous submissions. Prefers e-mail submissions if included in body of message. Seldom comments on rejected poems. Responds in 3 months. Pays 1 copy. Acquires one-time rights.

Advice: "Gather round, my children. Oh, come closer. Closer, don't be shy. Okay, scoot back, that's too close. Now listen carefully as there's something uncle Sammy wants to tell you. Billy, get those fingers out of your ears and listen. I'd like to give you a little advice about submissions. You see, kids, most people send me poems that just aren't funny. We're a *comedy* magazine, emphasis on the word 'comedy.' We're looking for things that make people laugh. Anything less than that demeans us both (but mostly you). So please make sure that whatever you send isn't just amusing or cute, but really, really, really hilarious."

⬤ **ILLUMINATIONS, AN INTERNATIONAL MAGAZINE OF CONTEMPORARY WRITING**, % Dept. of English, College of Charleston, 66 George St., Charleston SC 29424-0001. (843)953-1920. Fax: (843)953-3180. E-mail: lewiss@cofc.edu. Website: www.cofc.edu/Illuminations. Established 1982. **Editor:** Simon Lewis.

Magazine Needs: *Illuminations* is published annually "to provide a forum for new writers alongside already established ones." Open as to form and style. Do not want to see anything "bland or formally clunky." Has published poetry by Peter Porter, Michael Hamburger, Geri Doran, and Anne Born. *Illuminations* is 64-88 pages, digest-sized, offset-printed and perfect-bound with 2-color card cover, includes photos and engravings. Receives about 1,500 poems/year, accepts up to 5%. Press run is 400. Subscription: $15/2 issues. Sample: $10.

How to Submit: Submit up to 6 poems at a time. No previously published poems or simultaneous submissions. Accepts e-mail and fax submissions. Brief cover letter preferred. Time between accep-tance and publication "depends on when received. Can be up to a year." Publishes theme issues occasionally; "issue 16 [2000] was a Vietnamese special; issue 17 [2001] focused on Cuban and Latin American writing." Guidelines available by e-mail. Responds within 2 months. Pays 2 copies plus one subsequent issue. Acquires all rights. Returns rights on request.

⬤ **ILLYA'S HONEY**, % Dallas Poets Community, P.O. Box 700865, Dallas TX 75370. Website: www.dallaspoets.org. Established 1994, acquired by Dallas Poets Community in January 1998. **Man-aging Editor:** Ann Howells. **Contact:** Editor.

Magazine Needs: *Illya's Honey* is a quarterly journal of poetry and micro fiction. "All subjects and styles are welcome, but we admit a fondness for free verse. Poems may be of any length but should be accessible, thought-provoking, fresh, and should exhibit technical skill. Every poem is read by at least three members of our editorial staff, all of whom are poets. No didactic or overly religious verse, please." Recently published poetry by Lyn Lifshin, Joe Ahern, Seamus Murphy, Robert East-wood, and Brandon Brown. *Illya's Honey* is 40 pages, digest-sized, and saddle-stapled, glossy card cover with b&w photographs. Receives about 2,000 poems/year, accepts about 5-10%. Press run is 250 for 80 subscribers, 50 shelf sales. Subscription: $18. Current issue: $6. Sample: $4.

How to Submit: Submit 3-5 poems at a time. No previously published poems or simultaneous submissions. Cover letter preferred. Include short biography. Occasionally comments on rejected poems. Guidelines available for SASE. Responds in up to 5 months. Pays 1 contributor's copy.

Also Offers: Annual Dallas Poets Community Open Poetry Competition. Submit mss to above address between May 1 and July 15. Format: 1 poem per page, any subject, any length to 3 pages; include cover sheet with contact information and name(s) of poems. **Entry fee:** $5 per poem. Offers award of 1st prize: $300; 2nd prize: $200; 3rd prize: $100. Winners are published in *Illya's Honey*. Also see see listing for Dallas Poets Community under Organizations.

IMAGE: A JOURNAL OF ARTS & RELIGION (Specialized: religion), 3307 3rd Ave. W., Seattle WA 98119. E-mail: image@imagejournal.org. Website: www.imagejournal.org. Established 1989. **Publisher:** Gregory Wolfe.

Magazine Needs: *Image*, published quarterly, "explores and illustrates the relationship between faith and art through world-class fiction, poetry, essays, visual art, and other arts." Wants "poems that grapple with religious faith, usually Judeo-Christian." Has published poetry by Philip Levine, Scott Cairns, Annie Dillard, Mary Oliver, Mark Jarman, and Kathleen Norris. *Image* is 136 pages, 10×7, perfect-bound, acid free paper with glossy 4-color cover, averages 10 pages of 4-color art/issue (including cover), ads. Receives about 800 poems/year, accepts up to 2%. Has 4,000 subscribers of which 100 are libraries. Subscription: $36. Sample: $12.

How to Submit: Submit up to 4 poems at a time. No previously published poems. Cover letter preferred. No e-mail submissions. Time between acceptance and publication is 1 year. Guidelines available on website. Responds in 3 months. Always sends prepublication galleys. Pays 4 copies plus $2/line ($150 maximum). Acquires first North American serial rights. Reviews books of poetry in 2,000 words, single or multi-book format. Send materials for review consideration.

IMPLOSION PRESS; IMPETUS (Specialized: erotica, women), 4975 Comanche Trail, Stow OH 44224-1217. (330)688-5210. E-mail: impetus@aol.com. Website: www.mipogallery. com/impetus. Established 1984. **Poetry Editor:** Cheryl Townsend.

Magazine Needs: Publishes *Impetus*, a "somewhat" quarterly literary magazine, chapbooks and special issues. Would like to see "strong social protest with raw emotion. Material should be straight from the gut, uncensored and real. Absolutely no nature poetry or rhyme for the sake of rhyme, oriental, or 'Kissy, kissy I love you' poems. Any length as long as it works. All subjects OK, providing there are no 'isms.' *Impetus* is now also publishing annual erotica and all-female issues. Material should reflect these themes." Has published poetry by Ron Androla, Kurt Nimmo, Lyn Lifshin, and Lonnie Sherman. *Impetus* is now published online only (except for anthology published in December). Back issues: $5; make checks payable to Implosion Press.

How to Submit: Submit 3-8 poems at a time. "I prefer shorter, to-the-point work." Include name and address on each page. Accepts previously published work if it is noted when and where. "I always like a cover letter that tells me how the poet found out about my magazine." Accepts submissions by e-mail (in text box) and by postal mail. Generally a 5-month backlog. Guidelines available for SASE, by e-mail, on website, and in publication. Usually responds within 4 months. Pays 1 copy. Acquires one-time rights. Reviews books of poetry. Send materials for review consideration.

Advice: "Know your market. Request guidelines and/or a sample copy."

$ IN THE FAMILY (Specialized: gay/lesbian/bisexual/transgender), 7850 N. Silverbell Rd. #114-188, Tucson AZ 85743. (520)579-8043. E-mail: lmarkowitz@aol.com. Website: http://inthefamily.com. Established 1995. **Fiction Editor:** Helena Lipstadt.

Magazine Needs: *In the Family* is a quarterly "magazine exploring clinical issues for queer people and their families." We're open to anything but it must refer to a gay/lesbian/bisexual/transgender theme. No long autobiography. No limericks." Has published poetry by Benjamin Goldberg, Penny Perry, and Katrina Gonzalez. *In the Family* is 32 pages, magazine-sized, offset-printed and saddle-stapled with 2-color cover, includes art and ads. Receives about 50 poems/year, accepts approximately 5%. Press run is 5,000 for 3,000 subscribers of which 10% are libraries, 5% shelf sales; 10% distributed free to direct mail promos. Subscription: $24. Sample: $6. Make checks payable to ITF.

How to Submit: Submit 5 poems at a time. Accepts simultaneous submissions; no previously published poems. No e-mail submissions. Cover letter required. Time between acceptance and publication is up to 5 months. Poems are circulated to an editorial board. "Fiction editor makes recommendations." Publishes theme issues. Responds in 6 weeks. Always sends prepublication galleys. Pays

$35 and 5 copies. Acquires first rights. Reviews books of poetry. Send materials for review consideration to attn. Reviews.

IN THE GROVE (Specialized: regional, California), P.O. Box 16195, Fresno CA 93755. (559)442-4600, ext. 8469. Fax: (559)265-5756. E-mail: inthegrove@rocketmail.com. Website: http://leeherrick.tripod.com/itg. Established 1996. **Publisher:** Lee Herrick. **Editor:** Michael Roberts. **Poetry Editor:** Zay Guffy-Bill.

Magazine Needs: *In the Grove* appears 2 times/year and publishes "short fiction, essays, and poetry by new and established writers born or currently living in the Central Valley and throughout California." Wants "poetry of all forms and subject matter. We seek the originality, distinct voice and craftsmanship of a poem. No greeting card verse or forced rhyme. Be fresh. Take a risk." Has published poetry by Ruth Schwartz, Gillian Wegener, Andres Montoya, Loren Palsgaard, Amy Uyematsu, and Renny Christopher. *In The Grove* is 80-100 pages, digest-sized, photocopied and perfect-bound with heavy card stock cover, 4-5 pages of ads. Receives about 500 poems/year, accepts up to 10%. Press run is 150 for 50 subscribers, 75 shelf sales; 25 distributed free to contributors, colleagues. Subscription: $12. Sample: $6.

How to Submit: Submit 3-5 poems at a time. Accepts previously published poems and simultaneous submissions. Cover letter preferred. Time between acceptance and publication is up to 6 months. "Poetry editor reads all submissions and makes recommendations to editor, who makes final decisions." Seldom comments on rejected poems. Guidelines available for SASE or on website. Responds in 3 months. Pays 2 copies. Acquires first or one-time rights. Rights return to poets upon publication.

IN THE SPIRIT OF THE BUFFALO, Opportunity Assistance, 233 N. 48th St., Suite MBE 151, Lincoln NE 68504. (402)464-1994. Fax: (978)285-0331. E-mail: webmaster@opportunityassistance.com. Website: www.inthespiritofthebuffalo.com. Established 1996. **Publisher/Editor:** Keith P. Stiencke.

Magazine Needs: *In the Spirit of the Buffalo* is published 7 or 8 times a year an e-mail newsletter to "provide a forum for poets and authors of all experience levels to be a positive influence for social awareness and change through creative personal expression." Wants "poetry that awakens social consciousness while still being positive in tone. Motivational, inspirational, and spiritual writing is highly acceptable. No poetry that promotes racism; no hate poetry; pornographic content is not acceptable."

How to Submit: Submit up to 3 poems at a time. Accepts previously published poems; no simultaneous submissions. Accepts submissions on disk, by e-mail (in text box), by fax, or by regular mail. E-mail preferred. Cover letter preferred; "we would appreciate being able to publish your contact information, however it is not a requirement for publication." Time between acceptance and publication is 3-6 months. Seldom comments on rejected poems. Responds in up to 4 months. Acquires one-time rights. Send materials for review consideration.

INDEFINITE SPACE (Specialized: style/experimental), P.O. Box 40101, Pasadena CA 91114. Established 1992. **Editor:** Marcia Arrieta.

Magazine Needs: *Indefinite Space* appears annually. Wants experimental, visual, minimalistic poetry. Does not want rhyming poetry. Recently published poetry by Lisa Fishman, Dan Campion, Jeffrey Little, Crag Hill, W.B. Keckler, and Rob Cook. *Indefinite Space* is 36 pages, digest-sized, with b&w art. Single copy: $6; subscription: $10/2 issues. Sample: $6. Make checks payable to Marcia Arrieta.

How to Submit: Accepts simultaneous submissions; no previously published poems. No fax, e-mail, or disk submissions. Seldom comments on rejected poems. Guidelines available for SASE. Responds in up to 3 months. Copyright retained by poets.

INDIAN HERITAGE PUBLISHING; INDIAN HERITAGE COUNCIL QUARTERLY; NATIVE AMERICAN POETRY ANTHOLOGY (Specialized: ethnic/nationality, Native American; spirituality/inspirational); P.O. Box 2302, Morristown TN 37816. (423)581-4448 or (423)277-1103. Established 1986. **CEO:** Louis Hooban.

• *Indian Heritage Council Quarterly* received the Evergreen Award from the Consortium of International Environmental Groups.

Magazine Needs: *Indian Heritage Council Quarterly*, appearing quarterly, devotes 1 issue to poetry with a Native American theme. Wants "any type of poetry relating to Native Americans, their beliefs, or Mother Earth." Does not want "doggerel." Accepts poetry written by young writers. Has published poetry by Running Buffalo and Angela Evening Star Dempsey. *Indian Heritage Council Quarterly* is 6 pages, digest-sized (8½×11 folded sheet with 5½×8½ insert), photocopied. Receives about 300 poems/year, accepts up to 30%. Press run and number of subscribers vary, 50% shelf sales; 50 distributed free to Indian reservations. Subscription: $10. Sample: "negotiable." Make checks payable to Indian Heritage Council.

How to Submit: Submit up to 3 poems at a time. Accepts previously published poems (author must own rights only) and simultaneous submissions. Cover letter required. Time between acceptance and publication is 3 months to 1 year. Poems are circulated to an editorial board. "Our editorial board decides on all publications." Seldom comments on rejected poems. Charges criticism fees "depending on negotiations." Publishes theme issues. Guidelines and upcoming themes available for SASE and in publication. Responds within 3 weeks. Pay is negotiable. Acquires one-time rights. Staff reviews books or chapbooks of poetry or other magazines. Send materials for review consideration.

Book/Chapbook Needs & How to Submit: Indian Heritage Publishing publishes chapbooks of Native American themes and/or Native American poets. Has published *Crazy Horse's Philosophy of Riding Rainbows*, *Native American Predictions*, and *The Vision: an Anthology of Native American Poetry*. Format of chapbooks varies. Query first, with a few sample poems and cover letter with brief bio and publication credits. Responds to queries within 3 weeks, varies for mss. Pays 33-50% royalties. **Offers subsidy arrangements that vary by negotiations, number of poems, etc.** For sample chapbooks, write to the above address.

Also Offers: Sponsors a contest for their anthology, "if approved by our editorial board. Submissions are on an individual basis—always provide a SASE."

Advice: "Write from the heart and spirit and write so the reader can understand or grasp the meaning."

$🖉 INDIANA REVIEW, Ballantine Hall 465, 1020 E. Kirkwood Ave., Bloomington IN 47405-7103. (812)855-3439. E-mail: inreview@indiana.edu. Website: www.indiana.edu/~inreview. Established 1982. **Contact:** Danit Brown.

- Poetry published in *Indiana Review* has been frequently selected for inclusion in *The Best American Poetry* and in the *Pushcart Prize* anthology.

Magazine Needs: *Indiana Review* is a biannual of prose, poetry, and visual art. "We look for an intelligent sense of form and language, and admire poems of risk, ambition and scope. We'll consider all types of poems—free verse, traditional, experimental. Reading a sample issue is the best way to determine if *Indiana Review* is a potential home for your work. Any subject matter is acceptable if it is written well." Has published poetry by Philip Levine, Sherman Alexie, Lucia Perillo, Campbell McGrath, Charles Simic, Marilyn Chin, and Alberto Rios. The magazine uses about 40-60 pages of poetry in each issue (digest-sized, flat-spined, 160 pages, color matte cover, professional printing). Receives about 5,000 submissions/year, accepts up to 60. The magazine has 500 subscriptions. Sample: $8.

How to Submit: Submit 4-6 poems at a time, do not send more than 10 pages of poetry per submission. No electronic submissions. Pays $5/page ($10 minimum/poem), plus 2 copies and remainder of year's subscription. Acquires first North American serial rights only. "We try to respond to manuscripts in 3-4 months. Reading time is often slower during summer and holiday months." Brief book reviews are also featured. Send materials for review consideration. Holds yearly contests. Guidelines available for SASE.

◯ 🎯 INSECTS ARE PEOPLE TWO; PUFF 'N' STUFF PRODUCTIONS (Specialized: insects), P.O. Box 146486, Chicago IL 60614-6400. Established 1989. **Publisher:** H.R. Felgenhauer.

Magazine Needs: *Insects Are People Two* is an infrequent publication focusing solely on "poems about insects doing people things and people doing insect things." Accepts poetry written by children. Has published poetry by Bruce Boston, Steve Sneyd, Paul Wieneman, and Lyn Lifshin. *Insects Are People Two* is magazine-sized, with card cover, b&w art and graphics. Press run is 1,000. Sample: $6.

How to Submit: Accepts previously published poems and simultaneous submissions. Often comments on rejected poems. Publishes theme issues. Responds "immediately." Pay varies. Send materials for review consideration.

Book/Chapbook Needs & How to Submit: Puff 'N' Stuff Productions publishes 1 chapbook/year. Responds to queries and mss in 10 days. Pay is negotiable.

Advice: "Hit me with your best shot. Never give up—editors have tunnel-vision. The *BEST* mags you almost *NEVER* even hear about. Don't believe reviews. Write for yourself. Prepare for failure, not success."

⬤ INTERBANG; BERTYE PRESS, INC., P.O. Box 1574, Venice CA 90294. (310)450-6372. E-mail: heather@interbang.net. Website: www.interbang.net. Established 1995. **Editor:** Heather Hoffman.

Magazine Needs: *Interbang*, published quarterly, is "Dedicated to Perfection in the Art of Writing." Wants "enticing poetry of any length on any subject. Although we do not have strict standards regarding substance, texture, or structure, your craft, in tandem with your subject matter, should elicit a strong response in the reader: love, hate, shock, sorrow, revulsion, you name it. Write your name, address, and phone number on each page of your submission." Has published poetry by Rob Lipton, John Thomas, Linda Platt Mintz, David Centorbi, and Jessica Pompei. *Interbang* is 30 pages, 7½×8½, offset-printed and saddle-stapled with colored card stock cover, includes line art and photos. Receives about 500 poems/year, accepts up to 50%. Press run is 2,000 for 100 subscribers of which 10 are libraries, 20 shelf sales; 40 distributed free to other magazines, the rest distributed free at coffeehouses and bookstores in L.A. Send two stamps for a free sample copy.

How to Submit: Submit 5-15 poems at a time. Accepts previously published poems and simultaneous submissions. Accepts e-mail submissions; include text in body of message. Comments on rejected poems on request. *Interbang Writer's Guide* available by e-mail or on website. Responds in 6 months. Always sends prepublication galleys. Pays 5 copies. Reviews chapbooks of poetry and other magazines in 350-400 words, single book format. Send materials for review consideration.

⬤ THE INTERFACE; BUTTERMILK ART WORKS, % GlassFull Productions, P.O. Box 57129, Philadelphia PA 19111-7129. E-mail: madlove3000@excite.com. Website: www.baworks.com/Interface. Established 1997. **Publisher:** Earl Weeks.

Magazine Needs: *The INTERFACE* is published quarterly on the Internet and covers wrestling, comic books, trading cards, science fiction, and politics. Wants "all kinds of work—romantic, political, social commentary. We want poetry that comes from your heart, that makes tears come to the eye or forces one to want to mobilize the troops. No poems of hate or discrimination." Has published poetry by Mike Emrys, Sheron Regular, Cassandra Norris, and Monique Frederick. Receives about 20 poems/year, accepts up to 35%. Publishes 15 poems/issue.

How to Submit: Submit 7 poems at a time. Accepts previously published poems and simultaneous submissions. Accepts submissions by e-mail, through online submission form, and by regular mail. Cover letter preferred. Send all submissions % Earl Weeks. "We will consider accompanying illustration." Submit seasonal poems 6 months in advance. Time between acceptance and publication is 9 months. Poems are circulated to an editorial board. Occasionally publishes theme issues. Guidelines and upcoming themes available on website. Does not respond to submissions. Acquires two-time rights. "We also have a sister magazine, *The Maelan News*, available only on newsstands in Philly. If you wish not to be printed in the print mag, let us know." Reviews books and chapbooks of poetry and other magazines.

Also Offers: "We publish poetry, essays, videogame reviews, book reviews, fashion, science fiction, art, and more. We are trying to make *The INTERFACE* a meeting place for idea exchanges. We need your opinions and views, so submit them to us."

⬤ INTERIM, 5034 English Dept., University of Nevada, Las Vegas, Las Vegas NV 89154-5011. (702)895-3333. Fax: (702)895-4801. E-mail: keelanc@nevada.edu. or interim_unlv@yahoo.com. **Editor:** Claudia Keelan. **Member:** CLMP.

Magazine Needs: *Interim* is an annual magazine, appearing in early spring, that publishes poetry, short fiction, essays, and book reviews. "We seek submissions from writers who are testing the boundaries of genre." Has published poetry by Charles Bernstein, Robert Creeley, Alice Notley, April Ossman, and Wole Soyinka. *Interim* is 150 pages, digest-sized, professionally printed and perfect-bound with coated card cover. Press run is 400. Individual subscription: $12/year. Sample: $6 (back issue).

How to Submit: Submit 3-5 poems with brief bio and SASE. No simultaneous submissions. No fax or e-mail submissions. Reads mss from September to April. Responds in up to 3 months. Pays 2 copies. Acquires first serial rights. Poems may be reprinted elsewhere with a permission line noting publication in *Interim*.

○ ◎ **INTERNATIONAL BLACK WRITERS; BLACK WRITER MAGAZINE (Specialized: ethnic)**, 535 Logan Dr. #903, Hammond IN 46320. (312)458-5745. Established 1970. **President/CEO:** Mable Terrell.

Magazine Needs & How to Submit: *Black Writer* is a "quarterly literary magazine to showcase new writers and poets and provide educational information for writers. Open to all types of poetry." *Black Writer* is 30 pages, magazine-sized, offset-printed, with glossy cover. Press run is 1,000 for 200 subscribers. Subscription: $19/year. Sample: $1.50. Responds in 10 days, has 1 quarter backlog. Pays 10 contributor's copies.

Book/Chapbook Needs & How to Submit: For chapbook publication (40 pages), submit 2 sample poems and cover letter with short bio. Accepts simultaneous submissions. Pays copies. For sample chapbook, send SASE with book rate postage.

Also Offers: Offers awards of $100, $50, and $25 for the best poems published in the magazine and presents them to winners at annual awards banquet. International Black Writers is open to all writers.

⊘ ◎ **INTERNATIONAL POETRY REVIEW (Specialized: translations)**, Dept. of Romance Languages, UNC-Greensboro, Greensboro NC 27402-6170. (336)334-5655. Fax: (336)334-5358. E-mail: k_mather@uncg.edu or kathleenkoestler@gbronline.com. Website: www.uncg.edu/rom/ipr.htm. Established 1975. **Editor:** Kathleen Koestler.

Magazine Needs: *International Poetry Review* is a biannual primarily publishing translations of contemporary poetry with corresponding originals (published on facing pages) as well as original poetry in English. Recently published work by Richard Exner, René Char, Alvaro Mutis, and Tony Barnstone. *International Poetry Review* is 100 pages, digest-sized, professionally printed and perfect-bound with 2-3 color cover. "We accept 5% of original poetry in English and about 30% of translations submitted." Press run is 500 for 200 subscribers. Subscription: $12/$20/$30 (for one, two, and three years respectively) for individuals, $20/$35/$50 for institutions. Sample: $5. Make checks payable to *International Poetry Review*.

How to Submit: Submit no more than 6 pages of poetry. Accepts simultaneous submissions; no previously published poems. Reads submissions between September 1 and April 30. Seldom comments on rejected poems. Guidelines and upcoming themes available for SASE. Responds in up to 6 months. Pays 1 copy. All rights revert to authors and translators. Occasionally reviews books of poetry. Send materials for review consideration.

Advice: "We strongly encourage contributors to subscribe. We prefer poetry in English to have an international or cross-cultural theme."

★ ⊕ ⊘ **INTERPRETER'S HOUSE; BEDFORD OPEN POETRY COMPETITION**, 10 Farrell Rd., Wootton, Bedfordshire MK43 9DU United Kingdom. Established 1996. **Contact:** Merryn Williams.

Magazine Needs: *Interpreter's House* appears 3 times/year (February, June, October) and publishes short stories and poetry. Wants "good poetry (and short stories), not too long. No Christmas-card verse or incomprehensible poetry." Has published poetry by Dannie Abse, Tony Curtis, Pauline Stainer, Alan Brownjohn, Peter Redgrove, and R.S. Thomas. *Interpreter's House* is 74 pages, A5 with attractive cover design. Receives about 1,000 poems/year, accepts up to 5%. Press run is 300 for 200 subscribers. Subscription: £10.00. Sample: £3 plus 44 p.

How to Submit: Submit 5 poems at a time. No previously published poems or simultaneous submissions. Cover letter preferred. Time between acceptance and publication is 2 weeks to 8 months. Often comments on rejected poems. Guidelines available for SASE or SAE and IRC. Responds "fast." Pays 1 copy.

Also Offers: Sponsors the Bedford Open Poetry Competition. Send SAE and IRC for details.

★ ◐ ◎ **INVERTED-A, INC. (form/style, traditional); INVERTED-A HORN**, 900 Monarch Way, Northport AL 35473-2663. E-mail: amnfn@well.com. Established 1977. **Editors:** Netz Katz and Aya Katz.

Magazine Needs: *Inverted-A Horn* is an irregular periodical. Wants traditional poetry with meter and rhyme, and welcomes political topics, science fiction, and social issues. Does not want to see anything "modern, formless, existentialist." *Inverted-A Horn* is usually 9 pages, magazine-sized, offset-printed; press run is 300.

How to Submit: Accepts simultaneous submissions. Accepts submissions by postal mail and as ASCII file. Responds to queries in 1 month, to mss in 4 months. Pays 1 copy plus a 40% discount on additional copies. Samples: SASE with postage for 2 ounces (subject to availability).

Book/Chapbook Needs & How to Submit: Inverted-A, Inc. is a very small press that evolved from publishing technical manuals for other products. "Our interests center on freedom, justice, and honor." Publishes 1 chapbook/year.

Advice: "I strongly recommend that would-be contributors avail themselves of this opportunity to explore what we are looking for. Most of the submissions we receive do not come close."

🌐 ◐ **IOTA**, 1 Lodge Farm, Snitterfield, Warwicks CV37 0LR United Kingdom. Phone: 01789 730358. Fax: 01789 730320. E-mail: iotapoetry@aol.com. Website: www.iotapoetry.co.uk. Established 1988. **Editors:** Janet Murch and Bob Mee.

Magazine Needs: *Iota* is a quarterly wanting "any style and subject; no specific limitations as to length." Has published poetry by Don Winter, John Robinson, Tony Petch, Donna Pucciani, Brian Daldorph, and Michael Kriesel. *Iota* is 60 pgs., professionally printed and saddle-stapled with light colored card cover. Publishes about 300 of 6,000 poems received. Press run is 300 with 150 subscribers of which 8 are libraries. Subscription: $24 (£12). Sample: $6 (£3).

How to Submit: Submit 4-6 poems at a time. Prefers name and address on each poem, typed. No simultaneous submissions or previously published poems. Accepts e-mail submissions (in text box); no fax submissions. Responds in 3 weeks (unless production of the next issue takes precedence). "No SAE, no reply." Pays 1 copy. Reviews books of poetry. Send materials for review consideration.

Also Offers: "The editors also run Ragged Raven Press which publishes poetry collections, nonfiction, and an annual anthology of poetry linked to an international competition." Website: www.ragged raven.co.uk.

Advice: "Read poetry, particularly contemporary poetry. Edit your own poems to tighten and polish."

$ ◐ **THE IOWA REVIEW; THE TIM McGINNIS AWARD; THE IOWA AWARD; THE REVIEW STAFF AWARD**, 308 EPB, University of Iowa, Iowa City IA 52242. (319)335-0462. E-mail: iowa-review@uiowa.edu. Website: www.iowa.edu/~iareview. Established 1970. **Editor:** David Hamilton. **Contact:** editor.

● Poetry published in *The Iowa Review* has been frequently included in *The Best American Poetry* and the *Pushcart Prize* anthologies.

Magazine Needs: *The Iowa Review* appears 3 times/year and publishes fiction, poetry, essays, reviews, interviews, and autobiographical sketches. "We simply look for poems that at the time we read and choose, we admire. No specifications as to form, length, style, subject matter, or purpose. There are around 40 pages of poetry in each issue and we like to give several pages to a single poet. Though we print work from established writers, we're always delighted when we discover new talent." *The Iowa Review* is 200 pages, professionally printed, flat-spined. Receives about 5,000 submissions/year, accepts up to 100. Press run is 2,900 with 1,000 subscribers of which about half are libraries; 1,500 distributed to stores. Subscription: $18. Sample: $6.

How to Submit: Submit 3-6 poems at a time. No e-mail submissions. Cover letter (with title of work and genre) encouraged and SASE required. Reads submissions "from Labor Day to April Fool's Day or until we fill our next volume year's issues." Time between acceptance and publication is "around a year. Sometimes people hit at the right time and come out in a few months." Occasionally comments on rejected poems or offers suggestions on accepted poems. Responds in up to 4 months. Pays $20/page for the first page and $15 for each subsequent page, 2 copies, and a 1-year subscription. Acquires first North American serial rights, non-exclusive anthology rights, and non-exclusive electronic rights.

Also Offers: Sponsors the Tim McGinnis Award. "The award, in the amount of $500, is given irregularly to authors of work with a light or humorous touch. We have no separate category of submissions to be considered alone for this award. Instead, any essay, story, or poem we publish will automatically be under consideration for the McGinnis Award. This year, 2003, we are also instituting two new awards. 1) An Iowa Award in Poetry, Fiction, and Essay. The entry fee is $15. The deadline February 1. Outside Judges for finalists. Winners will receive $1,000 and publication. Several runners up may also be published. 2) A Review Staff Award, again in the amount of $1,000, given to a former contributor who returns to our pages, in any genre, and whose work is most admired by our student staff members."

IRIS: A JOURNAL ABOUT WOMEN (Specialized: women/feminism), P.O. Box 800588, University of Virginia, Charlottesville VA 22908. (434)924-4500. Website: http://iris.virginia .edu. Established 1980. **Coordinating Editor:** Kimberley Roberts. **Poetry Editor:** Nura Yingling.

Magazine Needs: *Iris* is a semiannual magazine appearing in April and November that "focuses on issues concerning women worldwide. It features quality poetry, prose and artwork—mainly by women, but will also accept work by men if it illuminates some aspect of a woman's reality. It also publishes translations. Form and length are unspecified. The poetry staff consists of experienced poets with a diversity of tastes who are looking for new and original language and diverse perspectives in well-crafted poems." Poets who have appeared in *Iris* include Sharon Olds, Mary Oliver, Charlotte Matthews, Rebecca B. Rank, Lisa Russ Spaar, and Gregory Orr. *Iris* is 78 pages, magazine-sized, professionally printed on heavy, glossy stock, saddle-stapled with a full-color glossy card cover, using graphics and photos. Press run is over 2,000 for about 40 library subscriptions, 1,000 shelf sales. Single copy: $5; subscription: $9/year; $17/2 years. Sample: $6.50.

How to Submit: Submit no more than 5 poems at a time. Simultaneous submissions are discouraged. Name, address, phone number should be listed on every poem. Cover letter should include list of poems submitted and a brief bio. Publishes theme issues. Next theme issue appearing in October 2003 is "Passion." Upcoming themes available for SASE, on website, and in publication. Guidelines available for SASE and on website. Responds in 6 months. Pays 5 copies. Acquires first rights.

Advice: "The poetry staff at *Iris* is interested in pieces exploring all aspects of women's lives—especially the lives of younger women. Because many poems are on similar topics, freshness of imagery and style are even more important."

ITALIAN AMERICANA; JOHN CIARDI AWARD (Specialized: ethnic, Italian), URI/ CCE, 80 Washington St., Providence RI 02903-1803. (401)277-5306. Fax: (401)277-5100. E-mail: bonomoal@ital.uri.edu. Website: www.uri.edu/prov/italian/italian.html. Established 1974. **Editor:** Carol Bonomo Albright. **Poetry Editor:** Dana Gioia.

Magazine Needs: *Italian Americana* appears twice/year using 16-20 poems of "no more than three pages. No trite nostalgia; no poems about grandparents." Has published poetry by Mary Jo Salter and Joy Parini. It is 150-200 pages, digest-sized, professionally printed and flat-spined with glossy card cover. Press run is 1,000 for 900 subscribers of which 175 are libraries, 175 shelf sales. Singly copy: $10; subscription: $20/year, $35/2 years. Sample: $6.

How to Submit: Submit 3 poems at a time. No previously published poems or simultaneous submissions. Cover letter not required "but helpful." Name on first page of ms only. Do not submit poetry in July, August or September. Occasionally comments on rejected poems. Responds in 6 weeks.

Acquires first rights. Reviews books of poetry in 600 words, multi-book format. Send materials for review consideration to Prof. John Paul Russo, English Dept., University of Miami, Coral Gables FL 33124.

Also Offers: Along with the National Italian American Foundation, *Italian Americana* co-sponsors the annual $1,000 John Ciardi Award for Lifetime Contribution to Poetry. *Italian Americana* also presents $250 fiction or memoir award annually; and $1,500 in history prizes.

Advice: "Single copies of poems for submissions are sufficient."

$ ⊚ ITALICA PRESS (Specialized: bilingual/foreign language, translations), 595 Main St., #605, New York NY 10044-0047. (212)935-4230. Fax: (212)838-7812. E-mail: inquiries@italica press.com. Website: www.italicapress.com. Established 1985. **Publishers:** Eileen Gardiner and Ronald G. Musto.

Book/Chapbook Needs: Italica is a small press publisher of English translations of Italian works in paperbacks, averaging 175 pages. Has published *Contemporary Italian Women Poets*, a dual-language (English/Italian) anthology edited and translated by Anzia Sartini Blum and Lara Trubowitz, and *Women Poets of the Italian Renaissance*, a dual-language anthology, edited by Laura Anna Stortoni, translated by Laura Anna Stortoni and Mary Prentice Lillie.

How to Submit: Query with 10 sample translations of medieval and Renaissance Italian poets. Include cover letter, bio, and list of publications. Accepts simultaneous submissions, but translation should not be "totally" previously published. Accepts e-mail submissions (in text box and as attachment); no fax submissions. Responds to queries in 3 weeks, to mss in 3 months. Always sends prepublication galleys. Pays 7-15% royalties plus 10 author's copies. Acquires English language rights.

◪ JACK MACKEREL MAGAZINE; ROWHOUSE PRESS, P.O. Box 23134, Seattle WA 98102-0434. Established 1992. **Editor:** Greg Bachar.

Magazine Needs: *Jack Mackerel*, published quarterly, features poetry, fiction, and art. Has published poetry by Bell Knott, John Rose, and William D. Waltz. *Jack Mackerel* is 40-60 pages, digest-sized, printed on bond paper, with glossy card coverstock, b&w illustrations and photos. Press run is 1,000. Subscription: $12. Sample: $5. Make checks payable to Greg Bachar.

How to Submit: No previously published poems or simultaneous submissions. Cover letter preferred. Poems are circulated to an editorial board. Seldom comments on rejected poems. Responds in 1 month. Pays with copies. Send materials for review consideration.

◪ ALICE JAMES BOOKS; NEW ENGLAND/NEW YORK AWARD, BEATRICE HAWLEY AWARD, University of Maine at Farmington, 238 Main St., Farmington ME 04938. Phone/fax: (207)778-7071. E-mail: ajb@umf.maine.edu. Website: www.alicejamesbooks.org. Established 1973. **Contest Coordinator:** Aimee Beal.

Book/Chapbook Needs: "The mission of Alice James Books, a cooperative poetry press, is to seek out and publish the best contemporary poetry by both established and beginning poets, with particular emphasis on involving poets in the publishing process." Has published poetry by Jane Kenyon, Jean Valentine, B.H. Fairchild, and Matthea Harvey. Publishes flat-spined paperbacks of high quality, both in production and contents, no children's poetry or light verse. Publishes 6 books, 80 pages, each year in editions of 1,500, paperbacks—no hardbacks.

How to Submit: "Manuscripts are selected through two annual competitions—the Beatrice Hawley Award, a national award for poets living anywhere in the U.S., with no cooperative commitment, and the New England/New York Competition, where winners become members of the cooperative with a three-year commitment to the editorial board and receive a 1-month fellowship residing at the Vermont Studio Center. The winners in both competitions receive a cash award of $2,000. Competition deadlines are in early fall and winter. Send SASE or check website for guidelines." No phone queries. Send 2 copies of the ms, SASE for notification, and submission fee. Accepts simultaneous submissions, but "we would like to know immediately when a manuscript is accepted elsewhere." Responds in 4 months.

◪ JEOPARDY MAGAZINE, 132 College Hall, Bellingham WA 98225. (360)650-3118. E-mail: jeopardy@cc.wwu.edu. Website: http://jeopardy.wwu.edu. Established 1965. **Editor-in-Chief:** Nicole Albright.

Magazine Needs: *Jeopardy Magazine* appears annually in June or July. Seeks originality, command of vocabulary, interesting perspectives, creativity. Recently published poetry by Galway Kinnell, James Bertolino, David Wagoner, Knute Skinner, and Omar S. Castañeda. *Jeopardy Magazine* is 80-150 pages, digest-sized, press-printed, book binding, color, hard stock cover, with photo, drawings, paintings, prints. Receives about 200 poems/year, accepts about 10%. Press run is 1,500 for 50 subscribers of which 30 are libraries; distributed free to students and community. Sample: $5. Make checks payable to *Jeopardy*.

How to Submit: Submit 6 poems at a time. Line length for poetry is 10 pages maximum. Accepts simultaneous submissions; no previously published poems. No disk or e-mail submissions. Cover letter is required. Include SASE. Reads submissions December 1-April 1. Time between acceptance and publication is 3 months. Poems are circulated to an editorial board. "Assistant editors read, the head editors make decision." Never comments on rejected poems. Occasionally publishes theme issues. Upcoming themes available by e-mail. Guidelines are available for SASE and on website. Responds in 3 months. Pays 2 contributor's copies. Acquires one-time rights.

JEWISH CURRENTS (Specialized: themes, religious; ethnic/nationality), 22 E. 17th St., Suite 601, New York NY 10003-1919. (212)924-5740. Fax: (212)414-2227. E-mail: jewish.c urrents@verizon.net. Website: www.jewishcurrents.org. Established 1946. **Editor:** Lawrence Bush.

Magazine Needs: *Jewish Currents* is a magazine appearing 6 times/year that publishes articles, reviews, fiction, and poetry pertaining to Jewish subjects or presenting a Jewish point of view on an issue of interest, including translations from the Yiddish and Hebrew (original texts should be submitted with translations). Accepts poetry written by children. *Jewish Currents* is 40 pages, magazine-sized, offset, saddle-stapled. Press run is 2,500 for 2,100 subscribers of which about 10% are libraries. Subscription: $30/year. Sample: $5.

How to Submit: Submit 1 poem at a time, typed, double-spaced, with SASE. Include brief bio with author's publishing history. No previously published poems or simultaneous submissions. Accepts fax submissions. Cover letter required. Publishes theme issues. Upcoming themes include November: Jewish Book Month; December: Hanuka; February: Black History Month; March: Jewish Music Season, Purim, International Women's Day; April: Holocaust Resistance, Passover; May: Israel; July/August: Soviet Jewish History. Deadlines for themes are 6 months in advance. Guidelines available for SASE. Time between acceptance and publication is 2 years. Seldom comments on rejected poems. Responds in up to 1 year. Always sends prepublication galleys. Pays 6 copies. Reviews books of poetry.

Advice: "Be intelligent, original, unexpected. Don't write doggerel."

$ JEWISH WOMEN'S LITERARY ANNUAL (Specialized: ethnic, women), 820 Second Ave., New York NY 10017. (212)751-9223. Fax: (212)935-3523. Established 1994. **Editor:** Dr. Henny Wenkart.

Magazine Needs: *Jewish Women's Literary Annual* appears annually in April and publishes poetry and fiction by Jewish women. Wants "poems by Jewish women on any topic, but of the highest literary quality." Has published poetry by Alicia Ostriker, Savina Teubal, Grace Herman, Enid Dame, Marge Piercy, and Lesléa Newman. *Jewish Women's Literary Annual* is 160 pages, digest-sized, perfect-bound with a laminated card cover, b&w art and photos inside. Receives about 500 poems/year, accepts about 15%. Press run is 1,500 for 480 subscribers. Subscription: $18/3 issues. Sample: $7.50.

How to Submit: No previously published poems. No fax submissions. Poems are circulated to an editorial board. Often comments on rejected poems. Responds in up to 5 months. Pays 3 copies plus a small honorarium. Rights remain with the poet.

Advice: "It would be helpful, but not essential, if poets would send for a sample copy of our annual before submitting."

JOEL'S HOUSE PUBLICATIONS; WILLIAM DEWITT ROMIG POETRY CONTEST (Specialized: religious/Christian; spirituality; recovery), P.O. Box 328, Beach Lake PA 18405-0328. (570)729-8709. Fax: (570)729-7246. E-mail: newbeginmin@ezaccess.net. Website: http://newbeginningmin.org. Established 1997. **Editor:** Kevin T. Coughlin.

Magazine Needs: *Joel's Hosue Publications* appears quarterly. Produced by New Beginning Ministry, Inc., a nonprofit corporation, *Joel's House Publications* is a newsletter featuring poetry, articles, and original art. Wants poetry that is related to recovery, spirituality; also Christian poetry. Will consider any length, positive topic, and structure. No poetry which is inappropriately sexually graphic or discriminatory in nature. Recently published poetry by Cynthia Brackett-Vincent, John Wadding-ton-Feather, Wendy Apgar, K.F. Homer, Melanie Schurr, and William DeWitt Romig. *Joel's House Publications* is 10-20 pages, digest-sized, offset-printed, saddle-stapled, card stock cover, with original and clip art. Receives about 25-50 poems/year, accepts about 25%. Publishes about 25-50 poems/issue. Press run is 1,000 for 100 subscribers; 200 distributed free to mailing list. Single copy: $3; subscription: $12/1 year, 1 issue. Sample: $2 plus p&h. Make checks payable to New Beginning Ministry, Inc.

How to Submit: Submit 3-5 poems at a time. No previously published poems or simultaneous submissions. Accepts submissions by fax, e-mail, postal mail, and on disk. Cover letter is preferred. "Always send a SASE, typed manuscript with name and address on each poem." Reads submissions all year. Time between acceptance and publication is up to 1 year. Seldom comments on rejected poems. Guidelines available for SASE. Responds in up to 6 weeks. Always sends prepublication galleys. Pays 2 contributor's copies. Acquires first rights.

Also Offers: Poetry contest (send SASE for details) and writing retreats (check website for details). "Poetry contest will be held every December. The William DeWitt Romig poetry award will be given to the poet who best demonstrates life through the art of poetry."

Advice: "Keep writing—revise, revise, revise! If you write poetry, you are a poet. Be true to your craft."

⊘ THE JOHNS HOPKINS UNIVERSITY PRESS, 2715 N. Charles St., Baltimore MD 21218. Website: www.press.jhu.edu. Established 1878. "One of the largest American university presses, Johns Hopkins is a publisher mainly of scholarly books and journals. We do, however, publish short fiction and poetry in the series Johns Hopkins: Poetry and Fiction, edited by John Irwin. Unsolicited submissions are not considered."

◆ ⊘ JONES AV.; OEL PRESS, 88 Dagmar Ave., Toronto ON M4M 1W1 Canada. (416)461-8739. E-mail: oel@interlog.com. Website: www.interlog.com/~oel. Established 1994. **Editor/Publisher:** Paul Schwartz.

Magazine Needs: *Jones Av.* is published quarterly and contains "poems from the lyric to the ash can; starting poets and award winners." Wants poems "up to 30 lines mostly, concise in thought and image. Prose poems sometimes. Rhymed poetry is very difficult to do well these days, it better be good." Has published poetry by Bert Almon, Michael Estabrook, John Grey, Bernice Lever, B.Z. Niditch, and Elane Wolff. *Jones Av.* is 24 pages, digest-sized, photocopied and saddle-stapled with card cover, uses b&w graphics. Receives about 300 poems/year, accepts 30-40%. Press run is 100 for 40 subscribers. Subscription: $8. Sample: $2. Make checks payable to Paul Schwartz

How to Submit: Submit 5-8 poems at a time. No previously published poems or simultaneous submissions. Cover letter required. Accepts submissions by e-mail (in text box), and by postal mail. Include e-mail submissions in body of message. Time between acceptance and publication is up to 12 months. Often comments on rejected poems. Publishes theme issues occasionally; upcoming themes available in publication. Guidelines available for SASE or on website. "Remember, US stamps cannot be used in Canada." Responds in 3 months. Pays 1 copy. Acquires first rights. Staff reviews books and chapbooks of poetry and other magazines in 50-75 words, multi-book format. Send materials for review consideration.

Advice: "Request and study a sample issue of the publication if you are not familiar with the editor's taste."

★ ⊕ ⊘ THE DAVID JONES JOURNAL; THE DAVID JONES SOCIETY, 48 Sylvan Way, Sketty, Swansea, W. Glam SA2 9JB Wales. Phone: (01792)206144. Fax: (01792)205305. E-mail: anne.price-owen@sihe.ac.uk. Established 1997. **Editor:** Anne Price-Owen.

Magazine Needs: *The David Jones Journal* annually publishes "material related to David Jones, the Great War, mythology and the visual arts." Wants "poetry which evokes or recalls themes and/or images related to the painter/poet David Jones (1895-1974)." Has published poetry by John Mole, R.S. Thomas, Seamus Heaney and John Montague. The journal is about 160 pages, digest-sized, camera-ready printed and perfect-bound with full cover card cover, includes b&w illustrations. Receives about 12 poems/year, accepts approximately 8%. Press run is 400 for 300 subscribers. Single copy: $12; subscription: $35. Sample: $10. Make checks payable to The David Jones Society.

How to Submit: Submit 1 poem at a time. Accepts simultaneous submissions; no previously published poems. Accepts e-mail and disk submissions. Cover letter preferred. Time between acceptance and publication is 6 months. Poems are circulated to an editorial board. "Two editors agree on publication." Publishes theme issues occasionally. Obtain guidelines via e-mail. Responds in 6 weeks. Sometimes sends prepublication galleys. Pays 2 copies. Acquires first rights. Reviews books and chapbooks of poetry and other magazines in 750 words, single book format. Open to unsolicited reviews. Poets may also send books for review consideration.

$ ◘ **THE JOURNAL**, Dept. of English, Ohio State University, 164 W. 17th Ave., Columbus OH 43210. (614)292-4076. Fax: (614)292-7816. E-mail: thejournal@osu.edu. Website: www.english.ohio-state.edu/journals/the_journal/. Established 1972. **Co-Editors:** Kathy Fagan and Michelle Herman.

Magazine Needs: *The Journal* appears twice yearly with reviews, essays, quality fiction, and poetry. "We're open to all forms; we tend to favor work that gives evidence of a mature and sophisticated sense of the language." Has published poetry by Beckian Fritz Goldberg, Terrance Hayes, Bob Hicok, and Carol Potter. *The Journal* is digest-sized, professionally printed on heavy stock, 128-144 pages, of which about 60 in each issue are devoted to poetry. Receives about 4,000 submissions/year, accepts about 200, and have a 3- to 6-month backlog. Press run is 1,900. Subscription: $12. Sample: $7.

How to Submit: No submissions via fax. On occasion editor comments on rejected poems. Occasionally publishes theme issues. Pays 2 copies and an honorarium of $25-50 when funds are available. Acquires all rights. Returns rights on publication. Reviews books of poetry.

Advice: "However else poets train or educate themselves, they must do what they can to know our language. Too much of the writing we see indicates poets do not in many cases develop a feel for the possibilities of language, and do not pay attention to craft. Poets should not be in a rush to publish—until they are ready."

🌐 ◘ **THE JOURNAL; ORIGINAL PLUS PRESS**, Flat 3, 18 Oxford Grove, Ilfracombe, Devon EX34 9HQ United Kingdom. E-mail: smithsssj@aol.com. Website: http://members.aol.com/smithsssj/index.html. Established 1994. **Contact:** Sam Smith.

Magazine Needs: *The Journal* features English poetry or English translations, reviews, and articles. Wants "new poetry howsoever it comes, translations and original English language poems." Does not want "staid, generalized, all form no content." Accepts poetry written by children. Has published poetry by David H. Grubb, Gary Allen, and Ozdemir Asaf. *The Journal* is 40 pages, A4, offset printed, stapled. Receives about 1,000 poems/year, accepts approximately 5%. Press run is 100-150 for 80 subscribers of which 12 are libraries. Single copy: £2.50. For three issues: £7. Sample: £2 or £3 (sterling). Make checks payable to Sam Smith.

How to Submit: Submit up to 6 poems. Accepts previously published poems and simultaneous submissions. Accepts e-mail submissions. Cover letter preferred. "Please send hard copy submissions with 2 IRCs." Time between acceptance and publication is up to 1 year. Often comments on rejected poems. Guidelines available for SASE (or SAE and IRC). Responds in 1 month. Always sends prepublication galleys. Pays 1 contributor's copy.

Also Offers: In 1997, Original Plus began publishing collections of poetry. Has published books by Richard Wonnacott, James Turner, Don Ammons, Idris Caffrey, and RG Bishop. Send SASE (or SAE and IRC) for details.

Advice: "I prefer poetry that has been written with thought—both to what it is saying and how it is being said."

◎ **JOURNAL OF AFRICAN TRAVEL-WRITING (Specialized)**, P.O. Box 346, Chapel Hill NC 27514. Website: www.unc.edu/~ottotwo. Established 1996. **Contact:** Poetry Editor.

Magazine Needs: *Journal of African Travel-Writing*, published annually, "presents and explores past and contemporary accounts of African travel." Wants "poetry touching on any aspect of African travel. Translations are also welcome." Published poets include José Craveirinha, Theresa Sengova, Charles Hood, and Sandra Meek. *Journal of African Travel-Writing* is 192 pages, 7 × 10, professionally printed, perfect-bound, coated stock cover with cover and illustrative art, ads. Press run is 600. Subscription: $10. Sample: $6.

How to Submit: Submit up to 6 poems at a time. Include SASE. Accepts simultaneous submissions; no previously published poems. Cover letter preferred. Time between acceptance and publication is up to 1 year. "The poetry editor usually makes these selections." Sometimes comments on rejected poems. Guidelines available for SASE or on website. Publishes theme issues. Responds in up to 6 weeks. Always sends prepublication galleys. Pays 5 copies. Acquires first international publication rights. Reviews books, chapbooks or magazines of poetry. Send materials for review consideration.

⚡ $◎ JOURNAL OF ASIAN MARTIAL ARTS (Specialized: sports/recreation), 821 W. 24th St., Erie PA 16502. (814)455-9517. Fax: (814)526-5262. E-mail: info@goviamedia.com. Website: www.goviamedia.com. Established 1991. **Editor-in-Chief:** Michael A. DeMarco.

Magazine Needs: *JAMA* is a quarterly "comprehensive journal on Asian martial arts with high standards and academic approach." Wants poetry about Asian martial arts and Asian martial art history/culture. No restrictions provided the poet has a feel for, and good understanding of, the subject. Doesn't want poetry showing a narrow view. "We look for a variety of styles from an interdisciplinary approach." The journal is 124 pages, magazine-sized, professionally printed on coated stock and perfect-bound with soft cover, b&w illustrations, computer and hand art and ads. Press run is 12,000 for 1,500 subscribers of which 50 are libraries, the rest mainly shelf sales. Single copy: $9.75; subscription: $32/year, $55/2 years. Sample: $10.

How to Submit: Accepts previously published poems; no simultaneous submissions. Accepts e-mail submissions. Cover letter required. Often comments on rejected poems. Send SASE for guidelines or request via e-mail or fax. Responds in 2 months. Sometimes sends prepublication galleys. Pays $1-100 and/or 1-5 copies on publication. Buys first world and reprint rights. Reviews books of poetry "if they have some connection to Asian martial arts; length is open." Open to unsolicited reviews. Poets may send material for review consideration.

Advice: "We offer a unique medium for serious poetry dealing with Asian martial arts. Any style is welcome if there is quality in thought and writing."

◐ ◎ JOURNAL OF NEW JERSEY POETS (Specialized: regional, New Jersey), English Dept., County College of Morris, 214 Center Grove Rd., Randolph NJ 07869-2086. (973)328-5471. Fax: (973)328-5425. E-mail: szulauf@ccm.edu. Website: www.ccm.edu. Established 1976. **Editor:** Sander Zulauf. **Associate Editors:** North Peterson, Gretna Wilkinson, Sara Pfaffenroth, and Debra DeMattio.

Magazine Needs: Published annually, *Journal of New Jersey Poets* is "not necessarily about New Jersey—but of, by, and for poets from New Jersey." Wants "serious work that is regional in origin but universal in scope." Has published poetry by Amiri Baraka, X.J. Kennedy, Tina Kelley, Gerald Stern, Renée and Ted Weiss, and J. Chester Johnson. *Journal of New Jersey Poets* is digest-sized, offset-printed, with an average of 72 pages. Press run is 900. Single copy: $10; subscription: $16/2 issues; institutions: $16/issue; students/senior citizens: $10/2 issues. Sample: $5.

How to Submit: Send up to 3 poems; SASE with sufficient postage required for return of mss. Accepts e-mail and fax submissions "but they will not be acknowledged or returned." Annual deadline: September 1. Responds in up to 1 year. Time between acceptance and publication is within 1 year. Pays 5 copies and 1-year subscription. Acquires first North American serial rights. Only using solicited reviews. Send materials for review consideration.

Advice: "Read the *Journal* before submitting. Realize we vote on everything submitted, and rejection is more an indication of the quantity of submissions received and the enormous number of poets submitting quality work."

◐ ◎ JOURNAL OF THE AMERICAN MEDICAL ASSOCIATION (JAMA) (Specialized: health concerns, themes), 515 N. State, Chicago IL 60610. Fax: (312)464-5824. E-mail: charlene_breedlove@ama-assn.org. Website: www.jama.com. Established 1883. **Associate Editor:** Charlene Breedlove.

Magazine Needs: *JAMA*, a weekly journal, has a poetry and medicine column and publishes poetry "in some way related to a medical experience, whether from the point-of-view of a health care worker or patient, or simply an observer. No unskilled poetry." Has published poetry by Aimée Grunberger,

Floyd Skloot, and Walt McDonald. *JAMA* is magazine-sized, flat-spined, with glossy paper cover. Accepts about 7% of 750 poems received/year. Has 360,000 subscribers of which 369 are libraries. Subscription: $66. Sample: free. "No SASE needed."

How to Submit: Accepts simultaneous submissions, if identified; no previously published poems. "I always appreciate inclusion of a brief cover letter with, at minimum, the author's name and address clearly printed. Mention of other publications and special biographical notes are always of interest." Accepts fax submissions (include in body of message with postal address). "Poems sent via fax will be responded to by postal service." Accepts e-mail submissions; include in body of message. Publishes theme issues. Theme issues include AIDS, violence/human rights, tobacco, medical education, access to care, and end-of-life care. "However, we would rather that poems relate obliquely to the theme." A list of upcoming themes is available on website. Pays 1 contributor's copy, more by request. "We ask for a signed copyright release, but publication elsewhere is always granted free of charge."

◉ JUBILAT, Dept. of English, Bartlett Hall, University of Massachusetts, Amherst MA 01003-0515. (413)577-1064. E-mail: jubilat@english.umass.edu. Website: www. jubilat.org. Established 2000. **Editors:** Robert Casper, Christian Hawkey, Kelly LeFave, Michael Teig. **Managing Editor:** Lisa Olstein.

● Poetry published in *Jubilat* has been included in the 2001 *Best American Poetry* and the 2003 Pushcart Prize Anthology.

Magazine Needs: *Jubilat* appears biannually as an "international poetry journal that bases itself on the notion that, to poetry, everything is relevant. To this end we publish an arresting mix of poetry, prose, art, and interviews." Wants "high quality submissions of poetry, as well as poetic prose that may or may not have anything to do with poetry per se but captures a quality of poetic thought. We publish quality work by established and emerging writers regardless of school, region, or reputation." Recently published poetry by John Ashbery, Jane Miller, Vasko Popa, Anne Carson, Reginald Shepard, and Dean Young. *Jubilat* is 150 pages, digest-sized, offset-printed, perfect-bound, 4-color glossy cover, with fine art features. Receives about 3,000 submissions/year, accepts about 2%. Publishes about 20-30 poems/issue. Press run is 2,000 for 1,000 subscribers of which 100 are libraries, 1,000 shelf sales. Single copy: $8; subscription: $14/1 year, $26/2 years, $38/3 years. Sample: $8. Make checks payable to University of Massachusetts/*Jubilat*.

How to Submit: Submit 3-5 poems at a time. Accepts simultaneous submissions if noted in cover letter and informed of acceptance elsewhere; no previously published poems. No fax, e-mail, or disk submissions. Brief cover letter preferred. "We strongly encourage poets to read an issue and look at our website before submitting." Reads submissions year round. Time between acceptance and publication varies. Poems are circulated to an editorial board. "*Jubilat* is collectively edited. All submissions are reviewed by at least one, often four editors." Seldom comments on rejected poems. Guidelines available for SASE and on website. Responds in up to 6 months. Always sends prepublication galleys. Acquires first North American serial rights; rights revert to author.

✦ ◉ ◎ KAIMANA: LITERARY ARTS HAWAII; HAWAII LITERARY ARTS COUNCIL (Specialized: regional), P.O. Box 11213, Honolulu HI 96828. Established 1974. **Editor:** Tony Quagliano.

● Poets in *Kaimana* have received the Pushcart Prize, the Hawaii Award for Literature, the Stefan Baciu Award, Cades Award, and the John Unterecker Award.

Magazine Needs: *Kaimana*, an annual, is the magazine of the Hawaii Literary Arts Council. Poems with "some Pacific reference are preferred—Asia, Polynesia, Hawaii—but not exclusively." Has published poetry by Howard Nemerov, John Yau, Reuel Denney, Haunani-Kay Trask, Anne Waldman, Joe Balaz, Susan Schultz, and Joseph Stanton. *Kaimana* is 64-76 pages, 7½×10, saddle-stapled, with high-quality printing. Press run is 1,000 for 600 subscribers of which 200 are libraries. Subscription: $15, includes membership in HLAC. Sample: $10.

How to Submit: Cover letter with submissions preferred. Sometimes comments on rejected poems. Responds with "reasonable dispatch." Guidelines available in the publication. Pays 2 contributor's copies.

Advice: "Hawaii gets a lot of 'travelling regionalists,' visiting writers with inevitably superficial observations. We also get superb visiting observers who are careful craftsmen anywhere. *Kaimana* is interested in the latter, to complement our own best Hawaii writers."

$ ⊚ KALEIDOSCOPE: EXPLORING THE EXPERIENCE OF DISABILITY THROUGH LITERATURE AND FINE ARTS (Specialized: disability themes), 701 S. Main St., Akron OH 44311-1019. (330)762-9755. Fax: (330)762-0912. E-mail: mshiplett@udsakron.org. Website: www.udsak ron.org. Established 1979. **Senior Editor:** Gail Willmott.

Magazine Needs: Published in January and July, *Kaleidoscope* is based at United Disability Services, a nonprofit agency. Poetry should deal with the experience of disability but not limited to that when the writer has a disability. "*Kaleidoscope* is interested in high-quality poetry with vivid, believable images, and evocative language. Works should not use stereotyping, patronizing, or offending language about disability." Has published poetry by Sandra J. Lindow, Gerald R. Wheeler, Desire Vail, and Sheryl L. Nelms. *Kaleidoscope* is 64 pages, magazine-sized, professionally printed and saddle-stapled with 4-color semigloss card cover, b&w art inside. Press run is 1,500, including libraries, social service agencies, health-care professionals, universities, and individual subscribers. Single copy: $6; subscription: $10 individual, $15 agency. Sample: $5.

How to Submit: Submit up to 6 poems at a time. Send photocopies with SASE for return of work. Accepts previously published poems and simultaneous submissions, "as long as we are notified in both instances." Accepts fax and e-mail submissions. Cover letter required. All submissions must be accompanied by an autobiographical sketch and "should be double-spaced, pages numbered, and with author's name on each page." Deadlines: March 1 and August 1. Publishes theme issues. Themes for 2004 include "Perspectives on Aging: I am Still Learning" in January and "Mental Illness" in July. Upcoming themes and guidelines available for SASE, by fax, by e-mail, and on website. Upcoming themes also announced in publication. Responds in 3 weeks; acceptance or rejection may take 6 months. Pays $10-25 plus 2 copies. Rights return to author upon publication. Staff reviews books of poetry. Send materials for review consideration to Gail Willmott, senior editor.

⊘ THE KALEIDOSCOPE REVIEW, P. O. Box 16242, Pittsburgh PA 15242-0242. Established 2000. **Editor:** Rebecca Chembars.

Magazine Needs: *The Kaleidoscope Review* appears bimonthly as a forum for fresh, creative poetry. "We tend to prefer shorter poetry. Two pages are dedicated to haiku. One (the last) page is dedicated to witty and/or humorous submissions. Writing must be effective and interesting. No preferred style, form, or school." Does not want graphic violence or pornography. *The Kaleidoscope Review* is 16 pages, digest-sized, laser-printed, saddle-stapled, card stock cover. Receives about 900 poems/year, accepts about 20%. Publishes about 30 poems/issue. Press run is 100 for 20 subscribers; 70 are distributed free to "friends and local business for distribution to the public." Single copy: $2; subscription: $12. Sample: $2 plus SASE. Make checks payable to *The Kaleidoscope Review*.

How To Submit: Submit 3 poems at a time, 5 if all haiku or very short poems. Line length is 35 maximum. Accepts previously published poems and simultaneous submissions. No fax, e-mail, or disk submissions. "Name and address on each sheet. Include SASE. Short cover letter highly preferred." Submit seasonal poems 3 months in advance. Time between acceptance and publication is 2-4 months. Often comments on rejected poems. "Submissions not returned to author unless SASE included." Occasionally publishes theme issues. Upcoming themes and guidelines available for SASE and in publication. Responds in up to 8 weeks. Pays 1 contributor's copy; 2 subscriber/contributor's copies. Acquires one-time rights.

Advice: "Life *is* poetry in motion. Refocus!"

$ ⊘ ⊚ KALLIOPE, A JOURNAL OF WOMEN'S LITERATURE & ART (Specialized: women, translations, themes); SUE SANIEL ELKIND POETRY CONTEST, South Campus, 11901 Beach Blvd., Jacksonville FL 32246. (904)646-2081. Website: www.fccj.org/kalliope. Established 1978. **Editor:** Mary Sue Koeppel.

Magazine Needs: Appearing in fall and spring, *Kalliope* is a literary/visual arts journal published by Florida Community College at Jacksonville; the emphasis is on women writers and artists. "We like the idea of poetry as a sort of artesian well—there's one meaning that's clear on the surface and another deeper meaning that comes welling up from underneath. We'd like to see more poetry from Black, Hispanic, and Native American women. Nothing sexist, racist, conventionally sentimental.

Write for specific guidelines." Poets published include Denise Levertov, Marge Piercy, Martha M. Vertreace, Karen Subach, Maxine Kumin, and Tess Gallagher. *Kalliope* calls itself "a journal of women's literature and art" and publishes fiction, interviews, drama, and visual art in addition to poetry. Appearing 2 times/year, *Kalliope* is 7¼ × 8¼, flat-spined, handsomely printed on white stock, glossy card cover and b&w photographs of works of art. Average number of pages is 120. Press run is 1,600 for 400-500 subscribers of which 100 are libraries, 800 shelf sales. Subscription: $16/year or $27/2 years. Sample: $9.

How to Submit: Submit poems in batches of 3-5 with brief bio note, phone number, and address. No previously published poems. Accepts submissions by postal mail only. Reads submissions September through April only. SASE required. Because all submissions are read by several members of the editing staff, response time is usually up to 4 months. Publication will be within 6 months after acceptance. Criticism is provided "when time permits and the author has requested it." Guidelines and upcoming themes available on website or for SASE. Guidelines also published in journal. Pays $10 if grant money available, subscription if not. Acquires first publication rights. Reviews books of poetry, "but we prefer groups of books in one review." Send materials for review consideration.

Also Offers: Sponsors the Sue Saniel Elkind Poetry Contest. 1st Prize: $1,000; runners up published in *Kalliope*. Deadline: November 1. Details available for SASE or on website.

Advice: "*Kalliope* is a carefully stitched patchwork of how women feel, what they experience, and what they have come to know and understand about their lives . . . a collection of visions from or about women all over the world. Send for a sample copy, to see what appeals to us, or better yet, subscribe!"

◗ **KARAMU**, Dept. of English, Eastern Illinois University, Charleston IL 61920. Established 1966. **Editor:** Olga Abella.

• *Karamu* has received grants from the Illinois Arts Council and has won recognition and money awards in the IAC Literary Awards competition.

Magazine Needs: *Karamu* is an annual, usually published by May, whose "goal is to provide a forum for the best contemporary poetry and fiction that comes our way. We especially like to print the works of new writers. We like to see poetry that shows a good sense of what's being done with poetry currently. We like poetry that builds around real experiences, real images, and real characters and that avoids abstraction, overt philosophizing, and fuzzy pontifications. In terms of form, we prefer well-structured free verse, poetry with an inner, sub-surface structure as opposed to, let's say, the surface structure of rhymed quatrains. We have definite preferences in terms of style and form, but no such preferences in terms of length or subject matter. Purpose, however, is another thing. We don't have much interest in the openly didactic poem. We don't want poems that preach against or for some political or religious viewpoint. The poem should first be a poem." Has published poetry by Allison Joseph, Katharine Howd Machan, and Joanne Mokosh Riley. The format is 120 pages, digest-sized, matte cover, handsomely printed (narrow margins), attractive b&w art. Receives submissions from about 500 poets each year, accepts 40-50 poems. Sometimes about a year—between acceptance and publication. Press run is 350 for 300 subscribers of which 15 are libraries. Sample: $7.50.

How to Submit: Poems—in batches of no more than 5—may be submitted to Olga Abella. "We don't much like, but do accept simultaneous submissions. We read September 1 through March 1 only, for fastest decision submit January through March. Poets should not bother to query. We critique a few of the better poems. We want the poet to consider our comments and then submit new work." Publishes occasional theme issues. Upcoming themes available for SASE. Pays 1 copy. Acquires first serial rights.

**FOR EXPLANATIONS OF THESE SYMBOLS,
SEE THE INSIDE FRONT COVER OF THIS BOOK.**

Advice: "Follow the standard advice: Know your market. Read contemporary poetry and the magazines you want to be published in. Be patient."

⊘ **KATYDID BOOKS**, 1 Balsa Rd., Santa Fe NM 87505. Website: http://katydidbooks.com. Established 1973. **Editors/Publishers:** Karen Hargreaves-Fitzsimmons and Thomas Fitzsimmons.
Book/Chapbook Needs & How to Submit: Katydid Books publishes 2 paperbacks and 2 hardbacks/year. "We publish two series of poetry: Asian Poetry in Translation (distributed by University of Hawaii Press) and American Poets." Currently not accepting submissions.

⊕ ⊘ ◉ **KAVYA BHARATI; STUDY CENTRE FOR INDIAN LITERATURE IN ENGLISH AND TRANSLATION (SCILET) (Specialized: poetry from India or on Indian themes)**, SCILET, American College, Post Box 63, Madurai 625 002 India. Phone: (091)452-533609. Fax: (091)452-531056. E-mail: scilet@md2.vsnl.net.in. Website: www.scilet.org. Established 1988. **Director:** Paul L. Love. **Editor:** R.P. Nair.
Magazine Needs: *Kavya Bharati* annually publishes "Indian poetry originally written in English and English translations from regional languages of India. We want to see poetry that makes you see life with a new pair of eyes and affirms values." Has published work by Cyril Baby Deen, Kamala Suraiya, Ranjit Hoskote, Suniti Namjoshi, Hoshang Merchant, and Eunice de Souza. *Kavya Bharati* is digest-sized, photo typeset and hard-bound with cardboard cover. Receives about 90 poems/year, accepts approximately 20%. Publish 30 poems/issue. Press run is 1,000 for 200 subscribers of which 60 are libraries. Sample (including guidelines): $15. Make checks payable to Study Centre, *Kavya Bharati*.
How to Submit: Submit 6 poems at a time. No previously published poems or simultaneous submissions. Accepts e-mail submissions (as attachment). Cover letter with bio required. Reads submissions January through June only. Submit seasonal poems 6 months in advance. Time between acceptance and publication is 6 months. Poems are circulated to an editorial board. "A three member advisory board selects all poems." Often comments on rejected poems. Publishes theme issues occasionally. Guidelines available in publication. Responds in 6 months. Pays 2 copies. Acquires first rights. Reviews books of poetry. Send materials for review consideration.
Also Offers: Conducts an annual creative writing workshop. Write for details.
Advice: "Be original and affirm values."

◐ ◉ **KELSEY REVIEW (Specialized: regional, Mercer County)**, Mercer County Community College, P.O. Box B, Trenton NJ 08690. (609)586-4800, ext. 3326. Fax: (609)586-2318. E-mail: kelsey.review@mccc.edu. Website: www.mccc.edu. Established 1988. **Editor-in-Chief:** Robin Schore.
Magazine Needs: *Kelsey Review* is an annual published in September by Mercer County Community College. It serves as "an outlet for literary talent of people living and working in Mercer County, New Jersey only." Has no specifications as to form, length, subject matter or style, but does not want to see poetry about "kittens and puppies." Accepts poetry written by children. Has published poetry by Pat Hardigree, Bill Waters, Betty Lies, Helen Gorenstein, Ron McCall, and Shirley Wright. *Kelsey Review* is about 80 glossy pages, 7×11, with paper cover and line drawings; no ads. Receives about 60 submissions/year, accepts 6-10. Press run is 2,000. All distributed free to contributors, area libraries, bookstores, and schools.
How to Submit: Submit up to 6 poems at a time, typed. No previously published poems or simultaneous submissions. No fax or e-mail submissions. Deadline: May 1. Always comments on rejected poems. Information available for e-mail. Responds in June of each year. Pays 5 copies. All rights revert to authors.

★ ⊘ **KENNESAW REVIEW**, Dept. of English, Building 27, Kennesaw State University, 1000 Chastain Rd., Kennesaw GA 30144-5591. E-mail: kr@kennesaw.edu. Website: www.kennesaw.edu/kr. Established 1987 as print journal; 2002 online. **Managing Editors:** Amy Whitney and Maren Blake.
Magazine Needs: *Kennesaw Review* is an online literary journal appearing 3 times/year and publishing poetry, short fiction, essays, and reviews. Wants exceptional poetry, short fiction, and essays. "Our goal is to publish the best we can find, whether by experienced or emerging writers. We are

open to both formal poems and free verse." Recently published poetry by Kathryn Kirkpatrick, Luivette Resto, and Matthew W. Schmeer. *Kennesaw Review* is published online only. Publishes about 15 poems/issue.

How to Submit: Submit up to 5 poems at a time. Accepts simultaneous submissions if noted in cover letter; no previously published poems. No fax, e-mail, or disk submissions. Cover letter is preferred. "Submissions are by hard copy. Include your name, address, telephone number, e-mail address, and SASE for our response. Manuscripts must be typed, no smaller than 12 point. Do not send disks or e-mail attachments. Submissions will not be returned and will be recycled; therefore, do not send us your only copy." Reads submissions year round. Time between acceptance and publication is 3-6 months. Poems are circulated to an editorial board. "Poems are read and discussed in weekly editorial meetings." Seldom comments on rejected poems. Occasionally publishes theme issues. List of upcoming themes and guidelines available on website. Responds in 2 months. "The *Kennesaw Review* reserves rights for first online publication and for possible publication as a compiled annual edition in CD or print format, or both. Copyright remains with author." Reviews books and chapbooks of poetry and other magazines/journals in 500 words, single book format. Poets may send materials for review consideration to Jeff Cebulski, Review Editor.

Also Offers: Possible print or CD annual.

Advice: "Review the poetry on our site before submitting your work for our consideration."

$ ⊘ THE KENYON REVIEW; THE WRITERS WORKSHOP, Kenyon College, Gambier OH 43022. (740)427-5208. Fax: (740)427-5417. E-mail: kenyonreview@kenyon.edu. Website: www. KenyonReview.org. Established 1939. **Editor:** David Lynn.

- ● "Because of editorial sabbatical, unsolicited manuscripts will *not* be read until September 2004."

Magazine Needs: *Kenyon Review* is a triquarterly review containing poetry, fiction, essays, criticism, reviews, and memoirs. It features all styles and forms, lengths and subject matters, but this market is more closed than others because of the volume of submissions typically received during each reading cycle. Issues contain work by such poets as Billy Collins, Diane Ackerman, John Kinsella, Carol Muske-Dukes, Diane di Prima, and Seamus Heaney. *Kenyon Review* is 180 pages, digest-sized, flat-spined. Press run is 5,000 for both subscribers and newsstand sales. Receives about 4,000 submissions/year, accepts 50 pages of poetry in each issue, has a 1-year backlog. The editor urges poets to read a few copies before submitting to find out what they are publishing. Sample: $10 includes postage.

How to Submit: Unsolicited mss will not be read until September 2004. Typical reading period September 1 through March 31. Writers may contact by phone, fax, or e-mail, but may submit mss by mail only. Responds in 3 months. Pays $15/page for poetry, $10/page for prose and 2 copies. Acquires first North American serial rights. Reviews books of poetry in 2,500-7,000 words, single or multi-book format. "Reviews are primarily solicited—potential reviewers should inquire first."

Also Offers: Also sponsors The Writers Workshop, an annual 8-day event in June. Location: the campus of Kenyon College. Average attendance is 12 per class. Open to writers of fiction, nonfiction and poetry. Conference is designed to provide intensive conversation, exercises and detailed readings of participants' work. Past speakers have included Erin Belieu, Allison Joseph, P.F. Kluge, Wendy MacLeod, Pamela Painter, Nancy Zafris, David Baker, and Reginald McKnight. Other special features include a limited-edition anthology produced by workshop writers and *The Kenyon Review* that includes the best writing of the session. College and non-degree graduate credit is offered. Application available for SASE and on website. Early application is encouraged as the workshops are limited.

Advice: "Editor recommends reading recent issues to get familiar with the type and quality of writing being published before submitting your work."

▢ ⊘ ◎ THE KERF (Specialized: animals, nature/ecology), College of the Redwoods, 883 W. Washington Blvd., Crescent City CA 95531. Established 1995. **Editor:** Ken Letko.

Magazine Needs: *The Kerf*, annually published in May, features "poetry that speaks to the environment and humanity." Wants "poetry that exhibits an environmental consciousness." Accepts poetry written by children. Has published poetry by Ruth Daigon, Meg Files, James Grabill, and George Keithley. *The Kerf* is 40 pages, digest-sized, printed via Docutech, saddle-stapled with CS2 coverstock. Receives about 2,000 poems/year, accepts up to 3%. Press run is 400, 150 shelf sales; 100 distributed free to contributors and writing centers. Sample: $5. Make checks payable to College of the Redwoods.

How to Submit: Submit up to 5 poems (up to 7 pages) at a time. No previously published poems or simultaneous submissions. Reads submissions January 15 through March 31 only. Time between acceptance and publication is 3 months. Poems are circulated to an editorial board. "Our editors debate (argue for or against) the inclusion of each manuscript." Seldom comments on rejected poems. Guidelines available for SASE. Responds in 2 months. Sometimes sends prepublication galleys. Pays 1 copy. Acquires first North American serial rights.

KIMERA: A JOURNAL OF FINE WRITING, 1316 Hollis, Spokane WA 99201. E-mail: kimera@js.spokane.wa.us. Website: www.js.spokane.wa.us/kimera/. Established 1996. **Publisher:** Jan Strever. **Contact:** Derek Moss.

Magazine Needs: *Kimera* is a biannual online journal (appears yearly in hard copy) and "attempts to address John Locke's challenge—'where is the head with no chimeras.' " Wants poetry that "attempts to 'capture the soul in motion.' No flabby poems." Has published poetry by Gail Zwirn, Tom Gribble, Iris Gribble-Neal, John Gilgun, Heather MacLeod, and Robert Cooperman. Accepts about 10% of poems/year. Press run is 300 for 200 subscribers. Single copy: $7; subscription: $14. Sample: $7.

How to Submit: Submit 3-6 poems at a time. Accepts simultaneous submissions; no previously published poems. Accepts submissions on disk, as e-mail attachment, in e-mail text box, via online submission form, and by postal mail. Cover letter required. Poems are circulated to an editorial board. Seldom comments on rejected poems. Guidelines available on website. Responds in 3 months. Pays 1 copy. Acquires first rights.

Also Offers: Hosts an annual contest, alternating years between poetry and fiction (2004, fiction; 2005, poetry; 2006, fiction etc.). Contact for more information.

Advice: "Attune yourself to the now. Think of the poem as a distillation of the moment. Everything of importance is here right now in this breath we take, the sound we here. Listen . . ."

N KING LOG. E-mail: davidcase@earthlink.net. Website: www.angelfire.com/il/kinglog. Established 1997. **Editors:** David Starkey, Carolie Parker-Lopez, David Case.

Magazine Needs: *King Log* appears quarterly. Wants "accomplished poetry by American and Anglophone writers, whether experimental, confessional, or formalist. We are especially interested in poetry that captures the confusion of work/writing, romantic attachments, popular and high culture, history, and political and philosophical idealism and disillusion—comedy, irony, and passion." Does not want gushy, sentimental, macho, or precious work. Recently published poetry by Jim Daniels, Barry Spacks, Katherine Swiggart, Walt McDonald, Evelyn Perry, and Paul Willis. *King Log* is 30 pages, published online with illustrations from *Aesop's Fables*. Receives about 400 poems/year, accepts about 60. Publishes about 20 poems/issue.

How to Submit: Submit 3-5 poems at a time. No previously published poems or simultaneous submissions. Accepts e-mail submissions; no disk submissions. Cover letter is required. Reads submissions all year. Time between acceptance and publication is 3 months. Poems are circulated to an editorial board. "Development of consensus among three editors who, broadly, share a sensibility and do not often disagree." Seldom comments on rejected poems. Guidelines available on website. Responds in 3 weeks. No payment. Acquires one-time rights.

$ THE KIT-CAT REVIEW; GAVIN FLETCHER MEMORIAL PRIZE FOR POETRY, 244 Halstead Ave., Harrison NY 10528-3611. (914)835-4833. Established 1998. **Editor:** Claudia Fletcher.

Magazine Needs: *The Kit-Cat Review* appears quarterly and is "named after the 18th century Kit-Cat Club whose members included Addison, Steele, Congreve, Vanbrugh, Garth, etc. Purpose: to promote/discover excellence and originality." Wants quality work—traditional, modern, experimental. Has published poetry by Coral Hull, Virgil Suárez, Margret J. Hoehn, Louis Phillips, Chayym Zeldis, and Romania's Nobel Prize nominee Marin Sorescu. *The Kit-Cat Review* is 75 pages, digest-sized, laser printed/photocopied, saddle-stapled with colored card cover, includes b&w illustrations.

Receives about 1,000 poems/year. Press run is 500 for 200 subscribers. Subscription: $25. Sample: $7. Make checks payable to Claudia Fletcher.

How to Submit: Submit any number of poems at a time. Accepts previously published poems and simultaneous submissions. "Cover letter should contain relevant bio." Time between acceptance and publication is 2 months. Responds within 2 months. Pays up to $100 a poem and 2 copies. Acquires first or one-time rights.

Also Offers: Sponsors the annual Gavin Fletcher Memorial Prize for Poetry of $1,000. "Deadline June 31 for publication in autumn issue."

★ ◑ KNUCKLE MERCHANT: THE JOURNAL OF NAKED LITERARY AGGRESSION, 116 Oak Grove #205, Minneapolis MN 55403. E-mail: knucklemerchant@hotmail.com. Website: www.lostprophetpress.com. Established 2000. **Editor:** Christopher Jones.

Magazine Needs: *Knuckle Merchant: The Journal of Naked Literary Aggression* "is a bimonthly knife in the ribs of the Man." Published by Lost Prophet Press (see separate listing in this section). "We want the voice of this country (and this world) the way it should be: awake, rebellious, and vibrant. Tell us what makes you angry, joyous, frenzied, and alive; we'll put it all together and Reauchambeau Big Brother on your behalf 'cause, damn, we just don't like that guy.' " Send work "liberally seasoned with political/justice/labor flavors—particularly tasty to the merchant in these dark days." *Knuckle Merchant* is 28-32 pages, digest-sized, docutech-printed, type of binding: stapled, b&w cardstock cover, with b&w photos and art, and ads. Accepts about 5% of submissions. Press run is 200. Single copy: $5; subscription: $15. Make checks payable to *Knuckle Merchant*.

How to Submit: Submit 5 poems at a time. Accepts previously published poems and simultaneous submissions. Accepts fax and e-mail submissions. "Have some manners, send a cover letter." Time between acceptance and publication is 2 months. Often comments on rejected poems. Guidelines are available for SASE. Pays 1-2 copies. Acquires first rights or one-time rights. Send materials for review consideration to Christopher Jones.

Also Offers: See also Lost Prophet Press in this section.

★ ◑ KOTAPRESS; KOTAPRESS POETRY JOURNAL. (206)251-6706. E-mail: editor@kota press.com. Website: www.kotapress.com. Established 1999. **Editor:** Kara L.C. Jones.

Magazine Needs: *KotaPress Poetry Journal* is a monthly online e-zine "seeking to publish new as well as seasoned poets. We seek to publish the best poetry that comes to us and then to support the poet in whatever ways he or she may need. While form is sometimes important, we are more interested in content. We want to know what you have to say. We are interested in the honesty and conviction of your poems. Give us accessibility over form any day. Seeing tankas, for instance, in 5-7-5-7-7 form can be interesting and accessible, but do not send us words that you have stuffed into a form just to say you could write in form." Has published poetry by Charles Fishman, Ruth Daigon, Claudia Mauro, Patricia Wellingham-Jones, and John Fox.

How to Submit: Submit 4 poems at a time. Accepts previously published poems; no simultaneous submissions. Accepts e-mail submissions *only*, but no attachments. Cover letter required. "Previously-published poems must include credit to prior publication. We accept e-mail submissions only; include text in body of message. Please include bio info in e-mail message. Be sure to give us contact info so we can get back to you." Accepts submissions year-round on a rolling basis. Time between acceptance and publication is 1-2 months. Guidelines available on website. Responds in 2 months. Acquires one-time electronic rights and archive rights. "We do not remove works from our archives."

Also Offers: "We offer an annual contest that result in print books, so please see Poetry section of site for guidelines. Because we are an Internet magazine, we are able to provide writers with resources and support through links, articles and services—as well as producing a high-quality poetry journal. Please see our website at www.kotapress.com to find out more about us and about what we offer. We look forward to hearing from you and reading your poetry."

Advice: "If you want to be a published writer you must submit your work again and again and again to anywhere and everywhere. For every 100 rejections, you will quite possibly get 1 or 2 acceptances, but you won't get rejected or accepted if you don't submit in the first place!"

⊕ ◑ ◎ KRAX (Specialized: humor), 63 Dixon Lane, Leeds, Yorkshire LS12 4RR England. Established 1971. **Editor:** Andy Robson.

Editor Andy Robson says the main concern for choosing *Krax*'s cover image was its striking appearance. Of artist Gail Schilke's artwork, Robson says, "The implication is that it is seeking to find and also striving to contain the urban heart, which seems relevant to the time." Layout for Issue No. 39 was by *Krax* Editorial.

Magazine Needs: *Krax* appears twice yearly, and publishes contemporary poetry from Britain and America. Wants poetry which is "light-hearted and witty; original ideas. Undesired: haiku, religious, or topical politics." 2,000 words maximum. All forms and styles considered. Has published poetry by Mandy Precious, Toby Litt, Patricia Prime, and Bob Eccleston. *Krax* is digest-sized, 64 pages of which 30 are poetry, saddle-stapled, offset-printed with b&w cartoons and graphics. Receives up to 1,000 submissions/year, accepts about 6%, has a 2- to 3-year backlog. Single copy: £3.50 ($7); subscription: £10 ($20). Sample: $1 (75p).

How to Submit: "Submit maximum of six pieces. Writer's name on same sheet as poem. Sorry, we cannot accept material on disk. SASE or SAE with IRC encouraged but not vital." No previously published poems or simultaneous submissions. Brief cover letter preferred. Responds in 2 months. Pays 1 copy. Reviews books of poetry (brief, individual comments; no outside reviews). Send materials for review consideration.

Advice: "Write pieces that you would want to read for yourself and not ones which you think will please your English teacher or that are parodies of classic works."

⊘ KUMQUAT MERINGUE; PENUMBRA PRESS, P.O. Box 736, Pine Island MN 55963. (507)367-4430. E-mail: moodyriver@aol.com. Website: www.kumquatcastle.com. Established 1990. **Editor:** Christian Nelson.

Magazine Needs: *Kumquat Meringue* appears on an irregular basis, using "mostly shorter poetry about the small details of life, especially the quirky side of love and sex. We want those things other magazines find just too quirky. Not interested in rhyming, meaning of life or high-flown poetry." The magazine is "dedicated to the memory of Richard Brautigan." Has published works by Gina Bergamino, T. Kilgore Splake, Antler, Monica Kershner, Lynne Douglass, and Ianthe Brautigan. *Kumquat Meringue* is 40-48 pages, digest-sized, "professionally designed with professional typography and nicely printed." Press run is 600 for 250 subscribers. Subscription: $12/3 issues. Sample: $6.

How to Submit: "We like cover letters but prefer to read things about who you are, rather than your long list of publishing credits. Accepts previously published and simultaneous submissions are, but please let us know." Often comments on submissions. No fax or e-mail submissions. "Please don't forget your SASE or you'll never hear back from us. E-mail address is for 'hello, praise, complaints, threats, and questions' only." Guidelines available for SASE and on website. Usually responds in 3 months. Pays 1 copy. Acquires one-time rights.

Advice: "Read *Kumquat Meringue* and anything by Richard Brautigan to get a feel for what we want, but don't copy Richard Brautigan, and don't copy those who have copied him. We just want that same feel. We also have a definite weakness for poems written 'to' or 'for' Richard Brautigan.

Reviewers have called our publication iconoclastic, post-hip, post-beat, post-antipostmodern; and our poetry, carefully crafted imagery. When you get discouraged, write some more. Don't give up. Eventually your poems will find a home. We're very open to unpublished writers, and a high percentage of our writers had never been published anywhere before they submitted here."

KWIL KIDS PUBLISHING; KWIL KIDS QUARTERLY; LIBRARY CARD NOT INCLUDED (Specialized: children/teen/young adult), Box 29556, Maple Ridge BC V2X 2V0 Canada. E-mail: kwil@telus.net or Leef@telus.net. Established 1996. **Publisher:** Kwil.

Magazine Needs: *Kwil Kids* is a quarterly newsletter "publishing stories/poems to encourage and celebrate writers in the Kwil Club." Wants poetry that is "gentle; with compassionate truth and beauty; peace; humor; for children, by children, about children. No profane, hurtful, violent, political, or satirical work. Has published poetry by Darlene Slevin (adult), Gord Brandt (adult), Wendy Matthews (adult), Torrey Janzen (age 10), Carol McNaughton (age 6), and Ben Stoltz (age 11). *Kwil Kids* is 8 pages, includes b&w graphics. Receives about 400 poems/year, accepts about 80%. Publish 8 poems/issue. Press run is 200 for 150 subscribers. Subscription: $25 (cost includes membership to the Kwil Club). Sample: SASE (or SAE and IRC) and $2. Make checks payable to Kwil Kids Publishing.

How to Submit: Submit 5 poems at a time. Include SASE and parent's signature. Cover letter preferred. Accepts e-mail submissions; include in body of message, no attachments. Submit seasonal poems 3 months in advance. Time between acceptance and publication is up to 3 months. Always comments on rejected poems. "Kwil always provides encouragement and personalized response with SASE (or SAE and IRC)." Publishes theme issues occasionally. Guidelines available for SASE by e-mail. Responds in April, August, and December. Pays 1 copy. Acquires one-time rights.

Also Offers: Also sponsors The Kwil Club—a club for readers, writers, and artists of all ages. Membership features include newsletter, newspaper, and greeting card publishing opportunities; a free subscription to Kwil's e-mail poetry list; reading, writing, and publishing tips and encouragement galore. Membership fee: $25. Also publishes *Library Card NOT Included*, "a quarterly newsletter that celebrates the love of literature, language, lyrics, legends, and lore."

Advice: "Kwil's motto: Keep your pencil moving (and your keyboard tapping!) Just be who you are, and do what you do. Miracles happen . . . when *you* love *you*."

LA JOLLA POET'S PRESS; NATIONAL POETRY BOOK SERIES; SAN DIEGO POET'S PRESS; AMERICAN BOOK SERIES, P.O. Box 8638, La Jolla CA 92038. **Editor/Publisher:** Kathleen Iddings.

Book Needs: La Jolla Poet's Press and San Diego Poet's Press are nonprofit presses that publish only poets who "have published widely. No beginners here." Has published 36 individual poet's books including *Slow Dance on Stilts* by Marie Gordon (2002), and 5 poetry anthologies featuring poetry by Allen Ginsberg, Carolyn Kizer, Galway Kinnell, Tess Gallagher, Robert Pinsky, and Carolyn Forche. Most books are approximately 100 pages, digest-sized, perfect-bound, with laminated covers. Sample: $14.

How to Submit: Send 6 sample poems and SASE. "Please do not send entire manuscript. Editor will request manuscript if 6 poems are excellent." Accepts submissions by postal mail only. Poets receive 100 copies.

Advice: "I publish poets who have been getting a lot of individual poems published in poetry magazines and journals, not beginners."

LACTUCA, 159 Jewett Ave., Jersey City NJ 07304-2003. (201)451-5411. Fax: (201)451-1044. E-mail: lactuca@mindspring.com. Website: www.mindspring.com/~lactuca. Established 1986. **Editor/Publisher:** Mike Selender.

Magazine Needs: *Lactuca* appears up to once/year. "Our bias is toward work with a strong sense of place, a strong sense of experience, a quiet dignity, and an honest emotional depth. Dark and disturbing writings are preferred over safer material. No haiku, poems about writing poems, poems using the poem as an image, light poems, or self-indulgent poems. Readability is crucial. We publish poetry that readily transposes between the spoken word and printed page. First English language translations are welcome provided that the translator has obtained the approval of the author." Has published poetry by Sherman Alexie, Joe Cardillo, Christy Beatty, and Kathleen ten Haken. *Lactuca* will resume publication with a new format: 200 pages, perfect-bound. Sample back issues: $4. Make checks payable to Stone Buzzard Press.

How to Submit: "*Lactuca* is currently dormant. Query to find out if we're accepting new submissions. Unsolicited manuscripts will not be responded to promptly." Queries accepted via e-mail and postal mail. Submit 4-5 poems at a time. No previously published material or simultaneous submissions. "We comment on rejected poems when we can. However the volume of mail we receive limits this." Always sends prepublication galleys. Pays 1-2 copies. Acquires first rights. Reviews books of poetry. Send materials for review consideration.

Advice: "The purpose of *Lactuca* is to be a small literary magazine publishing high-quality poetry, fiction, and b&w drawings. Much of our circulation goes to contributors' copies and exchange copies with other literary magazines. *Lactuca* is not for poets expecting large circulation. Poets appearing here will find themselves in the company of other good writers."

LAKE EFFECT, School of Humanities & Social Sciences, Penn State Erie, Station Rd., Erie PA 16563-1501. (814)898-6281. Fax: (814)898-6032. E-mail: gol1@psu.edu. Established 1978 as *Tempus*; renamed *Lake Effect* in 2001. **Editor-in-Chief:** George Looney. Member: CLMP.

Magazine Needs: *Lake Effect* is published annually in March/April "to provide an aesthetic venue for writing that uses language precisely to forge a genuine and rewarding experience for our readers. *Lake Effect* wishes to publish writing that rewards more than one reading, and to present side-by-side the voices of established and emerging writers." Wants "poetry aware of, and wise about, issues of craft in forming language that is capable of generating a rich and rewarding reading experience." Does not want "sentimental verse reliant on clichés." Recently published poetry by Virgil Suarez, Allison Joseph, Liz Beasley, Ryan G. Van Cleave, David Starkey, and Al Maginnes. *Lake Effect* is 150 pages, digest-sized, offset-printed, perfect-bound, gloss by-flat film lamination cover. Receives about 300 poems/year, accepts about 10%. Publishes about 25-30 poems/issue. Press run is 800 for 300 shelf sales; 300 distributed free to contributors and writing programs. Single copy: $6; subscription: $6. Make checks payable to *Lake Effect*.

How to Submit: Submit 3-5 poems at a time. No previously published poems; accepts simultaneous submissions. No fax, e-mail, or disk submissions. Cover letter is required. Reads submissions year round. Time between acceptance and publication is up to 4 months. Poems are circulated to an editorial board. "The poetry staff reads the poems, meets and discusses them to come to a consensus. Poetry editor, along with editor-in-chief, makes final decisions." Seldom comments on rejected poems. Guidelines available in magazine. Responds in up to 4 months. Pays 2 contributor's copies. Acquires first North American serial rights.

Advice: "*Lake Effect* strives to provide an attractive venue for the good work of both established and emerging writers. We care about the integrity of poetry, and care for the poems we accept."

LAKE SHORE PUBLISHING; SOUNDINGS (Specialized: anthology), 498 Riverside Dr., Burley ID 83318-5419. (208)678-6378. Established 1983. **Poetry Editor:** Carol Spelius.

Magazine Needs: *Soundings* is an effort "to put out decent, economical volumes of poetry." **Reading fee:** $1/page. Accepts poetry in any form or length, as long as it's "understandable and moving, imaginative with a unique view, in any form. Make me laugh or cry or think. I'm not so keen on gutter language or political dogma—but I try to keep an open mind. No limitations in length." Accepts poetry written by children. Has published poetry by Constance Vogel, Ivan Podulka, Tod Palmer, Gertrude Rubin, and June Shipley. The first 253-page anthology, including over 100 poets, is a paperback, at $7.95 (add $1 p&h), which was published (in 1985) in an edition of 2,000. *Soundings* is flat-spined, photocopied from typescript, with glossy, colored card cover with art.

How to Submit: Submit 5 poems at a time, with $1/page **reading fee**, and a cover letter telling about your other publications, biographical background, personal or aesthetic philosophy, poetic goals and principles. Accepts simultaneous submissions. Accepts submissions by postal mail on disk. "Reads submissions anytime, but best in fall." Upcoming themes available for SASE. Responds in 1 year. Pays 1 copy and half-price for additional copies. "All rights return to poet after first printing."

Book/Chapbook Needs & How to Submit: The editor will read chapbooks, or full-length collections, with the possibility of sharing costs if Lake Shore Publishing likes the book (**$1/page reading fee**). "I split the cost if I like the book." Sample copy of anthology or random choice of full-length collections to interested poets: $5.

✪ ⊕ $ ◎ LANDFALL: NEW ZEALAND ARTS AND LETTERS (Specialized: regional), University of Otago Press, P.O. Box 56, Dunedin, New Zealand. Phone: 0064 3 479 8807. Fax: 0064 3 479 8385. E-mail: landfall@otago.ac.nz. Established 1947. Originally published by Caxton Press, then by Oxford University Press, now published by University of Otago Press. **Editor:** Justin Paton.

Magazine Needs: *Landfall* appears twice/year (in May and November). "Apart from occasional commissioned features on aspects of international literature, *Landfall* focuses primarily on New Zealand literature and arts. It publishes new fiction, poetry, commentary, and interviews with New Zealand artists and writers, and reviews of New Zealand books." Single issue: NZ $24.95; subscription: NZ $45 for 2 issues for New Zealand subscribers, A $30 for Australian subscribers, US $30 for other overseas subscribers.

How to Submit: Submissions must be typed and include SASE. "Once accepted, contributions should if possible also be submitted on disk." No fax or e-mail submissions. Publishes theme issues. Guidelines and upcoming themes available for SASE. New Zealand poets should write for further information.

Ⓝ ◯ ◎ LANGUAGE AND CULTURE.NET, (Specialized: translations, bilingual), 4000 Pimlico Dr., Suite 114-192, Pleasanton CA 94588. E-mail: review@languageandculture.net. Website: www.languageandculture.net. Established 2001. **Editor:** Liz Fortini.

Magazine Needs: *Language and Culture.net* is a quarterly, "exclusively online publication publishing translations of contemporary poetry with originals in Spanish, French, German, Portuguese, or Italian. Russian under review." Also accepts translations without original language versions of poems as well as original poetry in English. No restrictions on form, subject matter (except profanity), or style. Does not want profanity, greeting card verse, or predictable rhyme. Recently published poetry by Heike Gerber-Yeralan and Jeff Colvin. *Language and Culture.net* is published online only. Receives a varied number of poems/year. Publishes about 15-20 poems/issue (5% English, 40% translation).

How to Submit: Submit 3 poems at a time. Line length for poetry is 3 minimum, 50 maximum. Accepts previously published poems and simultaneous submissions. Accepts e-mail submissions; no fax or disk submissions. Cover letter is preferred. "All submissions must be in the body of the e-mail, not as an attachment." Reads submissions "yearly." Time between acceptance and publication is up to 3 months. Poems are circulated to an editorial board. "Area linguists of specified languages edit yearly." Seldom comments on rejected poems. Occasionally publishes theme issues. List of upcoming themes and guidelines available on website. No payment. Acquires one-time rights.

Also Offers: *Language and Culture* Poetry in Translation Contest. Offers annual award of 1st Prize: $25; 2nd Prize: $15; 3rd Prize: $10. Submit up to 3 poems, maximum 40 lines each. Must be dual-language; include English translation. Guidelines available on website. **Entry fee:** $5 for up to 3 poems. **Postmark deadline:** February 25, 2004. Also offers local scholarship.

Advice: "Enrich your lives with different perspectives and poetry styles."

⊕ ◗ THE LANTERN REVIEW, 17 Sea Rd., Galway, County Galway, Ireland. E-mail: patjourda n@eircom.net. Established 2002. **Editor:** Pat Jourdan.

Magazine Needs: *The Lantern Review* appears quarterly. Originally founded to promote the work of a Galway writers' group but welcomes submissions from others as well. Wants modern, unforced, "preferably honest and bright" poetry. Does not want rampant rhyme, cutesy nature clichés; no sexist or sentimental poetry. *The Lantern Review* is 40 pages, digest-sized, stapled, paper cover. Receives about 500 poems/year, accepts about 25%. Publishes about 30 poems/issue. Press run is 100. Single copy: € 3.50; subscription: € 10. Sample: € 3.50. Make checks payable to Pat Jourdan.

How to Submit: Submit 3 poems at a time. Line length for poetry is 30 maximum. No previously published poems or simultaneous submissions. No fax, e-mail, or disk submissions. Send poems "preferably by letterpost only, IRCs enclosed, SAEs also." Reads submissions all year. Submit seasonal poems 3 months in advance. Time between acceptance and publication is 3 months. In choosing poems, "members of the writing group have precedence; invited poets are given several pages; others then included." Never comments on rejected poems. Guidelines available in magazine. Responds in 2 months. Pays 1 contributor's copy. Acquires first rights. Reviews books of poetry and other magazines/journals in 100 words, single book format. Poets may send materials for review consideration to Pat Jourdan.

Advice: "Try to write on what you see around you—not from other people's poetry. Go out and walk around, read the dictionary now and again to improve your vocabulary. Enjoy your own writing and others will, too."

★ ⊕ ◑ ◎ **LAPWING PUBLICATIONS (Specialized: ethnic/nationality, Ireland)**, 1 Ballysillan Dr., Belfast BT14 8HQ United Kingdom. Phone/fax: (01232)391240. Established 1989. Director/Editor: Dennis Greig. Director/Editor: Rene Greig.
Book/Chapbook Needs: Lapwing publishes "emerging Irish poets and poets domiciled in Ireland, plus the new work of a suitable size by established Irish writers." Publishes 6-10 chapbooks/year. Wants poetry of all kinds. But, "no crass political, racist, sexist propaganda even of a positive or 'pc' tenor." Has published poetry by Robert Greacen, James Simmons, Padraig Fiacc, Jack Holland, and Desmond O'Grady. Chapbooks are usually 44-52 pages, A5, Docutech printed and saddle-stapled with colored card cover, includes occasional line art.
How to Submit: "Submit 6 poems in the first instance, depending on these, an invitation to submit more may follow." Accepts simultaneous submissions; no previously published poems. Cover letter required. Poems are circulated to an editorial board. "All submissions receive a first reading. If these poems have minor errors or faults, the writer is advised. If poor quality, the poems are returned. Those 'passing' first reading are retained and a letter of conditional offer is sent." Often comments on rejected poems. Responds to queries in 1 month; to mss in 2 months. Pays 25 author's copies (out of a press run of 250).
Also Offers: Sponsors the new imprint Ha'Penny Press and Prize. Send SASE for details.
Advice: "Due to limited resources, material will be processed well in advance of any estimated publishing date. All accepted material is strictly conditional on resources available, no favoritism. The Irish domestic market is small, the culture is hierarchical, poet/personality culture predominates, literary democracy is limited."

◐ ◎ **LAURELS; WEST VIRGINIA POETRY SOCIETY (Specialized: membership)**, Rt. 2, Box 13, Ripley WV 25271. E-mail: mbush814@aol.com. Established 1996. **Editor:** Jim Bush.
Magazine Needs: *Laurels* is the quarterly journal of the West Virginia Poetry Society containing poetry, line drawings, and a critical article on a poet or form in each issue. Only considers work from WVPS members. Wants traditional forms and good free verse. "If it's over 39 lines it must be very, very good. No porn, off-color language, shape poems, doggerel, or 'broken prose.' " Also accepts poetry written by children, if members. *Laurels* is 62 pages, saddle-stapled with paper cover. No ads. Receives about 2,000 poems/year, accepts about 80%. Press run is 275 for 210 subscribers. Membership: $15 to Carla Bumgardner, membership secretary, 524 Henderson Ave., Williamstown WV 26187 (checks payable to WVPS treasurer). Sample: $4 to Jim Bush at above address.
How to Submit: Submit 4-5 poems at a time. Accepts previously published poems. Accepts e-mail submissions. Cover letter preferred, including brief bio. Time between acceptance and publication is up to 1 year. *Replies "only if revision is needed or if poetry is not acceptable."* Issue deadlines are March 15, May 15, August 15, and November 15. Guidelines available for SASE. Sometimes sends prepublication galleys. Acquires one-time rights.
Also Offers: Sponsors a 35-category annual contest for members. Entry fee: no fee to current WVPS members or K-12 students. Guidelines available to nonmembers for SASE.
Advice: "Our purpose is to encourage and aid amateur poets who believe that words can be used to communicate meaning and to create beauty."

★ $◐ ◎ **LEADING EDGE (Specialized: science fiction/fantasy)**, 3146 JKHB, Provo UT 84602. E-mail: tle@byu.edu Website: http://tle.clubs.byu.edu. **Editor:** Kristina Kugler.
Magazine Needs: *The Leading Edge* is a magazine appearing 2 times/year. Wants "high quality poetry reflecting both literary value and popular appeal and dealing with science fiction and fantasy. We accept traditional science fiction and fantasy poetry, but we like innovative stuff. No graphic sex, violence, or profanity." Has published poetry by Michael Collings, Tracy Ray, Susan Spilecki, and Bob Cook. *Leading Edge* is 120 pages, digest-sized, using art. Accepts about 4 out of 60 poems received/year. Press run is 400, going to 100 subscribers (10 of them libraries) and 300 shelf sales. Single copy: $4.95; subscription: $12.50 (3 issues). Sample: $5.50.
How to Submit: Submit 1 or more poems with name and address at the top of each page. "Please

include SASE with every submissions." No simultaneous submissions or previously published poems. No e-mail submissions. Cover sheet with name, address, phone number, length of poem, title, and type of poem preferred. Guidelines available for SASE. Responds in 4 months. Always sends prepublication galleys. Pays $10 for the first 1-4 typeset pages, $4.50 for each additional page; plus 2 contributor's copies. Acquires first North American serial rights.

Advice: "Poetry is given equal standing with fiction and is not treated as filler, but as art."

○ **LEAPINGS LITERARY MAGAZINE; LEAPINGS PRESS**, P.O. Box 2510, Mendocino CA 95460. Fax: (707)937-3146. E-mail: 72144.3133@compuserve.com. Website: http://home.inreach. com/editserv/leapings.html. Established 1998. **Editor:** S.A. Warner.

Magazine Needs: *Leapings* is a semiannual literary magazine that publishes essays, book reviews, b&w artwork, literary and genre fiction, and poetry. "Open to any form, but prefer shorter verse. No rhymed for rhyming sake; no pornography." Accepts poetry written by children. Has published poetry by Kit Knight, Kenneth Pobo, Anselm Brocki, John Grey, Leslie Woolf Hedley, and John Taylor. *Leapings* is 35-50 pages, digest-sized, laserjet printed and saddle-stapled with cardstock cover, uses b&w graphics. Receives about 1,000 poems/year, accepts about 10%. Press run is 200 for 25 subscribers of which 5 are libraries, about 50 shelf sales. Single copy: $6; subscription: $10/year. Sample: $5. Make checks payable to S.A. Warner.

How to Submit: Submit up to 6 poems at a time. No previously published poems or simultaneous submissions. Accepts e-mail (poetry, only in body of message) and fax submissions. Cover letter preferred. "Poetry manuscripts may be submitted single-spaced and e-mailed." SASE with sufficient postage required for return of ms sent via regular mail. Time between acceptance and publication is 1 year. Often comments on rejected poems. Guidelines available for SASE, by e-mail, or on website. Responds in 3 months. Pays 2 copies. Acquires first rights. Reviews books and chapbooks of poetry and other magazines in 300 words, single book format. Send materials for review consideration.

◐ **THE LEDGE**, 78-44 80th St., Glendale NY 11385. E-mail: tkmonaghan@aol.com. Established 1988. **Editor-in-Chief/Publisher:** Timothy Monaghan. **Co-Editor:** George Held. **Associate Editor:** Laura M. Corrado. **Assistant Editor:** Kimberlee A. Rohleder.

Magazine Needs: "We publish the best poems we receive. We seek poems with purpose, poems we can empathize with, powerful poems. Excellence is the ultimate criterion." Contributors include Elton Glaser, Vivian Shipley, Tony Gloeggler, Sherry Fairchok, Neil Carpathios, Marilyn L. Taylor, and Doug Goetsch. *The Ledge* is 128 pages, digest-sized, typeset and perfect-bound with b&w glossy cover. Accepts 3% of poetry submissions. Press run is 1,200, including 750 subscribers. Single copy: $8.95; subscription: $15/2 issues, $27/4 issues or $36/6 issues.

How to Submit: Submit 3-5 poems with SASE. Accepts simultaneous submissions; no previously published work. Reads submissions September through May only. Responds in 3 months. Pays 1 copy. Acquires one-time rights.

Also Offers: *The Ledge* sponsors an annual poetry chapbook contest, as well as an annual poetry contest. Details available for SASE or e-mail.

◐ ◎ **LEFT CURVE (Specialized: political, social issues)**, P.O. Box 472, Oakland CA 94604-0472. (510)763-7193. E-mail: editor@leftcurve.com. Website: www.leftcurve.com. Established 1974. **Editor:** Csaba Polony.

Magazine Needs: *Left Curve* appears "irregularly, about every ten months." The journal "addresses the problem(s) of cultural forms, emerging from the crisis of modernity, that strives to be independent from the control of dominant institutions, and free from the shackles of instrumental rationality." Wants poetry that is "critical culture, social, political, 'post-modern,' not purely formal, too self-centered, poetry that doesn't address in sufficient depth today's problems." Has published poetry by Jon Hillson, Devorah Major, W.K. Buckley, and Jack Hirschman. *Left Curve* is about 140 pages,

---

OPENNESS TO SUBMISSIONS: ○ beginners; ◐ beginners and experienced; ◖ mostly experienced, few beginners; ◎ specialized; ◯ closed to all submissions.

magazine-sized, offset-printed, perfect-bound with Durosheen cover, photos and ads. Press run is 2,000 for 200 subscribers; 50 are libraries, 1,500 shelf sales. Subscription: $30/3 issues (individuals); $45/3 issues (institutions). Sample: $10.

How to Submit: Submit up to 5 poems at a time. "Most of our published poetry is one page in length, though we have published longer poems of up to 8 pages. We will look at any form of poetry, from experimental to traditional." Accepts submissions on disk, by e-mail (in text box and as attachment). Cover letter explaining "why you are submitting" required. Publishes theme issues. Guidelines and upcoming themes available for SASE. by e-mail, or on website. Responds in up to 6 months. Pays 3 copies. Send materials for review consideration.

⭐ ⊘ **LIFTOUTS MAGAZINE; PRELUDIUM PUBLISHERS**, 520 SE Fifth St., Suite 4, Minneapolis MN 55414-1628. Fax: (612)305-0655. E-mail: barcass@mr.net. Established 1971. **Poetry Editor:** Barry Casselman. *Liftouts* appears irregularly as a "publisher of experimental literary work and work of new writers in translation from other languages." Currently not accepting unsolicited material.

⊘ **LIGHT**, Box 7500, Chicago IL 60680. Website: www.lightquarterly.com. Established 1992. **Editor:** John Mella.

Magazine Needs: *Light* is a quarterly of "light and occasional verse, satire, wordplay, puzzles, cartoons, and line art." Does not want "greeting card verse, cloying or sentimental verse." *Light* is 64 pages, perfect-bound, including art and graphics. Single copy: $6; subscription: $20. Sample: $5 (back issues) with an additional $2 for first-class postage.

How to Submit: Submit 1 poem on a page with name, address, poem title and page number on each page. No previously published poems or simultaneous submissions. Seldom comments on rejected poems. Guidelines available for #10 SASE. Responds in 3 months or less. Always sends prepublication galleys. Pays 2 copies to domestic contributors, 1 copy to foreign contributors. Send materials for review consideration.

⊘ **THE LIGHTNING BELL**, 3300 Dawn Ridge Court, Greensboro NC 27403. E-mail: rfoley@lightningbell.org or gcupper3@lightningbell.org. Website: www.lightningbell.org/. Established 2001. **Co-Editors:** Ruth Foley and George Upper.

Magazine Needs: *The Lightning Bell* appears 3-4 times/year. "We aim to publish the best poetry we can find and especially like to see well-written formal poetry, but publish free verse poems as well. Extremely long poems and concrete poetry have very little chance with us, but we will read everything with an open mind." *The Lightning Bell* is published online. Receives about 1,250 poems/ year, accepts about 5%. Publishes about 20 poems/issue. Sample free to anyone with an Internet connection.

How to Submit: Submit 2-4 poems at a time. Accepts simultaneous submissions "if notified and kept informed"; no previously published poems. Accepts e-mail submissions; no fax or disk submissions. Cover letter is preferred. "No snail mail submissions—online submissions only. See website for details." Reads submissions year round. Submit seasonal poems 5 months in advance. Time between acceptance and publication is up to 4 months. "The co-editors read every poem and only accept those that appeal to both of them." Seldom comments on rejected poems. Guidelines available on website. Responds in up to 1 month. Acquires first rights.

Advice: "Please read the poems on the website to see if *The Lightning Bell* is an appropriate place for your work. Poetry takes work—if your poems did not take work, please send them elsewhere."

⭐ ◎ **LILITH MAGAZINE (Specialized: women, ethnic)**, 250 W. 57th St., Suite 2432, New York NY 10107. (212)757-0818. Fax: (212)757-5705. E-mail: lilithmag@aol.com. Website: www.lilithmag.com. Established in 1976. **Editor-in-Chief:** Susan Weidman Schneider. **Poetry Editor:** Marge Piercy.

Magazine Needs: *Lilith* "is an independent magazine with a Jewish feminist perspective" which uses poetry by Jewish women "about the Jewish woman's experience. Generally we use short rather than long poems. Run four poems/year. Do not want to see poetry on other subjects." Has published poetry by Irena Klepfisz, Lyn Lifshin, Marcia Falk, and Adrienne Rich. *Lilith Magazine* is 48 pages, magazine-sized, glossy. "We use colors. Covers are very attractive and professional-looking (one has won an award). Generous amount of art. It appears 4 times/year, circulation about 10,000, about 6,000 subscriptions." Subscription: $21 for 4 issues. Sample: $6.

How to Submit: Send up to 3 poems at a time; advise if simultaneous submission. Editor "sometimes" comments on rejected poems. Guidelines available for SASE or on website.

Advice: "(1) Read a copy of the publication before you submit your work. (2) Please be patient; it takes up to 6 months for a reply. (3) Short cover letters only. Copy should be neatly typed and proofread for typos and spelling errors."

LILLIPUT REVIEW (Specialized: form, ten lines or less), 282 Main St., Pittsburgh PA 15201-2807. Website: http://donw714.tripod.com/lillieindex.html. Established 1989. **Editor:** Don Wentworth.

Magazine Needs: *Lilliput* is a tiny (4½×3.6 or 3½×4¼), 12- to 16-page magazine, appearing irregularly and using poems in any style or form no longer than 10 lines. Has published *The Future Tense of Ash* by Miriam Sagan and *No Choice* by Cid Corman and poetry by Pamela Miller Ness, Albert Huffstickler, Ed Baker, and Jen Besemer. *Lilliput Review* is laser-printed on colored paper and stapled. Press run is 250. Sample: $1 or SASE. Make checks payable to Don Wentworth.

How to Submit: Submit up to 3 poems at a time. Currently, every fourth issue is a broadside featuring the work of one particular poet. Guidelines available for SASE. Responds within 3 months. Pays 2 copies/poem. Acquires first rights. Editor comments on submissions "occasionally—always try to establish human contact."

Book/Chapbook Needs & How to Submit: Started the Modest Proposal Chapbook Series in 1994, publishing 1 chapbook/year, 18-24 pages in length. Chapbook submissions are by invitation only. Query with standard SASE. Sample chapbook: $3. Chapbook publications include *Half Emptied Out* by Lonnie Sherman.

Advice: "A note above my desk reads 'Clarity & resonance, not necessarily in that order.' The perfect poem for *Lilliput Review* is simple in style and language and elusive/allusive in meaning and philosophy. *Lilliput Review* is open to all short poems in approach and theme, including any of the short Eastern forms, traditional or otherwise."

LIMITED EDITIONS PRESS; ART: MAG, P.O. Box 70896, Las Vegas NV 89170. (702)734-8121. E-mail: magman@iopener.net. Established 1982. **Editor:** Peter Magliocco.

Magazine Needs: *ART:MAG* has "become, due to economic and other factors, more limited to a select audience of poets as well as readers. We seek to expel the superficiality of our factitious culture, in all its drive-thru, junk-food-brain, commercial-ridden extravagance—and stylize a magazine of hard-line aesthetics, where truth and beauty meet on a vector not shallowly drawn. Conforming to this outlook is an operational policy of seeking poetry from solicited poets primarily, though unsolicited submissions will be read, considered and perhaps used infrequently. Sought from the chosen is a creative use of poetic styles, systems and emotional morphologies other than banally constricting." Has published poetry by Lucinda Mason, Tricia Yost, Barry Ballard, T.J. O'Donnell, Pearl Mary Wilshaw, and J. Lyndon Smith. *ART: MAG*, appearing in 1-2 large issues of 100 copies/year, is limited to a few poets. Subscription: $8 (2 issues). Sample: $3 or more. Make checks payable to Peter Magliocco.

How to Submit: Submit 5 poems at a time with SASE. "Submissions should be neat and use consistent style format (except experimental work). Cover letters are optional." Accepts simultaneous submissions; sometimes previously published poems. No fax or e-mail submissions. Sometimes comments on rejected poems. Publishes theme issues. Guidelines and upcoming themes available for SASE. Responds within 3 months. Pays 1 copy. Acquires first rights. Staff occasionally reviews books of poetry. Send materials for review consideration.

Book/Chapbook Needs & How to Submit: "Recently published (in cooperation with Trafford Publishing) the novel *Nu-Evermore* by Peter Magliocco. For any other press chapbook possibilities, query the editor before submitting any manuscript."

Advice: "The mag is seeking a futuristic aestheticism where the barriers of fact and fiction meet, where inner- and outer-space converge in the realm of poetic consciousness in order to create a more productively viable relationship to the coming *Nu-Evermore* of the 21st century."

★ ✿ \$◑ ◎ **THE LINK & VISITOR (Specialized: nationality, religious, women)**, 30 Arlington Ave., Toronto ON M6G 3K8 Canada. (416)651-7192. Fax: (416)651-0438. E-mail: linkvis @ibaptistwomen.com. Established 1878.

Magazine Needs: *The Link & Visitor* provides bimonthly "encouragement, insight, inspiration for Canadian Christian women; Baptist, mission and egalitarian slant. Poetry must relate to reader's experience; must be grounded in a biblical Christian faith; contemporary in style and language; upbeat but not naive. We do not want to see anything that has already been better said in the Bible or traditional hymns." *The Link & Visitor* is 24 pages, magazine-sized, offset-printed with self cover. Receives about 20 poems/year, accepts about 30%. "We have a few poets we use regularly because their work fits our mix." Press run is 4,000. Subscription: \$16 (Canadian), \$25 (US and overseas airmail). Sample: \$2.75 (Canadian).

How to Submit: Submit up to 5 poems at a time. Line length for poetry is 8 minimum, 30 maximum. Accepts previously published poems and simultaneous submissions. Accepts e-mail submissions. Cover letter required. Include SASE with Canadian stamps. Time between acceptance and publication is up to 2 years. Seldom comments on rejected poems. Usually publishes theme issues. Guidelines and upcoming themes are available for SASE. Pays \$10-25 (Canadian). Acquires one-time rights.

Advice: "Canadian writers only, please."

🌐 ◑ **LINKS**, Bude Haven, 18 Frankfield Rise, Tunbridge Wells TN2 5LF United Kingdom. E-mail: linksmag@supanet.com. Established 1992. **Editor:** Bill Headdon.

Magazine Needs: *Links* is published annually in February and contains good quality poetry and reviews. Wants "contemporary, strong poetry to 80 lines." Has published poetry by Gross, Bartlett, and Shuttle. *Links* is up to 32 pages, A5, photocopied and saddle-stapled with card cover. Receives about 2,000 poems/year, accepts 7%. Press run is 200 for 150 subscribers of which 5 are libraries, 30 shelf sales. Subscription: £4/year (overseas £6), £7.50/2 years (overseas £10). Sample (with guidelines): £2 (£3 outside UK).

How to Submit: Submit 5-6 poems at a time. No previously published poems or simultaneous submissions. No fax or e-mail submissions. Cover letter preferred. "No long bios or list of previous publications." Time between acceptance and publication is up to 10 months. Sometimes comments on rejected poems. Guidelines available for SASE or by e-mail. Responds in up to 1 month. Pays 1 copy. Acquires first rights. Reviews books and chapbooks of poetry and other magazines in 200 to 400 words, single or multi-book format. Send materials for review consideration.

★ 🌐 ◯ **LINKWAY MAGAZINE**, The Shieling, The Links, Burry Port, Carms SA16 0H6 S. Wales United Kingdom. Established 1995. **Editor:** Fay C. Davies.

Magazine Needs: "*Linkway* is a quarterly general interest magazine for writers and friends. It publishes new writers alongside established ones and includes poetry, articles, stories, tips and other items." Wants all types of poetry, any topic or style. No erotica or crude language. Also accepts work by children under 16. "Please state age." Has published poetry by Ken Ross (Scotland), Andy Boteril (UK) and Justin Swanton (South Africa). *Linkway* is up to 60 pages, magazine-sized, cardboard cover, includes illustrations. Receives about 500 poems/year, accepts approximately 50%. Press run is 500. Subscription: £15 (sterling). Free sample. Make checks payable to F. C. Davies.

How to Submit: Submit 1-4 poems at a time. Line length for poetry is 42 maximum. Prefers poems "printed in single-line spacing, with double-spacing between verses." No previously published poems. Cover letter preferred. "Poem must be clearly typed or printed, can be hand printed. Writer's notes requested, name and address on each submission. Please send brief details for writers notes." Time between acceptance and publication is 3 months. Often comments on rejected poems. Publishes theme issues occasionally. Upcoming themes and guidelines available in publication, guidelines also available for SAE and IRC. Responds in 3 weeks. Reviews books and chapbooks of poetry and other magazines in 500 words. Poets may send material for review consideration.

Also Offers: "Prizes awarded for the best item in each category."

◎ **LINTEL**, 24 Blake Lane, Middletown NY 10940. (845)342-5224. Established 1977. **Poetry Editor:** Walter James Miller.

Book/Chapbook Needs: "We publish poetry and innovative fiction of types ignored by commercial presses. We consider any poetry except conventional, traditional, cliché, greeting card types, i.e., we consider any artistic poetry." Has published poetry by Sue Saniel Elkind, Samuel Exler, Adrienne Wolfert, Edmund Pennant, and Nathan Teitel. "Typical of our work" is Teitel's book, *In Time of Tide*, 64 pages, digest-sized, professionally printed in bold type, flat-spined, hard cover stamped in gold, jacket with art and author's photo on back.

How to Submit: Not currently accepting unsolicited mss.

LIPS, Box 1345, Montclair NJ 07042. (201)662-1303. Fax: (201)861-2888. E-mail: LBOSS7 9270@aol.com. Established 1981. **Poetry Editor:** Laura Boss.

Magazine Needs: *Lips* "is a quality poetry magazine that is published twice/year and takes pleasure in publishing previously unpublished poets as well as the most established voices in contemporary poetry. We look for quality work: the strongest work of a poet; work that moves the reader; poems take risks that work. We prefer clarity in the work rather than the abstract. Poems longer than six pages present a space problem." Has published poetry by Allen Ginsberg, Gregory Corso, Michael Benedikt, Maria Gillan, Stanley Barkan, Lyn Lifshin, Marge Piercy, Warren Woessner, David Ignatow, and Ishmael Reed. *Lips* is 150 pages (average), digest-sized, flat-spined. Receives about 8,000 submissions/year, accepts approximately 1%, have a 6-month backlog. Circulation is 1,000 for 200 subscriptions, approximately 100 are libraries. Sample: $10, add $2 for postage.

How to Submit: Poems should be submitted between September and March only, 6 pages, typed, no query necessary. Responds in 1 month but has gotten backlogged at times. Sometimes sends prepublication galleys. Pays 1 copy. Acquires first rights. Send SASE for guidelines.

Advice: "Remember the 2 T's: Talent *and* Tenacity."

THE LISTENING EYE, Kent State Geauga Campus, 14111 Claridon-Troy Rd., Burton OH 44021. (440)286-3840. E-mail: grace_butcher@msn.com. Website: www.geocities.com/Athens/3716. Established 1970 for student work, 1990 as national publication. **Editor:** Grace Butcher. **Assistant Editors:** Jim Wohlken and Joanne Speidel.

Magazine Needs: *The Listening Eye* is an annual publication, appearing in late summer/early fall, of poetry, short fiction, creative nonfiction, and art that welcomes both new and established poets and writers. Wants "high literary quality poetry. Prefer shorter poems (less than two pages) but will consider longer if space allows. Any subject, any style. No trite images or predictable rhyme." Accepts poetry written by children if high literary quality. Has published poetry by Alberta Turner, Virgil Suarez, Walter McDonald, and Simon Perchik. *The Listening Eye* is 52-60 pages, digest-sized, professionally printed and saddle-stapled with card stock cover with b&w art. Receives about 200 poems/year, accepts about 5%. Press run is 300. Single copy: $4. Sample: $4. Make checks payable to Kent State University.

How to Submit: Submit up to 4 poems at a time, typed, single-spaced, 1 poem/page—name, address phone, and e-mail in upper left-hand corner of each page—with SASE for return of work. Previously published poems occasionally accepted; no simultaneous submissions. Cover letter required. No e-mail submissions. Reads submissions January 1 through April 15 only. Time between acceptance and publication is up to 6 months. Poems are circulated to the editor and 2 assistant editors who read and evaluate work separately, then meet for final decisions. Occasionally comments on rejected poems. Guidelines available for SASE and in publication. Responds in 3 months. Pays 2 copies. Acquires first or one-time rights. Also awards $30 to the best sports poem in each issue.

Advice: "I look for tight lines that don't sound like prose, unexpected images or juxtapositions; the unusual use of language, noticeable relationships of sounds; a twist in viewpoint, an ordinary idea in extraordinary language, an amazing and complex idea simply stated, play on words and with words, an obvious love of language. Poets need to read the 'Big 3'—cummings, Thomas, Hopkins—to see the limits to which language can be taken. Then read the 'Big 2'—Dickinson to see how simultaneously tight, terse, and universal a poem can be, and Whitman to see how sprawling, cosmic, and personal. Then read everything you can find that's being published in literary magazines today and see how your work compares to all of the above."

THE LITERARY REVIEW: AN INTERNATIONAL JOURNAL OF CONTEMPORARY WRITING, Fairleigh Dickinson University, 285 Madison Ave., Madison NJ 07940. (973)443-8564. Fax: (973)443-8364. E-mail: tlr@fdu.edu. Website: www.theliteraryreview.org. Established 1957. **Editor-in-Chief:** René Steinke. **Contact:** William Zander.

Magazine Needs: *The Literary Review*, a quarterly, seeks "work by new and established poets which reflects a sensitivity to literary standards and the poetic form." No specifications as to form, length, style, subject matter, or purpose. Has published poetry by David Citino, Rick Mulkey, Virgil Suarez, Gary Fincke, and Dale M. Kushner. *The Literary Review* is 200 pages, digest-sized, professionally printed and flat-spined with glossy color cover, using 50-75 pages of poetry in each issue. Press run is 2,500 with 900 subscriptions of which one-third are overseas. Receives about 1,200 submissions/year, accepts 100-150, have a 12- to 16-month backlog. Sample: $5 domestic, $6 outside US, request a "general issue."

How to Submit: Submit up to 5 typed poems at a time. Accepts simultaneous submissions. No fax or e-mail submissions. Do not submit during the summer months of June, July, and August. At times the editor comments on rejected poems. Publishes theme issues. Responds in 3 months. Always sends prepublication galleys. Pays 2 copies. Acquires first rights. Reviews books of poetry in 500 words, single book format. Send materials for review consideration.

Also Offers: Website features original work. Has published poetry by Renée Ashley and Catherine Kasper. Website contact is Louise Stahl.

Advice: "Read a general issue of the magazine carefully before submitting."

◖ LITTLE BROWN POETRY, P.O. Box 4533, Portsmouth NH 03802. Fax: (240)282-6418. E-mail: editor@littlebrownpoetry.com. Website: www.littlebrownpoetry.com. Established 1998. **Editor:** Sam Siegel.

Magazine Needs: *Little Brown Poetry* is an online literary magazine with collected print anthologies. Wants "good quality emotional poetry, any style, any form." Has published poetry by Ric Masten, David Sutherland, Jarrett Keene, Janet Buck, Walt McDonald, Simon Perchik, John Sweet, and Virgil Suarez. The upcoming *Little Brown Poetry* anthology will be over 170 pages, journal-sized, perfect-bound with original cover art. Receives about 3,500 poems/year, accepts about 15%. Press run is 1,000 for 350 subscribers. Sample: $8.50. "Price varies for each anthology; check website or e-mail."

How to Submit: Submit at least 3 poems at a time. Accepts previously published poems and simultaneous submissions. "Please let us know to whom else you have submitted your work (the same piece of work you are submitting), and with whom else you have published your work." Accepts submissions by e-mail (as attachment or in text box), by fax, and through regular mail. Cover letter preferred. Publishes theme issues. Guidelines and upcoming themes available for SASE, by e-mail, or on website. Responds in up to 3 months. Pays 1 copy. Acquires one-time rights.

Advice: "Submit your best work. Spend more time on your poetry than your cover letter and read the poetry here before submitting and please read the guidelines on our website for more detailed information."

◔ LONE STARS MAGAZINE; "SONGBOOK" POETRY CONTEST, 4219 Flinthill, San Antonio TX 78230. Established 1992. **Editor/Publisher:** Milo Rosebud.

Magazine Needs: *Lone Stars*, published 3 times/year, features "contemporary poetry." Wants poetry that holds a continuous line of thought. No profanity. Has published poetry by Sheila Roark, Tom Hendrix, and Patricia Rourke. *Lone Stars* is 25 pages, magazine-sized, photocopied, with some hand-written poems, saddle-stapled, bound with tape, includes clip art. Press run is 200 for 100 subscribers of which 3 are libraries. Single copy: $5; subscription: $15. Sample: $4.50.

How to Submit: Submit 3-5 poems at a time with "the form typed the way you want it in print." **Charges reading fee of $1 per poem.** Accepts previously published poems and simultaneous submissions. Cover letter preferred. Time between acceptance and publication is 2 months. Publishes theme issues. Guidelines and upcoming themes available for SASE. Responds within 3 months. Acquires one-time rights.

Also Offers: Sponsors annual "Songbook" (song-lyric poems) Poetry Contest. Details available for SASE.

◎ LONG ISLAND QUARTERLY (Specialized: regional), P.O. Box 114, Northport NY 11768. E-mail: Liquarterly@aol.com. Website: www.poetrybay.com. Established 1990. **Editor/Publisher:** George Wallace.

Magazine Needs: *Long Island Quarterly* uses poetry (mostly lyric free verse) by people on or from Long Island. "Surprise us with fresh language. No conventional imagery, self-indulgent confessionalism, compulsive article-droppers." Has published poetry by Edmund Pennant and David Ignatow. *Long Island Quarterly* is 28 pages, digest-sized, professionally printed on quality stock and saddle-stapled with matte card cover. Press run is 250 for 150 subscribers of which 15 are libraries, 50-75 shelf sales. Subscription: $15. Sample: $4.

How to Submit: Submit 3 poems at a time. Name and address on each page. Accepts e-mail submissions in text box; no attachments. Cover letter including connection to Long Island region required. Submissions without SASE are not returned. Responds in 3 months. Sometimes sends prepublication galleys. Pays 1 copy.

Book/Chapbook Needs & How to Submit: Wants serious contemporary poetry of merit. Publishes up to 5 chapbooks per year. Chapbooks are usually 24-32 pages. Reviews books and chapbooks of poetry. Send materials for review consideration. Terms vary.

Advice: "(1) Go beyond yourself; (2) Don't be afraid to fictionalize; (3) Don't write your autobiography—if you are worth it, maybe someone else will."

⊘ LONGHOUSE; SCOUT; ORIGIN PRESS, 1604 River Rd., Guilford VT 05301. E-mail: poetry@sover.net. Website: www.longhousepoetry.com. Established 1973. **Editor:** Bob Arnold.

Magazine Needs & How to Submit: *Longhouse* is a literary annual using poems "from the serious working poet" from any region in any style. Has published poetry by Hayden Carruth, Janine Pommy Vega, Bobby Byrd, Sharon Doubiago, John Martone, and James Koller. *Longhouse* appears as a thick packet of looseleaf 8½ × 14 sheets, photocopied from typescript, in a handsomely printed matte cover. Press run is 100-300. Sample: $12. Pays 2 copies. Reviews books of poetry.

Book/Chapbook Needs & How to Submit: Publishes chapbooks and books (solicited manuscripts only) under the imprints of Longhouse and Scout. Has published *Together* by Cid Corman, *A Folder for L.N.* by Theodore Enslin, *The New Heaven Now* by Franks Samperi, *The Instant of My Death* by Maurice Blanchot, and *Path* by John Phillips, as well as booklets by Michael Casey, Joanne Kyger, and Alan Chong Lau. Pays 15% of print run.

Also Offers: "We are also a bookshop and mail-order business for modern first editions and modern poetry and small presses. We encourage poets and readers looking for collectible modern first editions and scarce—and not so scarce—books of poetry and small press magazines to locate our website."

Advice: "Origin Press is best known as Cid Corman's press. One of the quiet giants in American poetry plus the wide scope of international work. Established in the early 1950s in Boston, it has moved around as Cid went with his life: France, Italy, Boston, for many years now in Kyoto, Japan. Cid has merged with *Longhouse* in that we now edit and publish a few items together. He continues to edit, translate, and publish from Kyoto. His own books are heavily based in our bookshop and mail-order catalog."

★ ⊘ ◎ LOONFEATHER ANNUAL; LOONFEATHER PRESS (Specialized: regional), P.O. Box 1212, Bemidji MN 56619-1212. (218)444-4869. E-mail: brossi@paulbunyan.net. Established 1979. **Poetry Editors:** Betty Rossi and Gail Rixen.

Magazine Needs & How to Submit: The literary magazine *Loonfeather* appears annually, "primarily but not exclusively for Minnesota writers. Prefer short poems of not over 42 lines, accepts some traditional forms if well done, no generalizations on worn-out topics." *Loonfeather* is 98 pages, digest-sized, professionally printed in small type with matte card cover, using b&w art and ads. Subscription: $10/year. Pays 2 copies. Query with 2-3 sample poems, cover letter, and previous publications. Reads submissions accepted October, November, and December only.

Book/Chapbook Needs & How to Submit: Loonfeather Press publishes a limited number of quality poetry books. Has published *Green Journey Red Bird* by Mary Kay Rummel, *Dark Lake* by Kathryn Kysar, and *Outside After Dark: New and Selected Poems* by Susan Carol Hauser. "Currently have a backlog of accepted material for publication." Query with up to 10 sample poems, cover letter and previous publications. Responds to queries in 6 months. Time between acceptance and publication is up to 2 years. Pays 10% royalties.

◑ LOS, 150 N. Catalina St., No. 2, Los Angeles CA 90004. E-mail: lospoesy@earthlink.net. Website: http://home.earthlink.net/~lospoesy. Established 1991. **Contact:** the Editors.

Magazine Needs: *Los*, published 4 times/year, features poetry. Has published poetry by Taj Jackson, Jara Jones, Heather Lowe, Gregory Jerozal, Peter Layton, and Ed Orr. *Los* is digest-sized and saddle-stapled. Press run is 100. Sample: $2. Make checks payable to Heather J. Lowe.

How to Submit: Accepts submissions by e-mail (text box or attachment) and by postal mail. Guidelines available on website. Time between acceptance and publication is up to 6 months. Responds in 2 months. Pays 1 copy.

⊘ **LOTUS PRESS, INC.**, P.O. Box 21607, Detroit MI 48221. (313)861-1280. Fax: (313)861-4740. E-mail: lotuspress@aol.com. Established 1972. **Editor:** Naomi Long Madgett. **Contact:** Constance Withers.

- "We are presently not accepting submissions except for the Naomi Long Madgett Poetry Award." (See separate listing in Contests & Awards section.)

Advice: "Read some of the books we have published, especially award winners. Read a lot of good contemporary poetry."

⊘ ⊚ **LOUISIANA LITERATURE; LOUISIANA LITERATURE PRIZE FOR POETRY (Specialized: regional)**, SLU-792, Southeastern Louisiana University, Hammond LA 70402. (504) 549-5022. E-mail: lalit@selu.edu. Website: www.selu.edu/orgs/lalit. **Editor:** Jack Bedell.

Magazine Needs: *Louisiana Literature* appears twice/year. "Receives mss year round although we work through submissions more slowly in summer. We consider creative work from anyone though we strive to showcase our state's talent. We appreciate poetry that shows firm control and craft, is sophisticated yet accessible to a broad readership. We don't use highly experimental work." Has published poetry by Claire Bateman, Elton Glaser, Gray Jacobik, Vivian Shipley, D.C. Berry, and Judy Longley. *Louisiana Literature* is 150 pages, 6¾ × 9¾, flat-spined, handsomely printed on heavy matte stock with matte card cover. Single copies: $8 for individuals; subscription: $12 for individuals, $12.50 for institutions.

How to Submit: Submit up to 5 poems at a time. Send cover letter, including bio to use in the event of acceptance. No simultaneous submissions. Enclose SASE "and specify whether work is to be returned or discarded." No fax or e-mail submissions. Publishes theme issues. Guidelines and upcoming themes available for SASE or on website. Sometimes sends prepublication galleys. Pays 2 copies. Send materials for review consideration; include cover letter.

Also Offers: The Louisiana Literature Prize for Poetry offers a $400 award. Guidelines available for SASE. Website includes submission guidelines, special announcements, journal contents and notes from editor.

Advice: "It's important to us that the poets we publish be in control of their creations. Too much of what we see seems arbitrary."

⊛ ⊚ **THE LOUISIANA REVIEW (Specialized: regional, Louisiana)**, % Division of Liberal Arts, Louisiana State University at Eunice, P.O. Box 1129, Eunice LA 70535. (337)550-1328. E-mail: mgage@lsue.edu. Website: www.lsue.edu/LA-Review/. Established 1999. **Editor:** Dr. Maura Gage. **Associate Editor:** Dr. Susan LeJeune. **Assistant Editor:** Ms. Barbara Deger.

Magazine Needs: *The Louisiana Review* appears annually in the fall semester. "We wish to offer Louisiana poets, writers, and artists a place to showcase their most beautiful pieces. Others may submit Louisiana-related poetry, stories, interviews with Louisiana writers, and art. We want to publish the highest-quality poetry, fiction, art, and drama. For poetry we like strong imagery, metaphor, and evidence of craft, but we do not wish to have sing-song rhymes, abstract, religious or overly sentimental work." Has published poetry by Gary Snyder, Antler, David Cope, and Catfish McDaris. *The Louisiana Review* is 100-225 pages, magazine-sized, professionally printed and perfect-bound, includes photographs/artwork. Receives about up to 2,000 poems/year, accepts 40-50 poems. Press run is 300-600. Single copy: $8.

How to Submit: Submit up to 5 poems at a time. No previously published poems. No fax or e-mail submissions. Include cover letter indicating your association with Louisiana. Name and address should appear on each page. Reads submissions January 15 through March 31 only. Time between acceptance and publication is between 10 months and two years. Pays 1 copy. Poets retain the rights.

Advice: "Be true to your own voice and style."

⊘ **LOUISIANA STATE UNIVERSITY PRESS**, P.O. Box 25053, Baton Rouge LA 70894-5053. (578)388-6294. Fax: (578)388-6461. Established 1935. **Poetry Editor:** Sylvia Frank Rodriguez. A

insider report

A late, but strong start

If you're waiting until grand inspiration strikes to begin writing poetry, your approach may have merit. Lisel Mueller, who at 29 was sparked into action by the death of her mother, didn't publish her first poetry collection, *Dependencies* (Louisiana State University Press, 1965), until she was 41.

Mueller's late start, far from hindering her career, was a strong and true start. Noted as a contemporary master of free verse, she has published seven collections of poetry and won many awards, including the National Book Award in 1980 and the Pulitzer Prize in 1997. In 2002, the Modern Poetry Association bestowed upon Mueller one of the most prestigious literary honors in the English language, the Ruth Lilly Poetry Prize. The $100,000 award is one of the largest given to poets in the United States.

Lisel Mueller

Although Mueller did tinker with poetry while she was an undergraduate at the University of Evansville in Indiana, with her first attempts published in the college newspaper, Mueller says she abandoned poetry for ten years. When she decided to start writing again, she had to teach herself the craft.

"I would get books from the library about prosody and set myself exercises to do various forms and rhythms and rhyme schemes. So I was writing very formally," Mueller says. "Later on, I decided that my poetry was too imitative of poets like Keats. I couldn't hear my own voice very well in those poems. Of course, it takes time to develop your own voice. At that point, I abandoned formal verse."

Mueller's earliest influence was Carl Sandburg, whom she discovered in high school while reading on her own. She had a hard time with poets such as Keats and Shelley, especially since she was still learning English at the time, having emigrated from Germany when she was 15.

"I was emboldened by reading Sandburg," says Mueller. "His poetry was very accessible and, of course, it was free verse and ordinary language. I thought, well, I would like to try that. And I did—those were the poems printed in the college newspaper."

After graduating with a degree in sociology from Evansville in 1944, Mueller continued on to Indiana University, where she studied comparative literature, concentrating in mythology and folklore. In the mid-1950s, she began meeting with a poetry group in Evanston, Illinois, a stepping-stone that Mueller considers integral to her development as a poet.

"They were at the same stage that I was, just beginning, and we got together every few weeks, read to each other, discussed poetry, and talked about what we had read," Mueller says. "A community of writers is very important to beginning writers especially. I know my daughter, who has been in the Iowa MFA program, has a hard time writing when she's not in a program, because it spurs you on, you have to produce. So it's good to have other writers. You make friends."

Mueller, who still resides in the Chicago area and is a founding member of the city's Poetry Center, says finding a tightly knit poets' group isn't the most important thing for skill development. It's reading.

Photo by Tom Maday

"I read poetry because there were no schools for writing at the time. After college there was this hiatus where I didn't write at all, but used the library a lot," says Mueller. "I got every month's issue of the best journals—mostly it was *Poetry* magazine and *Chicago*, and they published all the new poets of the time. So I think reading is what really educates you as to what poetry is all about and what people have written."

It may have taken 41 years for her to gather the knowledge and skill for her first collection, but Mueller's second soon followed. *Life of a Queen* was published by Juniper Press in 1970. In 1977, Mueller became an instructor in the MFA program at Goddard College, and she started regularly producing collections and translations until her most recent in 1996, *Alive and Together* (Louisiana State University Press), which won the 1997 Pulitzer Prize.

Mueller says it was advantageous for her to start late. However, with age, her poetry has changed a great deal.

"My poetry has become more spare, more pared down all the time. Age has done that and I don't know why. My first book is much more baroque than subsequent books. More and more they have become very pared down. There doesn't seem to be anything that I can do about it. It just happened."

Although she hasn't done much writing to speak of in recent years, it would be wrong to conclude that Mueller is finished with poetry, perhaps because she has no writing ritual, no specific process.

"I do it when the spirit hits me, when something, when a couple of images or ideas come together in my head," says Mueller. "And I see something differently than I have before."

—*Jane Friedman*

highly respected publisher of collections by poets such as Lisel Mueller, Margaret Gibson, Fred Chappell, Marilyn Nelson, and Henry Taylor. Currently not accepting poetry submissions; "fully committed through 2005."

THE LOUISVILLE REVIEW, Spalding University, 851 S. Fourth St., Louisville KY 40203. (502)585-9911, ext. 2777. E-mail: louisvillereview@spalding.edu. Website: www.louisvillereview.org. Established 1976. **Contact:** Poetry Editor.

Magazine Needs: *The Louisville Review* appears twice/year. Uses any kind of poetry except translations; has a section devoted to children's poetry (grades K-12) called The Children's Corner. Recently published poetry by Wendy Bishop, Gary Fincke, Michael Burkard, and Sandra Kohler. *The Louisville Review* is 100 pages, digest-sized, flat-spined. Receives about 700 submissions/year, accepts about 10%. Single copy: $8; subscription: $14. Sample: $4.

How to Submit: Include SASE; no electronic submissions. Reads submissions year round. "We look for the striking metaphor, unusual imagery, and fresh language. Submissions are read by three readers; time to publication is two to three months after acceptance. Poetry by children must include permission of parent to publish if accepted." Guidelines available on website. Pays 2 contributor's copies.

LOW-TECH PRESS, 30-73 47th St., Long Island City NY 11103. Established 1981. **Editor:** Ron Kolm. Has recently published *Bad Luck* by Mike Topp and *Goodbye Beautiful Mother* Tsaurah Litzky. "We only publish solicited mss."

LSR, P.O. Box 440195, Miami FL 33144. Established 1990. **Editor/Publisher:** Nilda Cepero.

Magazine Needs: "Appearing 2 times per year, *LSR* publishes poetry, book reviews, interviews, and line artwork. Style, subject matter, and content of poetry open; we prefer contemporary with meaning and message. No surrealism, no porn, or religious poetry. Reprints are accepted." Has published poetry by Catfish McDaris, Mike Catalano, Janine Pommey-Vega, Margarita Engle, and Evangeline Blanco. *LSR* is 20 pages, magazine-sized, offset-printed and saddle-stapled with a 60 lb. cover, includes line work, with very few ads. Receives about 300 poems/year, accepts about 30%. Publish 40-50 poems/issue. Press run is 3,000 for more than 100 subscribers of which 20 are libraries; the rest distributed free to selected bookstores in the US, Europe and Latin America. Single copy: $4; subscription: $6. Sample: $5, including postage.

How to Submit: Submit 4 poems at a time. Line length for poetry is 5 minimum, 45 maximum. Accepts previously published poems; no simultaneous submissions. Accepts disk submissions. Cover letter required. "We only accept disk submissions with print-out. Include SASE and bio." Reads submissions February 1 through October 31 only. Time between acceptance and publication is 1 year. Poems are circulated to an editorial board. "Three rounds by different editors. Editor/Publisher acts on recommendations." Guidelines available for SASE. Responds in 9 months. Pays 2 contributor's copies. Acquires one-time rights. Reviews books. "We will not write reviews; however, will consider those written by others to 750 words."

Advice: "Read as many current poetry magazines as you can."

LUCID MOON, 67 Norma Rd., Hampton NJ 08827. (908)735-4447. E-mail: ralphy@lucid moonpoetry.com. Website: www.lucidmoonpoetry.com. Established 1997. **Editor:** Ralph Haselmann Jr.

Magazine Needs: An online journal updated monthly, *Lucid Moon* wants "underground Beat poetry and heartfelt, romantic love poetry, humor, moon-themed poetry and poems with references to pop culture." Does not want "indeciperable experimental poetry or annoying religious poetry." Has published poetry by Antler, Ana Christy, Kevin M. Hibshman, Herschel Silverman, Allen Ginsberg, Gerald Locklin, and Charles Plymell. *Lucid Moon* is published online though "I'm planning on resurrecting my *Lucid Moon* magazine in book format."

How to Submit: Submit up to 6 poems at a time. Accepts previously published poems and simultaneous submissions. Accepts postal mail, e-mail, and disk submissions. "Put name and address under each poem. Cover letter with 3- to 6-sentence bio required (open cover letter with date, editor's name, journal title and mailing address, e-mail, website). Handwritten cover letters, cover letters addressed to 'Whom It May Concern,' and poems with copyright symbols will be thrown out." Time between acceptance and posting on website is 3 months. Guidelines available on website. Responds same day. Rights revert to author upon posting. Poets may send poetry chapbooks, CDs, and broadsides for possible review.

Advice: "Read other poets and back issues of *Lucid Moon* to get a feel for the style wanted. Keep cursing and sexual situations to a minimum because I'd like to have grade school and high school students view this material. Check out my *Lucid Moon* website and sign my guestbook!"

$☐ LUCIDITY; BEAR HOUSE PUBLISHING, 14781 Memorial Dr., #10, Houston TX 77079-5210. (281)920-1795. E-mail: tedbadger1@yahoo.com. Established 1985. **Editor:** Ted O. Badger.

Magazine Needs: *Lucidity* is a semiannual journal of poetry. **Submission fee required**—$1/poem for "juried" selection by a panel of judges or $2/poem to compete for cash awards of $15, $10, and $5. Other winners paid in both cash and in copies. Also publishes 6 pages of Succint Verse—poems of 12 lines or less—in most issues. "We expect them to be pithy and significant and there is no reading/entry fee if sent along with Cash Award or Juried poems. Just think of all poetic forms that are 12 lines or less: the cinquain, limerick, etheree, haiku, senryu, lune, etc., not to mention quatrain, triolet and couplets." In addition, the editor invites a few guest contributors to submit to each issue. Contributors are encouraged to subscribe or buy a copy of the magazine. The magazine is called *Lucidity* because, the editor says, "I have felt that too many publications of verse lean to obscurity." "Open as to form, 36-line limit due to format. We look for poetry that is life-related and has clarity and substance." Purpose: "We dedicate our journal to publishing those poets who express their thoughts, feelings and impressions about the human scene with clarity and substance." Does not want "religious, nature or vulgar poems." Published poets include Barbara Vail, Tom Padgett, John Gorman, Penny Perry, and Katherine Zauner. The magazine is 72 pages, digest-sized, photocopied from typescript and saddle-stapled with matte card cover. Publishes about 60 poems in each issue. Press run is 350 for 220 subscribers. Subscription: $6. Sample (including guidelines): $3.

How to Submit: Submit 3-5 poems at a time. Accepts simultaneous submissions. No e-mail submissions. Time between acceptance and publication is 4 months. Guidelines available for SASE. Responds in 4 months. Pays 1 copy plus "cash." Acquires one-time rights.

Book/Chapbook Needs & How to Submit: Bear House Press is a self-publishing arrangement by which poets can pay to have booklets published in the same format as *Lucidity,* prices beginning at 100 copies of 32 pages for $336. Publishes 8 chapbooks/year.

Also Offers: Sponsors the Lucidity Poets' Ozark Retreat, a 3-day retreat held during the month of April.

Advice: "Small press journals offer the best opportunity to most poets for publication."

N $◐ LULLABY HEARSE, 26 Fifth St., Bangor ME 04401. (207)990-5839. E-mail: editor@lullabyhearse.com. Website: www.lullabyhearse.com. Established 2002. **Editor:** Sarah Ruth Jacobs.

Magazine Needs: *Lullaby Hearse* appears quarterly and publishes writing, art, poetry, and vintage movie reviews, with emphasis on work with an edge. Wants "vivid, pained poetry within the genres of horror, experimental, urban, rural, erotic, and personal verse. We read for talent, solidity of voice, and loyalty to vision over fancy." Does not want "poems about writing, bland odes to nature, clumsy/ heavy-handed rhyme, self-pitying lyrics, or far-out fantasy. Shocking poetry is fine, when it isn't created from a place of self-imposed ignorance. We prefer crudity over bombast." *Lullaby Hearse* is 20-30 pages, digest-sized, photocopied, saddle-stapled, color card cover with art. Receives about 300 poems/year, accepts about 15. Press run is 200 for 70 subscribers of which 10 are libraries, 100 shelf sales. Single copy: $5; subscription: $15. Make checks payable to Sarah Ruth Jacobs.

How to Submit: Submit 3-10 poems at a time. Accepts simultaneous submissions; no previously published poems. Accepts e-mail submissions. Cover letter is preferred. "Include a SASE with all hard copy submissions." Reads submissions year round. Time between acceptance and publication is up to 3 months. "I seldom postpone poems for the second upcoming issue. Instead I may delay in replying until all or a substantial amount of submissions have been received." Seldom comments on rejected poems. Guidelines available for SASE or on website. Responds in 6 weeks. Pays $5/poem and 1 contributor's copy. Acquires one-time rights. Reviews books and chapbooks of poetry and other magazines/journals in 1,000 words. Poets may send materials for review consideration to Sarah Ruth Jacobs.

◑ LULLWATER REVIEW; LULLWATER PRIZE FOR POETRY, Emory University, P.O. Box 22036, Atlanta GA 30322. (404)727-6184. E-mail: LullwaterReview@yahoo.com. Established 1990. **Poetry Editors:** Gwyneth Driskill and Laurel DeCou.

Magazine Needs: "Appearing in May and December, the *Lullwater Review* is Emory University's nationally distributed literary magazine publishing poetry, short fiction, and artwork." Seeks poetry of any genre with strong imagery, original voice, on any subject. No profanity or pornographic material. Has published poetry by Amy Greenfield, Peter Serchuk, Katherine McCord, Virgil Suarez, and Ha Jin. *Lullwater Review* is 104-120 pages, magazine-sized, full color cover, includes b&w pictures. Press run is 2,500. Subscription: $12. Sample: $5.

How to Submit: "Limit the number of submissions to 6 poems or fewer." Prefers poems single-spaced with name and contact info on each page. "Poems longer than 1 page should include page numbers." Accepts simultaneous submissions; no previously published poems. Accepts submissions on disk, as e-mail attachment, or by postal mail. Cover letter preferred. "We must have a SASE with which to reply. Poems may not be returned." Reads submissions September 1 through May 15 only. Time between acceptance and publication is up to 6 months. Poems are circulated to an editorial board. "A poetry editor selects approximately 16 poems per week to be reviewed by editors, who then discuss and decide on the poem's status." Seldom comments on rejected poems. Guidelines and

USE THE GENERAL INDEX in the back of this book to find the page number of a specific market. Also, markets listed in the 2003 edition but not included in this edition appear in the General Index with a code explaining their absence from the listings.

upcoming themes available for SASE. Responds in 5 months maximum. Pays 3 contributor's copies. Acquires first North American serial rights.

Also Offers: Sponsors the annual Lullwater Prize for Poetry. Award is $500 and publication. Deadline: November 1st. Guidelines available for SASE. Entry fee: $8.

Advice: "Keep writing, find your voice, don't get frustrated. Please be patient with us regarding response time. We are an academic institution."

$⬤📀◎ LUMMOX PRESS; LUMMOX JOURNAL; LITTLE RED BOOKS SERIES; LUMMOX SOCIETY OF WRITERS; DUFUS (Specialized: writing; biography), P.O. Box 5301, San Pedro CA 90733-5301. E-mail: lumoxraindog@earthlink.net. Website: http://home.earthlink.net/~lumoxraindog/. Established 1994 (press), 1996 (journal). **Editor/Publisher:** RD Armstrong.

Magazine Needs: *Lummox Journal* appears monthly and "explores the creative process through interviews, articles, and commentary." Wants "genuine and authentic poetry—socially conscious, heartfelt, honest, insightful, experimental. No angst-ridden confessional poetry; no pretentious, pompous, racist, and/or sexist work." Has published poetry by over 500 poets including Janet Buck, Philomene Long, John Thomas, Rebecca Morrison, and Raindog. *Lummox Journal* is up to 24 pages, digest-sized, photocopied and saddle-stapled with 60 lb. paper cover, includes art and ads. Receives about 1,000 poems/year, accepts about 10%. Press run is 180 for 150 subscribers. Subscription: $22/12 issues, $25 for institutions (US) and $35 (overseas). Sample: $2. Make checks payable to *Lummox*.

How to Submit: Submit 3 poems at a time. Line length for poetry is 40 lines maximum. Accepts previously published poems and simultaneous submissions. Prefers e-mail submissions (in text box); accepts submissions on disk (PC Win 98). Cover letter with bio preferred. Reads submissions from February to July. Time between acceptance and publication is up to 6 months. Seldom comments on rejected poems. Criticism fees: $10 to critique, $25 to advise, $50 to tutor. Guidelines and upcoming themes available for SASE or by e-mail. Responds in 2 weeks. Pays 1 copy. Acquires one-time rights. Reviews books chapbooks, CDs of poetry/music, and other magazines. Send materials for review consideration. "Inquire first."

Magazine Needs & How To Submit: *Dufus*, a poetry journal online at www.geocities.com/lumoxraindog/dufus.html is "fast becoming the main poetry outlet for the *Lummox Journal*. E-mail 3 poems (any length up to 75 lines), no attachments please. Issue of *Dufus* appear every 2-3 months (1,800 visitors in 2002)."

Book/Chapbook Needs & How to Submit: Lummox Press is no longer accepting unsolicited mss for the imprint Little Red Books. "The LRB series attempts to honor the poem as well as the poet." Publishes 6 to 8 books per year. Books are usually 48 pages, ¼ sheet-sized, photocopied/offset-printed, saddle-stapled/perfect-bound. Offers subsidy arrangements (under the imprint of Plug Nickel Press) for the cost of printing and distribution plus ISBN #, $2.50 per book. Send check for $6 to Lummox for sample package.

Also Offers: "Lummox Society of Writers (LSW) includes a newsletter (twice yearly) listing submission guidelines and addresses for magazines and presses that the editor recommends. Future newsletters will offer helpful tips on submitting, presentation, and updates." Subscription is $6.

📀◎ LUNA BISONTE PRODS; LOST AND FOUND TIMES (Specialized: style), 137 Leland Ave., Columbus OH 43214-7505. Established 1967. **Poetry Editor:** John M. Bennett.

Magazine Needs: *Lost and Found Times* publishes experimental and avant-garde writing. Wants "unusual poetry, naive poetry, surrealism, experimental, visual poetry, collaborations—no poetry workshop or academic pabulum." Has published poetry by J. Leftwich, Sheila Murphy, J.S. Murnet, Peter Ganick, I. Argüelles, and A. Ackerman. *Lost and Found Time* is digest-sized, 60-pages, photoreduced typescript with wild graphics, matte card cover with graphics. Press run is 350 with 75 subscribers of which 30 are libraries. Subscription: $30 for 5 numbers. Sample: $7.

How to Submit: Submit anytime—preferably camera-ready (but this is not required). Responds in 2 days. Pays 1 contributor's copy. All rights revert to authors upon publication. Staff reviews books of poetry. Send materials for review consideration.

Book/Chapbook Needs & How to Submit: Luna Bisonte also will consider book submissions: query with samples and cover letter (but "keep it brief"). Chapbook publishing usually depends on grants or other subsidies and is usually by solicitation. Will also consider subsidy arrangements on

negotiable terms. A sampling of various Luna Bisonte Prods products—from posters and audio cassettes to pamphlets and chapbooks—available for $10.
Advice: "Be blank."

LUNGFULL! MAGAZINE, 316 23rd St., Brooklyn NY 11215. E-mail: lungfull@rcn.com. Website: http://users.rcn.com/lungfull. Established 1994. **Editor/Publisher:** Brendan Lorber.
 • *LUNGFULL!* was the recipient of a multi-year grant from the New York State Council for the Arts.
Magazine Needs: *LUNGFULL!*, published annually, prints "the rough draft of each poem, in addition to the final so that the reader can see the creative process from start to finish." Wants "any style as long as its urgent, immediate, playful, probing, showing great thought while remaining vivid and grounded. Poems should be as interesting as conversation." Does not want "empty poetic abstractions." Has published poetry by Alice Notley, Allen Ginsberg, Lorenzo Thomas, Tracie Morris, Hal Sirowitz, Sparrow, Eileen Myles, and Bill Berkson. *LUNGFULL!* is 200 pages, 8½×7, offset-printed, perfect-bound, desktop-published, glossy 2 color cover with lots of illustrations and photos and a few small press ads. Receives about 1,000 poems/year, accepts 5%. Press run is 1,000 for 150 subscribers, 750 shelf sales; 100 distributed free to contributors. Single copy: $7.95; subscription: $31.80/4 issues, $15.90/2 issues. Sample: $9.50. Make checks payable to Brendan Lorber.
How to Submit: "We recommend you get a copy before submitting." Submit up to 6 poems at a time. Accepts previously published poems and simultaneous submissions (with notification). "However, other material will be considered first and stands a much greater chance of publication." Accepts e-mail submissions. "We prefer hard copy by USPS—but e-submissions can be made in the body of the e-mail itself or in a file saved as text." Cover letter preferred. Time between acceptance and publication is up to 8 months. "The editor looks at each piece for its own merit and for how well it'll fit into the specific issue being planned based on other accepted work." Guidelines available by e-mail. Responds in 6 months. Pays 2 copies.
Also Offers: "Each copy of *LUNGFULL! Magazine* now contains a short poem, usually from a series of six, printed on a sticker—they can be removed from the magazine and placed on any flat surface to make it a little less flat. Innovatively designed and printed in black & white, previous stickers have had work by Sparrow, Rumi, Julie Reid, Donna Cartelli, Joe Maynard, and Jeremy Sharpe, among others."
Advice: "Failure demands a certain dedication. Practice makes imperfection and imperfection makes room for the amazing. Only outside the bounds of acceptable conclusions can the astounding transpire, can writing contain anything beyond twittering snack food logic and the utilitarian pistons of mundane engineering."

THE LUTHERAN DIGEST (Specialized: humor, nature/rural/ecology, religious, inspirational), P.O. Box 4250, Hopkins MN 55343. (952)933-2820. Fax: (952)933-5708. E-mail: tldi@lutherandigest.com. Website: www.lutherandigest.com. Established 1953. **Editor:** David Tank.
Magazine Needs: *The Lutheran Digest* appears quarterly "to entertain and encourage believers and to subtly persuade non-believers to embrace the Christian faith. We publish short poems (24 lines or less) that will fit in a single column of the magazine. Most are inspirational, but that doesn't necessarily mean religious. No avant-garde poetry or work longer than 25 lines." Has published poetry by Kathleen A. Cain, William Beyer, Margaret Peterson, Florence Berg, and Erma Boetkher. *The Lutheran Digest* is 64 pages, digest-sized, offset-printed and saddle-stapled with 4-color paper cover, includes b&w photos and illustrations, local ads to cover cost of distribution. Receives about 200 poems/year, accepts 20%. Press run is 110,000; 105,000 distributed free to Lutheran churches. Subscription: $14/year, $22/2 years. Sample: $3.50.
How to Submit: Submit 3 poems at a time. Line length for poetry is 25 maximum. Accepts previously published poems and simultaneous submissions. Accepts submissions by fax, as e-mail attachment, and by postal mail. Cover letter preferred. "Include SASE if return is desired." Time between acceptance and publication is up to 9 months. Poems are circulated to an editorial board. "Selected by editor and reviewed by publication panel." Guidelines available for SASE or on website. Responds in 3 months. Pays credit and 1 copy. Acquires one-time rights.
Advice: "Poems should be short and appeal to senior citizens. We also look for poems that can be sung to traditional Lutheran hymns."

$☐ LYNX EYE; SCRIBBLEFEST LITERARY GROUP, 542 Mitchell Dr., Los Osos CA 93402. (805)528-8146. Fax: (805)528-7876. E-mail: pamccully@aol.com. Established 1994. **Contact:** Pam McCully.

Magazine Needs: *Lynx Eye* is the quarterly publication of the ScribbleFest Literary Group, an organization dedicated to the development and promotion of the literary arts. *Lynx Eye* is "dedicated to showcasing visionary writers and artists, particularly new voices." Each issue contains a special feature called Presenting, in which an unpublished writer of prose or poetry makes his/her print debut. No specifications regarding form, subject matter, or style of poetry. Has published poetry by Bruce Curley, Dani Montgomery, Michael Neal Morris, and Whitman McGowan. *Lynx Eye* is about 120 pages, digest-sized, perfect-bound with b&w artwork. Receives about 2,000 poetry submissions/year and have space for about 75. Press run is 500 for 250 subscribers, 200 shelf sales. Subscription: $25/year. Sample: $7.95. Make checks payable to ScribbleFest Literary Group.

How to Submit: Submissions must be typed and include phone number, address, and an SASE. Accepts simultaneous submissions; no previously published poems. No fax or e-mail submissions. Name, address, and phone number on each piece. Guidelines available for SASE and by e-mail. Responds in up to 3 months. Pays $10/piece and 3 copies. Acquires first North American serial rights.

Ⓝ ✖ $☐ ◎ LYNXFIELD PUBLISHING (Specialized: anthology; themes), P.O. Box 216, Pittsfield NH 03263. Phone/fax: (603)798-5461. E-mail: brown006@tds.net. Established 1999. **Editor/Publisher:** Mary Brown.

Book/Chapbook Needs: Lynxfield Publishing produces the *Messages* series of small anthology collections of essays, poetry, quotes, and short stories. Most recent title was *Messages from Mothers to Sons*. Wants positive poems celebrating relations (family, friends, etc.). Does not want negative poetry in poor taste. Recently published poetry by Michele Bardsley, Eleanor Hartmann, Maureen Cannon, Laura May Duplessis, and Humphrey Brown. Lynxfield Publishing publishes 1 anthology/year. Manuscripts are selected through open submission. Anthologies are usually 50 pages, 4×5½, perfect-bound. Receives about 200 poems/year, accepts about 5. Publishes about 6-10 poems/issue. Sample: $5.

How to Submit: Line length for poetry is 24 maximum. Accepts previously published poems and simultaneous submissions. Accepts e-mail submissions; no fax or disk submissions. Reads submissions year round. Regularly publishes theme issues. Guidelines available for SASE. Responds in 6 months. Pays $25 on publication and 3 contributor's copies.

◎ THE LYRIC; LESLIE MELLICHAMP AWARD, 65 VT. SR 15, Jericho VT 05465. Phone/fax: (802)899-3993. E-mail: Lyric@sover.net. Established 1921 ("the oldest magazine in North America in continuous publication devoted to the publication of traditional poetry"). **Editor:** Jean Mellichamp-Milliken.

Magazine Needs: *The Lyric* uses about 55 poems each quarterly issue. "We use rhymed verse in traditional forms, for the most part, with an occasional piece of blank or free verse. Forty lines or so is usually our limit. Our themes are varied, ranging from religious ecstasy to humor to raw grief, but we feel no compulsion to shock, embitter or confound our readers. We also avoid poems about contemporary political or social problems—grief but not grievances, as Frost put it. Frost is helpful in other ways: If yours is more than a lover's quarrel with life, we're not your best market. And most of our poems are accessible on first or second reading. Frost again: Don't hide too far away." Has published poetry by Rhina P. Espaillat, Maureen Cannon, Alfred Dorn, Paul Petrie, R.L. Cook, and Lionel Willis. *The Lyric* is 32 pages, digest-sized, professionally printed with varied typography, matte card cover. Press run is 800 for 600 subscribers of which 40 are libraries. Receives about 3,000 submissions/year, accepts 5%. Subscription: $12 US, $14 Canada and other countries (in US funds only). Sample: $3.

How to Submit: Submit up to 6 poems at a time. Will read simultaneous submissions; no previously published poems or translations. "Cover letters often helpful, but not required." Guidelines available for SASE and by e-mail. Responds in 3 months (average). Pays 1 copy, and all contributors are eligible for quarterly and annual prizes totaling $750. "Subscription will not affect publication of submitted poetry."

Also Offers: "Among the yearly prizes awarded, we have recently added the Leslie Mellichamp Award of $100."

Advice: "Our raison d'être has been the encouragement of form, music, rhyme, and accessibility in poetry. As we witness the growing dissatisfaction with the modernist movement that ignores these things, we are proud to have provided an alternative for 82 years that helps keep the roots of poetry alive."

N **○** **LYRIC POETRY REVIEW**, P.O. Box 980814, Houston TX 77098. (713)942-2169. E-mail: lyricreview@ev1.net. Website: www.lyricreview.org. Established 2001. **Editor:** Mira Rosenthal. Member: Council of Literary Magazines and Presses (CLMP).
   • *Lyric Poetry Review* was a Pushcart Prize winner for 2003

Magazine Needs: *Lyric Poetry Review* appears biannually and presents poetry by Americans and translations of both little-known and celebrated poets from around the world. Also publishes literary essays. Wants "poems with singing power, poems with fresh energy to delight and awaken deep feeling. Lyric essays that use poetic logic and relate a mosaic of ideas." Does not want reviews or poems of more than 500 words. Recently published poetry by Linda Gregg, Marilyn Hacker, David St. John, Tomaz Salamun, Czeslaw Milosz, and John Felstiner. *Lyric Poetry Review* is 64 pages, digest-sized, offset-printed, perfect-bound, full-color cover with original artwork. Receives about 200 poems/year, accepts about 5%. Publishes about 40 poems/issue. Press run is 1,000. Single copy: $8; subscription: $14/year (subscribers outside US add $5 postage). Make checks payable to *Lyric Poetry Review*.

How to Submit: Submit 3-6 poems at a time. Accepts simultaneous submissions if notified; no previously published poems. No fax, e-mail, or disk submissions. Cover letter is required. Reads submissions year round. Time between acceptance and publication is 1-6 months. Poems are circulated to an editorial board. "Editorial decisions are made collectively by all associated editors. We strongly advise that those submitting work read a recent issue first." Seldom comments on rejected poems. Occasionally publishes theme issues. List of upcoming themes available by e-mail. Guidelines available in magazine, for SASE, or on website. Responds in up to 3 months. Always sends prepublication proofs. Pays 3 copies. Acquires first rights.

○ **M.I.P. COMPANY (Specialized: foreign language, erotica)**, P.O. Box 27484, Minneapolis MN 55427. (763)544-5915. Fax: (612)871-5733. E-mail: mp@mipco.com. Website: www.mipco.com. Established in 1984. **Contact:** Michael Peltsman.

Book/Chapbook Needs & How to Submit: M.I.P. Company publishes 3 paperbacks/year. Publishes only Russian erotic poetry and prose written in Russian. Has published poetry collections by Mikhail Armalinsky and Aleksey Shelvakh. Accepts simultaneous submissions; no previously published poems. Responds to queries in 1 month. Seldom comments on rejected poems.

○ **MAD POETS REVIEW; MAD POETS REVIEW POETRY COMPETITION; MAD POETS SOCIETY**, P.O. Box 1248, Media PA 19063-8248. E-mail: madpoets@comcast.com. Website: www.madpoetssociety.com. Established 1987. **Editor:** Eileen M. D'Angelo. **Associate Editor:** Camelia Nocella.

Magazine Needs: *Mad Poets Review* is published annually in October/November. "Our primary purpose is to promote thought-provoking, moving poetry, and encourage beginning poets. We don't care if you have a 'name' or a publishing history, if your poetry is well-crafted." "Anxious for work with 'joie de vivre' that startles and inspires." No restrictions on subject, form, or style. "Just because our name is *Mad Poets Review* doesn't mean we want mad ramblings masquerading under the guise of poetry." No obsenities simply for shock value. Has published poetry by Gerald Stern, Naomi Shihab Nye, Greg Djanikian, Harry Humes, Maria Mazziotti Gillan, Nathalie Anderson. *Mad Poets Review* is about 140 pages, digest-sized, attractively printed and perfect-bound with textured card cover. Receives about 1,000 poems/year, accepts 800. Press run is 300. Single copy: $10. Sample: $12. Make checks payable to either Mad Poets Society or *Mad Poets Review*.

How to Submit: Submit 6 poems at a time. "We accept first class mail or e-mail submissions (no certified or Registered Mail). For e-mail, attach a Microsoft Word document (format is Times New Roman, 12 pt.). We will need a mailing address to send out a proof of the poem prior to publication, and 3-4 line bio. Poems without an SASE with adequate postage will not be returned or acknowledged." Accepts previously published poems and simultaneous submissions. Cover letter not necessary, but "include 3-4 sentences about yourself suitable for our Bio Notes section. Mark envelope 'contest' or 'magazine.' " Reads submissions January 1 through June 1 only. Time between acceptance and publication is 8 months. Often comments on rejected poems. Responds in 3 months. Pays 1 contributor's copy. Acquires one-time rights.

Also Offers: Sponsors the annual *Mad Poets Review* Poetry Competition. "All themes and styles of poetry are welcome, no line limit, previously unpublished work only." Complete contest guidelines available for SASE. Winners published in *Mad Poets Review*. Cash prizes awarded. "The Mad Poets Society is an active organization in Pennsylvania. We run several poetry series; have monthly meetings for members for critique and club business; coordinate a children's contest through Del. Co. School system; run an annual poetry festival the first Sunday in October; sponsor Mad Poets Bonfires for local poets and musicians; publish an annual literary calendar and newsletters that offer the most comprehensive listing available anywhere in the tri-state area. We send quarterly newsletters to members, as well as PA Poetry Society news covering state and national events."

Advice: "It is advised that if someone is going to submit they see what kind of poetry we publish."

THE MADISON REVIEW, University of Wisconsin, Dept. of English, Helen C. White Hall, 600 N. Park St., Madison WI 53706. (608)263-2566. E-mail: madreview@mail.student.org.wisc .edu. Website: http://mendota.english.wisc.edu/~MadRev. Established 1978. **Contact:** Poetry Editor.

Magazine Needs: *The Madison Review*, published in May and December, wants poems that are "smart and tight, that fulfill their own propositions. Spare us: religious or patriotic dogma and light verse." Has published work by Simon Perchik, Amy Quan Barry, Mitch Raney, Erica Meitner, and Henry B. Stobbs. Selects 15-20 poems from a pool of 750. Sample: $5.

How to Submit: Submit up to 6 poems at a time. No simultaneous submissions. No e-mail submissions. Guidelines available for SASE, by e-mail, on website, and in publication. Usually responds in 9 months. Pays 2 contributor's copies.

Also Offers: See listing for the Phyllis Smart Young Prize in Poetry in the Contests & Awards section.

Advice: "Contributors: Know your market! Read before, during, and after writing. Treat your poems *better* than job applications!"

MAELSTROM, HC #1 Box 1624, Blakeslee PA 18610. E-mail: lmaelstrom@aol.com. Website: www.geocities.com/~readmaelstrom. Established 1997. **Editor:** Christine L. Reed. **Art Editor:** Jennifer Fennell.

Magazine Needs: *Maelstrom*, a quarterly, "tries to be a volatile storm of talents throwing together

Anton Orlov's "Long Way Home" graces the cover of the Spring 2002 issue of *The Madison Review*. Fiction Editor Elizabeth Staudt says, "This image is reflective as well as visually engaging. Simply put, we like the way it looks." The editors agreed collectively on the cropping of the image and integrating the bar code, "our first issue with that consideration. We think it looks great."

art, poetry, short fiction, comedy and tragedy." Wants any kind of poetry, "humor appreciated. No pornography." Has published poetry by Grace Cavalieri, Mekeel McBride, Daniela Gioseffi, and B.Z. Niditch. *Maelstrom* is 40-50 pages, 7×8½, saddle-stapled with color cover, includes b&w art. Receives about 600 poems/year, accepts about 20%. Press run is 500 for 100 subscribers. Single copy: $5; subscription: $20. Sample: $4.

How to Submit: Submit up to 4 poems at a time. Accepts previously published poems and simultaneous submissions. Accepts e-mail submissions "in the body of the e-mail message. Please do not send attached files." Cover letter preferred. Include name and address on every page. Send sufficient SASE for return of work. "There is no reading fee, however, submissions accompanied by a $1 donation will be answered immediately, all others will be answered in the order they are received." Time between acceptance and publication is up to 3 months. Seldom comments on rejected poems. Guidelines available by e-mail or on website. Responds in up to 3 months. Pays 1 contributor's copy. Acquires first North American serial or one-time rights. Staff reviews chapbooks of poetry and other magazines. Send materials for review consideration. "Material cannot be returned."

Also Offers: Also publishes a year anthology, *Poetography.* "Send $1 and SASE for more info."

THE MAGAZINE OF FANTASY & SCIENCE FICTION, P.O. Box 3447, Hoboken NJ 07030. E-mail: FandSF@aol.com. Website: www.fsfmag.com. Established 1949. **Editor:** Gordon Van Gelder.

- *The Magazine of Fantasy & Science Fiction* is a past winner of the Hugo Award and World Fantasy Award.

Magazine Needs: *The Magazine of Fantasy & Science Fiction* appears monthly, 11 times/year. "One of the longest-running magazines devoted to the literature of the fantastic." Wants only poetry that deals with the fantastic or the science-fictional. Has published poetry by Rebecca Kavaler, Elizabeth Bear, and Robert Frazier. *The Magazine of Fantasy & Science Fiction* is 160 pages, digest-sized, offset-printed, perfect-bound, glossy cover, has ads. Receives about 20-40 poems/year, accepts about ½-1%. Publishes about 1-2 poems/year. Press run is 35,000 for 20,000 subscribers. Single copy: $3.95; subscription: $32.97. Sample: $5. Make checks payable to *The Magazine of Fantasy & Science Fiction*.

How to Submit: Submit 1-3 poems at a time. No previously published poems or simultaneous submissions. No fax, e-mail, or disk submissions. Time between acceptance and publication is 3-9 months. "I buy poems very infrequently—just when one hits me right." Seldom comments on rejected poems. Guidelines available for SASE or on website. Responds in up to 1 month. Always sends prepublication galleys. Pays 2 contributor's copies. Acquires first North American serial rights.

$ ◑ ◎ THE MAGAZINE OF SPECULATIVE POETRY (Specialized: horror, science fiction, science), P.O. Box 564, Beloit WI 53512. Established 1984. **Editor:** Roger Dutcher.

Magazine Needs: *The Magazine of Speculative Poetry* is a biannual magazine that features "the best new speculative poetry. We are especially interested in narrative form, but interested in variety of styles, open to any form, length (within reason). We're looking for the best of the new poetry utilizing the ideas, imagery, and approaches developed by speculative fiction and will welcome experimental techniques as well as the fresh employment of traditional forms." Has published poetry by Mark Rudolph, Tracina Jackson-Adams, Mario Milosevic, Duane Ackerson, and Laurel Winter. *The Magazine of Speculative Poetry* is 24-28 pages, digest-sized, offset-printed, saddle-stapled with matte card cover. Accepts less than 5% of some 500 poems received/year. Press run is 150-200, for nearly 100 subscribers. Subscription: $19/4. Sample: $5.

How to Submit: Submit 3-5 poems at a time, double-spaced with a "regular old font." "We are a small magazine, we can't print epics. Some poems run 2 or 3 pages, but rarely anything longer." No previously published poems or simultaneous submissions. "We like cover letters but they aren't necessary. We like to see where you heard of us; the names of the poems submitted; a statement if the poetry ms is disposable; a big enough SASE; and if you've been published, some recent places." Editor comments on rejected poems "on occasion." Guidelines available for SASE. Responds in up to 2 months. Pays 3¢/word, minimum $5, maximum $25, plus copy. Acquires first North American serial rights. "All rights revert to author upon publication, except for permission to reprint in any 'Best of' or compilation volume. Payment will be made for such publication." Reviews books of speculative poetry. Query on unsolicited reviews. Send materials for review consideration.

🌐 ○ **MAGMA POETRY MAGAZINE**, 43 Keslake Rd., London NW6 6DH United Kingdom. E-mail: magmapoems@aol.com. Website: www.champignon.net/Magma. Established 1994. **Editorial Secretary:** David Boll.

Magazine Needs: *Magma* appears 3 times/year and contains "modern poetry, reviews and interviews with poets." Wants poetry that is "modern in idiom and shortish (two pages maximum). Nothing sentimental or old fashioned." Has published poetry by Thomas Lynch, Thom Gunn, Michael Donaghy, John Burnside, Vicki Feaver, and Roddy Lumsden. *Magma* is 64 pages, 8×8, photocopied and stapled, includes b&w illustrations. Receives about 3,000 poems/year, accepts 4-5%. Press run is about 500. Single copy: £4 UK and Ireland, £5 Europe; outside Europe, £6 airmail, £5 surface mail. Subscription: £11/3 issues UK and Ireland, £14.50 Europe; outside Europe, £17.50 airmail, £14.50 surface. Make checks payable to *Magma.* For subscriptions contact Helen Nicholson, distribution secretary, 82 St. James's Dr., London SW17 7RR.

How to Submit: Submit up to 6 poems at a time. Accepts simultaneous submissions. Accepts submissions by e-mail (as attachment or in text box) and by post. Cover letter preferred. Reads submissions September through November and February through July only. Time between acceptance and publication is maximum 3 months. Poems are circulated to an editorial board. "Each issue has an editor who submits his/her selections to a board for final approval. Editor's selection very rarely changed." Occasionally publishes theme issues. Responds in 4 months. Always sends prepublication galleys. Pays 1 contributor's copy.

Also Offers: "We hold a public reading in London three times/year, to coincide with each new issue, and poets in the issue are invited to read."

◪ **MAIN STREET RAG**, 4416 Shea Ln., Charlotte NC 28227. (704)573-2516. E-mail: editor@mainstreetrag.com. Website: www.MainStreetRag.com. Established 1996. **Publisher/Editor:** M. Scott Douglass.

Magazine Needs: *Main Street Rag,* is a quarterly that publishes "poetry, short fiction, essays, interviews, reviews, photos, art, cartoons, (political, satirical), and poetry collections as well as books—we are now a full service bindery with an online bookstore. We like publishing good material from people who are interested in more than notching another publishing credit, people who support small independent publishers like ourselves." *Main Street Rag* "will consider almost anything but prefer writing with an edge—either gritty or bitingly humorous." Has recently published work by Serena Fusek, Keith Flynn, Joy Harjo, Lisa Boylan, and David Plumb. *Main Street Rag* is approximately 96 pages, digest-sized, perfect bound with 100 lb. laminated color cover. Publishes 30-40 poems and one short story per issue out of 2,500 submissions/year. Press run is over 1,000 for 300 subscribers of which 15 are libraries. "Sold nationally in bookstores." Single copy: $7; subscription: $20/year, $35/2 years. Sample: $5.

How to Submit: Submit 6 pages of poetry at a time. No previously published poems or simultaneous submissions. No e-mail submissions. Cover letter preferred with a brief bio "about the poet, not their credits." Has backlog of up to 1 year. Guidelines available for SASE and by e-mail. Responds within 6 weeks. Pays 1 copy and contributor's discount for the issue in which work appears. Acquires one-time rights.

Also Offers: Book-length poetry contest (48-84 pages). Deadline: January 31. 1st Prize: $1,000 and 50 copies. Entry fee: $20. Also offers chapbook contest. Deadline: May 31. 1st Prize: $100 and 200 copies. Entry fee: $15. Previous winners: David Chorltan, Alan Catlin, Dede Wilson, Nancy Kenney Connolly, Pam Bernard.

Advice: "Small press independent exist by and for writers. Without their support (and the support of readers) we have no means or reason to publish. Sampling is always appreciated."

🔖 $◪ **THE MALAHAT REVIEW; LONG POEM PRIZE**, P.O. Box 1700, STN CSC, University of Victoria, Victoria BC V8W 2Y2 Canada. (250)721-8524. E-mail: malahat@uvic.ca. Website: www.malahatreview.ca. Established 1967. **Editor:** Marlene Cookshaw.

Magazine Needs: *The Malahat Review* is "a high quality, visually appealing literary quarterly which has earned the praise of notable literary figures throughout North America. Its purpose is to publish and promote poetry and fiction of a very high standard, both Canadian and international. We are interested in various styles, lengths, and themes. The criterion is excellence." Has published poetry by Karen Solie and Don McKay. Uses 50 pages of poetry in each issue, have 1,000 subscribers of which 300 are libraries. Receives about 2,000 poems/year, accepts approximately 100. Subscription: $40 Canadian (or US equivalent). Sample: $8 US.

How to Submit: Submit 5-10 poems, addressed to editor Marlene Cookshaw. Include SASE with Canadian stamps or IRC with each submission. Guidelines available for SASE (or SAE and IRC). Responds within 3 months. Pays $30/anticipated magazine page plus 2 copies and year's subscription. Acquires first world serial rights. Reviews Canadian books of poetry.

Also Offers: Sponsors the Long Poem Prize, two awards of $400 plus publication and payment at their usual rates (entry fee is a year's subscription) for a long poem or cycle 5-15 pages (flexible minimum and maximum), deadline March 1 of alternate years (2003, 2005, etc.). Entry fee: $40 Canadian or US equivalent. Include name and address on a separate page.

$ ☑ MAMMOTH BOOKS; MAMMOTH PRESS INC., 7 Juniata St., DuBois PA 15801. E-mail: guidelines@mammothbooks.com (for guidelines) or info@mammothbooks.com (for questions). Website: www.mammothbooks.com. Established 1997. **Publisher:** Antonio Vallone.

Book/Chapbook Needs: MAMMOTH books, an imprint of MAMMOTH press inc., publishes 2-4 paperbacks/year of creative nonfiction, fiction, and poetry through annual competitions. "We are open to all types of literary poetry." Has published *The House of Sages* by Philip Terman; *The Never Wife* by Cynthia Hogue; *These Happy Eyes* by Liz Rosenberg; and *Subjects for Other Conversations* by John Stigall. Books are usually 5×7 or digest-sized, digitally-printed and perfect-bound, covers vary (1-4 color), include art.

How to Submit: Send mss to contest. Not currently reading outside of contests. For poetry mss, submit a collection of poems or a single long poem. Translations are accepted. "Manuscripts as a whole must not have been previously published. Some or all of each manuscript may have appeared in periodicals, chapbooks, anthologies, or other venues. These must be identified. Authors are responsible for securing permissions." Accepts simultaneous submissions. No e-mail submissions. Submit mss by postal mail only. Poetry mss should be single-spaced, no more than 1 poem/page. Reads submissions September 1 through February 28/29. Entry fee: $20. Make checks payable to MAMMOTH books. Time between acceptance and publication is up to 2 years. Poems are circulated to an editorial board. "Finalists will be chosen by the staff of MAMMOTH books in consultation with an outside editorial board and/or guest editor. Manuscripts will be selected based on merit only." Seldom comments on rejected poems. "Pays royalties: 10% of books printed." Other finalist manuscripts may be selected for publication and offered a standard royalty contract and publication of at least 500 trade paperback copies. Finalists will be announced within 1 year from the end of each submission period. MAMMOTH press inc. reserves the right not to award a prize if no entries are deemed suitable. Complete rules are available for SASE or by e-mail to guidelines@mammothbooks.com. Order sample books by sending for information to their mailing address or e-mail.

Advice: "Read big. Write big. Publish small. Join the herd."

◘ MANDRAKE POETRY REVIEW; THE MANDRAKE PRESS, Box 792, Larkspur CA 94977-0792. E-mail: mandrake@a4.pl. Website: www.mandrake.a4.pl/. Established 1993 in New York. **Editor:** Leo Yankevich. **Editor:** David Castleman.

Magazine Needs: *Mandrake Poetry Review* appears at least twice/year. Seeks poetry in translation as well as content concerning ethnicity/nationality, politics, and social issues. Accepts poetry written by children. Has published poetry by Michael Daugherty, George Held, Hugh Fox, Errol Miller, Simon Perchik, and Joan Peternel. *Mandrake Poetry Review* is 76-150 pages, A5, offset-printed and flat-spined with glossy white card cover. Accepts about 10% of the poetry received. Press run is 500 for 100 subscribers from 3 continents. Single copy: $5 (by airmail); subscription: $20/2 years. Make checks payable to David Castleman.

How to Submit: Submit up to 7 poems at a time. "Send only copies of your poems, as we do not return poems with our reply." Accepts previously published poems and simultaneous submissions. Accepts e-mail submissions (in text box). Cover letter preferred. Guidelines available for SASE. Responds in 2 months. Pays 2 contributor's copies "sometimes more." All rights revert to author. "Poets are encouraged to send their books for review consideration to David Castleman. All editors and publishers whose books/chapbooks are selected for review will receive one copy of the issue in which the review appears. We publish 50-100 reviews yearly."

◢ ◎ **THE MANHATTAN REVIEW (Specialized: translations)**, 440 Riverside Dr., Apt. 38, New York NY 10027. (212)932-1854. Established 1980. **Poetry Editor:** Philip Fried.

Magazine Needs: *The Manhattan Review* "publishes American writers and foreign writers with something valuable to offer the American scene. We like to think of poetry as a powerful discipline engaged with many other fields. We want to see ambitious work. Interested in both lyric and narrative. Not interested in mawkish, sentimental poetry. We select high-quality work from a number of different countries, including the U.S." Has published poetry by Zbigniew Herbert, D. Nurkse, Baron Wormser, Penelope Shuttle, Marilyn Hacker, and Peter Redgrove. *The Manhattan Review* is now "an annual with ambitions to be semiannual." 64 pages, digest-sized, professionally printed with glossy card cover, photos and graphics. Press run is 500 for 400 subscribers of which 250 are libraries. Distributed by Bernhard DeBoer, Inc. Receives about 300 submissions/year, uses few ("but I do read everything submitted carefully and with an open mind"). "I return submissions as promptly as possible." Single copy: $5; subscription: $10. Sample: $6.35 with 6×9 envelope.

How to Submit: Submit 3-5 pages of poems at a time. No simultaneous submissions. Cover letter with short bio and publications required. Editor sometimes comments "but don't count on it." Responds in 3 months if possible. Pays contributor's copies. Staff reviews books of poetry. Send materials for review consideration.

Advice: "Always read the magazine first to see if your work is appropriate."

★ ◢ **MANKATO POETRY REVIEW**, English Dept., 230 Armstrong Hall, Minnesota State University, Mankato MN 56001. (507)389-5511. E-mail: roger.sheffer@mankato.msus.edu. Website: www.english.mnsu.edu/publications/masthead.html. Established 1984. **Editor:** Roger Sheffer.

Magazine Needs: *Mankato Poetry Review* is a semiannual magazine that is "open to all forms and themes, though we seldom print 'concrete poetry,' religious, or sentimental verse. We frequently publish first-time poets." Has published poetry by Edward Micus, Gary Fincke, Judith Skillman, and Walter Griffin. *Mankato Poetry Review* is 30 pages, digest-sized, typeset on 60 lb. paper, saddle-stapled with buff matte card cover printed in one color. It appears usually in May and December and has a press run of 200. Subscription: $5/year. Sample: $2.50.

How to Submit: Submit up to 6 poems at a time. Line length for poetry is 60 maximum. "Please include biographical note on separate sheet. Poems not accompanied by SASE will not be returned." However, do not submit mss in summer (May through August). No previously published poems or simultaneous submissions. Cover letter required. Guidelines available for SASE. Deadlines are April 15 (May issue) and November 15 (December issue). Responds in about 2 months; "We accept only what we can publish in next issue." Pays 2 contributor's copies.

Advice: "We're interested in looking at longer poems—up to 60 lines, with great depth of detail relating to place (landscape, townscape)."

★ $◢ **MĀNOA: A PACIFIC JOURNAL OF INTERNATIONAL WRITING**, 1733 Donaghho Rd., Honolulu HI 96822. Fax: (808)956-7808. E-mail: mjournal-1@hawaii.edu. Website www.hawaii.edu/mjournal. Established 1989. **Poetry Editor:** Frank Stewart.

   • Poetry published in *Mānoa* has also been selected for inclusion in the 1995 and 1996 volumes of *The Best American Poetry*.

Magazine Needs: *Mānoa* appears twice/year. "We are a general interest literary magazine and consider work in many forms and styles, regardless of the authors' publishing history. However, we are not for the beginning writer. It is best to look at a sample copy of the journal before submitting." Has published poetry by Arthur Sze, Linda Gregg, Linda Hogan, and John Haines. *Mānoa* is 240 pages, 7×10, offset printed, flat-spined using art and graphics. Receives about 1,000 poems/year, accepts 2%. Press run is over 2,500 for several hundred subscribers of which 100 are libraries, 400 shelf sales. "In addition, *Manoa* is available through Project Muse to about 600 institutional subscribers throughout the world." Subscription: $22/year. Sample: $10.

How to Submit: Query by mail or e-mail. Submit 3-5 poems at a time. Guidelines available for SASE. Responds in 6 weeks. Always sends prepublication galleys. Pay "competitive" plus 2 copies.

Seldom comments on rejected poems. Reviews current books and chapbooks of poetry. Send materials for for review consideration, attn. reviews editor.

Advice: "We are not a regional journal, but each issue features a particular part of Asia or the Pacific; these features, which include poetry, are assembled by guest editors. The rest of each issue features work by poets from the U.S. and elsewhere. We welcome the opportunity to read poetry from throughout the country, but we are not interested in genre or formalist writing for its own sake or in casual impressions of the Asia-Pacific region."

MANY MOUNTAINS MOVING; MANY MOUNTAINS MOVING LITERARY AWARDS, 420 22nd St., Boulder CO 80302. (303)545-9942. E-mail: mmm@mmminc.org. Website: www.mmminc.org. Established 1994. **Editor:** Naomi Horii. **Poetry Editor:** Debra Bokur.

• Poetry published in *Many Mountains Moving* has also been included in volumes of *The Best American Poetry* and *The Pushcart Prize*.

Magazine Needs: Published 6 times/year, *Many Mountains Moving* is "a literary journal of diverse contemporary voices that welcomes previously unpublished fiction, poetry, nonfiction, and art from writers and artists of all walks of life. We publish the world's top writers as well as emerging talents." Open to any style of poetry, but they do not want any "Hallmark-y" poetry. Accepts poetry by children, "but quality would have to be on par with other accepted work." Has published poetry by Robert Bly, W.S. Merwin, Sherman Alexie, Lawson Fusao Inada, Allen Ginsberg, and Adrienne Rich. *Many Mountains Moving* is about 88 pages, magazine-sized, web offset and perfect-bound with four-color cover and b&w art and photos inside. Receives 4,000 poems/year, accepts .1%. Press run is 1,500. Single copy: $3.99; subscription: $18/year.

How to Submit: Submit 3-10 poems at a time, typed with SASE. Accepts only mailed submissions. Accepts simultaneous submissions; no previously published poems. Cover letter preferred. Poems are circulated to an editorial board. "Poems are first read by several readers. If considered seriously, they are passed to the poetry editor for final decision." Seldom comments on rejected poems. Occasionally publishes theme issues. Upcoming themes and guidelines are available for SASE or on website. Responds within 1 month, "if we are seriously considering a submission, we may take longer." Sends prepublication galleys. Pays 3 copies, additional copies available at $2/copy. Acquires first North American serial rights and "rights to publish in a future edition of the *Best of Many Mountains Moving Anthology*."

Also Offers: Sponsors an annual book contest, which awards an honorarium and publication of ms in book form, and the Many Mountains Moving Literary Awards, which awards $200 plus publication in the categories of poetry, fiction, and essay. Entry fee: $15 (includes subscription). Details available for SASE.

Advice: "Although we have featured a number of established poets, we encourage new writers to submit. However, we recommend that poets read through at least one issue to familiarize themselves with the type of work we generally publish."

MANZANITA QUARTERLY, P.O. 9289, Sante Fe NM 87504-9289. E-mail: authenticj@aol. com Website: www.manzanitaquarterly.com. Established 1998. **Editor:** Mariah Hegarty.

Magazine Needs: *Manzanita Quarterly* is a quarterly that publishes quality, accessible poetry. Does not want porn, rhyming poems, or Hallmark-type verse. Recently published poetry by Elizabeth Biller Chapman, Joan Logghe, Judith Barrington, Paulann Petersen, Peter Pereira, and Roger Weaver. *Manzanita Quarterly* is 75 pages, digest-sized, perfect-bound, printed card stock cover with photo. Receives about 1,000 poems/year, accepts about 25%. Publishes about 45 poems/issue. Press run is 250 for 70 subscribers of which 5 are libraries, 30 shelf sales; 10 are distributed free to libraries, reviewers. Single copy: $9 and $1 for postage; subscription: $30. Sample: $9 and $1 for postage. Make checks payable to *Manzanita Quarterly*.

How to Submit: Submit 5 poems at a time. No previously published poems or simultaneous submissions. Accepts submissions by regular mail only; no e-mail. Cover letter is preferred. "Send SASE, cover letter with short, serious bio, name and address on each page." Reads submissions all year. Deadlines: February 7, May 9, August 12, November 15. Submit seasonal poems 2 months in advance. Time between acceptance and publication is 2 months. Seldom comments on rejected poems. Guidelines are available in magazine, for SASE, on website, and by e-mail. Responds in 3 months from each deadline. Pays 1 contributor's copy. Acquires first North American serial rights.

Advice: "I look for vivid images, fresh language, and quality, well-crafted writing. Poetry should be accessible; I like poetry that is evocative, poignant, vital, humorous, and thoughtful. Send your best."

◐ MARGIE/THE AMERICAN JOURNAL OF POETRY; THE MARJORIE J. WILSON AWARD FOR EXCELLENCE IN POETRY, P.O. Box 250, Chesterfield MO 63006-0250. Website: www.margiereview.com. Established 2001. **Editor:** Robert Nazarene.

Magazine Needs: *MARGIE/The American Journal of Poetry* appears annually in September. "*MARGIE* publishes superlative poetry. No limits to school, form, subject matter. Imaginative, risk-taking poetry which disturbs and/or consoles is of paramount interest. A distinctive voice is prized." Recently published poetry by Emmylou Harris, Stephen Dunn, Ted Kooser, Jane Mead, Sherod Santos, and David Wagoner. *MARGIE* is 300 pages, digest-sized, professionally-printed, perfect-bound, glossy cover with art/graphics, has ads. Receives about 15,000 poems/year, accepts less than 1%. Publishes about 150 poems/issue. Press run is 2,000 (circulation). Single copy: $9.95; subscription: $9.95 individual; $14.95 institution and outside US (all one year/one issue). Make checks payable to *MARGIE*.

How to Submit: Submit 3-5 poems at a time. Line length for poetry is 90 maximum. Accepts simultaneous submissions (notify in cover letter); no previously published poems. No fax, e-mail, or disk submissions. Cover letter is required. "A short bio is useful, but not required." Open reading: June 1-October 15. "Subscribers *only* may submit year round. Identify yourself as 'subscriber' on outside of submission envelope." Time between acceptance and publication is up to 1 year. Poems are circulated to an editorial board. "The editorial board meets quarterly. Recommendations are made to the editor. Editor makes final decision." *Sometimes* comments on rejected poems. Guidelines available for SASE or on website. Responds in up to 3 months. Sometimes sends prepublication galleys. Pays 2 contributor's copies. Acquires first rights. All rights revert to poet upon publication.

Also Offers: The Marjorie J. Wilson Award for Excellence in Poetry; send SASE for contest guidelines.

Advice: "Invest 90% of your literary life: reading, reading, reading; 10% of your time: writing. Be audacious, innovative, distinctive. Never, never, never give up."

★ ◐ ◎ MARGIN: EXPLORING MODERN MAGICAL REALISM (Specialized: magical realism). E-mail: smike10@qwest.net. Website: www.magical-realism.com. Established 2000. **Contact:** Poetry Editor.

- "*Margin's* staff is on a reading hiatus through 2003 except submissions concerning the 2003 special theme—Caribbean magical realism. Writers should inquire about the opening of a new general reading period before submitting."

Magazine Needs: *Margin: Exploring Modern Magical Realism* is the world's only continuous survey of contemporary literary magical realism. We want accessible poetry where metamorphoses are authentic, and where the magical and mundane coexist. Metaphor alone does not qualify as magical realism. No light verse, forced rhyme, or language poetry, and *no* New Age, Wiccan, or science fiction." *Margin* is published online. Receives "thousands" of poems/year, accepts about 2%. Publishes about 3-4 poems/issue ("publishing as we find good poetry—no schedule"). Circulation is 2,000-3,000 hits/month. Single copy: free; subscription: free, automated, private. Sample: visit website.

How to Submit: Submit up to 6 poems at a time. "No preferred line length, but our bias runs to shorter rather than longer." Accepts previously published poems and simultaneous submissions (if notified). Accepts e-mail submissions (*no* attachments). "Poems submitted without SASE will not be read or returned." Reads submissions September 1 through April 30. Time between acceptance and publication is usually 6 months. Poems are circulated to an editorial board. "Editors live in

---

THE SUBJECT INDEX in the back of this book helps you identify potential markets for your work.

separate cities in the US and Canada. We nominate for Pushcart." Seldom comments on rejected poems ("Only when they are good poems but not magical realism. Send reading list of top 10 favorite magical realist poets or authors, plus bio and short definition of 'magical realism.' ") Occasionally publishes theme issues. Guidelines and upcoming themes available on website. Responds in 6 months. Usually sends prepublication galleys as URL form. Pays "perpetual global exposure, nominates for literary prizes." Rights acquired are negotiable. Reviews books and chapbooks of poetry in under 500 words ("but we are flexible"), single book and multi-book format. Poets may send material for review consideration to Poetry Editor ("Nothing academic!"). Also interested in articles, essays on poetry as magical realism, interviews of magical realist poets, and critical discussions of magical realist work by poets from around the world.

Also Offers: "Broad global exposure has benefited many of our published writers."

Advice: *"Understand* what magical realism is *first* before submitting. For criteria see website guidelines."

N ⊘ MARSH HAWK PRESS, P.O. Box 220, Stuyvesant Station, New York NY 10009. E-mail: MarshHawkPress@cs.com. Website: www.MarshHawkPress.org. Established 2001.

Book/Chapbook Needs & How to Submit: Marsh Hawk Press publishes books of "quality poetry of any lineage—post-Imagist-Objectivist, New York School, surrealist, experimental, language, concrete, etc." Recently published poetry by Eileen Tabios, Sandy McIntosh, Ed Foster, Harriet Zinnes, Sharon Dolin, and Martha King. Publishes 3-4 poetry books/year. Manuscripts are selected through open submission. Books are 64-110 pages, photo offset-printed, perfect-bound, 4-color cover. Marsh Hawk Press currently accepts submissions only through its annual competition, the Marsh Hawk Press Prize. "The press is a collective whose author-members agree to work with the press on all aspects of book production, including editing, design, distribution, sales, advertising, publicity, and fund raising."

Advice: "See our website for our manifesto and information."

◑ ◎ MARYMARK PRESS (Specialized: form/style), 45-08 Old Millstone Dr., East Windsor NJ 08520. (609)443-0646. Website: www.experimentalpoet.com. Established 1994. **Editor/Publisher:** Mark Sonnenfeld.

Book/Chapbook Needs: Marymark Press's goal is "to feature and promote experimental poets. I will most likely be publishing only broadsides and samplers; no books at this time. I want to see experimental poetry of the outer fringe. Make up words, sounds, whatever, but say something you thought never could be explained. Disregard rules if need be." No traditional, rhyming or spiritual verse; no predictable styles. Has published poetry by Robert Pomerhin, Steve Kostecke, John Crouse, Leah Angstman, Joe Speer, and Ric Cafagna.

How to Submit: Submit 3 poems at a time. Accepts previously published poems and simultaneous submissions. Cover letter preferred. "Copies should be clean, crisp, and camera-ready. I do not have the means to accept electronic submissions. A SASE should accompany all submissions, and a telephone number if at all possible." Guidelines available for SASE. Time between acceptance and publication is 2 months. Seldom comments on rejected poems. Responds to queries and mss in up to 2 months. Pays at least 10 author's copies (out of a press run of 200-300). May offer subsidy arrangements. "I am new at this. And so it all depends upon my financial situation at the time. Yes, I might ask the author to subsidize the cost. It could be worth their while. I have good connections in the small press." Order sample publications by sending a 6×9 SAE. "There is no charge for samples."

Advice: "Experiment with thought, language, the printed word."

$ ◘ THE MASSACHUSETTS REVIEW, South College, University of Massachusetts, Amherst MA 01003. (413)545-2689. E-mail: massrev@external.umass.edu. Website: www.massreview.org. Established 1959. **Poetry Editors:** Paul Jenkins and Anne Halley.

● Work published in this review has been frequently included in volumes of *The Best American Poetry.*

Magazine Needs: Appearing quarterly, *The Massachusetts Review* publishes "fiction, essays, artwork, and excellent poetry of all forms and styles." Has published poetry by Marilyn Hacker, Virgil Suarez, and Miller Williams. *The Massachusetts Review* is digest-sized, offset-printed on bond paper, perfect-bound with color card cover with occasional art and photography sections. Receives about

2,500 poems/year, accepts about 50. Press run is 1,600 for 1,100-1,200 subscribers of which 1,000 are libraries, the rest for shelf sales. Subscription: $22/year (US), $30 outside US, $30 for libraries. Sample: $8 (US), $11 outside US.

How to Submit: No simultaneous submissions or previously published poems. Reads submissions October 1 through June 1 only. Guidelines available for SASE and on website. Responds in 6 weeks. Pays minimum of $10, or 35¢/line, plus 2 copies.

$ ⊘ ◎ MATURE YEARS (Specialized: senior citizen, Christian), P.O. Box 801, 201 Eighth Ave. S., Nashville TN 37202. (615)749-6292. Fax: (615)749-6512. E-mail: matureyears@ump ublishing.org. Established 1954. **Editor:** Marvin W. Cropsey.

Magazine Needs: *Mature Years* is a quarterly. "The magazine's purpose is to help persons understand and use the resources of Christian faith in dealing with specific opportunities and problems related to aging. Poems are usually limited to 16 lines and may, or may not, be overtly religious. Poems should not poke fun at older adults, but may take a humorous look at them. Avoid sentimentality and saccharine. If using rhymes and meter, make sure they are accurate." *Mature Years* is 112 pages, magazine-sized, perfect-bound, with full-color glossy paper cover. Press run is 55,000. Sample: $5.

How to Submit: Line length for poetry is 16 lines of up to 50 characters maximum. Accepts fax submissions; prefers e-mail submissions. Submit seasonal and nature poems for spring during December through February; for summer, March through May; for fall, June through August; and for winter, September through November. Guidelines available for SASE. Responds in 2 months; sometimes a year's delay before publication. Pays $1/line upon acceptance.

⊘ ◎ MAUSOLEUM: MORTIS ES VERITUS (Specialized: horror, dark fantasy), 6324 Locust, NE, Albuquerque NM 87113-1011. E-mail: c_ravenscar@hotmail.com. Website: www.geocit ies.com/crowravenscar. Established 1994. **Editor/Publisher:** Kelly Ganson (aka Crow Ravenscar).

Magazine Needs: *Mausoleum* appears annually in October, publishing fiction, poetry, and artwork. Wants "horror, Gothic horror, Wicca, dark fantasy and Renaissance horror for subject matter or genre. Free verse, rhyming verse, haiku, or humorous. Halloween themed is good. Absolutely no exploitation, sexual, graphic, or pornographic, cruelty to people or animals. If I see this, it'll be returned." Accepts poetry by young writers over age 16. Recently published poetry by John Grey, R. David Fulcher, Kelly Gunter Atlas, Leah Angstman, and Rain Oubliette. *Mausoleum* is 30 pages, digest-sized, photocopied, saddle-stapled, b&w cardstock/colored cardstock cover, with all original artwork, some computer graphics. Receives about 20 poems/year, accepts about 8%. Publishes about 14-16 poems/issue. Press run is 40 for 8 subscribers, 20 shelf sales; 10 distributed free to contributors. Single copy: $6.50 US. Sample: $5. Make checks payable to Kelly Ganson.

How to Submit: Submit 5 poems at a time. Line length for poetry is 10 minimum, 20 maximum. Accepts previously published poems and simultaneous submissions. No fax, e-mail, or disk submissions. Cover letter is required. "Name, address, e-mail, bio, etc., in cover letter. Always include SASE or I cannot respond." Reads submissions all year. Submit seasonal poems 3 months in advance (Halloween themed especially). Time between acceptance and publication is up to 1 year (annual publication). "I read the poems; if accepted, a release form and acceptance letter are sent to contributor. If rejected, a rejection notice goes to contributor." Always comments on rejected poems. "I *do* ask that a contributor buy a sample copy of the magazine or ask for guidelines before submitting poetry, fiction, or art." Occasionally publishes theme issues, "mostly Halloween themes, but sometimes vampires or werewolves." Upcoming themes available for SASE; guidelines available for SASE and on website. Responds in 3 weeks. Sometimes sends prepublication galleys. Pays 1 contributor's copy with discounts available on additional copies. Acquires one-time rights. Reviews other magazines/journals in 1-2 paragraphs. Poets may send magazines/journals for review consideration to *Mausoleam*.

Also Offers: SevenSkulls Entertainment/Gothia Graphics, "which will, in the future, be publishing books, chapbooks, novellas, and collections of horror, fantasy/sword & sorcery, dark fantasy, vampire fiction, and werewolf fiction. Poetry accepted." For guidelines and more detailed information, contact Kelly Ganson (above) or Rose Titus, 5 Fisk Rd., Andover MA 01810.

Advice: "Don't be afraid to submit! And if I do reject your work, it doesn't mean you are not good enough. It just means I couldn't use your work. Try again and keep trying!"

◉ ◯ **MAYPOLE EDITIONS**, 22 Mayfair Ave., Ilford, Essex IG1 3DQ England. (0181)252-0354.

Book/Chapbook Needs: Maypole Editions publishes 3 hardbacks/year of fiction and poetry, including anthologies. Wants "poems broadly covering social concerns, ethnic minorities, feminist issues, romance, lyric." Does not want "politics." Has published poetry by A. Lee Firth, Samantha Willow, Sam Smith, Brian Jeffry, Mindy Cresswell, Denise Bell, and Paul Amphlet. Sample: £7.95, add £2.50 US.

How to Submit: Query first with a few sample poems approximately 30 lines long and cover letter with brief bio and publication credits. Accepts submissions on disk (3.5 floppy) and by postal mail. Obtain samples of books by sending £1 and an A5 SAE for a catalog.

$ ◯ ◎ **MEADOWBROOK PRESS (Specialized: anthologies, children, humor)**, 5451 Smetana Dr., Minnetonka MN 55343. Website: www.meadowbrookpress.com. Established 1975.
Contact: Read 'Em, Rate 'Em editor.

Book/Chapbook Needs: Meadowbrook Press "is currently seeking poems to be posted on website and to be considered for future funny poetry book anthologies for children." Wants humorous poems aimed at children ages 6-12. "Poems should be fun, light and refreshing. We're looking for new, hilarious, contemporary voices in children's poetry that kids can relate to." Accepts poetry written by children "only for website contests—not for publication in books." Has published poetry by Shel Silverstein, Jack Prelutsky, Jeff Moss, Kenn Nesbitt, and Bruce Lansky. Anthologies have included *Kids Pick the Funniest Poems*; *A Bad Case of the Giggles*; and *Miles of Smiles*.

How to Submit: "Please take time to read our guidelines, and send your best work." Submit up to 10 poems; 1 poem to a page with name and address on each. Line length for poetry is 15 maximum. Include SASE with submission. Accepts simultaneous submissions. Cover letter required "just to know where the poet found us." Time between acceptance and publication is 1-2 years. Poems are tested in front of grade school students before being published. Guidelines available for SASE and on website. Pays $50-100/poem plus 1 copy.

◉ **MEDICINAL PURPOSES LITERARY REVIEW; MARILYN K. PRESCOTT MEMORIAL POETRY CONTEST; POET TO POET, INC.**, 86-37 120th St., #2D, Richmond Hill NY 11418. (718)776-8853 or (718)847-2150. E-mail: dunnmiracle@juno.com. Established 1994.
Executive Editor: Robert Dunn. **Managing Editor:** Thomas M. Catterson. **Associate Editor/Poetry Editor:** Leigh Harrison. **Prose Editor:** Anthony Scarpantonio.

Magazine Needs: *Medicinal Purposes* appears biannually and wants "virtually any sort of quality poetry (3 poems, up to 60 lines/poem). Please, no pornography, gratuitous violence, or hate mongering." Accepts poetry written by children for the young writers' column. Has published poetry by X.J. Kennedy, Rhina P. Espaillat, Maureen Holm, Ellen Peckham, and Philip Carwin. *Medicinal Purposes* is 40 pages, magazine-sized, professionally printed and perfect-bound with card stock cover with b&w illustration, b&w illustrations also inside. Receives 1,200 poems/year, accepts about 10%. Press run is 1,000 for 270 subscribers of which 6 are libraries, 30% shelf sales. Single copy: $9; subscription: $16/year. Sample: $6. Make checks payable to Poet to Poet.

How to Submit: Submit 3 poems at a time, up to 60 lines per poem, typed with SASE. No previously published poems or simultaneous submissions. Accepts e-mail submissions (in text box, no attachments). Cover letter preferred. Time between acceptance and publication is up to 16 months. Often comments on rejected poems. Guidelines available for SASE or by e-mail. Responds in 3 months. Always sends prepublication galleys. Pays 2 contributor's copies. Acquires first rights.

Also Offers: Produces a poetry/folk music public access cable show called "Poet to Poet." Also sponsors an annual poetry contest, 1st Prize $100. Submit 3 poems of 6-16 lines each with a $5 entry fee by June 15. Winners will be published in the year's end issue. Additionally they sponsor a chapbook contest. Also administers the Marilyn K. Prescott Memorial Poetry Contest. Details available for SASE.

Advice: "Poetry cannot be created out of a vacuum. Read the work of others, listen to performances, learn the difference between the universal and the generic, and most important—Get A Life! Do Things! If you get struck by lightning, then share the light. Only then do you stand a chance of finding your own voice."

★ ◑ MELLEN POETRY PRESS, P.O. Box 450, Lewiston NY 14092-0450. (716)754-2266. Fax: (716)754-4056. E-mail: mellen@wzrd.com. Website: www.mettenpress.com. Established 1973. **Poetry Editor:** Patricia Schultz.

Book/Chapbook Needs: "Mellen Poetry Press is a division of The Edwin Mellen Press, a scholarly press. We do not have access to large chain bookstores for distribution, but depend on direct sales and independent bookstores." Pays 5 copies, royalties "after 500 copies are sold for 5 years. We require no author subsidies. However, we encourage our authors to seek grants from Councils for the Arts and other foundations because these add to the reputation of the volume." Wants "original integrated work—living unity of poems, preferably unpublished, encompassable in one reading." Has published poetry by Andrew Oerke and James Sutton. Books are up to 128 pages, digest-sized, hardcover binding, no graphics. Price: $39.95.

How to Submit: Submit 70-120 sample poems with cover letter including bio and publications. "We do not print until we receive at least 50 prepaid orders. Successful marketing of poetry books depends on the author's active involvement. We send out free review copies to journals or newspapers when requested. An author may, but is not required to, purchase books that count toward the needed pre-publication sales."

Advice: "We seek to publish volumes unified in mood, tone, theme."

★ $ ◎ THE MENNONITE (Specialized: Christian), P.O. Box 347, Newton KS 67114-0347. (316)283-5100. Fax: (316)283-0454. E-mail: gordonh@themennonite.org. Website: www.themennonite.org. Established 1885. **Associate Editor:** Gordon Houser.

Magazine Needs: *The Mennonite* is published twice per month and wants "Christian poetry—usually free verse, not too long, with multiple layers of meaning. No sing-song rhymes or poems that merely describe or try to teach a lesson." Has published poetry by Jean Janzen and Julia Kasdorf. *The Mennonite* is 32 pages, magazine-sized, full color cover, includes art and ads. Receives about 200 poems/year, accepts about 5%. Press run is 16,500 for 16,000 subscribers. Single copy: $2; subscription: $38.75. Sample: $1.

How to Submit: Submit up to 4 poems at a time. Accepts previously published poems and simultaneous submissions. E-mail submissions preferred. Cover letter preferred. Time between acceptance and publication is up to 6 months. Seldom comments on rejected poems. Publishes theme issues occasionally. Guidelines and upcoming themes are available for SASE. Responds in 2 weeks. Pays $50-75 plus 2 copies. Acquires first or one-time rights.

★ $ ◑ MERIDIAN, University of Virginia, P.O. Box 400145, Charlottesville VA 22904-4145. (434)989-5793. E-mail: meridian@virginia.edu. Website: www.engl.virginia.edu/meridian. Established 1998. **Contact:** Poetry Editor.

Magazine Needs: *Meridian* appears biannually publishing poetry, fiction, interviews, and reviews. Recently published poetry by David Kirby, Charles Wright, and Joelle Biele. *Meridian* is 190 pages, digest-sized, offset-printed, perfect-bound, color cover, internal art. Receives about 2,500 poems/year, accepts about 30 (less than 1%). Publishes about 15 poems/issue. Press run is 1,000 for 750 subscribers of which 15 are libraries, 200 shelf sales; 150 are distributed free to writing programs. Single copy: $7; subscription: $10/year. Make checks payable to *Meridian*.

How to Submit: Submit 1-5 poems at a time. Accepts simultaneous submissions; no previously published poems. No fax, e-mail, or disk submissions. Cover letter is preferred. Reads submissions September-May primarily. Time between acceptance and publication is 1-2 months. Seldom comments on rejected poems. Guidelines available on website. Responds in up to 2 months. Sometimes sends prepublication galleys. Pays $15/page ($250 maximum, as long as funding is available) and 2 contributor's copies (additional copies available at discount). Reviews books of poetry.

▢ ◎ MERIDIAN ANTHOLOGY OF CONTEMPORARY POETRY; RACHEL BENT-LEY POETRY COMPETITION, P.O. Box 970309, Boca Raton FL 33497. E-mail: LetarP@aol.com. Website: www.Meridiananthology.com. Established 2002. **Editor/Publisher:** Phyliss L. Geller.

Magazine Needs: *Meridian Anthology of Contemporary Poetry* appears annually in November and wants "poetry that is contemporary, insightful, and illuminating, that touches the nerves. It should have color, content, and be deciphering of existence." Does not want vulgarity, clichés. Has published poetry by June Owens, John Grey, Richard St. John, Gerald Zipper, and Brenda Serratte. *Meridian*

Anthology is up to 96 pages (possibly more), digest-sized, offset-printed, perfect-bound, soft cover. Publishes about 75-90 poems/issue. Press run is 1,000. Single copy: $14 for soft cover. Make checks payable to *Meridian Anthology*.

How to Submit: Submit 1-5 poems at a time. Line length for poetry is 39 maximum. Accepts simultaneous submissions and previously published poems. No fax, e-mail, or disk submissions. Cover letter is preferred. Must include SASE. Reads submissions year round. Submit seasonal poems 6 months in advance. Time between acceptance and publication is up to 1 year. Seldom comments on rejected poems. Guidelines available for SASE or on website. Responds in "3 weeks to 3 months, depending on backlog." Pays 1 contributor's copy. Acquires one-time rights.

Also Offers: Rachel Bentley Poetry Competition awards $200 for 1st Place, plus winner will be featured with bio in an upcoming issue (3-4 line bio must be included with entry). Also awards 2nd Place: $50 and publication, 3rd Place: $25 and publication. **Entry fee:** $10 for 3 poems. **Deadline:** October 15.

Advice: "A poem must have a reason for existence, some universal tendril."

Ø MIAMI UNIVERSITY PRESS, English Dept., Miami University, Oxford OH 45056. (513)529-5110. Website: www.muohio.edu/mupress/. Established 1992. **Editor:** James Reiss.

Book/Chapbook Needs & How to Submit: Publishes 2 books/year in paperback and cloth editions by poets who have already published at least one full-length book of poems. Recent titles include *Ariadne's Island* by Molly Bendall, Winter 2002; *Gender Studies* by Jeffrey Skinner, Winter 2002; *Burning the Aspern Papers*, by John Drury, Winter 2003; *Beside Ourselves*, by Nance Van Winckel, Winter 2003. Currently closed to unsolicited poetry.

$Ø MICHIGAN QUARTERLY REVIEW; LAURENCE POETRY AWARD, Dept. PM, 3574 Rackham Bldg., University of Michigan, 915 E. Washington St., Ann Arbor MI 48109. (734)764-9265. E-mail: mqr@umich.edu. Website: www.umich.edu/~mqr. Established 1962. **Editor-in-Chief:** Laurence Goldstein.

• Poetry published in the *Michigan Quarterly Review* is frequently included in volumes of *The Best American Poetry* and has been selected for the 2002 *Pushcart Prize* anthology.

Magazine Needs: *Michigan Quarterly Review* is "an interdisciplinary, general interest academic journal that publishes mainly essays and reviews on subjects of cultural and literary interest." Uses all kinds of poetry except light verse. No specifications as to form, length, style, subject matter, or purpose. Has published poetry by Susan Hahn, Carl Phillips, Mary Oliver, and Yusef Komunyakaa. *Michigan Quarterly Review* is 160 pages, digest-sized, flat-spined, professionally printed with glossy card cover, b&w photos and art. Receives about 1,400 submissions/year, accepts about 30, has a 1-year backlog. Press run is 2,000, with 1,200 subscribers of which half are libraries. Single copy: $7; subscription: $25. Sample: $5 plus 2 first-class stamps.

How to Submit: Prefers typed mss. No previously published poems or simultaneous submissions. No fax or e-mail submissions. Cover letter preferred; "it puts a human face on the manuscript. A few sentences of biography is all I want, nothing lengthy or defensive." Publishes theme issues. Theme for autumn 2002 is "Jewish in America." Responds in 6 weeks. Always sends prepublication galleys. Pays $8-12/page. Acquires first rights only. Reviews books of poetry. "All reviews are commissioned."

Also Offers: The Laurence Poetry Award, an annual cash prize of $1,000 give to the author of the best poem to appear in *Michigan Quarterly* during the calendar year. "Established in 2002, the prize is sponsored by the Office of the President of the University of Michigan."

Advice: "There is no substitute for omnivorous reading and careful study of poets past and present, as well as reading in new and old areas of knowledge. Attention to technique, especially to rhythm and patterns of imagery, is vital."

$▢ ◎ THE MID-AMERICA PRESS, INC.; THE MID-AMERICA POETRY REVIEW; THE MID-AMERICA PRESS WRITING AWARD COMPETITION (Specialized: regional), P.O. Box 575, Warrensburg MO 64093-0575. (660)747-4602. Press established 1976. **Editor:** Robert C. Jones.

Magazine Needs: *Mid-America Poetry Review* appears 3 times/year and publishes "well-crafted poetry primarily from—but not limited to—poets living in Missouri, Illinois, Arkansas, Oklahoma,

Kansas, Nebraska, and Iowa. We are open to all styles and forms; what we look for is poetry by writers who know both what they are doing and why. We have a prejudice against work with content that is primarily self-indulgent or overly private." Has published poetry by David Anstaett, Brian Daldorph, Carol Hamilton, Simon Perchik, Jane Sasser, Jim Thomas, and Barbara Van Noord. *The Mid-America Poetry Review* is 60-70 pages, digest-sized, offset-printed and perfect-bound with matte-paper cover. Receives about 700-1,000 poems/year, accepts about 20%. Press run is 750. Single copy: $6; subscription: $30/2 years. Sample: $6. Make checks payable to The Mid-America Press, Inc.

How to Submit: Submit 1-3 poems at a time. No previously published poems or simultaneous submissions. Cover letter useful. "Type submissions, single- or double-spaced, on 8½×11 white paper; name, address, telephone number, and e-mail address (if available) in top left or right corner. Keep copy of your manuscript—unused submissions will be recycled; send SASE for notification. One-page cover letter (if included) should list items to be considered; contain brief paragraphs of information about author and previous publications." Time between acceptance and publication is up to 9 months. Sometimes comments on rejected poems. Guidelines available for SASE. Responds within 2 months. Sends prepublication galleys. Pays $5/poem and 2 contributor's copies. Acquires first North American serial rights. Staff occasionally reviews books of poetry. Send materials for review consideration.

Book/Chapbook Needs & How to Submit: The Mid-America Press, Inc. publishes 2-6 paperbacks per year with 1 book selected through The Mid-America Press Writing Award Competition. "At present—with the exception of entries for the competition—the Press is not reading unsolicited book-length poetry mss. The competition is limited to 48- to 148-page poetry mss (previously unpublished in book form) by poets living in Missouri, Arkansas, Oklahoma, Kansas, Nebraska, Iowa, or Illinois." Entry fee: $20. Entry guidelines and deadline date available for SASE. The winner of Writing Award 2001 was *The Graveyard Picnic*, by William Ford. Mid-America Press, Inc. award-winning publications include *Red Silk* (1999) by Maryfrances Wagner (winner of the 2000 Thorpe Menn Award for Writing Excellence) and *Living Off the Land, A Gathering of Writing from The Warrensburg Writers Circle* (1999) edited by Robert C. Jones (First Place in The 2000 Walter Williams Major Work Award, from the Missouri Writers' Guild). Other publications include *Outcasts, Poems* (2000), by Brian Daldorph; *Memories & Memoirs, Essays, Poems, Stories, Letters by Contemporary Missouri Authors* (2000), edited by Sharon Kinney Hanson; *Dreaming the Bronze Girl* (2002) by Sevina Allison Hearn; and *Light and Chance* (2001) by Ardyth Bradley. Obtain sample books by sending $13.95 per book (For *Memories & Memoirs*, send $18.95).

N ⓓ **MIDNIGHT MIND MAGAZINE**, P.O. Box 146912, Chicago IL 60614. (312)545-6129. E-mail: submissions@midnightmind.com. Website: www.midnightmind.com. Established 2000. **Editor:** Brett Van Emst.

Magazine Needs: *Midnight Mind Magazine*, a cultural review, appears biannually. Wants poetry of any style, any form. Does not want "poems about flowers" or seasonal poems. Recently published poetry by David Ray, Marion Boyer, Phillip Corwin, Audrianne Hill, Tim Kahl, and Tom Short. *Midnight Mind Magazine* is 180 pages, digest-sized, offset-printed, perfect-bound, cardstock cover with photography, includes ads. Receives about 300 poems/year, accepts about 10%. Publishes about 10 poems/issue. Press run is 2,000 for 150 subscribers, 500 shelf sales; 100 are distributed free to the press, advertisers, and bookstores. Single copy: $10 (includes postage); subscription: $12/year, $20/2 years. Make checks payable to 3 A.M. Publishing.

How to Submit: Submit any number poems at a time. Line length is open. Accepts simultaneous submissions; no previously published poems. Accepts e-mail submissions; no fax or disk submissions. Cover letter is preferred. "No crazy fonts!" Reads submissions year round. Time between acceptance and publication is 3-6 months. Poems are circulated to an editorial board. "There is a poetry editor, general editor, and advisory board—ALL are involved." Seldom comments on rejected poems. Regularly publishes theme issues. List of upcoming themes available by e-mail or on website. Guidelines available in magazine, for SASE, by e-mail, or on website. Responds in up to 6 months. Always sends prepublication galleys. Pays 2 contributor's copies. Acquires first North American serial rights. Reviews books and chapbooks of poetry and other magazines/journals in 500 words, single book format. Poets may send materials for review consideration to Brett Van Emst.

Advice: "Just write and send it out."

$ ◎ MIDSTREAM: A MONTHLY ZIONIST REVIEW (Specialized: ethnic), 633 Third Ave., 21st Floor, New York NY 10017. (212)339-6040. Fax: (212)318-6176. E-mail: midstreamTHF @aol.com. Website: www.midstreamTHF.com. **Editor:** Leo Haber.

Magazine Needs: *Midstream* is an international journal appearing 8 times/year. Wants short poems with Jewish themes or atmosphere. Has published poetry by Yehuda Amichai, Marge Piercy, Abraham Sutzkever, Liz Rosenberg, and John Hollander. *Midstream* is 48 pages, about magazine-sized, saddle-stapled with colored card cover. Each issue includes 4 to 5 poems (which tend to be short, lyric, and freestyle expressing seminal symbolism of Jewish history and Scripture). Receives about 300 submissions/year, accepts 5-10%. Press run is 10,000. Single copy: $3; subscription: $21.

How to Submit: Submit 2 poems at a time. Accepts e-mail submissions. Time between acceptance and publication is within 1 year. Publishes theme issues; "Our April issue centers on Holocaust material. Our July/August issue centers on Yiddish and Ladino." Responds in 6 months. Pays $25/ poem and 3 contributor's copies. Acquires first rights.

$ ◐ MIDWEST POETRY REVIEW, 7443 Oak Tree Lane, Springhill FL 34607-2324. (352)688-8116. E-mail: mariasingh@cs.com. Established 1980. **Editor/Publisher:** Pariksith Singh and Maria Scunziano.

Magazine Needs: *Midwest Poetry Review* appears annually in July, with no other support than subscriptions, contest entry fees, and an occasional advertisement. Looking for "quality, accessible verse. Evocative and innovative imagery with powerful adjectives and verbs. Poetry that opens the door to the author's feelings through sensory descriptions. We are attempting to encourage the cause of poetry by purchasing the best of modern poetry. Any subject is considered, if handled with skill and taste. No pornography. Nothing which arrives without SASE is read or gets a reply. We are open to new poets, but they must show talent." Accepts poetry written by children. "Must be good writing." Has published poetry by Rukmini Callamchi, B.R. Culbertson, Junette Fabian, Glenna Holloway, Mikal Lofgren, and Bettie Sellers. *Midwest Poetry Review* is 56 pages, professionally printed, digest-sized, saddle-stapled with matte card cover. Subscription: $20. Sample: $7 (when available).

How to Submit: Submit up to 5 poems at a time, 1 poem/page. Line length for poetry is 100 maximum. No previously published poems or simultaneous submissions. No bios or credit lists. Accepts disk and e-mail (in text box or as attachment) submissions. Guidelines are available for SASE, by e-mail, and in publication. "We will critique up to 10 of your poems at a time." Criticism fee: $10 plus SASE. Responds in 6 to 9 months due to the high volume of submissions. Pays $50/ poem. Acquires first rights.

Also Offers: Has varied contests in each issue, with prizes ranging from $10-250, with "unbiased, non-staff judges for all competitions." Contests have entry fees. Details available for SASE.

◐ THE MIDWEST QUARTERLY, Pittsburg State University, Pittsburg KS 66762. (316)235-4689. Fax: (316)235-4686. E-mail: smeats@pittstate.edu. Website: www.pittstate.edu/engl/midwest.h tml. Established 1959. **Poetry Editor:** Stephen Meats.

Magazine Needs: *Midwest Quarterly* "publishes articles on any subject of contemporary interest, particularly literary criticism, political science, philosophy, education, biography, and sociology, and each issue contains a section of poetry usually 15 poems in length. I am interested in well-crafted, though not necessarily traditional poems that explore the inter-relationship of the human and natural worlds in bold, surrealistic images of a writer's imaginative, mystical experience. Sixty lines or less (occasionally longer if exceptional)." Has published poetry by David Baker, Fleda Brown, Jim Daniels, Naomi Shibab Nye, Grey Kuzma, Walt McDonald, Jeanne Murray Walker, and Peter Cooley. *Midwest Quarterly* is 130 pages, digest-sized, professionally printed and flat-spined with matte cover. Press run is 650 for 600 subscribers of which 500 are libraries. Receives about 4,000 poems/year, accepts about 60. Subscription: $12. Sample: $5.

How to Submit: Mss should be typed with poet's name on each page, 10 poems or fewer. Accepts simultaneous submissions; no previously published poems. No fax or e-mail submissions. Occasionally publishes theme issues. Guidelines and upcoming themes available for SASE, by fax, or by e-mail. Responds in 2 months, usually sooner. "Submissions without SASE cannot be acknowledged." Pays 3 contributor's copies. Acquires first serial rights. Editor comments on rejected poems "if the poet or poems seem particularly promising." Reviews books of poetry by *Midwest Quarterly* published poets only.

Advice: "Keep writing; read as much contemporary poetry as you can lay your hands on; don't let the discouragement of rejection keep you from sending your work out to editors."

◎ ⊘ **MIDWEST VILLAGES & VOICES (Specialized: regional)**, P.O. Box 40214, St. Paul MN 55104. (612)822-6878. Established 1979.
Book/Chapbook Needs & How to Submit: Midwest Villages & Voices is a cultural organization and small press publisher of Midwestern poetry and prose. "We encourage and support Midwestern writers and artists. However, at this time submissions are accepted by invitation only. Unsolicited submissions are not accepted."

◎ **MIDWIFERY TODAY (Specialized: childbirth)**, P.O. Box 2672, Eugene OR 97402-0223. (541)344-7438. Fax: (541)344-1422. E-mail: editorial@midwiferytoday.com. Website: www.midwife rytoday.com. Established 1986. **Editor-in-Chief:** Jan Tritten. **Editor:** Jessica Cagle.
Magazine Needs: *Midwifery Today* is a quarterly that "provides a voice for midwives and childbirth educators. We are a midwifery magazine. Subject must be birth or birth profession related." Does not want poetry that is "off subject or puts down the subject." *Midwifery Today* is 75 pages, magazine-sized, offset-printed, saddle-stapled, with glossy card cover with b&w photos and b&w artwork photos, and ads inside. Uses about 1 poem/issue. Press run is 5,000 for 3,000 subscribers, 1,000 shelf sales. Subscription: $50. Sample: $10.
How to Submit: No previously published poems. Accepts e-mail submissions (as attachment or in text box). Cover letter required. Time between acceptance and publication is 1-2 years. Seldom comments on rejected poems. Publishes theme issues. Past theme issues include Spring 2003: Tear Prevention (deadline: December 1, 2002); Summer 2003: Birth Environment (deadline: March 1, 2003); Fall 2003: Fear in Midwifery and Birth (deadline: June 1, 2003). Upcoming themes available on website. Guidelines available for SASE and on website. Responds in 6 months. Pays 2 contributor's copies. Acquires first rights.
Advice: "With our publication *please* stay on the subject."

◢ **MILKWEED EDITIONS**, 1011 Washington Ave. S., Suite 300, Minneapolis MN 55415-1246. (612)332-3192. Fax: (612)215-2550. E-mail: editor@milkweed.org. Website: www.milkweed.org. Established 1979. **Contact:** Poetry Reader.
Book/Chapbook Needs: Milkweed Editions is "looking for poetry manuscripts of high quality that embody humane values and contribute to cultural understanding." Not limited in subject matter, though poetry about natural world preferred for "The World As Home: Literature About the Natural World" publishing program. Open to writers with previously published books of poetry or a minimum of 6 poems published in nationally distributed commercials or literary journals. Accepts translations and bilingual mss. Published books of poetry include *Turning Over the Earth*, by Ralph Black; *Song of the World Becoming*, by Pattiann Rogers; and *The Porcelain Apes of Moses Mendelssohn*, by Jean Nordhaus.
How to Submit: Submit 60 pages or more, typed on good quality white paper. Do not send originals. No submissions by fax or e-mail. Include SASE for our reply. Unsolicited mss read in January and June *only*. "Milkweed can no longer return manuscripts in stamped book mailers. In the event that manuscripts are not accepted for publication, we prefer to recycle them. If you need your work returned, *please enclose a check for $5* rather than a stamped mailer." Guidelines available for SASE. Responds in up to 6 months. Catalog available on request, with $1.50 in postage.

◢ **MILKWOOD REVIEW**, Georgia College and State University, CBX 44, Dept. of English, Speech, and Journalism, Milledgeville GA 31061. E-mail: milkwoodreview@yahoo.com. Website: www.milkwoodreview.com. Established 2000. **Editors:** Joel Peckham and Susan Atefat Peckham.
Magazine Needs: *The Milkwood Review* is constantly updated and available year round in annual issues online. "*The Milkwood Review* is an interdisciplinary journal that seeks to create a web environment in which poetry, fiction, nonfiction, speculative essays, short scholarly articles, etc., are presented in a form appropriate to the material. All creative work appears with audio samples." Will consider "any kind of poetry from narrative to lyric, from traditional to experimental—no length or line-length restrictions. Because of the journal's commitment to real-audio technology, we favor work that concentrates on poetry as a musical form of literature in which sound is as important as meaning."

Does not want "work that is uncrafted or facile." Recently published poetry by Minnie Bruce Pratt, Charles Fishman, and Timothy Skeen.

The Milkwood Review is published online with a fine art cover and art/graphics. Accepts about 10% of poems submitted. Publishes 15-30 poems/issue.

How to Submit: Submit 4-8 poems at a time. Accepts previously published poems and simultaneous submissions. Accepts submissions by e-mail (as attachment or in text box) and by postal mail. Cover letter is required. "Each poem printed in *Milkwood* will include an audio file. Once a poem has been accepted (not before) we will require the author to submit a recorded version of the piece." Reads submissions year-round. Submit seasonal poems anytime. Time between acceptance and publication is up to 6 months. "Poems are read by both editors and full staff. Final decisions on the publication of work in *Milkwood* rest with the founding editors." Often comments on rejections. Occasionally publishes theme issues. A list of upcoming themes is available for SASE. Guidelines are available for SASE and on website. Sometimes sends prepublication galleys. No pay; publication only. Acquires first North American serial or one-time rights, reverts to poet upon publication. Reviews books, and chapbooks of poetry and other magazines, open length, in single and multibook format. Send materials for review consideration to the editors.

Advice: "Read poetry—but also, *listen to it*. Pay attention not only to the precise and intentional placement of words but to the momentum they create, the surge and urge of the poem."

$⬛ MILLER'S POND; LOELLA CADY LAMPHIER PRIZE FOR POETRY; H&H PRESS, RR 2, Box 241, Middlebury Center PA 16935. (570)376-3361. Fax: (570)376-2674. E-mail: publisher@millerspondpoetry.com. Website: http://millerspondpoetry.com. Established 1987. **Publisher:** C.J. Houghtaling. **Editor:** David Cazden. **Web Editor:** Julie Damerell

Magazine Needs: Published in January, *miller's pond* is an annual magazine featuring contemporary poetry, interviews, reviews, and markets. "We want contemporary poetry that is fresh, accessible, energetic, vivid, and flows with language and rhythm. No religious, horror, pornographic, vulgar, rhymed, preachy, lofty, trite, or overly sentimental work." Has published poetry by Vivian Shipley, Robert Cooperman, Terese Coe, and Reid Bush. *miller's pond* is 48 pages, digest-sized, offset-printed and saddle-stapled with cardstock cover. Receives about 200 poems/year, accepts 20-25 poems/issue. Press run is 200. Single copy: $10. Sample (back issue) including guidelines: $8. Make checks payable to H&H Press.

How to Submit: Submit 3-5 poems at a time. Line length for poetry is 40 maximum. Accepts previously published poems and simultaneous submissions. Accepts submissions by postal mail and through online submission form. Cover letter preferred. "No returns without SASE." Reads submissions May 1 through November 1 only. Time between acceptance and publication is up to 1 year. Seldom comments on rejected poems. Guidelines available for SASE, on website, or in publication. Responds in up to 11 months; "although we try to respond sooner, we are not always able to." Sometimes sends prepublication galleys. Pays $2/poem and 1 copy for work that appears in hard copy version. Acquires one-time rights. Reviews books of poetry in up to 500 words, single book format.

Also Offers: H&H Press sponsors the Loella Lamphier Prize for Poetry. Awards $100 for 1st Place, $50 for 2nd Place and $25 3rd Place. Guidelines available on website. Send SASE. "*miller's pond* will be holding a chapbook competition. All updates will be posted on the website." Also, website features original content not found in magazine. Accepts submissions through an online submission form only. Contact web editor Julie Damerell.

Book/Chapbook Needs & How to Submit: "H&H Press is a micro-publisher of poetry chapbooks and how-to-write books, with plans to expand into nonfiction and specialty books." Publishes 1 paperback and 1 chapbook per year. Books are usually 24-36 pages, magazine-sized, offset-printed and saddle-stapled with cardstock cover, includes some art. "By invitation only; do not query. My requirements are simple—the poem/poetry must speak to me on more than one level and stay with me for more than just those few brief moments I'm reading it." Responds in 4 months. Pays royalties of 7% minimum, 12% maximum and 25 author's copies (out of a press run of 200). Books are available for sale via website, phone, or fax.

Advice: "Believe in yourself. Perseverance is a writer's best 'tool.' Study the contemporary masters: Vivian Shipley, Billy Collins, Maxine Kumin, Colette Inez, Hayden Carruth. Please check our website before submitting."

⊘ MIND PURGE, 6001 Skillman St., Apt. #163, Dallas TX 75231. E-mail: mind_purge@yahoo.c om. Established 1994. **Editor:** Jason Hensel.

Magazine Needs: *Mind Purge* is a biannual literary and art magazine appearing in April and October that publishes poetry, short fiction, one-act plays, short screenplays, essays, book reviews, and art. Wants poetry that is "well-crafted, insightful, imagistic. No specifications as to form, length, subject matter, or style. However no greeting card verse, hackneyed themes or poetry that says nothing or goes nowhere." Has published poetry by Lyn Lifshin, Robert Cooperman, Wayne Hogan, B.Z. Niditch, and Ryan G. Van Cleave. *Mind Purge* is 36-52 pages, digest-sized, neatly printed and saddle-stapled with matte card stock cover with b&w or color photo. Receives about 100 poems/year, accepts 10%. Press run is 100 for 10 subscribers. Subscription: $10. Sample: $4. Make checks payable to Jason Hensel.

How to Submit: Submit up to 5 poems or 10 pages at a time, name and address on each page. No previously published poems or simultaneous submissions. Accepts e-mail submissions (in body of message). Cover letter preferred. Seldom comments on rejected poems. Responds within 3 months. Pays 1 contributor's copy. Reviews books of poetry in 200 words, single book format. Send materials for review consideration.

Advice: "Read, read, read everything!"

Ⓝ ○ MINDBEND; FLAXENMULLET PRESS, Box 4871, Newark OH 43058. E-mail: grimm amanda@hotmail.com. Established 2003. **Editor:** Amanda Grimm.

Magazine Needs: "*Mindbend* is a new biannual publication looking to support the arts outside of academia. I'm committed to publishing new and up-and-coming artists as well as those already well published in the small press world." Wants "poetry that I can taste. Art that I can touch. I want vivid images, daring form." Does not want "anything dull." *Mindbend* is digest-sized, professionally-printed, saddle-stapled, cardstock cover with color artwork, includes b&w internal art; will swap ads. Single copy: $5. Make checks payable to Amanda Grimm.

How to Submit: Submit 3-5 poems at a time. Accepts simultaneous submissions; no previously published poems. No fax, e-mail, or disk submissions. Cover letter is preferred. Include a short bio and SASE. "As editor, I alone will review submitted work. I will choose works that seem the most honest and uncompromising. I will avoid work that tries too hard to fit into a category." Seldom comments on rejected poems. Guidelines available by e-mail. Sometimes sends prepublication galleys. Pays 1 contributor's copy. Acquires one-time rights.

Ⓝ ○ Ⓖ MINDPRINTS, A LITERARY JOURNAL (Specialized: writers & artists with disabilities), Learning Assistance Program, Allan Hancock College, 800 South College Dr., Santa Maria CA 93454-6399. (805)922-6966, ext. 3274. Fax: (805)922-3556. E-mail: pafahey@hancock.cc. ca.us. Website: www.hancockcollege.edu (click on Student Services, then Learning Assistance Program, then Mindprints). Established 2000. **Editor:** Paul Fahey.

  ● *Mindprints* was named one of the Top 30 Short Story Markets by *Writer's Digest* (June 2002)

Magazine Needs: "*Mindprints, A Literary Journal* is a national annual publication of flash fiction, flash memoir, poetry, and black-and-white artwork. The journal is created as a forum for writers and artists with disabilities, but we also invite those who work in the field or have an interest in the population to submit their work. *Mindprints* takes great pride in showcasing new artists and giving voice to new writers. We also welcome and encourage established writers and artists." Wants all kinds of poetry. "We love anything short: haiku, haibun, cinquain; prose and rhyming poetry with unusual imagery." Recently published poetry by Barbara Crooker, LaVonne Schoneman, Margaret Davidson, Marganit Alverez, Denize Lavoie Cain, and Joan C. Fingon. *Mindprints* is digest-sized, perfect-bound, gloss laminated cover, with internal b&w and digital artwork and photography. Receives about 150 poems/year, publishes about 22/issue. Press run is 600. "We sell copies at book fairs and to the community out of our office." Single copy: $6 plus $2 first class postage. Make checks payable to Allan Hancock College.

How to Submit: Submit up to 3 poems per reading period. Line length for poetry is 34 maximum. Accepts previously published poems and simultaneous submissions. Accepts e-mail submissions **only if poet resides outside the States**; accepts disk submissions only once the poems are accepted; no fax submissions. Cover letter is required. "Please send cover letter and SASE. In cover letter, tell us something about yourself, previous publications, if applicable, and tell us why you are submitting to

Mindprints." Accepts submissions year-round and begins reading collected submissions April 1; contributors are notified in late May. Time between acceptance and publication is 3-4 months. Poems are circulated to an editorial board. "We have a poetry editor who is an established poet and instructor at the college who reads the poetry and ranks it. (All identifying information has been removed.)" Seldom comments on rejected poems. Guidelines available in magazine, for SASE, or on website. Pays 1 contributor's copy. Acquires one-time rights.

Advice: "We are one of the few national community college journals devoted to celebrating the work of artists and writers with disabilities. We look for a strong voice, unusual point of view, and rich imagery and description."

THE MINNESOTA REVIEW: A JOURNAL OF COMMITTED WRITING (Specialized: political, social issues), English Dept., University of Missouri-Columbia, 110 Tate Hall, Columbia MO 65211. Fax: (573)882-5785. E-mail: WilliamsJeff@missouri.edu. Established 1960. **Editor:** Jeffrey Williams.

Magazine Needs: *The Minnesota Review* is a biannual literary magazine wanting "poetry which explores some aspect of social or political issues and/or the nature of relationships. No nature poems, and no lyric poetry without the above focus." Has published poetry by Hollander and Fuentes Lemus. *The Minnesota Review* is about 200 pages, digest-sized, flat-spined, with b&w glossy card cover and art. Press run is 1,500 for 800 subscribers. Subscription: $30/2 years to individuals; $45/1 year to institutions. Sample: $12.

How to Submit: Address submissions to "Poetry Editor" (not to a specific editor). No fax or e-mail submissions. Cover letter including "brief intro with address" preferred. SASE with sufficient postage required for return of mss. Publishes theme issues. Upcoming themes available for SASE. Responds in up to 4 months. Pays 2 contributor's copies. Acquires all rights. Returns rights upon request.

$ THE MIRACULOUS MEDAL (Specialized: religious, Catholic), 475 E. Chelten Ave., Philadelphia PA 19144-5785. (215)848-1010. Established 1928. **Editor:** Rev. James O. Kiernan, C.M.

Magazine Needs: *Miraculous Medal* is a religious quarterly. "Poetry should reflect solid Catholic doctrine and experience. Any subject matter is acceptable, provided it does not contradict the teachings of the Roman Catholic Church. Poetry must have a religious theme, preferably about the Blessed Virgin Mary." Has published poetry by Gladys McKee. *Miraculous Medal* is 32 pages, digest-sized, saddle-stapled, 2-color inside and cover, no ads. *Miraculous Medal* is used as a promotional piece and is sent to all clients of the Central Association of the Miraculous Medal. Circulation is 250,000.

How to Submit: Sample and guidelines free for postage. Line length for poetry is 20 maximum, double-spaced. No simultaneous submissions or previously published poems. Responds in up to 3 years. Pays 50¢ and up/line, on acceptance. Acquires first North American rights.

$ THE MISSING FEZ; THE RED FELT AWARD, P.O. Box 57310, Tucson AZ 85711. E-mail: missingfez@hotmail.com. Website: www.missingfez.com. Established 1999. **Poetry Editor:** Alan Brich.

Magazine Needs: Appearing in January and July, *The Missing Fez* is "a forum for the abnormal in literature. We want poems that embody some form of strangeness or oddity in either style, content, or language. Give us something different. No poems that rhyme or are about pets, or would meet parental approval." Has published poetry by Matthew Scrivner, Elise Mandernack, Ruby Jetts, Jefferson Carter, and Ian Gill. *The Missing Fez* is 100 pages, digest-sized, photocopied on laser quality paper and perfect-bound, includes b&w photos and illustrations. Receives about 150 poems/year, accepts 15%. Publish 3-5 poems/issue. Press run is 1,000 for 800 subscribers, 600 shelf sales; 100

THE GEOGRAPHICAL INDEX in the back of this book helps you locate markets in your region.

distributed free to sponsored reading series. Single copy: $10; subscription: $15/year. Sample: $5. Make checks payable to Red Felt Publishing.

How to Submit: Submit 3-5 poems at a time with **$3 reading fee**. Accepts previously published poems and simultaneous submissions. No fax or e-mail submissions. Cover letter preferred. "We do require $3 reading fee and SASE since we comment on all submissions and pay on acceptance." Time between acceptance and publication is 3-6 months. Always comments on rejected poems. Occasionally publishes theme issues. Guidelines and a list of upcoming themes available for SASE or on website. Responds in up to 3 months. Pays $15 for 2-3 poems plus 2 copies. Acquires one-time rights.

Also Offers: Sponsors the annual Red Felt Award. 1st Prize winner receives $250. Complete guidelines available for SASE or on website.

Advice: "Don't write safe poetry—if you do, don't send it to us."

MISSISSIPPI REVIEW, University of Southern Mississippi, Box 5144, Hattiesburg MS 39406-5144. (601)266-4321. Fax: (601)266-5757. E-mail: fbx@comcast.net or rief@netdoor.com. Website: www.mississippireview.com. **Editor:** Frederick Barthelme. **Managing Editor:** Rie Fortenberry.

Magazine Needs & How to Submit: Literary publication for those interested in contemporary literature. Publishes 2 issues annually; one, edited by a guest editor, uses only solicited material while the other publishes contest finalists. "The guest editors for upcoming issues will always be listed on the home page of the magazine. If you can find no editor and issue listed there, then the magazine is not reading new work for the moment." Submissions accepted by e-mail (either as Word or RTF attachment or in text box). Guidelines available on website.

Also Offers: The Mississippi Review Prize. Contest open to all US writers except current or former students and employees of USM. Submit up to 3 poems (10 pages maximum). Does not accept previously published material. "Entrants should put 'MR Prize,' name, address, phone, e-mail, and title on page one of entry." No limit to number of entries. Reads submissions April 1 to October 1, 2003. **Fee:** $15 per entry. **Postmark Deadline:** October 1, 2003. Prize: publication and $1,000. Finalists published in prize issue. Each entrant receives a copy of prize issue. No mss returned. Winners announced late January 2004 and published April 2004. Judges for 2003: Angela Ball (poetry) and both Mary Robison and Frederick Barthelme (fiction).

$ MISSOURI REVIEW; TOM MCAFEE DISCOVERY FEATURE; LARRY LEVIS EDITORS' PRIZE IN POETRY, 1507 Hillcrest Hall, University of Missouri, Columbia MO 65211. (573)882-4474. E-mail: marta@moreview.org. Website: www.morereview.org. Established 1978. **Contact:** Poetry Editor.

Magazine Needs: *Missouri Review* appears 3 times/year, publishing poetry features only—6-14 pages for each of 3 to 5 poets/issue. "By devoting more editorial space to each poet, *Missouri Review* provides a fuller look at the work of some of the best writers composing today." Has published poetry by Quan Barry, Anna Meek, Timothy Liu, Bob Hicok, George Bilgere, and Camille Dungy. Subscription: $22. Sample: $8.

How to Submit: Submit 6-12 poems at a time. No previously published poems or simultaneous submissions. Include SASE. Reads submissions year round. Responds in up to 3 months. Sometimes sends prepublication galleys. Pays 3 copies and $25/page, $200 maximum. Acquires all rights. Returns rights "after publication, without charge, at the request of the authors." Staff reviews books of poetry.

Also Offers: Offers the Tom McAfee Discovery Feature at least once a year to showcase an outstanding young poet who has not yet published a book; poets are selected from regular submissions at the discretion of the editors. Also offers the Larry Levis Editors' Prize in Poetry. 1st Prize: $2,000; and publication. Three finalists receive a minimum of $100, or consideration for publication at regular rates. Enter any number of poems up to 10 pages. Guidelines available for SASE or on website. Entry fee: $15.

Advice: "We remain dedicated to publishing at least one younger or emerging poet in every issue."

MÖBIUS, P.O. Box 7544, Talleyville DE 19803-0544. E-mail: mobiusmag@aol.com. Website: www.mobiuspoetry.com. Established 1982. **Editor:** Jean Hull Herman.

Magazine Needs: *Möbius* is published twice/year, on Memorial Day and Thanksgiving. Looks for "the informed mind responding to the challenges of reality and the expression of the imagination in poetry that demonstrates intelligence and wit. Poets should say significant, passionate things about the larger world outside themselves, using all the resources of the English language. Preference is given to poetry that pleases the ear as well as the intellect and soul; strong preference is given to work that is fine, structured, layered, as opposed to untitled, unpunctuated jottings. General topics include usage of language and the forms of poetry; the great philosophical questions; romance; relationships; war/peace; science and technology; everyday life; and humor (the editor has a weakness for humorous lines). The magazine claims no rights to poems. Delaware's only poetry magazine, Möbius has published poetry not only from 50 states but also from all seven continents." Has published poetry by Gerald Zipper, Simon Perchik, Ellaraine Lockie, Karen Springer, Earl Maxwell Coleman, and Suellen Lawish. *Möbius* is 60-70 pages, magazine-sized, professionally printed and perfect-bound. Single copy: $10; subscription: $8/year (2 issues). Sample: $10.

How to Submit: Submit up to 4 poems at a time, typed with name and address on each poem, 1 submission/issue. Simultaneous submissions accepted. Accepts submissions by e-mail from poets outside US; domestic submissions by postal mail only. Submissions read year-round. Responds in 3 months. Comments on rejected poems. Pays 1 contributor's copy. Guidelines available for SASE, on website, and in publication.

Advice: "Fine poetry will be as strong on the printed page as it will if being read aloud. Use all the resources of the English language, including the basics of grammar as well as poetic diction."

$ ☐ ◎ MODERN HAIKU; FOUR HIGH SCHOOL SENIOR SCHOLARSHIPS (Specialized: translations; form, haiku/senryu/haibun), P.O. Box 68, Lincoln IL 62656. Website: www.modernhaiku.org. Established 1969. Poetry Editor: Lee Gurga.

Magazine Needs: *Modern Haiku* appears 3 times/year in February, June, and October and "is the foremost international journal of English language haiku and criticism. We are devoted to publishing only the very best haiku being written and also publish articles on haiku and have the most complete review section of haiku books. Issues average 90 pages." Wants "contemporary haiku in English (including translations into English) that incorporate the traditional aesthetics of the haiku genre, but which may be innovative as subject matter, mode of approach or angle of perception, and form of expression. Haiku, senryu, and haibun only. No tanka or other forms." Accepts poetry written by children. Has published haiku by Cor van den Heuvel, Billy Collins, and Jane Hirschfield. The digest-sized magazine appears 3 times/year, printed on heavy quality stock with cover illustrations especially painted for each issue by the staff artist. Receives about 12,000-14,000 submissions/year, accepts about 500. There are over 150 poems in each issue. Press run is 1,000. Subscription: $21. Sample: $8.

How to Submit: Submit on "any size sheets, any number of haiku on a sheet; but name and address on each sheet." Include SASE. No previously published haiku or simultaneous submissions. Guidelines available for SASE. Responds in 2 weeks. Pays $1/haiku (but no contributor's copy). Acquires first North American serial rights. Staff reviews books of haiku in 350-1,000 words, single book format. Send materials for review consideration.

Also Offers: Offers 4 annual scholarships for the best haiku by high school seniors. Scholarships range from $200-500 (total $1,400). Deadline is mid-March. Rules available for SASE. Also offers $200 Best of Issue Awards.

Advice: "Study what haiku really are. We do not want sentimentality, pretty-pretty, or pseudo-Japanese themes. Juxtaposition of seemingly disparate entities that nonetheless create harmony is very desirable."

◖ MOJO RISIN'; JOSH SAMUELS ANNUAL POETRY COMPETITION, P.O. Box 268451, Chicago IL 60626-8451. Established 1995. Editor: Ms. Josh Samuels.

Magazine Needs: *mojo risin'*, published biannually in February and August, features "poetry, prose, short stories, articles, and black & white artwork in each issue." Wants "any form or style." Does not want "incest, racism, blatant sex, or anything written for shock value." Has published poetry by A.D. Winans, Alan Catlin, T.K. Splake, B.Z. Niditch, James Metlicka, and Gene Mahoney. *mojo risin'* is 36 pages, magazine-sized, photocopied, saddle-stapled with colored cardstock cover and b&w artwork. Receives about 500 poems/year, accepts 30%. Press run is 300 for 200 subscribers. Subscription: $20/year; $30/2 years. Sample: $7.

How to Submit: Subscription not required for acceptance. Submit 3-5 poems (2 pages maximum) at a time. No previously published poems or simultaneous submissions. Cover letter preferred. Time between acceptance and publication is up to 6 months. The editor is solely responsible for all aspects of editing and publishing. Guidelines available for SASE. Responds within 10 days. Manuscripts not returned. Acquires first North American serial rights.

Also Offers: Sponsors the Josh Samuels Annual Poetry Competition. 1st Place: $100; 2nd Place: $75; 3rd Place $50. Entry fee: $10/5 poems maximum. Any form, style or subject. No previously published poems or simultaneous submissions. Mss not returned. Deadline: November 30. Submissions read March through November only. Winners published and paid in February. Guidelines available for SASE.

Advice: "Writers should never use form letters or preprinted cover letters with their submissions. I am offended by them and will likely reject the work. Also, always re-type previously rejected work from other editors. I don't want to know that I'm receiving work that no one else wants because I will usually follow suit."

MONAS HIEROGLYPHICA, 58 Seymour Rd., Hadleigh, Benfleet, Essex SS7 2HL United Kingdom. E-mail: monas_hieroglyphica@postmaster.co.uk. Website: www.geocities.com/terribleport/. Established 1994. **Contact:** Mr. Jamie Spracklen.

Magazine Needs: *Monas Hieroglyphica* appears quarterly. Wants poetry concerning social issues, spirituality, the psychic/occult, and horror. No racist or sexist work. Accepts poetry written by children. Has published poetry by Sean Russell Friend and Steve Sneyd. *Monas Hieroglyphica* is 30 pages, magazine-sized, photocopied and bound with paper cover, includes art/graphics and ads. Receives about 100 poems/year, accepts 25%. Press run is 500 for 400 subscribers. Single copy: £5; subscription: £20, English funds only please. Make checks payable to Jamie Spracklen.

How to Submit: Submit 3 poems at a time. Line length for poetry is 60 maximum. Accepts simultaneous submissions; no previously published poems. Accepts submissions by e-mail (as attachment), on disk, and by post. Cover letter required. "Poems must be typed on size A4 paper and in English." Time between acceptance and publication is 3 months. Seldom comments on rejected poems. Occasionally publishes theme issues. Upcoming themes and guidelines available on website and in publication. Responds in 2 weeks. Pays 1 copy. "Rights stay with author." Reviews books and chapbooks of poetry and other magazines in 20 words, multi-book format. Send materials for review consideration.

MONKEY'S FIST; PATHFINDER PRESS, P.O. Box 316, Madison ME 04950-0316. Established 2001. **Co-editors:** Robin Merrill, Heidi Parker.

Magazine Needs: *Monkey's Fist* appears 2-3 times/year. Wants "edgy, sassy, accessible poetry that lives in the real world. We accept all forms and styles, but modern free verse dominates our pages. Have something to say and say it well." NOTE: "Our journal has nothing to do with monkeys and we have two female editors. Keep these things in mind." Recently published poetry by Nancy A. Henry, Louis McKee, Jennifer Stanley, and Karl Koweski. *Monkey's Fist* is 60 pages, digest-sized, photocopied, saddle-stapled, cardstock cover with b&w art. Receives hundreds of poems/year, accepts about 5%. Publishes about 15-20 poems/issue. Press run is 100 for 50 subscribers. Single copy: $3; subscription: $6. Make checks payable to Robin Merrill.

How to Submit: Submit 3 poems at a time. Accepts previously published poems and simultaneous submissions. No fax, e-mail, or disk submissions. Cover letter is " absolutely mandatory. Have some manners. In your letter, name your favorite small press publication." Poems should be submitted one/page on plain white 8½ × 11 paper, name and address on each page. "Send in white #10 envelope and include SASE. We like creases and dislike big brown envelopes and wasted stamps." Reads submissions January 1 through February 28 **only**. Time between acceptance and publication is up to 1 year. "Poems are read by two editors who duke it out." Often comments on rejected poems. Occasionally publishes theme issues. List of upcoming themes and guidelines available in magazine. "Do not send for guidelines. Just be courteous and professional and follow the guidelines here." Responds in up to 2 months. Sometimes sends prepublication galleys. Pays 1 contributor's copy. Acquires one-time rights. Reviews chapbooks of poetry. Poets may send materials for review consideration to Robin Merrill.

Book/Chapbook Needs & How to Submit: Pathfinder Press publishes occasional chapbooks by poets published in *Monkey's Fist*. Publishes 1-2 chapbooks/year. Chapbooks are photocopied, saddle-stapled, b&w cardstock covers. Query first, with a few sample poems and a cover letter with brief bio and publication credits. Chapbook mss may include previously published poems. "Our chaps are generally solicited, but if you have something that's going to take our heads off, we want to see it." Pays 20 author's copies (out of a press run of 50). Order sample chapbooks by sending $3 to Robin Merrill.

Also Offers: Prizes awarded to winner of the "Reader's Choice Award" of each issue.

Advice: "Submit to *Monkey's Fist*. We don't care if we've never heard of you."

✖ 🄌 MOTHER EARTH INTERNATIONAL JOURNAL; NATIONAL POETRY ASSOCIATION; POETRY FILM FESTIVAL,

% National Poetry Association, 934 Brannan St., 2nd Floor, San Francisco CA 94103. (415)552-9261. Fax: (415)552-9271. Website: www.nationalpoetry.org. *Mother Earth International Journal* established 1991, National Poetry Association in 1976. **Editor/Publisher:** Herman Berlandt.

Magazine Needs: "*Mother Earth International* is the only on-going anthology of contemporary poetry in English translation from all regions of the world. *Mother Earth International Journal* provides a forum to poets to comment in poetic form on political, economic, and ecological issues." Wants "bold and compassionate poetry that has universal relevance with an emphasis on the world's current political and ecological crisis. No self-indulgent or prosaic stuff that lacks imagination." Has published poetry by Lawrence Ferlinghetti (USA), Tanure Ojaide (Nigeria), Marianne Larsen (Denmark), Ping Hsin (China), Simon Ortiz (USA), and Takashi Arima (Japan). *Mother Earth International Journal* is 60 pages, tabloid-sized, offset-printed, includes graphics and photographs. Receives about 4,000 poems/year, accepts 15%. Press run is 2,000 for 1,200 subscribers of which 280 are libraries. Subscription: $12/year. Sample: $3.75. Make checks payable to Uniting the World Through Poetry. "We encourage the purchase of a copy or a year's subscription."

How to Submit: Submit 4 poems at a time. Accepts previously published poems and simultaneous submissions. No fax or e-mail submissions. Cover letter preferred. Time between acceptance and publication is 4 months. Occasionally publishes theme issues. Guidelines and upcoming themes available for SASE. Responds in 3 months. Sometimes sends prepublication galleys. Pays 2 copies. All rights revert to the author.

Also Offers: Sponsors a $50 prize to the best of "Your Two Best Lines," a benefit collage poem which will list all entries as a collective poem. As an entry fee, "a $5 check should be enclosed with submission." Also offers the National Poetry Association, currently working to establish an International Poetry Museum in San Francisco. For more information, check out www.internationalpoetrymuseum.org.

Advice: "*Mother Earth International* is an ongoing anthology of world contemporary poetry. For subscribers we reduced the subscription from $18 to $12/year. While all future issues will include an American section, we hope that all who send in entries will subscribe to *Mother Earth International Journal* to get a truly world perspective of universal concerns."

🄌 MOUNT OLIVE COLLEGE PRESS; MOUNT OLIVE REVIEW; LEE WITTE POETRY CONTEST,

634 Henderson St., Mount Olive NC 28365. (919)658-2502. Established 1987 (*Mount Olive Review*), 1990 (Mount Olive College Press). **Editor:** Dr. Pepper Worthington.

Magazine Needs: *Mount Olive Review*, features "literary criticism, poetry, short stories, essays, and book reviews." Wants "modern poetry." *Mount Olive Review* is 7½×10. Receives about 2,000 poems/year, accepts 8%. Press run is 1,000. Single copy: $25. Make checks payable to Mount Olive College Press.

How to Submit: Submit 6 poems at a time. No previously published poems or simultaneous submissions. Cover letter preferred. Time between acceptance and publication varies. Poems are circulated to an editorial board. Seldom comments on rejected poems. Publishes theme issues. A list of upcoming themes and guidelines available for SASE. Responds in 3 months. Sometimes sends prepublication galleys. Acquires first rights. Reviews books and chapbooks of poetry and other magazines. Send materials for review consideration.

Book/Chapbook Needs & How to Submit: Mount Olive Press publishes 2 books/year and sponsors the Lee Witte Poetry Contest. Write to above address for guidelines. Books are usually digest-sized. Submit 12 sample poems. Responds to queries and mss in 3 months. Obtain sample books by writing to the above address.

◎ ⦿ MOVING PARTS PRESS (Specialized: bilingual/foreign language, regional), 10699 Empire Grade, Santa Cruz CA 95060-9474. (831)427-2271. E-mail: frice@movingpartspress.com. Website: www.movingpartspress.com. Established 1977. **Poetry Editor:** Felicia Rice. Does not accept unsolicited mss. Published *Codex Espangliensis: from Columbus to the Border Patrol* (1998) with performance texts by Guillermo Gómez-Peña and collage imagery by Enrique Chagoya.

★ ◐ MUDLARK: AN ELECTRONIC JOURNAL OF POETRY & POETICS, Dept. of English, University of North Florida, Jacksonville FL 32224-2645. (904)620-2273. Fax: (904)620-3940. E-mail: mudlark@unf.edu. Website: www.unf.edu/mudlark. Established 1995. **Editor:** William Slaughter.
Magazine Needs: *Mudlark* appears "irregularly but frequently. *Mudlark* has averaged, from 1995-1999, three issues and six posters per year. *Mudlark* publishes in three formats: issues of *Mudlark* are the electronic equivalent of print chapbooks; posters are the electronic equivalent of print broadsides; and flash poems are poems that have news is them, poems that feel like current events. The poem is the thing at *Mudlark* and the essay about it. As our full name suggests, we will consider accomplished work that locates itself anywhere on the spectrum of contemporary practice. We want poems, of course, but we want essays, too, that make us read poems (and write them?) differently somehow. Although we are not innocent, we do imagine ourselves capable of surprise. The work of hobbyists is not for *Mudlark*." Has published poetry by Sheila E. Murphy, Chris Semansky, Diane Wald, Frances Driscoll, Van K. Brock, Robert Sward, and James Brook. *Mudlark* is archived and permanently on view at www.unf.edu.
How to Submit: Submit any number of poems at a time. No simultaneous submissions. Accepts e-mail and disk submissions. "Previously published poems: Inasmuch as issues of *Mudlark* are the electronic equivalent of print chapbooks, some of the individual poems in them might, or might not, have been previously published; if they have been, that previous publication must be acknowledged. Only poems that have not been previously published will be considered for *Mudlark* posters, the electronic equivalent of print broadsides, or for *Mudlark* flash poems." Cover letter optional. Time between acceptance and publication is up to 3 months. Seldom comments on rejected poems. Guidelines available for SASE, by e-mail, or on website. Responds in 1 month. Always sends prepublication galleys, "in the form of inviting the author to proof the work on a private website that *Mudlark* maintains for that purpose." Does not pay. However, "one of the things we can do at *Mudlark* to 'pay' our authors for their work is point to it here and there. We can tell our readers how to find it, how to subscribe to it, and how to buy it . . . if it is for sale. Toward that end, we maintain A-Notes (on the authors) we publish. We call attention to their work." Acquires one-time rights.
Advice: "*Mudlark* has been reviewed well and often. At this early point in its history, *Mudlark* has established itself, arguably, as one of the few serious rivals in the first generation of the electronic medium, to print versions of its kind. Look at *Mudlark*, visit the website (www.unf.edu/mudlark) spend some time there. Then make your decision: to submit or not to submit."

◻ MUSE'S KISS LITERARY 'ZINE, P.O. Box 703, Lenoir NC 28645. Fax: (208)247-4747. E-mail: museskiss@aol.com or museskiss@yahoo.com. Website: http://members.aol.com/museskiss. Established 1998. **Editor:** Alex Reeves. **Publisher:** L.S. Bush. **Contact:** Anthony Scott.
Magazine Needs: "*Muse's Kiss* is a free annual webzine. It contains experimental and traditional poetry and short stories. We will consider general fiction, science fiction, historical fiction, and mystery for short stories and anything except erotica or haiku for poetry. Prefers free verse and literary poetry and fiction. Please do not send love poems or 'Hallmark' verse. We are not interested in rhyming or love poetry." Accepts poetry written by children 12 and older. Has published poetry by Duane Locke, L.B. Sedlacek, Robert Klein Engler, James C. Speegle, Janet Buck, Taylor Graham. Receives about 400 poems/year, accepts about 15%. Sample: $3 (by mail, online version free). Make checks payable to L.S. Bush.
How to Submit: Submit 5 poems at a time. Line length for poetry is 8 minimum, 60 maximum. No previously published poems. Cover letter with brief bio preferred. No fax submissions, but submissions by e-mail (in text box) and by postal mail accepted. "Poems must be typed in body of e-mail—

no attachments. Use plain fonts, like Arial, and single space. If you prefer, you may submit offline by sending your poems and a cover letter. If you submit offline, there is a reading fee of $1 for up to 10 poems." Time between acceptance and publication is 3 months. Guidelines available for SASE, by blank e-mail to museskiss@sendfree.com, and on website. Responds in 3 months. Acquires one-time electronic rights. Payment is publication; small honorarium "of $2 when funds are available."

Advice: "Please check our free issues to see what other poetry we've published and read and follow our guidelines. If you have not followed our guidelines, it shows! If you show care with your submission then we will show you the same care in return."

THE MUSING PLACE (Specialized: poets with a history of mental illness), 2700 N. Lakeview, Chicago IL 60614. (773)281-3800, ext. 2465. Fax: (773)281-8790. E-mail: sford@threshol ds.org. Website: http://thresholds.org. Established 1986. **Editor:** Shannon Ford.

Magazine Needs: *The Musing Place* is an annual magazine "written and published by people with a history of mental illness. All kinds and forms of poetry are welcome." *The Musing Place* is 32 pages, magazine-sized, typeset, and stapled with art also produced by people with a history of mental illness. Receives about 300 poems/year, accepts about 40. Press run is 1,000. Single copy: $3.

How to Submit: Accepts simultaneous submissions; no previously published poems. Accepts fax submissions. Cover letter required. "Poets must prove and explain their history of mental illness." Time between acceptance and publication is up to 1 year. "The board reviews submissions and chooses those that fit into each issue." Seldom comments on rejected poems. Responds within 6 months. Pays 1 copy.

$ 🖉 ◎ MYTHIC DELIRIUM (Specialized: science fiction, fantasy, horror, surreal, cross-genre), P.O. Box 13511, Roanoke VA 24034-3511. E-mail: mythicdelirium@dnapublications. com. Website: www.dnapublications.com/delirium/. Established 1998. **Editor:** Mike Allen. Member: Science Fiction Poetry Association, Science Fiction & Fantasy Writers of America.

Magazine Needs: *Mythic Delirium* appears biannually as "a journal of speculative poetry for the new millennium. All forms considered. Must fit within the genres we consider, though we have published some mainstream verse." Does not want "forced rhyme, corny humor, jarringly gross sexual material, gratuitous obscenity, handwritten manuscripts." Recently published poetry by Ian Watson, Darrell Schweitzer, Laurel Winter, Amy Sterling Casil, and Wendy Rathbone. *Mythic Delirium* is 32 pages, digest-sized, saddle-stapled, color cover art, with b&w interior, uses house ads. Receives about 300 poems/year, accepts about 15%. Publishes about 18 poems/issue. Press run is 150. Subscription: $9 (2 issues), $16 (4 issues). Sample: $5. Make checks payable to DNA Publications, P.O. Box 2988, Radford VA 24143-2988 (subscription address **only**).

How to Submit: No previously published poems or simultaneous submissions. No fax, e-mail, or disk submissions. Cover letter is preferred. Time between acceptance and publication is 9 months. Often comments on rejected poems. Guidelines available for SASE, by e-mail, or on website. Responds in 5 weeks. Pays $5 for poems up to 40 lines, $10 for poems over 40 lines, plus 1 contributor's copy. Acquires first North American serial rights.

Advice: "*Mythic Delirium* isn't easy to get into, but we publish newcomers in every issue. Show us how ambitious you can be, and don't give up."

🖉 ◎ NADA PRESS; BIG SCREAM (Specialized: form/style), 2782 Dixie SW, Grandville MI 49418. (616)531-1442. E-mail: decope@yahoo.com. Established 1974. **Poetry Editor:** David Cope.

Magazine Needs: *Big Scream* appears annually in January or February and is "a brief anthology of unknown and established poets. We are promoting a continuation of objectivist tradition begun by Williams and Reznikoff. We want objectivist-based short works; some surrealism; basically short, tight work that shows clarity of perception and care in its making." Has published poetry by Antler, Richard Kostelanetz, Andy Clausen, Dianne DiPrima, Anne Waldman, and Jim Cohn. *Big Scream* is 50 pages, magazine-sized, xerograph on 60 lb. paper, side-stapled, "sent gratis to a select group of poets and editors." Receives "several hundred (not sure)" unsolicited submissions/year, use "very few." Press run is 100. Subscription to institutions: $10/year. Sample: $10.

How to Submit: Submit after March. Send 10 pages. No cover letter. "If poetry interests me, I will ask the proper questions of the poet." Accepts simultaneous submissions. Accepts submissions on disk (formatted in MS Word and accompanied by a hardcopy), as an e-mail attachment (in .doc format), and by postal mail. Comments on rejected poems "if requested and ms warrants it." Responds in up to 2 months. Sometimes sends prepublication galleys. Pays 2 copies.

Advice: "Read Pound's essay, 'A Retrospect,' then Reznikoff and Williams; follow through the Beats and NY School, especially Denby & Berrigan, and you have our approach to writing well in hand. I expect to be publishing *Big Scream* regularly ten years from now, same basic format."

NANNY FANNY; FELICITY PRESS, 2524 Stockbridge Dr. #15, Indianapolis IN 46268-2670. E-mail: nightpoet@prodigy.net. Established 1998. **Editor:** Lou Hertz.

Magazine Needs: *Nanny Fanny* appears 3 times/year and "publishes accessible, high quality poetry. Some artwork wanted (b&w 5″ square for cover)." Wants "external, extroverted observations and character studies. Most poems published are free verse. Formal poetry discouraged. Prefer 30 lines or less. No internalized, self-pitying poetry. Nothing under 8 lines or over 30 unless exceptional. No pornography, extremes of violence or language. No political or overly religious poems." Accepts poetry written by children. Has published poetry by B.Z. Niditch, Nancy A. Henry, Lamar Thomas, and John Grey. *Nanny Fanny* is 36-40 pages, digest-sized, laser-printed and side-stapled with colored 67 lb. cover, includes cover art and some b&w line drawings inside. Receives about 1,000 poems/year, accepts about 10%. Press run is 120 for 35 subscribers, 2 of which are libraries; 40 distributed free to contributors, etc. Subscription: $10/3 issues. Sample: $4. Make checks payable to Lou Hertz. "Query first about reviews."

How to Submit: Submit 3-8 poems at a time, 1 poem/page with name and address on each. Accepts previously published poems ("if writer gives credit for previous appearance"); no simultaneous submissions. No e-mail submissions. Accepts disk submissions. Cover letter with brief bio preferred. Time between acceptance and publication is up to 6 months. Usually comments on rejected poems. Guidelines available for SASE or by e-mail. Responds in up to 2 months. Sends prepublication galleys on request. Pays 1 contributor's copy. Acquires one-time rights.

Book/Chapbook Needs: Felicity Press is not currently open for submissions.

Advice: "I want good quality poetry that the average person will be able to understand and enjoy. Let's use poetic imagery to draw them in, not scare them away."

$ THE NATION; "DISCOVERY"/THE NATION POETRY CONTEST, 33 Irving Place, New York NY 10003. Established 1865. **Poetry Editor:** Grace Schulman.

• Poetry published by *The Nation* has been included in *Best American Poetry*.

Magazine Needs & How to Submit: *The Nation*'s only requirement for poetry is "excellence," which can be inferred from the list of poets they have published: Marianne Moore, Robert Lowell, W.S. Merwin, Maxine Kumin, Donald Justice, James Merrill, Richard Howard, May Swenson, Amy Clampitt, Edward Hirsch, and Charles Simic. Pays $1/line, not to exceed 35 lines, plus 1 copy. Accepts submissions only by postal mail and only with SASE.

Also Offers: The magazine co-sponsors the Lenore Marshall Prize for Poetry which is an annual award of $10,000 for an outstanding book of poems published in the US in each year. For details, write to the Academy of American Poets, 584 Broadway, #1208, New York NY 10012 (also see separate listing in the Contests & Awards section). Also co-sponsors the "Discovery"/*The Nation* Poetry Contest ($300 each plus a reading at The Unterberg Poetry Center, 1395 Lexington Ave., New York NY 10128). Deadline: mid-February. Guidelines available for SASE, on www.92ndsty.org, or by calling (212)415-5759. (See separate listing for Unterberg Poetry Center in the Organizations section.)

N THE NATIONAL POETRY REVIEW, P.O. Box 640625, San Jose CA 95164-0625. Website: www.nationalpoetryreview.com. Established 2003. **Editor:** C.J. Sage.

Magazine Needs: "*The National Poetry Review* is a selective journal of contemporary verse appearing twice per year. It is open to well-crafted poetry in both formal and free verse modes but is especially fond of rich sound, image play *within* form, and unique diction and syntax. (E.E. Cummings' 'somewhere I have never travelled, gladly beyond' or 'it may not always be so; and I say'; Stuart Lishan's 'Eurydice and Loverboy'; Anna Rabinowitz's 'Ecosystem'; and Kathleen Jamie's 'Skeins o Geese' are just a few examples. More classical verse is also welcome; John Brehm's 'Songbird' is a good example." Does not want "confessional poetry, simple autobiography, narratives without musicality, prose poems, or vulgarity." *The National Poetry Review* is about 50 pages, digest-sized, 4-color cover. Anticipates accepting about 1% of submissions. Publishes about 30-40 poems/issue. **First issue due out in fall 2003.** Single copy: $6; subscription: $10/year. Make checks payable to C.J. Sage.

How to Submit: Submit 3-5 poems at a time. Accepts simultaneous submissions with notification ONLY; no previously published poems. No fax, e-mail, or disk submissions. Cover letter is preferred. "Submit poems double-spaced, with brief bio, contact information including e-mail address if you have one (e-mail addresses will be kept confidential), and SASE. Please write *your own* address in the return address area of your SASE as well as in the addressee area." Reads submissions all year. Time between acceptance and publication is no more than 6 months. "The editor makes all publishing decisions." Seldom comments on rejected poems. Guidelines available in magazine or on website. Responds in up to 2 months. Pays 1 contributor's copy. Acquires first rights.

Also Offers: Offers a cash prize for best poem published in *The National Poetry Review* each year.

Advice: "Send only your very best work."

○ ◎ **NATIVE TONGUE; NATIVE TONGUE PRESS (Specialized: ethnic, African-American)**, P.O. Box 822, Eufaula AL 36072-0822. (334)616-7722. E-mail: ntp59@hotmail.com. Established 1998. **Submissions Editor:** Anthony Canada.

Magazine Needs: *Native Tongue* is published quarterly "to keep the voices and history of the black poet historic, and expand an audience for new black poets." Wants poetry "on or about the African-American experience. Open to all forms, subject matter, styles or purpose. Interested in poems which emphasize but are not limited to cultural issues, the exploration of self-esteem, and personal empower-ment, and the exploration of the direction of African-American people. No submissions that do not deal with the African-American experience." *Native Tongue* is 7-10 pages, 8½ × 11 sheets, 3-column format, stapled. Receives about 150 poems/year, accepts about 85%. Press run is 200 for 55 subscrib-ers, 45 shelf sales; 100 distributed free to the public, colleges, poetry groups. Subscription: $11. Sample: $3. Make checks payable to Anthony G. Canada.

How to Submit: Submit up to 5 poems at a time. Accepts previously published poems and simulta-neous submissions. Accepts submissions by e-mail (as attachment) and by postal mail. Cover letter required. "In cover letter include basic poet information—name, address, occupation, experience, previous publishings, books, etc." SASE required for return of submitted poems. Past theme issues include Romance/Love (Spring 2003) and Erotica (Summer 2003). Time between acceptance and publication is 3 months. Poems are circulated to an editorial board. "Submissions reviewed by board; published pieces selected by committee." Often comments on rejected poems. Responds in 3 months. Pays 4 contributor's copies. Acquires one-time rights. Reviews books and chapbooks of poetry in 200 words, single book format. Send materials for review consideration.

Advice: "The aim and goal of this newsletter is to open up to a wider audience the poetic voices of our many talented brothers and sisters. The African-American community has always had a historic and rich poetic legacy. We at *Native Tongue* wish to continue and expand upon this great tradition of African-American poets. So brothers and sisters take pen to paper, and continue to make our history historic. Let your voices by heard!"

✪ $ ◎ **NAZARENE INTERNATIONAL HEADQUARTERS; STANDARD; LISTEN; (Specialized: religious, children)**, 6401 The Paseo, Kansas City MO 64131. (816)333-7000.

Magazine Needs & How to Submit: Each of the magazines published by the Nazarenes has a separate editor, focus, and audience. *Standard*, press run 135,000, is a weekly inspirational "story paper" with Christian leisure reading for adults. Free samples and guidelines available for SASE with 2 first-class stamps. Uses 2 poems each week. Submit maximum of 5 poems, no more than 30 lines each. Pays 25¢ a line. For *Listen* and *Holiness Today*, write individually for guidelines and samples.

◉ **THE NEBRASKA REVIEW; THE NEBRASKA REVIEW AWARDS**, Creative Writing Program, FA, University of Nebraska, Omaha NE 68182-0324. (402)554-3159. Fax: (402)554-3436. Established 1973. **Fiction and Managing Editor:** James Reed. **Poetry Editor:** Coreen Wees.

● Poetry published in *The Nebraska Review* has been included in the 2001 *Best American Poetry* and the 2002 *Pushcart Prize* anthology.

Magazine Needs: *The Nebraska Review* is a semiannual literary magazine publishing fiction and poetry with occasional essays. Wants "lyric poetry from 10-200 lines, preference being for under 100 lines. Subject matter is unimportant, as long as it has some. Poets should have mastered form, meaning poems should have form, not simply 'demonstrate' it." Doesn't want to see "concrete, inspirational, didactic, or merely political poetry." Has published poetry by Angela Ball, Virgil Suarez, James Reiss, and Katharine Whitcomb. *The Nebraska Review* is 108 pages, digest-sized, nicely printed and flat-spined with glossy card cover. It is a publication of the Writer's Workshop at the University of Nebraska at Omaha. Press run is 500 for 380 subscribers of which 85 are libraries. Single copy: $8; subscription: $15/year. Sample: $4.50.

How to Submit: Submit 4-6 poems at a time. "Clean typed copy strongly preferred." No fax submissions. Reads open submissions January 1 through April 30 only. Responds in 4 months. Time between acceptance and publication is up to 12 months. Pays 2 contributor's copies and 1-year subscription. Acquires first North American serial rights.

Also Offers: Submissions for The Nebraska Review Awards are read from September 1 through November 30 only. The Nebraska Review Awards of $500 each in poetry, creative nonfiction, and fiction are published in the spring issue. Entry fee: $15, includes discounted subscription. You can enter as many times as desired. Deadline: November 30.

Advice: "Your first allegiance is to the poem. Publishing will come in time, but it will always be less than you feel you deserve. Therefore, don't look to publication as a reward for writing well; it has no relationship."

⊘ NEDGE, P.O. Box 2321, Providence RI 02906. Website: www.nedgemagazine.com. Established 1994. **Editor:** Henry Gould.

Magazine Needs: *Nedge* is published by the Poetry Mission, a nonprofit arts organization. Includes poetry, fiction, reviews, and essays. Circulation is 300. Subscription: $12/2 issues. Sample: $6. Back issues available for $3.

How to Submit: Currently not accepting unsolicited submissions.

✖ ⊘ THE NEOVICTORIAN/COCHLEA, P.O. Box 55164, Madison WI 53705. E-mail: eacam @execpc.com. Website: www.pointandcircumference.org. Established 1995. **Editor:** Esther Cameron.

Magazine Needs: *The Neovictorian/Cochlea* appears biannually and "seeks to promote a poetry of introspection, dialogue, and social concern." Wants "poetry of beauty and integrity with emotional and intellectual depth, commitment to subject matter as well as language, and the courage to ignore fashion. Welcome: well-crafted formal verse, social comment (including satire), love poems, philosophical/religious poems, poems reflecting dialogue with other writers (in particular: responses to the work of Paul Celan)." Very rarely accepts poetry by children. Has published poetry by Ida Fasel, Carolyn Stoloff, Joseph Salemi, Richard Moore, Constance Rowell Mastores, and Michael Burch. *The Neovictorian/Cochlea* is 28-32 pages, magazine-sized, photocopied and saddle-stapled with cardstock cover, occasional graphics, no ads. Press run is 250 for 50 subscribers. Single copy: $6; subscription: $10.

How to Submit: Submit 3-5 poems at a time. Accepts simultaneous submissions and "on rare occasions a previously published poem." Accepts e-mail submissions (include in text box), but prefers postal mail. Cover letter "not necessary. Poets whose work is accepted will be asked for titles of books available, to be published in the magazine." Time between acceptance and publication is up to 12 months. Often comments on rejected poems. Does not offer guidelines because "the tradition is the only 'guideline.' We do encourage contributors to write for a sample." Responds in up to 4 months. Pays 2 contributor's copies. Acquires first rights. *The Neovictorian/Cochlea* publishes the addresses of poets who would welcome correspondence. "Poets can also submit longer selections of work for publication on the 'Point and Circumference' website."

THE OPENNESS TO SUBMISSIONS INDEX in the back of this book lists markets according to the level of writing they prefer to see.

Advice: "Like all our social functioning, poetry today suffers from a loss of community, which translates into a lack of real intimacy with the reader. Poets can work against this trend by remaining in touch with the poetry of past generations and by forming relationships in which poetry can be employed as the language of friendship. Publication should be an afterthought."

◻ ◉ **NERVE COWBOY; LIQUID PAPER PRESS**, P.O. Box 4973, Austin TX 78765. Website: www.onr.com/user/jwhagins/nervecowboy.html. Established 1995. **Co-Editors:** Joseph Shields and Jerry Hagins.

Magazine Needs: *Nerve Cowboy* is a biannual literary journal featuring contemporary poetry, short fiction and b&w drawings. "Open to all forms, styles and subject matter preferring writing that speaks directly, and minimizes literary devices. We want to see poetry of experience and passion which can find that raw nerve and ride it. We are always looking for that rare writer that inherently knows what word comes next." Has published poetry by Charles H. Webb, Thomas Michael McDade, Heather Abner, Julie Lechevsky, and Fred Voss. *Nerve Cowboy* is 64 pages, $7 \times 8\frac{1}{2}$, attractively printed and saddle-stapled with matte card cover with b&w cover art. Currently accepts about 5% of the submissions received. Press run is 300 for 125 subscribers. Subscription: $16/4 issues. Sample: $5.

How to Submit: Submit 3-7 poems at a time, name on each page. Accepts previously published poems with notification; no simultaneous submissions. Informal cover letter with bio credits preferred. Seldom comments on rejected poems. Guidelines available for SASE. Responds in 2 months. Pays 1 copy. Acquires first or one-time rights.

Book/Chapbook Needs & How to Submit: Liquid Paper Press publishes 2-3 chapbooks/year but will not be accepting unsolicited chapbook mss in the foreseeable future. Only chapbook contest winners and solicited mss will be published in the next couple of years. For information on *Nerve Cowboy*'s annual chapbook contest, please send a SASE. Deadline is January 31 of each year. Entry fee: $10. Cash prizes and publication for 1st and 2nd place finishers. Chapbooks are 24-40 pages, digest-sized, photocopied with some b&w artwork. Recent winners include Lori Jakiela, Ralph Dranow, Christopher Jones, and Belinda Subraman. Publications include *The Regulars* by Lori Jakiela; *Hoeing Cotton in High Heels* by Wilma Elizabeth McDaniel; *Broke-Down Shotgun Blues* by James Edward O'Brien; *Everyone, Exquisite* by Bob Pajich; *The Back East Poems* by Gerald Locklin; and *Learning to Lie* by Albert Huffstickler. Send SASE for a complete list of available titles.

$ ◉ **NEW ENGLAND REVIEW**, Middlebury College, Middlebury VT 05753. (802)443-5075. Fax: (802)443-2088. E-mail: nereview@middlebury.edu. Website: www.middlebury.edu/~nereview/ . Established 1978. **Editor:** Stephen Donadio.

● Work published in this review is frequently included in volumes of *The Best American Poetry*.

Magazine Needs: *New England Review* is a prestigious, nationally distributed literary quarterly, 180 pages, 7×10, flat-spined, elegant make-up and printing on heavy stock, glossy cover with art. Receives 3,000-4,000 poetry submissions/year, accepts about 70-80 poems/year; has a 3-6 month backlog between time of acceptance and publication. The editors urge poets to read a few copies of the magazine before submitting work. Has published poetry by Nick Flynn, Henri Cole, Debora Greger, and Pimone Triplett. Subscription: $25. Sample: $8.

How to Submit: Submit up to 6 poems at a time. Address submissions to Poetry Editor. No previously published poems. "Brief cover letters are useful. All submissions by mail. Accepts questions by e-mail." Reads submissions September 1 through May 31 only. Response time is 12 weeks. Always sends prepublication galleys. Pays $10/page, $20 minimum, plus 2 contributor's copies. Also features essay-reviews. Send materials for review consideration.

◉ **NEW ISSUES PRESS; NEW ISSUES PRESS POETRY SERIES; NEW ISSUES PRESS FIRST BOOK POETRY PRIZE; THE GREEN ROSE PRIZE IN POETRY FOR ESTABLISHED POETS**, Dept. of English, Western Michigan University, Kalamazoo MI 49008-5331. (269)387-8185. Fax: (269)387-2562. E-mail: herbert.scott@wmich.edu. Website: www.wmich.edu/newissues. Established 1996. **Editor:** Herbert Scott.

Book/Chapbook Needs: New Issues Press First Book Prize publishes 3-6 first books of poetry per year, one through its annual New Issues Poetry Prize. Additional mss will be selected from those submitted to the competition for publication in the series. "A national judge selects the prize winner and recommends other manuscripts. The editors decide on the other books considering the judge's recommendation, but are not bound by it." Past judges include Philip Levine, C.D Wright, C.K. Williams, Campbell McGrath, Brenda Hillman, and Marianne Boruch. Books are published on acid free paper in editions of 1,500.

How to Submit: Open to "poets writing in English who have not previously published a full-length collection of poems in an edition of 500 or more copies." Submit 48- to 72-page ms with 1-paragraph bio, publication credits (if any), and $15 entry fee. No e-mail or fax submissions. Reads submissions June 1 through November 30 only. Complete guidelines available for SASE. Winner will be notified the following April. Winner receives $2,000 plus publication of manuscript. "We offer 33⅓% discounts on our books to competition entrants."

Also Offers: New Issues Press also sponsors the Green Rose Prize in Poetry. Award is $2,000 and publication for a book of poems by an established poet who has published one or more full-length collections of poetry. Entry fee: $20/ms. Mss accepted May 1 through September 30. Winner announced in January. Winners include *When the Moon Knows You're Wandering* by Ruth Ellen Kocher (2001); Christopher Bursk (2002); and both Gretchen Mattox for *Buddha Box* and Christine Hume for *Alaskaphrenia* (2003). Other Green Rose poets include Michael Burkard, Maurice Kilwein Guevara, Mary Ann Samyn, Jim Daniels. Guidelines available for SASE, by fax, by e-mail, or on website.

Advice: "Our belief is that there are more good poets writing than ever before. Our mission is to give some of the best of these a forum. Also, our books have been reviewed in *Publishers Weekly*, *Booklist*, and the *Library Journal* as well as being featured in the *Washington Post Book World* and the *New York Times Book Review* during 2000 and 2001. New Issues books are advertised in *Poets & Writers*, *APR*, *American Poet*, *The Bloomsbury Review*, etc. We publish 8-12 books of poems a year. New Issues Press is profiled in the May/June 2000 issue of *Poets & Writers*."

$ ☑ NEW LETTERS; NEW LETTERS LITERARY AWARD, University of Missouri-Kansas City, Kansas City MO 64110. (816)235-1168. Fax: (816)235-2611. E-mail: newletters@umkc.edu. Website: www.newsletters.org. Established 1934 as *University Review*, became *New Letters* in 1971. **Editor:** Robert Stewart.

Magazine Needs: *New Letters* "is dedicated to publishing the best short fiction, best contemporary poetry, literary articles, photography, and artwork by both established writers and new talents." Wants "contemporary writing of all types—free verse poetry preferred, short works are more likely to be accepted than very long ones." Has published poetry by Marilyn Hacker, Miller Williams, James Tate, Robin Becker, Amiri Baraka, and Tony Whedon. *New Letters* is digest-sized, flat-spined, professionally printed quarterly, glossy 2-color cover with art, uses about 40-45 (of 120) pages of poetry in each issue. Press run is 2,500 with 1,800 subscriptions of which about 40% are libraries. Receives about 7,000 submissions/year, accepts less than 1%, has a 6-month backlog. Poems appear in a variety of styles exhibiting a high degree of craft and universality of theme (rare in many journals). Subscription: $17. Sample: $5.50.

How to Submit: Send no more than 6 poems at a time. No previously published poems or simultaneous submissions. Short cover letter preferred. "We strongly prefer original typescripts and we don't read between May 15 and October 15. No query needed." Upcoming themes and guidelines available for SASE, by e-mail, and on website. Responds in up to 10 weeks. Pays a small fee plus 2 copies.

Also Offers: The New Letters Literary Award is given annually for a group of 3-6 poems. Entry guidelines available for SASE. Deadline: May 15.

Advice: "Write with originality and freshness in language, content, and style. Avoid clichés in imagery and subject."

☑ ◎ NEW NATIVE PRESS (Specialized: translations), P.O. Box 661, Cullowhee NC 28723. (828)293-9237. E-mail: newnativepress@hotmail.com. Established 1979. **Publisher:** Thomas Rain Crowe.

Book/Chapbook Needs: New Native Press has "selectively narrowed its range of contemporary 20th century literature to become an exclusive publisher of writers in marginalized and endangered languages. All books published are bilingual translations from original languages into English." Publishes on average 2 paperbacks/year. Recently published *Kenneth Patchen: Rebel Poet in America* by Larry Smith and Gaelic, Welsh, Breton, Cornish, and Manx poets in an all-Celtic language anthology of contemporary poets from Scotland, Ireland, Wales, Brittany, Cornwall, and Isle of Man entitled

Writing The Wind: A Celtic Resurgence (The New Celtic Poetry). Books are sold by distributors in four foreign countries and in the US by library vendors and Small Press Distribution. Books are typically 80 pages, offset-printed and perfect-bound with glossy 120 lb. stock with professionally-designed color cover.

How to Submit: Not currently accepting submissions. For specialized translations only—authors should query first with 10 sample poems and cover letter with bio and publication credits. Accepts previously published poems and simultaneous submissions. Time between acceptance and publication is up to 12 months. Always comments on rejected poems. Responds in 2 weeks. Pays copies, "amount varies with author and title."

Advice: "We are still looking for work indicative of rare talent—unique and original voices using language experimentally and symbolically, if not subversively."

☑ NEW ORLEANS POETRY JOURNAL PRESS, 2131 General Pershing St., New Orleans LA 70115. (504)891-3458. Established 1956. **Publisher/Editor:** Maxine Cassin. **Co-Editor:** Charles de Gravelles.

Book/Chapbook Needs: "We prefer to publish relatively new and/or little-known poets of unusual promise or those inexplicably neglected." Does not want to see "cliché or doggerel, anything incomprehensible or too derivative, or workshop exercises. First-rate lyric poetry preferred (not necessarily in traditional forms)." Has published books by Vassar Miller, Everette Maddox, Charles Black, Malaika Favorite, Raeburn Miller, Martha McFerren, Ralph Adamo, and Charles de Gravelles.

How to Submit: This market is currently closed to all submissions.

Advice: "1) Read as much as possible! 2) Write only when you must, and 3) Don't rush into print! No poetry should be sent without querying first! Publishers are concerned about expenses unnecessarily incurred in mailing manuscripts. *Telephoning is not encouraged.*"

★ $☑ NEW ORLEANS REVIEW, Box 195, Loyola University, New Orleans LA 70118. (504)865-2295. Fax: (504)865-2294. Website: www.loyno.edu/~noreview. Established 1968. **Editor:** Christopher Chambers. **Poetry Editor:** Sophia Stone. **Book Review Editor:** Mary McCay.

Magazine Needs: *New Orleans Review* publishes "poetry of all types, fiction, and essays. We're looking for dynamic writing that demonstrates attention to the language, and a sense of the medium, writing that engages, surprises, moves us. We suscribe to the belief that in order to truly write well, one must first master the rudiments: grammar and syntax, punctuation, the sentence, the paragraph, the line, the stanza." Has published poetry by Jack Gilbert, Rodney Jones, Besmilr Brigham, Mark Halliday, and Moira Crone. *New Orleans Review* is 120-200 pages, perfect-bound, elegantly printed with glossy card cover. Receives about 3,000 mss/year, publishes 5%. Press run is 1,700. Sample: $5. Single copy: $7.

How to Submit: Submit 3-5 poems at a time. No previously published work. Brief cover letter preferred. Accepts simultaneous submissions "if we're notified immediately upon acceptance elsewhere." Does not accept e-mail or fax submissions. Guidelines available on website. Responds in up to 4 months. Pays 2 copies and modest stipend. Acquires first North American serial rights.

❀ ☑ NEW ORPHIC REVIEW; NEW ORPHIC PUBLISHERS, 706 Mill St., Nelson BC V1L 4S5 Canada. (250)354-0494. Fax: (250)352-0743. Established New Orphic Publishers (1995), New Orphic Review (1998). **Editor-in-Chief:** Ernest Hekkanen.

Magazine Needs: "Appearing 2 times/year, *New Orphic Review* is run by an opinionated visionary who is beholden to no one, least of all government agencies like the Canada Council or institutions of higher learning. He feels Canadian literature is stagnant, lacks daring, and is terribly incestuous." *New Orphic Review* publishes poetry, novel excerpts, mainstream and experimental short stories, and articles on a wide range of subjects. Each issue also contains a *Featured Poet* section. "*New Orphic Review* publishes authors from around the world as long as the pieces are written in English and are accompanied by an SASE with proper Canadian postage and/or US dollars to offset the cost of postage." Prefers "tight, well-wrought poetry over leggy, prosaic poetry. No 'fuck you' poetry; no rambling pseudo Beat poetry." Has published poetry by Catherine Owen, Steven Michael Berzensky (aka Mick Burrs), Robert Wayne Stedingh, John Pass, and Susan McCaslin. *New Orphic Review* is 120-140 pages, magazine-sized, laser printed and perfect-bound with color cover, includes art/graphics and ads. Receives about 400 poems/year, accepts about 10%. Press run is 500 for 250 subscribers

of which 20 are libraries. Subscription: $25 (individual), $30 (institution). Sample: $15.
How to Submit: Submit 6 poems at a time. Line length for poetry is 5 minimum, 30 maximum. Accepts simultaneous submissions; no previously published poems. Cover letter preferred. "Make sure a SASE (or SAE and IRC) is included." Time between acceptance and publication is up to 8 months. Poems are circulated to an editorial board. The managing editor and associate editor refer work to the editor-in-chief. Seldom comments on rejected poems. Occasionally publishes theme issues. Guidelines available for SASE (or SAE and IRC). Responds in 2 months. Pays 1 contributor's copy. Acquires first North American serial rights.
Also Offers: New Orphic Publishers publishes 4 paperbacks/year. However, all material is solicited.

$ ☑ THE NEW RENAISSANCE, 26 Heath Rd. #11, Arlington MA 02474-3645. E-mail: wmich aud@gwi.net. Established 1968. **Editor-in-Chief:** Louise T. Reynolds. **Poetry Editor:** Frank Finale.
Magazine Needs: *the new renaissance* is "intended for the 'renaissance' person—the generalist, not the specialist. Publishes the best new writing and translations and offers a forum for articles on political, sociological topics; features established as well as emerging visual artists and writers, highlights reviews of small press, and offers essays on a variety of topics from visual arts and literature to science. Open to a variety of styles, including traditional." Has published poetry by Anita Susan Brenner, Ann Struther, Miguel Torga (trans. Alexis Levetin), Stephen Todd Booker, Rabindranath Togore (trans. Wendy Barker and S. Togore). *the new renaissance* is 144-182 pages, digest-sized, flat-spined, professionally printed on heavy stock, glossy, color cover, using 24-40 pages of poetry in each issue. Receives about 650 poetry submissions/year, accepts about 40; has about a 1½- to 2-year backlog. Usual press run is 1,500 for 760 subscribers of which 132 are libraries. Single copy: $11.50 (recent), $12.50 (current), $7.50 (back issue). Subscriptions: $30/3 issues US, $35 Canada, $38 all others. All checks in US $. "A 3-issue subscription covers 18-22 months."
How to Submit: Submit 3-6 poems at a time, "unless a long poem—then one." Accepts simultaneous submissions, if notified; no previously published poems "unless magazine's circulation was under 250." Always include SASE or IRC. Accepts submissions by postal mail only; "when accepted, we ask if a disk is available, and we prefer accepted translations to be available in the original language on disk. All poetry submissions are tied to our Awards Program for poetry published in a three-issue volume; judged by independent judges. **Entry fee:** $16.50 for nonsubscribers, $11.50 for subscribers, for which they receive two back issues or a recent issue or an extension of their subscription. Submissions without entry fee are *returned unread*." In 2003, reading period was January 2 through June 30. Guidelines available for SASE. Responds in 5 months. Pays $21-40, more for the occasional longer poem, plus 1 copy/poem. Acquires all rights but returns rights provided *the new renaissance* retains rights for any *the new renaissance* collection. Reviews books of poetry. The Awards Program gives 3 awards of $250, $125, and $60, with 3 Honorable Mentions of $25 each.
Advice: "Read, read, read! And support the literary magazines that support serious writers and poets." *tnr* adds that "in 2002, more than 350 separate submissions came in, all without the required fee. Since our *tnr* Poetry Awards Program has been in effect since 1995, and since we've notified all markets about our guidelines and entry fee, this just shows an indifferent, careless reading of our magazine's requirements."

◪ ◯ NEW RIVERS PRESS; MINNESOTA VOICES PROJECT; HEADWATERS LITERARY COMPETITION, MSU Moorehead, 1104 Seventh Ave. S., Moorhead MN 56563. E-mail: nrp@mnstate.edu. Website: www.mnstate.edu/newriverspress. Established 1968. **Editor:** Eric Braun.
Book/Chapbook Needs: Publishes collections of poetry, novels or novellas, translations of contemporary literature, collections of short fiction. "We will continue to publish books regularly by new and emerging writers, especially those with a connection to the midwest or to New York City, but we also welcome the opportunity to read work of every character and to publish the best literature available in America (the Many Americas Project, the American Fiction Project) and abroad (the New Rivers Abroad Project)." Has published *Pieces from the Long Afternoon* by Monica Ochtrup, *Wolves* by Jim Johnson, *Nothern Latitudes* by Lawrence Millman, and *Divining the Landscape* by Diane Jarvenpa. New and emerging authors living in Minnesota are eligible for the Minnesota Voices Project (MVP).
How to Submit: Book-length mss of poetry, short fiction, novellas, or creative nonfiction are all

accepted. Guidelines and catalog available on website. No fax or e-mail submissions.

Also Offers: The Minnesota Voices Project (MVP). Awards $500 and publication of ms by New Rivers Press. Competition open only to residents of the Upper Midwest who have not had a book by a commercial or major university press nor have had more than 2 books published by small presses (excludes chapbooks). Entrants may only submit one ms to one New Rivers Press competition annually. Send 2 copies of complete ms (between 40 and 70 pages) placed in either a binder or a plain manila folder. Name and address should appear on outside and on title page; pages must be numbered. All previously published poems must be acknowledged. No co-authored mss. "Simultaneous submissions are okay if noted as such. If your manuscript is accepted elsewhere during the judging, you must notify New Rivers Press immediately. If you do not give such notification and your manuscript is selected, your signature on the entry form gives New Rivers Press permission to go ahead with publication." Entry form and guidelines available on website. **Deadline:** In 2003, postmarked between March 1 and April 30.

A NEW SONG; NEW SONG PRESS; NEW SONG CHAPBOOK COMPETITION (Specialized: religious, spirituality), P.O. Box 629, W.B.B., Dayton OH 45409-0629. E-mail: nsongpress@aol.com. Website: www.NewSongPress.com. Established 1995. **Editor/Publisher:** Susan Jelus.

Magazine Needs: *A New Song* is published 2 times/year, in January and June, and "exhibits contemporary American poetry that speaks to the faith journey and enriches the spiritual lives of its readers. Includes poetry that takes a fresh approach and uses contemporary, natural language." Wants "free verse that addresses spiritual life through a wide range of topics and vivid imagery. No rhyming, sing-song, old-fashioned 'religious' poetry." Has published poetry by Claude Wilkinson, Janet McCann, Herbert W. Martin, and John Grey. *A New Song* is 40-50 pages, digest-sized, usually Docutech- or offset-printed, saddle-stapled, cardstock cover, photo or artwork on cover. Receives about 600 poems/year, accepts about 20%. Press run is 300 for 150 subscribers, 100 shelf sales; 50-75 distributed free to reviewers, bookstores, editors, professors, pastors. Single copy: $6.95; subscription: $12.95. Sample back issue: $5. Make checks payable to New Song Press.

How to Submit: Submit 3-5 poems at a time with short bio and SASE. Accepts simultaneous submissions; no previously published poems. Accepts e-mail submissions if included in body of message, "up to 3 poems only and must have a mailing address and bio." Also accepts disk submissions. Send SASE with regular mail submissions. Time between acceptance and publication is up to 18 months. Poems are circulated to an editorial board. Often comments on rejected poems. Occasionally publishes theme issues. Guidelines available for SASE, by e-mail, or on website. Responds in 3 months. Pays 1 copy. Acquires first North American serial rights. Sometimes reviews books of poetry in 750-1,000 words, single book format. Send materials for review consideration.

Book/Chapbook Needs & How to Submit: New Song Press's goals are "to help develop a genre of contemporary spiritual poetry." Publishes 1 chapbook per year. Has published *Remembered into Life* by Maureen Tolman Flannery. Chapbooks are usually 20-40 pages, digest-sized, usually Docutech-printed, sometimes offset-printed color cover, saddle-stapled, cardstock cover, includes art/graphics. Query first, with a few sample poems and a cover letter with brief bio and publication credits. Responds to queries in 3 months; to mss in 6 months. Payment varies.

Also Offers: Sponsors chapbook contest every other year or so (odd-numbered years only). Prize: $150 plus copies. Deadline: July 1st. Two runners-up also recognized. Entry fee for chapbook contest entries: $18, which includes a 1-year subscription to *A New Song*.

NEW WELSH REVIEW (Specialized: Ethnic), P.O. Box 170, Aberystwyth, Ceredigion SY23 1WZ Wales, United Kingdom. Phone: (0)1970-626230. E-mail: nwr@welshnet.co.uk. Established 1988. **Editor:** Francesca Rhydderch.

Magazine Needs: *New Welsh Review* is a literary quarterly publishing articles, short stories, and poems. *New Welsh Review* is an average of 104 pages, glossy paper in three colors, laminated cover, using photographs, graphics, and ads. Press run is 1,000. Subscription: £20 (£28.50 overseas airmail via cheque, Visa, or MasterCard). Sample: £7.50.

How to Submit: Submit poems double-spaced. No simultaneous submissions or previously published poems. Accepts submissions by postal mail only. Responds in 3 months. Publication within 7 months. Reviews books of poetry.

🌐 **$** 🖉 **THE NEW WRITER; THE NEW WRITER PROSE AND POETRY PRIZES**, P.O. Box 60, Cranbrook TN17 2ZR England. Phone: 01580 212626. Fax: 01580 212041. Website: www.thenewwriter.com. E-mail: admin@thenewwriter.com. Established 1996. **Poetry Editor:** Abi Hughes-Edwards.

Magazine Needs: Published 6 times/year, *"The New Writer* is the magazine you've been hoping to find. It's *different* and it's aimed at writers with a serious intent; who want to develop their writing to meet the high expectations of today's editors. The team at *The New Writer* are committed to working with their readers to increase the chances of publication. That's why masses of useful information and plenty of feedback is provided. More than that, we let you know about the current state of the market with the best in contemporary fiction and cutting-edge poetry backed up by searching articles and in-depth features in every issue. We are interested in short fiction, 2,000 words max.; subscribers' only; short and long unpublished poems, provided they are original and undeniably brilliant; articles that demonstrate a grasp of contemporary writing and current editorial/publishing policies; news of writers' circles, new publications, competitions, courses, workshops, etc." No "problems with length/ form but anything over two pages (150 lines) needs to be brilliant. Cutting edge shouldn't mean inaccessible. No recent disasters—they date. No my baby/doggie poems; no God poems that sound like hymns, dum-dum rhymes, or comic rhymes (best left at the pub)." *The New Writer* is 56 pages, A4, professionally printed and saddle-stapled with paper cover, includes clipart and b&w photos. Press run is 1,500 for 1,350 subscribers; 50 distributed free to publishers, agents. Single copy: £3.95; subscription: £33 in US. Sample: £3.95 or equivalent in IRCs. "A secure server for subscriptions and entry into the annual Prose & Poetry Prizes on the website. Monthly e-mail newsletter now included free of charge in the subscription package."

How to Submit: Submit up to 6 poems at a time. Accepts previously published poems. Accepts e-mail submissions if included in body of message. Time between acceptance and publication is up to 6 months. Often comments on rejected poems. Offers criticism service: £12/6 poems. Guidelines available for SASE (or SAE with IRC) or on website. Pays £3 voucher plus 1 copy. Acquires first British serial rights. Reviews books and chapbooks of poetry and other magazines. Send materials for review consideration.

Also Offers: Sponsors the New Writer Prose & Poetry Prizes. An annual prize, "open to all poets writing in the English language, who are invited to submit an original, previously unpublished poem or collection of six to ten poems. Up to 25 prizes will be presented as well as publication for the prize-winning poets in an anthology plus the chance for a further 10 shortlisted poets to see their work published in *The New Writer* during the year." Rules available by e-mail.

$ 🖉 ◎ **NEW WRITER'S MAGAZINE (Specialized: humor, writing)**, P.O. Box 5976, Sarasota FL 34277-5976. (941)953-7903. E-mail: newriters@aol.com. Website: www.newriters.com. Established 1986. **Editor:** George S. Haborak.

Magazine Needs: *New Writer's Magazine* is a bimonthly magazine "for aspiring writers, and professional ones as well, to exchange ideas and working experiences." Open to free verse, light verse and traditional, 8-20 lines, reflecting upon the writing lifestyle. "Humorous slant on writing life especially welcomed." Does not want poems about "love, personal problems, abstract ideas or fantasy." *New Writer's Magazine* is 28 pages, magazine-sized, offset printed, saddle-stapled, with glossy paper cover, b&w photos and ads. Receives about 300 poems/year, accepts 10%. Press run is 5,000. Subscription: $15/year, $25/2 years. Sample: $3.

How to Submit: Submit up to 3 poems at a time. No previously published poems or simultaneous submissions. No e-mail submissions. Time between acceptance and publication is up to 1 year. Guidelines available for SASE or by e-mail. Responds in 2 months. Pays $5/poem. Acquires first North American serial rights. Each issue of this magazine also includes an interview with a recognized author, articles on writing and the writing life, tips, and markets.

⭐ **$** 🖉 **NEW YORK QUARTERLY**, P.O. Box 693, Old Chelsea Station, New York NY 10113. Website: www.nyquarterly.com. Established 1969. **Poetry Editor:** Raymond Hammond.

Magazine Needs: *New York Quarterly* appears 3 times/year. Seeks to publish "a cross-section of the best of contemporary American poetry" and, indeed, have a record of publishing many of the best and most diverse of poets, including Charles Bukowski, James Dickey, Lola Haskins, Lyn Lifshin,

Elisavietta Ritchie, and W.D. Snodgrass. *New York Quarterly* appears in a digest-sized, flat-spined format, thick, elegantly printed, glossy color cover. Subscription: $20.
How to Submit: Submit 3-5 poems at a time with your name and address; include SASE. Accepts simultaneous submissions with notification. Responds within 1 month. Pays contributor's copies.

$ ◐ THE NEW YORKER, 4 Times Square, New York NY 10036. E-mail: poetry@newyorker.com. Website: www.newyorker.com. Established 1925. **Contact:** Poetry Editor.
  • Poems published in *The New Yorker* have been frequently included in volumes of *The Best American Poetry*.
Magazine Needs: *The New Yorker* appears weekly and publishes poetry of the highest quality (including translations). A recent edition featured poetry by Kathleen Jamie, Paul Muldoon, and Hugh Seidman. Subscription: $46/46 issues (one year), $76/92 issues (2 years).
How to Submit: Submit up to 6 poems at one time. "We prefer to receive no more than two submissions per writer per year, and generally cannot reply to more." No simultaneous submissions or previously published poems. Does not accept submissions by fax or by regular mail; send poems by e-mail only (in text box, no attachments). Mss are not read during the summer. Responds in up to 3 months. Pays top rates.

◐ NEW ZOO POETRY REVIEW; SUNKEN MEADOWS PRESS, P.O. Box 36760, Richmond VA 23235. Website: http://members.aol.com/newzoopoet. Established 1997. **Editor:** Angela Vogel.
Magazine Needs: *New Zoo Poetry Review* is published annually in January and "tends to publish free verse in well-crafted lyric and narrative forms. Our goal is to publish established poets alongside lesser-known poets of great promise. *New Zoo Poetry Review* wants serious, intellectual poetry of any form, length or style. Rhyming poetry only if exceptional. No light verse, song lyrics or greeting card copy. If you are not reading the best of contemporary poetry, then *New Zoo Poetry Review* is not for you." Has published poetry by Heather McHugh, Diane Glancy, D.C. Berry, Natasha Sajé, and Martha Collins. *New Zoo Poetry Review* is 40 pages, digest-sized, photocopied and saddle-stapled with glossy card cover with b&w photography. Receives about 2,000 poems/year, accepts approximately 5%. Press run is 200. Single copy: $5; subscription: $8/2 years.
How to Submit: Submit 3-5 poems at a time. Accepts simultaneous submissions; no previously published poems. Cover letter with brief bio required. Seldom comments on rejected poems. Responds in 2 months. Pays 1 contributor's copy. Acquires first North American serial rights. "Poets are discouraged from submitting more than once in a 12-month period. Please do not write to us for these submission guidelines."

◻ ◎ NEWSLETTER INAGO (Specialized: free-verse), P.O. Box 26244, Tucson AZ 85726-6244. Established 1979. **Poetry Editor:** Del Reitz.
Magazine Needs: *Newsletter Inago* is a monthly newsletter-format poetry journal. "Free verse and short narrative poetry preferred. Rhymed poetry must be truly exceptional (nonforced) for consideration. Due to format, 'epic' and monothematic poetry will not be considered. Cause specific, political, or religious poetry stands little chance of consideration. A wide range of short poetry, showing the poet's preferably eclectic perspective is best for *Newsletter Inago*. No haiku, please." Has published poetry by Dana Thu, Kate Fuller-Niles, Jack Coulehan, Padma Jared-Thornlyre, Corina K. Cook, and Tom Rich. *Newsletter Inago* is 4-5 pages, corner-stapled. Press run is approximately 200 for subscriptions. No price is given for the newsletter, but the editor suggests a donation of $3.50 an issue or $18.50 annually ($3.50 and $21 Canada, £8 and £21 UK). Make checks payable to Del Reitz. Copyright is retained by authors.
How to Submit: Submit 10-15 poems at a time. "Poetry should be submitted in the format in which the poet wants it to appear, and cover letters are always a good idea." Accepts simultaneous submissions and previously published poems. Sometimes comments on rejected poems. Guidelines available for SASE. Responds ASAP (usually within 2 weeks). Pays in contributor copies.

★ ◐ NEXUS, WO16A Student Union, Wright State University, Dayton OH 45435. (937)775-5533. E-mail: nexus_magazine@hotmail.com. Established 1967. **Editors:** Donna M. Marbury.
Magazine Needs: "*Nexus* is a student operated magazine of mainstream and street poetry; also

essays on environmental and political issues. We're looking for truthful, direct poetry. Open to poets anywhere. We look for contemporary, imaginative work." *Nexus* appears 3 times/year—fall, winter and spring, using about 40 pages of poetry (of 80-96) in each issue. Receives about 1,000 submissions/year, accepts approximately 30-50. Circulation is 1,000. For a sample, send a 10×15 SAE with 5 first-class stamps and $5.

How to Submit: Submit 4-6 pages of poetry with bio. Reads submissions September through May only. Accepts simultaneous submissions, "but due to short response time we want to be told it's a simultaneous submission." Editor sometimes comments on rejected poems. Past themes include Passion (winter 2003) and Rhythm & Movement (spring 2003). Upcoming themes and guidelines available for SASE, by e-mail, and in publication. Responds in 5 months except summer months. Pays 2 copies. Acquires first rights.

Ⓓ NIMROD: INTERNATIONAL JOURNAL OF POETRY AND PROSE; NIMROD/ HARDMAN AWARD; PABLO NERUDA PRIZE FOR POETRY, University of Tulsa, 600 S. College, Tulsa OK 74104-3189. (918)631-3080. Fax: (918)631-3033. E-mail: nimrod@utulsa.edu. Website: www.utulsa.edu/nimrod/. Established 1956. **Editor-in-Chief:** Francine Ringold. **Poetry Editor:** Manly Johnson.

● Poetry published in *Nimrod* has been included in *The Best American Poetry 1995*.

Magazine Needs: *Nimrod* "is an active 'little magazine,' part of the movement in American letters which has been essential to the development of modern literature. *Nimrod* publishes 2 issues/year, an awards issue in the fall featuring the prize winners of their national competition and a thematic issue each spring." Wants "vigorous writing that is neither wholly of the academy nor the streets, typed mss." Has published poetry by Diane Glancy, Judith Strasser, Steve Lautermilch, Reeves Kegworth, and Robin Chopman. *Nimrod* is 160 pages, digest-sized, flat-spined, full-color glossy cover, professionally printed on coated stock with b&w photos and art, uses 50-90 pages of poetry in each issue. Poems in non-award issues range from formal to freestyle with several translations. Receives about 2,000 submissions/year, accepts 1%; has a 3- to 6-month backlog. Press run is 3,500 of which 200 are public and university libraries. Subscription: $17.50/year inside USA; $19 outside. Sample: $10. Specific back issues available.

How to Submit: Submit 5-10 poems at a time. No fax or e-mail submissions. Publishes theme issues. Guidelines and upcoming themes available for SASE, by e-mail, or on website. Responds in up to 12 weeks. Pays 2 contributor's copies plus reduced cost on additional copies. "Poets should be aware that during the months that the Ruth Hardman Awards Competition is being conducted, reporting time on non-contest manuscripts will be longer."

Also Offers: Send business-sized SASE for rules for the Ruth G. Hardman Award: Pablo Neruda Prize for Poetry ($2,000 and $1,000 prizes). Entries accepted January 1 through April 30 each year. The $20 entry fee includes 2 issues. Also sponsors the Nimrod/Hardman Awards Workshop, a 1-day workshop held annually in October. Cost is approximately $50. Send SASE for brochure and registration form.

Ⓓ 96 INC MAGAZINE, P.O. Box 15559, Boston MA 02215. (617)267-0543. Fax: (617)262-3568. Website: www.96inc.com. Established 1992. **Editors:** Julie Anderson, Vera Gold, and Nancy Mehegan.

Magazine Needs: *96 Inc* is an annual literary magazine appearing in July that focuses on new voices, "connecting the beginner to the established, a training center for the process of publication." Wants all forms and styles of poetry, though "shorter is better." Also accepts poetry written by teens. Has published poetry by Jennifer Barber, Peter Desmond, Dana Elder, Andrew Glaze, Judy Katz-Levine, and Patricia Li. *96 Inc* is 60-69 pages, magazine-sized, saddle-stapled with coated card cover and b&w photos and graphics. Receives around 2,000 submissions/year, accepts approximately 5%. Press run is 3,000 for 500 subscribers of which 50 are libraries, 1,500 shelf sales. Single copy: $5; subscription: $15. Sample: $7.50.

How to Submit: Accepts simultaneous submissions; no previously published poems. Time between acceptance and publication is 1 year or longer. Poems are circulated to an editorial board. Guidelines available for SASE. Responds in 6-12 months. Pays 4 copies, subscription, and modest fee (when funds are available). Copyright reverts to author 2 months after publication. Occasionally, staff reviews books of poetry. Send materials for review consideration, attn: Andrew Dawson.

Advice: "*96 Inc* is an artists' collaborative and a local resource. It often provides venues and hosts readings in addition to publishing a magazine."

★ ◎ ∅ **NINETY-SIX PRESS (Specialized: regional)**, Furman University, Greenville SC 29613. (864)294-3156. Fax: (864)294-2224. E-mail: bill.rogers@furman.edu. Established 1991. **Editors:** William Rogers and Gilbert Allen.

Book/Chapbook Needs & How to Submit: Publishes 1-2 paperback books of poetry/year. "The name of the press is derived from the old name for the area around Greenville, South Carolina—the Ninety-Six District. The name suggests our interest in the writers, readers, and culture of the region." Books are usually 45-70 pages, digest-sized, professionally printed and perfect-bound with coated stock cover. For a sample, send $10. "We currently accept submissions by invitation only. At some point in the future, however, we hope to be able to encourage submissions by widely published poets who live in South Carolina."

∅ **NO EXIT**, P.O. Box 454, South Bend IN 46624-0454. Fax: (801)650-3743. Established 1994. **Editor:** Mike Amato.

Magazine Needs: *No Exit* is a quarterly forum "for the experimental as well as traditional excellence." Wants "poetry that takes chances in form or content. Form, length, subject matter and style are open. No poetry that's unsure of why it was written. Particularly interested in long (not long-winded) poems." Has published poetry by David Lawrence, Gregory Fiorini, and Ron Offen. *No Exit* is 32 pages, saddle-stapled, digest-sized, card cover with art. Accepts 10-15% of the submissions received. Press run is less than 500. Subscription: $12. Sample: $4.

How to Submit: Submit up to 5 poems ("send more if compelled, but I will stop reading after the fifth"). "No handwritten work, misspellings, colored paper, multiple type faces, typos, long-winded cover letters and lists of publication credits." Accepts simultaneous submissions; no previously published poems. No e-mail submissions. Time between acceptance and publication can vary from 1 month to 1 year. Sometimes comments on rejected poems, "if the poem strikes me as worth saving. No themes. But spring issues are devoted to a single poet. Interested writers should submit 24 pages of work. Don't bother unless of highest caliber. There are no other guidelines for single-author issues." Guidelines available for SASE. Responds in up to 3 months. Pays 1 contributor's copy plus 4-issue subscription. Acquires first North American serial rights plus right to reprint once in an anthology. "Also looking for articles, critical in nature, on poetry/poets."

Advice: "Presentation means something; namely, that you care about what you do. Don't take criticism, when offered, personally. I'll work with you if I see something solid to focus on."

∅ ◎ **NOCTURNAL LYRIC, JOURNAL OF THE BIZARRE (Specialized: horror)**, P.O. Box 542, Astoria OR 97103. E-mail: nocturnallyric@melodymail.com. Website: www.angelfire.com/ca/nocturnallyric. Established 1987. **Editor:** Susan Moon.

Magazine Needs: *Nocturnal Lyric* is a quarterly journal "featuring bizarre fiction and poetry, primarily by new writers." Wants "poems dealing with the bizarre: fantasy, death, morbidity, horror, gore, etc. Any length. No 'boring poetry.' " Has published poetry by Carrie L. Clark, J. Kevilus, Stan Morner, Richard Geyer, Stephen Kopel, Linda Rosenkrans. *Nocturnal Lyric* is 40 pages, digest-sized, photocopied, saddle-stapled, with trade ads and staff artwork. Receives about 200 poems/year, accepts about 35%. Press run is 400 for 40 subscribers. Single copy: $3 within US, $5 for non-US addresses. Make checks payable to Susan Moon.

How to Submit: Submit up to 4 poems at a time. Accepts previously published poems and simultaneous submissions. No e-mail submissions. Seldom comments on rejected poems. Guidelines available for SASE, on website, and in publication. Responds in up to 6 months. Pays 50¢ "discount on subscription" coupons. Acquires one-time rights.

Advice: "Don't follow the trends. We admire the unique."

∅ **NOMAD'S CHOIR**, % Meander, 30-15 Hobart St. F4H, Woodside NY 11377. Established 1989. **Editor:** Joshua Meander.

Magazine Needs: *Nomad's Choir* is a quarterly. "Subjects wanted: love poems, protest poems, mystical poems, nature poems, poems of humanity, poems with solutions to world problems and inner conflict. 9-30 lines, poems with hope. Simple words, careful phrasing. Free verse, rhymed poems, sonnets, half-page parables, myths and legends, song lyrics. No curse words in poems, little or no name-dropping, no naming of consumer products, no two-page poems, no humor, no bias writing, no poems untitled." Has published poetry by Viviana Grell, Matthew Anish, Pethia Garabediah, and Jimmy Burns. *Nomad's Choir* is 12 pages, magazine-sized, typeset and saddle-stapled with 3 poems/page. Receives about 150 poems/year, accepts 50. Press run is 400; all distributed free. Subscription: $5. Sample: $1.50. Make checks payable to Joshua Meander.

How to Submit: Responds in 2 months. Pays 1 contributor's copy. Publishes theme issues. Guidelines and upcoming themes available for SASE.

Advice: "Mail four copies each on a different topic. Social commentary with beauty and hope gets first consideration."

$✉ NORTH AMERICAN REVIEW; JAMES HEARST POETRY PRIZE, University of Northern Iowa, Cedar Falls IA 50614-0516. (319)273-6455. Fax: (319)273-4326. E-mail: nar@uni.e du. Website: http://webdelsol.com/NorthAmReview/NAR. Established 1815. **Editor:** Vince Gotera.

Magazine Needs: *North American Review* is a slick magazine-sized bimonthly of general interest, 48 pages average, saddle-stapled, professionally printed with glossy full-color paper cover, publishing poetry of the highest quality. Has published poetry by Debra Marquart, Nick Carbó, Yusef Komunya-kaa, Virgil Suárez, Nance Van Winckel, and Dara Wier. Receives about 7,000 poems/year, accepts 100. Press run is 2,500 for 1,500 subscribers of which 1,000 are libraries. Writer's subscription: $18. Sample: $5.

How to Submit: Include SASE. No simultaneous submissions or previously published poems. Accepts submissions by regular mail and by e-mail (in text box or as attachment). No fax submissions. Time between acceptance and publication is up to 1 year. Guidelines available for SASE, by e-mail, on website, and in publication. Responds in 3 months. Always sends prepublication galleys. Pays $1/ line ($20 minimum) and 2 contributor's copies. Acquires first North American serial rights only. Rights revert after publication.

Also Offers: North American Review sponsors the annual James Hearst Poetry Prize. First prize $1000. Postmark deadline is October 31. Rules are available for SASE, by e-mail, by fax, or on website.

✴ ◐ NORTH DAKOTA QUARTERLY, Box 7209, University of North Dakota, Grand Forks ND 58202-7209. E-mail: robert-lewis@und.nodak.edu. Website: www.und.hodak.edu/org/ndq/index. html. Established 1910. **Editor:** Robert Lewis.

Magazine Needs: *North Dakota Quarterly* is published by the University of North Dakota and includes material in the arts and humanities—essays, fiction, interviews, poems, and visual art. "We want to see poetry that reflects an understanding not only of the difficulties of the craft, but of the vitality and tact that each poem calls into play." Has published poetry by Edward Kleinschmidt, Alane Rollings, and Robert Wrigley. *North Dakota Quarterly* is digest-sized, about 200 pages, perfect-bound, professionally designed and often printed with full-color artwork on a white card cover. Publishes almost every kind of poem—avant-garde to traditional. Typically the work of about 5 poets is included in each issue. Press run is 850 for 650 subscribers. Subscription: $25/year. Sample: $8.

How to Submit: Submit 5 poems at a time, typed. No previously published poems or simultaneous submissions. No fax or e-mail submissions. Time between acceptance and publication varies. Responds in up to 6 weeks. Always sends prepublication galleys. Pays 1 contributor's copy. Acquires first serial rights.

Advice: "We look to publish the best fiction, poetry, and essays that in our estimation we can. Our tastes and interests are best reflected in what we have been recently publishing, and we suggest that you look at some current numbers."

MARKETS LISTED in the 2003 edition of *Poet's Market* that do not appear this year are identified in the General Index with a code explaining their absence from the listings.

◒ **NORTHEAST ARTS MAGAZINE**, P.O. Box 4363, Portland ME 04101. Established 1990. **Publisher/Editor:** Mr. Leigh Donaldson.

Magazine Needs: *Northeast Arts Magazine* is a biannual using poetry, short fiction, essays, reviews, art, and photography that is "honest, clear, with a love of expression through simple language, under 30 lines. We maintain a special interest in work that reflects cultural diversity in New England and throughout the world." Has published poetry by Steve Lutrell, Eliot Richman, Elizabeth R. Curry, Bob Begieburg, and Alisa Aran. *Northeast Arts Magazine* is 32 or more pages, digest-sized, professionally printed with 1-color coated card cover. Accepts 10-20% of submissions. Press run is 500-1,000 for 150 subscribers of which half are libraries, 50 to arts organizations. An updated arts information section and feature articles are included. Subscription: $10. Sample: $4.50.

How to Submit: Reads submissions September 1 through February 28 only. "A short bio is helpful." Guidelines available for SASE. Responds in 3 months. Pays 2 copies. Acquires first North American serial rights.

◖ **NORTHERN STARS MAGAZINE; NORTH STAR PUBLISHING**, N17285 Co. Rd. 400, Powers MI 49874. Website: http://members.aol.com/WriterNet/NorthStar.html. Established 1997. **Editor:** Beverly Kleikamp.

Magazine Needs: *Northern Stars* is published bimonthly and "welcomes submissions of fiction, nonfiction, and poetry on any subject or style. The main requirement is good clean family reading material. Nothing you can't read to your child or your mother. No smut or filth." Accepts poetry written by children. Has published poetry by Terri Warden, Gary Edwards, Paul Truttman, and Sarah Jense. Has published poetry chapbooks as well, including *Spiraling Beyond Clouds* by Nancy M. Ryan and *Capable of Anything* by Paul Truttman. *Northern Stars Magazine* is 32 pages, magazine-sized, photocopied and saddle-stapled with cardstock cover, may include b&w line drawings and photographs. "Send SASE for subscription information." Single copy: $5; subscription: $21. Make checks payable to Beverly Kleikamp or *Northern Stars Magazine*.

How to Submit: Submit up to 5 poems at a time, no more than 25 lines each. Accepts previously published poems and simultaneous submissions. Cover letter preferred. "Manuscripts must be typed—please do not submit handwritten material." Often comments on rejected poems. Occasionally publishes theme issues. "No payment, but nonsubscribers are notified of publication." No fee for regular subscribers. All rights return to authors on publication.

Also Offers: Sponsors monthly alternating issues contest for poetry and fiction/nonfiction (i.e., poetry contest in March-April issue, fiction/nonfiction in May-June). Entry fee: $2.50/poem for nonsubscribers, $1/poem for subscribers. Deadline: 20th of month preceding publication. Guidelines available for SASE. Publishes an annual chapbook of contest winners and honorable mentions. "I do publish many chapbooks for others now for an 'affordable' price to the writer." 100 copies or less available; sample available $5. Also has a "Somewhere In Michigan" regular column featuring people/places/events, etc., tied in with Michigan. Also prints chapbooks for a fee. Prices and information available for SASE.

Advice: "Just keep it clean and send me your best work. I do favor shorter poems over very long ones."

◒ **NORTHWEST REVIEW**, 369 PLC, University of Oregon, Eugene OR 97403. (541)346-3957. Fax: (541)346-1509. E-mail: jwitte@oregon.uoregon.edu. Website: http://darkwing.uoregon.edu/engl/deptinfo/NWR.html. Established 1957. **Poetry Editor:** John Witte.

• Poetry published by *Northwest Review* has been included in the 2001 volume of *Best American Poetry*.

Magazine Needs: "*Northwest Review* is a triannual publication appearing in May, September, and January. "The only criterion for acceptance of material for publication is that of excellence. There are no restrictions on length, style, or subject matter. But we smile on originality." Has published poetry by Alan Dugan, Charles Bukowski, Ted Hughes, Olga Broumas, Gary Snyder, and William Stafford. *Northwest Review*, a digest-sized, flat-spined magazine, appears 3 times/year and uses 25-40 pages of poetry in each issue. Receives about 3,500 submissions/year, accepts about 4%; has up to a 4-month backlog. Press run is 1,300 for 1,200 subscribers of which half are libraries. Sample: $4. Single copy: $8; subscription: $20 (3 issues).

How to Submit: Submit 6-8 poems clearly reproduced. No simultaneous submissions. Accepts submissions by postal mail only. Guidelines available on website. Responds within 3 months. Pays 3 copies.

Advice: "Persist."

$ ◙ NORTHWOODS PRESS, THE POET'S PRESS; NORTHWOODS JOURNAL, A MAGAZINE FOR WRITERS; C.A.L. (CONSERVATORY OF AMERICAN LETTERS), P.O. Box 298, Thomaston ME 04861-0298. (207)354-0998. Fax: (207)354-8953. E-mail: cal@americ anletters.org. Website: www.americanletters.org. Northwoods Press established 1972, *Northwoods Journal, a magazine for writers* 1993. **Editor:** Robert Olmsted.

Magazine Needs & How to Submit: *Northwoods Journal, a magazine for writers* is a quarterly literary magazine that publishes fiction, reviews, nonfiction, and poetry. "The journal is interested in all writers who feel they have something to say and who work to say it well. We have no interest in closet writers, or credit seekers. All writers seeking an audience, working to improve their craft, and determined to 'get it right' are welcome here." Accepts poetry written by children though standards are the same. *Northwoods Journal* is about 40 pages, digest-sized. Subscription: $12.50/year. Membership to C.A.L. ($25/year) includes subscription. Sample: $5.50 with 6×9 SAE and $1.09 in postage. **Reading fee:** $1/2 poems for C.A.L. members, $1/poem for nonmembers. Make reading fee checks payable to C.A.L. "C.A.L. offers one free read (up to 5 poems) per year if poetry is submitted simultaneously with membership or renewal." No simultaneous submissions or previously published poems. No e-mail submissions; accepts postal mail submissions only. Guidelines available for SASE or on website; "see guidelines before submitting anything." Pays 10¢/line on average; "We do not provide free issues."

Book Needs & How to Submit: "We consider books by *working* writers only. No subsidy permitted. All books are accepted with a CD of the author (or others) reading the book, or selections from the book. Original CD to be produced by author as we have no recording studio. No reading fee for book-length works. We would like to publish up to 12 books per year, but never receive enough quality manuscripts." Also publishes books through the Annual Poetry Contest. Offers $100 and a publishing contract to the 3 best mss. "No more than 10% of the ms (by line count) may have been previously published. Manuscript must be complete, with color cover (or design), all front matter including dedication, copyright page, title page, contents, or whatever you envision. Blank pages should also be included where desired." Entry fee: $10 for nonmembers, $8 for members. **Deadline:** December 31, annually. "If your manuscript is one of the best three, we will hold it until it is beaten. Once beaten, it will be returned with a sincere thank you." Previous winners include *The Mushroom Papers* by Anne Harding Woodworth, *What Rough Beast* by S.M. Hall III, and *Adventures through Time and Space, The Northwest Corner of the North American Continent and Other Matters, With the Help of My Favorite White Goddess Aphrodite* by Erik Peterson. "Ultimately, manuscript must be on disk, but do not submit on disk."

Also Offers: *The Northwoods Anthology.* The Spring 2004 will be the first annual edition. Accepts poetry, fiction, photography. Guidelines available for #10 SASE and on website. Pays cash on acceptance.

Advice: "Reading fees hold submissions down to a level that someone with 'yes' authority can actually read. They limit competition in a big way. We never get enough of anything. Reading this blurb does not equal 'knowing your market.' Read a few issues. Anyone who submits to a magazine they've never seen deserves what they get."

◙ ◎ NOSTALGICALLY (Specialized: nostalgia), (formerly *Nostalgia*), P.O. Box 2224, Orangeburg SC 29116. E-mail: cnostalgia@aol.com. Established 1986. **Poetry Editor:** Connie Lakey Martin.

Magazine Needs: *Nostalgically* is a quarterly newsletter with "stories of true personal experience . . . and not necessarily events that happened so long ago. 'Yesterday' can mean last week, last month. Reflective and insightful accounts of your faith, encounters, calamity, and fate. Try not to dwell solely on memories of parents, relatives, pets, holidays, etc." Wants "modern prose, but short poems, never longer than one page, no profanity, no ballads." *Nostalgically* is 12 pages. Press run is 1,000. Subscription: $8. Sample: $2.

How to Submit: "If material is previously published, please advise." No e-mail submissions. Include SASE and put name and address on each poem. Guidelines available for SASE. All rights revert to author upon publication.

Advice: "I offer criticism to most rejected poems, but I suggest sampling before submitting."

NOTRE DAME REVIEW, Creative Writing Program, Dept. of English, University of Notre Dame, Notre Dame IN 46556. (574)631-6952. Fax: (574)631-4268. E-mail: english.ndreview.1@nd.edu. Website: www.nd.edu/~ndr/review.htm. Established 1994. **Contact:** Poetry Editor.

Magazine Needs: Appearing biannually, *Notre Dame Review*'s "goal is to present a panoramic view of contemporary art and literature—no one style is advocated over another. We are especially interested in work that takes on big issues by making the invisible seen." Has published poetry by Ken Smith, Robert Creeley, and Denise Levertov. *Notre Dame Review* is 170 pages, magazine-sized, perfect-bound with 4-color glossy cover, includes art/graphics and ads. Receives about 400 poems/year, accepts 10%. Press run is 2,000 for 500 subscribers of which 150 are libraries, 1,000 shelf sales; 350 distributed free to contributors, assistants, etc. Single copy: $8; subscription: $15/year. Sample: $6. "Read magazine before submitting."

How to Submit: Submit 3-5 poems at a time. Accepts simultaneous submissions; no previously published poems. Cover letter required. Reads submissions September-November and January-April only. Time between acceptance and publication is 3 months. Seldom comments on rejected poems. Publishes theme issues. Guidelines and upcoming themes available on website. Responds in 3 months. Always sends prepublication galleys. Pays 2 copies. Acquires first rights. Staff reviews books of poetry in 500 words, single and multi-book format. Send materials for review consideration.

Also Offers: Sponsors the Ernest Sandeen Prize for Poetry, a book contest open to poets with at least one other book publication. Send SASE for details.

NOVA EXPRESS (Specialized: science fiction, fantasy, horror), P.O. Box 27231, Austin TX 78755. E-mail: lawrence@io.com. Website: www.io.com/~lawrence/nova.html. Established 1987. **Editor:** Lawrence Person.

● **"There will only be 2 more print issues of *Nova Express* so we will not accept submissions beyond 2004."**

Magazine Needs: *Nova Express* appears "irregularly (at least once/year) with coverage of cutting edge science fiction, fantasy and horror literature, with an emphasis on post-cyperpunk and slipstream. We feature interviews, reviews, poetry, and serious (but nonacademic) critical articles on important issues and authors throughout the entire science fiction/fantasy/horror/slipstream field. *Nova Express* is no longer a market for unsolicited fiction, but we still look at poetry." Wants "poetry relating to literature of the fantastic in some way." Has published poetry by Alison Wimsatt and Mark McLaughlin. *Nova Express* is 48 pages, magazine-sized, stapled, desktop-published with b&w graphics and line art. Receives about 40-50 poems/year, accepts 1-2. Press run is 500 for 200 subscribers, 100 shelf sales; 100 distributed free to science fiction industry professionals. Subscription: $15. Sample: $5.

How to Submit: Submit up to 5 poems at a time. No previously published poems or simultaneous submissions. Cover letter preferred. E-mail submissions (in body of message) preferred. Time between acceptance and publication is 3 months. Often comment on rejected poems. Publishes theme issues. Upcoming themes available by e-mail. Guidelines available for SASE or by e-mail. Responds in up to 6 months. "Response will be slow until the slush pile is cleaned out." Sometimes sends prepublication galleys. Pays 2 copies plus 4-issue subscription. Acquires one-time rights.

Advice: "We are not interested in any poetry outside the science fiction/fantasy/horror genre. *Nova Express* is read widely and well regarded by genre professionals."

NOW & THEN (Specialized: regional, themes), ETSU, P.O. Box 70556, Johnson City TN 37614-1707. (423)439-5348. Fax: (423)439-6340. E-mail: woodsidj@mail.etsu.edu. Website: http://.cass.etsu.edu/n&t. Established 1984. **Editor-in-Chief:** Jane Woodside. **Poetry Editor:** Linda Parsons Marion.

Magazine Needs: *Now & Then* is a regional magazine that covers Appalachian issues and culture. It contains fiction, poetry, articles, interviews, essays, memoirs, reviews, photos, and drawings. Wants poetry related to the region. "Each issue focuses on one aspect of life in the Appalachian region (anywhere hilly from Northern Mississippi on up to Southern New York). Previous theme issues have featured architecture, Appalachian lives, transportation, poetry, food, and religion. We want genuine, well-crafted voices, not sentimentalized stereotypes." Has published poetry by Fred Chappell, Maggie Anderson, Robert Morgan, and Lynn Powell. *Now & Then* appears 3 times/year and is 42 pages, magazine-sized, saddle-stapled, professionally printed, with matte card cover. Press run is 1,250-1,500 for 900 members of the Center for Appalachian Studies and Services, of which 100 are libraries. Accepts 6-10 poems an issue. Center membership is $25; the magazine is one of the membership benefits. Sample: $5 postage.

How to Submit: Will consider simultaneous submissions; they occasionally use previously published poems. Submit up to 5 poems, with SASE and cover letter including "a few lines about yourself for a contributor's note and whether the work has been published or accepted elsewhere." Put name, address and phone number on every poem. Accepts fax submissions. No e-mail submissions. Deadlines: March 1, July 1 and November 1. Publishes theme issues. Upcoming themes include "Appalachian Crafts" (Deadline March 1) and "The New Immigrants" (July 1). Guidelines and upcoming themes available for SASE or on website. Editor prefers fax or e-mail to phone calls. Responds within 6 months. Sends prepublication galleys. Pays $20/poem plus 2 copies. Acquires all rights. Reviews books of poetry in 750 words. Send poetry directly to poetry editor Linda Parsons Marion, 2909 Fountain Park Blvd., Knoxville TN 37917. E-mail for correspondence lpmarion@utk.edu. Send materials for review consideration to Marianne Worthington, book review editor, Communication and Theatre Arts Dept., Cumberland College, 600 College Station Dr., Williamsburg KY 40769. E-mail: mworthin@cc.cumber.edn.

Also Offers: Sponsors a biennial poetry competition. Guidelines can be found at www.cass.etsu.edu/n&t/contest.htm.

⬤ ◎ **NUTHOUSE; TWIN RIVERS PRESS (Specialized: humor)**, P.O. Box 119, Ellenton FL 34222. Website: http://hometown.aol.com/Nuthouse499/index2.html. Press established 1989, magazine established 1993. **Editor:** Ludwig Von Quirk.

Magazine Needs: *Nuthouse*, "amusements by and for delightfully diseased minds," appears every 2 months using humor of all kinds, including homespun and political. Wants "humorous verse; virtually all genres considered." Has published poetry by Holly Day, Daveed Garstenstein-Ross, and Don Webb. *Nuthouse* is 12 pages, digest-sized and photocopied from desktop-published originals. Receives about 500 poems/year, accepts approximately 100. Press run is 100 for 50 subscribers. Subscription: $5/5 issues. Sample: $1.25. Make checks payable to Twin Rivers Press.

How to Submit: Accepts previously published poems and simultaneous submissions. Time between acceptance and publication is 6-12 months. Often comments on rejected poems. Responds within 1 month. Pays 1 copy/poem. Acquires one-time rights.

⬤ ◎ **THE OAK; THE ACORN (Specialized: children); THE GRAY SQUIRREL (Specialized: senior citizens); THE SHEPHERD (Specialized: religious; inspirational)**, 1530 Seventh St., Rock Island IL 61201. (309)788-3980. **Poetry Editor:** Betty Mowery.

Magazine Needs & How to Submit: *The Oak*, established in 1990, is a "publication for writers with poetry and fiction." Wants poetry of "no more than 35 lines and fiction of no more than 500 words. No restrictions as to types and style, but no pornography or love poetry." *The Oak* appears quarterly. Established 1991, *The Gray Squirrel* is now included in *The Oak* and takes poetry of no more than 35 lines fiction up to 500 words from poets 60 years of age and up. Uses more than half of about 100 poems received each year. Include a SASE or mss will not be returned. Press run is 250, with 10 going to libraries. Subscription: $10. Sample: $3. Make all checks payable to *The Oak*. Submit 5 poems at a time. Accepts simultaneous submissions and previously published poems. Responds in 1 week. *"The Oak* does not pay in dollars or copies but you need not purchase to be published."* Acquires first or second rights. *The Oak* holds several contests. Guidelines available for SASE.

Magazine Needs & How to Submit: *The Acorn*, established in 1988, is a "newsletter for young authors and teachers or anyone else interested in our young authors. Takes mss from kids K-12th grades. Poetry no more than 35 lines. It also takes fiction of no more than 500 words." *The Acorn* appears 4 times/year and "we take well over half of submitted mss." Press run is 100, with 6 going to libraries. Subscription: $10. Sample: $3. Make all checks payable to *The Oak*. Submit 5 poems at a time. Accepts simultaneous submissions and previously published poems. Responds in 1 week. *"The Acorn* does not pay in dollars or copies but you need not purchase to be published." Acquires first or second rights. Young authors, submitting to *The Acorn*, should put either age or grade on manuscripts. *The Shepherd*, established in 1996, is a quarterly publishing inspirational poetry from all ages. Poems may be up to 35 lines and fiction up to 500 words. "We want something with a message but not preachy." Subscription: $10 (4 issues). Sample: $3. Make checks payable to *The Oak*. Include SASE with all submissions.

Also Offers: Sponsors numerous contests. Guidelines available for SASE.

Advice: "Write tight poems with a message; don't write about lost loves or crushes. Study the markets for word limit and subject. Always include SASE or rejected manuscripts will not be returned. Please make checks for *all* publications payable to *The Oak*."

$ ◑ OASIS, P.O. Box 626, Largo FL 33779-0626. (727)345-8505. E-mail: oasislit@aol.com. Established 1992. **Editor:** Neal Storrs.

Magazine Needs: *Oasis* is a quarterly forum for high quality literary prose and poetry written almost exclusively by freelancers. Usually contains 6 prose pieces and the work of 4-5 poets. Wants "to see poetry of stylistic beauty. Prefer free verse with a distinct, subtle music. No superficial sentimentality, old-fashioned rhymes or rhythms." Has published poetry by Carolyn Stoloff and Simon Perchik. *Oasis* is about 75 pages, 7×10, attractively printed on heavy book paper, perfect-bound with medium-weight card cover, no art. Receives about 2,000 poems/year. Press run is 300 for 90 subscribers of which 5 are libraries. Subscription: $20/year. Sample: $7.50.

How to Submit: Submit any number of poems. Accepts simultaneous submissions; rarely accepts previously published poems. Accepts e-mail submissions (include in body of message). Cover letter preferred. Time between acceptance and publication is usually 4 months. Seldom comments on rejected poems. Guidelines available for SASE. Responds "the same or following day more than 99% of the time." Sends prepublication galleys on request. Pays $5/poem and 1 contributor's copy. Acquires first or one-time rights.

⊕ ◔ OASIS BOOKS; OASIS MAGAZINE, 12 Stevenage Rd., London SW6 6ES England. Established 1969. **Editor/Publisher:** Ian Robinson.

Magazine Needs: *Oasis Magazine* appears 3 times/year and publishes short fiction and poetry as well as occasional reviews and other material. "No preference for style or subject matter; just quality. No long poems; *Oasis* is a very short magazine. Also, usually no rhyming poetry." Has published poetry by Andrea Moorhead, Michael Heller (USA), Nathaniel Tarn (USA), Toby Olson (USA), and August Kleinzahler (USA). *Oasis* is international A5 size, litho, folded sheets. Receives 500-600 poems/year, accepts approximately 4 or 5. Press run is 500 for 400 subscribers of which 10 are libraries. Subscription: $30/4 issues. Sample: $3.50 (US). Make checks in American funds payable to Robert Vas Dias. "Dollar bills accepted."

How to Submit: Submit up to 6 poems at a time. Accepts previously published poems sometimes; simultaneous submissions "if work comes from outside the U.K." Include SAE and 4 IRCs for return (US postage is not valid). Seldom comments on rejected poems. Publishes theme issues occasionally. Responds in 1 month. Pays up to 5 copies.

Book/Chapbook Needs & How to Submit: Oasis Books publishes 2-3 paperbacks and 2-3 chapbooks/year. Has published *Among Memory's Ruins* by Zdenek Vanicek; *From Far Away* by Harry Gilonis and Tony Baker; *Flecks* by Ralph Hawkins; *Anxious to Please* by Nicholas Moore; and *3,600 Weekends* by Ken Edwards. Responds to queries and mss in 1 month. For sample books or chapbooks, write for catalog. "No more book or chapbook publications are planned for the next two years (i.e., for 2003 and 2004)."

Advice: "One IRC (U.S. postage is not valid) is not enough to ensure return airmail postage; three will, provided manuscript is not too thick. No return postage will ensure that the ms is junked. It's best to write first before submitting (include 2 IRCs for reply)."

$ ◑ ◎ OCEAN VIEW BOOKS (Specialized: form/style, surrealism), P.O. Box 9249, Denver CO 80209. Established 1981. **Editor:** Lee Ballentine.

Book/Chapbook Needs: Ocean View Books publishes "books of poetry by poets influenced by

surrealism." Publishes 2 paperbacks and 2 hardbacks/year. No "confessional/predictable, self-referential poems." Has published poetry by Anselm Hollo, Janet Hamill, and Tom Disch. Books are
usually 100 pages, digest-sized, offset-printed and perfect-bound with 4-color card cover, includes
art. "Our books are distinctive in style and format. Interested poets should order a sample book for
$8 (in the US) for an idea of our focus before submitting."

How to Submit: Submit a book project query including 5 poems. Accepts previously published
poems and simultaneous submissions. Cover letter preferred. Time between acceptance and publication is up to 2 years. "If our editors recommend publication, we may circulate manuscripts to distinguished outside readers for an additional opinion. The volume of submissions is such that we can
respond to queries only if we are interested in the project. If we're interested we will contact you
within 4 months." Pays $100 honorarium and a number of author's copies (out of a press run of
500). "Terms vary per project."

Advice: "In 15 years, we have published about 50 books—most consisted of previously published
poems from good journals. A poet's 'career' must be well-established before undertaking a book."

○ OFFERINGS, P.O. Box 1667, Lebanon MO 65536-1667. Established 1994. **Editor:** Velvet
Fackeldey.

Magazine Needs: *Offerings* is a poetry quarterly. "We accept traditional and free verse from established and new poets, as well as students. Prefer poems of less than 30 lines. No erotica." Currently
overstocked with nature themes. Accepts poetry written by children. Has published poetry by Tom
Harmon, G.G. Gilchrist, B.Z. Niditch, Nancy M. Ryan, and Robert H. Demaree Jr. *Offerings* is 50-
60 pages, digest-sized, neatly printed and saddle-stapled with paper cover. Receives about 500 poems/
year, accepts about 25%. Press run is 100 for 75 subscribers, 25 shelf sales. Single copy: $5; subscrip-
tion: $16. Sample: $3.

How to Submit: Submit typed poems with name and address on each page. Students should also
include grade level. SASE required. No simultaneous submissions. Seldom comments on rejected
poems. Guidelines available for SASE. Responds in up 1 month. All rights revert to author after
publication.

Advice: "We are unable to offer payment at this time (not even copies). We welcome beginning
poets."

⊕ ○ OFFERTA SPECIALE; BERTOLA CARLA PRESS, Corso De Nicola 20, 10-128 Torino
Italy. Established 1988. **Director/Editor:** Bertola Carla. **Co-Director:** Vitacchio Alberto.

Magazine Needs: *Offerta Speciale* is a biannual international journal appearing in May and November. Has published poetry by Federica Manfredini (Italy), Bernard Heidsieck (France), Richard Kostelanetz, and E. Mycue (US). *Offerta Speciale* is 56 pages, digest-sized, neatly printed and saddle-
stapled with glossy card cover. Receives about 300 poems/year, accepts about 40%. Press run is 500
for 60 subscribers. Single copy: $25; subscription: $100. Make checks payable to Carla Bertola.

How to Submit: Submit 3 poems at a time. No previously published poems or simultaneous submissions. Time between acceptance and publication is 1 year. Often comments on rejected poems. Guidelines available for SASE (or SAE and IRC). Pays 1 contributor's copy.

○ ◎ OFFICE NUMBER ONE (Specialized: form), 1708 S. Congress Ave., Austin TX 78704.
Established 1988. **Editor:** Carlos B. Dingus.

Magazine Needs: Appearing 2-4 times/year, *Office Number One* is a "humorous, satirical zine of
news information and events from parallel and alternate realities." In addition to stories, they want
limericks, 3-5-3 or 5-7-5 haiku, and rhymed/metered quatrains. "Poems should be short (2-12 lines)
and make a point. No long rambling poetry about suffering and pathos. Poetry should be technically
perfect." Accepts poetry written by children, "if it stands on its own." As for a sample, the editor
says, "No one poem provides a fair sample." *Office Number One* is 12 pages, magazine-sized,
computer set in 10 pt. type, saddle-stapled, with graphics and ads. Uses about 40 poems/year. Press
run is 2,000 for 75 subscribers, 50 shelf sales; 1,600 distributed free locally. Single copy: $1.85;
subscription: $8.82/6 issues. Sample: $2.

How to Submit: Submit up to 5 pages of poetry at a time. Accepts previously published poems
and simultaneous submissions. "Will comment on rejected poems if comment is requested." Publishes theme issues occasionally. Guidelines and upcoming themes available for SASE or by e-mail.

Responds in 2 months. Pays "23¢" and 1 copy. Acquires rights for "use in any *Officer Number One* publication."
Advice: "Say something that a person can use to change his life."

⬛ **THE OLD RED KIMONO**, Humanities Division, P.O. Box 1864, Floyd College, Rome GA 30162. E-mail: napplega@mail.fc.peachnet.edu. Website: www.fc.peachnet.edu/ork/. Established 1972. **Poetry Editors:** La Nelle Daniel, Dr. Nancy Applegate, and Erskine Thompson.
Magazine Needs: Appearing annually, *Old Red Kimono* has the "sole purpose of putting out a magazine of original, high-quality poetry and fiction. *Old Red Kimono* is looking for submissions of three to five short poems and/or one short story." Has published poetry by Walter McDonald, Peter Huggins, Midred Greear, John C. Morrison, Jack Stewart, Kirsten Fox, and Al Braselton. *Old Red Kimono* is 72 pages, magazine-sized, professionally printed on heavy stock with b&w graphics, colored matte cover with art, using approximately 40 pages of poetry (usually 1 or 2 poems to the page). Receives about 1,000 submissions/year, accepts approximately 60-70. Sample: $3.
How to Submit: Submit 3-5 poems. Accepts submissions by e-mail (in text box) and by regular mail. Reads submissions September 1 through March 1 only. Guidelines available for SASE and on website. Responds in 3 months. Pays 2 copies. Acquires first publication rights.

⬛ **ONTHEBUS; BOMBSHELTER PRESS**, P.O. Box 481266, Bicentennial Station, Los Angeles CA 90048. (323)651-5488. Fax: (323)651-5132. E-mail: jgrapes@attbi.com. Website: www.bombshelterpress.com. Established 1975. **Editor:** Jack Grapes (magazine). **Poetry Editors:** Jack Grapes and Michael Andrews (press).
Magazine Needs: *ONTHEBUS*, appearing biannually, uses "contemporary mainstream poetry—no more than six (ten pages total) at a time. No rhymed, 19th Century traditional 'verse.'" Has published poetry by Charles Bukowski, Albert Goldbarth, Ai, Norman Dubie, Kate Braverman, Stephen Dobyns, Allen Ginsberg, David Mura, Richard Jones, and Ernesto Cardenal. *ONTHEBUS* is 275 pages, offset printed, flat-spined, with color card cover. Press run is 3,500 for 600 subscribers of which 40 are libraries, 1,200 shelf sales ("500 sold directly at readings"). Subscription: $28/3 issues; Issue #17/18, special double issue: $15. Sample (including guidelines): $12.
How to Submit: Submit 3-6 poems at a time to the above address (send all other correspondence to: 6684 Colgate Ave., Los Angeles CA 90048). Accepts simultaneous submissions and previously published poems, "if I am informed where poem has previously appeared and/or where poem is also being submitted. I expect neatly-typed, professional-looking cover letters with list of poems included plus poet's bio. Sloppiness and unprofessional submissions do not equate with great writing." Do not submit mss between November 1 and March 1 or between June 1 and September 1. Submissions sent during those times will be returned unread. Responds in "anywhere from two weeks to two years." Pays 1 copy. Acquires one-time rights. Reviews books of poetry in 400 words (chapbooks in 200 words), single format. Send materials for review consideration.
Book/Chapbook Needs & How to Submit: Bombshelter Press publishes 4-6 flat-spined paperbacks and 5 chapbooks/year. Query first. Primarily interested in Los Angeles poets. "We publish very few unsolicited mss." Responds in 3 months. Pays 50 copies. Also publishes the *ONTHEBUS* Poets Anthology Series. Send SASE for details.
Advice: "My goal is to publish a democratic range of American poets and ensure they are read by striving to circulate the magazine as widely as possible. It's hard work and a financial drain. I hope the mag is healthy for poets and writers, and that they support the endeavor by subscribing as well as submitting."

⬛ **ONCE UPON A TIME (Specialized: poetry about writing or illustrating)**, 553 Winston Court, St. Paul MN 55118. (651)457-6223. Fax: (651)457-9151. E-mail: audreyouat@aol.com. Website: http://members.aol.com/ouatmag. Established 1990. **Editor/Publisher:** Audrey B. Baird.
Magazine Needs: Published quarterly, *Once Upon A Time* is a support magazine for children's writers and illustrators. Poetry should be 20 lines maximum—writing or illustration-related. "No poems comparing writing to giving birth to a baby. Very overdone!" *Once Upon A Time* is 32 pages, magazine-sized, stapled with glossy cover, includes art/graphics and a few ads. Receives about 40 poems/year, accepts about 60%. Press run is 1,000 for 900 subscribers. Single copy: $6; subscription: $25. Sample: $5. Make checks payable to Audrey B. Baird.

How to Submit: Submit no more than 6 poems at a time. Accepts previously published poems and simultaneous submissions. Cover letter preferred. Time between acceptance and publication "can be up to 2 years. Short poems usually printed in less than 1 year." Often comments on rejected poems. Guidelines available for SASE or on website. Responds in 1 month. Pays 2 contributor's copies. Acquires one-time rights.

Advice: "Don't send your piece too quickly. Let it sit for a week or more. Then re-read it and see if you can make it better. If you're writing rhyming poetry, the rhythm has to work. Count syllables! Accents, too, have to fall in the right place! Most rhyming poetry I receive has terrible rhythm. Don't forget SASE!"

⊘ **ONE TRICK PONY; BANSHEE PRESS**, P.O. Box 11186, Philadelphia PA 19136. (215)331-7389. E-mail: lmckee4148@aol.com. Established 1997. Editor: Louis McKee.

Magazine Needs: *One Trick Pony* is published biannually and contains "poetry and poetry related reviews and essays (for reviews, essays, interviews, etc.—please query)." No limitations. Has published poetry by William Heyen, Naomi Shihab Nye, Denise Duhamel, David Kirby, and Michael Waters. *One Trick Pony* is 60 pages, digest-sized, offset printed and saddle-stapled, glossy cover with art. Receives about 750 poems/year, accepts approximately 10%. Press run is 400 for over 150 subscribers of which 12 are libraries, 150 shelf sales. Single copy: $5; subscription: $10/2 issues. Sample: $5. Make checks payable to Louis McKee.

How to Submit: Submit 3-6 poems at a time. No simultaneous submissions or previously published poems. Responds in 1 month. Pays 2 copies. Acquires first rights. Reviews books and chapbooks of poetry. Send materials for review consideration.

Book/Chapbook Needs: Banshee Press publishes 1 chapbook/year. Chapbooks are *by invitation only.*

⊘ **OPEN HAND PUBLISHING INC.**, P.O. Box 20207, Greensboro NC 27420. (336)292-8585. Fax: (336)292-8588. E-mail: info@openhand.com. Website: www.openhand.com. Established 1981. **Publisher:** Richard Koritz. Open Hand is a "literary/political book publisher bringing out flat-spined paperbacks as well as cloth cover editions about African-American and multicultural issues." Has published *Where Are the Love Poems for Dictators?* by E. Ethelbert Miller, *Old Woman of Irish Blood* by Pat Andrus, and *Stone on Stone: Poetry by Women of Diverse Heritages* edited by Zoë Anglesey. Does not consider unsolicited mss.

⊠ ◎ **OPEN MINDS QUARTERLY; THE WRITER'S CIRCLE ONLINE (Specialized: individuals who have experienced mental illness)**, The Writer's Circle, 680 Kirkwood Dr., Building 2, Sudbury ON P3E 1X3 Canada. (705)675-9193, ext. 8286. Fax: (705)675-3501. E-mail: openminds@nisa.on.ca. Website: www.nisa.on.ca/literaryprograms.htm. Established 1997. **Editor:** Barb Dubé, M.A.

Magazine Needs: *Open Minds Quarterly* provides a "venue for individuals who have experienced mental illness to express themselves via poetry, short fiction, essays, first-person accounts of living with mental illness, book/movie reviews." Wants unique, well-written, provocative poetry. No overly graphic or sexual violence. Recently published poetry by Derek Day, Alexander Radway, Sydney B. Smith, and Gail Kroll. *Open Minds Quarterly* is 24 pages, magazine-sized, saddle-stapled, 100 lb. stock cover with original artwork back/front, approximately 3-6 ads/issue. Receives about 125 poems/year, accepts about 65%. Publishes about 5-10 poems/issue. Press run is 1,000 for 550 subscribers of which 4-5 are libraries, 5 shelf sales; 400 distributed free to potential subscribers, published writers, advertisers. Single copy: $5 Canadian, $3.50 US; subscription: $35 Canadian, $28.25 US (special rates also available). Sample: $3.50 US, $5 Canadian. Make checks payable to NISA/Northern Initiative for Social Action.

How to Submit: Submit 1-5 poems at a time. Accepts previously published poems and simultaneous submissions. Accepts fax, e-mail, and disk submissions. Cover letter is required. "Info in cover letter: indication as to 'consumer/survivor' of the mental health system status." Reads submissions all year. Submit seasonal poems at least 8 months in advance. Time between acceptance and publication is 6-18 months. "Poems are accepted/rejected by the editor. Sometimes, submissions are passed on to a second or third party for input or a 'second opinion.' " Seldom comments on rejected poems. Guidelines available in magazine (once a year), for SASE, by fax, by e-mail, or on website. Responds in up to 4 months. Sometimes sends prepublication galleys. "All authors own their work—if another publisher seeks to reprint from our publication, we request them to cite the source."

Also Offers: "All material not accepted for our magazine/journal will be considered for *The Writer's Circle Online*, our Internet publication forum. Same guidelines apply. Same contact person."

Advice: "We are unique in that our outlets help to reduce the stigma surrounding mental illness by illustrating the creative talents of individuals suffering from mental illness."

⬛ ◎ **OPENED EYES POETRY & PROSE MAGAZINE (Specialized: membership/sub-scription; senior citizen; students; African-American, Caribbean); KENYA BLUE POETRY AWARD CONTEST**, P.O. Box 21708, Brooklyn NY 11202-1708. (718)703-4008. E-mail: kenyablue@excite.com. Established 1998. **Editor-in-Chief:** Kenya Blue.

Magazine Needs: Appearing 3 times/year, *Opened Eyes* is a "venue for seniors, known poets, novice poets, and minority poets; offering a supportive environment and challenging environment." Wants "free verse, traditional forms; prose—all styles; all subject matter; short, poetic stories. No hate or sexually explicit/graphic poetry." Accepts poetry written by children. Has published poetry by Nicole Davis, McGuffy Ann Morris, and Carol D. Meeks. *Opened Eyes* is magazine-sized, photo-copied and either strip-bound or comb-bound with cardstock cover, includes art/graphics and ads. Receives about 100 poems/year, accepts about 95%. Publish up to 30 poems/issue. Press run is 100 for 50 subscribers, 24 shelf sales. Subscription: $18/year. Sample: $7. Make checks payable to K. Blue.

How to Submit: Submit 1-3 poems at a time with *$3 reading fee if nonsubscriber.* Line length for poetry is 30 maximum. Accepts previously published poems and simultaneous submissions. Accepts e-mail submissions; include in body of message. "Type name, address, and e-mail in upper left hand corner. Submit typed poem in desired format for magazine and editor will try to accommodate." Time between acceptance and publication is up to 2 months. "Poems are circulated to editor and poetry consultant." Occasionally publishes theme issues; upcoming themes available for SASE. Guidelines available for SASE, by e-mail, and in publication. Responds in 3 weeks. Pays 5 copies. Acquires one-time rights.

Also Offers: "Sponsors the Kenya Blue Poetry Award contest. Winner paid in copies of magazine. Kenya Blue Award topics change yearly.

Advice: "Challenge yourself and take a first step in being creative via literature and via poetry."

⬛ ⬛ **$**⬜ **ORBIS: AN INTERNATIONAL QUARTERLY OF POETRY AND PROSE**, 17 Greenhow Ave., W. Kirby, Wirral CH48 5EL United Kingdom. E-mail: carolebaldock@hotmail.com. Established 1968. **Editor:** Carole Baldock.

Magazine Needs: *Orbis*, appearing quarterly, publishes "fiction and the occasional upbeat poem. Looking for more work from young people (this includes 20-somethings) and women writers." Features "news, reviews, views, letters, prose, and quite a lot of poetry." *Orbis* is 80 pages, digest-sized, flat-spined, professionally printed with glossy card cover. Receives "thousands" of submissions/year. Single copy: £4 (€9, $9); subscription: £15/4 issues (€32, $32). Send books for review consideration to Rupert Loydell, 11 Sylvan Rd., Exeter, Devon EX4 6EW, United Kingdom. Send magazines for review consideration to Matt Bryden, 28A Tadcaster Rd., Dringhouses, York YO24 1LQ United Kingdom.

How to Submit: Submit up to 4 poems (1 poem per page). Accepts e-mail submissions from outside UK only (only 2 poems, no attachments). Enclose 2 IRCs for all correspondence, not US postage. Responds in up to 1 month.

Also Offers: Prizes in each issue—$80 for featured writer (3 poems) and $80 "Reader's Award" for piece receiving the most votes (with $80 split between 4 runner-ups).

VISIT THE WRITER'S DIGEST WEBSITE at www.writersdigest.com for books, markets, newsletter sign-up, and a special poetry page.

$ ◙ **ORCHISES PRESS**, P.O. Box 20602, Alexandria VA 22320-1602. E-mail: lathbury@gmu.e
du. Website: http://mason.gmu.edu/~rlathbur. Established 1983. **Poetry Editor:** Roger Lathbury.
Book/Chapbook Needs: Orchises is a small press publisher of literary and general material in flat-
spined paperbacks and in hardcover. "Although we will consider mss submitted, we prefer to seek
out the work of poets who interest us." Regarding poetry, Orchises has "no restrictions; it must be
technically proficient and deeply felt. I find it unlikely that I would publish a ms unless a fair
proportion of its contents has appeared previously in respected literary journals." Has published
Chokecherries by Peter Klappert and *The Travelling Library* by David Kirby. Publishes about 4 flat-
spined paperbacks of poetry a year, averaging 96 pages, and some casebound books. Most paperbacks
are $14.95. Hardbacks are $20-21.95 each.
How to Submit: Submit 5-6 poems at a time. No e-mail submissions. When submitting, "tell where
poems have previously been published." Brief cover letter preferred. Guidelines available on website.
Responds in 1 month. Pays 36% of money earned once Orchises recoups its initial costs and has a
"generous free copy policy."

◖ ◎ **OSIRIS, AN INTERNATIONAL POETRY JOURNAL/UNE REVUE INTERNA-
TIONALE (Specialized: translations, bilingual)**, P.O. Box 297, Deerfield MA 01342-0297.
Established 1972. **Poetry Editor:** Andrea Moorhead.
Magazine Needs: *Osiris* is a semiannual that publishes contemporary poetry in English, French,
and Italian without translation and in other languages with translation, including Polish, Danish, and
German. Wants poetry which is "lyrical, non-narrative, multi-temporal, post-modern, well-crafted.
Also looking for translations from non-IndoEuropean languages." Has published poetry by Tahar
Bekri (France), John Falk (USA), Françoise Han (France), Karl Lubomirski (Austria), Herberto Hel-
der (Portugal), and Warren Woessner (USA). *Osiris* is 40-48 pages, digest-sized, saddle-stapled with
graphics and photos. There are 15-20 pages of poetry in English in each issue of this publication.
Print run is 500 with 50 subscription copies sent to college and university libraries, including foreign
libraries. Receives 200-300 submissions/year, accepts about 12. Single copy: $7.50; subscription:
$15. Sample: $3.
How to Submit: Submit 4-6 poems at a time. "Poems should be sent regular mail." Include short
bio and SASE with submission. "Translators should include a letter of permission from the poet or
publisher as well as copies of the original text." Responds in 1 month. Sometimes sends prepublication galleys. Pays 5 contributor's copies.
Advice: "It is always best to look at a sample copy of a journal before submitting work, and when
you do submit work, do it often and do not get discouraged. Try to read poetry and support other
writers."

◙ **OSRIC PUBLISHING; THE WHITE CROW**, P.O. Box 4501, Ann Arbor MI 48106-4501.
E-mail: chris@osric.com. Website: http://osric.com and http://wcrow.com. Established 1993. **Editor:**
Christopher™ Herdt. **Assistant Editor:** Mrrranda L. Tarrow.
Magazine Needs: *The White Crow* is a quarterly "literate, not literary journal. It contains poetry
and fiction that is meaningful and that will appeal to an educated, but not necessarily high-brow
audience. Something that even an electrical engineer might enjoy." Wants "nothing bigger than a
breadbox. No one-pagers that use the word black more than four times and no 'throbbing, beefy
torpedo' poems." Has published poetry by David Offut, Alan Catlin, Stepan Chapman, and Eileen
Doherty. *The White Crow* is 32 pages, digest-sized, sometimes photocopied, sometimes offset-printed,
saddle-stapled with cardstock, black only cover, includes art and graphics. Receives about 2,000
poems/year, accepts 5%. Press run is 400 for 50 subscribers, 200 shelf sales; 50 distributed free to
reviewers and associates. Single copy: $2.50; subscription: $8. Sample (including guidelines): $2.50.
Make checks payable to Osric Publishing.
How to Submit: Submit 5 poems at a time. Accepts previously published poems and simultaneous
submissions. No e-mail or disk submissions. Cover letter preferred. Time between acceptance and
publication is about 1 month. Poems are circulated to an editorial board. "The editors all get together
and drink heavily, eat some food, and rate and berate the submissions." Guidelines are available for
SASE or on website. Responds in about 6 months. Pays 1 contributor's copy. Acquires first rights.
Staff reviews books and chapbooks of poetry and other magazines in 100 words, single book format.
Send materials for review consideration to Christopher™ Herdt.

Book/Chapbook Needs & How to Submit: Osric Publishing seeks "poetry and short fiction for the literate, not literary." Publishes 1 chapbook/year. Has published *Bench Marks* by David Offutt. Books are usually 24 pages, 8½ × 5½, photocopied or offset-printed and saddle-stapled with cardstock cover, uses art/graphics. Query first, with a few sample poems and a cover letter with brief bio and publication credits. Responds to queries and mss in 6 months. Pays 20 author's copies (out of a press run of 200). Order sample books by sending $2 to Osric Publishing.

Advice: "No poems about poetry, no poems about writing poetry, no stories about writing stories."

$ ☑ ◎ THE OTHER SIDE MAGAZINE (Specialized: Christian, political, social issues), 300 W. Apsley St., Philadelphia PA 19144. (215)849-2178. Website: www.theotherside.org. Established 1965. **Poetry Editor:** Jeanne Minahan.

Magazine Needs: "*The Other Side* is an independent ecumenical magazine that seeks to advance a broad Christian vision that's biblical and compassionate, appreciative of the creative arts, and committed to the intimate intertwining of personal spirituality and social transformation. We weave together first-person essays, insightful analyses, biblical reflection, interviews, fiction, poetry, and an inviting mix of visual art. We strive to nurture, uplift, and challenge readers with personal, provocative writing that reflects the transformative, liberating Spirit of Jesus Christ." *The Other Side* publishes 1-2 poems/issue. "Poetry submissions should include strong imagery, fresh viewpoints, and lively language, while avoiding versifications of religious instruction or syrupy piety. Be warned that only 0.5% of the poems reviewed are accepted." Has published poetry by Kathleen Norris, Paul Ramsey, Carol Hamilton, and John Knoepfle. *The Other Side* is magazine-sized, professionally printed on quality pulp stock, 64 pages, saddle-stapled, with full-color paper cover. Circulation is 13,000 to that many subscriptions. Subscription: $24. Sample: $4.50.

How to Submit: Submit 3 poems at a time. Line length for poetry is 50 maximum. No previously published poems or simultaneous submissions. Accepts submissions by postal mail only. Editor "almost never" comments on rejected poems. Guidelines available for SASE. Responds in 3 months. Pays $15 plus 2 copies and 2-year subscription.

◖ ◎ OUTER DARKNESS: WHERE NIGHTMARES ROAM UNLEASHED (Specialized: horror, mystery, science fiction, dark fantasy), 1312 N. Delaware Place, Tulsa OK

Pennsylvania artist Allen Koszowski provided the artwork for *Outer Darkness*, Issue No. 25. Editor Dennis Kirk, who designed the cover layout, says, "While this drawing doesn't necessarily reflect the contents of this issue, it, like most of Allen's work, reflects very well the imaginative nature of *Outer Darkness* itself—a magazine of horror and science fiction."

74110. E-mail: odmagazine@aol.com. Established 1994. **Editor:** Dennis Kirk.

Magazine Needs: *Outer Darkness* is a quarterly magazine featuring short stories, poetry, and art in the genres of horror, dark fantasy, and science fiction (and also mystery with a horror/gothic slant). Wants "all styles of poetry, though traditional rhyming verse is preferred. Send verse that is dark and melancholy in nature. Nothing experimental—very little of this type of verse is published in *Outer Darkness.*" Has published poetry by Kendall Evans, Richard William Pearce, Michelle Scalise, and Louise Webster. *Outer Darkness* is 40-60 pages, digest-sized, photocopied, saddle-stapled, glossy cover, includes cover art, cartoons and illustrations and runs ads for other publications. Receives about 200 poems/year, accepts 20%. Press run is 250, 25% to subscribers, 25% to contributors, 25% sample copy sales, 25% to advertisers, free copies, etc. Single copy: $3.95; subscription: $11.95.

How to Submit: Submit up to 3 poems at a time, no longer than 60 lines each. Accepts simultaneous submissions; no previously published poems. Accepts submissions by postal mail. Cover letter preferred. "Poets are encouraged to include cover letters with their submissions, with biographical information, personal interests, past publishing credits, etc. I strongly prefer hardcopy submissions rather than disks." Always comments on rejected poems. Guidelines available for SASE. Responds in up to 6 weeks. Sends prepublication galleys, when requested. Pays 2 copies. Acquires one-time rights.

Advice: "Take your time when composing verse. Pick and choose your words carefully. I receive many poems which seem forced or clumsy in places. And don't be afraid to experiment with different forms of rhyme. When you've produced the best work you can, submit—keep submitting. What may not work for one editor may work very well for another."

OUTRIDER PRESS, 937 Patricia Lane, Crete IL 60417-1362. (708)672-6630. Fax: (708)672-5820. E-mail: outriderpr@aol.com. Website: www.outriderpress.com. Established 1988. **Senior Editor:** Whitney Scott.

Book/Chapbook Needs: Outrider publishes 1-3 novels/anthologies/chapbooks annually in August. Wants "poetry dealing with the terrain of the human heart and plotting inner journeys; growth and grace under pressure. No bag ladies, loves-that-never-were, please." Has published poetry by David T. Lloyd, Albert DeGenova, Vivian Shipley, Michele Cooper, Maureen Connolly, and Lynn Lifshin. Anthologies are 250-300 pages, digest-sized, attractively printed and perfect-bound with glossy card cover, $15.95 to $17.95.

How to Submit: Submit 3-4 poems at a time with SASE. Include name, address, phone/fax number, and e-mail address on every poem. Accepts simultaneous submissions, if specified. Accepts submissions on disk, by e-mail (in text box), and by postal mail. Guidelines and upcoming themes available for SASE, and by e-mail. Cover letter preferred. Responds to queries in 1 month, to mss in 2 months. Pays 1 copy.

Also Offers: Outrider publishes a themed anthology annually in August, with cash prizes for best poetry and short fiction. Submit up to 8 poems, no longer than 24 lines in length. **Reading fee:** $16.50, $12 for Tallgrass Writers Guild members. Guidelines available for SASE. Deadline: February 28, 2004. Published in August 2004. 2004 theme: "Things That Go Bump . . ."—Apparitions, Ghosts, Familiars, and Hauntings of all kinds. The press is affiliated with the Tallgrass Writers Guild, an international organization open to all who support equality of voices in writing. Annual membership fee: $40. Information available for SASE or on website.

Advice: "We look for visceral truths expressed without compromise, coyness, or cliché. Go for the center of the experience. Pull no punches."

$ "OVER THE BACK FENCE" MAGAZINE (Specialized: regional), 14 S. Paint St., Suite 169, P.O. Box 756, Chillicothe OH 45601. (740)772-2165. Fax: (740)773-7626. E-mail: backfenc@bright.net. Website: www.backfence.com/. Established 1994. **Managing Editor:** Sarah Williamson.

Magazine Needs: A quarterly regional magazine "serving nineteen counties in southern Ohio and 10 counties in Northern Ohio, *'Over The Back Fence'* has a wholesome, neighborly style that is appealing to readers from young adults to seniors." Wants rhyming or free verse poetry, 24 lines or less; open to subject matter, "but seasonal works well"; friendly or inspirational work. "Since most of our readers are not poets, we want something simple and likeable by the general public. No profanity or erotic subject matter, please." *"Over The Back Fence"* is 68 pages, published on high gloss paper, saddle-stapled with b&w and color illustrations and photos, includes ads. Receives less than 200 poems/year, accepts approximately 4-10. Press run is 15,000 for about 4,000 subscribers in Southern Ohio and 2,000 in Northern Ohio, 40% shelf sales. Single copy: $2.95; subscription: $9.97/ year. Sample: $4. Make checks payable to Panther Publishing, Inc.

How to Submit: Submit up to 4 poems at a time. Accepts previously published poems and simultaneous submissions, "if identified as such." Cover letter preferred. "Since we prefer reader-submitted poetry, we would like for the cover letter to include comments about our magazine or contents." Computer disk submissions should be saved in an ASCII text format or Microsoft Word file. Disk should be labeled with your name, address, daytime phone number, name of format and name of file. Time between acceptance and publication is 6-12 months. Seldom comments on rejected poems. "We do not publish theme issues, but do feature specific Ohio counties quarterly. Send or call for specific areas." Guidelines available for SASE. Responds in up to 3 months. Pays 10¢/word, $25 minimum. Acquires one-time North American print rights.

Advice: "While we truly appreciate the professional poet, most of our published poetry comes from beginners or amateurs. We strive for reader response and solicit poetry contributions through the magazine."

◍ OVER THE TRANSOM, P.O. Box 423528, San Francisco CA 94142-3528. (415)928-3965. E-mail: jsh619@earthlink.net. Established 1997. **Editor:** Jonathan Hayes.

Magazine Needs: *Over The Transom*, a free publication of art and literature, appears 2 times/year. Open to all styles of poetry. Recently published poetry by B.Z. Niditch, A.D. Winans, Garret Caples, Donald P. Hilla, Jr., Marie Kazalia, and Glen Chesnut. *Over The Transom* is 32 pages, magazine-sized, saddle-stapled, cardstock cover, with b&w art. Receives about 1,000 poems/year, accepts about 20%. Publishes about 25 poems/issue. Press run is 700 for 100 subscribers; 500 distributed free to cafes, bookstores, and bars. Single copy: free. Sample: $2 to cover postage. Make checks payable to Jonathan Hayes.

How to Submit: Submit 5 poems at a time. Accepts previously published poems and simultaneous submissions. Accepts e-mail submissions; no fax or disk submissions. Cover letter is required. Must include a SASE. Reads submissions all year. Time between acceptance and publication is 2-6 months. Poems are circulated to an editorial board. "We look for the highest quality poetry that best fits the issue." Never comments on rejected poems. Occasionally publishes theme issues. Guidelines available for SASE or by e-mail. Responds in 2 months. Sometimes sends prepublication galleys. Pays 1 contributor's copy. Acquires first rights.

Advice: "All editors have differing tastes, so don't be upset by early rejection; but please ensure you always send a SASE for response, whatever it may be."

★ ◐ OXFORD MAGAZINE, 856 Bachelor Hall, Miami University, Oxford OH 45056. (513)529-1274. E-mail: oxmag@muohio.edu. Established 1984. **Editor:** Brian Seidman. **Contact:** Poetry Editor.

● Work published in *Oxford Magazine* has been included in the *Pushcart Prize* anthology.

Magazine Needs: *Oxford Magazine* appears annually, in the spring. "We are open in terms of form, content, and subject matter. We have eclectic tastes, ranging from New Formalism to Language poetry to Nuyorican poetry." Has published poetry by Eve Shelnutt, Denise Duhamel, and Walter McDonald. Sample: $7.

How to Submit: Submit 3-5 poems at a time. Accepts simultaneous submissions; no previously published poems. No e-mail submissions. Cover letter preferred. Reads submissions September 1 through December 31. Pays copies only. Acquires first North American serial rights.

★ ◐ OYEZ REVIEW, School of Liberal Studies, Roosevelt University, 430 S. Michigan Ave., Chicago IL 60605. (312)341-2157. Fax: (312)341-2156. E-mail: oyezreview@roosevelt.edu. Website: www.roosevelt.edu/oyezreview. Established 1965/66. **Editor/Publisher:** Janet Wondra.

Magazine Needs: *Oyez Review* is an annual appearing in January published by Roosevelt University's MFA Program in Creative Writing. It "receives submissions from across the nation and around the world. We're open to poetic sequences and longer poems provided they hold the reader's attention. We welcome skilled and polished work from newcomers as well as poems from established authors.

The quality of the individual poem is key, not the poet's reputation." Has published poetry by Grace Marie Grafton, Paul Grant, John McKernan, Marjorie Power, J.P. Dancing Bear, and Walter Bargen. *Oyez* is 90 pages, digest-sized, includes photos and drawings. Accepts 5% of poems received. Publishes 15-20 poems per issue. Press run is 500. Single copy: $4; subscription: $8/2 issues.

How to Submit: Submit up to 5 poems or 10 pages at a time. Discourages simultaneous submissions. "Be sure to include a cover letter with a 3 to 5 sentence biography and complete contact information, including phone and e-mail." Does not accept submissions on disk, by fax, or by e-mail. Reads submissions August 1 through October 1 only. Time between acceptance and publication is 2 months. Guidelines available for SASE or on website. Responds in 3 months. Pays 2 copies. Acquires first North American serial rights.

Advice: "Our major goal is to foster the development of student and beginning authors."

OYSTER BOY REVIEW; OFF THE CUFF BOOKS, P.O. Box 83, Chapel Hill NC 27514. E-mail: editors@oysterboyreview.com. Website: www.oysterboyreview.com. Established 1993. **Poetry Editor:** Jeffery Beam.

Magazine Needs: *Oyster Boy Review* appears 2 times/year in March and October. "We're interested in the underrated, the ignored, the misunderstood, and the varietal. We'll make some mistakes. 'All styles are good except the boring kind'—Voltaire." Accepts poetry written by children; "We're about to publish a three year-old." Has published poetry by Jonathan Williams, Cid Corman, Lyn Lifshin, and Paul Dilsaver. *Oyster Boy Review* is 60 pages, 6½×11, Docutech printed and stapled with paper cover, includes photography and ads. Receives about 1,500 poems/year, accepts 2%. Press run is 200 for 30 subscribers, 100 shelf sales; 30 distributed free to editors, authors. Subscription: $20.

How to Submit: Submit up to 5 poems at a time. No previously published poems or simultaneous submissions. Accepts e-mail submissions if poems are included in body of message. Cover letter preferred. Postal submissions require SASE. Do not submit mss in late December. "Upon acceptance, authors asked to provide electronic version of work and a biographical statement." Time between acceptance and publication is 6 months. Seldom comments on rejected poems. Guidelines are available by e-mail and on website. Responds in 3 months. Pays 2 copies. Reviews books and chapbooks of poetry in 250-500 words (1st books only), in single or multi-book format. Send materials for review consideration.

Book/Chapbook Needs: *Off the Cuff is not open to submissions or solicitations.* Off the Cuff Books publishes "longer works and special projects of authors published in *Oyster Boy Review.*"

Advice: "*Oyster Boy Review* responds to freshness—to the unschooled enthusiasm that leads to fresh idioms and subjects—without kowtowing to any camps, mainstream or not."

O!!ZONE (Specialized: visual poetry, photography, collage), 1266 Fountain View, Houston TX 77057-2204. (713)784-2802. Fax: (713)784-0284. E-mail: HarryBurrus@earthlink.net. Established 1993. **Editor/Publisher:** Harry Burrus.

Magazine Needs: *O!!Zone* is "an international literary-art zine featuring visual poetry, travel pieces, interviews, haiku, manifestos, and art. We are particularly intrigued by poets who also do photography (or draw or paint). We also do broadsides, publish small, modest saddle-stapled collections, and will consider book-length collections (on a collaborative basis) *as time and dinero permits.*" Wants visual poetry and collage. "I am interested in discovery and self-transcendence." No academic, traditional, or rhyming poetry. "Not for prudes, the politically correct, ultra conservatives, or the judgemental—those who believe they can decide what is right and proper for others. If you're easily offended by unusual lifestyles, nudity, and provocative words, don't bother." Has published poetry by Dmitry Babenko, Patricia Salas, Anthony Zantra, Sasha Surikov, Willi Melnikov, Laura Ryder, and Joel Lipman. *O!!Zone* is 80-100 pages, magazine-sized, desktop-published, loaded with graphics. "Write for a catalog listing our titles. Our *O!!Zone 97, International Visual Poetry* ($25) and *O!!Zone 98* ($25) and *O!!Zone 99-00* ($25) are three anthologies that cover what's going on in international visual poetry."

How to Submit: Submit 3-6 poems at a time. No previously published poems or simultaneous submissions. No fax submissions. "Submissions of visual poetry via snail mail; textual poems may come by e-mail." Inquire before submitting via e-mail. Cover letter preferred. Has a large backlog, "but always open to surprises." Seldom comments on rejected poems. Guidelines available for SASE. Responds "soon." Pays 1-2 contributor's copies.

P.D.Q. (POETRY DEPTH QUARTERLY), 5836 North Haven Dr., North Highlands CA 95660. (916)331-3512. E-mail: poetdpth@aol.com Website: www.angelfire.com/biz/PoetsGuild/guide.html. Established 1995. **Contact:** G. Elton Warrick, publisher. **Editor:** Joyce Odam.

- *"P.D.Q.* editor submits nominations for the Pushcart Prize."

Magazine Needs: Published quarterly, *P.D.Q.* wants "original poetry that clearly demonstrates an understanding of craft. All styles accepted." Does not want "poetry which is overtly religious, erotic, inflammatory, or demeans the human spirit." Has published poetry by Jane Blue, Taylor Graham, Simon Perchik, Carol Hamilton, B.Z. Niditch, and Danyen Powell. *P.D.Q.* is 35-60 pages, digest-sized, coated and saddle-stapled with a glossy color cover and original art. Receives 1,800-2,000 poems/year, accepts about 10%. Press run is 200 of which 5 subscribers are libraries. Single: $5; subscription: $18.50 (add $10/year for foreign subscriptions). Make checks payable to G. Elton Warrick.

How to Submit: Submit 3-5 poems of any length, "typewritten and presented exactly as you would like them to appear," maximum 52 characters/line (including spaces), with name and address on every page. All submissions require SASE (or SAE with IRC) and cover letter with short 3-10 line bio. "Manuscripts without SASE or sufficient postage will not be read or returned." No simultaneous submissions. Accepts previously published poems "occasionally" with publication credits. Accepts e-mail submissions, include "legal name and postal address included with each page of poetry. No download submissions accepted." Guidelines available for SASE, by e-mail, or on website. Responds in 3 months. Pays 1 contributor's copy.

Advice: "Read the contemporary poetry publications. Read, read, read. Spell-check before submission. Always offer your best work."

$ PACIFIC COAST JOURNAL, P.O. Box 56, Carlsbad CA 92018. E-mail: paccoastj@french breadpublications.com. Website: www.frenchbreadpublications.com/pcj. Established 1992. **Editor:** Stillson Graham.

Magazine Needs: *Pacific Coast Journal* is an "unprofessional quarterly literary magazine. Whatever you think that means, go with it." Wants "off beat and off-beat. Ask the question 'why is it poetry?'" Has published poetry by Paul B. Roth, Allison Joseph, and Patrick Hartigan. *Pacific Coast Journal* is 56 pages, digest-sized, photocopied and saddle-stapled with a card stock cover and b&w photos and artwork. Receives 400-500 poems/year, accepts about 5-10%. Press run is 200 for 100 subscribers. Single copy: $3; subscription: $12. Sample: $2.50.

How to Submit: Submit up to 6 poems or 12 pages at a time. Accepts simultaneous submissions; no previously published poems. No e-mail submissions. Cover letter preferred. Time between acceptance and publication is up to 18 months. Seldom comments on rejected poems. Guidelines available for SASE or by e-mail. Responds in 4 months. Pays 1 contributor's copy. Acquires one-time rights.

Advice: "Shock people by saying something true."

PAINTBRUSH: A JOURNAL OF POETRY & TRANSLATION (Specialized: translation, themes, writing), MC 335, Truman State University, Kirksville MO 63501. (660)785-4185. Fax: (660)785-7486. E-mail: bbennani@truman.edu. Website: www.paintbrush.org. Established 1974. **Editor:** Ben Bennani.

Magazine Needs: *Paintbrush* appears annually in the Fall and is 250-300 pages, digest-sized, using quality poetry. Circulation is 500. Sample: $15.

How to Submit: No submissions June, July, and August. No e-mail submissions. Send SASE with inquiries and request for samples. Pays 2 copies. Reviews books of poetry.

PALANQUIN; PALANQUIN POETRY SERIES, Dept. of English, University of South Carolina-Aiken, 471 University Pkwy., Aiken SC 29801. E-mail: phebed@aiken.sc.edu. Established 1988. **Editor:** Phebe Davidson.

Book/Chapbook Needs: The press no longer sponsors annual contests, but continues to publish occasional chapbooks and longer books of poetry. Does not want "sentimental, religious, consciously academic" poetry. Has published poetry by Lois Marie Harrod, Robert King, and Doughtry "Doc" Long. Sample copy: $12 paper; $18 hardback. Make checks payable to Palanquin Press.

How to Submit: Send sample of 6-10 poems with query letter and SASE. Accepts submissions by e-mail (as attachment). Responds in 3 months.

Advice: "Read what you write; send finished work only."

▣ ◻ ◉ **PAPER WASP: A JOURNAL OF HAIKU (Specialized: form/style, haiku/tonka/ haibun); SOCIAL ALTERNATIVES (Specialized: social issues); POST PRESSED**, 14 Fig Tree Pocket Rd., Chapel Hill Q 4069 Australia. E-mail: ksamuelowicz@optusnet.com.au. Website: http://users.bigpond.net.au/ReportWright/PaperWasp/PaperWasp.html. *Paper Wasp* established 1972, *Social Alternatives* established 1971. **Manager:** Katherine Samuelowicz.

Magazine Needs: "*paper wasp* quarterly publishes haiku, senryu, renga, and tanka in a range of fresh tones and voices. We acknowledge a range of forms and styles from one-liners to the conventional 5-7-5 form, and variations such as development or neglect of seasonal words for regional contexts." Wants haiku, senryu, tanka, renga, linked verse, and haibun. Has published poetry by Janice Bostok, Carla Sari, Cornelis Vleeskens, Ross Clark, Tony Beyer, and Bernard Gadd. *paper wasp* is 16 pages, digest-sized, desktop-published and saddle-stapled, cardboard cover, includes art/ graphics. Receives about 2,000 submissions/year, accepts 15%. Publishes about 50 haiku/issue. Press run is 200 for 67 subscribers of which 12 are libraries. Single copy: $6 AUD within Australia, $8 US elsewhere. Subscription: $20 AUD within Australia, $26 US elsewhere. Make checks payable to *paper wasp*. "Due to very high bank charges on overseas cheques, we prefer cash or IRCs for single copies. Copies of relevant pages only are sent to published contributors who are not subscribers or who do not pay for the relevant copy."

Magazine Needs: "*Social Alternatives* is a quarterly multidisciplinary journal which seeks to analyse, critique, and review contemporary social, cultural, and economic developments and their implications at local, national, and global levels." Has published poetry by MTC Cronin, Jules Leigh Koch, ouyang yu, John O'Connor, Gina Mercer, and Michael Sariban. *Social Alternatives* is 76 pages, magazine-sized, desktop-published, saddle-stapled with cardboard cover, includes art/graphics, ads. Receives about approximately 1,200 submissions, accepts about 15%. Publishes about 30 poems/ issue. Press run is about 800 for 587 subscribers of which 112 are libraries. Single copy: $8. Subscription: $30, plus $40 for overseas airmail.

How to Submit: Submit up to 12 poems at a time for *paper wasp*, up to 6 poems (36 lines maximum) for *Social Alternatives*. No previously published poems or simultaneous submissions. Accepts regular mail, e-mail (in text box), and disk submissions (IBM format with Word files, plus hard copy). Cover letter required. "If mailed within Australia, send SASE, otherwise SAE plus IRCs. Unless requested with SASE, copy is not returned." Time between acceptance and publication is up to 6 months. Poems are circulated to an editorial board. "Read by two editors." Sometimes comments on rejected poems. Responds within 6 months. *paper wasp* does not pay except one copy for poets publishing with them for the first time. *Social Alternatives* pays 1 contributor's copy. Copyright remains with authors.

◉ **PARADOXISM; XIQUAN PUBLISHING HOUSE; PARADOXISM ASSOCIATION (Specialized: form)**, University of New Mexico, Gallup NM 87301. E-mail: smarand@unm.edu. Website: www.gallup.unm.edu/~smarandache/a/paradoxism.htm. Established 1990. **Editor:** Florentin Smarandache.

Magazine Needs: *Paradoxism* is an annual journal of "avant-garde poetry, experiments, poems without verses, literature beyond the words, anti-language, non-literature and its literature, as well as the sense of the non-sense; revolutionary forms of poetry. Paradoxism is based on excessive use of antitheses, antinomies, contradictions, paradoxes in creation. It was made up in the 1980s by the editor as an anti-totalitarianism protest." Wants "avant-garde poetry, one to two pages, any subject, any style (lyrical experiments). No classical, fixed forms." Has published poetry by Paul Georgelin, Titu Popescu, Ion Rotaru, Michéle de LaPlante, and Claude LeRoy. *Paradoxism* is 52 pages, digest-sized, offset-printed, soft cover. Press run is 500. "It is distributed to its collaborators, U.S. and Canadian university libraries, and the Library of Congress as well as European, Chinese, Indian, and Japanese libraries."

How to Submit: No previously published poems or simultaneous submissions. Do not submit mss in the summer. "We do not return published or unpublished poems or notify the author of date of publication." Responds in up to 3 weeks. Pays 1 contributor's copy.

Book/Chapbook Needs & How to Submit: Xiquan Publishing House also publishes 2 paperbacks and 1-2 chapbooks/year, including translations. The poems must be unpublished and must meet the requirements of the Paradoxism Association. Responds to queries in 2 months, to mss in up to 3 weeks. Pays 50 author's copies. Sample e-books available on website.

Advice: "We mostly receive traditional or modern verse, but not avant-garde (very different from any previously published verse). We want anti-literature and its literature, style of the non-style, poems without poems, non-words and non-sentence poems, very upset free verse, intelligible unintelligible language, impersonal texts personalized, transformation of the abnormal to the normal. Make literature from everything; make literature from nothing!"

PARIS/ATLANTIC, The American University of Paris, 31 Avenue Bosquet, Paris 75007, France. Phone: (33 1)01 40 62 05 89. Fax: (33 1)01 45 89 13. E-mail: auplantic@hotmail.com. Established 1982. **Contact:** Editor.

Magazine Needs: *Paris/Atlantic* appears biannually and is "a forum for both new and established artists/writers that is based in Paris and is distributed internationally. The contents vary; we publish poetry, prose, paintings, sculpture, sketches, etc." Has published poetry by Ben Wilensky, Ryan G. Van Cleave, Margo Berdeshevsky and Susan Maurer. *Paris/Atlantic* is 100-200 pages, professionally published with sewn binding and softcover, includes ads. Receives about 400-500 poems/year, accepts approximately 40%. Press run is 1,000-1,500; distributed free to bookstores, universities, literary societies, other poets, etc.

How to Submit: Submit any number of poems at a time. "There are no requirements aside from a biography and international postage so we can forward 2 free copies of *Paris/Atlantic* if your work is published." Accepts previously published poems and simultaneous submissions. No e-mail submissions. "Please cut and paste e-mail submissions. No attachments!" Cover letter including author's name, return address with telephone number, e-mail address or fax number and a short biography required. Reads submissions September 1 through November 1 and January 1 through April 1 only. Poems are circulated to an editorial board. "The editorial board reviews work in a roundtable discussion." Send SASE (or SAE and IRC) for guidelines or request via fax or e-mail. Pays 2 copies. Acquires first rights. Rights revert to author upon publication.

Advice: "Be heard! The *Paris/Atlantic* Reading Series of Poetry and Prose takes place once a month, for which we invite two poets to perform their work in the Amex Café of The American University of Paris, followed by open mikes. Take advantage to listen and be heard in this international forum, and contact us if you would like to participate."

PARNASSUS LITERARY JOURNAL, P.O. Box 1384, Forest Park GA 30298-1384. (404)366-3177. Established 1975. **Editor:** Denver Stull.

Magazine Needs: "Our sole purpose is to promote poetry and to offer an outlet where poets may be heard. We welcome well-constructed poetry, but ask that you keep it uplifting, and free of language that might be offensive to one of our readers. We are open to all poets and all forms of poetry, including Oriental, 24-line limit, maximum 3 poems." No erotica or translations. Accepts poetry written by children. Has published poetry by David Bernatchez, Jean Calkins, Rod Farmer, David Hay, Simon Perchik, and T.K. Splake. *Parnassus Literary Journal*, published 3 times/year, is 84 pages, photocopied from typescript, saddled-stapled, colored card cover, with an occasional drawing. Receives about 1,500 submissions/year, accepts 350. Currently have about a 1-year backlog. Press run is 300 for 200 subscribers of which 5 are libraries. Circulation includes Japan, England, Greece, India, Korea, Germany, and Netherlands. Single copy: $7 US and Canada, $9.50 overseas; subscription: $18 US and Canada, $25 overseas. Sample: $3. Offers 20% discount to schools, libraries and for orders of 5 copies or more. Make checks or money orders payable to Denver Stull.

How to Submit: Submit up to 3 poems, up to 24 lines each, with #10 SASE. Include name and address on each page of ms. "I am dismayed at the haphazard manner in which work is often submitted. I have a number of poems in my file containing no name and/or address. Simply placing your name and address on your envelope is not enough." Accepts previously published poems and simultaneous submissions. Cover letter including something about the writer preferred. "Definitely" comments on rejected poems. "We do not respond to submissions or queries not accompanied by SASE." Guidelines available for SASE. Responds within 1 week. "We regret that the ever-rising costs of publishing forces us to ask that contributors either subscribe to the magazine, or purchase a copy of the issue in which their work appears." Pays 1 copy. All rights remain with the author. Readers vote on best of each issue.

Advice: "Write about what you know. Read your work aloud. Does it make sense? Rewrite, rewrite, rewrite."

$⬛ PARNASSUS: POETRY IN REVIEW; POETRY IN REVIEW FOUNDATION, 205 W. 89th St., #8F, New York NY 10024-1835. (212)362-3492. Fax: (212)875-0148. Website: www.par nassuspoetry.com. Established 1972. **Poetry Editor:** Herbert Leibowitz.

Magazine Needs: *Parnassus* provides "comprehensive and in-depth coverage of new books of poetry, including translations from foreign poetry. We publish poems and translations on occasion, but we solicit all poetry. Poets invited to submit are given all the space they wish; the only stipulation is that the style be non-academic." Has published work by Alice Fulton, Eavan Boland, Mary Karr, Debora Greger, William Logan, Seamus Heaney, and Rodney Jones. Subscriptions are $24/year, $46/year for libraries; has 1,250 subscribers, of which 550 are libraries.

How to Submit: Not open to unsolicited poetry. However, unsolicited essays are considered. In fact, this is an exceptionally rich market for thoughtful, insightful, non-academic essay-reviews of contemporary collections. It is strongly recommended that writers study the magazine before submitting. Multiple submissions disliked. Cover letter required. Upcoming themes available for SASE. Responds to essay submissions within 10 weeks (response takes longer during the summer). Pays $25-250 plus 2 gift subscriptions—contributors can also take one themselves. Editor comments on rejected poems—from 1 paragraph to 2 pages. Send for a sample copy (prices of individual issues can vary) to get a feel for the critical acumen needed to place here.

Advice: "Contributors are urged to subscribe to at least one literary magazine. There is a pervasive ignorance of the cost of putting out a magazine and no sense of responsibility for supporting one."

⬛ PARTING GIFTS; MARCH STREET PRESS, 3413 Wilshire, Greensboro NC 27408. E-mail: rbixby@aol.com. Website: http://members.aol.com/marchst/. Established 1987. **Editor:** Robert Bixby.

Magazine Needs: *Parting Gifts* is published biannually in July and November. "I want to see everything. I'm a big fan of Jim Harrison, C.K. Williams, Amy Hempel, and Janet Kauffman." Has published poetry by Eric Torgersen, Lyn Lifshin, Elizabeth Kerlikowske, and Russell Thorburn. *Parting Gifts* is 72 pages, digest-sized, photocopied, with colored matte card cover, appearing twice/year. Press run is 200. Subscription: $18. Sample: $9.

How to Submit: Submit in groups of 3-10 with SASE. Accepts simultaneous submissions; no previously published poems. "I like a cover letter because it makes the transaction more human. Best time to submit mss is early in the year." Guidelines available for SASE or on website. Responds in 2 weeks. Sometimes sends prepublication galleys. Pays 1 copy.

Book/Chapbook Needs & How to Submit: March Street Press publishes chapbooks. **Reading fee:** $20.

Advice: "Read our online archives."

⬛ $⬛ ◎ PASSEGGIATA PRESS (Specialized: ethnic, regional, translations, women/feminism), P.O. Box 636, Pueblo CO 81002. (719)544-1038. Fax: (719)546-7889. E-mail: passeggia ta@compuserve.com. Established 1973. **Poetry Editor:** Donald Herdeck.

Book/Chapbook Needs: "Published poets only welcomed and only non-European and non-American poets . . . We publish literature by creative writers from the non-western world (Africa, the Middle East, the Caribbean and Asia/Pacific)—poetry only by non-western writers or good translations of such poetry if original language is Arabic, French, African vernacular, etc." Has published *An Ocean of Dreams* by Mona Saudi, *Sky-Break* by Lyubomir Levchev, *The Right to Err* by Nina Iskreuko, and *The Journey of Barbarus* by Ottó Orbán. Also publishes anthologies and criticisms focused on relevant themes.

How to Submit: Query with 4-5 samples, bio, publication credits. Responds to queries in 2-4 weeks, to submissions (if invited) in 1-2 weeks. Always sends prepublication galleys. Offers 7.5% royalty contract (5% for translator) with $100-200 advance plus 10 copies. Acquires worldwide English rights. Send SASE for catalog to buy samples.

◙ PATERSON LITERARY REVIEW; ALLEN GINSBERG POETRY AWARDS; THE PATERSON POETRY PRIZE; THE PATERSON PRIZE FOR BOOKS FOR YOUNG PEOPLE; PASSAIC COUNTY COMMUNITY COLLEGE POETRY CENTER LIBRARY, Poetry Center, Passaic County Community College, Cultural Affairs Dept., 1 College Blvd., Paterson NJ 07505-1179. (973)684-6555. Fax: (973)684-5843. E-mail: mgillan@pccc.cc.nj.us. Website: www.pccc.cc.nj.us/poetry. Established 1979. **Editor and Director:** Maria Mazziotti Gillan.

Magazine Needs & How to Submit: A wide range of activities pertaining to poetry are conducted by the Passaic County Community College Poetry Center, including the annual *Paterson Literary Review* (formerly *Footwork: The Paterson Literary Review*) using poetry of "high quality" under 100 lines; "clear, direct, powerful work." Has published poetry by Diane di Prima, Ruth Stone, Marge Piercy, and Laura Boss. *Paterson Literary Review* is 320 pages, magazine-sized, saddle-stapled, professionally printed with glossy card 2-color cover, using b&w art and photos. Press run is 1,000 for 100 subscribers of which 50 are libraries. Sample: $10. Send up to 5 poems at a time. Accepts simultaneous submissions. Reads submissions December through March only. Responds in 1 year. Pays 1 contributor's copy. Acquires first rights.

Also Offers: The Poetry Center of the college conducts the Allen Ginsberg Poetry Awards Competition each year. Entry fee: $13. Prizes of $1,000, $200, and $100. Deadline: April 1. Rules available for SASE. Also publishes a *New Jersey Poetry Resources* book and the *New Jersey Poetry Calendar*. The Paterson Poetry Prize of $1,000 is awarded each year to a book of poems published in the previous year. Also sponsors the Paterson Prize for Books for Young People. Awards $500 to one book in each category (Pre-K-Grade 3, Grades 4-6, Grades 7-12). Books must be published in the previous year and be submitted by the publisher. Publishers should write with SASE for application form to be submitted by February 1 (for Poetry Prize) and March 15 (for Books for Young People Prize). Passaic County Community College Poetry Center Library has an extensive collection of contemporary poetry and seeks small press contributions to help keep it abreast. The Distinguished Poetry Series offers readings by poets of international, national, and regional reputation. Poetryworks/USA is a series of programs produced for UA Columbia-Cablevision.

◙ PAVEMENT SAW; PAVEMENT SAW PRESS; PAVEMENT SAW PRESS CHAPBOOK AWARD; TRANSCONTINENTAL POETRY AWARD, P.O. Box 6291, Columbus OH 43206-0291. E-mail: info@pavementsaw.org. Website: www.pavementsaw.org. Established 1992. **Editor:** David Baratier.

Magazine Needs: *Pavement Saw*, which appears annually in August, wants "letters and short fiction, and poetry on any subject, especially work. Length: one or two pages. No poems that tell, no work by a deceased writer and no translations." Dedicates 10-15 pages of each issue to a featured writer. Has published poetry by Simon Perchik, Dana Curtis, Sofia Starres, Alan Catlin, Tony Gloeggler, Sean Killian, and Tracy Philpot. *Pavement Saw* is 88 pages, digest-sized, perfect-bound. Receives about 14,500 poems/year, accepts less than 1%. Press run is 550 for about 300 subscribers, about 250 shelf sales. Single copy: $6; subscription: $12. Sample: $5. Make checks payable to Pavement Saw Press.

How to Submit: Submit 5 poems at a time. "No fancy typefaces." Accepts simultaneous submissions, "as long as poet has not published a book with a press run of 1,000 or more"; no previously published poems. No e-mail submissions. Cover letter required. Seldom comments on rejected poems. Guidelines available for SASE. Responds in 4 months. Sometimes sends prepublication galleys. Pays 2 copies. Acquires first rights.

Book/Chapbook Needs & How to Submit: The press also publishes books of poetry. "Most are by authors who have been published in the journal." Published "seven titles in 2000 and nine titles in 2001, eight are full-length books ranging from 72 to 612 pages."

Also Offers: Sponsors the Transcontinental Poetry Award. "Each year, Pavement Saw Press will seek to publish at least one book of poetry and/or prose poems from manuscripts received during this competition. Competition is open to anyone who has not previously published a volume of poetry or prose. Writers who have had volumes of poetry and/or prose under 40 pages printed or printed in limited editions of no more than 500 copies are eligible. Submissions are accepted during June and July only." Entry fee: $15. Awards publication, $1,000 and a percentage of the press run. Include stamped postcard and SASE for ms receipt acknowledgement and results notification. Guidelines available for SASE. Also sponsors the Pavement Saw Press Chapbook Award. Submit up to 32 pages of poetry with a cover letter. Entry fee: $7. Awards publication, $500 and 10% of print run. "Each entrant will receive a chapbook provided a 9×12 SAE with 5 first-class stamps is supplied." Deadline: December 31. Guidelines available for SASE.

PEACE & FREEDOM; EASTERN RAINBOW; PEACE & FREEDOM PRESS (Specialized: subscribers), 17 Farrow Rd., Whaplode Drove, Spalding, Lincs PE12 OTS England. E-mail: p_rance@yahoo.co.uk. Website: http://geocities.com/p_rance/pandF.htm. Established 1985. **Editor:** Paul Rance.

Magazine Needs: *Peace & Freedom* is a magazine appearing 2 times/year. "We are looking for poems up to 32 lines particularly from U.S. poets who are new to writing, especially women. The poetry we publish is pro-animal rights, anti-war, environmental; poems reflecting love; erotic, but not obscene poetry; humorous verse and spiritual, humanitarian poetry. With or without rhyme/metre." Accepts poetry written by children. Has published poetry by Dorothy Bell-Hall, Freda Moffat, Bernard Shough, Mona Miller, and Andrew Savage. *Peace & Freedom*'s format varies but publishes at least 30 poems in each issue. Sample: US $5; UK £1.75. "Sample copies can only be purchased from the above address, and various mail-order distributors too numerous to mention. Advisable to buy a sample copy first. Banks charge the equivalent of $5 to cash foreign cheques in the U.K., so please only send bills, preferably by registered post." Subscription: US $20, UK £10/6 issues.

How to Submit: No simultaneous submissions or previously published poems. No fax or e-mail submissions. Poets are requested to send in bios. Reads submissions all through the year. Publishes theme issues. Upcoming themes available for SAE with IRC, by e-mail, on website, and in publication. Responds to submissions normally under a month, with IRC/SAE. "Work without correct postage will not be responded to or returned until proper postage is sent." Pays 1 copy. Reviews books of poetry.

Also Offers: Also publishes anthologies. Details on upcoming anthologies and guidelines are available for SAE with IRC. "*Peace & Freedom* now holds regular contests as does one of our other publications, *Eastern Rainbow*, which is a magazine concerning 20th century popular culture using poetry up to 32 lines. Subscription: US $20; UK £10/6 issues. Further details of competitions and publications for SAE and IRC."

Advice: "Too many writers have lost the personal touch and editors generally appreciate this. It can make a difference when selecting work of equal merit."

PEARL; PEARL POETRY PRIZE; PEARL EDITIONS, 3030 E. Second St., Long Beach CA 90803-5163. (562)434-4523 or (714)968-7530. E-mail: pearlmag@aol.com. Website: www.pearl mag.com. Established 1974. **Poetry Editors:** Joan Jobe Smith, Marilyn Johnson, and Barbara Hauk.

Magazine Needs: *Pearl* is a literary magazine appearing 2 times/year in April and November. "We are interested in accessible, humanistic poetry that communicates and is related to real life. Humor and wit are welcome, along with the ironic and serious. No taboos stylistically or subject-wise. We don't want to see sentimental, obscure, predictable, abstract, or cliché-ridden poetry. Our purpose is to provide a forum for lively, readable poetry, that reflects a wide variety of contemporary voices, viewpoints and experiences—that speaks to real people about real life in direct, living language, profane, or sublime. Our Fall/Winter issue is devoted exclusively to poetry, with a 12-15 page section featuring the work of a single poet." Has published poetry by Fred Voss, David Hernandez, Denise Duhamel, Kim Addonizio, Jim Daniels, and Nin Andrews. *Pearl* is 96-121 pages, digest-sized, perfect-bound, offset-printed, with glossy cover. Press run is 700 for 150 subscribers of which 7 are libraries. Subscription: $18/year includes a copy of the winning book of the Pearl Poetry Prize. Sample: $7.

How to Submit: Submit 3-5 poems at a time. No previously published poems. "Simultaneous submissions must be acknowledged as such." Prefer poems no longer than 40 lines, each line no more

THE ◎ SYMBOL indicates a market with a specific or unique focus. This specialized area of interest is listed in parentheses behind the market title.

than 10-12 words to accommodate page size and format. "Handwritten submissions and unreadable printouts are not acceptable." No e-mail submissions. "Cover letters appreciated." Reads submissions September through May only. Time between acceptance and publication is up to 1 year. Guidelines available for SASE or on website. Responds in 2 months. Sometimes sends prepublication galleys. Pays 1 contributor's copy. Acquires first serial rights.

Book/Chapbook Needs: Pearl Editions "only publishes the winner of the Pearl Poetry Prize. All other books and chapbooks are *by invitation only.*"

Also Offers: "We sponsor the Pearl Poetry Prize, an annual book-length contest, judged by one of our more well-known contributors. Winner receives publication, $1,000 and 25 copies. Entries accepted May 1 to July 15. There is a $20 entry fee, which includes a copy of the winning book." Complete rules and guidelines are available for SASE or on website. Recent books include *From Sweetness* by Debra Marquart, *Trigger Finger* by Micki Myer, *Bus Ride to a Blue Movie* by Anne-Marie Levine, and *Little Novels* by Denise Duhamel and Maureen Seaton.

Advice: "Advice for beginning poets? Just write from your own experience, using images that are as concrete and sensory as possible. Keep these images fresh and objective. Always listen to the music."

PEGASUS, P.O. Box 61324, Boulder City NV 89006. Established 1986. **Editor:** M.E. Hildebrand.

Magazine Needs: *Pegasus* is a poetry quarterly "for serious poets who have something to say and know how to say it using sensory imagery." Avoid "religious, political, pornographic themes." Has published poetry by John Grey, Elizabeth Perry, Diana K. Rubin, Lyn Lifshin, Robert K. Johnson, and Nikolas Macioci. *Pegasus* is 32 pages, digest-sized, desktop-published, saddle-stapled with colored paper cover. Publishes 10-15% of the work received. Circulation is 200. Subscription: $20. Sample: $6.

How to Submit: Submit 3-5 poems, 3-40 lines. Accepts previously published poems, provided poet retains rights; no simultaneous submissions. Guidelines available for SASE. Responds in 2 weeks. Publication is payment. Acquires first or one-time rights.

THE PEGASUS REVIEW (Specialized: themes), P.O. Box 88, Henderson MD 21640-0088. (410)482-6736. Established 1980. **Editor:** Art Bounds.

Magazine Needs: "*The Pegasus Review* is a bimonthly, in a calligraphic format and each issue is based on a specific theme. Since themes might be changed it is suggested to inquire as to current themes. With a magazine in this format, strictly adhere to guidelines—brevity is the key. Poetry—not more than 24 lines (the shorter the better); fiction (short short—about 2½ pages would be ideal); essays and cartoons. All material must pertain to indicated themes only. Poetry may be in any style (rhyming, free verse, haiku)." Has published poetry by Robert H. Deluty, A.C. Brocki, Marijane G. Ricketts, and Frieda Levinstky. Press run is 120 for 100 subscribers, of which 2 are libraries. Subscription: $12. Sample: $2.50.

How to Submit: Submit 3-5 poems with name and address on each page. Accepts previously published poems, if there is no conflict or violation of rights agreement and simultaneous submissions, but author must notify proper parties once specific material is accepted. Brief cover letter with specifics as they relate to one's writing background welcome. Upcoming themes only available for SASE. Responds within a month, often with a personal response. Pays 2 copies.

Also Offers: Offers occasional book awards throughout the year.

Advice: "Although the publishing marketplace is changing, continue to improve your work as well as market it. It needs to be shared."

$ ☑ ◎ PELICAN PUBLISHING COMPANY (Specialized: children, regional), Box 3110, Gretna LA 70054-3110. Website: www.pelicanpub.com. Established 1926. **Editor-in-Chief:** Nina Kooij.

Book/Chapbook Needs: Pelican is a "moderate-sized publisher of cookbooks, travel guides, regional books, and inspirational/motivational books," which accepts poetry for "hardcover children's books only, preferably with a regional focus. However, our needs for this are very limited; we do twelve juvenile titles per year, and most of these are prose, not poetry." Accepts poetry written by children. Has published *The Firefighter's Night Before Christmas* by Kimbra Cutlip. Books are 32-

page, large-format (magazine-sized) with illustrations. Two of their popular series are prose books about Gaston the Green-Nosed Alligator by James Rice and Clovis Crawfish by Mary Alice Fontenot. Has a variety of books based on "The Night Before Christmas" adapted to regional settings such as Cajun, prairie, and Texas. Typically Pelican books sell for $14.95. Write for catalog to buy samples.

How to Submit: *Currently not accepting unsolicited mss.* Query first with cover letter including "work and writing backgrounds and promotional connections." No previously published poems or simultaneous submissions. Guidelines available for SASE and on website. Responds to queries in 1 month, to mss (if invited) in 3 months. Always sends prepublication galleys. Pays royalties. Acquires all rights. Returns rights upon termination of contract.

Advice: "We try to avoid rhyme altogether, especially predictable rhyme. Monotonous rhythm can also be a problem."

⊕ $ ☺ **PEN&INC; REACTIONS; PRETEXT,** School of English & American Studies, University of East Anglia, Norwich, Norfolk NR4 7TJ United Kingdom. Phone: (01603)592 783. Fax: (01603)507 728. E-mail: info@penandinc.co.uk. Website: www.penandinc.co.uk. Established 1999. **Editor** (*Reactions*): Esther Morgan; Managing Editor (*Pretext*): Katri Skala.

Magazine Needs & How to Submit: "*Pen&inc* is a small pocket of resistance and a statement of independence as part of the new wave of community-based publications which offer a fresh perspective on the writers and writing that are important at the start of the 21st century. Pen&inc aims to publish good writing, as simple as that, whether it be in poetry, short fiction, essays, criticism, or novel form." Publishes 3 perfect-bound paperbacks/year selected through both open submission and competition. Books are usually 150-200 pages, glue-bound, full color or b&w gloss cover on card, with original image or photograph (color/b&w). Query first, with a few sample poems and cover letter with brief bio and publication credits. Responds to queries in 3 months. Order books/publications by sending "cover price to Pen&inc address above. UK Sterling only accepted. Transactions by debit/credit card fine also."

Magazine Needs & How to Submit: *Reactions* is "a round-up of the best new poets fromaround the UK and abroad. Partly selected from open submission and partly commissioned, *Reactions* features the work of poets who are at a first collection stage or working towards it and contains work by over 40 UK and international poets. The emphasis is on emerging writers." Recently published poetry by Liz Almond, Anne Berkeley, Roy Blackman, Frank Dullaghan, Margaret Gillio, Stephanie Norgate, and Robert Seatter. "Submissions are invited from writers who have had a first collection or pamphlet published (but not a single) and from those who have not yet reached that stage. If you are interested in submitting work, please send to Esther Morgan. Must be accompanied by a covering letter which lists the titles of your poems, plus a short biography of nomore than 70 words. Single copy: £9.99 (USA/ROW), £8.99 (Europe) and £7.99 (UK), all including postage and packing. Submit a maximum of 5 poems at a time. Accepts original, unpublished poems. Accepts postal and disk submissions. Covering letter is required. "Poems must be your own original work and must not be accepted for publication by any other magazine or anthology. Enclose an SAE. Poems submitted in electronic format should be on a floppy disk, readable by PC and Mac and be formatted in latest version on Word, or at least Word 98." Reads submissions on an ongoing basis. Time between acceptance and publication is dependent on publication date of book. Guidelines available in magazine, by e-mail, on website or send SAE. Responds in 3 months. Pays fee of £50 and one contributor's copy. **Advice:** "Write well and good and do not despair. Try and try again. If you write well, you will be recognized one day."

Magazine Needs & How to Submit: *Pretext,* appearing biannually in May and November, is "the international literary magazine from the acclaimed creative writing institution of the University of East Anglia. With over 200 pages of new poetry, short fiction, essays, criticism, and novel extracts from new and established writers, it provides a cutting-edge platform for creative writing from Great Britain and beyond. There are no editorial restrictionson subject or style, just an insistence on quality and perspective that the work strongly asserts where it's coming from and is well realized on the page." Recently published poetry by Margaret Atwood, Hilary Davies, Alan Jenkins, Graham Mort, and Egon Schiele. *Pretext* is 200 pages, book-sized magazine, litho-printed, glue-bound, full color gloss cover, with 3-5 photographs/images (b&w) within the book to illustrate text, includes ads. Receives about 500 poems/year, accepts about 25%. Publishes about 5 poems per issue. Print run is

1,000 for 100 subscribers of which 10 are libraries, 500 shelf sales; 100 distributed free to contributors/ reviewers. Single copy: £9.99 (USA/ROW including postage and packing), £7.99 (UK including p&p), £8.99 (Europe including p&p); subscription: (1 year/2 issues) £14 UK including p&p, £18 USA/ROW including p&p, £16 Europe including p&p. Make checks payable to The University of East Anglia. Regularly publishes theme issues (Rancour and Havoc are recent themes). Upcoming themes available on website. Guidelines available in magazine, by e-mail, on website or send SAE. Responds in 3 months. Always send pre-publication galleys. Pays £50 fee and 1 contributor's copy. UK and international copyright remains with author at all times. See submission details above for *Reactions*. "Poems are received and passed to the editorial board for relevant publication. Consultation process involving editors and contributing editors occurs. Poems are accepted or rejected, or passed back to poet for rewriting if deemed necessary."

PENNINE INK, % Mid Pennine Arts, The Gallery, Yorke St., Burnley BB11 1HD Great Britain. Phone: (01282)703657. E-mail: sheridans@casanostra.p3online.net. Established 1983. **Editor:** Laura Sheridan.
Magazine Needs: *Pennine Ink* appears annually in January using poems and short prose items. Wants "poetry up to 40 lines maximum. Consider all kinds." *Pennine Ink* is 48 pages, A5, with b&w illustrated cover, small local ads and 3 or 4 b&w graphics. Receives about 400 poems/year, accepts approximately 40. Press run is 500. "Contributors wishing to purchase a copy of *Pennine Ink* should enclose £3 ($6 US) per copy."
How to Submit: Submit up to 6 poems at a time. Accepts previously published poems and simultaneous submissions. Accepts submissions by e-mail. Seldom comments on rejected poems. Responds in 3 months. Pays 1 copy.
Advice: "Prose and poetry should be accompanied by a suitable stamped, addressed envelope (SASE or SAE with IRCs) for return of work."

PENNINE PLATFORM, Frizingley Hall, Frizinghall Rd., Bradford, West Yorkshire BD9 4LD United Kingdom. Established 1973. **Poetry Editor:** Nicholas Bielby.
Magazine Needs: *Pennine Platform* appears 2 times/year. Wants any kind of poetry but concrete ("lack of facilities for reproduction"). No specifications of length, but poems of less than 40 lines have a better chance. "All styles—effort is to find things good of their kind. Preference for religious or sociopolitical awareness of an acute, not conventional kind." Has published poetry by Joolz, Gaia Holmes, Milner Place, Seán Body, and Ian Parks. *Pennine Platform* is 48 pages, digest-sized, photocopied from typescript, perfect-bound, with matte card cover with graphics. Circulation is 400 for 300 subscribers of which 16 are libraries. Receives about 300 submissions/year, accepts approximately 60, has about a 6-month backlog. Subscription: £10 for 2 issues (£15 abroad; £25 if not in sterling). Sample: £5.
How to Submit: Submit up to 6 poems, typed. Responds in about 3 months. No pay. Acquires first serial rights. Editor occasionally comments on rejected poems. Reviews books of poetry in 500 words, multi-book format. Send materials for review consideration.

PENNSYLVANIA ENGLISH, Penn State DuBois, DuBois PA 15801-3199. (814)375-4814. E-mail: ajv2@psu.edu. Established 1988 (first issue in March, 1989). **Editor:** Antonio Vallone.
Magazine Needs: *Pennsylvania English*, appearing annually in winter, is "a journal sponsored by the Pennsylvania College English Association." Wants poetry of "any length, any style." Has published poetry by Liz Rosenberg, Walt MacDonald, Amy Pence, Jennifer Richter, and Jeff Schiff. *Pennsylvania English* is up to 200 pages, digest-sized, perfect-bound with a full color cover. Press run is 500. Subscription: $10/year.
How to Submit: Submit 3 or more typed poems at a time. Include SASE. Considers simultaneous submissions but not previously published poems. Guidelines available for SASE. Responds in 6 months. Pays 3 copies.
Advice: "Poetry does not express emotions; it evokes emotions. Therefore, it should rely less on statements and more on images."

THE PENWOOD REVIEW (Specialized: spirituality), P.O. Box 862, Los Alamitos CA 90720-0862. E-mail: penwoodreview@charter.net. Website: http://webpages.charter.net/penwood review/penwood.htm. Established 1997. **Editor:** Lori M. Cameron.

Magazine Needs: *The Penwood Review*, published biannually, "seeks to explore the spiritual and sacred aspects of our existence and our relationship to God." Wants "disciplined, high-quality, well-crafted poetry on any subject. Prefer poems be less than two pages. Rhyming poetry must be written in traditional forms (sonnets, tercets, villanelles, sestinas, etc.)" Does not want "light verse, doggerel, or greeting card-style poetry. Also, nothing racist, sexist, pornographic, or blasphemous." Has published poetry by Kathleen Spivack, Anne Babson, Hugh Fox, Anselm Brocki, Nina Tassi, and Gary Guinn. *The Penwood Review* has about 40 pgs, magazine-sized, saddle-stapled with heavy card cover. Press run is 50-100. Single copy: $6; subscription: $12.

How to Submit: Submit 3-5 poems, 1/page with the author's full name, address and phone number in the upper right hand corner. No previously published poems or simultaneous submissions. Accepts e-mail submissions in body of message. Cover letter preferred. Time between acceptance and publication is up to 18 months. "Submissions are circulated among an editorial staff for evaluations." Seldom comments on rejected poems. Responds in up to 6 months. For payment, offers subscription discount of $10 to published authors and one additional free copy in which author's work appears. Acquires one-time rights.

$ ◖ THE PEOPLE'S PRESS, 4810 Norwood Ave., Baltimore MD 21207-6839. Phone/fax: (410)448-0254. Press established 1997, firm established 1989. **Contact:** Submissions Editor.

Book/Chapbook Needs: "The goal of the types of material we publish is simply to move people to think and perhaps act to make the world better than when we inherited it." Wants "meaningful poetry that is mindful of human rights/dignity." Has published *Sweet Somethings* by Garrett Flagg and Marvin Pirila, *Braids* by Rasheed Adero Merritt, and *Country Potatoes and Queens* by Shirley Richburg, *Tokarski Meets Acevedo* by Henry J. Tokarski and Judith Acevedo; *The Patient Presents* Kelley Jean White, MD; and *60 Pieces of My Heart* by Jennifer Closs. Accepts poetry written by children; parental consent is mandatory for publication. Books are usually 50 pages, digest-sized, photocopied, perfect-bound and saddle-stapled with soft cover, includes art/graphics.

How to Submit: Query first with 1-5 sample poems and a cover letter with brief bio and publication credits. SASE required for return of work and/or response. No submissions by fax. Time between acceptance and publication is 6-12 months. Seldom comments on rejected poems. Publishes theme issues. Guidelines available for SASE. Responds to queries in 2-6 weeks; to mss in 1-3 months. Pays royalties of 5-20% and 30 author's copies (out of a press run of 500). Order sample books by sending $8.

Also Offers: The People's Press sponsors an annual Poetry Month Contest in April. "Prizes and/or publication possibilities vary from contest to contest." Details available for SASE.

◖ THE PERALTA PRESS, 333 E. Eighth St., Oakland CA 94606. (510)748-2340. Website: www.peraltapress.org. Established 2000. **Editor:** Jay Rubin.

Magazine Needs: *The Peralta Press* appears annually in January. Provides a podium for a diverse blend of both established and emerging twenty-first century voices cutting across race, gender, ethnic, age, religious, political, and sexually oriented boundaries. Wants all forms up to 30 lines (including stanza breaks); no poetry over 30 lines. *The Peralta Press* is 144 pages, digest-sized, perfect-bound. Receives about 400 poems/year, accepts about 15%. Publishes about 50-60 poems/issue. Press run is 1,500. Single copy: $10. Sample: $12. Make checks payable to PCCD.

How to Submit: Submit 3 poems at a time. Line length for poetry is 30 maximum. No previously published poems or simultaneous submissions. No fax, e-mail, or disk submissions. Cover letter is required. Reads submissions August 25-September 15. Time between acceptance and publication is 4 months. Poems are circulated to an editorial board. "Editor makes first cut, teams of judges then determine contest winners." Never comments on rejected poems. "Submit through annual contests. Entry fee: $10 for 3 poems includes free copy." Guidelines available in magazine, for SASE, or on website. Responds in 1 month. Pays 1 contributor's copy, plus cash prize for winning poem. Acquires one-time print and Internet rights.

Advice: "Edit, revise, edit, revise. Preview journals before mass mailing."

◖ PEREGRINE; AMHERST WRITERS & ARTISTS, P.O. Box 1076, Amherst MA 01004-1076. Phone/fax: (413)253-7764. E-mail: awapress@aol.com. Website: www.amherstwriters.com. Established 1984. **Managing Editor:** Nancy Rose.

Magazine Needs: *Peregrine*, published annually in October, features poetry and fiction. Open to all styles, forms and subjects except greeting card verse. Has published poetry by Sofía Arroyo, Charles Atkinson, Aliki Caloyeras, Allen C. Fisher, John Grey, Susan Terris, Dianalee Velie, and Jane Yolen. *Peregrine* is 104 pages, digest-sized, professionally printed, perfect-bound with glossy cover. Each issue includes at least one poem in translation and reviews. Press run is 1,000. Single copy: $12; subscription: $25/3 issues; $35/5 issues; $250/lifetime. Sample: $10. Make checks payable to AWA Press.

How to Submit: Submit 3-5 poems, no more than 70 lines (and spaces) each. Accepts simultaneous submissions; no previously published work. Include cover letter with bio, 40 word maximum. No e-mail submissions. "Each ms is read by several readers. Final decisions are made by the poetry editor." Guidelines available for #10 SASE or on website. Reads submissions October through April only. Postmark deadline: April 1. Pays 2 copies. Acquires first rights.

Also Offers: The Peregrine Prize, an annual fiction and/or poetry contest will not be offered in 2004. The AWA Chapbook Series is *closed* to unsolicited submissions.

PERSPECTIVES (Specialized: religious), Dept. of English, Hope College, Holland MI 49422-9000. Established 1986. **Co-Editors:** Roy Anker, Leanne Van Dyk, and Dave Timmer. **Poetry Editor:** Francis Fike (send poetry submissions to Francis Fike at Dept. of English, Hope College, Holland MI 49422-9000).

Magazine Needs: *Perspectives* appears 10 times/year. The journal's purpose is "to express the Reformed faith theologically; to engage issues that Reformed Christians meet in personal, ecclesiastical, and societal life, and thus to contribute to the mission of the church of Jesus Christ." Wants "both traditional and free verse of high quality, whether explicitly 'religious' or not. Prefer traditional form. Publish one or two poems every other issue, alternating with a Poetry Page on great traditional poems from the past. No sentimental, trite, or 'inspirational' verse, please." Has published poetry by R.L. Barth, David Middleton, Paul Willis, Frederik Zydek, and Sandi Van Doren. *Perspectives* is 24 pages, magazine-sized, web offset and saddle-stapled, with paper cover containing b&w illustration. Receives about 50 poems/year, accepts 6-10. Press run is 3,300 for 3,000 subscribers of which 200 are libraries. Subscription: $30. Sample: $3.50.

How to Submit: No previously published poems or simultaneous submissions. No e-mail submissions. Cover letter preferred. Include SASE. Time between acceptance and publication is 12 months or less. Occasionally comments on rejected poems. Responds in up to 3 months. Pays 5 contributor's copies. Acquires first rights.

PERUGIA PRESS (Specialized: women), P.O. Box 60364, Florence MA 01062. E-mail: info@perugiapress.com. Website: www.perugiapress.com. Established 1997. **Director:** Susan Kan.

Book/Chapbook Needs: "Perugia Press publishes one collection of poetry each year, by a woman at the beginning of her publishing career (first or second books only). Our books appeal to people who have been reading poetry for decades, as well as those who might be picking up a book of poetry for the first time. Slight preference for narrative poetry." Has published *Red* by Melanie Braverman, *The Work of Hands* by Catherine Anderson, *Finding the Bear* by Gail Thomas, *Impulse to Fly* by Almitra David, *A Wound on Stone* by Faye Gore, and *Reach* by Janet E. Aalfs. Books average 88 pages, digest-sized, offset-printed and perfect-bound with 2-color card cover with photo or illustration. Print run 500-750.

How to Submit: Perugia Press is now accepting mss through annual contest only. Send 48-72 pages on white 8½×11 paper "with legible typeface, pagination, and fastened with a removable clip. Include *two* cover pages: one with title of manuscript, name, address, telephone number, and e-mail address and one with just manuscript title. Include table of contents and acknowledgments page." Cover letter and bio not required. Individual poems may be previously published. Accepts simultaneous submissions if notified of acceptance elsewhere. No translations or self-published books. "Poet must be a living, U.S. resident." Entry fee: $20/ms. Make checks payable to Perugia Press. Postmark between August 1 and November 15, 2003; "No FedEx or UPS." SASE for April 1 notification only; mss will be recycled. Judges: panel of Perugia authors, booksellers, scholars, etc. Prize: $1,000 and publication. No e-mail submissions. Guidelines available on website. Order sample books by sending $14.

⊘ PHI KAPPA PHI FORUM, 129 Quad Center, Mell St., Auburn University AL 36849-5306. (334)844-5200. Fax: (334)844-5994. E-mail: kaetzjp@auburn.edu. Website: www.auburn.edu/natfor um. Established 1915. **Editor:** James P. Kaetz. **Contact:** poetry editors.
Magazine Needs: *Phi Kappa Phi Forum* is the quarterly publication of Phi Kappa Phi using quality poetry. *Phi Kappa Phi Forum* is 48 pages, magazine-sized, professionally printed, saddle-stapled, with full-color paper cover and interior. Receives about 300 poems/year, accepts about 20. Press run is 115,000 for 113,000 subscribers of which 300 are libraries. Subscription: $25.
How to Submit: Submit 3-5 short (one page or less in length) poems at a time, including a biographical sketch with recent publications. Accepts e-mail submissions. Reads submissions approximately every 3 months. Responds in about 4 months. Pays 10 contributor's copies.

⊘ ◎ PHOEBE: JOURNAL OF FEMINIST SCHOLARSHIP THEORY AND AESTHET-ICS (Specialized: women/feminism), Women's Studies Dept., Suny-College at Oneonta, Oneonta NY 13820-4015. (607)436-2014. Fax: (607)436-2656. E-mail: omarakk@oneonta.edu. Established 1989. **Poetry Editor:** Marilyn Wesley. **Editor:** Kathleen O'Mara.
Magazine Needs: *Phoebe* is published semiannually. Wants "mostly poetry reflecting women's experiences; prefer 3 pages or less." Has published poetry by Barbara Crooker, Graham Duncan, and Patty Tana. *Phoebe* is 120 pages, digest-sized, offset-printed on coated paper and perfect-bound with glossy card cover, includes b&w art/photos and "publishing swap" ads. Receives about 500 poems/year, accepts 8%. Press run is 500 for 120 subscribers of which 52 are libraries. Single copy: $7.50; subscription: $15/year or $25/year institutional. Sample: $5.
How to Submit: No previously published poems. Accepts fax submissions. Cover letter preferred. Reads submissions October through January and May through July only. Time between acceptance and publication is 3 months. Seldom comments on rejected poems. Publishes theme issues occasionally. Guidelines available for SASE. Responds in up to 14 weeks. Sometimes sends prepublication galleys. Pays 1 contributor's copy. Staff reviews books and chapbooks of poetry in 500-1,000 words, single book format. Send materials for review consideration.

⊘ ◎ PIANO PRESS; "THE ART OF MUSIC" ANNUAL WRITING CONTEST (Specialized: music-related topics), P.O. Box 85, Del Mar CA 92014-0085. (619)884-1401. Fax: (858)459-3376. E-mail: pianopress@aol.com. Website: www.pianopress.com. Established 1998. **Owner:** Elizabeth C. Axford, M.A. Member: The American Academy of Poets.
Book/Chapbook Needs: Piano Press regularly publishes anthologies using "poems on music-related topics to promote the art of music." Publishes 50-100 poems every 2 years. "We are looking for poetry on music-related topics only. Poems can be of any length and in any style." Accepts poetry by children aged 4 and older; any poet under eighteen must provide parents' signed permission. Recently published *The Art of Music: A Collection of Writings Vol. I*. Includes poetry by Robert Cooperman, Gelia Dolci Mascolo, Arthur McMaster, Alana Merritt Mahattey, Bobbi Sinha-Morey, and Gerald Zipper. Chapbooks are usually 64 pages, digest-sized with paper cover, includes some art/graphics. Anthology is $9.95 and $1.50 p&h.
How to Submit: Query first, with a few sample poems and cover letter with brief bio and publication credits. Accepts previously published poems and simultaneous submissions. Accepts submissions by e-mail (attachment or in textbox) and by postal mail. SASE required for reply. Reads submissions September 1 through June 30 only. Time between acceptance and publication is up to 18 months. Poems are circulated to an editorial board. "All submissions are reviewed by several previously published poets." Often comments on rejected poems. Responds to queries and mss in up to 3 months. Pays author's copies. Order sample chapbooks online or by sending SASE for order form.
Also Offers: Sponsors an annual writing contest for poetry, short stories, and essays on music. Open to ages 4 and up. Entry fee: $20. Entry form available online.
Advice: "Please do not send poems if they are not on music-related topics. Otherwise, all music-related poems will be considered."

$⊘ ◎ PIG IRON SERIES; KENNETH PATCHEN COMPETITION (Specialized: themes), P.O. Box 237, Youngstown OH 44501. (330)747-6932. Fax: (330)747-0599. E-mail: pigiro npress@cboss.com. Established 1975. **Poetry Editor:** Jim Villani.
Magazine Needs: Pig Iron Press publishes a literary annual as part of the *Pig Iron Series*. Wants

poetry "up to 300 lines; free verse and experimental; write for current themes." Does not want to see "traditional" poetry. Has published poetry by Frank Polite, Larry Smith, Howard McCord, Andrena Zawinski, Juan Kincaid, and Coco Gordon. *Pig Iron* is 128 pages, magazine-sized, flat-spined, typeset on good stock with glossy card cover using b&w graphics and art, no ads. Press run is 1,000 for 200 subscribers of which 50 are libraries. Single copy: $12.95. Subscription: $12.95/year. Sample: $5. (Include $1.75 postage.)

How to Submit: Include SASE with submission. Accepts submissions by postal mail only. Responds in 3 months. Time between acceptance and publication is 12-18 months. Publishes theme issues. Next theme issue: "Family: The Possibility of Endearment." Deadline: October 2003. Theme for volume 22 of the *Pig Iron Series* is "Jazz Tradition," deadline: June 3, 2004. Guidelines and upcoming themes available for SASE. Responds in up to 4 months. Pays $5/poem plus 2 copies (additional copies at 50% retail). Acquires one-time rights.

Also Offers: Sponsors the annual Kenneth Patchen Competition. Details available for SASE.

Advice: "Reading the work of others positions one to be creative and organized in his/her own work."

PIKEVILLE REVIEW, Humanities Dept., Pikeville College, Pikeville KY 41501. (606)218-5002. Fax: (606)218-5225. E-mail: eward@pc.edu. Website: www.pc.edu. Established 1987. **Editor:** Elgin M. Ward.

Magazine Needs: "There's no editorial bias though we recognize and appreciate style and control in each piece. No emotional gushing." *Pikeville Review* appears annually in July, accepting about 10% of poetry received. *Pikeville Review* is 94 pages, digest-sized, professionally printed and perfect-bound with glossy card cover with b&w illustration. Press run is 500. Sample: $4.

How to Submit: No simultaneous submissions or previously published poems. Editor sometimes comments on rejected poems. Guidelines available for SASE or on website. Pays 5 contributor's copies.

PINCHGUT PRESS, 6 Oaks Ave., Cremorne, Sydney, NSW 2090 Australia. Phone: (02)9908-2402. Established 1948. Publishes Australian poetry but is not currently accepting poetry submissions.

$ PINE ISLAND JOURNAL OF NEW ENGLAND POETRY (Specialized: regional, New England), P.O. Box 317, West Springfield MA 01090-0317. Established 1998. **Editor:** Linda Porter.

Magazine Needs: *Pine Island* appears 2 times/year "to encourage and support New England poets and the continued expression of New England themes." Wants poems of "up to thirty lines, haiku and other forms welcome, especially interested in New England subjects or themes. No horror, no erotica." Has published poetry by Larry Kimmel, Roy P. Fairfield, and Carol Purington. *Pine Island* is 50 pages, digest-sized, desktop-published and saddle-stapled, cardstock cover with art. Press run is 200 for 80 subscribers. Subscription: $10. Sample: $5. Make checks payable to Pine Island Journal.

How to Submit: "Writers must be currently residenced in New England." Submit 5 poems at a time. Line length for poetry is 30 maximum. No previously published poems or simultaneous submissions. Cover letter preferred. "Include SASE, prefer first time submissions to include cover letter with brief bio." Time between acceptance and publication is 6 months. Seldom comments on rejected poems. Responds in up to 2 months. Pays $1/poem and 1 contributor's copy. Acquires first rights.

PINK CADILLAC: THE MAGAZINE OF CREATIVE THOUGHT, 2822 Beale Ave., Altoona PA 16601-1708. Website: http://hometown.aol.com/ikey95/myhomepage/business.html.

● **At press time we learned *Pink Cadillac* is suspending publication.**

Magazine Needs: *Pink Cadillac* is a quarterly forum for new and established writers. Wants any style, up to 50 lines. "No vulgar, pornographic or overly sentimental, sappy drivel." Has published poetry by Stephen Klein, Karen R. Porter, Elizabeth Fuller, and Mary Rudbeck Stanko. *Pink Cadillac* is 20 pages, magazine-sized, includes line art and reading/writing related ads. Subscription: $10/4 issues. Sample: $2.50.

How to Submit: Submit 4-8 typed poems at a time. "Nothing handwritten." Line length for poetry is 3 minimum, 50 maximum. Accepts previously published poems and simultaneous submissions.

Accepts e-mail submissions. Cover letter preferred. Time between acceptance and publication is 6 months. Guidelines available for SASE or by e-mail. Responds in 6 months. Pays 1 copy. Acquires one-time rights. Reviews books and chapbooks of poetry and other magazines. Send materials for review consideration.

Advice: "Read contemporary poetry. Write, revise, rewrite. Listen!"

◻ **THE PINK CHAMELEON—ONLINE**. E-mail: dpfreda@juno.com. Website: www.geocities. com/thepinkchameleon/index.html. Established 1985 (former print version), 1999 (online version). **Editor:** Dorothy P. Freda.

Magazine Needs: *Pink Chameleon—Online* wants "family-oriented, upbeat, any genre in good taste that gives hope for the future. For example, poems about nature, loved ones, rare moments in time. No pornography, no cursing, no swearing, nothing evoking despair." *The Pink Chameleon* is published online with public domain illustrations and Yahoo ads. Receives about 50 poems/year, accepts about 50%. Publishes about 25 poems/issue.

How to Submit: Submit 1-4 poems at a time. Line length for poetry is 6 minimum, 24 maximum. Accepts previously published poems; no simultaneous submissions. "Only e-mail submissions considered. Please, *no attachments*. Include work in the body of the e-mail itself. Use plain text. Include a brief bio." Reads submissions all year. Time between acceptance and publication is 2 months. "As editor, I reserve the right to edit for grammar, spelling, sentence structure, flow, omit redundancy and any words or material I consider in bad taste. No pornography, no violence for the sake of violence, no curse words. Remember this is a family-oriented electronic magazine." Often comments on rejected poems. Guidelines available by e-mail or on website. Responds in 1 month. No payment. Acquires one-time, one-year publication rights. All rights revert to poet one year after publication online.

Advice: "Always keep a typed hard copy or a back-up disk of your work for your files. Mail can go astray. And I'm human, I can accidentally delete or lose the submission."

◻ ◎ **THE PIPE SMOKER'S EPHEMERIS (Specialized: pipes and pipe smoking)**, 20-37 120th St., College Point NY 11356-2128. Established 1964. **Editor/Publisher:** Tom Dunn.

Magazine Needs: "The *Ephemeris* is a limited edition, irregular quarterly for pipe smokers and collectors and anyone else who is interested in its varied contents. Publication costs are absorbed by the editor/publisher, assisted by any contributions—financial or otherwise—that readers might wish to make." Wants poetry with themes related to pipes and pipe smoking. Issues range from 76-116 pages, and are magazine-sized, offset, saddle-stapled, with coated stock covers and illustrations. Has also published collections covering the first and second 15 years of the *Ephemeris* and issues a triennial "Collector's Dictionary."

How to Submit: Accepts submissions on disk. Cover letter required with submissions; include any credits. Pays 1-2 contributor's copies. Staff reviews books of poetry. Send materials for review consideration.

◖ **PITCHFORK; PITCHFORK PRESS**, 2002 A Guadalupe St. #461, Austin TX 78705. Established 1998. **Editor:** Christopher Gibson.

Magazine Needs: *Pitchfork* is a biannual publishing "freaky goodness." Wants post-beat and surreal poetry—"erotic, psychotic and surreal poetry. No hack work." Has published poetry by Gerald Nicosia, Doug Draime, Lawrence Welsh, and Steve Dalachinsky. *Pitchfork* is 60-80 pages, digest-sized, photocopied and saddle-stapled with colored paper cover. Press run varies. Sample: $3. Single copy: $4; subscription: $10 (includes 2 issues and a chapbook of choice). Make checks payable to Christopher Gibson.

How to Submit: Submit 3-7 poems at a time. Accepts previously published poems and simultaneous submissions "but let us know." Cover letter preferred. "Include name and address on each page; always include SASE." Time between acceptance and publication is 6 months. Seldom comments on rejected poems. Response time varies. Pays 1 copy. Acquires all rights. Returns rights.

Book/Chapbook Needs & How to Submit: Pitchfork Press publishes 2 chapbooks per year. Has published *Mountains* by t. kilgore splake, *Our Wounds* by Thomas Michael McDade, *Factory Stiff* by William Hart. Chapbooks are usually 40-60 pages, digest-sized, photocopied and side-stapled. However, they are not accepting unsolicited mss at this time.

PITT POETRY SERIES; UNIVERSITY OF PITTSBURGH PRESS; AGNES LYNCH STARRETT POETRY PRIZE, 3400 Forbes Ave., Pittsburgh PA 15260. (412)383-2456. Fax: (412)383-2466. Website: www.pitt.edu/~press. Established 1968. **Poetry Editor:** Ed Ochester.

Book/Chapbook Needs: Publishes 6 books/year by established poets, and 1 by a new poet—the winner of the Starrett Poetry Prize competition. Wants "poetry of the highest quality; otherwise, no restrictions—book mss minimum of 48 pages." Poets who have previously published books should query. Accepts simultaneous submissions. Always sends prepublication galleys. Has published books of poetry by Lynn Emanuel, Larry Levis, Billy Collins and Alicia Ostriker. Their booklist also features such poets as Etheridge Knight, Sharon Olds, Ronald Wallace, David Wojahn and Toi Derricotte.

How to Submit: Unpublished poets or poets "who have published chapbooks or limited editions of less than 750 copies" must submit through the Agnes Lynch Starrett Poetry Prize (see below). For poetry series, submit "entire manuscripts only." Cover letter preferred. Reads submissions from established poets in September and October only. Seldom comments on rejected poems.

Also Offers: Sponsors the Agnes Lynch Starrett Poetry Prize. "Poets who have not previously published a book should send SASE for rules of the Starrett competition ($20 handling fee), the only vehicle through which we publish first books of poetry." The Starrett Prize consists of cash award of $5,000 and book publication. Entries must be postmarked between March 1 and April 30. Competition receives 1,000 entries.

PLAINSONGS, Dept. of English, Hastings College, Hastings NE 68902-0269. (402)461-7352. Fax: (402)461-7756. E-mail: dm84342@alltel.net. Established 1980. **Editor:** Dwight C. Marsh.

Magazine Needs: *Plainsongs* is a poetry magazine that "accepts manuscripts from anyone, considering poems on any subject in any style but free verse predominates. Plains region poems encouraged." Has published Jeffrey Kuczmarski, Sarah E. Lamers, Andy Macera, Judith Tato O'Brien, and Tom Rich. *Plainsongs* is 40 pages, digest-sized, set on laser, printed on thin paper and saddle-stapled with one-color matte card cover with generic black logo. "Published by the English department of Hastings College, the magazine is partially financed by subscriptions. Although editors respond to as many submissions with personal attention as they have time for, the editor offers specific observations to all contributors who also subscribe." The name suggests not only its location on the Great Plains, but its preference for the living language, whether in free or formal verse. *Plainsongs* is committed to poems only, to make space without visual graphics, bio, reviews, or critical positions. Subscription: $12/3 issues. Sample: $4.

How to Submit: Submit up to 6 poems at a time with name and address on each page. Deadlines are August 15 for fall issue; November 15 for winter; March 15 for spring. Notification is mailed 5-6 weeks after deadlines. Pays 2 contributor's copies and 1-year subscription, with 3 award poems in each issue receiving $25. "A short essay in appreciation accompanies each award poem." Acquires first rights.

Advice: "We like to hear tension in the lines, with nothing flaccid."

$ PLANET: THE WELSH INTERNATIONALIST, P.O. Box 44, Aberystwyth, Ceredigion SY23 3ZZ, Wales. Phone: 01970-611255. Fax: 01970-611197. E-mail: planet.enquiries@planet magazine.org.uk. Website: http://planetmagazine.org.uk. Established 1970. **Editor:** John Barnie.

Magazine Needs: *Planet* is a bimonthly cultural magazine, "centered on Wales, but with broader interests in arts, sociology, politics, history and science." Wants "good poetry in a wide variety of styles. No limitations as to subject matter; length can be a problem." Has published poetry by Nigel Jenkins, Anne Stevenson, and Mertyl Morris. *Planet* is 128 pages, A5 size, professionally printed and perfect-bound with glossy color card cover. Receives about 500 submissions/year, accepts approximately 5%. Press run is 1,550 for 1,500 subscribers of which about 10% are libraries, 200 shelf sales. Single copy: £3.25; subscription: £15 (overseas: £16). Sample: £4.

How to Submit: No previously published poems or simultaneous submissions. Accepts submissions on disk, as e-mail attachment, and by postal mail. SASE or SAE with IRCs essential for reply. Time between acceptance and publication is 6-10 months. Seldom comments on rejected poems. Send SASE (or SAE and IRCs if outside UK) for guidelines. Responds within a month or so. Pays £25 minimum. Acquires first serial rights only. Reviews books of poetry in 700 words, single or multi-book format.

◐ **THE PLASTIC TOWER**, P.O. Box 702, Bowie MD 20718. Established 1989. **Editors:** Carol Dyer and Roger Kyle-Keith.

Magazine Needs: *The Plastic Tower* is a quarterly using "everything from iambic pentameter to silly limericks, modern free verse, haiku, rhymed couplets—we like it all! Only restriction is length— under 40 lines preferred. So send us poems that are cool or wild, funny or tragic—but especially those closest to your soul." Has published poetry by "more than 400 different poets." *The Plastic Tower* is 38-54 pages, digest-sized, saddle-stapled; "variety of typefaces and b&w graphics on cheap photocopy paper. Line drawings also welcome." Press run is 200. Subscription: $8/year. Copy of current issue: $2.50. "We'll send a back issue free for a large (at least 6×9) SAE with 2 first-class stamps attached."

How to Submit: Submit up to 10 poems at a time. Accepts previously published poems and simultaneous submissions. Accepts submissions by postal mail only. Often comment on submissions. Guidelines available for SASE. Responds in up to 1 year. Pays 1 contributor's copy. Send materials for review consideration.

Advice: "*The Plastic Tower* is an unpretentious little rag dedicated to enjoying verse and making poetry accessible to the general public as well as fellow poets. We don't claim to be the best, but we try to be the nicest and most personal. Over the past several years, we've noticed a tremendous upswing in submissions. More people than ever are writing poetry and submitting it for publication, and that makes it tougher for individual writers to get published. But plenty of opportunities still exist (there are thousands of little and literary magazines in the U.S. alone), and the most effective tool for any writer right now is not talent or education, but persistence. So keep at it!"

⊕ ◐ ◎ **THE PLAZA (Specialized: bilingual)**, U-Kan, Inc., Yoyogi 2-32-1, Shibuya-ku, Tokyo 151-0053, Japan. Phone: 81-3-3379-3881. Fax: 81-3-3379-3882. E-mail: plaza@u-kan.co.jp. Website: http://u-kan.co.jp. Established 1985. **Contact:** editor.

Magazine Needs: *The Plaza* is a quarterly, currently published only online (http://u-kan.co.jp), which "represents a borderless forum for contemporary writers and artists" and includes poetry, fiction, and essays published simultaneously in English and Japanese. Wants "highly artistic poetry dealing with being human and interculturally related. Nothing stressing political, national, religious, or racial differences. *The Plaza* is edited with a global view of mankind." Has published poetry by Al Beck, Antler, Charles Helzer, Richard Alan Bunch, Morgan Gibson, and Bun'ichirou Chino. *The Plaza* is 50 full color pages. Available free to all readers on the Internet. Receives about 2,500 poems/ year, accepts 8%. Proofs of accepted poems are sent to the authors 1 month before online publication.

How to Submit: Accepts simultaneous submissions; no previously published poems. Accepts e-mail and fax submissions. "No attachments. Cover letter required. Please include telephone and fax numbers or e-mail address with submissions. As *The Plaza* is a bilingual publication in English and Japanese, it is sometimes necessary, for translation purposes, to contact authors. Japanese translations are prepared by the editorial staff." Seldom comments on rejected poems. Responds within 2 months. Reviews books of poetry, usually in less than 500 words. Send materials for review consideration.

Advice: "*The Plaza* focuses not on human beings but humans being human in the borderless world."

$◐ **PLEIADES; LENA-MILES WEVER TODD POETRY SERIES; PLEIADES PRESS**, Dept. of English and Philosophy, Central Missouri State University, Warrensburg MO 64093. (660)543-8106. E-mail: kdp8106@cmsu2.cmsu.edu. Website: www.cmsu.edu/englphil/pleiades.html. Established in 1990. **Editors:** Kevin Prufer.

Magazine Needs: *Pleiades* is a semiannual journal, appearing in April and October, which publishes poetry, fiction, literary criticism, belles lettres (occasionally), and reviews. It is open to all writers. Wants "avant-garde, free verse and traditional poetry, and some quality light verse. Nothing pretentious, didactic, or overly sentimental." Has published poetry by James Tate, Joyce Carol Oates, Brenda Hillman, Dara Wier, Rafael Campo, and David Lehman. *Pleiades* is 160 pages, digest-sized, perfect-bound with a heavy coated cover and color cover art. Receives about 3,000 poems/year,

---

◆ **INDICATES A MARKET** that did not appear in the 2003 edition.

accepts 1-3%. Press run is 2,500-3,000, about 200 distributed free to educational institutions and libraries across the country, several hundred shelf sales. Single copy: $6; subscription: $12. Sample: $5. Make checks payable to Pleiades Press.

How to Submit: Submit 3-5 poems at a time. Accepts simultaneous submissions with notification; no previously published poems. Cover letter with brief bio preferred. Time between acceptance and publication can be up to 1 year. Each poem published must be accepted by 2 readers and approved by the poetry editor. Seldom comments on rejected poems. Guidelines available for SASE or on website. Responds in up to 3 months. Payment varies. Acquires first and second serial rights and requests rights for *Wordbeat*, a TV/radio show featuring work published in *Pleiades*.

Also Offers: Sponsors the Lena-Miles Wever Todd Poetry Series. "We will select one book of poems in open competition and publish it in our Pleiades Press Series. Louisiana State University Press will distribute the collection." Has published *A Sacrificial Zinc* by Matthew Cooperman and *The Light in Our Houses* by Al Maginnes. Entry fee: $15. Postmark deadline: September 30 annually. Complete guidelines available for SASE.

$◐ PLOUGHSHARES, Emerson College, 120 Boylston St., Boston MA 02116. (617)824-8753. Website: www.pshares.org. Established 1971.

● Work published in *Ploughshares* is frequently selected for inclusion in volumes of *The Best American Poetry*.

Magazine Needs: *Ploughshares* is "a journal of new writing guest-edited by prominent poets and writers to reflect different and contrasting points of view." Editors have included Carolyn Forché, Gerald Stern, Rita Dove, Chase Twichell, and Marilyn Hacker. Has published poetry by Donald Hall, Li-Young Lee, Robert Pinsky, Brenda Hillman, and Thylias Moss. The triquarterly is 250 pages, digest-sized. Press run is 6,000. Receives about 2,500 poetry submissions/year. Subscription: $24 domestic; $36 foreign. Sample: $10.95 current issue, $8.50 sample back issue.

How to Submit: "We suggest you read a few issues before submitting." Simultaneous submissions acceptable. Do not submit mss from April 1 to July 31. Responds in up to 5 months. Always sends prepublication galleys. Pays $25/printed page per poem ($50 min, $250 max), plus 2 copies and a subscription.

▓ $○ THE PLOWMAN, The Plowman Ministries—A Mission for Christ, Box 414, Whitby ON L1N 5S4 Canada. (905)668-7803. Established 1988. **Editor:** Tony Scavetta.

Magazine Needs: *The Plowman* appears annually in July or August using "didactic, eclectic poetry; all forms. We will also take most religious poetry except satanic and evil. We are interested in work that deals with the important issues in our society. Social and environment issues are of great importance." Has published poetry by Larry Prouty, K.L. Haley, Ari Zepkin, Luther C. Hanson, and Angela Galipeau. *The Plowman* is 20 pages, magazine-sized, photocopied, unbound, contains clip art and market listings. Accepts 70% of the poetry received. Press run is 15,000 for 1,200 subscribers of which 500 are libraries. Single copy: $5; subscription: $10. Sample free.

How to Submit: Submit up to 5 poems (preferably 38 lines or less). Accepts previously published poems and simultaneous submissions. Cover letter required. No SASE necessary. Always comments on rejected poems. Guidelines available for SASE. Responds in up to 2 weeks. Always sends prepublication galleys. Pays 1 copy. Reviews books of poetry.

Book/Chapbook Needs & How to Submit: Also publishes 125 chapbooks/year. Responds to queries and mss in 1 month. **Reading fee:** $25/book. Pays 20% royalties. Has published *Coloring Outside the Lines* by Ellaraine Lackie, *As Girlfriends Do, As Women Will* by Donna Michele Hill, *Glissando Surprise* by Thomas M. Snyder, *Brenda's World* by d.n. summers, *His Word in Me* by Michael Salerno, and *On the Tompson* by Gordon Watts.

Also Offers: Offers monthly poetry contests. Entry fee: $2/poem. 1st Prize: 50% of the proceeds; 2nd: 25%; 3rd: 10%. The top poems are published. "Balance of the poems will be used for anthologies."

◖ POEM; HUNTSVILLE LITERARY ASSOCIATION, P.O. Box 2006, Huntsville AL 35804. Established 1967. **Editor:** Rebecca Harbor.

Magazine Needs: *Poem*, appears twice/year, consisting entirely of poetry. "We are open to traditional as well as non-traditional forms, but we favor work with the expected compression and intensity of good lyric poetry and a high degree of verbal and dramatic tension. We equally welcome submissions from established poets as well as from less-known and beginning poets." Has published poetry by Robert Cooperman, Andrew Dillon, and Scott Travis Hutchison. *Poem* is a flat-spined, digest-sized, 90-page journal that contains more than 60 poems (mostly lyric free verse under 50 lines) generally featured 1 to a page on good stock paper with a clean design and a classy matte cover. Press run is 400 (all subscriptions, including libraries). Sample: $5.

How to Submit: "We do not accept translations, previously published works, or simultaneous submissions. Best to submit December through March and June through September. We prefer to see a sample of three to five poems at a submission, with SASE. We generally respond within a month. We are a nonprofit organization and can pay only in copy to contributors." Pays 2 contributor's copies. Acquires first serial rights.

POEM DU JOUR, P.O. Box 416, Somers MT 59932. Established 1999. **Editor:** Asta Bowen.
Magazine Needs: *Poem du Jour* is a "weekly one-page broadside circulated in the retail environment." Wants "accessible but not simplistic poetry; seasonal work encouraged; humorous, current events, slam favorites; topical work (rural, mountain, outdoors, environmental, Northwest). No erotica, forced rhyme, or poems of excessive length." Press run is 20-50. Sample: $2. Make checks payable to Asta Bowen—PDJ.
How to Submit: Submit up to 5 poems at a time. Line length for poetry is 50 maximum. Accepts previously published poems and simultaneous submissions. Cover letter preferred. "Prefer poems typed with name, address and phone on each page." Time between acceptance and publication varies. Seldom comments on rejected poems. Guidelines available for SASE. Responds in 2 months. Sometimes sends prepublication galleys. Pays 1 contributor's copy. Acquires one-time rights.
Advice: "New/young writers encouraged."

POEMS & PLAYS; THE TENNESSEE CHAPBOOK PRIZE, English Dept., Middle Tennessee State University, Murfreesboro TN 37132. (615)898-2712. Established 1993. **Editor:** Gaylord Brewer.
Magazine Needs: *Poems & Plays* is an annual "eclectic publication for poems and short plays," published in April. No restrictions on style or content of poetry. Has published poetry by Naomi Wallace, Kate Gale, Richard Newman, Ron Koertge, and Moira Egan. *Poems & Plays* is 88 pages, digest-sized, professionally printed and perfect-bound with coated color card cover and art. "We receive 1,500 poems per issue, typically publish 30-35." Press run is 800. Subscription: $10/2 issues. Sample: $6.
How to Submit: No previously published poems or simultaneous submissions (except for chapbook submissions). Reads submissions October 1 through December 31 only. "Work is circulated among advisory editors for comments and preferences. All accepted material is published in the following issue." Usually comments on rejected poems. Responds in 2 months. Pays 1 contributor's copy. Acquires first publication rights only.
Also Offers: "We accept chapbook manuscripts (of poems or short plays) of 20-24 pages for The Tennessee Chapbook Prize. Any combination of poems or plays, or a single play, is eligible. The winning chapbook is printed as an interior chapbook in *Poems & Plays* and the author receives 50 copies of the issue. SASE and $10 (for reading fee and one copy of the issue) required. Dates for contest entry are the same as for the magazine (October 1 through December 31). Past winners include Julie Lechevsky, David Kirby, Angela Kelly, and Rob Griffith. The chapbook competition annually receives over 150 manuscripts from the U.S. and around the world."

POESY MAGAZINE, P.O. Box 7823, Santa Cruz CA 95061. (831)460-1048. E-mail: info@poesy.org. Website: www.posey.org. Established 1994. **Editor/Publisher:** Brian Morrisey.
Magazine Needs: *POESY Magazine* appears quarterly. "*POESY* is an anthology of American poetry. *POESY*'s main concentration is Boston, MA and Santa Cruz, CA, two thriving homesteads for poets, beats, and artists of nature. Our goal is to unite the two scenes, updating poets on what's happening across the country. We like to see poems that express atmosphere and observational impacts of both Santa Cruz and Boston. Acceptence is based on creativity, composition, and relation to the goals of *POESY*. Please do not send poetry with excessive profanity. We would like to endorse creativity beyond the likes of everyday babble." Recently published poetry by Lawrence Ferlinghetti,

Edward Sanders, Herschel Silverman, Linda Lerner, Simon Perchik, and Corey Mesler. *POESY* is 16 pages, magazine-sized, newsprint, glued/folded, with computer generated and quarter-page ads. Receives about 1,000 poems/year, accepts about 10%. Publishes about 30 poems/issue. Press run is 1,000, most distributed free to local venues. Single copy: $1; subscription: $12/year. Sample: $2. Make checks payable to Brian Morrisey.

How to Submit: Submit 4-6 poems at a time. Line length for poetry is 32 maximum. No previously published poems or simultaneous submissions. Accepts e-mail and disk submissions; no fax submissions. Cover letter preferred. "Snail mail submissions are preferred with a SASE." Reads submissions year round. Time between acceptance and publication is 1 month. "Poems are accepted by the Santa Cruz editor and the publisher based on how well the poem stimulates our format." Often comments on rejected poems. Guidelines are available in magazine, for SASE, and by e-mail. Responds in 1 month. Sometimes sends prepublication galleys. Pays 3 contributor's copies. Acquires one-time rights. Reviews books and chapbooks of poetry and other magazines/journals in 1,000 words, single book format. Send materials for review consideration to *POESY*, % Brian Morrisey.

Advice: "Branch away from typical notions of love and romance. Become one with your surroundings and discover a true sense of natural perspective."

$ ○ A POET BORN PRESS, P.O. Box 24238, Knoxville TN 37933. E-mail: wm.tell.us@apoetborn.com. Website: www.apoetborn.com. Established 1998. **Contact:** Laura Skye.

Book/Chapbook Needs: A Poet Born Press publishes 6-8 paperbacks per year. Wants any style or form of poetry, 45 lines or less, including spaces. "Poems should be descriptive of the 20th Century, its people and its issues." No profanity. Has published poetry by Robin Moore, Dwhisperer, and Skye. Books are usually 50-150 pages, digest-sized, perfect-bound with 80 lb. coverstock, 1 color or full bleed color covers, includes some photographs, some drawings.

How to Submit: Query first with 1-2 sample poems and cover letter with brief bio and publication credits. Line length for poetry is 45 maximum including spaces. Accepts previously published poems and simultaneous submissions. Accepts e-mail and disk submissions. "All poetry must be accompanied by author's name and address, as well as by e-mail address and URL if applicable. Also, author must specify what submission is for: contest, certain publications or call for poems, etc." Time between acceptance and publication is up to 6 months. Poems are circulated to an editorial board. "The editorial staff reviews all submissions for publication and makes their recommendations to the Senior Editor who makes the final selections." Often comments on rejected poems. "We charge for criticism only on manuscript-length work. Price varies depending on length of manuscript. E-mail for complete details." Responds to queries in 2 months. Pays 5-35% royalties "depending on individual contract." 50% of books are author-subsidy published each year. "We have four different subsidy programs. Program is dependent upon work, audience, sales track, and author/press choice. Contracts are specifically tailored to individual authors and their work. No royalties are paid for poems accepted for anthologies."

Also Offers: Sponsors three contests per year. 1st Place: $100 plus a brass plaque of poem; 2nd Place: brass plaque of poem; 3rd Place: A Poet Born coffee mug. "All winners receive web publication within 6 weeks of contest and print publication within one year." Entry fee: $5/poem. Website includes complete contest guidelines and submission form, Call for Poems section and permission form, Winners Circle and archive of previous winning poems, Poetry Night listings, poetry news and events, resource links and Teacher's Corner. "Teacher's Corner features lessons in poetry provided by published poets, authors, professors, editors and more. Recent appearances in the Teacher's Corner include: Robert Pinsky; Robin Moore, author of the *French Connection* and *The Green Berets*; Eugene McCarthy, statesman and published poet; and Michael Bugeja, author of *The Art and Craft of Poetry*."

○ POET LORE, The Writer's Center, 4508 Walsh St., Bethesda MD 20815. (301)654-8664. Fax: (301)654-8667. E-mail: postmaster@writer.org. Website: www.writer.org. Established 1889. **Editors:** Rick Cannon, E. Ethelbert Miller, and Jody Bolz. **Contact:** Jo-Ann Billings.

Magazine Needs: *Poet Lore* is a biannual dedicated "to the best in American and world poetry and objective and timely reviews and commentary. We look for fresh uses of traditional form and devices, but any kind of excellence is welcome. Has published poetry by Martin Galvin, Eliot Khalil Wilson, Herman Asarnow, Carrie Etter, Geri Rosenzweig, and Maria Terrone. *Poet Lore* is digest-sized,

120 pages, perfect-bound, professionally printed with glossy card cover. Circulation includes 600 subscriptions of which 200 are libraries. Receives about 3,000 poems/year, accepts 125. Single copy: $9; subscription: $18. "Add $5 postage for subscriptions outside U.S."

How to Submit: Submit typed poems, author's name and address on each page, SASE required. No simultaneous submissions. Guidelines available for SASE, by fax, by e-mail, on website. Upcoming themes available in publication. Responds in 3 months. Pays 2 contributor's copies. Reviews books of poetry. Send materials for review consideration.

POETCRIT (Specialized: membership), Maranda, H.P. 176 102 India. Phone: 01894-238277. E-mail: dcchambrial@indiatimes.com. Established 1988. **Editor:** Dr. D.C. Chambial.

Magazine Needs: *Poetcrit* appears each January and July "to promote poetry and international understanding through poetry. Purely critical articles on various genres of literature are also published." Wants poems of every kind. Has published poetry by Ruth Wilder Schuller (US), Danae G. Papastratau (Greece), Shiv K. Kumar (India), Joy B. Cripps (Australia), and O.P. Bhatnagar (India). *Poetcrit* is 100 pages, magazine-sized, offset-printed with simple paper cover, includes ads. Receives about 1,000 poems/year, accepts 20%. Press run is 1,000 for 500 subscribers of which 100 are libraries, 200 shelf sales; 400 distributed free to new members. Single copy: $9; subscription: $15. Sample: $10. Make checks payable to Dr. D.C. Chambial. Membership required for consideration.

How to Submit: Submit 3 poems at a time. Line length for poetry is 25 maximum. Accepts simultaneous submissions; no previously published poems. Cover letter required. Reads submissions September 1 through 20 and March 1 through 20. Poems are circulated to an editorial board. "All poems reviewed by various editors and selected for publication." Occasionally publishes theme issues. Guidelines and upcoming themes are available for SASE or SAE with IRC. Responds in about 1 month. Pays 1 contributor's copy. Acquires one-time rights. Reviews books and chapbooks of poetry and other magazines in 1,000 words, single book format.

Advice: "Beginners should meditate well on their themes before writing."

POETIC HOURS, 43 Willow Rd., Carlton, Nolts NG4 3BH England. E-mail: erranpublishing@hotmail.com. Website: www.poetichours.homestead.com. Established 1993. **Editor:** Nicholas Clark.

Magazine Needs: *Poetic Hours*, published biannually, "is published to encourage and publish new poets, i.e., as a forum where good but little known poets can appear in print and to raise money for Third World charities. The magazine features articles and poetry by subscribers and others." Wants "any subject, rhyme preferred but not essential; suitable for wide ranging readership, 30 lines maximum." Does not want "gothic, horror, extremist, political, self-interested." *Poetic Hours* is 36 pages, A4, printed, saddle-stapled and illustrated throughout with Victorian woodcuts. Receives about 500 poems/year, accepts about 40%. Press run is 400 of which 12 are for libraries, 300 shelf sales. Subscription: £7, overseas payments in sterling or US dollars ($20). For a subscription send bankers checks or cash. Sample: £3.75. Make checks payable to Erran Publishing. "Subscribe online at our site at www.poetichours.homestead.com."

How to Submit: "Poets are encouraged to subscribe or buy a single copy, though not required." Submit up to 5 nonreturnable poems at a time. Accepts previously published poems; no simultaneous submissions. Prefers e-mail submissions in attachments; accepts disk submissions. Cover letter required. Time between acceptance and publication is 3 months. "Poems are read by editors and if found suitable, are used." Always comments on rejected poems. Publishes theme issues. Upcoming themes listed in magazine. Responds "immediately, whenever possible." Acquires one-time rights.

Also Offers: "Poetic Hours Online" at www.poetichours.homestead.com features original content by invitation of editor only.

Advice: "We welcome newcomers and invite those just starting out to have the courage to submit work. The art of poetry has moved from the hands of book publishers down the ladder to the new magazines. This is where all the best poetry is found." *Poetic Hours* is non-profit-making and all proceeds go to various national charities, particularly Oxfam and Amnesty International. A page of *Poetic Hours* is set aside each issue for reporting how money is spent.

POETIC LICENSE POETRY MAGAZINE, P.O. Box 1095, Peoria IL 61653-1095. E-mail: poeticlicense99@hotmail.com. Website: www.poeticlicense.net. Established 1996. **Editor:** Denise Felt.

Magazine Needs: *Poetic License Poetry Magazine* is a quarterly publication with "the purpose of giving new and experienced poets a chance to be published. It includes articles and contests that challenge poets to grow in their craft. We want the best free verse and rhymed poetry by adults and children. No profane, vulgar, pornographic, or sloppy work accepted." Has published poetry by Gary Edwards, Terri Warden, William Middleton, and Robert Hentz. *Poetic License Poetry Magazine* is 80 pages, magazine-sized, magazine-bound with full color cover, includes graphic art and ads. Receives over 4,000 poems/year, accepts about 95%. Press run is 150/issue. Subscription: $48/year. Sample: $5.50. Make checks payable to *Poetic License*.

How to Submit: Submit up to 5 poems at a time. Accepts previously published poems. Accepts e-mail submissions in body of message. Cover letter preferred. "Send double-spaced typed poems with name and address in upper right hand corner. Age required if poet is 18 or younger." Time between acceptance and publication is up to 3 months. "I judge poems on a 25-point system. Adult submissions with 15 points or less are rejected. Children's submissions with 10 points or less are rejected." Publishes theme issues. Responds in 1 month. Acquires one-time rights. Guidelines and upcoming themes available for SASE, by e-mail, or on website.

Advice: "The most important thing poets should concern themselves with is excellence. Whether a poem is rewritten twice or twenty times, it shouldn't matter. The goal is to bring the poem to life. Then it's fit for publication. There is more talent in literate people of all ages than the poets of past centuries could have dreamed. Our goal is to encourage that talent to grow and flourish through exposure to the public."

POETIC MATRIX PRESS; POETIC MATRIX, A PERIODIC LETTER; POETIC MATRIX SLIM VOLUME SERIES, P.O. Box 1223, Madera CA 93639. (559)673-9402. E-mail: poetic matrix@yahoo.com. Website: www.geocities.com/poeticmatrix. Established 1997 in Yosemite. **Editor/Publisher:** John Peterson.

Magazine Needs: *Poetic Matrix, a periodic letteR* appears periodically 2-4 times/year. Wants poetry that "creates a 'place in which we can live' rather than telling us about the place. Poetry that draws from the imaginal mind and is rich in the poetic experience—hence the poetic matrix." Does not want poetry that talks about the experience. Recently published poetry by Jeff Mann, Grace Marie Grafton, Tony White, Kathryn Kruger, James Downs, and Brandon Cesmat. *Poetic Matrix* is 4-12 pages, newsletter format, photocopied, saddle-stapled, with b&w art. Publishes about 10-20 poems/issue. Press run is 500 for 250 subscribers; 150 distributed free to interested parties, etc. Subscription: $12/4 issues. Make checks payable to *Poetic Matrix*.

How to Submit: Submit through Slim Volume Series. Accepts previously published poems and simultaneous submissions. Accepts submissions by postal mail only. Cover letter is required. Charges reading fee for yearly Slim Volume series submissions *only*. "Poems for *letteR* are generally, but not always drawn from the call for manuscripts for the *Poetic Matrix* Slim Volume Series." Often comments on rejected poems. Guidelines available for SASE or by e-mail. Responds in 2 months. Pays 25 contributor's copies. Acquires one-time rights. Reviews books and chapbooks of poetry and other magazines/journals in 500-1,000 words, single and multi-book format. Send materials for review consideration to John Peterson, editor.

Book/Chapbook Needs & How to Submit: Poetic Matrix Press publishes books (60-90 pages), slim volumes (44-55 pages, perfect-bound), and chapbooks (20-30 pages). "Poetic Matrix Press hosts a new Slim Volume Series call for submissions of manuscripts 45-55 pages. The manuscript selected will be published with full-color cover, perfect binding, and ISBN. The selected poet will receive 50 copies of the completed book and a $200 honorarium." Full guidelines and submission dates available for SASE. For chapbook and book information, contact the publisher. Order sample copies from Poetic Matrix Press.

Advice: "If poets and lovers of poetry don't write, publish, read, purchase poetry books, etc., then we will have no say in the quality of our contemporary culture and no excuses for the abuses of language, ideas, truth, beauty, and love in our cultural life."

POETICA (Specialized: Jewish), Box 11014, Norfolk VA 23517. E-mail: poeticamag@aol.com. Established 2002. Publisher: Michael Mahgerefteh. **Editor:** Meira Swain.

Magazine Needs: *Poetica* appears 3 times/year. "We seek energetic poetry that builds around real experience and real characters on Jewish subjects or presenting a Jewish point of view." Does not want long pieces, haiku, rhyming poetry. Accepts poetry by young poets grades 9-12. *Poetica* is 40 pages, digest-sized, desktop-published, saddle-stapled, with card stock cover (glossy with art/graphics) with b&w internal art/graphics, ads. Receives about 200 poems/year, accepts about 60%. Publishes 30 poems/issue. Press run is 200 for 30 subscribers. Single copy: $4; subscription: $12. Make checks payable to Poetica Publishing Company.

How to Submit: Submit 3 poems at a time. Accepts simultaneous submissions. No e-mail or disk submissions. Cover letter is preferred. "Poems no longer than two pages; short stories no longer than two pages." Reads submissions year round. Time between acceptance and publication is 6-12 months. Seldom comments on rejected poems. **Charges criticism fee of $3/poem, 3 poems at a time. Send Attention: Meira Swain, Editor.** Occasionally publishes theme issues: January 2004—Family, May 2004—Israel, September 2004—Sephardic Heritage, January 2005—Spirituality. Upcoming themes available for SASE or by e-mail. Guidelines available in magazine, for SASE, or by e-mail. Responds in 1 month. Sometimes sends prepublication galleys. Pays 1 contributor's copy. Acquires one-time rights.

Advice: "We are interested in poetry that has a spiritual content. 'A fierce light beats upon the Jew'—reflect it in your writings."

N ◯ POETREE MAGAZINE. E-mail: mcintosh@comrev.com. Website: www.poetreemagazine .org/. Established 2002. **Editor:** Jennifer R. McIntosh.

Magazine Needs: *Poetree Magazine* appears quarterly online. Open to poets of all ages and skills. Wants "all styles and forms about interesting topics. Looking for creativity." Does not want "porn or obscenity. Overly religious work. Puppy love poems you'd be embarrassed by 10 years from now." Accepts poetry written by young writers. "Please include age or grade with submission." Recently published poetry by Hamida Owusu. *Poetree Magazine* is published online. Publishes about 6 poems/ issue.

How to Submit: Accepts previously published poems and simultaneous submissions. Accepts e-mail submissions; no disk submissions. Cover letter is preferred. "Must include name and contact method (either valid e-mail or phone number). Only original work." Reads submissions continuously. Time between acceptance and publication is 2 weeks. "I am the sole editor. If a poem moves me, I publish it." Guidelines available on website. Responds in 2 months ("depends on how busy I am"). Poets retain rights after publication.

Book/Chapbook Needs & How to Submit: *Poetree Magazine* publishes e-chapbooks, "online collections of poems by one author." Publishes 4 chapbooks/year. Manuscripts are selected through open submission. Chapbooks are published online with clip art illustrations. May include previously published poems. Responds to queries in weeks.

Advice: "Don't give up! Keep writing. Use your local library to find great resources on writing and publishing."

$ ◪ POETRY; THE MODERN POETRY ASSOCIATION; BESS HOKIN PRIZE; LEVINSON PRIZE; FREDERICK BOCK PRIZE; J. HOWARD AND BARBARA M.J. WOOD PRIZE; RUTH LILLY POETRY PRIZE; RUTH LILLY POETRY FELLOWSHIP; JOHN FREDERICK NIMS PRIZE; THE FRIENDS OF LITERATURE PRIZE, 60 W. Walton St., Chicago IL 60610-3380. E-mail: poetry@poetrymagazine.org. Website: www.poetrymagazine.org. Established 1912. **Editor:** Joseph Parisi.

• Work published in *Poetry* is frequently selected for inclusion in volumes of *The Best American Poetry* and *Pushcart Prize* anthology.

Magazine Needs: *Poetry* "is the oldest and most distinguished monthly magazine devoted entirely to verse. Established in Chicago in 1912, it immediately became the international showcase that it has remained ever since, publishing in its earliest years—and often for the first time—such giants as Ezra Pound, Robert Frost, T.S. Eliot, Marianne Moore, and Wallace Stevens. *Poetry* has continued to print the major voices of our time and to discover new talent, establishing an unprecedented record. There is virtually no important contemporary poet in our language who has not at a crucial stage in his career depended on *Poetry* to find a public for him: John Ashbery, Dylan Thomas, Edna St. Vincent Millay, James Merrill, Anne Sexton, Sylvia Plath, James Dickey, Thom Gunn, David Wagoner—only a partial list to suggest how *Poetry* has represented, without affiliation with any movements or schools, what Stephen Spender has described as 'the best, and simply the best' poetry being written." *Poetry* is an elegantly printed, flat-spined, 5½ × 9 magazine. Receives over 90,000 submissions/year, accepts about 300-350; has a backlog up to 9 months. Press run is 12,400 for 8,200 subscribers of which 33% are libraries. Single copy: $3.75; subscription: $35, $38 for institutions. Sample: $5.50.

How to Submit: Submit up to 4 poems at a time with SASE. No e-mail submissions. No simultaneous submissions. Guidelines available for SASE. Responds in 4 months—longer for mss submitted during the summer. Pays $2 a line. Acquires all rights. Returns rights "upon written request." Reviews books of poetry in multi-book formats of varying lengths. Poets may send books to Stephen Young, senior editor, for review consideration.

Also Offers: Six prizes (named in heading) ranging from $300 to $5,000 are awarded annually to poets whose work has appeared in the magazine that year. Only verse already published in *Poetry* is eligible for consideration and no formal application is necessary. *Poetry* also sponsors the Ruth Lilly Poetry Prize, an annual award of $100,000, and the Ruth Lilly Poetry Fellowship, two annual awards of $15,000 to undergraduate or graduate students to support their further studies in poetry/creative writing.

POETRY & PROSE ANNUAL, P.O. Box 1175, Seaside OR 97138. E-mail: poetry@poetrypro seannual.com. Website: www.poetryproseannual.com. Established 1996. **Editor:** Sandra Claire Foushe é.

Magazine Needs: *Poetry & Prose Annual*, appearing in May, "publishes work that focuses on the nature of consciousness and enlightens the human spirit. A general selection of poetry, fiction, nonfiction and photography. We are looking for excellence and undiscovered talent in poems of emotional and intellectual substance. Poems should be original with rhythmic and lyric strength. Innovation and fresh imagery encouraged. Metrical ingenuity recognized. Open to all forms." Has published poetry by Anita Endrezze, Mary Crow, Nancy McCleery, Renate Wood, Mark Christopher Eades, Donna K. Wright, and Carlos Reyes. *Poetry & Prose Annual* is approximately 82 pages, 7 × 8½, offset-printed and perfect-bound with glossy card cover, cover photograph, contains line art and photos inside. Press run is about 1,000. Subscription: $15. Sample copy: $10 (includes postage).

How to Submit: A $20 entry fee is required (includes subscription and entry into the Gold Pen Award contest). "Any work submitted without submission fee or SASE will not be returned or read. " Submit no more than 200 lines of poetry at a time, typed, with line count, name, address and phone number on first page. Include SASE and brief bio. Accepts previously published poems "if author holds copyright"and simultaneous submissions. Guidelines available for SASE. Responds after deadline. Sometimes sends prepublication galleys. Pays 2 contributor's copies. Acquires one-time and reprints rights. Work may also appear in the *Poetry & Prose Annual* website.

Also Offers: The online journal contains original content not found in the print edition. "From poetry submissions we may use some original material on the website which may/may not be published in the Annual. Poetry needs are the same as for the journal. Several new writers will also be chosen from the general selection to be featured in *American Portfolio*—a special section within the journal showcasing work of several authors in a portfolio."

THE POETRY EXPLOSION NEWSLETTER (THE PEN) (Specialized: ethnic, love, subscription, nature), P.O. Box 4725, Pittsburgh PA 15206-0725. (412)886-1114. E-mail: arthurford@hotmail.com. Established 1984. **Editor:** Arthur C. Ford Sr.

Magazine Needs: *The Pen* is a "quarterly newsletter dedicated to the preservation of poetry." Arthur Ford wants "poetry—40 lines maximum, no minimum. All forms and subject matter with the use of good imagery, symbolism and honesty. Rhyme and non-rhyme. No vulgarity." Accepts poetry written by children; "if under 18 years old, parent or guardian should submit!" Recently published poetry by Justin Scott, Margaret A. Brennan, and Iva Fedorka. *The Pen* is 12-16 pages, saddle-stapled, mimeographed on both sides. Receives about 300 poems/year, accepts 80. Press run is 850 for 525 subscribers of which 5 are libraries. Subscription: $20. Send $4 for sample copy and more information. Make checks payable to Arthur C. Ford.

How to Submit: Submit up to 5 poems at a time (40 lines maximum) with $1 **reading fee**. Also include large SASE if you want work returned. Accepts simultaneous submissions and previously published poems. No e-mail submissions. Sometimes publishes theme issues. "We announce future dates when decided. July issue is usually full of romantic poetry." Guidelines and upcoming themes available for SASE. Responds in up to 3 weeks. Editor comments on rejected poems "sometimes, but not obligated." Pays 1 contributor's copy. Poetry critiques available for 15¢ a word. Send materials for review consideration.

Advice: "Be fresh, honest, and legible!"

POETRY FORUM; THE JOURNAL (Specialized: subscription, mystery, science fiction/fantasy, social issues); HEALTHY BODY-HEALTHY MINDS (Specialized: health concerns), 5713 Larchmont Dr., Erie PA 16509. E-mail: 75562.670@compuserve.com Website: www.thepoetryforum.com. **Editor:** Gunvor Skogsholm.

Magazine Needs: *Poetry Forum* appears 3 times/year. "We are open to any style and form. We believe new forms ought to develop from intuition. Length up to 50 lines accepted. Would like to encourage long themes. No porn or blasphemy, but open to all religious persuasions." Accepts poetry written by children ages 10 and under. Has published poetry by Marshall Myers, Dana Thu, Joseph Veranneau, Ray Greenblatt, Jan Haight, and Mark Young. *Poetry Forum* is 7 × 8½, 38 pages, saddle-stapled with card cover, photocopied from photoreduced typescript. Sample: $3.

How to Submit: Accepts simultaneous submissions and previously published poems. Accepts submissions by fax, on disk, by postal mail, and e-mail (text box). Editor comments on poems "if asked, but respects the poetic freedom of the artist." Publishes theme issues. Guidelines available for SASE, by fax, by e-mail, and in publication. Sometimes sends prepublication galleys. Gives awards of $25, $15, $10, and 3 honorable mentions for the best poems in each issue. Acquires one-time rights. Reviews books of poetry in 250 words maximum. Send materials for review consideration.

Magazine Needs & How to Submit: *The Journal*, which appears twice/year, accepts experimental poetry of any length from subscribers only. Sample: $3. *Healthy Body-Healthy Minds* is a biannual publication concerned with health issues. Accepts essays, poetry, articles, and short-shorts on health, fitness, mind, and soul. Details available for SASE.

Also Offers: Offers a poetry chapbook contest. Handling fee: $12. Prize is publication and 20 copies. Send SASE for information.

Advice: "I believe today's poets should experiment more and not feel stuck in the forms that were in vogue 300 years ago. I would like to see more experimentalism—new forms will prove that poetry is alive and well in the mind and spirit of the people."

$ POETRY HARBOR; NORTH COAST REVIEW (Specialized: regional, Upper Midwest), P.O. Box 103, Duluth MN 55801-0103. (218)525-1854. Established 1989. **Director:** Patrick McKinnon.

Magazine Needs: Poetry Harbor is a "nonprofit, tax-exempt organization dedicated to fostering literary creativity through public readings, publications, radio and television broadcasts, and other artistic and educational means." Its main publication, *North Coast Review*, is a regional magazine appearing 2 times/year with poetry and prose poems by and about Upper Midwest people, including those from Minnesota, Wisconsin, North Dakota, and the upper peninsula of Michigan. "No form/style/content specifications, though we are inclined toward narrative, imagist poetry. We do not want to see anything from outside our region, not because it isn't good, but because we can't publish it due to geographics." Has published poetry by Robert Bly, Katri Sipila, and Freya Manfred. *North Coast Review* is 56 pages, 7 × 8½, offset and saddle-stapled, paper cover with various b&w art, ads at back. Receives about 500 submissions/year, accepts 100-150. Press run is 1,000 for 300 subscribers of which 20 are libraries, 300 shelf sales. Subscription: $19.95/4 issues. Sample: $4.95.

How to Submit: Submit 3-5 pages of poetry, typed single-spaced, with name and address on each page. Accepts previously published poems and simultaneous submissions, if noted. Cover letter with brief bio ("writer's credits") required. "We read three times a year, but our deadlines change from time to time. Write to us for current deadlines for our various projects." Guidelines available for SASE. Responds in up to 5 months. Pays $10 plus 2-4 contributor's copies. Acquires one-time rights.

Book/Chapbook Needs & How to Submit: Poetry Harbor also publishes 1 perfect-bound paperback of poetry and 4-8 chapbooks each biennium. "Chapbooks are selected by our editorial board from the pool of poets we have published in *North Coast Review* or have worked with in our other projects. We suggest you send a submission to *North Coast Review* first. We almost always print chapbooks and anthologies by poets we've previously published or hired for readings." Anthologies include *Nitaawichige: Poetry and Prose by 4 Anishinaabe Writers*, *Poets Who Haven't Moved to St. Paul*, and *Days of Obsidian, Days of Grace*, selected poetry and prose by four Native American writers. Complete publications list available upon request.

Also Offers: Poetry Harbor also sponsors a monthly reading series ("poets are paid to perform"), a weekly TV program (4 different cable networks regionally), various radio programming, and other special events.

Advice: "Poetry Harbor is extremely committed to cultivating a literary community and an appreciation for our region's literature within the Upper Midwest. Poetry Harbor projects are in place to create paying, well-attended venues for our region's fine poets. Poets are now OK to people up here, and literature is thriving. The general public is proving to us that they *do* like poetry if you give them some that is both readable and rooted in the lives of the community."

POETRY INTERNATIONAL, Dept. of English, San Diego State University, San Diego CA 92182-8140. (619)594-1523. Fax: (619)594-4998. E-mail: fmoramar@mail.sdsu.edu. Website: http://poetryinternational.sdsu.edu. Established 1996. **Editor:** Fred Moramarco.

Magazine Needs: *Poetry International*, published annually in November, is "an eclectic poetry magazine intended to reflect a wide range of poetry being written today." Wants "a wide range of styles and subject matter. We're particularly interested in translations." Does not want "cliché-ridden, derivative, obscure poetry." Has published poetry by Adrienne Rich, Robert Bly, Hayden Carruth, Kim Addonizio, Maxine Kumin, Billy Collins, and Gary Soto. *Poetry International* is 200 pgs, perfect bound, with coated card stock cover. Press run is 1,000. Single copy: $12; subscription: $24/2 years.

How to Submit: Submit up to 5 poems at a time. Accepts simultaneous submissions "but prefer not to"; no previously published poems. No fax or e-mail submissions. Reads submissions September 1 through December 30 only. Time between acceptance and publication is 8 months. Poems are circulated to an editorial board. Seldom comments on rejected poems. Responds in up to 4 months. Pays 2 contributor's copies. Acquires all rights. Returns rights "50/50," meaning they split with the author any payment for reprinting the poem elsewhere. "We review anthologies regularly."

Advice: "We're interested in new work by poets who are devoted to their art. We want poems that matter—that make a difference in people's lives. We're especially seeking good translations and prose by poets about poetry."

$ POETRY IRELAND REVIEW; POETRY IRELAND, Bermingham Tower, Dublin Castle, Dublin 2, Ireland. Phone: (353)(1)6714632. Fax: (353)(1)6714634. E-mail: poetry@iol.ie. Website: www.poetryireland.ie. Established 1979. **Director:** Joseph Woods.

Magazine Needs: *Poetry Ireland Review*, the magazine of Ireland's national poetry organization, "provides an outlet for Irish poets; submissions from abroad also considered. No specific style or subject matter is prescribed. We strongly dislike sexism and racism." Has published poetry by Seamus Heaney, Michael Longley, Denise Levertov, Medbh McGuckian, and Charles Wright. Occasionally publishes special issues. *Poetry Ireland Review* is 6×8 and appears quarterly. Press run is 1,200 for 800 subscriptions. Receives up to 8,000 submissions/year, accepts about 3%; has a 2-month backlog. Prints 60 pages of poetry in each issue. Single copy: IR£5.99; subscription: IR£24 Ireland and UK; IR£32 overseas (surface). Sample: $10.

How to Submit: Submit up to 6 poems at a time. Include SASE (or SAE with IRC). "Submissions not accompanied by SAEs will not be returned." No previously published poems or simultaneous submissions. No submissions by e-mail. Time between acceptance and publication is up to 3 months. Seldom comments on rejected poems. Send SASE (or SAE with IRCs) for guidelines. Responds in 2 months. Pays IR£25/poem or 1-year subscription. Reviews books of poetry in 500-1,000 words.

Also Offers: *Poetry Ireland Review* is published by Poetry Ireland, an organization established to "promote poets and poetry throughout Ireland." Poetry Ireland offers readings, an information service, an education service, library and administrative center, and a bimonthly newsletter giving news, details of readings, competitions, etc. for IR£6/year. Also sponsors an annual poetry competition. Details available for SASE (or SAE with IRCs).

Advice: "Keep submitting: Good work will get through."

⊕ ◢ **POETRY KANTO**, Kanto Gakuin University, Kamariya-cho 3-22-1, Kanazawa-Ku, Yoko-
hama 236-8502, Japan. Established 1984. **Editor:** William I. Elliott.
Magazine Needs: *Poetry Kanto* appears annually in August and is published by the Kanto Poetry
Center. The magazine publishes well-crafted original poems in English and in Japanese. Wants "anything except pornography, English haiku and tanka, and tends to publish poems under 30 lines." Has
published work by A.D. Hope, Peter Robinson, Naomi Shihab Nye, Nuala Ni Dhomhnaill, and
Christopher Middleton. *Poetry Kanto* is 60-80 pages, digest-sized, nicely printed (the English poems
occupy the first half of the issue, the Japanese poems the second), saddle-stapled, matte card cover.
Press run is 700, of which 400 are distributed free to schools, poets and presses; it is also distributed
at poetry seminars. The magazine is unpriced. For sample, send SAE with IRCs.
How to Submit: Interested poets should query from February through March with SAE and IRCs
before submitting. No previously published poems or simultaneous submissions. Often comments on
rejected poems. Responds to mss in 2 weeks. Pays 3 contributor's copies.
Advice: "Read a lot. Get feedback from poets and/or workshops. Be neat, clean, legible, and polite
in submissions. SAE with IRCs absolutely necessary when requesting sample copy."

★ ⊕ ◙ ◎ **POETRY LIFE (Specialized: subscription)**, 1 Blue Ball Corner, Water Lane,
Winchester, Hampshire SO23 0ER England. E-mail: adrian.abishop@virgin.net. Website: http://frees
pace.virgin.net/poetry.life/. Established 1994. **Editor:** Adrian Bishop.
Magazine Needs: *Poetry Life*, published 3 times/year, describes itself as "Britain's sharpest poetry
magazine with serious articles about the poetry scene." Wants "poets who have passion, wit, style,
revelation, and loads of imagination." Does not want "poems on pets." Has published articles on
James Fenton, Carol Ann Duffy, Les Murray, Benjamin Zephaniah, and Simon Armitage. *Poetry Life*
is printed on A4 paper. Accepts about 1% of submissions received. Press run is 1,500. Single copy:
£3, £5 overseas.
How to Submit: Accepts previously published poems and simultaneous submissions. Cover letter
required. "In common with most poetry magazines we now only accept recordings of the poets work
on CD. Please do not send manuscripts. If we like what we hear then we will ask for a manuscript."
Time between acceptance and publication is 6 months. Poems are circulated to an editorial board.
Guidelines available for SAE with IRCs. Responds in 6 months. Reviews books or other magazines.
Send materials for review consideration.
Also Offers: Sponsors open poetry competitions. Send SAE with IRCs for guidelines.

★ ◙ **POETRY MIDWEST**, Dept. of English, Modern Languages, & Philosophy, Francis Marion
University, P.O. Box 100547, Florence SC 29505-0547. (843)661-1503. E-mail: editors@poetrymidw
est.org (queries); submit@poetrymidwest.org (submissions). Website: www.poetrymidwest.org. Established 2000. **Editor/Publisher:** Matthew W. Schmeer.
Magazine Needs: *Poetry Midwest* appears 3 times/year (winter, spring/summer, fall) and features
poetry, nongenre microfiction, and brief creative nonfiction from new and established writers. Wants
free verse, traditional Western forms, traditional Asian forms other than haiku and senryu, prose
poems, long poems, nongenre microfiction (up to 300 words), and brief creative nonfiction (up to
300 words). Does not want science fiction, fantasy, inspirational, religious, or children's verse or
fiction; anything of an overtly political or religious nature; or spoken word poetry. Recently published
poetry by A.D. Winans, Ryan G. Van Cleave, Robin Reagler, Suzanne Burns, Joseph Somoza, and
Richard Garcia. *Poetry Midwest* is 20-100 pages, published online as a downloadable Adobe Acrobat
PDF file. Receives about 1,500 poems/year, accepts about 7%. Publishes about 25-40 poems/issue
("varies per quality of submissions"). Copies distributed free online through PDF file.
How to Submit: Submit 3 poems at a time. Line length for poetry is 3 minimum; no more than 10
pages maximum. Accepts simultaneous submissions; no previously published poems. Accepts e-mail
submissions; no submissions by fax or by postal mail. "Submit via e-mail only. Submissions should

---

NEED HELP? To better understand and use the information in these listings, see the
introduction to this section.

be pasted into the body of an e-mail message with 'Poetry Midwest Submission' in subject line (omit quotation marks). Absolutely no e-mail file attachments." Reads submissions year round. Submit seasonal poems 3-6 months in advance. Time between acceptance and publication is 3 months to 1 year. "I read submissions as they are received, deciding whether or not to use a piece based on its own literary merits and whether it fits in with other poems selected for an issue in progress." Seldom comments on rejected poems. Guidelines available by e-mail or on website. Responds in up to 6 months. Acquires first rights or first North American serial rights as well as First Electronic Rights, Reprint Rights, and Electronic Archival Rights.

Advice: "Since *Poetry Midwest* is freely available online, there is no excuse for not reading an issue to sample the type of work the journal tends to feature. Poets should do their research before submitting to any journal; otherwise, they may be wasting not only their time, but the editor's time, too. Online journals are deluged with submissions, and following the posted guidelines will let the editor know you want your submission seriously considered."

◻ POETRY MOTEL; POETRY MOTEL WALLPAPER BROADSIDE SERIES, P.O. Box 103, Duluth MN 55801-0103. Established 1984. **Editors:** Patrick McKinnon, Bud Backen, and Linda Erickson.

Magazine Needs: *Poetry Motel* appears "every 260 days." Poetry magazine with some fiction and memoire. Wants poetry of "any style, any length." Recently published poetry by Adrian C. Louis, Ron Androla, Todd Moore, Ellie Schoenfeld, and Serena Fusek. *Poetry Motel* is 52 pages digest-sized, offset-printed, stapled, wallpaper cover, with collages. Receives about 1,000 poems/year, accepts about 5% Publishes about 50 poems/issue. Press run is 1,000 for 400 subscribers of which 10 are libraries. Single copy: $8.95; subscription: $26/3 issues, $99/forever. Make checks payable to *Poetry Motel*.

How to Submit: Submit 3-6 pages at a time. Accepts previously published poems and simultaneous submissions. No fax, e-mail, or disk submissions. "Include SASE or brief bio." Reads submissions all year. Time between acceptance and publication varies. Never comments on rejected poems. Guidelines are available in magazine and for SASE. Responds in "1 week to never." Pays 1-5 contributor's copies. Acquires no rights. Reviews books and chapbooks of poetry and other magazines/journals in varied lengths. Poets may send material for review consideration to Linda Erickson.

Advice: "All work submitted is considered for both the magazine and the broadside series."

⊕ ◻ POETRY NOTTINGHAM INTERNATIONAL; NOTTINGHAM OPEN POETRY COMPETITION; NOTTINGHAM POETRY SOCIETY, P.O. Box 6740, Nottingham NG5 1QG United Kingdom. Website: http://nottinghampoetrysociety.co.uk. Established 1946. **Editor:** Julie Lumsden.

Magazine Needs: Nottingham Poetry Society meets monthly for readings, talks, etc., and publishes quarterly its magazine, *Poetry Nottingham International*, which is open to submissions from anyone. Has published poetry by Vernon Scannell, Lotte Kramer, Bruno Anthony, E.D. Paul, and Mark Mansfield. *Poetry Nottingham International* features 56 pages of poetry in each issue of the 6 × 8 magazine, professionally printed with articles, letters, news, reviews, glossy art paper cover. Receives about 1,500 submissions/year, accepts approximately 120, usually has a 1- to 3-month backlog. Press run is 275 for 200 subscribers. Single copy: £2.75 ($9.75 US); subscriptions: £17 sterling or $34 US.

How to Submit: Submit up to 6 poems at any time, or articles up to 500 words on current issues in poetry. No previously published poems. Send SAE and 3 IRCs for stamps. No need to query but requires cover letter. Responds in 2 months. Pays 1 copy. Staff reviews books of poetry. Send material for review consideration.

Book/Chapbook Needs & How to Submit: Nottingham Poetry Society publishes collections by individual poets who are members of Nottingham Poetry Society.

Also Offers: Nottingham Open Poetry Competition offers cash prizes, annual subscriptions and publication in *Poetry Nottingham International*. Open to all. Check website for address and details. Contact for website and Nottingham Poetry Society is Jeremy Duffield, 71 Saxton Ave., Heanor, Derbyshire DE75 7PZ United Kingdom.

Advice: "Poems most often rejected due to: use of tired language and imagery, use of clichés and inversions, old treatment of an old subject. Write lively free verse."

◘ **POETRY OF THE PEOPLE**, 3341 SE 19th Ave., Gainesville FL 32641. (352)375-0244. E-mail: poetryforaquarter@yahoo.com. Website: www.angelfire.com/fl/poetryofthepeople. Established 1986. **Poetry Editor:** Paul Cohen.

Magazine Needs: *Poetry of the People* is a leaflet that appears monthly. "We take all forms of poetry but we like humorous poetry, love poetry, nature poetry, and fantasy. No racist or highly ethnocentric poetry will be accepted. I do not like poetry that lacks images or is too personal or contains rhyme to the point that the poem has been destroyed. All submitted poetry will be considered for posting on website which will be updated every month." Also accepts poetry written in French and Spanish. Accepts poetry written by children. Has published poetry by Laura Stamps, Dan Matthews, Jenica Deer, Shannon Dixon, Kristi Castro, and Peggy C. Hall. *Poetry of the People* is 4 pages, magazine-sized, sometimes on colored paper. Issues are usually theme oriented. Samples: $4 for 11 pamphlets. "New format is being devised."

How to Submit: Submit "as many poems as you want." Include SASE. Accepts submissions on disk, by e-mail (as attachment or in text box), and by postal mail. Cover letter with biographical information required with submissions. "I feel autobiographical information is important in understanding the poetry." Poems returned within 6 months. Editor comments on rejected poems "often." Upcoming themes available for SASE. Guidelines available by e-mail and on website. Pays 10 contributor's copies for poetry published in leaflet. Acquires first rights.

Advice: "You should appeal to as broad an audience as possible. Nature makes people happy."

◎ **POETRY PROTOCOL; SYNDICATE (Specialized: members only)**, P.O. Box #6221, Tulsa OK 74148-0221. (918)836-5539. Fax: (918)665-4586. E-mail: amccl25089@aol.com. Website: http://hometown.aol.com/jymmeemak1/myhomepage. Established 1991. **President/Co-editor:** Alton McCloud.

Magazine Needs & How to Submit: *Poetry Protocol* appears quarterly "to provide an outlet to unknown poets for international recognition." Also publishes short stories and columns. Accepts all forms; prefers free verse (20 lines or less), acrostics, haiku. Does not want very long (essay) poems. Accepts poetry from young writers over age 14. Recently published poetry by Shiela Roark, dn simmers, Sylvia Lukeman, Mel Guenther, Gayle Crowder, and Ashok Chakavarthy. *Poetry Protocol* is sponsored by the North Tulsa Literary Guild, Inc., a nonprofit organization that also hosts local open mic readings and an international relationship with Poets Who Care of Liverpool, England. *Poetry Protocol* accepts submissions from members only. Guidelines available for SASE. Contact Alton C. McCloud for information.

Also Offers: "We sponsor two contests/year that award 1st Prize: $50, 2nd Prize: $30, 3rd Prize: $20, also Honorable Mention certificates."

Advice: "*Poetry Protocol* provides an outlet for beginning poets. If your work is not accepted by us, always try again with a different form/genre of poetry. And remember that neatness and presentation count."

⊕ **$** ◙ **POETRY REVIEW; NATIONAL POETRY COMPETITION; THE POETRY SOCIETY**, 22 Betterton St., London WC2H 9BU United Kingdom. Phone: (0044)207 420 9880. Fax: (0044)207 240 4818. E-mail: poetryreview@poetrysociety.org.uk. Website: www.poetrysociety. org.uk. Established 1909. **Editor:** Peter Forbes.

Magazine Needs: *Poetry Review*, published quarterly, strives "to be a serious and generous space in which a wide variety of English-language poetry (and foreign poetry in translation) can be displayed, circulated, appreciated, and discussed. We publish poetry, reviews, essays, and art." Wants "poems which resist cliché and tweak convention; nothing is ruled-out or ruled-in but there has to be evidence of commitment, intelligence, vivacity, passion, integrity, generosity, curiousity, humility, sensuality, adventure." Does not want "anecdote or diary entry artlessly rendered, nor sentimental doggerel or twee verse." Has published poetry by John Ashbery, Geoffrey Hill, Medbh McGuckian, Michael Haslam, Lee Harwood, Susan Wheeler, and Peter Reading. *Poetry Review* is 120 pages, digest-sized, paperback, with cartoons and photos.

How to Submit: Submit 6 poems at a time. No previously published poems or simultaneous submissions. No fax or e-mail submissions. Time between acceptance and publication is 3 months. Poems are selected by the editors. Seldom comments on rejected poems. Responds in up to 3 months.

Sometimes sends prepublication galleys. Pays £40 plus 1 copy. Acquires UK first publication rights. **Also Offers:** Sponsors the annual National Poetry Competition run by the Poetry Society. 1st Prize: £5,000; 2nd Prize: £1,000; 3rd Prize: £500. Entry fee: £5 for first poem, £3/poem thereafter. Deadline: October 31. Guidelines available for SASE (or SAE and IRC). "The Poetry Society promotes poetry, assists poets and campaigns for poets wherever possible." Offers "Poetry Prescription" reading service: £40 for 100 lines.

POETRY SALZBURG; POETRY SALZBURG REVIEW; UNIVERSITY OF SALZBURG PRESS, University of Salzburg, Dept. of English and American Studies, Akademiestrasse 24, A-5020 Salzburg Austria. Phone: 0049662 8044 4422. Fax: 0049 662 80 44 167. E-mail: editor@poetrysalzburg.com. Website: www.poetrysalzburg.com. Established 1971. **Editor:** Dr. Wolfgang Goertschacher.

Magazine Needs: *Poetry Salzburg Review* appears twice/year and contains "articles on poetry, mainly contemporary, and 60 percent poetry. Also includes prose, reviews, and translations. We tend to publish selections by authors who have not been taken up by the big poetry publishers. Nothing of poor quality." Has published poetry by Desmond O'Grady, James Kirkup, Dermot Bolger, Daniel Weissbrot, Alice Notley, Georgie Scott, Anne MacLeod, and Rupert Loydell. *Poetry Salzburg Review* is about 170 pages, A5, professionally printed and perfect-bound with illustrated card cover, sometimes includes art. Receives about 5,000 poems/year, accepts 10%. Press run is 500 for 150 subscribers of which 30% are libraries. Single copy: about $11; subscription: $20 (cash only for those sending US funds). Make checks payable to Wolfgang Goertschacher. "No requirements, but it's a good idea to subscribe to *Poetry Salzburg Review*."

How to Submit: No previously published poems or simultaneous submissions. Accepts submissions by fax, on disk, by e-mail (as attachment), or by regular mail. Time between acceptance and publication is 6 months. Seldom comments on rejected poems. Occasionally publishes theme issues. Responds in 2 months. Payment varies. Acquires first rights. Reviews books and chapbooks of poetry and other magazines. Send materials for review consideration.

Book/Chapbook Needs & How to Submit: Poetry Salzburg publishes "collections of at least 100 pages by mainly poets not taken up by big publishers." Publishes 6-20 paperbacks/year. Books are usually 100-700 pages, A5, professionally printed and perfect-bound with card cover, includes art. Query first, with a few sample poems and a cover letter with brief bio and publication credits. Suggests authors publish in *Poetry Salzburg Review* first. Responds to queries in 2 weeks; to mss in about 1 month. Payment varies.

POETRYBAY, P.O. Box 114, Northport NY 11768. (631)427-1950. Fax: (631)367-0038. E-mail: poetrybay@aol.com Website: www.poetrybay.com. Established 2000. **Editor:** George Wallace.

Magazine Needs: *Poetrybay* appears quarterly and "seeks to add to the body of great contemporary American poetry by presenting the work of established and emerging writers. Also, we consider essays and reviews." Recently published poetry by Robert Bly, Yevgeny Yevtushenko, Marvin Bell, Diane Wakoski, Cornelius Eady, and William Heyen. *Poetrybay* is an online publication. Publishes about 24 poems/issue.

How to Submit: Submit 5 poems at a time. Accepts simultaneous submissions; no previously published poems. Accepts e-mail submissions; no disk submissions. "We prefer e-mail with text in body. No attachments." Time between acceptance and publication is 2 months. Seldom comments on rejected poems. Occasionally publishes theme issues. Guidelines available on website. Sometimes sends prepublication galleys. Acquires first time electronic rights. Reviews books and chapbooks of poetry and other magazines/journals. Send materials for review consideration.

POETS ON THE LINE, P.O. Box 020292, Brooklyn NY 11202-0007. E-mail: llerner@mindspring.com. Website: www.echonyc.com/~poets. Established 1995. **Editor:** Linda Lerner. Currently not accepting unsolicited work.

POETS' PODIUM, 2-3265 Front Rd., E. Hawksbury ON K6A 2R2 Canada. E-mail: kennye1@hotmail.com. Website: http://geocities.com/poetspodium/. Established 1993. **Associate Editors:** Ken Elliott, Catherine Heaney Barrowcliffe, Robert Piquette.

Magazine Needs: *Poets' Podium* is a quarterly newsletter published "to promote the reading and

writing of the poetic form, especially among those being published for the first time." Poetry specifications are open. However, does not want poetry that is gothic, erotic/sexual, gory, bloody, or that depicts violence. Publish 25 poems/issue. Subscription: $10 (US). Sample: $3 (US). "Priority is given to valued subscribers. Nevertheless, when there is room in an issue we will publish nonsubscribers."
How to Submit: Submit 3 poems at a time. Line length for poetry is 4 minimum, 25 maximum. Accepts previously published poems and simultaneous submissions. Cover letter required. Include SASE (or SAE and IRC), name, address, and telephone number; e-mail address if applicable. Time between acceptance and publication varies. Guidelines available for SASE (or SAE with IRC), by fax, or by e-mail. Pays 3 copies. All rights remain with the author.
Advice: "Poetry is a wonderful literary form. Try your hand at it. Send us the fruit of your labours."

⬤ PORCUPINE LITERARY ARTS MAGAZINE, P.O. Box 259, Cedarsburg WI 53012. E-mail: ppine259@aol.com. Website: members.aol.com/ppine259. Established 1996. **Managing Editor:** W.A. Reed.
Magazine Needs: *Porcupine*, published biannually, contains featured artists, poetry, short fiction, and visual art work. "There are no restrictions as to theme or style. Poetry should be accessible and highly selective. If a submission is not timely for one issue, it will be considered for another." Has published poetry by Carol Hamilton, James Grabill, and George Wallace. *Porcupine* is 100-150 pages, digest-sized, offset, perfect-bound with full-color glossy cover and b&w photos and art (occasionally use color inside, depending on artwork). Receives about 500 poems/year, accepts 10%. Press run is 1,500 for 500 subscribers of which 50 are libraries, 500 shelf sales; 100 distributed free. Single copy: $8.95; subscription: $15.95. Sample: $5.
How to Submit: Submit up to 3 poems, 1/page with name and address on each. Include SASE. "The outside of the envelope should state: 'Poetry.' " No previously published poems or simultaneous submissions. Accepts e-mail submissions (include in text box). Time between acceptance and publication is 6 months. "Poems are selected by editors and then submitted to managing editor for final approval." Seldom comments on rejected poems. Guidelines available for SASE or on website. Responds in 3 months. Pays 1 contributor's copy. Acquires one-time rights.

◪ ⬤ PORTLAND REVIEW, Box 347, Portland State University, Portland OR 97207-0347. (503)725-4533. Fax: (503)725-5860. E-mail: review@vanguard.vg.pdx.edu. Website: www.portlandr eview.org ("our website is a general introduction to our magazine with samples of our poetry, fiction, and art."). Established 1954. **Editor:** Rebecca Rich Goldweber.
Magazine Needs & How to Submit: *Portland Review* is a literary quarterly published by Portland State University. "Experimental poetry welcomed." The quarterly is about 75 pages. Accepts about 30 of 1000 poems received each year. "Press run is 1000 for subscribers, libraries, and bookstores throughout Oregon and Washington." Sample: $6. Accepts simultaneous submissions. Accepts e-mail submissions in body. Guidelines available for SASE and on website. Pays 1 contributor's copy.

⬤ ◎ THE POST-APOLLO PRESS (Specialized: form/style, women), 35 Marie St., Sausalito CA 94965. (415)332-1458. Fax: (415)332-8045. E-mail: tpapress@rcn.com. Website: http://users.r cn.com/tpapress. Established 1982. **Publisher:** Simone Fattal.
Book/Chapbook Needs & How to Submit: The Post-Apollo Press publishes "quality paperbacks by experimental poets/writers, mostly women, many first English translations." Publishes 2-3 paperbacks/year. "Please note we are *not* accepting manuscripts at this time due to full publishing schedule."

◻ POTLUCK CHILDREN'S LITERARY MAGAZINE (Specialized: children/teen), P.O. Box 546, Deerfield IL 60015-0546. (847)948-1139. Fax: (847)317-9492. E-mail: susan@potluckmag azine.org. Website: http://potluckmagazine.org. Established 1997. **Editor:** Susan Napoli Picchietti.
Magazine Needs: *Potluck* is published quarterly "to provide a forum which encourages young writers to share their voice and to learn their craft. Open to all styles, forms, and subjects—we just want well crafted works that speak to the reader. No works so abstract they only have meaning to the writer. Violent, profane, or sexually explicit works will not be accepted." *Potluck* is about 40 pages, digest-sized, photocopied and saddle-stapled with 60 lb. paper cover, includes original artwork on covers. Receives about 350 poems/quarter. Publish 10-15 poems/issue. Press run is over 1,110 for

150 subscribers, 625 shelf sales. Single copy: $5.80 ($7.80 Canada); subscription: $18 ($26 Canada). Sample (including guidelines): $4.25.

How to Submit: Submit up to 3 poems at a time. Line length for poetry is 30 maximum. No previously published poems or simultaneous submissions. Accepts submissions by fax, by e-mail (in text box), and by regular mail. Cover letter optional. "Works without a SASE or an e-mail address will not be considered." Submit seasonal poems 3 months in advance. Time between acceptance and publication is 4-6 weeks. Poems are circulated to an editorial board. "We each review each poem—make remarks on page then discuss our view of each—the best works make the issue." Always comments on rejected poems. Guidelines available for SASE, by fax, by e-mail, in publication, or on website. Responds 6 weeks after deadline. Pays 1 contributor's copy. Acquires first rights. Reviews chapbooks of poetry.

Advice: "Be present; write what you see, hear, taste, smell, observe and what you feel/experience. Be honest, clear, and choose your words with great care. Enjoy."

⬤ POTOMAC REVIEW: A JOURNAL OF ARTS & HUMANITIES, Montgomery College, Paul Peck Humanities Institute, 51 Mannakee St., Rockville MD 20850. (301)610-4100. Fax: (301)738-1745. Website: www.montgomerycollege.edu/potomacreview. Established 1994. **Editor:** Myrna Goldberg.

Magazine Needs: Appearing in November and May, "*Potomac Review* is a regionally rooted semi-annual at the heart of the nation with a national and international range. *Potomac Review* seeks poets from all quarters and focuses." Has published poetry by Judith McCombs, Virgil Suarez, and Hugh Fox. *Potomac Review* is 248 pages, biannual, digest-sized, offset-printed, perfect-bound, with medium card cover, b&w graphic art, photos and ads. Receives about 1,000 poems/year, accepts 5%. Press run is 2,000 for 1,000 subscribers plus about 400 shelf sales. Subscription: $18/year and $18.90/year for MD residents (includes 2 double issues); $30/2 years. Sample: $8.

How to Submit: Submit up to 3 poems, 5 pages at a time with SASE. Accepts simultaneous submissions; no previously published poems. Cover letter preferred with brief bio and SASE. Time between acceptance and publication is up to 1 year. Poems are read "in house," then sent to poetry editor for comments and dialogue. Often comments on rejected poems. Publishes theme issues. Fall 2003-2004 will be "Beyond." Guidelines and upcoming themes available for SASE or on website. Responds in 3 months. Pays 2 contributor's copies and offers discount on additional copies. Acquires

Sculptor Komelia Hongja Okim created "Winter Walk #1" and photographed it as well for Issue 34 of *Potomac Review*. The sculpture was one of a series by the artist featured in the issue's art portfolio, says Christa Watters, senior editor. "We try to alternate between photography and art for the cover images of our twice-yearly magazine." Magazine design was by Jane Knaus; cover design by Ken Jassie and Jon Goell.

first North American serial rights. Reviews books of poetry; write first for review consideration.

Also Offers: Sponsors annual poetry contest, open January through March 15. 1st Prize: $1,000; winner's poem and some runners-up are published in fall/winter. To enter, send $18 (provides 1-year subscription), up to 3 poems, any subject, any form. Deadline: March 15. Competition receives about 150 entries. Guidelines available for SASE, in fall/winter issue, or on website.

POTPOURRI; DAVID RAY POETRY AWARD, P.O. Box 8278, Prairie Village KS 66208. (913)642-1503. Fax: (913)642-3128. E-mail: PotpourriEditor@aol.com. Website: www.Potpourri.org. Established 1989. **Poetry Editor:** Terry Hoyland. **Haiku Editor:** Jeri Ragan.

Magazine Needs: *Potpourri* is a quarterly magazine "publishing works of writers, including new and unpublished writers. We want strongly voiced original poems in either free verse or traditional. Traditional work must represent the best of the craft. No religious, confessional, racial, political, erotic, abusive, or sexual preference materials. No concrete/visual poetry (because of format)." Has published poetry by Lyn Lifshin, David Ray, Richard Moore, Leslie Mcilroy, Robert Cooperman, and Carol Hamilton. *Potpourri* is 80 pages, magazine-sized, professionally printed, saddle-stapled with 2-color art on glossy cover, drawings, photos and ads inside. Press run is 1,500 for 850 subscribers. Subscription: $16. Sample: $6.95 include 9 × 12 envelope; $9.25 overseas.

How to Submit: Submit up to 3 poems at a time, one to a page, length to 75 lines (approximately 30 preferred). Address haiku and related forms to Jeri Ragan. Accepts submissions on disk, by e-mail (in text box), and by regular mail. Guidelines available for SASE, by fax, by e-mail, or on website. Responds in up to 10 weeks at most. Pays 1 contributor's copy. Acquires first North American serial rights.

Also Offers: The David Ray Poetry Award ($100 or more, depending upon grant monies) is given annually for best of volume. Another annual award is sponsored by the Council on National Literatures and offers $100 and publication in *Potpourri* for selected poem or short story; alternating years (2003 poetry). Official guidelines available for SASE. Deadline was September 1, 2002. Website includes back issues, biographies, submission guidelines, sample writings and literary links.

Advice: "Keep your new poems around long enough to become friends with them before parting. Let them ripen, and, above all, learn to be your own best editor. Read them aloud, boldly, to see how they ripple the air and echo what you mean to say. Themes of unrequited love, children, grandchildren, and favorite pets find little chance here."

$ POTTERSFIELD PORTFOLIO; POTTERSFIELD PORTFOLIO SHORT POEM COMPETITION (Specialized: regional, Canadian), P.O. Box 40, Station A, Sydney NS B1P 6G9 Canada. Website: www.magomania.com. Established 1979. **Editor:** Douglas A. Brown. **Contact:** Poetry Editor.

Magazine Needs: Appearing in July and December, *Pottersfield Portfolio* is a "literary magazine publishing fiction, poetry, essays and reviews by authors from Canada. No restrictions on subject matter or style. However, we will not use religious, inspirational, or children's poetry. No doggerel or song lyrics." Has published poetry by David Zieroth, Don Domanski, Jean McNeil, and Alden Nowlan. *Pottersfield* is 90 pages, magazine-sized, professionally printed and perfect-bound with b&w cover, includes photos and ads. Receives about 3,000 poems/year, accepts 5%. Press run is 1,500 for 250 subscribers of which 25 are libraries, 750 shelf sales. Single copy: $9; subscription: $26. Sample: $9. "Subscribers from outside Canada please remit in U.S. dollars."

How to Submit: Canadian poets submit 6 poems at a time. No previously published poems. Include SAE with IRCs. Cover letter strongly preferred. "Submissions should be on white paper of standard dimensions (8½ × 11). Only one poem per page." Time between acceptance and publication is 3 months. Guidelines available for SASE (or SAE with IRC) and on website. "Note: U.S. stamps are no good in Canada." Responds in 5 months. Pays $10/printed page to a maximum of $50 plus 1 contributor's copy. Acquires first Canadian serial rights.

Also Offers: Sponsors the *Pottersfield Portfolio* Short Poem Competition. Deadline: May 1 each year. Entry fee: $20 for 3 poems, which must be no more than 20 lines in length. Fee includes subscription. Write for details or consult website.

Advice: "Only submit your work in a form you would want to read yourself. Subscribe to some literary journals. Read lots of poetry."

■ $ ▨ ◎ THE PRAIRIE JOURNAL; PRAIRIE JOURNAL PRESS (Specialized: regional, prairie; themes), P.O. Box 61203, Brentwood Post Office, 217-3630 Brentwood Rd. NW, Calgary AB T2L 2K6 Canada. E-mail: prairiejournal@yahoo.com. Website: www.geocities.com/prairiejournal. Established 1983. **Editor:** A. Burke.

Magazine Needs: For *The Prairie Journal*, the editor wants to see poetry of "any length, free verse, contemporary themes (feminist, nature, urban, non-political), aesthetic value, a poet's poetry." Does not want to see "most rhymed verse, sentimentality, egotistical ravings. No cowboys or sage brush." Has published poetry by Liliane Welch, Cornelia Hoogland, Sheila Hyland, Zoe Lendale, and Chad Norman. *Prairie Journal* is 40-60 pages, 7 × 8½, offset, saddle-stapled with card cover, b&w drawings and ads, appearing twice/year. Receives about 1,000 poems/year, accepts 10%. Press run is 600 for 200 subscribers of which 50% are libraries, the rest are distributed on the newsstand. Subscription: $8 for individuals, $15 for libraries. Sample: $8 ("Use postal money order").

How to Submit: No simultaneous submissions or previously published poems. Does not accept e-mail submissions. Guidelines available for postage (but "no U.S. stamps, please"—get IRCs from the Post Office) or on website. "We will not be reading submissions until such time as an issue is in preparation (twice yearly), so be patient and we will acknowledge, accept for publication, or return work at that time." Sometimes sends prepublication galleys. Pays $10-50 plus 1 copy. Acquires first North American serial rights. Reviews books of poetry "but must be assigned by editor. Query first."

Book/Chapbook Needs & How to Submit: For chapbook publication, Canadian poets only (preferably from the region) should query with 5 samples, bio, publications. Responds to queries in 2 months, to mss in 6 months. Payment in modest honoraria. Has published *Voices From Earth*, selected poems by Ronald Kurt and Mark McCawley, and *In the Presence of Grace*, by McCandless Callaghan. "We also publish anthologies on themes when material is available."

Also Offers: Publishes "Poems of the Month" online. Submit up to 4 poems for $1 reading fee.

Advice: "Read recent poets! Experiment with line length, images, metaphors. Innovate."

◗ PRAIRIE SCHOONER; STROUSSE PRIZE; LARRY LEVIS PRIZE; GLENNA LU-SCHEI AWARD; SLOTE PRIZE; FAULKNER AWARD; HUGH J. LUKE AWARD; STANLEY AWARD; JANE GESKE AWARD; READERS' CHOICE AWARDS, 201 Andrews, University of Nebraska, Lincoln NE 68588-0334. (402)472-0911. Fax: (402)472-9771. E-mail: eflanagan 2@unl.edu. Website: www.unl.edu/schooner/psmain.htm (features writer's guidelines, names of editors, subscription info, history, table of contents, and excerpts from current issue). Established 1926. **Editor:** Hilda Raz.

● Poetry published in *Prairie Schooner* has also been selected for inclusion in *The Best American Poetry 1996* and the *Pushcart Prize* anthology.

Magazine Needs: *Prairie Schooner is* "one of the oldest literary quarterlies in continuous publication; publishes poetry, fiction, personal essays, interviews, and reviews." Wants "poems that fulfill the expectations they set up." No specifications as to form, length, style, subject matter, or purpose. Has published poetry by Alicia Ostriker, Marilyn Hacker, D.A. Powell, Stephen Dunn, and David Ignatow. *Prairie Schooner* is 200 pages, digest-sized, flat-spined and uses 70-80 pages of poetry in each issue. Receives about 4,800 mss (of all types)/year, uses 300 pages of poetry. Press run is 3,100. Single copy: $9; subscription: $26. Sample: $6.

How to Submit: Submit 5-7 poems at a time. No simultaneous submissions. No fax or e-mail submissions. "Clear copy appreciated." Considers mss from September through May only. Publishes theme issues. Guidelines available for SASE. Responds in 4 months; "sooner if possible." Always sends prepublication galleys. Pays 3 contributor's copies. Acquires all rights. Returns rights upon request without fee. Reviews books of poetry. Send materials for review consideration. Editor Hilda Raz also promotes poets whose work has appeared in her pages by listing their continued accomplishments in a special section (even when their work does not concurrently appear in the magazine).

Also Offers: The Strousse Award for poetry ($500), the Bernice Slote Prize for beginning writers ($500), Hugh J. Luke Award ($250), the Edward Stanley Award for Poetry ($1000), the Virginia Faulkner Award for Excellence in Writing ($1,000), the Glenna Luschei Prize for Literary Distinction ($1,000), the Jane Geske Award ($250), and the Larry Levis Prize for Poetry ($1,000). Also, each year 4-8 Readers' Choice Awards ($250 each) are given for poetry, fiction, and nonfiction. All contests are open only to those writers whose work was published in the magazine the previous year. Editors serve as judges.

⊞ ◯ ◎ **PRAKALPANA LITERATURE; KOBISENA (Specialized: bilingual, form)**, P-40 Nandana Park, Kolkata 700034, West Bengal, India. Phone: (91)(033)2403-0347. E-mail: prakalpana@rediffmail.com. Website: http://prakalpana.tripod.com. *Kobisena* established 1972; *Prakalpana Literature* press 1974; magazine 1977. **Editor:** Vattacharja Chandan.

Magazine Needs: "We are small magazine which publish only Prakalpana (a mixed form of prose, poetry, graphics, and art), Sarbangin (whole) poetry, experimental b&w art and photographs, essays on the Prakalpana movement and the Sarbangin poetry movement, letters, literary news and very few books on Prakalpana and Sarbangin literature. Purpose and form: for advancement of poetry in the super-space age, the poetry must be really experimental using mathematical signs and symbols and visualizing the pictures inherent in the alphabet (within typography) with sonorous effect accessible to people. That is Sarbangin poetry. Length: within 30 lines (up to 4 poems). Prakalpana is a mixed form of prose, poetry, essay, novel, story, play with visual effect and it is not at all short story as it is often misunderstood. Better send six IRCs to read *Prakalpana Literature* first and then submit. Length: within 16 pages (up to 2 prakalpanas) at a time. Subject matter: society, nature, cosmos, humanity, love, peace, etc. Style: own. We do not want to see traditional, conventional, academic, religious, mainstream, and poetry of prevailing norms and forms." Has published poetry by Dilip Gupta, Margarita Engle, Satya Ranjan Biswas, Jim DeWitt, Utpal, and Nikhil Bhowmick. *Prakalpana Literature*, an annual, is 72 pages, $7 \times 4\frac{1}{2}$, saddle-stapled, printed on thin stock, matte card cover. *Kobisena*, which also appears once/year, is 16 pages, digest-sized, newsletter format, no cover. Both use both English and Bengali. Receive about 400 poems/year, accept approximately 10%. Press run is 1,000 for each, and each has about 500 subscribers of which 50 are libraries. Samples: 60 rupees for *Prakalpana*, 4 rupees for *Kobisena*. Overseas: 6 IRCs and 3 IRCs respectively or exchange of avant-garde magazines.

How to Submit: Submit 4 poems at a time. Accepts submissions by e-mail (as attachment or in text box), on disk, or by postal mail. Cover letter with short bio and small photo/sketch of poet/writer/artist required; camera-ready copy ($4 \times 6\frac{1}{2}$) preferred. Time between acceptance and publication is within a year. After being published in the magazines, poets may be included in future anthologies with translations into Bengali/English if and when necessary. "Joining with us is welcome but not a pre-condition." Editor comments on rejected poems "if wanted." Guidelines available for SAE with IRC. Pays 1 copy. Reviews books of poetry, fiction, and art, "but preferably experimental books." Poets, writers, and artists may send material for review consideration.

Advice: "We believe that only through poetry, fiction, and art, the deepest feelings of humanity as well as nature and the cosmos can be best expressed and conveyed to the peoples of the ages to come. And only poetry can fill up the gap in the peaceless hearts of dispirited peoples, resulted from the retreat of god and religion with the advancement of hi-tech. So, in an attempt, since the inception of Prakalpana Movement in 1969, to reach that goal in the experimental way we stand for Sarbangin poetry. And to poets and all concerned with poetry we wave the white handkerchief saying (in the words of Vattacharja Chandan), 'We want them who want us.' "

◯ ◎ **PRAYERWORKS (Specialized: religious; senior citizen)**, P.O. Box 301363, Portland OR 97294-9363. (503)761-2072. E-mail: jay4prayer@aol.com. Established 1988. **Editor:** V. Ann Mandeville.

Magazine Needs: Established as a ministry to people living in retirement centers, *PrayerWorks* is a weekly newsletter encouraging "elderly people to recognize their value to God as prayer warriors." Features "prayer, ways to pray, stories of answered prayer, teaching on a Scripture portion, articles that build faith, and poems." *PrayerWorks* is 4 pages, digest-sized, photocopied, desktop-published, folded. Receives about 50 poems/year, accepts approximately 25%. Press run is 1,000 for 1,000 subscribers. Subscription: free.

How to Submit: Submit 5 poems, 1/page. Accepts previously published poems and simultaneous submissions. Accepts e-mail submissions (Wordperfect or Microsoft Word files). Cover letter preferred. Time between acceptance and publication is usually within 1 month. Seldom comments on rejected poems. Publishes theme issues relating to the holidays (submit holiday poetry 2 months in advance). Guidelines available for SASE. Responds in 3 weeks. Pays 5 or more copies.

◯ **PREMIERE GENERATION INK**, P.O. Box 2056, Madison WI 53701-2056. E-mail: poetry@premieregeneration.com. Website: www.premieregeneration.com. Established 1998. **Contact:** poetry editor.

Magazine Needs: *Premiere Generation Ink* appears twice yearly and publishes "high quality, honest poetry in a magazine/journal format and also in a multimedia format via website. We are also looking for art, photos, live recordings of poetry (audio or video) to be put on the Web and to be used in the journal. We also want experimental video poetry which can be mailed by VHS cassette. We would like to see poetry that is less concerned with being poetry than it is with being honest and true. We welcome any length, format, style or subject matter. We do not want to see pretentious and contrived poetry." Has published poetry by Ruth Stone, Liz Rosenberg, and Virgil Suarez. *Premiere Generation Ink* is 30-40 pages, magazine-sized, photocopied in color and saddle-stapled, cover is color or b&w "depending on issue," includes art/graphics. Single copy: $5; subscription: $18. Sample: $5.

How to Submit: Submit 5 poems at a time. Accepts previously published poems and simultaneous submissions. Accepts e-mail submissions (either in body or as attachment). Website features online submission as well. Cover letter preferred. Cover letters need not be formal, we prefer casual and personal. Time between acceptance and publication is up to 8 months. Poems are circulated to an editorial board. "Editorial staff reviews all submissions and a collective decision is reached." Often comments on rejected poems; "Tries to comment on first submission. Requests that author purchases sample copy before resubmitting. Comments on electronic submissions if author sends SASE." Guidelines available for SASE, by e-mail, or on website. Responds in 6 months. Pays 2-5 copies. Acquires first or reprint rights.

Also Offers: "We would like to publish books in cooperation with an author. *Premiere Generation Ink* will chiefly be a means for writers to distribute their art to a larger audience via the Web and the poetry journal. The sales proceeds will go to cover the costs associated with production. Any net profit will be divided equally between the author and the publisher. The main goal of this company is not profit, but rather to distribute quality art to a larger audience. We expect to work closely with the author on the format and layout of the book, and we hope eventually they will become just as much a part of the company as the founders." Order sample books via regular mail or online. "Prior to submitting for chapbook publication, a sample copy must be purchased." *Premiere Generation Ink* is "actively seeking people to help with distribution of books journals, promotional material as well as people to help with website, multimedia, and print products."

THE PRESBYTERIAN RECORD (Specialized: inspirational, religious), 50 Wynford Dr., North York ON M3C 1J7 Canada. (416)441-1111. Fax: (416)441-2825. E-mail: tdickey@presbyterian.ca. Established 1876.

Magazine Needs: *The Presbyterian Record* is "the national magazine that serves the membership of The Presbyterian Church in Canada (and many who are not Canadian Presbyterians). We seek to stimulate, inform, inspire, to provide an 'apologetic' and a critique of our church and the world (not necessarily in that order!)." Wants poetry which is "inspirational, Christian, thoughtful, even satiric but not maudlin. No 'sympathy card' type verse à la Edgar Guest or Francis Gay. It would take a very exceptional poem of epic length for us to use it. Shorter poems, 10-30 lines, preferred. Blank verse OK (if it's not just rearranged prose). 'Found' poems. Subject matter should have some Christian import (however subtle)." Has published poetry by Margaret Avison, Wendy Turner Swanson, Fredrick Zydek, John Grey, T.M. Dickey, and Charles Cooper. *The Presbyterian Record* appears 11 times/year. Press run is 55,000. Subscription: $15.

How to Submit: Submit 3-6 poems at a time; seasonal work 6 weeks before month of publication. Accepts simultaneous submissions; rarely accepts previously published poems. Poems should be typed, double-spaced. Accepts fax and e-mail submissions "but will not necessarily reply to unsolicited faxes or e-mails." Pays $30-50/poem. Acquires one-time rights.

PRESENCE (Specialized: form), 12 Grovehall Ave., Leeds LS11 7EX United Kingdom. E-mail: martin.lucas@talk21.com. Website: http://freespace.virgin.net/haiku.presence. Established 1995. **Contact:** Dr. Martin Lucas.

HAVE A COLLECTION OF POETRY you want to publish? See the Chapbook Publishers Index or Book Publishers Index in the back of this book.

Magazine Needs: *Presence*, published 3 times/year, features haiku, senryu, renga, tanka, etc. Wants "haiku or haiku-related/haiku-influenced work. Maximum length: 16 lines (including title and spaces)." Does not want "anything longer than 16 lines (except renga)." Has published poetry by Owen Bullock, Gary Hotham, Cicely Hill, and Carrie Etter. *Presence* is 52-60 pages, A5, photocopied, perfect-bound, with brushdrawn art on card cover and illustrations. Receives about 2,000 poems/year, accepts about 10%. Press run is 200 for 150 subscribers of which 5 are libraries, 10 shelf sales. Subscription: £10 ($20 US) for 3 issues by air mail. £3.50 ($7 US) per single issue by air mail. Sample: £3 ($6 US). Please pay in US bills (no checks).

How to Submit: Submit 4-12 poems at a time. "Please ensure that separate poems can be identified, and not mistaken for a sequence." No previously published poems or simultaneous submissions. Accepts e-mail submissions in body of message. Cover letter preferred. Time between acceptance and publication is 4 months. Comments on rejected poems if requested. Guidelines available for SASE (or SAE with IRC) or on website. Responds within 1 month. Pays 1 contributor's copy. Copyright remains with authors. Staff reviews books or chapbooks of poetry or other magazines in 100-1,500 words, single format. Poets may send material for review consideration.

Advice: "The more you read the better you'll write. Those who subscribe to read make better poets than those who are motivated solely by seeing their own name in print."

THE PRESS OF THE THIRD MIND (Specialized: form), 1301 North Dearborn #1007, Chicago IL 60610. (312)337-3122. E-mail: b_seidman@hotmail.com. Website: www.thepressofthe3rdmindink.org. Established 1985. **Poetry Editor:** Bradley Bongwater.

Book/Chapbook Needs: Press of the Third Mind is a small press publisher of artist books, poetry, and fiction. "We are especially interested in found poems, Dada, surrealism, written table-scraps left on the floors of lunatic asylums by incurable psychotics, etc." Has published poetry by Anthony Stark, Jorn Barger, Michael Kaspar, Patrick Porter, Tom Vaultonburg, and Eric Forsburg. Press run is 1,000 with books often going into a second or third printing. Sample for $1.43 postage.

How to Submit: For book publication submit up to 20 sample poems. "No anthologized mss where every poem has already appeared somewhere else." Accepts simultaneous submissions, if noted. No submissions by e-mail. "Cover letter is good, but we don't need to know everything you published since you were age nine in single-spaced detail." Upcoming themes available for SASE. "Authors are paid as the publication transcends the break-even benchmark." The press has released an 80-page anthology entitled *Empty Calories* and published a deconstructivist novel about the repetition compulsion called *The Squeaky Fromme Gets the Grease.*

PRISM INTERNATIONAL, Creative Writing Program, University of British Columbia, Vancouver BC V6T 1Z1 Canada. E-mail: prism@interchange.ubc.ca. Website: http://prism.arts.ubc.ca. Established 1959. **Contact:** Editor (rotating title).

• *PRISM international* is known in literary circles as one of the top journals in Canada.

Magazine Needs: "*PRISM* is an international quarterly that publishes poetry, drama, short fiction, imaginative nonfiction, and translation into English in all genres. We have no thematic or stylistic allegiances: Excellence is our main criterion for acceptance of mss. We want fresh, distinctive poetry that shows an awareness of traditions old and new. We read everything." Accepts poetry by young writers—"Excellence is the only criterion." Has published poetry by Matt Robinson, Carmen Rodriguez, Jann Conn, Esta Spalding, Karen Connelly, and Derek Wynand. *PRISM* is 96 pages, digest-sized, elegantly printed, flat-spined with original color artwork on a glossy card cover. Circulation is for 1,100 subscribers of which 200 are libraries. Receives 1,000 submissions/year, accepts about 80; has a 3 to 4 month backlog. Subscription: $18, $27/2 years. (Please note: Canadian subscribers add GST; all others, please pay in US $). Sample: $5.

How to Submit: Submit up to 6 poems at a time, any print so long as it's typed. Include SASE (or SAE with IRCs). No previously published poems or simultaneous submissions. Accepts fax submissions. Cover letter with brief introduction and previous publications required. "Translations must be accompanied by a copy of the original." Guidelines available for SASE (or SAE with IRCs), by e-mail, or on website. Responds in up to 6 months. Pays $40/printed page plus subscription; plus an additional $10/printed page to selected authors for publication online. Editors sometimes comment on rejected poems. Acquires first North American serial rights.

Advice: "While we don't automatically discount any kind of poetry, we prefer to publish work that challenges the writer as much as it does the reader. We are particularly looking for poetry in translation."

N ○ PROSE AX, P.O. Box 22643, Honolulu HI 96823. E-mail: prose_ax@attbi.net. Website: www.proseax.com. Established 2000. **Editor:** J. Salazar. Member: CLMP.
- *Prose Ax* won Honorable Mention in the *Writer's Digest* Zine Competition for 2000 and 2001.

Magazine Needs: *Prose Ax* appears 3 times/year, showcasing "prose, poetry, and visual arts with an edge from emerging and established artists." Wants well crafted free verse. "We usually lean toward poems that 'tell stories' versus poems that 'paint a landscape.' " Does not want haiku, rhyming poetry, epic poems, or poems in Old English. Recently published poetry by Richard Jordan, Eric Paul Shaffer, Cyril Wong, and C.R. Garza. *Prose Ax* is 24-36 pages, 8½×7, digital copies, stapled, with 60 lb. b&w cover, various art/graphics; also published online. Receives about 240 poems/year, accepts about 30. Publishes about 8 poems/issue. Press run is 500. Single copy: $2/issue; subscription: $6 for 3 issues. Make checks payable to *Prose Ax*.

How to Submit: Submit 3-6 poems at a time. Accepts previously published poems and simultaneous submissions. Accepts e-mail submissions; no disk submissions. Cover letter is preferred ("but doesn't have to be formal"). "Prefer e-mail submissions, pasted into body of e-mail, attached if there are formatting issues." Reads submissions year round. Time between acceptance and publication is 1-3 months. Poems are circulated to an editorial board (reviewed between editor and assistant editor). Often comments on rejected poems (if asked). Guidelines available for SASE, by e-mail, or on website. Responds in up to 3 months. Always sends prepublication galleys. Pays 2 contributor's copies. Acquires one-time rights.

Advice: "At the least, read the poems online to see what our tastes are."

$ ○ PROVINCETOWN ARTS; PROVINCETOWN ARTS PRESS, 650 Commercial St., Provincetown MA 02657-1725. (508)487-3167. Fax: (508)487-4791. E-mail: cbusa@mediaone.net. Established 1985. **Editor:** Christopher Busa.

Magazine Needs: An elegant annual using quality poetry, "*Provincetown Arts* focuses broadly on the artists and writers who inhabit or visit the tip of Cape Cod and seeks to stimulate creative activity and enhance public awareness of the cultural life of the nation's oldest continuous art colony. Drawing upon a century-long tradition rich in visual art, literature, and theater, *Provincetown Arts* publishes material with a view towards demonstrating that the artists' colony, functioning outside the urban centers, is a utopian dream with an ongoing vitality." Has published poetry by Bruce Smith, Franz Wright, Sandra McPherson, and Cyrus Cassells. *Provincetown Arts* is about 170 pages, magazine-sized, perfect-bound with full-color glossy cover. Press run is 10,000 for 500 subscribers of which 20 are libraries, 6,000 shelf sales. Sample: $10.

How to Submit: Submit up to 3 typed poems at a time. All queries and submissions should be via regular mail. Reads submissions October through February. Guidelines available for SASE. Responds in 3 months. Usually sends prepublication galleys. Pays $25-100/poem plus 2 contributor's copies. Acquires first rights. Reviews books of poetry in 500-3,000 words, single or multi-book format. Send materials for review consideration.

Book/Chapbook Needs & How to Submit: The Provincetown Arts Press has published 8 volumes of poetry. The Provincetown Poets Series includes *At the Gate* by Martha Rhodes, *Euphorbia* by Anne-Marie Levine, a finalist in the 1995 Paterson Poetry Prize, and *1990* by Michael Klein, co-winner of the 1993 Lambda Literary Award.

★ ○ THE PUCKERBRUSH PRESS; THE PUCKERBRUSH REVIEW, 76 Main St., Orono ME 04473-1430. (207)866-4868 or 581-3832 Press established 1971. *Review* established 1978. **Poetry Editor:** Constance Hunting.

Magazine Needs & How to Submit: *The Puckerbrush Review* is a literary, twice-a-year magazine. Looks for freshness and simplicity, but does not want to see "confessional, religious, sentimental, dull, feminist, incompetent, derivative" poetry. Has published Wolly Swist and Muska Nagel. For the review, submit 5 poems at a time. Pays 2 copies.

Book/Chapbook Needs & How to Submit: The Puckerbrush Press is a small press publisher of flat-spined paperbacks of literary quality. Recently published *Revelation* by Robert Taylor, *At Fifteen* by May Sarton (early journal), and *Catching Beauty* by Mary Sarton. For book publication, query with 10 samples. Prefers no simultaneous submissions. Offers criticism for a fee: $100 is usual. Pays 10% royalties plus 10 copies.

Advice: "Just write the best and freshest poetry you can."

PUDDING HOUSE PUBLICATIONS; PUDDING MAGAZINE: THE INTERNATIONAL JOURNAL OF APPLIED POETRY; PUDDING HOUSE CHAPBOOK COMPETITIONS; PUDDING HOUSE BED & BREAKFAST FOR WRITERS; PUDDING HOUSE WRITERS INNOVATION CENTER (Specialized: political, social issues, popular culture), 60 N. Main St., Johnstown OH 43031. (740)967-6060. E-mail: pudding@johnstown.net. Website: www.puddinghouse.com. Established 1979. **Editor:** Jennifer Bosveld.

Magazine Needs: Pudding House Publications provides "a sociological looking glass through poems that speak to the pop culture, struggle in a consumer and guardian society and more—through 'felt experience.' Speaks for the difficulties and the solutions. Additionally a forum for poems and articles by people who take poetry arts into the schools and the human services." Publishes *Pudding* every several months, also chapbooks, anthologies, broadsides. "Wants what hasn't been said before. Speak the unspeakable. Don't want preachments or sentimentality. Don't want obvious traditional forms without fresh approach. Long poems OK as long as they aren't windy. Interested in receiving poetry on popular culture, rich brief narratives, i.e. 'virtual journalism.' (sample sheet $1 plus SASE)." Has published poetry by Knute Skinner, David Chorlton, Mary Winters, and Robert Collins. Uses up to 60 pages of poetry in each issue—digest-sized, 70 pages, offset-composed on Microsoft Word PC. Press run is 2,000 for 1,400 subscribers. Subscription: $22/3 issues. Sample: $7.95.

How to Submit: Submit 3-10 poems at a time with SASE. "Submissions without SASEs will be discarded." No postcards. No simultaneous submissions. Previously published submissions respected but include credits. Likes cover letters and "cultivates great relationships with writers." Sometimes publishes theme issues. Guidelines available for SASE. Responds on same day (unless traveling). Pays 1 copy; to featured poet $10 and 4 copies. Returns rights "with *Pudding* permitted to reprint." Send materials for review consideration or listing as recommended. "See our website for vast calls for poems for magazine, chapbooks, and anthologies; for poetry and word games, and essays and workshop announcements."

Book/Chapbook Needs & How to Submit: Has recently published *Dancing with the Switchman* by Conrad Squires, *When I Had it Made* by Will Nixon, and *Subject Apprehended* by Hans Ostrom. Chapbooks considered outside of competitions, no query. **Reading fee:** $10. Send complete ms and cover letter with publication credits and bio. Editor sometimes comments, will critique on request for $4/page of poetry or $85 an hour in person.

Also Offers: Pudding House is the publisher of the nationwide project POETS' GREATEST HITS—an invitational. They have over 250 chapbooks and books in print. Pudding House offers 2 annual chapbook competitions—each requires a $10 reading fee with entry. Deadlines: June 30 and September 30. The competitions award $100, publication, and 20 free copies. Pudding House Bed & Breakfast for Writers offers "pretty, comfortable, clean rooms with desk and all the free paper you can use" as well as free breakfast in large comfortable home 1 block from conveniences. Location of the Pudding House Writers Innovation Center and Library on Applied Poetry. Bed & Breakfast is $85 single or double/night, discounts to writers. Reservations recommended far in advance. Details available for SASE. "Our website is one of the greatest poetry websites in the country—calls, workshops, publication list/history, online essays, games, guest pages, calendars, poem of the month, poet of the week, much more." The website also links to the site for The Unitarian Universalist Poets Cooperative and American Poets Opposed to Executions, both national organizations.

Advice: "Editors have pet peeves. I won't respond to postcards. I require SASEs. I don't like cover letters that state the obvious, poems with trite concepts, or meaning dictated by rhyme. Thoroughly review our website; it will give you a good idea about our publication history and editorial tastes."

THE PUDDIN'HEAD PRESS (Specialization: regional/Chicago), P.O. Box 477889, Chicago IL 60647. (708)656-4900. E-mail: phbooks@compuserve.com. Established 1985. **Editor-in-Chief:** David Gecic.

Book/Chapbook Needs: The Puddin'head Press is interested in "well-rounded poets who can support their work with readings and appearances. Most of our poets are drawn from the performance poetry community." Wants "quality poetry by active poets. We occasionally publish chapbook-style anthologies and let poets on our mailing lists know what type of work we're interested in for a particular project." Does not want experimental, overly political poetry, or poetry with overt sexual content; no shock or novelty poems. Recently published poetry by John Dickson, Nina Corwin, JJ Jameson, and Jeff Helgeson.

How to Submit: Puddin'head Press publishes 1 book and 1 chapbook/year. Books/chapbooks are 30-100 pages, perfect-bound or side-stapled ("we use various formats"). Responds to queries in 1 month; to mss in 3 months. Poets must include SASE with submission. Pays various royalty rates "depending on the publication. We usually have a press run of 500 books." **About 25% of books are author-subsidy published.** Terms vary. Order sample books/chapbooks by sending $10 (price plus postage) to The Puddin'head Press (also available through Amazon).

Also Offers: "We prefer to work closely with poets in the Chicago area. There are numerous readings and events which we sponsor. We do our own distribution, primarily in the Midwest, and also do distribution for other small presses. Please send a SASE for a list of our current publications and publication/distribution guidelines."

Advice: "It is difficult to find a quality publisher. Poets must have patience and find a press that will work with them. The most important part of publication is the relationship between poet and publisher. Many good books will never be seen because the poet/publisher relationship is not healthy. If a poet is involved in the literary world, he will find a publisher, or a publisher will find him."

⊘ PUERTO DEL SOL, Box MSC3, New Mexico State University, Las Cruces NM 88003-8001. E-mail: puerto@nmsu.edu. Website: www.nmsu.edu/~puerto/welcome.html. Established 1972 (in present format). **Poetry Editor:** Kathleene West. **Editor-in-Chief:** Kevin McIlvoy.

Magazine Needs: "We publish a literary magazine twice per year. Interested in poems, fiction, essays, photos, originals, and translations, usually from the Spanish. Also (generally solicited) reviews and interviews with writers. We want top quality poetry, any style, from anywhere. We are sympathetic to Southwestern writers, but this is not a theme magazine. Excellent poetry of any kind, any form." Has published poetry by Judith Sornberger, Ana Castillo, Marilyn Hacker, John Repp, and Lois-Ann Yamanaka. *Puerto del Sol* is digest-sized, flat-spined, professionally printed, matte card cover with art. Press run is 1,250 for 300 subscribers of which 25-30 are libraries. Devotes 40-50 pages to poetry in each 150-page issue. Uses about 50 of the 900 submissions (about 6,000 poems) received each year to fill up the 90 pages of poetry the 2 issues encompass. Subscription: $10/2 issues. Sample: $8.

How to Submit: Submit 3-6 poems at a time, 1 poem to a page. Accepts simultaneous submissions. No e-mail submissions. Brief cover letter welcome. "Do not send publication vitae." Reads mss September 1 to March 1 only. Offers editorial comments on most mss. Responds in 6 months. Sometimes sends prepublication galleys. Pays 2 contributor's copies.

Advice: "Read the magazine before submitting work."

⊕ ⊘ PULSAR POETRY MAGAZINE; LIGDEN PUBLISHERS, 34 Lineacre, Grange Park, Swindon, Wiltshire SN5 6DA United Kingdom. Phone: (01793)875941. E-mail: david.pike@virgin.n et. Website: www.pulsarpoetry.com. Established 1992. **Editor:** David Pike. **Editorial Assistant:** Jill Meredith.

Magazine Needs: *Pulsar*, published quarterly, "encourages the writing of poetry from all walks of life. Contains poems, reviews and editorial comments." Wants "hard-hitting, thought-provoking work; interesting and stimulating poetry." Does not want "racist material. Not keen on religious poetry." Has published poetry by Merryn Williams, Liz Atkin, Li Min Hua, Virgil Suarez, and Michael Newman. *Pulsar* is 36 pages, A5, professionally printed, saddle-stapled, glossy 2-color cover with photos and ads. Press run is 300 for 100 subscribers of which 40 are libraries; several distributed free to newspapers, etc. Subscription: $30 (£12 UK). Sample: $7. Make checks payable to Ligden Publishers.

How to Submit: Submit 3 poems at a time "preferably typed." No previously published poems or simultaneous submissions. Send no more than 2 poems via e-mail; file attachments will not be read.

Cover letter preferred; include SAE with IRCs. "Poems can be published in next edition if it is what we are looking for. The editor and assistant read all poems." Time between acceptance and publication is about 1 month. Seldom comments on rejected poems. Guidelines available for SASE (or SAE with IRC) and on website. Responds within 3 weeks. Pays 1 contributor's copy. "Originators retain copyright of their poems." Acquires first rights. Staff reviews poetry books and poetry audio tapes (mainstream); word count varies. Send materials for review consideration.

Advice: "Give explanatory notes if poems are open to interpretation. Be patient and enjoy what you are doing. Check grammar, spelling, etc. (should be obvious). Note: we are a non-profit making society."

⊕ ◑ PURPLE PATCH; THE FIRING SQUAD, 25 Griffiths Rd., West Bromwich B7I 2EH England. E-mail: ppatch@hotmail.com. Established 1975. **Editor:** Geoff Stevens.

Magazine Needs: *Purple Patch* a quarterly poetry and short prose magazine with reviews, comment and illustrations. "All good examples of poetry considered, but prefer 40 lines max. Do not want poor rhyming verse, non-contributory swear words or obscenities, hackneyed themes." Has published poetry by Joyce Metzger, M.T. Nowak, Jodi Azzouni, Eamen O'Keefe, Peter Tomlinson, and Geoffrey Clarke. *Purple Patch* is 24 pages, digest-sized, photocopied and side-stapled with cover on the same stock with b&w drawing. Receives about 2,500 poems/year, accepts approximately 8%. Publish 40 poems/issue. Circulation "varies." Subscription: £5 UK/3 issues; US price is $20 (submit dollars). Make checks (sterling only) payable to G. Stevens.

How to Submit: "Send 2 or more poems with return postage paid." Accepts submissions by postal mail only. Cover letter with short self-introduction preferred with submissions. Time between acceptance and publication is 4 months. Publishes theme issues occasionally. Upcoming themes available for SASE (or SAE and IRCs). Guidelines available in publication. Comments on rejected poems. Response time is 1 month to Great Britain, can be longer to US. Overseas contributors have to buy a copy to see their work in print. Acquires first British serial rights. Staff reviews poetry chapbooks, short stories and tapes in 30-300 words. Send materials for review consideration.

Also Offers: *The Firing Squad* is a broadsheet of short poetry of a protest or complaint nature, published at irregular intervals. "All inquiries, submissions of work, etc., must include SASE or SAE and IRCs or $1 U.S./Canadian for return postage/reply."

$◑ QED PRESS; CYPRESS HOUSE, 155 Cypress St., Fort Bragg CA 95437. (707)964-9520. Fax: (707)964-7531. E-mail: qedpress@mcn.org. Website: www.cypresshouse.com. Established 1985. **Editor:** John Shaw.

Book/Chapbook Needs: "QED Press seeks clear, clean, intelligent, and moving work." Publishes 1-2 paperbacks/year. Wants "concrete, personal and spare writing. No florid rhymed verse." Has published poetry by Victoria Greenleaf, Luke Breit, Paula Tennant (Adams), and Cynthia Frank. Books are usually around 100 pages, digest-sized, offset printed, perfect-bound, full-color CS1 10 pt. cover.

How to Submit: "We prefer to see all the poems (about 100 pages worth or 75-80 poems) to be bound in a book." Accepts previously published poems and simultaneous submissions. Cover letter required. "Poets must have prior credits in recognized journals, and a minimum of 50% new material." Time between acceptance and publication is 6-12 months. Poems are circulated to an editorial board. "We publish only 1-2 poetry books each year—by consensus." Seldom comments on rejected poems. Responds to queries and mss in 3 months. Pays royalties of 7½-12% and 25 author's copies (out of a press run of 500-1,000). Order sample books by sending SASE for catalog.

Also Offers: Through the imprint Cypress House, they offer subsidy arrangements and "provide typesetting, design, marketing, and promotion services for independent presses and self-publishers. We are not a vanity press." 50% of books are author-subsidy published each year.

⊕ $◻ QUANTUM LEAP; Q.Q. PRESS, York House, 15 Argyle Terrace, Rothesay, Isle of Bute PA20 0BD Scotland, United Kingdom. Established 1997. **Editor:** Alan Carter.

Magazine Needs: *Quantum Leap* is a quarterly poetry magazine. Wants "all kinds of poetry—free verse, rhyming, whatever—as long as it's well written and preferably well punctuated, too. We rarely use haiku." Also accepts poetry written by children. Has published poetry by Pamela Constantine, Ray Stebbing, Leigh Eduardo, Sam Smith, Sky Higgins, Norman Bissett, and Gordon Scapens. *Quan-*

tum Leap is 40 pages, digest-sized, desktop-published and saddle-stapled with card cover, includes clip art and ads for other magazines. Receives about 2,000 poems/year, accepts about 15%. Press run is 200 for 180 subscribers. Single copy: $10; subscription: $34. Sample: $9. Make checks payable to Alan Carter. "All things being equal in terms of a poem's quality, I will sometimes favor that of a subscriber (or someone who has at least bought an issue) over a nonsubscriber, as it is they who keep us solvent."

How to Submit: Submit 6 poems at a time. Line length for poetry is 36 ("normally"). Accepts previously published poems (indicate magazine and date of first publication) and simultaneous submissions. Cover letter required. "Within the UK, send a SASE, outside it, send IRCs to the value of what has been submitted." Time between acceptance and publication is usually 3 months "but can be longer now, due to magazine's increasing popularity." Sometimes comments on rejected poems. Guidelines available for SASE (or SAE and IRC). Responds in 3 weeks. Pays £2 sterling. Acquires first or second British serial rights.

Book/Chapbook Needs: Under the imprint "Collections," Q.Q. Press offers subsidy arrangements "to provide a cheap alternative to the 'vanity presses'—poetry only." Charges £130 sterling for 50 32-page books (A4), US $260 plus postage. Please write for details. Order sample books by sending $12 (postage included). Make checks payable to Alan Carter.

Also Offers: Sponsors open poetry competitions and competitions for subscribers only. Send SAE and IRC for details.

Advice: "Submit well-thought-out, well-presented poetry, preferably well punctuated, too. If rhyming poetry, make it flow and don't strain to rhyme. I don't bite, and I appreciate a short cover letter, but not a long, long list of where you've been published before! Please do not add U.S. stamps to IRCs. They have no validity here. If you want to increase the value, just send extra IRCs."

QUARTER AFTER EIGHT; PROSE WRITING CONTEST (Specialized: form/ style), Ellis Hall, Ohio University, Athens OH 45701. (740)593-2827. Fax: (740)593-2818. E-mail: quarteraftereight@hotmail.com. Website: www.quarteraftereight.org. Established 1993. **Editors-in-Chief:** William Breeze and Hayley Mitchell Haugen.

• "The Art of the Snake Story" by Amy England was selected for inclusion in the 2001 volume of *Best American Poetry*.

Magazine Needs: *Quarter After Eight* is "an annual journal of prose and commentary devoted to the exploration of prose in all its permutations. We are interested in reading fiction, sudden fiction, prose poetry, creative and critical non-fiction, interviews, reviews, letters, memoirs, translations, and drama. We do not publish traditional (lineated) poetry, but we do welcome work that provocatively explores—even challenges—the prose/poetry distinction. Our primary criteria in evaluating submissions are freshness of approach and an address to the prose form." Has published poetry by Colette Inez, Maureen Seaton, Virgil Suarez, Cecilia Pinto, and Matthew Cooperman. *Quarter After Eight* is 286 pages, digest-sized, professionally printed and perfect-bound with glossy card cover, includes b&w photos and ads. Receives about 1,000 poems/year, accepts 3%. Press run is 800 for 200 subscribers of which 50 are libraries, 300 shelf sales. Sample: $10.

How to Submit: Submit 4-6 poems at a time. Accepts simultaneous submissions; no previously published poems. Accepts disk submissions with hard copy. "Include publishing history. We encourage readers/submitters to obtain a copy of the magazine." Reads submissions September 15 through March 15 only. Poems are circulated to an editorial board. "Editorial board makes final decisions; a pool of readers handles first reads and commentary/input on editorial decisions." Often comments on rejected poems. Guidelines available for SASE or on website. Responds in up to 4 months. Pays 2 contributor's copies. Acquires first North American serial rights. Reviews books of poetry in 800-1,200 words, single or multi-book format. Send material for review consideration to Lisa Schroot-Mitchum, Book Review Editor.

Also Offers: Sponsors an annual Prose Writing Contest with $300 cash award. Reading fee: $15 (includes subscription). Winner is published in subsequent issue. Maximum length 10,000 words—can be a sequence of prose poems. Guidelines available for SASE or on website.

Advice: "*Quarter After Eight* is a somewhat specialized niche. Check out the magazine and explore the boundaries of genre."

$ ⊚ ELLERY QUEEN'S MYSTERY MAGAZINE (Specialized: mystery), 475 Park Ave. S, 11th Floor, New York NY 10016. E-mail: elleryqueen@dellmagazines.com. Website: www.themyst eryplace.com. Established 1941. **Contact:** Janet Hutchings.

Magazine Needs: *Ellery Queen's Mystery Magazine*, appearing 11 times/year, uses primarily short stories of mystery, crime, or suspense. *Ellery Queen's Mystery Magazine* is 144 pages, digest-sized, professionally printed on newsprint, flat-spined with glossy paper cover. Subscription: $39.97. Sample: $3.50 (available on newsstands).

How to Submit: Accepts simultaneous submissions; no previously published poems. Accepts submissions by postal mail only. Include SASE with submissions. Guidelines available for SASE and on website. Responds in 3 months. Pays $15-65 plus 3 contributor's copies.

🍁 $ ⬙ ⊚ QUEEN'S QUARTERLY: A CANADIAN REVIEW (Specialized: regional), Queen's University, Kingston ON K7L 3N6 Canada. (613)533-2667. Fax: (613)533-6822. E-mail: qquarter@post.queensu.ca. Website: www.info.queensu.ca/quarterly. Established 1893. **Editor:** Boris Castel.

Magazine Needs: *Queen's Quarterly* is "a general interest intellectual review featuring articles on science, politics, humanities, arts and letters, extensive book reviews, some poetry and fiction. We are especially interested in poetry by Canadian writers. Shorter poems preferred." Has published poetry by Evelyn Lau, Sue Nevill, and Raymond Souster. Each issue contains about 12 pages of poetry, digest-sized, 224 pages. Press run is 3,500. Receives about 400 submissions of poetry/year, accepts 40. Subscription: $20 Canadian, $25 US for US and foreign subscribers. Sample: $6.50 US.

How to Submit: Submit up to 6 poems at a time. No simultaneous submissions. Submissions can be sent on hard copy with a SASE (no replies/returns for foreign submissions unless accompanied by an IRC) or by e-mail and will be responded to by same. Responds in 1 month. Pays usually $50 (Canadian)/poem, "but it varies," plus 2 copies.

⭐ ⬙ QUEST, Freiburger Hall, Lynn University, 3601 N. Military Trail, Boca Raton FL 33431. E-mail: jmorgan@lynn.edu. Established 1997. **Editor:** Dr. Jeff Morgan.

Magazine Needs: *Quest* is an annual literary and arts journal published in April. "We want poems with a clear voice that use careful diction to create poetry in which sound and sense work together, creating fresh perception. We do not want poems that rely on profanity or shock value." Recently published poetry by Eugene Martel, Andrea Best, Fred Cichocki, Johanne Perron, and Diane Richard-Allerdyce. *Quest* is digest-sized, laser copy-printed, saddle-stapled, 32# bright white coverstock printed with 4-color process, includes original student art laid out with Photoshop/QuarkXPress. Receives about 100 poems/year, accepts about 25. Publishes about 25 poems/issue. Press run is 200 for one subscriber (library); 150 distributed free to Lynn University faculty, staff, and students. Single copy: $5. Make checks payable to Jeff Morgan.

How to Submit: Submit up to 5 poems at a time. No previously published poems or simultaneous submissions. No fax, e-mail, or disk submissions. Cover letter is preferred. "Include adequate SASE if you want work returned." Reads submissions mid-September to mid-January. **Charges $1 reading fee; criticism fee of 15 cents/word.** Time between acceptance and publication is up to 7 months. Poems are circulated to an editorial board. "English Department faculty review submissions." Seldom comments on rejected poems. Guidelines available for SASE. Responds in up to 2 months. Pays 1 contributor's copy. Acquires one-time rights.

Advice: "Even the freest of verse has its roots in the formal elements."

⬗ ⊚ RADIX MAGAZINE (Specialized: poetry that expresses a Christian world-view), P.O. Box 4307, Berkeley CA 94704. E-mail: radixmag@aol.com. Website: www.radixmagazine.com. Established 1969. **Editor:** Sharon Gallagher. **Poetry Editor:** Luci Shaw.

Magazine Needs: *Radix* wants poems "that reflect a Christian world-view, but aren't preachy." Recently published poetry by John Leax, Walter McDonald, Evangeline Paterson, and Luci Shaw. *Radix* is 32 pages, magazine-sized, offset-printed, saddle-stapled, self cover 60 lb. Receives about 50 poems/year, accepts about 20%. Publishes about 2-3 poems/issue. Press run varies. Sample: $5. Make checks payable to *Radix Magazine*.

How to Submit: Submit 1-4 poems at a time. No previously published poems or simultaneous submissions. Prefers e-mail submissions; no fax or disk submissions. Submit seasonal poems 6 months in advance. Time between acceptance and publication is 3 months-3 years. "We have a serious backlog. The poetry editor accepts or rejects poems and sends the accepted poems to the editor. The editor then publishes poems in appropriate issues. If more than one poem is accepted from any poet, there will probably be a long wait before another is published, because of our backlog of accepted poems." Seldom comments on rejected poems. "Familiarity with the magazine is helpful, but not required." Occasionally publishes theme issues. Responds in 2 months. Pays 2 contributor's copies. Acquires first rights. Returns rights upon request. Reviews books of poetry.

Advice: "*Radix* has a distinctive voice and often receives submissions that are completely inappropriate. Familiarity with the magazine is recommended before sending any submissions."

THE RAINTOWN REVIEW, P.O. Box 40851, Indianapolis IN 46240. Website: http://members.iquest.net/~pkanouse. Established 1996. **Editor:** Patrick Kanouse.

Magazine Needs: *The Raintown Review* is published irregularly and contains only poetry. Wants well-crafted poems—metered, syllabic, or free-verse. "While attention is paid to formal verse, *The Raintown Review* does publish all kinds of poetry. The one criteria: quality." Has published poetry by William Baer, Dorothy Stone, Annie Finch, Len Roberts, and Ted Simmons. *The Raintown Review* is about 60 pages, chapbook-sized, desktop-published and saddle-stapled with card cover. Receives about 900 poems/year, accepts 10-15%. Press run is about 200 with most going to subscribers and contributors. Subscription: $24/year. Sample: $6.50.

How to Submit: Submit up to 4 poems at a time. No length restrictions. Accepts previously published poems (with acknowledgement of previous publication) and simultaneous submissions. No e-mail submissions. Cover letter preferred. "We prefer contributors write for guidelines before submitting work." Guidelines available for SASE and in publication. Responds in up to 3 months. Pays 1 contributor's copy and 2 issue subscription. Acquires one-time rights.

RALPH'S REVIEW (Specialized: horror, nature/rural/ecology, psychic/occult, science fiction/fantasy), 129A Wellington Ave., Albany NY 12203. E-mail: rcpub@juno.com. Established 1988. **Editor:** R. Cornell.

Magazine Needs: *Ralph's Review*, published quarterly, contains "mostly new writers, short stories and poems." Wants "horror/fantasy, environmental. No more than 30 lines." Does not want "rape, racial, political poems." Has published "Moods of Madness" by R. Cornell and poetry by Joanne Tolson, Joseph Danoski, Jim Sullivan, and Brendan J. MacDonald. *Ralph's Review* is 20-35 pages, magazine-sized, photocopied, sometimes with soft cover, with art, cartoons and graphics. Receives about 80-100 poems/year, accepts 40%. Press run is 75-100 for 35 subscribers of which 3 are libraries; 30-40 distributed free to bookstores, toy stores, antique, and coffee shops. Single copy: $2; subscription: $15. Make checks payable to R. Cornell.

How to Submit: Submit up to 5 poems, with a **50¢/poem reading fee** and SASE. Accepts previously published poems and simultaneous submissions. No e-mail submissions. Cover letter required. Time between acceptance and publication is 2-4 months. Seldom comments on rejected poems. Publishes theme issues. Guidelines and upcoming themes available for SASE or by e-mail. Responds in 3 weeks. Pays 1 copy. Acquires all rights. Returns rights 1 year after acceptance.

Advice: "Write good stuff, no foul language, be descriptive, colorful, short to the point, with an active ending."

$ RATTAPALLAX; RATTAPALLAX PRESS, 532 La Guardia Place, Suite 353, New York NY 10012. (212)560-7459. E-mail: info@rattapallax.com. Website: www.rattapallax.com. Established 1998. **Editor-in-Chief:** Martin Mitchell.

Magazine Needs: "A biannual journal of contemporary literature, *Rattapallax* is Wallace Steven's word for the sound of thunder." Wants "extraordinary work in poetry and short fiction—words that are well-crafted and sing, words that recapture the music of the language, words that bump into each other in extraordinary ways and leave the reader touched and haunted by the experience. We do not want ordinary words about ordinary things." Has published poetry by Anthony Hecht, Sharon Olds, Lou Reed, Marilyn Hacker, Billy Collins, and Glyn Maxwell. *Rattapallax* is 128 pages, magazine-sized, offset-printed, perfect-bound, with 12 pt. C1S cover, includes photos, drawings, and CD with poets. Receives about 5,000 poems/year, accepts 2%. Press run is 2,000 for 100 subscribers of which 50 are libraries, 1,200 shelf sales; 200 distributed free to contributors, reviews, and promos. Single copy: $7.95; subscription: $14/1 year. Sample (including guidelines): $7.95. Make checks payable to *Rattapallax*.

How to Submit: Submit 3-5 poems at a time. Accepts simultaneous submissions; no previously published poems. Accepts e-mail submissions from outside of the US and Canada; all other submissions must be sent via postal mail. "SASE is required and e-mailed submissions should be sent as simple text." Cover letter preferred. Reads submissions all year; issue deadlines are June 1 and December 1. Time between acceptance and publication is 6 months. Poems are circulated to an editorial board. "The editor-in-chief, senior editor, and associate editor review all the submissions then decide on which to accept every week. Near publication time, all accepted work is narrowed and unused work is kept for the next issue." Often comments on rejected poems. Guidelines available by e-mail or on website. Responds in 2 months. Always sends prepublication galleys. Pays 2 contributor's copies. Acquires first rights.

Book/Chapbook Needs & How to Submit: Rattapallax Press publishes "contemporary poets and writers with unique powerful voices." Publishes 5 paperbacks and 3 chapbooks/year. Books are usually 64 pages, digest-sized, offset-printed and perfect-bound with 12 pt. C1S cover, include drawings and photos. Query first with a few sample poems and cover letter with brief bio and publication credits and SASE. Requires authors to first be published in *Rattapallax*. Responds to queries in 1 month; to mss in 2 months. Pays royalties of 10-25%. Order sample books by sending SASE and $7.

◖ RATTLE, 12411 Ventura Blvd., Studio City CA 91604. (818)986-3274. E-mail: stellasueL@aol.com. Website: www.rattle.com. Established 1994. **Editor:** Alan Fox. **Poetry Editor:** Stellasue Lee. Address submissions to Stellasue Lee.

Magazine Needs: *RATTLE* is a biannual poetry publication (appearing in June and December) which also includes interviews with poets, essays, and reviews. Wants "high quality poetry of any form, three pages maximum. Nothing unintelligible." Accepts some poetry written by children ages 10 to 18. Has published poetry by Lucille Clifton, Charles Simic, Mark Doty, Sharon Olds, Billy Collins, and Stephen Dunn. *RATTLE* is 196 pages, digest-sized, neatly printed and perfect-bound with 4-color coated card cover. Receives about 8,000 submissions/year, accepts 250. Press run is 4,000. Subscription: $28/2 years. Sample: $8. Make checks payable to *RATTLE*.

How to Submit: Submit up to 5 poems at a time with name, address, and phone number on each page in upper right hand corner. Include SASE. No previously published work or simultaneous submissions. Accepts submissions by e-mail (in text box) and by fax. Cover letter and e-mail address, if possible, is required as well as a bio. Guidelines available by e-mail, on website, and in publication.

Artist Marcia Reich created an image "at once thoughtful, yet strong; enduring," says Stellasue Lee, editor of *RATTLE*. "After painting, the artist went outside to water her garden. She noticed how the shadow of the window cut through the painting, made something of a frame. I thought it perfectly represented the pose of a writer," an apt image for the Summer 2002 tribute to Pulitzer Prize winners. Cover designer was Tony Donegan.

Reads submissions all year. Seldom comments on rejected poems unless asked by the author. Responds in up to 2 months. Pays 2 contributor's copies. Rights revert to authors upon publication. Welcomes essays up to 2,000 words on the writing process and book reviews on poetry up to 250 words. Send materials for review consideration.

RAW DOG PRESS; POST POEMS, 151 S. West St., Doylestown PA 18901-4134. (215)345-6838. Website: www.freeyellow.com/members/rawdog. Established 1977. **Poetry Editor:** R. Gerry Fabian.

Magazine Needs: "Publishes Post Poems annual—a postcard series. We want short poetry (three to seven lines) on any subject. The positive poem or the poem of understated humor always has an inside track. No taboos, however. All styles considered. Anything with rhyme had better be immortal." Has published poetry by Don Ryan, John Grey, and the editor, R. Gerry Fabian.

How to Submit: Submit 3-5 poems at a time. Prefers shorter poetry. Send SASE for catalog to buy samples. Always comments on rejected poems. Guidelines available on website. Pays contributor's copies. Acquires all rights. Returns rights on mention of first publication. Sometimes reviews books of poetry.

Book/Chapbook Needs & How to Submit: Raw Dog Press welcomes new poets and detests second-rate poems from 'name' poets. We exist because we are dumb like a fox, but even a fox takes care of its own."

Also Offers: Offers criticism for a fee; "if someone is desperate to publish and is willing to pay, we will use our vast knowledge to help steer the ms in the right direction. We will advise against it, but as P.T. Barnum said. . . ."

Advice: "I get poems that do not fit my needs. At least one quarter of all poets waste their postage because they do not read the requirements. Also, these are too many submissions without a SASE and they go directly into the trash!"

RB'S POETS' VIEWPOINT, Box 940, Eunice NM 88231. Established 1989. **Editor:** Robert Bennett.

Magazine Needs: *RB's Poets' Viewpoint* published bimonthly, features poetry and cartoons. Wants "general and religious poetry, sonnets, and sijo with a 21-line limit." Does not want "vulgar language." Has published poetry by Marion Ford Park, Ruth Ditmer Ream, Ruth Halbrooks, and Delphine Ledoux. *RB's Poets' Viewpoint* is 34 pages, digest-sized, photocopied, saddle-stapled with drawings and cartoons. Receives about 400 poems/year, accepts about 90%. Press run is 60. Subscription: $8. Sample: $2. Make checks payable to Robert Bennett.

How to Submit: Submit 3 poems typed single space. **Reading fee:** $1.50/poem. Accepts previously published poems and simultaneous submissions. Reads submissions February, April, June, August, October, and December only. Time between acceptance and publication is 1 month. "Poems are selected by one editor." Often comments on rejected poems. Guidelines available for SASE. Responds in 1 month. Pays 1 contributor's copy. Acquires one-time rights.

Also Offers: Sponsors contests for general poetry, religious poetry, sonnets, and sijo with 1st Prizes of $20, $6, and $5, respectively, plus publication in *RB's Poets' Viewpoint*. There is a $1.50 per poem entry fee, except the sijo category, which has a 50¢ per poem fee. Guidelines available for SASE.

RE:AL—THE JOURNAL OF LIBERAL ARTS, Dept. PM, Box 13007, Stephen F. Austin State University, Nacogdoches TX 75962. (409)468-2059. Fax: (409)468-2190. E-mail: f_real@titan. sfasu.edu. Website: www.libweb.sfasu.edu/real/default.htm. Established 1968. **Editor:** W. Dale Hearell.

Magazine Needs: *RE:AL*, printed in fall and spring, is a "Liberal Arts Forum" using short fiction, reviews, criticism, and poetry and also contains editorial notes and personalized "Contributors' Notes." Aims "to use from 90 to 110 pages of poetry per issue, typeset in editor's office. *RE:AL* welcomes all styles and forms that display craft, insight, and accessibility." Accepts poetry written by children. Receives between 60-100 poems/week. "We need a better balance between open and generic forms. We're also interested in critical writings on poems or writing poetry and translations with a bilingual format (permissions from original author)." *RE:AL* is handsomely printed, "reserved format," perfect-bound with line drawings and photos. Circulation approximately 400, "more than half of which are major college libraries." Subscriptions also in Great Britain, Ireland, Italy, Holland, the Phillipines, Puerto Rico, Brazil, Croatia, and Canada. Subscription: $40 for institutions, $30 individual. Sample: $15.

How to Submit: Submit original and copy. "Editors prefer a statement that ms is not being simultaneously submitted; however, this fact is taken for granted when we receive a ms." Writer's guidelines available for SASE. *RE:AL* acknowledges receipt of submissions and strives for a 1-month decision. Submissions during summer semesters may take longer. Pays 2 contributor's copies. Reviews are assigned, but queries about doing reviews are welcome.

N ◯ REARVIEW QUARTERLY. E-mail: rearviewquarterly@yahoo.com. Website: http://rearview.domynoes.net. Established 2002. **Editors:** Erica Mayyasi, Laura Arellano-Weddleton.

Magazine Needs: *Rearview Quarterly* publishes poetry, short prose, and b&w artwork and photography. Wants all poetry, especially narrative poetry. Does not want erotica or overly religious poetry. Recently published poetry by Helen Losse and Janet Buck. *Rearview Quarterly* is 16 pages, digest-sized, photocopied, hand-bound, cardstock cover with illustration, includes b&w internal art/graphics. Receives about 500 poems/year, accepts about 3%. Publishes about 12 poems/issue. Press run is 50 for 10 subscribers, 25 shelf sales; 15 are distributed free to contributors. Single copy: $2.50; subscription: $10. Sample: $2. Make checks payable to *Rearview Quarterly*.

How to Submit: Submit 7 poems at a time. Accepts previously published poems and simultaneous submissions. Accepts e-mail submissions **only**; no fax or disk submissions. Cover letter is preferred. Reads submissions year round. Submit seasonal poems 3 months in advance. Time between acceptance and publication is less than 3 months. Poems are circulated to an editorial board. "Poems are read individually by both editors. If we both like the poem, it is 'first-cut.' The first-cut poems are then looked at as a group and the final decision is made based on how the poems read together." Seldom comments on rejected poems. Guidelines available for SASE, by e-mail, or on website. Responds in up to 6 weeks. Pays 1 contributor's copy. Acquires first North American serial rights.

Advice: "Take chances and tell it like it is. We want to read about life—real life, not something sugar-coated."

⬛ RED BOOTH REVIEW; RED BOOTH CHAPBOOKS. E-mail: rbr@wtp62.com. Website: http://wtp62.com/rbr.htm. Established 1998. **Contact:** W. T. Pfefferle.

Magazine Needs: *Red Booth Review* appears 3 times/year online, 1 time/year in print. Publishes "best poetry we see, moving poems about driving, meagre love, compact and focused." Recently published poetry by Joseph Hutchins, Carol Borzyskowski, Amy Pence, and David McNaron. *Red Booth Review* print edition is 64 pages, digest-sized, digitally-printed, perfect-bound, slick cover, with some art/graphics. Receives about 1,200 poems/year, accepts about 5%. Publishes about 20 poems/issue online, about 40 in print. Press run is 250 for 30 subscribers; 220 are distributed free to writers and editors. E-mail editor for sample copy prices.

How to Submit: Submit 4-10 poems at a time with bio and mailing address. Accepts simultaneous submissions; no previously published poems. No postal mail submissions; accepts e-mail submissions only (as attachment or in text box). Cover letter is preferred. Reads submissions all year. Time between acceptance and publication is 1 week. Usually one editor and one guest editor select poems. Often comments on rejected poems. Guidelines are available on website. Responds in 1 week. Pays 1 contributor's copy for print issue. Acquires first North American serial rights; rights revert to author upon publication.

Book/Chapbook Needs & How to Submit: Red Booth Chapbooks prefers moving and compact poetry. Publishes 1-2 chapbooks/year. Chapbooks are chosen through contest 2 times/year. Winners include Michael Cadnum, Julie Chisholm, and Terry J. England. Chapbooks are usually 30 pages, digitally-printed, saddle-stapled, slick cover, with art/graphics. Responds to queries in 1 month; to

---

WAIT! Don't mail your submission or correspondence without enclosing a SASE (self-addressed stamped envelope). If sending outside your own country, include SAE and IRCs (International Reply Coupons) instead.

mss in 4 months. Pays winner $250 plus 25 copies of the finished chapbook. Order sample books/chapbooks from website.

THE RED CANDLE PRESS; CANDELABRUM POETRY MAGAZINE (Specialized: form/style, metrical and rhymed), Rose Cottage, Threeholes Bridge, Wisbech, PE14 9JR England. E-mail: rcp@poetry7.fsnet.co.uk. Website: www.members.tripod.com/redcandlepress. Established 1970. **Editor:** M.L. McCarthy, M.A.

Magazine Needs: Red Candle Press "is a formalist press, specially interested in metrical and rhymed poetry, though free verse is not excluded. We're more interested in poems than poets: that is, we're interested in what sort of poems an author produces, not in his or her personality." Publishes the magazine, *Candelabrum*, twice yearly (April and October). Wants "good-quality metrical verse, with rhymed verse specially wanted. Elegantly cadenced free verse is acceptable. Accepts 5-7-5 haiku. No weak stuff (moons and Junes, loves and doves, etc.) No chopped-up prose pretending to be free verse. Any length up to about 40 lines for *Candelabrum*, any subject, including eroticism (but not porn)—satire, love poems, nature lyrics, philosophical—any subject, but nothing racist, ageist, or sexist." Has published poetry by Pam Russell, Ryan Underwood, David Britton, Alice Evans, Jack Harvey, Nick Spargo. *Candelabrum* is digest-sized, staple-spined, small type, exemplifies their intent to "pack in as much as possible, wasting no space, and try to keep a neat appearance with the minimum expense." Uses about 40 pages (some 70 poems) in each issue. Receives about 2,000 submissions/year, of which 10% is accepted, usually holds over poems for the next year. Press run is 900 for 700 subscribers of which 22 are libraries. Sample: $6 in bills only; non-sterling checks not accepted.

How to Submit: "Submit anytime. Enclose one IRC for reply only; three IRCs if you wish manuscript returned. If you'd prefer a reply by e-mail, without return of unwanted manuscript, please enclose one British first-class stamp, IRC, or U.S. dollar bill to pay for the call. Each poem on a separate sheet please, neat typescripts or neat legible manuscripts. Please no dark, oily photostats, no colored ink (only black or blue). Author's name and address on each sheet, please." No simultaneous submissions. No e-mail submissions. Guidelines available on website. Responds in about 2 months. Pays 1 contributor's copy.

Advice: "Traditional-type poetry is much more popular here in Britain, and we think also in the United States, now than it was in 1970, when we established *Candelabrum*. We always welcome new poets, especially traditionalists, and we like to hear from the U.S.A. as well as from here at home. General tip: Study the various outlets at the library, or buy a copy of *Candelabrum*, or borrow a copy from a subscriber, before you go to the expense of submitting your work. The Red Candle Press regrets that, because of bank charges, it is unable to accept dollar cheques. However, it is always happy to accept U.S. dollar bills."

RED DRAGON PRESS, P.O. Box 19425, Alexandria VA 22320-0425. Website: www.reddragonpress.com. Established 1993. **Editor/Publisher:** Laura Qa.

Book/Chapbook Needs: Red Dragon Press publishes 3-4 chapbooks/year. Wants "innovative, progressive, and experimental poetry and prose using literary symbolism, and aspiring to the creation of meaningful new ideas, forms, and methods. We are proponents of works that represent the nature of man as androgynous, as in the fusing of male and female symbolism, and we support works that deal with psychological and parapsychological topics." Has published *Spectator Turns Witness* by George Karos and *The Crown of Affinity* by Laura Qa. Chapbooks are usually 64 pages, digest-sized, offset-printed, perfect-bound on trade paper with 1-10 illustrations.

How to Submit: Submit up to 5 poems at a time with SASE. Accepts previously published poems and simultaneous submissions. Cover letter preferred with brief bio. **Reading fee:** $5 for poetry and short fiction, $10 for novels; check or money order payable to Red Dragon Press. Time between acceptance and publication is 8 months. Poems are circulated to an editorial board. "Poems are selected for consideration by the publisher, then circulated to senior editor and/or poets previously published for comment. Poems are returned to the publisher for further action; i.e., rejection or acceptance for publication in an anthology or book by a single author. Frequently submission of additional works is required before final offer is made, especially in the process for a book by a single author." Often comments on rejected poems. Charges criticism fee of $10 per page on request.

Responds to queries in 10 weeks, to mss in 1 year. For sample books, purchase at book stores or mail order direct from Red Dragon Press at the above address.

$ ☑ RED HEN PRESS; RED HEN POETRY CONTEST, P.O. Box 3537, Granada Hills CA 91394. Fax: (818)831-6659. E-mail: editors@redhen.org. Website: www.redhen.org. Established 1993. **Publisher:** Mark E. Cull. **Editor:** Kate Gale.

Book/Chapbook Needs: Red Hen Press wants "good literary fiction and poetry" and publishes 10 paperbacks, one selected through a competition. "Translations are fine. No rhyming poetry." Has published poetry by Dr. Benjamin Saltman, Robert Peters, Eloise Klein Healy, and Terry Wolverton. Books are usually 64-96 pages, digest-sized, professionally printed and perfect-bound with trade paper cover, includes paintings and photos.

How to Submit: Submit 5 poems at a time. Accepts previously published poems and simultaneous submissions. Cover letter preferred. Time between acceptance and publication is 1 year. Poems are circulated to an editorial board. "One main poetry editor plus three to four contributing editors review the work." Seldom comments on rejected poems. Responds to queries in 1 month. Pays 10% royalties and 50 author's copies. To obtain sample books "write to our address for a catalog."

Also Offers: Sponsors the Benjamin Saltman Poetry Contest for a full-length collection (46-68 pages). Deadline is October 31.

Advice: "Be willing to help promote your own book and be helpful to the press. Writers need to help small presses survive."

$ ☑ ◎ RED MOON PRESS; THE RED MOON ANTHOLOGY; CONTEMPORARY HAIBUN (Specialized: form/style, haiku) (formerly *American Haibun & Haiga*), P.O. Box 2461, *Winchester VA 22604-1661. (540)722-2156. Fax: (708)810-8992. E-mail: redmoon@shentel.net. Website: www.haikuworld.org/books/redmoon. Established 1994, American Haibun & Haiga* established 1999. **Editor/Publisher:** Jim Kacian.

Magazine Needs: *Contemporary Haibun* (formerly *American Haibun & Haiga*), published annually in April, is the first western journal dedicated to haibun and haiga and is 128 pages, digest-sized, offset-printed on quality paper with heavy stock four-color cover. Receives several hundred submissions per year, accepts approximately 5%. Recently published Michael McClintock, Linda Jeanette Ward, David Cobb, William Ramsey, Ban'ya Natsuishi, and Dimitar Awakiev. Accepts poetry written by children. Expected print run is 1,000 for subscribers and commercial distribution. Subscription: $15 plus $3 shipping and handling. A brief sample of the form will be available for SASE or via return e-mail.

How to Submit: Submit up to 3 haibun or haiga at a time with SASE. Considers previously published work. Accepts submissions by fax, on disk, by e-mail (as attachment or in text box), or by regular mail. Guidelines available for SASE, by e-mail, and in publication. Submissions will be read by editorial board. Time between acceptance and publication varies according to time of submission. Pays $1/page. Acquires first North American serial rights. "Only haibun and haiga will be considered. If the submitter is unfamiliar with the form, consult *Journey to the Interior*, edited by Bruce Ross, or previous issues of *Contemporary Haibun*, for samples and some discussion."

Book/Chapbook Needs: Red Moon Press "is the largest and most prestigious publisher of English-language haiku and related work in the world." Publishes *The Red Moon Anthology*, an annual volume, the finest English-language haiku and related work published anywhere in the world in the previous 12 months. *The Red Moon Anthology* is 160 pages, digest-sized, offset-printed, perfect-bound, glossy 4-color heavy-stock cover. Inclusion is by nomination of the editorial board only. The press also publishes 6-8 volumes per year, usually 3-5 individual collections of English-language haiku, as well as 1-3 books of essays, translation, or criticism of haiku. Under other imprints the press also publishes chapbooks of various sizes and formats.

How to Submit: Query with book theme and information, and 30-40 poems, or draft of first chapter. Responds to queries in 2 weeks, to mss (if invited) in 2-3 months. "Each contract separately negotiated."

Advice: "Haiku is a burgeoning and truly international form. It is nothing like what your fourth-grade teacher taught you years ago, and so it is best if you familiarize yourself with what is happening in the form (and its close relatives) today before submitting. We strive to give all the work we publish plenty of space in which to resonate, and to provide a forum where the best of today's practitioners can be published with dignity and prestige. All our books have either won awards or are awaiting notification."

Ø RED RAMPAN' PRESS; RED RAMPAN' REVIEW; RED RAMPAN' BROADSIDE SE-RIES, Bishop House, 518 East Court St., Dyersburg TN 38024-4714. Established 1981. **Poetry Editor:** Larry D. Griffin. Presently not accepting poetry.

Ø RED RIVER REVIEW, E-mail: Editor@RedRiverReview.com. Website: www.RedRiverReview .com. Established 1999. **Editor:** Bob McCranie.
Magazine Needs: "Published quarterly, *Red River Review* is a fully electronic literary journal. Our purpose is to publish quality poetry using the latest technology. *Red River* is a journal for poets who have studied the craft of writing and for readers who enjoy being stirred by language." Wants "poetry which speaks to the human experience in a unique and accessible way. No rhyming poetry or poetry that is annoyingly obscure." Has published poetry by Marin Sorescu, Padi Harman, Barbara F. Lefcowitz, Deborah DeNicola, Ed Madden, and Jeanne P. Donovan. Receives about 2,500 poems/year, accepts about 10%.
How to Submit: Submit 4-6 poems at a time. No previously published poems or simultaneous submissions. Accepts submissions through online submission form only, no e-mail. Cover letter preferred. Time between acceptance and publication is 3 months. Often comments on rejected poems. Guidelines available on website. Responds in 3 months. Sometimes sends prepublication galleys. Acquires first rights and anthology rights, "if we want to do a *Red River Review Anthology*." Contact by e-mail for address and query information.
Advice: "Write about who you are and who we are in the world. Read other writers as much as possible."

Ø RED ROCK REVIEW; RED ROCK POETRY AWARD, English Dept. J2A, Community College of Southern Nevada, 3200 E. Cheyenne Ave., North Las Vegas NV 89030. (702)651-4094. Fax: (702)651-4639. E-mail: richard_logsdon@ccsn.nevada.edu. Website: www.ccsn.nevada.edu/eng lish/redrockreview/index.html. Established 1994. **Editor-in-Chief:** Dr. Rich Logsdon. **Associate Editor:** Todd Moffett.
Magazine Needs: *Red Rock Review* appears biannually in May and December and publishes "the best poetry available." Also publishes fiction, creative nonfiction, and book reviews. Has published poetry by Dorianne Laux, Kim Addonizio, Ellen Bass, Cynthis Hogue, and Dianne di Prima. *Red Rock Review* is about 130 pages, magazine-sized, professionally printed and perfect-bound with 10 pt. cornwall, C1S cover. Accepts about 15% of poems received/year. Press run is 1,000. Sample: $5.50.
How to Submit: Submit 2-3 poems at a time, "mailed flat, not folded, into a letter sized envelope." Line length for poetry is 80 maximum. Accepts simultaneous submissions; no previously published poems. Accepts disk submissions. Cover letter with SASE required. Do not submit mss June 1 through August 31. Time between acceptance and publication is 3 months. Poems are circulated to an editorial board. "Poems go to poetry editor, who then distributes them to three readers." Seldom comments on rejected poems. Guidelines available for SASE or on website. Responds in 2 months. Pays 2 contributor's copies. Acquires first North American serial rights. Reviews books and chapbooks of poetry in 500-1,000 words, multi-book format. Send materials for review consideration.
Also Offers: Sponsors the annual Red Rock Poetry Award. Winner receives $500 plus publication in the *Red Rock Review*. Submit up to 3 poems of not more than 20 lines each, typed on 8½×11 white paper. Reading fee: $6/entry (3 poems). Deadline: October 31. Complete rules available for SASE.

Ø RED WHEELBARROW, De Anza College, 21250 Stevens Creek Blvd., Cupertino CA 95014. (408)864-8600. E-mail: SplitterRandolph@fhda.edu. Website: www.deanza.fhda.edu/RedWheelbarr ow. Established 1976. **Editor:** Randolph Splitter.
• "Note: We are not affiliated with Red Wheelbarrow Press or any similarly named publication."
Magazine Needs: This college-produced magazine appears annually in summer. *Red Wheelbarrow*

has published poetry by Steve Fellner, Virgil Suarez, Al Young, Amber Coverdale Sumrall, Mario Susko, and Morton Markus. *Red Wheelbarrow* is up to 220 pages, digest-sized, well-printed on heavy stock with b&w graphics, perfect-bound. Press run is 500. Single copy: $5.

How to Submit: Submit 3-5 poems at a time. "Before submitting, writers are strongly urged to purchase a sample copy." Accepts e-mail submissions. Best submission times: September through January. Annual deadline: December 31. Responds in up to 6 months, depending on backlog. Include SASE or e-mail address for reply. "We cannot return manuscripts." Pays 2 contributor's copies.

◑ ◎ **THE REDNECK REVIEW, an online poetry journal (Specialized: regional/Southern literary tradition)**, PMB 167, 931 Monroe Dr. NE, Suite 102, Atlanta GA 30308-1778. E-mail: editor@redneckreview.com. Website: www.redneckreview.com. Established 2000. **Editor:** Penya Sandor.

Magazine Needs: *The Redneck Review* is a biannual online poetry journal "born out of the rich literary tradition of the South. We are looking for writing that is interesting, has energy, and doesn't feel like homework." Recently published poetry by Denise Duhamel, Marie Howe, Walt McDonald, Hal Sirowitz, Ben Satterfield, and Jean Trounstine. *The Redneck Review* is published online. Publishes about 15-20 poems/issue.

How to Submit: Submit no more than 5 poems at a time. Accepts previously published poems and simultaneous submissions. Accepts e-mail and disk submissions; no fax submissions. Cover letter is preferred. "If mailing submissions, include SASE unless you have an e-mail address. Poems won't be returned." Time between acceptance and publication "depends. *I* read the poems." Often comments on rejected poems. Guidelines available on website. Response time varies. Sometimes sends prepublication galleys. No payment. "Authors retain rights, but we ask they mention our journal if they publish the poem again." Send materials for review consideration to *The Redneck Review*.

Advice: "There are many respectable literary journals that publish well written but dull writing. We would prefer to read literature that is electric, not just technically well crafted."

◑ ◎ **REFLECT (Specialized: form/style)**, 1317-D Eagles Trace Path, Chesapeake VA 23320. Established 1979. **Poetry Editor:** W.S. Kennedy. **Assistant Editor:** Clara Holton.

Magazine Needs: Uses "spiral poetry: featuring an inner-directed concern with sound (euphony), mystical references or overtones, and objectivity—rather than personal and emotional poems. No love poems, pornography, far left propaganda; nothing overly sentimental." Has published poetry by Marikay Brown, H.F. Noyes, Joe Malone, Ruth Wildes Schuler, and Joan Payne Kincaid. The quarterly is 48 pages, digest-sized, saddle-stapled, typescript. Subscription: $8. Sample: $2.

How to Submit: Submit 4 or 5 poems at a time. All submissions should be single-spaced and should fit on one typed page. No previously published poems or simultaneous submissions. Sometimes comments on rejected poems. Issue deadlines: fall—September 12 for October 15 publication; winter—December 12 for January 15 publication; spring—March 12 for April 15 publication; summer—June 12 for July 15 publication. Guidelines available for SASE. Responds within a month. Pays 1 copy to nonsubscribers, 2 copies to subscribing contributors. Acquires first rights.

Advice: "Get a sample copy in order to understand the type of poetry we publish as to subjects and length."

⬥ ◑ **REFLECTIONS LITERARY JOURNAL**, P.O. Box 1197, Roxboro NC 27573. (336)599-1181 ext. 428. E-mail: thrasht@piedmont.cc.nc.us. Established 1999. **Editor:** Tami Sloane Thrasher.

Magazine Needs: *Reflections Literary Journal* appears annually in June publishing poetry, short fiction, and creative nonfiction. Wants any styles and forms of poetry, including translations, of any length. Does not want material using obscenities and culturally insensitive material ("these tend to be rejected by our editorial panel"). Recently published poetry by J.E. Bennett, Fred Chappell, Sara Claytor, Betsy Humphreys, Sheri Narin, and Lynn Veach Sadler. *Reflections Literary Journal* is 128-144 pages, digest-sized. Receives about 200 poems/year, accepts about 10%. Publishes about 20 poems/issue. Press run is 500 for 20 subscribers of which 4 are libraries, 150 shelf sales; 100 are distributed free to contributors, editors, advisors, local schools, and cultural sites. Single copy: $7; subscription: $7. Sample: $5 for back issue. Make checks payable to *Reflections Literary Journal*.

How to Submit: Submit 3-5 poems at a time. Accepts previously published poems and simultaneous submissions (if notified). Accepts disk submissions in rich text format; no fax or e-mail submissions.

Cover letter is optional. "Include a 50-word brief bio with submission. Include one copy with name and address and one copy without. Single-space poetry submissions. Affix adequate postage to SAE for return of manuscript if desired, or use first class stamps on SAE for notification." Reads submissions August 1 through December 31. Time between acceptance and publication is 10 weeks. Poems are circulated to an editorial board. "Our 10-12 member editorial board ranks the submissions through 'blind' readings. Every board member reads and ranks every submission, with the exception of board members who are also submitting work, who then refrain from ranking their own submissions." Seldom comments on rejected poems. Guidelines available in magazine, for SASE, or by e-mail. Responds in up to 9 months (in March or April). Pays 1 contributor's copy. Acquires first North American serial rights (if poem is unpublished) or one-time rights (if poem is previously published).

⬤ **THE "REJECTION NOTICE" ZINE**, 231 E. 22nd St., Paterson NJ 07514-2109. (973)279-7610. E-mail: pheekuh@aol.com. Established 1993. **Editor:** Ron Emolo.
Magazine Needs: *The "Rejection Notice" Zine* wants "any" kind of poetry. Recently published poetry by Don Kommit, Christine Conforti, and Joe Ruffilo. *"Rejection Notice"* is 4-8 pages, magazine-sized, photocopied, stapled, with drawings on cover. Receives about 100 poems/year, accepts about 5%. Publishes about 5 poems/year. Press run is 80 copies distributed free to all for SASE.
How to Submit: Submit any number of poems. Accepts previously published poems and simultaneous submissions. No fax, e-mail, or disk submissions. Cover letter preferred. Include SASE. Reads submissions anytime. Time between acceptance and publication is 4-6 weeks. "I enjoy unusual poems. Anything different. I publish what moves me. Also, I'm looking for experimental poems." Never comments on rejected poems. Guidelines and upcoming themes available for SASE. Responds in 3 weeks. "Authors responsible for copywriting their work." Send materials for review consideration to *"Rejection Notice" Zine*.
Advice: "I will work with young and new writers, if they ask."

⬤ ◎ **REMUDA (Specialized: horses, cowboy lifestyle)**, (formerly *Literally Horses*) Equestrienne Ltd., 208 Cherry Hill St., Kalamazoo MI 49006. (269)345-5915. E-mail: literallyhorses@aol.com. Website: www.literallyhorses.com/index.html. Established 1999. **Editor:** Laurie A. Cerny.
Magazine Needs: *Remuda* is "an annual venue for creative poetry/fiction and essays that have a horse/western lifestyle theme. Any style is acceptable. Nothing sexually explicit; nothing offensive; no curse words or racial overtones." Accepts poetry by children but "under 18 needs signed permission by parents." Has published poetry by Mary K. Herbert, Rod Miller, Michele F. Cooper, Mary Ruthart, Thomas Michael McDade, and Tena Bastian. *Remuda* is about 80 pages, digest-sized, desktop-published and saddle-stapled with b&w paper cover, includes simple drawings, classified ads. Receives about 200 poems/year, accepts about 75%. Press run is 1,000. Single copy: $4.25; subscription: $9.95. Sample (including guidelines): $4.25. Make checks payable to Equestrienne Ltd.
How to Submit: Submit 1-3 poems at a time. Line length for poetry is 5 minimum, 75 maximum. Accepts previously published poems and simultaneous submissions. No fax or e-mail submissions. Cover letter required. "Cover letters with bio and release/permission to use poems. Include SASE for return of poems and acceptance." Time between acceptance and publication is 3 months. Often comments on rejected poems. Responds in 3 months. Pays 2 copies. Acquires one-time rights. Reviews books and chapbooks of poetry in 150 words. Send materials for review consideration.
Also Offers: "Annual poetry contest. Submit up to 3 poems (under 50 lines each), bio, SASE. No entry fee required. First place: $25. Numerous smaller awards; "over 25 awards were given in the 2001 contest." Deadline: July 31 of every year. Winning entries are published in winter issue."
Advice: "Know horses and their world. The cowboy poetry I see is very good . . . so if submitting cowboy poetry, know what others are writing."

🌐 $ ◎ **RENDITIONS: A CHINESE-ENGLISH TRANSLATION MAGAZINE (Specialized: translations)**, Research Center for Translation, CUHK, Shatin, NT, Hong Kong. Phone: 852-2609-7399. Fax: 852-2603-5110. E-mail: renditions@cuhk.edu.hk. Website: www.renditions.org. **Editor:** Dr. Eva Hung.
Magazine Needs: *Renditions* appears twice/year in May and November. "Contents exclusively translations from Chinese, ancient and modern." Also publishes a hardback series (called Renditions Books) and a paperback series (called Renditions Paperbacks) of Chinese literature in English transla-

tion. Has published translations of the poetry of Yang Lian, Gu Cheng, Shu Ting, Mang Ke, and Bei Dao. *Renditions* is about 150 pages, magazine-sized, elegantly printed, perfect-bound, all poetry with side-by-side Chinese and English texts, using some b&w and color drawings and photos, with glossy card cover. Annual subscription: $28/1 year; $45/2 years: $62/3 years. Single copy: $17.

How to Submit: Accepts e-mail and fax submissions. "Chinese originals should be sent by regular mail because of formatting problems. Include 2 copies each of the English translation and the Chinese text to facilitate referencing." Publishes theme issues. Guidelines and upcoming themes available on website. Responds in 2 months. Pays "honorarium" plus 5 contributor's copies. Use British spelling. "Will consider" book mss. Query with sample translations. Submissions should be accompanied by Chinese originals. Books pay 10% royalties plus 10 copies. Mss usually not returned. Editor sometimes comments on rejected translations.

REVISTA/REVIEW INTERAMERICANA (Specialized: ethnic, regional), Inter-American University of Puerto Rico, Box 5100, San Germán, Puerto Rico 00683. Phone: (787)264-1912, ext. 7229 or 7230. Fax: (787)892-6350. E-mail: reinter@sg.inter.edu. **Editor:** Anibal José Aponte.

Magazine Needs: Published online, *Revista/Review* is a bilingual scholarly journal oriented to Puerto Rican, Caribbean, and Hispanic American and inter-American subjects, poetry, short stories, and reviews.

How to Submit: Submit at least 5 poems, but no more than 7, in Spanish or English, blank verse, free verse, experimental, traditional, or avant-garde, typed exactly as you want them to appear in publication. Name should not appear on the poems, only the cover letter. No simultaneous submissions. Accepts fax and e-mail submissions. Cover letter with brief personal data required.

RFD: A COUNTRY JOURNAL FOR GAY MEN EVERYWHERE (Specialized: gay), P.O. Box 68, Liberty TN 37095. (615)536-5176. E-mail: mail@rfdmag.org. Website: www.rfdmag.org. Established 1974. **Contact:** Poetry Editor.

Magazine Needs: *RFD* "is a quarterly for gay men with emphasis on lifestyles outside of the gay mainstream—poetry, politics, profiles, letters." Wants poetry that "illuminates the uniqueness of the gay experience. Themes that will be given special consideration are those that explore the rural gay experience, the gay perspective on social and political change, and explorations of the surprises and mysteries of relationships." Has published poetry by Antler, James Broughton, Gregory Woods and Winthrop Smith. *RFD* has a circulation of 3,000 for 700 subscribers. Single copy: $7.75; subscription: $37 first class, $25 second class. Sample: $7.75.

How to Submit: Submit up to 5 poems at a time. Accepts simultaneous submissions. Guidelines available for SASE and on website. Editor sometimes comments on rejected poems. Responds in up to 9 months. Pays 1 copy. Open to unsolicited reviews.

Advice: "*RFD* looks for interesting thoughts, succinct use of language and imagery evocative of nature and gay men and love in natural settings."

RHINO, P.O. Box 591, Evanston IL 60204. Website: www.rhinopoetry.org. Established 1976. **Editors:** Deborah Rosen, Alice George, Kathleen Kirk, and Helen Degen Cohen.

● "*RHINO* recently won three Illinois Arts Council Literary Awards."

Magazine Needs: *RHINO* "is an annual poetry journal, appearing in March, which also includes short-shorts and occasional essays on poetry. Translations welcome. The editors delight in work which reflects the author's passion, originality, and artistic conviction. We also welcome experiments with poetic form, sophisticated wit, and a love affair with language. Prefer poems under 100 lines." Has published poetry by Maureen Seaton, James McManus, Floyd Skoot, Lucia Getsi, and Richard Jones. *RHINO* is 100 pages, digest-sized, card cover with art, on high-quality paper. Receives 1,500 submissions/year, accepts 60-80. Press run is 1,000. Single copy: $10. Sample: $7.

How to Submit: Submit 3-5 poems with SASE. Accepts simultaneous submissions with notification; no previously published submissions. Submissions are accepted April 1 through October 1. Guidelines available for SASE or on website. Responds in up to 6 months. Pays 2 contributor's copies. Acquires first rights only.

$ THE RIALTO, P.O. Box 309, Alysham, Norwich, Norfolk NR11 6LN England. Website: www.therialto.co.uk. Established 1984. **Editor:** Michael Mackmin.

Magazine Needs: *The Rialto* appears 3 times/year and "seeks to publish the best new poems by established and beginning poets. *The Rialto* seeks excellence and originality." Has published poetry by Alice Fulton, Jenny Joseph, Les Murray, Penelope Shuttle, George Szirtes, Philip Gross, and Ruth Padel. *The Rialto* is 56 pages, A4 with full color cover, occasionally includes art/graphics. Receives about 12,000 poems/year, accepts about 1%. Publishes 50 poems/issue. Press run is 1,500 for 1,000 subscribers of which 50 are libraries. Subscription: £18. Sample: £6.50. Make checks payable to *The Rialto*. "Checks in sterling only please."

How to Submit: Submit 6 poems at a time. Accepts simultaneous submissions; no previously published poems. Cover letter preferred. "SASE or SAEs with IRCs essential. U.S. readers please note that U.S. postage stamps are invalid in U.K." Time between acceptance and publication is up to 4 months. Seldom comments on rejected poems. Responds in up to 4 months. "A large number of poems arrive every week, so please note that you will have to wait at least 10 weeks for yours to be read." Pays £20/poem. Poet retains rights.

Also Offers: "*The Rialto* has recently commenced publishing first collections by poets. Andrew Waterhouse's book *In* won the 2000 Forward/Whetherstone's Best First Collection prize. Please *do not* send book length manuscripts. Write first enquiring." Sponsors an annual young poets competition as well. Details available on website and in publication.

Advice: Before submitting, "you will probably have read many poems by many poets, both living and dead. You will probably have put aside each poem you write for at least 3 weeks before considering it afresh. You will have asked yourself, 'Does it work technically?' Checked the rhythm, the rhymes (if used), and checked that each word is fresh and meaningful in its context, not jaded and tired. You will hopefully have read *The Rialto*."

RIO: A JOURNAL OF THE ARTS, P.O. Box 165, Port Jefferson NY 11777. E-mail: rioarts@angelfire.com. Website: www.engl.uic.edu/rio/rio.html and www.rioarts.com. Established 1997. **Editors:** Cynthia Davidson, Susan Pilewski, Wilbur Farley, and Gail Lukasik.

Magazine Needs: *Rio* is a biannual online journal containing "poetry, essays of interest to artists, creative nonfiction, scannable artwork/photography, and book reviews. Query for anything else." Wants poetry of any length or form. "Experiments encouraged with voice, image, or language. No greeting card verse or sentimentality." Has published poetry by Virgil Suarez, Thomas Robert Barnes, Ron Overton, Camincha, Ruth E. Foley, George Wallace, and Carol Frith. Accepts about 20% of poems received/year. Back issues are available on the website.

How to Submit: Submit 5-8 poems at a time. Accepts previously published poems and simultaneous submissions "as long as you inform us of publication elsewhere." Accepts e-mail submissions. "For electronic submissions, use text (ASCII) or Macintosh attachments, or e-mail submissions in body of e-mail message." Cover letter preferred. "Unaccepted entries without the SASE will be discarded." Time between acceptance and publication is up to 6 months. Sometimes comments on rejected poems. Guidelines available website. Responds in up to 6 months. Acquires all rights. Rights revert to authors immediately upon publication. Reviews books and chapbooks of poetry in 500-1,200 words, single book format. Send materials for review consideration.

Advice: "We're looking for writers who do not fall into an easy category or niche."

RIO GRANDE REVIEW, 105 East Union, El Paso TX 79968-0622. Website: www.utep.edu/rdr. **Contact:** Poetry Editor.

Magazine Needs: *Rio Grande Review*, a annual student publication from the University of Texas at El Paso appearing in March, contains poetry; flash, short, and nonfiction; short drama; photography and line art. *Rio Grande Review* is 168 pages, digest-sized, professionally printed and perfect-bound with card cover with line art, line art inside. Subscription: $8/year, $15/2 years.

How to Submit: Include bio information with submission. "Submissions are recycled regardless of acceptance or rejection." SASE for reply only. Guidelines available for SASE and on website. Pays 2 copies. "Permission to reprint material remains the decision of the author. However, *Rio Grande Review* does request it be given mention."

RIVER CITY, English Dept., University of Memphis, Memphis TN 38152. (901)678-4591. Fax: (901)678-2226. E-mail: rivercity@memphis.edu. Website: www.people.memphis.edu/~rivercity. Established 1980. **Editor:** Dr. Mary Leader.

Magazine Needs: *River City* appears biannually (winter and summer) and publishes fiction, poetry, interviews, and essays. Has published poetry by Marvin Bell, Maxine Kumin, Jane Hirshfield, Terrance Hayes, Paisley Rekaal, S. Beth Bishop, and Virgil Suarez. *River City* is 160 pages, 7×10, perfect-bound, professionally printed with 4-color glossy cover. Publishes 40-50 pages of poetry/issue. Subscription: $12. Sample: $7. Press run is 2,000.

How to Submit: Submit no more than 5 poems at a time with SASE. Accepts submissions by e-mail (as attachment). Include SASE. Does not read mss June through August. *River City* no longer publishes theme issues. Guidelines available for SASE and by e-mail. Responds in up to 3 months. Pays 2 contributor's copies.

$ ◖ RIVER CITY PUBLISHING, 1719 Mulberry St., Montgomery AL 36106. E-mail: sales@riverpublishing.com. Website: www.rivercitypublishing.com. Established 1989. **Editor:** Jim Davis. **Contact:** Staff Editor.

Book/Chapbook Needs: "We publish serious or academic poetry; no religious, romantic, or novelty material. We are not a good market for inexperienced authors." Publishes 1-3 poetry hardbacks/year. Has published *Prepositional Heaven* by Thomas Rabbitt, *White for Harvest*, by Jeanie Thompson, *The Map That Lies Between Us* by Anne George, *Blue Angels* by Peter Huggins, *Haiku: The Travelers of Eternity* by Charles Ghigna, and *Enemies of the State* by Thomas Rabbitt.

How to Submit: "Experienced poets should submit high-quality collections of at least forty poems." Most mss selected by nationally known poet, others by staff. Responds in several weeks. "E-mail submissions are permitted but not encouraged." Guidelines available for SASE, by fax, by e-mail, and on website. Pays industry-standard royalties and author's copies.

Also Offers: "We can manufacture paperback books. We accept suitable poetry projects from authors interested in partially or totally financing the project. Contact the Staff Editor for more information."

◖ RIVER KING POETRY SUPPLEMENT, P.O. Box 122, Freeburg IL 62243. (618)234-5082. Fax: (618)355-9298. E-mail: riverkng@icss.net. Established 1995. **Editors:** Wayne Lanter, Donna Biffar, Phil Miller, Emily Lambeth.

Magazine Needs: *River King Poetry Supplement*, published biannually in August and February, features "all poetry with commentary about poetry." Wants "serious poetry." Does not want inspirational or prose poetry and no prose cut into short lines. Has published poetry by Alan Catlin, R.G. Bishop, Phil Dacey, John Knoepfle, P.F. Allen, David Ray, and Lyn Lifshin. *River King* is 8-12 pages, tabloid-sized, press printed, folded with line art. Receives about 6,000 poems/year, accepts approximately 2%. Press run is 5,000 of which 600 are for libraries.

How to Submit: Submit 3-6 poems at a time. No simultaneous submissions or previously published poems. Accepts fax and e-mail submissions. Cover letter preferred. Time between acceptance and publication is up to 6 months. Often comments on rejected poems. Responds in up to 6 months. Pays 10 copies.

★ ◖ RIVER OAK REVIEW, P.O. Box 3127, Oak Park IL 60303. (708)524-8725. E-mail: info@riveroakarts.org. Website: www.riveroakarts.org/home.html. Established 1993.

Magazine Needs: *River Oak Review* is a biannual literary magazine publishing high quality short fiction, creative nonfiction and poetry. Regarding work, they say, "quality is primary, but we probably wouldn't publish poems longer than 100 lines or so." Has published poetry by Billy Collins, Kathleen Norris, Steve Lautermilch and Maureen Seaton. *River Oak Review* is 128 pages, digest-sized, neatly printed and perfect-bound with glossy 4-color card cover with art. Receives about 1,500-2,500 poems/year, publishes approximately 1-2%. Press run is 1,000 for 500 subscribers, 200 shelf sales. Single copy: $10; subscription: $15/year, $25/2 years. Sample: $8. Make checks payable to River Oak Arts.

How to Submit: Submit 4-6 poems at a time. Accepts simultaneous submissions if notified; no previously published poems. Cover letter preferred. No e-mail submissions. Poems are circulated to readers, then an editorial board, then the editor. Seldom comments on rejected poems. Guidelines available for SASE. Responds in up to 5 months. Always sends prepublication galleys. Pays 2 copies. Acquires first North American serial rights.

Also Offers: Also sponsors a poetry contest in December with an award of $500 and publication in the spring issue of *River Oak Review*. Submit up to 4 poems at a time (maximum 500 lines total); typed, double spaced; with name, address, phone on cover letter only. Entries are not returned. Send postcard for notification of receipt and SASE for winners. Winners will be announced in spring. Guidelines available for SASE.

Advice: "Read literary magazines; read new poetry books; only submit if it's excellent."

$⬚ RIVER STYX MAGAZINE; BIG RIVER ASSOCIATION, 634 N. Grand Ave., 12th Floor, St. Louis MO 63103. Website: www.riverstyx.org. Established 1975. **Editor:** Richard Newman. **Managing Editor:** Melissa Gurley Banks.

• Poetry published in *River Styx* has been selected for inclusion in past volumes of *The Best American Poetry*, *Beacon Best*, and *Pushcart Prize* anthologies.

Magazine Needs: *River Styx*, published 3 times/year (April, August, December), is "an international, multicultural journal publishing both award-winning and previously undiscovered writers. We feature poetry, short fiction, essays, interviews, fine art and photography." Wants "excellent poetry—original, energetic, musical and accessible. Please don't send us chopped prose or opaque poetry that isn't about anything." Has published work by Louis Simpson, Molly Peacock, Marilyn Hacker, Yusef Komunyakaa, Andrew Hudgins, and Catie Rosemurgy. *River Styx* is 100 pages, digest-sized, professionally printed on coated stock, perfect-bound with color cover and b&w art, photographs, and ads. Receives about 8,000 poems/year, accepts 60-75. Press run is 2,500 for 1,000 subscribers of which 80 are libraries. Sample: $7. Subscription: $20/year, $35/2 years.

How to Submit: Submit 3-5 poems at a time, "legible copies with name and address on each page." Time between acceptance and publication is within 1 year. Reads submissions May 1 through November 30 only. Publishes theme issues once a year. Guidelines available for SASE or on website. Editor sometimes comments on rejected poems. Responds in up to 5 months. Pays 2 contributor's copies plus 1-year subscription plus $15/page if funds available. Acquires one-time rights.

Also Offers: Sponsors annual poetry contest. Past judges include Miller Williams, Ellen Bryant Voigt, Marilyn Hacker, Philip Levine, Mark Doty, Naomi Shihab Nye, Billy Collins, and Molly Peacock. Deadline: May 31. Guidelines available for SASE.

⬚ RIVERSTONE, A PRESS FOR POETRY; RIVERSTONE POETRY CHAPBOOK AWARD, P.O. Box 1421, Carefree AZ 85377. Established 1992. **Contact:** Editor.

Book/Chapbook Needs: Riverstone publishes 1 perfect-bound chapbook/year through an annual contest. Recent chapbooks includ *Reading the Night Sky* by Margo Stever, *A Record* by Anita Barrows, *Dragon Lady: Tsukimi* by Martha Modena Vertreace, *Everything Speaking Chinese* by G. Timothy Gordon, *Balancing on Light* by Margaret Hoen. The 2002 winner, Lisa Rhoades' *Into Grace*, is 44 pages, digest-sized, attractively printed on 80 lb. paper and perfect-bound with spruce green endleaves and a stippled beige card stock cover.

How to Submit: To be considered for the contest, submit $8 entry fee and chapbook ms of 24-36 pages, "including poems in their proposed arrangement, title page, contents, and acknowledgments. All styles welcome." Accepts previously published poems, multiple entries, and simultaneous submissions. Include 6×9 SASE or larger for notification and copy of last year's chapbook. Guidelines available for SASE. Contest deadline: June 30 postmark. Winner receives publication, 50 author's copies, and a cash prize of $100. Sample: $5.

⬚ ROANOKE REVIEW, English Dept., Roanoke College, 221 College Lane, Salem VA 24153. Established 1968. **Poetry Editor:** Paul Hanstedt.

Magazine Needs: *Roanoke Review* is an annual literary review which uses poetry that is "grounded in strong images and unpretentious language." Has published poetry by David Citino, Jeff Daniel Marion, and Charles Wright. *Roanoke Review* is 200 pages, digest-sized, professionally printed with matte card cover with full-color art. Uses 25-30 pages of poetry in each issue. Press run is 250-300 for 150 subscribers of which 50 are libraries. Receives 400-500 submissions of poetry/year, accepts 40-60. Subscription: $8. Sample: $5.

Also Offers: Biannual Poetry Competition (2004, 2006, etc.). Send up to 3 poems. Deadline: December 31. Entry fee: $10. Make checks payable to Roanoke College.

How to Submit: Submit original typed mss, no photocopies. Responds in 3 months. No pay.

Advice: "Be real. Know rhythm. Concentrate on strong images."

🔳 **THE ROCKFORD REVIEW; ROCKFORD WRITERS' GUILD**, 7721 Venus St., Loves Park IL 61111. E-mail: haikupup@aol.com or Dragonlady@prodigy.net. Website: http://writersguild1 .tripod.com. Established 1971. **Editor:** Cindy Guentherman.

Magazine Needs: *The Rockford Review* is a publication of the Rockford Writers' Guild which appears 3 times/year, publishing their poetry and prose, that of other writers throughout the country and contributors from other countries. *The Rockford Review* seeks experimental or traditional poetry of up to 50 lines. "We look for the magical power of the words themselves, a playfulness with language in the creation of images and fresh insights on old themes, whether it be poetry, satire, or fiction." Accepts poetry by younger writers, but warns they would be competing with adults. Has published poetry by John Grey, Richard Luftig, and Laura Wilson. *The Rockford Review* is about 50 pages, digest-sized, professionally printed and saddle-stapled with card cover with b&w illustration. Press run is 350. Single copy: $6; subscription: $20 (3 issues plus the Guild's monthly newsletter, *Write Away*).

How to Submit: Submit up to 3 poems at a time with SASE. Accepts simultaneous submissions; no previously published poems. No electronic submissions; accepts submissions by postal mail only. "Include a cover letter with your name, address, phone number, e-mail address (if available), a three-line bio, and an affirmation that the submission is unpublished in print or electronically." Guidelines available for SASE and on website. Responds in 2 months. Pays 1 contributor's copy and "you will receive an invitation to be a guest of honor at a Contributors' Reading & Reception in the spring." Acquires first North American serial rights.

Also Offers: Offers Editor's Choice Prizes of $25 for prose, $25 for poetry each issue. Also sponsors a Spring Stanzas Contest and a Fall Short Story Contest with cash prizes and publication in *The Rockford Review*. Accepts work by children for both contests. The Rockford Writers' Guild is a nonprofit, tax-exempt corporation established "to encourage, develop and nurture writers and good writing of all kinds and to promote the art of writing in the Rockford area." Offers lectures by Midwest authors, editors, and publishers, conducts several workshops and publishes a monthly newsletter. Membership: $30/year. Further information available for written request or on website.

Advice: "We look for poems that appeal to a general readership. If we don't understand it, neither will our readers. Although we do see and publish many 'sad' poems, we love to see those that celebrate the joys of life. We love juicy drippy details. Leave vagueness and generality at home under the bed."

⭐ 🌐 🔘 **ROMANTIC OUTSIDER**, 44 Spa Croft Rd., Ossett, West Yorkshire WF5 0HE United Kingdom. Phone: (01924)275814. E-mail: susandarlington@ukonline.co.uk. Established 1997. **Editor:** Susan Darlington.

Magazine Needs: "*Romantic Outsider* appears 2-3 times/year and provides exposure to new writers (and musicians); celebrates the social outsider." Wants "anything with passion. No overly sentimental or bigoted work." Has published poetry by Giovanni Malito, Jacqueline Disler, and Ian Sawicki. *Romantic Outsider* is about 40 pages, A5, photocopied and stapled with colored paper cover and occasional illustrations. Receives about 100 poems/year, accepts about 30%. Press run is about 100. Sample: $4 US, (£1 in UK). Make checks (sterling only) payable to Susan Darlington.

How to Submit: Submit 5 poems maximum at a time. Accepts previously published poems and simultaneous submissions. Accepts disk submissions (Word format) and e-mail submissions (attachments preferred). "Reply not guaranteed unless SAE/IRC included." Time between acceptance and publication is up to 5 months. Often comments on rejected poems. Responds in 1 month. Pays 1 contributor's copy. Reviews books and chapbooks of poetry in 250 words, single book format. Send materials for review consideration.

Advice: "More submissions from women especially welcome."

◐ **ROMANTICS QUARTERLY (Specialized: form/style)**, 318 Indian Trace #183, Weston FL 33326. E-mail: mar62451@aol.com. Website: www.thehypertexts.com/Romantics%20Quarterly.htm. Established 2000. **Editor:** Mary Rae. **Assistant Editor:** Skadi Macc Beorh.

Magazine Needs: "The vision of *Romantics Quarterly*, while continuing the tradition of the Great Romantics such as Blake, Wordswroth, Shelley, Yeats, and Housman, is to secure the place of formal verse, both rhymed and blank, in today's poetic arena. We are not collectors of oddities and discarded flights of fancy. Instead, we ask for well-crafted poetry, poetry in translation, short stories, and essays inspired by the muse and then wrought in the fires of discipline. *Romantics Quarterly* provides a home for the poet who may have been working alone with his or her craft, building an understanding of the past, even in the face of Postmodern critics." Translations must be accompanied by original. Has published by work by Rhina Espaillat, Richard Moore, Gail White, Michael R. Burch, Kevin N. Roberts, and Tim Myers. *Romantics Quarterly* is 75 pages, digest-sized, full-color original art on cover. Accepts 10% of poems submitted. Single copy: $6; subscription: $24. Sample: $5.

How to Submit: Submit up to 5 poems at a time. Considers but does not encourage previously published poems. Accepts submissions by postal mail; "E-mail submissions are acceptable, but those sent without a courteous note will not be read. We will not acknowledge e-mails redirecting us to a website." Cover letter preferred. Upcoming themes and guidelines available for SASE. Responds in 2 months. Pays 1 contributor's copy. Acquires one-time rights.

Advice: "We advise all contributors to consider subscribing, or to buy a copy of the journal before sending work. We publish many wonderful poets, and are delighted to consider the work of those who actually have a solid idea of what we are looking for."

◐ ◎ **ROOK PUBLISHING (Specialized: style/rhyming poetry)**, 1805 Calloway Dr., Clarksville TN 37042. (931)648-6225. Fax: (931)552-3050. Established 1996. **Publisher:** Edgar A. Lawson.

Book/Chapbook Needs & How to Submit: Rook Publishing's goal is "to secure and to re-introduce meaningful sonnet/rhyming poetry in published paperback books of 100-150 pages." Wants "rhyming/sonnet poetry on any subject. We would love poems for children; 10-50 lines seem to work well, open to any style. No profanity, religion-bashing, gay/lesbian subject matter, vampires, gore, aliens, pornography, haiku, free verse, or poems in poor taste." Recently published poetry by Mary Louise Westbrook, Stephen Scaer, and Byron Von Rosenberg. Rook Publishing publishes 2 paperbacks/year. Books are usually 100-120 pages, 5×7, photocopied, perfect-bound, 4-color cover, with original/in-house art. Accepts submissions by postal mail only. "No query letter will be necessary, published poems are fine with us." Responds to queries in 10 weeks. Pays royalties of 15-25%, $100, and 3 author's copies (out of a press run of 300-500); or 5 author's copies (out of a press run of 500). Order sample books by sending $8.50 to Rook Publishing.

Advice: "We do not believe the well of great rhyming poetry has been drained. We do believe that a growing generation will be visiting it more often than ever. We seek those writers, therefore, who write and believe in this form of poetry and the challenge that it offers."

★ ⬇ $◐ ◎ **ROOM OF ONE'S OWN (Specialized: women)**, P.O. Box 46160 Station D, Vancouver BC V6J 5G5 Canada. E-mail: contactus@roommagazine.com. Website: www.roommagazine.com. Established 1975.

Magazine Needs: *Room of One's Own* is a quarterly using "poetry by and about women, written from a feminist perspective. Nothing simplistic, clichéd. Short fiction also accepted." *Room of One's Own* is 96 pages, digest-sized. Press run is 1,000 for 420 subscribers of which 50-100 are libraries; 350 shelf sales. Subscription: $22 ($32 US or foreign). Sample: $8 plus IRCs.

How to Submit: "We prefer to receive 5-6 poems at a time, so we can select a pair or group." Include bio note. No simultaneous submissions. The mss are circulated to a collective, which "takes time." Publishes theme issues. Guidelines and upcoming themes available for SAE and 1 IRC. Responds in 6 months. Pays honorarium plus 2 copies. Acquires first North American serial rights. "We solicit reviews." Send material for review consideration, attn. book review editor.

◐ **ROSE ALLEY PRESS**, 4203 Brooklyn Ave. NE #103A, Seattle WA 98105. (206)633-2725. E-mail: rosealleypress@juno.com. Established 1995. **Publisher/Editor:** David D. Horowitz. "We presently do not read unsolicited manuscripts."

★ ☑ ◎ **ROSEBUD (Specialized: themes)**, P.O. Box 459, Cambridge WI 53523. (907)822-5146 or (800)786-5669. Website: www.rsbd.net. Established 1993. **Editor:** Rod Clark. **Poetry Editor:** Ron Ellis.

Magazine Needs: *Rosebud* is an attractive quarterly "for people who enjoy good writing." It is "a reader's feast for the eye, ear and heart" which has rotating themes/departments. Wants contemporary poetry with "strong images, real emotion, authentic voice; well crafted, literary quality. No inspirational verse." *Rosebud* is 136 pages, 7×10, offset-printed and perfect-bound with full-color coated card cover, art, graphics and ads. Receives about 700 poems/year, accepts 1%. Press run is 10,000 for 2,000 subscribers, 8,000 shelf sales. Subscription: $22. Sample: $6.95.

How to Submit: Submit 3-5 poems at a time. Accepts previously published poems and simultaneous submissions. Sometimes comments on rejected poems. Guidelines and explanation of themes/departments available for SASE. Responds in 3 months. Pays 3 copies. Acquires one-time rights.

Advice: "We are seeking stories, articles, profiles and poems of love, alienation, travel, humor, nostalgia and unexpected revelation. And something has to 'happen' in the pieces we choose."

☑ **ROSEWATER PUBLICATIONS; THROUGH SPIDER'S EYES**, 223 Chapel St., Leicester MA 01524-1115. (508)615-1095. E-mail: rosewaterbooks@yahoo.com. Established 1997. **Editor:** April M. Ardito.

Magazine Needs: *Through Spider's Eyes*, appearing annually, is "a showcase of the best of what RoseWater Publications receives. The best art is about art or has a strong message. We prefer coffeehouse and slam style poems, work that is just as powerful spoken as written. Multi-layered work always appreciated. Prefer modern and experimental work. Rhymed poetry must be exceptional; biased against 'God is great' and 'See the pretty trees and flowers' poetry." Recently published poetry by Timothy McCoy, Gwen Ellen Rider, Ed Fuqua, Jay Walker, Craig Nelson, and Alex Stolis. *Through Spider's Eyes* is 20-36 pages, digest-sized, photocopied b&w. Receives and accepts varied number of poems/year. Publishes about 10-40 poems/issue. Press run is 50. Single copy: $4.50. Make checks payable to April M. Ardito.

How to Submit: Submit up to 5 poems at a time. Line length for poetry is 3 minimum, 250 maximum. Accepts previously published poems; no simultaneous submissions. Accepts e-mail submissions, either as attachment (.txt or .doc format) or in textbox. Cover letter is preferred. Likes "disposable manuscripts; casual, personal cover letter; SASE required." Reads submissions year round. Does not publish seasonal poems. Accepts personal checks, money orders, or PayPal for all samples and subscriptioins. Time between acceptance and publication is up to 1 year. "Editor always attempts to read all submissions personally, but has a few people who help out when submissions get overwhelming." Seldom comments on rejected poems. "Prefer that poets submit a full chapbook-length manuscript. Responds in up to 6 months. Pays 1 copy per accepted poem. Acquires one-time rights and reprint rights (possible inclusion in an anthology at a later date). Reviews books and chapbooks of poetry and other magazines/journals in less than 1 page, single book format. Send materials for review consideration to April M. Ardito.

Book/Chapbook Needs & How to Submit: RoseWater Publications "wants to create an aesthically pleasing product for poets who spend as much time on the stage as with the page." Hopes to publish full-length anthologies in the future. Publishes 5-10 chapbooks/year. Chapbooks are usually 20-64 pages, photocopied b&w, stapled, colored paper, cardstock, or business stock cover with original cover design. "Please send full manuscript (16-60 pages). We do not wish to see queries. We would prefer to see a poet's full vision." Responds to mss in up to 6 months. Pays 50% of copies (out of a press run of 50-100). **Approximately 10% of titles are author-subsidy published.** "Poet pays for layout and editing fees. RoseWater Publications would like to discontinue subsidy publishing in the next 1-2 years." Order sample books/chapbooks by sending $4.50 to April M. Ardito.

Also Offers: Also publishes poetry for vending machines. Send full ms (up to 120 lines), titled. Press run of 40, author receives 20 copies. Format is 8½×11 sheet folded in eighths.

Advice: "Spend a lot of time reading and re-reading, writing and re-writing. Always try to keep one finger on the pulse of contemporary poetry, as much to know what isn't working as what is. Stay true to yourself and your vision. Use your words to lure others into your experiences."

▢ ◎ **RUAH; POWER OF POETRY (Specialized: spirituality)**, Dominican School of Philosophy/Theology, 2401 Ridge Rd., Berkeley CA 94709. Fax: (510)596-1860. E-mail: cjrenzop@yah oo.com. Established 1990. **General Editor:** C.J. Renz, O.P. **Editor:** Ann Applegarth.

Magazine Needs: *Ruah*, an annual journal published in June, "provides a 'non-combative forum' for poets who have had few or no opportunities to publish their work. Theme: spiritual poetry. The journal has three sections: general poems, featured poet, and chapbook contest winners." Wants "poetry which is of a 'spiritual nature,' i.e., describes an experience of the transcendent. No religious affiliation preferences; no style/format limitations. No 'satanic verse'; no individual poems longer than four typed pages." Has published poetry by Benjamin Alire Saens, Jean Valentine, Alberto Rios, and Luci Shaw. *Ruah* is 60-80 pages, digest-sized, photocopied and perfect-bound, glossy card stock cover, color photo, includes occasional b&w sketches of original artwork. Receives about 350 poems/year, accepts 10-20%. Press run is 150 for about 100 subscribers of which 7 are libraries, 10 shelf sales; 50 distributed free to authors, reviewers and inquiries. Subscription: $10 plus $1.50 p&h. Sample: $5 plus $1.50 postage/handling. Make checks payable to Power of Poetry/DSPT.

How to Submit: Submit 3-5 poems at a time. Accepts simultaneous submissions; no previously published poems. Accepts submissions by e-mail (MS Word 97 file attachments or in text box), by fax, on disk, by regular mail. Chapbooks, however, cannot be submitted by e-mail. "Do not mail submissions to publisher's address. Contact general editor via e-mail for current address or send written inquiries to Dominican School." Reads submissions December through March only. Time between acceptance and publication is up to 6 months. Poems are circulated to an editorial board. "Poems reviewed by writers and/or scholars in field of creative writing/literature." Guidelines available for SASE or by e-mail. Responds in 2 weeks. Pays 1 copy/poem. Acquires first rights.

Book/Chapbook Needs & How to Submit: Power of Poetry publishes 1 chapbook of spiritual poetry through their annual competition. Chapbooks are usually 24 pages, and are included as part of *Ruah*. "Poets should e-mail General Editor for contest guidelines and submission address or write to Dominican School." Entry fee: $10. Deadline: December 30. Responds to queries in up to 6 weeks; to mss in up to 6 months. Winner receives publication in a volume of *Ruah* and 25 author's copies (out of a press run of 250).

Advice: "*Ruah* is a gathering place in which new poets can come to let their voice be heard alongside of and in the context of 'more established' poets. The journal hopes to provide some breakthrough experiences of the Divine at work in our world."

RUNES, A REVIEW OF POETRY, Arctos Press, P.O. Box 401, Sausalito CA 94966-0401. (415)331-2503. Fax: (415)331-3092. E-mail: RunesRev@aol.com. Website: http://members.aol.com/Runes. Established 2000. **Editors:** Susan Terris and CB Follett. Member: SPAN, BAIPA.

Magazine Needs: *RUNES, A Review Of Poetry* appears annually. "Our taste is eclectic, but we are looking for excellence in craft." Wants "poems that have passion, originality, and conviction. We are looking for narrative and lyric poetry that is well-crafted and has something surprising to say. No greeting card verse." Recently published poetry by Norman Dubie, Jane Hirshfield, Shirley Kaufman, Li-Young Lee, David St. John. *RUNES* is 144 pages, digest-sized, professionally-printed, flat-spined, glossy card cover, with art/graphics. Receives about 6,000 poems/year, accepts about 100. Press run is 1,000. Single copy: $12; subscription: $12. Sample: $10. Make checks payable to Arctos Press.

How to Submit: Submit no more than 5 poems at a time. Prefers poems under 100 lines. Accepts simultaneous submissions if notified; no previously published poems. No e-mail or disk submissions. SASE required. Reads submissions April 1-May 31 only. Time between acceptance and publication is 6 months. Seldom comments on rejections. Publishes theme issues regularly. Themes will be "Storm" in 2004, "Signals" in 2005. Guidelines and themes available for SASE, by e-mail, in publication, or on website. Responds in 4 months. Sometimes sends prepublication galleys. Pays 1 contributor's copy. Acquires first North American serial rights.

Also Offers: Poetry competition for 2003 will have same theme as magazine—"Storm." 2004 judge will be Jane Hirshfield. "Three poems plus a one-year subscription for $15. For publication in *Runes*, it is *not* necessary to enter competition. All submitted poems will be read." Make checks payable to Arctos Press. (See separate listing for Arctos Press in this section.)

Advice: "No one can write in a vacuum. If you want to write good poetry, you must read good poetry—classic as well as modern work."

S.W.A.G., THE MAGAZINE OF SWANSEA'S WRITERS AND ARTISTS; S.W.A.G. NEWSLETTER, Dan-y-Bryn, 74 CWM Level Rd., Brynhyfryd, Swansea SA5 9DY

Wales, United Kingdom. Established 1992. **Chairman/Editor:** Peter Thabit Jones.

Magazine Needs: *S.W.A.G.* appears biannually and publishes poetry, prose, articles, and illustrations. "Our purpose is to publish good literature." Wants "first-class poetry—up to 40 lines, any style." Has published poetry by Adrian Mitchell, Alan Llwyd, Mike Jenkins, and Dafydd Rowlands. *S.W.A.G.* is 48 pages, A4, professionally printed on coated paper and saddle-stapled with glossy paper cover, photos and illustrations. Accepts 12-20 poems/issue. Press run is 500 for 120 subscribers of which 50 are libraries. Subscription: £5. Sample (including guidelines): £2.50 plus postage.

How to Submit: "Interested poets should obtain sample beforehand (to see what we offer)." Submit 6 poems, typed. No previously published poems or simultaneous submissions. Cover letter required. Time between acceptance and publication is 4-6 months. Poems are circulated to an editorial board. "Editor chooses/discusses choices with board." Guidelines available for SASE (or SAE with IRCs). Responds ASAP. Pays 2 contributor's copies plus a copy of S.W.A.G.'s newsletter. Staff reviews books or poetry (half page to full). Send materials for review consideration.

Also Offers: The Swansea Writers and Artists Group (S.W.A.G.) also publishes a newsletter containing information on the group's events. Send SASE for details on the organization. "We also publish Welsh language poetry."

$ 🖂 ◎ SACHEM PRESS (Specialized: translations, bilingual), P.O. Box 9, Old Chatham NY 12136-0009. Established 1980. **Editor:** Louis Hammer.

Book/Chapbook Needs: Sachem, a small press publisher of poetry and fiction, both hardcover and flat-spined paperbacks. Wants to see "strong, compelling, even visionary work, English-language or translations." Has published poetry by Cesar Vallejo, Yannis Ritsos, 24 leading poets of Spain (in an anthology), Miltos Sahtouris, and Louis Hammer. The paperbacks average 120 pages and the anthology of Spanish poetry contains 340 pages. Each poem is printed in both Spanish and English, and there are biographical notes about the authors. The small books cost $6.95 and $9.95 and the anthology $24.

How to Submit: No new submissions, only statements of projects, until January 2004. Submit mss January through April only. Royalties are 10% maximum, after expenses are recovered, plus 50 author's copies. Rights are negotiable. Book catalog is free "when available," and poets can purchase books from Sachem "by writing to us, 33⅓% discount."

◐ ◎ SACRED JOURNEY: THE JOURNAL OF FELLOWSHIP IN PRAYER (Specialized: Christian), 291 Witherspoon St., Princeton NJ 08542. (609)924-6863. Fax: (609)924-6910. E-mail: editorial@sacredjourney.org. Website: www.sacredjourney.org. Established 1950. **Contact:** Editor.

Magazine Needs: *Sacred Journey* is an interfaith bimonthly "concerned with prayer, meditation and spiritual life" using short poetry "with deep religious (or spiritual) feeling." *Sacred Journey* is 48 pages, digest-sized, professionally printed, saddle-stapled with glossy card cover. Accepts about 10% of submissions received. Press run is 10,000. Subscription: $18. Sample free.

How to Submit: Submit 5 poems at a time, double-spaced. Accepts simultaneous submissions and "sometimes" previously published poems. Accepts submissions on disk, by e-mail (in text box), and by regular mail. Cover letter preferred. Responds in 2 months. Pays 5 copies.

◐ ◎ SAHARA (Specialized: regional/Central New England), P.O. Box 20705, Worcester MA 01602. (508)798-5672. E-mail: SaharaJournal@aol.com. Established 2000. **Managing Editor:** Lydia Mancevice.

Magazine Needs: *Sahara* appears biannually in June and December. "We are dedicated to the poetry of our region, Central New England." Wants "unaffected, clear writing in any style. Poems may exist, but they should mean something, too. No pointless obscenities." Accepts poetry written by children. Recently published poetry by Dennis Brutus, Robert Cording, Martin Espada, Laura Jehn Menides, Judith Ferrar, and Lyn Lifshin. *Sahara* is 90 pages, digest-sized, offset-printed, perfect-bound, b&w printed card cover with graphics. Receives about 600 poems/year, accepts about 10%. Publishes about 30-40 poems/issues. Press run is 300 for 70 subscribers of which 10 are libraries, 100-150 shelf sales. Single copy: $10; subscription: $18. Sample: $11.50. Make checks payable to Elizabethan Press.

How to Submit: Submit 5 poems at a time. No previously published poems or simultaneous submissions. No fax, e-mail, or disk submissions. Cover letter is required. "Please state the titles of the poems and include a bio." Reads submissions continually. Submit seasonal poems 6 months in advance. Time between acceptance and publication is 6 months. "Material is circulated among several editors and must find at least one strong advocate to be considered." Seldom comments on rejected poems. "Subscribers are preferred." Responds in up to 4 months. Sometimes sends prepublication galleys. Pays 1 contributor's copy. Acquires one-time rights. Reviews books and chapbooks of poetry in 300-600 words. Send materials for review consideration to *Sahara*.

Advice: "Keep revising and submitting your work."

$ ☐ ◎ ST. ANTHONY MESSENGER (Specialized: religious, Catholic), 28 W. Liberty St., Cincinnati OH 45210-1298. Fax: (513)241-0399. Website: www.americancatholic.org. **Poetry Editor:** Christopher Heffron.

Magazine Needs: *St. Anthony Messenger* is a monthly 56-page magazine, press run 340,000, for Catholic families, mostly with children in grade school, high school, or college. Some issues feature a poetry page that uses poems appropriate for their readership. Poetry submissions are always welcome despite limited need. Accepts poetry by young writers, age 14 and up.

How to Submit: "Submit seasonal poetry (Christmas/Easter/nature poems) several months in advance. Submit a few poems at a time; do not send us your entire collection of poetry. We seek to publish accessible poetry of high quality. Poems must be original, under 25 lines, spiritual/inspirational in nature a plus, but not required. We do not publish poems that have already been published— must be first run. Please include your social security number with your submission." Accepts submissions by fax or by e-mail (as attachment or in text box). Guidelines available by fax and for standard SASE, free sample for 9 × 12 SASE. Pays $2/line on acceptance and 2 copies. Acquires first worldwide serial rights. *St. Anthony Messenger* poetry occasionally receives awards from the Catholic Press Association Annual Competition.

$ ◎ ◎ ST. JOSEPH MESSENGER & ADVOCATE OF THE BLIND (Specialized: religious), 537 Pavonia Ave., P.O. Box 288, Jersey City NJ 07303. Established 1898. **Poetry Editor:** Sister Mary Kuiken, C.S.J.P.

Magazine Needs: *St. Joseph Messenger* is semiannual and publishes "brief but thought-filled poetry; do not want lengthy and issue-filled." Most of the poets they have used are previously unpublished. Receives 400-500 submissions/year, accepts about 50. *St. Joseph Messenger* is 16 pages, magazine-sized, and prints about 2 pages of poetry/issue. Press run 14,000. Subscription: $5.

How to Submit: Currently oversupplied; not accepting submissions. Sometimes comments on rejected poems. Publishes theme issues. Guidelines, a free sample, and upcoming themes available for SASE. Responds within 1 month. Pays $10-20/poem and 2 copies.

★ ◎ SALT HILL; SALT HILL POETRY PRIZE; SALT HILL SHORT SHORT FICTION PRIZE, English Dept., Syracuse University, Syracuse NY 13244-1170. (315)443-1984. E-mail: salthill@cas.syr.edu. Website: http://students.syr.edu/salthill/. Established 1994. **Editor:** Ellen Litman. **Contact:** Poetry Editor.

Magazine Needs: *Salt Hill*, published biannually, features "high-quality contemporary writing including poetry, fiction, essays, book reviews, and artwork." Also seeks hypertext submissions for online issues. E-mail url to letthewordsout@aol.com. or visit website for more information. "*Salt Hill* has an open aesthetic and a revolving editorialship. Imagination, technical innovation, and a sense of humor are all appreciated, but we publish good poems of all varieties." Recently published poetry by Campbell McGrath, Dean Young, Kim Addonizio, and James Tate. *Salt Hill* is 120-150 pages, digest-sized, perfect-bound, with art, photography and ads. Receives about 3,000 poems/year, accepts approximately 2%. Press run is 1,000. Subscription: $15. Sample: $8.

How to Submit: Submit 5 poems at a time. Accepts simultaneous submissions; no previously published poems. Cover letter preferred with a brief bio. Time between acceptance and publication is 2-8 months. Seldom comments on rejected poems. Guidelines available for SASE. Responds in up to 6 months. Pays 2 copies. Acquires one-time rights. Reviews books or chapbooks of poetry or other magazines in 900-3,000 words and/or essay reviews of single/multi book format. Send material for review consideration to Book Review Editor, at the above address.

Also Offers: Sponsors annual *Salt Hill* Poetry Prize, awarding $500 1st Prize and publication, $250

2nd Prize and publication and $100 3rd Prize and publication. Submit unpublished poems with name, address and phone on each. Entry fee is $5 for up to 150 lines (1-3 poems); $3 extra for every additional 100 lines. Include SASE. Postmark deadline May 1. Also sponsors *Salt Hill* Fiction Prize, awarding $500 1st Prize and publication, $250 2nd Prize and publication, $100 3rd Prize and publication. "Submit original unpublished fiction up to 1,500 words with a $10 entry fee. Include SASE. Postmark deadline: January 15th."

✪ ❍ ◎ **SAMSARA (Specialized: suffering/healing)**, P.O. Box 467, Ashburn VA 20147. E-mail: rdfgoalie@aol.com. Website: http://samsara.cjb.net. Established 1993. **Editor:** R. David Fulcher.

Magazine Needs: *Samsara* is a biannual publication of poetry and fiction dealing with suffering and healing. "Both metered verse and free verse poetry is welcome if dealing with the theme of suffering/healing." Has published poetry by Michael Foster and Jeff Parsley. *Samsara* is 80 pages, magazine-sized, desktop published, with a colored card stock cover and b&w art. Receives about 200 poems/year, accepts approximately 15%. Publishes about 6-10 poems/issue. Press run is 300 for 200 subscribers. Single copy: $5.50. Subscription: $10. Make checks payable to *Samsara*.

How to Submit: Submit up to 5 poems at a time. Line length for poetry is 3 minimum, 100 maximum. No previously published or simultaneous submissions. Accepts submissions by postal mail only. Time between acceptance and publication is 3 months. Seldom comments on rejected poems. Guidelines available for SASE and on website. Responds in 2 months. pays 1 contributor's copy. Acquires one-time rights. Reviews books nd chapbooks of poetry in 500 words, single book format. Send material for review consideration to editor.

❍ **SANSKRIT**, UNC Charlotte, Cone University Center, Charlotte NC 28223. (704)687-2326. Fax: (704)687-3394. E-mail: sanskrit@email.uncc.edu. Website: www.uncc.edu/life/smp/smp-sanskrit.life/smp/smp_sanskrit.html. Established 1965. **Editor:** Jénice Bastien. **Literary Editor:** Sarah Feinman.

Magazine Needs: *Sanskrit* is a literary annual appearing in April that uses poetry. "No restrictions as to form or genre, but we do look for maturity and sincerity in submissions. Nothing trite or sentimental." Has published poetry by Kimberleigh Luke-Stallings. Seeks "to encourage and promote beginning and established artists and writers." *Sanskrit* is 60-65 pages, magazine-sized, flat-spined, printed on quality matte paper with heavy matte card cover. Press run is 3,500 for about 100 subscribers of which 2 are libraries. Sample: $10.

How to Submit: Submit up to 15 poems at a time. Accepts simultaneous submissions. Accepts submissions by e-mail (as attachment or in text box) and by postal mail. Cover letter with 30-70 word bio required (please do not list previous publications as a bio). Guidelines available for SASE or by e-mail. Submission deadline is the first Friday in November. Editor comments on submissions "infrequently." Responds in 2 months. Pays 1 contributor's copy.

$ ◙ **SARABANDE BOOKS, INC.; THE KATHRYN A. MORTON PRIZE IN POETRY**, 2234 Dundee Rd., Suite 200, Louisville KY 40205. (502)458-4028. Fax: (502)458-4065. E-mail: sarabandeb@aol.com. Website: www.SarabandeBooks.org. Established 1994. **Editor-in-Chief:** Sarah Gorham.

Book/Chapbook Needs: Sarabande Books publishes books of poetry and short fiction. Wants "poetry of superior artistic quality. Otherwise no restraints or specifications." Has published poetry by Eleanor Lerman, Frank Bidart, Ralph Angel, Belle Waring, and Afaa Michael Weaver.

How to Submit: Query with 10 sample poems during the month of September only. No fax or e-mail submissions. SASE must always be enclosed. Accepts previously published poems if acknowledged as such and simultaneous submissions "if notified immediately of acceptance elsewhere." Seldom comments on rejected poems. Responds to queries in 3 months, to mss (if invited) in 6 months. Guidelines available for SASE. Pays 10% royalties and author's copies.

Also Offers: The Kathryn A. Morton Prize in Poetry is awarded to a book-length ms (at least 48 pages) submitted between January 1 and February 15. $20 handling fee and entry form required. Guidelines available in November for SASE or on website. Winner receives a $2,000 cash award, publication, and a standard royalty contract. All finalists are considered for publication. "At least half of our list is drawn from contest submissions." Entry fee: $20. Reads entries January 1 through

February 15 only. Competition receives 1,200 entries. Most recent contest winner was Connie St. George Comer for *The Unrequited*. Judge was Stephen Dunn.

Ⓩ SATURDAY PRESS, Box 43548, Upper Montclair NJ 07043. (973)256-5053. Fax: (973)256-4987. E-mail: saturdaypr@aol.com. Established 1975. **Editor:** S. Ladov. "We do not plan to read manuscripts in the foreseeable future."

✪ $Ⓩ SCIENCE FICTION POETRY ASSOCIATION; STAR*LINE (Specialized: science fiction, horror); THE RHYSLING ANTHOLOGY, P.O. Box 13222, Berkeley CA 94712-4222. (205)553-2284. E-mail: timpratt@sff.net. Website: www.dm.net/~bejay/sfpa.htm. Established 1978. **Editor:** Tim Pratt.

Magazine Needs: The Association publishes *Star*Line*, a bimonthly newsletter and poetry magazine. "Open to all forms—free verse, traditional forms, light verse—so long as your poetry shows skilled use of the language and makes a good use of science fiction, science, fantasy, horror or speculative motifs." The Association also publishes *The Rhysling Anthology*, a yearly collection of nominations from the membership "for the best science fiction/fantasy long and short poetry of the preceding year." Also accepts poetry written by children. The magazine has published poetry by Lawrence Schimel, Kendall Evans, Charlie Jacob, Terry A. Garey and Timons Esaias. The digest-sized magazine and anthology are saddle-stapled, photocopied, with numerous illustrations and decorations. Has 250 subscribers of which 1 is a library. Subscription: $13/6 issues. Sample: $2. Send requests for copies/membership information to John Nichols, Secretary-Treasurer, 6075 Bellevue Dr., North Olmstead OH 44070. Submissions to *Star*Line* only. Receives about 300-400 submissions/year, accepts approximately 80—mostly short (under 50 lines).

How to Submit: Send 3-5 poems/submission, typed. No simultaneous submissions or queries. Accepts e-mail submissions "as part of the e-mail message, no attachments." Include brief cover letter. Responds in 1 month. Pays 5¢/line plus 1¢/word and a copy. Buys first North American serial rights. Reviews books of poetry "within the science fiction/fantasy field" in 50-500 words. Open to unsolicited reviews. Poets may send material for review consideration to Todd Earl Rhodes, 735 Queensbury Loop, Winter Garden FL 34787-5808.

Ⓩ Ⓩ SCORE MAGAZINE; SCORE CHAPBOOKS AND BOOKLETS (Specialized: form), 1111 E. Fifth, Moscow ID 83843. (208)892-8826. E-mail: orion@pullman.com. **Poetry Editor:** Crag Hill.

Magazine Needs: Score Chapbooks and Booklets is a small press publisher of visual poetry in the annual magazine *Score*, booklets, postcards, and broadsides. Wants "poetry which melds language and the visual arts such as concrete poetry; experimental use of language, words, and letters—forms. The appearance of the poem should have as much to say as the text. Poems on any subject; conceptual poetry; poems which use experimental, non-traditional methods to communicate their meanings." Doesn't want "traditional verse of any kind—be it free verse or rhymed." Has published poetry by Joel Lewis, Nico Vassilakis, Jono Schneider, Michael Basinski, and Sheila Murphy. Editor says that it is impossible to quote a sample because "some of our poems consist of only a single word—or in some cases no recognizable words." *Score* is 48-72 pages, magazine-sized, offset-printed, saddle-stapled, using b&w graphics, 2-color matte card cover. Press run is 200 for 25 subscribers, of which 6 are libraries, about 50-60 shelf sales. Sample: $10.

How to Submit: We strongly advise looking at a sample copy before submitting if you are not familiar with visual poetry. Accepts previously published poems "if noted"; no simultaneous submissions. Guidelines available for SASE. Pays 2 contributor's copies. Send materials for review consideration.

Book/Chapbook Needs & How to Submit: For chapbook consideration send entire ms. No simultaneous submissions. Almost always comments on rejected poems. Pays 25% of the press run. Subsidy publishing available "if author requests it."

Ⓒ SCRIPT MAGAZINE; BROWNISLANDPUBLISHING.COM, 6818 N. Wayne, Chicago IL 60626. E-mail: brwneyz24@hotmail.com. Website: http://brownislandpublishing.com. Established 2002. **Editor:** Godfrey Logan.

Magazine Needs: Appearing 4 or 5 times/year online, *Script Magazine* publishes "a large number of poems per issue because we believe that there are a lot of poets who would like to go beyond writing for a hobby and would like to be given a chance to get published. We still look for quality." Print version is desk jet-printed, stapled, newsletter format cover, with photos. Accepts about 90% of poems received. Publishes 10-20 poems/issue. Single copy: $3, subscription: $12.

How to Submit: Charges $2 reading fee for more than 10 poems. Accepts print and online submissions with background information/inspiration. Reads submissions year round. "I read over poems myself with a keen open mind." Does not respond to rejected submissions. Occasionally publishes theme issues. Guidelines available on website. Pays for featured author ("entire issue dedicated to author") and photos ("$5 or more per print, $50 for featured artist honor"). Also pays 1 contributor's copy. Acquires one-time rights. Reviews books of poetry in single book format **(charges $5 for book reviews)**. Poets may send material for review consideration to the editor.

Also Offers: Annual "end-of-year, best-of-year anthology," 30-60 pages, spiral-bound, cardstock cover with photo or artwork.

Advice: "Poetry is beauty and pain, ironies, sentiment. The single most beautiful thing in the world."

★ ✂ ◪ **SCRIVENER**, Poetry Dept., McGill University, 853 Sherbrooke St. W., Montreal QC H3A 2T6 Canada. (514)398-6588. E-mail: scrivenermag@hotmail.com. Established 1980. **Contact:** Katie Franklin and John Woodside.

Magazine Needs: *Scrivener* is an annual review of contemporary literature and art published in April by students at McGill University. With a circulation throughout North America, *Scrivener* publishes the best of new Canadian and American poetry, short fiction, criticism, essays, reviews, and interviews. "*Scrivener* is committed to publishing the work of new and unpublished writers." Recently published poetry by Nicola Little, Shane Neilson, Giovanni Malito, and Sharon Desmarais. *Scrivener* is perfect-bound, 8½×7, 120 pages, with 25 pages of b&w photography printed on coated paper. Text and graphics are printed in b&w duotone cover. Subscription: $9 Canadian in Canada, $11 Canadian in US and $13 Canadian anywhere else. Prices include postage.

How to Submit: January 15 deadline for submissions; contributors encouraged to submit in early fall. Send 5-10 poems, one poem/page; be sure that each poem is identified separately, with titles, numbers, etc. Accepts e-mail submissions (attachments or within text box). Submissions require SASE for return. Comments or questions regarding back issues or submissions may be sent to scrivene rmag@hotmail.com. *Scrivener* only operates fully between September and April. Responds in 6 months. Pays 1 copy (multiple copies available upon request).

★ 🌐 ◪ **SEAM**, 10 Collingwood Rd., South Woodham Ferrers, Chelmsford CM3 5YB, United Kingdom. Established 1994. **Editor:** Frank Dullaghan.

Magazine Needs: *Seam* appears twice/year (in January and July) to publish "good contemporary poetry." Wants "high quality poems that engage the reader in any length." Has published poetry by Annemarie Austin, Vernon Scannell, Kim Bridgford, Morgan Kenney, Caroline Natzler, and Angus Macmillan. *Seam* is 64 pages, A5, folded with b&w cover photo. Receives about 2,000 poems/year, accepts about 5%. Press run is 300. Subscription: £6/year, £10 overseas. Sample: £3, £5 overseas.

How to Submit: Submit 5-6 poems at a time; each poem on 1 sheet of paper (A4 size). No poems previously published in UK or simultaneous submissions. Sometimes comments on rejected poems. Pays 1 contributor's copy.

Also Offers: Essex Poetry Festival Competition. Annual, send for details.

SEAWEED SIDESHOW CIRCUS, P.O. Box 234, Jackson WI 53037. (414)791-1109. Fax: (262)677-0896. E-mail: sscircus@aol.com. Website: http://hometown.aol.com/SSCircus/sscweb.ht ml. Established 1994. **Editor:** Andrew Wright Milam.

Book/Chapbook Needs: Seaweed Sideshow Circus is "a place for young or new poets to publish a chapbook." Has published *Main Street* by Steven Paul Lansky and *The Moon Incident* by Amy McDonald. Publishes 1 chapbook/year. Chapbooks are usually 30 pages, digest-sized, photocopied and saddle-stapled with cardstock cover. Send 5-10 sample poems and cover letter with bio and credits. Responds to queries in 3 weeks; to mss in 3 months. Pays royalties of 10 author's copies (out of a press run of 100). Order sample chapbooks by sending $6.

How to Submit: Accepts fax, postal mail, and e-mail submissions (include in body); no fax submissions. Include SASE and name and address on each page. Cover letter preferred. Time between acceptance and publication is 1-2 months. Often comments on rejected poems. Guidelines available for SASE. Responds in 2 months. Pays 1 contributor's copy. Rights revert to author upon publication.

🌐 🖉 **SECOND AEON PUBLICATIONS**, 19 Southminster Rd., Roath, Cardiff CF23 SAT Wales. Phone/fax: (02920)493093. E-mail: peter@peterfinch.co.uk. Website: www.peterfinch.co.uk. Established 1966. **Poetry Editor:** Peter Finch. Does not accept unsolicited mss.

🖉 **SEEMS**, P.O. Box 359, Lakeland College, Sheboygan WI 53082-0359. (920)565-1276 or (920)565-3871. Fax: (920)565-1206. E-mail: kelder@excel.net. Website: www.1.lakeland.edu/seems. Established 1971. **Editor:** Karl Elder.

Magazine Needs: *Seems* is published irregularly. This is a handsomely printed, nearly square (7 × 8¼) magazine, saddle-stapled, generous with white space on heavy paper. Two of the issues are considered chapbooks, and the editor suggests sampling *Seems #14, What Is The Future Of Poetry?* for $5, consisting of essays by 22 contemporary poets, and "If you don't like it, return it and we'll return your $5." *Explain That You Live: Mark Strand with Karl Elder* (#29) is available for $3. There are usually about 20 pages of poetry/issue. Has recently published poetry by Bruce Dethlefsen, Doug Flaherty, Janet McCann, Kevin McFadden, and Craig Paulenich. Print run is 500 for over 250 subscribers of which 20 are libraries. Single copy: $4; subscription: $16/4 issues.

How to Submit: There is a 1- to 2-year backlog. "People may call or fax with virtually any question, understanding that the editor may have no answer." No simultaneous submissions. No fax or e-mail submissions. Guidelines available on website. Responds in up to 3 months (slower in summer). Pays 1 copy. Acquires first North American serial rights and permission to publish online. Returns rights upon publication.

Advice: "Visit the new Seems website."

🖉 **SENSATIONS MAGAZINE (Specialized: membership/subscription, themes)**, 2 Radio Ave., A5, Secaucus NJ 07094. Website: www.sensationsmag.com. Established 1987. **Publisher/Executive Editor:** David Messineo.

Magazine Needs: "*Sensations Magazine* is celebrating its 16th anniversary of independent publishing with a four issue salute to the arts. We are interested in well-crafted poetry: accent on *craft*. Beginning writers should know what a sonnet, a sestina, a pantoum, and a villanelle are (and preferably have attempted to write one of each) before submitting material to us." Has published work by Robert Bovino, Kerri M. Habben, Helen M. Malcom, Faith Vicinanza, and Vicki Moss. *Sensations Magazine* is "printed from a 600 dpi printer, hand collated and bound" with full-color photography. See website for purchasing information. Sample issues: $15 or $30.

How to Submit: "Be aware that we charge a nominal entry fee for nonsubscribers, and detailed critiques (one of our specialties) are offered only to full-year subscribers." Upcoming themes and guidelines available for SASE and on website. Since 1994 has offered $3.25/line "for the top poem published every year."

Advice: "Remember to spell check your work and *always* be courteous to the publisher."

$ 🖉 **THE SEWANEE REVIEW**, University of the South, Sewanee TN 37383-1000. (931)598-1246. E-mail: rjones@sewanee.edu. Website: www.sewanee.edu/sreview/home.html. Established 1892, thus being our nation's oldest continuously published literary quarterly. **Editor:** George Core.

Magazine Needs: Fiction, criticism, and poetry are invariably of the highest establishment standards. Many of our major poets appear here from time to time. *Sewanee Review* has published poetry by Wendell Berry, Catherine Savage Brosman, Debora Greger, Peter Makuck, David Mason, and Kathryn Starbuck. Each issue is a hefty paperback of nearly 200 pages, conservatively bound in matte paper, always of the same typography. Open to all styles and forms: formal sequences, metered verse, structured free verse, sonnets, and lyric and narrative forms—all accessible and intelligent. Press run is 3,200. Sample: $8.50 (US), $9.50 (foreign). Subscription: $24/year, $30/year (institutions).

How to Submit: Submit up to 6 poems at a time. Line length for poetry is 40 maximum. No simultaneous submissions. No electronic submissions. "Unsolicited works should not be submitted between June 1 and August 31. A response to any submission received during that period will be greatly delayed." Guidelines available for SASE, by e-mail, and on website. Responds in 6 weeks.

Pays 60¢/line, plus 2 copies (and reduced price for additional copies). Also includes brief, standard, and essay-reviews.

Also Offers: Presents the Aiken Taylor Award for Modern American Poetry to established poets. Poets *cannot* apply for this prize.

Advice: "Please keep in mind that for each poem published in *Sewanee Review*, approximately 250 poems are considered."

SHADES OF DECEMBER, P.O. Box 786, Natick MA 01760. E-mail: fiction@shadesofdecember.com or poetry@shadesofdecember.com. Website: www.shadesofdecember.com. Established 1998. **Poetry Editor:** Alexander C.P. Danner. **Fiction Editor:** Brandy L. Danner.

Magazine Needs: Published quarterly, *Shades of December* "provides a forum that is open to all forms of writing (poetry, prose, drama, etc.). Topics and tones range from the academic to the whimsical. We are open to any genre and style. No trite greeting-card verse." Has published poetry by Joe Lucia, William Doreski, Virgil Suarez, and Claudia Grinnell. *Shades of December* has discontinued print publication in favor of publishing exclusively online.

How to Submit: Submit 3-7 poems at a time. Accepts simultaneous submissions; no previously published poems. Accepts e-mail submissions in an attached file. Cover letter preferred. "Cover letter should include brief 75-word bio listing previous publications/noteworthy facts. Include SASE. All electronic submissions should be in an IBM-recognizable format (any version MS Word, Corel Word Perfect)." Time between acceptance and publication is 1-4 months. Seldom comments on rejected poems. Guidelines available for SASE or on website. Responds in up to 6 months. Sometimes sends prepublication galleys. Acquires one-time rights.

SHEMOM (Specialized: motherhood), 2486 Montgomery Ave., Cardiff CA 92007. E-mail: pdfrench@cox.net. Established 1997. **Editor:** Peggy French.

Magazine Needs: "Appearing 2-4 times/year, *Shemom* celebrates motherhood and the joys and struggles that present themselves in that journey. It includes poetry, essays, book and CD reviews, recipes, art, and children's poetry. Open to any style, prefer free verse. We celebrate motherhood and related issues. Haiku and native writing also enjoyed. Love to hear from children." *Shemom* is a 10-20-page zine. Receives about 70 poems/year, accepts 50%. Press run is 50 for 30 subscribers. Single copy: $3; subscription: $12/4 issues. Sample: $3.50. Make checks payable to Peggy French.

How to Submit: Submit 3 poems at a time. Accepts previously published poems and simultaneous submissions included in body of message. Accepts e-mail submissions (as attachment or in text box). "Prefer e-mail submission, but not required if material is to be returned, please include a SASE." Guidelines available for SASE or by e-mail. Time between acceptance and publication is 3 months. Responds in 2 months. Pays 1 copy. Acquires one-time rights.

SHENANDOAH; THE JAMES BOATWRIGHT III PRIZE FOR POETRY, Troubadour Theater, 2nd Floor, Washington and Lee University, Lexington VA 24450-0303. (540)458-8765. E-mail: lleech@wlu.edu. Website: http://shenandoah.wlu.edu. Established 1950. **Editor:** R.T. Smith.

● Poetry published in *Shenandoah* has been included in the 1999 and 2000 volumes of *The Best American Poetry*.

Magazine Needs: Published at Washington and Lee University, *Shenandoah* is a quarterly literary magazine. Has published poetry by Mary Oliver, Ted Kooser, W.S. Merwin, and Marilyn Hacker. *Shenandoah* is 160 pages, digest-sized, perfect-bound, professionally printed with full-color cover.

FOR EXPLANATIONS OF THESE SYMBOLS,
SEE THE INSIDE FRONT COVER OF THIS BOOK.

Generally, it is open to all styles and forms. Press run is 1,900. Subscription: $22/year; $35/2 years; $45/3 years. Sample: $5.

How to Submit: All submissions should be typed on one side of the paper only. Your name and address must be clearly written on the upper right corner of the the ms. Does not accept e-mail submissions. Include SASE. Reads submissions September 1 through May 30 only. Responds in 3 months. Pays $2.50/line, 1-year subscription, and 1 contributor's copy. Acquires first publication rights. Staff reviews books of poetry in 7-10 pages, multi-book format. Send material for review consideration. Most reviews are solicited.

Also Offers: Sponsors the James Boatwright III Prize For Poetry. A $1,000 prize awarded annually to the author of the best poem published in *Shenandoah* during a volume year.

○ **SHIP OF FOOLS; SHIP OF FOOLS PRESS**, Box 1028, University of Rio Grande, Rio Grande OH 45674-9989. (740)992-3333. Website: http://meadhall.homestead.com. Established 1983. **Editor:** Jack Hart. **Assistant Editor:** Catherine Grosvenor. **Review Editor:** James Doubleday.

Magazine Needs: *Ship of Fools* is "more or less quarterly." Wants "coherent, well-written, traditional or modern, myth, archetype, love—most types. No concrete, incoherent or greeting card poetry." Has published poetry by Rhina Espaillat, Paula Tatarunis, Simon Perchik, and Lyn Lifshin. *Ship of Fools* as digest-sized, saddle-stapled, offset printed with cover art and graphics. Press run is 190 for 43 subscribers of which 6 are libraries. Subscription: $8/4 issues. Sample: $2.

How to Submit: No previously published poems or simultaneous submissions. Cover letter preferred. Guidelines available for SASE. Often comments on rejected poems. Responds in 1 month. "If longer than six weeks, write and ask why." Pays 1-2 copies. Reviews books of poetry.

Book/Chapbook Needs & How to Submit: "We have no plans to publish chapbooks in the next year due to time constraints."

Advice: "Forget yourself; it is not you that matters, but the words."

◎ **SHIRIM, A JEWISH POETRY JOURNAL (Specialized: ethnic)**, 4611 Vesper Ave., Sherman Oaks CA 91403. (310)476-2861. Established 1982. **Editor:** Marc Dworkin.

Magazine Needs: *Shirim* appears biannually and publishes "poetry that reflects Jewish living without limiting to specific symbols, images, or contents." Has published poetry by Robert Mezcy, Karl Shapiro, and Grace Schulmon. *Shirim* is 40 pages, 4 × 5, desktop-published, saddle-stapled with card stock cover. Press run is 200. Subscription: $7. Sample: $4.

How to Submit: Submit 4 poems at a time. No previously published poems or simultaneous submissions. Cover letter preferred. Seldom comments on rejected poems. Publishes theme issues regularly. Responds in 3 months. Acquires first rights.

Ⓝ ◔ **SHŌ**, P.O. Box 31, Prescott AZ 86302. Established 2002. **Editor:** Clélia Cordova.

Magazine Needs: *Shō* is a biannual journal "that makes people want to read poetry. We look for poetry written with clarity and energy. Any school, any style." Does not want "strange, infantile Christian fanatacism." Recently published poetry by Fred Voss, A.D. Winans, Todd Moore, Gerald Locklin, Joan Jobe Smith, and Andrew Schelling. *Shō* is 80-100 pages, digest-sized, perfect-bound, glossy cover with original artwork, sometimes includes internal art/graphics. Receives about 1,000 poems/year, accepts about 140. Publishes about 70 poems/issue. Press run is 500 for 30 subscribers, 100 shelf sales; 100 are distributed free to reviewers and potential contributors. Single copy: $10; subscription: $20. Make checks payable to HSMLLC.

How to Submit: Submit 3-6 poems at a time. Accepts simultaneous submissions; no previously published poems. No fax, e-mail, or disk submissions. Cover letter is preferred. Reads submissions year round. Time between acceptance and publication is 6 months. "At this time, *Shō* is a one-person operation. The editor reads everything." Seldom comments on rejected poems. Guidelines available in magazine or for SASE. Responds in up to 3 months. Pays 1 contributor's copy. Acquires first rights and one-time rights.

Ⓝ $◔ **SIDEREALITY: A JOURNAL OF SPECULATIVE & EXPERIMENTAL POETRY; SIDEREALITY PUBLISHING**, Columbia SC. E-mail: managingeditor@sidereality.com. Website: www.sidereality.com. Established 2002. **Managing Editor:** Clayton A. Couch.

Magazine Needs: *sidereality: a journal of speculative & experimental poetry* appears quarterly as an Internet-only e-journal. "We consider a broad range of styles and forms, but we are looking specifically for poems which challenge reader expectations and imbue the English language with vitality and 'newness.' " Does not want cliched, non-specific, or vague poetry. Recently published poetry by Joel Chace, Eileen Tabios, Charles Fishman, Susan Terris, Vernon Frazer, and John Amen. *sidereality* is 40-50 pages, published online with a web page cover with digital art. Receives about 550-600 poems/year, accepts about 15-20%. Publishes 30-35 poems/issue.

How to Submit: Submit 1-10 poems at a time. No previously published poems or simultaneous submissions. Accepts e-mail submissions; no disk submissions. Cover letter is preferred. "*sidereality* accepts only e-mail submissions. Send to poetryeditor@sidereality.com with poems in the body of the message or in an attached file (.doc or .rtf format)." Reads submissions all year. Time between acceptance and publication is 2-5 months. Often comments on rejected poems. Guidelines available on website. Responds in up to 1 month. Sometimes sends prepublication galleys. Pays $2/poem. "We purchase first printing world exclusive rights for three months, after which time you may republish your work elsewhere, so long as *sidereality* is noted as the original publisher. We hope that you will allow *sidereality* to maintain your work in its archives indefinitely, but should you decide to remove it, contact Clayton A. Couch with the request." Reviews books and chapbooks of poetry and other magazines/journals. Poets may send materials for review consideration to Steven J. Stewart, Reviews Editor, stevenj1@hotmail.com.

Book/Chapbook Needs & How to Submit: Beginning in 2003, the editors of sidereality Publishing intend to publish 2-4 poetry-related e-books per year. E-books will be 25-75 pages with digital covers with art/graphics. Query first, with a few sample poems and a cover letter with brief bio and publication credits. Book/chapbook mss may include previously published poems. "Since we're new to the e-books world, please contact Clayton A. Couch to inquire about the status of our e-books line." Responds to queries in up to 2 months. Payment to be announced.

Advice: "Read, read as much as you can. Take risks with your writing, and most importantly, allow your poems room to grow."

SILVER WINGS/MAYFLOWER PULPIT (Specialized: religious, spirituality/inspirational); POETRY ON WINGS, INC., P.O. Box 1000, Pearblossom CA 93553-1000. (661)264-3726. E-mail: wilcoxmyflwrplpt@aol.com. Established 1983. Published by Poetry on Wings, Inc. **Poetry Editor:** Jackson Wilcox.

Magazine Needs: "As a committed Christian service we produce and publish *Silver Wings/Mayflower Pulpit*, a bimonthly poetry magazine. We want poems with a Christian perspective, reflecting a vital personal faith and a love for God and man. Will consider poems from 3-20 lines. Short poems are preferred. Poems over 20 lines will not even be read by the editor. Quite open in regard to meter and rhyme." Accepts poetry by children but it is only rarely used. Has published poetry by Dave Evans, C. David Hay, and Phillip Kolin. *Silver Wings/Mayflower Pulpit* is 16 pages, digest-sized, offset with cartoon-like art. Each issue contains a short inspirational article or sermon plus 15-20 poems. Receives about 1,500 submissions/year, accepts about 260. Press run is 250 with 200 subscribers, 50 shelf sales. Subscription: $10. Sample: $2.

How to Submit: Submit typed ms, double-spaced. Include SASE. Accepts simultaneous submissions; no previously published poems. Accepts submissions by postal mail only. Time between acceptance and publication can be up to 2 years. Guidelines and upcoming themes available for SASE. Responds in 3 weeks, providing SASE is supplied. Pays 1 contributor's copy. "We occasionally offer an award to a poem we consider outstanding and most closely in the spirit of what *Silver Wings* seeks to accomplish." Acquires first rights.

Also Offers: Sponsors an annual contest. For theme and details send SASE.

Advice: "We are interested in poetry that has a spiritual content and may be easily understood by people of humble status and simple lifestyle."

$ SILVERFISH REVIEW PRESS; GERALD CABLE BOOK AWARD, (formerly *Silverfish Review*), P.O. Box 3541, Eugene OR 97403. (541)344-5060. E-mail: sfrpress@earthlink.net. Established 1979. **Editor:** Rodger Moody.

Book/Chapbook Needs & How to Submit: Silverfish Review Press sponsors the *Gerald Cable Poetry Contest*. A $1,000 cash award and publication is awarded annually to the best book-length ms *or* original poetry by an author who has not yet published a full-length collection. No restrictions on the kind of poetry or subject matter; translations not acceptable. Has published *Why They Grow Wings* by Nin Andrews, *Odd Botany* by Thorpe Moeckel, *Bodies that Hum* by Beth Gylys, and *Inventing Difficulty* by Jessica Greenbaum. Books are $12 and $3.50 p&h. A $20 entry fee must accompany the ms; make checks payable to Silverfish Review Press. Guidelines available for SASE or by e-mail. Pays 10% of press run (out of 1,000).

◉ SIMPLYWORDS, 605 Collins Ave., Centerville GA 31028. Phone/fax: (478)953-9482 (between 10 a.m. and 5 p.m. only). E-mail: simplywords@att.net. Website: www.simplywords.i.am. Established 1991. **Editor:** Ruth Niehaus.

Magazine Needs: *SimplyWords* is a quarterly magazine open to all types, forms, and subjects. "No foul language or overtly sexual works." Accepts poetry written by children; "there are no reading fees for children." Has published poetry by Helen McIntosh Gordon, Sarah Jensen, Barbara Cagle Ray, Betty Tuohy, Sheila B. Roark, Donald Harmande, and Daniel Green. *SimplyWords* is 34-38 pages, magazine-sized, deskjet printed and spiral-bound, photo on cover, uses clip art. Receives about 500 poems/year, accepts about 90%. Press run is 60-100 depending on subscriptions and single issue orders in house." Subscription: $21.50/year. Sample: $6.

How to Submit: Send SASE for guidelines before submitting and write 'guidelines' in big block letters on left hand corner of envelope. No e-mail submissions. Line length for poetry is 28 maximum. "Name, address, phone number, e-mail, and line count must be on each page submitted." SASE required. Guidelines available for SASE, by fax, and on website. **Reading fee:** $1/poem. Time between acceptance and publication "depends on what issue your work was accepted for."

Advice: "It is very important that you send for guidelines before you submit to any publication. They all have rules and expect you to be professional enough to respect that. So learn the ropes— read, study, research your craft. If you want to be taken seriously prove that you are by learning your chosen craft."

⊕ ◉ SKALD, 2 Greenfield Terrace, Menai Bridge, Anglesey LL59 5AY Wales, United Kingdom. Phone: 1248-716343. E-mail: submissions@skald.co.uk. Website: www.skald.co.uk. Established 1994. **Contact:** Zoë Skoulding and Ian Davidson.

Magazine Needs: *Skald* appears 2 times/year and publishes "poetry and prose in Welsh or English. "It aims to publish a broad range of writing, including the innovative and experimental, and it is interested in the connections and differences between the local and the international, the visual and the verbal." Features reviews and artwork. *Skald* is 30-40 pages, A5, professionally printed and saddle-stapled with textured card cover, contains b&w artwork. Receives about 300 poems/year, accepts about 25%. Press run is 300 for 20 subscribers, 250 shelf sales; 20 distributed free to other magazines, art boards. Single copy: £3; subscription: £6/year (payments in sterling only).

How to Submit: Submit 6 poems at a time. No previously published poems or simultaneous submissions. Brief cover letter preferred. Time between acceptance and publication is 4 months. Often comments on rejected poems. Responds in 1 month. Pays 1 contributor's copy.

★ ◉ SKANKY POSSUM, 2925 Higgins St., Austin TX 78722. E-mail: skankypossum@hotmail. com. Website: www.skankypossum.com. Established 1998. **Editors:** Dale Smith and Hoa Nguyen.
   • *Skanky Possum* was a recipient of the Fund for Poetry Awards, with work included in *Best of American Poetry 2002*

Magazine Needs: *Skanky Possum* appears 2 times/year. "We love *Didelphis Marsupialis*. And that skanked-out gutter-feeder is our hero. Viva la skank!" Wants "skank! Not your everyday, run-of-the-mill skankiness, but down-and-dirty, licking-the-flies-off-my-furry-back skank. You got skank—we got ears." Does not want: "Don't make us play dead!" Recently published poetry by Clayton Eshleman, Tom Clark, Eileen Myles, Tom Devaney, Lee Ann Brown, and Carol Szamatowicz. *Skanky Possum* is digest-sized, photocopied, stapled, linen stock cover stamped, offset-printed, or handpainted, includes ads. Receives about 400-500 poems/year, accepts about 2-6%. Publishes about 40-60 poems/issue. Press run is 300. Single copy: $6.50; subscription: $20. Make checks payable to Dale Smith or Hoa Nguyen.

How to Submit: Submit 2-5 poems at a time. Accepts simultaneous submissions; no previously published poems. No fax, e-mail, or disk submissions. Cover letter is preferred. Reads submissions

January-June. Time between acceptance and publication is 6-8 months. "It's difficult to explain the editorial process of a marsupial. What possum wants, possum gets." Seldom comments on rejected poems. Guidelines available on website. Responds in up to 8 months. Sometimes sends prepublication galleys. Pays 2 contributor's copies. Acquires one-time rights. Reviews books and chapbooks of poetry and other magazines/journals. Poets may send materials for review consideration to Dale Smith.

Advice: "Start your own small press. Publish or perish. Get the work out any way you can. Vive le Poss!"

⬤ SKIDROW PENTHOUSE, 44 Four Corners Rd., Blairstown NJ 07825. (908)362-6808 or (212)286-2600. Established 1998. **Editor:** Rob Cook. **Editor:** Stephanie Dickinson.

Magazine Needs: *Skidrow Penthouse* is published "to give emerging and idiosyncratic writers a new forum in which to publish their work. We are looking for deeply felt authentic voices, whether surreal, confessional, New York School, formal, or free verse. Work should be well crafted: attention to line-break and diction. We want poets who sound like themselves, not workshop professionals. We don't want gutless posturing, technical precision with no subject matter, explicit sex and violence without craft, or abstract intellectualizing. We are not impressed by previous awards and publications." Has published poetry by Lisa Jarnot, Christopher Edgar, Aase Berg, Karl Tierney, James Grinwis, and Tom Savage. *Skidrow Penthouse* is 250 pages, digest-sized, professionally printed and perfect-bound with 4-color cover, includes original art and photographs as well as contest announcements, magazine advertisements. Receives about 500 poems/year, accepts 3%. Publish 35-40 poems/issue. Press run is 300 for 50 subscribers; 10% distributed free to journals for review consideration. Single copy: $12.50; subscription: $20. Make checks payable to Rob Cook or Stephanie Dickinson.

How to Submit: Submit 3-5 poems at a time. Accepts previously published poems and simultaneous submissions. "Include a legal sized SASE; also name and address on every page of your submission. No handwritten submissions will be considered." Time between acceptance and publication is 1 year. Seldom comments on rejected poems. Responds in 2 months. Pays 1 contributor's copy. Acquires one-time rights. Reviews books and chapbooks of poetry and other magazines in 1,500 words, single book format. Send materials for review consideration.

Also Offers: "We're trying to showcase a poet in each issue by publishing up to 60 page collections within the magazine." Send query with SASE.

Advice: "We get way too many anecdotal fragments posing as poetry; too much of what we receive feels like this mornings inspiration mailed this afternoon. The majority of those who submit do not seem to have put in the sweat a good poem demands. Also, the ratio of submissions to sample copy purchases is 50:1. Just because our name is Skidrow Penthouse does not mean we are a repository for genre work or 'eat, shit, shower, and shave' poetry."

◢ ◎ SKIPPING STONES: A MULTICULTURAL CHILDREN'S MAGAZINE; ANNUAL YOUTH HONOR AWARDS (Specialized: bilingual, children/teen, ethnic/nationality, nature/ecology, social issues), P.O. Box 3939, Eugene OR 97403. (541)342-4956. E-mail: editor@skippingstones.org. Website: www.skippingstones.org. Established 1988. **Editor:** Arun Toké.

Magazine Needs: *Skipping Stones* is a "nonprofit magazine published bimonthly during the school year (5 issues) that encourages cooperation, creativity and celebration of cultural and ecological richness." Wants poetry by young writers under 18; 30 lines maximum on "nature, multicultural and social issues, family, freedom . . . uplifting." No work by adults. *Skipping Stones* is magazine-sized, saddle-stapled, printed on recycled paper. Receives about 500-1,000 poems/year, accepts 10%. Press run is 2,500 for 1,700 subscribers. Subscription: $25. Sample: $5.

How to Submit: Submit up to 3 poems at a time. Accepts simultaneous submissions; no previously published poems. Accepts e-mail submissions included in body of message. Cover letter preferred. "Include your cultural background, experiences and what was the inspiration behind your creation." Time between acceptance and publication is up to 9 months. Poems are circulated to a 3-member editorial board. "Generally a piece is chosen for publication when all the editorial staff feel good about it." Seldom comments on rejected poems. Publishes theme issues. Guidelines and upcoming themes available for SASE. Responds in up to 4 months. Pays 1 contributor's copy, offers 25% discount for more. Acquires all rights. Returns rights after publication, but "we keep reprint rights."

Also Offers: Sponsors Annual Youth Honor Awards for 7-17 year olds. Theme for Annual Youth Honor Awards is "Multicultural and Nature Awareness." Deadline: January 20. Entry fee: $3 which includes free issue featuring winners. Details available for SASE.

◙ SLANT: A JOURNAL OF POETRY, Box 5063, University of Central Arkansas, 201 Donaghey Ave., Conway AR 72035-5000. (501)450-5107. Website: www.uca.edu/divisions/academic/english/Slant/HOMPAGE.html. Established 1987. **Editor:** James Fowler.
Magazine Needs: *Slant* is an annual using *only* poetry. Uses "traditional and 'modern' poetry, even experimental, moderate length, any subject on approval of Board of Readers; purpose is to publish a journal of fine poetry from all regions of the United States and beyond. No haiku, no translations." Accepts poetry written by children ("although we're not a children's journal.") Has published poetry by Richard Broderick, William Doreski, Twyla Hansen, Sandra Kohler, Alfred Nicol, and Mary Winkers. *Slant* is 120 pages, professionally printed on quality stock, flat-spined, with matte card cover. Receives about 1,500 poems/year, accepts 70-80. Press run is 200 for 70-100 subscribers. Sample: $10.
How to Submit: Submit up to 5 poems of moderate length with SASE between September and mid-November. "Put name, address (including e-mail if available) and phone on the top of each page." No simultaneous submissions or previously published poems. Editor comments on rejected poems "on occasion." Allow 3-4 months from November 15 deadline for response. Pays 1 contributor's copy.
Advice: "I would like to see more formal and narrative verse."

◯ SLAPERING HOL PRESS, 300 Riverside Dr., Sleepy Hollow NY 10591-1414. (914)332-5953. Fax: (914)332-4825. E-mail: info@writerscenter.org. Website: www.writerscenter.org. Established 1990. **Contact:** Stephanie Strickland and Margo Stever.
Book/Chapbook Needs: "Slapering Hol Press is the small press imprint of The Hudson Valley Writers' Center, created in 1990 to provide publishing opportunities for emerging poets who have not yet published a book or chapbook, and to produce anthologies of a thematic nature. Chapbooks are selected for publication on the basis of an annual competition." Recently published poetry by *Islands* by Andrew Krivak, *The Last Campaign* by Rachel Loden, *No Pinetree in this Forest is Perfect* by Ellen Goldsmith, *The Landscape of Mind* by Jianqing Zheng, *Freight* by Sondra Upham, and *Scottish Café* by Susan Case. Slapering Hol Press publishes 1 chapbook/year. Chapbooks are usually less than 40 pages, offset-printed, hand sewn, 80 lb. cover weight cover.
How to Submit: Submit 16-20 pages with a $10 entry fee and SASE by May 15. Guidelines available for SASE, by fax, by e-mail, and on website. For further information see separate listing for Slapering Hol Press Chapbook competition in the Contests & Awards section. Order sample chapbooks by sending $13.50 postage paid to Hudson Valley Writers' Center.

★ ◯ ◎ SLATE & STYLE (Specialized: blind writers), Dept. PM, 2704 Beach Dr., Merrick NY 11566. (516)868-8718. Fax: (516)868-9076. E-mail: LoriStay@aol.com. **Editor:** Loraine Stayer.
Magazine Needs: *Slate & Style* is a quarterly for blind writers available on cassette, in large print, Braille and e-mail, "including articles of interest to blind writers, resources for blind writers. Membership/subscription is $10 per year, all formats. Division of the National Federation of the Blind." Poems may be "5-36 lines. Prefer contributors to be blind writers, or at least writers by profession or inclination. New writers welcome. No obscenities. Will consider all forms of poetry including haiku. Interested in new talent." Accepts poetry by young writers, but please specify age. Has published poetry by Mary Brunoli, Kerry Elizabeth Thompson, John Gordon Jr., Katherine Barr, and Nancy Scott. The print version of *Slate & Style* is 28-32 pages, magazine-sized, stapled, with a fiction and poetry section. Press run is 200 for 160 subscribers of which 4-5 are libraries. Subscription: $10/year. Sample: $2.50.
How to Submit: Submit 3 poems once or twice/year. No simultaneous submissions or previously published poems. Accepts submissions by e-mail (include in text box) and by postal mail. Cover letter preferred. "On occasion we receive poems in Braille. I prefer print, since Braille slows me down. Typed is best." Do not submit mss in July. Editor comments on rejected poems "if requested." Guidelines available for SASE, by e-mail, on website, and in publication. Responds in "two weeks if I like it." Pays 1 contributor's copy. Reviews books of poetry. Send materials for review consideration.

insider report

Finding time for poetry

Margo Stever

Photo by Mark Sadan

As a poet, you're probably aware of the endless opportunities available for you in the writing world. Whether it's sharing your work by publishing in journals or books, or participating in the poetry community by joining workshops or going to readings, the life of a poet can be very exciting. It can also be overwhelming, especially since you still have to find time to write. Poet Margo Stever knows first hand all that's involved in being a poet, yet she takes the challenge head-on by striving to succeed in every area of a poet's life.

Stever literally has immersed herself in poetry. In addition to founding The Hudson Valley Writers' Center and helping coordinate their impressive reading series, she is co-editor of Slapering Hol Press, which runs an annual chapbook competition for new poets and publishes anthologies. Her own poems have appeared in such prestigious journals as the *New England Review*, *The Seattle Review*, *Connecticut Review*, *Rattapallax*, *Ironwood*, and *Poet Lore*. Riverstone Press published her chapbook, *Reading the Night*, and, more recently, her book *Frozen Spring* has just been released from Mid-List Press.

Stever's successes in these different areas of poetry didn't happen without effort and determination. In fact, she pushed herself very hard to get where she is today, gathering knowledge along the way on a variety of topics, from forming a community of writers to getting published, that she now shares gladly with other poets.

Like many new writers, when Stever first started putting pen to paper, she didn't even realize she was writing poetry. "I was writing these 'things' out of my own need and with a great sense of urgency," Stever recalls. "There were a lot of difficulties in my family: My father died when I was 12, my stepfather died when I was 18, and my mother was a manic depressive alcoholic. I started to write just to resolve what I saw in the world. But I didn't really understand that I was writing poetry."

At Harvard University, a friend saw Stever's writing and suggested she take a class at MIT with poet Denise Levertov. "Denise was able to see I was writing poetry," says Stever. "She was incredibly inspirational as a teacher and she stayed a friend throughout her whole life." That class changed Stever forever; she now saw herself as a poet.

As an emerging poet, she longed to join a community of writers where she could share her work and her love of poetry. But, as many poets often experience, finding this community wasn't easy, especially after Stever's husband took a job at Pace Law School. Their move to the New York suburbs of North Tarrytown, now called Sleepy Hollow, caused Stever much apprehension. "Many of the women were in garden clubs, and some even wore white gloves, harkening back to the 1950s. I was worried about feeling the extreme alienation and the stifling experiences of living in the suburbs." Not content to live life feeling like an outsider, Stever decided to start a poetry series to help bring writers together. In 1983, the Sleepy Hollow Poetry Series was born.

If you've ever thought about starting a local reading series, consider following the steps Stever took as a guide. She first applied for a Decentralization Grant from her local Westchester Arts Council. Grants are frequently available to writers and range from city to state to even national levels. Information about grants can be found by consulting state or local arts councils, or by looking at the *Foundation Center Directory* or the PEN American Center's annual *Grants and Awards Available to American Writers*. With her grant, Stever worked in close conjunction with the local Warner Library in Tarrytown, which not only provided great resources but served as the site of the first reading series.

Although she didn't know many local writers, Stever did know poet Maxine Kumin, who agreed to be one of the series's first readers. The initial readings were not only successful, they also allowed Stever to network with other area writers. "When Maxine came to read," says Stever, "I met some people who were instrumental in helping me find writers around the local area and who helped bring in writers from around the country as well."

Stever strongly believes that an important part of any poet's development is being surrounded by people who support writing. "You have to have a community—whether it's a group of poets, your spouse, or a grocer—who will support you and provide the conditions for you to grow as a poet." From a desire for a bigger community, Stever decided to branch out from her successful reading series and start an entire writing center.

In 1988, her new network of writers founded The Hudson Valley Writers' Center. Today their membership is around 300 strong and has boasted impressive members, such as U.S. Poet Laureate Billy Collins, who is also on the Center's advisory board. In addition to the reading series, the Writers' Center presents writing workshops and an outreach program that has provided workshops and literacy programs to nursing homes, schools for children with severe emotional problems, homeless shelters, and AIDS-related community service organizations. One of their on-going projects is restoring the formerly abandoned Philipse Manor Railroad Station to serve as home for the Writers' Center. "The station was on the brink of falling into the tracks," says Stever. "You couldn't even walk on the floor." Now it's a gorgeous building that hosts many creative endeavors.

A key benefit of a strong writing community is having a range of people who can critique one another's work, and writing workshops are an important part of The Hudson Valley Writers' Center. Stever believes that "workshops can be extremely helpful, depending on how the workshop is run. Some workshops, however, can be a negative and almost destructive experience." Whether poets can take something useful away from a workshop frequently depends on their ability to sort through the criticism they've received.

"Criticism is one of the most important elements of a writer's development," says Stever. "But it's also important for a poet to be able to figure out which criticism is actually valuable. On one hand it's important to listen to your audience, but on the other hand it's important to maintain your authorial identity. No matter who is critiquing your work, whether it's a great writer or even a trusted friend, that person may say something about your work that isn't going to make sense. If you bow down to whatever anybody says and change too much, you just lose your identity and the heart and soul of your work."

Of course, finding time for workshops, and for writing itself, can be a challenge for any poet. When it came to discipline, Stever admits, "I was always distracted by things of the world, like starting a writing center and making sure my kids were okay. Oddly enough, I wrote the best when my children were young and I didn't have a babysitter. I had to write when they took naps, and I was really prolific in my writing because I had to be there." Stever strongly believes that poets must try their hardest to make time to write, even if it's for a short amount of time. "You don't have to sit somewhere for three hours a day. You can write on the train or duck into a corner, but you have to do it. If you are a gifted writer, that's great, but you have to be there to provide the time. The gift may come to you, but if you aren't there it will never happen. You have to show up for anything to happen."

Discipline also means sending your work out regularly, even if you get rejected. Although Stever had been published in several literary journals, getting her book published required an extreme resolve. "My manuscript was the finalist or semi-finalist for 15 contests. It was depressing for me. I thought it would never get published. It became an obsession for me because I just kept sending it out." Her determination paid off when her manuscript won the Mid-List Press's First Series Award for Poetry. Part of the prize was the publication of her book, *Frozen Spring*, which has been featured in *The New York Times*.

"Lamentation: School Bus in Morning"

They say this is normal, the calm
he had about leaving for kindergarten,
his desire to take the bus.
She saw his foot against the backdrop of the door,
and then only a vapor trail.

If the toilets hadn't run,
hadn't made gurgling sounds,
pressing against the crevices
of her innermost ear, she would be
wild with worry over the child,
her small child, his crayons
on the chair, his books
smelling of dusk and smoke.

The uneasy creaking of the empty
house—the inside,
black and crenellated, drawn out
like geese against the clouds,
the inside, new with emptiness,
comes out against the outside.

Instead, the toilet, and then
the fall rain. So much rain
she forgot about the child leaving,
about how like screaming
the rain came down.

(from *Frozen Spring* (Mid-List Press, 2002); reprinted with permission of the author)

Because Stever experienced firsthand the challenges of getting published, she decided to work with The Hudson Valley Writers' Center to start a new press. So on top of everything else she was doing, in 1990 Stever founded the Slapering Hol Press, which gets its unusual name from "the old Dutch words for Sleepy Hollow," says Stever. With her co-editor, Stephanie Strickland, Stever has published several anthologies and now runs an annual chapbook competition, which is open to all poets. Every year the competition receives 200 to 300 submissions, and past winners have received an honorarium of $500, a reading at The Hudson Valley Writers' Center, and the publication of their chapbooks. (For information and guidelines, see the listing for the Slapering Hol Press Chapbook Competition in the Contests & Awards section, or check out www.writerscenter.org.)

Stever stresses when sending out submissions, poets should look for a press that publishes work similar to what they are doing. Nevertheless, she recognizes that this can be a challenging task for any busy writer. "You hear that you should go read literary magazines and see what the press is like," says Stever. "It can be extremely difficult to find the time to really figure out what they want. But it's true, every press has its orientation. If you can figure that out, then you're way ahead of the game. You end up wasting a lot less time."

Slapering Hol Press focuses on collections that address issues regarding the environment, women, and even the international community. "One of the winning chapbooks, *No Pine Tree in This Forest is Perfect*, was written about a woman who had breast cancer. *The Scottish Café*, the 2002 chapbook winner, is about some Polish mathematicians in Lvov who are able to keep doing meaningful work during World War II when everything was basically falling apart around them."

Poets must also present their work in a professional manner, which is something Stever learned the hard way. "I was always revising my manuscript and redoing the page numbers by typing them in. It didn't look professional," Stever recalls. "I joked I'd been a finalist or a semi-finalist so many times, and it was only after I put my manuscript on the computer and got automatic pagination that it got published. Maybe it was a coincidence—maybe it wasn't."

Stever's final advice to poets is, "Don't put pressure on yourself to produce. You may write two lines today that can later be transformed into something good. You also can't put all of your eggs in one basket. Even now I'm working on an anthology, my own poetry, projects at the Writer's Center and at the Press, and a film." With this attitude, Stever hopes she'll always be successful in at least one area of the poet's life.

—*Donya Dickerson*

Also Offers: Offers an annual poetry contest. Entry fee: $5/poem. Deadline: June 1. Write for details. Also holds a contest for blind children; write for details.
Advice: "Before you send us a poem, read it aloud. Does is sound good to you? We put our poetry into tape format, so we want it to sound and look good."

SLIPSTREAM, Box 2071, New Market Station, Niagara Falls NY 14301-0071. (716)282-2616 (after 5PM, EST). E-mail: editors@slipstreampress.org. Website: www.slipstreampress.org. Established 1980. **Poetry Editors:** Dan Sicoli, Robert Borgatti, and Livio Farallo.
Magazine Needs: *Slipstream* is a "small press literary mag published in the spring and is about 90% poetry and 10% fiction/prose, with some artwork. Likes new work with contemporary urban flavor. Writing must have a cutting edge to get our attention. We like to keep an open forum, any length, subject, style. Best to see a sample to get a feel. Like city stuff as opposed to country. Like poetry that springs from the gut, screams from dark alleys, inspired by experience." No "pastoral, religious, traditional, rhyming" poetry. Has published poetry by M. Scott Douglass, Johnny Cordova, Douglas Goetsch, Gerald Locklin, Alison Miller, Jim Daniels, James Snodgrass, and Chrys Darkwater. *Slipstream* appears 1-2 times/year in a $7 \times 8\frac{1}{2}$ format, 80-100 pages, professionally printed, perfect-bound, using b&w photos and graphics. It contains mostly free verse, some stanza patterns. Receives over 2,500 submissions of poetry/year, accepts less than 10%. Press run is 500 for 400 subscribers of which 10 are libraries. Subscription: $20/2 issues and 2 chapbooks. Sample: $7.
How to Submit: No e-mail submissions. Editor sometimes comments on rejected poems. Publishes

theme issues, but "reading for a general issue through 2004." Guidelines and upcoming themes available for SASE and on website. "Reading for a general issue through 2002." Responds in up to 2 months, "if SASE included." Pays 1-2 copies.

Also Offers: Annual chapbook contest has December 1 deadline. **Entry fee:** $15. Submit up to 40 pages of poetry, any style, previously published work OK with acknowledgments. Guidelines available for SASE and on website. Winner receives $1,000 and 50 copies. All entrants receive copy of winning chapbook and an issue of the magazine. Past winners have included Rene Christopher, Gerald Locklin, Alison Pelegrin, Laurie Mezzaferro, Ronald Wardall, and most recently J.P. Dancing Bear for *What Language*.

Advice: "Do not waste time submitting your work 'blindly.' Sample issues from the small press first to determine which ones would be most receptive to your work."

$ ◐ SLOPE; SLOPE EDITIONS, 2350 Kensington Ave., Amherst NY 14226. E-mail: ethan@sl ope.org (for magazine) or info@slope.org (for press). Website: www.slope.org (for magazine) or www.slopeeditions.org (for press). Established 1999. **Editor-in-Chief:** Ethan Paquin. **Senior Editor:** Christopher Janke. **Managing Editor:** Molly Dorozenski. Member: CLMP.

Magazine Needs: *Slope* "is a quarterly, online journal of poetry featuring work that is challenging, dynamic, and innovative. We encourage new writers while continuing to publish award-winning and established poets from around the world." Wants "no particular style. Interested in poetry in translation." Recently published poetry by Forrest Gander, Paul Hoover, Eleni Sikelianos, James Tate, Bruce Beasley, and Charles Bernstein.

How to Submit: Submit 3-6 poems at a time. No previously published poems; or simultaneous submissions. Accepts submissions by e-mail only (as attachments). "Submit poems via e-mail to the address at the website." Reads submissions year round. Time between acceptance and publication is 3-6 months. Seldom comments on rejections. Guidelines available by e-mail or on website. Responds in 3 months. Acquires one-time rights. Reviews books and chapbooks of poetry in 400 words, single book format. Send materials for review consideration; "query first."

Book/Chapbook Needs: "Slope Editions publishes books of innovative poetry." Wants "writing of superior quality, of no particular style. As an offshoot of the online journal *Slope*, Slope Editions believes in actively promoting and supporting its authors, especially via the web." Has published *The Body* by Jenny Boully, *Bivouac* by Laura Solomon, and *Maine* by Jonah Winter. Books are professionally-printed paperbacks, perfect-bound, 60-120 pages.

How to Submit: Query with 10-15 sample poems and SASE during July and August only. Accepts simultaneous submissions if notified of acceptance elsewhere. Submit book mss by postal mail only. Responds to queries in 3 months, to mss (if solicited) within 6 months. Guidelines available for SASE and on website. Pays up to 10% royalties and authors' copies.

Also Offers: The Slope Edition Book Prize (see separate listing in Contests & Awards section).

◐ SMALL POND MAGAZINE OF LITERATURE, P.O. Box 664, Stratford CT 06615. (203)378-4066. Established 1964. **Editor:** Napoleon St. Cyr.

Magazine Needs: *Small Pond Magazine of Literature* is a literary triquarterly that features poetry "and anything else the editor feels is interesting, original, important." Poetry can be "any style, form, topic, except haiku, so long as it is deemed good, but limit of about 100 lines." Wants "nothing about cats, pets, flowers, butterflies, etc. Generally nothing under eight lines." Has published poetry by Marvin Solomon, Ruth Moon Kempher, Carol Hamilton, Herb Coursen, and Lynn Lifshin. *Small Pond* is 40 pages, digest-sized, offset from typescript on off-white paper, with colored matte card cover, saddle-stapled, artwork both on cover and inside. Press run is 300, of which about a third go to libraries. Subscription: $10/3 issues. Sample (including guidelines): $3 for a random selection, $4 current. "Random back issue for $2; same quality, famous editor's comments."

How to Submit: Doesn't want 60 pages of anything; "dozen pages of poems max." Name and

---

OPENNESS TO SUBMISSIONS: ○ beginners; ◐ beginners and experienced; ◑ mostly experienced, few beginners; ◉ specialized; ⦸ closed to all submissions.

address on each page. No previously published poems or simultaneous submissions. Brief cover letter preferred. Time between acceptance and publication is up to 15 months. Responds in up to 30 days. Pays 2 copies. Acquires all rights. Returns rights with written request including stated use. "One-time use per request." All styles and forms are welcome here. Guidelines available for SASE and in publication. Responds quickly, often with comments to guide poets whose work interests him.

SMARTISH PACE; ERSKINE J. POETRY PRIZE, P.O. Box 22161, Baltimore MD 21203. Website: wwwsmartishpace.com. Established 1999. **Editor:** Stephen Reichert.

Magazine Needs: *Smartish Pace*, published in spring and fall, contains poetry, translations, essays on poetry, reviews, and interviews with poets. "*Smartish Pace* is an independent poetry journal and is not affiliated with any institution." No restrictions on style or content of poetry. Has published poetry by Diane Wakoski, Irving Feldman, Mark Jarman, Rachel Hadas, Sherod Santos, Allen Grossman, and X.J. Kennedy. *Smartish Pace* is about 80 pages, digest-sized, professionally printed and perfect-bound with color, heavy stock cover. Receives about 3,000 poems/year, accepts 4%; publishes 50-60 poems/issue. Press run is 500 for 300 subscribers. Subscription: $12. Sample: $6.

How to Submit: Submit no more than 6 poems at a time. Accepts simultaneous submissions; no previously published poems. "Please provide prompt notice when poems have been accepted elsewhere. Cover letter with bio and SASE is required. Electronic submissions to www.smartishpace.com are encouraged." Submit seasonal poems 8 months in advance. Time between acceptance and publication is up to 1 year. Guidelines available for SASE or on website. Responds in up to 8 months. Pays 1 copy. Acquires first rights. Encourages unsolicited reviews, essays, interviews. Poets and publishers encouraged to send review copies. All books received will also be listed in the books received sections of each issue and at the website along with ordering information and a link to the publisher's website.

Also Offers: "*Smartish Pace* hosts the annual Erskine J. Poetry Prize. Submit 3 poems with $5 entry fee in either check or money order made payable to *Smartish Pace*. Additional poems may be submitted for $1 per poem. No more than 8 poems may be submitted (8 poems = $5 + $5 = $10). Winners receive cash prizes and publication. Recent winners Mark DeFoe, Gaylord Brewer, and Susan Cavanaugh. See website for complete information."

SMOKE, First Floor, Liver House, 96 Bold St., Liverpool L1 4HY England. Phone: (0151)709-3688. Website: www.windowsproject.demon.co.uk. Established 1974. **Editor:** Dave Ward.

Magazine Needs: *Smoke* is a biannual publication of poetry and graphics. Wants "short, contemporary poetry, expressing new ideas through new forms." Has published poetry by Carol Ann Duffy, Roger McGough, Jackie Kay, and Henry Normal. *Smoke* is 24 pages, A5, offset-litho printed and stapled with paper cover, includes art. Receives about 3,000 poems/year, accepts about 40 poems. Press run is 750 for 350 subscribers of which 18 are libraries, 100 shelf sales; 100 distributed free to contributors/other mags. Subscription: $5 (cash). Sample: $1. Make checks payable to Windows Project (cash preferred/exchanges rate on cheques not viable).

How to Submit: Submit 6 poems at a time. Accepts previously published poems and simultaneous submissions. Cover letter preferred. Time between acceptance and publication is 6 months. Seldom comments on rejected poems. Responds in 2 weeks. Pays 1 copy.

$ SNOWY EGRET (Specialized: animals, nature), P.O. Box 29, Terre Haute IN 47808. Established 1922 by Humphrey A. Olsen. **Contact:** Editors.

Magazine Needs: Appearing in spring and autumn, *Snowy Egret* specializes in work that is "nature-oriented: poetry that celebrates the abundance and beauty of nature or explores the interconnections between nature and the human psyche." Has published poetry by Conrad Hilberry, Lynn Lifshin, Gayle Eleanor, and Patricia Hooper. *Snowy Egret* is 60-page, magazine-sized format, offset, saddle-stapled, with original graphics. Receives about 500 poems/year, accepts about 30. Press run is 800 for 500 subscribers of which 50 are libraries. Sample: $8; subscription: $15/year, $25/2 years.

How to Submit: Guidelines available for #10 SASE. Responds in 1 month. Always sends prepublication galleys. Pays $4/poem or $4/page plus 2 copies. Acquires first North American and one-time reprint rights.

Advice: "First-hand, detailed observation gives poetry authenticity and immediacy."

�𝄢 ◎ SO TO SPEAK: A FEMINIST JOURNAL OF LANGUAGE AND ART (Specialized: women/feminism), George Mason University, 4400 University Dr., MS 2D6, Fairfax VA 22030-4444. (703)993-3625. E-mail: sts@gmu.edu. Website: www.gmu.edu/org/sts. Established 1991. **Poetry Editor:** Renee Angle.

Magazine Needs: *So to Speak* is published 2 times/year. "We publish high-quality work about women's lives—fiction, nonfiction (including book reviews and interviews), b&w photography, artwork, collaborations, lyrical essays, and other genre-questioning texts, as well as poetry. We look for poetry that deals with women's lives, but also lives up to a high standard of language, form and meaning. We are most interested in experimental, high-quality work. There are no formal specifications. We like work that takes risks successfully. No unfinished/unpolished work." Has published poetry by Eleni Sikelianos, Hannah Wiener, Harryette Mullen, Marcella Durand, Jean Donnelly, Heather Fuller, and Carolyn Forché. *So To Speak* is 100-128 pages, digest-sized, photo-offset printed and perfect-bound, with glossy cover, includes b&w photos and art, ads. Receives about 300 poems/year, accepts 10%. Press run is 1,000 for 40 subscribers, 50 shelf sales; 500 distributed free to students/submitters. Subscription: $12. Sample: $6.

How to Submit: Submit 3-5 poems at a time. Accepts simultaneous submissions; no previously published poems. Cover letter preferred. "Please submit poems as you wish to see them in print. We do have an e-mail address but do not accept e-mail submissions. Be sure to include a cover letter with full contact info, publications credits, and awards received." Reads submissions August 15 through October 15 and December 31 through March 15. Time between acceptance and publication is 6-8 months. Seldom comments on rejected poems. Occasionally publishes theme issues. Guidelines and upcoming themes available for SASE. Responds in 3 months if submissions are received during reading period. Pays 2 copies. Acquires one-time rights. Reviews books and chapbooks of poetry and other magazines in 750 words, single book format. Send materials for review consideration.

Also Offers: *So to Speak* runs an annual poetry contest. "Our 2002 judge was Eileen Myles."

Advice: "We are looking for poetry that, through interesting use of language, locates experiences of women. We particularly appreciate poems that challenge tradition but remain cohesive and meaningful."

○ SO YOUNG!; ANTI-AGING PRESS, INC., P.O. Box 141489, Coral Gables FL 33114. (305)662-3928. Fax: (305)661-4123. E-mail: julia2@gate.net. Established 1992 press, 1996 newsletter. **Editor:** Julia Busch.

Magazine Needs: *So Young!* is a bimonthly newsletter publishing "anti-aging/holistic health/humorous/philosophical topics geared to a youthful body, attitude, and spirit." Wants "short, upbeat, fresh, positive poetry. The newsletter is dedicated to a youthful body, face, mind and spirit. Work can be humorous, philosophical fillers. No off color, suggestive poems or anything relative to first night, or unrequited love affairs." *So Young!* is 12 pages, magazine-sized (11 × 17 sheets folded), unbound. Receives several hundred poems/year, accepts 6-12. Press run is 700 for 500 subscribers. Subscription: $35. Sample: $6.

How to Submit: Submit up to 10 poems at a time. Accepts previously published poems and simultaneous submissions. Accepts e-mail submissions (in text box). Cover letter preferred. Time between acceptance and publication "depends on poem subject matter—usually 6-8 months." Guidelines available for SASE. Responds in 2 months. Pays 10 copies. Acquires one-time rights.

�𝄢 ◎ THE SOCIETY OF AMERICAN POETS (SOAP); IN HIS STEPS PUBLISHING COMPANY; THE POET'S PEN; PRESIDENT'S AWARD FOR SUPERIOR CHOICE (Specialized: religious), P.O. Box 3563, Macon GA 31205-3563. (478)788-1848. Fax: (478)788-0925. E-mail: DrRev@msn.com. Established 1984. **Editor:** Dr. Charles E. Cravey.

Magazine Needs: *The Poet's Pen* is a literary quarterly of poetry and short stories. "Open to all styles of poetry and prose—both religious and secular. No gross or 'X-rated' poetry without taste or character." Accepts poetry written by children. Has published poetry by Najwa Salam Brax, Henry Goldman, Henry W. Gurley, William Heffner, Linda Metcalf, and Charles Russ. *The Poet's Pen* uses poetry primarily by members and subscribers, but outside submissions are also welcomed. Sample copy: $15. Membership: $30/year; $25/students.

How to Submit: Submit 3 poems per quarter, include name and address on each page. "Submissions or inquiries will not be responded to without a #10 business-sized SASE. We do stress originality and have each new poet and/or subscriber sign a waiver form verifying originality." Accepts simultaneous submissions and previously published poems, if permission from previous publisher is included. Publishes seasonal/theme issues. Upcoming themes and guidelines available for SASE, by fax, in publication, or by e-mail. Sometimes sends prepublication galleys. Editor "most certainly" comments on rejected poems.

Book/Chapbook Needs & How to Submit: In His Steps publishes religious and other books. Also publishes music for the commercial record market. Query for book publication.

Also Offers: Sponsors several contests each quarter which total $100-250 in cash awards. Editor's Choice Awards each quarter. President's Award for Superior Choice has a prize of $50; deadline is November 1. Also publishes a quarterly anthology that has poetry competitions in several categories with prizes of $25-100.

Advice: "Be honest with yourself above all else. Read the greats over and again and study styles, grammar, and what makes each unique. Meter, rhythm, and rhyme are still the guidelines that are most acceptable today."

⚡ $◎ SOJOURNERS (Specialized: religious, political), 2401 15th St. NW, Washington DC 20009. (202)328-8842. E-mail: sojourners@sojo.net. Website: www.sojo.com. Established 1975. **Poetry Editor:** Rose Berger.

Magazine Needs: *Sojourners* appears 6 times/year, "with approximately 40,000 subscribers. We focus on faith, politics and culture from a radical Christian perspective. We publish one or two poems/month depending on length. All poems must be original and unpublished. We look for seasoned, well-crafted poetry that reflects the issues and perspectives covered in our magazine. We highly discourage simplistic, rhyming poetry. Poetry using non-inclusive language (any racist, sexist, homophobic poetry) will not be accepted." *Sojourners* is about 70 pages, magazine-sized, offset printed and saddle-stapled with 4-color paper cover, includes photos and illustrations throughout. Receives about 400 poems/year, accepts approximately 6-8. Press run is 50,000 for 40,000 subscribers of which 500 are libraries, 2,000 shelf sales. Single copy: $4; subscription: $30. Sample: free.

How to Submit: Submit up to 3 poems at a time. Line length for poetry is 50 maximum. Accepts submissions by postal mail only. Cover letter with brief (3 sentences) bio required. Editor occasionally comments on submissions. Guidelines available on website. Responds in up to 6 weeks. Pays $25/poem plus 5 copies. "We assume permission to grant reprints unless the author requests otherwise."

Advice: "Read the magazine first to familiarize yourself with our perspective."

Ⓝ $⊘ ◎ SONG OF THE SIREN: MYTHOPOEIC CREATIVE WORKS (Specialized: mythopoeic), P.O. Box 172, Lebanon NH 03766. E-mail: editor@song-of-the-siren (inquiries); poetry@song-of-the-siren (submissions). Website: www.song-of-the-siren.net. Established 2003. **Editor:** Linda Jeanne.

Magazine Needs: *Song of the Siren* is a monthly online journal of poetry, fiction, nonfiction, and visual art inspired by mythology, folklore, and dream. Wants all styles and forms "as long as it works and ties fundamentally back to the journal's theme. Show me a unique point of view or insight, something that speaks with potency." *Song of the Siren* is published online only. Publishes about 4 poems/issue.

How to Submit: Submit up to 5 poems at a time. Accepts previously published poems and simultaneous submissions ("please let me know when and where poems were published/submitted"). Accepts e-mail submissions; no fax or disk submissions. Cover letter is preferred. "E-mail submissions to poetry@song-of-the-siren.net. For snail mail, send SASE or IRC for response and return of manuscript ." Submit seasonal poems 3 months in advance. Time between acceptance and publication is 1-3 months. Seldom comments on rejected poems. Occasionally publishes theme issues. List of upcoming themes and guidelines available on website. Responds in up to 6 weeks. Pays $5/page ($2 minimum). Acquires non-exclusive electronic rights. Reviews books and chapbooks of poetry and other magazines/journals. Poets may send materials for review consideration to Linda Jeanne.

◐ SOUL FOUNTAIN, 90-21 Springfield Blvd., Queens Village NY 11428. Phone/fax: (718)479-2594. E-mail: davault@aol.com. Website: www.TheVault.org. Established 1997. **Editor:** Tone Bellizzi.

Magazine Needs: *Soul Fountain* appears 4 times/year and publishes poetry, art, photography, short fiction, and essays. "Open to all. Our motto is 'Fear no Art.' We publish all quality submitted work, and specialize in emerging voices. We are particularly interested in visionary, challenging and consciousness-expanding material. We are especially seeking poetry from North and South Dakota, Utah, Vermont, Alaska, Nevada, and Kansas for our 50 states issue. We're hungry for artwork, particularly small black on white drawings." Accepts poetry written by teenage writers. Has published poetry by Robert Dunn, Thomas Catterson, Jay Chollick, and Paula Curci. *Soul Fountain* is 28 pages, magazine-sized, offset-printed and saddle-stapled. Subscription: $20. Sample: $5. Make checks payable to Hope for the Children Foundation.

How to Submit: Submit 2-3 "camera-ready" poems at a time. One page in length for each piece maximum. No cover letters necessary. Accepts previously published poems and simultaneous submissions. Accepts e-mail submissions (include in body of message); when e-mailing a submission, it is necessary to include your mailing address. Time between acceptance and publication is up to 2 years. Publishes theme issues. Guidelines and upcoming themes is available for SASE. Pays 1 copy. "For each issue there is a release/party/performance, 'Poetry & Poultry in Motion,' attended by poets, writers, artists, etc., appearing in the issue."

Also Offers: *Soul Fountain* is published by The Vault, "a not-for-profit arts project of the Hope for the Children Foundation; a growing, supportive community committed to empowering young and emerging artists of all disciplines at all levels to develop and share their talents through performance, collaboration, and networking."

Advice: "Fear no art—stretch."

SOUR GRAPES: ONLINE VINE FOR REJECTED WRITERS AND OTHER TORMENTED SOULS (Specialized), 26 Sheridan St., Woburn MA 01801-3542. E-mail: sandyberns@attbi.com. Website: www.sourgrapesnewsletter.com. Hardcopy established 1995, discontinued 1998, website established 1997. **Editor/Publisher:** Sandy Bernstein.

Needs: *Sour Grapes* website, published "haphazardly," is "dedicated to the discouraged, disgruntled, disillusioned, and dejected writers of the universe." Wants "insightful verse that is thought-provoking, creates an image or stirs a feeling. Poems don't have to be gripe-related, but should be of normal length—no epics, please. Almost any form style or subject is acceptable." Doesn't want " 'Experimental Poems' such as lines printed horizontally and vertically. If it looks like a crossword puzzle, don't send it here. No 'Gratuitous Profanity,' show us poetic language—not street talk."

How to Submit: Submit no more than 5 poems at one time (limit for haiku, 10; limit for very short verse, 7). Prefer e-mail submissions ("text in the body of the e-mail is preferred"), but accepts by postal mail. Please include cover letter with short bio and credits. Regular mail submissions should include SASE for return of mss. Often comments on rejected poems. Guidelines available for SASE or on website. Response time "may vary but will not be unreasonable." Guidelines available on the website, check frequently to see updated reading periods. Pays 1 copy (include SASE).

Advice: "Only submissions that follow our guidelines will be considered."

SOUTH–A POETRY MAGAZINE FOR THE SOUTHERN COUNTIES, P.O. Box 5369, Poole BH14 0XN United Kingdom. E-mail: south@martinblyth.co.uk. Website: http://martinblyth.co.uk. Established 1990. **Contact:** Poetry Editor.

Magazine Needs: *South* is published biannually in April and October. "Poets from or poems about the South region are particularly welcome, but poets from all over the world are free to submit work on all subjects." Has published poetry by Ian Caws, Stella Davis, Finola Holiday, Elsa Corbluth, and Brian Hinton. *South* is 68 pages, digest-sized, litho-printed and saddle-stapled with gloss laminated, duotone cover. Receives about 1,500 poems/year, accepts about 10%. Press run is 250 for 160 subscribers. Single copy: £5.60; subscription: £10/1 year, £18/2 years. Make checks (in sterling) payable to *South Poetry Magazine*.

How to Submit: Submit up to 6 poems at a time. No previously published poems or simultaneous submissions. Accepts submissions on disk (if accompanied by hard copy) and by postal mail. Deadline for April issue: November 30; for October issue: May 31. "Selection does not begin prior to the deadline and may take 6 weeks or more from that date." Time between acceptance and publication is up to 5 months.

Advice: "Buy the magazine. Then it will still be there to consider and publish your work and you'll get the idea of the sort of work we publish. These are basic steps, and both are essential."

$⃝ THE SOUTH BOSTON LITERARY GAZETTE, P.O. Box 443, South Boston MA 02127. Website: www.thesouthbostonliterarygazette.org. Established 1999. **Editor:** Dave Connolly.
Magazine Needs: *The South Boston Literary Gazette* appears quarterly, dedicated to "promoting quality work by both new and established writers from South Boston, from Greater Boston, from anywhere if writing is good. Very open to diversity in style, content, age groups." Does not want "acid ramblings; no extreme pornography (although foul language with a purpose is considered); amateurish, grammatically disordered writing." Accepts poetry written by children. Recently published poetry by Leonard Peltier, W.D. Ehrhardt, Michael Brown, Nancy A. Henry, Linda Lerner, and David Connolly. *The South Boston Literary Gazette* is 70 pages, magazine-sized, on 70 lb. gloss paper, spiral-bound, 80 lb. 4-color high gloss cover. Also published in online format. Receives about 400 poems/year, accepts about 25%. Publishes about 25 poems/issue. Press run is 500 for 100 subscribers, 150 shelf sales; 50 are distributed free to contributors and donors. Single copy: $10 (includes p&h); subscription: $25/year (4 issues). Make checks payable to *The South Boston Literary Gazette*.
How to Submit: *The South Boston Literary Gazette* Submit up to 4 poems at a time. Maximum length for poetry is 3,000 words. Accepts previously published poems and simultaneous submissions. Accepts submissions by postal mail. Cover letter "is preferred with name, address, phone, e-mail, and short bio, if possible; name and number on each page of submission." Reads submissions at all times. Submit seasonal poems well in advance. **Reading Fee:** $5; work not accompanied by reading fee will not be read. "We are a nonprofit existing on grants, donations, subscriptions, and these fees." Time between acceptance and publication is 1-3 months. Poems are circulated to an editorial board, "four editors; independent reviews using a 1-3 grading system; roundtable discussions follow." Guidelines available in magazine, for SASE, by e-mail, or on website. Responds in up to 3 months. Sometimes sends prepublication galleys. Pays 1 contributor's copy. "*The South Boston Literary Gazette* reserves the right to republish work as part of a volume."
Also Offers: Each issue awards at least two $50 prizes, one for poetry and one for prose.

⭐ ◐ ◎ SOUTH DAKOTA REVIEW (Specialized: regional, themes), University of South Dakota, Vermillion SD 57069. (605)677-5184 or 677-5966. Fax: (605)677-6409. E-mail: bbedard@us d.edu. Website: www.usd.edu/SDR. Established 1963. **Editor:** Brian Bedard.
Magazine Needs: *South Dakota Review* is a "literary quarterly publishing poetry, fiction, criticism, scholarly and personal essays. When material warrants, an emphasis on the American West; writers from the West; Western places or subjects; frequent issues with no geographical emphasis; periodic special issues on one theme, one place or one writer. Looking for originality, sophistication, significance, craft—i.e., professional work." Uses 15-20 poems/issue. Press run is 500-600 for 450 subscribers of which half are libraries. Single copy: $6; subscription: $18/year, $30/2 years. Sample: $5.
How to Submit: Submit 3-6 poems at one time. Editor comments on submissions "occasionally." Publishes theme issues. Guidelines available for SASE. Responds in 2 months. Reads submissions year round. Pays in copies and 1-year subscription. Acquires first and reprint rights.
Advice: "We tend to favor the narrative poem, the concrete crafted lyric, the persona poem and the meditative place poem. Yet we try to leave some room for poems outside those parameters to keep some fresh air in our selection process."

⭐ ◎ THE SOUTH 666 BITCH (Specialized: form/style beat, gay, horror, erotica, psychic/occult, social issues), Box 3756, Erie PA 16508. Established 1997. **Editor:** "That Bitch."
Magazine Needs: *The South 666 Bitch* appears 2-4 times/year and is "eager to offend those (what be) easily offended! 'That Bitch' prefers pro-anti, pro-beat, pro-morbid, pro-street poetry; 3-40 lines." Does not want to see "anything pretentious." Has published poetry by R.L. Nichols, Jim Delavern, Kevin M. Hibshman, Shane Allison, and Mark Sonnenfeld. *Bitch* is 6-12 pages, magazine-sized, photocopied and side-stapled with plenty of art and lots of ads. Accept approximately 2-10% of poems received. Press run is 66 for subscribers, 2 of which are universities. Sample: $1. Make checks payable to Robert L. Nichols.
How to Submit: Submit 3-6 poems at a time. Previously published poems and simultaneous submissions preferred. "Check your work for typos and uncorrect grammar (if unintentional)." Reads sub-

missions January 2 through October 27 only. **Reading fee:** $1/3 poems. Time between acceptance and publication is 6 months. Seldom comments on rejected poems. Publishes theme issues occasionally. Halloween issue: October 30, 2000 deadline; possible Christmas issue: October 27, 2000 deadline. Responds in 6 months. Pays 1-2 copies.

Advice: " 'That Bitch' publishes only six poets per issue."

◘ **THE SOUTHEAST REVIEW; SUNDOG CHAPBOOK AWARD**, English Dept., Florida State University, 216 Williams Bldg., Tallahassee FL 32306. (850)644-2773. E-mail: southeastreview @english.fsu.edu. Website: http://english.fsu.edu/southeastreview/. Established 1979. **Editor:** James Kimbrell.

Magazine Needs: *The Southeast Review* appears twice a year. "We look for the very best poetry by new and established poets." *The Southeast Review* is 160 pages, digest-sized. Receives about 5,000 poems/year, accepts less than 10%. Publishes about 50 poems/issue. Press run is 1,200 for 800 subscribers of which 100 are libraries, 200 shelf sales; 200 are distributed free. Single copy: $10; subscription: $8/year. Sample: $5. Make checks payable to *The Southeast Review*.

How to Submit: Submit 3-5 poems at a time. Accepts simultaneous submissions; no previously published poems. No fax, e-mail, or disk submissions. Cover letter is preferred. Include SASE. Reads submissions September through May. Time between acceptance and publication up to 1 year. Seldom comments on rejected poems. Occasionally publishes theme issues. List of upcoming themes available by e-mail. Guidelines available for SASE, by e-mail, or on website. Responds in up to 5 months. Pays 2 contributor's copies. Acquires first North American serial rights. Reviews books and chapbooks of poetry. Poets may send material for review consideration to the editor, *The Southeast Review*.

Also offers: Sundog Chapbook Award. Submissions must be typed, single-spaced. 1st prize: $500 and publication in the following spring issue; many finalists published as well. **Entry fee:** $10/entry (15-20 poems). **Annual Deadline:** Submit between September 1 and November 30.

◓ ◎ **THE SOUTHERN CALIFORNIA ANTHOLOGY (Specialized: anthology); ANN STANFORD POETRY PRIZES**, c/o Master of Professional Writing Program, WPH 404, University of Southern California, Los Angeles CA 90089-4034. (213)740-3252. Established 1983.

Magazine Needs: *The Southern California Anthology* is an "annual literary review of serious contemporary poetry and fiction. Very open to all subject matters except pornography. Any form, style OK." Has published poetry by Robert Bly, Donald Hall, Allen Ginsberg, Lisel Mueller, James Ragan, Nikki Giovanni, W.S. Merwin, and John Updike. *The Southern California Anthology* is 144 pages, digest-sized, perfect-bound, with a semi-glossy color cover featuring one art piece. Press run is 1,500, 50% going to subscribers of which 50% are libraries, 30% are for shelf sales. Sample: $5.95.

How to Submit: Submit 3-5 poems between September 1 and January 1 only. No simultaneous submissions or previously published poems. All decisions made by mid-February. Guidelines available for SASE. Responds in 4 months. Pays 2 contributor's copies. Acquires all rights.

Also Offers: The Ann Stanford Poetry Prizes ($1,000, $200, and $100) have an April 15 deadline, $10 fee (5 poem limit), for unpublished poems. Include cover sheet with name, address, and titles as well as SASE for contest results. All entries are considered for publication, and all entrants receive a copy of *The Southern California Anthology*.

◓ **SOUTHERN HUMANITIES REVIEW; THEODORE CHRISTIAN HOEPFNER AWARD**, 9088 Haley Center, Auburn University, Auburn AL 36849-5202. E-mail: shrengl@auburn. edu. Website: www.auburn.edu/english/shr/home.htm. Established 1967. **Co-Editors:** Dan Latimer and Virginia M. Kouidis.

Magazine Needs: *Southern Humanities Review* is a literary quarterly "interested in poems of any length, subject, genre. Space is limited, and brief poems are more likely to be accepted. Translations welcome, but also send written permission from the copyright holder." Has published poetry by Donald Hall, Andrew Hudgins, Margaret Gibson, Stephen Dunn, Walt McDonald, and R.T. Smith. *Southern Humanities Review* is 100 pages, digest-sized, press run 700. Subscription: $15/year. Sample: $5.

How to Submit: "Send 3-5 poems in a business-sized envelope. Include SASE. Avoid sending faint computer printout." No previously published poems or simultaneous submissions. No e-mail submissions. Responds in 2 months, possibly longer in summer. Always sends prepublication galleys.

Pays 2 copies. Copyright reverts to author upon publication. Reviews books of poetry in approximately 750-1,000 words. Send materials for review consideration.

Also Offers: Sponsors the Theodore Christian Hoepfner Award, a $50 award for the best poem published in a given volume of *Southern Humanities Review*.

Advice: "For beginners we'd recommend study and wide reading in English and classical literature, and, of course, American literature—the old works, not just the new. We also recommend study of or exposure to a foreign language and a foreign culture. Poets need the reactions of others to their work: criticism, suggestions, discussion. A good creative writing teacher would be desirable here, and perhaps some course work too. And then submission of work, attendance at workshops. And again, the reading: history, biography, verse, essays—all of it. We want to see poems that have gone beyond the language of slippage and easy attitudes."

$○ THE SOUTHERN REVIEW, 43 Allen Hall, Louisiana State University, Baton Rouge LA 70803-5005. (225)578-5108. Fax: (225)578-5098. E-mail: bmacon@lsu.edu. Website: www.lsu.edu/thesouthernreview. Established 1935 (original series), 1965 (new series). **Editor:** James Olney. **Associate Editor:** John Easterly.

  • Work published in this review has been frequently included in *The Best American Poetry* and appeared in *The Beacon's Best of 1999*.

Magazine Needs: *The Southern Review* "is a literary quarterly that publishes fiction, poetry, critical essays, and book reviews, with emphasis on contemporary literature in the U.S. and abroad, and with special interest in southern culture and history. Selections are made with careful attention to craftsmanship and technique and to the seriousness of the subject matter. We are interested in any variety of poetry that is well crafted, though we cannot normally accommodate excessively long poems (say 10 pages and over)." Has published poetry by Mary Oliver, Sharon Olds, Reynolds Price, and Ellen Bryant Voigt. *The Southern Review* is digest-sized, 240 pages, flat-spined, matte card cover. Receives about 6,000 submissions of poetry/year. All styles and forms seem welcome, although accessible lyric and narrative free verse appear most often in recent issues. Press run is 2,500 for 2,100 subscribers of which 70% are libraries. Subscription: $25. Sample: $8.

How to Submit: "We do not require a cover letter but we prefer one giving information about the author and previous publications." Prefers submissions of up to 6 pages. No fax or e-mail submissions. Guidelines available for SASE or on website. Responds in 1 month. Pays $20/printed page plus 2 contributor's copies. Acquires first North American serial rights. Staff reviews books of poetry in 3,000 words, multi-book format. Send material for review consideration.

$○ SOUTHWEST REVIEW; ELIZABETH MATCHETT STOVER MEMORIAL AWARD; MORTON MARR POETRY PRIZE, 307 Fondren Library West, P.O. Box 750374, Southern Methodist University, Dallas TX 75275-0374. (214)768-1037. Fax: (214)768-1408. E-mail: swr@mail.smu.edu. Website: www.southwestreview.org. Established 1915. **Editor:** Willard Spiegelman.

  • Poetry published in *Southwest Review* has been included in the 1995 and 1998 volumes of *The Best American Poetry* as well as the 2002 *Pushcart Prize* anthology.

Magazine Needs: *Southwest Review* is a literary quarterly that publishes fiction, essays, poetry, and interviews. "It is hard to describe our preference for poetry in a few words. We always suggest that potential contributors read several issues of the magazine to see for themselves what we like. But some things may be said: We demand very high quality in our poems; we accept both traditional and experimental writing, but avoid unnecessary obscurity and private symbolism; we place no arbitrary limits on length but find shorter poems easier to fit into our format than longer ones. We have no specific limitations as to theme." Has published poetry by Albert Goldbarth, John Hollander, Mary Jo Salter, James Hoggard, Dorothea Tanning, and Michael Rosen. *Southwest Review* is digest-sized, 144 pages, perfect-bound, professionally printed, with matte text stock cover. Receives about 1,000 submissions of poetry/year, accepts about 32. Poems tend to be lyric and narrative free verse combining a strong voice with powerful topics or situations. Diction is accessible and content often conveys a strong sense of place. Circulation is 1,500 for 1,000 subscribers of which 600 are libraries. Subscription: $24. Sample: $6.

How to Submit: No simultaneous submissions or previously published work. Guidelines available for SASE and on website. Responds within a month. Always sends prepublication galleys. Pays cash plus copies.

Also Offers: The $250 Elizabeth Matchett Stover Memorial Award is awarded annually for the best poems, chosen by editors, published in the preceding year. The $1,000 Morton Marr Poetry Prize gives an annual award to a poem by a writer who has not yet published a first book; poems submitted should be in a "traditional" form. Details available on website.

★ ⏺ ◎ SOUTHWESTERN AMERICAN LITERATURE (Specialized: regional), Center for the Study of the Southwest, 601 University Dr., San Marcos TX 78666. (512)245-2232. Fax: (512)245-7462. E-mail: mb13@swt.edu. Website: www.english.swt.edu/css/cssindex.htm. Established 1971. **Editor:** Dr. Mark Busby. **Editor:** Dr. Dick Heaberlin.

Magazine Needs: *Southwestern American Literature* is "a biannual scholarly journal that includes literary criticism, fiction, poetry, and book reviews concerning the Greater Southwest. While we are a regional journal, we enjoy seeing poetry of all subject matters, not just about tumbleweeds, longhorns, and urban cowboys." Has published poetry by Naomi Shihab Nye, Alberto Rios, Alison Deming, and Simon J. Ortiz. *Southwestern American Literature* is 100-125 pages, digest-sized, professionally printed and perfect-bound with 80 lb. embossed bond cover. Receives about 200 poems/year, accepts approximately 10%. Press run is 400 for 225 subscribers of which 80 are libraries. Subscription: $14/year. Sample: $7.

How to Submit: Submit 5 poems at a time. Accepts simultaneous submissions; no previously published poems. Cover letter preferred. "Two copies of manuscript should be submitted along with SASE." No e-mail submissions. Time between acceptance and publication is 2-6 months. Poems are circulated to an editorial board. "Each poem that is accepted has been recommended by at least two members of our editorial board." Seldom comments on rejected poems. Publishes theme issues occasionally. Guidelines available for e-mail. Responds in 6 weeks. Pays 1 copy. Acquires all rights. Returns rights upon publication. Staff reviews books of poetry in 500-1,000 words, single or multibook format. Send material for review consideration.

★ ⏺ SOU'WESTER, Box 1438, Southern Illinois University, Edwardsville IL 62026. (618)650-3190. Fax: (618)650-3509. E-mail: sw@siue.edu. Website: www.siue.edu/ENGLISH/SW. Established 1960. **Co- Editors:** Allison Funk and Geoff Schmidt.

Magazine Needs: *Sou'wester* appears biannually in December and June. "We lean toward poetry with strong imagery, successful association of images, and skillful use of figurative language." Has published poetry by Robert Wrigley, Beckian Fritz Goldberg, Eric Pankey, Betsy Sholl, and Angie Estes. *Sou'wester* has 30-40 pages of poetry in each digest-sized, 100-page issue. *Sou'wester* is professionally printed, flat-spined, with textured matte card cover, press run is 300 for 500 subscribers of which 50 are libraries. Receives 3,000 poems (from 600 poets) each year, accepts 36-40, has a 6-month backlog. Subscription: $12/2 issues. Sample: $6.

How to Submit: Accepts simultaneous submissions. Reads submissions from September 1 through May 31. Responds in 3 months. Pays 2 copies and 1-year subscription. Acquires all rights. Returns rights. Editor comments on rejected poems "usually, in the case of those that we almost accept."

⏺ THE SOW'S EAR POETRY REVIEW, 355 Mount Lebanon Rd., Donalds SC 29638-9115. (864)379-8061. E-mail: errol@kitenet.net. Established 1988. **Contact:** Errol Hess, managing editor. **Editor:** Kristin Camitta Zimet.

Magazine Needs: *The Sow's Ear* is a quarterly. "We are open to many forms and styles, and have no limitations on length. We try to be interesting visually, and we use graphics to complement the poems. Though we publish some work from our local community of poets, we are interested in poems from all over. We publish a few by previously unpublished poets." Has recently published poetry by Andrea Carter Brown, Corrine Clegg Hales, Jerry McGuire, Virgil Suarez, Susan Terris, and Franz Wright. *The Sow's Ear Poetry Review* is 32 pages, magazine-sized, saddle-stapled, with matte card cover, professionally printed. Receives about 2,000 poems/year, accepts about 100. Press run is 600 for 500 subscribers of which 15 are libraries, 20-40 shelf sales. Subscription: $10. Sample: $5.

How to Submit: Submit up to 5 poems at a time with SASE. Accepts simultaneous submissions if you tell them promptly when work is accepted elsewhere; no previously published poems. Enclose brief bio. No e-mail submissions. Guidelines available for SASE or by e-mail. Responds in up to 6 months. Pays 2 copies. Acquires first publication rights. Most prose (reviews, interviews, features) is commissioned.

Also Offers: Offers an annual contest for unpublished poems, with fee of $2/poem, prizes of $1,000, $250, and $100, and publication for 15-20 finalists. For contest, submit poems in September/October, with name and address on a separate sheet. Submissions of 5 poems/$10 receive a subscription. Include SASE for notification. 2001 Judge: Dabney Stuart. Also sponsors a chapbook contest in March/April with $10 fee, $1,000 1st Prize, publication, 25 copies and distribution to subscribers; 2nd Prize $200 and 3rd Prize $100. Send SASE or e-mail for chapbook contest guidelines.

Advice: "Four criteria help us judge the quality of submissions: Does the poem make the strange familiar or the familiar strange or both? Is the form of the poem vital to its meaning? Do the sounds of the poem make sense in relation to the theme? Does the little story of the poem open a window on the Big Story of the human situation?"

$ □ ◎ SPACE AND TIME (Specialized: science fiction/fantasy, horror), 138 W. 70th St. (4B), New York NY 10023-4468. Established 1966. **Poetry Editor:** Linda Addison.

Magazine Needs: *Space and Time* is a biannual that publishes "primarily science fiction/fantasy/ horror; some related poetry and articles. We do not want to see anything that doesn't fit science fiction/ fantasy/weird genres." Has published poetry by Lyn Lifshin, Susan Spilecki, Mark Kreighbaum, and Cynthia Tedesco. The issue of *Space and Time* we received was about 100 pages, digest-sized, perfect-bound, however, the magazine will be reformatted to 48 pages, magazine-sized, web press printed on 50 lb. stock and saddle-stapled with glossy card cover and interior b&w illustrations. Receives about 500 poems/year, accepts 5%. Press run is 2,000 for 200 subscribers of which 10 are libraries, 1,200 shelf sales. Single copy: $5; subscription: $10. Sample: $6.25.

How to Submit: Submit up to 4 poems at a time. No previously published poems or simultaneous submissions. Time between acceptance and publication is up to 9 months. Often comments on rejected poems. Poets may send SASE for guidelines "but they won't see more than what's here." Responds in up to 6 weeks, "longer if recommended." Pays 1¢/word ($5 minimum) plus 2 copies. Acquires first North American serial rights.

□ SPILLWAY, P.O. Box 7887, Huntington Beach CA 92615-7887. (714)968-0905. Website: www.t ebothach.org. Established 1991. **Editors:** Mifanwy Kaiser and J.D. Lloyd.

Magazine Needs: *Spillway* is a biannual journal, published in March and September, "celebrating writing's diversity and power to affect our lives. Open to all voices, schools, and tendencies. We publish poetry, translations, reviews, essays and b&w photography." Has published poetry by John Balaban, Sam Hamill, Robin Chapman, Richard Jones, and Eleanor Wilner. *Spillway* is about 176 pages, digest-sized, attractively printed, perfect-bound, with 2-color or 4-color card cover. Press run is 2,000. Single copy: $9; subscription: $16/2 issues, $28/4 issues. Sample (including guidelines): $10. Make checks payable to *Spillway*.

How to Submit: Submit 3-6 poems at a time, 10 pages total. Accepts previously published work ("say when and where") and simultaneous submissions ("say where also submitted"). Accepts submissions on disk, by e-mail (as a Word attachment or in text box), and by postal mail. Cover letter including brief bio and SASE required. Reads submissions year-round. "No cute bios." Responds in up to 6 months. Pays 1 copy. Acquires one-time rights. Reviews books of poetry in 500-2,500 words maximum. Send materials for review consideration.

Advice: "We have no problem with simultaneous or previously published submissions. Poems are murky creatures—they shift and change in time and context. It's exciting to pick up a volume, read a poem in the context of all the other pieces, and then find the same poem in another time and place. And, we don't think a poet should have to wait until death to see work in more than one volume. What joy to find out that more than one editor values one's work. Our responsibility as editors,

---

USE THE GENERAL INDEX in the back of this book to find the page number of a specific market. Also, markets listed in the 2003 edition but not included in this edition appear in the General Index with a code explaining their absence from the listings.

collectively, is to promote the work of poets as much as possible—how can we do this if we say to a writer you may only have a piece published in one volume and only one time?"

★ ◎ **SPINDRIFT**, Shoreline Community College, 16101 Greenwood Ave. N., Seattle WA 98133. (206)546-5864. Established 1962. **Faculty Advisor:** currently Gary Parks.

Magazine Needs: *Spindrift*, published annually, is open to all varieties of poetry except greeting card style. Has published poetry by Lyn Lifshin, Mary Lou Sanelli, James Bertolino, Edward Harkness, and Richard West. *Spindrift* is 125 pages, handsomely printed in an 8″ square, flat-spined, includes visual art as well as literature. Press run is 500. Single copy: $8. Sample: $2.

How to Submit: "Submit two copies of each poem, six lines maximum. The author's name should not appear on the submitted work. Include SASE and cover letter with 2-3 lines of biographical information including name, address, phone number, e-mail address, and a list of all materials sent. We accept submissions postmarked between September and January; editorial responses are mailed by March 15." Guidelines available for SASE. Pays 2 copies. All rights revert to author upon publication.

Advice: "Read the magazine. Be distinctive, love language, work from the heart but avoid sentimentality."

◎ **SPINNING JENNY**, Black Dress Press, P.O. Box 1373, New York NY 10276. Website: www.blackdresspress.com. Established 1994. **Editor:** C.E. Harrison.

Magazine Needs: *Spinning Jenny* appears once/year in April. Has published poetry by Tina Cane, Sara Fox, Matthew Lippman, and Ian Randall Wilson. *Spinning Jenny* is 112 pages, digest-sized, perfect-bound with heavy card cover. "We accept less than 5% of unsolicited submissions." Press run is 1,000. Single copy: $8; subscription: $15/2 issues. Sample: $8.

How to Submit: No previously published poems or simultaneous submissions. Accepts e-mail submissions (include in body of message). Seldom comments on rejected poems. Guidelines available for SASE or on website. Responds within 2 months. Pays 5 contributor copies. Authors retain rights.

★ ◎ **SPITBALL: THE LITERARY BASEBALL MAGAZINE; CASEY AWARD (Specialized: sports/recreation, baseball)**, 5560 Fox Rd., Cincinnati OH 45239. (513)385-2268. Established 1981. **Poetry Editor:** William J. McGill.

Magazine Needs: *Spitball* is "a unique literary magazine devoted to poetry, fiction, and book reviews exclusively about baseball. Newcomers are very welcome, but remember that you have to know the subject. We do and our readers do. Perhaps a good place to start for beginners is one's personal reactions to the game, a game, a player, etc. and take it from there." *Spitball* is 96-pages, digest-sized biannual, computer typeset and perfect-bound. Receives about 1,000 submissions/year, accepts about 40. "Many times we are able to publish accepted work almost immediately." Circulation is 1,000 for 750 subscribers of which 25 are libraries. Subscription: $12. Sample: $6. "**We now require all first-time submitters to purchase a sample copy for $6**. This is a one-time only fee, which we regret but economic reality dictates that we insist those who wish to be published in *Spitball* help support it, at least at this minimum level."

How to Submit: "We are not very concerned with the technical details of submitting, but we do prefer a cover letter with some bio info. We also like batches of poems and prefer to use several of same poet in an issue rather than a single poem." Pays 2 copies.

Also Offers: "We sponsor the Casey Award (for best baseball book of the year) and hold the Casey Awards Banquet every January. Any chapbook of baseball poetry should be sent to us for consideration for the 'Casey' plaque that we award to the winner each year."

Advice: "We encourage anyone interested to submit to *Spitball*. We are always looking for fresh talent. Those who have never written 'baseball poetry' before should read some first probably before submitting. Not necessarily ours."

🌐 ○ **SPLIZZ**, 4 St. Marys Rise, Burry Port, Carms SA16 0SH Wales. E-mail: a_jmorgan@yahoo. co.uk. Website: www.stmarys4.freeserve.co.uk/Splizz.htm. Established 1993. **Editor:** Amanda Morgan.

Magazine Needs: *Splizz*, published quarterly, features poetry, prose, reviews of contemporary music and background to poets. Wants "any kind of poetry. We have no restrictions regarding style, length, subjects." However, they do not want "anything racist or homophobic." Has published Colin Cross

(UK), Anders Carson (Canada), Paul Truttman (US), Jan Hansen (Portugal), and Gregory Arena (Italy). *Splizz* is 40-44 pages, A5, saddle-stapled with art and ads. Receives about 200-300 poems/year, accepts about 90%. Press run is 150 for 35 subscribers. Single copy: £1.30, 5 IRCs elsewhere; subscription: £5 UK, £10 elsewhere. Sample: £1.30 UK, 5 IRCs elsewhere. Make checks payable to Amanda Morgan (British checks only).

How to Submit: Submit 5 poems, typed submissions preferred. Name and address must be included on each page of submitted work. Include SAE with IRCs. Does not accept previously published poems or simultaneous submissions. Accepts e-mail submissions in attached file. Cover letter required with short bio. Time between acceptance and publication is 4 months. Often comments on rejected poems. Charges criticism fee: "Just enclose SAE/IRC for response, and allow one to two months for delivery." Guidelines available for SASE (or SAE and IRC), by e-mail, or in publication. Responds in 2 months. Sometimes sends prepublication galleys. Reviews books or chapbooks of poetry or other magazines in 50-300 words. Send materials for review consideration. E-mail for further enquiries.

Advice: "Beginners seeking to have their work published, send your work to *Splizz*, as we specialize in giving new poets a chance."

THE SPOON RIVER POETRY REVIEW; EDITORS' PRIZE CONTEST, 4240/English

Dept., Illinois State University, Normal IL 61790-4240. Website: www.litline.org/spoon. Established 1976. **Editor:** Lucia Getsi.

Magazine Needs: *Spoon River Poetry Review* is a a biannual "poetry magazine that features newer and well-known poets from around the country and world." Also features 1 Illinois poet/issue at length for the magazine's Illinois Poet Series. "We want interesting and compelling poetry that operates beyond the ho-hum, so-what level, in any form or style about anything; language that is fresh, energetic, committed, filled with a strong voice that grabs the reader in the first line and never lets go." Also uses translations of poetry. Has published poetry by Stuart Dybek, Robin Behn, Dave Smith, Beth Ann Fennelly, Dorothea Grünzweig, and Alicia Ostriker. *Spoon River Poetry Review* is 128 pages, digest-sized, laser set with card cover using photos, ads. Receives about 3,000 poems/month, accepts 1%. Press run is 1,500 for 800 subscribers, of which 100 are libraries. Subscription: $16. Sample (including guidelines): $10.

How to Submit: "No simultaneous submissions unless we are notified immediately if a submission is accepted elsewhere. Include name and address on every poem." Do not submit mss May 1 through September 1. Editor comments on rejected poems "many times, if a poet is promising." Guidelines available on website and in publication. Responds in 2 months. Pays a year's subscription. Acquires first North American serial rights. Reviews books of poetry. Send materials for review consideration.

Also Offers: Sponsors the Editor's Prize Contest for previously unpublished work. One poem will be awarded $1,000 and published in the fall issue of *Spoon River Poetry Review*, and two runners-up will receive $100 each and publication in the fall issue. Entries must be previously unpublished. **Entry fee:** $16, including 1-year subscription. **Deadline:** April 15. Write for details. Past winners were Marilyn Krysl and Aleida Rodríguez.

Advice: "Read. Workshop with poets who are better than you. Subscribe to at least 5 literary magazines a year, especially those you'd like to be published in."

SPOUT MAGAZINE, P.O. Box 581067, Minneapolis MN 55458-1067. Website: www.spoutpress.com. Established 1989. **Editors:** John Colburn and Michelle Filkins.

Magazine Needs: *Spout* appears approximately 3 times/year providing "a paper community of unique expression." Wants "poetry of the imagination, poetry that surprises. We enjoy the surreal, the forceful, the political, the expression of confusion." No light verse, archaic forms or language. Has published poetry by Gilian McCain, Larissa Szporluck, Dan Raphael, Sheila E. Murphy, and Jeffrey Little. *Spout* is 40-60 pages, saddle-stapled, card stock or glossy cover is a different color each issue. Receives about 400-450 poems/year, accepts approximately 10%. Press run is 200-250 for 35-40 subscribers, 100-150 shelf sales. Single copy price: $4; subscription: $15. Sample: $4.

How to Submit: Submit up to 6 poems at a time. Accepts previously published poems and simultaneous submissions. Cover letter preferred. Time between acceptance and publication is 2-3 months. Poems are circulated to an editorial board. "Poems are reviewed by two of three editors, those selected for final review are read again by all three." Seldom comments on rejected poems. Send SASE for guidelines. Responds in 4 months. Pays 1 copy.

⬐ ◎ **SPRING: THE JOURNAL OF THE E.E. CUMMINGS SOCIETY (Specialized: membership/subscription)**, 33-54 164th St., Flushing NY 11358-1442. (718)353-3631 or (718)461-9022. Fax: (718)353-4778. E-mail: EECSPRINGNF@aol.com. Website: www.gvsu.edu/english/Cummings/Index.html. **Editor:** Norman Friedman.

Magazine Needs: *Spring* is an annual publication, usually appearing in fall, designed "to maintain and broaden the audience for Cummings and to explore various facets of his life and art." Wants poems in the spirit of Cummings, primarily poems of one page or less. Nothing "amateurish." Has published poetry by John Tagliabue, Jacqueline Vaught Brogan, and Gerald Locklin. *Spring* is about 180 pages, digest-sized, offset and perfect-bound with light card stock cover. Press run is 500 for 200 subscribers of which 15 are libraries, 300 shelf sales. Subscription or sample: $17.50.

How to Submit: No previously published poems or simultaneous submissions. Accepts submissions by fax and by e-mail (as attachment). Cover letter required. Reads submissions January through March only. Seldom comments on rejected poems. Guidelines available for SASE. Responds in 6 months. Pays 1 copy.

Advice: "Contributors are required to subscribe."

$⬐ ◎ SPS STUDIOS, INC., PUBLISHERS OF BLUE MOUNTAIN ARTS® (Specialized: greeting cards and gift books), Dept. PM, P.O. Box 1007, Boulder CO 80306-1007. Fax: (303)447-0939. E-mail: editorial@spsstudios.com. Website: www.sps.com. Established 1971. **Contact:** editorial staff.

Book/Chapbook Needs: SPS Studios publishes greeting cards, books, calendars, prints, and mugs. Looking for poems, prose, and lyrics ("usually non-rhyming") appropriate for publication on greeting cards and in poetry anthologies. Also actively seeking "book-length manuscripts that would be appropriate for book and gift stores. We are also very interested in receiving book and card ideas that would be appropriate for college stores, as well as younger buyers. Poems should reflect a message, feeling, or sentiment that one person would want to share with another. We'd like to receive creative, original submissions about love relationships, family members, friendships, philosophies, and any other aspect of life. Poems and writings for specific holidays (Christmas, Valentine's Day, etc.) and special occasions, such as graduation, anniversary, and get well are also considered. Only a small portion of the material we receive is selected each year and the review process can be lengthy, but be assured every manuscript is given serious consideration."

How to Submit: Submissions must be typewritten, 1 poem/page or sent via e-mail (no attachments). Enclose SASE if you want your work returned. Simultaneous submissions "discouraged but OK with notification." Accepts submissions by e-mail (in text box), by fax, and by postal mail. Submit seasonal material at least 4 months in advance. Guidelines available for SASE or by e-mail. Responds in up to 6 months. Pays $300/poem all rights for each of the first 2 submissions chosen for publication (after which payment scale escalates), for the worldwide, exclusive right, $50/poem for one-time use in an anthology.

Advice: "We strongly suggest that you familiarize yourself with our products before submitting material, although we caution you not to study them too hard. We do not need more poems that sound like something we've already published. Overall, we're looking for poetry that expresses real emotions and feelings."

⬐ **SPUNK**, Box 55336, Hayward CA 94545. (415)974-8980. Established 1996. **Editor:** Violet Jones.

Magazine Needs: Appearing 2 times/year, *Spunk: The Journal of Unrealized Potential* contains "writings and artwork of every nature. We are an outlet for spontaneous expressions only. Save the self-satisfied, over-crafted stuff for *Paris Review*, please." Accepts poetry written by children. *Spunk* is up to 70 pages though "its size varies; silkscreened and photocopied, hand bound, no ads." Receives about 800-1,000 poems/year, accepts less than 5%. Press run is 500; all distributed free to anyone who really, really wants them. Sample: $1. No checks.

How to Submit: Submit any number of poems at a time. No previously published poems or simultaneous submissions. Cover letter preferred. "Just make us happy we opened the envelope—how you do this is up to you." Time between acceptance and publication is up to 1 year. Often comments on rejected poems. Occasionally publishes theme issues. Guidelines and upcoming themes available for

SASE. Responds in up to 1 year. Pays 1 contributor's copy. Acquires first North American serial rights. Staff occasionally reviews books and chapbooks of poetry and other magazines in 100-500 words, single book format. Send materials for review consideration. "Our review section has expanded, we run reviews every issue now."

STAPLE, Padley Rise, Nether Padley, Grindleford, Hope Valley, Derbys S32 2HE United Kingdom or 35 Carr Rd., Walkley, Sheffield S6 2WY United Kingdom. Phone: 01433-631949. Established 1982 (redesigned 2001). **Co-Editors:** Ann Atkinson and Elizabeth Barrett.
Magazine Needs: *Staple* appears 3 times/year and "accepts poetry, short fiction, and articles about the writing process." *Staple* is 100 pages, perfect-bound. Press run is 500 for 350 subscribers. Single copy: £3.50, subscription: £15/year. Sample: £3.
How to Submit: Submit 6 poems at a time. No simultaneous submissions or previously published poems. Cover letter preferred. Include 2 IRCs and SAE. Editors sometimes comment on rejected poems. Submission deadlines are end of March, July, and November. Responds in up to 3 months. Sometimes sends prepublication galleys. Pays either £5/poem (£10/story or article) or free annual subscription to *Staple*.

$ STICKMAN REVIEW: AN ONLINE LITERARY JOURNAL, 2890 N. Fairview Dr., Flagstaff AZ 86004. (928)913-0869. E-mail: editors@stickmanreview.com. Website: www.stickmanr eview.com. Established 2001.
Magazine Needs: *Stickman Review* is a biannual online literary journal dedicated to publishing great poetry, fiction, nonfiction, and artwork. Wants poetry "that is literary in intent, no restrictions on form, subject matter, or style. We would prefer not to see rhyming poetry." Publishes about 15 poems/issue.
How to Submit: Submit 5 poems at a time. Accepts simultaneous submissions; no previously published poems. Accepts e-mail submissions *only*; no fax or disk submissions. Cover letter is preferred. Reads submissions year round. Time between acceptance and publication is 2 months. "Currently, the editors-in-chief review all submissions." Often comments on rejected poems. Guidelines available on website. Responds in 2 months. Pays $10/poem up to $20 per author. Acquires first rights.
Advice: "Keep writing and submitting. A rejection is not necessarily a reflection upon the quality of your work. Be persistent, trust your instincts, and sooner or later, good things will come."

$ STONE SOUP, THE MAGAZINE BY YOUNG WRITERS AND ARTISTS; THE CHILDREN'S ART FOUNDATION (Specialized: children), P.O. Box 83, Santa Cruz CA 95063. (831)426-5557. Fax: (831)426-1161. E-mail: editor@stonesoup.com. Website: www.stoneso up.com. Established 1973. **Editor:** Ms. Gerry Mandel.
 • *Stone Soup* has received both Parents' Choice and Edpress Golden Lamp Honor Awards.
Magazine Needs: *Stone Soup* publishes writing and art by children through age 13; wants free verse poetry but no rhyming poetry, haiku, or cinquain. *Stone Soup*, published 6 times/year, is magazine-sized, professionally printed on heavy stock with 10-12 full-color art reproductions inside and a full-color illustration on the coated cover, saddle-stapled. A membership in the Children's Art Foundation at $33/year includes a subscription to the magazine. Receives 5,000 poetry submissions/year, accepts about 12. There are 2-4 pages of poetry in each issue. Press run is 20,000 for 14,000 subscribers, 5,000 to bookstores, 1,000 other. Sample: $5.
How to Submit: Submissions can be any number of pages, any format. Include name, age, home address, and phone number. Don't include SASE; responds only to those submissions under consideration and cannot return mss. Do not send original artwork. No simultaneous submissions. No e-mail submissions. Guidelines available for SASE, by e-mail, or on website. Responds in up to 6 weeks. Pays $40, a certificate, and 2 copies plus discounts. Acquires all rights. Returns rights upon request. Open to reviews by children.

STORY LINE PRESS; NICHOLAS ROERICH POETRY PRIZE, Three Oaks Farm, P.O. Box 1240, Ashland OR 97520-0055. (541)512-8792. Fax: (541)512-8793. E-mail: mail@storylinepre ss.com. Website: www.storylinepress.com. Established 1985. **Executive Director:** Robert McDowell.
 • Books published by Story Line Press have recently received such prestigious awards as the

insider report

The market for young poets

The market for young writers is a strange and challenging obstacle course, but the prize for completion is wonderful. No thrill could rival opening your contributor's copy and finding your poem smack in the middle of page 42 and knowing others will find it (and read it), too.

This is probably what drove writers like Ernest Hemingway, Sylvia Plath, Langston Hughes, and Louisa May Alcott to publish work before they reached their 18th birthday (Plath when she was only 8). If your 8th year has already come and gone, don't panic; French poet Arthur Rimbaud didn't publish his first piece until he was 16, only to retire from writing at age 20.

How can *you* get started? Get to know the publishing opportunities available to young writers, including the raft of sites online, and investigate their age requirements. You'll find most of those journals and websites welcome submissions from teen writers exclusively, while a handful accept submissions from pre-teens only. Rarely will you find a magazine that accepts poetry from both age groups.

Some of the magazines that consider and publish work by young poets include *Claremont Review*, *Merlyn's Pen*, *Stone Soup*, and *Word Dance*. The editors can select the best poetry submitted by the best young poets, and the quality of their magazines shows that they do. This means you're in for some stiff competition when you submit to these markets. *Stone Soup*, for example, publishes only writers aged 8 through 13, yet editor Gerry Mandel is flooded with more submissions than she can possibly use.

"At *Stone Soup* we get 300 submissions a week," Mandel explains. "That's 15,000 a year, and more than half of those submissions are poems. Now, keep in mind, we publish only 10 to 12 poems a year." She adds, "We'd like to publish two poems every issue, but that doesn't always happen." Mandel receives phone calls from 14-year-olds on a regular basis, begging the magazine to let them submit their work. She usually directs them to the links page on the *Stone Soup* website, which lists several children- and teen-friendly markets.

When searching for publishing opportunities, Kathy Henderson, author of *The Young Writer's Guide to Getting Published* (Writer's Digest Books), says, "Look locally. Kids who are beginning should look to local groups and newspapers." Her own local paper prints a weekly column that frequently publishes poetry by kids. "Putting together a chapbook locally is also a great start," Henderson says. "Get your friends to go in on it or talk to your teachers about it."

If you're serious about your poetry, strive to make each poem well crafted, and ready for a challenge, perhaps it's time to approach adult-level magazines. Remember, though, your poetry will be judged against poems submitted by adults, who are probably more experienced and skilled. However, Henderson points out, "I've been working with some nine- and ten-year-olds who can write the pants off some adults."

Michael Hathaway, editor of the literary journal *Chiron Review*, admits a younger writer will be given more consideration when he or she submits to his journal. "I can be more sympathetic because it's a little unusual," Hathaway says, but he stresses that quality still matters. Most of the submissions he receives are from teenagers who "usually write about teenage stuff like angst, trying to fit in, puppy love. I want to see them going outside of themselves."

Whether you're submitting poetry for local publication, submitting to magazines for and by kids, or submitting to adult literary journals, you're in competition with other poets. Aside from writing excellent, powerful poetry, what would give you the edge over other young writers? Over adults?

First, remember this: The quickest path to rejection is an unprofessional-looking manuscript. Check out the formatting instructions in "Frequently Asked Questions" in the front of this book. Unless a magazine's guidelines tell you differently, use our suggested format to set up your manuscript.

A neat, professional manuscript really does make a difference. Let's say an editor receives a brilliant poem. At least he *thinks* it's brilliant—smeared ballpoint ink makes the tiny handwriting impossible to read. The poem's sort of scrawled on a piece of lined paper ripped from a spiral-bound notebook. There's no cover letter with the submission, no SASE, just a name and a phone number squeezed into the bottom corner of the page.

Quite simply, the editor's not going to publish that poem. Despite its brilliance, such a submission falls squarely into the too-much-trouble-to-bother-with category. No matter where you're submitting your work, do it right. Make sure your manuscript is neatly typed or computer-generated on white paper, with no typos or painful grammatical mistakes, and with your contact information presented clearly.

Wait, back up to those "magazine guidelines" mentioned above. What are those? Guidelines spell out all the requirements for submission: word or line count, format, number of poems to submit, and other important information. Guidelines may be available from a magazine for a SASE (self-addressed stamped envelope) or on the magazine's website.

Note that ignoring guidelines is another surefire way to get rejected. "We do not publish formula verse," says *Stone Soup*'s Mandel, yet every visit from the mailman brings limericks, ballads, and all manner of rhyming poetry. Formula verse is an automatic disqualifier; *Stone Soup* publishes only free verse because the editors feel it's the most sincere form. "With rhyming poetry, you get the word 'glee' a lot because it rhymes with 'me,' " says Mandel. "Not to say rhyming poetry isn't a valuable exercise at school or at home, because it is, but we publish free verse only." *Stone Soup* also recently changed their submission policy, asking poets not to include SASEs with their manuscripts anymore because the editors can reply only when work is accepted for publication. Poets who don't consult the submission guidelines won't know about this important change.

Another example is *The Louisville Review*, which publishes poetry by young writers in a section called "The Children's Corner" but doesn't accept poetry electronically. So, obviously, don't submit your work by e-mail! *Highlights* publishes poetry by young writers, but offers payment only to writers over age 16 and won't publish work containing "sex, violence, or unmitigated pessimism." So, if your poem touches on suicide, *Highlights* isn't the market for it.

"Find out the individual guidelines," Henderson recommends. "You'll get further along that way than by breaking the rules."

Guidelines can only tell you so much about a journal, though. It's an excellent idea to purchase a sample copy of a publication, primarily to see if your poetry would suit it—but also to see if the journal suits your poetry. Shelling out two or three dollars for a sample copy (usually a back issue) will be worth it if you wind up deciding you don't want your work to appear in a journal that's been photocopied badly and paper-clipped together. (If a journal that interests you isn't available in your local bookstore or at the library, check online for ordering information.)

The preceding rules apply to adult as well as young writers, but there's one area that generally doesn't concern adults: Should you include your age in the cover letter?

Chiron Review's Hathaway believes you probably should include it, because it might bring benefits. "I'm far more likely to give attention, advice, or encouragement to a young writer, even if I don't accept their work for publication." Hathaway also likes to know if he needs to get a parent's permission before he publishes your work—especially if that issue of the journal features more "mature" material.

Henderson, however, takes the opposite stance. "I advise kids, and their teachers and parents, not to tell their age unless guidelines specify they should. Editors want good work, not good work by 9-year-olds or good work by 35-year-olds." If a poem is accepted, *then* tell the editors your age.

"Have your parents' support and permission," Henderson advises. That way, if your poem is accepted and the editor of the journal *does* want your parents' okay, you can take care of everything professionally, without any fuss. There's no need to include your parents' permission with your manuscript (unless the guidelines expressly instruct you to). If your poetry is accepted, you might need to have your parents write you a note or fill out a contract. Then again, you might not need them to do anything at all except sit back and wait for your contributor's copy to arrive.

If you're 13 or older, you're the one who should handle the actual submission process. Hathaway says *Chiron Review* has received a few submissions sent by parents, but "for the experience, the kids ought to do it themselves."

As far as who submits the actual work to *Stone Soup*, Mandel says it "runs the whole gamut. More teachers and kids, though, than parents."

Henderson is adamant about copyright for kids when the adults get involved. "I am totally against parents and teachers sending work in without the poet's permission," she says. "If you're squeamish about someone reading your work, then don't publish it." Seeking publication should be the poet's choice and no one else's.

Henderson says if you're submitting a classroom exercise to an editor, either with the rest of your class or on your own, "Keep in mind that when teachers are reviewing poetry, they're judging by completely different criteria than a magazine editor. You receive an A for understanding the concepts and putting them into practice, but your friend—who maybe doesn't shine grammatically—is published in venues everywhere because he's taking risks, writing from his heart, trying new things, pushing boundaries in his writing." Henderson points out the difference between writing poetry for school and writing for yourself or for publication: "School is about learning how to do it; art is about learning how to do it better."

Whether you're looking to publish to satisfy a class assignment or to take your first steps on the path to a writing career, submit only work you are proud of. Even if your work is not accepted, mastering the submission process puts you light years ahead of your peers and is an accomplishment in itself.

—*Vanessa Lyman*

Lenore Marshall Prize, the Whiting Award, and the Harold Morton Landon Prize.

Book/Chapbook Needs: Story Line Press publishes each year the winner of the Nicholas Roerich Poetry Prize ($1,000 plus publication and a paid reading at the Roerich Museum in New York; a runner-up receives a full Story Line Press Scholarship to the Wesleyan Writers Conference in Middletown, CT [see listing in Conferences and Workshops section]; $20 entry and handling fee). The press also publishes books about poetry and has published collections by such poets as Alfred Corn, Annie Finch, Donald Justice, Mark Jarman, and David Mason.

How to Submit: Deadline for Nicholas Roerich Poetry Prize competition is October 31st. Complete guidelines available for SASE.

Also Offers: Story Line Press annually publishes 10-15 books of poetry, literary criticism, memoir, fiction, and books in translation. Query first.

◑ **THE STORYTELLER**, 2441 Washington Rd., Maynard AR 72444. (870)647-2137. E-mail: storyteller1@cox-internet.com. Website: www.freewebz.com/fossilcreek. Established 1996. **Editor:** Regina Williams.

Magazine Needs: *The Storyteller*, a quarterly magazine, "is geared to, but not limited to new writers and poets." Wants "any form up to 40 lines, any matter, any style, but must have a meaning. Do not throw words together and call it a poem. Nothing in way of explicit sex, violence, horror or explicit language. I would like it to be understood that I have young readers, ages 9-18." Accepts poetry by young readers of all ages. Has published poetry by W.C. Jameson, Bryan Byrd, and Sol Rubin. *Storyteller* is 64 pages, magazine-sized, desktop-published with slick cover, original pen & ink drawings on cover, ads. Receives about 300 poems/year, accepts about 40%. Press run is 600 for over 500 subscribers. Subscription: $20; $24 Canada & foreign; $8 Canada & foreign. Sample: $6 (if available).

How to Submit: Submit 2 poems at a time, typed and double-spaced. Accepts previously published poems and simultaneous submissions, "but must state where and when poetry first appeared." Send submissions by postal mail only. Cover letter preferred. **Reading fee:** $1/poem. Time between acceptance and publication is 9 months. Poems are circulated to an editorial board. "Poems are read and discussed by staff." Sometimes comments on rejected poems. Occasionally publishes theme issues. Upcoming themes and guidelines available for SASE; guidelines also available on website. Responds in up to 5 weeks. Acquires first or one-time rights. Reviews books and chapbooks of poetry by subscribers only. Send materials for review consideration to associate editor Ruthan Riney.

Also Offers: Sponsors a quarterly contest. "Readers vote on their favorite poems. Winners receive copy of magazine and certificate suitable for framing. We also nominate for the Pushcart Prize."

Advice: "Be professional. Do not send four or five poems on one page. Send us poetry written from the heart."

$ ◪ **THE STRAIN**, 11702 Webercrest, Houston TX 77048. **Poetry Editor:** Norm Stewart Jr.

Magazine Needs: *The Strain* is a monthly magazine using "experimental or traditional poetry of very high quality." Does not include sample lines of poetry here as they "prefer not to limit style of submissions."

How to Submit: Accepts simultaneous submissions and previously published poems. Guidelines issue: $5 and 8 first-class stamps. Pays "no less than $5. We would prefer you submit before obtaining the guidelines issue which mostly explains upcoming collections and collaborations." Send materials for review consideration.

◪ **STRAY DOG; PRILLY & TRU PUBLICATIONS, INC.**, P.O. Box 713, Amawalk NY 10501. E-mail: straydog@bestweb.net. Website: www.prillyandtru.com. Established 2000. **Editor/Publisher:** j.v. morrissey.

Magazine Needs: *Stray Dog* appears annually in June or July and seeks "to publish the best, most powerful work we can find," including contemporary poetry, short-shorts, and art. "We print high-quality poetry, short-shorts and b&w art in any form or style. We're looking for work that is evocative and incisive, work that will leave skid marks on the reader's emotional highway. Prior publication credits admired but not required." Does not want to see anything "preachy, whiny, obscure, pornographic, gratuitously violent, or trite." Recently published poetry by A.D. Winans, Virgil Suarez, Richard Kostelanetz, Stephanie Dickinson, Joan P. Kincaid, t. kilgore spake, and Marco North. *Stray Dog* is 64 pages, digest-sized, Docutech printed, saddle-stitched, glossy card cover with b&w art.

Receives about 400 poems/year, accepts 10%. Publishes about 40-45 poems/issue. Press run is 250. Single copy: $6; subscription: $6/year. Sample: $5. Make checks payable to Stray Dog.

How to Submit: Submit 3-5 poems at a time. Line length for poetry is 2 pages maximum. Accepts simultaneous submissions; no previously published poems. No e-mail or disk submissions. Cover letter is preferred. "All submissions and correspondence must be accompanied by SASE for response and return of work; name/address/phone number on each page. No handwritten work. Include 2-3 line bio." Reads submissions year round. Time between acceptance and publication is within 1 year. Sometimes comments on rejected poems. Guidelines available by fax, by e-mail, on website, or for SASE. Responds in up to 5 months. Pays 2 copies. Acquires first North American serial rights.

Book/Chapbook Needs & How to Submit: Prilly & Tru Publications, Inc. is "not publishing books or chapbooks at this time, but plans to in the future."

Advice: "Surprise me! Blow me away! Knock the neon-striped toe socks off my feet! Think 'indie' film, not network TV."

STRIDE PUBLICATIONS, 11 Sylvan Rd., Exeter, Devon EX4 6EW England. E-mail: editor@stridebooks.co.uk. Website: www.stridebooks.co.uk and www.stridemagazine.co.uk. Established 1982. **Managing Editor:** R.M. Loydell.

Book/Chapbook Needs: Stride Publications publishes poetry, poetry sequences, experimental prose, and an online magazine. Wants to see any poetry that is "new, inventive, nothing self-oriented, emotional, no narrative or fantasy, rhyming doggerel, light verse, or the merely-confessional." Has published work by Peter Redgrove, William Everson, Sheila E. Murphy, Peter Finch, and Charles Wright. Stride Publications publishes paperbacks 60-100 pages of poetry, plus a few novels and anthologies.

How to Submit: Unsolicited submissions for book publication are accepted. "All submissions must be typewritten/word-processed and have an SAE included" with IRCs. Authors should obtain submission guidelines first via e-mail or by sending SASE with return postage or IRCs. Cover letter required with bio, summary, and review quotes. Queries will be answered in 6 weeks and mss reported on in 3 months or more. Pays minimum 30 author's copies. Magazine reviews books and tapes of poetry in 100-200 words, multi-book format. Send books etc. for review consideration.

STRUGGLE: A MAGAZINE OF PROLETARIAN REVOLUTIONARY LITERA-TURE (Specialized: social issues), P.O. Box 13261, Detroit MI 48213-0261. (313)273-9039. E-mail: timhall11@yahoo.com. Established 1985. **Editor:** Tim Hall.

Magazine Needs: *Struggle* is a "literary quarterly, content: the struggle of the working people and all oppressed against the rich. Issues such as: racism, poverty, women's rights, aggressive wars, workers' struggle for jobs and job security, the overall struggle for a non-exploitative society, a genuine socialism." The poetry and songs printed are "generally short, any style, subject matter must criticize or fight—explicitly or implicitly—against the rule of the billionaires. We welcome experimentation devoted to furthering such content. We are open to both subtlety and direct statement." Has published poetry by Katisha Burt, Phil Goldvarg, Jon Mathewson, Grace Stevenson, Naomi Wolf Budbill, Sonja Haughton-Bloetner, Jennifer Edwards, Timothy McCoy, and Luis Cuanhtemoc Berrizabal. *Struggle* is 36 pages, digest-sized, photocopied with occasional photos or artwork, short stories, and short plays as well as poetry and songs. "We need more fiction, artwork, and cartoons." Subscription: $10 for 4 issues. Sample: $3. Make checks payable to "Tim Hall—Special Account."

How to Submit: Submit up to 8 poems at a time. "Writers must include SASE. Name and address must appear on the opening page of each poem." Accepts e-mail submissions in body of message (no attachments), but prefers postal mail. Accepted work usually appears in the next or following issue. Editor tries to provide criticism "with every submission." Tries to respond in 4 months, but often becomes backlogged. Pays 2 copies. "If you are unwilling to have your poetry published on our website, please inform us."

Also Offers: "Coming soon: website at STRUGGLEMAGAZINE.org."

Advice: "Show passion and fire. Humor also welcome. Prefer powerful, colloquial language over academic timidity. Look to Neruda, Lorca, Bly, Whitman, Braithwaite, Tupac Shakur, Muriel Rukeyser. Experimental, traditional forms both welcome. Especially favor: works reflecting rebellion by the working people against the rich; works against racism, sexism, militarism, imperialism; works critical of our exploitative culture; works showing a desire for—or fantasy of—a non-exploitative society; works attacking the Republican 'anti-terrorism' war frenzy and the Democrats' surrender to it."

⭐ $◎ **STUDENT LEADERSHIP JOURNAL (Specialized: college students, Christian)**, Dept. PM, P.O. Box 7895, Madison WI 53707-7895. (608)274-4823, ext. 425 or 413. Website: www.ivcf.org/slj. **Editor:** Jeff Yourison.

Magazine Needs: *Student Leadership* appears 3 times/year and is a "magazine for Christian student leaders on secular campuses. We want poetry with solid Biblical imagery, not preachy or trite. We get too many prayer-poems. Also, we accept little rhymed poetry; it must be very, very good." *Student Leadership* is 32 pages, magazine-sized, full color, with no advertising, 70% editorial, 30% graphics/art. Press run is 10,000 going to college students in the US and Canada. Subscription: $12. Sample: $4.

How to Submit: Accepts previously published poems; no simultaneous submissions. "Would-be contributors should read us to be familiar with what we publish." Best time to submit mss is March through July ("We set our year's editorial plan"). Editor "occasionally" comments on rejected poems. Guidelines available for SASE. Responds in 3 months. Time between acceptance and publication is 1-24 months. Pays $25-50/poem plus 2 copies. Acquires first or reprint rights.

Advice: "Try to express feelings through images and metaphor. Religious poetry should not be overly didactic, and it should never moralize!"

🌐 ◨ ◎ **STUDIO, A JOURNAL OF CHRISTIANS WRITING (Specialized: Christian, spirituality)**, 727 Peel St., Albury, New South Wales 2640 Australia. Phone/fax: 61 2 6021 1135. E-mail: pgrover@bigpond.com. Established 1980. **Publisher:** Paul Grover.

Magazine Needs: *Studio* is a quarterly journal publishing "poetry and prose of literary merit, offering a venue for previously published, new and aspiring writers, and seeking to create a sense of community among Christians writing." The journal also publishes occasional articles as well as news and reviews of writing, writers, and events of interest to members. In poetry, the editors want "shorter pieces but with no specification as to form or length (necessarily less than 200 lines), subject matter, style, or purpose. People who send material should be comfortable being published under this banner: *Studio, A Journal of Christians Writing.*" Has published poetry by John Foulcher and other Australian poets. *Studio* is 36 pages, digest-sized, professionally printed on high-quality recycled paper, saddle-stapled, matte card cover, with graphics and line drawings. Press run is 300, all subscriptions. Subscription: $48 (Aud) for overseas members. Sample available (airmail to US) for $8 (Aud).

How to Submit: Submissions must be typed and double-spaced on one side of A4 white paper. Accepts simultaneous submissions. Name and address must appear on the reverse side of each page submitted. Cover letter required; include brief details of previous publishing history, if any. SASE (or SAE with IRC) required. Response time is 2 months and time to publication is 9 months. Pays 1 contributor's copy. Acquires first Australian rights. Reviews books of poetry in 250 words, single format. Send materials for review consideration.

Also Offers: The magazine conducts a biannual poetry and short story contest.

Advice: "The trend in Australia is for imagist poetry and poetry exploring the land and the self. Reading the magazine gives the best indication of style and standard, so send for a sample copy before sending your poetry. Keep writing, and we look forward to hearing from you."

⭐ ◨ **STUDIO ONE**, Haehn Campus Center, College of St. Benedict, St. Joseph MN 56374. E-mail: studio1@csbsju.edu. Established 1976. Editor changes yearly.

Magazine Needs: *Studio One* an annual literary and visual arts magazine appearing in May is designed as a forum for local, regional, and national poets/writers. No specifications regarding form,

---

THE SUBJECT INDEX in the back of this book helps you identify potential markets for your work.

subject matter or style of poetry submitted. However, poetry no more than 2 pages stands a better chance of publication. Accepts poetry written by children. Has published poetry by Bill Meissner, Eva Hooker, and Larry Schug. *Studio One* is 50-80 pages, soft cover, typeset. Includes 1-3 short stories, 22-30 poems and 10-13 visual art representations. Receives 600-800 submissions/year. No subscriptions, but a sample copy can be obtained by sending a self-addressed stamped manilla envelope and $6 for p&h. Make checks payable to *Studio One*.

How to Submit: Accepts simultaneous submissions, no more than 5 per person. Does not accept previously published poems. Accepts e-mail submissions included in body of message; clearly show page breaks and indentations. Deadline: February 1 for spring publication. Seldom comments on rejected poems. Send SASE for results.

THE STYLES, P.O. Box 7171, Madison WI 53707. E-mail: timothy@thestyles.org. Website: www.thestyles.org. Established 2000. **Poetry Editor:** Amara Verona.

Magazine Needs: *THE STYLES* appears biannually. Publishes "ambitious original and creative ideas and standards of what writing should be. *THE STYLES* encourages new ideas about how writing should be written, read, evaluated, and what it should accomplish. Experimental work." Looking for "highly experimental poetry. Most of the poetry we publish is prose poetry." Does not want "anything sentimental." Recently published poetry by Jennie Trivanovich, Sarah Lindsay, Laura Mullen, Scott Bently, Mark Terrill, and Brian Johnson. *THE STYLES* is over 100 pages, 8 × 8, offset-printed, perfect-bound, soft point-spot laminated color cover. Accepts about 3% of poems submitted. Publishes 12-20 poems/issue. Press run is 2,000. Single copy: $10; subscription: $16/year (2 issues). Sample: $10. Make checks payable to *THE STYLES*.

How to Submit: Submit 3 or more poems at a time. Line length for poetry is open. Accepts simultaneous submissions; no previously published poems. No fax, e-mail, or disk submissions. Cover letter is preferred. "Always send a SASE. Cover letters and bios are appreciated, but not required." Reads submissions all year. Time between acceptance and publication is 1-12 months. Often comments on rejected poems. Guidelines are available in magazine, for SASE, or on website. Responds in 4 months. Sometimes sends prepublication galleys. Pays 1 contributor's copy. Acquires first North American serial rights. Send materials for review consideration. "We will make 'comments,' quotes, and advanced comments for books, chapbooks, and other magazines. We don't have a section in our publication for reviews."

Advice: "We publish very little poetry in each issue. We are looking for poets who are using language in new ways. Read our publication. Our readers enjoy work that is accessible and yet still challenging."

SULPHUR RIVER LITERARY REVIEW, P.O. Box 19228, Austin TX 78760-9228. (512)292-9456. Established 1978, reestablished 1987. **Editor/Publisher:** James Michael Robbins.

Magazine Needs: Appearing in March and September, *Sulphur River* is a semiannual of poetry, prose, and artwork. "No restrictions except quality." Does not want poetry that is "trite or religious or verse that does not incite thought." Has published poetry by Willie James King, Alan Britt, Nicole Melanson, Jen Besemer, Tom Chandler, and Geri Rosenzweig. *Sulphur River* is digest-sized, perfect-bound, with glossy cover. Receives about 2,000 poems/year, accepts 4%. Press run is 400 for 200 subscribers, 100 shelf sales. Subscription: $12. Sample: $7.

How to Submit: No previously published poems or simultaneous submissions. Often comments on rejected poems, although a dramatic increase in submissions has made this increasingly difficult. Responds in 1 month. Always sends prepublication galleys. Pays 2 contributor's copies.

Also Offers: "*Sulphur River* also publishes full-length volumes of poetry; latest book: *Like a Pilot: Selected Poems of Rolf Dieter Brinkman*."

Advice: "Poetry is, for me, the essential art, the ultimate art, and there can be no compromise of quality if the poem is to be successful."

$ SUMMER STREAM PRESS, P.O. Box 6056, Santa Barbara CA 93160-6056. (805)962-6540. E-mail: geehossiffer@aol.com. Established 1978. **Poetry Editor:** David D. Frost.

Book/Chapbook Needs: Publishes a series of books (Box Cars) in hardcover and softcover, each presenting 6 poets, averaging 70 text pages for each poet. "The mix of poets represents many parts of the country and many approaches to poetry. The poets previously selected have been published, but that is no requirement. We welcome traditional poets in the mix and thus offer them a chance for publication in this world of free-versers. The six poets share a 15% royalty. We require rights for our editions worldwide and share 50-50 with authors for translation rights and for republication of our editions by another publisher. Otherwise all rights remain with the authors." Has published poetry by Virginia E. Smith, Sandra Russell, Jennifer MacPherson, Nancy Berg, Lois Shapley Bassen, and Nancy J. Wallace.

How to Submit: To be considered for future volumes in this series, query with about 12 sample poems, no cover letter. No e-mail submissions. Responds to query in 6 months, to submission (if invited) in 1 year. Accepts previously published poetry and simultaneous submissions. Editor usually comments on rejected poems. Always sends prepublication galleys. Pays 6 contributor's copies plus royalties.

Advice: "We welcome both traditional poetry and free verse. However, we find we must reject almost all the traditional poetry received simply because the poets exhibit little or no knowledge of the structure and rules of traditional forms. Much of it is rhymed free verse."

A SUMMER'S READING, 409 Lakeview Dr., Sherman IL 62684. (217)496-3012. E-mail: t_morrissey@hotmail.com. Established 1996. **Contact:** Ted Morrissey.

Magazine Needs: *A Summer's Reading*, published annually in June, strives "to provide one more well edited, attractive outlet for new and emerging writers, poets and artists. Willing to look at all kinds of poetry, prefer free verse or blank verse with clear images and ideas." Does not want "sappy 'greeting card' stuff." Has published poetry by Robert Cooperman, Fernand Roqueplan, Patty Dickson Pieczka, and Dianalee Velie. *A Summer's Reading* is approximately 80 pages, offset-printed, with color cover, b&w artwork. Press run is 200 for 50 subscribers. Subscription: $6. Sample: $4.

How to Submit: Submit up to 10 poems with name, address, phone, and line count on each. Accepts simultaneous submissions if so noted. Cover letter preferred with brief bio and publishing history. Time between acceptance and publication is 3-12 months. Sometimes comments on rejected poems. Guidelines available for SASE. Responds in 3 months. Always sends prepublication galleys. Pays 2 copies. Acquires one-time rights plus request for acknowledgement if reprinted. May include staff-written reviews of poetry books in the future. Poets may send material for review consideration.

Advice: "Don't hesitate to submit—we will be respectful and fair to your work. We strive to publish newcomers with emerging and established artists. We would like to see more translations (include original text)."

SUN POETIC TIMES, P.O. Box 790526, San Antonio TX 78279-0526. (210)349-8216. E-mail: sunpoets@hotmail.com. Website: http://clik.to/SunPoets. Established 1994. **Editor:** Rod C. Stryker.

Magazine Needs: *Sun Poetic Times, a literary & artistic magazine*, appears quarterly to "publish all types of literary and visual art from all walks of life. We take all types. Our only specification is length—1 page in length if typed, 2 pages if handwritten (legibly)." Has published poetry by Naomi Shihab Nye, Chris Crabtree, Trinidad Sanchez, Jr., and Garland Lee Thompson, Jr. *Sun Poetic Times* is 24-28 pages, magazine-sized, attractively printed and saddle-stapled with glossy card stock cover, uses b&w line drawings/halftones. Receives about 700 poems/year, accepts about 30%. Press run is 300, 200 shelf sales. Subscription: $10 for 2 issues, $20/1 year (4 issues). Sample: $5 and SASE. Make checks payable to Sun Poetic Times.

How to Submit: Submit 3-5 poems at a time. Accepts simultaneous submissions; no previously published poems. Accepts e-mail submissions included in body of message (no attached files). Cover letter preferred. "In cover letters, we like to hear about your publishing credits, reasons you've taken up the pen, and general B.S. like that (biographical info)." Time between acceptance and publication is up to 8 months. Seldom comments on rejected poems. Occasionally publishes theme issues. Guidelines and upcoming themes available for SASE or by e-mail. E-mail queries welcome. Responds in up to 8 months. Pays 1 contributor's copy. Rights revert back to author upon publication.

SUPERIOR POETRY NEWS (Specialized: translations; regional, Rocky Mountain West); SUPERIOR POETRY PRESS, P.O. Box 424, Superior MT 59872. Established 1995. **Editors:** Ed and Guna Chaberek.

Magazine Needs: *Superior Poetry News* appears quarterly and "publishes the best and most interesting of new poets, as well as established poets, we can find. Also, we encourage lively translation into English from any language." Wants "general, rural, Western, or humorous poetry; translations; 40 lines or under. Nothing graphically sexual; containing profanity." Accepts poetry by young writers; the only restriction is quality, not age. Has published poetry by makyo, Simon Perchik, Harland Ristau, and Bill "Dusty" Powell. *Superior Poetry News* is 12-24 pages, digest-sized, photocopied. Receives about 2,000 poems/year, accepts 10-20%. Press run is 75-100 for 50 subscribers; 3-5 distributed free to libraries. Single copy: "free with a stamp (sweethearts send two)."

How to Submit: Submit 3-5 poems at a time. No previously published poems or simultaneous submissions (unless stated). Cover letter with short bio preferred. Time between acceptance and publication is 3 months. Seldom comments on rejected poems. Guidelines available for SASE. Responds in 1 week. Pays 1 copy. Acquires first rights. Staff reviews books and chapbooks of poetry and other magazines in 50 words, single book format. Send mataerial for review consideration with return postage (overseas contributors please include two IRCs).

Also Offers: " 'Montana: Ways, Winds, Whispers' as part of *Superior Poetry News*' regular format. This section is devoted exclusively to Montana poets. We also publish one to three 'special' issues per year which primarily serve as a showcase/sampler for Montana poets. Liks 'SPN,' we now offer these for a stamp. Send proposals to *Superior Poetry News*."

◑ ◎ SUZERAIN ENTERPRISES; LOVE'S CHANCE MAGAZINE (Specialized: love/ romance); FIGHTING CHANCE MAGAZINE (Specialized: horror, mystery, science fiction/fantasy), P.O. Box 60336, Worcester MA 01606. Established 1994. **Editor/Publisher:** Milton Kerr.

Magazine Needs: *Love's Chance Magazine* and *Fighting Chance Magazine* are each published 3 times/year to "give unpublished writers a chance to be published and to be paid for their efforts." *Love's Chance* deals with romance; *Fighting Chance* deals with dark fiction, horror, and science fiction. "No porn, ageism, sexism, racism, children in sexual situations." Has published poetry by Gary McGhee, T.R. Barnes, Dan Buck, Sebastian Daez, Cecil Boyce, and Ellaraine Lockie. Both magazines are 15-30 pages, magazine-sized, photocopied and side-stapled, computer-designed paper cover. Both receive about 500 poems/year, accept about 10%. Press runs are 100 for 70-80 subscribers. Subscription: $12/year for each. Samples: $4 each. Make checks payable to Suzerain Enterprises.

How to Submit: For both magazines, submit 3 poems at a time. Line length for poetry is 20 maximum. Accepts previously published poems and simultaneous submissions. Cover letter preferred. "Proofread for spelling errors, neatness; must be typewritten in standard manuscript form. No handwritten manuscripts." Time between acceptance and publication is 3 months. Often comments on rejected poems. Guidelines available in publication. Responds in 6 weeks. Acquires first or one-time rights.

Advice: "Proofread and edit carefully, send proper postage, always include a SASE. Don't let rejection slips get you down. Don't be afraid to write something different. Keep submitting and don't give up."

◗ SWEET ANNIE & SWEET PEA REVIEW, 7750 Highway F-24 W, Baxter IA 50028. (515)792-3578. Fax: (515)792-1310. E-mail: anniespl@netins.net. Established 1995. **Editor/Publisher:** Beverly A. Clark.

Magazine Needs: *Sweet Annie & Sweet Pea Review*, published quarterly, features short stories and poetry. Wants "poems of outdoors, plants, land, heritage, women, relationships, olden times—simpler times." Does not want "obscene, violent, explicit sexual material, obscure, long-winded materials, no overly religious materials." Has published poetry by Anne Carol Betterton, Mary Ann Wehler, Ellaraine Lockie, Celeste Bowman, Dick Reynolds, and Susanne Olson. *Sweet Annie & Sweet Pea Review* is 30 pages, digest-sized, offset-printed, saddle-stapled, bond paper with onion skin page before title page, medium card cover, and cover art. Receives about 200 poems/year, accepts 25-33%. Press run is 40. Subscription: $24. Sample: $7. Make checks payable to Sweet Annie Press.

How to Submit: Submit 6-12 poems at a time. "Effective 2001, **reading fee** $5/author submitting. Strongly recommend ordering a sample issue prior to submitting and preference is given to poets and writers following this procedure and submitting in accordance with the layout used consistently by this Press." Accepts simultaneous submissions; no previously published poems. No e-mail submissions. Cover letter preferred with personal comments about yourself and phone number. Time between acceptance and publication is 9 months. Often comments on rejected poems. Publishes theme issues occasionally. "We select for theme first, select for content second; narrow selections through editors." Pays 1 contributor's copy. Acquires all rights. Returns rights with acknowledgment in future publications. Will review chapbooks of poetry or other magazines of short length, reviews 500 words or less. Send materials for review consideration.

SYCAMORE REVIEW, Dept. of English, Purdue University, 500 Oval Dr., West Lafayette IN 47907-2038. (765)494-3783. Fax: (765)494-3780. E-mail: sycamore@purdue.edu. Website: www.sla. purdue.edu/sycamore/. Established 1988 (first issue May, 1989). **Contact:** Poetry Editor.

● Poetry published by *Sycamore Review* was selected for inclusion in the 2002 *Pushcart Prize* anthology.

Magazine Needs: *Sycamore Review* is published biannually in January and June. "We accept personal essays, short fiction, drama, translations, and quality poetry in any form. We aim to publish many diverse styles of poetry from formalist to prose poems, narrative, and lyric." Has published poetry by Denise Levertov, Mark Halperin, Brigit Pegeen Kelly, Mark Halliday, Billy Collins, and Ed Hirsch. *Sycamore Review* is semiannual in a digest-sized format, 160 pages, flat-spined, professionally printed, with matte, color cover. Press run is 1,000 for 500 subscribers of which 50 are libraries. Subscription: $12; $14 outside US. Sample: $7. Make checks payable to Purdue University (Indiana residents add 5% sales tax.)

How to Submit: Submit 3-6 poems at a time. Name and address on each page. Accepts simultaneous submissions, if notified immediately of acceptance elsewhere; no previously published poems except translations. No submissions accepted via fax or e-mail. Cover letters not required but invited; include phone number, short bio and previous publications, if any. "We read August 1 through March 1 only." Guidelines available for SASE. Responds in 4 months. Pays 2 copies. Acquires first North American rights. After publication, all rights revert to author. Staff reviews books of poetry. Send books to editor-in-chief for review consideration.

Advice: "Poets who do not include SASE do not receive a response."

$ ◨ SYNERGEBOOKS, 1235 Flat Shoals Rd., King NC 27021. (888)812-2533. Fax: (336)994-8403. E-mail: Inquiries@synergebooks.com. Website: www.synergebooks.com. Established 1999. **Acquisitions Editor:** Allie McCormack. Member: EPPRO, SPAN, EPC, PMA.

Book/Chapbook Needs: SynergEbooks specializes in quality works by talented new writers in every available digital format, including CD-ROMs and paperback. "Poetry must have a unique twist or theme and must be edited." Will accept historical, romantic, poetry from teens, etc. Does not want unedited work. Recently published poetry by Theresa Jodray, Brenda Roberts, Vanyell Delacroix, S.A. Shaw, Joel L. Young, and Minerva Bloom. SynergEbooks publishes up to 40 titles/year, 2-5 of them poetry. Books are usually 45-150 pages, print-on-demand with paperback binding.

How to Submit: Query first by e-mail, with a few sample poems and cover letter with brief bio and publication credits. "We prefer no simultaneous submission, but inform us if this is the case." Accepts submissions on disk or by e-mail (as attachment) only. Responds to queries in 1 month; to mss in up to 5 months. Pays royalties of 35-40%.

Advice: "We are inundated with more poetry than prose every month; but we will accept the occasional anthology with a unique twist that is original and high quality. New poets welcome."

★ ○ TACENDA, P.O. Box 259, Marshfield MO 65706. (417)353-3680. E-mail: tacenda77@yahoo.com. Established 1990. **Editor-in-Chief:** Penny Lynn Dunn.

Magazine Needs *Tacenda* appears 2-3 times/year but is "a literary *quarterly* by intent, with poetry, featured artist(s), short fiction, opinion, photography, black and white art, and reviews." No limitations in style or form; special interest in environmental and political themes. Does not want short stories or poems intended for romance or women's magazines. Recently published poetry by Robert Johnson, David Lloyd Whited, Richard Downing, Phoenix Lyndon, and Frank Palmisano. *Tacenda* is 64 pages, magazine-sized, stapled, cardstock with half tone cover, includes art/graphics. Receives about 500 poems/year, accepts about 120. Publishes about 30 poems/issue. Press run is 500 for 30 subscribers with a variable number of shelf sales; 100 are distributed free to authors and publishers. Single copy: $7; subscription: $20. Make checks payable to James Dunn, Managing Editor.

How to Submit: Submit 3-5 poems at a time. Accepts previously published poems and simultaneous submissions. Accepts e-mail submissions; no fax or disk submissions. Cover letter is preferred. Reads submissions August 16-June 14. Time between acceptance and publication is 3 weeks-3 months. Poems are circulated to an editorial board. "All poems considered for acceptance reviewed by editor(s)." Often comments on rejected poems. "Quality is our only requirement." Occasionally publishes theme issues. List of upcoming themes available by e-mail. Guidelines available for SASE. Responds in 2 months. Pays 2 contributor's copies. Acquires first North American serial rights or one-time rights. Reviews books and chapbooks of poetry and other magazines/journals in 750 words. Query for reviews.

Also Offers: Hopes to sponsor contests in the future.

Advice: "Not interested in 'confessional' poetry; prefer work with perspective on issues affecting our world."

TAK TAK TAK, BCM Tak, London WC1N 3XX England. Website: www.taktaktak.com. Established 1986. **Editors:** Andrew and Tim Brown. *Tak Tak Tak* appears occasionally in print and on cassettes. "However, we are currently not accepting submissions."

TAKAHE, P.O. Box 13 335, Christchurch, New Zealand. (03)359-8133. Established 1990. **Poetry Editor:** Victoria Broome.

Magazine Needs: "*Takahe* appears three to four times/year, and publishes short stories and poetry by both established and emerging writers. The publisher is the Takahe Collective Trust, a nonprofit organization formed to help new writers and get them into print. While insisting on correct British spelling (or recognized spellings in foreign languages), smart quotes, and at least internally consistent punctuation, we, nonetheless, try to allow some latitude in presentation. Any use of foreign languages must be accompanied by an English translation." No style, subject, or form restrictions. Length: "A poem can take up to two pages, but we have published longer." Has published poetry by John O'Connor, John Allison, Patricia Prime, Jennifer Compton, David Eggleton, Mark Pirie, and James Norcliff. *Takahe* is 60 pages, A4. Receives about 250 poems/year, accepts about 30%. Press run is 340 for 250 subscribers of which 30 are libraries, 40 shelf sales. Single copy: $NZ6; subscription: $NZ25 within New Zealand, $NZ35 elsewhere.

How to Submit: Accepts previously published poems; no simultaneous submissions. Accepts IBM compatible disk submissions. Cover letter required. Time between acceptance and publication is 4 months. Often comments on rejected poems. Guidelines available for SASE. Responds in 4 months. "Payment varies but currently NZ$30 total for any and all inclusions in an issue plus 2 copies." Acquires first or one-time rights.

TALE SPINNERS; MIDNIGHT STAR PUBLICATIONS (Specialized: rural/pastoral), R.R. #1, Ponoka AB T4J 1R1 Canada. (403)783-2521. Established 1996. **Editor/Publisher:** Nellie Gritchen Scott.

Magazine Needs: *Tale Spinners* is a quarterly " 'little literary magazine with a country flavour,' for writers who love country and all it stands for." Wants poetry, fiction, anecdotes, personal experiences, etc. pertaining to country life. Children's poetry welcome." No "scatological, prurient or sexually explicit or political content." Accepts poetry written by children, ages 6 and up. Published poetry by Daniel Green, A.H. Ferguson, C. David Hay, Don Melcher, Melvin Sandberg, and Richard Arnold. *Tale Spinner* is 48 pages, digest-sized, photocopied and saddle-stapled with light cardstock cover, uses clip art or freehand graphics. Receives about 100 poems/year, accepts about 80%. Press run is 75 for 50 subscribers. Subscription: $20. Sample: $5.

How to Submit: Submit up to 6 poems at a time. Accepts previously published poems. Cover letter ensures a reply. Include a SAE and IRC. "Short poems preferred, but will use narrative poems on occasion." Time between acceptance and publication is 3 months. Often comments on rejected poems. Guidelines available for SASE. Responds in 2 weeks. Pays 1 copy.

Book/Chapbook Needs & How to Submit: "Midnight Star Publications is not accepting chapbook manuscripts at present."

Advice: "Read the guidelines before submitting! Include return postage or IRC."

TALVIPÄIVÄNSEISAUS SPECIALS, (formerly *Muuna Takeena*), Oritie 4C24, FIN-01200 Vantaa Finland. E-mail: palonen@mbnet.fi. Established 1987. **Editor:** Timo Palonen.
Magazine Needs: *Talvipäivänseisaus Specials* appear annually now that the editor has retired *Muuna Takeena*. Does not want to see experimental poems. *Talvipäivänseisaus Specials* are about 30 pages, magazine-sized, photocopied and stapled, cover includes photo/drawing, also includes photos/drawings inside, some paid ads. Receives about 50 poems/year, accepts 90%. Press run is 200. Sample: $3. "No checks."
How to Submit: Submit 3 poems at a time. Accepts simultaneous submissions; no previously published poems. Accepts e-mail submissions (in text box). Cover letter required. Time between acceptance and publication is 6 months. Pays 1 contributor's copy. Staff reviews books and chapbooks of poetry and other magazines in up to 100 words, single book format. Send materials for review consideration.
Advice: "I read, if I like, it could be printed. If I do not like, I send forward to other zine makers."

TAMEME (Specialized: bilingual, regional), 199 First St., #335, Los Altos CA 94022. Website: www.tameme.org. Established 1999. **Contact:** Poetry Editor.
• *Tameme* was awarded a grant from the Rockefeller/Bancomer Fund for US—Mexico Culture.
Magazine Needs: "*Tameme* is an annual literary magazine dedicated to publishing new writing from North America in side-by-side English-Spanish format. *Tameme*'s goals are to play an instrumental role in introducing important new writing from Canada and the United States to Mexico, and vice versa, and to provide a forum for the art of literary translation. By 'new writing' we mean the best work of serious literary value that has been written recently. By 'writing from North America' we mean writing by citizens or residents of Mexico, the United States, and Canada." Has published poetry by Alberto Blanco, Jaime Sabines, T. Lopez Mills, Marianne Toussaint, and W.D. Snodgrass. *Tameme* is 225 pages, digest-sized. Receives about 200 poems/year, accepts 1%. Press run is 2,000. Subscription: $14.95. Sample: $14.95. Make checks payable to Tameme, Inc.
How to Submit: *Tameme* is currently closed to unsolicited mss.

TAPESTRIES (Specialized: senior citizen; anthology), MWCC Life Program, 444 Green St., Gardner MA 01440. (978)630-9176. Fax: (978)632-6155. E-mail: davpat@myexcel.com or L-Wickman@mwcc.mass.edu. Established 2001. **Editor:** Patricia B. Cosentino, Life Program, Mount Wachusett Community College.
Magazine Needs: *Tapestries* appears annually in October as "an anthology for senior citizens of poetry, short stories, features on family, heritage, tradition, and folklore. Our anthology is subsidized by Mount Wachusett Community College through a grant from Massachusetts Cultural Council for senior citizen writers and poets." Wants any style poetry, no restrictions on form "but must be no longer than 24 lines." Does not want "political, propaganda, pornographic or sexually explicit material as this is a 'family' magazine. We do not exclude religious poems but they must have non-sectarian universality." Recently published poetry by Maxine Kumin, Victor Howes, Diana Der-Hovanessian, John Tagliabue, BG Thurston, and Robert D. Wetmore. *Tapestries* is 100 pages, magazine-sized, offset-printed (high speed Xerox), tape-bound, with card stock/offset cover. Receives about 250 poems/year, accepts about 10%. Publishes about 25-30 poems/issue. Press run is 500. Single copy: $5 plus $3 postage. Make checks payable to MWCC Life Program.
How to Submit: Submit 3-5 poems at a time. Line length is 24 maximum. Accepts previously published poems and simultaneous submissions. Accepts e-mail and disk submissions; no fax submissions. Cover letter is preferred (only if work is previously published). "Prefer hard copy submissions. Send SASE to MWCC Life Program for guidelines." Deadline for submissions is March 31. Time between acceptance and publication is 1 month. Poems are circulated to an editorial board of 3-4 judges. For 2002, the judges were Prof. Arthur Marley, Prof. John Hogden, and poet Nazaleem Smith. Occasionally publishes theme issues. List of upcoming themes available for SASE, by e-mail, or on website. Guidelines available for SASE, by fax, e-mail, or on website. Responds in 1 month. Does not pay. Acquires first North American serial rights.
Advice: "As an anthology we accept original and/or previously published material, but prefer original. Our authors range in age from 50-92 in our most recent issue. We want humor and wisdom in our writings."

TAPROOT LITERARY REVIEW; TAPROOT WRITER'S WORKSHOP ANNUAL WRITING CONTEST, P.O. Box 204, Ambridge PA 15003. (724)266-8476. E-mail: taproot10@aol.com. Established 1986. **Editor:** Tikvah Feinstein.

Magazine Needs: *Taproot* is an annual publication, open to beginners. "We publish some of the best poets in the U.S. *Taproot* is a very respected anthology with increasing distribution. We enjoy all types and styles of poetry from emerging writers to established writers to those who have become valuable and old friends who share their new works with us." Writers published include Sally Levine, Judith R. Robinson, Tikvah Feinstein, Ellen Hyatt, Ace Boggess, and Ellaraine Lockie. *Taproot Literary Review* is approximately 95 pages, offset-printed on white stock with one-color glossy cover, art and no ads. Circulation is 500, sold at bookstores, barnesandnoble.com, amazon.com. readings and through the mail. Single copy: $8.95; subscriptions $7.50. Sample: $5.

How to Submit: Submit up to 5 poems, "no longer than 30 lines each." Nothing previously published or pending publication will be accepted. Accepts e-mail submissions (no attached files); "we would rather have a printed copy. 'We would rather have a hard copy. Also, we cannot answer without a SASE." Cover letter with general information required. Submissions accepted between September 1 and December 31 only. Guidelines available for SASE. Sometimes sends prepublication galleys. Pays 2 contributor's copies; additional copies are $6.50. Open to receiving books for review consideration. Send query first.

Also Offers: Sponsors the annual Taproot Writer's Workshop Annual Writing Contest. 1st Prize: $25 and publication in *Taproot Literary Review*; 2nd Prize: publication; and 3rd Prize: publication. Submit 5 poems of literary quality, any form and subject except porn. Entry fee: $10/5 poems (no longer than 35 lines each), provides copy of review. Deadline: December 31. Winners announced the following March.

Advice: "We publish the best poetry we can in a variety of styles and subjects, so long as it's literary quality and speaks to us. We love poetry that stuns, surprises, amuses, and disarms."

TAR RIVER POETRY, English Dept., East Carolina University, Greenville NC 27858-4353. (252)328-6046. Website: www.ecu.edu/journals. Established 1960. **Editor:** Peter Makuck.

Magazine Needs: "We are not interested in sentimental, flat-statement poetry. What we would like to see is skillful use of figurative language." *Tar River* is an "all-poetry" magazine that accepts dozens of poems in each issue, providing the talented beginner and experienced writer with a forum that features all styles and forms of verse. Has published poetry by Ronald Wallace, Deborah Cummins, Jonathon Holden, Susan Meyers, Thomas Reiter, and Cathy Smith Bowers. *Tar River* appears twice yearly and is 60 pages, digest-sized, professionally printed on salmon stock, some decorative line drawings, matte card cover with photo. Receives 6,000-8,000 submissions/year, accepts 150-200. Press run is 900 for 500 subscribers of which 125 are libraries. Subscription: $10. Sample: $5.50.

How to Submit: Submit 3-6 poems at a time. "We do not consider previously published poems or simultaneous submissions. Double or single-spaced OK. Name and address on each page. We do not consider mss during summer months." Reads submissions September 1 through April 15 only. Editors will comment "if slight revision will do the trick." Guidelines available for SASE or on website. Responds in 6 weeks. Pays 2 contributor's copies. Acquires first rights. Reviews books of poetry in 4,000 words maximum, single or multi-book format. Send materials for review consideration.

Advice: "Read widely and deeply in traditional and contemporary poetry. Subscribe to three or four literary journals every year."

TARPAULIN SKY, P.O. Box 883, Everson WA 98247-0883. E-mail: info@tarpaulinsky.com (inquiries) or poetry@tarpaulinsky.com (submissions). Website: www.tarpaulinsky.com. Established 2002. **Poetry Editors:** Christian Peet, Lizzie Harris, and Jonathan Livingston.

Magazine Needs: *Tarpaulin Sky* is a quarterly online literary journal "publishing highest quality poetry, prose, art, photography, interviews, and reviews. We are open to all styles and forms, providing they appear inevitable and/or inextricable from the work." Recently published poetry by Barry Gifford, Louis Jenkins, Kenneth Rosen, Mark Turpin, Connie Wanek, and Anne Winters. *Tarpaulin Sky* is published online only. Receives about 600 poems/year, accepts about 4% of unsolicited work. Publishes about 10-20 poems/issue.

How to Submit: Submit 3 or more poems at a time. Accepts simultaneous submissions; no previously published poems. Accepts e-mail submissions; no fax or disk submissions. Cover letter is preferred. "E-mail submissions are best received as attached word processor documents." Reads submissions year round. Time between acceptance and publication is 1 month. "All poems are read by three poetry editors. We aim for consensus." Often comments on rejected poems. Guidelines available for SASE, by e-mail, or on website. Responds in 3 months. Always sends prepublication galleys (electronic). Acquires first rights. Reviews books and chapbooks of poetry.

TEARS IN THE FENCE, 38 Hodview, Stourpaine, Nr. Blandford Forum, Dorset DT11 8TN England. Phone: 0044 1258-456803. Fax: 0044 1258-454026. E-mail: westrow@cooperw.fsnet.co.uk. Website: www.wanderingdog.co.uk. Established 1984. **General Editor:** David Caddy.

Magazine Needs: *Tears in the Fence* is a "small press magazine of poetry, fiction, interviews, articles, reviews and graphics. We are open to a wide variety of poetic styles. Work that is unusual, perceptive, risk-taking as well as imagistic, lived, and visionary will be close to our purpose. However, we like to publish a variety of work." Has published poetry by Ed Ochester, Christopher Locke, Joan Jobe Smith, Lee Harwood, Jeremy Reed, and Sharon Mesmer. *Tears in the Fence* appears 3 times/year, is 128 pages, A5, docutech printed on 110 gms. paper and perfect-bound with matte card cover and b&w art and graphics. Press run is 800, of which 512 go to subscribers. Subscription: $20/4 issues. Sample: $7.

How to Submit: Submit 6 typed poems with IRCs. Accepts submissions by e-mail (in text box), on disk, and by postal mail. Cover letter with brief bio required. Publishes theme issues. Upcoming themes available for SASE. Responds in 3 months. Time between acceptance and publication is 10 months "but can be much less." Pays 1 contributor's copy. Reviews books of poetry in 2,000-3,000 words, single or multi-book format. Send materials for review consideration.

Also Offers: The magazine is informally connected with the East Street Poets literary promotions, workshops and events, including the annual Wessex Poetry Festival and the annual East Street Poets International Open Poetry Competition. Also publishes books. Books published include *Hanging Windchimes In A Vacuum*, by Gregory Warren Wilson, *Heart Thread* by Joan Jobe Smith, and *The Hong Kong/Macao Trip* by Gerald Locklin.

Advice: "I think it helps to subscribe to several magazines in order to study the market and develop an understanding of what type of poetry is published. Use the review sections and send off to magazines that are new to you."

TEBOT BACH, P.O. Box 7887, Huntington Beach CA 92615-7887. (714)968-0905. E-mail: info@tebotbach.org. Website: www.tebotbach.org. **Editors/Publishers:** Mifanwy Kaiser

Book/Chapbook Needs & How to Submit: Tebot Bach (Welsh for "little teapot") publishes books of poetry. Titles include *Cantatas* by Jeanette Clough, *48 Questions* by Richard Jones, *The Way In* by Robin Chapman, and *Written in Rain: New and Selected Poems 1985-2000* by M.L. Liebler. Query first with sample poems and cover letter with brief bio and publication credits. Include SASE. Responds to queries and mss, if invited, in 1 month. Time between acceptance and publication is up to 2 years. Write to order sample books.

Also Offers: An anthology of California poets, published annually in April. Must be current or former resident of California in order to submit, but no focus or theme required for poetry. Deadline for submission is in August, annually. Submit up to 6 poems with "California Anthology" written on lower left corner of envelope. Accepts submissions by e-mail (as attachment in Word or in text box).

TEEN VOICES (Specialized: teen, women), P.O. Box 120-027, Boston MA 02112-0027. (617)426-5505. E-mail: teenvoices@teenvoices.com. Website: www.teenvoices.com. Established 1988; first published 1990. **Contact:** Submission Director.

Magazine Needs: *Teen Voices*, published quarterly, is a magazine written by, for, and about teenage girls. Regular features are family, cultural harmony, surviving sexual assault, teen motherhood, and all other topics of interest to our writers and readers. Accepts poetry written by young women ages 13-19. *Teen Voices* is 64 pages, with glossy cover, art and photos. "We accept 10% of the poems we receive, but can't afford to publish all of them timely." Press run is 25,000. Single copy: $3.50; subscription: $19.95. Sample: $5. Make checks payable to *Teen Voices*.

How to Submit: Submit any number of poems with name, age and address on each. Accepts simultaneous submissions; no previously published poems. Accepts submissions by fax, postal mail, online submission form, and by e-mail (as attachment and in text box). Cover letter preferred. "Confirmation of receipt of submission sent in 6-8 weeks." Poems are circulated to a teen editorial board. Pays 5 contributor's copies. Open to unsolicited reviews.

$ **TEMPORARY VANDALISM RECORDINGS; THE SILT READER**, P.O. Box 6184, Orange CA 92863-6184. E-mail: tvrec@yahoo.com. Website: http://members.aol.com/aphasiapress. Established 1991 (Temporary Vandalism Recordings), 1999 (*The Silt Reader*). **Editors:** Robert Roden and Barton M. Saunders.

Magazine Needs: *The Silt Reader*, is published biannually in January and August. "Form, length, style and subject matter can vary. It's difficult to say what will appeal to our eclectic tastes." Does not want "strictly rants, overly didactic poetry." Has published poetry by M. Jaime-Becerra, Gerald Locklin, Simon Perchik, Margaret Garcia, and Don Winter. *The Silt Reader* is 32 pages, 4¼ × 5½, saddle-stapled, photocopied with colored card cover and some ads. Accepts less than 10% of poems received. Press run is 500. Sample: $2. Make checks payable to Robert Roden.

How to Submit: Submit 5 neatly typed poems at a time. Accepts previously published poems and simultaneous submissions. Does not accept e-mail submissions. Cover letter preferred. Time between acceptance and publication is 6 months. "Two editors' votes required for inclusion." Seldom comments on rejected poems. Responds in up to 6 months. Guidelines available for SASE and on website. Pays 2 contributor's copies. Acquires one-time rights.

Book/Chapbook Needs & How to Submit: Temporary Vandalism Recordings publishes 2 chapbooks/year. Chapbooks are usually 40 pages, photocopied, saddle-stapled, press run of 100 intially, with reprint option if needed. Submit 10 sample poems, with SASE for response. "Publication in some magazines is important, but extensive publishing is not required." Responds in 6 months. Pays 50% royalty (after costs recouped) and 5 author's copies (out of a press run of 100). For sample chapbooks send $5 to the above address.

10TH MUSE, 33 Hartington Rd., Southampton, Hants SO14 0EW England. E-mail: andyj@noplace.screaming.net. Established 1990. **Editor:** Andrew Jordan.

Magazine Needs: *10th Muse* "includes poetry and reviews, as well as short prose (usually no more than 2,000 words) and graphics. I prefer poetry with a strong 'lyric' aspect. I enjoy experimental work that corresponds with aspects of the pastoral tradition. I have a particular interest in the cultural construction of landscape." Has published poetry by Peter Riley, Andrew Duncan, Richard Caddel, Ian Robinson, John Welch, and Jeremy Hooker. *10th Muse* is 48-72 pages, A5, photocopied, saddle-stapled, with card cover, no ads. Press run is 200. "U.S. subscribers—send $8 in bills for single copy (including postage)."

How to Submit: Submit up to 6 poems. Include SASE (or SAE with IRCs). Accepts submissions by postal mail and in e-mail text box. Often comments on rejected poems. Responds in 3 months. Pays 1 contributor's copy. Staff reviews books of poetry. Send materials for review consideration.

Advice: "Poets should read a copy of the magazine first."

TERMINUS: A JOURNAL OF LITERATURE AND ART, 1034 Hill St. SE, Atlanta GA 30315. E-mail: Terminusmag@aol.com. Website: www.Terminusmagazine.com. Established 2001. **Editors:** Chad Prevost and Travis Denton.

Magazine Needs: Appearing in March and September, *Terminus* publishes poetry, fiction, creative nonfiction, and art. Strives "to achieve a balance between high creativity and supreme quality. We seek the best writing nationwide mostly from established writers but some from emerging writers." Wants poetry "which is quality and accessible. Innovative images. Original objects and forms welcome. Any subject, especially when handled with skill and taste." *Terminus* is 96-200 pages, digest-sized, perfect bound, glossy cover. Single copy: $12; subscription: $24/year. Sample: $8.

How to Submit: Submit 3-5 poems at a time. Accepts simultaneous submissions ("just please notify us as soon as you have news of publication elsewhere"); no previously published poems. No e-mail submissions "though queries and requests are welcome." Cover letter is preferred. "Manuscripts without SASE cannot be returned." Reads submissions September 1 through April 30 only. Time between acceptance and publication is 3-9 months. Usually comments on returned poems "if we'd like to see more." Responds in up to 4 months. Pays 2 contributor's copies. Acquires first rights.

Also Offers: Annual chapbook contest. Reads from September 1 to January 31. Entry fee: $20. Open to all forms, styles, and genres—fiction, poetry, creative nonfiction. Publishes winning chapbook, up to 48 pages. 2003 Winner: Christopher Buckley.

Advice: "For each issue we seek to publish a journal that readers will want to come back to again and again. Please send only the work you feel most strongly about. Support us and also learn about the kind of work we accept by picking up a copy or subscribing."

◙ TERRA INCOGNITA, A BILINGUAL LITERARY REVIEW; TERRA INCOGNITA—ENCUENTRO CULTURAL BILINGÜE (Specialized: Bilingual, Spanish/English), P.O. Box 150585, Brooklyn NY 11215-0585. (718)492-3508. E-mail: terraincognitamagazine@yahoo.com. Website: www.terra-incognita.com. Established 1998 (first issue published in summer 2000). **US Poetry Editor:** Alexandra van de Kamp. **Spanish Poetry Editor:** Luciano Priego. Member: CLMP.

Magazine Needs: *Terra Incognita, A Bilingual Literary Review* appears annually in autumn. Goal is "to print the best work we can find from established and emerging writers in English and Spanish on both sides of the Atlantic and to act as a cultural bridge between the various Spanish and English-speaking communities. We are open to all forms and subject matter except for that of pornography and material with racist/sexist themes. We're looking for work with guts and intelligence that shows a love of the craft. We do not want to see poetry that asks only so much of itself." Recently published poetry by Billy Collins, Virgil Suarez, José Hierro, Phillip Korbylarz, Sarah Kennedy, and Amalia Serna Iglesias. *Terra Incognita* is 90 pages, magazine-sized, printed, perfectly-bound, card stock cover, with b&w photos, sketches, and selective ads for mainly independent presses and companies. Accepts about 3% of poems submitted. Publishes about 25-30 poems/issue. Press run is 1,000. Single copy $7.50; subscription: $9/year or $17/2 years (includes postage). Sample: $7 plus $2 postage. Make checks payable to Alexandra van de Kamp.

How to Submit: Submit 5 poems at a time. Line length per poem is 100 maximum. Accepts simutaneous submissions with notification; no previously published poems. Accepts submissions by postal mail only. Cover letter is preferred. Note: **Submissions in Spanish should be sent to Apartado 14.401, 28080, Madrid, Spain with 2-3 IRCs.** Reads *Spanish* submissions all year; reads *English* submissions September 1 to April 1 only. Time between acceptance and publication is 2-10 months. "The final decision on poetry submissions lies with the poetry editor, but other editors are consulted as well." Sometimes comments on rejected poems. Guidelines are available for SASE, by e-mail, or on website. Responds in up to 3 months. Sometimes sends prepublication galleys. Pays 2 contributor's copies. Acquires first North American serial rights. Reviews books and chapbooks of poetry in 1,000 words, single book format. Send materials for review consideration to Alexandra van de Kamp, "but we ask that you look at our website and the kind of poetry we publish first."

Also Offers: *Terra Incognita* is part of a larger cultural association that does bilingual readings and encourages cultural exchanges.

Advice: "We look for poetry that is not merely good or capable, but which is actually exciting and thrilling to read—something that bubbles up from deeper, more complex sources. Beginners, ask yourself why your poem or piece *needs* to be in the world."

⊠ ◙ TEXAS REVIEW; TEXAS REVIEW PRESS; X.J. KENNEDY POETRY COMPETITION, % English Dept., Box 2146, Sam Houston State University, Sam Houston Huntsville TX 77341-2146. (936)294-1992. Fax: (936)294-3070. E-mail: eng_pdr@shsu.edu. Website: www.shsu.edu/~www_trp/. Established 1976.

Magazine Needs: *The Texas Review*, published biannually, is a "scholarly journal publishing poetry, short fiction, essays and book reviews." Has published poetry by Donald Hall, X.J. Kennedy, and Richard Eberhart. *The Texas Review* is 152 pages, digest-sized, offset printed, perfect-bound, bond paper with 4-color cover and ads. Press run is 1,000 for 500 subscribers of which 250 are libraries. Single copy: $12; subscription: $24. Sample: $5. Make checks payable to Friends of *Texas Review*.

THE GEOGRAPHICAL INDEX in the back of this book helps you locate markets in your region.

How to Submit: No previously published poems or simultaneous submissions. Include SASE. Reads submissions September 1 through June 1 only. Time between acceptance and publication is 6 months. Poems are circulated to an editorial board. Seldom comments on rejected poems. Responds in a few months. Pays 1 year subscription and 1 copy (may request more). Acquires all rights. Returns rights "for publication in anthology."

Also Offers: Sponsors the X.J. Kennedy Poetry Competition. Winning mss will be published. For contest guidelines send SASE specifying "for poetry/fiction contest guidelines." Website includes catalog, contest guidelines and editors.

TEXAS TECH UNIVERSITY PRESS (Specialized: series), P.O. Box 41037, Lubbock TX 79409-1037. (806)742-2982. Fax: (806)742-2979. E-mail: ttup@ttu.edu. Website: www.ttup.ttu.edu. Established 1971. **Editor:** Judith Keeling. Does not read unsolicited manuscripts.

$ THEMA (Specialized: themes), Thema Literary Society, P.O. Box 8747, Metairie LA 70011-8747. E-mail: thema@home.com. Website: http://members.cox.net/thema. Established 1988. **Editor:** Virginia Howard. **Poetry Editor:** Gail Howard. Address poetry submissions to Gail Howard.

 • *THEMA* is supported by a grant from the Louisiana Division of the Arts, Office of Cultural Development, Department of Culture, Recreation and Tourism, in cooperation with the Louisiana State Arts Council as administered by Art Council of New Orleans.

Magazine Needs: *THEMA* is a triannual literary magazine using poetry related to specific themes. "Each issue is based on an unusual premise. Please, please send SASE for guidelines before submitting poetry to find out the upcoming themes. Upcoming themes (and submission deadlines) include: *Stone, Paper, Scissors* (November 1, 2003), *While You Were Out . . .* (March 1, 2004), *Hey, Watch This!* (July 1, 2004). No scatologic language, alternate life-style, explicit love poetry." Poems will be judged with all others submitted. Has published poetry by James Penha, Susan Terris, Nancy G. Westerfield, Kay Bache-Snyder. *THEMA* is 200 pages, digest-sized, professionally printed, with matte card cover. Receives about 400 poems/year, accepts about 8%. Press run is 500 for 270 subscribers of which 30 are libraries. Subscription: $16. Sample: $8.

How to Submit: Submit up to 3 poems at a time with SASE. All submissions should be typewritten and on standard 8½×11 paper. Submissions are accepted all year, but evaluated after specified deadlines. Guidelines and upcoming themes available for SASE, on website, by e-mail, and in publication. Editor comments on submissions. Pays $10/poem plus 1 contributor's copy. Acquires one-time rights.

Advice: "Do *not* submit to *THEMA unless* you have one of *THEMA*'s upcoming themes in mind. Tell us which one!"

$ THESE DAYS (Specialized: mainstream Christian), 100 Witherspoon St., Louisville KY 40202-1396. E-mail: vpatton@presbypub.com. Established 1969. **Editor:** Vince Patton.

Magazine Needs: *These Days* is a quarterly magazine of daily devotions and devotional resources published by the Presbyterian Church (USA) in partnership with the Cumberland Presbyterian Chuch, The Presbyterian Church in Canada, The United Church of Canada, and the United Church of Christ. We publish only short religious poetry of high quality that has a contemporary but not erudite feel. We especially need church holiday and seasonal poems. We do not want to see nonreligious, nonliterary, obscure work or poetry that is outdated in form." Has published poetry by Anne Shotwell, Katherine Stewart, Sara A. DuBose, Richard Nystrom, Gordon E. Jowers and Ruth Hunt. *These Days* is 104 pages, magazine-sized, offset printed and stapled with soft, glossy cover, includes full color cover art. Receives about 500 poems/year, accepts approximately 1%. Publish 1 poem/issue. Press run is 200,000 for 195,000 subscribers. Subscription: $6.95 regular print, $8.10 large print; Canada: $10.40 regular, $10.80 large print. Sample: 77¢ postage and 5×7 envelope.

How to Submit: Submit 5 poems maximum at a time. Line length for poetry is 3 minimum, 15 maximum. Accepts previously published poems. Cover letter preferred. "Please include a SASE for reply and return of submissions." Accepts submissions by e-mail (either as attachment or in text box). Submit seasonal poems 8 months in advance. Time between acceptance and publication is 1 year. Seldom comments on rejected poems. Guidelines available for SASE or by e-mail. Responds in 3 months. Pays $10 for cover poems and 5 copies. Acquires one-time rights.

Advice: "Study the publication thoroughly. If possible, subscribe and do the devotions daily."

★ ◑ **THIN COYOTE; LOST PROPHET PRESS**, 116 Oak Grove #205, Minneapolis MN 55403. E-mail: knucklemerchant@hotmail.com. Established 1992. **Publisher/Editor:** Christopher Jones.

Magazine Needs: *Thin Coyote* is a quarterly magazine "churning up whirlwinds of creative endeavor by the planet's scofflaws, mule skinners, seers, witchdoctors, maniacs, alchemists, and giant-slayers. Get in touch with your inner shapeshifter and transcribe his howls, growls, and wails. No singsong rhyming crap; no greeting card devotional stuff or I'll come over to your house and put a terrible hurtin' on you." Has published poetry by Jonis Agee, John Millett, Pat McKinnon, and Paul Weinman. *Thin Coyote* is 40-60 pages, magazine-sized, docutech printed and perfect-bound with b&w cardstock cover, includes b&w photos and ads. Receives about 3,000 poems/year, accepts 2-5%. Press run is 300 for 30 subscribers of which 20 are libraries, 270 shelf sales. Single copy: $6; subscription: $18. Sample: $6. Make checks payable to Christopher Jones/*Thin Coyote*.

How to Submit: Submit 5 poems at a time. Accepts previously published poems and simultaneous submissions. Accepts e-mail submissions. Cover letter preferred. Time between acceptance and publication is 4 months. Often comments on rejected poems. Guidelines available for SASE. Responds in 1 month. Pays 1 contributor's copy. Acquires first or one-time rights. Reviews books and chapbooks of poetry and other magazines. Send materials for review consideration to Christopher Jones.

Book/Chapbook Needs & How to Submit: Lost Prophet Press publishes "primarily poetry, some short stories." Publishes 2-3 chapbooks/year. Chapbooks are usually 30-40 pages, digest-sized, offset-printed and saddle-stapled with cardstock cover, includes art. Query first, with a few sample poems and a cover letter with brief bio and publication credits. Responds to queries in 1 month; to mss in 2 weeks. Pays advance or 25% of run.

Also Offers: See listing for *Knuckle Merchant* in the Publishers of Poetry section.

◑ **THIRD COAST**, Dept. of English, Western Michigan University, Kalamazoo MI 49008-5092. (616)387-2675. Fax: (616)387-2562. Website: www.wmich.edu/thirdcoast. Established 1995. **Editors:** Cody Todd and Amanda Warner. **Contact:** Poetry Editors.

Magazine Needs: *Third Coast* is a biannual national literary magazine of poetry, prose, creative nonfiction, and translation. Wants "excellence of craft and originality of thought. Nothing trite." Has published poetry by Billy Collins, Chris Buckley, Margot Schlipp, Mark Halliday, Philip Levine, and Bai Hua. *Third Coast* is 140 pages, digest-sized, professionally printed and perfect-bound with a 4-color cover with art. Receives about 2,000 poems/year, accepts approximately 3-5%. Press run is 1,000 for 100 subscribers of which 20 are libraries, 350 shelf sales. Single copy: $6; subscription: $11/year, $20/2 years, $29/3 years.

How to Submit: Submit up to 5 poems at a time. Poems should be typed and single-spaced, with the author's name on each page. Stanza breaks should be double-spaced. No previously published poems or simultaneous submissions. No electronic submissions. Cover letter with bio preferred. Poems are circulated to assistant poetry editors and poetry editors; poetry editors make final decisions. Seldom comments on rejected poems. Guidelines available for SASE and on website. Responds in 4 months. Pays 2 copies and 1-year subscription. Acquires first rights.

★ ◑ ◎ **13TH MOON (Specialized: women about women)**, English Dept., University at Albany, State University of New York, Albany NY 12222. (518)442-5593. E-mail: moon13@csc.alba ny.edu. Website: www.albany.edu/13thMoon. Established 1973. **Editor:** Judith Emlyn Johnson.

Magazine Needs: *13th Moon* is a feminist literary magazine appearing yearly (one double issue). Beyond a doubt, a real selection of forms and styles is featured here. For instance, free verse has appeared with formal work, concrete poems, long poems, stanza patterns, prose poems, a crown of sonnets, prose, translations, poetics. *13th Moon* is a digest-sized, flat-spined, handsomely printed format with glossy card cover, using photographs and line art. Press run is 1,500 for 70 subscribers. Subscription: $10. Sample: $15 (vintage edition posters available with back issues).

How to Submit: Submit 3-5 poems at a time. No previously published poems or simultaneous submissions. Reads submissions September 1 through May 30 only. Publishes theme issues. Guidelines and upcoming themes available for SASE. Theme for 2003 was "Women's Reflections of Popular Global Culture for the New Millenium"

■✖ ✖ **$**◎ **THISTLEDOWN PRESS LTD. (Specialized: regional)**, 633 Main St., Saskatoon SK S7H 0J8 Canada. (306)244-1722. Fax: (306)244-1762. E-mail: edit@thistledown.sk.ca. Website: www.thistledown.sk.ca. Established 1975. **Editor-in-Chief:** Patrick O'Rourke.

Book/Chapbook Needs: Thistledown is "a literary press that specializes in quality books of contemporary poetry by Canadian authors. Only the best of contemporary poetry that amply demonstrates an understanding of craft with a distinctive use of voice and language. Only interested in full-length poetry manuscripts with 53-71 pages minimum." Publishes *Wormwood Vermouth*, *Warphistory* by Charles Noble and *Zhivago's Fire* by Andrew Wreggitt.

How to Submit: Do not submit unsolicited mss. Canadian poets must query first with letter, bio and publication credits. No e-mail or fax queries or submissions. Submission guidelines available upon request. Responds to queries in 2-3 weeks, to submissions (if invited) in 3 months. No authors outside Canada. No simultaneous submissions. "Please submit quality laser-printed or photocopied material." Always sends prepublication galleys. Contract is for 10% royalty plus 10 copies.

Advice: "Poets submitting mss to Thistledown Press for possible publication should think in 'book' terms in every facet of the organization and presentation of the mss: Poets presenting mss that read like good books of poetry will have greatly enhanced their possibilities of being published. We strongly suggest that poets familiarize themselves with some of our poetry books before submitting a query letter."

◙ **THORNY LOCUST**, P.O. Box 32631, Kansas City MO 64171-5631. E-mail: skoflersilvia@net scape.net. Website: www.thornylocust.com. Established 1993. **Editor:** Silvia Kofler. **Managing Editor:** Celeste Kuechler.

Magazine Needs: *Thorny Locust*, published quarterly, is a "literary magazine that wants to be thought-provoking, witty, and well-written." Wants "poetry with some 'bite' e.g., satire, epigrams, black humor and bleeding-heart cynicism." Does not want "polemics, gratuitous grotesques, sombre surrealism, weeping melancholy, or hate-mongering." Has published poetry by Virgil Suarez, Patricia Cleary Miller, Simon Perchik, and Brian Daldorph. *Thorny Locust* is 28-32 pages, $7 \times 8\frac{1}{2}$, desktop-published, saddle-stapled with medium coverstock, drawings and b&w photos. Receives about 350-400 poems/year, accepts about 35%. Press run is 150-200 for 30 subscribers of which 6 are libraries; 60 distributed free to contributors and small presses. Single copy: $4; subscription: $15. Sample: $3. Make checks payable to Silvia Kofler.

How to Submit: Submit 3 poems at a time. "If you do not include a SASE with sufficient postage, your submission will be pitched!" Accepts simultaneous submissions; no previously published poems. Cover letter preferred. "Poetry and fiction must be typed, laser-printed or in a clear dot-matrix." Time between acceptance and publication is 2 months. Seldom comments on rejected poems. Guidelines available for SASE and on website. Responds in 3 months. Pays 1 contributor's copy. Acquires one-time rights.

Advice: "Never perceive a rejection as a personal rebuke, keep on trying. Take advice."

◙ ◎ **THOUGHTS FOR ALL SEASONS: THE MAGAZINE OF EPIGRAMS (Specialized: form, humor, themes)**, % editor Prof. Em. Michel Paul Richard, 478 NE 56th St., Miami FL 33137-2621. Established 1976. **Contact:** Editor.

Magazine Needs: *Thoughts for All Seasons* "is an irregular serial: designed to preserve the epigram as a literary form; satirical. All issues are commemorative." Rhyming poetry and nonsense verse with good imagery will be considered although most modern epigrams are prose—no haiku. *Thoughts for All Seasons* is 80 pages, offset from typescript and saddle-stapled with full-page illustrations, card cover. Accepts about 20% of material submitted. Press run is 500-1,000. There are several library subscriptions but most distribution is through direct mail or local bookstores and newsstand sales. Single copy: $6 (includes postage and handling).

How to Submit: "Submit at least one or two pages of your work, 10-12 epigrams, or two-four poems." Include SASE. Accepts simultaneous submissions, but not previously published epigrams "unless a thought is appended which alters it." Editor comments on rejected poems. Publishes theme issues including "Time Travel" and "New Lyrics for Old Songs." Guidelines available for SASE and in publication. Responds in 1 month. Pays 1 contributor's copy.

THREE CANDLES, E-mail: editor@threecandles.org. Website: www.threecandles.org. Established 1999. **Editor:** Steve Mueske.

Magazine Needs: *Three Candles* is published online ("post updates when qualified poetry is available, generally once or twice a week"). "Though I am not particular about publishing specific forms of poetry, I prefer to be surprised by the content of the poems themselves. I believe that poetry should have some substance and touch, at least tangentially, on human experience." Does not want poems that are "overtly religious, sexist, racist, or unartful." Recently published poetry by Jeffrey Levine, Deborah Keenan, Joyce Suthpen, Susan Steger Welsh, and Paul Perry. *Three Candles* is a "high-quality online journal, professionally designed and maintained." Receives about 3,000 poems/year. Publishes "approximately 4-6 poets/month, about 10 poems. Many poems I publish are solicited directly from poets." Receives 35,000 hits/month.

How to Submit: Submit 3-5 poems at a time. No simultaneous submissions or previously published poems. Accepts *only* e-mail submissions; no disk submissions. Send poems "as the body of the text or, if special formatting is used, as attachments in Word or rich text format. In the body of the e-mail, I want a short bio, a list of previous publications, the certification statement that appears on the 'information' page on the site, and a brief note about what writing poetry means to you as an artist." Accepts submissions year round. Time between acceptance and publication is about 6 weeks. "Reading the journal is important to get an idea of the level of craft expected." Guidelines available on website. Responds within 2 months. Does not send prepublication galleys but "allows author to make any necessary changes before a formal announcement is e-mailed to the mailing list." No payment "at this time." Acquires first rights. Copyright reverts to author after publication.

Advice: "The online poetry community is vital and thriving. Take some time and get to know the journals that you are submitting to. Don't send work that is like what is published. Send work that is as good but different in a way that is uniquely your own."

3 CUP MORNING; SOMETIMES I SLEEP WITH THE MOON . . . ELECTRONIC PUBLICATION, 13865 Dillabough Rd., Chesterville ON K0C 1H0 Canada. Fax: (613)448-1478. E-mail: threecupmorning@hotmail.com. Website: http://3cupmorning.8k.com. Established 1999. **Editor:** Gen O'Neil.

Magazine Needs: Published bimonthly online, *3 cup morning* is "a platform for the beginning and novice poet to showcase their work. We firmly believe that seeing your work in print is the single greatest encouragement needed to continue. Every poet should have the opportunity to see their work in print—at least once anyway." Accepts all types of poetry, haiku, traditional, experimental, free form, etc. No graphic violence, hate, profanity, or graphic sex. Has published poetry by Robert Hogg, Valerie Poynter, J. Kevin Wolfe, Mary-Ann Hazen, and Ruth Witter. *3 cup morning* is an online journal, publishing hardcopies for subscribers only. Subscription: $20 Canadian, $25 US, $30 all others. Make checks (Canada and US only) or International Money Order payable to Gen O'Neil.

How to Submit: Submit 5 poems at a time. Line length for poetry is 3 minimum, 40 maximum. Accepts previously published poems and simultaneous submissions. Prefers e-mail submissions but accepts "anything that is neatly typed or printed." Electronic submissions can be sent in html or plain text. "All work must be neatly typed on white paper with your name and address on every page. SAE with an IRC must be included if you want to have work returned or a review of your work sent to you. Would prefer to have an e-mail address to send critique to." Submit seasonal poems well in advance. Time between acceptance and publication is 4 months. Poems are circulated to an editorial board. Guidelines available on website. "We guarantee that at least one poem from each submission will be printed in our publication. If you would like to be published on the web, please say so in your cover letter." Does not pay; send personal check (Canada and US only) or International Money Order for $2 for contributor's copy.

Advice: "We look for poetry that is visible. Poetry you can see and touch and feel."

360 DEGREES, 3810 Deckford Place, Charlotte NC 28211. E-mail: threesixtydegreesreview@yahoo.com. Website: www.threesixtydegreesreview.com. Established 1993. **Managing Editor:** Karen Kinnison.

Magazine Needs: *360 Degrees* is a biannual review, containing literature and artwork. "We are dedicated to keeping the art of poetic expression alive." "No real limits" on poetry, "only the limits of the submitter's imagination." However, does not want to see "greeting card verse, simplified emotions, or religious verse." Accepts poetry written by children. Has published poetry by David Demarest, Sean Brendan-Brown, Lyn Lifshin, and Rochelle Holt. *360 Degrees* is 40 pages, digest-sized, neatly printed and saddle-stapled. Receives about 1,000 poems/year, accepts about 100. Press run is 200 for 100 subscribers and one library. Subscription: $6. Sample: $3.

How to Submit: Submit 3-6 poems at a time. Include SASE. Accepts simultaneous submissions; no previously published poems. "Just let us know if a particular piece you have submitted to us has been accepted elsewhere." Accepts submissions by e-mail (as attachment or in text box). Cover letter preferred. Seldom comments on rejected poems. Guidelines available for SASE, by e-mail, on website, and in publication. Responds within 3 months. Pays 1 contributor's copy.

Advice: "The quality of the poetry we publish is often very high, often very innovative, and thought-provoking."

$⬤ THE THREEPENNY REVIEW, P.O. Box 9131, Berkeley CA 94709. (510)849-4545. Website: www.threepennyreview.com. Established 1980. **Poetry Editor:** Wendy Lesser.
  • Work published in this review has also been included in *The Best American Poetry* and *Pushcart Prize* anthologies.

Magazine Needs: *Threepenny Review* "is a quarterly review of literature, performing and visual arts, and social articles aimed at the intelligent, well-read, but not necessarily academic reader. Nationwide circulation. Want: formal, narrative, short poems (and others). Prefer under 100 lines. No bias against formal poetry, in fact a slight bias in favor of it." Has published poetry by Thom Gunn, Frank Bidart, Seamus Heaney, Czeslaw Milosz, and Louise Glück. Features about 10 poems in each 36-page tabloid issue. Receives about 4,500 submissions of poetry/year, accepts about 12. Press run is 10,000 for 8,000 subscribers of which 150 are libraries. Subscription: $25. Sample: $12.

How to Submit: Submit up to 5 poems at a time. Do not submit mss June through August. Guidelines available for SASE or on website. Responds in up to 2 months. Pays $100/poem plus year's subscription. Acquires first serial rights. "Send for review guidelines (SASE required)."

◨ $⬤ TICKLED BY THUNDER, HELPING WRITERS GET PUBLISHED SINCE 1990, 14076-86A Ave., Surrey BC V3W 0V9 Canada. E-mail: info@tickledbythunder.com. Website: www.tickledbythunder.com. Established 1990. **Publisher/Editor:** Larry Lindner.

Magazine Needs: *Tickled by Thunder*, appears up to 4 times/year, using poems about "fantasy particularly, about writing or whatever. Require original images and thoughts. Keep them short (up to 40 lines)—not interested in long, long poems. Nothing pornographic, childish, unimaginative. Welcome humor and creative inspirational verse." Has published poetry by Laleh Dadpour Jackson and Helen Michiko Singh. *Tickled by Thunder* is 24 pages, digest-sized, published on Macintosh. 1,000 readers/subscribers. Subscription: $12/4 issues. Sample: $2.50.

How to Submit: Include 3-5 samples of writing with queries. No e-mail submissions. Cover letter required with submissions; include "a few facts about yourself and brief list of publishing credits." Responds in up to 6 months. Guidelines available for SASE. Pays 2¢/line to $2 maximum. Acquires first rights. Editor comments on rejected poems "80% of the time." Reviews books of poetry in up to 300 words. Open to unsolicited reviews. Send materials for review consideration.

Also Offers: Offers a poetry contest 4 times/year. Deadlines: the 15th of February, May, August, and October. Entry fee: $5 for 1 poem; free for subscribers. Prize: cash, publication, and subscription. Publishes author-subsidized chapbooks. "We are interested in student poetry and publish it in our center spread: *Expressions*." Send SASE (or SAE and IRC) for details.

⬤ TIMBER CREEK REVIEW, 8969 UNCG Station, Greensboro NC 27413. (336)334-2952. E-mail: timber_creek_review@hoopsmail.com. Established 1994. **Editor:** John M. Freiermuth. **Associate Editor:** Roslyn Willett.

Magazine Needs: *Timber Creek Review* appears quarterly publishing short stories, literary nonfiction, and poetry. Wants all types of poetry. Does not want religious, pornography. Recently published Mike Dockins, Jane Stuart, Scott Welvaert, Elsie Pankowski, William V. Davis, Elain McHenry, Fred Chappell, and Simon Perchik. *Timber Creek Review* is 80-92 pages, digest-sized, laser-printed, stapled, colored paper cover with graphics. Receives about 800 poems/year, accepts about 5%. Publishes about 11-13 poems/issue. Press run is 150 for 120 subscribers of which 2 are libraries, 30 shelf sales.

Single copy: $4.50; subscription: $16. Sample: $4.50. Make checks payable to J.M. Freiermuth.
How to Submit: Submit 3-6 poems at a time. Line length for poetry is 3 minimum. Accepts simultaneous submissions; no previously published poems. No fax, e-mail, or disk submissions. Cover letter is required. Reads submissions year round. Submit seasonal poems 10 months in advance. Time between acceptance and publication is 3-6 months. Never comments on rejected poems. Occasionally publishes theme issues. Guidelines available for SASE or by e-mail. Responds in up to 6 months. Pays 1 contributor's copy. Acquires first North American serial rights.

$ ☑ **TIMBERLINE PRESS**, 6281 Red Bud, Fulton MO 65251. (573)642-5035. Established 1975. **Poetry Editor:** Clarence Wolfshohl.
Book/Chapbook Needs: "We do limited letterpress editions with the goal of blending strong poetry with well-crafted and designed printing. We lean toward natural history or strongly imagistic nature poetry but will look at any good work. Also, good humorous poetry." Has published *Annuli* by William Heyen, *Trance Arrows* by James Bogan, *Time Travel Reports* by Charles Fishman, and *Harmonic Balance* by Walter Bargen. Sample copies may be obtained by sending $7.50, requesting sample copy, and noting you saw the listing in *Poet's Market*. Responds in under 1 month. Pays "50-50 split with author after Timberline Press has recovered its expenses."
How to Submit: Query before submitting full ms.

★ ◻ ◎ **TIMBOOKTU (Specialized: ethnic/nationality)**, P.O. Box 933, Mobile AL 36601-0933. E-mail: editor@timbooktu.com. Website: www.timbooktu.com. Established 1996. **Editor:** Memphis Vaughan, Jr.
Magazine Needs: *TimBookTu* is a monthly online journal. Wants "positive, creative, and thought-provoking poetry that speaks to the diverse African-American culture and the African diaspora." Has published poetry by Zamounde Allie, Jamal Sharif, B.T. Bonner, Trina Williams-Emigh, Tameko Bernette, and Richard "Rip" Parks. Receives about 2,500 poems/year, accepts about 75%.
How to Submit: Submit 3 poems at a time. Accepts previously published poems and simultaneous submissions. Accepts e-mail and disk submissions; no fax submissions. Cover letter preferred. Time between acceptance and publication is 2 months. Always comments on rejected poems. Guidelines available for SASE. Responds in up to 2 months. Send materials for review consideration.

★ ✿ ◻ ◎ **TIME FOR RHYME (Specialized: form/style)**, P.O. Box 1055, Battleford SK S0M 0E0 Canada. (306)445-5172. Established 1995. **Editor:** Richard W. Unger.
Magazine Needs: *Time for Rhyme*, published quarterly, aims to "promote traditional rhyming poetry. Other than short editorial, contents page, review page, PoeMarkets (other markets taking rhyme), this magazine is all rhyming poetry." Wants "any rhyming poetry in any form up to about 32 lines on nearly any subject." Does not want poetry that is "obscene (4-letter words), pornographic, profane, racist, or sexist. No e.e. cummings' style either." Accepts poetry by younr writers. Has published poetry by R. Wayne Edwards, Elizabeth Symon, R.L.Cook, Marion Young, C. David Hay, and Virginia Frey. *Time for Rhyme* is 32 pages, 4 × 5½, photocopied, hand-bound with thread, hand press printed cover, with clip art, handmade rubber stamps, letterpress art and ads. Receives several hundred poems/year, accepts about 10%. Subscription: $12. Sample: $3.25.
How to Submit: "Preference given to subscribers, however, no requirements." Accepts previously published poems ("But must ensure poet retained rights on it. Prefer unpublished"). No simultaneous submissions. Cover letter preferred, list titles submitted and if first submission here give brief list of publications poet has been published in. No poems published yet? Send some general information." Often comments on rejected poems. Guidelines available for SASE (or SAE with IRC). "Americans submitting can save money by sending SAE and $1 U.S. bill (cheaper than IRC). Please no SASE with U.S. stamps." Responds ASAP. Pays 1 copy. Acquires first North American serial rights—will consider second serial rights. Staff reviews books/magazines containing mostly or all rhyming poetry. Reviews vary in length but up to about 100 words. Send materials for review consideration.
Advice: "Though non-rhyming poetry can be excellent, *Time for Rhyme* was created to be a platform for poets who prefer rhyme and as a source for those who prefer to read it. Old-fashioned values popular here too. Might be best to read a back issue before submitting."

TIME OF SINGING, A MAGAZINE OF CHRISTIAN POETRY (Specialized: religious), P.O. Box 149, Conneaut Lake PA 16316. E-mail: timesing@toolcity.net. Website: www.timeofsinging.bizland.com. Established 1958-1965, revived 1980. **Editor:** Lora H. Zill.

Magazine Needs: *Time of Singing* appears 4 times/year. "Collections of uneven lines, series of phrases, preachy statements, unstructured 'prayers,' and trite sing-song rhymes usually get returned. We look for poems that 'show' rather than 'tell.' The viewpoint is unblushingly Christian—but in its widest and most inclusive meaning. Moreover, it is believed that the vital message of Christian poems, as well as inspiring the general reader, will give pastors, teachers, and devotional leaders rich current sources of inspiring material to aid them in their ministries. Would like to see more forms. Has published poetry by Tony Cosier, John Grey, Luci Shaw, Bob Hostetler, Evelyn Minshull, Frances P. Reid, Barbara Crooker, and Charles Waugaman. *Time of Singing* is 44 pages, digest-sized, offset from typescript with decorative line drawings scattered throughout. The bonus issues are not theme based. Receives over 800 submissions/year, accepts about 175. Press run is 300 for 150 subscribers. Single copy: $6; subscription: $15 US, $18 Canada, $27 overseas. Sample: $4.

How to Submit: Submit up to 5 poems at a time, single-spaced. "We prefer poems under 40 lines, but will publish up to 60 lines if exceptional." Accepts simultaneous submissions and previously published poems. Accepts e-mail submissions, include in body of message. Time between acceptance and publication is up to 1 year. Editor comments with suggestions for improvement if close to publication. Publishes theme issues "quite often." Guidelines and upcoming themes are available for SASE, by e-mail, and on website. Responds in 2 months. Pays 1 contributor's copy.

Also Offers: Sponsors several theme contests for specific issues. Contest rules available by e-mail and for SASE.

Advice: "Study the craft. Be open to critique—a poet is often too close to their work and needs a critical, honest eye."

TITAN PRESS; MASTERS AWARDS, Box 17897, Encino CA 91416. E-mail: ucla654@yahoo.com. Website: www.titanpress.info. Established 1980. **Publisher:** Stephanie Wilson.

Book/Chapbook Needs & How to Submit: Titan Press is "a small press presently publishing 6-7 works per year including poetry, photojournals, calendars, novels, etc. We look for quality, freshness, and that touch of genius." In poetry, "we want to see verve, natural rhythms, discipline, impact, etc. We are flexible but verbosity, triteness, and saccharine make us cringe. *We now read and publish only mss accepted from the Masters Award.*" Has published books by Bebe Oberon, Walter Calder, Exene Vida, Carlos Castenada, and Sandra Gilbert. Their tastes are for poets such as Adrienne Rich, Li-Young Lee, Charles Bukowski, and Czeslaw Milosz. "We have strong liaisons with the entertainment industry and like to see material that is media-oriented and au courant."

Also Offers: "We sponsor the Masters Awards, established in 1981, including a $1,000 grand prize annually plus each winner (and the five runners-up in poetry) will be published on website or in a clothbound edition and distributed to selected university and public libraries, news mediums, etc. There is a one-time only $15 administration and reading fee per entrant. Submit a maximum of five poems or song lyric pages (no tapes) totaling no more than 150 lines. Any poetic style or genre is acceptable, but a clear and fresh voice, discipline, natural rhythm, and a certain individuality should be evident. Further application and details available with a #10 SASE."

Advice: "Please study what we publish before you consider submitting."

TORRE DE PAPEL (Specialized: ethnic/nationality), 111 Phillips Hall, Iowa City IA 52242-1409. (319)335-0487. E-mail: torredepapel@uiowa.edu. Website: www.uiowa.edu/~spanport. Established 1991. **Editor:** Peter Watt.

Magazine Needs: Appearing 3 times/year, *Torre de Papel* is a "journal devoted to the publication of critical and creative works related to Hispanic and Luso-Brazilian art, literature, and cultural production. We are looking for poetry written in Spanish, Portuguese, or languages of these cultures; translations of authors writing in these languages; or poems in English representative of some aspect of Hispanic or Luso-Brazilian culture." Does not want to see "poetry for children; no religious or esoterical work." *Torre de Papel* is 110 pages, 8¾ × 11½. Press run is 200 for 50 subscribers of which 25 are libraries. Single copy: $7; subscription: $21. Sample: $10.

How to Submit: Submit up to 5 poems at a time. No previously published poems or simultaneous submissions. Accepts e-mail submissions, include as attached file. Cover letter with brief bio required. Include e-mail address. Submit 3 copies of each poem and a Macintosh or IBM diskette of the work. Reads submissions September through April only. Poems are circulated to an editorial board for review. "We send creative work to three readers of our advisory board for comments. However, since we publish articles and stories as well, space for poetry can be limited." Responds in 6 months. Pays 1 contributor's copy.

TRAINED MONKEY PRESS; TRAINED MONKEY BROADSIDES, 918 York St., 1st Floor, Newport KY 41071. E-mail: trainedmonkeypress@amish2000.com. Established 2000. **Editor:** Vic Grunkenmeyer.

Magazine Needs: Trained Monkey Broadsides appear bimonthly and include poetry, album reviews, short fiction, photos. They are given away free at distribution points, and by mail for $1. Trained Monkey Broadsides are 10 pages, digest-sized, saddle-stapled, paper cover, with art/graphics and business card size and flyer size ads. Receives about 100 poems/year, accepts about 20%. Publishes about 4 poems/issue. Press run is 200 for 20 subscribers; 150 are distributed free to bars, businesses, music stores. Single copy: $1; subscription: $10/year. Sample: $1.

How to Submit: Submit 3-6 poems at a time. Line length for poetry is 1 minimum, 50 maximum. No previously published poems or simultaneous submissions. Accepts e-mail submissions; no fax or disk submissions. Cover letter is preferred. "Always use SASEs when submitting." Reads submissions year round. Time between acceptance and publication is 2 months. Submissions may be circulated within the editorial board. Seldom comments on rejected poems. Guidelines available in magazine or by e-mail. Responds in 2 weeks. Pays 1 contributor's copy. Acquires one-time rights. Reviews books and chapbooks of poetry and other magazines/journals in 200 words, single book format. Poets may send materials for review consideration to Trained Monkey Press.

Book/Chapbook Needs & How to Submit: The goal of Trained Monkey Press publications is "to get people to pick them up and read. We look for strong words; good poetry in any form that is about something. Satire is encouraged." Does not want "didactic, preachy, wishy-washy whining." Recently published poetry by Joey Shannanagins, Tom Case, David Garza, Cliff Spisak, Julie Judge, and Mr. Spoons. Trained Monkey Press publishes 5-7 chapbooks/year. Chapbooks are usually 30 pages, saddle-stapled, with stock cover and art/graphics. Query first, with a few sample poems and a cover letter with brief bio and publication credits. Responds to queries in 2 weeks; to mss in 2 months. Pays 5 author's copies (out of a press run of 100). Order sample chapbooks by sending $5 to Trained Monkey Press.

Advice: "Get it out . . . submit to the monkey."

**Transcendent Visions Fall 2002
Celebrating Ten Years of Mad Art**

Editor David Kime wanted a special cover to celebrate ten years of *Transcendent Visions*, a journal which provides a creative outlet for psychiatric survivors and ex-mental patients. The artist, Robert Bullock, is Director of Coalition Ingenu, an association of self-taught artists in Philadelphia.

◐ ◎ **TRANSCENDENT VISIONS (Specialized: psychiatric survivors, ex-mental patients)**, 251 S. Olds Blvd. 84-E, Fairless Hills PA 19030-3426. (215)547-7159. Established 1992. **Editor:** David Kime.

Magazine Needs: *Transcendent Visions* appears 1-2 times/year "to provide a creative outlet for psychiatric survivors/ex-mental patients." Wants "experimental, confessional poems; strong poems dealing with issues we face. Any length or subject matter is OK but shorter poems are more likely to be published. No rhyming poetry." Has published poetry by Gindy Elizabeth Houston, James Michael Ward, David Beard, and B.Z. Niditch. *Transcendent Visions* is 24 pages, magazine-sized, photocopied and corner-stapled with paper cover, b&w line drawings. Receives about 100 poems/ year, accepts 20%. Press run is 200 for 50 subscribers. Subscription: $6. Sample: $2. Make checks payable to David Kime.

How to Submit: Submit 5 poems at a time. Accepts previously published poems and simultaneous submissions. Cover letter preferred. "Please tell me something unique about you, but I do not care about all the places you have been published." Time between acceptance and publication is 6 months. Responds in 4 months. Pays 1 contributor's copy of issue in which poet was published. Acquires first or one-time rights. Staff reviews books and chapbooks of poetry and other magazines in 20 words. Send materials for review consideration.

Also Offers: "I also publish a political zine called *Crazed Nation*, featuring essays concerning mental illness."

★ $ ◎ **TRAVEL NATURALLY; INTERNATURALLY, INC. PUBLISHING (Specialized: nude recreation)**, P.O. Box 317, Newfoundland NJ 07435-0317. (973)697-3552. Fax: (973)697-8313. E-mail: naturally@internaturally.com. Website: www.internaturally.com. Established 1981. **Editor/Publisher:** Bern Loibl.

Magazine Needs: *Travel Naturally* is a quarterly magazine devoted to family nudism and naturism. Wants poetry about the naturalness of the human body and nature, any length. *Travel Naturally* is 72 pages, magazine-sized, printed on glossy paper and saddle-stapled with full-color photos throughout. Receives about 30 poems/year, accepts approximately 4. Press run is 16,000 for 6,500 subscribers, 8,500 shelf sales. Single copy: $7.50; subscription: $24.95. Sample: $11.75 postpaid.

How to Submit: Accepts previously published poems and simultaneous submissions. Accepts e-mail and fax submissions. "Name and address must be submitted with e-mail." Often comments on rejected poems. Guidelines available for SASE or by e-mail. Responds in 2 months. Pays $20 and 1 copy. Acquires first North American serial or one-time rights.

★ ◎ **TULANE REVIEW**, 122 Norman Mayer, New Orleans LA 70118. (504)865-5160. Fax: (504)862-8958. E-mail: litsoc@tulane.edu. Website: www.tulane.edu/~litsoc. Established 1988. **Editor:** Claire Kiefer.

• *Tulane Review* is the recipient of an AWP Literary Magazine Design Award

Magazine Needs: *Tulane Review* is a national biannual literary journal seeking quality submissions of prose, poetry, and art. "We consider all types of poetry, but prefer poems between one and two pages. We favor imaginative poems with bold, inventive images." Recently published poetry by Virgil Suarez, Tom Chandler, Gaylord Brewer, and Ryan Van Cleave. *Tulane Review* is 80 pages, 7×9, perfect-bound, 100# cover with full-color artwork, includes 10-12 pieces of internal art and ads for literary journals. Receives about 600 poems/year, accepts about 30. Publishes about 15 poems/ issue. Single copy: $5; subscription: $10. Make checks payable to *Tulane Review*.

How to Submit: Submit up to 6 poems at a time. Accepts simultaneous submissions; no previously published poems. No fax, e-mail, or disk submissions. Cover letter is required. "Include brief biography." Reads submissions year round. Time between acceptance and publication is 2 months. Poems are circulated to an editorial board. "Poems are reviewed anonymously by a review board under a poetry editor's supervision. Recommendations are given to the editor, who makes final publication decisions." Often comments on rejected poems. Guidelines available in magazine, for SASE, by e-mail, or on website. Responds in 2 months. Pays 3 contributor's copies. Acquires first North American serial rights.

Also Offers: "We have contests periodically that present cash awards to poets, writers, and artists."

⊘ **TURKEY PRESS**, 6746 Sueno Rd., Isla Vista CA 93117-4904. Established 1974. **Poetry Editors:** Harry Reese and Sandra Reese. "We do not encourage solicitations of any kind to the press. We seek out and develop projects on our own."

$⊘ **TURNROW**, English Dept., The University of Louisiana at Monroe, Monroe LA 71209. (318)342-1510. Fax: (318)342-1491. E-mail: ryan@ulm.edu or heflin@ulm.edu. Website: http://turnr ow.ulm.edu. Established 2000. **Editors:** Jack Heflin, William Ryan.
Magazine Needs: *turnrow* appears biannually and seeks submissions of nonfiction of a general interest, short fiction, poetry, translations, interviews, art, and photography. Recently published poetry by CD Wright, Mary Ruefle, Christopher Howell, Gonzalo Rojas, James Haug, and Karen Donovan. *turnrow* is 130 pages, digest-sized, offset-printed, perfect-bound, full color cover, with art, graphics, photography. Receives about 5,000 poems/year, accepts about .01%. Publishes about 6-10 poems/ issue. Press run is 1,000 for 100 subscribers of which 15 are libraries, 400 shelf sales. Single copy: $7; subscription: $12/1 year, $20/2 years. Sample: $7. Make checks payable to *turnrow*.
How to Submit: Submit 3 poems at a time. Line length for poetry is open. No previously published poems or simultaneous submissions. No fax, e-mail, or disk submissions. Cover letter is preferred. Reads submissions September 15 through May 15. Time between acceptance and publication is 6 months. Seldom comments on rejected poems. Occasionally publishes theme issues. A list of upcoming themes available for SASE or on website. Guidelines available for SASE. Responds in 2 months. Sometimes sends prepublication galleys. Pays $50 and 2 contributor's copies. Acquires first rights.

▨ $◉ **TURNSTONE PRESS LIMITED (Specialized: regional)**, 607-100 Arthur St., Winnipeg MB R3B 1H3 Canada. (204)947-1555. Fax: (204)942-1555. E-mail: editor@turnstonepress.mb. ca. Website: www.TurnstonePress.com. Established 1976. **Contact:** Acquisitions Editor-Poetry.
  ● Books published by Turnstone Press have won numerous awards, including the McNally Robinson Book of the Year Award, the Canadian Author's Association Literary Award for Poetry and the Lampert Memorial Awards.
Book/Chapbook Needs: "Turnstone Press publishes Canadian authors/landed immigrants with special priority to prairie interests/themes." Publishes 3 paperbacks/year. Has published poetry by Di Brandt, Catherine Hunter, Patrick Friesen, and Dennis Cooley. Books are usually digest-sized, offset-printed and perfect-bound with quality paperback cover.
How to Submit: Query first with 10 sample poems and cover letter with brief bio and publication credits. No simultaneous submissions. Cover letter preferred. No e-mail submissions. "Please enclose SASE (or SAE with IRC) and if you want the submission back, make sure your envelope and postage cover it." Time between acceptance and publication is 1 year. Poems are circulated to an editorial board. "The submissions that are approved by our readers go to the editorial board for discussion." Receives more than 1,200 unsolicited mss/year, about 5% are given serious consideration. Responds to queries in 3 months; to mss in 4 months. Pays royalties of 10% plus advance of $200 and 10 author's copies.
Advice: "Competition is extremely fierce in poetry. Most work published is by poets working on their craft for many years."

⊘ **24.7; RE-PRESST**, 30 Forest St., Providence RI 02906. (401)521-4728. Established 1994. **Poetry Editor:** David Church. Currently not accepting submissions.

⊘ **TWILIGHT ENDING**, 21 Ludlow Dr., Milford CT 06460-6822. (203)877-3473. Established 1995. **Editor/Publisher:** Emma J. Blanch. **Co-Editor:** Martin Goorhigian.
Magazine Needs: *Twilight Ending* appears 3 times/year publishing "poetry and short fiction of the highest caliber, in English, with universal appeal." Has featured the work of poets from the US, Canada, Europe, Middle East, Japan, and New Zealand. Wants "poems with originality in thought and in style, reflecting the latest trend in writing, moving from the usual set-up to a vertical approach. We prefer unrhymed poetry, however we accept rhymed verse if rhymes are perfect. We look for the unusual approach in content and style with clarity. No haiku. No poems forming a design. No foul words. No translations. No bio. No porn." *Twilight Ending* is digest-sized, "elegantly printed on white linen paper with one poem with title per page (12-30 lines)." Receives about 1,500 poems/ year, accepts 10%. Press run is 120 for 50 subscribers of which 25 are libraries. Sample: $6 US,

$6.50 Canada, $7 Europe, $8 Middle East, Japan, and New Zealand. Make checks payable to Emma J. Blanch.

How to Submit: Submit only 3-4 poems at a time. "Use standard 8½ × 11 white paper. Type each poem, single-spaced, one poem per page. Each poem must have a title. No abbreviation. Type name, address, and zip code on top right page." No previously published poems or simultaneous submissions nor poems submitted to contests while in consideration for *Twilight Ending*. Include white stamped business envelop for reply (overseas contributors should include 2 IRCs). No fax or e-mail submissions. "When accepted, poems and fiction will not be returned so keep copies." Submission deadlines: mid-December for Winter issue, mid-April for Spring/Summer issue, mid-September for Fall issue. No backlog, "all poems are destroyed after publication." Often comments on rejected poems. Guidelines available for SASE and in publication. Responds in 1 week. Pays nothing—not even a copy. Acquires first rights.

Advice: "If editing is needed, suggestions will be made for the writer to rework and resubmit a corrected version. The author always decides; remember that you deal with experts."

☺ TWO RIVERS REVIEW, P.O. Box 158, Clinton NY 13323. E-mail: tworiversreview@juno.com. Website: http://trrpoetry.tripod.com. Established 1998. **Editor:** Philip Memmer.

Magazine Needs: *Two Rivers Review* appears biannually and "seeks to print the best of contemporary poetry. All styles of work are welcome, so long as submitted poems display excellence." Has published poetry by Billy Collins, Gary Young, Lee Upton, Baron Wormser, and Olga Broumas. *Two Rivers Review* is 44-52 pages, digest-sized, professionally printed on cream-colored paper, with card cover. Subscription: $10. Sample: $5. "Poets wishing to submit work may obtain a sample copy for the reduced price of $4."

How to Submit: Submit no more than 4 poems at a time with cover letter (optional) and SASE (required). Simultaneous submissions are considered with notification. No e-mail submissions. Guidelines available for SASE, by e-mail, or on website. Responds to most submissions within 1 month. Acquires first rights.

Also Offers: Sponsors the annual *Two Rivers Review* Poetry Prize. In 2002, the *Two Rivers Review* chapbook series will also be introduced, with books chosen through a competition. Guidelines available for SASE or on website.

☺ U.S. I WORKSHEETS; U.S. I POETS' COOPERATIVE, P.O. Box 127, Kingston NJ 08528-0127. Website: www.geocities.com/princetonpoets2001/index.html. Established 1973. **Contact:** Poetry Editors. **Managing Editor:** Winifred Hughes.

Magazine Needs: *U.S. 1 Worksheets* is a literary annual, double issue December or January, circulation 400, which uses high-quality poetry and fiction. "We use a rotating board of editors; it's wisest to query when we're next reading before submitting. A self-addressed, stamped postcard will get our next reading period dates (usually in the spring)." Has published poetry by Alicia Ostriker, James Richardson, Frederick Tibbetts, Lois Marie Harrod, James Haba, Charlotte Mandel, and David Keller. *U.S. 1 Worksheets* is 72 pages, digest-sized, saddle-stapled, with color cover art. "We read a lot but take very few. Prefer complex, well-written work." Subscription: $7, $12/2 years.

How to Submit: Submit 5 poems at a time. Include name, address, and phone number in upper right-hand corner. No simultaneous submissions; rarely accepts previously published poems. Requests for sample copies, subscriptions, queries, back issues, and all mss should be addressed to the editor (address at beginning of listing). Guidelines available for SASE. Pays 1 contributor's copy.

$☺ U.S. CATHOLIC; CLARETIAN PUBLICATIONS, 205 W. Monroe St., Chicago IL 60606. (312)236-7782. E-mail: aboodm@claretianpubs.org. Website: www.uscatholic.org. Established 1935. **Literary Editor:** Maureen Abood.

Magazine Needs: "Published monthly, *U.S. Catholic* engages a broad range of issues as they affect

THE OPENNESS TO SUBMISSIONS INDEX in the back of this book lists markets according to the level of writing they prefer to see.

the everyday lives of Catholics." Has no specifications for poetry, but does not necessarily want poems religious in nature. No light verse. Has published poetry by Naomi Shihab Nye. *U.S. Catholic* is 51 pages, magazine-sized, printed in 4-color and stapled, includes art/graphics. Receives about 1,000 poems/year, accepts about 12 poems. Publishes 1 poem/issue. Press run is 50,000. Subscription: $22.

How to Submit: Submit 3 poems at a time. Line length for poetry is 50 maximum. Accepts simultaneous submissions; no previously published poems. Accepts e-mail submissions (include in body of message); no fax submissions. Cover letter preferred. Always include SASE. Time between acceptance and publication is 3 months. Poems are circulated to an editorial board. Seldom comments on rejected poems. Guidelines available for SASE. Responds in 3 months. Pays $75 and 5 contributor's copies. Acquires first North American serial rights.

◻ **THE U.S. LATINO REVIEW; HISPANIC DIALOGUE PRESS**, P.O. Box 150009, Kew Gardens NY 11415. E-mail: andrescastro@aol.com or editor@uslatinoreview.org. Website: www.usla tinoreview.org. Established 1999. **Managing Editor:** Andrés Castro.

Magazine Needs: "*U.S. Latino Review* is an annual literary review for Latinos, our friends, and critics. It is indeed a labor of love dedicated to promoting the best we as a community of creative artists have to offer. We expect truth, excellence and passion from contributors and ourselves. We include poetry, short short story, essay, sketch art and other forms considered if queried. Submissions of all content and form are considered, but writers and artists should understand that we heavily favor work that focuses concretely on the urgent social, political, economic and ecological issues of our time. We stress that *U.S. Latino Review* is not exclusionary—we are won over easily by care, craft and conscience." Has published poetry by Alma Luz Villianueva, L.S. Asekoff, Jack Agüeros, Cornelius Eady, Virgil Suarez, Kimiko Hahn, and Ray Gonzalez. Published in September, *U.S. Latino Review* is 64 pages, digest-sized, printed on 100% recycled 24 lb. stock and flat-spined with semi-gloss card cover, includes black ink sketch art/prints. Receives about 500 poems/year, accepts 3-5%. Press run is 1,000 for 100 subscribers, 700 shelf sales. Single copy: $7.50 US; subscription: $12 US; $22 US/2 years. Make checks payable to *The U.S. Latino Review*.

How to Submit: Submit 3-5 poems at a time. Accepts previously published poems and simultaneous submissions. Accepts e-mail submissions in body of message (no attachments). Cover letter preferred. "SASE must accompany submissions. A short bio is requested but not necessary for contributors page." Time between acceptance and publication is up to 6 months. Poems are circulated to an editorial board. "Editor does early screening and poems forwarded to editorial board of at least three others for final selection." Guidelines available for SASE, by e-mail, on website, or in publication. Responds in up to 6 months. Sends prepublication galleys if requested. Pays 5 contributor copies. Acquires first rights.

Advice: "Please, send your best."

◪ **UMBRIATE**, 710 Old Farm Rd., Point Pleasant NJ 08742-4046. (732)701-0656. E-mail: e.lovela nd@att.net. Established 2000. **Editors:** Emile Gustave and Eric Loveland.

Magazine Needs: *UMBRIATE* appears biannually. Wants "daring conceptual, concrete, or lyric poetry of which the form is driven by the content." Does not want "sloppy poetry, mawkish nonsense, bad surrealism, adolescent angst." Recently published poetry by Emile Gustave, Eric Geist, Dan Buck, and Joe Felice. *UMBRIATE* is 20-25 pages, computer-generated/photocopied, saddle-stapled, with card stock cover and b&w art. Receives about 100 poems/year, accepts about 40%. Press run is 100-150; most are distributed free to poets, libraries, bookstores. Single copy: $2 or price of postage; subscription: $4 or price of postage. Sample: $1. Make checks payable to Eric Loveland.

How to Submit: Submit 3-6 poems at a time. Accepts simultaneous submissions; no previously published poems. Accepts e-mail and disk submissions. Cover letter preferred. Reads submissions all year long. Time between acceptance and publication is up to 6 months. "Poems are circulated to three members of staff and chosen by consensus." Seldom comments on rejected poems. Guidelines available in magazine. Responds in 6 weeks. Sometimes sends prepublication galleys. Pays 2 contributor's copies. Acquires one-time rights. Reviews chapbooks of poetry and other magazines/journals in 50-70 words. Send materials for review consideration to Eric Loveland.

Advice: "Think, write, rewrite—then think, write, rewrite."

☒ $UNIVERSITY OF ALBERTA PRESS, Ring House 2, Edmonton AB T6G 2E1 Canada. (780)492-3662. Fax: (780)492-0719. E-mail: uap@ualberta.ca. Website: www.uap.ualberta.ca. Established 1969. **Managing Editor:** Leslie Vermeer. **Contact:** Michael Luski, acquisitions editor.
Book/Chapbook Needs: "The University of Alberta Press is a scholarly press, generally publishing nonfiction plus some literary titles." Publishes 1-2 paperback poetry titles per year. Looking for "mature, thoughtful work—nothing too avant-garde. No juvenile or 'Hallmark verse.' " Has published *Bloody Jack* by Dennis Cooley and *The Hornbooks of Rita K* by Robert Kroetsch.
How to Submit: Query first, with 10-12 sample poems and cover letter with brief bio and publication credits. "Do not send complete manuscript on first approach." Accepts previously published poems. Accepts e-mail and disk submissions. Time between acceptance and publication is 6-10 months. Poems are circulated to an editorial board. "The process is: acquiring editor to editorial group meeting to two external reviewers to press committee to acceptance." Seldom comments on rejected poems. Responds to queries in 3 months. Pays royalties of 10% of net plus 10 author's copies. See website to order sample books.

☑ UNIVERSITY OF CENTRAL FLORIDA CONTEMPORARY POETRY SERIES, % English Dept., University of Central Florida, Orlando FL 32816-1346. (407)823-2212. Established 1968. **Poetry Editor:** Judith Hemschemeyer.
Book/Chapbook Needs: Publishes two 50- to 80-page hardback or paperback collections each year. "Strong poetry on any theme in the lyric-narrative tradition." Has published poetry by Robert Cooperman, Katherine Soniat, and John Woods.
How to Submit: Submit complete paginated ms with table of contents and acknowledgement of previously published poems. Accepts simultaneous submissions. "Please send a SASE for return of ms and a self-addressed postcard for acknowledgment of receipt of ms." Reads submissions September through April only. **Reading fee:** $7, make checks payable to the UCF Contemporary Poetry Series. Responds in 3 months. Time between acceptance and publication is 1 year.

☑ UNIVERSITY OF GEORGIA PRESS; CONTEMPORARY POETRY SERIES, 330 Research Dr., Suite B100, University of Georgia, Athens GA 30602-4901. Website: www.uga.edu/ugapress. Press established 1938, series established 1980. **Series Editor:** Bin Ramke. **Poetry Competition Coordinator:** Erin McElroy.
   ● Poetry published by University of Georgia Press has been included in the 2002 *Pushcart Prize* anthology.
Book/Chapbook Needs: Through its annual competition, the press publishes 4 collections of poetry/year, 2 of which are by poets who have not had a book published, in paperback editions. Has published poetry by Marjorie Welish, Arthur Vogelsang, C.D. Wright, Martha Ronk, and Paul Hoover.
How to Submit: "Writers should query first for guidelines and submission periods. Please enclose SASE." There are no restrictions on the type of poetry submitted, but "familiarity with our previously published books in the series may be helpful." No fax or e-mail submissions. $20 submission fee required. Make checks payable to University of Georgia Press. Manuscripts are *not* returned after the judging is completed.

☑ UNIVERSITY OF IOWA PRESS; THE IOWA POETRY PRIZES, 100 Kuhl House, 119 West Park Rd., Iowa City IA 52242-1000. Fax: (319)335-2055. E-mail: rhonda-wetjen@uiowa.edu. Website www.uiowapress.org.
Book/Chapbook Needs: The University of Iowa Press offers annually the Iowa Poetry Prizes for book-length mss (50-150 pages) by new or established poets. Winners will be published by the Press under a standard royalty contract. Winning entries for 2002 were *Small Boat* by Leslie Lewis and *Thieves' Latin* by Peter Jay Shippy.
How to Submit: Mss are received annually in April only. All writers of English are eligible. Poems from previously published books may be included only in mss of selected or collected poems, submissions of which are encouraged. Accepts simultaneous submissions if press is immediately notified if the book is accepted by another publisher. $20 entry fee is charged; mss will not be returned. Include name on the title page only.
Advice: "These awards have been initiated to encourage all poets, whether new or established, to submit their very best work."

◙ **THE UNIVERSITY OF MASSACHUSETTS PRESS; THE JUNIPER PRIZE**, P.O. Box 429, Amherst MA 01004-0429. (413)545-2217. Fax: (413)545-1226. E-mail: info@umpress.umass.e du. Website: www.umass.edu/umpress. Established 1964. **Contact:** Alice I. Maldonado, assistant editor and web manager.

Book/Chapbook Needs: The press offers an annual competition for the Juniper Prize, in alternate years to first and subsequent books. In even-numbered years (2000, 2002, etc.) only subsequent books will be considered: mss whose authors have had at least one full-length book or chapbook of poetry published or accepted for publication. Such chapbooks must be at least 30 pages, and self-published work is not considered to lie within this "books and chapbooks" category. In odd-numbered years (1999, 2001, etc.) only "first books" will be considered: mss by writers whose poems may have appeared in literary journals and/or anthologies but have not been published, or been accepted for publication, in book form. Has published *The Double Task* by Gray Jacobik; *Song of the Cicadas* by Mông-Lan; *Heartwall* by Richard Jackson; *At the Site of Inside Out* by Anna Rabinowitz; *Cities and Towns: Poems* by Arthur Vogelsang; and *Fugitive Red* by Karen Donovan. "Poetry books are approximately $14 for paperback editions and $24 for cloth."

How to Submit: Submissions must not exceed 70 pages in typescript. Include paginated contents page; provide the title, publisher and year of publication for previously published volumes. A list of poems published or slated for publication in literary journals and/or anthologies must also accompany the ms. Such poems may be included in the ms and must be identified. "Mss by more than one author, entries of more than one ms simultaneously or within the same year, and translations are not eligible." Entry fee: $15 plus SASE for return of ms or notification. Entries must be postmarked not later than September 30. The award is announced in April/May and publication is scheduled for the following spring. The amount of the prize is $1,000 and is in lieu of royalties on the first print run. Poet also receives 12 copies in one edition or 6 copies each if published in both hardcover and paperbound editions. Fax, call or send SASE for guidelines and/or further information to the above address. Entries are to be mailed to Juniper Prize, University of Massachusetts, Amherst MA 01003.

◙ **UNIVERSITY OF WISCONSIN PRESS; BRITTINGHAM PRIZE IN POETRY; FELIX POLLAK PRIZE IN POETRY**, Dept. of English, 600 N. Park St., University of Wisconsin, Madison WI 53706. Website: www.wisc.edu/wisconsinpress/index.html. Brittingham Prize inaugurated in 1985. **Poetry Editor:** Ronald Wallace.

Book/Chapbook Needs: The University of Wisconsin Press publishes primarily scholarly works, but they offer the annual Brittingham Prize and the Felix Pollak Prize, both $1,000 plus publication. These prizes are the only way in which this press publishes poetry. Rules available for SASE or on website. Qualified readers will screen all mss. Winners will be selected by "a distinguished poet who will remain anonymous until the winners are announced in mid-February." Past judges include Rita Dove, Alicia Ostriker, Mark Doty, Ed Hirsch, Kelly Cherry, and Robert Bly. Winners include Tony Hoagland, Stephanie Strickland, Derick Burleson, Cathy Colman, Greg Rappleye, Roy Jacobstein, and Anna Meek.

How to Submit: For both prizes, submit between September 1 and September 30, unbound ms volume of 50-80 pages, with name, address, and telephone number on title page. No translations. Poems must be previously unpublished in book form. Poems published in journals, chapbooks, and anthologies may be included but must be acknowledged. There is a non-refundable $20 entry fee which must accompany the ms. (Checks to University of Wisconsin Press.) Mss will not be returned. Contest results available for SASE. "Previous winners of the prizes may submit subsequent book manuscripts between November 1 and November 30."

Advice: "Each submission is considered for both prizes (one entry fee only)."

◻ **THE UNKNOWN WRITER**, P.O. Box 698, Ramsey NJ 07446. E-mail: unknown_writer_200 0@yahoo.com. Website: http://munno.net/unknownwriter/. Established 1995. **Poetry Editor:** Amy Munno.

Magazine Needs: "We are a quarterly print magazine publishing poetry and fiction by up-and-coming writers who have small-press credits. We also delight in giving quality writers a start with their first publication. Send us strong, rich poetry with attention to imagery, emotion, and detail. We enjoy the traditional and structured forms like sonnet and haiku as much as experimental and modern free verse. Any subject matter is acceptable as long as the poem makes a direct connection with the reader. Keep the work fresh, intelligent, and mindful." Does not want forced rhyme, limericks, or vulgar work. No profane or sexually explicit material and no graphic violence. Accepts poetry from young adults (16 or older). *The Unknown Writer* is usually 40 pages, digest-sized, saddle-stapled, cardstock cover and b&w line art and photos (when possible). Publishes up to 7 poems/issue. Single copy: $4, subscription: $15 (4 issues).

How to Submit: Submit 3-5 poems at a time. Line length for poetry is 2 minimum, 100 maximum. Accepts simultaneous submissions; no previously published poems. "Please be respectful and tell us if a poem is accepted elsewhere." Accepts e-mail (as attachment but prefers in text box) and disk submissions. Cover letter is preferred. "Through postal mail, include a SASE, full address and e-mail address. Through e-mail, attach poems as a file or include them in the message body. With e-mail submissions, include full contact information and introduce yourself in a short note; don't just send poems. Tell us if the submission is simultaneous." Reads submissions all year. Submit seasonal poems 4 months in advance. Time between acceptance and publication is up to 9 months. Poem may be read by some or all of editorial board members." Guidelines available by e-mail, for SASE, or on website. Responds in 4 months. Pays 2 copies. Acquires first worldwide rights.

Advice: "We want to discover new, talented writers who need their first break or have a handful of previous acceptances, but new does not mean clichéd or careless. Write about your passion with rich language. Read your poems to others and get feedback. Support and participate in local poetry readings. Then revise and proofread. Writing is a practice and a craft. If we reject your first submission but tell you to submit again, we mean it. Keep trying."

★ ◯ UNLIKELY STORIES: A COLLECTION OF LITERARY ART. (770)422-9731. E-mail: unlikely@flash.net (prefers to be contacted through e-mail). Website: http://go.to/unlikely. Established 1998. **Editor:** Jonathan Penton.

Magazine Needs: "*Unlikely Stories* is a monthly online publication containing poetry, fiction, and nonfiction which falls under my own highly subjective definition of 'literary art.' I especially like work that has trouble finding publication due to adult, offensive, or weird content." Wants "any subject matter, including those normally considered taboo. I like informal poetry, but am open to formal poetry that demonstrates an understanding of good meter. No emotionless poetry, lies. 'I'll love you forever' is a lie; spare me." Has published poetry by Scott Holstad, Wendy Carlisle, Laurel Ann Bogen, and Elisha Porat. Receives about 500 poems/year, accepts about 30%.

How to Submit: Submit 3 or more poems at a time. Accepts previously published poems and simultaneous submissions. Accepts e-mail and disk submissions. Cover letter preferred. "*Unlikely Stories* is designed to promote acquaintanceship between readers and authors therefore, only multiple submissions will be accepted. I greatly prefer to see a bio; there is no maximum length." Time between acceptance and publication is 1 month. Often comments on rejected poems, if requested. Guidelines available for SASE, by e-mail, or on website. Responds in up to 6 weeks. Acquires one-time rights.

Also Offers: "If a contributor asks me a question, or for editorial or business advise, I'll answer. I have edited full manuscripts for a fee."

Advice: "Write from the heart, if you must, but write from that part of you which is unique."

✿ ♥ UNMUZZLED OX, 43B Clark Lane, Staten Island NY 10304 or Box 550, Kingston ON K7L 4W5 Canada. (212)226-7170. Established 1971. **Poetry Editor:** Michael Andre.

Magazine Needs & How to Submit: *Unmuzzled Ox* is a tabloid literary biannual. Each edition is built around a theme or specific project. "The chances of an unsolicited poem being accepted are slight since I always have specific ideas in mind." Has published poetry by Allen Ginsberg, Robert Creeley, and Denise Levertov. "Only unpublished work will be considered, but works may be in French as well as English." Subscription: $20.

Advice: "I suggest contributors read carefully an issue before sending in unsolicited manuscript."

◉ UNWOUND, P.O. Box 835, Laramie WY 82073. (307)755-0669. E-mail: unwoundmagazine@juno.com. Website: www.FyUoCuK.com/unwound. Established 1998. **Editor:** Lindsay Wilson.

Magazine Needs: *Unwound* appears annually. "Looking for work that is informal and relatable that has concerns for the image. Take a risk—if not, don't send. Looking for poetry that is honest and visual. Quality is a must. Growing more and more into the surreal image. I'm not interested in formal or Hallmark poetry. If it's strange just to be strange, or if I had to be there, don't send it." Recently published poetry by Leonard Cirino, Nathan Graziano, Daniel Crocker, Simon Perchik, Taylor Graham, and C.C. Russell. *Unwound* is 56 pages, digest-sized, copied, stapled, laser copy/silk screen cover, with b&w/silk screen art and ads. Receives about 2,500 poems/year, accepts about 2%. Publishes about 25 poems/issue. Press run is 200 for 50 subscribers of which 4 are libraries, 12 shelf sales; 50 distributed free to readings and friends, or left places. Single copy: $4; subscription: $7. Sample: $4. Make checks payable to Lindsay Wilson.

How to Submit: Submit 5 poems at a time. No previously published poems or simultaneous submissions. No fax, e-mail, or disk submissions. Cover letter is preferred. "No SASE, no chance." Does not read submissions in July. Time between acceptance and publication is 1-5 months. "I read all the poems and decide on my own. Seldomly I refer poems to a co-editor." Seldom comments on rejected poems. Guidelines available on website. Responds in up to 5 months. Sometimes sends prepublication galleys. Pays 1 contributor's copy. Acquires one-time rights. Reviews books and chapbooks of poetry and other magazines/journals in 1,000 words, single book format. Send materials for review consideration to Lindsay Wilson.

Advice: "At least check out the website and see if your work will fit in *Unwound*. If your gut has questions about what you're sending, listen to it and don't send. Please take a risk with your work—only send your best."

✪ ✇ ◯ **URBAN GRAFFITI**, P.O. Box 41164, Edmonton AB T6J 6M7 Canada. E-mail: cogwheels@worldgate.com. Established 1993. **Editor:** Mark McCawley.

Magazine Needs: Appearing 2 times/year, *Urban Graffiti* is "a litzine of transgressive, discursive, post-realist writing concerned with hard-edged urban living, alternative lifestyles, deviance—presented in their most raw and unpretentious form." Wants "free verse, prose poetry; urban themes and subject matter; transgressive, discursive, post-realist and confessional work. No metaphysical, religious or Hallmark verse." Has published poetry by Lyn Lifshin, Carolyn Zonailo, Beth Jankalo, Daniel Jones and Allan Demeule. *Urban Graffiti* is 28 pages, magazine-sized, photocopied and saddle-stapled with paper cover, includes art/graphics. Receives about 100 poems/year, accepts approximately 10-15%. Press run is 250. Single copy: $5; subscription: $10/3 issues. Make checks payable to Mark McCawley.

How to Submit: Submit 5-8 poems at a time. No previously published poems or simultaneous submissions. Does not accept e-mail submissions. Cover letter "with creative bio" required. Time between acceptance and publication is 6-12 months. Seldom comments on rejected poems. Send SASE for guidelines. Responds in up to 6 months. Pays 5 copies. Acquires first North American serial and first anthology rights. Reviews books and chapbooks of poetry and other magazines in 500-1,000 words, multi-book format. Send materials for for review consideration.

Advice: "If it's raunchy, realistic, angry, sarcastic, caustic, funny, frightening, brutally honest . . . then that's what we're looking for at *UG*."

⊕ ◑ ◎ **URTHONA MAGAZINE (Specialized: Buddhism)**, 9A Auckland Rd., Cambridge CB5 8DW United Kingdom. Phone: (01223) 309470. E-mail: urthona.mag@virgin.net. Website: www.urthona.com. Established 1992. **Contact:** Poetry Editor.

Magazine Needs: *Urthona*, published biannually, explores the arts and western culture from a Buddhist perspective. Wants "poetry rousing the imagination." Does not want "undigested autobiography, political, or New-Agey poems." Has published poetry by Peter Abbs, Robert Bly, and Peter Redgrove. *Urthona* is 60 pages, A4, offset-printed, saddle-stapled with 4-color glossy cover, b&w photos, art and ads inside. Receives about 300 poems/year, accepts about 40. Press run is 900 for 50 subscribers of which 4 are libraries, 500 shelf sales; 50 distributed free to Buddhist groups. Subscription: £8.50 (surface), £11.50 (airmail)/2 issues; £15 (surface), £22 (airmail)/4 issues. Sample (including guidelines): £3.50.

How to Submit: Submit 6 poems at a time. No previously published poems or simultaneous submissions. Accepts submissions by e-mail (as attachment). Cover letter preferred. Time between acceptance and publication is 8 months. Poems are circulated to an editorial board and read and selected by poetry editor. Other editors have right of veto. Responds in 6 months. Pays 1 contributor's copy.

Acquires one-time rights. Reviews books or chapbooks of poetry or other magazines in 600 words. Send materials for review consideration.

◎ UTAH STATE UNIVERSITY PRESS; MAY SWENSON POETRY AWARD, Logan UT 84322-7800. (435)797-1362. Fax: (435)797-0313. E-mail: mspooner@upress.usu.edu. Website: www .usu.edu/usupress. Established 1972. **Poetry Editor:** Michael Spooner. Publishes poetry only through the May Swenson Poetry Award competition annually. Has published *Dear Elizabeth* and *May Out West* by May Swenson; *Plato's Breath* by Randall Freisinger; *The Hammered Dulcimer* by Lisa Williams; *The Owl Question* by Faith Shearin; *Borgo of the Holy Ghost* by Stephen McLeod. See website for details.

✿ $◎ VALLUM MAGAZINE, P.O. Box 48003, 5678 du Parc, Montreal QC H2V 4S8 Canada. E-mail: vallummag@sympatico.ca. Website: www.vallummag.com. Established 2000. **Editors:** Joshua Auerbach, Helen Zisimatos.
Magazine Needs: *Vallum Magazine* appears biannually. "We are looking for poetry that's fresh and edgy, something that reflects contemporary experience and is also well-crafted. Open to most styles. We publish new and established poets." Recently published poetry by D.G. Jones, Erin Mouré, Rhoda Jenzen, B.Z. Niditch, and Eamon Grennan. *Vallum Magazine* is 80 pages, $7 \times 8\frac{1}{2}$, digitally-printed, perfect-bound, color images on coated stock cover, with art/graphics. Publishes about 40 poems/ issue. Press run is 1,750. Single copy: $8 ($1.50 p&h); subscription: $16.50 ($3 p&h). Make checks payable to *Vallum Magazine*.
How to Submit: Submit 5-8 poems at a time. No previously published poems or simultaneous submissions. No fax or e-mail submissions. "Accepted work must be sent to us on IBM diskette." Cover letter is preferred. Include SASE. Time between acceptance and publication is up to 1 year. Sometimes comments on rejected poems. Occasionally publishes theme issues. Guidelines and up-coming themes available on website. Responds in 3 months. Pays $10 honorarium and 1 contributor's copy. Acquires first North American serial rights. Reviews books and chapbooks of poetry in 250-500 words. Send materials for review consideration to *Vallum Magazine*.
Advice: "Hone your craft, read widely, be original."

◎ VALPARAISO POETRY REVIEW, Dept of English, Valparaiso University, Valparaiso IN 46383-6493. (219)464-5278. Fax: (219)464-5511. E-mail: vpr@valpo.edu. Website: www.valpo.edu/ english/vpr/. Established 1999. **Editor:** Edward Byrne.
Magazine Needs: *Valparaiso Poetry Review: Contemporary Poetry and Poetics* is "a biannual online poetry journal accepting submissions of unpublished or previously published poetry, book reviews, author interviews, and essays on poetry or poetics that have not yet appeared online and for which the rights belong to the author. Query for anything else." Wants poetry of any length or style, free verse or traditional forms. Recently published poetry by Charles Wright, Jonathan Holden, Reginald Gibbons, Janet McCann, Laurence Lieberman, Beth Simon, and Margot Schilpp. *Valparaiso Poetry Review* is published online only. Receives about 500 poems/year, accepts about 7%. Publishes about 17 poems/issue.
How to Submit: Submit 3-5 poems at a time. Accepts previously published poems ("original publication must be identified to ensure proper credit") and simultaneous submissions. Accepts e-mail submissions (but prefers postal mail); no fax or disk submissions. Cover letter is preferred. Include SASE. For e-mail submissions, include text in body of message rather than as an attachment. Submit no more than 5 poems at a time. Reads submissions year round. Time between acceptance and publication is 6-12 months. Seldom comments on rejected poems. Guidelines available on website. Responds in up to 6 weeks. Acquires one-time rights. "All rights remain with author." Reviews books of poetry in single book and multi-book format. Send materials for review consideration to Edward Byrne, editor.

◎ VEGETARIAN JOURNAL; THE VEGETARIAN RESOURCE GROUP (Specialized: children/teens, vegetarianism), P.O. Box 1463, Baltimore MD 21203. Website: www.vrg.org. Established 1982.
Magazine Needs: The Vegetarian Resource Group is a publisher of nonfiction. *Vegetarian Journal*

is a quarterly, 36 pages, magazine-sized, saddle-stapled and professionally printed with glossy card cover. Press run is 20,000. Sample: $3.

How to Submit: "Please no submissions of poetry from adults; 18 and under only."

Also Offers: The Vegetarian Resource Group offers an annual contest for ages 18 and under, $50 savings bond in 3 age categories for the best contribution on any aspect of vegetarianism. "Most entries are essay, but we would accept poetry with enthusiasm." Postmark deadline: May 1. Details available for SASE.

★ ✿ ♡ ◎ VEHICULE PRESS; SIGNAL EDITIONS (Specialized: regional), P.O. Box 125 Station Place du Parc, Montreal QC H2X 4A3 Canada. (514)844-6073. Fax: (514)844-7543. E-mail: vp@vehiculepress.com. Website: www.vehiculepress.com. **Poetry Editor:** Carmine Starnino. **Publisher:** Simon Dardick.

Book/Chapbook Needs: Vehicle Press is a "literary press with a poetry series, Signal Editions, publishing the work of Canadian poets only." Publishes flat-spined paperbacks and hardbacks. Has published *White Stone: The Alice Poems* by Stephanie Bolster (winner of the 1998 Governor-General's Award for Poetry); *Araby* by Eric Ormsby; and *Fielder's Choice* by Elise Partridge. Publishes Canadian poetry which is "first-rate, original, content-conscious."

How to Submit: Query before submitting.

★ ⊕ ◐ VERANDAH, c/o Faculty of Arts, Deakin University, 221 Burwood Hwy., Burwood, Victoria, Australia 3125. Phone: 61.3.9251.7134. Fax: 61.3.9244.6755. E-mail: verandah@deakin.edu .au. Website: www.deakin.edu.au/~ctgeorge/verandah. Established 1986. **Contact:** Verandah Poetry Editor.

Magazine Needs: *Verandah* appears annually in October and is "a high-quality literary journal edited by professional writing students. It aims to give voice to new and innovative writers and artists." Has published poetry by Christos Tsiolka, Dorothy Porter, Seamus Heaney, Les Murray, Ed Burger, and Joh Muk Muk Burke. *Verandah* is 120 pages, flat-spined with full-color glossy card cover, professionally printed on glossy stock. Sample: A$17.50.

How to Submit: Annual deadline: May 31. Accepts submissions by fax, by postal mail, and on disk. Charges A$5 reading fee; Deakin University students exempted. Pays 1 contributor's copy. Acquires first Australian publishing rights.

◐ VERSE, Dept. of English, University of Georgia, Athens GA 30602. Website: www.versemag.o rg. Established 1984. **Editors:** Brian Henry and Andrew Zawacki.

● Poetry published in *Verse* also appeared in *The Best American Poetry* and *Pushcart Prize* anthology.

Magazine Needs: *Verse* appears 3 times/year and is "an international poetry journal which also publishes interviews with poets, essays on poetry, and book reviews." Wants "no specific kind; we look for high-quality, innovative poetry. Our focus is not only on American poetry, but on all poetry written in English, as well as translations." Has published poetry by Heather McHugh, John Ashbery, James Tate, Mark Strand, Matthew Rohrer, and Eleni Sikelianos. *Verse* is 128-416 pages, digest-sized, professionally printed and perfect-bound with card cover. Receives about 5,000 poems/year, accepts 1%. Press run is 1,000 for 600 subscribers of which 200 are libraries, 200 shelf sales. Subscription: $18 for individuals, $36 for institutions. Current issue $9. Sample: $6.

How to Submit: Submit up to 3 poems at a time. Accepts simultaneous submissions; no previously published poems. Cover letter required. Time between acceptance and publication is up to 18 months. Guidelines available on website. Responds in 6 months. Often comments on rejected poems. "The magazine often publishes special features—recent features include younger American poets, Mexican poetry, Scottish poetry, Latino poets, prose poetry, women Irish poets, and Australian poetry—but does not publish 'theme' issues." Always sends prepublication galleys. Pays 2 contributor's copies plus a one-year subscription. Send materials for review consideration.

◐ VIA DOLOROSA PRESS; ERASED, SIGH, SIGH. (Specialized: "dark" poetry and death), 701 E. Schaaf Rd., Cleveland OH 44131-1227. Phone/fax: (216)459-0896. E-mail: viadoloro sapress@aol.com. Website: www.angelfire.com/oh2/dolorosa. Established 1994. **Editor:** Ms. Hyacinthe L. Raven.

Magazine Needs: *Erased, Sigh, Sigh* appears biannually in January and July. Literary journal "showcasing free verse poetry/fiction with a dark tinge. Our theme is death/suicide." Prefers "free verse poetry that is very introspective and dark. We do not publish light-hearted works. No traditional or concrete poetry. Vampire poems will be thrown away." Recently published poetry by John Sweet, Karen Porter, Scott Urban, and Lara Haynes. *Erased, Sigh, Sigh* is about 40 pages, digest-sized, Xerox-printed, saddle-stapled/hand-bound, parchment paper cover and pages, with pen & ink drawings, print-ready ads accepted. Receives 200 poems/year, accepts about 25%. Publishes about 30 poems/issue. Press run is 500-1,000 of which 75% are shelf sales; 25% are distributed free to "other journals for review and also to charity organizations." Single copy: $4 and p&h, subscription rates available on request. Sample copy: $4 postage paid. Make checks and money orders payable to Via Dolorosa Press.

How to Submit: Submit any number of poems at a time. Line length for poetry is open. Accepts previously published poems and simultaneous submissions. No fax, e-mail, or disk submissions. Cover letter is preferred. "SASE required for response; we do not respond by e-mail." Subscription rates available on request. Reads submissions any time. Submit seasonal poems 6 months in advance. Time between acceptance and publication is up to 1 year. "Poems are chosen by the editor. Writers will receive an acceptance/rejection letter usually within a month of receipt." Often comments on rejected poems. Publishes theme issues on "death, poets, and suicide. We publish dark poetry on these themes in every issue." Guidelines are available for 6×9 SASE with 2 first-class stamps. "Send for submission guidelines! We are strict about our theme and style. We also recommend reading a couple issue prior to considering us." Responds in 1 month. Pays 1 contributor's copy. Acquires one-time rights.

Book/Chapbook Needs & How to Submit: Via Dolorosa Press publishes "poetry, fiction, and nonfiction with an existential/humanist feel. Darker works preferred." Has published *Seasons of Rust* by John Sweet, *Ghostwhispers* by Karen Porter, and *Sestina* by Lara Haynes. Publishes 2-10 chapbooks/year. Chapbooks are usually 10-50 pages, photocopied or offset-printed, saddle-stapled or hand-bound, card stock, parchment, or other cover, with pen & ink drawings. "We ask that poets request our submission guidelines first. Then, if they think their work is fitting, we prefer to read the entire manuscript to make our decision." Responds to queries in 1 month; to mss in 2 months. Pays royalties of 25% plus 10% of press run. "See submission guidelines—our payment terms are listed in there." Send for free catalog.

Advice: "If you are repeatedly rejected because editors label your work as 'too depressing,' try us before you give up! We want work that makes us cry and that makes us think."

★ ⊕ ◑ **VIGIL; VIGIL PUBLICATIONS,** 12 Priory Mead, Bruton, Somerset BA10 ODZ England. Established 1979. **Poetry Editor:** John Howard Greaves.

Magazine Needs: *Vigil* appears 2 times/year. Wants "poetry with a high level of emotional force or intensity of observation. Poems should normally be no longer than 40 lines. Color, imagery and appeal to the senses should be important features. No whining self-indulgent, neurotic soul-baring poetry. Form may be traditional or experimental." Has published poetry by Michael Newman, Claudette Bass, David Flynn, Sheila Murphy, and Karen Rosenberg. *Vigil* is 40 pages, digest-sized, saddle-stapled, professionally printed with colored matte card cover. Receives about 400 poems/year, accepts about 60. Press run is 250 for 85 subscribers of which 6 are libraries. Subscription: £8. Sample: £3.

How to Submit: Submit up to 6 poems at a time in typed form. No previously published poems. Guidelines available for SASE (or SAE and IRC). Sometimes sends prepublication galleys. Pays 1 contributor's copy. Sometimes comments on rejected poems.

Book/Chapbook Needs & How to Submit: Query regarding book publication by Vigil Publications. Offers "appraisal" for £10 for a sample of a maximum of 6 poems.

$ ◐ **THE VIRGINIA QUARTERLY REVIEW; EMILY CLARK BALCH PRIZE,** 1 West Range, P.O. Box 400223, Charlottesville VA 22904-4223. (434)924-3124. Fax: (434)924-1397. Website: http://virginia.edu\vqr. Established 1925.

Magazine Needs: *The Virginia Quarterly Review* uses about 15 pages of poetry in each issue, no length or subject restrictions. Issues have largely included lyric and narrative free verse, most of which features a strong message or powerful voice. *The Virginia Quarterly Review* is 220 pages, digest-sized, flat-spined. Press run is 4,000.

How to Submit: Submit up to 5 poems and include SASE. "You will *not* be notified otherwise." No simultaneous submissions. Responds in 3 months or longer "due to the large number of poems we receive." Guidelines and upcoming themes available for SASE, by e-mail, and on website; do not request by fax. Pays $1/line.

Also Offers: Also sponsors the Emily Clark Balch Prize, an annual prize of $500 given to the best poem published in the review during the year.

◐ ◎ **VOCE PIENA (specialized: experimental); ONE THOUSAND BUDDHAS (specialized: Buddhist poetry)**, 1011½ W. Micheltorena, Santa Barbara CA 93101. (805)962-7068. E-mail: dslaght@aol.com. Established 2000. **Contact:** Deborah Slaght, editor.

Magazine Needs: *Voce Piena* appears annually in October. Publishes experimental poetry. *Voce Piena* is magazine-sized, desktop-published, white glossy 90 lb. paper cover, with abstract art. Receives varied number of poems/year. Publishes about 15-20 poems/issue. Single copy: $10; subscription: $10. Make checks payable to *Voce Piena*.

How to Submit: Submit 3-5 poems at a time. Length for poetry is 4 lines minimum, 3 pages maximum. Accepts previously published poems; no simultaneous submissions. Cover letter is required. "If there are graphics in poem, include an explanation of how the graphics should be reproduced." Reads submissions June-August. Time between acceptance and publication is up to 4 months. Never comments on rejected poems. Responds in 1 week. Pays 1 contributor's copy. Acquires first North American serial rights.

Magazine Needs: *One Thousand Buddhas* appears annually in December and publishes Buddhist poetry. *One Thousand Buddhas* is desk-top published and features Buddhist art. Receives about 15-20 poems/year. Press run varies. Single copy: $10. Make checks payable to Deborah Slaght.

How to Submit: Submit 3-5 poems at a time. Length per poem is 1 page minimum and 2 pages maximum. Accepts previously published poems and simultaneous submissions. Accepts submissions on disk. Reads submissions August through December. Time between acceptance and publication is up to 4 months. Regularly publishes theme issues. Upcoming themes available for SASE. Responds in 3 months. Pays 1 copy. Acquires one-time rights.

Advice: "Do not send any submissions using profanity. All experimental poetry, including experimental lyricism are read and considered thoughtfully."

⊕ ◐ ◎ **VOICES ISRAEL (Specialized: anthology); REUBEN ROSE POETRY COMPETITION; MONTHLY POET'S VOICE (Specialized: members)**, P.O. Box 661, Metar Israel 85025. Phone: 972-7-6519118. Fax: 972-7-6519119. E-mail: aschatz@bgumail.bgu.ac.il. Website: http://members.tripod.com/~VoicesIsrael. Established 1972. **Editor-in-Chief:** Amiel Schotz; with an editorial board of 7.

Magazine Needs: "*Voices Israel* is an annual anthology of poetry in English coming from all over the world. You have to buy a copy to see your work in print. Submit all kinds of poetry (up to 4 poems), each no longer than 40 lines, in seven copies." Has published poetry by Yehuda Amichai, Hsi Muren, Alexander Volovick, Péter Kántor, and Ada Aharoni. *Voices Israel* is approximately 121 pages, digest-sized, offset from laser output on ordinary paper, flat-spined with varying cover. Press run is 350. Subscription: $15. Sample back copy: $10. Contributor's copy: $15 airmail. "All money matters—including $35 annual membership—must be handled by the treasurer, Mel Millman, 15 Shachar St., Jerusalem, Israel 96263."

How to Submit: Accepts previously published poems, "but please include details and assurance that copyright problems do not exist." No simultaneous submissions. Accepts submissions on disk, as e-mail attachment, by fax, and by postal mail. Cover letter with brief biographical details required with submissions. Deadline: end of November; responds as per receipt.

Also Offers: Sponsors the annual Reuben Rose Poetry Competition. Prizes: $300, $150, $100, and $50 as well as honorable mentions. Published and distributed together with the *Voices Israel* anthology

MARKETS LISTED in the 2003 edition of *Poet's Market* that do not appear this year are identified in the General Index with a code explaining their absence from the listings.

as separate booklet. Send poems of up to 40 lines each, plus $5/poem to P.O. Box 236, Kiriat Ata, Israel. Poet's name and address should be on a separate sheet with titles of poems. *The Monthly Poet's Voice*, a broadside edited by Ezra Ben-Meir, is sent only to members of the Voices Group of Poets in English.

Advice: "To achieve a universality, your poem must be extremely personal. Images should be fresh and immediate. Moral generalizations about, say, the horrors of war, tend to be banal. The reader does not need the poet to tell him or her that the death of a child is tragic. So avoid preachiness. Rhyme is a wonderful servant, but a terrible master. Finally, don't be lazy and let one inappropriate or weak phrase or image spoil what otherwise is a good poem."

★ ⊕ $ ⬛ ◎ VOICEWORKS MAGAZINE (Specialized: youth culture), 42 Courtney St., North Melbourne, VIC 3051 Australia. Phone: (03)9326 8367. Fax: (03)9326 8076. E-mail: vworks@vicnet.net.au. Website: www.expressmedia.org.au. Established 1985. **Editor:** Kelly Chander.

Magazine Needs: *Voiceworks* appears 4 times/year to publish "young," "new," "emerging" writers under 25 years of age. "We have no specifications for poetry. Only the poets must be under 25 years of age. No racist, stolen, or libelous work." *Voiceworks* is 80 pages, magazine-sized, perfect-bound, includes art/graphics and ads. Receives about 400 poems/year, accepts 14%. Publish 14 poems/issue. Press run is 1,000. Single copy: $7; subscription: $25.50/year. Sample: $4. Make checks payable to Express Media/*Voiceworks Magazine*.

How to Submit: Submit no more than 8 poems at a time. Accept simultaneous submissions; no previously published poems. Accepts e-mail and disk submissions. Cover letter required. "We need a short bio and SASE (or SAE and IRC). If giving a disk or submitting by e-mail save the file as a Rich Text format." Reads submissions January 4 through 11, April 4 through 11, July 4 through 11, and October 4 through 11 only. Time between acceptance and publication is 2 months. Poems are circulated to an editorial board. "We all read the submissions, make comments and decide what to publish." Often comments on rejected poems. Publishes theme issues. Guidelines and upcoming themes are available for SASE (or SAE with IRCs), by fax, or by e-mail. Responds in 2 months. Pays $50. Poets retain rights. Staff reviews books and chapbooks of poetry and other magazines. Send materials for review consideration.

◐ VOICINGS FROM THE HIGH COUNTRY; HIGH COUNTRY WORD CRAFTERS, 4920 South Oak St., Casper WY 82601. Established 2000. **Editor:** Ella J. Cvancara.

Magazine Needs: *Voicings from the High Country* appears annually in the spring. Accepts "poetry with substance, not just pretty words; understandable, rather than obscure; poetry that goes beyond the self. The editor is biased toward free verse that is worldly rather than introspective, tells a story, and uses many/most/all of the five senses. Also accepts haiku for a haiku page. No rhyming, pornography, violent language, 'Hallmark' verse, political poems, or overtly religious poetry. No poetry that's unsure of why it was written, is demeaning to the human spirit, or untitled." Recently published poetry by Jean Goedicke, Mervin Mecklenberg, and Christine Valentine. *Voicings from the High Country* is 35-40 pages, digest-sized, computer-generated, stapled, 110 lb. cardstock cover, with in-house artistic photography. Receives about 100 poems/year, accepts about 25%. Publishes about 25 poems/issue. Press run is 75 of which 45 are shelf sales; 30 distributed free to contributors. Single copy: $5. Make checks payable to Ella J. Cvancara.

How to Submit: Submit 3 poems at a time. Accepts previously published poems; no simultaneous submissions. No fax, e-mail, or disk submissions. Cover letter is required with a 3-5 line biography. "Submit each poem on a separate page with name/address in upper right corner; typed or computer-generated; 35 lines or less; include a SASE for a response." Reads submissions July 1 through February 1 *only*. Submit seasonal poems 3 months in advance. Time between acceptance and publication is 3 months. "Poems are circulated to a 3-member editorial board with the names of the poets removed. They are ranked according to a ranking system." Seldom comments on rejected poems. Guidelines available for SASE. Responds in 6 months. Pays 1 contributor's copy. Acquires one-time rights.

Advice: "Beginners often write about themselves. Reach beyond yourself, avoid clichés, search for fresh language. Use metaphor and simile. Strike a spark with words. Nothing is off limits to the poet."

○ **VOODOO SOULS QUARTERLY**, P.O. Box 4117, Lawrence KS 66046. E-mail: Meredith.Say ers@jocoks.com. Established 2000. **Editor:** Meredith Sayers.

Magazine Needs: *Voodoo Souls Quarterly* is "a place where quality writing—poetry, essays, and short fiction—can find a home, regardless of the fame of its author. I've no real inclination toward a particular school of poetry. To be accepted, it will need to be precise, meaningful, and possess a sense of its own power. Innovation and clarity are appreciated." Does not want "inspirational, gratuitously violent, watered-down, imitations, or just plain poorly-written." Accepts poetry written by children. Recently published poetry by Simon Perchik, Jill Atherton, Alan Britt, Anne Gatschet, Stephen Meats, and Paul B. Roth. *Voodoo Souls Quarterly* is 20-40 pages, digest-sized, high-quality photocopied, saddle-stapled, cardstock cover with b&w art/graphics. Receives about 100 poems/year, accepts about 50%. Publishes about 5-10 poems/issue. Press run is 50 for 10 subscribers of which 1 is a library, 30 shelf sales; 10 are distributed free to contributors. Single copy: $4; subscription: $12. Sample: $4. Make checks payable to Meredith Sayers.

How to Submit: Submit 3-5 poems at a time. No previously published poems or simultaneous submissions. No fax, e-mail, or disk submissions. Cover letter is preferred. "Include SASE and bio. Please tell a bit about yourself—not just your publications!" Reads submissions year round. Submit seasonal poems 6 months in advance. Time between acceptance and publication is 3-6 months. Often comments on rejected poems. Guidelines are available in magazine and for SASE. Responds in 3 months. Always sends prepublication galleys. Pays 1 contributor's copy. "Any submission without SASE will not be read or returned. Submission is considered permission to publish in *Voodoo Souls Quarterly*. Rights revert to authors upon publication." Reviews books and chapbooks of poetry in single book format. Send materials for review consideration to Meredith Sayers.

Advice: "Put your ego on the line and send what you love. Don't bother checking popular literary mags to see if you're following the current trend. Set your own!"

○ ◎ **VORTEX OF THE MACABRE; DARK GOTHIC (Specialized: horror, vampires, magical/occult themes)**, 1616 E. Barringer St., Philadelphia PA 19150-3304. E-mail: serae37378 @yahoo.com. Established 1996. **Editor/Publisher:** Ms. Cinsearae S.

Magazine Needs: Publishes two annuals, *Dark Gothic* and *Vortex of the Macabre*. "*Dark Gothic* is a vampire-themed zine of dark, erotic, and romantic poetry, art, and short stories. *Vortex of the Macabre* publishes weird, insane, gross poetry and art, reviews, and short-short stories. If it's twilight-zoneish, tales from the crypt-ish, insane, kooky, or just plain weird, I want it! Freestyle, prose, it doesn't matter since poetry is an art. No line limits here. No fuzzy-bunny stuff!" Has published poetry by Steven Bohn, Andrew Okoski, Mary Louise Westbrook, John Picinich, and Douglas M. Stokes. The publications are 10-20 pages (*Dark Gothic*), 20-25 pages (*Vortex of the Macabre*), magazine-sized, photocopied and side-stapled with b&w paper cover, includes "art of an eerie or morbid tone," also ads. Receives about 80-90 poems/year, accepts approximately 95%. Press run is 100. Subscription: $14 for both, otherwise $9 for *Vortex of the Macabre*, $6 for *Dark Gothic*. Sample: $4.50 for *Vortex of the Macabre*, $3 for *Dark Gothic*. Make checks payable to Ms. Cinsearae S. "Purchase of copy is strongly encouraged. I sometimes get things too grossly obscene and almost criminal sounding! Also, contributors must send SASE with any works."

How to Submit: Submit 5 poems at a time. Accepts previously published poems and simultaneous submissions. Accepts submissions by e-mail (as attachment or in text box), on disk, or by postal mail. Cover letter preferred. "Poems should be single-spaced, as well as any short stories submitted to *Dark Gothic*. Send 'friendly' cover letter about you; I don't care all that much about your 'credentials.' " Time between acceptance and publication is 5 months. Often comments on rejected poems. Publishes theme issues occasionally. Guidelines and upcoming themes available for SASE and by e-mail. Responds in 3 months. Pays 1 copy. Acquires one-time rights. Reviews books and chapbooks of poetry and other magazines in up to 174 words. Poets may send material for review consideration to the editor, % *Vortex of the Macabre* only.

Advice: "If writing is your passion and one true joy, then it is all you need in a passionless world. The right people will hear your voice and read your words, and these people will be your kindred spirits."

◎ VQONLINE (Specialized: volcanoes and volcanology), 8009 18th Lane SE, Lacey WA 98503. (360)455-4607. E-mail: jmtanaka@webtv.net. Website: http://community.webtv.net/JMTan aka/VQ. Established 1992. **Editor:** Janet M. Cullen Tanaka.

Magazine Needs: *VQOnline* is an "interest" publication for professional and amateur volcanologists and volcano buffs. Wants "any kind of poetry as long as it is about volcanoes and/or the people who work on them." Does not want "over-emotive, flowery stuff or anything not directly pertaining to volcanoes." Accepts poetry written by children. Has published poetry by Dane Picard and C. Martinez. Free on the Internet, no subscription costs.

How to Submit: Submit any number of poems. Accepts previously published poems with permission of the original copyright holder and simultaneous submissions. Accepts disk (ASCII compatible) and e-mail submissions in body of message, no attachments. Time between acceptance and publication is 6 months. Always comments on rejected poems. "I try not to outright reject, preferring to ask for a rewrite." Guidelines available for SASE, by e-mail, or on website. Responds in 1 month. Pays up to 5 copies. "Contributors may copyright in the usual fashion. But there is as yet no mechanism on the Internet to keep users honest. We also need written permission to publish on the Internet." Reviews books or chapbooks of poetry or other magazines by guest reviewers. Send materials for review consideration if subject is volcanoes.

Advice: "I want to concentrate on the positive aspects of volcanoes—gifts from God, 'partners' in creation, resources, beauty, awe, etc."

✡ $◎ WAKE FOREST UNIVERSITY PRESS (Specialized: bilingual/foreign language, ethnic/nationality), P.O. Box 7333, Winston-Salem NC 27109. (336)758-5448. Fax: (336)758-5636. E-mail: wfupress@wfu.edu. Website: www.wfu.edu/wfupress. Established 1976. **Director/ Poetry Editor:** Jefferson Holdridge. **Advisory Editor:** Dillon Johnston.

Book/Chapbook Needs: "We publish only poetry from Ireland. I am able to consider only poetry written by native Irish poets. I must return, unread, poetry from American poets." Has published *Collected Poems* by John Montague; *Ghost Orchid* by Michael Longley; *Selected Poems* by Medbh McGuckian; and *The Wake Forest Book of Irish Women's Poetry.*

How to Submit: Query with 4-5 samples and cover letter. No simultaneous submissions. Responds to queries in 1-2 weeks, to submissions (if invited) in 2-3 months. Sometimes sends prepublication galleys. Publishes on 10% royalty contract with $500 advance, 6-8 author's copies. Buys North American or US rights.

Advice: "Because our press is so circumscribed, we get few direct submissions from Ireland. Our main problem, however, is receiving submissions from American poets, whom we do not publish because of our very limited focus here. I would advise American poets to read listings carefully so they do not misdirect to presses such as ours, work that they, and I, value."

◎ WAKE UP HEAVY (WUH); WAKE UP HEAVY PRESS, P.O. Box 4668, Fresno CA 93744-4668. E-mail: wuheavy@yahoo.com. Established 1998. **Editor/Publisher:** Mark Begley.

Magazine Needs: *Wake Up Heavy* is not currently publishing magazine issues, nor accepting submissions for the magazine. The first 4 issues of *Wake Up Heavy* included poetry/prose by Laura Chester, Wanda Coleman, Fielding Dawson, Edward Field, Michael Lally, and Diane Wakoski. "These out-of-print issues are available through the Web at www.abebooks.com. Many of the poems published have been reprinted in major collections by these authors, most notably three poems by Wanda Coleman that originally appeared in the premier issue of the magazine, and were later reprinted in her National Book Award nominated book *Mercurochrome* (Black Sparrow Press, 2001). Any other questions about future magazine publications should be sent to the above e-mail address."

How to Submit: *Wake Up Heavy* **is not currently accepting submissions of any kind, and the magazine has been halted indefinitely.**

Book/Chapbook Needs & How to Submit: "Chapbooks and broadsides by single authors have become our main focus. Wake Up Heavy Press has published chapbooks/pamphlets of single poems (Michael Lally's long, prose poem *¿Que Pasa Baby?*; Diane Wakoski's *Trying to Convince Robert and Inviting John & Barbara*), groups of poems, stories (Wanda Coleman's *Crabs for Breakfast*; Fielding Dawson's *The Dirty Blue Car* and *Backtalk*), memoirs (Wanda Coleman's Pushcart Prize-nominated *Love-ins with Nietzsche*), and chapters from novels (Laura Chester's *Kingdom Come*)."

Wake Up Heavy Press publishes 2-3 chapbooks/pamphlets per year. Chapbooks/pamphlets are usually copied/offset-printed, saddle-stapled, heavy coverstock, some contain drawings or photos, and most include a signed/numbered edition. "Again, these titles are available via the Web at www.abebooks.com. Also, you can e-mail about upcoming publications/the availability of past ones. Chapbooks, pamphlets, and broadsides are *strictly from solicitations. Please do not send mss for these publications.*" Wake Up Heavy Press pays authors in copies, 50% of the press run, which is usually between 130-200 copies. Inquire about samples at the above e-mail address.

◯ **WARTHOG PRESS**, 29 South Valley Rd., West Orange NJ 07052. (973)731-9269. Established 1979. **Poetry Editor:** Patricia Fillingham.
Book/Chapbook Needs: Warthog Press publishes paperback books of poetry "that are understandable, poetic." Has published *From the Other Side of Death* by Joe Lackey; *Wishing for the Worst* by Linda Portnay; *Enemies of Time* by Donald Lev; and *Hanging On* by Joe Benevento.
How to Submit: Query with 5 samples, cover letter, and SASE. "A lot of the submissions I get seem to be for a magazine. I don't publish anything but books." Accepts simultaneous submissions. Ms should be "readable." Comments on rejected poems, "if asked for. People really don't want criticism."
Advice: "The best way to sell poetry still seems to be from poet to listener."

⊕ ◯ ◎ **WASAFIRI (Specialized: ethnic/nationality)**, Dept. of English, Queen Mary, University of London, Mile End Rd., London E1 4NS United Kingdom. Phone/fax: +44 020 7882 3120. E-mail: wasafiri@qmw.ac.uk. Website: www.wasafiri.org. Established 1984. **Editor:** Susheila Nasta. **Managing Editor:** Richard Dyer.
Magazine Needs: *Wasafiri*, (published in March, July, and November) "promotes new writing and debate on African, Asian, Caribbean, and associated literatures." Wants "African, Asian, Caribbean, diaspora, post-colonial, innovative, high-quality poetry." Has published poetry by Vikram Seth, Fred D'Aguiar, Marlene Nourbese Philip, and Kamau Brathwaite. *Wasafiri* is 80 pages, A4, professionally-printed on coated stock, perfect-bound, with full color glossy cover, graphics, photos, and ads. Receives about 350 poems/year, accepts about 30%. Press run is 1,500 for 1,000 subscribers of which 450 are libraries, 300 shelf sales; 50 distributed free to arts council literature panel and education board. Single copy: £7; subscription: £21 individuals; £27 institutions/overseas; £42 UK institutions, £54 overseas institutions.
How to Submit: Submit 3 poems at a time. No simultaneous submissions. Cover letter required. Accepts disk submissions by postal mail and on disk (Word or WordPerfect). Time between acceptance and publication is 6-12 months. Poems are circulated to an editorial board. "Poems are considered by the editor and managing editor. Where guest editors are involved, poetry is considered by them also. Associate editors with expertise are asked to participate also." Often comments on rejected poems. Publishes theme issues. Guidelines and upcoming themes available for SAE and IRC, by e-mail, or on website. Themes for future issues include "Translation and Film" and "African Literature." Responds in up to 6 months. Sometimes sends prepublication galleys. Pays 1 copy. Acquires all rights. Returns rights with editor's permission. Reviews books or chapbooks of poetry or other magazines. Send materials for review consideration.

◑ **WASHINGTON SQUARE, A JOURNAL OF THE ARTS**, 19 University Place, Room 219, New York University Graduate Creative Writing Program, New York NY 10003. E-mail: washington.square.journal@nyu.edu. Website: www.nyu.edu/gsas/program/cwp/wsr.htm. Established 1994 as *Washington Square* (originally established in 1979 as *Ark/Angel*). **Editor:** Sarah Kain. **Contact:** Katherine Dimma.
Magazine Needs: Published in December and May, *Washington Square* is "a non-profit literary journal publishing fiction, poetry and essays by new and established writers. It's edited and produced by the students of the NYU Creative Writing Program." Wants "all poetry of serious literary intent." Has published poetry by Billy Collins, Rick Moody, A.E. Stalling, Dana Levin, Timothy Lin, and Arthur Sze. *Washington Square* is about 150 pages. Press run is 2,000. Subscription: $12. Sample: $6.
How to Submit: Submit up to 6 poems at a time; name and contact information should appear on every page. Accepts simultaneous submissions if noted. Accepts submissions by postal mail only.

Cover letter with short bio required. Reads submissions September through April only. Time between acceptance and publication is up to 6 months. Poems are circulated to an editorial board. "The poetry editors and editorial staff read all submissions, discuss and decide which poems to include in the journal." Sometimes comments on rejected poems. Guidelines available for SASE or by e-mail. Responds in up to 4 months. Pays 2 copies and a 1 year subscription. Acquires first North American serial rights. Sometimes reviews books and chapbooks of poetry and other magazines in 300 words. Send materials for review consideration.

Ø WATER MARK PRESS, 138 Duane St., New York NY 10013. Established 1978. **Editor:** Coco Gordon. Currently does not accept any unsolicited poetry.
  ● Note: Please do not confuse Water Mark Press with the imprint Watermark Press, used by other businesses.

$□ WATERBEARER PRESS; ABOVE WATER, P.O. Box 933, Buffalo NY 14201-0933. (716)937-7732. E-mail: tgardner@waterbearerpress.com. Website: www.waterbearerpress.com. Established 2000. **Editor-in-Chief:** Tam'e Gardner.
Magazine Needs: *Above Water* is a bimonthly newsletter containing comments from the editor, upcoming events, a Featured Artist section and articles. No limitations to form or content. Artists are "free to express as they see fit." Recently published poetry by Tam'e Gardner, Brian A. Menzies, and Raymond L. Waldron. *Above Water* is about 16 pages, magazine-sized, desktop-published, stapled, with photography. Publishes up to 10 poem/issue. Subscription: $5/12 months (6 editions). First copy (sample) is complimentary. Make checks payable to Waterbearer Press.
How to Submit: Accepts previously published poems and simultaneous submissions. No fax, e-mail, or disk submissions. Cover letter is preferred. Reads submissions upon receipt. Time between acceptance and publication is within 1 year. Editor reviews all poetry and decides "if it will be published and when and where (newsletter, website)." May publish theme issues. "We send a proof and then the artist receives a complimentary copy of the newsletter they are published in." Acquires one-time rights.
Book/Chapbook Needs & How to Submit: Waterbearer Press mainly publishes poetry and short stories by beginning artists in all genres. "We are also interested in artwork such as painting and photography." Publishes 2 titles/year; format depends on what artist wants. "We work with the artist to determine goals and try to best reach them." Query first, with a few sample poems and cover letter with brief bio and publication credits. Responds to queries and mss in up to 6 months. Royalties negotiated by contract.
Advice: "Waterbearer Press is specifically designed to assist authors of poetry and short stories, as well as support artists who paint, draw, or utilize photography or other means for expression. Our goal is to work *with* the artist to accomplish *their* goals."

□ ◎ WATERWAYS: POETRY IN THE MAINSTREAM (Specialized: themes); **TEN PENNY PLAYERS** (Specialized: children/teen/young adult); **BARD PRESS**, 393 St. Paul's Ave., Staten Island NY 10304-2127. (718)442-7429. E-mail: tenpennyplayers@SI.RR.com. Website: www.tenpennyplayers.org. Established 1977. **Poetry Editors:** Barbara Fisher and Richard Spiegel.
Magazine Needs: Ten Penny Players "publishes poetry by adult poets in a magazine [*Waterways*] that is published 11 times/year. We do theme issues and are trying to increase an audience for poetry and the printed and performed word. The project produces performance readings in public spaces and is in residence year round at the New York public library with workshops and readings. We publish the magazine *Waterways*, anthologies, and chapbooks. We are not fond of haiku or rhyming poetry; never use material of an explicit sexual nature. We are open to reading material from people we have never published, writing in traditional and experimental poetry forms. While we do 'themes,' sometimes an idea for a future magazine is inspired by a submission so we try to remain open to poets' inspirations. Poets should be guided however by the fact that we are children's and animal rights advocates and are a NYC press." Has published poetry by Ida Fasel, Albert Huffstickler, Joy Hewitt Mann, and Will Inman. *Waterways* is 40 pages, 4¼×7, photocopied from various type styles, saddle-stapled, using b&w drawings, matte card cover. Uses 60% of poems submitted. Press run is 150 for 58 subscribers of which 12 are libraries. Subscription: $25. Sample: $2.60.
How to Submit: Submit less than 10 poems for first submission. Accepts simultaneous submissions.

Accepts e-mail submissions (in text box). Guidelines for approaching themes are available for SASE. "Since we've taken the time to be very specific in our response, writers should take seriously our comments and not waste their emotional energy and our time sending material that isn't within our area of interest. Sending for our theme sheet and for a sample issue and then objectively thinking about the writer's own work is practical and wise. Manuscripts that arrive without a return envelope are not sent back." Editors sometimes comment on rejected poems. Responds in less than a month. Pays 1 copy. Acquires one-time publication rights.

Book/Chapbook Needs & How to Submit: Chapbooks published by Ten Penny Players are "by children and young adults only—*not by submission*; they come through our workshops in the library and schools. Adult poets are published through our Bard Press imprint, *by invitation only*. Books evolve from the relationship we develop with writers we publish in *Waterways* and whom we would like to give more exposure."

Advice: "We suggest that poets attend book fairs and check our website. It's a fast way to find out what we are publishing. Without meaning to sound 'precious' or unfriendly, the writer should understand that small press publishers doing limited editions and all production work inhouse are working from their personal artistic vision and know exactly what notes will harmonize, effectively counterpoint and meld. Many excellent poems are sent back to the writers by *Waterways* because they don't relate to what we are trying to create in a given month."

WAVELENGTH: POEMS IN PROSE AND VERSE, 1753 Fisher Ridge Rd., Horse Cave KY 42749-9706. Established 1999. **Editor/Publisher:** David P. Rogers.

Magazine Needs: *Wavelength: Poems in Prose and Verse* appears 3 times/year. "We want poems approximately 30 lines or less that use lively images, intriguing metaphor, and original language. Rhyme is almost always a liability. All subjects and styles considered as long as the poem is thought-provoking or uses language in an innovative way. Prose poems are fine." Does not want "rhymed, very religious—anything that sacrifices creativity for convention." Recently published poetry by Robert Cooperman, Lyn Lifshin, Francis Blessington, Ann Taylor, Albert Haley, and Virgil Suarez. *Wavelength* is 35 pages, digest-sized, laser-printed, perfect-bound with heavy cardstock cover and cover illustration. Receives about 450 poems/year, accepts 5-10%. Publishes about 30 poems/issue. Press run is 150 for 25 subscribers, 20-25 shelf sales; 100 distributed free to the public. Single copy: $6; subscription: $15. Sample: $6. Make checks payable to Dr. David P. Rogers.

How to Submit: Submit 1-10 poems at a time. Line length for poetry is 30 maximum. Accepts no previously published poems and simultaneous submissions, "but please do *not* withdraw the poem after we've accepted it." No e-mail or disk submissions. Cover letter is preferred. "SASE or no response. Brief bio preferred. Poet's name and address must appear on every page. Poets who want poems returned should include sufficient postage." Submit seasonal poems 3 months in advance. Time between acceptance and publication is up to 1 year. "Read and write every day. We like to publish new and young poets." Seldom comments on rejected poems. "Please do *not* write for guidelines. Just send a courteous submission following the guidelines in the *Poet's Market* entry." Responds in 4 months. Pays 1 copy. Acquires one-time rights. Reviews books and chapbooks of poetry in 100-150 words, single book format. Send materials for review consideration to David P. Rogers.

Advice: "Read and write every day. If a poem still seems good a year after you wrote it, send it out. Be original. Say something clever, and ask what will the *reader* get out of it?"

WAYNE LITERARY REVIEW, % Dept. of English, Wayne State University, Detroit MI 48202. Established 1960. **Editor:** Richard Brixton.

Magazine Needs: *Wayne Literary Review* appears biannually. "Our philosophy is to encourage a diversity of writing styles. Send your favorites. If you like them, others probably will, too." Does not want "lack of craft, gratuitous sex and violence." *Wayne Literary Review* is 75 pages, digest-sized. Receives about 1,000 poems/year, accepts about 5%. Publishes about 25 poems/issue. Press run is 500 which are distributed free to the public.

How to Submit: Submit 3 poems at a time. No previously published poems or simultaneous submissions. No fax, e-mail, or disk submissions. Cover letter is preferred. "Send SASE with proper postage." Reads submissions anytime. Submit seasonal poems 6 months in advance. Time between acceptance and publication is 6 months. Poems are circulated to an editorial board. Seldom comments on rejected poems. Guidelines are available for SASE. Responds in 3 months. Pays 2 contributor's copies. Acquires first North American serial rights.

$ ◖ W͞eBER STUDIES—VOICES AND VIEWPOINTS OF THE CONTEMPORARY WEST, 1214 University Circle, Weber State University, Ogden UT 84408-1214. (801)626-6473. E-mail: weberstudies@weber.edu. Website: http://weberstudies.weber.edu. Established 1983. **Editor:** Brad L. Roghaar.

● Poetry published here has appeared in *The Best American Poetry*.

Magazine Needs: *Weber Studies* appears 3 times/year and publishes fiction, poetry, criticism, personal essays, nonfiction, and interviews. It is an interdisciplinary journal interested in relevant works covering a wide range of topics. Wants "three or four poems; we publish multiple poems from a poet." Does not want "poems that are flippant, prurient, sing-song, or preachy." Has published poetry by William Kloefkorn, Gailmarie Pahmeier, Mark Strand, Janet Sylvester, David Lee, and Katharine Coles. *Weber Studies* is 140 pages, 7½×10, offset-printed on acid-free paper, perfect-bound, with color cover. Receives about 150-200 poems/year, accepts 30-40. Press run is 1,200 for 1,000 subscribers of which 90 are libraries. Subscription: $20, $20 institutions. Sample: $7-8.

How to Submit: Submit 3-4 poems, 2 copies of each (one without name). Accepts simultaneous submissions; no previously published poems. Cover letter preferred. Time between acceptance and publication is 15 months. Poems are selected by an anonymous (blind) evaluation. Seldom comments on rejected poems. Publishes theme issues. Upcoming themes and guidelines available for SASE, by e-mail, on website, or in publication. Responds in up to 6 months. Always sends prepublication galleys. Pays 2 copies and $20-25/page; depending on fluctuating grant monies. Acquires all rights. Copyright reverts to author after first printing.

Also Offers: Cash award given every three years for poems published in *Weber Studies*. Only poetry published in *Weber Studies* during 3-year interval considered.

Advice: "This journal is referred by established poets—beginners not encouraged."

$ ◖ ◎ WEIRD TALES (Specialized: fantasy and horror), 123 Crooked Lane, King of Prussia PA 19406-2570. (610)275-4463. E-mail: owlswick@netaxs.com. Established 1923. **Editor:** George Scithers.

Magazine Needs: *Weird Tales* appears quarterly. Publishes "fantasy and horror fiction with some poetry on those subjects." Wants poetry touching on fantasy or horror, mostly serious. Some humor accepted including limericks and double dactyls. Does not want poetry on mundane subjects. *Weird Tales* is 52 pages, magazine-sized, offset-printed, saddle-stapled, process color cover, with art/graphics and ads. Receives about 120 poems/year, accepts about 10%. Publishes about 3 poems/issue. Press run is 10,000. Single copy: $4.95; subscription: $16. Sample: $5. Make checks payable to Terminus Publishing Co.

How to Submit: Submit up to 5 poems at a time. No previously published poems or simultaneous submissions. No fax, e-mail, or disk submissions. "Double line-space poems. Include author address on every poem." Time between acceptance and publication is very irregular. Poems are circulated to an editorial board. Very seldom comments on rejected poems. Very occasionally publishes theme issues. List of upcoming themes not available. Guidelines available for SASE or by e-mail. Responds in 2 months. Always sends prepublication galleys. Pays $1 or less/line and 2 contributor's copies. Acquires first North American serial rights.

Advice: "Follow standard manuscript format."

◖ ◎ WELLSPRING: A JOURNAL OF CHRISTIAN POETRY (Specialized: Christian, spirituality/inspirational). E-mail: wellspringjournal@hotmail.com. Website: www.angelfire.com/wa2/wellspring. Established 1999. **Editor:** Deborah Beachboard.

Magazine Needs: "*Wellspring* is an online journal featuring quality Christian poetry by various authors. Poems are published on an ongoing basis. I am looking for poetry that touches every aspect of Christian living—from the worship of God to the activities of daily life. No pornography, no senseless violence, nothing New Age." Has published poetry by Peter Vetrano, Frank Atanasia, Jane Hutto, Elizabeth Pearson, and Monique Nicole Fox. Accepts about 80% of poems received per year.

How to Submit: Submit 5 poems at a time. Accepts previously published poems and simultaneous

submissions. Accepts e-mail submissions included in body of message. "Currently I am accepting submissions by e-mail only. When submitting, indicate it is for *Wellspring*. Include address and name with each poem submitted." Cover letter preferred. Accepts submissions September through May only. No submissions accepted June, July, or August. Time between acceptance and publication is 2 months. Seldom comments on rejected poems. Guidelines available on website. Responds in 1 month. Sometimes sends prepublication galleys. Acquires one-time rights.
Also Offers: *Dayspring*, bimonthly e-zine of contemporary Christian poetry and *The Beehive*, a place for poetry by women named Deborah, in any variation of the name.
Advice: "Heartfelt poetry is wonderful, but quality poetry will show an understanding of the craft of poetry. Learn how to incorporate poetic device into your poetry even when writing free verse!"

$ ⬤ WESLEYAN UNIVERSITY PRESS, 110 Mt. Vernon, Middletown CT 06459. (860)685-2420. Established 1957. **Editor-in-Chief:** Suzanna Tamminen.
Book/Chapbook Needs: Wesleyan University Press is one of the major publishers of poetry in the nation. Publishes 4-6 titles/year. Has published poetry by James Dickey, Joy Harjo, James Tate, and Yusef Komunyakaa.
How to Submit: Query first with SASE. Considers simultaneous submissions. Guidelines available for SASE. Responds to queries in 2 months; to mss in 4 months. Pays royalties plus 10 copies. Poetry publications from Wesleyan tend to get widely (and respectfully) reviewed.

⬤ WEST ANGLIA PUBLICATIONS, P.O. Box 2683, La Jolla CA 92038. **Editor:** Wilma Lusk.
Book Needs: West Anglia Publications wants only the best poetry and publishes 1 paperback/year. Wants "contemporary poems, well wrought by poets whose work has already been accepted in various fine poetry publications. This is not a press for beginners." Has published poetry by Gary Morgan, Kathleen Iddings, and John Theobald. Books are usually 75-100 pages, digest-sized, perfect-bound. Sample book: $10 plus $1.50 postage and handling.
How to Submit: Query with 6 poems, cover letter, professional bio, and SASE. "Don't send entire manuscript unless requested by Editor." Pays 100 copies.

$ ◿ WEST BRANCH, Bucknell Hall, Bucknell University, Lewisburg PA 17837-2123. E-mail: westbranch@bucknell.edu. Website: www.bucknell.edu/westbranch. Established 1977. **Editor:** Paula Closson Buck. **Managing Editor:** Andrew Ciotola. Member: CLMP.
Magazine Needs: Appearing biannually, *West Branch* is "an aesthetic conversation between the traditional and the innovative in poetry, fiction, and nonfiction. It brings writers, both new and established, to the rooms where they will be heard, and where they will, no doubt, rearrange the furniture." Wants "well-structured verse that is both formally interesting and emotionally engaging; short lyric, prose poetry, and longer meditative and narrative poetry. We are especially interested in prose poetry." No confessional, genre, workshop, or slam poetry; no greeting card verse. Has published poetry by Margaret Gibson, John Haines, Ted Kooser, David St. John, and Wayne Dodd. *West Branch* is 120 pages, digest-sized, press run 1,000. Subscription: $10/year, $16/2 years. Sample: $3.
How to Submit: Submit 3-6 poems. Simultaneous submissions accepted if clearly marked as such; "ASAP notification of publication elsewhere." No disk or e-mail submissions. Reads September through April only. Time between acceptance and publication is up to 8 months. Guidelines available for SASE or on website. Responds within 2 months. Pays 3 copies and $10/page ($20 minimum/$100 maximum). Acquires first rights. Rights revert to author on publication.
Advice: *West Branch* "publishes less than 3% of submissions—always send your best work."

▟ $ ◿ ◎ WEST COAST LINE, 2027 EAA, Simon Fraser University, Burnaby BC V5A 1S6 Canada. (604)291-4287. Fax: (604)291-4622. E-mail: wcl@sfu.ca. Website: www.sfu.ca/west-coast-line. Established 1990. **Editors:** Glen Lowry and Jarold Zaslove. **Managing Editor:** Roger Farr.
Magazine Needs: *West Coast Line* is published 3 times/year and "favors work by both new and established Canadian writers, but it observes no borders in encouraging original creativity. Our focus is on contemporary poetry, short fiction, criticism, and reviews of books." Has published poetry by Bruce Andrews, Dodie Bellamy, Clint Burnham, Lisa Robertson, Aaron Vidaver, and Rita Wong. *West Coast Line* is 144 pages, digest-sized, handsomely printed on glossy paper and flat-spined. Receives 500-600 poems/year, accepts about 20. Approximately 40 pages of poetry/issue. Press run

is 800 for 500 subscribers of which 350 are libraries, 150 shelf sales. Single copy: $12; subscription: $30.

How to Submit: Submit poetry ". . . in extended forms; excerpts from works in progress; experimental and innovative poems; to 400 lines." No previously published poetry or simultaneous submissions. No e-mail submissions. Time between acceptance and publication is up to 8 months. Publishes theme issues. Guidelines available on website or by e-mail. Responds in 4 months. Pays $10 (Canadian)/printed page plus a 1-year subscription and 2 copies. Mss returned only if accompanied by sufficient Canadian postage or IRC.

Advice: "We have a special concern for contemporary writers who are experimenting with, or expanding the boundaries of, conventional forms of poetry, fiction, and criticism. That is, poetry should be formally innovative. We recommend that potential contributors send a letter of inquiry before submitting a manuscript."

⭐ ◎ WEST END PRESS (Specialized: social/political concerns; multicultural), P.O. Box 27334, Albuquerque NM 87125. (505)345-5729. Established 1976. **Publisher:** John Crawford.

Book/Chapbook Needs & How to Submit: West End Press publishes poetry, fiction, and drama with a social/cultural interest. Open as to form. Does not want "purely aesthetic, precious, self-involved poetry." Recently published poetry by Julia Stein, Ken Waldman, William Witherup, Duane Niatum, and Laura Tohe. Publishes 2 poetry books/year; occasional chapbooks and anthologies. Books/chapbooks are 48-96 pages, offset-printed, perfect-bound, glossy 4-color cover. Query first, with a few sample poems and a cover letter with brief bio and publication credits. Book/chapbook mss may include previously published poems. Responds to queries in 6 weeks; to mss in 3 months. Pays royalties of 6%; 10% author's copies (out of a press run of 600-1,500). Order sample books/chapbooks postage free by sending $8.95 to West End Press.

Advice: "May you live in interesting times."

⭐ 🌐 $◻ WESTERLY; PATRICIA HACKETT PRIZE, Dept. of English, University of Western Australia, Crawley, Western Australia 6009. Phone: (08)9380-2101. Fax: (08) 9380-1030. E-mail: westerly@cyllene.uwa.edu.au. Website: http://westerly.uwa.edu.au. Established 1956. **Editors:** Dennis Haskell and Delys Bird. **Poetry Editor:** Marcella Polain.

Magazine Needs: *Westerly* is a literary and cultural annual, appearing in November, which publishes quality short fiction, poetry, literary critical, socio-historical articles, and book reviews with special attention given to Australia and the Indian Ocean region. "We don't dictate to writers on rhyme, style, experimentation, or anything else. We are willing to publish short or long poems. We do assume a reasonably well-read, intelligent audience. Past issues of *Westerly* provide the best guides. Not consciously an academic magazine." *Westerly* is 200 pages, digest-sized, "electronically printed," with some photos and graphics. Press run is 1,200. Subscription: $13.50 (US), $23.95 (AUS).

How to Submit: Submit up to 6 poems at a time. Accepts fax and e-mail submissions in an attached file, Word 6; if submission is short, include in body of e-mail. "Please do not send simultaneous submissions. Covering letters should be brief and nonconfessional." Deadline for inclusion in *Westerly* is June 30. Time between acceptance and publication is 3 months. Occasionally publishes theme issues. Responds in 3 months. Pays minimum of AU $50 plus 1 contributor's copy. Acquires first publication rights; requests acknowledgment on reprints. Reviews books of poetry in multi-book format. Poets may send material to Reviews Editor for review consideration.

Also Offers: The Patricia Hackett Prize (value approx. AU $750) is awarded in March for the best contribution published in *Westerly* during the previous calendar year.

Advice: "Be sensible. Write what matters for you but think about the reader. Don't spell out the meanings of the poems and the attitudes to be taken to the subject matter—i.e., trust the reader. Don't be swayed by literary fashion. Read the magazine if possible before sending submissions."

◻ ◎ WESTERN ARCHIPELAGO REVIEW; WESTERN ARCHIPELAGO PRESS (Specialized: ethnic/nationality, regional), P.O. Box 803282, Santa Clarita CA 91380. (661)799-0694. E-mail: adorxyz@aol.com or jjero809@earthlink.net. Established 1999. **Editor:** Jovita Ador Lee.

Magazine Needs: *Western Archipelago Review* "publishes verse with a focus on the civilizations of Asia and the Pacific. All types of verse considered." *Western Archipelago Review* is 12 pages, digest-sized, with glossy cover. Press run is 40. Subscription: $36. Sample: $7. Make checks payable to GoodSAMARitan Press

How to Submit: Submit 3 poems at a time. Accepts previously published poems and simultaneous submissions. Accepts submissions by e-mail and by postal mail . Cover letter with SASE required. Reads submissions September to June. Time between acceptance and publication is 6 weeks. Poems are circulated to an editorial board. Guidelines available for SASE. Responds in 6 weeks. Reviews books and chapbooks of poetry and other magazines in 100 words. Send materials for review consideration.

$◙ WESTERN HUMANITIES REVIEW, University of Utah, 255 S. Central Campus Dr., Room 3500, Salt Lake City UT 84112-0494. (801)581-6070. Fax: (801)585-5167. E-mail: whr@mail. hum.utah.edu. Website: www.hum.utah.edu/whr. Established 1947. **Managing Editor:** Paul Ketzle.
   • Poetry published in this review has been selected for inclusion in the 1995 and 1998 volumes of *The Best American Poetry* as well as the 2002 *Pushcart Prize* anthology.

Magazine Needs: Appearing in April and October, *Western Humanities Review* is a semiannual publication of poetry, fiction, and a small selection of nonfiction. Wants "quality poetry of any form, including translations." Has published poetry by Scott Cairns, Philip Levine, Bin Ramke, Lucie Brock-Broido, Timothy Liu, and Pattiann Rogers. *Western Humanities Review* is 96-125 pages, digest-sized, professionally printed on quality stock and perfect-bound with coated card cover. Receives about 900 submissions/year, accepts less than 10%, publishes approximately 60 poets. Press run is 1,100 for 1,000 subscribers of which 900 are libraries. Subscription: $16 to individuals in the US. Sample: $10.

How to Submit: "We do not publish writer's guidelines because we think the magazine itself conveys an accurate picture of our requirements." Accepts simultaneous submissions; no previously published poems. No fax or e-mail submissions. Reads submissions October 1 through May 31 only. Time between acceptance and publication is 1-4 issues. Managing editor makes an initial cut then the poetry editor makes the final selections. Seldom comments on rejected poems. Occasionally publishes special issues. Responds in up to 6 months. Pays $5/published page and 2 copies. Acquires first serial rights.

Also Offers: Also offers an annual spring contest for Utah poets.

◙ WESTVIEW: A JOURNAL OF WESTERN OKLAHOMA, 100 Campus Dr., SWOSU, Weatherford OK 73096. (580)774-3168. Established 1981. **Editor:** Fred Alsberg.

Magazine Needs: *Westview* is a semiannual publication that is "particularly interested in writers from the Southwest; however, we are open to work of quality by poets from elsewhere. We publish free verse, prose poems and formal poetry." Has published poetry by Carolynne Wright, Miller Williams, Walter McDonald, Robert Cooperman, Alicia Ostriker, and James Whitehead. *Westview* is 64 pages, magazine-sized, perfect-bound, with glossy card cover in full-color. Receives about 500 poems/year, accepts 7%. Press run is 700 for 300 subscribers of which about 25 are libraries. Subscription: $10/2 years. Sample: $5.

How to Submit: Submit 5 poems at a time. Cover letter including biographical data for contributor's note requested with submissions. "Poems on 3.5 computer disk are welcome so long as they are accompanied by the hard copy and the SASE has the appropriate postage." Editor comments on submissions "when close." Mss are circulated to an editorial board; "we usually respond within two to three months." Pays 1 copy.

Also Offers: C. Michael Mikinarey Poetry Contest. Offers a cash prize and publication. Entry fee: $15 (includes 2 year subscription).

◙ WHISKEY ISLAND MAGAZINE, English Dept., Cleveland State University, Cleveland OH 44115. (216)687-2056. Fax: (216)687-6943. E-mail: whiskeyisland@csuohio.edu. Website: www.csu ohio.edu/whiskey_island. Established 1968. Student editors change yearly. **Contact:** Poetry Editor.

Magazine Needs: *Whiskey Island* appears biannually in January and July and publishes poetry, fiction, nonfiction, and art. Wants "advanced writing. We want a range of poetry from standard to experimental and concrete poetry. Thought provoking." Has published poetry by Maj Ragain, E. Maxwell, Christopher Franke, Jim Lang, Ye Qin, and Doug Manson. *Whiskey Island Magazine* is 86-120 pages, digest-sized, professionally printed and perfect-bound with glossy stock cover and b&w art. Receives 1,000-1,500 poetry mss/year, accepts 6%. Press run is 1,200 for 200 subscribers of which 20 are libraries, about 300 shelf sales. Subscription: $12, $20 overseas. Sample: $6. Make checks payable to *Whiskey Island Magazine*.

How to Submit: Submit up to 10 pages of poetry at a time. Include SASE for reply/ms return. Include name, address, e-mail, fax, and phone number on each page. No previously published poems. Include cover letter with brief bio. Accepts fax and e-mail submissions for mss outside of US; send as Rich Text format (.RTF) or ASCII files. Reads submissions September through April only. "Poets may fax inquiries and work that runs a few pages (longer submissions should be mailed). They may e-mail requests for submission and contest information." Poems are circulated to an editorial committee. Guidelines available for SASE, by e-mail, in publication, or on website. Responds within 4 months. Pays 2 contributor's copies, and 1 year subscription.

Also Offers: Sponsors an annual poetry contest. 1st Prize: $300; 2nd Prize: $200; 3rd Prize: $100. Entry fee: $10. Entries accepted October 1 through January 31. Query regarding contest for 2002.

Advice: "Include SASEs and your name, address, and phone for reply. List contents of submission in a cover letter."

WHITE EAGLE COFFEE STORE PRESS; FRESH GROUND, P.O. Box 383, Fox River Grove IL 60021-0383. E-mail: wecspress@aol.com. Website: http://members.aol.com/wecspress. Established 1992.

Magazine Needs & How to Submit: *Fresh Ground* is an annual anthology, appearing in November, that features "some of the best work of emerging poets. We're looking for edgy, crafted poetry. Poems for this annual are accepted during May and June only."

Book/Chapbook Needs: White Eagle is a small press publishing 5-6 chapbooks/year. "Alternate chapbooks are published by invitation and by competition. Author published by invitation becomes judge for next competition." "Open to any kind of poetry. No censorship at this press. Literary values are the only standard. Generally not interested in sentimental or didactic writing." Has published poetry by Timothy Russell, Connie Donovan, Scott Lumbard, Linda Lee Harper, Scott Beal, and Jill Peláez Baumgaertner. Sample: $5.95.

How to Submit: Submit complete chapbook ms (20-24 pages) with a brief bio, 125-word statement that introduces your writing and $10 reading fee. Accepts previously published poems and simultaneous submissions, with notice. No e-mail submissions. Deadline: September 30. Guidelines available for SASE or on website. "Each competition is judged by either the author of the most recent chapbook published by invitation or by previous competition winners." Seldom comments on rejected poems. Responds 3 months after deadline. All entrants will receive a copy of the winning chapbook. Winner receives $200 and 25 copies.

Advice: "Poetry is about a passion for language. That's what we're about. We'd like to provide an opportunity for poets of any age who are fairly early in their careers to publish something substantial. We're excited by the enthusiasm shown for this press and by the extraordinary quality of the writing we've received."

WHITE HERON; WHITE HERON PRESS, 2079 SW Hillsborough Ave., Arcadia FL 34266. E-mail: wheditor@hotmail.com or editor@whiteheron-press.com. Established 1997. **Editor:** Kevin Hull.

Magazine Needs: *White Heron* is published annually in July. "We are interested in lyric poetry, vivid imagery, open form, natural landscape, philosophical themes but not at the expense of honesty and passion; model examples: Wendell Berry, Gabriela Mistral, and Issa." Has published poetry by Bill Witherup, Corrinne Lee, Georgette Perry, Ken Meisel, and Michael Hannon. *White Heron Review* is 30 pages, digest-sized, professionally printed and saddle-stapled with card stock cover, sometimes includes art. Single copy: $7; subscription: $10. Make checks payable to Kevin Hull.

How to Submit: Submit up to 3 poems at a time. "Long poems, because of space, are rarely taken." Accepts previously published poems "by request only" and simultaneous submissions. Accepts submissions by e-mail (in text box), on disk, and by postal mail. Time between acceptance and publication is up to 6 months. Guidelines available by e-mail and on website. Pays 1 contributor's copy.

Book/Chapbook Needs & How to Submit: White Heron Press also considers chapbook publication. "Each manuscript considered on its own merits, regardless of name recognition. Basic production costs variable. Query or send manuscript and I'll respond."

Also Offers: The *White Heron* Poetry Contest. Submit 24 pages of poetry and $15 entry fee between March 1 and June 15 (include SASE for return of ms if desired). Prize: $500 and 50 copies. For The Short Poem Contest, send 16 pages of poetry, a $10 entry fee, and SASE for return of ms if desired between August 1 and October 15. Further guidelines available for SASE and on website.

Advice: "Do the work. Get used to solitude and rejection."

WHITE PELICAN REVIEW, P.O. Box 7833, Lakeland FL 33813. Established 1999. **Editor:** Nancy J. Wiegel.

Magazine Needs: *White Pelican Review* is a biannual literary journal, appearing in April and October, dedicated to publishing poetry of the highest quality. "Although a relatively new publication, *White Pelican Review* seeks to attract writing that goes beyond competency to truly masterful acts of imagination and language. To this end, the Lake Hollingsworth prize of $100 is offered to the most distinguished poem in each issue." Has published poetry by Trent Busch, Barbara Lefcowitz, Virgil Suarez, and Peter Meinke. *White Pelican Review* is about 48 pages, digest-sized, photocopied from typescript and saddle-stapled with matte cardstock cover. Receives about 3,000 poems/year, accepts 3%. Press run is 250 for 100 subscribers of which 10 are libraries. Subscription: $8, sample: $4. Make checks payable to *White Pelican Review.*

How to Submit: Submit 3-5 poems at a time. Length: 60 lines maximum. No previously published poems or simultaneous submissions. Cover letter and SASE required. "Please include name, address, telephone number, and e-mail address when available on each page. No handwritten poems." Time between acceptance and publication is 3 months. Poems are circulated to an editorial board which reviews all submissions. Seldom comments on rejected poems. Guidelines available for SASE. Responds in 6 months. Pays 1 contributor's copy. Acquires one-time rights.

WHITE PINE PRESS; THE WHITE PINE PRESS POETRY PRIZE, P.O. Box 236, Buffalo NY 14201. E-mail: wpine@whitepine.org. Website: www.whitepine.org. Established 1973. **Editor:** Dennis Maloney. **Managing Director:** Elaine LaMattina.

Book/Chapbook Needs & How to Submit: White Pine Press publishes poetry, fiction, literature in translation, essays—perfect-bound paperbacks. "We accept unsolicited work *only* for our annual competition—the White Pine Poetry Prize—and work in translation. We are always open to submissions of poetry in translation." Competition awards $1,000 plus publication to a book-length collection of poems by a US author. Entry fee: $20. Deadline: November 30. Guidelines available for SASE and on website. No e-mail submissions. Has published *My Father Sings, to My Embarassment* by Sandra Castillo (winner of the White Pine Poetry Prize), *Miracles & Mortifications* by Morton Marcus, and *Woman in Her Garden: Selected Poems of Dulce Maria Loynaz.*

WHITE WALL REVIEW, Dept. of English, 5th Floor Jorgenson Hall, 350 Victoria St., Toronto ON M5B 2K3 Canada. E-mail: whitewal@acs.ryerson.ca. Established 1976. Editors change every year.

Magazine Needs: *White Wall Review* is an annual, appearing in August, "focused on publishing clearly expressed, innovative poetry and prose. No style is unacceptable." Has published poetry by Vernon Mooers and David Sidjak. *White Wall Review* is between 90-144 pages, digest-sized, professionally printed and perfect-bound with glossy card cover, using b&w photos and illustrations. Press run is 250. Subscription: $9 in Canada, $9.50 in US and elsewhere. Sample: $5.

How to Submit: Submit up to 5 poems at a time. Length: 5 pages/piece maximum. Accepts submissions on disk, by fax, and by postal mail. Cover letter required; include short bio. Guidelines available for SASE, by e-mail, and in publication. Responds "as soon as possible." Pays 1 contributor's copy. "Innovative work is especially appreciated."

TAHANA WHITECROW FOUNDATION; CIRCLE OF REFLECTIONS (Specialized: Native American, animals, nature, spirituality/inspirational), 2350 Wallace Rd. NW, Salem OR 97304. (503)585-0564. Fax: (503)585-3302. E-mail: tahana@open.org. Website: www.open.org/tahana. Established 1987. **Executive Director:** Melanie Smith.

Magazine Needs & How to Submit: The Whitecrow Foundation conducts one spring/summer poetry contest on Native American themes in poems up to 30 lines in length. Deadline for submissions: May 31. No haiku, Seiku, erotic or porno poems. **Reading fee:** $3/poem, $10/4poems. Winners, honorable mentions and selected other entries are published in a periodic anthology, *Circle of Reflections*. Winners receive free copies and are encouraged to purchase others for $6.95 plus $2 handling in order to "help ensure the continuity of our contests." No fax or e-mail submissions. Guidelines available for SASE. Pays at least 2 copies.

Advice: "We seek unpublished Native American writers. Poetic expressions of full-bloods, mixed bloods, and empathetic non-Indians need to be heard. Future goals include chapbooks. Advice to new writers: Practice, practice, practice to tap into your own rhythm and to hone and sharpen material; don't give up."

WILD VIOLET, P.O. Box 39706, Philadelphia PA 19106-9706. E-mail: wildvioletmagazine@yahoo.com. Website: www.wildviolet.net. Established 2001. **Editor:** Alyce Wilson.

Magazine Needs: *Wild Violet* appears quarterly online. "Our goal is to democratize the arts: to make the arts more accessible and to serve as a creative forum for writers and artists." Wants "poetry that is well crafted, that engages thought, that challenges or uplifts the reader. We have published free verse, haiku, and blank verse. If the form suits the poem, we will consider any form." Does not want "abstract, self-involved poetry; poorly managed form; excessive rhyming; self-referential poems that do not show why the speaker is sad, happy, or in love." Recently published poetry by Erik Kestler, Jules St. John, Sam Vaknin, Leanne Kelly, John Haag, Jim DeWitt, and Rich Furman. *Wild Violet* is published online with photos, artwork, and graphics. Accepts about 20% of work submitted. Publishes about 10-15 poems/issue.

How to Submit: Submit 3-5 poems at a time. Accepts simultaneous submissions; no previously published poems. Accepts e-mail submissions; no fax or disk submissions. Cover letter is preferred. "Include poem(s) in body of e-mail or send as a text or Microsoft Word attachment." Reads submissions year round. Submit seasonal poems 3 months in advance. Time between acceptance and publication is 3 months. "Decisions on acceptance or rejection are made by the editor. Contests are judged by an independent panel." Seldom comments on rejected poems; comments given if requested. Occasionally publishes theme issues. Upcoming themes and guidelines available by e-mail. Responds in up to 6 weeks. Pays by providing a bio and link on contributor's page. All rights retained by author. Reviews books and chapbooks of poetry in 250 words, single book format. Send materials for review consideration to Alyce Wilson, editor.

Also Offers: Holds a contest with first prize being $100 and publication in *Wild Violet*. **Entry fee:** $5. E-mail for full details.

Advice: "Read voraciously; experience life and share what you've learned. Write what is hardest to say; don't take any easy outs."

WILLARD & MAPLE, 163 South Willard St., Freeman 302, Box 34, Burlington VT 05401. E-mail: willardandmaple@champlain.edu. Established 1996. **Contact:** Poetry Editor.

Magazine Needs: *Willard & Maple* appears annually in April and is "a student-run literary magazine from Champlain College that publishes a wide array of poems, short stories, creative essays, short plays, pen and ink drawings, black and white photos, and computer graphics." Wants "creative work of the highest quality." Does not want any submissions over 5 typed pages in length; all submissions must be in English. Recently published poetry by P-R Smith, Francine Page, Cheryl Burghdurf, Bill Everts, and Charles Ballantyne. *Willard & Maple* is 100 pages, digest-sized, digitally-printed, saddle-stapled, with b&w internal art/graphics. Receives about 500 poems/year, accepts about 20%. Publishes about 50 poems/issue. Press run is 500 for 80 subscribers of which 4 are libraries; 200 are distributed free to the Champlain College writing community. Single copy: $8.50. Make checks payable to Champlain College.

How to Submit: Submit up to 5 poems at a time. Line length for poetry is 100 lines maximum. Accepts simultaneous submissions; no previously published poems. Accepts e-mail and disk submissions; no fax submissions. Cover letter is required. "Please provide current contact information including an e-mail address. Single-space submissions, one poem/page." Reads submissions September 1-April 30. Time between acceptance and publication is less than 1 year. Poems are circulated to an editorial board. "All editors receive a blind copy to review. They meet weekly throughout the academic year. These meetings consist of the submissions being read aloud, discussed, and voted upon." Seldom comments on rejected poems. Occasionally publishes theme issues. List of upcoming themes available by e-mail. Responds in 2 months. Pays 2 contributor's copies. Acquires one-time rights. Reviews books and chapbooks of poetry and other magazines/journals in 1,200 words. Poets may send materials for review consideration to the Poetry Editor.

Advice: "Work hard, be good, never surrender!"

THE WILLIAM AND MARY REVIEW, Campus Center, College of William and Mary, P.O. Box 8795, Williamsburg VA 23187-8795. (757)221-3290. Established 1962. **Poetry Editors:** Philip Clark and Stephanie Insley.

Magazine Needs: *The William and Mary Review* is a 120-page annual, appearing in May, "dedicated to publishing new work by established poets as well as work by new and vital voices." Has published poetry by Cornelius Eady, Minnie Bruce Pratt, Edward Field, Dan Bellm, Forrest Gander, and Walter Holland. *The William and Mary Review* is about 120 pages, digest-sized, professionally printed on coated paper and perfect-bound with 4-color card cover, includes 4-color artwork and photos. Receives about 5,000 poems/year, accepts 12-15. Press run is 3,500. Has 250 library subscriptions, about 500 shelf sales. Sample: $5.50.

How to Submit: Submit 1 poem/page, batches of up to 6 poems addressed to Poetry Editors. Cover letter required; include address, phone number, e-mail address (if available), past publishing history, and brief bio note. Reads submissions September 1 through February 15 *only*. Responds in approximately 4 months. Pays 5 contributor's copies.

Advice: "If you lie in your cover letter, we usually figure it out. Submit considered, crafted poetry or don't bother. No guidelines, just send poems."

WILLOW REVIEW; COLLEGE OF LAKE COUNTY READING SERIES, College of Lake County, 19351 W. Washington St., Grayslake IL 60030-1198. (847)223-6601, ext. 2956. Fax: (847)543-3956. E-mail: mlatza@clcillinois.edu. Established 1969. **Editor:** Michael F. Latza.

Magazine Needs: "We are interested in poetry and fiction of high quality with no preferences as to form, style or subject." Has published poetry by Lisel Mueller, Lucien Stryk, David Ray, Louis Rodriguez, John Dickson, and Garrett Hongo and interviews with Gregory Orr, Diane Ackerman, and Li-Young Lee. *Willow Review* is an 88- to 96-page, flat-spined annual, digest-sized, professionally printed with a 4-color cover featuring work by an Illinois artist. Editors are open to all styles, free verse to form, as long as each poem stands on its own as art and communicates ideas. Press run is 1,000, with distribution to bookstores nationwide. Subscription: $15 for 3 issues, $25 for 5 issues. Sample back issue: $4.

How to Submit: Submit up to 5 poems or short fiction/creative nonfiction up to 4,000 words. Accepts submissions on disk and by postal mail. Reads submissions from September to May. Sometimes sends prepublication galleys. Pays 2 contributor's copies. Acquires first North American serial rights. Prizes totaling $400 are awarded to the best poetry and short fiction/creative nonfiction in each issue.

Also Offers: The reading series, 4-7 readings/academic year, has included Angela Jackson, Thomas Lux, Charles Simic, Isabel Allende, Donald Justice, Gloria Naylor, David Mura, Galway Kinnell, Lisel Mueller, Amiri Baraka, Stephen Dobyns, Heather McHugh, Linda Pastan, Tobias Wolff, William Stafford, and others. One reading is for contributors to *Willow Review*. Readings are usually held on Thursday evenings, for audiences of about 150 students and faculty of the College of Lake County and other area colleges and residents of local communities. They are widely publicized in Chicago and suburban newspapers.

insider report

Tuning up to read poetry

How does one come to combine original poetry and Appalachian-style fiddling—on the page, in performance, and on CD? Ken Waldman, Alaska's Fiddling Poet, says poetry writing and fiddle playing "kind of got intertwined. I was playing fiddle before I wrote poems, but I was doing other writing."

Ken Waldman

Photo by Kate Salisbury

A Philadelphia native, Waldman first explored fiddling while living in Carrboro, North Carolina, near Chapel Hill. "I had a housemate who played clawhammer banjo, and a friend of his had a fiddle he wanted to get rid of," Waldman explains. "I bought it for $100." Waldman learned enough to "get beyond the initial part," but public performance lay far in the future.

So did poetry. Waldman moved to Seattle ("a hotbed for fiddle stuff") and continued his musical apprenticeship. Then, about a year later he applied to writing school in Fairbanks, Alaska. "I was in the program as a fiction writer," says Waldman, "but in workshops people were writing poems. I didn't know much about poetry but was intrigued enough to start writing some."

The long Fairbanks winters were ideal for dedicating himself to his fiddling as well as his writing. After three years, Waldman received his MFA with a fiction writing emphasis but continued to write poems as well. After graduation he wrote stories but found himself drawn more and more to poetry. "I also made the jump to being a decent old-time fiddle player," Waldman adds. The ensuing years found him writing and fiddling in Juneau, Sitka, and Nome.

"Village Fiddle"

I toted my junker, side seam already cracked,
an old cheap box of wood that would take
the steep banks of small planes aiming
for runways, the bumps and jostles of sleds
hooked to snowmachines, the ice, the wind,
nights in the villages. Higher education
missionary, I made rounds to students' homes
(where I visited, but never fit), to liaisons'
offices (where the state-issued equipment
sometimes worked), to the local high schools
and elementaries (where I volunteered service)—
fiddle closer to my heart than the backpack
full of books. Indeed, closer to my heart
than the frozen broken truth: a bloody pump
buried in utter darkness. Quick to unsnap
the case, I scratched tunes where no one had,
played real-life old-time music to Eskimos

and the odd whites in that weathered land.
The Pied Fiddler, I might have been, gently
placing the beat-up instrument in others' hands,
giving up the bow. Good for smiles and laughs.
Random questions and comments. A third-grader:
It must be like having a dog always making noise—
you must never get lonely. A high-schooler:
Is it hard to learn? One of my college students:
Why are you out here? Where is your family?

(from *Nome Poems* (West End Press, 2000); reprinted with permission of the author)

Waldman's job as visiting assistant professor increased his public exposure, which included doing readings. He added fiddle playing to his performances, and his reputation as a unique performing artist spread. Since 1994, the former college professor has appeared as Alaska's Fiddling Poet at leading clubs, universities, bookstores, and art festivals nationwide. Waldman is also popular as a visiting artist, teaching in classrooms and through academic residencies in more than 100 schools throughout the country.

Early on, self-publishing became a natural extension of Waldman's activities. "I had an invitation to do a program at the Bilingual Multicultural Education and Equity Conference in Anchorage," he says. "Since I included reading poems in my presentation, I thought it would be convenient to have a chapbook instead of coping with a sheaf of papers. The chapbooks also gave me something to sell and allowed me to get around to do occasional book fairs in the Northwest."

Waldman describes his move to self-publishing as proactive. "Instead of waiting to be 'annointed' by an editor, I decided to gather a collection of poems myself." Aware of the stigma associated with self-publishing, Waldman altered his viewpoint thanks to a book on independent scholars as well as the examples of James Joyce, Virginia Woolf, and Walt Whitman, who also published their own writing. "Self-publishing is respectable as far as literary tradition is concerned," he says, although Waldman also acknowledges self-publishing isn't for everyone. "I'd recommend it for the right person at the right time—if you want to, if you're confident enough." And he stresses that a poet has to get out there to promote and keep the momentum going. "If you have a chapbook, talk to your local library, talk to a café, get some friends together and write more poems so you can do another chapbook." In all, Waldman has put together 26 of his own chapbooks.

He points to another method poets can use to get the word out. "The music folks are playing these 'house concerts.' That's something poets could do." According to Waldman, someone with a large space in a private home will hire a musician or band to stage an intimate concert, drawing an audience from interested friends and family and charging a certain amount per head as a "donation" toward the evening's expenses. For Waldman, such occasions have resulted in sales of books and CDs in addition to his fee for performing. "I sold 15 copies of a book at one house concert, about $200 worth of stuff at another. Poets could do the same thing instead of waiting for the 'right' reading series or an opening at a café. One of the beauties is you can do it yourself or rent out a space and have someone else present it on your behalf." In addition to the monetary benefits, such opportunities provide welcome exposure and the chance to build an audience.

What do Waldman's audiences make of a poet who fiddles (or is it a fiddler who writes poetry)? "There isn't one response," Waldman observes. "Sometimes there's this attitude, 'If he's a musician, he must not be a serious poet,' and vice versa. Some people just want the poems, others just want the music." Once they see Waldman's skilled and energetic performance, though, audiences are usually won over, with new fans added to Waldman's following. "I like it when someone says, 'I wasn't expecting this, but it's pretty cool,' or 'I feel like I need to go to my atlas and look at Alaska.' "

For an artist who combines poetry reading with fiddle playing, the natural next step was putting together a CD. As with his chapbooks, Waldman chose to do the project himself. "In the music business, there's not the same stigma when artists do their own productions," he says. Getting airplay for his CDs is similar to having a poem accepted by a journal. "Radio people are like editors, in a sense, getting all these CDs, choosing to play this or that. And like poetry journals, many of these small stations are 'under the radar.' Often the on-air personalities are from the community itself. They can play only so many things in a given amount of time."

Even in such a competitive environment, Waldman's first CD, *A Week in Eek* (2000), was well received and got enthusiastic airplay nationwide. Accompanied by Vancouver musician Andrea Cooper (banjo and flute) and other guest artists, Waldman presented the same mix of original poetry and old-time fiddle tunes (some traditional, some his own compositions) he delivers onstage. *Burnt Down House* followed, with the new *Music Party* appearing in January, 2003. All three CDs were produced and released through Waldman's Nomadic Press.

Eventually Waldman had full-length poetry collections published by West End Press, reflecting material that originally appeared in his many self-published chapbooks. *Nome Poems* (2000) and *To Live on This Earth* (2002) are both in their second printings. Meanwhile, Waldman is a busy troubadour, staying on the road most of the year. 2002 took him to the AWP (Associated Writing Programs) Conference in New Orleans, BookExpo in New York (with a gig at The Knitting Factory, the famous NYC club), and the Dodge Poetry Festival in New Jersey (both as one of the "Poets Among Us" readers and as a wandering musician). He continues his ongoing appearances at a range of venues, large and small, that keep him crisscrossing the country.

He does most things from the road: writing and submitting poems, sending out press kits, networking, keeping up with phone messages left at his Alaska home number, and checking his e-mail from libraries and Internet cafes. Although he has an agent for some venues, Waldman books a lot of engagements himself, which takes plenty of time, energy, and legwork. Self-publishing required self-promotion, and Waldman credits that experience with building the savvy he applies to seeking and booking performances.

He notes that he works full time but not necessarily on his poetry. Waldman has had close to 400 poems published in national journals, but these days he's more likely to be sending out press kits than literary submissions. Still, Waldman describes himself as grounded in the William Stafford school of writing, "the idea that you get up every day and write. 'Lower your standards' and just write. 'The more you write, the luckier you get,' is how I paraphrase it."

This philosophy reassures Waldman he'll be productive when he needs to be, "when I have the time and energy. There's a time to write, but now it's my time to travel around the country doing this." In addition to his poetry, Waldman anticipates publishing a short story collection and a novel, as well as further poetry collections, all of which are already written. Also, he's planning to write a couple of nonfiction books, one about his times in Alaska, the other about his current troubadour lifestyle.

In the meantime, Waldman believes he's "doing it in a way that makes sense for me."
—*Nancy Breen*

For more information about Ken Waldman, see www.kenwaldman.com.

⊘ ◎ **WILLOW SPRINGS**, 705 W. First Ave., MS-1, Eastern Washington University, Spokane WA 99201. (509)623-4349. Fax: (509)623-4238. E-mail: willow.springs@mail.ewu.edu. Established 1977. **Editor:** Jennifer Davis.

Magazine Needs: "We publish quality poetry and fiction that is imaginative, intelligent, and has a concern and care for language. We are especially interested in translations from any language or period." Has published poetry by Michael Heffernan, Robert Gregory, Beckian Fritz-Goldberg, and Mark Halliday. *Willow Springs*, a semiannual, is one of the most visually appealing journals being published. *Willow Springs* is 128 pages, digest-sized, professionally printed, flat-spined, with glossy 4-color card cover with art. Receives about 4,000 poems/year, accepts approximately 1-2%. Editors seem to prefer free verse with varying degrees of accessibility (although an occasional formal poem does appear). Press run is 1,500 for 700 subscribers of which 30% are libraries. Subscription: $11.50/year, $20/2 years. Sample: $5.50.

How to Submit: Submit September 15 through May 15 only. "We do not read in the summer months." Include name on every page, address on first page of each poem. Brief cover letter saying how many poems on how many pages preferred. No simultaneous submissions. Accepts submissions by postal mail only. Guidelines available for SASE. Responds in up to 3 months. Pays 2 copies plus a copy of the succeeding issue, others at half price, and cash when funds available. Acquires all rights. Returns rights on release. Reviews books of poetry and short fiction in 200-500 words.

Also Offers: Has annual poetry and fiction awards ($400 and $500 respectively) for work published in the journal.

Advice: "We like poetry that is fresh, moving, intelligent and has no spare parts."

⊘ **WIND; JOY BALE BOONE POETRY AWARD; THE QUENTIN R. HOWARD CHAP-BOOK PRIZE**, P.O. Box 24548, Lexington KY 40524. (859)277-6849. E-mail: wind@wind.org. Website: www.wind.wind.org. Established 1971. **Editor:** Chris Green. **Poetry Editor:** Rebecca Howell.

Magazine Needs: *Wind* appears 3 times/year. "Using poetry, fiction, and nonfiction, *Wind* operates on the metaphor of neighborly conversation between writers about the differing worlds in which they live. Founded in 1971 in rural Kentucky, *Wind* looks to bring the vision and skill of writers from all concerns and walks of life into dialogue." *Wind*'s goal is "to publish a wide scope of literary work from diverse communities. Hence, we believe that each piece must be evaluated on its own terms based on its context. As not all poets and communities in America are like ourselves, and context does not travel with a poem, if you need to explain the rhetoric of your piece, please do!" Recently published poetry by Wendell Berry, James Baker Hall, Eleanor Lerman, Mariko Susko, Walter Griffin, and Donna J. Gelagotis Lee. *Wind* is 125 pages, digest-sized, perfect-bound, with line illustrations. Receives about 3,000 poems/year, accepts about 1%. Publishes 15 poems/issue. Press run is 400 for 200 subscribers of which 75 are libraries, 100 shelf sales. Single copy: $6; subscription: $15/year or $25/2 years. Sample: $4.50. Make checks payable to *Wind*.

How to Submit: Submit up to 5 poems at a time. Accepts simultaneous submissions; no previously published poems. No e-mail or disk submissions. Cover letter is preferred. Include "a brief letter of introduction letting us know a little bit about your place in life and the world." Reads submissions year round. Time between acceptance and publication is 1-2 months. "Staff readers review each manuscript. Poetry editor makes final selection." Comments on rejections "when near misses." Guidelines available for SASE and on website. Responds in 4 months. Pays 1 contributor's copy and discount on extras. Acquires first North American serial rights. Reviews books of poetry and other magazines in 250-500 words, single books format. Send materials for review consideration to Chris Green, *Wind*.

Also Offers: Joy Bale Boone Poetry Award, $500, deadline: March 1st; The Quentin R. Howard Chapbook Prize, published as summer issue of magazine, $100 and 25 copies, deadline: October 31st. Guidelines available for SASE. Each issue of *Wind* also features community spotlight. "We highlight literary communities in the greater Ohio Valley—anywhere from Indianapolis to Knoxville, from the Mississippi to the Appalachians. Write '*Wind:* Literary Community Portraits' for guidelines."

Advice: "Be honest and relentless. There are hundreds of different poetries being written in America. As a way of selecting the appropriate place to submit work, find the community to which your voice and vision belong. Want to read every poem in whatever journal you submit to, then read them and join the conversation.''

◻ ◎ **WINDHOVER: A JOURNAL OF CHRISTIAN LITERATURE (Specialized: Christian)**, 900 College St., Box 8008, University of Mary Hardin-Baylor, Belton TX 76513. (254)295-4561. E-mail: windhover@umhb.edu. Established 1996. **Editor:** Audell Shelburne.

Magazine Needs: *"Windhover* annually publishes poetry and fiction by writers of faith. We're open to all types of poetry. Nothing trite or didactic.'' Has published poetry by Walt McDonald, Marjorie Maddox, David Brendan Hopes, and Kelly Cherry. *Windhover* is 160 pages, magazine-sized, perfect-bound. Receives about 150 poems/year, accepts approximately 10%. Press run is 500 for 50 subscribers. Subscription: $8/year. Sample: $6. Make checks payable to *Windhover.*

How to Submit: Submit 4 poems at a time. Accepts simultaneous submissions; no previously published poems. Accepts e-mail and disk submissions only. "We work best with e-mail submissions." Time between acceptance and publication is 4 months. Poems are circulated to an editorial board by e-mail. "We send poems to members of the editorial board for advisement. If poems are sent via e-mail, response time is shorter." Often comments on rejected poems. Guidelines available for SASE or by e-mail. Responds in 4 months. Sometimes sends prepublication galleys. Pays 2 copies. Acquires one-time rights. Reviews books and chapbooks of poetry in 300 words, single book format. Send materials for review consideration.

◪ $◪ **WINDSTORM CREATIVE**, 7419 Ebbert Dr. SE, Port Orchard WA 98367. Website: www.windstormcreative.com. Established 1989. **Senior Editor:** Ms. Cris Newport.

Book/Chapbook Needs: Windstorm Creative Ltd. publishes "thoughtful, quality work; must have some depth." Publishes 12 paperbacks/year. Wants "a minimum of 100 publishable, quality poems; book length. No sexually explicit material. You must be familiar with our published poetry before you submit work." Has published poetry by Jack Rickard, Vacirca Vaughn, and Rudy Kikel.

How to Submit: Current guidelines on website. "All submissions must have mailing label and submission form found on website." If invited, send entire mss, 100 poems minimum. Accepts previously published poems and simultaneous submissions. No e-mail queries. Cover letter preferred. "A bio with publishing history, a page about the collection's focus, theme, etc., will help in the selection process." Time between acceptance and publication is 2 years. Poems are circulated to an editorial board. "Senior editor reviews all work initially. If appropriate for our press, work given to board for review." Seldom comments on rejected poems. Responds to queries and to mss in 3 months. Pays 10-15% royalties.

◪ **WINGS MAGAZINE, INC.**, E-mail: pamwings@juno.com. Website: www.geocities.com/win gsmag2002. Established 1991. **Publisher/Poetry Editor:** Thomas Jones. **Associate Editor:** Pamela Malone.

Magazine Needs: *Wings* is an exclusively online publication. "We want to publish the work of poets who are not as widely known as those published in larger journals but who nevertheless produce exceptional, professional material. We also publish personal essays, fiction, and plays." Wants "poetry with depth of feeling. No jingly, rhyming poetry. Rhyming poetry must show the poet knows how to use rhyme in an original way. Poetry on any theme, 80 lines or less, any style." Receives about 500 poems/year. "No requirements, but we encourage poets to check out our website and get an idea of the kind of material we publish."

How to Submit: Submit up to 5 poems at a time. Accepts previously published poems but no simultaneous submissions. "We take submissions through e-mail only. Send e-mail to the above juno address. Copy and paste the poem and bio into the e-mail message. The bio should be five lines or less." Always responds to submissions. Guidelines available on website. Responds in 2 months. Staff reviews books and chapbooks of poetry in single book format. Send inquiries to pamwings@juno.com.

Also Offers: "Our needs are eclectic. Content can be on any topic as long as the poet shows mastery of subject matter and craft, as well as penetration into depths." Also, published a Best of Wings CD-ROM.

Advice: "We don't want doggerel. We want sincere, well-crafted work. Poetry has been reduced to second class status by commercial publishing, and we want to restore it to the status of fiction (novels) or plays."

WISCONSIN REVIEW; WISCONSIN REVIEW PRESS, 800 Algoma Blvd., University of Wisconsin-Oshkosh, Oshkosh WI 54901. (920)424-2267. E-mail: wireview@yahoo.com. Established 1966. **Contact:** Martin Brick or Andrew Osborne.

Magazine Needs: *Wisconsin Review* is published 3 times/year. "We like poems with vivid images and novel subject matter. Talk about something new, or at least talk in a very new way." Has published poetry by Virgil Suarez, Baron Wormser, Doug Flaherty, Len Roberts, and B.J. Buhrow. *Wisconsin Review* is 80-100 pages, digest-sized, elegantly printed on quality white stock, glossy card cover with color art, b&w art inside. Receives about 1,500 poetry submissions/year, accepts about 75; 40-50 pages of poetry in each issue. Press run is 1,600 for 40 subscribers of which 20 are libraries. Single copy: $4; subscription: $10.

How to Submit: Submit mss September 15 through May 15. Offices checked bimonthly during summer. Submit up to 4 poems at a time, one poem/page, single-spaced with name and address of writer on each page. Accepts simultaneous submissions, but previously unsubmitted works preferable. Cover letter required; include brief bio. Mss are not read during the summer months. Guidelines available for SASE. Responds in up to 9 months. Pays 2 contributor's copies.

$ ☑ ◎ A WISE WOMAN'S GARDEN (Specialized: women's issues, shamanism, mysticism, psychic, nature), P.O. Box 403, Racine WI 53401-0403. (262)632-2373. Established 1994. **Editor:** Katus Hortus (a.k.a. Katarzyna "Kat" Rygasiewicz).

Magazine Needs: *A Wise Woman's Garden*, an irregularly printed zine, is published "to connect readers with nature, landscape, metaphor magicks, the four elements (earth, water, air, fire) witnessed to in heart and mind." Wants "medicine-shield balanced poetry." Has published poetry by Antler, DyAnne Korda, Catherine Cofell, Melissa Pinol, Jeffrey Johannes, and Michael Thompson. *A Wise Woman's Garden* is 12-16 pages, 4¼×11, photocopied on colored paper, bound by hand, "corded 2-color classic 'J' book binder stitch," occasional sketches and cartoons. Press run is 450 for 70 subscribers; most distributed free through Racine and Kenosha WI coffeehouses, stores, soirees, libraries, and art galleries. Subscription: $22 regular; $17 libraries; $11 for poets accepted for printing. Sample (including guidelines): $2 in cash. "Issues are linked to sun-sign astrological imagery at month's beginning (example: March-Pisces). Please supply birthdate for appropriate astrological linkage."

How to Submit: Submit 3-7 poems at a time. Accepts previously published poems and simultaneous submissions. Cover letter preferred, with bio or "fantastickal anecdotes." Time between acceptance and publication is up to 18 months. Often comments on rejected poems. Guidelines available in publication. Responds in up to 4 months. Sometimes sends prepublication galleys. Pays $5/poem plus 10 copies ("if two or more poems used in same issue, subscription given also.") Acquires first or one-time rights.

Advice: " 'Earth' is usually capitalized (sacral respect). Poems automatically rejected for using the word 'dirt.' 'Soil' is a living organism. Find the magicks in your regional landscape and sculpt-sing them with all your knack. Biggest reason for rejection is for being mundane. Bring the reader into sacred space and the *non*-ordinary as a shaman would set the stage for healing. Ideal reader is perimenopausal woman or elder."

◯ ◎ THE WISHING WELL (Specialized: membership, women/feminism, lesbian/bisexual), P.O. Box 178440, San Diego CA 92177-8440. Phone/fax: (858)270-2779. E-mail: laddieww w@aol.com. Website: www.wishingwellwomen.com. Established 1974. **Editor/Publisher:** Laddie Hosler.

Magazine Needs: Appearing bimonthly, *The Wishing Well* is a "contact magazine for women who love women the world over; members' descriptions, photos, letters and poetry published with their permission only; resources, etc., listed. I publish writings only for and by members so membership is required." 1-2 pages in each issue are devoted to poetry, "which can be up to 8″ long—depending upon acceptance by editor, 3″ width column." *The Wishing Well* is 7×8½, offset printed from typescript, with soft matte card cover. Circulation is 100 members, 200 nonmembers. A sample is available for $5. Membership in *Wishing Well* is $25 for 3-5 months, $40 for 5-7 months, $60 for 7-9 months, $80 for 15 months.

How to Submit: Membership includes the right to publish poetry, a self description (exactly as you write it), to have responses forwarded to you, and other privileges. Accepts submissions by e-mail (as attachment or in text box), by fax, and by postal mail. Personal classifieds section, 50¢/word for members and $1/word for nonmembers.

Also Offers: Website includes membership application and introductory letter describing membership with *The Wishing Well*.

WOODLEY MEMORIAL PRESS (Specialized: regional), English Dept., Washburn University, Topeka KS 66621. (785)231-1010 ext. 1735. Fax: (785)231-1089. E-mail: amy.fleury@washburn.edu. Website: www.washburn.edu/reference/woodley-press. Established 1980. **Editor:** Amy Fleury. **President:** Larry McGurn. **Manuscript Editor:** Denise Low.

Book/Chapbook Needs: Woodley Memorial Press publishes 1-2 flat-spined paperbacks/year, about half being collections of poets from Kansas or with Kansas connections, "terms individually arranged with author on acceptance of ms." Has published *Horsetail* by Donald Levering, *The Gospel of Mary* by Michael Poage, *Kansas Poems of William Stafford* edited by Denise Low, *Killing Seasons* by Christopher Cokinos, and *Gathering Reunion* by David Tangeman. Samples may be individually ordered from the press for $5.

How to Submit: Guidelines available on website. Accepts e-mail queries. Responds to queries in 2 weeks, to mss in 6 months. Time between acceptance and publication is 1 year.

Advice: "We look for experienced writers who are part of their writing and reading communities."

WORCESTER REVIEW; WORCESTER COUNTY POETRY ASSOCIATION, INC. (Specialized: regional), 6 Chatham St., Worcester MA 01609. (508)797-4770. Website: www.geocities.com/Paris/LeftBank/6433. Established 1973. **Managing Editor:** Rodger Martin.

Magazine Needs: *Worcester Review* appears annually "with emphasis on poetry. New England writers are encouraged to submit, though work by other poets is used also." Wants "work that is crafted, intuitively honest and empathetic, not work that shows the poet little respects his work or his readers." Has published poetry by May Swenson, Robert Pinsky, and Walter McDonald. *Worcester Review* is 160 pages, digest-sized, flat-spined, professionally printed in dark type on quality stock with glossy card cover. Press run is 1,000 for 300 subscribers of which 50 are libraries, 300 shelf sales. Subscription: $20 (includes membership in WCPA). Sample: $5.

How to Submit: Submit up to 5 poems at a time. "I recommend three or less for most favorable readings." Accepts simultaneous submissions "if indicated." Previously published poems "only on special occasions." Editor comments on rejected poems "if ms warrants a response." Publishes theme issues. Guidelines and upcoming themes available for SASE. Responds in up to 9 months. Pays 2 copies. Acquires first rights.

Also Offers: Has an annual contest for poets who live, work, or in some way (past/present) have a Worcester County connection or are a WCPA member.

Advice: "Read some. Listen a lot."

WORD DANCE (Specialized: children/teen), P.O. Box 10804, Wilmington DE 19850. (302)894-1950. Fax: (302)894-1957. E-mail: playful@worddance.com. Website: www.worddance.com. Established 1989. **Director:** Stuart Ungar.

• "Listed as 'Best Bet' in *Instructor* magazine. Featured in *The New York Times*."

Magazine Needs: "Published quarterly, *Word Dance* magazine encourages the love of reading and writing in a nonthreatening, playful environment. It was created to give young people a quality vehicle for creative expression, a place where their voices can be heard. It includes short stories, poems, and artwork by kids in kindergarten through Grade 8." *Word Dance* features haiku, but accepts all forms of poetry. *Word Dance* is 32 pages, digest-sized, professionally printed and saddle-stapled, two-color card cover, includes two-color drawings. Subscription: $18/year US, $23 Canada, $28 other countries. Single copy/sample: $3.

How to Submit: Accepts poetry for four of their six sections. Field Trip accepts poems and stories about family and school trips; World Word accepts poems and short stories about the environment, war and peace, endangered species, etc.; for Haiku Corner send your Haiku poetry; Grab Bag accepts poems and short stories about any topic. "*Word Dance* receives many submissions for the Grab Bag section of the magazine, so competition is greater in this category. We recommend that students contribute to the other sections of the magazine to increase their chances of getting published." No previously published poems or simultaneous submissions. Accepts submissions by postal mail only; no fax or e-mail submissions. "Our submission form must be included with each submission." Submission form available in magazine, on website, by telephone, or by written request. Submission deadlines: February 25, May 25, August 25, November 25. Time between acceptance and publication is up to 9 months. Poems are circulated to an editorial board. Guidelines available for SASE, in publication, or on website. Copies are available at cost.

Advice: "A subscription is suggested to see examples of work. We are a nonprofit organization. Parents and teachers are encouraged to help their child/student revise and edit work."

$◑ WORD PRESS; WORD PRESS POETRY PRIZE; WORD PRESS FIRST BOOK PRIZE; WORD JOURNAL CHAPBOOK PRIZE; WORD JOURNAL POETRY PRIZE, P.O. Box 541106, Cincinnati OH 45254-1106. (513)474-3761. Fax: (513)474-9034. E-mail: connect@wor dtechweb.com. Website: www.word-press.com. Established 2000. **Editors:** Kevin Walzer and Lori Jareo.

Book/Chapbook Needs & How to Submit: Word Press "is an independent literary press devoted to publishing and distributing the best new poetry through annual contests and other channels." Pays winners $1,000 and 25 author's copies (out of a press run of 300-500). Runners-up receive 5 copies of their published book. Has published *When There Is No Shore* by Vivian Shipley, *The Gospel of Galore* by Tina Kelley, and *The Zydeco Tablets* by Alison Pelegrin. Publishes one paperback/year chosen through the Word Press Poetry Prize and Word Press First Book Prize. Books are 48-96 pages, offset-printed, perfect-bound, paper/laminated cover, with photos. "Submit at least 48 pages of poetry. Individual poems may be previously published, but manuscript may not." Open to both new and published poets. Guidelines available on website. Competition receives 100-200 entries/year. Judges are the Word Press staff. Annual deadline: December 1 for Word Press Poetry Prize; July 1 for Word Press First Book Prize. Copies of previous winning books are available from Word Press for $15.

Also Offers: *Word Journal*, which sponsors an annual chapbook contest and a contest for individual poems. Entry fee(s): $15 for chapbook or set of 4 poems. Chapbook and poem winners receive $250. Deadline: July 1.

Advice: "We look for books that have strongly crafted individual poems and that also resonate *as books*—that have a strong thematic, narrative, or lyric depth and focus."

◑ WORD SALAD, 2800 University Dr., Durham NC 27707. (919)493-3618. E-mail: whealton@ wordsalad.net. Website: http://wordsalad.net. Established 1995. **Publisher:** Bruce Whealton. **Editors:** Bruce Whealton, Jr. and Jean Jones.

Magazine Needs: Published quarterly online, *Word Salad* "continuously accepts original poetry. Although we do not restrict ourselves to one subject area or style, the Web allows us to receive a large number of poems and select the highest quality and we offer a world wide exposure. We are open to any form, style or subject matter; length should be no more than two typed pages. We especially like poetry dealing with oppressed/vulnerable populations, i.e., persons with mental illness, the poor/homeless. We accept poetry in Spanish to reflect the international nature of the Internet. No greeting card verse or forced rhyme; avoid love poems unless you have something original to say. We invite gay/lesbian/bisexual poetry." Has published poetry by Scott Urban, John Marshall, and Martin Kirby. Receives about 1,200 poems/year, accepts approximately 10%.

How to Submit: Submit 2 poems at a time. No previously published poems or simultaneous submissions. Accepts submissions on disk, in e-mail text box, via online submission form, and by postal mail. Cover letter preferred. Indicate whether submission is for publication, or contest (see below). "We receive 200-300 poems per quarter and publish 20-30. Most of the submissions are received via e-mail. We ask that poets read the submission guidelines on the Web." Time between acceptance and publication is about 3 months. Seldom comments on rejected poems. Publishes theme issues occasionally. Guidelines and upcoming themes available on website. Responds in about 3 months. Sometimes sends prepublication galleys. Open to unsolicited reviews.

Also Offers: Sponsors annual poetry contest. See website for announcements. Winners are announced June 15. Indicate whether submission is for publication or contest. "*Word Salad* is linked to a directory of online resources related to writing and creativity. Additionally, we have a web-based chat program that allows live chat discussions."

THE WORD WORKS; THE WASHINGTON PRIZE, P.O. Box 42164, Washington DC 20015. Fax: (703)527-9384. E-mail: editor@WORDSWORKSDC.com. Website: www.WORDWOR KSDC.com. Established 1974. **Editor-in-Chief:** Hilary Tham.

Book/Chapbook Needs: Word Works "is a nonprofit literary organization publishing contemporary poetry in single author editions usually in collaboration with a visual artist. We sponsor an ongoing poetry reading series, educational programs, the Capital Collection—publishing mostly metropolitan Washington, D.C. poets, and the Washington Prize—an award of $1,500 for a book-length manuscript by a living American poet." Previous winners include *Phoenix Suites* by Miles Waggoner, *One Hundred Children Waiting for a Train* by Michael Atkinson, *Last Heat* by Peter Blair; *Following Fred Astaire* by Nathalie Anderson; *Tipping Point* by Fred Marchant; and *Stalking the Florida Panther* by Enid Shomer. Submission open to any American writer except those connected with Word Works. Send SASE for rules. Entries accepted between February 1 and March 1. Postmark deadline is March 1. Winners are announced at the end of June. Publishes perfect-bound paperbacks and occasional anthologies and want "well-crafted poetry, open to most forms and styles (though not political themes particularly). Experimentation welcomed." "We want more than a collection of poetry. We care about the individual poems—the craft, the emotional content and the risks taken—but we want manuscripts where one poem leads to the next. We strongly recommend you read the books that have already won the Washington Prize. Buy them, if you can, or ask for your libraries to purchase them. (Not a prerequisite.)" Most books are $10.

How to Submit: "Currently we are only reading unsolicited manuscripts for the Washington Prize." Accepts simultaneous submissions, if so stated. Accepts submissions by postal mail only. Always sends prepublication galleys. Payment is 15% of run (usually of 1,000). Guidelines and catalog available for SASE or on website. Occasionally comments on rejected poems.

Also Offers: "We do have a contest for D.C.-area high school students who compete to read in our Miller Cabin Series." Young poets should submit ms with cover letter (detailing contact info, high school and grade, expected graduation date, and list of submitted poem titles) and SASE from January 1 to March 31. Send to Attn: W. Perry Epes. Two winners will receive an honorarium and a chance to read work.

Advice: "Get community support for your work, know your audience, and support contemporary literature by buying and reading the small press."

WORDS OF WISDOM, 8969 UNCG Station, Greensboro NC 27413. (336)334-2952. E-mail: Wowmail@hoopsmail.com. Established 1981. **Editor:** Mikhammad Abdel-Ishara.

Magazine Needs: *Words of Wisdom* appears quarterly with short stories, essays, and poetry. Wants all types of poetry. No religious, pornography. Recently published poetry by Patricia Prime, Esther Cameron, Michael Estabrook, Ulea, Millicent C. Borges, and Margene W. Hucek. *Words of Wisdom* is 76-88 pages, digest-sized, laser-printed, saddle-stapled, cover with art. Receives about 600 poems/year, accepts about 8-10%. Publishes about 10-12 poems/issue. Press run is 160 for 100 subscribers of which 2 are libraries, 50 shelf sales. Single copy: $4; subscription: $14. Sample: $4. Make checks payable to J.M. Freiermuth.

How to Submit: Submit 3-6 poems at a time. Line length for poetry is 30 maximum. Accepts simultaneous submissions; *absolutely no previously published poems*. No fax, e-mail, or disk submissions. Cover letter is required. Reads submissions all year. Submit seasonal poems 10 months in advance. Time between acceptance and publication is 6-9 months. Seldom comments on rejected poems. Occasionally publishes theme issues. Guidelines available for SASE or by e-mail. Responds in up to 6 months. Pays 1 contributor's copy. Acquires first North American serial rights.

Advice: "Turn off the Internet! Surf through a book of poetry."

$ ▢ ◎ WORDSONG; BOYDS MILLS PRESS (Specialized: children/teen/young adult), 815 Church St., Honesdale PA 18431. (800)490-5111. Website: www.boydsmillspress.com. Established 1990. **Editor:** Wendy Murray. **Editor-in-Chief:** Dr. Bernice E. Cullinan.

• Wordsong's *Been to Yesterdays* received the Christopher Award and was named a Golden Kite Honor Book.

Book/Chapbook Needs: Wordsong is the imprint under which Boyds Mills Press (a *Highlights for Children* company) publishes books of poetry for children of all ages. Seek "quality poetry that captures both the fun and nonsense of childhood as well as moments of wonder and quiet reflection. We publish poems for toddlers through sophisticated poems for young adults, but not poetry for adults. Themes of sexuality and violence are not our market. Themes that work in elementary and middle school curricula are a plus, but we seek inspired work, not work written for a particular market." Has published *The Alligator in the Closet* by David L. Harrison, *By Definition* by Sara Holbrook, *In the Spin of Things* by Rebecca Kai Dotlich, and *Horizons* by Jane Yolen.

How to Submit: "Wordsong prefers original work but will consider anthologies and previously published collections. We ask poets to send collections of 25-45 poems, preferably with a common theme, such as adolescence, or family relationships, or animals, but if it doesn't have a theme, it ought to have some overarching idea or organizing principles. Please send complete book manuscripts, not single poems. We publish on an advance-and-royalty basis." No fax or e-mail submissions. Always sends prepublication galleys.

Advice: "Wordsong favors poetry that makes music of language, whether the poems are free verse or rhyme, silly or serious. As you conceive of your book of poetry, define for yourself what makes your book unique. The best poetry for children may ignite the imagination; help children see the world in a new way; play to their love of nonsense; glimmer with a truth they recognize; give comfort; move child closer to finding the rhythm of oneself."

$ ◎ THE WRITE CLUB (Specialized: membership), P.O. Box 1454, Conover NC 28613. (828)256-3821. E-mail: poetsnet@juno.com. Established 2001. **Club President/Editor:** Nettie C. Blackwelder.

Magazine Needs: *The Write Club* appears quarterly. "We print *one* original poem from *each* of our members in *each* quarterly club booklet. These poems are voted on by all members. We pay $1 to each member for each vote his/her poem receives. Each booklet also contains four assignments for all members who want to do them (usually poetry assignments). Our poetry specifications are open as to form, subject matter, style, or purpose. Just send your best. We don't print anything indecent or offensive." Recently published poetry by Johnnie Elma Anderson, David Bell, Lou Ellen Hoffman, Vincent J. Tomeo, Bruce Tedder, and Sallie A. Hinds. *The Write Club* is 24 pages, 4¼ × 11, computer-printed, saddle-stapled, color, light-weight, laminated cover. Receives about 200 poems/year, accepts about 90%. Publishes about 40 poems/issue. Press run is 50 for 32 subscribers; 12 distributed free to anyone who requests information. Single copy: $2; subscription: $15 (membership). Sample: $1 (or 3 first-class stamps). Make checks payable to Nettie C. Blackwelder.

How to Submit: Submit 1 poem at a time. Line length for poetry is 3 minimum, 30 maximum. Accepts previously published poems and simultaneous submissions. Accepts e-mail submissions; no fax or disk submissions. Cover letter is preferred. "Send SAE and 3 first-class stamps (or $1) for information and sample booklet before submitting poetry." Reads submissions all year. Submit seasonal poems 3 months in advance. Time between acceptance and publication is 3 months. "Poems are voted on by our members. Each vote is worth $1 to that poem's author." **Membership required** (all members receive subscription to club booklet). Guidelines available for SASE or by e-mail. Responds in 3 months. Pays $1 per vote, per poem. Acquires one-time rights.

Advice: "Rhythm is the music of the soul and sets the pace of a poem. A clever arrangement of words means very little if they have no sense of 'stop' and 'go.' If you're not sure about the rhythm of a poem, reading it aloud a few times will quickly tell you which words don't belong or should be changed. My advice is rewrite, rewrite, rewrite until you love *every* word and phrase 'as is.' "

THE ◎ SYMBOL indicates a market with a specific or unique focus. This specialized area of interest is listed in parentheses behind the market title.

◢ **WRITE ON!! POETRY MAGAZETTE**, P.O. Box 901, Richfield UT 84701-0901. (435)896-6669. E-mail: jimnipoetry@yahoo.com. Website: www.fortunecity.com/victorian/stanmer/244/rpmag azette. Established 1998. **Editor:** Jim Garman.

Magazine Needs: *Write On!! Poetry Magazette* appears monthly and features "poetry from poets around the world." Wants poetry of "any style, all submissions must be suitable for all ages to read. No adult or vulgar material." Recently published poetry by Diane Ashley, Misty Lackey, and Benita Glickman. *Write On!!* is 24 pages, digest-sized, photostat-copied, saddle-stapled, with a color card cover. Receives about 500 poems/year, accepts about 50%. Publishes about 24 poems/issue. Press run is 50 for 10 subscribers of which 1 is a library, 10 shelf sales. Single copy: $4. Sample: $3. Make checks payable to Jim Garman.

How to Submit: Submit 1-6 poems at a time. Line length for poetry is 6 minimum, 28 maximum. Accepts previously published poems and simultaneous submissions. Accepts e-mail submissions (in text box); no fax or disk submissions. Reads submissions year round. Submit seasonal poems 2 months in advance. Time between acceptance and publication is 1 month. Never comments on rejected poems. Occasionally publishes theme issues. A list of upcoming themes available by e-mail. Guidelines available on website. Responds in 3 weeks. Acquires first rights.

Advice: "Send only your best material after it has been refined."

■ ○ ◎ **THE WRITE WAY (Specialized: writing); TAKING CARE OF YOURSELF (Specialized: health concerns); ANN'S ENTERPRISES**, P.O. Box 1734, Wilmington VT 05363. E-mail: annlarberg@hotmail.com. Established 1988. **Editor:** Ann Larberg.

Magazine Needs: *The Write Way* is a quarterly using poems of up to 20 lines on the theme of writing. *The Write Way* is an 6-page newsletter with articles on writing and ads. Single copy: $2; subscription: $6. Sample free with SASE.

How to Submit: Nonsubscribers must include $1 reading fee and SASE with submissions (up to 5 poems). Do not submit in summer. Reads submissions January 1 through June 30 only. Accepts e-mail submissions included in an attached file; 20 line limit. Publishes theme issues: winter, writing (the writing life); spring, nature; summer, travel; fall, greeting card rhymed verse. Upcoming themes and guidelines available for SASE. Responds in 6 weeks. Pays 1 copy. Send materials for review consideration.

Also Offers: *Awareness Newsletter*, published quarterly. Prints 1-2 short poems/issue on the theme of health. Sample free with SASE. Pays contributor's copies.

$ ◢ **WRITERS' JOURNAL**, P.O. Box 394, Perham MN 56573-0394. (218)346-7921. Fax: (218)346-7924. E-mail: writersjournal@lakesplus.com. Website: www.writersjournal.com. Established 1980. **Poetry Editor:** Esther M. Leiper.

Magazine Needs: *Writers' Journal* is a bimonthly magazine "for writers and poets that offers advice and guidance, motivation, inspiration, to the more serious and published writers and poets." Features 2 columns for poets: "Esther Comments," which specifically critiques poems sent in by readers, and "Every Day with Poetry," which discusses a wide range of poetry topics, often—but not always—including readers' work. Wants "a variety of poetry: free verse, strict forms, concrete, Oriental. But we take nothing vulgar, preachy or sloppily written. Since we appeal to those of different skill levels, some poems are more sophisticated than others, but those accepted must move, intrigue or otherwise positively capture me. 'Esther Comments' is never used as a negative force to put a poem or a poet down. Indeed, I focus on the best part of a given work and seek to suggest means of improvement on weaker aspects." Accepts poetry written by school-age children. Has published poetry by Lawrence Schug, Diana Sutliff, and Eugene E. Grollmes. *Writers' Journal* is 64 pages (including paper cover), magazine-sized, professionally printed, using 4-5 pages of poetry in each issue, including columns. Circulation is 26,000. Receives about 900 submissions/year, accepts approximately 25 (including those used in columns). Single copy: $3.99; subscription: $19.97/year (US), Canada/Mexico add $15, Europe add $30, all others $35. Sample: $5.

How to Submit: "Short is best: 25-line limit, we rarely use longer. Three to four poems at a time is just right." No query. Accepts submissions by postal mail only. Responds in up to 5 months. Pays $5/poem plus 1 copy.

Also Offers: The magazine also has poetry contests for previously unpublished poetry. Submit up to 6 poems on any subject or in any form, 25 line limit. "Submit in duplicate, one with name and address, one without." Send SASE for guidelines only. Deadlines: April 30, August 30 and December 30. Reading fee for each contest: $3 per poem. Competition receives 1,000 entries/year. Winners announced in *The Writers' Journal* and on website.

WRITING FOR OUR LIVES; RUNNING DEER PRESS (Specialized: women, feminism), 647 N. Santa Cruz Ave., The Annex, Los Gatos CA 95030-4350. Established 1991. **Editor/Publisher:** Janet McEwan.

Magazine Needs: Appearing annually, "*Writing For Our Lives* serves as a vessel for poems, short fiction, stories, letters, autobiographies, and journal excerpts from the life stories, experiences, and spiritual journeys of women." Wants poetry that is "personal, women's real life, life-saving, autobiographical, serious—but don't forget humorous, silence-breaking, many styles, many voices. Women writers only, please." Has published poetry by Sara V. Glover, Kennette Harrison, Sara Regina Mitcho, and Eileen Tabios. *Writing For Our Lives* is 80-92 pages, 5¼×8¼, printed on recycled paper and perfect-bound with matte card cover. Receives about 400 poems/year, accepts 5%. Press run is 500. Subscription: $15.50/2 issues. (CA residents add 8.25% sales tax). Back issues and overseas rates available, send SASE for info. Sample: $8, $11 overseas.

How to Submit: Submit up to 5 typed poems with name and phone number on each page. Accepts previously published poems ("sometimes") and simultaneous submissions. Include 2 SASEs; "at least one of them should be sufficient to return manuscripts if you want them returned." Closing date is August 15. Usually responds in 3 days, occasionally longer. "As we are now shaping 2-4 issues in advance, we may ask to hold certain poems for later consideration over a period of 18 to 24 months." Seldom comments on rejected poems. Guidelines available for SASE and in publication. Pays 2 contributor's copies, discount on additional copies, and discount on 2-issue subscription. Acquires first world-wide English language serial (or one-time reprint) rights.

Advice: "Our contributors and circulation are international. We welcome new writers, but cannot often comment or advise. We do not pre-announce themes. Subscribe or try a sample copy—gauge the fit of your writing with *Writing For Our Lives*—support our ability to serve women's life-sustaining writing."

XAVIER REVIEW, Box 110C, Xavier University, New Orleans LA 70125. (504)483-7303. Fax: (504)485-7917. E-mail: rskinner@xula.edu. Established 1961. **Editors:** Thomas Bonner, Jr. and Richard Collins. **Managing Editor:** Robert E. Skinner.

Magazine Needs: *Xavier Review* is a biannual that publishes poetry, fiction, nonfiction, and reviews (contemporary literature) for professional writers, libraries, colleges, and universities. Wants writing dealing with African/Americans, the South, and the Gulf/Caribbean Basin. Has published *I Am New Orleans* by Marcus Christian and *Three Poets in New Orleans* by Lee Grue as well as poetry by Biljiana Obradovic and Patricia Ward. Press run is 500.

How to Submit: Submit 3-5 poems at a time with SASE. Accepts submissions by postal mail only. No e-mail or fax submissions. Pays 2 contributor's copies.

YALOBUSHA REVIEW, University of Mississippi, Dept. of English, P.O. Box 1848, University MS 38677-1848. E-mail: yalobush@olemiss.edu. Established 1995. **Contact:** Poetry Editor.

Magazine Needs: *Yalobusha Review* appears annually in April "to promote new writing and art, creative nonfiction, fiction, and poetry." Does not want anything over 10 pages. Recently published poetry by Claude Wilkinson, Ann Fisher-Wirth, and Jim Nagal. *Yalobusha Review* is 126 pages, digest-sized, glossy cover, with b&w photos and drawings. Receives 300-400 poems/year, accepts about 15%. Publishes about 30 poems/issue. Press run is 500; 50 are distributed free to chosen writers/artists. Single copy: $10. Sample: $8. Make check payable to *Yalobusha Review*.

How to Submit: Submit 10 poems at a time. Length for poetry is 1 page minimum, 10 pages maximum. No previously published poems. Accepts disk submissions; no fax or e-mail submissions. Cover letter is required. Include SASE. Reads submissions August 15-January 15. Submit seasonal poems 4 months in advance. Time between acceptance and publication is 4 months. Poems are circulated to an editorial board: reader to specific editor (prose/poetry) to editor-in-chief to editorial board (including advisors). Never comments on rejected poems. Occasionally publishes theme issues.

Guidelines available by e-mail. Responds in up to 6 months. Pays 2 contributor's copies. Acquires all rights. Returns full rights upon request.

Advice: "It seems as though poetry has become so regional, leaving us to wonder, 'Where is the universal?' "

YA'SOU! A CELEBRATION OF LIFE, P.O. Box 77463, Columbus OH 43207. Established 2000. **Editor:** David D. Bell.

Magazine Needs: *Ya'sou! A celebration of life* appears quarterly. "Our purpose is to celebrate life. We like thought-provoking and uplifting material in any style and subject matter. We would like to see poetry essays, short stories, articles, and b&w artwork." Does not want "sexually explicit, violence. I'd like more poetry written by children." Recently published poetry by C. David Hay, B.Z. Niditch, Doug Lowney, Geri Ahearn, and Daphne Baumbach. *Ya'Sou!* is 25-35 pages, magazine-sized, photocopied, side-stapled, paper cover with color photo, with art/graphics, classified ads, recipes. Receives about 200 poems/year, accepts about 75%. Publishes about 40-50 poems/issue. Press run is 50 for 25 subscribers; 10 are distributed free. Single copy: $5; subscription: $10/year. Make checks payable to David D. Bell.

How to Submit: Submit 5 poems at a time. Length: 30 lines maximum. "Your name and complete address should be at the top left-hand corner of every poem." Accepts previously published poems and simultaneous submissions. Cover letter is preferred. **Reading fee:** $1/poem. "Work submitted by regular mail should be camera-ready. SASE required." Reads submissions all year. Time between acceptance and publication varies. "All work is read and chosen by the editor." Never comments on rejected poems. "Subscribers will receive preference. Subscribers only also receive special editions throughout the year." Guidelines are available for SASE. Responds in 1 week. Pays 1 contributor's copy. Acquires one-time rights.

Advice: "Let your own unique voice be heard. Remember, express your heart, live your soul, and celebrate life."

YAWP MAGAZINE; YAWP'S POETRY AND SHORT STORY CONTESTS, P.O. Box 5998, Pittsburgh PA 15210. E-mail: poetrysubmissions@hotmail.com. Website: www.yawpmagazine. com. Established 1999. **Poetry Contact:** Eric Bliman, editor.

Magazine Needs: *Yawp Magazine* appears biannually in winter and summer. "*Yawp* shocases the works of approximately 15-20 poets and generally a few story writers; also, *Yawp* publishes approximately 10-12 b&w reproductions of artwork, photography, and illustrations of high quality in each issue. Often, there will be a featured poet and/or artist appearing in a special section or sprinkled throughout, with a number of his or her works. *Yawp* publishes experienced and beginning poets, based solely upon the quality of the written work received." Wants "poetry that is both challenging and rewarding, stirring and intelligent, with or without a 'message'; mature voices aware of themselves and the postage stamp of earth they live on; i.e., the stuff that makes your feet tingle and your hair stand on end; joyful, desperate, confident, etc. All forms of poetry considered, only the best published. We want our readers to think and be moved; not preached or talked down to. Poems that haven't fermented for at least a month, and been revised a minimum of 10 times should not leave the house without supervision, with rare exceptions." Recently published poetry by Vivian Shipley, Andrena Zawinski, Jeff O'Brien, Jim Daniels, Allison Joseph, and John Sokol. *Yawp* is 80-130 pages, digest-sized, laser-copied, flat-spined, printed, tape-bound, heavy card stock cover with b&w illustration or photography, b&w art/graphics only. Receives about 750 poems/year, accepts about 15%. Publishes about 25-40 poems/issue. Press run is 450 for 100 subscribers of which 20 are libraries, 100 shelf sales; 100 are distributed free to contest entrants only. Single copy: $7 plus $1.50 s&h; subscription: $17/year, 2 issues. Sample: $6 includes shipping, no handling charge. Make checks payable to Yawp Magazine, Inc.

How to Submit: Submit 3-6 poems at a time. Line length for poetry is 175 maximum. Accepts previously published poems and simultaneous submissions. Accepts e-mail and disk submissions; no fax submissions. Cover letter is preferred. "Poems should be single-spaced, typed or word-processed. Brief bio of fewer than 60 words suggested but not required. Though we do accept poetry via poetrysubmissions@hotmail.com, poets should treat this medium as a convenience, not a shortcut to publication. If you use it, use it wisely and sparingly." Reads submissions March-June and September-

December. Submit seasonal poems 2-4 months in advance. Time between acceptance and publication is 2-3 months. "Content of magazine is determined solely by the editors of *Yawp Magazine*; less of a process than a madness." Seldom comments on rejected poems. "No fees for noncontest submitters, but we request that our readers and contributors help keep us afloat if they like what we're doing by purchasing a subscription, as we receive no grants or university support. Also, we strongly recommend that anyone considering submitting to *Yawp* buy a subscription first, to learn what we're all about, before sending any work." Guidelines available in magazine, by e-mail, or on website. Responds in up to 4 months. Sometimes sends prepublication galleys. Pays 1 contributor's copy. Acquires first rights. Reviews books of poetry in 500 words, single book format (query first).

Also Offers: "*Yawp* holds 2 contests each year for poetry, and sometimes short stories. Grand prize: $500. Check our website periodically for all contest-related updates and guidelines."

Advice: "Read everything you can get your hands on, first; and when you do sit down to write, don't distract yourself by thinking of all the magazine editors, teachers, friends, or family members that might or might not like it. Be wary of people who give too much advice about how to write poetry. Don't rush to publish."

○ YEFIEF, P.O. Box 8505, Santa Fe NM 87504-8505. (505)753-3648. Fax: (505)753-7039. E-mail: arr@imagesformedia.com. Established 1993. **Editor:** Ann Racuya-Robbins.

Book/Chapbook Needs: *yefief* is a serial imprint of Images For Media that was originally designed "to construct a narrative of culture at the end of the century." Wants "innovative visionary work of all kinds and have a special interest in exploratory forms and language. There is no set publication schedule." Has published poetry by Michael Palmer, Simon Perchik, and Carla Harryman. *yefief* is 250 pages, printed on site and perfect-bound with color coated card cover with color and b&w photos, art and graphics inside. Initial artbook press run is 500. Single copy: $24.95. Write for information on obtaining sample copies.

How to Submit: Submit 3-6 poems at a time. Accepts previously published poems and simultaneous submissions. Responds in 2 months. Pays 2-3 contributor's copies. Poets may send material for review consideration.

○ YELLOW BAT REVIEW; RICHARD GEYER, PUBLISHER, 1338 W. Maumee, Idlewilde Manor #136, Adrian MI 49221. E-mail: ybreview@yahoo.com. Website: www.geocities.com/rgeyer_2000/index.html. Established 2001. **Editor:** Craig Sernotti.

Magazine Needs: *Yellow Bat Review* appears semiannually as "a pocket-sized journal of eclectic writing, primarily poetry but also including some very short prose. *Yellow Bat Review* hopes to be *the* home for all types of poetry from subtle to humorous to strange and anything in between." Open to all schools and genres. No restrictions on form or content. Likes offbeat, surreal, gritty work. Nothing sentimental, no weak lines, no teenage angst. Has published work by Brian Evenson, Charlee Jacob, John Sweet, John Grey, Lyn Lifshin, and Duane Locke. *Yellow Bat Review* is 20-30 pages, pocket-sized (4¼×5½), photocopied, saddle-stapled, glossy, b&w card stock cover. Accepts less thn 5% of submission. Single copy: $2.50; subscription: $8 (4 issues). Sample: $2.50. Make checks payable to Richard Geyer.

How to Submit: Submit up to 4 poems at a time. Line length for poetry is 20 maximum (accepts prose up to 500 words). Accepts previously published poems (rarely); no simultaneous submissions. Accepts e-mail submissions; no fax or disk submissions. Cover letter is preferred. Strongly prefers e-mail submissions. Poems must be given as text in the body of the message. Time between acceptance and publication is 1-6 months. Often comments on rejected poems. Occasionally publishes theme issues. Guidelines available on website or by e-mail. Responds in up to 2 months. Always sends prepublication galleys. Pays 1 contributor's copy. Acquires first North American serial rights.

Book/Chapbook Needs & How to Submit: Richard Geyer, Publisher publishes pocket-sized chapbooks of dark poetry. Chapbook submissions are by invitation only. Publishes 2-4 chapbooks/year. Chapbooks are usually 10-30 pages, photocopied, saddle-stapled, glossy, b&w card stock cover. Order sample chapbooks by sending $2 to Richard Geyer.

Advice: "To beginners, try us, try everything. Experience only comes if you try. To everyone, we hope *Yellow Bat Review* will be a breath of fresh air in a world of dry lit mags. We don't care about being 'safe.' If the work is fresh and lively it will be published, regardless of school or style. Whether the poet is an 'unknown' or a 'well-known' is meaningless; it's the poem that counts."

YEMASSEE; YEMASSEE AWARDS, Dept. of English, University of South Carolina, Columbia SC 29208. (803)777-2085. E-mail: yemassee@gwm.sc.edu. Website: www.cla.sc.edu/ENGL/yem assee. Established 1993. **Co-Editors:** Carl Jenkinson and Jill Carroll.

Magazine Needs: *Yemassee* appears semiannually and "publishes primarily fiction and poetry, but we are also interested in one-act plays, brief excerpts of novels, essays, reviews, and interviews with literary figures. Our essential consideration for acceptance is the quality of the work; we are open to a variety of subjects and writing styles." Accepts 10-25 poems/issue. "No poems of such a highly personal nature that their primary relevance is to the author; bad Ginsberg." Has published poetry by Nick Finney, Kwame Dawes, Virgil Saurez, Phoebe Davidson, Pamela McClure, Rafael Campo, David Kirby, and Susan Ludvigson. *Yemassee* is 80-100 pages perfect-bound. Receives about 400 poems/year, accepts about 10%. Press run is 750 for 120 subscribers, 10 shelf sales; 275-300 distributed free to English department heads, creative writing chairs, agents and publishers. Subscription (2 issues): $10 for students, $15 regular. Sample: $5. Make checks payable to Education Foundation/ English Literary Magazine Fund.

How to Submit: Submit up to 5 poems at a time. Line length for poetry is fewer than 50, "but poems of exceptional quality are considered regardless of length." No previously published poems. No fax or e-mail submissions. Cover letter required. "Each issue's contents are determined on the basis of blind selections. Therefore we ask that all works be submitted, without the author's name or address anywhere on the typescript. Include this information along with the title(s) of the work(s) in a cover letter. For longer submissions, please include an approximate word count." Reads submissions August 15 to May 15. Time between acceptance and publication is up to 4 months. "Staff reads and votes on 'blind' submissions." Often comments on rejected poems. Guidelines available for SASE or on website. Responds in up to 2 months after submission deadline. Pays 2 contributor's copies with the option to purchase additional copies at a reduced rate. Acquires first rights.

Also Offers: Sponsors the *Yemassee* Awards when funding permits. Awards $400/issue, usually $200 each for poetry and fiction. Details of annual poetry competition posted on website in early spring: $500 1st prize.

YORKSHIRE JOURNAL (Specialized: regional), Ilkley Rd., Otley, West Yorkshire LS2 3JP England. Phone: (01943)467958. Fax: (01943)850057. E-mail: sales@smith-settle.co.uk. Established 1992. **Editor:** Mark Whitley.

Magazine Needs: *Yorkshire Journal* is a quarterly general interest magazine about Yorkshire. Wants poetry no longer than 25 lines with some relevance to Yorkshire. Has published poetry by Vernon Scannell, Anna Adams, Ted Hughes, Andrew Motion, and Simon Armitage. *Yorkshire Journal* is 120 pages, highly illustrated. Receives about 200 poems/year, accepts approximately 10%. Press run is 3,000 for 700 subscribers, 2,300 shelf sales. Subscription: £12. Sample: £2.95. Make checks payable to SMITH Settle Ltd.

How to Submit: Submit up to 6 poems at a time. Accepts previously published poems and simultaneous submissions. Accepts submissions by fax and e-mail (in text box). Cover letter required including biographical information. Has a large backlog. Time between acceptance and publication varies. Sometimes comments on rejected poems. Guidelines available for SASE (or SAE and IRC). Responds within 1 month maximum. Pays 1 copy.

ZILLAH: A POETRY JOURNAL, P.O. Box 202, Port Aransas TX 78373-0202. E-mail: lightni ngwhelk@msn.com. Established 2001. **Editor/Publisher:** Pamela M. Smith.

Magazine Needs: Appearing quarterly, *Zillah* is " 'not your mother's poetry.' Simply put, in the year 3999 an archaeologist's dig produces a copy of *Zillah* in situ and, reading it, the treasure hunter knows what it was like to live during the second and third millenia." Does not want pornography, gratuitous violence, evil or devil worship, or anything that lacks quality. *Zillah* is 40-50 pages, $7 \times 8\frac{1}{2}$, stapled, 80 lb. coverstock, with b&w original art or graphics. Receives about 1,200 poems/year. Single copy: $3; subscription: $12. Make checks payable to Pamela M. Smith.

How to Submit: Submit 5-6 poems at a time. Line length for poetry is 60 maximum. Accepts previously published poems and simultaneous submissions. Accepts submissions by e-mail (in text box); no fax submissions. "SASE essential, typed, double-spaced, one poem to a page." Reads submissions all year. Submit seasonal poems 6 months in advance. Time between acceptance and publication is up to 1 year. Never comments on rejected poems. Responds in 2 months. Pays 1 contributor's copy. Acquires first North American serial rights or second reprint rights; rights revert to author after publication.

Also Offers: The *Zillah* Poetry Contest. Winners will be published and receive 2 copies of magazine. Guidelines available for SASE.

Advice: "Everyone should write, everyone should write poetry. Take a leap of faith. Think of writing as a natural state of being. Let go from a stream of consciousness, from the heart, from depth—edit and refine later."

ZINE ZONE, 47 Retreat Place, London E9 6RH United Kingdom. Phone: (+44)20-85100157. Fax: (+44)20-85331028. E-mail: getzz@zinezone.co.uk. Website: www.zinezone.co.uk. Established 1992. **Contact:** "editorial."

Magazine Needs: *Zine Zone* appears 8 times/year and publishes "a chaotic mix of illustrative works with poetry, short stories, music reviews, etc." For their poetry wants, they say, "anything goes. Although, we mostly publish obscure unpublished poets and students." *Zine Zone* is 44 pages, A4, photocopied and stapled with b&w paper cover, b&w graphics. Receives about 200 poems/year, accepts 50-70%. Press run is 500 for 120 subscribers. Single copy: £1.95 ($4 US); subscription: £18 ($32 US)/8 copies, £11 ($30 US)/4 copies. Sample: £3 ($5 US).

How to Submit: Accepts previously published poems and simultaneous submissions. Accepts submissions on disk, by fax, and by postal mail. Cover letter preferred. Time between acceptance and publication is 2 months. Reviews books and chapbooks of poetry and other magazines, single book format.

Also Offers: "Poetry nights organized in and around London (UK) where poets read their work to an audience."

ZOO PRESS, P.O. Box 22990, Lincoln NE 68542. Fax: (402)614-6302. E-mail: editors@zoopre ss.org. Website: www.zoopress.org. Established 2000.

Book/Chapbook Needs: "Zoo Press aims to publish the best emerging writers writing in the English language, and will endeavor to do it at the rate of at least 12 manuscripts of admirable quality a year (in print and electronic formats as they become available), providing we can find them. We're confident we can. By quality we mean originality, an awareness of tradition, formal integrity, rhetorical variety (i.e., invective, satire, argument, irony, etc.), an impressive level of difficulty, authenticity, and, above all, beauty." Wants high quality poetry mss. Does not want mss written by those who do not regularly read poetry. Recently published poetry by Kate Light, Judith Taylor, Talvikki Ansel, Ben Downing, Kathy Fagan, Scott Cairns, and Therese Svoboda. Zoo Press publishes 12 paperbacks/year through open submissions and competition. Books are usually 50-100 pages, perfect-bound, 2-4 color matte covers.

How to Submit: "We only accept open submissions in July. The best way for a first-book poet to be published here is through our contest. Send only one copy of each manuscript, and do not send queries. Manuscripts of poetry should be between 50 and 100 pages, typed single-spaced, with no more than one poem per page. All manuscripts must be paginated and contain a table of contents. Illustrations are not accepted. Handwritten manuscripts will not be considered. A cover letter must be included with each submission. Submit a title page with each manuscript that includes the author's name, address, telephone number, e-mail if available, and the manuscript title. Each manuscript should be fastened with a single staple or binder clip. Writers who wish Zoo to acknowledge receipt of their manuscripts must enclose a self-addressed, stamped postcard. Also, a self-addressed, stamped, business-sized envelope must be enclosed in order to receive word about our decision, or an appropriately stamped envelope must be included for return of the entire manuscript, otherwise the manuscript will be discarded." Responds to mss in up to 2 months. Pays royalties of 10%, advance (varies), and 10 author's copies (out of a press run of 1,500-2,000). Order sample books by sending $10 to Zoo Press.

Also Offers: Sponsors The Paris Review Prize in Poetry and The Kenyon Review Prize in Poetry for a First Book (see separate listings in the Contest & Awards section). Also sponsors The Parnassus Prize in Poetry Criticism (contact for details).

Advice: "Please read our books or magazines published by our partners to get a feel for the quality and substance of poetry being published here."

ZUZU'S PETALS QUARTERLY ONLINE, P.O. Box 4853, Ithaca NY 14852. (607)539-1141. E-mail: info@zuzu.com. Website: www.zuzu.com. Established 1992. **Editor:** T. Dunn.

Magazine Needs: "We publish high-quality fiction, essays, poetry, and reviews on our award-winning website, which was featured in *USA Today Online*, *Entertainment Weekly*, *Library Journal*, and *Newsday*. Becoming an Internet publication allows us to offer thousands of helpful resources and addresses for poets, writers, editors, and researchers, as well as to greatly expand our readership. Free verse, blank verse, experimental, visually sensual poetry, etc. are especially welcome here. We're looking for a freshness of language, new ideas, and original expression. No 'June, moon, and spoon' rhymed poetry. No light verse. I'm open to considering more feminist, ethnic, alternative poetry, as well as poetry of place." Has published poetry by Ruth Daigon, Robert Sward, Laurel Bogen, W.T. Pfefferle, and Kate Gale. *Zuzu's Petals* averages 70-100 pages, using full-color artwork, and is an electronic publication available free of charge on the Internet. "Many libraries, colleges, and coffee-houses offer access to the Internet for those without home Internet accounts." Receives about 3,000 poems/year, accepts about 10%. Copies free online, printed sample: $5.

How to Submit: Submit up to 4 poems at a time. Accepts previously published poems and simultaneous submissions. Submissions via e-mail are welcome, as well as submissions in ASCII (DOS IBM) format on 3½″ disks. Include e-mail submissions in the body of the message. "Cover letters are not necessary. The work should speak for itself." Seldom comments on rejected poems. Guidelines available for SASE, by e-mail, in publication, or on website. Responds in up to 2 months. Acquires one-time electronic rights. Staff reviews books of poetry in approximately 200 words. Send material for review consideration.

Also Offers: Publishes digital poetry videos. "Please e-mail for details before sending."

Advice: "Read as much poetry as you can. Go to poetry readings, read books and collections of verse. Eat poetry for breakfast, cultivate a love of language, then write!"

Contests & Awards

This section contains a wide array of poetry competitions and literary awards. These range from state poetry society contests with a number of modest monetary prizes to prestigious honors bestowed by private foundations, elite publishers, and renowned university programs. Because there's such a variety of skill levels and degrees of competitiveness, it's important to read these listings carefully and note the requirements for each. *Never* enter a contest without consulting the guidelines and following directions to the letter (including manuscript formatting, number of lines or pages of poetry accepted, amount of entry fee, entry forms needed, and other details).

WHERE TO ENTER?

While it's perfectly okay to "think big" and aim high, being realistic actually may improve your chances of winning a prize for your poetry. Many of the listings in the Contests & Awards section begin with symbols that reflect their level of difficulty:

Contests ideal for beginners and unpublished poets are coded with the (❑) symbol. That's not to say these contests won't be highly competitive—there may be a very large number of entries. However, you may find these entries are more on a level with your own, increasing your chances of being "in the running" for a prize. Don't assume these contests reward low quality, though. If you submit less than your best work, you're wasting your time and money (in postage and entry fees).

Contests for poets with more experience are coded with the (◑) symbol. Beginner/unpublished poets are usually still welcome to enter, but the competition is keener here. Your work may be judged against that of widely published, prize-winning poets, so consider carefully whether you're ready for this level of competition. (Of course, nothing ventured, nothing gained—but those entry fees *do* add up.)

Contests for accomplished poets are coded with the (●) symbol. These may have stricter entry requirements, higher entry fees, and other conditions that signal these programs are not intended to be "wide open" to all poets.

Specialized contests are coded with the (◉) symbol. These may include regional contests; awards for poetry written in a certain form or in the style of a certain poet; contests for women, gay/lesbian, ethnic, or age-specific poets (for instance, children or older adults); contests for translated poetry only; and many others.

There are also symbols that give additional information about contests. The (N) symbol indicates the contest is newly established and new to this edition; the (✖) symbol indicates this contest did not appear in the 2003 edition; the (✖) symbol identifies a Canadian contest or award and the (⊕) symbol an international listing. Sometimes Canadian and international contests require that entrants live in certain countries, so pay close attention when you see these symbols.

ADDITIONAL CONTESTS & AWARDS

Often magazines and presses prefer to include their contests within their listings in the Publishers of Poetry section. Therefore, we provide a supplement at the end of this section as a cross reference to these opportunities. For details about a contest associated with a market in this list, go to that market's page number.

WHAT ABOUT ENTRY FEES?

Most contests charge entry fees, and these are usually quite legitimate. The funds are used to cover expenses such as paying the judges, putting up prize monies, printing prize editions of magazines and journals, and promoting the contest through mailings and ads. If you're concerned about a poetry contest or other publishing opportunity, see Poet Beware! on page 21 for advice on some of the more questionable practices in the poetry world.

OTHER RESOURCES

Be sure to widen your search for contests beyond those listed in *Poet's Market*. Many Internet writer's sites have late-breaking announcements about competitions old and new (see Websites of Interest on page 509). Often these sites offer free electronic newsletter subscriptions, so sign up! Information will come right to you via your e-mail inbox.

The writer's magazines at your local bookstore regularly include listings for upcoming contests, as well as deadlines for artist's grants at the state and national level. (See Publications of Interest on page 504 for a few suggestions; also, State & Provincial Grants on page 460.) Associated Writing Programs (AWP) is a valuable resource, including its publication, *Writer's Chronicle*. (See Organizations, page 485.) State poetry societies are listed throughout this book; they offer many contests as well as helpful information for poets (and mutual support). To find a specific group, search the General Index for listings under your state's name or look under "society"; also consult the Geographical Index on page 530.

Finally, don't overlook your local connections. City and community newspapers, radio and TV announcements, bookstore newsletters and bulletin boards, and your public library can be terrific resources for competition news, especially regional contests.

N **$** **MARIE M. ANDERSON POETRY AWARD**, P.O. Box 16368, Encino CA 91416-6368. Established 2003. **Award Director:** Amber N. Husted. Offers annual award of 1st Prize: $100; other prizes to be determined. For US residents only. Submissions must be unpublished and may be entered in other contests. Submit up to 2 poems; "we are open to all styles, from free form to traditional." Poems should be double-spaced, with name and address on each page; cover sheet preferred. Accepts submissions by regular mail only. No entry fee. **Deadline:** May 15. 2004 judges will be Amber N. Husted and Candis T. Smock. Winners will be announced by June 15; include SASE with entry for announcement by return mail. "We have founded this award in order to promote and acknowledge the works of beginning and established poets."

ARIZONA LITERARY & BOOK AWARDS, Arizona Authors Association, P.O. Box 87857, Phoenix AZ 85080-7857. (602)769-2066. Fax: (623)780-0468. E-mail: contest@azauthors.com. Website: www.azauthors.com. **Contact:** Vijaya Schartz, president. Arizona Authors Association sponsors annual literary contest in poetry, short story, essay, unpublished novels, and published books (fiction and nonfiction). Awards publication in *Arizona Literary Magazine*, radio interview, publication of novel by 1stbooks.com in e-book and print-on-demand, and $100 1st Prize in each category. Pays winners from other countries by International Money Order. Does not accept entry fees in foreign currencies. Poetry submissions must be unpublished and may be entered in other contests. Submit any number of poems on any subject up to 42 lines. Entry form and guidelines available for SASE. **Entry fee:** $10/poem. **Submission period:** January 1 through July 1. Competition receives 1,000 entries/year. Recent poetry winners include Ellaraine Lockie, Lynn Veach Sadler, and Betty Brownlow. Judges are Arizona authors, editors, reviewers, and readers. Winners will be announced at an award banquet in Phoenix by November 15. (For further information about Arizona Authors Association, see listing in Organizations section.)

$ **ARIZONA STATE POETRY SOCIETY ANNUAL CONTEST; THE SANDCUTTERS**, 7041 W. Cavalier Dr., Glendale AZ 85303. Website www.azpoetry.org/. **Contact:** Kristen A. Kerrick. **ASPS President:** Dorothy Zahner. Offers a variety of cash prizes in several categories ranging from $10-125; 1st, 2nd, and 3rd place winners are published in *The Sancutter*, ASPS's quarterly publication, which also lists names of Honorable Mention winners. See guidelines for detailed submission information (available for SASE or on website). **Entry fee:** varies according to category; see guidelines. **Postmark Deadline:** August 31. Competition receives over 1,000 entries/year. Membership information available from George Gilcrease, Membership Chair, 4726 W. Rosewood Drive, Glendale AZ 85304. "ASPS sponsors a variety of monthly contests for members. Membership is available to anyone anywhere."

◻ ARKANSAS POETRY DAY CONTEST; POETS' ROUNDTABLE OF ARKANSAS, 605 Higdon, Apt. 109, Hot Springs AR 71913. (501)321-4226. E-mail: vernalee@lpt.net. **Contact:** Verna Lee Hinegardner. Over 25 categories, many open to all poets. Brochure available in June; deadline in September; awards given in October. Guidelines available for SASE.

◼ $◻ ART COOPERATIVE FELLOWSHIP IN POETRY, 1124 Columbia NE, Albuquerque NM 87106. E-mail: art_coop@yahoo.com. Website: www.geocities.com/art_coop. Established 1996. **Contact:** Editor-in-Chief. Offers annual fellowship in poetry. Open to poets everywhere. Awards cash prize (not less than $250) and publication. Pays winners from other countries by cashier's check. Include cover sheet, bio, and list of publications. Guidelines and information available for SASE, by e-mail, or on website. Entry fee: $15 for up to 3 poems, $2 each thereafter. Does not accept entry fees in foreign currencies. "For flat $15 fee and SASE, feedback on poems provided." **Postmark Deadline:** by December 1 annually. Competition received 20 entries last year.

◼ $◿ "ART IN THE AIR" POETRY CONTEST, Inventing the Invisible/"Art in the Air" Radio Show, 3128 Walton Blvd., PMB 186, Rochester Hills MI 48309. Fax: (248)693-7344. E-mail: lagapvp@aol.com. Website: www.inventingtheinvisible.com. Established 1991. **Award Director:** Margo LaGattuta. Offers biannual award of 1st Prize: $100; 2nd Prize: $50; and 4 Honorable Mentions. Pays winners from other countries by check. ("All winners read poems on the radio.") Submissions may be previously published and may be entered in other contests. Submit 3 poems maximum in any form, typed, single-spaced, limit 2 pages per poem. Guidelines available for SASE or on website. Accepts inquiries by fax or e-mail. **Entry fee:** $5 for up to 3 poems. Accepts entry fees in US currency only. **Deadlines:** October 30 and April 30. Competition receives over 600 entries/year. Past contest winners include Simone Muench, Marilyn Krysi, Julie Moulds, Elizabeth Rosner, Bill Rudolph, Jenny Brown, and Wyatt Townley. Past judges include Mary Jo Firth Gillett and Margo LaGattuta. Winners will be announced 2 months after deadline. Copies of winning poems or books may be obtained by sending a SASE to the Inventing the Invisible address. "'Art in the Air' is an interview radio show on WPON, 1460 AM, in Bloomfield Hills, MI, hosted by Margo LaGattuta and may be heard on the website Fridays at 1:00 pm EST. The theme is creativity and the creative process, especially featuring writers both local and national. Send only your best work—well crafted and creative. Judges look for excellence in content and execution."

$◻ ◉ ARTIST TRUST; ARTIST TRUST GAP GRANTS; ARTIST TRUST/WSAC FELLOWSHIPS (Specialized: regional/WA), 1835 12th Ave., Seattle WA 98122. (206)467-8734. Fax: (206)467-9633. E-mail: info@artisttrust.org. Website: www.artisttrust.org. **Program Director:** Susan Myers. Artist Trust is a nonprofit arts organization that provides grants to artists (including poets) who are residents of the state. Accepts inquiries by mail, fax, and e-mail. **Deadline:** varies each year. Each competition receives 350-600 entries/year. Contest winners include Esperanza Feria, Kathleen Flenniken, T. Louise Freeman-Toole, Dennis Held, Eryn Huntington, Jeffrey Klausman, Tod Marshal, Sati Mookherjee, Emily Pitkin, Steve Wing, and Eileen Yoshina. Also publishes, 3 times/year, a journal of news about arts opportunities and cultural issues.

THE ATLAS FUND, The Academy of American Poets, 588 Broadway, Suite 604, New York NY 10012-3210. (212)274-0343. Fax: (212)274-9427. E-mail: academy@poets.org. Website: www.poets. org. Established 1934. **Executive Director:** Tree Swenson. The Atlas Fund assists noncommercial publishers of poetry. Since its inception, the Atlas Fund has supported the publication of more than 50 books of poetry. Guidelines available for SASE or on website. (For further information about The Academy of American Poets, see separate listing in the Organizations section.)

$ ⬚ THE BACKWATERS PRIZE, The Backwaters Press, 3502 N. 52nd St., Omaha NE 68104-3506. (402)451-4052. E-mail: gkosm62735@aol.com. Website: www.thebackwaterspress.homestead. com. Established 1998. **Contest Director:** Greg Kosmicki. Offers annual prize of $1,000 plus publication, promotion, and distribution. "Submissions may be entered in other contests and this should be noted in cover letter. Backwaters Press must be notified if manuscripts are accepted for publication at other presses." Submit up to 80 pages on any subject, any form. "Poems must be written in English. No collaborative work accepted. Parts of the manuscript may be previously published in magazines or chapbooks, but entire manuscript may not have been previously published." Manuscript should be typed (or word processed) in standard poetry format—single-spaced, one poem per page, one side only. Guidelines available for SASE, by e-mail, or on website. **Entry fee:** $25. Does not accept entry fees in foreign currencies. Send postal money order or personal check in US dollars. **Deadline:** postmarked by June 4. Competition receives 350-400 entries/year. Most recent contest winner was Susan Fiver (2001). Judges have included CarolAnn Russell (2001) and Hilda Raz (2002). Winner will be announced in AWP *Chronicle* ad and in *Poets & Writer's* "Recent Winners." Copies of winning books available through The Backwaters Press or Amazon.com. "The Backwaters Press is a nonprofit press dedicated to publishing the best new literature we can find. Send your best work."

◎ BAY AREA BOOK REVIEWERS ASSOCIATION AWARDS (BABRA); FRED CODY AWARD (Specialized: regional/Northern California), 1450 Fourth St., #4, Berkeley CA 94710. (510)525-5476. Fax: (510)525-6752. Website: www.poetryflash.org. Established 1981. **Executive Director:** Joyce Jenkins. Offers annual awards to recognize "the best of Northern California (from Fresno north) fiction, poetry, nonfiction, and children's literature." Submissions must be books published in the calendar year. Submit 3 copies of each book entered. The authors of the submitted books must live in Northern California. Guidelines available for SASE or on website. **Deadline:** December 1. Most recent poetry nominees were George Evans, Barbara Guest, Juan Felipe Herrera, Joanne Kyger, and Jack Marshall. BABRA also sponsors the Fred Cody Award for lifetime achievement given to a Northern California writer who also serves the community. Also gives, on an irregular basis, awards for outstanding work in translation and publishing. In 2003 the Cody Award was presented to Ronald Takaki. **Note:** *The Fred Cody Award does not accept applications.*

$ ◉ GEORGE BENNETT FELLOWSHIP, Phillips Exeter Academy, 20 Main St., Exeter NH 03833-2460. Website: www.exeter.edu. Established 1968. **Selection Committee Coordinator:** Charles Pratt. Provides an annual $10,000 fellowship plus residency (room and board) to a writer with a ms in progress. The Fellow's only official duties are to be in residence while the academy is in session and to be available to students interested in writing. The committee favors writers who have not yet published a book-length work with a major publisher. Application materials and guidelines available for SASE or on website. **Entry fee:** $5. Does not accept entry fees in foreign currencies; accepts cash, money order, or check in US dollars. **Deadline:** December 1. Competition receives 190 entries. Recent award winners were Laura Moriarty (2000-2001), Anne Campisi (2001-2002), and Maggie Dietz (2002-2003). Winners will be announced by mail. "Please, no telephone calls or e-mail inquiries."

$ ◎ BEST OF OHIO WRITERS WRITING CONTEST (Specialized: regional/Ohio residents), P.O. Box 91801, Cleveland OH 44101. (216)421-0403. E-mail: PWLGC@msn.com. Offers annual contest for poetry, fiction, creative nonfiction, and "Writers on Writing" (any genre). 1st Prize: $150, 2nd Prize: $50, plus publication for first-place winner of each category in a special edition of *Ohio Writer*. Submit up to 3 typed poems, no more than 2 pages each, unpublished mss only. Open only to Ohio residents. "Entries will be judged anonymously, so please do not put name or other identification on manuscript. Attach entry form (or facsimile) to submission. Manuscripts will not be returned." Include SASE for list of winners. Entry form and guidelines available for SASE or by e-mail. **Entry fee:** $15/first entry in each category (includes 1-year subscription or renewal to *Ohio Writer*); $2 for each additional entry in same category (limit 3/category). **Deadline:** July 31. Judges have included Larry Smith, Richard Hague, Ron Antonucci, and Sheila Schwartz. Winners announced in the November/December issue of *Ohio Writer*.

N ◎ BINGHAMTOM UNIVERSITY MILT KESSLER POETRY BOOK AWARD (Specialized: poets over 40), Binghamton University Creative Writing Program, P.O. Box 6000, Binghamton NY 13865. (607)777-2713. Fax: (607)777-2408. E-mail: cwpro@binghamton.edu. Website: http://english.binghamton.edu/cwpro/. Established 2001. **Award Director:** Maria Mazziotti Gillan. Offers annual award of $1,000 and a reading at the university for a book of poetry judged best of those published that year by a poet over the age of 40. "Submit books published that year; do not submit manuscripts." Entry form and guidelines available for SASE, by e-mail, or on website. **Entry fee:** None; "just submit three copies of book." **Deadline:** March 1. Competition receives 500 books/year. Most recent winner was Lilla Lyons (2002). 2002 judge was Dorianne Laux. Winner will be announced in June in *Poets & Writers* and on website, or by SASE if provided. (NOTE: Not to be confused with the Milton Kessler Memorial Prize for Poetry; see listing for *Harpur Palate* in the Publishers of Poetry section.)

$ ◪ BLUESTEM PRESS AWARD, Emporia State University, English Dept., Box 4019, Emporia KS 66801-5087. (620)341-5216. Fax: (620)341-5547. Website: www.emporia.edu/bluestem/index.htm. Established 1989. **Director:** Philip Heldrich. Offers annual award of $1,000 and publication for an original book-length collection of poems. Submissions must be unpublished and may be entered in other contests (with notification). Submit a typed ms of at least 48 pages on any subject in any form with a #10 SASE for notification. Guidelines and information available for SASE. **Entry fee:** $18. Does not accept entry fees in foreign currencies; send US check or money order. **Deadline:** March 1. Competition receives 500-700 entries/year. Most recent award winner was Elizabeth Tibbetts. Judge was Elizabeth Dodd. Winner will be announced in summer by SASE to participants, online, and in the trade media. Copies of winning poems or books available from the Bluestem Press at the above number. "Enter early to avoid missing the deadline; manuscripts will *not* be accepted after the deadline and will not be returned. Also, looking at the different winners from past years would help."

⊕ $ ◎ THE BOARDMAN TASKER AWARD (Specialized: mountain literature), The Boardman Tasker Charitable Trust. Phone/fax: 44 01792 386215. E-mail: margaretbody@lineone.net. Established 1983. **Contact:** Margaret Body (Pound House, Llangennith, Swansea, West Glamorgan SA3 1JQ Wales). Offers prize of £2,000 to "the author or authors of the best literary work, whether fiction, nonfiction, drama, or poetry, the central theme of which is concerned with the mountain environment. Entries for consideration may have been written by authors of any nationality but the work must be published or distributed in the United Kingdom between November 1 and October 31. (If not published in the U.K., please indicate name of distributor.) The work must be written or have been translated into the English language." Submit ms in book format. "In a collection of essays or articles by a single author, the inclusion of some material previously published but now in book form for the first time will be acceptable." *Submissions accepted from the publisher only.* Four copies of entry must be submitted with application. Accepts inquiries by fax or e-mail. **Deadline:** August 1. Competition receives about 25 entries. Most recent winner was *Fatal Mountaineer* by Robert Rober, published by St. Martin's Press.

◣ $ ◎ BP NICHOL CHAPBOOK AWARD (Specialized: regional/Canada), 316 Dupont St., Toronto ON M5R 1V9 Canada. (416)964-7919. Fax: (416)964-6941. Established 1985. Offers $1,000 (Canadian) prize for the best poetry chapbook (10-48 pages) in English published in Canada. Submit 3 copies (not returnable) and a brief curriculum vitae of the author. Accepts inquiries by fax. **Deadline:** March 31. Competition receives between 40-60 entries on average.

⊕ $□ THE BRIDPORT PRIZE; INTERNATIONAL CREATIVE WRITING COMPETITION, Bridport Arts Centre, South St., Bridport, Dorset DT6 3NR United Kingdom. Phone: (01308) 459444. E-mail: info@bridport-arts.com. Website: www.bridportprize.org.uk. Established 1980. **Contact:** Frances Everitt, competition secretary. Offers annual award for an original poem of not more than 42 lines and an original story of not more than 5,000 words. 1st Prize: £3,000, 2nd Prize: £1,500, and 3rd Prize: £500 in each category plus small supplementary prize. Prize-winning entries also published in anthology. Submissions must be previously unpublished and not submitted to any other competition. Open as to subject or form. Use online submission form to enter or submit by regular mail. Entry form and guidelines available on website. **Entry fee:** £6 sterling/

entry. Accepts foreign entry fees by VISA, Mastercard. **Deadline:** June 30 of each year. Competition receives approximately 8,000 entries. 2002 poetry winner was Christopher James. 2003 poetry judge was U A Fanthorpe. Winners will be announced at the end of November. Copies of winning anthologies available by sending £14.50 sterling to Competition Secretary at the above address (VISA and Mastercard also accepted).

■ $⌀ BRIGHT HILL PRESS POETRY BOOK AWARD, P.O. Box 193, 94 Church St., Treadwell NY 13846-0193. (607)829-5055. Fax: (607)829-5056. E-mail: wordthur@catskill.net. Website: www.brighthillpress.org. Established 1992. **Award Director:** Bertha Rogers. Offers annual award of $1,000 and publication for a poetry ms of 48-64 pages. Prize includes 25 author's copies (out of a press run of 600) and a reading at the Word Thursdays reading series. Pays winners from other countries by certified check or International Money Order. Submissions may be entered in other contests. Submit ms of 48-64 pages, paginated (includes bio, contents, acknowledgments, two title pages—one with name, address, and phone number, one with title of manuscript only) and secured with bulldog clip. Include SASE for results only; mss not returned. Guidelines available for SASE or by e-mail. **Entry fee:** $20. Does not accept entry fees in foreign currencies; US International Money Order only. **Postmark deadline:** November 30. Competition receives over 300 entries/year. Past winners include Richard Deutch (2000). Past judges have included Colette Inez, Michael Waters, Richard Foerster, Carol Frost, and Maurice Kenny. Winners will be announced in summer of the year following the contest. Copies of winning books available for $12 plus $3.05 postage from BHP Sample Books at the address above. "Publish your poems in literary magazines before trying to get a whole manuscript published. Publishing individual poems is the best way to hone your complete manuscript." (For further information about Bright Hill Press activities, see listing in Publishers of Poetry section.)

■ $⌀ BRIGHT HILL PRESS POETRY CHAPBOOK AWARD, P.O. Box 193, 94 Church St., Treadwell NY 13846-0193. (607)829-5055. Fax: (607)829-5056. E-mail: wordthur@catskill.net. Website: www.brighthillpress.org. Established 1992. **Award Director:** Bertha Rogers. Offers annual award of $250 and publication for a poetry ms of 16-24 pages. Prize includes 25 author's copies. Pays winners from other countries by certified check or International Money Order. Submissions may be entered in other contests. Submit ms of 16-24 pages, paginated (includes bio, contents, acknowledgments, two title pages—one with name, address, and phone number, one with title of manuscript only) and secured with bulldog clip. Include SASE for results only; mss not returned. Guidelines available for SASE or by e-mail. **Entry fee:** $10. Does not accept entry fees in foreign currencies; US International Money Order only. **Postmark deadline:** July 31. Competition receives over 300 entries/year. Recent winners include Barry Ballard (2001) and Matthew J. Spireng (2000). Winners will be announced in summer of the year following the contest. Copies of winning chapbook available for $6 plus $2.50 postage from BHP Sample Books at the address above. "Publish your poems in literary magazines before trying to get a whole manuscript published. Publishing individual poems is the best way to hone your complete manuscript." (For further information about Bright Hill Press activities, see listing in Publishers of Poetry section.)

■ $◎ CALIFORNIA BOOK AWARDS OF THE COMMONWEALTH CLUB OF CALIFORNIA (Specialized: regional), 595 Market St., San Francisco CA 94105. (415)597-6700. Fax: (415)597-6729. E-mail: cwc@sirius.com. Website: www.commonwealthclub.org. Established 1931. **Contact:** Barbara Lane, director. Annual awards "consisting of not more than two gold and eight silver medals" plus $2,000 cash prize to gold medal winners and $300 to silver medal winners. For books of "exceptional literary merit" in poetry, fiction, and nonfiction (including work related to California and work for children), plus 2 "outstanding" categories. Submissions must be previously published. Submit at least 3 copies of each book entered with an official entry form. (Books may be submitted by author or publisher.) Open to books, published during the year prior to the contest, whose author "must have been a legal resident of California at the time the manuscript was submitted for publication." Entry form and guidelines available for SASE or on website. **Deadline:** December 31. Competition receives approximately 50 poetry entries/year. Most recent award winners were Czeslaw Milosz and Carolyn Kizer.

⧈ $ ◎ ◿ CANADIAN AUTHORS ASSOCIATION AWARDS FOR ADULT LITERA-TURE (Specialized: regional); CCA JACK CHALMERS POETRY AWARD; CANADIAN AUTHORS ASSOCIATION, Box 419, Campbellford ON K0L 1L0 Canada. (705)653-0323. Fax: (705)653-0593. E-mail: canauth@redden.on.ca. Website: www.CanAuthors.org. **Administrator:** Alec McEachern. The CAA Awards for Adult Literature offers $2,500 and a silver medal in each of 5 categories (fiction, poetry, short stories, Canadian history, Canadian biography) to Canadian writers, for a book published during the year. The CCA Jack Chalmers Poetry Award is given for a volume of poetry by one poet. **Entry fee:** $20/title. **Deadline:** December 15; except for works published after December 1, in which case the postmark deadline is January 15. Competition receives 300 entries/ year. Most recent poetry award winners were Lynn Coady (2001) and Tim Bowling (2002). All awards are given at the CAA Awards Banquet at the annual conference.

$ ◎ CAVE CANEM POETRY PRIZE (Specialized: ethnic/African American); CAVE CANEM FOUNDATION, INC., 39 Jane St. GB, New York NY 10014. Fax: (434)977-8106. E-mail: cavecanempoets@aol.com. Website: www.cavecanempoets.org. Award established 1999; organization 1996. **Award Director:** Carolyn Micklem, Cave Canem director. Offers "annual first book award dedicated to presenting the work of African American poets who have not been published by a professional press. The winner will receive $500 cash, publication, and 50 copies of the book." **US poets only.** "Send two copies of manuscript of 50-75 pages. The author's name should not appear on the manuscript. Two title pages should be attached to each copy. The first must include the poet's name, address, telephone, and the title of the manuscript; the second should list the title only. Number the pages. Manuscripts will not be returned, but a SASE postcard can be included for notice of manuscript receipt. Simultaneous submissions should be noted. If the manuscript is accepted for publication elsewhere during the judging, immediate notification is requested." Guidelines available for SASE or on website. There is no entry fee. **Deadline:** May 15 of each year. Send ms to Cave Canem, P.O. Box 4286, Charlottesville, VA 22905-4286. Received 125 entries in 2002. Most recent award winners were Tracy K. Smith (2002), Lyrae Van Clief-Stefanan (2001), and Major Jackson (2000). Most recent judges were Quincy Troupe (2003), Kevin Young (2002), and Marilyn Nelson (2001). Winners will be announced by press release in October of year of contest. Copies of winning books are available from "any bookseller, because the publishers are Graywolf Press ('99 and '02), University of Georgia ('00 and '03), and University of Pittsburgh ('01 and '04). Cave Canem sponsors a week-long workshop/retreat each summer and regional workshops in New York City and Minnesota. (See Cave Canem listing in Conferences & Workshops section.) It sponsors readings in cities in various parts of the country. The winner of the Prize and the judge are featured in an annual reading." Recommends "since this is a highly competitive contest, you should be at a stage in your development where some of your poems have already been published in literary journals. Manuscripts not adhering to guidelines will not be forwarded to judge nor returned to applicant."

$ ◿ THE CENTER FOR BOOK ARTS' ANNUAL POETRY CHAPBOOK COMPETITION, 28 W. 27th St., 3rd Floor, New York NY 10001. (212)481-0295. E-mail: info@centerforbookarts.org. Website: www.centerforbookarts.org/. Established 1995. **Executive Director:** Rory Golden. Offers $500 cash prize, a $500 reading honorarium, and publication of winning manuscript in a limited edition letterpress-printed and handbound chapbook. Pays winners from other countries in US dollars. Submissions may be previously published and entered in other contests. Submit no more than 500 lines or 24 pages on any subject, in any form; collection or sequence of poems or a single long poem. Entry form and guidelines available for SASE, by e-mail, or on website. **Entry fee:** $15/ ms (fee will be credited toward the purchase of the winning chapbook). Does not accept entry fees in foreign currencies; accepts US check, cash, or VISA/MasterCard number. **Postmark deadline:** December 1. Competition receives 500-1,000 entries/year. Most recent contest winner was Jack Ridl. 2004 judges will be C.K. Williams and Sharon Dolin. Winner will be contacted in April by telephone. Each contestant receives a letter announcing the winner. Copies of winning chapbooks available for $25. Make checks payable to The Center for Book Arts. "Center for Book Arts is a nonprofit organization dedicated to the traditional crafts of bookmaking and contemporary interpretations of the book as an art object. Through the Center's Education, Exhibition, and Workspace Programs we ensure that the ancient craft of the book remains a viable and vital part of our civilization."

$ ▣ ◎ CHICANO/LATINO LITERARY PRIZE (Specialized: bilingual/English, Spanish), Dept. of Spanish & Portuguese, 322 Humanities Hall, University of California at Irvine, Irvine CA 92697-5275. E-mail: cllp@uci.edu. Website: www.humanities.uci.edu/spanishandportuguese/contest.html. Established 1974. **CLLP Director:** Prof. Juan Bruce-Novoa. **Contact:** Prize Coordinator. Annual contest focusing on 1 of 4 genres each year: novel (2003), short story (2004), poetry (2005), and drama (2006). 1st Prize: $1,000, publication of work if not under previous contract, and transportation to Irvine to receive the award; 2nd Prize: $500; 3rd Prize: $250. Work may be in English or Spanish. Only one entry/author. Open to US citizens or permanent residents of the US. Guidelines available for SASE, by e-mail, or on website. **Deadline:** June 1. Winners will be notified in October.

$ ▢ CNW/FFWA FLORIDA STATE WRITING COMPETITION, Florida Freelance Writers Association, P.O. Box A, North Stratford NH 03590-0167. (603)922-8338. E-mail: contest@writers-editors.com. Website: www.writers-editors.com. Established 1978. **Award Director:** Dana K. Cassell. Offers annual awards for nonfiction, fiction, children's literature, and poetry. Awards for each category are: 1st Prize: $100 plus certificate, 2nd Prize: $75 plus certificate, 3rd Prize: $50 plus certificate, plus Honorable Mention certificates. Submissions must be unpublished. Submit any number of poems on any subject in traditional forms, free verse, or children's. Entry form and guidelines available for SASE or on website. Accepts inquiries by e-mail. **Entry fee:** $3/poem (members), $5/poem (nonmembers). **Deadline:** March 15. Competition receives 350-400 entries/year. Competition is judged by writers, librarians, and teachers. Winners will be announced on May 31 by mail and on website.

$ ▢ DANA AWARD IN POETRY, 7207 Townsend Forest Ct., Browns Summit NC 27214. (336)656-7009. E-mail: danaawards@pipeline.com (for emergency questions only). Website: www.danaawards.com. Established 1996. **Award Chair:** Mary Elizabeth Parker. Offers annual award of $1,000 for the best group of 5 poems. Pays winners from other countries by check in US dollars. Submissions must be unpublished and not under promise of publication when submitted; may be simultaneously submitted elsewhere. Submit 5 poems on any subject, in any form; no light verse. Entries by regular mail only. Include SASE for winners list. No mss will be returned. Include separate cover sheet with name, address, phone, e-mail address, and titles of poems. Guidelines available for SASE, by e-mail, or on website. **Entry fee:** $15/5 poems. Does not accept entry fees in foreign currencies; accepts bank draft, International Money Order, or check in US dollars only, drawn on US bank. No personal checks written on foreign banks. **Postmark deadline:** October 31. Competition receives 400-500 poetry entries. Recent judges were Enid Shomer and Michael White. Winner will be announced in early spring by phone, letter, and e-mail.

$ ▢ DANCING POETRY CONTEST; DANCING POETRY FESTIVAL, Artists Embassy International, 704 Brigham Ave., Santa Rosa CA 95404-5245. (707)528-0912. E-mail: jhcheung@aol.com. Website: www.DANCINGPOETRY.com. Established 1993. **Contest Chair:** Judy Cheung. Annual contest offers three Grand Prizes of $100, five 1st Prizes of $50, 10 2nd Prizes of $25, 20 3rd Prizes of $10. The 3 Grand Prize-winning poems will be choreographed, costumed, premiered, and videotaped at the annual Dancing Poetry Festival at Palace of the Legion of Honor, San Francisco; Natica Angilly's Poetic Dance Theater Company will perform the 3 Grand Prize-winning poems. In addition, "all prizes include an invitation to read your prize poem at the festival and a certificate suitable for framing." Pays winners from other countries by International Money Order with US value at the time of the transaction. Submissions must be unpublished or poet must own rights. Submit 2 copies of any number of poems, 40 lines maximum (each), with name, address, phone number on one copy only. Foreign language poems must include English translations. Include SASE for winners list. Entry form available for SASE. No inquiries or entries by fax or e-mail. **Entry fee:** $5/poem or $10/3 poems. Does not accept entry fees in foreign currencies; send International Money Order in US dollars. **Deadline:** June 15. Competition receives about 500-800 entries. 2002 Grand Prize winners were Gretchen Fletcher, Laverne Frith, and John Rowe. Most recent contest winners include Raynette Eitel, Bonnie Nish, and Hope Vilsick-Greenwell. Judges for upcoming contest will be members of Artists Embassy International. Winners will be announced by mail; Grand Prize winners will be contacted by phone. Ticket to festival will be given to all winners. Artist Embassy International has been a nonprofit educational arts organization since 1951, "Furthering intercultural understanding and peace through the universal language of the arts."

🌐 $⬜ **THE DAVID ST. JOHN THOMAS CHARITABLE TRUST COMPETITIONS & AWARDS**, The David St. John Thomas Charitable Trust, P.O. Box 6055, Nairn IV12 4YB Scotland. Phone: (01667) 453351. Established 1990. **Contact:** Lorna Edwardson (Competition & Awards Manager). "We run what we believe is the largest single program of writing competitions and awards in the English-speaking world, with prizes totalling £20,000-30,000. There are some regulars, such as the annual ghost story and love story competitions (each 1,600-1800 words with £1,000 first prize) and open poetry competition (poems up to 32 lines, total prize money £1,200). Publication of winning entries is guaranteed, usually in *Writers' News/Writing Magazine* and/or annual anthology. Awards are led by the annual Self-Publishing Awards, open to anyone who has self-published a book during the preceding calendar year. There are four categories, each with £250 prize; the overall winner is declared Self-Publisher of the Year with a total award of £1,000 (established 1993). For full details of these and many others, including an annual writers' groups anthology and Letter-Writer of the Year, please send large SAE."

🆕 😊 **DREAM HORSE PRESS NATIONAL POETRY CHAPBOOK PRIZE**, P.O. Box 640746, San Jose CA 95164-0746. E-mail: dreamhorsepress@yahoo.com. Website: www.dreamhorse press.com. Established 1999. Offers annual award of a cash prize and multiple copies of a handsomely printed chapbook (amounts change yearly, check website for current information). Submissions may be previously published in magazines/journals but not in books or chapbooks. May be entered in other contests with notification. "Submit 16-24 paginated pages of poetry in a readable font with acknowledgments, bio, SASE for results, and entry fee." Multiple submissions acceptable (with separate fee for each entry). Poet's name should not appear anywhere on ms. All mss will be recycled. **Entry fee:** changes annually; check website. Fees accepted by check or money order. **Deadline:** check website; 2002 deadline was August 31. Most recent winner was Ryan G. Van Cleave for *The Florida Letters* (2001). Copies of winning chapbooks available from Dream Horse Press and Amazon.com.

🌐 $🖉 **T.S. ELIOT PRIZE (Specialized: regional/UK, Ireland)**, The Poetry Book Society, Book House, 45 East Hill, London SW18 20Z United Kingdom. Phone: (020)8874 6361. Fax: (020)8870 0865. E-mail: info@poetrybooks.co.uk. Website: www.poetrybooks.co.uk. Established 1993. **Award Director:** Clare Brown. Offers annual award for the best poetry collection published in the UK/Republic of Ireland each year. Prize: £10,000 (donated by Mrs. Valerie Eliot). Pays winners from other countries through publisher. Submissions must be previously published and may be entered in other contests. **Book/ms must be submitted by publisher** and have been published (or scheduled to be published) the year of the contest. Entry form and guidelines available for SASE or by fax or e-mail. Accepts inquiries by fax and e-mail. **Deadline:** early August. Competition receives 100 entries/year. Most recent contest winner was Anne Carson. Recent judges include Michael Longley, Fred D'Aguiav, and Deryn Rees-Jones. Winner will be announced in January.

$🖉 **T.S. ELIOT PRIZE FOR POETRY; TRUMAN STATE UNIVERSITY PRESS**, 100 E. Normal, Kirksville MO 63501-4221. (660)785-7199. Fax: (660)785-4480. E-mail: tsup@truman.edu. Website: http://tsup.truman.edu. Press established 1986. **Director:** Paula Presley. Offers annual award of $2,000, publication, and 10 copies as first prize. Submit 60-100 pages, include 2 title pages, 1 with name, address, phone, and ms title; the other with only the title. Individual poems may have been previously published in periodicals or anthologies, but the collection must not have been published as a book. Include SASE if you wish acknowledgement of receipt of your ms. Manuscripts will not be returned. Guidelines available for SASE or on website. Accepts inquiries by fax and e-mail. **Entry fee:** $25. **Deadline:** October 31. Competition receives 500 entries/year. Recent contest winners were James Gurley (2002), Christopher Bakken (2001), and H.L. Hix (2000).

⬤ ◎ **EMERGING VOICES (Specialized: writers from minority, immigrant, and under-served communities)**, PEN USA, 672 S. Lafayette Park Place, Suite 42, Los Angeles CA 90057. (213)365-8500. Fax: (213)365-9616. E-mail: ev@penusa.org. Website: www.penusa.org. **Contact:** Literary Programs Coordinator. Annual program offering $1,000 stipend and 8-month fellowship to writers in the early stages of their literary careers. Program includes one-on-one sessions with mentors, seminars on topics such as editing or working with agents, courses in the Writers' Program at UCLA Extension, and literary readings. Participants selected according to potential, experience, and goals. No age restrictions; selection is *not* based solely on economic need. Participants need not be published, but "the program is directed toward poets and writers of fiction and creative nonfiction with clear ideas of what they hope to accomplish through their writing. Mentors are chosen from PEN's comprehensive membership of professional writers and beyond. Participants are paired with established writers sharing similar writing interests and often with those of the same ethnic and cultural backgrounds." Program gets underway in January. **Deadline:** September 5, 2003 (for 2004 cycle). "All materials must arrive in the PEN offices by the submission deadline—no exceptions." See website for brochure and complete guidelines.

$⬤ **THE WILLIAM FAULKNER CREATIVE WRITING COMPETITION; MARBLE FAUN PRIZE FOR POETRY; THE DOUBLE DEALER REDUX**, The Pirate's Alley Faulkner Society, Inc., 632 Pirate's Alley, New Orleans LA 70116. (504)586-1609 or (504)529-3450. E-mail: faulkhouse@aol.com. Website: www.wordsandmusic.org. Established 1992. **Award Director:** Rosemary James. Offers annual publication in *The Double Dealer Redux*, cash prize of $750, gold medal, and trip to New Orleans from any continental US city. "Foreign nationals are eligible but the society pays transportation to awards ceremony from US cities only. Winners must be present at annual meeting to receive award." Submissions must be unpublished. Submit 1 poem of no more than 750 words on any subject in any English language form. Entry form (required) and guidelines available for SASE and on website. Accepts inquiries by e-mail. **Entry fee:** $25/entry. **Deadline:** April 30. Competition receives 1,000 (for 5 categories) entries/year. Most recent contest winner was John Cantney Knight (2002). Winners will be announced on the society's website. "Do not send us multiple poems and expect us to select one. The entry is a single poem. Competition is keen. Send your best work."

⬤ **THE FELLOWSHIP OF THE ACADEMY OF AMERICAN POETS**, The Academy of American Poets, 588 Broadway, Suite 604, New York NY 10012-3210. (212)274-0343. Fax: (212)274-9427. E-mail: academy@poets.org. Website: www.poets.org. Established 1934. **Executive Director:** Tree Swenson. **Awards Coordinator:** Ryan Murphy. The Fellowship of the Academy of American Poets awards $35,000 to a distinguished American poet at mid-career. **No applications are accepted.** 2001 winner was Ellen Bryan Voigt. (For further information about The Academy of American Poets, see separate listing in the Organizations section.)

$⬤ **THE ROBERT FROST FOUNDATION ANNUAL POETRY AWARD**, The Robert Frost Foundation, Heritage Place, 439 S. Union St., Lawrence MA 01843. (978)725-8828. E-mail: mejaneiro@aol.com. Website: www.frostfoundation.org. Established 1997. **Award Director:** Mary Ellen Janeiro. Offers annual award of $1,000. Pays winners from other countries in dollars (US). Submissions may be entered in other contests. Submit up to 3 poems of not more than 3 pages each, written in the spirit of Robert Frost. Guidelines available for SASE and on website. **Entry fee:** $10/poem. Does not accept entry fees in foreign currencies. **Deadline:** September 1 of each year. Competition receives over 200 entries/year. 2002 winner was Deborah Warren. Winners will be announced at the annual Frost Festival and by SASE following the Festival (late October). Winning poem can be viewed on website.

✽ ◯ ◎ **JOHN GLASSCO TRANSLATION PRIZE (Specialized: translation, regional/Canadian)**, Literary Translators' Association of Canada, Université Concordia, SB 335, 1455, boul.

de Maisonneuve Ouest, Montreal QC H3G 1M8 Canada. (514)848-8702. Fax: (514)848-4514. E-mail: ltac@alcor.concordia.ca. Website: www.geocities.com/Athens/Oracle/9070. **Contact:** Kathleen Merken, membership secretary. $1,000 awarded annually for a translator's first book-length literary translation into French or English, published in Canada during the previous calendar year. The translator must be a Canadian citizen or landed immigrant. Eligible genres include fiction, creative nonfiction, poetry, published plays, and children's books. Write for application form. Accepts inquiries by e-mail. **Deadline:** June 30. Competition receives 15 entries/year. Most recent prize winner was Ook Chung. Winner will be announced by e-mail to members and by press release after formal presentation of award on International Translation Day (end of September).

$◻ GLIMMER TRAIN'S APRIL POETRY OPEN, Glimmer Train Press, 710 SW Madison St., Suite 504, Portland OR 97205-2900. (503)221-0836. Fax: (503)221-0837. E-mail: linda@glimmertrain (for online-submission questions) and eds@glimmertrain (for all other questions). Website: www.glimmertrain.com. Established 1998. **Co-Editor:** Linda Swanson-Davies. Offers annual prizes. 1st Prize: $500, publication in *Glimmer Train Stories*, and 20 copies of that issue; 2nd Prize: $250; 3rd Prize: $100. Pays winners from other countries by check in US dollars. Submissions must be unpublished. No subject or form restrictions. **Entry fee:** $6/poem. **How to submit:** Use online submission procedure at www.glimmertrain.com during the month of April. Competition receives "several hundred" entries/year. 2002 winners were Ionna Carlsen, Brittney Corrigan, and Monica Berlin. Judged by the editors of Glimmer Train Press. Winners will be contacted by September 1. Glimmer Train Press publishes the quarterly *Glimmer Train Stories*, available through Amazon or most independent booksellers, and through website.

$◻ GLIMMER TRAIN'S OCTOBER POETRY OPEN, Glimmer Train Press, 710 SW Madison St., Suite 504, Portland OR 97205-2900. (503)221-0836. Fax: (503)221-0837. E-mail: linda@glimmertrain (for online-submission questions) and eds@glimmertrain (for all other questions). Website: www.glimmertrain.com. Established 1998. **Co-Editor:** Linda Swanson-Davies. Offers annual prizes. 1st Prize: $500, publication in *Glimmer Train Stories* and 20 copies of that issue; 2nd Prize: $250; 3rd Prize: $100. Pays winners from other countries by check in US dollars. Submissions must be unpublished. No subject or form restrictions. **Entry fee:** $6/poem. **How to submit:** Use an easy online submission procedure at www.glimmertrain.com during the month of October. Competition receives "several hundred" entries/year. 2002 winners were Zoë Griffith-Jones, Patricia Murphy, and Jennifer Meleana. Judged by the editors of Glimmer Train Press. Winners will be contacted by March 1. Glimmer Train Press publishes the quarterly *Glimmer Train Stories*, available through Amazon or most independent booksellers, and through website.

⬛ GOVERNOR GENERAL'S LITERARY AWARDS, The Canada Council for the Arts, P.O. Box 1047, 350 Albert St., Ottawa ON K1P 5V8 Canada. (613)566-4414, ext. 5576. Fax: (613)566-4410. E-mail: joanne.larocque-poirier@canadacouncil.ca. Website: www.canadacouncil.ca/prizes/GGLA. Established by Parliament in 1957, the Canada Council for the Arts "provides a wide range of grants and services to professional Canadian artists and art organizations in dance, media arts, music, theater, writing, publishing, and the visual arts." The Governor General's Literary Awards, valued at $15,000 (Canadian) each, are given annually for the best English-language and best French-language work in each of seven categories, including poetry. Non-winning finalists each receive $1,000 (Canadian). Books must be first-edition trade books written, translated, or illustrated by Canadian citizens or permanent residents of Canada and published in Canada or abroad during the previous year (September 1 through the following September 30). Collections of poetry must be at least 48 pages long and at least half the book must contain work not published previously in book form. In the case of translation, the original work must also be a Canadian-authored title. Books must be submitted by publishers with a Publisher's Submission Form, which is available from the Writing and Publishing Section. Guidelines and current deadlines available for SASE or by fax or e-mail.

$◻ GROLIER POETRY PRIZE; ELLEN LA FORGE MEMORIAL POETRY FOUNDATION, INC., 6 Plympton St., Cambridge MA 02138. (617)253-4452. E-mail: jjhildeb@mit.edu. Website: www.grolierpoetrybookshop.com. Established 1974. **Contact:** John Hildebidle. The Grolier Poetry Prize is open to all poets who have not published either a vanity, small press, trade, or chapbook of poetry. Two poets receive an honorarium of $200 each. Pays winners from other countries by money order. Up to 4 poems by each winner and 1-2 by each of 4 runners-up are chosen for publication in the *Grolier Poetry Prize Annual*. Submissions must be unpublished and may not be simultaneously submitted. Submit up to 5 poems, not more than 10 double-spaced pages. Submit one ms in duplicate, without name of poet. On a separate sheet give name, address, phone number, and titles of poems. Only 1 submission/contestant; mss are not returned. **Entry fee:** $7, includes copy of *Annual*. Make checks payable to the Ellen La Forge Memorial Poetry Foundation, Inc. Does not accept entry fees in foreign currencies; send money order. Enclose self-addressed stamped postcard if acknowledgement of receipt is required. Opens January 15 of each year. **Deadline:** May 1. Winners and runners-up will be selected and informed in early June. For update of rules, send SASE to Ellen La Forge Memorial Poetry Foundation before submitting mss. Competition receives approximately 500 entries. Recent award winners include Maggie Dietz, Natasha Trethewey, and Babo Kamel. The Ellen La Forge Memorial Poetry Foundation sponsors a reading series, generally 10/semester, held on the grounds of Harvard University. Poets who have new collections of poetry available are eligible. Honoraria vary. Such poets as Philip Levine, Susan Kinsolving, Donald Hall, and Molly McQuade have given readings. Foundation depends upon private gifts and support for its activities. Copies of the *Annual* available from the Book Shop at the above address.

$ ☑ ◎ J.C. AND RUTH HALLS AND DIANE MIDDLEBROOK FELLOWSHIPS IN POETRY (Specialized: MFA or equivalent degree in creative writing), Wisconsin Institute for Creative Writing, English Dept., 600 North Park St., Madison WI 53706. Website: http://creativew riting.wisc.edu. Established 1986. **Director:** Jesse Lee Kercheval. Offers annual fellowships, will pay $25,000 for one academic year. Applicants will teach one creative writing class per semester at U. of Wisconsin and give a public reading at the end of their stay. Submissions may be entered in other contests. Submit 10 poems maximum on any subject in any form. *Applicants must have a MFA or equivalent degree in creative writing.* Applicants cannot have published a book (chapbooks will not disqualify an applicant). Guidelines available for SASE or on website. **Deadline:** Applications must be received in the month of February. Competitions receive 200 entries/year. Judges are faculty of creative writing program. Results will be sent to applicants by May 1. "The fellowships are administered by the Program in Creative Writing at the University of Wisconsin-Madison. Funding is provided by the Jay C. and Ruth Halls Writing Fund and the Carl Djerassi and Diane Middlebrook Fund through the University of Wisconsin Foundation."

★ ⊕ ◎ FELICIA HEMANS PRIZE FOR LYRICAL POETRY (Specialized: membership, students), The University of Liverpool, P.O. Box 147, Liverpool L69 38X England. Phone: (0151)794 2458. Fax: (0151)794 3765. E-mail: wilderc@liv.ac.uk. Established 1899. **Contact:** Registrar, University of Liverpool. Offers annual award of £30. Submissions may be entered in other contests. Submit 1 poem. Open to past or present members and students of the University of Liverpool. Guidelines available for SASE only. Accepts inquiries by fax and e-mail. **Deadline:** May 1. Competition receives 12-15 entries. Judges are "the two professors of English Literature in the University." The winner and all other competitors will be notified by mail in June.

$ ☑ THE HODDER FELLOWSHIP, The Council of the Humanities, Joseph Henry House, Princeton University, Princeton NJ 08544. (609)258-4717. E-mail: humcounc@princeton.edu. Website: www.princeton.edu/~humcounc. Awarded to humanists in the early stages of their careers. Recipients have usually written one book and are working on a second. Preference is given to applicants outside academia. "The Fellowship is designed specifically to identify and nurture extraordinary potential rather than to honor distinguished achievement." **Candidates for the Ph.D. are not eligible.** Hodder Fellows spend an academic year in residence at Princeton working on independent projects in the humanities. Stipend is approximately $52,000. Most recent Hodder Fellows were Andrea Ashworth and Marlys West. Submit a résumé, sample of previous work (10 pages maximum, not returnable), a project proposal of 2-3 pages, and SASE. Guidelines available on website. Announcement of the Hodder Fellow is made in February by the President of Princeton University. **Postmark deadline:** November 1.

★ $ ◪ INTRO PRIZE IN POETRY; FRIENDS OF WRITERS, INC., P.O. Box 535, Village Station, New York NY 10014. (212)619-1105. Fax: (212)406-1352. E-mail: four_way_editors@yahoo.com. Website: www.fourwaybooks.com. **Award Director:** Karen Clarke. Offers biennial contest with prizes including book publication, honorarium ($1,000), and a reading at one or more participating series. Open to US poets who have not yet published a book. "Submit one manuscript, 48-100 pages suggested. More than one manuscript may be submitted but each must be entered separately. Your name should appear on the entry form and the title page of the manuscript and nowhere else. Include SASE if you would like notification of the winner." Entry form and guidelines available for SASE or on website. **Entry fee:** $25. **Postmark deadline:** March 31, 2004. Receives about 1,000 entries/year. Most recent contest winner was Gwen Ebert (2000). Judge was Lynn Emanuel. Winner will be announced Labor Day in the same year as the entry date. "Winner announced by mail and on our website." Copies of winning books available through Four Way Books online and at bookstores (to the trade through University Press of New England). "Four Way Books is the publishing arm of Friends of Writers, Inc., a Vermont-based not-for-profit organization dedicated to encouraging, supporting, and promoting the craft of writing and identifying and publishing writers at decisive stages in ther careers." (See separate listing for Four Way Books in Publishers of Poetry section.)

$ ◪ ◎ JAPANESE LITERARY TRANSLATION PRIZE (Specialized: translation/Japanese into English), Donald Keene Center of Japanese Culture, Columbia University, 507 Kent Hall, New York NY 10027. (212)854-5036. Fax: (212)854-4019. E-mail: donald-keene-center@columbia.edu. Website: www.columbia.edu/cu/ealac/dkc. **Associate Director:** Becky LeGette. Established 1981. The Donald Keen Center of Japanese Culture at Columbia University annually awards $5,000 in Japan-U.S. Friendship Commission Prizes for the Translation of Japanese Literature. A prize is given for the best translation of a modern work of literature or for the best classical literary translation, or the prize is divided between a classical and a modern work. Pays winners from other countries in US dollars. "Special attention is given to new or unpublished translators, and citizens of all nationalities are eligible." Submissions may be previously published and entered in other contests. Translated works submitted for consideration in 2004 may include: a) unpublished mss; b) works in press; c) translations published after January 1, 2001. Submit 7 copies of book-length ms or published book. Entry form and guidelines available for SASE, by fax, e-mail, or on website. **Deadline:** February 1 each year. Competition receives 20-25 entries/year. Most recent award winner was Royall Tyler (classical literature; only one prize awarded in 2002). Winners will be announced through press releases and on website.

$ ◻ JOHN WOOD COMMUNITY COLLEGE ADULT CREATIVE WRITING CONTEST, (formerly the Quincy Writers Guild Writing Contest), John Wood Community College, 1301 S. 48th St., Quincy IL 62305. Website: www.jwcc.edu. Established 1990. **Contest Coordinator:** Sherry L. Sparks. Offers annual award for original, unpublished poetry (serious poetry and light poetry), fiction, and nonfiction. Cash prizes based on dollar amount of entries. 1st, 2nd, and 3rd Prizes awarded in all categories. Guidelines available for SASE or on website. **Entry fee:** $3/poem; $5/nonfiction or fiction piece. Does not accept entry fees in foreign currencies; accepts cash in US dollars as well as Western Union and American Express checks. **Deadline:** entries accepted January 1 through April 1. Competition receives 150-175 entries. Contest is in coordination with the Mid Mississippi River Writers Conference.

$ ◻ ◎ HELEN VAUGHN JOHNSON MEMORIAL HAIKU AWARD (Specialized: forms/haiku); LONG POEM CONTEST; POETRY FOR PETS (Specialized: animals), Hutton Publications, P.O. Box 2907, Decatur IL 62524. Established 2001. **Award Director:** Linda Hutton. Offers annual award for traditional haiku. 1st Prize: $25; 2nd Prize: $15; 3rd Prize: $10. Pays winners from other countries by money order. Submissions may be entered in other contests. Submit unlimited number of poems of 5 lines about nature in traditional 5-7-5 haiku format; must not refer to people; no title. Name, address, and phone number should appear in upper righthand corner of each page. Guidelines available for SASE. **Entry fee:** $1/haiku. Accepts entry fees in foreign currencies. **Deadline:** January 17 annually. Competition receives 100 entries. Judge is Linda Hutton. Winners will be announced February 20 annually. "Study traditional haiku; we do not accept anything but 5-7-5." Also offers the Long Poem Contest. Awards 1st Prize: $25; 2nd Prize: $15; 3rd Prize: $10.

Submit unlimited number of poems, no length limit, any style or theme. Include name and address on poem, mail flat with #10 SASE for contest results. No entries will be returned or published. **Entry fee:** $1/poem. **Deadline:** July 1 annually. Also offers Poetry for Pets, an annual prize of $25 each in 2 categories (rhymed and unrhymed poetry). Submissions may be previously published, must be your own work. Submit any number of poems, no more than 24 lines each (excluding title) on the subject of "pets." Entries must be typed and titled, with poet's name and address on back of page. Include #10 SASE for list of winners. **Entry fee:** $2/poem, or 3 poems for $5. **Postmark Deadline:** June 1. "Two winners will be published in a special flyer. After paying prizes and expenses of contest, the remainder of the entry fees will be donated to The Humane Society of the United States." Make all checks payable to Linda Hutton.

$ ☑ KENYON REVIEW PRIZE IN POETRY FOR A FIRST BOOK, % Zoo Press, P.O. Box 22990, Lincoln NE 68542. (402)770-8104. Fax: (402)614-6302. E-mail: editors@zoopress.org. Website: www.zoopress.org. Established 2000. **Contact:** Award Director. Offers annual award of $3,500 and publication. Pays winners from other countries the equivalent of $3,500 in their own currency, unless they prefer American dollars. Entrants must never have published a full-length collection of poetry. Contestants should send only one copy of a ms of between 50 and 100 pages, typed single-spaced, with no more than one poem/page. Manuscripts must be paginated and contain a table of contents. Illustrations are not accepted. Handwritten mss will not be accepted. Contestants who have published poems in magazines may include those in the ms submitted, along with a page of acknowledgements. Submissions may be entered in other contests. Guidelines available for SASE, by e-mail, or on website. **Entry fee:** $25/submission. Does not accept entry fees in foreign currencies; American dollars only. **Deadline:** April 15. Competition receives 500-1,000 entries/year. 2002 winner was Christopher Cessac (*Republic Sublime*). Winners will be announced in the spring of the following year. Copies of winning books are available from local bookstores, online vendors, or through www.zoopress.org. "Zoo Press is a literary publisher of poetry, fiction, drama, and essay. Please see our Paris Review Prize in Poetry [in this section] and our Parnassus Prize for a Book of Poetry Criticism." Advises, "David Baker, the prize's recurring judge, is an eclectic editor with an eye for quality. We define quality in poetry as an awareness of tradition, formal integrity, rhetorical variety (i.e., invective, satire, argument, irony, etc.), an impressive level of difficulty in the project undertaken, authenticity, and, above all, beauty. All poetry manuscripts should aspire to these ideals."

$ ☑ ◎ HAROLD MORTON LANDON TRANSLATION AWARD, The Academy of American Poets, 588 Broadway, Suite 604, New York NY 10012-3210. (212)274-0343. Fax: (212)274-9427. E-mail: academy@poets.org. Website: www.poets.org. Established 1934. **Executive Director:** Tree Swenson. **Awards Coordinator:** Ryan Murphy. Offers one $1,000 award each year to a US citizen for translation of a book-length poem, a collection of poems, or a verse-drama translated into English from any language. Guidelines available for SASE or on website. **Deadline:** December 31 of year in which book was published. 2002 winner was David Ferry for *The Epistles of Horace*, chosen by Carolyn Forché. (For further information about The Academy of American Poets, see separate listing in the Organizations section.)

$ ☑ THE JAMES LAUGHLIN AWARD, The Academy of American Poets, 588 Broadway, Suite 604, New York NY 10012-3210. (212)274-0343. Fax: (212)274-9427. E-mail: academy@poets.org. Website: www.poets.org. Established 1934. **Executive Director:** Tree Swenson. **Awards Coordinator:** Ryan Murphy. Offers $5,000 prize for a poet's second book (ms must be under contract to a publisher). Submissions must be made by a publisher in ms form. The Academy of American Poets distributes over 10,000 copies of the Laughlin Award-winning book to its members. Poets must be American citizens. Entry form, signed by the publisher, required; entry form and guidelines available for SASE or on website. **Deadline:** submissions accepted between January 1 and May 1. Winners announced in August. 2002 winner was Karen Volkman for *Spar*, chosen by Daniel Hall, Campbell McGrath, and Mary Jo Bang. (For further information about The Academy of American Poets, see separate listing in the Organizations section.)

✿ ◎ THE STEPHEN LEACOCK MEMORIAL MEDAL FOR HUMOUR (Specialized: humor, regional/Canada); THE NEWSPACKET, Stephen Leacock Associates, P.O. Box 854,

Orillia ON L3V 3P4 Canada. (705)835-7061. Fax: (705)835-7062. E-mail: spruce@encode.com. Website: www.leacock.ca. **Contact:** Marilyn Rumball (corresponding secretary). **Award Chairman:** Judith Rapson. Annual prize presented for a book of humor in prose, verse, drama, or any book form—by a Canadian citizen. "Book must have been published in the current year and no part of it may have been previously published in book form." Submit 10 copies of book, 8×10 b&w photo, bio, and entry fee. **Entry fee:** $50 CAN. Prize: Silver Leacock Medal for Humour and Laurentian Bank of Canada cash award of $10,000. **Deadline:** December 31. Competition receives 40-50 entries. The 2002 winner was *Happiness TM* (originally published as *Generica*) by Will Ferguson. The committee also publishes *The Newspacket* 4 times/year, with the 4th issue being a special literary issue.

$◻ THE LEAGUE OF MINNESOTA POETS CONTEST, P.O. Box 1173, Brainerd MN 56401-1173. **Contest Chair:** Mary Larkin. Annual contest offers 18 different categories, with 3 prizes in each category ranging from $10-125. See guidelines for poem lengths, forms, and subjects. Guidelines available for #10 SASE. **Nonmember fee:** $1/poem per category; $2/poem (limit 6) for Grand Prize category. **Members fee:** $5 for 17 categories; $1/poem (limit 6) for Grand Prize category. Make checks payable to LOMP Contest. **Deadline:** July 31. Nationally known, non-Minnesota judges.

▨ $◪ LEVIS POETRY PRIZE; FRIENDS OF WRITERS, INC., P.O. Box 535, Village Station, New York NY 10014. (212)619-1105. Fax: (212)406-1352. E-mail: four_way_editors@yaho o.com. Website: www.fourwaybooks.com. **Award Director:** Karen Clarke. Offers biennial contest with prizes including book publication, honorarium ($1,000), and a reading at one or more participating series. Open to any US poet. "Submit one manuscript, 48-100 pages suggested. More than one manuscript may be submitted but each must be entered separately. Your name should appear on the entry form and the title page of the manuscript and nowhere else. Include SASE if you would like notification of the winner." Entry form and guidelines available for SASE and on website. **Entry fee:** $25. **Postmark deadline:** March 31, 2005. Receives about 1,000 entries/year. Most recent contest winner was Noelle Kocot (1999). Judge was Michael Ryan. Winner will be announced Labor Day in the same year as the entry date. "Winner announced by mail and on our website." Copies of winning books available through Four Way Books online and at bookstores (to the trade through University Press of New England). "Four Way Books is the publishing arm of Friends of Writers, Inc., a Vermont-based not-for-profit organization dedicated to encouraging, supporting, and promoting the craft of writing and identifying and publishing writers at decisive stages in ther careers." (See separate listing for Four Way Books in Publishers of Poetry section.)

Ⓝ $◎ LITERARY GIFT OF FREEDOM; A ROOM OF HER OWN (Specialized: US women poets; women in arts), P.O. Box 778, Placitas NM 87043. E-mail: info@aroomofherownf oundation.org. Website: www.aroomofherownfoundation.org. Established 2001. **Award Director:** Darlene Chandler Bassett. Offers biennial award of "up to $50,000 over two years, with a mentor for advice and dialogue and access to the Advisory Council for professional and business consultation." NOTE: Literary Award granted every other year, but poetry rotates with other writing genres. Open to US citizens only. Submissions may be previously published and may be entered in other contests. "The successful applicant will have a well articulated creative project concept and a clear plan for how it may be accomplished." Applicant must submit detailed application with attachments. Application form and guidelines available by e-mail or on website (application available November of each grant cycle). **Entry fee:** $25/application, US dollars only. **Postmark deadline:** on or before February 1, 2004. Receives 420 applications/grant cycle. Most recent winner was Jennifer Tseng (2002). Judges for the 2002 award were Dorothy Allison, R.S. Gwynn, Ramona King, and Charles E. Little. A new panel is chosen for each grant cycle. Recipient is contacted personally by telephone. Award recipients and finalists plus excerpts are posted on website. "A Room Of Her Own provides innovative arts patronage for women writers and artists through Gift of Freedom Awards. A Room Of Her Own Foundation is a 501(c)(3) nonprofit organization, organized and operated to further the vision of Virginia Woolf and bridge the often fatal gap between a woman's economic reality and her artistic creation. Even in this millennium, many women artists lack the privacy and financial stability essential to artistic output." Advice: "Read our entire website, read application, instructions, and hints and follow instructions exactly."

N ○ THE LITTLE BITTY POETRY COMPETITION, Shadow Poetry, P.O. Box 125, Excelsior Springs MO 64024. Fax: (208)977-9114. E-mail: shadowpoetry@shadowpoetry.com. Website: www.shadowpoetry.com. Established 2000. **Award Director:** James Summers. Offers quarterly award of 1st Prize: $40; 2nd Prize: $20; 3rd Prize: $10; plus the top 3 winners also receive a certificate, printed copy of their poem, and a ribbon. Pays winners from other countries in US dollars only by International Money Order. Submissions may be previously published and may be entered in other contests. Submit unlimited number of poems of 3-12 lines on any subject, in any form. "Entry form must be present with mail-in entries; name, address, phone number, and e-mail address (when available) on upper left-hand corner of each poem submitted. Enclose SASE for winners list. Include an additional SASE for entry receipt (optional). If no SASE is included for receipt, Shadow Poetry will e-mail an entry confirmation to the contestant, if applicable." Entry form and guidelines available for SASE or on website. **Entry fee:** $1.50/poem. Does not accept entry fees in foreign currencies; accepts International Money Order, cash (US dollars), or payments through PayPal for foreign entries. **Deadlines:** March 31, June 30, September 30, and December 31. Winners will be announced "15 days after each quarterly contest ends, by e-mail and to those who requested a winners list. Results will also be posted on the Shadow Poetry website."

◐ ◎ NAOMI LONG MADGETT POETRY AWARD (Specialized: ethnic/African-American), Lotus Press, P.O. Box 21607, Detroit MI 48221. (313)861-1280. Fax: (313)861-4740. E-mail: lotuspress@aol.com. Established 1972. **Contact:** Constance Withers. Offers annual award of $500 and publication by Lotus Press, Inc. for a poetry book ms by an African-American poet. Poems in submission may be previously published individually; "no poems published in a collection of your own work, self-published or not, should be included. Please do not submit a manuscript which you have submitted, or which you plan to submit during the period of consideration, to another publisher. However, you may enter another competition as long as you notify us that you have done or plan to do so. If you are notified that your manuscript has won another award or prize, you must inform us of this immediately." Manuscripts should total approximately 60-80 pages, exclusive of table of contents or other optional introductory material; begin each poem on a new page, no matter how short the poem, and number the pages. Submit 3 complete copies of ms, typed or computer-generated on white letter-sized paper, pages consecutively numbered. Do not include your name on pages. Each copy should include: 1) a cover sheet containing the title of the collection only; 2) another sheet listing title of ms; your name, address, telephone number(s), and e-mail address (if available); and brief statement signed with your legal name indicating all poems are original and previously uncollected and you are African-American. Enclose stamped, self-addressed postcard to confirm receipt of material; no SASE as mss will not be returned. Mail by First Class Priority; no Certified, Federal Express, or other mail requiring a signature. Guidelines available for SASE or by fax or e-mail. **Deadline:** entries must be received between April 1 and June 1. Recent winners include Peggy Ann Tartt for *Among Bones* (2001) and Monifa A. Love for *Dreaming Underground* (2002). Winner and judges announced no later than September 1. All participants will be notified in writing. Copies of winning books available from Lotus Press at the address above. "If you have already had a book published by Lotus Press, you are ineligible. However, inclusion in a Lotus Press anthology, such as *Adam of Ifé: Black Women in Praise of Black Men*, does not disqualify you. Those who have worked over a period of years at developing their craft will have the best chance for consideration. The work of novices is not likely to be selected."

⚑ $ ◑ ◎ MARIN ARTS COUNCIL INDIVIDUAL ARTIST GRANTS (Specialized: regional/Marin Co. CA), 650 Las Gallinas Ave., San Rafael CA 94903. (415)499-8350. Fax: (415)499-8537. E-mail: grants@marinarts.org. Website: www.marinarts.org. Established 1987. **Grants Program Director:** Lance Walker. Offers biennial grants starting at $2,000 to residents of Marin County, CA only. Submissions must have been completed within last 3 years. Submit 10 pages

---

MARKETS LISTED in the 2003 edition of *Poet's Market* that do not appear this year are identified in the General Index with a code explaining their absence from the listings.

on any subject in any form. ***Open to Marin County residents only***—"must have lived in Marin County for one year prior to application, be 18 or over and not in an arts degree program." Entry form and guidelines available for SASE or on website. Accepts inquiries by fax and e-mail. **Deadline:** January. Winners will be announced June of each year. "The Marin Arts Council offers grants in 13 different categories to individual artists living in Marin County. Deadlines and categories alternate each year. Call for more information." Competition receives 50-100 entries.

$ ☑ THE LENORE MARSHALL POETRY PRIZE, The Academy of American Poets, 588 Broadway, Suite 604, New York NY 10012-3210. (212)274-0343. Fax: (212)274-9427. E-mail: acade my@poets.org. Website: www.poets.org. Established 1934. **Executive Director:** Tree Swenson. **Awards Coordinator:** Ryan Murphy. Offers $10,000 for the most outstanding book of poems published in the US in the preceding year. Contest is open to books by living American poets published in a standard edition (40 pages or more in length with 500 or more copies printed). **Self-published books are not eligible.** Publishers may enter as many books as they wish. Four copies of each book must be submitted and none will be returned. Guidelines available for SASE or on website. **Deadline:** entries must be submitted between April 1 and June 15. Finalists announced in September; winner announced in October. 2002 winner was Madeline DeFrees for *Blue Dusk*, chosen by Joy Harjo, Michael S. Harper, and Lawson Fusao Inada. (For further information about The Academy of American Poets, see separate listing in the Organizations section.)

⊕ $□ ◎ MELBOURNE POETS UNION ANNUAL NATIONAL POETRY COMPE-TITION (Specialized: regional/Australian poets), Melbourne Poets Union, P.O. Box 266, Flinders Lane, Victoria 8009 Australia. Established 1977. **Contact:** Leon Shann. Offers annual prizes to a total of $1,000. Pays winners from other countries "with a cheque in foreign currency, after negotiation with winner." Submissions must be unpublished. Submit unlimited number of poems on any subject in any form. "Open to Australian residents living in Australia or overseas." Entry form and guidelines available for SASE (or SAE and IRC). **Entry fee:** AUS $5/poem; AUS $12/3 poems. Accepts entry fees in foreign currencies. **Deadline:** October 31. Competition receives over 500 entries/year. Recent winners include Kathryn Lomer, John West, and Susan Kruss. Winners will be announced on the last Friday of November by newsletter, mail, and phone. "The $1,000 prize money comes directly from entry money, the rest going to paying the judge and costs of running the competition."

$ ☑ MID-LIST PRESS FIRST SERIES AWARD FOR POETRY, Mid-List Press, 4324 12th Ave. S., Minneapolis MN 55407-3218. E-mail: guide@midlist.org. Website: www.midlist.org. Established 1990. "The First Series Award for Poetry is an annual contest we sponsor for poets who have never published a book of poetry. The award includes publication and a $500 advance against royalties." Individual poems within the book ms may be previously published and may be entered in other contests. Submit at least 60 single-spaced pages. "Note: We do not return manuscripts. Other than length we have no restrictions, but poets are encouraged to read previous award winners we have published." Recent award winners include Rustum Kozain, Margo Stever, Katherine Starke, and Adam Sol. Submissions are circulated to an editorial board. Guidelines are available for #10 SASE or on website; no inquiries by fax or e-mail. **Entry fee:** $30 US; must include entry form (available online). Does not accept entry fees in foreign currencies. **Deadline:** accepts submissions October 1 through February 1. Competition receives 350 entries/year. "The First Series Award contest is highly competitive. We are looking for poets who have produced a significant body of work but have never published a book-length collection. (A chapbook is not considered a 'book' of poetry.)"

◪ $□ MILFORD FINE ARTS COUNCIL NATIONAL POETRY CONTEST; HIGH TIDE, Milford Fine Arts Council, 40 Railroad Ave., South, Milford CT 06460. Established 1976. **Contest Chairpersons:** Lynne Connors and Martin Goorhigian. Offers annual award of 1st Prize: $100; 2nd Prize: $50; 3rd Prize: $25; plus winners will be published in MFAC's annual publication, *High Tide*. Submissions must be unpublished and not under consideration by any other publication or contest. Poems entered may not have won any other prizes or honorable mentions. "Poems must be typed single spaced on white standard paper, 10-30 lines (including title), no more than 48 characters/line, on any subject, in any style, rhymed or unrhymed. Use standard font, clear and legible, one poem/page, no script or fax. No bio or date, only the words 'Unpublished Original' typed above the poem. Type your name, address, and ZIP code in the middle back of the submitted poem, no identifying information on the front of the page. Poems will be judged on form, clarity, originality, and universal appeal. Poems will not be returned, so please keep copies. After winners are notified, poems will be destroyed." Guidelines available for SASE. **Entry fee:** $3 for one poem, $5 for 2 poems. Contestants may enter an unlimited number of poems. Check or money order accepted, no cash. **Deadline:** March 31. For a list of winners, send SASE with the word NOTIFICATION printed on the bottom left corner of the envelope. "Entries may be considered for publication in *High Tide*. If you do not want your poems considered for publication, then you *must* print on the back of the poem (below your name, address, and ZIP code) 'For National Poetry Contest Only.' "

$ ⊚ MONEY FOR WOMEN (Specialized: women/feminism); GERTRUDE STEIN AWARD; FANNIE LOU HAMER AWARD, Barbara Deming Memorial Fund, Inc., P.O. Box 630125, Bronx NY 10463. **Executive Director:** Susan Pliner. Offers biannual small grants of up to $1,500 to feminists in the arts "whose work addresses women's concerns and/or speaks for peace and justice from a feminist perspective." Pays Canadian winners in US dollars. Submissions may be previously published and entered in other contests. Application form available for SASE. Applicants must be citizens of US or Canada. **Application fee:** $10. Accepts entry fees by postal money order or checks drawn on US funds. **Deadline:** June 30. Competition receives 400 entries/year. Recent award winners were Kelle Groom, Danielle Montgomery, Lisa J. Parker, and Michele Thorsen. Winners will be announced in May and October. Also offers the Gertrude Stein Award for outstanding work by a lesbian, and the "Fannie Lou Hamer Award" for work which combats racism and celebrates women of color. "Entrants must use the current (within 6 months) entry form."

⊚ MONTANA ARTS; MARY BRENNEN CLAPP MEMORIAL POETRY CONTEST (Specialized: regional), P.O. Box 1872, Bozeman MT 59771. Biennual contest. Open to Montana poets or former Montana poets only, for 3 unpublished poems up to 100 lines total. Awards prizes of $100, $80, $60, and $40. Submit 3 poems and cover letter. Guidelines available for SASE. **Deadline:** September in even-numbered years.

◧ $ ◖ JENNY McKEAN MOORE WRITER IN WASHINGTON, Dept. of English, George Washington University, Washington DC 20052. (202)994-6515. Fax: (202)994-7915. E-mail: dmca@gwu.edu. Website: www.gwu.edu/~english. Offers fellowship for a visiting lecturer in creative writing, about $50,000 for 2 semesters. Apply by November 15 with résumé and writing sample of 25 pages or less. Awarded to poets and fiction writers in alternating years.

$ ◖ SAMUEL FRENCH MORSE POETRY PRIZE, English Dept., 406 Holmes, Northeastern University, Boston MA 02115. (617)373-4546. Fax: (617)373-2509. E-mail: g.rotella@neu.edu. Website: www.casdn.neu.edu/~english/. **Editor:** Prof. Guy Rotella. Offers book publication (ms 50-70 pages) by Northeastern University Press and an annual award of $1,000. Open to US poets who have published no more than 1 book of poetry. Entry must be unpublished in book form but may include poems published in journals and magazines. Guidelines available on website (under "Publications"). Accepts inquiries by e-mail. **Entry fee:** $15. **Deadline:** August 1 for inquiries; September 15 for single copy of ms. Manuscripts will not be returned. Competition receives approximately 400 entries/year. Most recent award winners include Jennifer Atkinson, Ted Genoways, and Catherine Sasanov. Most recent judge was Rosanna Warren.

$ ◻ NASHVILLE NEWSLETTER POETRY CONTEST, P.O. Box 60535, Nashville TN 37206-0535. Established 1977. **Editor/Publisher:** Roger Dale Miller. Offers quarterly prizes of $50, $25, and $10 plus possible publication in newsletter (published poets receive 3 copies of *Newsletter* in which their work appears), and at least 50 Certificates of Merit. Pays winners from other countries with check in US funds. Submit one unpublished poem to a page, any style or subject up to 40 lines, with name and address in upper left corner. Send large #10 SASE for more information and/or extra entry forms for future contests. **Entry fee:** $5 for up to 3 poems. Must be sent all at once for each contest. Does not accept entry fees in foreign currencies; accepts check/money order in US funds. "All other nonwinning poems will be considered for possible publication in future issues." Competition receives over 700 entries/year. Most recent winners were Dan Goldstein, Lisa Moran, Stan Morner, and Christina Moran. Recent judges were Hazel Kirby and Judy Craddock. Winners will be announced by mail. Sample: $3. Responds in up to 10 weeks.

$☑ NATIONAL BOOK AWARD, National Book Foundation, 95 Madison Ave., Suite 709, New York NY 10016. (212)685-0261. E-mail: natbkfdn@mindspring.com. Website: www.nationalbo ok.org. Offers annual grand prize of $10,000 in each of 4 categories plus 4 finalist awards of $1,000 in each category. Presents awards in fiction, nonfiction, poetry, and young people's literature. Submissions must be previously published and **must be entered by the publisher**. Entry form and guidelines available for SASE. **Entry fee:** $100/title. **Deadline:** early July. 2002 poetry winner was Ruth Stone (*In the Next Galaxy*).

◻ NATIONAL WRITERS UNION ANNUAL NATIONAL POETRY COMPETITION, P.O. Box 2409, Aptos CA 95001. E-mail: bonnie.thomas@att.net. Website: www.nwu.org. The 2003 competition is sponsored by Santa Cruz/Monterey Local 7 of the NWU. Guidelines available for SASE or on website. **Entry fee:** $4/poem. **Deadline:** November 30. Competition receives about 1,000 entries/year. 2002 winners were Janet K. Tracy Landman, Phyllis Collier, and Sam Friedman. Judge for the 2003 contest is Donald Hall. Winners will be announced in February, 2004.

◎ NEUSTADT INTERNATIONAL PRIZE FOR LITERATURE; WORLD LITERATURE TODAY, University of Oklahoma, 110 Monnet Hall, Norman OK 73019-4033. (405)325-4531. Fax: (405)325-7495. Website: www.ou.edu/worldlit/. **Executive Director:** Robert Con Davis-Undiano. Award of $50,000 given every other year in recognition of life achievement or to a writer whose work is still in progress; **nominations from an international jury only**. Most recent award winner was Alvaro Mutis (Colombia).

$◻ NEW MILLENNIUM AWARD FOR POETRY, NEW MILLENNIUM WRITINGS, P.O. Box 2463, Knoxville TN 37901. E-mail: mark@mach2.com. Website: www.mach2.com. **Editor:** Don Williams. Offers 2 annual awards of $1,000 each. Pays winners from other countries by money order. Submissions must be previously unpublished but may be entered in other contests. Submit up to 3 poems, 5 pages maximum. No restrictions on style or content. Include name, address, phone number, and a #10 SASE for notification. All contestants receive the next issue at no additional charge. Printable entry form on website. Manuscripts are not returned. Guidelines available for SASE. Accepts inquiries by e-mail. **Entry fee:** $17. Make checks payable to New Millennium Writings. Does not accept entry fees in foreign currencies; send money order drawn on US bank. **Deadlines:** June 17 and November 17. Competition receives 2,000 entries/year. "Two winners and selected finalists will be published." Most recent award winners include Jeff Walt and Larry Bradley. "Contests are not the only avenues to publication. We also accept—at no cost, no entry fee—general submissions for publication during the months of January and February only. These should be addressed to Editor. There are no restrictions as to style, form, or content. Submitters should enclose SASE for correspondence purposes."

$☑ NEW RIVER POETS QUARTERLY POETRY AWARDS, New River Poets, 5545 Meadowbrook St., Zephyrhills FL 33541-2715. Established 2000. **Awards Coordinator:** June Owens. Offers 1st Prize: $60; 2nd Prize: $40; 3rd Prize: $30 for each quarterly contest, plus 5 Honorable Mentions. Pays winners from other countries by International Bank Money Order. Submissions may be previously published and may be entered in other contests. Submit 1-3 poems of up to 42 lines each on any subject, in any form. "Send 2 copies each poem on 8½×11 white paper; poet's identification on only one copy of each. If previously published, state where/when. If in a traditional form, state form. Quarter for which work is submitted must appear upper right." Guidelines available for SASE. **Entry fee:** 1-3 poems for $4; $1 each additional; no limit. Prefers US funds. **Deadline:** November 15, February 15, May 15, August 15. Competition receives 800 entries/year. Most recent award winners were Glenna Holloway, Maureen Tolman Flannery, and Virginia H. McKinnie. Most recent contest judges were Catherine Moran, Ian Veitenheimer, Maureen Tolman Flannery, and Virginia H. McKinnie. (First Place winners are invited to judge a subsequent competition). Winners will be announced by mail within 45 days of deadline. "New River Poets is a chartered Chapter of Florida

State Poets Association, Inc. Its purpose is to acknowledge and reward outstanding poetic efforts. Its plans include the publication of an anthology, *Watermarks*, which will not only be open to general submissions but will offer each of our 1st, 2nd, and 3rd Place winners a modest honorarium for one-time use of his/her winning poem. Other plans include inviting student groups to participate and learn from specific NRP meetings. In July 2003, NRP sponsored and hosted 'Zinger in Zephyrhills' for FSPA's Quarterly Statewide Meeting. Also, we now contribute, from each quarter's entry fees, a portion to The Nature Conservancy, an international organization husbanding the environment and land conservation." Advises to "send your best. Always include SASE. Our 'rules' are quite wide open, but please adhere. Remember that competition is not only good for the cause of poetry but for the poetic soul, a win-win situation."

$ ☑ NEWBURYPORT ART ASSOCIATION ANNUAL SPRING POETRY CONTEST, 12 Charron Dr., Newburyport MA 01950. E-mail: espmosk@juno.com. Website: www.newburyportar t.org. Established 1990. **Contest Coordinator:** Rhina P. Espaillat. Offers annual awards of 1st Prize: $200, 2nd Prize: $150, 3rd Prize: $100, plus a number of Honorable Mentions and certificates. All winners, including Honorable Mention poets, are invited to read their own entries at the Awards Day Reading on May 18. Open to anyone over 16 years old. Pays winners from other countries with NAA check. Submissions must be previously unpublished, may be entered in other contests. Submit any number of poems, each no more than 3 pages in length. Must be typed, single- or double-spaced, on white 8½×11 paper; each poem must have a title. Send 2 copies of each poem: one without identifica-tion, one bearing your name, address, e-mail, and telephone number. Include SASE for notification of contest results. Any number of poems accepted, but all must be mailed together in a single envelope with one check covering the total entry fee. Guidelines available for SASE, by e-mail, and on website. **Entry fee:** $3/poem. Does not accept entry fees in foreign currencies; send US cash, check, or money order. Make checks payable to NAA Poetry Contest (one check for all entries). **Postmark deadline:** March 15, 2004. Winners for the 2002 contest were Bill Coyle, Len Krisak, and Diana Lockward, plus 14 Honorable Mentions. Judge was Dr. Robert B. Shaw. Do not submit entries without first securing a copy of the guidelines, then follow them carefully.

NFSPS COMPETITIONS; STEVENS MANUSCRIPT COMPETITION; ENCORE PRIZE POEM ANTHOLOGY; NFSPS COLLEGE/UNIVERSITY-LEVEL POETRY COMPETI-TION. **50-Category Annual Contest Chairman:** Kathleen Pederzani, 121 Grande Blvd., Reading PA 19608-9680 (e-mail: pederzanik@aol.com). Website: www.nfsps.com. NFSPS sponsors a national contest with 50 different categories each year, including the NFSPS Founders Award of $1,500 for 1st Prize; 2nd Prize: $500; 3rd Prize: $250. **Entry fees for members:** $1/poem or $8 total for 8 or more categories, plus $5/poem for NFSPS Founders Award (limit 4 entries in this category alone). All poems winning over $15 are published in the *ENCORE Prize Poem Anthology*. Rules for all contests are given in a brochure available from Madelyn Eastlund, editor of *Strophes* newsletter, at 310 South Adams St., Beverly Hills FL 34465 (e-mail: verdure@digitalusa.net); or from Kathleen Pederzani at the address above; or on the NFSPS website. You can also write for the address of your state poetry society. NFSPS also sponsors the annual Stevens Manuscript Competition with a 1st Prize of $1,000 and publication. **Deadline:** October 15. **Contact:** Doris Stengel, 1510 South Seventh St., Brainerd MN 56401-4342 (e-mail: dpoet@brainerd.net). Information for the College/University-Level Poetry Competition available from Sybella Beyer-Snyder, 3444 South Dover Terrace, Inverness FL 34452-7116 (e-mail: sybella@digitalusa.net). (For further information about the National Federa-tion of State Poetry Societies [NFSPS], see listing in the Organizations section.)

$ ☐ ◎ FRANK O'HARA AWARD CHAPBOOK COMPETITION; THORNGATE ROAD PRESS (Specialized: gay/lesbian/bisexual), Dept. of English and Humanities, Pratt Insti-tute, 200 Willoughby Ave., Brooklyn NY 11205. (718)636-3790. Fax: (718)636-3573. E-mail: jelledg e@pratt.edu. Established 1996. **Award Director/Publisher:** Jim Elledge. Offers annual award of $500, publication, and 25 copies. Submissions may be a combination of previously published and unpublished work and may be entered in other contests. Submit 16 pages on any topic, in any form. Another 4 pages for front matter is permitted, making the maximum total of 20 pages. Poets must be gay, lesbian, or bisexual (any race, age, background, etc.). One poem/page. Guidelines available for SASE. Accepts inquiries by fax and e-mail. **Entry fee:** $15/submission. **Deadline:** February 1.

Competition receives 200-300 entries. Most recent contest winner was *Other Side of the Fence* by Michele Spring-Moore. Judge is a nationally recognized gay, lesbian, or bisexual poet. Judge remains anonymous until the winner has been announced (by April 15). Copies of winning books may be ordered by sending $6 to the above address made out to Thorngate Road Press. "Thorngate Road publishes at least two chapbooks annually, and they are selected by one of two methods. The first is through the contest. The second, the Berdache Chapbook Series, is by invitation only. We published chapbooks by Kristy Nielsen, David Trinidad, Reginald Shepherd, Karen Lee Osborne, Timothy Liu, and Maureen Seaton in the Berdache series." Although the contest is only open to gay, lesbian, bisexual, and transgendered authors, the content of submissions does not necessarily have to be gay, lesbian, bisexual, or transgendered.

$ 🖊 OHIO POETRY DAY CONTESTS, Ohio Poetry Day Association, 3520 St. Route 56, Mechanicsburg OH 43044. (937)834-2666. Established 1937. **Contest Chairman:** Amy Jo Zook. Offers annual slate of up to 40 contest categories. Prizes range from $75 on down; all money-award poems published in anthology (runs over 100 pages). Pays winners from other countries in cash. "The bank we use does not do *any* exchange at any price." Submissions must be unpublished. Submit 1 poem/category on topic and in form specified. Some contests open to everyone, but others open only to Ohio poets. "Each contest has its own specifications. Entry must be for a specified category, so entrants *need rules*." Entry form and guidelines available for SASE. **Entry fee:** $8 inclusive, unlimited number of categories. Does not accept entry fees in foreign currencies. **Deadline:** was May 24 for 2003. Competition receives up to 4,000 entries/year. Judges for most recent contest listed in winners' book. Judges are never announced in advance. Winners list available in August for SASE; prizes given in October. Copies of winning books available from Amy Jo Zook for $7-8 (prices can differ from year to year) plus $1.50 postage for 1 or 2 books. "Ohio Poetry Day is the umbrella. Individual contests are sponsored by poetry organizations and/or individuals across the state. OPD sponsors one, plus Poet of the Year and Student Poet of the Year; have 4 memorial funds." Advises to "revise, follow rules, look at individual categories for a good match."

$ 🔲 OHIOANA BOOK AWARDS; OHIOANA POETRY AWARD (Helen and Laura Krout Memorial); OHIOANA QUARTERLY; OHIOANA LIBRARY ASSOCIATION (Specialized: regional), Ohioana Library Association, 274 E. First Ave., Columbus OH 43201. (614)466-3831. Fax: (614)728-6974. E-mail: ohioana@SLOMA.state.oh.us. Website: www.oplin.lib. oh.us/ohioana. **Director:** Linda Hengst. Offers annual Ohioana Book Awards. Up to 6 awards may be given for books (including books of poetry) by authors born in Ohio or who have lived in Ohio for at least 5 years. The Ohioana Poetry Award of $1,000 (with the same residence requirements), made possible by a bequest of Helen Krout, is given yearly "to an individual whose body of published work has made, and continues to make, a significant contribution to poetry, and through whose work as a writer, teacher, administrator, or in community service, interest in poetry has been developed." **Deadline:** nominations to be received by December 31. Competition receives several hundred entries. Most recent award winners were Patricia Goedicke (poetry award) and Robert DeMott and Jerry Roscoe (book award/poetry). *Ohioana Quarterly* regularly reviews Ohio magazines and books by Ohio authors and is available through membership in Ohioana Library Association ($25/year).

$ 🖊 PARIS REVIEW PRIZE IN POETRY, % Zoo Press, P.O. Box 22990, Lincoln NE 68542. (402)770-8104. Fax: (402)614-6302. E-mail: editors@zoopress.org. Website: www.zoopress.org. Established 2000. **Contact:** Award Director. Offers annual award of $5,000, a reading in NYC, and publication by Zoo Press. Pays winners from other countries the equivalent of $5,000 in their own currency, unless they prefer American dollars. Contestants should send only one copy of each ms. Manuscripts must be between 50 and 100 pages, typed single-spaced, with no more than one poem/page. Manuscripts must be paginated and contain a table of contents. Illustrations are not accepted. Handwritten mss will not be accepted. Contestants who have published poems in magazines may include those in the ms submitted, along with a page of acknowledgements. Submissions may be entered in other contests. Guidelines available for SASE, by e-mail, or on website. **Entry fee:** $25/submission. Does not accept entry fees in foreign currencies; American dollars only. **Deadline:** October 31. Competition receives 500-1,000 entries/year. 2001 winner was Bryan D. Dietrich (*Krypton Nights*). Winners will be announced in the spring of the following year. Copies of winning books are available from local bookstores, online vendors, or through www.zoopress.org. "Zoo Press is a literary publisher of poetry, fiction, drama, and essay. Please see our Kenyon Review Prize in Poetry for a First Book [in this section] and our Parnassus Prize for a Book of Poetry Criticism." Advises, "Richard Howard, the prize's recurring judge, is one of the most eclectic editors of poetry in the United States, so it's difficult to qualify or quantify his aesthetic more than to say he will choose a high quality manuscript. We define quality in poetry as an awareness of tradition, formal integrity, rhetorical variety (i.e., invective, satire, argument, irony, etc.), an impressive level of difficulty in the project undertaken, authenticity, and, above all, beauty. All poetry manuscripts should aspire to these ideals."

$ ◐ PAUMANOK POETRY AWARD COMPETITION; THE VISITING WRITERS PROGRAM, SUNY Farmingdale, Farmingdale NY 11735. E-mail: brownml@farmingdale.edu. Website: www.farmingdale.edu/CampusPages/ArtsSciences/EnglishHumanities/paward.html. Established 1990. **Director:** Dr. Margery Brown. Offers a prize of $1,000 plus an all-expense-paid feature reading in their 2003-2004 series (*Please note:* travel expenses within the continental US only). Also awards two runner-up prizes of $500 plus expenses for a reading in the series. Pays winners from other countries in US dollars. Submit cover letter, 1-paragraph literary bio, up to 5 poems of up to 10 pages (published or unpublished). **Entry fee:** $25. **Postmark deadline:** by September 15. Make checks payable to SUNY Farmingdale Visiting Writers Program (VWP). Does not accept entry fees in foreign currencies. Send money order in US dollars. Send SASE for results (to be mailed by late December). Guidelines available for SASE or on website. Accepts inquiries by e-mail. Competition receives over 600 entries. Most recent contest winners include Greg Rappleye (winner) and Kathy Fagan and Lisa Rhoades (runners-up). Poets who have read in this series include Hayden Carruth, Allen Ginsberg, Linda Pastan, Marge Piercy, Joyce Carol Oates, Louis Simpson, and David Ignatow. The series changes each year, so entries in the 2002 competition will be considered for the 2003-2004 series, and so on.

★ $◯ ◎ JUDITH SIEGEL PEARSON AWARD (Specialized: women), Wayne State University/Family of Judith Siegel Pearson, 51 W. Warren, Detroit MI 48202. (313)577-2450. Fax: (313)577-8618. E-mail: rhellar@sun.science.wayne.edu. **Contact:** Robert Hellar. Offers an annual award of up to $250 for "the best creative or scholarly work on a subject concerning women." The type of work accepted rotates each year: 2003, Fiction; 2004, Plays & Nonfictional Prose; 2005, Poetry. Submissions must be unpublished. Submit 4-10 poems (20 pages maximum). Open to "all interested writers and scholars." Guidelines available for SASE or by fax or e-mail. **Deadline:** March 1. Most recent contest winners were Deborah Bernhardt, Erika Meitner, and Lynn Wagner. Judges for the most recent contest were Dr. William Harris and Dr. Terry Blackhawk. Winner announced in April by mail.

◎ PEN CENTER USA WEST LITERARY AWARD IN POETRY (Specialized: regional/ west of the Mississippi), PEN Center USA West, 672 S. Lafayette Park Place, #42, Los Angeles CA 90057. (213)365-8500. Fax: (213)365-9616. E-mail: awards@penusa.org. Website: www.penusa.org. **Contact:** Awards Coordinator. Offers annual $1,000 cash award to a book of poetry published during the previous calendar year. Open to writers living west of the Mississippi. Submit 4 copies of the entry. Entry form and guidelines available for SASE, by fax, e-mail, or on website. **Entry fee:** $25. **Deadline:** December 19. Most recent award winner was Norman Dubie. Judges were Eloise Klein Healy, Donna Frazier, and Martha Ronk. Winner will be announced in a May 2004 press release and honored at a ceremony in Los Angeles.

$ ◐ ◎ PENNSYLVANIA POETRY SOCIETY ANNUAL CONTEST. (610)374-5848. E-mail: aubade@bluetruck.net. Website: www.geocities.com/paperlesspoets. **Contact:** Steve Concert, 6 Kitchen Ave., Harvey's Lake PA 18618. Offers Annual Contest with grand prize awards of $100, $50, and $25; 3 poems may be entered for grand prize at $2 each for members and nonmembers alike. Also offers prizes in other categories of $25, $15, and $10 (one entry/category). A total of 17 categories open to all, 4 categories for members only. **Entry fee:** for members entering categories 2-21, $2.50 inclusive; for nonmembers entering categories 2-15 and 17-21, $1.50 each. Guidelines available for SASE or on website. **Deadline:** January 15. Also sponsors the Pegasus Contest **for PA students only**, grades 5-12. For information send SASE to Carol Clark Williams, Chairman, 445

North George St., York PA. **Deadline:** February 15, 2003. The Ferguson Environmental Contest is for all poets, offers prizes of $75, $25, $15, and $10. **Entry fee:** $1, 1 poem limit. **Deadline:** September 15. Carlisle Poets Contest open to all poets. **Deadline:** October 31. Guidelines available for SASE from Joy Campbell, Chairman, 10 Polecat Rd., Landisburg PA 17040. The Wine & Roses Contest is for **PA poets only. Deadline:** October 25. Guidelines available for SASE from Ray Fulmer, Director, 316 Park Ave., Quakertown PA 18951. The Society publishes a quarterly newsletter with member poetry and challenges, plus an annual soft-cover book of prize poems from the Annual Contest. Pegasus Contest-wining poems are published in a booklet sent to schools. PPS membership dues: $17/fiscal year. Make checks payable to PPS, Inc., mail to Richard R. Gasser, Treasurer, at 801 Spruce St., West Reading PA 19611-1448.

$ ◪ THE RICHARD PHILLIPS POETRY PRIZE, The Phillips Publishing Co., 2200 E. Mountain Rd., Poetry Building: i-102, Springdale AR 72764. Established 1993. **Award Director:** Richard Phillips, Jr. Annual award of $1,000, open to all poets. Submit 48-page ms, published or unpublished poems, any subject, any form. Guidelines available for SASE. **Entry fee:** $15/ms, payable to Richard Phillips Poetry Prize. Accepts entry fees in foreign currencies. Manuscripts are not returned. **Postmark deadline:** January 31. "Winner will be announced and check for $1,000 presented the first week in May. Press release in poet's city of residence. Also, announcements sent to each entrant for SASE." Publication is the following September. Competition receives approximately 200 entries. Most recent prize winners were: Helen Olsen (2002), Clark Doane (2001), and Patricia Lang (2000). "There are no anthologies to buy, no strings attached. The best manuscript will win the prize."

$ ◪ POETIC LICENSE CONTEST; MKASHEF ENTERPRISES, P.O. Box 688, Yucca Valley CA 92286-0688. E-mail: alayne@inetworld.net. Website: www.asidozines.com. Established 1998. **Poetry Editor:** Alayne Gelfand. Offers a biannual poetry contest. 1st Prize: $500, 2nd Prize: $100, 3rd Prize: $40, plus publication in anthology and 1 copy. Pays winners from other countries in US cash, by money order, or through PayPal. Five honorable mentions receive 1 copy; other poems of exceptional interest will also be included in the anthology. **Themes and deadlines available for SASE.** Submit any number of poems, any style, of up to 50 lines/poem (poems may have been previously published). Include name, address, and phone on each poem. Enclose a SASE for notification of winners. Accepts submissions by regular mail, on disk, or by e-mail (attachment or pasted within text of message). "Judges prefer original, accessible, and unforced works." Guidelines available for SASE or by e-mail. **Entry fee:** $1/poem. "We're looking for fresh word usage and surprising imagery. Please keep in mind that our judges prefer non-rhyming poetry. Each contest seeks to explode established definitions of the theme being spotlighted. Be sure to send SASE or e-mail for current theme and deadline."

✪ $ ◪ ◎ THE POETRY COUNCIL OF NORTH CAROLINA ANNUAL POETRY CONTEST (Specialized: Regional/NC); BAY LEAVES, Poetry Council of North Carolina, 3805 Meredith Dr., Greensboro NC 27408. Phone/fax: (336)282-4032. E-mail: janlsull@aol.com. **Award Director:** Nancy Adams. **President:** Janice L. Sullivan. The Poetry Council of North Carolina is "an organization whose sole purpose is to sponsor several poetry contests and to publish the winning poems in our book, *Bay Leaves*. There is no membership fee and our Poetry Day, where all winners are invited to read their poems, is in the fall of each year, either late September or early October." Open to residents and former residents of North Carolina (persons born in NC, transients from other states who either attend school or work in NC, and NC residents temporarily out of state). Offers several contests with prizes ranging from $10 to $15; all money-winning poems plus Honorable Mentions will be published in *Bay Leaves*. Guidelines available for SASE. **Entry fee:** $3/poem, one poem/contest. Accepts entry fees by check or cash in U.S. dollars. **Deadline:** May 1 annually. Competition receives 200 entries/year. Winners list available for SASE, also appears in *Bay Leaves*. Copies of winning books available from Poetry Council of North Carolina. "Please read the guidelines carefully. Only send your best work. You can enter only one poem in each contest."

✪ $ POETRY SOCIETY OF AMERICA AWARDS, Poetry Society of America, 15 Gramercy Park, New York NY 10003. (212)254-9628. Website: www.poetrysociety.org. Offers the following awards open to PSA members only: The Writer Magazine/Emily Dickinson Award ($250, for a poem inspired by Dickinson though not necessarily in her style); Cecil Hemley Memorial Award ($500, for a lyric poem that addresses a philosophical or epistemological concern); Lyric Poetry Award ($500, for a lyric poem on any subject); Lucille Medwick Memorial Award ($500, for an original poem in any form on a humanitarian theme); Alice Fay Di Castagnola Award ($1,000 for a manuscript-in-progress of poetry or verse-drama). The following awards are open to both PSA members and nonmembers: Louise Louis/Emily F. Bourne Student Poetry Award ($250, for the best unpublished poem by a student in grades 9-12 from the U.S.); George Bogin Memorial Award ($500, for a selection of 4-5 poems that use language in an original way to reflect the encounter of the ordinary and the extraordinary and to take a stand against oppression in any of its forms); Robert H. Winner Memorial Award ($2,500, to acknowledge original work being done in mid-career by a poet who has not had substantial recognition, open to poets over 40 who have published no more than one book). Entries for the Norma Farber First Book Award ($500) and the William Carlos Williams Award (purchase prize between $500 and $1,000, for a book of poetry published by a small press, nonprofit, or university press) must be submitted directly by publishers. The Frost Medal (for distinguished lifetime service to American poetry) and The Shelley Memorial Award (between $6,000 and $9,000 awarded to a living American poet, selected with reference to his/her genius and need) are by nomination only. Complete submission guidelines for all awards are available on website. **Entry fee:** all of the above contests are free to PSA members; nonmembers pay $15 to enter any or all of contests 6-8; $5 for high school students to enter single entries in the student poetry competition; high school teachers/administrators may submit unlimited number of students' poems (one entry/student) to student poetry award for $20. **Deadline:** submissions must be postmarked between October 1 and December 21. Additional information available on website. (See separate listing for Poetry Society of American in the Organizations section; see separate listing for the PSA Chapbook Fellowships in this section.)

$🔲 ◎ POETS' CLUB OF CHICAGO; HELEN SCHAIBLE SHAKESPEAREAN/PE-TRARCHAN SONNET CONTEST (Specialized: form/sonnet), 1212 S. Michigan Ave., Apt. 2702, Chicago IL 60605. (312)786-1959. **Chairperson:** Tom Roby. The annual Helen Schaible Shakespearean/Petrarchan Sonnet Contest is open to anyone **except** members of Poets' Club of Chicago. **For sonnets only!** Offers 1st Prize: $50; 2nd Prize: $35; 3rd Prize: $15. Submit only 1 entry (2 copies) of either a Shakespearean or a Petrarchan sonnet, which must be original and unpublished. Entry must be typed on 8½×11 paper, double-spaced. Name and address in the upper right-hand corner on only one copy. *All necessary guidelines appear in this listing.* **No entry fee.** Prizes of $50, $35, and $15 and 3 non-cash honorable mentions. **Postmark deadline:** September 1. Competition receives 120 entries/year. Most recent contest winners were Catherine Moran, Sheila K. Barksdale, and Ellin G. Anderson. Judges are Tom Roby and members of The Poets' Club. Winners will be notified by mail by October 15. Include SASE with entry to receive winners' list. The Poets' Club of Chicago meets monthly at the Harold Washington Library to critique their original poetry, which the members read at various venues in the Chicago area and publish in diverse magazines and books. Members also conduct workshops at area schools and libraries by invitation.

$🔲 POETS' DINNER CONTEST, 2214 Derby St., Berkeley CA 94705-1018. (510)841-1217. **Contact:** Dorothy V. Benson. **Contestant must be present to win.** Submit 3 anonymous typed copies of original, unpublished poems in not more than 3 of the 8 categories [Humor, Love, Nature, Beginnings & Endings, Spaces & Places, People, Theme (changed annually), and Poet's Choice] without fee. Winning poems (Grand Prize, 1st, 2nd, 3rd) are read at an awards banquet and honorable mentions are presented. Cash prizes awarded; Honorable Mention receives books. The event is nonprofit. Since 1927 there has been an annual awards banquet sponsored by the ad hoc Poets' Dinner Committee, currently at the Holiday Inn in Emaryville. Contest guidelines available for SASE. **Deadline:** January.

USE THE GENERAL INDEX in the back of this book to find the page number of a specific market. Also, markets listed in the 2003 edition but not included in this edition appear in the General Index with a code explaining their absence from the listings.

Competition receives about 300 entries. Recent contest winners include Sandy Stark (Grand Prize); Frank Taber, Tammy Durston, Audrey Allison, Karen Huff, Tanya Joyce, Ruth Levitan, Marcha Nicol, and Sheila Mohn (First Prizes). *Remembering*, an anthology of winning poems from the Poet's Dinner over the last 25 years is available by mail for $10.42 from Dorothy V. Benson at the contest address.

★ ◲ THE POETS' PRIZE, The Poets' Prize Committee, % the Nicholas Roerich Museum, 319 W. 107th St., New York NY 10025. (212)864-7752. Fax: (212)864-7704. E-mail: director@roerich.org. **Contact:** Daniel Entin. **Award Directors:** Robert McDowell, Frederick Morgan, and Louis Simpson. Annual cash award of $3,000 given for a book of verse by an American poet published in the previous year. The poet must be a US citizen. Poets making inquiries will receive an explanation of procedures. Accepts inquiries by fax. Books may be sent to the committee members. A list of the members and their addresses will be sent upon request with SASE. **Deadline:** August 1.

N $ THE PSA CHAPBOOK FELLOWSHIPS, Poetry Society of America, 15 Gramercy Park, New York NY 10003. (212)254-9628. Website: www.poetrysociety.org. Established 2002. Offers the PSA National Chapbook Fellowships and the PSA New York Chapbook Fellowships, with 4 prizes (2 for each fellowship) of $1,000, publication of the chapbook ms with distribution by the PSA, and an invitation to read at The PSA Festival of New American Poets in April. National Chapbook Fellowships open to any U.S. resident who has not published a full-length poetry collection; New York Chapbook Fellowships open to any New York City resident (in the 5 boroughs) who is 30 or under and has not published a full-length poetry collection. *Poets may apply to one contest only.* Complete submission guidelines for both fellowships available on website. **Entry fee:** $12 for both PSA members and nonmembers. Accepts entry fees in US dollars only, by check or money order to Poetry Society of American. **Deadline:** entries accepted between October 1 and December 21 (postmarked). Does not accept entries by fax or e-mail. 2002 judges were Carl Phillips and C.D. Wright (National Chapbook Fellowships); and John Ashbery and Eavan Boland (NY Chapbook Fellowships). Additional information available on website. (See separate listing for Poetry Society of America in the Organizations section; see separate listing for the Poetry Society of America Awards in this section.)

$ ◕ ◎ THE RAIZISS/DE PALCHI TRANSLATION AWARD (Specialized: Italian poetry translated into English), The Academy of American Poets, 588 Broadway, Suite 604, New York NY 10012-3210. (212)274-0343. Fax: (212)274-9427. E-mail: academy@poets.org. Website: www.poets.org. Established 1934. **Executive Director:** Tree Swenson. **Awards Coordinator:** Ryan Murphy. Awarded for outstanding translations of modern Italian poetry into English. A $5,000 book prize and a $20,000 fellowship are given in alternate years. **Book Prize Deadline:** submissions accepted in odd-numbered years September 1 through November 1. **Fellowship Deadline:** submissions accepted in even-numbered years September 1 through November 1. Guidelines and entry form available for SASE or on website. 2001 winner was Stephen Sartarelli for *Songbook: The Selected Poems of Umberto Saba*, chosen by Alfredo de Palchi, Dana Gioia, and Charles Wright. (For further information about The Academy of American Poets, see separate listing in the Organizations section.)

★ ◎ ROANOKE-CHOWAN POETRY AWARD (Specialized: regional/NC); NORTH CAROLINA LITERARY AND HISTORICAL ASSOCIATION, 4610 Mail Service Center, Raleigh NC 27699-4610. (919)733-9375. Fax: (919) 733-8807. E-mail: michael.hill@ncmail.net. Website: www.lib.unc.edu/ncc/onl/litawards.html. **Awards Coordinator:** Michael Hill. Offers annual award for "an original volume of poetry published during the twelve months ending June 30 of the year for which the award is given." Open to "authors who have maintained legal or physical residence, or a combination of both, in North Carolina for the three years preceding the close of the contest period." Submit 3 copies of each entry. Guidelines available for SASE or by fax or e-mail. **Deadline:** July 15. Competition receives about 15 entries. Winner will be announced by mail October 15.

◎ ◲ ANNA DAVIDSON ROSENBERG AWARD, FOR POEMS ON THE JEWISH EXPERIENCE (Specialized: ethnic), The Magnes Museum, 2911 Russell St., Berkeley CA 94705. (415)591-8800. Fax: (415)591-8815. E-mail: info@magnesmuseum.org. Website: www.magnesmuse

um.org/. Established 1987. Offers prizes of $100, $50, and $25, as well as Honorable Mentions, for unpublished poems (in English) on the Jewish Experience. "This award is open to all poets. You needn't be Jewish to enter."

● There was no award given in 2002 or in 2003; poets should query regarding the status of the award for 2004 before submitting. (**Note:** The Judah L. Magnes Museum and the Jewish Museum San Francisco merged as of January 1, 2002.)

$ ◙ SAN FRANCISCO FOUNDATION; JOSEPH HENRY JACKSON AWARD; JAMES D. PHELAN AWARD (Specialized: regional/CA, NV), % Intersection for the Arts, 446 Valencia St., San Francisco CA 94103. (415)626-2787. Fax: (415)626-1636. E-mail: info@theintersection.org. Website: www.theintersection.org. **Contact:** Awards Coordinator. Offers the Jackson Award ($2,000), established in 1955, to the author of an unpublished work-in-progress of fiction (novel or short stories), nonfictional prose, or poetry. Applicants must be residents of northern California or Nevada for 3 consecutive years immediately prior to the January 31 deadline and must be between the ages of 20 and 35 as of the deadline. Offers the Phelan Award ($2,000), established in 1935, to the author of an unpublished work-in-progress of fiction (novel or short stories), nonfictional prose, poetry, or drama. Applicants must be California-born (although they may now reside outside of the state), and must be between the ages of 20 and 35 as of the January 31 deadline. Manuscripts for both awards must be accompanied by an application form. The award judge will use a name-blind process. Manuscripts should be copied on the front and back of each page and must include a separate cover page that gives the work's title and the applicant's name and address. The applicant's name should only be listed on the cover page; do not list names or addresses on the pages of the ms. Applicants may, however, use the ms title and page numbers on the pages of the ms. Manuscripts with inappropriate identifying information will be deemed ineligible. Three copies of the ms should be forwarded with one properly completed current year's official application form to the address listed above. Guidelines available on website. Entries accepted November 15 through January 31. Competitions receive 150-180 entries. Recent contest winners include Richard Dry, Kristen Hanlon, and Angela Morales.

✪ ◉ ERNEST SANDEEN PRIZE IN POETRY, Creative Writing Program, Dept. of English, University of Notre Dame, Notre Dame IN 46556. (219)631-7526. Fax: (219)631-8209. E-mail: english.righter.1@nd.edu. Website: www.nd.edu/~alcwp. **Director of Creative Writing:** Valerie Sayers. Sponsored by the Creative Writing Program, Department of English, and the University of Notre Dame in conjunction with the University of Notre Dame Press. Offers a biannual award of $1,000 ($500 cash prize, $500 advance against royalties) and publication by the University of Notre Dame Press. Open to any author who has published at least one collection of poetry; however, "we will pay special attention to second volumes." Guidelines available for SASE or on website. **Entry fee:** $15 (every contestant receives a 1-year subscription to *Notre Dame Review* (see separate listing in Publishers of Poetry section). **Deadline:** accepts submissions May 1-September 30 biannually (see website for upcoming deadline). Competition receives 150 submissions per reading period. Most recent winner was John Latta (*Breeze*, 2003). Judges are the faculty of the Creative Writing Program. Winner will be announced in January following deadline and notified by phone and mail.

$ ◪ ◙ SARASOTA POETRY THEATRE PRESS; SOULSPEAK; EDDA POETRY CHAPBOOK COMPETITION FOR WOMEN; ANIMALS IN POETRY (Specialized: women/feminism; animals/pets), P.O. Box 48955, Sarasota FL 34230-6955. (941)366-6468. Fax: (941)954-2208. E-mail: soulspeak1@comcast.net. Website: www.soulspeak.org. Established 1994-1998. **Award Director:** Scylla Liscombe. Offers 2 annual contests for poetry with prizes ranging from 1st Prize: $50 plus publication in an anthology to 1st Prize: $100 plus 50 published chapbooks. Honorable Mentions also awarded. Pays winners from other countries in copies. Guidelines and details about theater available for SASE, by e-mail, or on website. Accepts queries by e-mail. **Entry fees:** range from $4/poem to $10/ms. **Postmark deadline:** Animals in Poetry, April 30 (winners notified in July); Edda Poetry Chapbook Competition for Women, February 28 (winners notified in May). Competitions receive an average of 600 entries/year. Judges for contests are the staff of the press and ranking state poets. Winners are notified by mail. "Sarasota Poetry Theatre Press is a division of SOULSPEAK/Sarasota Poetry Theatre, a nonprofit organization dedicated to encouraging poetry in all its forms through the Sarasota Poetry Theatre Press, Therapeutic SOULSPEAK for at-risk youth, and the SOULSPEAK Studio. We are looking for honest, not showy, poetry; use a good readable font. Do not send extraneous materials."

$☐ ◎ CLAUDIA ANN SEAMAN POETRY AWARD (Specialized: students grades 9-12), The Community Foundation of Dutchess County, 80 Washington St., Suite 201, Poughkeepsie NY 12601. (845)452-3077. Fax: (845)452-3083. Website: http://communityfoundationdc.org. **Program Director:** Karen Rudowski. Established 1983. Offers annual award of $500 (1st Prize) in national contest. Submissions must be unpublished but may be entered in other contests. Submit 1 or 2 poems on any subject, in any form. Open to US students grades 9-12. "Entry must contain student and school names, addresses, and phone numbers and the name of the English or writing teacher." Entry form and guidelines available for SASE or on website. **Deadline:** May 1. 2002 award winner was Aditi Gupts. 2002 judge was Edward Hirsch. Winner contacted by phone or in writing. Winner announced and recognized each year at the Barnes & Noble in Manhattan (announcement date August 1). Copies of last year's winning poem may be obtained by contacting The Community Foundation by phone or in writing. "The Community Foundation is a nonprofit organization serving Dutchess County, NY; it administers numerous grant programs, scholarship funds, and endowment funds for the benefit of the community. This is an excellent opportunity for young, previously unpublished poets to earn recognition for their work. Since there's no fee, there is little to lose; realize, however, that a national contest will have more entries than a regional competition."

[N] ◎ SHADOW POETRY SEASONAL POETRY COMPETITION (Specialized: themes/4 seasons), P.O. Box 125, Excelsior Springs MO 64024. Fax: (208)977-9114. E-mail: shadowpoetry@shadowpoetry.com. Website: www.shadowpoetry.com. Established 2000. **Award Director:** James Summers. Offers biannual award of $50 each in Winter, Spring, Summer, and Fall/Autumn categories. The top 4 winners also receive a certificate, printed copy of their poem, and an outstanding achievement ribbon. Pays winners from other countries in US dollars only by International Money Order. Submissions may be previously published and may be entered in other contests. Submit maximum of 10 poems/poet, 30 line limit/poem, must be written on the topics of Winter, Spring, Summer, or Fall/Autumn, in any form. "Entry form must be present with mail-in entries; name, address, phone number, e-mail address (when available) and seasonal category (Winter, Spring, Summer, Fall/Autumn) on upper left-hand corner of each poem submitted. Enclose SASE for winners list. Include an additional SASE for entry receipt (optional). If no SASE is included for receipt, Shadow Poetry will e-mail an entry confirmation to the contestant, if applicable." Entry form and guidelines available for SASE or on website. **Entry fee:** $3/poem. Does not accept entry fees in foreign currencies; accepts International Money Order, cash (US dollars), or payments through PayPal for foreign entries. **Deadlines:** June 30 and December 31. Winners will be announced "15 days after each contest ends, by e-mail and to those who requested a winners list. Results will also be posted on the Shadow Poetry website."

[N] $☐ SHADOW POETRY'S BI-ANNUAL CHAPBOOK COMPETITION, Shadows Ink Publications, P.O. Box 125, Excelsior Springs MO 64024. Fax: (208)977-9114. E-mail: shadowpoetry@shadowpoetry.com. Website: www.shadowpoetry.com. Established 2000. **Award Director:** James Summers. Offers biannual award $100, 50 copies of published chapbook with ISBN, and 20% royalties paid on each copy sold through Shadow Poetry (retail only). Pays winners from other countries in US dollars only by International Money Order. Submissions must be unpublished and may be entered in other contests. (Winning poet retains copyrights and may publish poems elsewhere later.) Submit ms of 16-40 pages, including poetry and acknowledgments, on any subject, in any form . "Cover letter required with name, address, phone, age, and e-mail address. Enclose cover letter, manuscript, and cover ideas/art, if applicable, in #90 (9 × 12) envelope. Include #10 SASE for winner notification." Guidelines available for SASE or on website. **Entry fee:** $10/ms. Does not accept entry fees in foreign currencies; accepts International Money Order, cash (US dollars) for foreign entries. **Deadlines:** June 30 and December 31. "Notification of winners no later than 20 days after deadline by SASE." Copies of winning or sample chapbooks available from Shadow Poetry for $6.25 (see website for titles).

N̄ $☐ SHADOWS INK POETRY CONTEST, Shadows Ink Publications, P.O. Box 125, Excelsior Springs MO 64024. Fax: (208)977-9114. E-mail: shadowpoetry@shadowpoetry.com. Website: www.shadowpoetry.com. Established 2000. **Award Director:** James Summers. Offers annual award of 1st Prize: $100 and chapbook publication; 2nd Prize: $75; 3rd Prize: $35; top 3 winners also receive a certificate, printed copy of their poem, and a ribbon. The top 40 placing poems will be published in a Shadows Ink Poetry Chapbook, and all poets appearing in this publication will receive one free copy (additional copies available for $5 each plus shipping). Pays winners from other countries in US dollars only by International Money Order. Submissions must be unpublished and may be entered in other contests. (Winning poets retain copyrights and may publish poems elsewhere later.) Submit maximum of 10 poems, 24 line limit each, on any subject, in any form. "Entry form must be present with mail-in entries; name, address, phone number, and e-mail address (when available) on upper left-hand corner of each poem submitted. Enclose SASE for winners list. Include an additional SASE for entry receipt (optional). If no SASE is included for receipt, Shadow Poetry will e-mail an entry confirmation to the contestant, if applicable." Entry form and guidelines available for SASE or on website. **Entry fee:** $5/poem. Does not accept entry fees in foreign currencies; accepts International Money Order, cash (US dollars), or payments through PayPal for foreign entries. **Deadline:** December 31. Competition receives 300 entries/year. "Winners will be announced February 1 by e-mail and to those who requested a winners list. Results will also be posted on the Shadow Poetry website."

$☐ SKY BLUE WATERS POETRY CONTESTS; SKY BLUE WATERS POETRY SOCIETY, 232 SE 12th Ave., Faribault MN 55021-6406. (507)332-2803. **Contact:** Marlene Meehl. Sponsors monthly contests with prizes of $40, $30, $20, $10, plus 3 paid Editors Choice Awards of $5 each. Pays winners from other countries by check. Accepts simultaneous submissions. Submit any number of poems on any subject. Guidelines available for SASE. **Entry fee:** $2 first poem, $1 each additional poem. Does not accept entry fees in foreign currencies; send check or money order. Winners will be announced by mail one month following deadline date. "The Sky Blue Waters Poetry Society is a group of Southern Minnesota poets who exist for the sheer 'love of writing.' Most members agree that writing is not just a love but a necessity. Keep writing. Keep submitting. Today's creation will be tomorrow's winner."

$☐ SLAPERING HOL PRESS CHAPBOOK COMPETITION, The Hudson Valley Writers' Center, 300 Riverside Dr., Sleepy Hollow NY 10591. (914)332-5953. Fax: (914)332-4825. E-mail: info@writerscenter.org. Website: www.writerscenter.org. Established 1990. **Coeditor:** Margo Stever. Offers annual award of $500, publication, 10 author's copies, and a reading at The Hudson Valley Writers' Center. Pays winners from other countries with check in US currency. Submissions must be from poets who have not previously published a book or chapbook. Submit 16-20 pages of poetry, any form or style. **Entry fee:** $10. "Manuscript should be anonymous with separate cover sheet containing name, address, phone number, a bio, and acknowledgements." Guidelines available for SASE, by fax, e-mail, or on website. **Deadline:** May 15. Competition receives 200-300 entries. Most recent contest winner was Susan H. Case, (*The Scottish Café*). Winner will be announced in September. Copies of winning books available through website.

$☐ KAY SNOW WRITING AWARDS; WILLAMETTE WRITERS; THE WILLAMETTE WRITER, 9045 SW Barbur Blvd., Suite 5A, Portland OR 97219-4027. (503)452-1592. Fax: (503)452-0372. E-mail: wilwrite@teleport.com. Website: www.willamettewriters.com. Established 1986. **Award Director:** Elizabeth Shannon. Offers annual awards of 1st Prize: $300, 2nd Prize: $150, 3rd Prize: $50 and publication of excerpt only in December issue of *The Willamette Writer*. Pays winners from other countries by postal money order. Submissions must be unpublished. Submit up to 2 poems (one entry fee), maximum 5 pages total, on any subject in any style or form, single spaced, one side of paper only. Entry form and guidelines available for SASE or on website. Accepts inquiries by fax and e-mail. **Entry fee:** $10 for members of Willamette Writers; $15 for nonmembers. Does not accept entry fees in foreign currencies; only accepts a check drawn on a US bank. **Deadline:** May 15. Competition receives 150 entries. Most recent winners were Rayette Eitel, Mary Peers, Deena Lindstedt, Carla Perry, and Katie Koerper. Winners will be announced July 31. "Write and send in your very best poem. Read it aloud. If it still sounds like the best poem you've ever heard, send it in."

✪ $◻ SOUTH DAKOTA STATE POETRY SOCIETY (SDSPS) ANNUAL POETRY CONTEST; PASQUE PETALS, South Dakota State Poetry Society, P.O. 136, Canova SD 57321-0136. (605)523-2486. Established 1975. **SDSPS Contest Chairman:** Martha Hegdahl. Offers annual awards for poetry in several categories; some are for South Dakota residents only, others are open to all poets. Grand Prize—1st Prize: $75, 2nd Prize: $50, 3rd Prize: $25; all other categories—1st Prize: $25, 2nd Prize: $15, 3rd Prize: $10 (unless otherwise specified by sponsor). Poems must be original, unpublished, and have won no more than $10 in competition. Send as many poems as desired for Grand Prize category; send only one poem/category for rest of competition. No poem may be entered in more than one category and, except where noted in guidelines, length is limited to 40 lines/poem. All poems except haiku and tanka must be titled. Send one original and one copy with the category on the upper left of both, and your name and address on the upper right of copy only. Entry form and guidelines (including list of categories and prizes) available for SASE. **Entry fees:** range from $2-7, depending on category and membership status; see guidelines for complete information. **Deadline:** mid-August. Competition receives about 300 entries/year. Most recent award winners were Clarence Socwell, Cynthia Stupnick, Maria V. Bakkum, Emma Dimit, Carlee Swann, and Glenna Holloway. Complete list of winners in all categories available for SASE after October 31. Judges are selected from National Federation of State Poetry Society members during their summer meeting. There were 13 individual judges from across the US for the 2002 contests, a different judge for each category. The contest chairman announces the winners during the SDSPS Fall Conference in October. Winners not present are notified by mail. Winning poems will be published in *Pasque Petals,* the SDSPS magazine—free to winners and available by request to others for a fee. (See separate listing for South Dakota State Poetry Society in the Organizations section.) "Send SASE for rules and regulations—*read thoroughly!*"

◎ THE WALLACE STEVENS AWARD, The Academy of American Poets, 588 Broadway, Suite 604, New York NY 10012-3210. (212)274-0343. Fax: (212)274-9427. E-mail: academy@poets.org. Website: www.poets.org. Established 1934. **Executive Director:** Tree Swenson. **Awards Coordinator:** Ryan Murphy. Awards $150,000 annually to a poet for proven mastery in the art of poetry. **No applications are accepted.** 2002 winner was Ruth Stone, chosen by Marie Howe, Galway Kinnell, Yusef Komunyakaa, Dorianne Laux, and Phillip Levine. (For further information about The Academy of American Poets, see separate listing in the Organizations section.)

$◪ ◎ TOWSON UNIVERSITY PRIZE FOR LITERATURE (Specialized: regional/ Maryland), Towson University, College of Liberal Arts, Towson MD 21252. (410)704-2128. Fax: (410)704-6392. **Award Director:** Dean of the College of Liberal Arts. Offers annual prize of $1,000 "for a single book or book-length manuscript of fiction, poetry, drama, or imaginative nonfiction by a young Maryland writer. The prize is granted on the basis of literary and aesthetic excellence as determined by a panel of distinguished judges appointed by the university. The first award, made in the fall of 1980, went to novelist Anne Tyler." Work must have been published within the 3 years prior to the year of nomination or must be scheduled for publication within the year in which nominated. Submit 5 copies of work in bound form or in typewritten, double-spaced ms form. Entry form and guidelines available for SASE. Accepts inquiries by e-mail. **Deadline:** June 15. Competition receives 8-10 entries. Most recent contest winners were Karren Alenier and Barbara Hurd (co-winners).

⊕ $◪ ◎ THE TREWITHEN POETRY PRIZE (Specialized: rural), Trewithen Poetry, Chy-An-Dour, Trewithen Moor, Stithians, Truro, Cornwall TR3 7DU England. Website: www.trewith enpoetry.co.uk. Established 1995. **Competition Administrator:** D. Atkinson. Offers biennial award of 1st Prize: £500, 2nd Prize: £150, 3rd Prize: £75, plus 3 runner-up prizes of £25 each. Pays winners from other countries by "sterling cheque" or draft only. Submissions may be entered in other contests "*but* must *not* previously have won another competition." Submit any number of poems on a rural theme in any form. Entry form available for SASE or on website (not available until April 2004). **Entry fee:** £3 for the first poem and £2 for each additional poem. Does not accept entry fees in foreign currencies; send "sterling cheque" or draft only. **Deadline:** October 31 of contest year (next competition in 2004). Competition receives 1,000-1,500 entries. Recent contest winners were Lesley Quayle, Mike Sharpe, Mike Barlow, and W.R. Chadwick. Judged by a panel of 3-4 working poets who remain anonymous. Winners will be announced at the end of December by results sheet, through poetry magazines and organizations, and on website. Copies of *The Trewithen Chapbook* may be obtained for $2 each by using order form on entry form, by writing direct to the secretary and enclosing a SAE with IRC, or on website. "We are seeking good writing with a contemporary approach, reflecting any aspect of nature or rural life in any country."

$🖉 KATE TUFTS DISCOVERY AWARD; KINGSLEY TUFTS POETRY AWARD, Poetic Gallery for the Kingsley and Kate Tufts Poetry Awards, Claremont Graduate University, 160 E. 10th St., Harper East B7, Claremont CA 91711-6165. (909)621-8974. Website: www.cgu.edu/tufts/. Established 1992 (Kingsley Tufts Award) and 1993 (Kate Tufts Award). Kate Tufts Discovery Award offers $10,000 annually "for a first or very early work by a poet of genuine promise." Kingsley Tufts Poetry Award offers $100,000 annually "for a work by an emerging poet, one who is past the very beginning but has not yet reached the acknowledged pinnacle of his/her career." Books for the 2004 prizes must have been published between September 15, 2002 and September 15, 2003. Entry form and guidelines available for SASE or on website. **Deadline:** September 15. Most recent award winners were Linda Gregerson (Kingsley Tufts, 2003) and Joanie Mackowski (Kate Tufts, 2003). Winners announced in February. Check website for updated deadlines and award information.

🌐 $🖉 VER POETS OPEN COMPETITION, Ver Poets, Haycroft, 61/63 Chiswell Green Lane, St. Albans, Hertfordshire AL2 3AL United Kingdom. Phone: (01727)867005. E-mail: may.bad man@virgin.net. Established 1974. **Organiser/Editor:** May Badman. Offers annual open competition with prizes totaling £1,000, plus a free copy of anthology, *Vision On* with winning and selected poems. Pays winners from other countries in sterling by cheque. Submissions must be unpublished. Submit any number of poems on any subject, "open as to style, form, content. Sincere writing of high quality and skill gets the prizes. Poem must be no more than 30 lines excluding title, typed on white A4 sheets. Entry forms provided, pseudonyms to be used on poems." Two copies of poems required. **Entry fee:** £3/poem. Entry form and guidelines available for SASE (or SAE and IRC) or by e-mail. Accepts entry fees in foreign currencies. **Deadline:** April 30. Competition receives about 1,000 entries/year. Most recent contest winners were Margaret Speak, John Monks, Daphne Schiller, and Michael Henry. Recent adjudicators include John Gohorry and Alan Brownjohn. Winners announced at an "Adjudication & Tea" event in June each year and by post. Copies of winning anthologies available from May Badman at the contest address. "We have local and postal members, meet regularly in St. Albans, study poetry and the writing of it, try to guide members to reach a good standard, arrange 3 competitions per year with prizes and anthologies for members only. Plus the annual open competition. We do expect a high standard of art and skill. We make a gift to a charity each year."

🌐 $◎ WESTERN AUSTRALIAN PREMIER'S BOOK AWARDS (Specialized: regional/Western Australia), State Library of Western Australia, Alexander Library Bldg., Perth Cultural Centre, Perth, Western Australia 6000 Australia. Phone: (61 8)9427 3330. Fax: (61 8)9427 3336. E-mail: jham@liswa.wa.gov.au. Website: www.liswa.wa.gov.au/pba.html. Established 1982. **Award Director:** Ms. Julie Ham. Offers annual poetry prize of AUS $7,500 for a published book of poetry. Winner also eligible for Premier's Prize of AUS $20,000. Submissions must be previously published. Open to poets born in Western Australia, current residents of Western Australia, or poets who have resided in Western Australia for at least 10 years at some stage. Entry form and guidelines available by mail or on website. Accepts inquiries by fax and e-mail. No entry fee. **2003 Deadline:** January 6. Competition receives about 10-15 entries in poetry category/year (120 overall). Most recent winner was *Halfway Up the Mountain* by Dorothy Hewett. 2002 judges were Prof. Vijay Mishra, Ms. Sue Wyche, Dr. Simon Adams, and Mr. Zolton Kovacs. Winners announced in June each year (i.e., June 2003 for 2002 awards) at a presentation dinner given by the Premier of Western Australia. "The contest is organized by the State Library of Western Australia, with money provided by the Western Australian State Government to support literature."

★ ☑ **WHITING WRITERS' AWARDS; MRS. GILES WHITING FOUNDATION**, 1133 Avenue of the Americas, 22nd Floor, New York NY 10036-6710. **Director:** Barbara K. Bristol. The Foundation makes awards of $35,000 each to up to 10 writers of fiction, nonfiction, poetry and plays chosen by a selection committee drawn from a list of recognized writers, literary scholars, and editors. Recipients of the award are selected from nominations made by writers, educators, and editors from communities across the country whose experience and vocations bring them in contact with individuals of unusual talent. The nominators and selectors are appointed by the foundation and serve anonymously. **Direct applications and informal nominations are not accepted by the foundation.**

$ ☑ **THE WALT WHITMAN AWARD**, The Academy of American Poets, 588 Broadway, Suite 604, New York NY 10012-3210. (212)274-0343. Fax: (212)274-9427. E-mail: academy@poets.org. Website: www.poets.org. Established 1934. **Executive Director:** Tree Swenson. **Awards Coordinator:** Ryan Murphy. Offers $5,000 plus publication of a poet's first book by Louisiana State University Press. The Academy of American Poets distributes over 10,000 copies of the Whitman Award-winning book to its members. Winner also receives a 1-month residency at the Vermont Studio Center. Submit mss of 50-100 pages. Poets must be American citizens. Entry form required; entry form and guidelines available for SASE or on website. **Entry fee:** $25. **Deadline:** submit between September 15 and November 15. 2002 winner was Sue Kwock Kim for *Notes from the Divided Country*, chosen by Yusef Komunyakaa. (For further information about The Academy of American Poets, see separate listing in the Organizations section.)

$ ☑ **STAN AND TOM WICK POETRY PRIZE**, Wick Poetry Program, Dept. of English, Kent State University, P.O. Box 5190, Kent OH 44242-0001. (330)672-2067. Fax: (330)672-2567. E-mail: wickpoet@kent.edu. Website: http://dept.kent.edu/wick. Established 1994. **Program Coordinator:** Maggie Anderson. Offers annual award of $2,000 and publication by Kent State University Press. Submissions must be unpublished as a whole and may be entered in other contests as long as the Wick program receives notice upon acceptance elsewhere. Submit 48-68 pages of poetry. Open to poets writing in English who have not yet published a full-length collection. Entries must include cover sheet with poet's name, address, telephone number, and title of ms. Guidelines available for SASE or on website. **Entry fee:** $20. Does not accept entry fees in foreign currencies; send money order or US check. **Deadline:** May 1. Competition receives 700-800 entries. 2002 contest winner was Eve Alexander. 2002 judge was C.K. Williams.

$ ◎ **THE RICHARD WILBUR AWARD (Specialized: American poets)**, Dept. of English, University of Evansville, 1800 Lincoln Ave., Evansville IN 47722. (812)479-2963. Website: http:// english.evansville.edu/english/WilburAwardGuidelines.htm. **Series Director:** William Baer. Offers a biennial award (even-numbered years) of $1,000 and book publication to "recognize a quality book-length manuscript of poetry." Submissions must be unpublished ("although individual poems may have had previous journal publications") original poetry collections and "public domain or permission-secured translations may comprise up to one-third of the manuscript." Submit ms of 50-100 typed pages, unbound, bound, or clipped. Open to all American poets. Manuscripts should be accompanied by 2 title pages: one with collection's title, author's name, address, and phone number; one with only the title. Include SASE for contest results. Submissions may be entered in other contests. Manuscripts are *not* returned. Guidelines available for SASE or on webiste. **Entry fee:** $25/ms. **Next postmark deadline:** December 2, 2004. Competition receives 300-500 entries. Recent contest winner was A.M. Juster. Judge for last contest was Charles Martin. The winning ms is published and copyrighted by the University of Evansville Press.

★ $ ☑ **OSCAR WILLIAMS & GENE DERWOOD AWARD**, New York Community Trust, 2 Park Ave., New York NY 10016. An award given annually to nominees of the selection committee "to help needy or worthy artists or poets." **Selection Committee for the award does not accept submissions or nominations.** Amount varies from year to year.

$ ☑ ◎ **WORLD ORDER OF NARRATIVE AND FORMALIST POETS (Specialized: subscription, form/metrical)**, P.O. Box 580174, Station A, Flushing NY 11358-0174. Established 1980. **Contest Chairman:** Dr. Alfred Dorn. Sponsors contests in a number of categories for traditional and contemporary poetic forms, including the sonnet, blank verse, ballade, villanelle, and new forms created by Alfred Dorn. Prizes total at least $5,000. **Entry fee:** None, but only subscribers to *The Formalist* are eligible for the competition. Complete contest guidelines available for SASE from Alfred Dorn. "Our focus is on metrical poetry characterized by striking diction and original metaphors. We do not want trite or commonplace language." **Deadline:** 2003 deadline was August 20. Competition receives about 3,000 entries. Past contest winners include Melissa Cannon, Rhina P. Espaillat, Len Krisak, Jennifer Reeser, Alfred Nicol, and Deborah Warren. (For more information on *The Formalist*, see listing in the Publishers of Poetry section.)

⊕ $◻ THE WRITERS BUREAU POETRY AND SHORT STORY COMPETITION, The Writers Bureau, Sevendale House, 7 Dale St., Manchester M1 1JB England. Phone: +44 161 228 2362. Fax: +44 161 228 3533. E-mail: comp@writersbureau.com. Website: www.writersbureau.com/resources.htm. Established 1994. **Contact:** Head of Student Services. Offers annual prizes of 1st Place: £1,000, 2nd: £400, 3rd: £200, 4th: £100, six 5th Place prizes of £50, and publication in *Freelance Market News*. Submissions must be unpublished. "Any number of entries may be sent. There is no set theme or form. Entries must be typed, and no longer than 40 lines." Accepts entries by regular mail or by fax. Entry form available for SASE or on website. Accepts inquiries by fax or e-mail. **Deadline:** late July. Recent contest judge was Alison Chisholm. Winner(s) will be announced in September. "The Writers Bureau is a distance learning college offering correspondence courses in Journalism, Creative Writing, and Poetry." (See listing for *Freelance Market News* in the Publications of Interest section.)

$◻ THE W.B. YEATS SOCIETY ANNUAL POETRY COMPETITION, W.B. Yeats Society of New York, National Arts Club, 15 Gramercy Park S, New York NY 10003. (212)780-0605. Website: www.YeatsSociety.org. Established 1994. **President:** Andrew McGowan. Offers annual $250 cash prize for 1st Place, $100 cash prize for 2nd Place, and optional Honorable Mentions. Open to beginner as well as established poets. Winners are invited to read their winning entries at the Taste of the Yeats Summer School, held each April in New York; also inducted as Honorary Members of the Society (a 501(c)(3) charitable organization). Judges have included poets Eamon Grennan, L.S. Asekoff, Campbell McGrath, Billy Collins, Harvey Shapiro, and Paul Muldoon. Submissions may be entered in other contests. Submit any number of unpublished poems in any style or form, up to 50 lines each, typed on letter-size paper without poet's name. Guidelines available for SASE or on website; no entry form required. **Reading fee:** $7 for first poem, $6 per additional poem. Attach a 3×5 card to each entry containing the poem's title along with the poet's name, address, and phone/fax/e-mail. **Annual deadline:** February 15. Winners selected by March 31 and announced in April. Winning entries and judge's report are posted on the Society's website. Printed report available for SASE. Receives 200-300 entries/year. Most recent winners were Geraldine Connolly (1st), Karen Drayne (2nd), and Susan Thomas and George Drew (Honorable Mention). (See separate listing for W.B. Yeats Society of New York in the Organizations section.)

◻ PHYLLIS SMART YOUNG PRIZE IN POETRY, *The Madison Review*, Dept. of English, 600 N. Park St., Helen C. White Hall, University of Wisconsin-Madison, Madison WI 53706. (608)263-2566. E-mail: madreview@mail.student.org.wisc.edu (inquiries only). Website: http://mendota.english.wisc.edu/~MadRev. Offers annual prize of $500 and publication in *The Madison Review* for "the best group of three unpublished poems submitted by a single author, any form." All entries will be considered as submissions to *The Madison Review*. Submissions must be unpublished. Submit 3 poems, any form, with SASE. Guidelines available for SASE and in announcement in *AWP* or *Poets & Writers* magazines. **Entry fee:** $5. Make checks or money orders payable to *The Madison Review*. **Deadline:** submissions accepted September 1-30 only. No mss returned; allow 9 months for response. Competition receives about 300 entries/year. (See listing for *The Madison Review* in the Publishers of Poetry section.)

◼ **INDICATES A MARKET** that did not appear in the 2003 edition.

N ◎ **ZEN GARDEN HAIKU CONTEST (Specialized: form/style, haiku)**, Shadow Poetry, P.O. Box 125, Excelsior Springs MO 64024. Fax: (208)977-9114. E-mail: shadowpoetry@shadowpoe try.com. Website: www.shadowpoetry.com. Established 2000. **Award Director:** James Summers. Offers annual award of 1st Prize: $100; 2nd Prize: $50; 3rd Prize: $25, plus the top 3 winners also receive a certificate, a printed copy of their poem, and a ribbon. Pays winners from other countries in US dollars only by International Money Order. Submissions may be previously published and may be entered in other contests. Submit any number of haiku on any subject . "Haiku entries must be typed on 8½×11 paper, submitted in duplicate. Poet's name, address, phone number, and e-mail address (if applicable) in the upper left-hand corner of one sheet. If submitting more than one haiku, each poem must be typed on separate sheets (3×5 index card entries welcome). Submit haiku entries in duplicate, neatly handwritten or typed, with poet information on the back of only one card. Repeat method for multiple submissions." Entry form and guidelines available for SASE or on website. **Entry fee:** $2/haiku. Does not accept entry fees in foreign currencies; accepts International Money Order, cash (US dollars), or payments through PayPal for foreign entries. **Deadline:** December 31. Winners will be announced February 1 each year "by e-mail and to those who requested a winners list. Results will also be posted on the Shadow Poetry website."

(See page 456 for Additional Contests & Awards.)

Additional Contests & Awards

The following listings also contain information about contests and awards. Turn to the page numbers indicated for details about their offerings.

State & Provincial Grants

Arts councils in the United States and Canada provide assistance to artists (including poets) in the form of fellowships or grants. These grants can be substantial and confer prestige upon recipients; however, **only state or province residents are eligible**. Because deadlines and available support vary annually, query first (with a SASE).

UNITED STATES ARTS AGENCIES

Alabama State Council on the Arts, *201 Monroe St., Montgomery AL 36130-1800. (334)242-4076. E-mail: staff@arts.state.al.us. Website: www.arts.state.al.us.*

Alaska State Council on the Arts, *411 W. Fourth Ave., Suite 1-E, Anchorage AK 99501-2343. (907)269-6610 or (888)278-7424. E-mail: aksca_info@eed.state.ak.us. Website: www.educ.state.ak.us/aksca.*

Arizona Commission on the Arts, *417 W. Roosevelt, Phoenix AZ 85003. (602)255-5882. E-mail: general@ArizonaArts.org. Website: www.ArizonaArts.org/.*

Arkansas Arts Council, *1500 Tower Bldg., 323 Center St., Little Rock AR 72201. (501)324-9766. E-mail: info@arkansasarts.com. Website: www.arkansasarts.com.*

California Arts Council, *1300 I St., Suite 930, Sacramento CA 95814. (916)322-6555 or (800)201-6201. Website: www.cac.ca.gov/.*

Colorado Council on the Arts, *750 Pennsylvania St., Denver CO 80203-3699. (303)894-2617. Website: www.coloarts.state.co.us/.*

Connecticut Commission on the Arts, *755 Main St., 1 Financial Plaza, Hartford CT 06103. (860)566-4770. E-mail: artsinfo@ctarts.org. Website: www.ctarts.org.*

Delaware State Arts Council, *Carvel State Office Bldg., 820 N. French St., Wilmington DE 19801. (302)577-8278 (New Castle Co.), (302)739-5304 (Kent or Sussex Counties). E-mail: delarts@state.de.us. Website: www.artsdel.org.*

District of Columbia Commission on the Arts & Humanities, *410 Eighth St., NW, 5th Floor, Washington DC 20004. (202)724-5613. Website: http://dcarts.dc.gov.*

Florida Arts Council, *Division of Cultural Affairs, Florida Dept. of State, 1001 DeSoto Park Dr., Tallahassee FL 32301. (850)245-6470. E-mail: info@florida-arts.org. Website: www.florida-arts.org.*

Georgia Council for the Arts, *260 14th St., Suite 401, Atlanta GA 30318. (404)685-2787. E-mail: gaarts@gaarts.org. Website: www.gaarts.org/.*

Guam Council on the Arts & Humanities Agency, *703 East Sunset Blvd., Tiyan GU. (671)475-2242. E-mail: Kaha1@kuentos.guam.net. Website: www.guam.net/gov/kaha/.*

Hawaii State Foundation on Culture & the Arts, *250 S. Hotel St., 2nd Floor, Honolulu HI 96813. (808)586-0300. E-mail: sfca@sfca.state.hi.us. Website: www.state.hi.us/sfca.*

Idaho Commission on the Arts, *P.O. Box 83720, Boise ID 83720-0008. (208)334-2119 or (800)278-3863. E-mail: bgarrett@ica.state.id.us. Website: www2.state.id.us/arts.*

Illinois Arts Council, *James R. Thompson Center, 100 W. Randolph, Suite 10-500, Chicago IL 60601. (312)814-6750. E-mail: info@arts.state.il.us. Website: www.state.il.us/agency/iac.*

Indiana Arts Commission, *402 W. Washington St., Indianapolis IN 46204-2739. (317)232-1268. E-mail: arts@state.in.us. Website: www.state.in.us/iac/.*

Iowa Arts Council, *600 E. Locust, Capitol Complex, Des Moines IA 50319-0290. (515)281-6412. Website: www.culturalaffairs.org/iac/.*

Kansas Arts Commission, *700 SW Jackson, Suite 1004, Topeka KS 66603-3761. (785)296-3335. E-mail: KAC@arts.state.ks.us. Website: http://arts.state.ks.us/.*

Kentucky Arts Council, *Old Capitol Annex, 300 W. Broadway, Frankfort KY 40601-1980. (502)564-3757. E-mail: kyarts@mail.state.ky.us. Website: www.kyarts.org.*

Louisiana Division of the Arts, *P.O. Box 44247, Baton Rouge LA 70804-4247. (225)342-8180. E-mail: arts@crt.state.la.us. Website: www.crt.state.la.us/arts/.*

Maine Arts Commission, *193 State St., 25 State House Station, Augusta ME 04333-0025. (207)287-2724. E-mail: mac.info@maine.gov. Website: www.mainearts.com.*

Maryland State Arts Council, *175 West Ostend St., Suite E, Baltimore MD 21230. (410)767-6555. E-mail: marylandstateartscouncil@msac.org. Website: www.msac.org/.*

Massachusetts Cultural Council, *10 St. James Ave., 3rd Floor, Boston MA 02116-3803. (617)727-3668. E-mail: web@art.state.ma.us. Website: www.massculturalcouncil.org/.*

Michigan Council for Arts & Cultural Affairs, *702 W. Kalamazoo, P.O. Box 30705, Lansing MI 48909. (517)241-4011. E-mail: artsinfo@michigan.gov. Website: www.michigan.gov/hal/0,1607,7-160-17445_19272---,00.html.*

Minnesota State Arts Board, *Park Square Court, 400 Sibley St., Suite 200, St. Paul MN 55101-1928. (651)215-1600 or (800)8MN-ARTS. E-mail: msab@state.mn.us. Website: www.arts.state.mn.us/.*

Mississippi Arts Commission, *239 N. Lamar St., Suite 207, Jackson MS 39201. (601)359-6030. Website: www.arts.state.ms.us/.*

Missouri Arts Council, *Wainwright State Office Complex, 111 N. Seventh St., Suite 105, St. Louis MO 63101-2188. (314)340-6845. E-mail: moarts@ded.state.mo.us. Website: www.missouriartscouncil.org.*

Montana Arts Council, *P.O. Box 202201, Helena MT 59620-2201. (406)444-6430. E-mail: mac@state.mt.us. Website: www.art.state.mt.us.*

National Assembly of State Arts Agencies, *1029 Vermont Ave., NW, 2nd Floor, Washington DC 20005. (202)347-6352. E-mail: nasaa@nasaa-arts.org. Website: www.nasaa-arts.org.*

Nebraska Arts Council, *Joslyn Carriage House, 3838 Davenport St., Omaha NE 68131-2329. (402)595-2122. E-mail: cmalloy@nebraskaartscouncil.org. Website: www.nebraskaartscouncil.org.*

Nevada Arts Council, *716 N. Carson St., Suite A, Carson City NV 89701. (775)687-6680. E-mail: kjodonne@clan.lib.nv.us. Website: http://dmla.clan.lib.nv.us/docs/arts/.*

New Hampshire State Council on the Arts, *40 N. Main St., Concord NH 03301-4974. (603)271-2789. Website: http://webster.state.nh.us/nharts.*

New Jersey State Council on the Arts, *P.O. Box 306, 225 W. State St., Trenton NJ 08625. (609)292-6130. E-mail: njsca@arts.sos.state.nj.us. Website: www.njartscouncil.org/.*

New Mexico Arts, *P.O. Box 1450, Santa Fe NM 87504-1450. (505)827-6490. Website: www.nmarts.org/.*

New York State Council on the Arts, *175 Varick St., 3rd Floor, New York NY 10014. (212)627-4455. Website: www.nysca.org.*

North Carolina Arts Council, *Dept. of Cultural Resources, Raleigh NC 27699-4632. (919)733-2111. E-mail: ncarts@ncmail.net. Website: www.ncarts.org/.*

North Dakota Council on the Arts, *418 E. Broadway, Suite 70, Bismarck ND 58501-4086. (701)328-3954. E-mail: comserv@state.nd.us. Website: www.state.nd.us/arts/.*

Ohio Arts Council, *727 E. Main St., Columbus OH 43205-1796. (614)466-2613. E-mail: bob.fox@oac.state.oh.us. Website: www.oac.state.oh.us/.*

Oklahoma Arts Council, *P.O. Box 52001-2001, Oklahoma City OK 73152-2001. (405)521-2931. E-mail: okarts@arts.state.ok.us. Website: www.arts.state.ok.us/.*

Oregon Arts Commission, *775 Summer St. NE, Suite 200, Salem OR 97301-1284. (503)986-0082. E-mail: oregon.artscomm@state.or.us. Website: www.oregonartscommission.org.*

Pennsylvania Council on the Arts, *Room 216, Finance Bldg., Harrisburg PA 17120. (717)787-6883. Website: www.artsnet.org/pca/.*

Institute of Puerto Rican Culture, *P.O. Box 9024184, San Juan PR 00902-4184. (787)725-5137. E-mail: iprac@aspira.org. Website: http://iprac.aspira/org/.*

Rhode Island State Council on the Arts, *83 Park St., 6th Floor, Providence RI 02903-1037. (401)222-3880. E-mail: info@risca.state.ri.us. Website: www.risca.state.ri.us/.*

South Carolina Arts Commission, *1800 Gervais St., Columbia SC 29201. (803)734-8696. E-mail: goldstsa@arts.state.sc.us. Website: www.state.sc.us/arts/.*

South Dakota Arts Council, *Office of the Arts, 800 Governors Dr., Pierre SD 57501-2294. (605)773-3131. E-mail: sdac@stlib.state.sd.us. Website: www.state.sd.us/deca/sdarts/.*

Tennessee Arts Commission, *Citizens Plaza, 401 Charlotte Ave., Nashville TN 37243-0780. (615)741-1701. E-mail: dennis.adkins@state.tn.us. Website: www.arts.state.tn.us.*

Texas Commission on the Arts, *P.O. Box 13406, Capitol Station, Austin TX 78711. (512)463-5535. E-mail: front.desk@arts.state.tx.us. Website: www.arts.state.tx.us/.*

Utah Arts Council, *617 E. South Temple St., Salt Lake City UT 84102. (801)236-7555. Website: www.dced.state.ut.us/arts/.*

Vermont Arts Council, *136 State St., Drawer 33, Montpelier VT 05633-6001. (802)828-3291. E-mail: info@vermontartscouncil.org. Website: www.vermontartscouncil.org.*

Virgin Islands Council on the Arts, *P.O. Box 103, St. Thomas VI 00804. (340)774-5984. E-mail: vicouncil@islands.vi.*

Virginia Commission for the Arts, *Lewis House, 2nd Floor, 223 Governor St., Richmond VA 23219-2010. (804)225-3132. E-mail: arts@state.va.us. Website: www.arts.state.va.us/.*

Washington State Arts Commission, *234 E. Eighth Ave., P.O. Box 42675, Olympia WA 98504-2675. (360)753-3860. Website: www.arts.wa.gov.*

West Virginia Commission on the Arts, *Cultural Center, 1900 Kanawha Blvd. E., Charleston WV 25305-0300. (304)558-0240. Website: www.wvculture.org/arts/.*

Wisconsin Arts Board, *101 E. Wilson St., 1st Floor, Madison WI 53702. (608)266-0190. E-mail: artsboard@arts.state.wi.us. Website: http://arts.state.wi.us.*

Wyoming Arts Council, *2320 Capitol Ave., Cheyenne WY 82002. (307)777-7742. E-mail: ebratt@state.wy.us. Website: http://wyoarts.state.wy.us/.*

CANADIAN PROVINCES ARTS AGENCIES

Alberta Foundation for the Arts, *901 Standard Life Centre, 10405 Jasper Ave., Edmonton AB T5J 4R7. (780)427-6315. Website: www.cd.gov.ab.ca/all_about_us/commissions/arts/index.asp.*

British Columbia Arts Council, *P.O. Box 9819, Stn. Prov. Govt., Victoria BC V8W 9W3. (250)356-1718. E-mail: Tracy.Black@gems1.gov.bc.ca. Website: www.bcartscouncil.gov.bc.ca.*

The Canada Council, *350 Albert St., P.O. Box 1047, Ottawa ON K1P 5V8. (613)566-4414. E-mail: info@canadacouncil.ca. Website: www.canadacouncil.ca/grants/publishing.*

Manitoba Arts Council, *525-93 Lombard Ave., Winnipeg MB R3B 3B1. (204)945-2237. E-mail: info@artscouncil.mb.ca. Website: www.artscouncil.mb.ca.*

New Brunswick Arts Board (NBAB), *634 Queen St., Suite 300, Fredericton NB E3B 1C2. E-mail: nbabcanb@nbab-canb.nb.ca. Website: www.artsnb.ca.*

Newfoundland & Labrador Arts Council, *P.O. Box 98, St. John's NL A1C 5H5. (709)726-2212. E-mail: nlacmail@newcomm.net. Website: www.nlac.nf.ca/.*

Nova Scotia Arts Council. *See Arms'Length Funding for the Arts (ALFA). E-mail: alfa1@chebucto.ns.ca. Website: http://alfa.chebucto.org.*

Ontario Arts Council, *151 Bloor St. W., 5th Floor, Toronto ON M5S 1T6. (416)969-7429. E-mail: info@arts.on.ca. Website: www.arts.on.ca/.*

Prince Edward Island Council of the Arts, *115 Richmond, Charlottetown PE C1E 1H7. (902)368-6176. E-mail: artscouncil@pei.aibn.com. Website: www.gov.pe.ca/infopei/onelisting.php3?number=44465.*

Quebec Council for Arts & Literature, *79 boul. René-Lévesque Est, 3e étage, Quebec QC G1R 5N5. (418)643-1707. Website: www.calq.gouv.qc.ca/.*

Saskatchewan Arts Board, *2135 Broad St., Regina SK S4P 3V7. (306)787-4056. E-mail: sab@artsboard.sk.ca. Website: www.artsboard.sk.ca.*

Yukon Arts Section, *Cultural Services Branch, Tourism & Culture, Government of Yukon, Box 2703, Whitehorse YT Y1A 2C6. (867)667-8589. E-mail: arts@gov.yk.ca. Website: www.btc.gov.yk.ca/cultural/arts/.*

Resources

Conferences & Workshops

As poets, we keep learning day to day. Perhaps a helpful comment on a rejection slip, feedback from a writer's group, or an enlightening essay by an admired master provides that special lesson we need to improve our writing just that much more.

However, there are times when we want to immerse ourselves in learning. Or perhaps we crave a change of scenery, the creative stimulation of being around other artists, or the uninterrupted productivity of time alone to work.

That's what this section of *Poet's Market* is all about. Not only will you find a selection of writing conferences and workshops, but also artist colonies and retreats, poetry festivals, and even a few opportunities to go travelling with your muse. These listings give the basics: contact information, a brief description of the event, lists of past presenters, and offerings that may be of special interest to poets. If an event interests you, get in touch with the director for additional information, including up-to-date costs and housing details. (Please note that most directors had not finalized their 2004 plans when we contacted them for this edition of *Poet's Market*. However, where possible, they provided us with their 2003 dates, costs, faculty names, or themes to give you a better idea of what each event has to offer.)

Before you seriously consider a conference, workshop, or other event, determine what you hope to get out of the experience. Would a general conference with one or two poetry workshops among many other types of sessions be acceptable? Or are you looking for something exclusively focused on poetry? Do you want to hear poets speak about poetry writing, or are you looking for a more participatory experience such as a one-on-one critiquing session or a group workshop? Do you mind being one of hundreds of attendees or do you prefer a more intimate setting? Are you willing to invest in the expense of travelling to a conference, or would something local better suit your budget? Keep these questions and others in mind as you read these listings, view websites, and study conference brochures.

Some listings are coded with symbols to provide certain "information at a glance." The (N) symbol indicates a newly established conference/workshop new to this edition; the (★) symbol indicates this conference/workshop did not appear in the 2003 edition; the (✦) symbol denotes a Canadian listing and the (⊕) symbol an international one.

⊕ **ANAM CARA WRITER'S AND ARTIST'S RETREAT**, Eyeries, Beara, West Cork, Ireland. Phone: 353 (0)27 74441. Fax: 353 (0)27 74448. E-mail: anamcararetreat@eircom.net. Website: www.anamcararetreat.com. **Director:** Sue Booth-Forbes. Offers several 1-2 week workshops annually for writers and artists. Length of workshop varies with subject and leader/facilitator. 2003 programs scheduled for February through October. Location: "Beara is a rural and hauntingly beautiful part of Ireland that is kept temperate by the Gulf Stream. The retreat sits on a hill overlooking Coulagh Bay, the mountains of the Ring of Kerry, and the Slieve Miskish Mountains of Beara. The village of Eyeries is a short walk away." Average attendance: 12/workshop; 5 residents at the retreat when working individually.
Purpose/Features: "Anam Cara is for novice as well as professional writers and artists. Applicants are asked to provide a written description on the focus of their work while on retreat. Residencies are on a first-come, first-deposit-in basis." 2003 workshops included Poetry, Writing Out Loud, Wordpainting, and Proprioceptive Writing.

Costs/Accommodations: 2003 individual retreat costs ranged from €445-670/week depending on room and season booked. Meals and other services included except phone and Internet use. Transportation details available on website. Accommodations include full room and board, laundry, sauna, Jacuzzi, 5 acres of gardens, meadows, riverbank and cascades, river island and swimming hole, and stone mill. Overflow from workshops stay in nearby B&Bs a short walk away.

Additional Info: Requests for specific information about rates and availability can be made through the website; also available by fax or e-mail. Brochure available on website or by request.

ASPEN SUMMER WORDS WRITING RETREAT & LITERARY FESTIVAL; ASPEN WRITERS' FOUNDATION, 110 E. Hallam St., Suite 116, Aspen CO 81611. (970)925-3122. Fax: (970)920-5700. E-mail: info@aspenwriters.org. Website: www.aspenwriters.org. **Executive Director:** Julie Comins. Established 1976. Annual 5-day writing retreat and concurrent 5-day literary festival. 2003 dates: June 21-25. Location: The Given Institute in Aspen. Average attendance: 72 for the retreat, over 200 for the festival.

Purpose/Features: Offers more than a dozen events for readers and writers. Retreat includes intensive workshops in poetry, fiction, creative nonfiction, advanced fiction, and magazine symposium. Offerings for poets include workshops, readings, publishing panels, and agent/editor meetings. 2003 faculty included Christopher Merrill (poetry); Amy Bloom, Ron Carlson, and Pam Houston (fiction); and Laura Fraser (magazine writing). Guest speakers included Ann Patchett, Patricia Schroeder, Adrienne Miller, and many more.

Costs/Accommodations: 2003 tuition for writing retreat was $375; for magazine symposium, $195. 2003 cost for the literary festival was $150; $30 discount for registering for both the festival and retreat or symposium. Meals and other services charged separately, "though we offer complimentary morning coffee and pastries for students and two wine and hors d'oeuvres receptions for ASW registrants." Information on overnight accommodations available for registrants. 2003 cost of accommodations: rooms started at $110/double.

Additional Info: Writing sample required with application. "We accept in advance poetry manuscripts that will be discussed during workshop." Brochure and application available by phone request, fax, e-mail (include regular mailing address with all e-mail inquiries), or on website.

BREAD LOAF WRITERS' CONFERENCE; BAKELESS LITERARY PUBLICATION PRIZES, Middlebury College, Middlebury VT 05753. (802)443-5286. Fax: (802)443-2087. E-mail: blwc@middlebury.edu. Website: www.middlebury.edu/~blwc. **Director:** Michael Collier. **Administrative Manager:** Noreen Cargill. Established 1926. Annual 11-day event usually held in mid-August. Location: mountain campus of Middlebury College. Average attendance: 230.

Purpose/Features: Conference is designed to promote dialogue among writers and provide professional critiques for students. Conference usually covers fiction, nonfiction, and poetry.

Costs/Accommodations: 2003 conference cost was $1,933 (contributor) or $1,856 (auditor), including tuition, room, and board. Fellowships and scholarships for the conference available. "Candidates for fellowships must have a book published. Candidates for scholarships must have published in major literary periodicals or newspapers. A letter of recommendation, application, and supporting materials due by March 1. See website for further details. Awards are announced in June for the conference in August." Taxis to and from the airport or bus station are available.

Additional Info: Individual critiques also available. Sponsors the Bakeless Literary Publication Prizes, an annual book series competition for new authors of literary works in poetry, fiction, and creative nonfiction. Details, conference brochure, and application form are available for SASE or on website. Accepts inquiries by fax and e-mail.

CAPE COD WRITERS' CENTER SUMMER CONFERENCE, % Cape Cod Writers' Center, P.O. Box 186, Barnstable MA 02630. (508)375-0516. Fax: (508)362-2718. E-mail: ccwc@capecod.net. Website: www.capecodwriterscenter.com. **Executive Director:** Jacqueline M. Loring. Established 1963. Annual week-long event held the third week of August. 2003 dates were August 17-22. Location: the Craigville Beach Conference Center in a rustic setting overlooking Nantucket Sound. Average attendance: 150.

Purpose/Features: Open to everyone. Covers poetry, fiction, mystery writing, nonfiction, children's writing, screenwriting, plus one-evening Master Class. Editor and agent in residence. Wednesday evening Poetry Reading by faculty and participants is open to the public. 2003 keynote speaker was Mary Higgins Clark.

Costs/Accommodations: Check website for updated costs. "It is recommended that participants stay at the Craigville Beach Conference Center ((508)775-1265—early registration necessary)." Other housing information available from Bed & Breakfast Cape Cod.

Additional Info: Manuscript evaluations and personal conferences also available. For ms evaluation, submit no more than 15 pages of prose or 6 pages of poetry to CCWC by July 1st. Cost is $75/ms and 30-minute conference. Cost, brochure, and registration form available for SASE or on website. Accepts inquiries by fax and e-mail. Sponsors workshops and seminars in the fall and spring.

CATSKILL POETRY WORKSHOP, Hartwick College, Oneonta NY 13820. (607)431-4448. Fax: (607)431-4457. E-mail: frostc@hartwick.edu. Website: www.hartwick.edu/library/catskill/poetry.htm. **Director:** Carol Frost. Annual week long event. 2003 dates were June 28-July 6. Location: Hartwick College, a small, private college in the Catskill Mountain area. Average attendance: up to 40.

Purpose/Features: Open to "talented adult writers." Workshops cover poetry only. Offerings include "traditional meters, free verse lineation and uses of metaphor; individual instruction." 2003 faculty included Dave Smith, Maurya Simon, Lynn Emanuel, Stephen Dunn, Carol Frost, Michael Waters, Marcia Southwick, Kimiko Hahn, and B.H. Fairchild.

Costs/Accommodations: 2003 cost was $850, including tuition, room and board. Housing available in on-site facilities. Cost for commuters was $650, tuition and lunch included. Deposit required of all attendees.

Additional Info: Two individual ms conferences scheduled for each participant. Registration forms available for SASE and on website. Accepts inquiries by fax and e-mail.

CAVE CANEM, P. O. Box 4286, Charlottesville VA 22905-4286. E-mail: cavecanempoets@aol.com. Website: www.cavecanempoets.org/. **Contact:** Carolyn Micklem, foundation director. Established 1996. Annual week-long workshop for African-American poets. Usually held last week in June. Location: University of Pittsburgh at Greensburg, PA. Average attendance: 50.

Purpose/Features: Open to African-American poets. Participants selected based on a sample of 6-8 poems. Offerings include workshops by fellows and faculty, evening readings. Participants are assigned to groups of about 8 and remain together throughout session, with different faculty leading each workshop. 2003 faculty included Toi Derricotte, Cornelius Eady, Nikky Finney, Yusef Komanyakaa, Marilyn Nelson, and Al Young, with guest poet Kwames Dawes.

Costs/Accommodations: 2003 cost was $495. Meals and other services included. For complete information, contact Cave Canem.

Additional Information: Poets should submit 6-8 poems with cover letter. 2003 postmark deadline was March 15, with accepted poets notified by April 30. Cave Canem Foundation also sponsors the Cave Canem Poetry Prize (see separate listing in Contest & Awards section). Brochure and registration information available for SASE and on website. Accepts inquiries by e-mail.

CENTRUM'S PORT TOWNSEND WRITERS' CONFERENCE, % Centrum, P.O. Box 1158, Port Townsend WA 98368. (360)385-3102. Fax: (360)385-2470. E-mail: info@centrum.org. Website: www.centrum.org. **Program Manager:** Sam Hamill. **Registrar:** Carla Vander Ven. Established 1974. Annual 10-day event held the second week in July. Location: Fort Worden State Park, historic seaside entrance to Puget Sound. Average attendance: 150.

Purpose/Features: Open to all serious writers. Conference usually covers fiction (no genre fiction), poetry, and creative nonfiction. Offerings include limited-enrollment critiqued workshops with private conference or open enrollment workshops. Also included are open mic readings, faculty readings, and technique classes. 2003 faculty included poets Erin Belieu, Olga Broumas, Primus St. John, and Eleanor Wilner.

Costs/Accommodations: 2003 cost was $495 for critiqued workshop tuition, $395 open enrollment workshop tuition; $200-350 room and board. Information on overnight accommodations available.

Additional Info: Members of critiqued workshops must submit no more than 10 pages of writing samples or as requested by the faculty member. Brochure and registration form available for SASE or on website.

CHENANGO VALLEY WRITERS' CONFERENCE, Office of Summer Programs, Colgate University, 13 Oak Dr., Hamilton NY 13346-1398. (315)228-7771. Fax: (315)228-7975. E-mail: mleone @mail.colgate.edu. Website: http://clark.colgate.edu/cvwritersconference. **Conference Director:** Matthew Leone. Established 1996. Annual week-long event usually held in the middle of June. 2003 dates were June 15-21. Location: Colgate University; has "an expansive campus, with classrooms, dormitories, libraries, and recreational facilities all in close proximity to each other." Average attendance: 75.

Purpose/Features: Open to "all serious writers or aspirants. Our purpose is to work on honing writing skills: fiction, poetry, and nonfiction prose are covered." 2003 staff included Bruce Smith, Peter Balakian, Justin Cronin, Karen Novak, and Kelly Cherry.

Costs/Accommodations: 2003 cost was $995 for tuition, room and board, $650 for day students; $895 and $595 before March 1; $875 and $575 for returnees. Discounts available through fellowships, typically $100-350. Applicants for fellowships must apply before the May 1 deadline. "Will pick up airport, bus, and train station arrivals with prior notification for $30/trip." Accommodations include air-conditioned residencies (single rooms available at no extra charge), shared bathrooms; board includes breakfast, lunch, and dinner.

Additional Info: Individual poetry critiques available. Submit poems in advance to Matthew Leone. Brochures and registration forms available for SASE or on website. Accepts inquiries by fax and e-mail.

COLORADO MOUNTAIN WRITERS' WORKSHOP, P.O. Box 85394, Tucson AZ 85754. (520)465-1520. Fax: (520)572-0620. E-mail: megfiles@compuserv.com. Website: www.sheilabender .com. **Director:** Meg Files. Established 1999. Annual 5-day event. 2003 dates were June 23-27. Location: Steamboat Springs, CO, on the mountaintop campus of Colorado Mountain College. Average attendance: 50.

Purpose/Features: Open to all writers, beginning and experienced. "The workshop includes sessions on writing and publishing fiction, nonfiction, and poetry, as well as manuscript workshops and individual critiques and writing exercises." Faculty includes Sheila Bender, Jack Heffron, and Meg Files. Other special features include "a beautiful high-country site, extensive and intensive hands-on activities, individual attention, and a supportive atmosphere."

Costs/Accommodations: 2003 cost was $375 for tuition; dorm rooms and meals available on site.

Additional Info: Individual critiques are available. Submit 5 poems in advance to Meg Files.

THE CONFERENCE ON TEACHING AND POETRY, Robert Frost Place, Franconia NH 03580. (603)823-5510. E-mail: donald.sheehan@dartmouth.edu. Executive Director: Donald Sheehan. **Co-Director of Teacher Conference:** Baron Wormser. Annual event held in late June. 2003 dates were June 23-27.

Purpose/Features: Intended for high school and middle school classroom teachers. Daily sessions include talks on poetry and teaching, workshops on teaching poems, workshops for teachers who write poems, and teacher sharing sessions as well as talks by working teachers on poetry in the curriculum. 2003 guest faculty included Christopher Jane Corkery, Thomas Chandler, Kate Rushin, and Douglas Goetsch. Resident staff: Baron Wormser, David Capella, and Donald Sheehan.

Costs/Accommodations: 2003 fee for 5-day program was $450 (NH teachers $350), plus $372 for 3 graduate credits from the University of New Hampshire College for Lifelong Learning. Room and board available locally.

MARKET CONDITIONS are constantly changing! If you're still using this book and it's 2005 or later, buy the newest edition of *Poet's Market* at your favorite bookstore or order directly from Writer's Digest Books (800)448-0915 or www.writersdigest.com.

Additional Info: To apply, send letter describing current teaching situation and literary interests, along with $15 processing fee. (See separate listings for Festival of Poetry and Frost Place Seminar in this section.)

DJERASSI RESIDENT ARTISTS PROGRAM, Applications 2005, 2325 Bear Gulch Rd., Woodside CA 94062. (650)747-1250. Fax: (650)747-0105. E-mail: drap@djerassi.org. Website: www.djera ssi.org. **Residency Coordinator:** Judy Freeland. Established 1979. Offers 4- to 5-week residencies, at no cost, for writers and other creative artists. Residencies available mid-March through mid-November. Location: In a spectacular rural setting in the Santa Cruz Mountains, one hour south of San Francisco. Average attendance: 60 artists each year.

Purpose/Features: Residencies are awarded competitively to emerging and mid-career artists as well as artists with established national or international reputations. Purpose is "to support and enhance the creativity of artists by providing uninterrupted time for work, reflection, and collegial interaction."

Costs/Accommodations: Artists selected are offered room, board, and studio space at no cost. "Three rooms in The Artists' House are set up to accommodate writers, each with a large desk, work space, and outdoor deck."

Additional Info: Deadline for accepting applications is February 15 each year (i.e., 2004) for a residency in the following year (2005). Requires $25 application fee. Application materials available for SASE and on website.

EASTERN KENTUCKY UNIVERSITY CREATIVE WRITING CONFERENCE, English Dept., Case Annex 467, Richmond KY 40475. (859)622-3091. E-mail: christine.delea@eku.edu. Website: www.english.eku.edu/conferences. **Conference Director:** Christine Delea. Established 1964. Annual 5-day event usually held Monday through Friday of the third week in June. Location: Eastern Kentucky University. Average attendance: 15.

Purpose/Features: Open to poetry and fiction. Provides lectures, workshops, and private conferences with visiting writers to "help writers increase their skills in writing poetry and fiction." A ms of 4-8 poems (8 pages maximum) must be submitted by May 20 and accepted before enrollment in conference is allowed. Offerings include workshop discussions and individual conferences. 2003 poetry faculty included Harry Brown, Christine Delea, and James Baker Hall.

Costs/Accommodations: Costs are $122 undergraduate and $176 graduate (in-state fees), $335 undergraduate and $487 graduate (out-of-state fees); participants responsible for their own meals, available on campus. Cost for housing in on-site facilities is $15/night single occupancy, $10/night double occupancy. "Must bring your own sheets, pillow, blanket."

Additional Info: Brochure available for SASE or request by e-mail. Additional information available on website.

FESTIVAL OF POETRY, Robert Frost Place, Franconia NH 03580. (603)823-5510. E-mail: donald .sheehan@dartmouth.edu. Executive Director: Donald Sheehan. **Director of Festival Admissions:** David Keller. Established 1978. Annual week-long event held late July and early August at Robert Frost's house and barn, made into a center for poetry and the arts. 2003 dates were July 27-August 1. Average attendance: 50-55.

Purpose/Features: Open to poets only. 2003 guest faculty included Adrienne Su, Robert Cording, Cleopatra Mathis, Laure-Anne Bosselaar, Gerald Stern, and Galway Kinnell.

Costs/Accommodations: 2003 cost was $665 (participant), plus a $25 reading fee. Auditor fee: $590. Room and board available locally; information sent upon acceptance to program.

Additional Info: Application should be accompanied by 3 pages of your own poetry. Brochure and registration form available for SASE. (See separate listings for The Conference on Teaching and Poetry and The Frost Place Seminar in this section.)

FINE ARTS WORK CENTER, 24 Pearl St., Provincetown MA 02657. (508)487-9960. Fax: (508)487-8873. E-mail: workshops@fawc.org. Website: www.fawc.org. Established 1968. The Fine Arts Work Center in Provincetown "is a nonprofit organization dedicated to providing emerging writers and visual artists with time and space in which to pursue independent work in a community of peers." 2003 fees were $480 for each week-long workshop and $235 for each weekend workshop.

Accommodations for 6 nights cost $460. Fellowships are awarded to poets and fiction writers in the emerging stages of their careers; professional juries make admissions decisions. See website for details and an application form.

✪ FROST PLACE SEMINAR, Robert Frost Place, Franconia NH 03580. (603)823-5510. E-mail: donald.sheehan@dartmouth.edu. **Seminar Co-Directors:** Baron Wormser and Donald Sheehan. Held annually in early August following the Festival of Poetry (see separate listing in this section). 2003 dates were August 4-8. Average attendance: limited to 16 participants.

Purpose/Features: Open to those who have participated in the Festival of Poetry at least once prior to the summer for which you are applying. Includes daily lecture/seminar on poetry of the past, workshops focusing on participant poems, evening readings. 2003 guest faculty: Margaret Rabb and Christopher Bursk.

Costs/Accommodations: 2003 fee was $575 (including room), plus $75 for two meals daily and $25 reading fee.

Additional Info: Admission competitive. To apply, send cover letter outlining goals for your participation and 3 pages of your own poetry. (See separate listings for Festival of Poetry and The Conference on Teaching and Poetry in this section.)

✪ GREEN LAKE WRITERS CONFERENCE, Green Lake Conference Center, W2511 State Highway 23, Green Lake WI 54941-9599. (800)558-8898. Fax: (920)294-3848. E-mail: program@gl cc.org. Website: www.glcc.org. **Vice President of Adult Programming:** Blythe Ann Cooper. Established 1946. Annual weeklong event. 2003 dates: June 28 to July 5. Location: "Attendees stay in one of our three hotels. The Inn overlooks beautiful Green Lake 30 miles southwest of Oshkosh. Large private bath, double occupancy rooms, with singles available, extra charge. Located on 1,000 acres and is the national conference center for American Baptists. Alcoholic beverages are not permitted." Average attendance: 65-80.

Purpose/Features: Open to regional and national participants. Conference covers writing for children, fiction, autobiography, inspirational/devotional, humor, and feature articles. 2003 instructors included Ellen Kort (poet laureate for Wisconsin), Carol Pierskalla, Barbara Smith, Sharon Addy, Sharon Sherbondy, and Patricia Lorenz. Editors also represented *Guideposts Magazine* and *Writer's Digest*.

Costs/Accommodations: 2003 cost was $105 program fee plus $485.50/person for double occupancy room with meals. Camping available. Shuttle service to and from the airport provided for an additional fee. Information on overnight accommodations available for registrants.

Additional Info: Individual critiques also available. Call for brochure and registration form. Accepts inquiries by fax and e-mail. "A past participant wrote, 'I would recommend this conference to anyone committed to writing and sharing their work in a spiritual atmosphere. What I found to be most incredible was the fact that everyone was friendly, willing to talk, and incredibly generous with their time.' "

HARVARD SUMMER WRITING PROGRAM, 51 Brattle St., Dept. S810, Cambridge MA 02138. (617)495-4024. Fax: (617)495-9176. E-mail: summer@hudce.harvard.edu. Website: www.su mmer.harvard.edu. Annual 8-week event. 2004 dates: June 28 through August 20. Location: Harvard University. Average attendance: 700.

Purpose/Features: Open to all levels, from beginner to published author. Course offerings include creative, expository, professional, and journalistic writing. Offerings include beginning, intermediate, and graduate level poetry courses. Other special features include small classes, undergraduate and graduate credit, individual conferences, access to the Writing Center at Harvard, visiting writers, student-faculty readings, and a published journal of student work. Instructors are writers, editors, and faculty members from Harvard as well as other universities.

Costs/Accommodations: 2003 conference cost, $1,950/course (2 courses considered full-time), plus $3,375 for room and board (dormitory housing).

Additional Info: See website. Accepts inquiries by e-mail.

HAYSTACK WRITING PROGRAM, Summer Session, Portland State University, P.O. Box 1491, Portland OR 97207. (800)547-8887, ext. 4186 or (503)725-4186. Fax: (503)725-4840. E-mail: snyder e@pdx.edu. Website: www.haystack.pdx.edu. **Coordinator:** Elizabeth Snyder. Established 1969. Annual summer program of week-long and weekend workshops held in July and August. Location: Canon Beach, OR, a small coastal community; some readings, lectures, concerts, and other activities. Average attendance: 10-15/class; 400 total.

Purpose/Features: Open to all writers. Workshops include poetry, craft, fiction, children's book writing, memoir, nonfiction, and garden writing. 2003 staff included Tom Spanbauer, Karen Karbo, Linda Zuckerman, and Eric Kimmel.

Costs/Accommodations: 2003 workshop cost was $225-485; participants pay for their own lodging and meals. Wide range of options for accommodations. List provided upon registration.

Additional Info: Brochure and registration form available by mail. Accepts inquiries by fax and e-mail.

■ HIGHLAND SUMMER WORKSHOP, P.O. Box 7014, Radford University, Radford VA 24142. (540)831-5366. Fax: (540)831-5951. E-mail: jasbury@radford.edu. **Director:** Grace Toney Edwards. Established 1977. Annual 2-week event held the first 2 weeks in June. Location: Radford University campus. Average attendance: 20-25.

Purpose/Features: Open to everyone. "The conference, a lecture-seminar-workshop combination, is conducted by well-known guest writers and offers the opportunity to study and practice creative and expository writing within the context of regional culture." Topics covered vary from year to year. Poetry, fiction, and essays (prose) are generally covered each year. The last workshop was led by Robert Morgan and Richard Hague.

Costs/Accommodations: Costs range from $630-1,275 plus $16/day for meals. Individual meals may also be purchased. On-site housing costs range from $19-28/night. On-site accommodations available at Norwood Hall. Accommodations also available at local motels.

Additional Info: Brochure and registration form available for SASE. Accepts inquiries by fax and e-mail.

■ HOFSTRA UNIVERSITY SUMMER WRITERS' CONFERENCE, Hofstra University, University College for Continuing Education, Hempstead NY 11549. (516)463-5016. Fax: (516)463-4833. E-mail: marion.flomenhaft@hofstra.edu. Website: www.hofstra.edu/Academics/UCCE/. **Director:** Marion Flomenhaft. Established 1972. Annual 10-day event usually starts the Monday after July 4th. Location: Hofstra University. Average attendance: 60-70.

Purpose/Features: Open to all writers. Conference covers fiction, poetry, and children's writing, and, on occasion, one other area (science fiction, mystery, etc.). Guest speakers (other than the workshop leaders) "usually come from the world of publishing." There are also "readings galore and various special presentations."

Costs/Accommodations: 2003 conference cost was $430. Additional fee of $350 for air-conditioned dorm room during conference. For those seeking credit, other fees apply.

Additional Info: Individual critiques also available. "Each writer receives a half hour one-on-one with each workshop leader." Does not sponsor a contest, but "we submit exceptional work to various progams sponsored by Writers Conferences and Festivals." Write for brochure and registration form (available as of April). Accepts inquiries by fax and e-mail.

INDIANA UNIVERSITY WRITERS' CONFERENCE, Ballantine Hall 464, Indiana University, Bloomington IN 47405. (812)855-1877. Fax: (812)855-9535. E-mail: writecon@indiana.edu. Website: www.indiana.edu/~writecon/. **Director:** Amy M. Locklin. Established 1940. Annual week-long event usually held the last week in June at the university student union. Average attendance: 100.

Purpose/Features: Open to all. Conference covers fiction, creative nonfiction, poetry, and sometimes scriptwriting. Offerings include workshops and classes. 2003 faculty included Marilyn Chin, Brenda Hillman, A. Loudermilk, and Kevin Young.

Costs/Accommodations: 2003 conference cost was $300 for conference and classes; $450 for conference, classes, and one workshop; plus $25 application fee. Information on overnight accommodations available. "Rooms available in the student union or in a dorm."

Additional Info: Individual critiques also available. Submit 10 pages of poetry in advance. Submit separate ms of 3-5 poems for scholarship consideration. "All manuscripts submitted by April 10 will be considered for scholarships." Brochure and registration form available for SASE. Accepts inquiries by fax and e-mail.

IOWA SUMMER WRITING FESTIVAL, University of Iowa, 100 Oakdale Campus, W310, Iowa City IA 52242-5000. (319)335-4160. Fax: (319)335-4039. E-mail: iswfestival@uiowa.edu. Website: www.uiowa.edu/~iswfest. **Director:** Amy Margolis. Established 1987. Annual event held each summer in June and July for six weeks. Includes one-week and weekend workshops at the University of Iowa campus. Average attendance: 150/week.
Purpose/Features: Open to "all adults who have a desire to write." Conference offers courses in nearly all writing forms. 2003 offerings included 21 classes for all levels. Poetry faculty included Bruce Bond, Michael Dennis Browne, Lisa Chavez, Vince Gotera, Jim Heynen, and Richard Jackson.
Costs/Accommodations: 2003 conference cost was $210 for a weekend course and $435-460 for a 1-week course. Participants are responsible for their own meals. Accommodations available at the Iowa House and the Sheraton. Housing in residence hall costs about $31/night.
Additional Info: Participants in week-long workshops will have private conference/critique with workshop leader. Send for brochure and registration form. Accepts inquiries by phone, fax, or e-mail.

THE IWWG SUMMER CONFERENCE, The International Women's Writing Guild, P.O. Box 810, Gracie Station, New York NY 10028. (212)737-7536. Fax: (212)737-9469. E-mail: dirhahn@aol. com. Website: www.iwwg.com. **Executive Director:** Hannelore Hahn. Established 1978. Annual week-long event. 2003 dates were June 13-20. Location: Skidmore College in Saratoga Springs, NY. Average attendance: over 500.
Purpose/Features: Open to all women. Seventy workshops offered. "At least four poetry workshops offered for full week."
Costs/Accommodations: Cost is $880 for conference program and room and board.
Additional Info: "Critiquing available throughout the week." Brochure and registration form available for SASE. Accepts inquiries by e-mail (include mailing address for response). The International Women's Writing Guild's bimonthly newsletter features hundreds of outlets for poets.

KALANI OCEANSIDE RETREAT, RR2, Box 4500, Pahoa Beach Road HI 96778-9724. (808)965-7828 or (800)800-6886. Fax: (808)965-0527. E-mail: kalani@kalani.com. Website: www.k alani.com. Established 1980. **Director:** Richard Koob.
Purpose/Features: Offers 2-week to 2-month residencies on a year-round basis for visual, literary, folk, and performing artists. "Kalani Honua is situated near Kalapana on the big island of Hawaii on 113 acres of secluded forest and dramatic coastline, 45 minutes from the city of Hilo and 5 minutes from Hawaii Volcanoes National Park. Visitors stay in 3 two-story wooden lodges and 16 private cottage units that provide comfortable accommodations." Accommodates 100 (generally about 5 artists-in-residence) at a time in private rooms with full meal service plus optional kitchen facilities and shared or private baths; private desks and access to computer ports and reference material available. Activities include a variety of yoga, dance, drawing, fitness, and mind/body classes; also available are an olympic pool, sauna, fitness room, and nearby beach and thermal springs.
Costs/Accommodations: Residency cost ranges from $105/night to $210/night (private cottage); plus $29/day for meals. Stipends are most available in the periods of May through July and September through December. Stipends provide for 50% of lodging costs; balance is responsibility of the artist (stipends may *not* be applied toward dorm lodging or camping, or reduction in food or transportation costs).
Additional Information: Application form and guidelines available for SASE, by e-mail, or on website. When sending application, include $10 fee.

THE GEOGRAPHICAL INDEX in the back of this book helps you locate markets in your region.

KEY WEST WRITERS' WORKSHOP, 5901 College Rd., Key West FL 33040. (305)296-9081, ext. 302. Fax: (305)292-2392. E-mail: weinman_i@firn.edu. Website: www.firn.edu/fkcc/kwww.htm. **Director:** Irving Weinman. Established 1996. Five annual weekend events usually held from late January to early March. Location: "the conference room of Key West's historic Old City Hall—a modernized 1890's landmark building in the heart of the old town. Subsidiary activities (introductory get-together and optional Literary Walking Tour) also held in Old Town, Key West." Average attendance: limited to 10 for poetry weekends, 12 for fiction.

Purpose/Features: Open to all. However, "**not for beginners**." Workshop's purpose is to "bring the best writers into an intimate workshop setting with serious writers at all but beginning stages of their writing careers. Workshops are offered in poetry and fiction." Leaders for past workshops have included John Ashbery, Robert Creeley, Carolyn Forché, Sharon Olds, and Richard Wilbur.

Costs/Accommodations: 2003 conference cost was $300/weekend, tuition only. Participants responsible for their own meals. Information on overnight accommodations available.

Additional Info: Brochure and registration form available for SASE, by e-mail, or on website. Accepts inquiries by fax and e-mail. "Interested poets will be put on our brochure mailing list for the upcoming season."

LEDBURY POETRY FESTIVAL, Town Council Offices, Church St., Ledbury, Herefordshire HR8 1DH United Kingdom. Phone: +44(0)1531 634 156. Fax: +44(0)1531 631193. E-mail: info@poetry-festival.com. Website: www.poetry-festival.com. **Festival Director:** Dr. Charles Bennett. Established 1987. Annual 2-week event. 2003 dates: July 4-13. Location: "Various venues in Ledbury (e.g., church, halls, schools). Ledbury is a small medieval market town nestled in the wooded and rolling hills of Southeast Herefordshire. Accessible by rail, bus, and car." Average attendance: 24,000.

Purpose/Features: Open to poets and "literature-interested writers and readers." Festival covers poetry for adults, children, and the elderly; also related music and drama events, walks and tours. Includes workshops, readings, and the free town party. Past speakers have included Tom Paulin, Carol Ann Duffy, Simon Armitage, and Alastair McGowan.

Costs/Accommodations: Costs vary; participants responsible for their own meals. Discounts available to students (20%). Information on overnight accommodations available. Accommodations include special rates at area hotels.

Additional Info: Brochure and registration form available. Accepts inquiries by fax and e-mail.

LIGONIER VALLEY WRITERS CONFERENCE; THE LOYALHANNA REVIEW, P.O. Box B, Ligonier PA 15658. (724)537-3341. Fax: (724)537-0482. E-mail: sarshi@wpa.net. Established 1986. Annual 2-day event. 2003 dates were July 11 & 12. Location: Ligonier, PA, "a relaxing, educational, inspirational conference in a scenic, small town." Average attendance: 40-50.

Purpose/Features: Open to anyone interested in writing. Conference covers fiction, creative nonfiction, and poetry. Faculty readings held Friday evening.

Costs/Accommodations: Conference cost is approximately $200. Participants responsible for their own dinner and lodging. Information on overnight accommodations available for registrants.

Additional Info: Send 9×6 SASE for brochure and registration form. Accepts inquiries by fax and e-mail. "We also publish *The Loyalhanna Review*, a literary journal, which is open to participants."

THE LITERARY FESTIVAL AT ST. MARY'S, St. Mary's College of Maryland, St. Mary's City MD 20686. E-mail: msglaser@smcm.edu. Website: www.smcm.edu/academics/litfest. **Contact:** Dr. Michael S. Glaser. Semiannual event held during the early summer in even years (i.e., 2004, 2006). Approximately 18 guest poets and artists participate in and lead workshops, seminars, and readings. Concurrent with the festival, St. Mary's College offers 2-week intensive writing workshops in poetry and fiction and a 10-day writer's community retreat.

Purpose/Features: The poetry and fiction workshop engages the participants in structured writing experiences. Intended for anyone with a serious interest in writing. Offers 4 college credits or may be taken as non-credit courses. The retreat, designed for the serious writer, offers individual plans for writing alone or in conjunction with other participants.

Additional Info: For application or more information on these workshops or the festival, write to Michael S. Glaser at the above address. Accepts inquiries by e-mail.

MOUNT HERMON CHRISTIAN WRITERS CONFERENCE, P.O. Box 413, Mount Hermon CA 95041. (831)335-4466. Fax: (831)335-9413. E-mail: dtalbott@mhcamps.org. Website: www.mou nthermon.org/writers. **Director of Adult Ministries:** David R. Talbott. Established 1970. Annual 5-day event held Friday through Tuesday over Palm Sunday weekend. 2003 dates were April 11-15. Location: Full hotel-service-style conference center in heart of California redwoods near San Jose. Average attendance: 350-450.

Purpose/Features: Open to "anyone interested in the Christian writing market." Conference is very broad based. Always covers poetry, fiction, article writing, writing for children, plus an advanced track for published authors. Offerings have included several workshops, sessions on the greeting card industry, and individual 1-hour workshops (including a workshop for songwriters in 2003). "We usually have 45-50 teaching faculty made up of publishing reps of leading Christian book and magaz ine publishers, plus selected freelancers." Other special features have included an advance critique service (no extra fee); residential conference, with meals taken family-style with faculty; private appointments with faculty; and an autograph party. "High spiritual impact."

Costs/Accommodations: 2003 conference cost was $940 deluxe; $780 standard; $635 economy; $560 student dormitory; including 13 meals, snacks, on-site housing, and $350 tuition fee. No-housing fee: $600. $25 airport, Greyhound, or Amtrack shuttle from San Jose, CA.

Additional Info: Brochure and registration form available on request. Accepts inquiries by fax and e-mail.

NAPA VALLEY WRITERS' CONFERENCE, Napa Valley College, 1088 College Ave., St. Hel ena CA 94574. (707)967-2900. E-mail: writecon@napavalley.edu. Website: www.napacommunityed. org/writersconf. **Poetry Director:** Nan Cohen. **Managing Director:** Anne Evans. Established 1981. Annual week-long event usually held the last week in July or first week in August. 2003 dates were July 27-August 1. Location: Napa Valley College's new facility in the historic town of St. Helena, 30 minutes north of Napa in the heart of the valley's wine growing community. Average attendance: 48 in poetry and 48 in fiction.

Purpose/Features: "The conference has maintained its emphases on process and craft, featuring a faculty as renowned for the quality of their teaching as for their work. It has also remained small and personal, fostering an unusual rapport between faculty writers and conference participants. The poetry session provides the opportunity to work both on generating new poems and on revising previously written ones. Daily workshops emphasize writing new poems—taking risks with new material and forms, pushing boundaries in the poetic process." The 2003 poetry faculty included Stephen Dunn, Jane Hirshfield, Dorianne Laux, and Marilyn Nelson. "Participants register for either the poetry or the fiction workshops, but panels and craft talks are open to all writers attending. Evenings feature readings by the faculty that are open to the public and hosted by Napa Valley wineries."

Costs/Accommodations: 2003 cost was $550, not including meals or housing. A limited number of scholarships are available. Information on overnight accommodations available. "Through the generosity of Napa residents, limited accommodations in local homes are available on a first-come, first-served basis for a fee of $30 for the week."

Additional Info: All applicants are asked to submit a qualifying ms with their registration (no more than 5 poems or 10-15 pages of fiction) as well as a brief description of their writing background. 2003 application deadline: May 23. Brochure and registration form available for SASE or on website.

★ NATIONAL COWBOY POETRY GATHERING; WESTERN FOLKLIFE CENTER, 501 Railroad St., Elko NV 89801. (775)738-7508. Fax: (775)738-2900. E-mail: tbaer@westernfolklif e.org. Website: www.westernfolklife.org. **Contact:** Gathering Manager. 2003 was the 19th annual 8-day Gathering of cowboy poets and musicians. Usually held end of January. 2003 dates: January 25-February 1. Location: Western Folklife Center or the Elko Convention Center, plus other venues.

Purpose Features: Consists of 2 components: 1) Early Gathering Activities (first weekend and early in week) feature workshops, evening performances, and exhibits; 2) the Gathering swings into full gear on Wednesday with concert and keynote address, followed by 3 days of poetry and music, exhibits, panel discussions, and videos/films. 2003 workshops included "The Ins and Outs of Poetry Writing" with Jim Brummels, as well as readings and poetry/music sessions.

Costs/Accommodations: 2003 advance ticket cost: $31 for 3-day Guest Pass (including program book and guest pass pin); $13 for Single Day Pass (program book purchased separately). Ticket cost does not include handling charge or credit card fee; prices increase for non-advance tickets. Participants responsible for own meals and housing (there are many motels and casinos in Elko). Advance reservations recommended. Elko is serviced by Skywest Airlines (a Delta Connection), Amtrak, and Greyhound Bus.

Additional Information: The Western Folklife Center distributes books and tapes of cowboy poetry and songs as well as other cowboy memorabilia; also sponsors a variety of other community programs throughout the year. Additional information available about the Center and the Gathering on website.

N NORTHWEST OKLAHOMA WRITERS WORKSHOP; ENID WRITERS CLUB; EWC TIMES, 2113 W. Walnut, Enid OK 73703. (580)233-6436. E-mail: okwriter@yahoo.com. Website: www.scribequill.com/enidwriters.html. **Contact:** Rita Hess, EWC President. Established 1991. Annual 1-day event usually held in March. Location: Cherokee Strip Conference Center, 123 W. Maine, Enid OK 73701. Average attendance: 25-35.

Purpose/Features: Open to writers of all genres. Provides general writing instruction. Offerings include a section on poetry.

Costs/Accommodations: 2001 cost was $45, including lunch. Discounts available for early registration ($40 if registered a week before the workshop).

Additional Info: Additional information available by e-mail or on website. Workshop sponsored by the Enid Writers Club, the oldest writing club in Oklahoma. Membership dues: $15/year. Publishes *EWC Times,* a quarterly newsletter for writers.

OAKLAND UNIVERSITY WRITERS' CONFERENCE, College of Arts and Sciences, 221 Varner Hall, Oakland University, Rochester MI 48309-4401. (248)370-3125. Fax: (248)370-4280. E-mail: casce@oakland.edu. Website: www.oakland.edu/contin-ed/writersconf/. **Director:** Gloria J. Boddy. Established 1961. Annual 2-day event. 2003 dates: October 17-18. Location: in the university student center, in meeting rooms and large dining/meeting areas, plus adjoining classroom buildings with lecture halls. Average attendance: 300.

Purpose/Features: Open to beginning through professional adult writers. "No restrictions as to geographic area." Designed to "help writers develop their skills; to provide information (and contact) for getting published; to provide a current picture of publishing markets; to furnish a venue for networking. All genres of writing are covered." Offers "critiques, both one-on-one and group, on Friday. On Saturday, 36 concurrent sessions dealing with all aspects of writing in a variety of genres are available in four time slots. A well-known professional writer is invited to be keynote speaker. A panel of the major speakers answers questions in the concluding session."

Costs/Accommodations: 2003 conference cost: $95; ms critique: $65; hands-on workshop: $55; one-day writing retreats: $95. Meals and other services charged separately. "Discounts are not offered." Information on overnight accommodations available.

Additional Info: "Submit ten pages of poetry two weeks in advance of conference. Poets will receive written feedback and have a twenty-minute one-on-one consultation with critiques on Friday." Brochure and registration form available each September 1 prior to the October conference for SASE, by fax, e-mail, or on website. Accepts inquiries by fax and e-mail. Also offers the Mary Kay Davis Scholarships for high school and college students to attend conference. Check website for details.

PENNWRITERS ANNUAL CONFERENCE; PENNWRITERS, INC.; IN OTHER WORDS CONTEST; PENNWRITERS POETRY CONTEST. . E-mail: mcrawmer@aol.com. Website: http://pennwriters.org. **Conference Coordinator:** Mike Crawmer. Established 1987. Annual 3-day event. 2003 dates were May 16-18. Location: Wyndham Pittsburgh Airport Hotel; check website for 2004 location. Average attendance: 200.

Purpose/Features: Open to all writers, novice to multi-published. Covers fiction, nonfiction, and poetry. Offers workshops/seminars, appointments with agents and editors, autograph party, contests— all multi-genre oriented. Theme for 2003 conference was "Write Here, Write Now!"

Costs/Accommodations: 2002 conference cost was $130 (members), $175 (nonmembers) for all days of conference, including some meals. Special meal events are additional. "Scholarship awards are presented to Pennwriter members who are winners in our annual writing contests." Information on overnight accommodations available. Housing in on-site facilities cost $70/night in 2003, single or double occupancy.

Additional Info: Pennwriters sponsors 2 contests open to poets: 1. In Other Words Contest, held during annual conference, open to conference attendees only. Divisions for poetry, fiction, and nonfiction. Complete rules on website. Awards prizes; judged by peers. 2. Pennwriters Poetry Contest, open to all; nonmembers pay slightly higher fee. Cash prizes of $50, $25, $10. Complete guidelines on website. Brochure and registration form available for SASE or on website. Accepts inquiries by fax and e-mail. "The Pennwriters Annual Conference is sponsored by Pennwriters, Inc., a nonprofit organization with goals to help writers get published."

PIMA WRITERS' WORKSHOP, Pima College, 2202 W. Anklam Rd., Tucson AZ 85709-0170. (520)206-6084. E-mail: mfiles@pimacc.pima.edu. **Director:** Meg Files. Established 1987. Annual 3-day event. 2003 dates were May 23-25. Location: Pima College's Center for the Arts, "includes a proscenium theater, a black box theater, a recital hall, and conference rooms, as well as a courtyard with amphitheater." Average attendance: 250.

Purpose/Features: Open to all writers, beginning and experienced. "The workshop includes sessions on all genres (nonfiction, fiction, poetry, writing for children and juveniles, screenwriting) and on editing and publishing, as well as manuscript critiques and writing exercises." Past faculty has included Robert Morgan, Sharman Apt Russell, Barbara Kingsolver, Larry McMurtry, Nancy Mairs, Peter Meinke, Steve Kowit, David Citino, and others. Other special features include "accessibility to writers, agents, and editors; and the workshop's atmosphere—friendly and supportive, practical and inspirational."

Costs/Accommodations: 2003 conference cost was $65. Participants responsible for their own meals. Information on overnight accommodations available.

Additional Info: Individual poetry critiques available. Submit 3 poems in advance to Meg Files. Brochure and registration form available for SASE or by fax or e-mail. Accepts inquiries by e-mail.

POETRY WEEKEND INTENSIVES, 40 Post Ave., Hawthorne NJ 07506. (973)423-2921. Fax: (973)523-6088. E-mail: mariagillan@msn.com. Website: www.pccc.cc.nj.us/poetry. **Executive Director:** Maria Mazziotti Gillan. Established 1997. Usually held 4 times/year in March, June, October, and December. Location: generally at St. Marguerite's Retreat House, an English manor house at the Convent of St. John the Baptist in Mendhan, NJ; also several other convents and monasteries. Average attendance: 26.

Purpose/Features: Open to all writers. "The purpose of this retreat is to give writers the space and time to focus totally on their own work in a serene and beautiful setting away from the pressures and distractions of daily life." Sample theme: "Writing Your Way Home—Poetry of Memory and Place." "Writing weekend poets will find support and encouragement, stimulating activities leading to the creation of new work, workshop leaders who are actively engaged in the writing life, opportunities to read their work aloud to the group, a circle of writer friends, and networking opportunities." Poetry Weekend Intensives are led by Maria Mazziotti Gillan and Laura Boss. Other special features include one-on-one conferences with lead poet faculty.

Costs/Accommodations: Cost for 2003 weekends: $325, including meals. Offers a $25 early bird discount. Housing in on-site facilities included in the $325 price.

Additional Info: Individual poetry critiques available. Poets should bring poems to weekend. Registration form available for SASE or by fax or e-mail. Accepts inquiries by fax and e-mail. Maria Mazziotti Gillan is the director of the Creative Writing Program of Binghamton University—State University of New York, executive director of the Poetry Center at Passaic County Community College, and edits *Paterson Literary Review*. Laura Boss is the editor of *Lips* magazine. Fifteen professional development credits are available for each weekend.

⭐ 🌐 🔄 **THE POETS' HOUSE/TEACH NA H'EIGSE**, Clonbarra, Falcarragh, Donegal, Ireland. Phone: (00353)74 65470. Fax: (00353)74 65471. E-mail: phouse@iol.ie. Website: www.poetsho

⭐ **INDICATES A MARKET** that did not appear in the 2003 edition.

use.ie. **Director:** Janice Fitzpatrick-Simmons. Established 1990. Annual 10-day events (offered 3 times/summer) usually held July through August. Location: Donegal Gaeltacht, 26 miles northwest of Letterkenny (northwest Ireland). Average attendance: 12-24/session.

Purpose/Features: Open to "all interested in writing poems and in Irish poetry; to apply send three poems." Designed to "bring Irish and American poets together." Offerings include a morning lecture, afternoon workshop, and an evening reading by the poet of the day. Faculty has included Seamus Heaney, Paul Durcan, Medbh McGuckian, Paula Meehan, William Matthews, and Ted Deppe.

Costs/Accommodations: 2003 cost was £450/session. B&B lodging £13-15/night.

Additional Info: Individual critiques available. Submit 10 poems in advance to the directors. Brochure and registration form available for SAS and IRC. Accepts inquiries by e-mail and fax. Also offers M.A. in Creative Writing (now in its 10th year); "year-long and intensive, validated by Lancaster University in England."

SAGE HILL FALL POETRY COLLOQUIUM, P.O. Box 1731, Saskatoon SK S7K 3S1 Canada. Phone/fax: (306)652-7395. E-mail: sage.hill@sasktel.net. Website: www.lights.com/sagehill/fall.html. **Executive Director:** Steven Ross Smith. Established 1995. Annual event. 2003 dates: November 11-December 1. Location: "The peaceful milieu of St. Peter's College, adjoining St. Peter's Abbey, in Muenster, 125 kilometers east of Saskatoon."

Purpose/Features: Offers "an intensive three-week working and critiquing retreat designed to assist poets with manuscripts-in-progress. Each writer will have a significant publishing record and will wish to develop his/her craft and tune a manuscript. There will be ample time for writing, one-on-one critiques, and group meetings to discuss recent thinking in poetics. The rural, reflective setting in Muenster, Saskatchewan is ideal for such work. Eight writers will be selected from applications. Writers from anywhere may apply. 2003 instructors include Fred Wah (facilitator) and Hilary Clark (guest poet)."

Costs/Accommodations: 2003 cost: $995, including tuition, accommodations, and meals. Van transportation from Saskatoon airport can be arranged as needed for a fee. Participants encouraged to provide own transportation.

Additional Info: Brochure and registration form available for SASE. Most recent application deadline: July 31, 2003.

SAGE HILL WRITING SUMMER EXPERIENCE, P.O. Box 1731, Saskatoon SK S7K 3S1 Canada. Phone/fax: (306)652-7395. E-mail: sage.hill@sasktel.net. Website: www.lights.com/sagehill. **Executive Director:** Steven Ross Smith. Established in 1990. Annual 10-day adult program usually held the end of July through the beginning of August. 2003 dates were July 28-August 7. Location: St. Michael's Retreat, "a tranquil facility in the beautiful Qu'Appelle Valley just outside the town of Lumsden, 25 kilometers north of Regina." Average attendance: 45, with participants broken into small groups of 5-11.

Purpose/Features: Open to writers, 19 years of age and older, who are working in English. No geographic restrictions. The retreat/workshops are designed to "offer a special working and learning opportunity to writers at different stages of development. Top quality instruction, a low instructor-writer ratio, and the rural Saskatchewan setting offers conditions ideal for the pursuit of excellence in the arts of fiction, poetry, playwriting, and creative nonfiction." Offerings include a poetry workshop and poetry colloquium. 2003 faculty included Betsy Warland, Robert Kroetsch, and David Carpenter.

Costs/Accommodations: 2003 conference cost was $795, including instruction, accommodations, and meals. Limited local transportation to the conference is available. "Van transportation from Regina airport to Lumsden will be arranged for out-of-province travellers." On-site accommodations offer individual rooms with a writing desk and washroom.

Additional Info: Individual critiques offered as part of workshop and colloquium. Writing sample required with application. 2003 application deadline was April 25. Brochure and registration form available for SASE.

SAN DIEGO STATE UNIVERSITY WRITERS' CONFERENCE, 5250 Campanile Dr., San Diego CA 92182-1920. (619)594-2517. Fax: (619)594-8566. E-mail: lkoch@mail.sdsu.edu. Website: www.ces.sdsu.edu. **Director of Noncredit Community Education:** Leslie Koch. Established 1984. Annual 3-day event. 2003 dates were January 17-19. Location: Doubletree Hotel (Mission Valley), 7450 Hazard Center Dr., San Diego. Average attendance: 400.

Purpose/Features: Open to writers of fiction, nonfiction, children's books, poetry, and screenwriting. "We have participants from across North America." Offers numerous workshops in fiction, nonfiction, general interest, children's books, screenwriting, magazine writing, and poetry. Speakers at last conference included Abby Zidie (assistant editor, Bantam Dell Publishing Group) and screenwriter Madeline DiMaggio. Other special features include networking lunch, editor/agent appointments and consultations, and novel writing workshops.

Costs/Accommodations: 2003 cost was $295-400 (before January 4), including one meal. Transportation to and from the event provided by the Doubletree Hotel. Information on overnight accommodations available. Accommodations include special rates at the Doubletree Hotel.

Additional Info: Individual poetry critiques available. See website for details. Contest sponsored as part of conference. "Editors and agents give awards for favorite submissions." Information and registration form available on website. Accepts inquiries by fax and e-mail.

THE SANDHILLS WRITERS CONFERENCE, Augusta State University, Augusta GA 30904. (706)737-1500. Fax: (706)667-4770. E-mail: akellman@aug.edu. Website: www.sandhills.aug.edu. **Conference Director:** Anthony Kellman. Established 1975. Annual 3-day event usually held the third weekend in March. 2003 dates were March 20-22. Location: campus of Augusta State University. Facilities are handicapped accessible. Average attendance: 100.

Purpose/Features: Open to all aspiring writers. Conference designed to "hone the creative writing skills of participants and provide networking opportunities. All areas are covered—fiction, poetry, children's literature, playwriting, screenwriting, and writing of song lyrics, also nonfiction." Offerings include craft lectures, ms evaluations, and readings. 2003 conference speakers included Doug Marlette (Pulitzer Prize winner and keynote speaker), Jake Elwell (literary agent), Robert Olstead (fiction writer), Rosemary Daniell (poet), Leslie Smith (singer-songwriter), and Jerrie Oughton (children's author).

Costs/Accommodations: 2003 cost was $156 full conference registration; $110 conference-only registration (no ms critique); $76 full conference student registration. Includes lunches; participants responsible for dinners only. Information on overnight accommodations available.

Additional Info: Individual poetry critiques available. Submit 6 poems with a limit of 15 pages. Contest sponsored as part of conference. "All registrants who submit a manuscript for evaluation are eligible for the contest determined by the visiting authors in each respective genre." Brochure and registration form available for SASE or on website. Accepts inquiries by fax and e-mail.

SANTA BARBARA WRITERS' CONFERENCE, P.O. Box 304, Carpinteria CA 93014. (805)684-2250. Fax: (805)684-7003. E-mail: s-ross@sbwc-online.com. Website: www.sbwc-online. com/. **Conference Director:** Barnaby Conrad. Established 1973. Annual event held the last week in June. 2003 dates were June 20-27. Location: Westmont College in Montecito. Average attendance: 350.

Purpose/Features: Open to everyone. Covers all genres of writing. Workshops in poetry offered. 2002 presenters included Ray Bradbury, David Lee, Gary Nale, Perie J. Longo, and Bill Wilkins.

Costs/Accommodations: 2002 conference cost including all workshops and lectures, 2 dinners, and room and board, was $1,290 single, $990 double occupancy; $400 day students. Rooms are located in the residence halls.

Additional Info: Individual poetry critiques available. Submit 1 ms of no more than 3,000 words in advance with SASE. Competitions with awards sponsored as part of conference. Brochure and registration form available for SASE or on website.

SEWANEE WRITERS' CONFERENCE, 310 St. Luke's Hall, 735 University Ave., Sewanee TN 37383-1000. (931)598-1141. E-mail: cpeters@sewanee.edu. Website: www.sewaneewriters.org. **Creative Writing Programs Manager:** Cheri B. Peters. Established 1990. Annual 12-day event held the last 2 weeks in July. Location: the University of the South ("dormitories for housing, Women's Center for public events, classrooms for workshops, Sewanee Inn for dining, etc."). Attendance: about 105.

Purpose/Features: Open to poets, fiction writers, and playwrights who submit their work for review in a competitive admissions process. "Genre, rather than thematic, workshops are offered in each of the three areas." 2003 faculty members included Tony Earley, Barry Hannah, Robert Hass, Randall Kenan, Romulus Linney, Jill McCorkle, Alice McDermott, Dan O'Brien, Janet Perry, Mary Jo Salter, Alan Shapiro, and Mark Strand. Other speakers include editors, agents, and additional writers.

Costs/Accommodations: 2003 conference cost was $1,325, including room and board. Each year scholarships and fellowships based on merit are available on a competitive basis. "We provide free bus transportation from the Nashville airport on the opening day of the conference and back to the airport on the closing day."

Additional Info: Individual critiques available. "All writers admitted to the conference will have an individual session with a member of the faculty." A ms should be sent in advance after admission to the conference. Write for brochure and application forms; no SASE necessary. Accepts inquiries by e-mail.

SINIPEE WRITERS WORKSHOP, Continuing Education, Loras College, Dubuque IA 52004-0178. (563)588-7139. Fax: (563)588-4962. E-mail: cneuhaus@loras.edu. **Contact:** Chris Neuhaus. Established 1986. Annual 1-day event scheduled to be held April 24, 2004. Location: the campus of Loras College. Average attendance: 50-100.

Purpose/Features: Open to anyone, "professional or neophyte," interested in writing. Conference covers fiction, poetry, and nonfiction.

Costs/Accommodations: Cost for the last workshop was $65 pre-registration, $75 at the door. Scholarships covering half of the cost are traditionally available to senior citizens and to full-time students, both college and high school. Cost includes handouts, coffee-and-donut break, lunch, snacks in afternoon, and book fair with authors in attendance available to autograph their books. Information on overnight accommodations available.

Additional Info: Annual contest for nonfiction, fiction, and poetry sponsored as part of workshop. There is a $5 reading fee for each entry (article/essay of 1,500 words, short story of 1,500 words, or poetry of 40 lines). 1st Prize in each category: $100 plus publication, 2nd Prize: $50, and 3rd Prize: $25. Competition receives 50-100 entries. Entrants in the contest may also ask for a written critique by a professional writer. The cost for critique is an additional $15/entry. Brochure and registration form available for SASE.

(S.O.M.O.S.) SOCIETY OF THE MUSE OF THE SOUTHWEST; CHOKECHERRIES, P.O. Box 3225, Taos NM 87571. (505)758-0081. Fax: (505)758-4802. E-mail: somos@laplaza.com. Website: www.somostaos.org. **Executive Director:** Dori Vinella. Established 1983. "We offer readings, special events, and workshops at different times during the year, many during the summer." Length of workshops varies. Location: various sites in Taos. Average attendance: 10-50.

Purpose/Features: Open to anyone. "We offer workshops in various genres—fiction, poetry, nature writing, etc.," including the 2-day Annual Taos Storytelling Festival the second weekend in September. Past workshop speakers have included Denise Chavez, Alfred Depew, Marjorie Agosin, Judyth Hill, Robin Becker, and Robert Westbrook. Other special features include writing in nature/nature walks and beautiful surroundings in a historic writer's region.

Costs/Accommodations: Cost for workshops ranges from $30-175, excluding room and board. Information on overnight accommodations available.

Additional Info: Additional information available by fax, e-mail, or on website. Accepts inquiries by fax and e-mail. "Taos has a wonderful community of dedicated and talented writers who make S.O.M.O.S. workshops rigorous, supportive, and exciting." Also publishes *Chokecherries*, an annual anthology.

SOUTHAMPTON COLLEGE WRITERS CONFERENCE, 239 Montauk Hwy., Southampton NY 11968. (631)287-8175. Fax: (631)287-8253. E-mail: writers@southampton.liu.edu. Website: www.southampton.liu.edu/summer/2002/wc2002.htm. **Summer Director:** Carla Caglioti. Established 1976. Annual 10-day event. 2003 dates were July 16-27. Location: Southampton College of Long Island University "in the heart of the Hamptons, one of the most beautiful and culturally rich resorts in the country." Average attendance: 12/workshop.

Purpose/Features: Open to new and established writers, graduate students, and upper-level undergraduate students. Conference covers poetry, fiction, short story, playwriting, and nonfiction. Offerings include a poetry workshop. 2003 faculty included Billy Collins, Jules Feiffer, Frank McCourt, Bharati Mukkherjee, Clark Blaise, and Roger Rosenblatt.

Costs/Accommodations: 2003 conference cost was $2,050 workshop, room and board; $1,650 tuition only. Accommodations include "Writers Residence Hall, single sex suites, shared room and lavatory. Some small singles available at extra cost on first-come basis."

Additional Info: "Evening events will feature regular faculty and award-winning visiting authors. Participants will also enjoy a rich schedule of formal and informal social gatherings—author receptions, open mic nights, and special literary events. Early registration is encouraged." Brochure and registration form available by e-mail or on website. Accepts inquiries by fax and e-mail.

SPLIT ROCK ARTS PROGRAM, University of Minnesota, 360 Coffey Hall, 1420 Eckles Ave., St. Paul MN 55108-6084. (612)625-8100. Fax: (612)624-6210. E-mail: srap@cce.umn.edu. Website: www.cce.umn.edu/splitrockarts/. **Program Associate:** Vivien Oja. Established 1983. Annual week-long workshops in creative writing, visual art, design, and creativity enhancement. 2003 dates were June 29-August 2. Location: Workshops are held on the University's Duluth campus near Lake Superior and in the forests of northern Minnesota. Average attendance: 550.

Purpose/Features: Open to "anyone over 18 years old who has an interest in the visual and literary arts. Participants are lifelong learners from all walks of life—novices, professionals, passionate hobbyists, and advanced amateurs. Away from the demands of daily life, Split Rock participants revel in having the time and space to explore art without interruption, and in belonging to a supportive artists' community. Split Rock workshops offer a variety of approaches to art forms, media, and methods. Areas of concentration include poetry, stories, memoirs, novels, and personal essays." 2003 program instructors included Sandra Benitz, Ray Gonzalez, Kate Green, Mickey Pearlman, Catherine Watson, and more.

Costs/Accommodations: 2003 cost was $490/workshop noncredit; participants are responsible for their own meals. Meal tickets are available. "Scholarships are available to help motivated, committed writers and artists attend Split Rock." Housing in on-site facilities; costs were $192-270 (shared), $540/week for private apartment.

Additional Info: Write or call for free catalog or visit website (registration forms available online beginning in early March of each year). Accepts inquiries by fax and e-mail.

SQUAW VALLEY COMMUNITY OF WRITERS POETRY WORKSHOP, P.O. Box 1416, Nevada City CA 95959. (530)470-8440. Fax: (530)470-8446. E-mail: svcw@oro.net. Website: www.s quawvalleywriters.org. **Executive Director:** Brett Hall Jones. Established 1969. Annual 7-day event usually held last full week in July. 2003 dates were July 19-26. Location: The Squaw Valley Ski Corporation's Lodge in the Sierra Nevada near Lake Tahoe. "The workshop takes place in the off-season of the ski area. Participants can find time to enjoy the Squaw Valley landscape." Average attendance: 64.

Purpose/Features: Open to talented writers of diverse ethnic backgrounds and a wide range of ages. "The Poetry Program differs in concept from other workshops in poetry. Our project's purpose is to help participants break through old habits and write something daring and difficult. Workshops are intended to provide a supportive atmosphere in which no one will be embarrassed, and at the same time to challenge the participants to go beyond what they have done before. Admissions are based on quality of the submitted manuscripts." Offerings include regular morning workshops, craft lectures, and staff readings. "Participants gather in daily workshops to discuss the work they wrote in the previous 24 hours." 2003 staff poets included Lucille Clifton, Brenda Hillman, Gerald Stern, Tom Sleigh, and Sharon Olds.

Costs/Accommodations: 2003 workshop cost was $675, included regular morning workshops, craft lectures, staff readings, and dinners. Accommodations extra; information on separate accommodations available. Scholarships available. "Requests for financial aid must accompany submission/

VISIT THE WRITER'S DIGEST WEBSITE at www.writersdigest.com for books, markets, newsletter sign-up, and a special poetry page.

application and will be granted on the perceived quality of manuscript submitted and financial need of applicant." Transportation to workshop available. "We will pick poets up at the Reno/Lake Tahoe Airport if arranged in advance. Also, we arrange housing for participants in local houses and condominiums. Participants can choose from a single room for $400/week or a double room for $300/week within these shared houses. We do offer inexpensive bunk bed accommodations on a first come, first served basis."

Additional Info: Individual conferences available. "Only work-in-progress will be discussed." Brochure available by e-mail (include mailing address for response) or on website. Accepts inquiries by e-mail. Also publishes the annual *Squaw Valley Community of Writers Omnium Gatherum and Newsletter* containing "news and profiles on our past participants and staff, craft articles, and book advertising."

STEAMBOAT SPRINGS WRITERS CONFERENCE, P.O. Box 774284, Steamboat Springs CO 80477. (970)879-8079. E-mail: MsHFreiberger@cs.com. **Director:** Harriet Freiberger. Established 1981. Annual 1-day event usually held mid-July. 2002 conference was July 20. Location: a "renovated train station, the Depot is home of the Steamboat Springs Arts Council—friendly, relaxed atmosphere." Average attendance: 35-40 (registration limited).

Purpose/Features: Open to anyone. Conference is "designed for writers who have limited time. Instructors vary from year to year, offering maximum instruction during a weekend at a nominal cost." 2002 speaker was Stephen Topping, editor-in-chief, Johnson Books.

Costs/Accommodations: 2002 cost was $35 (early enrollment prior to May 25), including lunch. "A variety of lodgings available."

Additional Info: Brochure and registration form available for SASE or by e-mail. Optional: Friday evening dinner (cost not included in registration fee); readings by participants (no cost).

TAOS SUMMER WRITERS' CONFERENCE, University of New Mexico, Dept. of English, Humanities Bldg. #255, Albuquerque NM 87131-1106. (505)277-6248. Fax: (505)277-5573. E-mail: taosconf@unm.edu. Website: www.unm.edu/~taosconf. **Director:** Sharon Oard Warner. Established 1999. Annual 7-day (weeklong) and 2-day (weekend) workshops usually held mid-July. Location: Sagebrush Inn in Taos. Average attendance: 125 total; 60 places available in weekend, 120 places available in weeklong workshops. Class size limited to 12/class, usually smaller.

Purpose/Features: Open to everyone, beginners to experienced. Minimum age is 18. Friendly, relaxed atmosphere with supportive staff and instructors. Offers both weekend and weeklong workshops in such areas as fiction, creative nonfiction, memoir, travel writing, magazine article writing, and poetry. 2003 workshop presenters included Blas Falconer, Lisa D. Chavez, Laurie Kutchins, Robert McDowell, and Diane Thiel. Special features include writers craft panels, open mic sessions, tours of the D.H. Lawrence Ranch, and a museum crawl.

Costs/Accommodations: 2003 conference cost was $240 for weekend, $490 for weeklong sessions, $660 combo. Includes workshop registration and special events. Nearest airport is Albuquerque Sunport. Taos is about 2½ hours north of Albuquerque. Information on overnight accommodations available. Sagebrush Inn and Comfort Suites offer special rates.

Additional Info: Offers 4 merit-based scholarships (2 for poetry, 2 for fiction) providing tuition remission for individual workshops at the conference. Applicants must be registered to apply. Brochure and registration form available by e-mail or on website. "Taos is a unique experience of a lifetime. The setting and scenery are spectacular; historical and natural beauty abound. Our previous attendees say they have been inspired by the place and by the friendly, personal attention of our instructors."

TŶ NEWYDD WRITERS' CENTRE, Taliesin Trust, Llanystumdwy, Cricieth, Gwynedd LL52 0LW Wales, Great Britain. Phone: 0441766 522811. Fax: 0441766 523095. E-mail: tynewydd@dial.pipex.com. Website: www.tynewydd.org. **Director:** Sally Baker. Established 1990. Holds 4½-day courses throughout the year, Monday evening through Saturday morning. Location: Tŷ Newydd, "a house of historical and architectural interest situated near the village of Llanystumdwy. It was the last home of Lloyd George, the former British prime minister." Average attendance: 12/course.

Purpose/Features: Open to anyone over 16 years of age. Courses are designed to "promote the writing and understanding of literature by providing creative writing courses at all levels for all ages. Courses at Tŷ Newydd provide the opportunity of working intimately and informally with two professional writers." Courses specifically for poets of all levels of experience and ability are offered throughout the year.

Costs/Accommodations: 2002 cost for a 4½-day course was £320 (inclusive), shared room; some weekend courses available, cost was £130 (inclusive). Transportation to and from Centre available if arranged at least a week in advance. Participants stay at Tŷ Newydd House in shared bedrooms or single bedrooms. "Vegetarians and people with special dietary needs are catered for but please let us know in advance. Course participants help themselves to breakfast and lunch and help to prepare one evening meal as part of a team. Participants should bring towels and their own writing materials. Some typewriters and word processors are available."

Additional Info: Brochure and registration form available for SASE. Accepts inquiries by fax and e-mail.

UND WRITERS CONFERENCE, University of North Dakota, Department of English, Grand Forks ND 58202-7209. (701)777-3321. Fax: (701)777-2373. E-mail: james_mckenzie@und.nodak.e du. Website: www.undwritersconference.org. **Director:** James McKenzie. Established 1970. Annual 4- to 5-day event. 2003 dates were March 25-29. Location: The "UND student Memorial Union, with occasional events at other campus sites, especially the large Chester Fritz Auditorium or the North Dakota Museum of Art." Average attendance: 3,000-5,000. "Some individual events have as few as 20, some over 1,000."

Purpose/Features: All events are free and open to the public. "The conference is really more of a festival, though it has been called a conference since its inception, with a history of inviting writers from all genres. The conference's purpose is public education, as well as a kind of bonus curriculum at the University. It is the region's premier intellectual and cultural event." 2003 guests included Natalie Angier, Rafael Campo, Devra Lee Davis, Alison Hawthorne Deming, Thomas Disch, Ted Mooney, Oliver Sacks, Patiann Rogers, and Julia Whitty. "They read, participate in panels, and otherwise make themselves available in public and academic venues." 2003 conference theme was "Art & Science." Other special features include open mic student/public readings every morning, informal meetings with writers, autograph sessions, dinners, and receptions.

Additional Info: Brochure available for SASE. Accepts inquiries by e-mail.

UNIVERSITY OF WISCONSIN-MADISON'S SCHOOL OF THE ARTS AT RHINELANDER, 715 Lowell Center, 610 Langdon St., Madison WI 53703-1195. Fax: (608)262-1694. E-mail: kberigan@dcs.wisc.edu. Website: www.dcs.wisc.edu/lsa/writing/index.html. **Administrative Coordinator:** Kathy Berigan. Established 1964. Annual 5-day event. 2003 session held July 28-August 1. Location: local junior high school. Average attendance: 300.

Purpose/Features: Open to all levels and ages. Offerings include poetry workshops and related workshops in creativity.

Costs/Accommodations: 2003 workshop cost ranged from $134-319; credit fees are additional. Information on overnight accommodations available.

Additional Info: Write for brochure and registration form or check website.

VICTORIA SCHOOL OF WRITING, Suite 306-620 View St., Victoria BC V8W 1J6 Canada. (250)595-3000. E-mail: vicwrite@islandnet.com. Website: www.islandnet.com/vicwrite/. **Director:** John Gould. Established 1996. Annual 5-day event. 2003 dates: July 13-18. Location: "Residential school in natural, park-like setting. Easy parking, access to university, downtown." Average attendance: 100.

Purpose/Features: "A three- to ten-page manuscript is required as part of the registration process, which is open to all. The general purpose of the workshop is to give hands-on assistance with better writing, working closely with established writers/instructors. We have workshops in fiction, poetry, and nonfiction; plus three other workshops which vary." Offerings include 2 of the intensive 5-day workshops (16 hours of instruction and one-on-one consultation). 2003 workshop leaders included Gregory Scofield (poetry); Lorna Jackson and Fred Stenson (fiction); Sharon Butala (memoirs); Tom Henry (nonfiction); and Harold Renisch (work-in-progress).

Costs/Accommodations: 2003 workshop cost was $575 Canadian; included opening reception, 5 lunches, and final-night banquet. Other meals and accommodations available on site. "For people who register with payment in full before May 1, the cost is $525 Canadian."

Additional Info: Contest sponsored as part of conference. Most recent winners were Maija Liinamaa, Robert G. Evans, and Elizabeth Mulley. Competition receives approximately 200 entries. Brochure and registration form available for SASE. Accepts inquiries by e-mail.

WESLEYAN WRITERS CONFERENCE, Wesleyan University, Middletown CT 06457. (860)685-3604. Fax: (860)685-2441. E-mail: agreene@wesleyan.edu. Website: www.wesleyan.edu/writing/conferen.html. **Director:** Anne Greene. Established 1956. Annual 5-day event usually held the third week in June. Location: the campus of Wesleyan University "in the hills overlooking the Connecticut River, a brief drive from the Connecticut shore. Wesleyan's outstanding library, poetry reading room, and other university facilities are open to participants." Average attendance: 100.

Purpose/Features: "The conference welcomes everyone interested in the writer's craft. Participants are a diverse, international group, including both experienced and new writers. You may attend any of the seminars, including poetry, the novel, short story, fiction techniques, literary journalism, and memoir." Recent special sessions included "The Poetry of Engagement," "The Writer's Life," "Writing Memoirs," and "Publishing." Offerings include ms consultations and daily seminars. Recent faculty include Honor Moore, C.D. Wright, Henry Taylor, Dana Gioia, Judy Jordan, Mark Doty, William Meredith, G.E. Patterson, John D'Agata, and Craig Arnold.

Costs/Accommodations: 2003 cost, including meals, was $725 (day rate); $850 (boarding rate). "Wesleyan has scholarships for journalists, fiction writers, nonfiction writers, and poets. Request brochure for application information." Information on overnight accommodations available. "Conference participants may stay in university dormitories or off campus in local hotels."

Additional Info: Individual ms critiques available. Registration for critiques must be made before the conference. Accepts inquiries by phone, fax, and e-mail.

WINTER POETRY & PROSE GETAWAY IN CAPE MAY, 18 North Richards Ave., Ventnor NJ 08406. (609)823-5076. E-mail: info@wintergetaway.com. Website: www.wintergetaway.com. **Founder/Director:** Peter E. Murphy. Established 1994. Annual 4-day event. 2004 dates: January 17-20. Location: The Grand Hotel on the Oceanfront in Historic Cape May, New Jersey. "Participants stay in comfortable rooms with an ocean view, perfect for thawing out the muse. Hotel facilities include a pool, sauna, and whirlpool, as well as a lounge and disco for late evening dancing for night people." Average attendance: 200.

Purpose/Features: Open to all writers, beginners and experienced, over the age of 18. "The poetry workshop meets for an hour or so each morning before sending you off with an assignment that will encourage and inspire you to produce exciting new work. After lunch, we gather together to read new drafts in feedback sessions led by experienced poet-teachers who help identify the poem's virtues and offer suggestions to strengthen its weaknesses. The groups are small and you receive positive attention to help your poem mature. In late afternoon, you can continue writing or schedule a personal tutorial session with one of the poets on staff." Previous staff have included Renee Ashley, Robert Carnevale, Cat Doty, Stephen Dunn, Kathleen Rockwell Lawrence, Charles Lynch, Peter Murphy, Jim Richardson, and Robbie Clipper Sethi. There are usually 10 participants in each poetry workshop and 7 in each of the prose workshops. Other special features include extra-supportive sessions for beginners.

Costs/Accommodations: 2003 conference cost was $425, including breakfast and lunch for 3 days, all sessions, as well as a double room; participants responsible for dinner only. Discounts available. "Early Bard" Discount: Deduct $25 if paid in full by November 15. Single-occupancy rooms available at additional cost.

Additional Info: Individual poetry critiques available. "Each poet may have a 20-minute tutorial with one of the poets on staff." Brochure and registration form available by mail or on website. "The Winter Getaway is known for its challenging, yet supportive atmosphere that encourages imaginative risk-taking and promotes freedom and transformation in the participants' writing."

◼ WISCONSIN REGIONAL WRITERS' ASSOCIATION INC.; WISCONSIN REGIONAL WRITER, 510 W. Sunset Ave., Appleton WI 54911-1139. (920)734-3724. Fax: (920)734-5146. E-mail: info@wrwa.net. Website: www.wrwa.net. Biannual conferences held first Saturday in

May and last weekend in September. Location: various hotel-conference centers around the state. Average attendance: 100-150.

Purpose/Features: Open to all writers, "aspiring, amateur, or professional." All forms of writing/ marketing presentations rotated between conferences. "The purpose is to keep writers informed and prepared to express and market their writing in a proper format." Fall 2003 conference will be held jointly with Wisconsin Fellowship of Poets in Oshkosh, WI. Book Fair held at the fall conference where members can sell their published works. Banquet also held at the fall conference Saturday and Sunday, where the Jade Ring writing contest winners from 6 categories receive awards. Winners of two additional writing contests also receive awards at the spring conference in May.

Costs/Accommodations: Spring conference is approximately $35-40, the 2-day fall conference approximately $40-60. Conferences also include Saturday morning buffet; fall conference offers hors d'oeuvres buffet at the Book Fair and entertainment at the Jade Ring Banquet. Meals (Saturday luncheon and dinner) are at an additional cost. Information about overnight accommodations available. "Our organization 'blocks' rooms at a reduced rate."

Additional Info: Sponsors 3 writing contests/year. Membership in the WRWA and small fee required. Brochure and registration form available for SASE or on website. "We are affiliated with the Wisconsin Fellowship of Poets and the Council of Wisconsin Writers. We also publish a newsletter, *Wisconsin Regional Writer*, four times a year for members."

WRITERS@WORK, Conference Registration, P.O. Box 540370, North Salt Lake UT 84054-0370. (801)292-9285. E-mail: lisa@writersatwork.org. Website: www.writersatwork.org/conference.html. **Contact:** Lisa Peterson. Established 1985. Annual event. 2003 dates were June 22-27. Location: the beautiful Westminster College campus in Salt Lake City. Average attendance: limited to 15/workshop.

Purpose/Features: Open to writers of all levels. Schedule includes workshops where students get feedback on mss; in-class writing sessions and craft discussions; and Blank Page workshops "where students can learn to spark their creativity when facing that blank page of paper." Offerings include week-long workshop, readings by faculty and other featured poets, and daily afternoon panels providing insight to the process of writing and submitting work. 2003 faculty included Deborah Digges, Lance Larsen, Sarah Kennedy, and Rod Smith.

Costs/Accommodations: 2003 cost was $395 for workshop, afternoon sessions (excluding "The Blank Page"), and 30-minute ms consultation. Six-hour Blank Page workshop cost $125. Roundtable Box Lunch discussion also available for $15 (for full workshop participants only). Limited number of Westminster residency suites available for $150/week (must be 18 years of age). Information on other overnight accommodations available.

Additional Information: Also offers the Writers@Work Fellowship Competition for fiction, non-fiction, and poetry. See website for complete details.

⊠ THE WRITERS' CENTER AT CHAUTAUQUA, Box 408, Chautauqua NY 14722. (610)791-4367 or (610)799-1542. Fax: (610)799-1159. E-mail: cfmyers@lccc.edu. Website: www.ci web.org. **Director:** Carrie Myers. Established 1988. Annual event held 9 weeks in summer from late June to late August. Participants may attend for 1 week or more. "We are an independent, cooperative association of writers located on the grounds of Chautauqua Institution." Average attendance: 60 for readings and speeches, 10 for workshops.

Purpose/Features: Readings and speeches open to anyone; workshops open to writers. Purpose is "to make creative writing one of the serious arts in progress at Chautauqua; to provide a vacation opportunity for Writers-in-Residence and their families; and to help learning writers improve their skills and vision." Workshops available all 9 weeks. Poetry Works meets 2 hours each day. 2003 leaders included Ted Gup, Margaret Gibson, Len Roberts, Ann Pancake, Geraldine Connolly, Kathleen Aguero, Gregory Donovan, Jane Ciabattari, and David Bouchier. Prose Works offers 2 hours/ day in fiction and nonfiction, writing for children, and Young Writers' Workshops. Poets are welcome to explore other fields. Other special features include 2 speeches/week and 1 reading by the Writers-In-Residence.

Costs/Accommodations: 2003 tuition was $90/workshop. Participants responsible for gate fees, housing, and meals. "May bring family; sports, concerts, activities for all ages. A week's gate ticket to Chautauqua is $190/adult (less if ordered early); housing cost varies widely, but is not cheap;

meals vary widely depending on accommodations—from fine restaurants to cooking in a shared kitchen." Access best by car or plane to Jamestown, NY.

Additional Info: Brochure and registration from available for SASE or by e-mail. "Chautauqua is a great place for family vacations; plenty to do for all ages. Participants in writers' workshops are busy only two hours per day and assignments, if any, are light. Or a writer may concentrate on work and go lightly on the main Chautauqua program."

YOSEMITE WINTER LITERARY CONFERENCE, Yosemite Association, P.O. Box 230, El Portal CA 95318. (209)379-2321. Fax: (209)379-2486. E-mail: info@yosemite.org. Website: www.yo semite.org. **Coordinator:** Beth Pratt. Annual 4-day event. 2003 dates were February 23-27. Location: Ahwahnee Hotel, Yosemite National Park. Average attendance: 100.

Purpose/Features: "The conference is designed for a variety of interest levels. Its goal is to attract and introduce writers and other artists to Yosemite and to engage them in literary contemplation, activity, and exchange." 2002 staff included Gary Snyder, Jane Hirshfield, and Pam Houston.

Costs/Accommodations: Cost is $535 ($500 for Yosemite Association members); participants are responsible for their own meals. Lodging is extra.

Additional Info: Call for brochures. "The Yosemite Association is a nonprofit organization dedicated to educating the public about Yosemite. We publish books, offer 70 field seminars, and give funding to the National Park Service from our book sales. We welcome new members and will honor the member fee for those individuals just joining." Currently has 8,600 total members. Membership dues: $30. Additional information available for SASE, by e-mail, or on website.

Organizations

There are many organizations of value to poets. These groups may sponsor workshops and contests, stage readings, publish anthologies and chapbooks, or spread the word about publishing opportunities. A few provide economic assistance or legal advice. The best thing organizations offer, though, is a support system where poets can turn for a pep talk, a hard-nosed (but sympathetic) critique of a manuscript, or simply the comfort of talking and sharing with others who understand the challenges (and joys) of writing poetry.

Whether national, regional, or as local as your library or community center, each organization has something special to offer. The listings in this section reflect the membership opportunities available to poets with a variety of organizations. Some groups provide certain services to both members and nonmembers.

Certain symbols may appear at the beginning of some listings. The (▓) symbol indicates a newly established organization new to this edition; the (✖) symbol indicates this organization did not appear in the 2003 edition; the (✿) symbol denotes a Canadian organization and the (🌐) symbol an international one.

Since some organizations are included in listings in the Publishers of Poetry, Contest & Awards, and Conferences & Workshops sections of this book, we've included these markets in a cross reference at the end of this section called Additional Organizations. For further details about an organization associated with a market in this list, go to that market's page number.

To find out more about groups in your area (including those that may not be listed in *Poet's Market*), contact your YMCA, community center, local colleges and universities, public library, and bookstores (and don't forget newspapers and the Internet). And if you can't find a group that suits your needs, consider starting one yourself. You might be surprised to find there are others in your locality who would welcome the encouragement, feedback, and moral support of a writer's group.

THE ACADEMY OF AMERICAN POETS; THE AMERICAN POET, 588 Broadway, Suite 604, New York NY 10012-3210. (212)274-0343. Fax: (212)274-9427. E-mail: academy@poets.org. Website: www.poets.org. **Executive Director:** Tree Swenson. Established 1934. Robert Penn Warren wrote in *Introduction to Fifty Years of American Poetry*, an anthology published in 1984 containing one poem from each of the 126 Chancellors, Fellows, and Award Winners of the Academy: "What does the Academy do? According to its certificate of incorporation, its purpose is 'To encourage, stimulate and foster the production of American poetry. . . .' The responsibility for its activities lies with the Board of Directors and the Board of Chancellors, which has included, over the years, such figures as Louise Bogan, W.H. Auden, Witter Bynner, Randall Jarrell, Robert Lowell, Robinson Jeffers, Marianne Moore, James Merrill, Robert Fitzgerald, F.O. Matthiessen and Archibald MacLeish—certainly not members of the same poetic church." Awards The Fellowship of the Academy of American Poets; The Walt Whitman Award; The James Laughlin Award; the Harold Morton Landon Translation Award; The Lenore Marshall Poetry Prize; The Atlas Fund; The Raiziss/de Palchi Translation Award; and The Wallace Stevens Award. (For further details, see individual listings in the Contests & Awards section.) *American Poet* is an informative periodical sent to those who contribute $25 or more/year. Membership: begins at $25/year "though those who join at higher levels receive complimentary copies of award books and other benefits. The Academy also sponsors National Poetry Month (April), an annual celebration of the richness and vitality of American poetry; the Online Poetry Classroom, an educational resource and online teaching community for high school teachers; and the Poetry Audio Archive, a collection of audio recordings of poetry readings. Additionally, the Academy maintains one of the liveliest and most comprehensive poetry sites on the Internet, at www.poets.org."

ADIRONDACK LAKES CENTER FOR THE ARTS, P.O. Box 205, Rte. 28, Blue Mountain Lake NY 12812. (518)352-7715. Fax: (518)352-7333. E-mail: alca@telenet.net. **Program Coordinator:** Darren Miller. Established in 1967 to promote "visual and performing arts through programs and services, to serve established professional and aspiring artists and the region through educational programs and activities of general interest." An independent, private, nonprofit educational organization open to everyone. Currently has 1,300 members. Levels of membership: individual, family, and business. Offerings include workshops for adults and children, reading performances, discussions, and lectures. Offers a "comfortable, cozy performance space—coffeehouse setting with tables, candles, etc." Computers available for members and artists. Publishes a triannual newsletter/schedule containing news, articles, photos, and a schedule of events. "All members are automatically sent the schedule and others may request a copy." Sponsors a few readings each year. "These are usually given by the instructor of our writing workshops. There is no set fee for membership, a gift of any size makes you a member." Members meet each July. Additional information available for SASE and by fax and e-mail.

■ **THE AMERICAN POETS' CORNER**, The Cathedral Church of St. John the Divine, Cathedral Heights, 1047 Amsterdam Ave., New York NY 10025. (212)316-7540. Website: www.stjohndivine. org/arts/ampoetscorn.html. Initiated in 1984 with memorials for Emily Dickinson, Walt Whitman, and Washington Irving. Similar in concept to the British Poets' Corner in Westminster Abbey, was established and dedicated to memorialize this country's greatest writers. A board of electors chooses one deceased author each year for inclusion in The American Poets' Corner; poets and novelists chosen in alternate years. The Cathedral is also home to the Muriel Rukeyser Poetry Wall, a public space for posting poems, which was dedicated in 1976 by Ms. Rukeyser and the Cathedral's Dean. Send poems for the Poetry Wall to the above address.

ARIZONA AUTHORS ASSOCIATION; ARIZONA LITERARY MAGAZINE; ARIZONA AUTHORS NEWSLETTER, P.O. Box 87857, Phoenix AZ 85080-7857. (602)769-2066. Fax: (623)780-0468. E-mail: info@azauthors.com. Website: www.azauthors.com. **Contact:** Vijaya Schartz, president. Established 1978 to provide education and referral for writers and others in publishing. State-wide organization. Currently has 150 total members. Levels of membership: Published, Unpublished (seeking publication), Professional (printers, agents, and publishers), and Student. Sponsors conferences, workshops, contests, awards. Sponsors annual literary contest in poetry, short story, essay, unpublished novels, and published books (fiction and nonfiction). (See separate listing for Arizona Literary & Book Awards in Contests & Awards section.) Publishes *Arizona Literary Magazine* and *Arizona Authors Newsletter*. Membership dues: $45/year for authors, $30/year students, $60/year professionals. Members meet bimonthly. Additional information available on website.

ASSOCIATED WRITING PROGRAMS; WRITER'S CHRONICLE; THE AWP AWARD SERIES; DONALD HALL PRIZE FOR POETRY, MS 1E3, George Mason University, Fairfax VA 22030. (703)993-4301. Fax: (703)993-4302. E-mail: awp@gmu.edu. Website: www.awpwriter.o rg. Established 1967. Offers a variety of services to the writing community, including information, job placement assistance (helps writers find jobs in teaching, editing, and other related fields), writing contests, literary arts advocacy, and forums. Annual individual membership: $59/year; $99/2 years; students who provide photocopy of valid student ID pay $37/year. Membership includes 6 issues of *The Writer's Chronicle* (containing information about grants and awards, publishing opportunities, fellowships, and writing programs) and *AWP Job List* (employment opportunity listings for writers). Other member benefits and opportunities available. *The Writer's Chronicle* is available by subscription only for $20/year (6 issues) or $32/2 years (12 issues). Also sponsors the AWP Award Series for poetry, fiction, and creative nonfiction, which includes the Donald Hall Prize for Poetry. Guidelines and additional information available on website.

THE AUTHORS GUILD, INC.; THE BULLETIN, 31 E. 28th St., New York NY 10016. (212)564-5904. Fax: (212)564-8363. E-mail: staff@authorsguild.org. Website: www.authorsguild.org and www.authorsguild.net. **Executive Director:** Paul Aiken. Established in 1912, it "is the largest association of published writers in the United States. The Guild focuses its efforts on the legal and business concerns of published authors in the areas of publishing contract terms, copyright, taxation, and freedom of expression. The Guild services for members include free book and magazine contract reviews, exclusive website-building software, deeply discounted website hosting and domain name reservation, and BackInPrint.com, a service that allows members to republish and sell their out-of-print books. The Guild also makes group health insurance available to members. Writers must be published by a recognized book publisher or periodical of general circulation to be eligible for membership. We do not work in the area of marketing mss to publishers nor do we sponsor or participate in awards or prize selections." Also publishes *The Bulletin*, a quarterly journal for professional writers. Additional information available by mail, phone, and e-mail.

BURNABY WRITERS' SOCIETY, 6584 Deer Lake Ave., Burnaby BC V5G 3T7 Canada. E-mail: lonewolf@portal.ca. Website: www.bws.bc.ca. **Contact:** Eileen Kernaghan. Established 1967. Corresponding membership in the society, including a newsletter subscription, is open to anyone, anywhere. Currently has 150 total members. Yearly dues: $30 regular, $20 students/seniors. Sample newsletter in return for SASE with Canadian stamp. Holds monthly meetings at The Burnaby Arts Centre (located at 6450 Deer Lake Ave.), with a business meeting at 7:30 followed by a writing workshop or speaker. Members of the society stage regular public readings of their own work. Sponsors open mic readings for the public. Sponsors a poetry contest open to British Columbia residents. Competition receives about 200-400 entries/year. Past contest winners include Mildred Tremblay, Frank McCormack, and Kate Braid. Additional information available on website.

THE WITTER BYNNER FOUNDATION FOR POETRY, INC., P.O. Box 10169, Santa Fe NM 87504. (505)988-3251. Fax: (505)986-8222. E-mail: bynnerfoundation@aol.com. Website: www .bynnerfoundation.org. **Executive Director:** Steven Schwartz. Awards grants, ranging from $1,000 to $15,000, exclusively to nonprofit organizations for the support of poetry-related projects in the area of: 1) support of individual poets through existing nonprofit institutions; 2) developing the poetry audience; 3) poetry translation and the process of poetry translation; and 4) uses of poetry. "May consider the support of other creative and innovative projects in poetry." Letters of intent accepted annually from August 1 through December 1; requests for application forms should be submitted to Steven Schwartz, executive director. Applications, if approved, must be returned to the Foundation postmarked by February 1. Additional information available by fax and e-mail.

CANADIAN POETRY ASSOCIATION; POEMATA; THE SHAUNT BASMAJIAN CHAPBOOK AWARD; CPA ANNUAL POETRY CONTEST, P.O. Box 22571, St. George PO, 264 Bloor St. W, Toronto ON M5S 1V8 Canada. (905)312-1779. Fax: (905)312-8285. E-mail: cpa@sympatico.ca. Website: www.mirror.org/cpa. Established 1985 "to promote all aspects of the reading, writing, publishing, purchasing, and preservation of poetry in Canada. The CPA promotes the creation of local chapters to organize readings, workshops, publishing projects, and other poetry-related events in their area." Membership is open to anyone with an interest in poetry, including publishers, schools, libraries, booksellers, and other literary organizations. Publishes a bimonthly magazine, *Poemata*, featuring news articles, chapter reports, poetry by new members, book reviews, markets information, announcements, and more. Sample: $3. Membership dues: $30/year; seniors and students: $20 (all dues Canadian dollars). Membership form available for SASE or on website. Also sponsors the following contests: The Shaunt Basmajian Chapbook Award offers $100 (Canadian) and publication, plus 50 copies. Guidelines available for SASE and on website. **Annual deadline:** April 30. The CPA Annual Poetry Contest offers prizes of $50, $40, $30, $20, $10, and $5, with up to 10 Honorable Mentions. Winning poems published in *Poemata* and on CPA website. **Postmark deadline:** June 30 annually. Guidelines available for SASE or on website.

COLUMBINE STATE POETRY SOCIETY OF COLORADO, P.O. Box 6245, Denver CO 80021. (303)431-6774. E-mail: anitajg5@aol.com. Website: http://members.aol.com/copoets. **Secretary/Treasurer:** Anita Jepson-Gilbert. Established in 1978 to promote the writing and appreciation of poetry throughout Colorado. State-wide organization open to anyone interested in poetry. Currently has 98 total members. Levels of membership: Members at Large, who do not participate in the local chapters but who belong to the National Federation of State Poetry Societies and at the state level; and Members, who belong to the national, state, and local chapter in Denver, Colorado. Offerings for the Denver Chapter include weekly workshops and monthly critiques. Sponsors contests, awards for students and adults. Sponsors the Annual Poets Fest where members and nationally known writers give readings and workshops that are open to the public. Also sponsors a chapbook contest in alternate years under Riverstone Press. Membership dues: $12 state and national; $35 local, state, and national. Members meet weekly. Additional information available for SASE, by e-mail, or on website.

COUNCIL OF LITERARY MAGAZINES AND PRESSES; CLMP NEWSWIRE; DIRECTORY OF LITERARY MAGAZINES, 154 Christopher St., Suite 3C, New York NY 10014. (212)741-9110. E-mail: info@clmp.org. Website: www.clmp.org. Established 1967. Dedicated "to supporting and actively promoting the field of independent literary publishing." Open to publishers who are primarily literary in nature, have published at least one issue/title prior to applying for membership, publish at least one issue/title annually on an ongoing basis, have a minimum print run of 500/issue or title, do not charge authors a fee, are not primarily self-publishing, and do not primarily publish children's/students' work. Currently has 347 total members. Membership levels and dues based on publishing organization's annual budget. See website for complete member application process. Benefits include free and discounted monographs, subscription to *CLMP Newswire*, annual copy of *Directory of Literary Magazines*, plus many valuable services. Additional information available by e-mail or on website.

GEORGIA POETRY SOCIETY; GEORGIA POETRY SOCIETY NEWSLETTER, 1473 Aycock Rd., Bishop GA 30621-1146. (706)769-5755. Website: http://pages.prodigy.net/elcampbell. **President:** Rosemary Mauldin. Established 1979 to further the purposes of the National Federation of State Poetry Societies, Inc. (NFSPS) to secure fuller public recognition of the art of poetry, stimulate an appreciation of poetry, and enhance the writing and reading of poetry. Statewide organization open to any person who is in accord with the objectives listed above. Currently has 172 total members. Levels of membership: Active, $20 ($35 family), fully eligible for all aspects of membership; Student, $10, does not vote or hold office, and must be full-time enrolled student through college level; Lifetime, same as Active but pays a one-time membership fee of $300, receives free anthologies each year, and pays no contest entry fees. Offerings include affiliation with NFSPS. At least one workshop is held annually. Contests are sponsored throughout the year, some for members only (complete guidelines available for SASE or on website). Accepts entry fees in US dollars only. Publishes *Georgia Poetry Society Newsletter*, a quarterly, also available to nonmembers on request or on website. At each quarterly meeting (open to the public) members have an opportunity to read their own poems. Sponsors Poetry in the Schools project. Additional information available on website.

GREATER CINCINNATI WRITERS' LEAGUE, 2735 Rosina Ave., Covington KY 41015. (859)491-2130. E-mail: karenlgeo@aol.com. **Contact:** Karen George. Established in the 1930s "to promote and support poetry and those who write poetry in the Cincinnati area and the attainment of excellence in poetry as an art and a craft. We believe in education and discipline, as well as creative freedom, as important components in the development of our own poetry and open, constructive critique as a learning tool." Regional organization open to anyone interested in and actively writing. Currently has 35 total members. Offerings include a monthly meeting/workshop or critique. Critics are published poets, usually faculty members from local universities, who critique poems submitted by members. The group also joins in the critique. Sponsors workshops, contests (none planned for 2003), awards with monetary prizes, and an anthology published every few years. Members give readings that are open to the public or sponsor open mic readings at bookstores and other locations. Membership dues: $25. Members meet monthly. Additional information available for SASE.

THE HUDSON VALLEY WRITERS' CENTER, 300 Riverside Dr., Sleepy Hollow NY 10591-1414. (914)332-5953. Fax: (914)332-4825. E-mail: info@writerscenter.org. Website: www.writerscenter.org. **Executive Director:** Dare Thompson. Established 1988. "The Hudson Valley Writers' Center is a nonprofit organization devoted to furthering the literary arts in our region. Its mission is to promote the appreciation of literary excellence, to stimulate and nurture the creation of literary works in all sectors of the population, and to bring the diverse works of gifted poets and prose artists to the attention of the public." Open to all. Currently has 350 total members. Levels of membership: individual, family, senior/student, and donor. Offerings include public readings by established and emerging poets/writers, workshops and classes, monthly open mic nights, paid and volunteer outreach opportunities, and an annual chapbook competition. (See separate listing for Slapering Hol Press in Publishers of Poetry section; see separate listing for Slapering Hol Press Chapbook Competition in the Contests & Awards section.) Membership dues: $35 individual, $45 family, and $20 senior/student. Additional information available for SASE, by fax, e-mail, or on website.

INDIANA STATE FEDERATION OF POETRY CLUBS; THE POETS RENDEZVOUS CONTEST; THE POETS SUMMER STANZAS CONTEST; THE POETS WINTERS FORUM CONTEST; INDIANA POET, 808 E. 32nd St., Anderson IN 46016. (765)642-3611. E-mail: poetgglee@aol.com. **Contact:** Eleanor Cranmer, president. Established in 1941 to unite poetry clubs in the state; to educate the public concerning poetry; and to encourage poet members. Statewide organization open to anyone interested in poetry. Currently has over 150 total members. Offerings include 2 conventions each year, and membership in NFSPS. Sponsors conferences, workshops. Sponsors The Poets Rendezvous Contest. Offers more than $1,200 in prizes for poems in more than 25 categories. **Entry fee:** $5. **Deadline:** August 15. Sponsors the Poets Winters Forum and The Poets Summer Stanzas contests, with prizes of $25, $15, and $10, plus 3 honorable mentions. **Entry fee:** $1/poem. Does not accept entry fees in foreign currencies. **Deadlines:** January 15 and June 15 (respectively). Send SASE for details. Competitions receive 150-200 entries. Publishes *Indiana Poet*, a bimonthly newsletter. Members or nationally known writers give readings that are open to the public. Membership dues: $15/year (includes national membership). Members meet monthly in various local clubs. Additional information available for SASE or by e-mail.

IOWA POETRY ASSOCIATION (Specialized: regional/Iowa residents); IPA NEWSLETTER; LYRICAL IOWA, 2325 61st St., Des Moines IA 50322. (515)279-1106. **Editor:** Lucille Morgan Wilson. Established 1945 "to encourage and improve the quality of poetry written by Iowans of all ages." Statewide organization open to "anyone interested in poetry, with a residence or valid address in the state of Iowa." Currently has over 400 total members. Levels of membership: Regular and Patron ("same services, but patron members contribute to cost of running the association"). Offerings include "semiannual workshops to which a poem may be sent in advance for critique; annual contest—also open to nonmembers—with no entry fee; *IPA Newsletter*, published 5 or 6 times/year, including a quarterly national publication listing of contest opportunities; and an annual poetry anthology, *Lyrical Iowa*, containing prize-winning and high-ranking poems from contest entries, available for purchase at production cost plus postage. No requirement for purchase to ensure publication." Membership dues: $8/year (Regular); $15 or more/year (Patron). "Semiannual workshops are the only 'meetings' of the Association." Additional information (Iowa residents only) available for SASE.

THE KENTUCKY STATE POETRY SOCIETY; PEGASUS; KSPS NEWSLETTER, 2602 Alanmede Rd., Louisville KY 40205. Website: http://windpub.org/ksps. **Contact:** Georgia Wallace, president. Established in 1966 to promote interest in writing poetry, improve skills in writing poetry, present poetry readings and poetry workshops, and publish poetry. Regional organization open to all. Currently has about 235 total members. Member of The National Federation of State Poetry Societies (NFSPS). Offerings include association with other poets, information on contests and poetry happenings across the state and nation; annual state and national contests; national and state annual conventions with workshops, selected speakers, and open poetry readings. Sponsors workshops, contests, awards. Membership includes the quarterly *KSPS Newsletter*. Also includes a quarterly newsletter, *Strophes*, of the NFSPS; and the KSPS journal, *Pegasus*, published 3 times yearly: a spring/summer and fall/winter issue which solicits good poetry for publication (need not be a member to submit), and a Prize Poems issue of 1st Place contest winners in over 40 categories. Members or nationally

MARKET CONDITIONS are constantly changing! If you're still using this book and it's 2005 or later, buy the newest edition of *Poet's Market* at your favorite bookstore or order directly from Writer's Digest Books (800)448-0915 or www.writersdigest.com.

known writers give readings that are open to the public. Membership dues: students $5; adults $20; senior adults $15. Other categories: Life; Patron; Benefactor. Members meet annually. Membership information available for SASE and on website.

🂱 🂱 THE LEAGUE OF CANADIAN POETS; GERALD LAMPERT MEMORIAL AWARD; PAT LOWTHER MEMORIAL AWARD, 54 Wolseley St., Toronto ON M5T 1A5 Canada. (416)504-1657. Fax: (416)504-0096. E-mail: league@poets.ca. Website: www.poets.ca. **Contact:** Edita Petrauskaite. Established 1966. A nonprofit national association of professional publishing and performing poets in Canada. Its purpose is "to enhance the status of poets and nurture a professional poetic community to facilitate the teaching of Canadian poetry at all levels of education and to develop the audience for poetry by encouraging publication, performance, and recognition of Canadian poetry nationally and internationally. As well as providing members and the public with many benefits and services, the League speaks for poets on many issues such as freedom of expression, Public Lending Right, CanCopy, contract advice, and grievance." Open to all Canadian citizens and landed immigrants; applications are assessed by a membership committee. Currently has 600 total members. Levels of membership: Full, Associate, Student, and Supporting. Membership benefits include reading opportunities, promotion of work through the League, a listing in the online membership directory, and other features. Sponsors The Pat Lowther Memorial Award (for a book of poetry by a Canadian woman published in the preceding year; $1,000 prize) and The Gerald Lampert Memorial Award (recognizes the best first book of poetry published by a Canadian in the preceding year; $1,000). Publishes a members' newsletter. Membership dues: $175 Full, $60 Associate, $40 Student, and $100 Supporting. Additional information available on website.

🂱 LIVING SKIES FESTIVAL OF WORDS; THE WORD, 250 Thatcher Dr. E., Moose Jaw SK S6J 1L7 Canada. (306)691-0557. Fax: (306)693-2994. E-mail: word.festival@sasktel.net. Website: www3.sk.sympatico.ca/praifes. **Operations Manager:** Lori Dean. "Established in 1996, the purpose/ philosophy of the organization is to celebrate the imaginative uses of languages. The Festival of Words is a registered nonprofit group of over 150 volunteers who present an enjoyable and stimulating celebration of the imaginative ways we use language. We operate year round bringing special events to Saskatchewan, holding open microphone coffeehouses for youth, and culminating in an annual summer festival in July which features activities centered around creative uses of language." National organization open to writers and readers. Currently has 285 total members. Offerings include "The Festival of Words programs with readings by poets, panel discussions, and workshops. In addition, poets attending get to share ideas, get acquainted, and conduct impromptu readings. The activities sponsored are held in the Moose Jaw Library/Art Museum complex, as well as in various venues around the city." Sponsors workshops as part of the Festival of Words. "We are also associated with *FreeLance* magazine, a publication of the Saskatchewan Writers' Guild. This publication features many useful articles dealing with poetry writing and writing in general." Also publishes *The Word*, a newsletter appearing approximately 6-7 times/year containing news of Festival events, fund-raising activities, profiles of members, reports from members. Available to nonmembers. First issue is free. Members and nationally known writers give readings that are open to the public. Sponsors open mic readings for members and for the public. Membership dues: $5, $15/3 years. Additional information available for SASE, by fax, e-mail, or on website.

MASSACHUSETTS STATE POETRY SOCIETY, INC.; BAY STATE ECHO; THE NATIONAL POETRY DAY CONTEST; THE GERTRUDE DOLE MEMORIAL CONTEST; AMBASSADOR OF POETRY AWARD; POET'S CHOICE CONTEST; THE NAOMI CHERKOFSKY MEMORIAL CONTEST; OF THEE I SING! CONTEST; ARTHUR (SKIP) POTTER MEMORIAL CONTEST, 64 Harrison Ave., Lynn MA 01905. **President:** Jeanette C. Maes. Established 1959, dedicated to the writing and appreciation of poetry and promoting the art form. State-wide organization open to anyone with an interest in poetry. Currently has 200 total members. Offerings include critique groups. Sponsors workshops, contests including The National Poetry Day Contest, with prizes of $25, $15, and $10 (or higher) for each of 30 categories. Pays winners from other countries in US currency. **Entry fee:** $8. **Deadline:** August 1. Competition receives about 2,000 entries/year. Also sponsors these contests: The Gertrude Dole Memorial Contest, with prizes of $25, $15, and $10. **Entry fee:** $3. **Deadline:** March 1. Ambassador of Poetry Award, with prizes of $50, $30, and $20. **Entry fee:** $3/poem. **Deadline:** April 15 annually. The Poet's Choice Contest, with prizes of $50, $25, and $15. **Entry fee:** $3/poem. **Deadline:** November 1. The Naomi Cherkofsky Memorial Contest, with prizes of $50, $30, and $20. **Entry fee:** $3/poem. **Deadline:** June 30. The "Of Thee I Sing!" Contest, with prizes of $50, $25, and $15. **Deadline:** January 15. Arthur (Skip) Potter Memorial Contest with prizes of $50, $30, and $20. **Entry fee:** $3. **Deadline:** December 15 annually. Does not accept entry fees in foreign currencies. Guidelines available for SASE. Publishes a yearly anthology of poetry and a yearly publication of student poetry contest winners. Also publishes *Bay State Echo*, a newsletter, 5 times/year. Members or nationally known writers give readings that are open to the public. Sponsors open mic readings for members and the public for National Poetry Day. Membership dues: $12/year. Members meet 5 times/year. Additional information available for SASE.

MISSISSIPPI POETRY SOCIETY, INC.; THE MAGNOLIA MUSE, 608 N. Pearl St., Iuka MS 38852-2223. E-mail: poet@vol.com. **State President:** Dr. Emory D. Jones. ("This changes annually when new officers are installed.") Established in 1932 "to foster interest in the writing of poetry through a study of poetry and poetic form; to provide an opportunity for, and give recognition to, individual creative efforts relating to poetry; and to create an audience for poetry; and suggest or otherwise make known markets and contests for poetry to its members." Statewide organization, affiliated with the National Federation of State Poetry Societies (NFSPS), consisting of three branches open to "anyone who writes poetry or is interested in fostering the interests of poetry." Currently has 100 total members. Levels of membership: Regular (in-state members), At-Large (out-of-state members), Student (kindergarten-undergraduate), and Honorary (older members who have performed special services). Offerings include monthly meetings, annual contests, an annual awards banquet, and opportunities to have poems critiqued in sessions at state and branch meetings. State also holds a 1-day Mini-Festival in the fall and an annual 2-day Spring Festival; includes noted speakers and contests. Publishes bimonthly newsletter *Magnolia Muse* (members who win places in contests are published in *The Mississippi Poetry Journal*; student winners are published in *Fledglings*). Branches publish newsletters and/or journals periodically. "The state organization publishes journals of all winning poems each year, and often of other special contests. There are occasionally 'featured poets,' and two or three of their poems are featured in an issue of *Magnolia Muse*." Members give readings that are open to the public. Membership dues: $20 (Regular), $12 (At-Large), $11 (Students). Members meet at various times (North, South, and Central Branches may meet monthly, bimonthly, or quarterly; state organization meets in the fall and spring). Additional information available for SASE or by e-mail.

NATIONAL FEDERATION OF STATE POETRY SOCIETIES, INC.; STROPHES. **Membership Chairman:** Sy Swann, 2736 Creekwood Lane, Ft. Worth TX 76123-1105. (817)292-8598 or (605)768-2127 (June and July). Fax: (817)531-6593. E-mail: JFS@flash.net. Website: www.nfsps.com. Established in 1959, "NFSPS is a nonprofit organization exclusively educational and literary. Its purpose is to recognize the importance of poetry with respect to national cultural heritage. It is dedicated solely to the furtherance of poetry on the national level and serves to unite poets in the bonds of fellowship and understanding." Currently has 6,000 total members. Any poetry group located in a state not already affiliated, but interested in affiliating, with NFSPS may contact the membership chairman. In a state where no valid group exists, help may also be obtained by individuals interested in organizing a poetry group for affiliation. Most reputable state poetry societies are members of the National Federation and advertise their various poetry contests through the quarterly bulletin, *Strophes*, available for SASE and $1, edited by Madelyn Eastlund, 310 South Adams St., Beverly Hills FL 34465 (e-mail: verdure@digitalusa.net). **Beware of organizations calling themselves state poetry societies (however named) that are not members of NFSPS,** as such labels are sometimes used by vanity schemes trying to sound respectable. NFSPS holds an annual meeting in a different city each year with a large awards banquet, addressed by a renowned poet and writer. Sponsors 50 national contests in various categories each year. (See separate listing for NFSPS competitions in the Contests & Awards section.) Additional information available by fax, e-mail, or on website.

NATIONAL WRITERS ASSOCIATION; AUTHORSHIP, 3140 S. Peoria, #295, Aurora CO 80014. (303)841-0246. Fax: (303)841-2607. Website: www.nationalwriters.com. **Executive Director:** Sandy Whelchel. Established 1937. National organization with regional affiliations open to writers. Currently has 3,000 total members. Levels of membership: Published Writers and Other Writers. Hosts an annual Summer Conference where workshops, panels, etc., are available to all attendees, including poets. Also offers a yearly poetry writing contest with cash awards of $100, $50, and $25. Pays winners from other countries by US check. **Entry fee:** $10/poem. Accepts entry fees in foreign currencies. **Deadline:** October 1. Send SASE for judging sheet copies. Publishes *Authorship*, an annual magazine. Sample copy available for 9 × 12 envelope with $1.21 postage. Available to nonmembers for $18. Membership dues: Professional $85; others $65. Members meet monthly. Additional information available for SASE or by fax or e-mail. Contest forms available on website.

NATIONAL WRITERS UNION; THE AMERICAN WRITER, 113 University Place, 6th Floor, New York NY 10003. (212)254-0279. E-mail: nwu@nwu.org. Website: www.nwu.org. Poets eligible for membership if they've published at least 5 poems, or if they've written 5 poems and are actively writing and trying to publish their work. Other standards apply for various forms of writing (see website). Offers members such services as a grievance committee, contract guidelines, health insurance, press credentials, and caucuses and trade groups for exchange of information about special markets. Members receive *The American Writer*, the organization's newsletter. Membership is $95 for those earning less than $5,000/year; $155 for those earning $5,000-25,000; $210 for those earning $25,000-50,000; and $260 for those whose writing income is more than $50,000/year. Membership form available online. See website for complete information.

NEVADA POETRY SOCIETY, P.O. Box 7014, Reno NV 89510. (775)322-3619. **President:** Sam Wood. Established in 1976 to encourage the writing and critiquing of poetry. State-wide organization. Currently has 30 total members. Levels of membership: Active and Emeritus. Offerings include membership in the National Federation of State Poetry Societies (NFSPS), including their publication, *Strophes*; monthly challenges followed by critiquing of all new poems; lessons on types of poetry. Members of the society are occasionally called upon to read to organizations or in public meetings. Membership dues: $10 (this includes membership in NFSPS). Members meet monthly. Additional information available for SASE. "We advise poets to enter their poems in contests before thinking about publication."

NEW HAMPSHIRE WRITERS' PROJECT; EX LIBRIS, P.O. Box 2693, Concord NH 03302-2693. (603)226-6649. Fax: (603)226-0035. E-mail: nhwp@rcn.com. Website: www.nhwriters project.org. **Executive Director:** Katie Goodman. Established in 1988 "to foster the literary arts community in New Hampshire, to serve as a resource for and about New Hampshire writers, to support the development of individual writers, and to encourage an audience for literature in New Hampshire." Statewide organization open to writers at all levels in all genres. Currently has 800 members. Offerings include workshops, seminars, an annual conference, a literary calendar, and a ms review service. Sponsors day-long workshops and 4- to 6-week intensive courses. Also sponsors biennial awards for outstanding literary achievement. Publishes *Ex Libris*, a bimonthly newsletter for and about New Hampshire writers. Members and nationally known writers give readings that are open to the public. Membership dues: $35/year; $20/year for seniors and students. Additional information available for SASE, by fax, e-mail, or on website.

THE NORTH CAROLINA POETRY SOCIETY; BROCKMAN/CAMPBELL BOOK AWARD CONTEST. (Officers change annually; please contact us through our website at www.slee pycreek.org/poetry.) Established 1932 to "foster the writing of poetry; to bring together in meetings of mutual interest and fellowship the poets of North Carolina; to encourage the study, writing, and publication of poetry; and to develop a public taste for the reading and appreciation of poetry." State-wide and out-of-state organization open to "all interested persons." Levels of membership: Regular ($25/year) and Student ($10/year). NCPS conducts 3 general meetings and numerous statewide workshops each year, sponsors annual poetry contests with categories for adults and students (open to anyone, with small fee for nonmembers; December/January deadline; cash prizes), publishes the contest-winning poems in the annual book *Award Winning Poems*; publishes a newsletter and supports other poetry activities. Also sponsors the annual Brockman/Campbell Book Award Contest for a book of poetry (over 20 pages) by a North Carolina poet (native-born or current resident for 3 years). Prize: $150 and a Revere-style bowl. **Entry fee:** $10 for nonmembers. **Deadline:** May 1. Competitions receive 300 entries/year. Most recent contest winners include Betty Adcock, Robert Morgan, and Kathryn Byer. Additional information available on website.

NORTH CAROLINA WRITERS' NETWORK; THE WRITERS' NETWORK NEWS; BLUMENTHAL WRITERS & READERS SERIES, P.O. Box 954, Carrboro NC 27510. (919)967-9540. Fax: (919)929-0535. E-mail: mail@ncwriters.org. Website: www.ncwriters.org. Established 1985. Supports the work of writers, writers' organizations, independent bookstores, little magazines and small presses, and literary programming statewide. Membership dues: $55 annually brings members *The Writers' Network News*, a 24-page bimonthly newsletter containing organizational news, national market information, and other literary material of interest to writers; and access to the NCWN Library & Resource Center, other writers, workshops, conferences, readings and competitions, and NCWN's critiquing and editing service. Currently has 1,600 total members. Annual fall conference features nationally known writers, publishers, and editors, held in a different North Carolina location each November. Sponsors competitions in short fiction, nonfiction, and poetry for North Carolina residents and NCWN members. Guidelines available for SASE or on website.

OHIO POETRY ASSOCIATION; OHIO POETRY ASSOCIATION NEWSLETTER, 1576 E. High St., Apt. 7, Springfield OH 45505. (937)324-2486. **President:** Renée Young. Established in 1929 as Verse Writers' Guild of Ohio to promote the art of poetry and further the support of poets and others who support poetry. "We sponsor contests, seminars, readings, and publishing opportunities for poets of all ages and abilities throughout and beyond Ohio." Statewide membership with additional members in several other states, Japan, and England. Affiliated with the National Federation of State Poetry Societies (NFSPS). Organization open to "poets and writers of all ages and ability, as well as to nonwriting lovers of poetry in all its forms." Currently has over 220 total members. Levels of membership: Regular, Student, Associate, Honorary Life, Paid Life, and Honorary. Member benefits include regular contests, meeting/workshop participation, assistance with writing projects, networking; twice-yearly magazine, *Common Threads*, 4 state newsletters, 4 NFSPS newsletters, membership in NFSPS and lower entry fee for their contests. Members are automatically on the mailing list for Ohio Poetry Day contest guidelines. "We are cosponsors of Ohio Poetry Day. Individual chapters regularly host workshops and seminars. We publish *Common Threads*, a semiannual, saddle-bound anthology of poetry (open to submission from **members only**)." (See separate listing for *Common Threads* in the Publishers of Poetry section; for Ohio Poetry Day in the Contests & Awards section.) Publishes the *Ohio Poetry Association Newsletter*, a quarterly which includes general news, member accomplishments, publishing opportunities, contests, editorials, items of interest to poets and writers. First issue is complementary to nonmembers. Members and nationally known writers give readings that are open to the public (at quarterly meetings; public is invited). Sponsors open mic readings for members and the public. Past readers have included Lisa Martinovic, David Shevin, Michael Bugeja, David Citino, and Danika Dinsmore. Membership dues: $12 senior; $15 regular; $5 associate and student. Members meet quarterly at the state level (local groups meet monthly). Additional information available for SASE. "All poets need an organization to share info, critique, publish, sponsor contests, and just socialize. We do all that."

THE OREGON STATE POETRY ASSOCIATION; VERSEWEAVERS, P.O. Box 602, West Linn OR 97068. (503)655-1274. E-mail: OSPA@oregonpoets.org. Website: www.oregonpoets.org. **President:** Marianne Klekacz. Established 1936 for "the promotion and creation of poetry." Member of the National Federation of State Poetry Societies, Inc. (NFSPS), sponsors workshops, readings, and seminars around the state and an annual contest for students (K-12). Currently has over 400 total members. Membership dues: $20, $12 (65 and older), $5 (18 and under). Publishes a quarterly *OSPA Newsletter*, annual *Verseweavers* book, and annual *Cascadia* book of Oregon student poetry. Sponsors contests twice yearly, awards prizes in October during Fall Poetry Conference and in April during Spring Poetry Festival, with total cash prizes of $1,000 each (no entry fee to members, $3/poem for nonmembers; out-of-state entries welcome). Pays winners from other countries by International Money Order. Does not accept entry fees in foreign currencies. Send International Money Order.

Themes and categories vary; special category for New Poets. Competition receives 1,600 entries/year. Most recent contest winners include Glenna Holloway, M.E. Hope, Allison Joseph, Lynn Veach Sadler, Barbara Schweitzer, Jon K. Sinclair, Toni Van Deusen, and Ellen Waterston. For details send SASE to OSPA, after June 1 and December 1 each year, or check website. Members and nationally known writers give readings that are open to the public. Sponsors open mic readings for members and the public during National Poetry Month (April).

PEN AMERICAN CENTER; PEN WRITERS FUND; PEN TRANSLATION PRIZE; GRANTS AND AWARDS, 568 Broadway, New York NY 10012. (212)334-1660. E-mail: pen@pen.org. Website: www.pen.org. PEN American Center "is the largest of more than 100 centers which comprise International PEN, established in London in 1921 by John Galsworthy to foster understanding among men and women of letters in all countries. Members of PEN work for freedom of expression wherever it has been endangered, and International PEN is the only worldwide organization of writers and the chief voice of the literary community." Total membership on all continents is approximately 10,000. The 2,700 members of the American Center include poets, playwrights, essayists, editors, novelists (for the original letters in the acronym PEN), as well as translators and those editors and agents who have made a substantial contribution to the literary community. Membership in American PEN includes reciprocal privileges in foreign centers for those traveling abroad. Branch offices are located in Cambridge, Portland/Seattle, New Orleans, and San Francisco. Among PEN's various activities are public events and symposia, literary awards, assistance to writers in prison and to American writers in need (grants and loans up to $1,000 from PEN Writers Fund). Medical insurance for writers is available to members. The quarterly *PEN News* is sent to all members. The PEN Translation Prize is sponsored by the Book-of-the-Month Club, 1 prize each year of $3,000 for works published in the current calendar year. Publishes *Grants and Awards* biennially, containing guidelines, deadlines, eligibility requirements, and other information in over a thousand listings of grants, awards, and competitions for poets and other writers: $19.50. Send SASE for booklet describing activities and listing publications, some of them available free.

PITTSBURGH POETRY EXCHANGE, P.O. Box 4279, Pittsburgh PA 15203. (412)481-POEM. Website: http://trfn.clpgh.org/forpoems/. **Coordinator:** Michael Wurster. Established in 1974 as a community-based organization for local poets, it functions as a service organization and information exchange, conducting ongoing workshops, readings, forums, and other special events. No dues or fees. "Any monetary contributions are voluntary, often from outside sources. We've managed not to let our reach exceed our grasp." Reading programs are primarily committed to local and area poets, with honorariums of $25-85. Sponsors a minimum of three major events each year in addition to a monthly workshop. Some of these have been reading programs in conjunction with community arts festivals, such as the October South Side Poetry Smorgasbord—a series of readings throughout the evening at different shops (galleries, bookstores). Poets from out of town may contact the Exchange for assistance in setting up readings at bookstores to help sell their books. Additional information available for SASE, by phone, or on website.

N POETRY IN THE ARTS, INC., 5801 Highland Pass, Austin TX 78731. (512)453-7920. E-mail: dearpita@poetryinarts.org. Website: www.poetryinarts.org. Established 1985. Promotes "the literary and fine arts through publishing and exhibition, and through donor-funded secondary school education in creative writing and the creative process, scholarships, and poetry contests." Membership is open to all. See website for full information on membership levels and prerequisites. "PITA bestows membership as an honorary title on donors and provides a surprisingly full list of publications and other artifacts in return for the donor's consideration." Click the "Join PITA" button on the website's index page to become a member. Sponsors contests and awards. Publishes *Poets & Artists*, a semiannual journal, and *Best of Poetry in the Arts*, an annual anthology of poetry and art competition

---

MARKETS LISTED in the 2003 edition of *Poet's Market* that do not appear this year are identified in the General Index with a code explaining their absence from the listings.

winners. Available to nonmembers for $7.95 (journal) and $11 (anthology). Nationally known writers give readings that are open to the public. Additional information available on website.

🌐 **THE POETRY LIBRARY**, Royal Festival Hall, London SE1 8XX United Kingdom. Phone: (0207)921 0943/0664. Fax: (0207)921 0939. E-mail: poetrylibrary@rfh.org.uk. Website: www.poetry library.org.uk. **Poetry Librarians:** Simon Smith and Tania Earnshaw, joint acting librarians. Established 1953 as a "free public library of modern poetry. It contains a comprehensive collection of all British poetry published since 1912 and an international collection of poetry from all over the world, either written in or translated into English. As the United Kingdom's national library for poetry, it offers loan and information service and large collections of poetry magazines, tapes, videos, records, poem posters, and cards; also press cuttings and photographs of poets." National center with "open access for all visitors. Those wishing to borrow books and other materials must be residents of U.K." Offerings include "library and information service; access to all recently published poetry and to full range of national magazines; only source of international poetry, including magazines; and information on all aspects of poetry." Offers browsing facilities and quieter area for study; listening facilities for poetry on tape, video record, and CD. Adjacent to "Voice Box" venue for literature readings. Nationally known writers give readings that are open to the public. "Separate administration for readings in 'The Voice Box'—a year-round program of readings, talks, and literature events for all writing. Contact the literature section, Royal Festival Hall." Additional information available on website. "Our focus is more on published poets than unpublished. No unpublished poems or manuscripts kept or accepted. Donations welcome but please write or call in advance." Opened 11-8 Tuesday-Sunday; closed to visitors on Mondays, buy may be telephoned.

POETRY SOCIETY OF AMERICA; CROSSROADS: THE JOURNAL OF THE POETRY SOCIETY OF AMERICA, 15 Gramercy Park, New York NY 10003. (212)254-9628. Website: www.poetrysociety.org. **Executive Director:** Alice Quinn. Established 1910, the PSA is a national nonprofit organization for poets and lovers of poetry. Sponsors readings and lectures as well as programs such as Poetry in Motion; partners with The Favorite Poem Project. Levels of Membership: Student ($25), Member ($45), Supporter ($65), Sustainer ($100), Patron ($250), Benefactor ($500), and Angel ($1,000). All paid members receive *Crossroads: The Journal of the Poetry Society of American*; additional benefits available as membership levels increase. Free to join PSA mailing list for news of upcoming events. PSA also sponsors a number of competitions for members and nonmembers (see separate listing for Poetry Society of America Awards in the Contests & Awards section).

POETRY SOCIETY OF NEW HAMPSHIRE; THE POET'S TOUCHSTONE, 282 Meaderboro Rd., Farmington NH 03835. (603)332-0732. E-mail: frisella@worldpath.net. **President:** Patricia L. Frisella. Established in 1964 as a statewide organization for anyone interested in poetry. Member of the National Federation of State Poetry Societies (NFSPS). Currently has 155 total members. Levels of membership: $10, Junior; $20, Regular; $100, "Angel." Offerings include annual subscription to quarterly magazine, *The Poet's Touchstone*, membership in NFSPS, critiques, contests and workshops, public readings, and quarterly meetings with featured poets. *The Poet's Touchstone* available to nonmembers for $3.50 (single issue), $14 (subscription); available to nonprofit organizations for $7/year. Members and nationally known writers give readings that are open to the public. Sponsors open mic readings for members and the public. "Once a year we have a members' open mic. This year we are working with three Borders bookstores to sponsor panels of featured readers followed by open mics for National Poetry Month." Additional information available for SASE or by e-mail. "We do sponsor a national contest four times a year with $100, $50, and $25 prizes paid out in each one. People from all over the country enter and win."

THE POETRY SOCIETY OF TEXAS; POETRY SOCIETY OF TEXAS BULLETIN; A BOOK OF THE YEAR, 7059 Spring Valley Rd., Dallas TX 75254. (972)233-6348. E-mail: bmahan @airmail.net. Website: http://members.tripod.com/psttx/. **Contact:** Budd Powell Mahan. Established 1921. "The purpose of the society shall be to secure fuller public recognition of the art of poetry, to encourage the writing of poetry by Texans, and to kindle a finer and more intelligent appreciation of poetry, especially the work of living poets who interpret the spirit and heritage of Texas." PST is a member of the National Federation of State Poetry Societies (NFSPS). Has 22 chapters in cities throughout the state. Offers " 'Active' membership to native Texans, Citizens of Texas, or former Citizens of Texas who were active members; 'Associate' membership to all who desire to affiliate." Currently has 400 total members. Levels of membership: Active Membership, Associate Membership, Sustaining Membership, Benefactors, Patrons of the Poets, and Student Membership. Offerings include annual contests with prizes in excess of $5,000 as well as monthly contests (general and humorous); 8 monthly meetings; annual awards banquet; annual summer conference in a different location each year; round-robin critiquing opportunities sponsored at the state level; and Poetry in Schools with contests at state and local chapter levels. "Our monthly state meetings are held at the Preston Royal Branch of the Dallas Public Library. Our annual awards banquet is held at the Harvey Hotel in Dallas. Our summer conference is held at a site chosen by the hosting chapter. Chapters determine their meeting sites." Publishes *A Book of the Year* which presents annual and monthly award-winning poems, coming contest descriptions, minutes of meetings, by-laws of the society, history, and information. Also publishes the *Poetry Society of Texas Bulletin*, a monthly newsletter that features statewide news documenting contest winners, state meeting information, chapter and individual information, news from the National Federation of State Poetry Societies (NFSPS), and announcements of coming activities and offerings for poets. "*A Book of the Year* is available to nonmembers for $8." Members and nationally known writers give readings. "All of our meetings are open to the public." Membership dues: $25 for Active and Associate Memberships, $10 for students. Members meet monthly. Additional information available for SASE, by e-mail, or on website.

POETS & WRITERS, INC.; POETS & WRITERS MAGAZINE; A DIRECTORY OF AMERICAN POETS AND FICTION WRITERS, 72 Spring St., Suite 301, New York NY 10012. (212)226-3586. Website: www.pw.org. Poets & Writers, Inc., was established in 1970 to foster the development of poets and fiction writers and to promote communication through the literary community. The largest nonprofit literary organization in the nation, it offers information, support, publications, and exposure to writers at all stages in their careers. Sponsors programs such as Writers Exchange (emerging poets and fiction writers are introduced to literary communities outside their home states), Readings/Workshops, and publication in print and online of *A Directory of American Poets & Fiction Writers*. Publishes *Poets & Writers Magazine* (print), plus *Poets & Writers Online* offers topical information, the Speakeasy writers' message forum, links to over 1,000 websites of interest to writers, and a searchable database of over 3,000 listings from the *Directory*.

POETS' AND WRITERS' LEAGUE OF GREATER CLEVELAND; OHIO WRITER; POETRY: MIRROR OF THE ARTS; WRITERS AND THEIR FRIENDS, 12200 Fairhill Rd., Townhouse 3-A, Cleveland OH 44120. (216)421-0403. Fax: (216)791-1727. E-mail: PWLGC@msn.com. Website: www.pwlgc.com. **Executive Director:** Darlene Montonaro. "Established in 1974 to foster a supportive community for poets and writers and to expand the audience for creative writing among the general public." Currently has 300 total members. In 2002, PWLGC opened a Literary Center, offering classes, meeting space, and a retreat center for writers. Conducts a monthly workshop where poets can bring their work for discussion. Publishes a monthly calendar of literary events in NE Ohio; a bimonthly magazine, *Ohio Writer*, which includes articles on the writing life, news, markets, and an annual writing contest in all genres (see separate listing for Best of *Ohio Writer* Writing Contest in the Contests & Awards section); and two chapbooks/year featuring an anthology of work by area poets. "The PWLGC also sponsors a dramatic reading series, *Poetry: Mirror of the Arts*, which unites poetry and other art forms performed in cultural settings; and *Writers & Their Friends*, a biennial literary showcase of new writing (all genres), performed dramatically by area actors, media personalities, and performance poets." Membership dues: $25/year, includes subscription to *Ohio Writer Magazine* and discounts on services and facilities at the new Literary Center. Additional information available for SASE or by fax or e-mail.

POETS HOUSE; DIRECTORY OF AMERICAN POETRY BOOKS; THE REED FOUNDATION LIBRARY; THE POETS HOUSE SHOWCASE; POETRY IN THE BRANCHES; NYC POETRY TEACHER OF THE YEAR, 72 Spring St., New York NY 10012. (212)431-7920. Fax: (212)431-8131. E-mail: info@poetshouse.org. Website: www.poetshouse.org. **Contact:** Tim Kindseth. Established 1985, Poets House is a 40,000-volume (noncirculating) poetry library of books, tapes, and literary journals, with reading and writing space available. Comfortably furnished literary center open to the public year-round. New expanded space provides conference room, exhibition space, and a Children's Poets House. Over 50 annual public events include 1) poetic programs of cross-cultural and interdisciplinary exchange, 2) readings in which distinguished poets discuss and share the work of other poets, 3) workshops and seminars on various topics led by visiting poets, 4) an annual $1,000 award for the designated NYC Poetry Teacher of the Year, and 5) the People's Poetry Gathering. In addition, Poets House continues its collaboration with public library systems, Poetry in The Branches, aimed at bringing poetry into communities through collection building, public programs, seminars for librarians, and poetry workshops for young adults (information available upon request). Finally, in April Poets House hosts the Poets House Showcase, a comprehensive exhibit of the year's new poetry releases from commercial, university, and independent presses across the country. Related Showcase events include receptions, panel discussions, and seminars which are open to the public and of special interest to poets, publishers, booksellers, distributers, and reviewers. (**Note: Poets House is not a publisher.**) Following each Showcase, copies of new titles become part of the library collection and comprehensive listings for each of the books are added to the online version of the *Directory of American Poetry Books*, accessible on www.poetshouse.org. "Poets House depends, in part, on tax-deductible contributions of its nationwide members." Membership levels begin at $40/year, and along with other graduated benefits each new or renewing member receives free admission to all regularly scheduled programs. Additional information available by fax, e-mail, or on website.

▚ QUINCY WRITERS GUILD, P.O. Box 433, Quincy IL 62306. (217)885-3327. E-mail: chilleb r@adams.net. **Contact:** Carol Hillebrenner, treasurer. Established 1989 "to encourage writers to write and, if they wish, get published." Regional organization open to all those who love to write and want mutual support in their passion. Currently has 18 total members. Offers "support, encouragement, whatever information we can gather for each other, and an occasional newsletter and special speakers on the writing craft." Meets at the local public library the first Monday of most months. Sponsors conferences/workshops. Publishes *December Diversions*, a chapbook of stories and poems by members meant to be sent as a Christmas card; also a newsletter about upcoming meetings and "anything the editor thinks might interest others." *December Diversions* available for $3.50; newsletter is free for 1 year. Membership dues: $15/year. Members meet monthly. Additional information available by e-mail.

⊕ SCOTTISH POETRY LIBRARY; SCHOOL OF POETS; CRITICAL SERVICE; SCOT-TISH POETRY INDEX, 5 Crichton's Close, Edinburgh EH8 8DT Scotland. Phone: (0131)557-2876. Fax: (0131)557-8393. E-mail: inquiries@spl.org.uk. Website: www.spl.org.uk. **Director:** Robyn Marsack. **Librarian:** Iain Young. A reference information source and free lending library, also lends by post and has a travelling van service lending at schools, prisons, and community centres. Arranges poetry-writing workshops throughout Scotland, mainly for young people. The library has a web-based catalogue available at www.spl.org.uk allowing searches of all the library's resources, including books, magazines, and audio material, over 20,000 items of Scottish and international poetry. Need not be a member to borrow material; memberships available strictly to support the library's work. Levels of membership: £20 individual, £10 concessionary, £30 organizational. Benefits include biannual newsletter, annual report, new publications listing, and use of members' room at the library. The School of Poets is open to anyone; "at meetings members divide into small groups in which each participant reads a poem which is then analyzed and discussed." Meetings normally take place at 7:30 p.m. on the second Tuesday of each month at the library. Also offers a Critical Service in which groups of up to 6 poems, not exceeding 200 lines in all, are given critical comment by members of the School: £15 for each critique (with SAE). Publishes the *Scottish Poetry Index*, a multi-volume indexing series, photocopied, spiral-bound, that indexes poetry and poetry-related material in selected Scottish literary magazines from 1952 to present, and an audio CD of contemporary Scottish poems, *The Jewel Box* (January 2000). Members and nationally known writers give readings that are open to the public. Additional information available by e-mail or on website.

SMALL PRESS CENTER/THE CENTER FOR INDEPENDENT PUBLISHING, Society of Mechanics & Tradesmen, 20 W. 44th, New York NY 10036. (212)764-7021. Fax: (212)354-5365.

E-mail: smallpress@aol.com. Website: www.smallpress.org. **Executive Director:** Karin Taylor. Established in 1984, "the Small Press Center is a nonprofit reference center devoted to publishing and membership organization of small press independent publishers, writers, and independent press enthusiasts." National organization open to "any person, company, or organization that supports the small press." Currently has 1,400 total members—400 Friends, 1,000 Publisher Members. Offerings include workshops, readings, publishing reference center, and "support of the organization." Offers "a place in which the public may examine and order the books of independent publishers, free from commercial pressures. The Center is open five days a week." Sponsors conferences/workshops and awards. Publishes a quarterly newsletter. Members give readings that are open to the public. Publisher Membership dues: $75. Writer Membership dues start at $50. Additional information available for SASE, by fax, e-mail, or on website.

SOUTH CAROLINA WRITERS WORKSHOP; THE QUILL, P.O. Box 7104, Columbia SC 29202. Website: www.scwriters.com. Established 1990 "to offer writers a wide range of opportunities to improve their writing, network with others, and gain practical 'how to' information about getting published." Statewide organization open to all writers. Currently has 280 total members. Offerings include "chapter meetings where members give readings and receive critiques; *The Quill*, SCWW's bimonthly newsletter which features writing competitions and publishing opportunities; an annual conference with registration discount for members; two free seminars each year; and an annual anthology featuring members' work." Chapters meet in libraries, bookstores, and public buildings. Sponsors 3-day annual conference at Myrtle Beach and literary competitions in poetry, fiction, and nonfiction. Members and nationally known writers give readings that are open to the public. Sponsors open mic reading for members and the public at the annual conference. Membership dues: $50/year Individual; $75/year Family. Chapters meet bimonthly or monthly. Additional information available on website.

SOUTH DAKOTA STATE POETRY SOCIETY; PASQUE PETALS, Box 398, Lennox SD 57039. (605)647-2447. **Membership Chair/Editor:** Verlyss V. Jacobson. Established 1926 to provide a place for members to publish their poetry. Regional organization open to anyone. Currently has 200-225 total members. Levels of membership: Regular, Patron, Foreign, Student. Sponsors conferences, workshops, and 2 annual contests, one for adults and one for students, with 12 categories. (See separate listing for South Dakota State Poetry Society competitions in Contests & Awards section.) **Deadlines:** August 15 for adults, February 1 for students. Competition receives 300-500 entries/year for both contests. Publishes the magazine *Pasque Petals* 4 times/year. Membership dues: $20 regular, $30 patron, $5 students. Members meet biannually. Additional information available for SASE.

UNIVERSITY OF ARIZONA POETRY CENTER, 1216 N. Cherry Ave., Tucson AZ 85719. (520)626-3765. Fax: (520)621-5566. E-mail: poetry@u.arizona.edu. Website: www.poetrycenter.arizona.edu. **Director:** Gail Brown. Established in 1960 "to maintain and cherish the spirit of poetry." Open to the public. The Center is located in 3 historic adobe houses near the main campus and contains a nationally acclaimed poetry collection that includes over 40,000 items. Programs and services include a library with a noncirculating poetry collection and space for small classes; poetry-related meetings and activities; facilities, research support, and referral information about poetry and poets for local and national communities; the Free Public Reading Series of 12-18 readings each year featuring poets, fiction writers, and writers of literary nonfiction; a guest house for residencies of visiting writers and for use by other University departments and community literary activities; a 1-month summer residency at the Center's guest house offered each year to an emerging writer selected by jury; and poetry awards, readings, and special events for high school, undergraduate, and graduate students. Publishes a biannual newsletter. Additional information available for SASE, by fax, e-mail, or on website. "We do not have a membership program, but one can become a 'Friend of the Poetry Center' by making an annual contribution."

THE UNTERBERG POETRY CENTER OF THE 92ND STREET Y; "DISCOVERY"/THE NATION POETRY CONTEST, 1395 Lexington Ave., New York NY 10128. (212)415-5759. E-mail: unterberg@92ndsty.org. Website: www.92ndsty.org. Offers annual series of readings by major literary figures (weekly readings late September through May), writing workshops, master classes in fiction and poetry, and lectures and literary seminars. Also co-sponsors the "Discovery"/*The Nation* Poetry Contest (see separate listing for *The Nation* in the Publishers of Poetry section). **Deadline:** January. Competition receives approximately 1,000 entries/year. Additional information available for SASE or on website.

UTAH STATE POETRY SOCIETY; POET TREE, Utah Arts Council & NEA, 864 N. Bonita Way, Centerville UT 84014. (801)292-0283. E-mail: poetkmm@msn.com. Website: www.utah poets.com. **Contact:** Kolette Montague. Established in 1950 to secure a wider appreciation of the poetry arts and to promote excellence in writing poetry. Statewide organization. Membership is open to all citizens of the State of Utah and to interested people from any other state in the union, without consideration of age, race, regional, religious, educational, or other backgrounds. Currently has about 200 members. Sponsors conferences, workshops, contests, awards. USPS publishes, biannually, work of members in a chapbook anthology. Publishes *Poet Tree*, a biannual newsletter (also available on website). Publishes one winning manuscript annually. Members or nationally known writers give readings/workshops that are open to the public. Chapters meet at least once a month, with open readings, critiques, lessons. Annual Awards Festival includes open reading. Membership dues: $20/year ($15 for students) including membership in National Federation of State Poetry Societies (NF-SPS) and their newsletter *Strophes*, copy of the Book of the Year and other publications, and full contest privileges. Additional information available for SASE and on website. "We welcome all potential members."

VIRGINIA WRITERS CLUB; THE VIRGINIA WRITER, P.O. Box 300, Richmond VA 23218. Phone/fax: (804)648-0357. E-mail: charfinley@mindspring.com. Website: www.virginiawritersclub. org. **Editor/Executive Director:** Charlie Finley. Established in 1918 "to promote the art and craft of writing; to serve writers and writing in Virginia." State-wide organization with 7 local chapters open to "any and all writers." Currently has 350 total members. Offerings include networking with other poets and writers, discussions on getting published, workshops, and a newsletter, *The Virginia Writer*, published 5 times/year. Nationally known writers give readings that are open to the public. Membership dues: $25/year. Members meet 5 times/year as well as at workshops and monthly chapter meetings. Additional information available for SASE, by fax, e-mail, or on website.

WISCONSIN FELLOWSHIP OF POETS; MUSELETTER; WISCONSIN POETS' CALENDAR, 1830 W. Glendale Ave., Appleton WI 54914. E-mail: khuston@new.rr.com. Website: www. wfop.org. **Membership Chair:** Karla Huston. **President:** Peter Sherrill. Established in 1950 for the creation, promotion, and dissemination of poetry in the state of Wisconsin. Statewide organization open to residents and former residents of Wisconsin who are interested in the aims and endeavors of the organization. Currently has 450 total members. Levels of membership: Active, Student. Sponsors biannual conferences, workshops, contests and awards. Publishes *Wisconsin Poets' Calendar*, poems of Wisconsin (resident) poets. Also publishes *Museletter*, a quarterly newsletter. Members or nationally known writers give readings that are open to the public. Sponsors open mic readings. Membership dues: Active $25, Student $12.50. Members meet biannually. Additional information available for SASE to WFOP membership chair at the above address. Also available by e-mail or on website; no inquiries by fax.

THE WORDSMITHS (CHRISTIAN POETRY GROUP); WORDSMITHS NEWSLETTER, 493 Elgar Rd., Mont Albert North, Victoria 3129 Australia. Phone/fax: (03) 9890 5885. **Leader:** Jean Sietzema-Dickson. Established 1987 to provide a meeting place where poets could share their work for critique and encouragement. "We have met monthly (except in January) since 1987 and began publishing in 1990. Our concern, as a group, has been to encourage the development of excellence in our writing and to speak out with a distinctive voice. **We do not accept unsolicited**

VISIT THE WRITER'S DIGEST WEBSITE at www.writersdigest.com for books, markets, newsletter sign-up, and a special poetry page.

manuscripts for publication. Our brief is to publish *Australian* **Christian poetry.**" Currently has 50 members, mostly from the greater Melbourne area. Offerings include monthly workshops, plus "we subscribe to several magazines, have occasional guest poets and a Quiet Day once a year when we meet from 10 a.m.-4 p.m. to spend some time together in directed silence and writing." Holds occasional public readings. Through publishing arm, Poetica Christi Press, has published 4 group anthologies of the writing of the Wordsmiths and the works of 7 individual poets. Also sends out the *Wordsmiths Newsletter*, appearing quarterly and available to members for AUS $20/year as part of membership. Additional information and catalogues available on request by fax or e-mail (to Janette Fernando at rogerfernando@aol.com).

THE WRITER'S CENTER; WRITER'S CAROUSEL, 4508 Walsh St., Bethesda MD 20815. (301)654-8664. E-mail: postmaster@writer.org. Website: www.writer.org. **Founder and Artistic Director:** Allan Lefcowitz. Established 1976, "the Writer's Center is a literary crossroads designed to encourage the creation and distribution of contemporary literature. To support these goals we offer a host of interrelated programs and services including: workshops in all genres, a gallery of books and journals, readings and conferences, publications, desktop publishing center, meeting and workspace, and information and communication center. We welcome all genres and levels of skill as well as the other arts. These activities take place seven days a week in a 12,200 square foot facility, a former community center." Some 2,600 members support the center with annual donations. Publishes *Writer's Carousel*, a bimonthly magazine of articles and writing news. Also publishes *Poet Lore*, America's oldest poetry journal. (See separate listing for *Poet Lore* in the Publishers of Poetry section). Membership dues: $40/year general, $25/year student, $50/year family. Additional information available by e-mail or on website.

WRITERS' FEDERATION OF NOVA SCOTIA; ATLANTIC POETRY PRIZE; ATLANTIC WRITING COMPETITION; EASTWORD, 1113 Marginal Rd., Halifax NS B3H 4P7 Canada. (902)423-8116. Fax: (902)422-0881. E-mail: talk@writers.ns.ca. Website: www.writers.ns.ca. **Executive Director:** Jane Buss. Established in 1975 "to foster creative writing and the profession of writing in Nova Scotia; to provide advice and assistance to writers at all stages of their careers; and to encourage greater public recognition of Nova Scotian writers and their achievements." Regional organization open to anybody who writes. Currently has 650 total members. Offerings include resource library with over 2,500 titles, promotional services, workshop series, annual festivals, manuscript reading service, and contract advice. Sponsors the Atlantic Writing Competition for unpublished works by beginning writers, and the annual Atlantic Poetry Prize for the best book of poetry by an Atlantic Canadian. Publishes *Eastword*, a bimonthly newsletter containing "a plethora of information on who's doing what, markets and contests, and current writing events and issues." Members and nationally known writers give readings that are open to the public. Membership dues: $35 annually ($15 students). Additional information available on website.

WRITERS INFORMATION NETWORK; THE WIN-INFORMER, The Professional Association for Christian Writers, P.O. Box 11337, Bainbridge Island WA 98110. (206)842-9103. Fax: (206)842-0536. E-mail: WritersInfoNetwork@juno.com. Website: www.bluejaypub.com/win. **Director:** Elaine Wright Colvin. Established in 1983 "to provide a much needed link between writers and editors/publishers of the religious publishing industry, to further professional development in writing and marketing skills of Christian writers, and to provide a meeting ground of encouragement and fellowship for persons engaged in writing and speaking." International organization open to anyone. Currently has 1,000 members. Offerings include market news, networking, editorial referrals, critiquing, and marketing/publishing assistance. Sponsors conferences and workshops around the country. Publishes a 32- to 36-page bimonthly magazine, *The Win-Informer* containing industry news and trends, writing advice, announcements, and book reviews. The magazine will also consider "writing-related poetry, up to 24 lines, with inspirational/Christian thought or encouragement. We accept first rights only." Sample copy: $10. Membership dues: $40 US/1 year, $75/2 years; $50/year in US equivalent funds for Canada and foreign, $95/2 years. Additional information available for SASE.

THE WRITERS ROOM, 10 Astor Place, 6th Floor, New York NY 10003. (212)254-6995. Fax: (212)533-6059. Website: www.writersroom.org. Established in 1978 to provide a "home away from home" for any writer who needs a place to work. Open 24 hours a day, 7 days a week, offering desk space, Internet access, storage, and comradery. Currently has 400 total members. Supported by the National Endowment for the Arts, the New York State Council on the Arts, the New York City Department of Cultural Affairs, and private sector funding. Membership dues: biannual fee of $450 (full time), $370 (mornings and evenings), or $270 (evenings only). Call for application or download from website.

W.B. YEATS SOCIETY OF NEW YORK; POET PASS BY!, National Arts Club, 15 Gramercy Park S, New York NY 10003. Website: www.YeatsSociety.org. **President:** Andrew McGowan. Established in 1990 "to promote the legacy of Irish poet and Nobel Laureate William Butler Yeats through an annual program of lectures, readings, poetry competition, and special events." National organization open to anyone. Currently has 450 total members. Offerings include an annual poetry competition (see separate listing for W.B. Yeats Society Annual Poetry Competition in the Contests & Awards section) and *Poet Pass By!*, an annual "slam" of readings, songs, and music by poets, writers, entertainers. Also sponsors conferences/workshops. Each April, presents an all-day Saturday program, "A Taste of the Yeats Summer School in Ireland." Nationally known writers give readings that are open to the public. Membership dues: $25/year; $15/year students. Members meet monthly, September to June. Additional information available for SASE or on website; no inquiries by fax or e-mail.

(See page 502 for Additional Organizations.)

Additional Organizations

The following listings also contain information about organizations. Turn to the page numbers indicated for details about their offerings.

Publications of Interest

This section lists publications of special interest to poets, with a focus on information about writing and publishing poetry. While there are few actual markets for your work, some of these publications do identify promising leads for your submission efforts. You'll also find advice on craft, poet interviews, reviews of books and chapbooks, events calendars, and other valuable information in these publications. We provide contact information, but you may also find these publications in your library or bookstore or be able to order them through your favorite online bookseller.

Certain symbols may appear at the beginning of some listings. The (N) symbol indicates a newly established publication new to this edition; the (◪) symbol indicates this publication did not appear in the 2003 edition; the (◪) symbol denotes a Canadian publication and the (⊕) symbol an international one.

Some listings in the Publishers of Poetry, Contests & Awards, and Conferences & Workshops sections include informative publications (such as handbooks and newsletters). We've included these markets in a cross reference at the end of this section called Additional Publications of Interest. To find out more about a publication of interest associated with one of these markets, go to that market's page number.

⊕ **THE BBR DIRECTORY**, P.O. Box 625, Sheffield S1 3GY United Kingdom. E-mail: directory@bbr-online.com. Website: www.bbr-online.com/directory. **Editor/Publisher:** Chris Reed. Established 1996. *The BBR Directory* "is a monthly e-mail newssheet for everyone involved with or interested in the small press. Providing accurate and up-to-date information about what's happening in independent publishing all over the world, *The BBR Directory* is the ideal starting point for exploring the small press and for keeping tabs on who exactly is publishing what, and when." To subscribe, send a blank e-mail to directory-subs-on@bbr-online.com or sign up through website. Accepts inquiries by e-mail. *The BBR Directory* also has a special website of resources for writers at www.bbr-online.com/writers.

DUSTBOOKS; INTERNATIONAL DIRECTORY OF LITTLE MAGAZINES AND SMALL PRESSES; DIRECTORY OF POETRY PUBLISHERS; SMALL PRESS REVIEW; SMALL MAGAZINE REVIEW, P.O. Box 100, Paradise CA 95967. (530)877-6110. Fax: (530)877-0222. E-mail: dustbooks@dcsi.net. Website www.dustbooks.com. Dustbooks publishes a number of books useful to writers. Send SASE for catalog or check website. Regular publications include *The International Directory of Little Magazines & Small Presses*, published annually with almost 5,000 entries. In addition to a wide range of magazine and book publisher listings (with full editorial information), *The International Directory* offers 1,000 pages of indexes plus sources of unique subject material for readers and researchers. *Directory of Poetry Publishers* has similar information for over 2,000 poetry markets. *Small Press Review* is a bimonthly newsprint magazine carrying updates of listings in *The International Directory*, small press needs, news, announcements, and reviews—a valuable way to stay abreast of the literary marketplace. Also incorporates *Small Magazine Review*. Additional information available by fax, e-mail, or on website.

FIRST DRAFT: THE JOURNAL OF THE ALABAMA WRITERS' FORUM; THE ALABAMA WRITERS' FORUM, Alabama State Council on the Arts, 201 Monroe St., Montgomery AL 36130-1800. (334)242-4076 ext. 233, Fax: (334)240-3269. E-mail: awf1@arts.state.al.us. Website: www.writersforum.org. **Editor:** Jay Lamar. Established 1992. Appears 4 times/year with news, features, book reviews, and interviews relating to Alabama writers. "We do not publish original poetry or fiction." *First Draft* is 40 pages, magazine-sized, professionally printed on coated paper and saddle-stapled with b&w photos inside and a full color cover. Lists markets for poetry, contests/

awards, and workshops. Sponsored by the Alabama Writers' Forum, "the official literary arts advocacy organization for the state of Alabama and a partnership program of the Alabama State Council on the Arts." Reviews books of poetry, fiction, and nonfiction by "Alabama writers or from Alabama presses." Subscription: $35/year plus membership. Sample: $3.

🌐 **FREELANCE MARKET NEWS**, Sevendale House, 7 Dale St., Manchester M1 1JB England. Phone: +44 161 228 2362. Fax: +44 161 228 3533. E-mail: fmn@writersbureau.com. Website: http://writersbureau.com. **Editor:** Angela Cox. Established 1968. A monthly newsletter providing market information for writers and poets, *Freelance Market News* is 16 pages, A4-sized. Lists markets for poetry, contests/awards, conferences/workshops, and features how-to articles. Associated with the Writers College which offers correspondence courses in poetry. Occasionally reviews books or chapbooks of poetry. Subscription: £29. Sample: £2.50. Accepts inquiries by fax and e-mail.

🌐 **HANDSHAKE; THE EIGHT HAND GANG**, 5 Cross Farm Station Rd., Padgate, Warrington, Cheshire WA2 0QG England. **Contact:** John Francis Haines. Established 1992. Published irregularly to "encourage the writing of genre poetry, to provide a source of news and information about genre poetry, to encourage the reading of poetry of all types, including genre, and to provide an outlet for a little genre poetry." *Handshake* is 1 A4-sized page, printed on front and back. Lists markets for poetry and contests/awards. Single copy available for SAE and IRC.

INDEPENDENT PUBLISHER ONLINE; INDEPENDENT PUBLISHER BOOK AWARDS, Jenkins Group Inc., 400 W. Front St., Suite 4A, Traverse City MI 49684. (800)706-4636 or (231)933-0445 (main). Fax: (231)933-0448. E-mail: jimb@bookpublishing.com. Website: www.independentpublisher.com. **Managing Editor:** Jim Barnes. For 20 years the mission at *Independent Publisher* has been to recognize and encourage the work of publishers who exhibit the courage and creativity necessary to take chances, break new ground, and bring about change in the world of publishing. The annual Independent Publisher Book Awards, conducted each year to honor the year's best independently published titles (including poetry), accept entries from independent publishers throughout North America, ranging from self-publishers to major university presses. The Awards were launched in 1996 to bring increased recognition to unsung titles published by independent authors and publishers. $5,000 in prize money is divided equally among the Ten Outstanding Books of the Year, and winners and finalists in 49 categories receive plaques, certificates, and gold seals. Winner and finalists appear for an entire year in the *Independent Publisher Online* webzine, which goes out monthly to over 40,000 subscribers worldwide, many of whom are agents, buyers, and librarians.

🌐 **LIGHT'S LIST**, 37 The Meadows, Berwick-Upon-Tweed, Northumberland TD15 1NY England. Phone: (01289)306523. E-mail: photon.press@virgin.net. **Editor:** John Light. Established 1986. *Light's List* is an annual publication "listing some 1,450 small press magazines publishing poetry, prose, market information, articles, and artwork with address and brief note of interests. All magazines publish work in English. Listings are from the United Kingdom, Europe, United States, Canada, Australia, New Zealand, South Africa, and Asia." *Light's List* is 66 pages, A5-sized, photocopied, saddle-stapled, card cover. Single copy: $7 (air $8). Accepts inquiries by e-mail.

🌐 **MILLENNIUM ARTS MAGAZINE**, (formerly Merseyside Arts Magazine), P.O. Box 21, Liverpool L19 3RX England. Phone: 0151 427 8297. Fax: 0151 291 6280. E-mail: mamuk@webspawner.com. Website: www.webspawner.com/users/mamuk/index.html. **Editor:** Bernard F. Spencer. Established 1995. Previously a printed publication, now primarily an art-associated News-'n'-Information website. Presents a spectrum of arts-related activities and events in the form of gallery/studio exhibitions (mainly across the UK North West, but will include neighbouring areas). Includes a literary arts section with readings, competitions, and other information.

OHIO WRITER. (See listing for Poets' and Writers' League of Greater Cleveland in the Organizations section.)

PARA PUBLISHING, Box 8206-240, Santa Barbara CA 93118-8206. (805)968-7277, orders (800)727-2782. Fax: (805)968-1379. E-mail: info@ParaPublishing.com. Website: www.parapublishi

ng.com (hundreds of pages of valuable book writing, publishing, and promoting information). Author/ publisher Dan Poynter offers how-to books on book publishing and self-publishing, including *The Self-Publishing Manual: How to Write, Print and Sell Your Own Book.* Also available are Special Reports on various aspects of book production, promotion, marketing, and distribution. Additional information available by phone, e-mail, or on website.

PERSONAL POEMS, % Jean Hesse, 56 Arapaho Dr., Pensacola FL 32507. (850)492-9828. Fax: (850)492-7369. E-mail: fjean@mindspring.com. F. Jean Hesse started a business in 1980 writing poems for individuals for a fee (for greetings, special occasions, etc.). Others started similar businesses after she began instructing them in the process, especially through a cassette tape training program and other materials. Send SASE for free brochure or $20 plus $5.50 p&h for training manual, *How to Make Your Poems Pay.* Has published a 400-page paperback book, *For His Good Pleasure,* a one-year collection of poems for daily reading "to comfort and inspire." Available for $12.95 plus $3.50 p&h. Make checks payable to F. Jean Hesse.

🌐 **POETRY BOOK SOCIETY; PBS BULLETIN**, Book House, 45 East Hill, London SW18 2QZ England. Phone: +44 (0)20 8870 8403. Fax: +44 (0)20 8877 1615. E-mail: info@poetrybooks. co.uk. Website: www.poetrybooks.co.uk. Established 1953 "to promote the best newly published contemporary poetry to as wide an audience as possible." A book club with an annual subscription rate of £42, which covers 4 books of new poetry, the *PBS Bulletin,* and a premium offer (for new members). The selectors also recommend other books of special merit, which are obtainable at a discount of 25%. The Poetry Book Society is subsidized by the Arts Council of England. Please write (Attn: Clare Brown), fax, or e-mail for details.

POETRY FLASH; BAY AREA BOOK REVIEWERS ASSOCIATION (BABRA), 1450 Fourth St. #4, Berkeley CA 94710. (510)525-5476. Fax: (510)525-6752. E-mail: info@poetryflash. org (NOTE: **does not respond by e-mail to poetry submissions**). Website: www.poetryflash.org. **Editor:** Joyce Jenkins. Established 1972. Appears 6 times/year. "*Poetry Flash,* a Poetry Review & Literary Calendar for the West, publishes reviews, interviews, essays, and information for writers. Poems, as well as announcements about submitting to other publications, appear in each issue." *Poetry Flash* focuses on poetry, but its comprehensive literary calendar also includes events celebrating all forms of creative writing, with a focus on the West Coast, particularly California. *Poetry Flash* also sponsors a weekly poetry reading series at Cody's Books in Berkeley and sponsors the Bay Area Book Reviewers Association Awards. (See separate listing in Contests & Awards section.) Subscription $16/6 issues; $30/12 issues. Sample available by submitting an online request form.

PUSHCART PRESS, Box 380, Wainscott NY 11975. Website: www.wwnorton.com/trade/affiliates. htm. **Editor:** Bill Henderson. The Pushcart Press, an affiliate publisher of W.W. Norton & Co., publishes the acclaimed annual *Pushcart Prize* anthology, Pushcart Editor's Book Award, and other quality literature, both fiction and nonfiction. "The most-honored literary series in America, *The Pushcart Prize* has been named a notable book of the year by the *New York Times* and hailed with Pushcart Press as 'among the most influential in the development of the American book business' over the past century.'

RAIN TAXI REVIEW OF BOOKS, P.O. Box 3840, Minneapolis MN 55403. E-mail: editor@raint axi.com or info@raintaxi.com. Website: www.raintaxi.com. **Editor:** Eric Lorberer. Established 1996. "*Rain Taxi Review of Books* is a quarterly publication available by subscription and free in bookstores nationwide. Our circulation is 20,000 copies. We publish reviews of books that are overlooked by mainstream media, and each issue includes several pages of poetry reviews, as well as author interviews and original essays." Devotes 20% of publication to poetry. "We review poetry books in every issue and often feature interviews with poets." *Rain Taxi* is 56 pages, magazine-sized, web offset-printed on newsprint, saddle-stapled. Poets may send books for review consideration. Subscription: $12. Sample: $3. Accepts inquiries by e-mail. "We DO NOT publish original poetry. Please don't send poems."

WORDWRIGHTS CANADA, P.O. Box 456 Station O, Toronto ON M4A 2P1 Canada. Fax: (416)752-0689. E-mail: susanio@sympatico.ca. Website: www3.sympatico.ca/susanio. **Director:** Susan Ioannou. Publishes "books on poetics in layman's, not academic terms, such as *A Magical Clockwork: The Art of Writing the Poem* (160 pages, perfect-bound, $16.95) and *The Workshop Guide: Poetry Writing Exercises and Resources*." Considers mss of such books for publication, paying $50 advance, 10% royalties, and 5% of press run.

WRITERS' BULLETIN; COMPETITIONS BULLETIN, Cherrybite Publications, Linden Cottage, 45 Burton Rd., Little Neston, Cheshire CH64 4AE United Kingdom. E-mail: helicon@global net.co.uk. Website: www.cherrybite.co.uk. **Editor:** Shelagh Nugent. Established 1997. "Published quarterly, *Writers' Bulletin* aims to give writers the most reliable and up-to-date information on markets for fiction, nonfiction, poetry, photographs, artwork, cartoons; information on resources, courses, and conferences; book reviews (books about writing); editors' moves, publishing news, address changes; advice and tips on writing. All markets are verified with the editor—no guesswork or second-hand information." *Writer's Bulletin* is about 28 pages, saddle-stapled, colored paper cover. Single copy: £2.40 Europe, £3 USA sterling only, £2 UK. Will accept the equivalent in US dollars (cash). Sample issue also available for 2 International Reply Coupons. Accepts inquiries by e-mail. "Because we are adding news right up to publication day, *Writers' Bulletin* has the most up-to-date information available in print." Also publishes *Competitions Bulletin*, a competition listing for writers. "Over £100,000 prize money in each issue. Bimonthly and regularly updated. Same format and price as *Writers Bulletin*."

WRITER'S DIGEST BOOKS, 4700 E. Galbraith Rd., Cincinnati OH 45236. (800)448-0915. Website www.writersdigest.com. Writer's Digest Books publishes a remarkable array of books useful to all types of writers. In addition to *Poet's Market*, books for poets include *You Can Write Poetry* by Jeff Mock, *Creating Poetry* by John Drury, *The Art and Craft of Poetry* by Michael J. Bugeja, *The Writer's Digest Writing Clinic* (which includes a poetry segment), and *The Pocket Muse* by Monica Wood (stimulating inspiration for all writers, including poets). Call or write for a complete catalog or log on to www.writersdigest.com, which includes individual web pages for fiction, nonfiction, children's, poetry, personal writing, and scriptwriting, plus markets, tips, and special content. **PLEASE NOTE:** *Writer's Digest Books does not publish poetry.*

WRITERS' NEWS; WRITING MAGAZINES; DAVID ST. JOHN THOMAS CHARITABLE TRUST, P.O. Box 168, Wellington St., Leeds LS1 1RF United Kingdom. Phone: +44(0113)2388333. Fax: +44(0113)2388330. E-mail: JanetEvans@ypn.co.uk. **Editor:** Derek Hudson. Established 1989. A monthly magazine containing news and advice for writers. Devotes up to 10% to poetry and regularly features a poetry workshop, critiques, "method and type explained," and annual and monthly competitions. *Writer's News* is 32-64 pages, A4-sized, saddle-stapled. Lists markets for poetry, contests/awards, conferences/workshops, and readings. Associated with the David St. John Thomas Charitable Trust (P.O. Box 6055, Nairn 1V12 54B) which sponsors poetry competitions. Occasionally reviews books and chapbooks of poetry and other magazines. Poets may send books for review consideration. Subscription: £49.90 overseas. Sample: £4.50. Accepts inquiries by fax and e-mail. *Writers' News* subscribers also receive *Writing Magazine*, published 6 times/year and available on newsstands.

(See page 508 for Additional Publications of Interest.)

Additional Publications of Interest

The following listings also contain information about instructive publications for poets. Turn to the page numbers indicated for details about their offerings.

Get America's #1 Poetry Resource Delivered to Your Door—and Save!

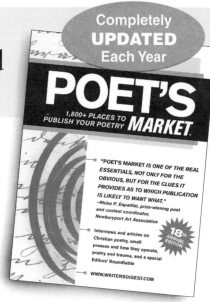

Finding the right outlets for your poetry is crucial to publishing success. With constant changes in the industry, it's not always easy to stay informed. That's why every year poets trust the newest edition of *Poet's Market* for the most up-to-date information on the people and places essential to getting their poetry published (more than 1,800 editors and publishers are included). This definitive resource also features insider tips from successful poets and editors to further increase your publishing opportunities.

2005 Poet's Market will be published and ready for shipment in August 2004.

Through this special offer, you can reserve your 2005 *Poet's Market* at the 2004 price—just $24.99. Order today and save!

Turn over for more books to help you write great poems and get them published!

More Great Books to Help You Write and Publish Your Poetry!

The Pocket Muse
by Monica Wood

It's a whole lot of inspiration — in a little bit of space! With hundreds of thought-provoking prompts, exercises and illustrations, *The Pocket Muse* will help you get started writing, overcome writer's block, think more creatively, and master important elements of the craft of writing.
#10806-K/$19.99/256 p/hc

Roget's Thesaurus of Phrases
by Barbara Ann Kipfer, Ph.D.

Sure, you go to the thesaurus when you need a synonym for a word, but now you can do the same for a phrase! Need to know a different way to say "crowning achievement" or "budget deficit?" Look no further than Kipfer's indispensable reference. You'll make your writing precise and colorful, with more than 10,000 multiword entries and example lists!
#10734-K/$22.99/432 p/hc

Word Painting
A guide to writing more descriptively
by Rebecca McClanahan

Explore and improve your descriptive writing techniques through 75+ creativity exercises. You'll learn by example from Toni Morrison, Truman Capote, Gustave Flaubert, and others! If you want to elevate your writing to new levels of richness and clarity, this book is for you!
#10709-K/$14.99/256 p/pb

Roget's Descriptive Word Finder
by Barbara Ann Kipfer

Make your work fresher and more evocative with this guide for choosing accurate, specific, descriptive words — the key to writing with precision and style. Flip through topic-by-topic to find just the right word or phrase. This is the perfect resource to help you capture those elusive words on the tip of your tongue!
#10834-K/$24.99/464 p/hc

Write Your Heart Out
by Rebecca McClanahan

Discover how to turn personal experiences, ideas, and emotions into stories, essays, poems, and memoirs. McClanahan will help you learn to write deeply, honestly, and imaginatively about the most important people, events, and emotions in your life, leading you on a path to both catharsis and self-discovery.
#10735-K/$17.99/224 p/pb

Websites of Interest

The resources for poetry on the Internet are growing daily, and there are far too many to list here. However, below you'll find those key sites every poet should bookmark. Content ranges from postal and copyright information to links, forums, articles, and reviews. (Although we confirmed every address at press time, URLs can become outdated; if a site comes up "not found," enter the name of the site in a search engine to check for a new address.)

SEARCH ENGINES:

Ask Jeeves: www.ask.com
Dogpile: www.dogpile.com
Google: www.google.com

RESOURCES:

Canadian Postal Service: www.canadapost.ca
IRS: www.irs.ustreas.gov/
US Copyright Office: www.loc.gov/copyright
US Postal Service: www.usps.gov

ESPECIALLY FOR POETS:

The Academy of American Poets: www.poets.org/
Alien Flower: www.alienflower.org
Cave Canem: www.cavecanempoets.org
Electronic Poetry Center: http://epc.buffalo.edu
National Federation of State Poetry Societies (NFSPS): www.nfsps.com
Poetic Voices: http://poeticvoices.com/
Poetry Daily: www.poems.com
Poetry Society of America: www.poetrysociety.org
Poetry Today Online: www.poetrytodayonline.com
Poets & Writers: www.pw.org
Slam News Service: www.slamnews.com

OTHER GREAT SITES FOR WRITERS:

Associated Writing Programs: www.awpwriter.org
Words Work Network (WoW Net): www.wow-schools.net
Writer Beware: www.sfwa.org/beware/
The Writer's Center: www.writer.org/
Writer's Digest: www.writersdigest.com (includes special poetry pages)
Writers Write®—The Write Resource™: www.writerswrite.com
Zuzu's Petals: www.zuzu.com

Poets in Education

Whether known as PITS (Poets in the Schools), WITS (Writers in the Schools), or similar names, programs exist nationwide that coordinate residencies, classroom visits, and other opportunities for experienced poets to teach students poetry writing. Many state arts agencies include such "arts in education" programs in their activities (see State & Provincial Grants on page 460 for contact information). Another good source is the National Assembly of State Arts Agencies (see below), which includes a directory of contact names and addresses for arts education programs state-by-state. Listed below is a mere sampling of programs and organizations that link poets with schools. Contact them for information about their requirements (some may insist poets have a strong publication history, others may prefer classroom experience) or check their websites where available.

The Academy of American Poets, *588 Broadway, Suite 604, New York NY 10012. E-mail: academy@poets.org. Website: www.poets.org (includes links to state arts in education programs).*

Arkansas Writers in the Schools, *WITS, 333 Kimpel Hall, University of Arkansas, Fayetteville AR 72701. E-mail: wits@cavern.uark.edu. Website: www.uark.edu/~wits/.*

California Poets in the Schools, *1333 Balboa St., Suite 3, San Francisco CA 94118. (415)221-4201. Toll free in CA (877)274-8764. Fax: (415)221-4301. E-mail: info@cpits.org. Website: www.cpits.org.*

e-poets.network, *a collective online cultural center that promotes education through videoconferencing (i.e., "distance learning"); also includes the* Voces y Lugares *project. Website: http://learning.e-poets.net/ (includes online contact form).*

Idaho Writers in the Schools, *Log Cabin Literary Center, 801 S. Capitol Blvd., Suite 100, Boise ID 83702. (208)331-8000. Website: www.logcablit.org/wits.html.*

Indiana Writers in the Schools, *University of Evansville, Dept. of English, 1800 Lincoln Ave., Evansville IN 47722. Website: http://english.evansville.edu/english/.*

Michigan Creative Writers in the Schools, *ArtServe Michigan, 17515 W. Nine Mile Rd., Suite 1025, Southfield MI 48075. E-mail: education@artservemichigan.org. Website: www.artservemichigan.org.*

National Assembly of State Arts Agencies, *1029 Vermont Ave., NW, 2nd Floor, Washington DC 20005. (202)347-6352. E-mail: nasaa@nasaa-arts.org. Website: www.nasaa-arts.org.*

"Pick-a-Poet," *The Humanities Project, Arlington Public Schools, 1426 N. Quincy St., Arlington VA 22207. Website: www.humanitiesproject.org/.*

Potato Hill Poetry, *6 Pleasant St. #2, S. Natick MA 01760. (508)652-9908. E-mail: info@potatohill.com. Website: www.potatohill.com (includes online contact form).*

Teachers & Writers Collaborative, Inc., *5 Union Square W., New York NY 10003-3306. (212)691-6590. E-mail: info@twc.org. Website: www.twc.org.*

Texas Writers in the Schools, *1523 W. Main, Houston TX 77006. (713)523-3877. E-mail: mail@writersintheschools.org. Website: www.writersintheschools.org.*

Writers & Artists in the Schools, *COMPAS, Landmark Center, 75 W. Fifth St., Suite 304, St. Paul MN 55102. (651)292-3249. E-mail: dei@compas.org. Website: www.compas.org.*

Glossary of Listing Terms

A3, A4, A5. Metric equivalents of $11\frac{3}{4} \times 16\frac{1}{2}$, $8\frac{1}{4} \times 11\frac{3}{4}$ and $5\frac{7}{8} \times 8\frac{1}{4}$ respectively.

Anthology. A collection of selected writings by various authors.

Attachment. A computer file electronically "attached" to an e-mail message.

b&w. Black & white (photo or illustration).

Bio. A short biographical statement often requested with a submission.

Camera-ready. Poems ready for copy camera platemaking; camera-ready poems usually appear in print exactly as submitted.

Chapbook. A small book of about 24-50 pages.

Circulation. The number of subscribers to a magazine/journal.

Contributor's copy. Copy of book or magazine containing a poet's work, sometimes given as payment.

Cover letter. Brief introductory letter accompanying a poetry submission.

Coverstock. Heavier paper used as the cover for a publication.

Digest-sized. About $5\frac{1}{2} \times 8\frac{1}{2}$, the size of a folded sheet of conventional printer paper.

Download. To "copy" a file, such as a registration form, from a website.

Electronic magazine. See *online magazine*.

E-mail. Mail sent electronically using computer and modem or similar means.

Euro. Currency unit for the 11 member countries of the European Union; designated by EUR or the € symbol.

FAQ. Frequently Asked Questions.

Font. The style/design of type used in a publication; typeface.

Galleys. First typeset version of a poem, magazine, or book/chapbook.

Honorarium. A token payment for published work.

Internet. A worldwide network of computers offering access to a variety of electronic resources.

IRC. International Reply Coupon; a publisher can exchange IRCs for postage to return a manuscript to another country.

Magazine-sized. About $8\frac{1}{2} \times 11$, the size of an unfolded sheet of conventional printer paper.

ms. Manuscript; **mss**. Manuscripts.

Multi-book review. Several books by the same author or by several authors reviewed in one piece.

Offset-printed. Printing method in which ink is transferred from an image-bearing plate to a "blanket" and then from blanket to paper.

Online magazine. Publication circulated through the Internet or e-mail.

p&h. Postage & handling.

p&p. Postage & packing.

"Pays in copies." See *contributor's copy.*

Perfect-bound. Publication with glued, flat spine; also called "flat-spined."

POD. See *print-on-demand.*

Press run. The total number of copies of a publication printed at one time.

Previously published. Work that has appeared before in print, in any form, for public consumption.

Print-on-demand. Publishing method that allows copies of books to be published as they're requested, rather than all at once in a single press run.

Publishing credits. A poet's magazine publications and book/chapbook titles.

Query letter. Letter written to an editor to raise interest in a proposed project.

Reading fee. A monetary amount charged by an editor or publisher to consider a poetry submission without any obligation to accept the work.

Rights. A poet's legal property interest in his/her literary work; an editor or publisher may acquire certain rights from the poet to reproduce that work.

ROW. "Rest of world."

Royalties. A percentage of the retail price paid to the author for each copy of a book sold.

Saddle-stapled. A publication folded, then stapled along that fold; also called "saddle-stitched."

SAE. Self-addressed envelope.

SASE. Self-addressed, stamped envelope.

Simultaneous submission. Submission of the same manuscript to more than one publisher at the same time.

Subsidy press. Publisher who requires the poet to pay all costs, including typesetting, production, and printing; sometimes called a "vanity publisher."

Tabloid-sized. 11 × 15 or larger, the size of an ordinary newspaper folded and turned sideways.

Text file. A file containing only textual characters (i.e., no graphics or special formats).

Unsolicited manuscript. A manuscript an editor did not ask specifically to receive.

Website. A specific address on the Internet that provides access to a set of documents (or "pages").

Glossary of Poetry Terms

This glossary is provided as a quick-reference only, briefly covering poetic styles and terms that may turn up in articles and listings in *Poet's Market*. For a full understanding of the terms, forms, and styles listed here, consult a solid textbook or handbook (ask your librarian or bookseller for recommendations).

Abstract poem: conveys emotion through sound, textures, and rhythm and rhyme rather than through the meanings of words.

Acrostic: initial letters of each line, read downward, form a word, phrase, or sentence.

Alphabet poem: arranges lines alphabetically according to initial letter.

American cinquain: derived from Japanese haiku and tanka by Adelaide Crapsey; counted syllabic poem of 5 lines of 2-4-6-8-2 syllables, frequently in iambic feet.

Anapest: foot consisting of 2 unstressed syllables followed by a stress (- - ').

Avant-garde: work at the forefront—cutting edge, unconventional, risk-taking.

Ballad: narrative poem often in ballad stanza (4-line stanza with 4 stresses in lines 1 and 3, 3 stresses in lines 2 and 4, which also rhyme).

Ballade: 3 stanzas rhymed *ababbcbC* (*C* indicates a refrain) with envoi rhymed *bcbC*.

Beat poetry: anti-academic school of poetry born in '50s San Francisco; fast-paced free verse resembling jazz.

Blank verse: unrhymed iambic pentameter.

Chant: poem in which one or more lines are repeated over and over.

Cinquain: any 5-line poem or stanza; also called "quintain" or "quintet." (See also *American cinquain*.)

Concrete poetry: see "emblematic poem."

Confessional poetry: work that uses personal and private details from the poet's own life.

Couplet: stanza of 2 lines; pair of rhymed lines.

Dactyl: foot consisting of a stress followed by 2 unstressed syllables (' - -).

Didactic poetry: poetry written with the intention to instruct.

Eclectic: open to a variety of poetic styles (as in "eclectic taste").

Ekphrastic poem: verbally presents something originally represented in visual art, though more than mere description.

Elegy: lament in verse for someone who has died, or a reflection on the tragic nature of life.

Emblematic poem: words or letters arranged to imitate a shape, often the subject of the poem.

Enjambment: continuation of sense and rhythmic movement from one line to the next; also called a "run-on" line.

Envoi: a brief ending (usually to a ballade or sestina) no more than 4 lines long; summary.

Epic poetry: long narrative poem telling a story central to a society, culture, or nation.

Epigram: short, witty, satirical poem or saying written to be remembered easily, like a punchline.

Experimental poetry: work that challenges conventional ideas of poetry by exploring new techniques, form, language, and visual presentation.

Foot: unit of measure in a metrical line of poetry.

Found poem: text lifted from a non-poetic source such as an ad and presented as a poem.

Free verse: unmetrical verse (lines not counted for accents, syllables, etc.).

Ghazal: Persian poetic form of 5-15 unconnected, independent couplets; associative jumps may be made from couplet to couplet.

Greeting card poetry: resembles verses in greeting cards; sing-song meter and rhyme.

Haibun: Japanese form in which prose and verse (specifically haiku) are interspersed, often in the form of a diary or travel journal.

Haikai no renga: see *renku*.

Haiku: Japanese form of 3 lines with 17 syllables, often arranged 5-7-5; essential elements include brevity, immediacy, spontaneity, imagery, nature, a season, and illumination.

Iamb: foot consisting of an unstressed syllable followed by a stress (- ').

Iambic pentameter: consists of 5 iambic feet per line.

Imagist poetry: short, free verse lines that present images without comment or explanation; strongly influenced by haiku and other Oriental forms.

Kyrielle: French form; 4-line stanza with 8-syllable lines, the final line a refrain.

Language poetry: attempts to detach words from traditional meanings to produce something new and unprecedented.

Limerick: 5-line stanza rhyming *aabba*; pattern of stresses/line is traditionally 3-3-2-2-3; often bawdy or scatalogical.

Line: basic compositional unit of a poem; measured in feet if metrical.

Linked poetry: written through the collaboration of 2 or more poets creating a single poetic work.

Long poem: exceeds length and scope of short lyric or narrative poem; defined arbitrarily, often as more than 2 pages or 100 lines.

Lyric poetry: expresses personal emotion; music predominates over narrative or drama.

Metaphor: 2 different things are likened by identifying one as the other (A=B).

Meter: the rhythmic measure of a line.

Modernist poetry: work of the early 20th century literary movement that sought to break with the past, rejecting outmoded literary traditions, diction, and form while encouraging innovation and reinvention.

Narrative poetry: poem that tells a story.

New Formalism: contemporary literary movement to revive formal verse.

Nonsense verse: playful, with language and/or logic that defies ordinary understanding.

Octave: stanza of 8 lines.

Ode: a songlike, or lyric, poem; can be passionate, rhapsodic, and mystical, or a formal address to a person on a public or state occasion.

Pantoum: Malayan poetic form of any length; consists of 4-line stanzas, with lines 2 and 4 of one quatrain repeated as lines 1 and 3 of the next; final stanza reverses lines 1 and 3 of the previous quatrain and uses them as lines 2 and 4; traditionally each stanza rhymes *abab*.

Petrarchan sonnet: octave rhymes *abbaabba*; sestet may rhyme *cdcdcd, cdedce, ccdccd, cddcdd, edecde,* or *cddcee.*

Prose poem: brief prose work with intensity, condensed language, poetic devices, and other poetic elements.

Quatrain: stanza of 4 lines.

Refrain: a repeated line within a poem, similar to the chorus of a song.

Regional poetry: work set in a particular locale, imbued with the look, feel, and culture of that place.

Renga: Japanese collaborative form in which 2 or more poets alternate writing 3 lines (haiku), then 2 lines (7 syllables each). (See also *linked poetry.*)

Renku: a popular version of the traditionally more aristocratic *renga*. (See also *linked poetry.*)

Rhyme: words that sound alike, especially words that end in the same sound.

Rhythm: the beat and movement of language (rise and fall, repetition and variation, change of pitch, mix of syllables, melody of words).

Rondeau: French form of usually 15 lines in 3 parts, rhyming *aabba aabR aabbaR* (*R* indicates a refrain repeating the first word or phrase of the opening line).

Senryu: short, humorous stanzas in haiku form, but more direct and to the point, aiming directly at human nature.

Sequence: a group or progression of poems, often numbered as a series.

Sestet: stanza of 6 lines.

Sestina: fixed form of 39 lines (6 unrhymed stanzas of 6 lines each, then an ending 3-line stanza), each stanza repeating the same 6 non-rhyming end-words in a different order; all 6 end-words appear in the final 3-line stanza.

Shakespearean sonnet: rhymes *abab cdcd efef gg*.

Simile: comparison that uses a linking word (*like, as, such as, how*) to clarify the similarities.

Sonnet: 14-line poem (traditionally an octave and sestet) rhymed in iambic pentameter; often presents an argument but may also present a description, story, or meditation.

Spondee: foot consisting of 2 stressed syllables (' ').

Stanza: group of lines making up a single unit; like a paragraph in prose.

Strophe: often used to mean "stanza"; also a stanza of irregular line lengths.

Surrealistic poetry: of the artistic movement stressing the importance of dreams and the subconscious, nonrational thought, free associations, and startling imagery/juxtapositions.

Tanka: Japanese form of 5 lines with 31 syllables (arranged 5-7-5-7-7); less concentrated and mysterious, more emotional and conversational than haiku.

Tercet: stanza or poem of 3 lines.

Terza rima: series of 3-line stanzas with interwoven rhyme scheme (*aba, bcb, cdc . . .*).

Trochee: foot consisting of a stress followed by an unstressed syllable (' -).

Villanelle: French form of 19 lines (5 tercets and a quatrain); line 1 serves as one refrain (repeated in lines 6, 12, 18), line 3 as a second refrain (repeated in lines 9, 15, 19); traditionally, refrains rhyme with each other and with the opening line of each stanza.

Visual poem: see "emblematic poem."

War poetry: poems written about warfare and military life; often written by past and current soldiers; may glorify war, recount exploits, or demonstrate the horrors of war.

Indexes
Chapbook Publishers

A poetry chapbook is a slim volume of 24-50 pages (although chapbook lengths can vary; some are even published as inserts in magazines). Many publishers and journals solicit chapbook manuscripts through competitions. Read listings carefully, check websites where available, and request guidelines before submitting. See Frequently Asked Questions on page 7 for further information about chapbooks and submission formats.

Book Publishers Index

The following are magazines and publishers that consider full-length book manuscripts (over 50 pages, often much longer). See Frequently Asked Questions on page 7 for further information about book manuscript submission.

Openness to Submissions Index

In this section, all magazines, publishers, and contests/awards with primary listings in *Poet's Market* are categorized according to their openness to submissions (as indicated by the symbols that appear at the beginning of each listing). Note that some markets are listed in more than one category.

❍ WELCOMES SUBMISSIONS FROM BEGINNING POETS

◑ PREFERS SUBMISSIONS FROM EXPERIENCED POETS, WILL CONSIDER WORK FROM BEGINNING POETS

◙ PREFERS SUBMISSIONS FROM SKILLED, EXPERIENCED POETS, FEW BEGINNERS

◎ MARKET WITH A SPECIALIZED FOCUS

Geographical Index

This section offers a breakdown of U.S. publishers and conferences/workshops arranged alphabetically by state or territory, followed by listings for Canada, Australia, France, Ireland, Japan, the United Kingdom, and other countries—a real help when trying to locate publishers in your region as well as conferences and workshops convenient to your area.

Conferences & Workshops

OTHER COUNTRIES

Publishers of Poetry

Subject Index

This index focuses on markets indicating a specialized area of interest, whether regional, poetic style, or specific topic (these markets show a ◎ symbol at the beginning of their listings). It also includes markets we felt offered special opportunities in certain subject areas. Subject categories are listed alphabetically, with additional subcategories indicated under the "Specialized" heading (in parentheses behind the market's name). Please note that this index only partially reflects the total markets in this book; many do not identify themselves as having specialized interests and so are not included here. Also, many specialized markets have more than one area of interest and will be found under multiple categories. Note, too, that when a market appears under a heading in this index, it does not necessarily mean it considers *only* poetry associated with that subject, poetry *only* from that region, etc. It's still best to read all listings carefully as part of a thorough marketing plan.

DISCOVER
A WORLD OF
WRITING
SUCCESS

Are you ready to be praised, published, and paid for your writing? It's time to invest in your future with *Writer's Digest*! Beginners and experienced writers alike have been enjoying *Writer's Digest*, the world's leading magazine for writers, for more than 80 years — and it keeps getting better! Each issue is brimming with:

- Inspiration from writers who have been in your shoes
- Detailed info on the latest contests, conferences, markets, and opportunities in every genre
- Tools of the trade, including reviews of the latest writing software and hardware
- Writing prompts and exercises to overcome writer's block and rekindle your creative spark
- Expert tips, techniques, and advice to help you get published
- And so much more!

That's a lot to look forward to every month. Let *Writer's Digest* put you on the road to writing success!

NO RISK!
Send No Money Now!

☐ **Yes!** Please rush me my 2 FREE issues of *Writer's Digest* — the world's leading magazine for writers. If I like what I read, I'll get a full year's subscription (12 issues, including the 2 free issues) for only $19.96. That's 67% off the newsstand rate! If I'm not completely happy, I'll write "cancel" on your invoice, return it and owe nothing. The 2 FREE issues are mine to keep, no matter what!

Name_____

Address_____

City_____

State_____ZIP_____

Annual newsstand rate is $59.88. Orders outside the U.S. will be billed an additional $10 (includes GST/HST in Canada.) Please allow 4-6 weeks for first-issue delivery.

www.writersdigest.com

Get 2 **FREE** TRIAL ISSUES of *Writer's* Digest

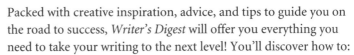

Packed with creative inspiration, advice, and tips to guide you on the road to success, *Writer's Digest* will offer you everything you need to take your writing to the next level! You'll discover how to:

- Create dynamic characters and page-turning plots
- Submit query letters that publishers won't be able to refuse
- Find the right agent or editor for you
- Make it out of the slush-pile and into the hands of the right publisher
- Write award-winning contest entries
- And more!

See for yourself by ordering your 2 FREE trial issues today!

Form/Style (Oriental)

Gay/Lesbian/Bisexual

Gothic/Horror

Humorous

Religious

Science Fiction

General Index

Markets that appeared in the *2003 Poet's Market* but are not included in this edition are identified by two-letter codes explaining their absence. These codes are: **(ED) editorial decision; (NP) no longer publishing poetry; (NR) no (or late) response to requested verification of information; (OB) out of business** (or, in the case of contests or conferences, cancelled); **(RR) removed by request of the market** (no reason given); **(UF) uncertain future; (UC) unable to contact;** and **(RP) restructuring/purchased.**